RAYMOND CHANDLER

RAYMOND CHANDLER

STORIES AND EARLY NOVELS
Pulp Stories
The Big Sleep
Farewell, My Lovely
The High Window

THE LIBRARY OF AMERICA

The paper used in this publication meets the
minimum requirements of the American National Standard for
Information Sciences—Permanence of Paper for Printed
Library Materials, ANSI Z39.48—1984.

Distributed to the trade in the United States
by Penguin Books USA Inc
and in Canada by Penguin Books Canada Ltd.

Library of Congress Catalog Number: 94–45462
For cataloging information, see end of Notes.
ISBN 1–883011–07–8

———

First Printing
The Library of America—79

Manufactured in the United States of America

FRANK MACSHANE
WROTE THE NOTES FOR THIS VOLUME

Contents

PULP STORIES

Contents

Blackmailers Don't Shoot

THE MAN in the powder-blue suit—which wasn't powder-blue under the lights of the Club Bolivar—was tall, with wide-set gray eyes, a thin nose, a jaw of stone. He had a rather sensitive mouth. His hair was crisp and black, ever so faintly touched with gray, as by an almost diffident hand. His clothes fitted him as though they had a soul of their own, not just a doubtful past. His name happened to be Mallory.

He held a cigarette between the strong, precise fingers of one hand. He put the other hand flat on the white tablecloth, and said:

"The letters will cost you ten grand, Miss Farr. That's not too much."

He looked at the girl opposite him very briefly; then he looked across empty tables towards the heart-shaped space of floor where the dancers prowled under shifting colored lights.

They crowded the customers around the dance-floor, so closely that the perspiring waiters had to balance themselves like tightrope walkers to get between the tables. But near where Mallory sat were only four people.

A slim, dark woman was drinking a highball across the table from a man whose fat red neck glistened with damp bristles. The woman stared into her glass morosely, and fiddled with a big silver flask in her lap. Farther along two bored, frowning men smoked long thin cigars, without speaking to each other.

Mallory said thoughtfully: "Ten grand does it nicely, Miss Farr."

Rhonda Farr was very beautiful. She was wearing, for this occasion, all black, except a collar of white fur, light as thistle-down, on her evening wrap. Except also a white wig which, meant to disguise her, made her look very girlish. Her eyes were cornflower blue, and she had the sort of skin an old rake dreams of.

She said nastily, without raising her head: "That's ridiculous."

"Why is it ridiculous?" Mallory asked, looking mildly surprised and rather annoyed.

Rhonda Farr lifted her face and gave him a look as hard as marble. Then she picked a cigarette out of a silver case that lay open on the table, and fitted it into a long slim holder, also black. She went on:

"The love letters of a screen star? Not so much any more. The public has stopped being a sweet old lady in long lace panties."

A light danced contemptuously in her purplish-blue eyes. Mallory gave her a hard look.

"But you came here to talk about them quick enough," he said, "with a man you never heard of."

She waved the cigarette holder, and said: "I must have been nuts."

Mallory smiled with his eyes, without moving his lips. "No, Miss Farr. You had a damn' good reason. Want me to tell you what it is?"

Rhonda Farr looked at him angrily. Then she looked away, almost appeared to forget him. She held up her hand, the one with the cigarette holder, looked at it, posing. It was a beautiful hand, without a ring. Beautiful hands are as rare as jacaranda trees in bloom, in a city where pretty faces are as common as runs in dollar stockings.

She turned her head and glanced at the stiff-eyed woman, beyond her towards the mob around the dance-floor. The orchestra went on being saccharine and monotonous.

"I loathe these dives," she said thinly. "They look as if they only existed after dark, like ghouls. The people are dissipated without grace, sinful without irony." She lowered her hand to the white cloth. "Oh yes, the letters, what makes them so dangerous, blackmailer?"

Mallory laughed. He had a ringing laugh with a hard quality in it, a grating sound. "You're good," he said. "The letters are not so much perhaps. Just sexy tripe. The memoirs of a school-girl who's been seduced and can't stop talking about it."

"That's lousy," Rhonda Farr said in a voice like iced velvet.

"It's the man they're written to that makes them important," Mallory said coldly. "A racketeer, a gambler, a fast money boy. And all that goes with it. A guy you couldn't be seen talking to—and stay in the cream."

"I don't talk to him, blackmailer. I haven't talked to him in years. Landrey was a pretty nice boy when I knew him. Most of us have something behind us we'd rather not go into. In my case it *is* behind."

"Oh yes? Make mine strawberry," Mallory said with a sudden sneer. "You just got through asking him to help you get your letters back."

Her head jerked. Her face seemed to come apart, to become merely a set of features without control. Her eyes looked like the prelude to a scream—but only for a second.

Almost instantly she got her self-control back. Her eyes were drained of color, almost as gray as his own. She put the black cigarette holder down with exaggerated care, laced her fingers together. The knuckles looked white.

"You know Landrey that well?" she said bitterly.

"Maybe I just get around, find things out. . . . Do we deal, or do we just go on snarling at each other?"

"Where did you get the letters?" Her voice was still rough and bitter.

Mallory shrugged. "We don't tell things like that in our business."

"I had a reason for asking. Some other people have been trying to sell me these same damned letters. That's why I'm here. It made me curious. But I guess you're just one of them trying to scare me into action by stepping the price."

Mallory said: "No; I'm on my own."

She nodded. Her voice was scarcely more than a whisper. "That makes it nice. Perhaps some bright mind thought of having a private edition of my letters made. Photostats. . . . Well, I'm not paying. It wouldn't get me anywhere. I don't deal, blackmailer. So far as I'm concerned you can go out some dark night and jump off the dock with your lousy letters!"

Mallory wrinkled his nose, squinted down it with an air of deep concentration. "Nicely put, Miss Farr. But it doesn't get us anywhere."

She said deliberately: "It wasn't meant to. I could put it better. And if I'd thought to bring my little pearl-handled gun I could say it with slugs and get away with it! But I'm not looking for that kind of publicity."

Mallory held up two lean fingers and examined them critically. He looked amused, almost pleased. Rhonda Farr put her slim hand up to her white wig, held it there a moment, and dropped it.

A man sitting at a table some way off got up at once and came towards them.

He came quickly, walking with a light, lithe step and swinging a soft black hat against his thigh. He was sleek in dinner clothes.

While he was coming Rhonda Farr said: "You didn't expect me to walk in here alone, did you? Me, I don't go to nightclubs alone."

Mallory grinned. "You shouldn't ought to have to, baby," he said dryly.

The man came up to the table. He was small, neatly put together, dark. He had a little black mustache, shiny like satin, and the clear pallor that Latins prize above rubies.

With a smooth gesture, a hint of drama, he leaned across the table and took one of Mallory's cigarettes out of the silver case. He lit it with a flourish.

Rhonda Farr put her hand to her lips and yawned. She said: "This is Erno, my bodyguard. He takes care of me. Nice, isn't it?"

She stood up slowly. Erno helped her with her wrap. Then he spread his lips in a mirthless smile, looked at Mallory, said: "Hello, baby."

He had dark, almost opaque eyes with hot lights in them.

Rhonda Farr gathered her wrap about her, nodded slightly, sketched a brief sarcastic smile with her delicate lips, and turned off along the aisle between the tables. She went with her head up and proud, her face a little tense and wary, like a queen in jeopardy. Not fearless, but disdaining to show fear. It was nicely done.

The two bored men gave her an interested eye. The dark woman brooded glumly over the task of mixing herself a highball that would have floored a horse. The man with the fat sweaty neck seemed to have gone to sleep.

Rhonda Farr went up the five crimson-carpeted steps to the lobby, past a bowing headwaiter. She went through looped-back gold curtains, and disappeared.

Mallory watched her out of sight, then he looked at Erno. He said: "Well, punk, what's on your mind?"

He said it insultingly, with a cold smile. Erno stiffened. His gloved left hand jerked the cigarette that was in it so that some ash fell off.

"Kiddin' yourself, baby?" he inquired swiftly.

"About what, punk?"

Red spots came into Erno's pale cheeks. His eyes narrowed to black slits. He moved his ungloved right hand a little, curled the fingers so that the small pink nails glittered. He said thinly:

"About some letters, baby. Forget it! It's out, baby, out!"

Mallory looked at him with elaborate, cynical interest, ran his fingers through his crisp black hair. He said slowly:

"Perhaps I don't know what you mean, little one."

Erno laughed. A metallic sound, a strained deadly sound. Mallory knew that kind of laugh; the prelude to gun-music in some places. He watched Erno's quick little right hand. He spoke raspingly.

"On your way, red hot! I might take a notion to slap that fuzz off your lip."

Erno's face twisted. The red patches showed startlingly in his cheeks. He lifted the hand that held his cigarette, lifted it very slowly, and snapped the burning cigarette straight at Mallory's face. Mallory moved his head a little, and the white tube arced over his shoulder.

There was no expression on his lean, cold face. Distantly, dimly, as though another voice spoke, he said:

"Careful, punk. People get hurt for things like that."

Erno laughed the same metallic, strained laugh. "Blackmailers don't shoot, baby," he snarled. "Do they?"

"Beat it, you dirty little wop!"

The words, the cold sneering tone, stung Erno to fury. His right-hand shot up like a striking snake. A gun whisked into it from a shoulder-holster. Then he stood motionless, glaring. Mallory bent forward a little, his hands on the edge of the table, his fingers curled below the edge. The corners of his mouth sketched a dim smile.

There was a dull screech, not loud, from the dark woman.

The color drained from Erno's cheeks, leaving them pallid, sunk in. In a voice that whistled with fury he said:

"Okey, baby. We'll go outside. March, you ——!"

One of the bored men three tables away made a sudden movement, of no significance. Slight as it was it caught Erno's eye. His glance flickered. Then the table rose into his stomach, knocked him sprawling.

It was a light table, and Mallory was not a lightweight. There was a complicated thudding sound. A few dishes clattered, some silver. Erno was spread on the floor with the table across his thighs. His gun settled a foot from his clawing hand. His face was convulsed.

For a poised instant of time it was as though the scene were imprisoned in glass, and would never change. Then the dark woman screeched again, louder. Everything became a swirl of movement. People on all sides came to their feet. Two waiters put their arms straight up in the air and began to spout violent Neapolitan. A moist, overdriven bus-boy charged up, more afraid of the headwaiter than of sudden death. A plump, reddish man with corn-colored hair hurried down steps, waving a bunch of menus.

Erno jerked his legs clear, weaved to his knees, snatched up his gun. He swiveled, spitting curses. Mallory, alone, indifferent in the center of the babble, leaned down and cracked a hard fist against Erno's flimsy jaw.

Consciousness evaporated from Erno's eyes. He collapsed like a half-filled sack of sand.

Mallory observed him carefully for a couple of seconds. Then he picked his cigarette case up off the floor. There were still two cigarettes in it. He put one of them between his lips, put the case away. He took some bills out of his trouser pocket, folded one lengthwise and poked it at a waiter.

He walked away without haste, towards the five crimson-carpeted steps and the entrance.

The man with the fat neck opened a cautious and fishy eye. The drunken woman staggered to her feet with a cackle of inspiration, picked up a bowl of ice cubes in her thin jeweled hands, and dumped it on Erno's stomach, with fair accuracy.

2

Mallory came out from under the canopy with his soft hat under his arm. The doorman looked at him inquiringly. He shook his head and walked a little way down the curving sidewalk that bordered the semicircular private driveway. He stood at the edge of the curbing, in the darkness, thinking hard. After a little while an Isotta-Fraschini went by him slowly.

It was an open phaeton, huge even for the calculated swank of Hollywood. It glittered like a Ziegfield chorus as it passed the entrance lights, then it was all dull gray and silver. A liveried chauffeur sat behind the wheel as stiff as a poker, with a peaked cap cocked rakishly over one eye. Rhonda Farr sat in the back seat, under the half-deck, with the rigid stillness of a wax figure.

The car slid soundlessly down the driveway, passed between a couple of squat stone pillars and was lost among the lights of the boulevard. Mallory put on his hat absently.

Something stirred in the darkness behind him, between tall Italian cypresses. He swung around, looked at faint light on a gun barrel.

The man who held the gun was very big and broad. He had a shapeless felt hat on the back of his head, and an indistinct overcoat hung away from his stomach. Dim light from a high-up, narrow window outlined bushy eyebrows, a hooked nose. There was another man behind him.

He said: "This is a gun, buddy. It goes boom-boom, and guys fall down. Want to try it?"

Mallory looked at him emptily, and said: "Grow up, flattie! What's the act?"

The big man laughed. His laughter had a dull sound, like the sea breaking on rocks in a fog. He said with heavy sarcasm:

"Bright boy has us spotted, Jim. One of us must look like a cop." He eyed Mallory, and added: "Saw you pull a rod on a little guy inside. Was that nice?"

Mallory tossed his cigarette away, watched it arc through the darkness. He said carefully:

"Would twenty bucks make you see it some other way?"

"Not tonight, mister. Most any other night, but not tonight."

"A C note?"

"Not even that, mister."

"That," Mallory said gravely, "must be damn' tough."

The big man laughed again, came a little closer. The man behind him lurched out of the shadows and planted a soft fattish hand on Mallory's shoulder. Mallory slid sidewise, without moving his feet. The hand fell off. He said:

"Keep your paws off me, gumshoe!"

The other man made a snarling sound. Something swished through the air. Something hit Mallory very hard behind his left ear. He went to his knees. He kneeled swaying for a moment, shaking his head violently. His eyes cleared. He could see the lozenge design in the sidewalk. He got to his feet again rather slowly.

He looked at the man who had blackjacked him and cursed him in a thick dull voice, with a concentration of ferocity that set the man back on his heels with his slack mouth working like melting rubber.

The big man said: "Damn your soul, Jim! What in hell'd you do that for?"

The man called Jim put his soft fat hand to his mouth and gnawed at it. He shuffled the blackjack into the side pocket of his coat.

"Forget it!" he said. "Let's take the —— and get on with it. I need a drink."

He plunged down the walk. Mallory turned slowly, followed him with his eyes, rubbing the side of his head. The big man moved his gun in a businesslike way and said:

"Walk, buddy. We're takin' a little ride in the moonlight."

Mallory walked. The big man fell in beside him. The man called Jim fell in on the other side. He hit himself hard in the pit of the stomach, said:

"I need a drink, Mac. I've got the jumps."

The big man said peacefully: "Who don't, you poor egg?"

They came to a touring car that was double-parked near the squat pillars at the edge of the boulevard. The man who had hit Mallory got in behind the wheel. The big man prodded Mallory into the back seat and got in beside him. He held his gun across his big thigh, tilted his hat a little further back, and got out a crumpled pack of cigarettes. He lit one carefully, with his left hand.

The car went out into the sea of lights, rolled east a short way, then turned south down the long slope. The lights of the city were an endless glittering sheet. Neon signs glowed and flashed. The languid ray of a searchlight prodded about among high faint clouds.

"It's like this," the big man said, blowing smoke from his wide nostrils. "We got you spotted. You were tryin' to peddle some phony letters to the Farr twist."

Mallory laughed shortly, mirthlessly. He said: "You flatties give me an ache."

The big man appeared to think it over, staring in front of him. Passing electroliers threw quick waves of light across his broad face. After a while he said:

"You're the guy all right. We got to know these things in our business."

Mallory's eyes narrowed in the darkness. His lips smiled. He said: "What business, copper?"

The big man opened his mouth wide, shut it with a click. He said:

"Maybe you better talk, bright boy. Now would be a hell of a good time. Jim and me ain't tough to get on with, but we got friends who ain't so dainty."

Mallory said: "What would I talk about, Lieutenant?"

The big man shook with silent laughter, made no answer. The car went past the oil well that stands in the middle of La Cienega Boulevard, then turned off on to a quiet street fringed with palm trees. It stopped half way down the block, in front of an empty lot. Jim cut the motor and the lights. Then he got a flat bottle out of the door-pocket and held it to his mouth, sighed deeply, passed the bottle back over his shoulder.

The big man took a drink, waved the bottle, said:

"We got to wait here for a friend. Let's talk. My name's Macdonald—detective bureau. You was tryin' to shake the Farr girl down. Then her protection stepped in front of her. You bopped him. That was nice routine and we liked it. But we didn't like the other part."

Jim reached back for the whiskey bottle, took another drink, sniffed at the neck, said: "This liquor is lousy."

Macdonald went on: "We was stashed out for you. But we don't figure your play out in the open like that. It don't listen."

Mallory leaned an arm on the side of the car, and looked out and up at the calm, blue, star-spattered sky. He said:

"You know too much, copper. And you didn't get your dope from Miss Farr. No screen star would go to the police on a matter of blackmail."

Macdonald jerked his big head around. His eyes gleamed faintly in the dark interior of the car.

"We didn't say how we got our dope, bright boy. So you *was* tryin' to shake her down, huh?"

Mallory said gravely: "Miss Farr is an old friend of mine. Somebody is trying to blackmail her, but not me. I just have a hunch."

Macdonald said swiftly: "What the wop pull a gun on you for?"

"He didn't like me," Mallory said in a bored voice. "I was mean to him."

Macdonald said: "Horse-feathers!" He rumbled angrily. The man in the front seat said: "Smack him in the kisser, Mac. Make the —— like it!"

Mallory stretched his arms downward, twisting his shoulders like a man cramped from sitting. He felt the bulge of his Luger under his left arm. He said slowly, wearily:

"You said I was trying to peddle some phoney letters. What makes you think the letters would be phoney?"

Macdonald said softly: "Maybe we know where the right ones are."

Mallory drawled: "That's what I thought, copper," and laughed.

Macdonald moved suddenly, jerked his balled fist up, hit him in the face, but not very hard. Mallory laughed again, then he touched the bruised place behind his ear with careful fingers.

"That went home, didn't it?" he said.

Macdonald swore dully. "Maybe you're just a bit too damn' smart, bright boy. I guess we'll find out after a while."

He fell silent. The man in the front seat took off his hat and scratched at a mat of gray hair. Staccato horn blasts came from the boulevard a half block away. Headlights streamed past the end of the street. After a time a pair of them swung around in a wide curve, speared white beams along below the palm trees. A dark bulk drifted down the half block, slid to the curb in front of the touring car. The lights went off.

A man got out and walked back. Macdonald said: "Hi, Slippy. How'd it go?"

The man was a tall thin figure with a shadowy face under a pulled-down cap. He lisped a little when he spoke. He said:

"Nothin' to it. Nobody got mad."

"Okey," Macdonald grunted. "Ditch the hot one and drive this heap."

Jim got into the back of the touring car and sat on Mallory's left, digging a hard elbow into him. The lanky man slid under the wheel, started the motor, and drove back to La Cienega, then south to Wilshire, then west again. He drove fast and roughly.

They went casually through a red light, passed a big movie palace with most of its lights out and its glass cashier's cage empty; then through Beverly Hills, over interurban tracks. The exhaust got louder on a long hill with high banks paralleling the road. Macdonald spoke suddenly:

"Hell, Jim, I forgot to frisk this baby. Hold the gun a minute."

He leaned in front of Mallory, close to him, blowing whiskey breath in his face. A big hand went over his pockets, down inside his coat around the hips, up under his left arm. It stopped there a moment, against the Luger in the shoulder-holster. It went on to the other side, went away altogether.

"Okey, Jim. No gun on bright boy."

A sharp light of wonder winked into being deep in Mallory's brain. His eyebrows drew together. His mouth felt dry.

"Mind if I light up a cigarette?" he asked, after a pause.

Macdonald said with mock politeness: "Now why would we mind a little thing like that, sweetheart?"

3

The apartment house stood on a hill above Westwood Village, and was new and rather cheap-looking. Macdonald and Mallory and Jim got out in front of it, and the touring car went on around the corner, disappeared.

The three men went through a quiet lobby past a switchboard where no one sat at the moment, up to the seventh floor in the automatic elevator. They went along a corridor, stopped before a door. Macdonald took a loose key out of his pocket, unlocked the door. They went in.

It was a very new room, very bright, very foul with cigarette smoke. The furniture was upholstered in loud colors, the carpet was a mess of fat green and yellow lozenges. There was a mantel with bottles on it.

Two men sat at an octagonal table with tall glasses at their elbows. One had red hair, very dark eyebrows, and a dead white face with deep-set dark eyes. The other one had a ludicrous big bulbous nose, no eyebrows at all, hair the color of the inside of a sardine can. This one put some cards down slowly and came across the room with a wide smile. He had a loose, good-natured mouth, an amiable expression.

"Have any trouble, Mac?" he said.

Macdonald rubbed his chin, shook his head sourly. He looked at the man with the nose as if he hated him. The man with the nose went on smiling. He said:

"Frisk him?"

Macdonald twisted his mouth to a thick sneer and stalked across the room to the mantel and the bottles. He said in a nasty tone:

"Bright boy don't pack a gun. He works with his head. He's smart."

He re-crossed the room suddenly and smacked the back of his rough hand across Mallory's mouth. Mallory smiled thinly, did not stir. He stood in front of a big bile-colored davenport spotted with angry-looking red squares. His hands hung down at his sides, and cigarette smoke drifted up from between his fingers to join the haze that already blanketed the rough, arched ceiling.

"Keep your pants on, Mac," the man with the nose said.

"You've done your act. You and Jim check out now. Oil the wheels and check out."

Macdonald snarled: "Who you givin' orders to, big shot? I'm stickin' around till this chiseler gets what's coming to him, Costello."

The man called Costello shrugged his shoulders briefly. The red-haired man at the table turned a little in his chair and looked at Mallory with the impersonal air of a collector studying an impaled beetle. Then he took a cigarette out of a neat black case and lit it carefully with a gold lighter.

Macdonald went back to the mantel, poured some whiskey out of a square bottle into a glass, and drank it raw. He leaned, scowling, with his back to the mantel.

Costello stood in front of Mallory, cracking the joints of long, bony fingers.

He said: "Where do you come from?"

Mallory looked at him dreamily and put his cigarette in his mouth. "McNeil's Island," he said with vague amusement.

"How long since?"

"Ten days."

"What were you in for?"

"Forgery." Mallory gave the information in a soft, pleased voice.

"Been here before?"

Mallory said: "I was born here. Didn't you know?"

Costello's voice was gentle, almost soothing. "No-o, I didn't know that," he said. "What did you come for—ten days ago?"

Macdonald heaved across the room again, swinging his thick arms. He slapped Mallory across the mouth a second time, leaning past Costello's shoulder to do it. A red mark showed on Mallory's face. He shook his head back and forth. Dull fire was in his eyes.

"Jeeze, Costello, this crumb ain't from McNeil. He's ribbin' you." His voice blared. "Bright boy's just a cheap chiseler from Brooklyn or K. C.—one of those hot towns where the cops are all cripples."

Costello put a hand up and pushed gently at Macdonald's shoulder. He said: "You're not needed in this, Mac," in a flat, toneless voice.

Macdonald balled his fist angrily. Then he laughed, lunged forward and ground his heel on Mallory's foot. Mallory said: "—— damn!" and sat down hard on the davenport.

The air in the room was drained of oxygen. Windows were in one wall only, and heavy net curtains hung straight and still across them. Mallory got out a handkerchief and wiped his forehead, patted his lips.

Costello said: "You and Jim check out, Mac," in the same flat voice.

Macdonald lowered his head, stared at him steadily through a fringe of eyebrow. His face was shiny with sweat. He had not taken his shabby, rumpled overcoat off. Costello didn't even turn his head. After a moment Macdonald barged back to the mantel, elbowed the gray-haired cop out of the way and grabbed at the square bottle of Scotch.

"Call the boss, Costello," he blared over his shoulder. "You ain't got the brains for this deal. For —— sake do something besides talk!" He turned a little towards Jim, thumped him on the back, said sneeringly: "Did you want just one more drink, copper?"

"What did you come here for?" Costello asked Mallory again.

"Looking for a connection." Mallory stared up at him lazily. The fire had died out of his eyes.

"Funny way you went about it, boy."

Mallory shrugged. "I thought if I made a play I might get in touch with the right people."

"Maybe you made the wrong kind of play," Costello said quietly. He closed his eyes and rubbed his nose with a thumb-nail. "These things are hard to figure sometimes."

Macdonald's harsh voice boomed across the close room. "Bright boy don't make mistakes, mister. Not with his brains."

Costello opened his eyes and glanced back over his shoulder at the red-haired man. The red-haired man swiveled loosely in his chair. His right hand lay along his leg, slack, half closed. Costello turned the other way, looked straight at Macdonald.

"Move out!" he snapped coldly. "Move out now. You're drunk, and I'm not arguing with you."

Macdonald ground his shoulders against the mantel and put his hands in the side pockets of his suit coat. His hat hung formless and crumpled on the back of his big, square head. Jim, the gray-haired cop, moved a little away from him, stared at him strainedly, his mouth working.

"Call the boss, Costello!" Macdonald shouted. "You ain't givin' me orders. I don't like you well enough to take 'em."

Costello hesitated, then moved across to the telephone. His eyes stared at a spot high up on the wall. He lifted the instrument off the prongs and dialed with his back to Macdonald. Then he leaned against the wall, smiling thinly at Mallory over the cup. Waiting.

"Hello . . . yes . . . Costello. Everything's oke except Mac's loaded. He's pretty hostile . . . won't move out. Don't know yet . . . some out-of-town boy. Okey."

Macdonald made a motion, said: "Hold it . . ."

Costello smiled and put the phone aside without haste. Macdonald's eyes gleamed at him with a greenish fire. He spit on the carpet, in the corner between a chair and the wall. He said:

"That's lousy. Lousy. You can't dial Montrose from here." Costello moved his hands vaguely. The red-haired man got to his feet. He moved away from the table and stood laxly, tilting his head back so that the smoke from his cigarette rose clear of his eyes.

Macdonald rocked angrily on his heels. His jawbone was a hard white line against his flushed face. His eyes had a deep, hard glitter.

"I guess we'll play it this way," he stated. He took his hands out of his pockets in a casual manner, and his blued service revolver moved in a tight, businesslike arc.

Costello looked at the red-haired man and said: "Take him, Andy."

The red-haired man stiffened, spit his cigarette straight out from between his pale lips, flashed a hand up like lightning.

Mallory said: "Not fast enough. Look at this one."

He had moved so quickly and so little that he had not seemed to move at all. He leaned forward a little on the davenport. The long black Luger lined itself evenly on the red-haired man's belly.

The red-haired man's hand came down slowly from his lapel, empty. The room was very quiet. Costello looked once at Macdonald with infinite disgust, then he put his hands out in front of him, palms up, and looked down at them with a blank smile.

Macdonald spoke slowly, bitterly. "The kidnapping is one too many for me, Costello. I don't want any part of it. I'm takin' a powder from this toy mob. I took a chance that bright boy might side me."

Mallory stood up and moved sidewise towards the red-haired man. When he had gone about half the distance the gray-haired cop, Jim, let out a strangled sort of yell and jumped for Macdonald, clawing at his pocket. Macdonald looked at him with quick surprise. He put his big left hand out and grabbed both lapels of Jim's overcoat tight together, high up. Jim flailed at him with both fists, hit him in the face twice. Macdonald drew his lips back over his teeth. Calling to Mallory, "Watch those birds," he very calmly laid his gun down on the mantel, reached down into the pocket of Jim's coat and took out the woven leather blackjack. He said:

"You're a louse, Jim. You always were a louse."

He said it rather thoughtfully, without rancor. Then he swung the blackjack and hit the gray-haired man on the side of the head. The gray-haired man sagged slowly to his knees. He clawed freely at the skirts of Macdonald's coat. Macdonald stooped over and hit him again with the blackjack, in the same place, very hard.

Jim crumpled down sidewise and lay on the floor with his hat off and his mouth open. Macdonald swung the blackjack slowly from side to side. A drop of sweat ran down the side of his nose.

Costello said: "Rough boy, ain't you, Mac?" He said it dully, absently, as though he had very little interest in what went on.

Mallory went on towards the red-haired man. When he was behind him he said:

"Put the hands way up, wiper."

When the red-haired man had done this, Mallory put his free hand over his shoulder, down inside his coat. He jerked a gun loose from a shoulder-holster and dropped it on the floor behind him. He felt the other side, patted pockets. He stepped back and circled to Costello. Costello had no gun.

Mallory went to the other side of Macdonald, stood where everyone in the room was in front of him. He said:

"Who's kidnaped?"

Macdonald picked up his gun and glass of whiskey. "The Farr girl," he said. "They got her on her way home, I guess. It was planned when they knew from the wop bodyguard about the date at the Bolivar. I don't know where they took her."

Mallory planted his feet wide apart and wrinkled his nose. He held his Luger easily, with a slack wrist. He said:

"What does your little act mean?"

Macdonald said grimly: "Tell me about yours. I gave you a break."

Mallory nodded, said: "Sure — for your own reasons. . . . I was hired to look for some letters that belong to Rhonda Farr." He looked at Costello. Costello showed no emotion.

Macdonald said: "Okey by me. I thought it was some kind of a plant. That's why I took the chance. Me, I want an out from this connection, that's all." He waved his hand around to take in the room and everything in it.

Mallory picked up a glass, looked into it to see if it was clean, then poured a little Scotch into it and drank it in sips, rolling his tongue around in his mouth.

"Let's talk about the kidnapping," he said. "Who was Costello phoning to?"

"Atkinson. Big Hollywood lawyer. Front for the boys. He's the Farr girl's lawyer, too. Nice guy, Atkinson. A louse."

"He in on the kidnaping?"

Macdonald laughed and said: "Sure."

Mallory shrugged, said: "It seems like a dumb trick — for him."

He went past Macdonald, along the wall to where Costello stood. He stuck the muzzle of the Luger against Costello's chin, pushed his head back against the rough plaster.

"Costello's a nice old boy," he said thoughtfully. "He wouldn't kidnap a girl. Would you, Costello? A little quiet extortion maybe, but nothing rough. That right, Costello?"

Costello's eyes went blank. He swallowed. He said between his teeth: "Can it. You're not funny."

Mallory said: "It gets funnier as it goes on. But perhaps you don't know it all."

He lifted the Luger and drew the muzzle down the side of Costello's big nose, hard. It left a white mark that turned to a red weal. Costello looked a little worried.

Macdonald finished pushing a nearly full bottle of Scotch into his overcoat pocket, and said:

"Let me work on the ——!"

Mallory shook his head gravely from side to side, looking at Costello.

"Too noisy. You know how these places are built. Atkinson is the boy to see. Always see the head man—if you can get to him."

Jim opened his eyes, flapped his hands on the floor, tried to get up. Macdonald lifted a large foot and planted it carelessly in the gray-haired man's face. Jim lay down again. His face was a muddy gray color.

Mallory glanced at the red-haired man and went over to the telephone stand. He lifted the instrument down and dialed a number awkwardly, with his left hand.

He said: "I'm calling the man who hired me. . . . He has a big fast car. . . . We'll put these boys in soak for a while."

4

Landrey's big black Cadillac rolled soundlessly up the long grade to Montrose. Lights shone low on the left, in the lap of the valley. The air was cool and clear, and the stars were very bright. Landrey looked back from the front seat, draped an arm over the back of the seat, a long black arm that ended in a white glove.

He said, for the third or fourth time: "So it's her own mouthpiece shaking her down. Well, well, well."

He smiled smoothly, deliberately. All his movements were smooth and deliberate. Landrey was a tall, pale man with white teeth and jet-black eyes that sparkled under the dome light.

Mallory and Macdonald sat in the back seat. Mallory said

nothing; he stared out of the car window. Macdonald took a pull at his square bottle of Scotch, lost the cork on the floor of the car, and swore as he bent over to grope for it. When he found it he leaned back and looked morosely at Landrey's clear, pale face above the white silk scarf.

He said: "You still got that place on Highland Drive?"

Landrey said: "Yes, copper, I have. And it's not doin' so well."

Macdonald growled. He said: "That's a damn' shame, Mr. Landrey." Then he put his head back against the upholstery and closed his eyes.

The Cadillac turned off the highway. The driver seemed to know just where he was going. He circled around into a land-scaped subdivision of rambling elaborate homes. Tree frogs sounded in the darkness, and there was a smell of orange blossoms.

Macdonald opened his eyes and leaned forward. "The house on the corner," he told the driver.

The house stood well back from a wide curve. It had a lot of tiled roof, an entrance like a Norman arch, and wrought iron lanterns lit on either side of the door. By the sidewalk there was a pergola covered with climbing roses. The driver cut his lights and drifted expertly up to the pergola.

Mallory yawned and opened the car door. Cars were parked along the street around the corner. The cigarette tips of a couple of lounging chauffeurs spotted the soft bluish dark.

"Party," he said. "That makes it nice."

He got out, stood a moment looking across the lawn. Then he walked over soft grass to a pathway of dull bricks spaced so that the grass grew between them. He stood between the wrought iron lanterns and rang the bell.

A maid in cap and apron opened the door. Mallory said:

"Sorry to disturb Mr. Atkinson, but it's important. Macdonald is the name."

The maid hesitated, then went back into the house, leaving the front door open a crack. Mallory pushed it open care-lessly, looked into a roomy hallway with Indian rugs on the floor and walls. He went in.

A few yards down the hallway a doorway gave on a dim room lined with books, smelling of good cigars. Hats and coats were spread around on the chairs. From the back of the house a radio droned dance music.

Mallory took his Luger out and leaned against the jamb of the door, inside.

A man in evening dress came along the hall. He was a plump man with thick white hair above a shrewd, pink, irritable face. Beautifully tailored shoulders failed to divert attention from rather too much stomach. His heavy eyebrows were drawn together in a frown. He walked fast and looked mad.

Mallory stepped out of the doorway and put his gun in Atkinson's stomach.

"You're looking for me," he said.

Atkinson stopped, heaved a little, made a choked sound in his throat. His eyes were wide and startled. Mallory moved the Luger up, put the cold muzzle into the flesh of Atkinson's throat, just above the V of his wing collar. The lawyer partly lifted one arm, as though to make a sweep at the gun. Then he stood quite still, holding the arm up in the air.

Mallory said: "Don't talk. Just think. You're sold out. Macdonald has ratted on you. Costello and two other boys are taped up at Westwood. We want Rhonda Farr."

Atkinson's eyes were dull blue, opaque, without interior light. The mention of Rhonda Farr's name did not seem to make much impression on him. He squirmed against the gun and said:

"Why do you come to me?"

"We think you know where she is," Mallory said tonelessly. "But we won't talk about it here. Let's go outside."

Atkinson jerked, sputtered. "No . . . no, I have guests."

Mallory said coldly: "The guest we want isn't here." He pressed on the gun.

A sudden wave of emotion went over Atkinson's face. He took a short step back and snatched at the gun. Mallory's lips tightened. He twisted his wrist in a tight circle, and the gun sight flicked across Atkinson's mouth. Blood came out on his lips. His mouth began to puff. He got very pale.

Mallory said: "Keep your head, fat boy, and you may live through the night."

Atkinson turned and walked straight out of the open door, stiffly, blindly.

Mallory took his arm and jerked him to the left, on to the grass. "Make it slow, mister," he said gratingly.

They rounded the pergola. Atkinson put his hands out in front of him and floundered at the car. A long arm came out of the open door and grabbed him. He went in, fell against the seat. Macdonald clapped a hand over his face and forced him back against the upholstery. Mallory got in and slammed the car door.

Tires squealed as the car circled rapidly and shot away. The driver drove a block before he switched the lights on again. Then he turned his head a little, said: "Where to, boss?"

Mallory said: "Anywhere. Back to town. Take it easy."

The Cadillac turned on to the highway again and began to drop down the long grade. Lights showed in the valley once more, little white lights that moved ever so slowly along the floor of the valley. Headlights.

Atkinson heaved up in the seat, got a handkerchief out and dabbed at his mouth. He peered at Macdonald and said in a composed voice:

"What's the frame, Mac? Shakedown?"

Macdonald laughed gruffly. Then he hiccoughed. He was a little drunk. He said thickly:

"Hell, no. The boys hung a snatch on the Farr girl tonight. Her friends here don't like it. But you wouldn't know anything about it, would you, big shot?" He laughed again, jeeringly.

Atkinson said slowly: "It's funny . . . but I wouldn't." He lifted his white head higher, went on: "Who are these men?"

Macdonald didn't answer him. Mallory lit a cigarette, guarding the match flame with cupped hands. He said slowly:

"That's not important, is it? Either you know where Rhonda Farr was taken, or you can give us a lead. Think it out. There's lots of time."

Landrey turned his head and looked back. His face was a pale blur in the dark.

"It's not much to ask, Mr. Atkinson," he said gravely. His voice was cool, suave, pleasant. He tapped on the seat-back with his gloved fingers.

Atkinson stared towards him for a while, then put his head

back against the upholstery. "Suppose I don't know anything about it," he said wearily.

Macdonald lifted his hand and hit him in the face. The lawyer's head jerked against the cushions. Mallory said in a cold, unpleasant voice:

"A little less of your crap, copper."

Macdonald swore at him, turned his head away. The car went on.

They were down in the valley now. A three-colored airport beacon swung through the sky not far away. There began to be wooded slopes and little beginnings of valley between dark hills. A train roared down from the Newhall tunnel, gathered speed and went by with a long shattering crash.

Landrey said something to his driver. The Cadillac turned off on to a dirt road. The driver switched the lights off and picked his way by moonlight. The dirt road ended in a spot of dead brown grass with low bushes around it. There were old cans and torn discolored newspapers faintly visible on the ground.

Macdonald got his bottle out, hefted it and gurgled a drink. Atkinson said thickly:

"I'm a bit faint. Give me one."

Macdonald turned, held the bottle out, then growled: "Aw, go to hell!" and put it away in his coat. Mallory took a flash out of the door pocket, clicked it on, and put the beam on Atkinson's face. He said:

"Talk, kidnaper."

Atkinson put his hands on his knees and stared straight at the beacon of the flashlight. His eyes were glassy and there was blood on his chin. He spoke.

"This is a frame by Costello. I don't know what it's all about. But if it's Costello, a man named Slippy Morgan will be in on it. He has a shack on the mesa by Baldwin Hills. They might have taken Rhonda Farr there."

He closed his eyes, and a tear showed in the glare of the flash. Mallory said slowly:

"Macdonald should know that."

Atkinson kept his eyes shut, said: "I guess so." His voice was dull and without any feeling.

Macdonald balled his fist, lurched sidewise and hit him in

the face again. The lawyer groaned, sagged to one side. Mallory's hand jerked; jerked the flash. His voice shook with fury. He said:

"Do that again and I'll put a slug in your guts, copper. So help me I will."

Macdonald rolled away, with a foolish laugh. Mallory snapped off the light. He said, more quietly:

"I think you're telling the truth, Atkinson. We'll case this shack of Slippy Morgan's."

The driver swung and backed the car, picked his way back to the highway again.

5

A white picket fence showed up for a moment before the headlights went off. Behind it on a rise the gaunt shapes of a couple of derricks groped towards the sky. The darkened car went forward slowly, stopped across the street from a small frame house. There were no houses on that side of the street, nothing between the car and the oil field. The house showed no light.

Mallory got to the ground and went across. A gravel driveway led along to a shed without a door. There was a touring car parked under the shed. There was thin worn grass along the driveway and a dull patch of something that had once been a lawn at the back. There was a wire clothes line and a small stoop with a rusted screen door. The moon showed all this.

Beyond the stoop there was a single window with the blind drawn; two thin cracks of light showed along the edges of the blind. Mallory went back to the car, walking on the dry grass and the dirt road surface without sound.

He said: "Let's go, Atkinson."

Atkinson got out heavily, stumbled across the street like a man half asleep. Mallory grabbed his arm sharply. The two men went up the wooden steps, crossed the porch quietly. Atkinson fumbled and found the bell. He pressed it. There was a dull buzz inside the house. Mallory flattened himself against the wall, on the side where he would not be blocked by the opening screen door.

Then the house door came open without sound, and a figure loomed behind the screen. There was no light behind the figure. The lawyer said mumblingly:

"It's Atkinson."

The screen hook was undone. The screen door came outward.

"What's the big idea?" said a lisping voice that Mallory had heard before.

Mallory moved, holding his Luger waist high. The man in the doorway whirled at him. Mallory stepped in on him swiftly, making a clucking sound with tongue and teeth, shaking his head reprovingly.

"You wouldn't have a gun, would you, Slippy," he said, nudging the Luger forward. "Turn slow and easy, Slippy. When you feel something against your spine go on in, Slippy. We'll be right with you."

The lanky man put his hands up and turned. He walked back into the darkness, Mallory's gun in his back. A small living-room smelled of dust and casual cooking. A door had light under it. The lanky man put one hand down slowly and opened the door.

An unshaded light bulb hung from the middle of the ceiling. A thin woman in a dirty white smock stood under it, limp arms at her sides. Dull, colorless eyes brooded under a mop of rusty hair. Her fingers fluttered and twitched in involuntary contractions of the muscles. She made a thin plaintive sound, like a starved cat.

The lanky man went and stood against the wall on the opposite side of the room, pressing the palms of his hands against the wallpaper. There was a fixed, meaningless smile on his face.

Landrey's voice said from behind: "I'll take care of Atkinson's pals."

He came into the room with a big automatic in his gloved hand. "Nice little home," he added pleasantly.

There was a metal bed in a corner of the room. Rhonda Farr was lying on it, wrapped to the chin in a brown army blanket. Her white wig was partly off her head, and damp golden curls showed. Her face was bluish-white, a mask in which the rouge and lip-paint glared. She was snoring.

Mallory put his hand under the blanket, felt for her pulse. Then he lifted an eyelid and looked closely at the upturned pupil.

He said: "Doped."

The thin woman in the smock wet her lips. "A shot of M," she said in a slack voice. "No harm done, mister."

Atkinson sat down on a hard chair that had a dirty towel on the back of it. His dress shirt was dazzling under the unshaded light. The lower part of his face was smeared with dry blood. The lanky man looked at him contemptuously, and patted the stained wallpaper with the flat of his hands. Then Macdonald came into the room.

His face was flushed and sweaty. He staggered a little and put a hand up along the door-frame. "Hi ho, boys," he said vacantly. "I ought to rate a promotion for this."

The lanky man stopped smiling. He ducked sidewise very fast, and a gun jumped into his hand. Roar filled the room, a great crashing roar. And again a roar.

The lanky man's duck became a slide and the slide degenerated into a fall. He spread himself out on the bare carpet in a leisurely sort of way. He lay quite still, one half-open eye apparently looking at Macdonald. The thin woman opened her mouth wide, but no sound came out of it.

Macdonald put his other hand up to the door-frame, leaned forward and began to cough. Bright red blood came out on his chin. His hands came down the door-frame slowly. Then his shoulder twitched forward, he rolled like a swimmer in a breaking wave, and crashed. He crashed on his face, his hat still on his head, the mouse-colored hair at the nape of his neck showing below it in an untidy curl.

Mallory said: "Two down," and looked at Landrey with a disgusted expression. Landrey looked down at his big automatic and put it away out of sight, in the side pocket of his thin dark overcoat.

Mallory stooped over Macdonald, put a finger to his temple. There was no heartbeat. He tried the jugular vein with the same result. Macdonald was dead, and he still smelled violently of whiskey.

There was a faint trace of smoke under the light bulb, an acrid fume of powder. The thin woman bent forward at the waist and scrambled towards the door. Mallory jerked a hard hand against her chest and threw her back.

"You're fine where you are, sister," he snapped.

Atkinson took his hands off his knees and rubbed them together as if all the feeling had gone out of them. Landrey went over to the bed, put his gloved hand down and touched Rhonda Farr's hair.

"Hello, baby," he said lightly. "Long time no see." He went out of the room, saying: "I'll get the car over on this side of the street."

Mallory looked at Atkinson. He said casually: "Who has the letters, Atkinson? The letters belonging to Rhonda Farr?"

Atkinson lifted his blank face slowly, squinted as though the light hurt his eyes. He spoke in a vague, far-off sort of voice.

"I—I don't know. Costello, maybe. I never saw them."

Mallory let out a short harsh laugh which made no change in the hard cold lines of his face. "Wouldn't it be funny as hell if that's true!" he said jerkily.

He stooped over the bed in the corner and wrapped the brown blanket closely around Rhonda Farr. When he lifted her she stopped snoring, but she did not wake.

6

A window or two in the front of the apartment house showed light. Mallory held his wrist up and looked at the curved watch on the inside of it. The faintly glowing hands were at half-past three. He spoke back into the car:

"Give me ten minutes or so. Then come on up. I'll fix the doors."

The street entrance to the apartment house was locked. Mallory unlocked it with a loose key, put it on the latch. There was a little light in the lobby, from one bulb in a floor lamp and from a hooded light above the switchboard. A wizened, white-haired little man was asleep in a chair by the switchboard, with his mouth open and his breath coming in long, wailing snores, like the sounds of an animal in pain.

Mallory walked up one flight of carpeted steps. On the second floor he pushed the button for the automatic elevator. When it came rumbling down from above he got in and pushed the button marked "7." He yawned. His eyes were dull with fatigue.

The elevator lurched to a stop, and Mallory went down the bright, silent corridor. He stopped at a gray olive wood door and put his ear to the panel. Then he fitted the loose key slowly into the lock, turned it slowly, moved the door back an inch or two. He listened again, went in.

There was light from a lamp with a red shade that stood beside an easy chair. A man was sprawled in the chair and the light splashed on his face. He was bound at the wrists and ankles with strips of wide adhesive tape. There was a strip of adhesive across his mouth.

Mallory fixed the door latch and shut the door. He went across the room with quick silent steps. The man in the chair was Costello. His face was a purplish color above the white adhesive that plastered his lips together. His chest moved in jerks and his breath made a snorting noise in his big nose.

Mallory yanked the tape off Costello's mouth, put the heel of one hand on the man's chin, forced his mouth wide open The cadence of the breathing changed a bit. Costello's chest stopped jerking, and the purplish color of his face faded to pallor. He stirred, made a groaning sound.

Mallory took an unopened pint bottle of rye off the mantel and tore the metal strip from the cap with his teeth. He pushed Costello's head far back, poured some whiskey into his open mouth, slapped his face hard. Costello choked, swallowed convulsively. Some of the whiskey ran out of his nostrils. He opened his eyes, focused them slowly. He mumbled something confused.

Mallory went through velour curtains that hung across a doorway at the inner end of the room, into a short hall. The first door led into a bedroom with twin beds. A light burned, and a man was lying bound on each of the beds.

Jim, the gray-haired cop, was asleep or still unconscious. The side of his head was stiff with congealed blood. The skin of his face was a dirty gray.

The eyes of the red-haired man were wide open, diamond

bright, angry. His mouth worked under the tape, trying to chew it. He had rolled over on his side and was almost off the bed. Mallory pushed him back towards the middle, said:

"Sorry, punk. It's all in the game."

He went back to the living-room and switched on more light. Costello had struggled up in the easy chair. Mallory took out a pocket knife and reached behind him, sawed the tape that bound his wrists. Costello jerked his hands apart, grunted, and rubbed the backs of his wrists together where the tape had pulled hairs out. Then he bent over and tore tape off his ankles. He said:

"That didn't do me any good. I'm a mouth breather." His voice was loose, flat and without cadence.

He got to his feet and poured two inches of rye into a glass, drank it at a gulp, sat down again and leaned his head against the high back of the chair. Life came into his face; glitter came into his washed-out eyes.

He said: "What's new?"

Mallory spooned at a bowl of water that had been ice, frowned and drank some whiskey straight. He rubbed the left side of his head gently with his finger tips and winced. Then he sat down and lit a cigarette.

He said: "Several things. Rhonda Farr is home. Macdonald and Slippy Morgan got gunned. But that's not important. I'm after some letters you were trying to peddle to Rhonda Farr. Dig 'em up."

Costello lifted his head and grunted. He said: "I don't have the letters."

Mallory said: "Get the letters, Costello. Now." He sprinkled cigarette ash carefully in the middle of a green and yellow diamond in the carpet design.

Costello made an impatient movement. "I don't have them," he insisted. "Straight goods. I never saw them."

Mallory's eyes were slate-gray, very cold, and his voice was brittle. He said: "What you heels don't know about your racket is just pitiful. . . . I'm tired, Costello. I don't feel like an argument. You'd look lousy with that big beezer smashed over on one side of your face with a gun barrel."

Costello put his bony hand up and rubbed the reddened skin around his mouth where the tape had chafed it. He glanced down the room. There was a slight movement of the velour curtains across the end door, as though a breeze had stirred them. But there was no breeze. Mallory was staring down at the carpet.

Costello stood up from the chair, slowly. He said: "I've got a wall safe. I'll open it up."

He went across the room to the wall in which the outside door was, lifted down a picture and worked the dial of a small inset circular safe. He swung the little round door open and thrust his arm into the safe.

Mallory said: "Stay just like that, Costello."

He stepped lazily across the room, and passed his left hand down Costello's arm, into the safe. It came out again holding a small pearl-handled automatic. He made a sibilant sound with his lips and put the little gun into his pocket.

"Just can't learn, can you, Costello?" he said in a tired voice.

Costello shrugged, went back across the room. Mallory plunged his hands into the safe and tumbled the contents out on to the floor. He dropped on one knee. There were some long white envelopes, a bunch of clippings fastened with a paper clip, a narrow, thick checkbook, a small photograph album, an address book, some loose papers, some yellow bank statements with checks inside. Mallory spread one of the long envelopes carelessly, without much interest.

The curtains over the end door moved again. Costello stood rigid in front of the mantel. A gun came through the curtains in a small hand that was very steady. A slim body followed the hand, a white face with blazing eyes—Erno.

Mallory came to his feet, his hands breast high, empty.

"Higher, baby," Erno croaked. "Much higher, baby!"

Mallory raised his hands a little more. His forehead was wrinkled in a hard frown. Erno came forward into the room. His face glistened. A lock of oily black hair drooped over one eyebrow. His teeth showed in a stiff grin.

He said: "I think we'll give it to you right here, two-timer."

His voice had a questioning inflection, as if he waited Costello's confirmation.

Costello didn't say anything.

Mallory moved his head a little. His mouth felt very dry. He watched Erno's eyes, saw them tense. He said rather quickly:

"You've been crossed, mugg, but not by me."

Erno's grin widened to a snarl, and his head went back. His trigger finger whitened at the first joint. Then there was a noise outside the door, and it came open.

Landrey came in. He shut the door with a jerk of his shoulder, and leaned against it, dramatically. Both his hands were in the side pockets of his thin dark overcoat. His eyes under the soft black hat were bright and devilish. He looked pleased. He moved his chin in the white silk evening scarf that was tucked carelessly about his neck. His handsome pale face was like something carved out of old ivory.

Erno moved his gun slightly and waited. Landrey said cheerfully:

"Bet you a grand you hit the floor first!"

Erno's lips twitched under his shiny little mustache. Two guns went off at the same time. Landrey swayed like a tree hit by a gust of wind; the heavy roar of his .45 sounded again, muffled a little by cloth and the nearness to his body.

Mallory went down behind the davenport, rolled and came up with the Luger straight out in front of him. But Erno's face had already gone blank.

He went down slowly; his light body seemed to be drawn down by the weight of the gun in his right hand. He bent at the knees as he fell, and slid forward on the floor. His back arched once, then went loose.

Landrey took his left hand out of his coat pocket and spread the fingers away from him as though pushing at something. Slowly and with difficulty he got the big automatic out of the other pocket and raised it inch by inch, turning on the balls of his feet. He swiveled his body towards Costello's rigid figure and squeezed the trigger again. Plaster jumped from the wall at Costello's shoulder.

Landrey smiled vaguely, said: "Damn!" in a soft voice. Then his eyes went up in his head and the gun plunged down from his nerveless fingers, bounded on the carpet. Landrey went down joint by joint, smoothly and gracefully, kneeled, swaying a moment before he melted over sidewise, spread himself on the floor almost without sound.

Mallory looked at Costello, and said in a strained, angry voice: "Boy, are you lucky!"

The buzzer droned insistently. Three little lights glowed red on the panel of the switchboard. The wizened, white-haired little man shut his mouth with a snap and struggled sleepily upright.

Mallory jerked past him with his head turned the other way, shot across the lobby, out of the front door of the apartment house, down the three marble-faced steps, across the sidewalk and the street. The driver of Landrey's car had already stepped on the starter. Mallory swung in beside him, breathing hard, and slammed the car door.

"Get goin' fast!" he rasped. "Stay off the boulevard. Cops here in five minutes!"

The driver looked at him and said: "Where's Landrey? . . . I heard shootin'."

Mallory held the Luger up, said swiftly and coldly: "Move, baby!"

The gears went in, the Cadillac jumped forward, the driver took a corner recklessly, the tail of his eye on the gun.

Mallory said: "Landrey stopped lead. He's cold." He held the Luger up, put the muzzle under the driver's nose. "But not from my gun. Smell that, punk! It hasn't been fired!"

The driver said: "Jeeze!" in a shattered voice, swung the big car wildly, missing the curb by inches.

It was getting to be daylight.

7

Rhonda Farr said: "Publicity, darling. Just publicity. Any kind is better than none at all. I'm not so sure my contract is going to be renewed and I'll probably need it."

She was sitting in a deep chair, in a large, long room. She looked at Mallory with lazy, indifferent purplish-blue eyes and moved her hand to a tall, misted glass. She took a drink.

The room was enormous. Mandarin rugs in soft colors swathed the floor. There was a lot of teakwood and red lacquer. Gold frames glinted high up on the walls, and the ceiling was remote and vague, like the dusk of a hot day. A huge carved radio gave forth muted and unreal strains.

Mallory wrinkled his nose and looked amused in a grim sort of way. He said:

"You're a nasty little rat. I don't like you."

Rhonda Farr said: "Oh yes, you do, darling. You're crazy about me."

She smiled and fitted a cigarette into a jade-green holder that matched her jade-green lounging pajamas. Then she reached out her beautifully shaped hand and pushed the button of a bell that was set into the top of a low nacre and teakwood table at her side. A silent, white-coated Japanese butler drifted into the room and mixed more highballs.

"You're a pretty wise lad, aren't you, darling?" Rhonda Farr said, when he had gone out again. "And you have some letters in your pocket you think are body and soul to me. Nothing like it, mister, nothing like it." She took a sip of the fresh highball. "The letters you have are phoney. They were written about a month ago. Landrey never had them. He gave *his* letters back a long time ago. . . . What you have are just props." She put a hand to her beautifully waved hair. The experience of the previous night seemed to have left no trace on her.

Mallory looked at her carefully. He said: "How do you prove that, baby?"

"The notepaper—if I have to prove it. There's a little man down at Fourth and Spring who makes a study of that kind of thing."

Mallory said: "The writing?"

Rhonda Farr smiled dimly. "Writing's easy to fake, if you have plenty of time. Or so I'm told. That's my story anyhow."

Mallory nodded, sipped at his own highball. He put his hand into his inside breast pocket and took out a flat manila envelope, legal size. He laid it on his knee.

"Four men got gunned out last night on account of these phoney letters," he said carelessly.

Rhonda Farr looked at him mildly. "Two crooks, a double-crossing policeman, make three of them. I should lose my sleep over that trash! Of course I'm sorry about Landrey."

Mallory said politely: "It's nice of you to be sorry about Landrey. Swell."

She said peacefully: "Landrey, as I told you once, was a pretty nice boy a few years ago, when he was trying to get into pictures. But he chose another business, and in that business he was bound to stop a bullet sometime."

Mallory rubbed his chin. He said: "It's funny he didn't remember he'd given you back your letters. Very funny."

"He wouldn't care, darling. He was that kind of actor, and he'd like the show. It gave him a chance for a swell pose. He'd like that terribly."

Mallory let his face get hard and disgusted. He said: "The job looked on the level to me. I didn't know much about Landrey, but he knew a good friend of mine in Chicago. He figured a way to the boys who were working on you, and I played his hunch. Things happened that made it easier—but a lot noisier."

Rhonda Farr tapped little bright nails against her little bright teeth. She said: "What are you back where you live, darling? One of those hoods they call private dicks?"

Mallory laughed harshly, made a vague movement and ran his fingers through his crisp dark hair. "Let it go, baby," he said softly. "Let it go."

Rhonda Farr looked at him with a surprised glance, then laughed rather shrilly. "It gets mad, doesn't it?" she cooed. She went on, in a dry voice: "Atkinson has been bleeding me for years, one way and another. I fixed the letters up and put them where he could get hold of them. They disappeared. A few days afterward a man with one of those tough voices called up and began to apply the pressure. I let it ride. I figured I'd hang a pinch on Atkinson somehow, and our two reputations put together would be good for a write-up that wouldn't hurt me too much. But the thing seemed to be spreading out, and I got scared. I thought of asking Landrey to help me out. I was sure he would like it."

Mallory said roughly: "Simple, straightforward kid, ain't you? Like hell!"

"You don't know much about this Hollywood racket, do you, darling?" Rhonda Farr said. She put her head on one side and hummed softly. The strains of a dance band floated idly through the quiet air. "That's a gorgeous melody. . . . It's swiped from a Weber sonata. . . . Publicity has to hurt a bit out here. Otherwise nobody believes it."

Mallory stood up, lifting the manila envelope off his knee. He dropped it in her lap.

"Five grand these are costing you," he said.

Rhonda Farr leaned back and crossed her jade-green legs. One little green slipper fell off her bare foot to the rug, and the manila envelope fell down beside it. She didn't stir towards either one.

She said: "Why?"

"I'm a business man, baby. I get paid for my work. Landrey didn't pay me. Five grand was the price. The price to him, and now the price to you."

She looked at him almost casually, out of placid, corn-flower-blue eyes, and said: "No deal . . . blackmailer. Just like I told you at the Bolivar. You have all my thanks, but I'm spending my money myself."

Mallory said curtly: "This might be a damn' good way to spend some of it."

He leaned over and picked up her highball, drank a little of it. When he put the glass down he tapped the nails of two fingers against the side for a moment. A small tight smile wrinkled the corners of his mouth. He lit a cigarette and tossed the match into a bowl of hyacinths.

He said slowly: "Landrey's driver talked of course. Landrey's friends want to see me. They want to know how come Landrey got rubbed out in Westwood. The cops will get around to me after a while. Someone is sure to tip them off. I was right beside four killings last night, and naturally I'm not going to run out on them. I'll probably have to spill the whole story. The cops will give you plenty of publicity, baby. Landrey's friends—I don't know what they'll do. Something that will hurt a lot, I should say."

Rhonda Farr jerked to her feet, fumbling with her toe for the green slipper. Her eyes had gone wide and startled.

"You'd . . . sell me out?" she breathed.

Mallory laughed. His eyes were bright and hard. He stared along the floor at a splash of light from one of the standing lamps. He said in a bored voice:

"Why the hell should I protect you? I don't owe you anything. And you're too damn' tight with your dough to hire me. I haven't a record, but you know how the law boys love my sort. And Landrey's friends will just see a dirty plant that got a good lad killed. —— sake, why should I front for a chiseler like you, baby?"

He snorted angrily and flung his cigarette at the bowl of hyacinths. Red spots showed in his tanned cheeks.

Rhonda Farr stood quite still and shook her head slowly from side to side. She said: "No deal, blackmailer . . . no deal." Her voice was small and tired, but her chin stuck out hard and brave.

Mallory reached out and picked up his hat. "You're a hell of a guy, baby," he said, grinning. "——! but you Hollywood frails must be hard to get on with!"

He leaned forward suddenly, put his left hand behind her head and kissed her on the mouth hard. Then he flipped the tips of his fingers across her cheek.

"You're a nice kid—in some ways," he said. "And a fair liar. Just fair. You didn't fake any letters, baby. Atkinson wouldn't fall for a trick like that." Rhonda Farr stooped over, snatched the manila envelope off the rug, and tumbled out what was in it—a number of closely written gray pages, deckle-edged, with thin gold monograms. She stared down at them with quivering nostrils.

She said slowly: "I'll send you the money."

Mallory put his hand against her chin, and pushed her head back.

He said rather gently:

"I was kidding you, baby. I have that bad habit. But there are two funny things about these letters. They haven't any envelopes, and there's nothing to show who they were written to—nothing at all. The second thing is, Landrey had them in his pocket when he was killed."

He nodded once, turned away. Rhonda Farr said sharply: "Wait!" Her voice was suddenly terrified. She flopped down into the chair, sat limp.

Mallory said: "It gets you when it's over, baby. Take a drink."

He went a little way down the room, turned his head. He said: "I have to go. Got a date with a big black spot. . . . Send me some flowers, baby. Wild, blue flowers, like your eyes."

He went out under an arch. A door opened and shut heavily. Rhonda Farr sat without moving for a long time.

8

Cigarette smoke laced the air. A group of people in evening clothes stood sipping cocktails at one side of a curtained opening that led to the gambling rooms. Beyond the curtains light blazed down on one end of a roulette table.

Mallory put his elbows on the bar, and the bartender left two young girls in party gowns and slid a white towel along the polished wood towards him. He said:

"What'll it be, chief?"

Mallory said: "A small beer."

The bartender gave it to him, smiled, went back to the two girls. Mallory sipped the beer, made a face, and looked into the long mirror that ran all the way behind the bar and slanted forward a little, so that it showed the floor all the way over to the far wall. A door opened in the wall and a man in dinner clothes came through. He had a wrinkled brown face and hair the color of steel wool. He met Mallory's glance in the mirror and came across the room nodding.

He said. "I'm Mardonne. Nice of you to come." He had a soft, husky voice, the voice of a fat man, but he was not fat.

Mallory said: "It's not a social call."

Mardonne said: "Let's go up to my office."

Mallory drank a little more of the beer, made another face, and pushed the glass away from him across the bar top. They went through the door, up a carpeted staircase that met another staircase halfway up. An open door shone light on the landing. They went in where the light was.

The room had been a bedroom, and no particular trouble had been taken to make it over into an office. It had gray walls, two or three prints in narrow frames. There was a big filing cabinet, a good safe, chairs. A parchment-shaded lamp stood on a walnut desk. A very blond young man sat on a corner of the desk swinging one leg over the other. He was wearing a soft hat with a gay band.

Mardonne said: "All right, Henry. I'll be busy."

The blond young man got off the desk, yawned, put his hand to his mouth with an affected flirt of the wrist. There was a large diamond on one of his fingers. He looked at Mallory, smiled, went slowly out of the room, closing the door.

Mardonne sat down in a blue leather swivel-chair. He lit a thin cigar and pushed a humidor across the grained top of the desk. Mallory took a chair at the end of the desk, between the door and a pair of open windows. There was another door, but the safe stood in front of it. He lit a cigarette, said:

"Landrey owed me some money. Five grand. Anybody here interested in paying it?"

Mardonne put his brown hands on the arms of his chair and rocked back and forth. "We haven't come to that," he said.

Mallory said: "Right. What have we come to?"

Mardonne narrowed his dull eyes. His voice was flat and without tone. "To how Landrey got killed."

Mallory put his cigarette in his mouth and clasped his hands together behind his head. He puffed smoke and talked through it at the wall above Mardonne's head.

"He crossed everybody up and then he crossed himself. He played too many parts and got his lines mixed. He was gun-drunk. When he got a rod in his hand he had to shoot somebody. Somebody shot back."

Mardonne went on rocking, said: "Maybe you could make it a little more definite."

"Sure . . . I could tell you a story . . . about a girl who wrote some letters once. She thought she was in love. They were reckless letters, the sort a girl would write who had more guts than was good for her. Time passed, and somehow the letters got on the blackmail market. Some workers started to shake the girl down. Not a high stake, nothing that would have bothered her, but it seems she liked to do things the hard way. Landrey thought he would help her out. He had a plan, and the plan needed a man who could wear a tux, keep a spoon out of a coffee-cup, and wasn't known in this town. He got me. I run a small agency in Chicago.

Mardonne swiveled towards the open windows and stared out at the tops of some trees. "Private dick, huh?" he grunted impassively. "From Chicago."

Mallory nodded, looked at him briefly, looked back at the same spot on the wall. "And supposed to be on the level, Mardonne. You wouldn't think it from some of the company I've been keeping lately."

Mardonne made a quick impatient gesture, said nothing.

Mallory went on: "Well, I gave the job a tumble, which was my first and worst mistake. I was making a little headway when the shakedown turned into a kidnaping. Not so good. I got in touch with Landrey and he decided to show with me. We found the girl without a lot of trouble. We took her home. We still had to get the letters. While I was trying to pry them loose from the guy I thought had them one of the bad boys got in the back way and wanted to play with his gun. Landrey made a swell entrance, struck a pose and shot it out with the hood, toe to toe. He stopped some lead. It was pretty, if you like that sort of thing, but it left me in a spot. So perhaps I'm prejudiced. I had to lam out and collect my ideas."

Mardonne's dull brown eyes showed a passing flicker of emotion. "The girl's story might be interesting, too," he said coolly.

Mallory blew a pale cloud of smoke. "She was doped and doesn't know anything. She wouldn't talk, if she did. And I don't know her name."

"I do," Mardonne said. "Landrey's driver also talked to me. So I won't have to bother you about that."

Mallory talked on, placidly. "That's the tale from the out-side, without notes. The notes make it funnier—and a hell of a lot dirtier. The girl didn't ask Landrey for help, but he knew about the shakedown. He'd once had the letters, because they were written to him. His scheme to get on their trail was for me to make a wrong pass at the girl myself, make her think *I* had the letters, talk her into a meeting at a night-club where we could be watched by the people who were working on her. She'd come, because she had that kind of guts. She'd be watched, because there would be an inside—maid, chauffeur or something. The boys would want to know about me. They'd pick me up, and if I didn't get conked out of hand, I might learn who was who in the racket. Sweet set-up, don't you think so?"

Mardonne said coldly: "A bit loose in places. . . . Go on talking."

"When the decoy worked I knew it was fixed. I stayed with it, because for the time being I had to. After a while there was another sour play, unrehearsed this time. A big flattie who was taking graft money from the gang got cold feet and threw the boys for a loss. He didn't mind a little extortion, but a snatch was going off the deep end on a dark night. The break made things easier for me, and it didn't hurt Landrey any, because the flattie wasn't in on the clever stuff. The hood who got Landrey wasn't either, I guess. That one was just sore, thought he was being chiseled out of his cut."

Mardonne flipped his brown hands up and down on the chair arms, like a purchasing agent getting restless under a sales talk. "Were you supposed to figure things out this way?" he asked with a sneer.

"I used my head, Mardonne. Not soon enough, but I used it. Maybe I wasn't hired to think, but that wasn't explained to me either. If I got wise, it was Landrey's hard luck. He'd have to figure an out to that one. If I didn't, I was the nearest thing to an honest stranger he could afford to have around."

Mardonne said smoothly: "Landrey had plenty of dough. He had some brains. Not a lot, but some. He wouldn't go for a cheap shake like that."

Mallory laughed harshly: "It wasn't so cheap to him, Mardonne. He wanted the girl. She'd got away from him, out of his class. He couldn't pull himself up, but he could pull her down. The letters were not enough to bring her into line. Add a kidnaping and a fake rescue by an old flame turned racketeer, and you have a story no rag could be made to softpedal. If it was spilled, it would blast her right out of her job. *You* guess the price for not spilling it, Mardonne."

Mardonne said: "Uh-huh," and kept on looking out of the window.

Mallory said: "But all that's on the cuff, now. I was hired to get some letters, and I got them—out of Landrey's pocket when he was bumped. I'd like to get paid for my time."

Mardonne turned in his chair and put his hands flat on the top of the desk. "Pass them over," he said. "I'll see what they're worth to me."

Mallory let out another harsh laugh. His eyes got sharp and bitter. He said: "The trouble with you heels is that you can't figure anybody to be on the up and up. . . . The letters are withdrawn from circulation, Mardonne. They passed around too much and they wore out."

"It's a sweet thought," Mardonne sneered. "For somebody else. Landrey was my partner, and I thought a lot of him. . . . So you give the letters away, and I pay you dough for letting Landrey get gunned. I ought to write that one in my diary. My hunch is you've been paid plenty already—by Miss Rhonda Farr."

Mallory said, sarcastically: "I figured it would look like that to you. Maybe *you'd* like the story better this way. . . . The girl got tired of having Landrey trail her around. She faked some letters and put them where her smart lawyer could lift them, pass them along to a man who was running a strong-arm squad the lawyer used in his business sometimes. The girl wrote to Landrey for help, and he got me. The girl got to me with a better bid. She hired me to put Landrey on the spot. I played along with him until I got him under the gun of a wiper that was pretending to make a pass at me. The wiper let him have it, and I shot the wiper with Landrey's gun, to make it look good. Then I had a drink and went home to get some sleep."

Mardonne leaned over and pressed a buzzer on the side of his desk. He said: "I like that one a lot better. I'm wondering if I could make it stick."

"You could try," Mallory said lazily. "I don't guess it would be the first lead quarter you've tried to pass."

9

The room door came open and the blond boy strolled in. His lips were spread in a pleased grin and his tongue came out between them. He had an automatic in his hand.

Mardonne said: "I'm not busy any more, Henry."

The blond boy shut the door. Mallory stood up and backed slowly towards the wall. He said grimly:

"Now for the funny stuff, eh?"

Mardonne put brown fingers up and pinched the fat part of his chin. He said curtly:

"There won't be any shooting here. Nice people come to this house. Maybe you didn't spot Landrey, but I don't want you around. You're in my way."

Mallory kept on backing until he had his shoulders against the wall. The blond boy frowned, took a step towards him. Mallory said:

"Stay right where you are, Henry. I need room to think. You might get a slug into me, but you wouldn't stop my gun from talking a little. The noise wouldn't bother me at all."

Mardonne bent over his desk, looking sidewise. The blond boy slowed up. His tongue still peeped out between his lips. Mardonne said:

"I've got some C notes in the desk here. I'm giving Henry ten of them. He'll go to your hotel with you. He'll even help you pack. When you get on the train East he'll pass you the dough. If you come back after that, it will be a new deal—from a cold deck." He put his hand down slowly and opened the desk drawer.

Mallory kept his eyes on the blond boy. "Henry might make a change in the continuity," he said unpleasantly. "Henry looks kind of unstable to me."

Mardonne stood up, brought his hand from the drawer. He dropped a packet of notes on top of the desk. He said:

"I don't think so. Henry usually does what he is told."

Mallory grinned tightly. "Perhaps *that's* what I'm afraid of," he said. His grin got tighter still, and crookeder. His teeth glittered between his pale lips. "You said you thought a lot of Landrey, Mardonne. That's hooey. You don't care a thin dime about Landrey, now he's dead. You probably stepped right into his half of the joint, and nobody around to ask questions. It's like that in the rackets. You want me out because you think you can still peddle your dirt—in the right place—for more than this small time joint would net in a year. But you can't peddle it, Mardonne. The market's closed. Nobody's going to pay you a plugged nickel either to spill it or not to spill it."

Mardonne cleared his throat softly. He was standing in the same position, leaning forward a little over the desk, both hands on top of it, and the packet of notes between his hands. He licked his lips, said:

"All right, master mind. Why not?"

Mallory made a quick but expressive gesture with his right thumb.

"I'm the sucker in this deal. *You're* the smart guy. I told you a straight story the first time and my hunch says Landrey wasn't in that sweet frame alone. *You* were in it up to your fat neck! . . . But you aced yourself backwards when you let Landrey pack those letters around with him. The girl can talk now. Not a whole lot, but enough to get backing from an outfit that isn't going to scrap a million-dollar reputation because some cheap gambler wants to get smart. . . . If your money says different, you're going to get a jolt that'll have you picking your eyeteeth out of your socks. You're going to see the sweetest cover-up even Hollywood ever fixed."

He paused, flashed a quick glance at the blond boy. "Something else, Mardonne. When you figure on gun play get yourself a loogan that knows what it's all about. The gay caballero here forgot to thumb back his safety!"

Mardonne stood frozen. The blond boy's eyes flinched down to his gun for a split second of time. Mallory jumped fast along the wall, and his Luger snapped into his hand. The blond boy's face tensed, his gun crashed. Then the Luger cracked, and a slug went into the wall beside the blond boy's gay felt hat. Henry faded down gracefully, squeezed lead again. The shot knocked Mallory back against the wall. His left arm went dead.

His lips writhed angrily. He steadied himself; the Luger talked twice, very rapidly.

The blond boy's gun arm jerked up and the gun sailed

against the wall high up. His eyes widened, his mouth came open in a yell of pain. Then he whirled, wrenched the door open and pitched straight out on the landing with a crash.

Light from the room streamed after him. Somebody shouted somewhere. A door banged. Mallory looked at Mardonne, saying evenly:

"Got me in the arm, ——! I could have killed the —— four times!"

Mardonne's hand came up from the desk with a blued revolver in it. A bullet splashed into the floor at Mallory's feet. Mardonne lurched drunkenly, threw the gun away like something red hot. His hands groped high in the air. He looked scared stiff.

Mallory said: "Get in front of me, big shot! I'm moving out of here."

Mardonne came out from behind the desk. He moved jerkily, like a marionette. His eyes were as dead as stale oysters. Saliva drooled down his chin.

Something loomed in the doorway. Mallory heaved sidewise, firing blindly at the door. But the sound of the Luger was overborne by the terrific flat booming of a shotgun. Searing flame stabbed down Mallory's right side. Mardonne got the rest of the load.

He plunged to the floor on his face, dead before he landed.

A sawed-off shotgun dumped itself in through the open door. A thick-bellied man in shirtsleeves eased himself down in the door-frame, clutching and rolling as he fell. A strangled sob came out of his mouth, and blood spread on the pleated front of a dress shirt.

Sudden noise flared out down below. Shouting, running feet, a shrilling off-key laugh, a high sound that might have been a shriek. Cars started outside, tires screeched on the driveway. The customers were getting away. A pane of glass went out somewhere. There was a loose clatter of running feet on a sidewalk.

Across the lighted patch of landing nothing moved. The blond boy groaned softly, out there on the floor, behind the dead man in the doorway.

Mallory plowed across the room, sank into the chair at the end of the desk. He wiped sweat from his eyes with the heel of his gun hand. He leaned his ribs against the desk, panting, watching the door.

His left arm was throbbing now, and his right leg felt like the plagues of Egypt. Blood ran down his sleeve inside, down on his hand, off the tips of two fingers.

After a while he looked away from the door, at the packet of notes lying on the desk under the lamp. Reaching across he pushed them into the open drawer with the muzzle of the Luger. Grinning with pain he leaned far enough over to pull the drawer shut. Then he opened and closed his eyes quickly, several times, squeezing them tight together, then snapping them open wide. That cleared his head a little. He drew the telephone towards him.

There was silence below stairs now. Mallory put the Luger down, lifted the phone off the prongs and put it down beside the Luger.

He said out loud: "Too bad, baby. . . . Maybe I played it wrong after all. . . . Maybe the louse hadn't the guts to hurt you at that . . . well . . . there's got to be talking done now."

As he began to dial, the wail of a siren got louder coming up the long hill from Sherman. . . .

10

The uniformed officer behind the typewriter desk talked into a dictaphone, then looked at Mallory and jerked his thumb towards a glass-paneled door that said: "Captain of Detectives. Private."

Mallory got up stiffly from a hard chair and went across the room, leaned against the wall to open the glass-paneled door, went on in.

The room he went into was paved with dirty brown linoleum, furnished with the peculiar sordid hideousness only municipalities can achieve. Cathcart, the captain of detectives, sat in the middle of it alone, between a littered roll-top desk that was not less than twenty years old and a flat oak table large enough to play ping-pong on.

Cathcart was a big shabby Irishman with a sweaty face and

a loose-lipped grin. His white mustache was stained in the middle by nicotine. His hands had a lot of warts on them.

Mallory went towards him slowly, leaning on a heavy cane with a rubber tip. His right leg felt large and hot. His left arm was in a sling made from a black silk scarf. He was freshly shaved. His face was pale and his eyes were as dark as slate.

He sat down across the table from the captain of detectives, put his cane on the table, tapped a cigarette and lit it. Then he said casually:

"What's the verdict, chief?"

Cathcart grinned. "How you feel, kid? You look kinda pulled down."

"Not bad. A bit stiff."

Cathcart nodded, cleared his throat, fumbled unnecessarily with some papers that were in front of him. He said:

"You're clear. It's a lulu, but you're clear. Chicago gives you a clean sheet—damn' clean. Your Luger got Mike Corliss, a two-time loser. I'm keepin' the Luger for a souvenir. Okey?"

Mallory nodded, said: "Okey. I'm getting me a .25 with copper slugs. A sharpshooter's gun. No shock effect, but it goes better with evening clothes."

Cathcart looked at him closely for a minute, then went on: "Mike's prints are on the shotgun. The shotgun got Mardonne. Nobody's cryin' about that much. The blond kid ain't hurt bad. That automatic we found on the floor had his prints and that will take care of him for a while."

Mallory rubbed his chin slowly, wearily. "How about the others?"

The captain raised tangled eyebrows, and his eyes looked absent. He said: "I don't know of nothin' to connect you there. Do you?"

"Not a thing," Mallory said apologetically. "I was just wondering."

The captain said firmly: "Don't wonder. And don't get to guessin', if anybody should ask you. . . . Take that Baldwin Hills thing. The way we figure it Macdonald got killed in the line of duty, takin' with him a dope-peddler named Slippy Morgan. We have a tag out for Slippy's wife, but I don't guess we'll make her. Mac wasn't on the narcotic detail, but it was his night off and he was a great guy to gum-shoe around on his night off. Mac loved his work."

Mallory smiled faintly, said politely: "Is that so?"

"Yeah," the captain said. "In the other one it seems this Landrey, a known gambler—he was Mardonne's partner too —that's kind of a funny coincidence—went down to West-wood to collect dough from a guy called Costello that ran a book on the Eastern tracks. Jim Ralston, one of our boys, went with him. Hadn't ought to, but he knew Landrey pretty well. There was a little trouble about the money. Jim got beaned with a blackjack and Landrey and some little hoof fogged each other. There was another guy there we don't trace. We got Costello, but he won't talk and we don't like to beat up an old guy. He's got a rap comin' on account of the blackjack. He'll plead, I guess."

Mallory slumped down in his chair until the back of his neck rested on top of it. He blew smoke straight up towards the stained ceiling. He said:

"How about night before last? Or was that the time the roulette wheel backfired and the trick cigar blew a hole in the garage floor?"

The captain of detectives rubbed both his moist cheeks briskly, then hauled out a very large handkerchief and snorted into it.

"Oh that," he said negligently, "that wasn't nothin'. The blond kid—Henry Anson or something like that—says it was all his fault. He was Mardonne's bodyguard, but that didn't mean he could go shootin' anyone he might want to. That takes care of him, but we let him down easy for tellin' a straight story."

The captain stopped short and stared at Mallory hard-eyed. Mallory was grinning. "Of course if you don't *like* his story . . ." the captain went on coldly.

Mallory said: "I haven't heard it yet. I'm sure I'll like it fine."

"Okey," Cathcart rumbled, mollified. "Well, this Anson says Mardonne buzzed him in where you and the boss were talkin'. You was makin' a kick about something, maybe a crooked wheel downstairs. There was some money on the desk and Anson got the idea it was a shake. You looked pretty fast to him, and not knowing you was a dick he gets kinda nervous. His gun went off. You didn't shoot right away, but the poor sap lets off another round and plugs you. Then, by —— you drilled him in the shoulder, as who wouldn't, only if it had been me, I'd of pumped his guts. Then the shotgun boy comes bargin' in, lets go without asking any questions, fogs Mardonne and stops one from you. We kinda thought at first the guy might of got Mardonne on purpose, but the kid says no, he tripped in the door comin' in. . . . Hell, we don't like for you to do all that shooting, you being a stranger and all that, but a man ought to have a right to protect himself against illegal weapons."

Mallory said gently: "There's the D.A. and the coroner. How about them? I'd kind of like to go back as clean as I came away."

Cathcart frowned down at the dirty linoleum and bit his thumb as if he liked hurting himself.

"The coroner don't give a damn about that trash. If the D.A. wants to get funny, I can tell him about a few cases his office didn't clean up so good."

Mallory lifted his cane off the table, pushed his chair back, put weight on the cane and stood up. "You have a swell police department here," he said. "I shouldn't think you'd have any crime at all."

He moved across towards the outer door. The captain said to his back:

"Goin' on to Chicago?"

Mallory shrugged carefully with his right shoulder, the good one. "I might stick around," he said. "One of the studios made me a proposition. Private extortion detail. Blackmail and so on."

The captain grinned heartily. "Swell," he said. "Eclipse Films is a swell outfit. They always been swell to me. . . . Nice easy work, blackmail. Oughtn't to run into any rough stuff."

Mallory nodded solemnly. "Just light work, Chief. Almost effeminate, if you know what I mean."

He went on out, down the hall to the elevator, down to the street. He got into a taxi. It was hot in the taxi. He felt faint and dizzy going back to his hotel.

Smart-Aleck Kill

THE DOORMAN at the Kilmarnock was six feet two. He wore a pale blue uniform, and white gloves made his hands look enormous. He opened the door of the Yellow taxi as gently as an old maid stroking a cat.

Mallory got out and turned to the red-haired driver. He said: "Better wait for me around the corner, Joey."

The driver nodded, tucked a tooth-pick a little farther back in the corner of his mouth, and swung his cab expertly away from the white-marked loading zone. Mallory crossed the sunny sidewalk and went into the enormous cool lobby of the Kilmarnock. The carpets were thick, soundless. Bellboys stood with folded arms and the two clerks behind the marble desk looked austere.

Mallory went across to the elevator lobby. He got into a paneled car and said: "End of the line, please."

The penthouse floor had a small quiet lobby with three doors opening off it, one to each wall. Mallory crossed to one of them and rang the bell.

Derek Walden opened the door. He was about forty-five, possibly a little more, and had a lot of powdery gray hair and a handsome, dissipated face that was beginning to go pouchy. He had on a monogrammed lounging robe and a glass full of whiskey in his hand. He was a little drunk.

He said thickly, morosely: "Oh, it's you. C'mon in, Mallory."

He went back into the apartment, leaving the door open. Mallory shut it and followed him into a long, high-ceilinged room with a balcony at one end and a line of French windows along the left side. There was a terrace outside.

Derek Walden sat down in a brown and gold chair against the wall and stretched his legs across a footstool. He swirled the whiskey around in his glass, looking down at it.

"What's on your mind?" he asked.

Mallory stared at him a little grimly. After a moment he said:

"I dropped in to tell you I'm giving you back my job."

Walden nodded again, still silent. He put his hands down on his knees and clutched them until his knuckles whitened.

Ricchio went on: "We'll play clean. Our racket wouldn't be worth a squashed bug if we didn't. You'll play clean too. If you don't your shamus will wake up on a pile of dirt. Only he won't wake up. Get it?"

Mallory said contemptuously: "And if he pays up—I suppose you turn me loose to put the finger on you."

Smoothly, without looking at him, Ricchio said: "There's an answer to that one, too. . . . Ten grand today, Walden. The other ten the first of the week. Unless we have trouble. . . . If we have, we'll get paid for our trouble."

Walden made an aimless, defeated gesture with both hands outspread. "I guess I can arrange it," he said hurriedly.

"Swell. We'll be on our way then."

Ricchio nodded shortly and put his gun away. He took a brown kid glove out of his pocket, put it on his right hand, moved across and took Mallory's Colt away from the sandy-haired man. He looked it over, slipped it into his side pocket and held it there with the gloved hand.

"Let's drift," he said with a jerk of his head.

They went out. Derek Walden stared after them bleakly.

The elevator car was empty except for the operator. They got off at the mezzanine and went across a silent writing-room past a stained glass window with lights behind it to give the effect of sunshine. Ricchio walked half a step behind on Mallory's left. The sandy-haired man was on his right, crowding him.

They went down carpeted steps to an arcade of luxury shops, along that, out of the hotel through the side entrance. A small brown sedan was parked across the street. The sandy-haired man slid behind the wheel, stuck his gun under his leg and stepped on the starter. Ricchio and Mallory got in the back. Ricchio drawled:

"East on the boulevard, Noddy. I've got to figure."

Noddy grunted. "That's a kick," he growled over his shoulder. "Ridin' a guy down Wilshire in daylight!"

"Drive the heap, bozo!"

The sandy-haired man grunted again and drove the small sedan away from the curb, slowed a moment later for the

Walden drank the whiskey out of his glass and put it down on the corner of a table. He fumbled around for a cigarette, stuck it in his mouth and forgot to light it.

"Tha' so?" His voice was blurred but indifferent.

Mallory turned away from him and walked over to one of the windows. It was open and an awning flapped outside. The traffic noise from the boulevard was faint.

He spoke over his shoulder:

"The investigation isn't getting anywhere—because you don't want it to get anywhere. *You* know why you're being blackmailed. *I* don't. Eclipse Films is interested because they have a lot of sugar tied up in film you have made."

"To hell with Eclipse Films," Walden said, almost quietly.

Mallory shook his head and turned around. "Not from my angle. They stand to lose if you get in a jam the publicity hounds can't handle. You took me on because you were asked to. It was a waste of time. You haven't cooperated worth a cent."

Walden said in an unpleasant tone: "I'm handling this my own way and I'm not gettin' into any jam. I'll make my own deal—when I can buy something that'll stay bought. . . . And all you have to do is make the Eclipse people think the situation's bein' taken care of. That clear?"

Mallory came part of the way back across the room. He stood with one hand on top of a table, beside an ash-tray littered with cigarette stubs that had very dark lip rouge on them. He looked down at these absently.

"That wasn't explained to me, Walden," he said coldly.

"I thought you were smart enough to figure it out," Walden sneered. He leaned sidewise and slopped some more whiskey into his glass. "Have a drink?"

Mallory said: "No, thanks."

Walden found the cigarette in his mouth and threw it on the floor. He drank. "What the hell!" he snorted. "You're a private detective and you're being paid to make a few motions that don't mean anything. It's a clean job—as your racket goes."

Mallory said: "That's another crack I could do without hearing."

Walden made an abrupt, angry motion. His eyes glittered.

The corners of his mouth drew down and his face got sulky. He avoided Mallory's stare.

Mallory said: "I'm not against you, but I never was for you. You're not the kind of guy I could go for, ever. If you had played with me, I'd have done what I could. I still will—but not for your sake. I don't want your money—and you can pull your shadows off my tail any time you like."

Walden put his feet on the floor. He laid his glass down very carefully on the table at his elbow. The whole expression of his face changed.

"Shadows? . . . I don't get you." He swallowed. "I'm not having you shadowed."

Mallory stared at him. After a moment he nodded. "Okey, then. I'll backtrack on the next one and see if I can make him tell who he's workin' for. . . . I'll find out."

Walden said very quietly: "I wouldn't do that, if I were you. You're—you're monkeying with people that might get nasty. . . . I know what I'm talking about."

"That's something I'm not goin' to let worry me," Mallory said evenly. "If it's the people that want *your* money, they were nasty a long time ago."

He held his hat out in front of him and looked at it. Walden's face glistened with sweat. His eyes looked sick. He opened his mouth to say something.

The door-buzzer sounded.

Walden scowled quickly, swore. He stared down the room but did not move.

"Too damn' many people come here without bein' announced," he growled. "My Jap boy is off for the day."

The buzzer sounded again, and Walden started to get up. Mallory said: "I'll see what it is for you. I'm on my way anyhow."

He nodded to Walden, went down the room and opened the door.

Two men came in with guns in their hands. One of the guns dug sharply into Mallory's ribs, and the man who was holding it said urgently:

"Back up, and make it snappy! This is one of those stick-ups you read about!"

He was dark and good-looking and cheerful. His face was as clear as a cameo, almost without hardness. He smiled.

The one behind him was short and sandy-haired. He scowled. The dark one said:

"This is Walden's dick, Noddy. Take him over and go through him for a gun."

The sandy-haired man, Noddy, put a short-barreled revolver against Mallory's stomach and his partner kicked the door shut, then strolled carelessly down the room towards Walden.

Noddy took a .38 Colt automatic from under Mallory's arm, walked around him and tapped his pockets. He put his own gun away and transferred Mallory's Colt to his business hand.

"Okey, Ricchio. This one's clean," he said in a grumbling voice. Mallory let his arms fall, turned and went back into the room. He looked thoughtfully at Walden. Walden was leaning forward with his mouth open and an expression of intense concentration on his face. Mallory looked at the dark stick-up and said softly:

"Ricchio?"

The dark boy glanced at him. "Over there by the table, sweetheart. I'll do all the talkin'."

Walden made a hoarse sound in his throat. Ricchio stood in front of him, looking down at him pleasantly, his gun dangling from one finger by the trigger-guard.

"You're too slow on the pay-off, Walden. Too damn' slow! So we came to tell you about it. Tailed your dick here too. Wasn't that cute?"

Mallory said gravely, quietly: "This punk used to be your bodyguard, Walden—if his name is Ricchio."

Walden nodded silently and licked his lips. Ricchio snarled at Mallory:

"Don't crack wise, dick! I'm not tellin' you again." He stared with hot eyes, then looked back at Walden, looked at a watch on his wrist.

"It's eight minutes past three, Walden. I figure a guy with your drag can still get dough out of the bank. We're giving you an hour to raise ten grand. Just an hour. And we're takin' your shamus along to arrange about delivery."

boulevard stop. An empty Yellow pulled away from the west curb, swung around in the middle of the block and fell in behind. Noddy made his stop, turned right and went on. The taxi did the same. Ricchio glanced back at it without interest. There was a lot of traffic on Wilshire.

Mallory leaned back against the upholstery and said thoughtfully:

"Why wouldn't Walden use his telephone while we were coming down?"

Ricchio smiled at him. He took his hat off and dropped it in his lap, then took his right hand out of his pocket and held it under the hat, with the gun in it.

"He wouldn't want us to get mad at him, dick."

"So he lets a couple of punks take me for the ride."

Ricchio said coldly: "It's not that kind of a ride. We need you in our business. . . . And we ain't punks, see?"

Mallory rubbed his jaw with a couple of fingers. He smiled slightly, said nothing. The sandy-haired man turned his head quickly and snapped:

"Straight ahead at Robertson?"

"Yeah. I'm still figuring," Ricchio said.

"What a brain!" the sandy-haired man sneered.

Ricchio grinned tightly and showed even white teeth. The light changed to red half a block ahead. Noddy slid the sedan forward and was first in the line at the intersection. The empty Yellow drifted up on his left. Not quite level. The driver of it had red hair. His cap was balanced on one side of his head and he whistled cheerfully past a toothpick.

Mallory drew his feet back against the seat and put his weight on them. He pressed his back hard against the upholstery. The tall traffic light went green and the sedan started forward, then hung a moment for a car that crowded into a fast left turn. The Yellow slipped forward on the left and the red-haired driver leaned over his wheel, yanked it suddenly to the right. There was a grinding, tearing noise. The riveted fender of the taxi plowed over the low-swung fender of the brown sedan, locked over its left front wheel. The two cars jolted to a stop.

Horn-blasts behind the two cars sounded angrily, impatiently.

Mallory's right fist crashed against Ricchio's jaw. His left hand closed over the gun in Ricchio's lap. He jerked it loose as Ricchio sagged in the corner. Ricchio's head wobbled. His eyes opened and shut flickeringly. Mallory slid away from him along the seat and slipped the Colt under his arm.

Noddy was sitting quite still in the front seat. His right hand moved slowly towards the gun under his thigh. Mallory opened the door of the sedan and got out, shut the door, took two steps and opened the door of the taxi. He stood beside the taxi and watched the sandy-haired man.

Horns of the stalled cars blared furiously. The driver of the Yellow was out in front tugging at the two cars with a great show of energy and with no result at all. His toothpick waggled up and down in his mouth. A motorcycle officer in amber glasses threaded the traffic, looked the situation over wearily, jerked his head at the driver.

"Get in and back up," he advised. "Argue it out somewhere else—we use this intersection."

The driver grinned and scuttled around the front end of his Yellow. He climbed into it, threw it in gear and worried it backwards with a lot of tooting and left arm waving. It came clear. The sandy-haired man peered woodenly from the sedan. Mallory got into the taxi and pulled the door shut.

The motorcycle officer drew a whistle out and blew two sharp blasts on it, spread his arms from east to west. The brown sedan went through the intersection like a cat chased by a police dog.

The Yellow went after it. Half a block on Mallory leaned forward and tapped on the glass.

"Let 'em go, Joey. You can't catch them and I don't want them. . . . That was swell routing back there."

The red-head leaned his chin towards the opening in the panel. "Cinch, chief," he said, grinning. "Try me on a hard one some time."

2

The telephone rang at twenty minutes to five. Mallory was lying on his back on the bed. He was in his room at the

Merrivale. He reached for the phone without looking at it, said: "Hello."

The girl's voice was pleasant and a little strained. "This is Mianne Crayle. Remember?"

Mallory took a cigarette from between his lips. "Yes, Miss Crayle."

"Listen. You must please go over and see Derek Walden. He's worried stiff about something and he's drinking himself blind. Something's got to be done."

Mallory stared past the phone at the ceiling. The hand holding his cigarette beat a tattoo on the side of the bed. He said slowly:

"He doesn't answer his phone, Miss Crayle. I've tried to call him a time or two."

There was a short silence at the other end of the line. Then the voice said:

"I left my key under the door. You'd better just go on in."

Mallory's eyes narrowed. The fingers of his right hand became still. He said slowly:

"I'll get over there right away, Miss Crayle. Where can I reach you?"

"I'm not sure. . . . At John Sutro's, perhaps. We were supposed to go there."

Mallory said: "That's fine." He waited for the click, then hung up and put the phone away on the night table. He sat up on the side of the bed and stared at a patch of sunlight on the wall for a minute or two. Then he shrugged, stood up. He finished a drink that stood beside the telephone, put on his hat, went down in the elevator and got into the second taxi in the line outside the hotel.

"Kilmarnock again, Joey. Step on it."

It took fifteen minutes to get to the Kilmarnock.

The tea dance had let out and the streets around the big hotel were a mess of cars bucking their way out from the three entrances. Mallory got out of the taxi half a block away and walked past groups of flushed debutantes and their escorts to the arcade entrance. He went in, walked up the stairs to the mezzanine, crossed the writing-room and got into an elevator full of people. They all got out before the penthouse floor.

Mallory rang Walden's bell twice. Then he bent over and looked under the door. There was a fine thread of light broken by an obstruction. He looked back at the elevator indicators, then stooped and teased something out from under the door with the blade of a pen-knife. It was a flat key. He went in with it. . . . stopped . . . stared. . . .

There was death in the big room. Mallory went towards it slowly, walking softly, listening. There was a hard light in his gray eyes and the bone of his jaw made a sharp line that was pale against the tan of his cheek.

Derek Walden was slumped almost casually in the brown and gold chair. His mouth was slightly open. There was a blackened hole in his right temple, and a lacy pattern of blood spread down the side of his face and across the hollow of his neck as far as the soft collar of his shirt. His right hand trailed in the thick nap of the rug. The fingers held a small, black automatic.

The daylight was beginning to fade in the room. Mallory stood perfectly still and stared at Derek Walden for a long time. There was no sound anywhere. The breeze had gone down and the awnings outside the French windows were still.

Mallory took a pair of thin suede gloves from his left hip pocket and drew them on. He kneeled on the rug beside Walden and gently eased the gun from the clasp of his stiffening fingers. It was a .32, with a walnut grip, a black finish. He turned it over and looked at the stock. His mouth tightened. The number had been filed off and the patch of file marks glistened faintly against the dull black of the finish. He put the gun down on the rug and stood up, walked slowly towards the telephone that was on the end of a library table, beside a flat bowl of cut flowers.

He put his hand towards the phone but didn't touch it. He let the hand fall to his side. He stood there a moment, then turned and went quickly back and picked up the gun again. He slipped the magazine out and ejected the shell that was in the breech, picked that up and pressed it into the magazine. He forked two fingers of his left hand over the barrel, held the cocking piece back, twisted the breech-block and broke the gun apart. He took the butt-piece over to the window.

The number that was duplicated on the inside of the stock had not been filed off.

He reassembled the gun quickly, put the empty shell into the chamber, pushed the magazine home, cocked the gun and fitted it back into Derek Walden's dead hand. He pulled the suede gloves off his hands and wrote the number down in a small notebook.

He left the apartment, went down in the elevator, left the hotel. It was half-past five and some of the cars on the boulevard had switched on their lights.

3

The blond man who opened the door at Sutro's did it very thoroughly. The door crashed back against the wall and the blond man sat down on the floor—still holding on to the knob. He said indignantly:

"Earthquake, by gad!"

Mallory looked down at him without amusement.

"Is Miss Mianne Crayle here—or wouldn't you know?" he asked.

The blond man got up off the floor and hurled the door away from him. It went shut with another crash. He said in a loud voice:

"Everybody's here but the Pope's tomcat—and he's expected."

Mallory nodded, said: "You ought to have a swell party."

He went past the blond man down the hall and turned under an arch into a big old-fashioned room with built-in china closets and a lot of shabby furniture. There were seven or eight people in the room and they were all flushed with liquor.

A girl in shorts and a green polo shirt was shooting craps on the floor with a man in dinner clothes. A fat man with nose-glasses was talking sternly into a toy telephone. He was saying: "Long Distance—Sioux City—and put some snap into it, sister!"

The radio blared: "Sweet Madness."

Two couples were dancing around carelessly, bumping into each other and the furniture. A man who looked like Al Smith was dancing all alone, with a drink in his hand and an absent expression on his face. A tall, white-faced blonde weaved towards Mallory, slopping liquor out of her glass. She shrieked:

"Darling! Fancy meeting you here!"

Mallory went around her, went towards a saffron-colored woman who had just come into the room with a bottle of gin in each hand. She put the bottles on the piano and leaned against it, looking bored. Mallory went up to her and asked for Miss Crayle.

The saffron-colored woman reached a cigarette out of an open box on the piano. "Outside—in the yard," she said tonelessly.

Mallory said: "Thank you, Mrs. Sutro."

She stared at him blankly. He went under another arch, into a darkened room with wicker furniture in it. A door led to a glassed-in porch and a door out of that led down steps to a path that wound off through dim trees. Mallory followed the path to the edge of a bluff that looked out over the lighted part of Hollywood. There was a stone seat at the edge of the bluff. A girl sat on it with her back to the house. A cigarette tip glowed in the darkness. She turned her head slowly and stood up.

She was small and dark and delicately made. Her mouth showed dark with rouge, but there was not enough light to see her face clearly. Her eyes were shadowed.

Mallory said: "I have a cab outside, Miss Crayle. Or did you bring a car?"

"No car. Let's go. It's rotten here, and I don't drink gin."

They went back along the path and passed around the side of the house. A trellis-topped gate let them out on the sidewalk, and they went along by the fence to where the taxi was waiting. The driver was leaning against it with one heel hooked on the edge of the running-board. He opened the cab door. They got in.

Mallory said: "Stop at a drug-store for some butts, Joey."

"Oke."

Joey slid behind his wheel and started up. The cab went down a steep, winding hill. There was a little moisture on the surface of the asphalt pavement and the store fronts echoed back the swishing sound of the tires.

After a while Mallory said: "What time did you leave Walden?"

The girl spoke without turning her head towards him. "About three o'clock."

"Put it a little later, Miss Crayle. He was alive at three o'clock—and there was somebody else with him."

The girl made a small, miserable sound like a strangled sob. Then, she said very softly: "I know—he's dead." She lifted her gloved hands and pressed them against her temples.

Mallory said: "Sure. Let's not get any more tricky than we have to. . . . Maybe we'll have to—enough."

She said very slowly, in a low voice: "I was there after he was dead."

Mallory nodded. He did not look at her. The cab went on and after a while it stopped in front of a corner drug-store. The driver turned in his seat and looked back. Mallory stared at him, but spoke to the girl.

"You ought to have told me more over the phone. I might have got in a hell of a jam. I may be in a hell of a jam now."

The girl swayed forward and started to fall. Mallory put his arm out quickly and caught her, pushed her back against the cushions. Her head wobbled on her shoulders and her mouth was a dark gash in her stone-white face. Mallory held her shoulder and felt her pulse with his free hand. He said sharply, grimly:

"Let's go on to Carli's, Joey. Never mind the butts. . . . This party has to have a drink—in a hurry."

Joey slammed the cab in gear and stepped on the accelerator.

4

Carli's was a small club at the end of a passage between a sporting goods store and a circulating library. There was a grilled door and a man behind it who had given up trying to look as if it mattered who came in.

Mallory and the girl sat in a small booth with hard seats and looped-back green curtains. There were high partitions between the booths. There was a long bar down the other side of the room and a big juke box at the end of it. Now and then, when there wasn't enough noise, the bartender put a nickel in the juke box.

The waiter put two small glasses of brandy on the table and Mianne Crayle downed hers at a gulp. A little light came into her shadowed eyes. She peeled a black and white gauntlet off her right hand and sat playing with the empty fingers of it, staring down at the table. After a little while the waiter came back with a couple of brandy highballs.

When he had gone away again Mianne Crayle began to speak in a low, clear voice, without raising her head:

"I wasn't the first of his women by several dozen. I wouldn't have been the last—by that many more. But he had his decent side. And believe it or not he didn't pay my room rent."

Mallory nodded, didn't say anything. The girl went on without looking at him:

"He was a heel in a lot of ways. When he was sober he had the dark blue sulks. When he was lit up he was vile. When he was nicely edged he was a pretty good sort of guy besides being the best smut director in Hollywood. He could get more smooth sexy tripe past the Hays office than any three other men."

Mallory said without expression: "He was on his way out. The sexy tripe is on its way out, and that was all he knew."

The girl looked at him briefly, lowered her eyes again and drank a little of her highball. She took a tiny handkerchief out of the pocket of her sports jacket and patted her lips.

The people on the other side of the partition were making a great deal of noise.

Mianne Crayle said: "We had lunch on the balcony. Derek was drunk and on the way to get drunker. He had something on his mind. Something that worried him a lot."

Mallory smiled faintly. "Maybe it was the twenty grand somebody was trying to pry loose from him—or didn't you know about that?"

"It might have been that. Derek was a bit tight about money."

"His liquor cost him a lot," Mallory said dryly. "And that motor cruiser he liked to play about in—down below the Line."

The girl lifted her head with a quick jerk. There were sharp lights of pain in her dark eyes. She said very slowly:

"He bought all his liquor at Ensenada. Brought it in himself. He had to be careful—with the quantity he put away."

Mallory nodded. A cold smile played about the corners of his mouth. He finished his drink and put a cigarette in his mouth, felt in his pocket for a match. The holder on the table was empty.

"Finish your story, Miss Crayle," he said.

"We went up to the apartment. He got two fresh bottles out and said he was going to get good and drunk. . . . Then we quarreled. . . . I couldn't stand any more of it. I went away. When I got home I began to worry about him. I called up but he wouldn't answer the phone. I went back finally . . . and let myself in with the key I had . . . and he was dead in the chair."

After a moment Mallory said: "Why didn't you tell me some of that over the phone?"

She pressed the heels of her hands together, said very softly: "I was terribly afraid. . . . And there was something . . . wrong."

Mallory put his head back against the partition, stared at her with his eyes half-closed.

"It's an old gag," she said. "I'm almost ashamed to spring it. But Derek Walden was left-handed. . . . I'd know about that, wouldn't I?"

Mallory said very softly: "A lot of people must have known that—but one of them might have got careless."

Mallory stared at Mianne Crayle's empty glove. She was twisting it between her fingers.

"Walden was left-handed," he said slowly. "That means he didn't suicide. The gun was in his other hand. There was no sign of a struggle and the hole in his temple was powder-burned, looked as if the shot came from about the right angle. That means whoever shot him was someone who could get in there and get close to him. Or else he was paralyzed drunk, and in that case whoever did it had to have a key."

Mianne Crayle pushed the glove away from her. She clenched her hands. "Don't make it any plainer," she said sharply. "I know the police will think I did it. Well—I didn't. I loved the poor damn' fool. What do you think of that?"

Mallory said without emotion: "You *could* have done it, Miss Crayle. They'll think of that, won't they? And you might be smart enough to act the way you have afterwards. They'll think of that, too."

"That wouldn't be smart," she said bitterly. "Just smart-aleck."

"Smart-aleck kill!" Mallory laughed grimly. "Not bad." He ran his fingers through his crisp hair. "No, I don't think we can pin it on you—and maybe the cops won't know he was left-handed . . . until somebody else gets a chance to find things out."

He leaned over the table a little, put his hands on the edge as if to get up. His eyes narrowed thoughtfully on her face.

"There's one man downtown that might give me a break. He's all cop, but he's an old guy and don't give a damn about his publicity. Maybe if you went down with me, let him size you up and hear the story, he'd stall the case a few hours and hold out on the papers."

He looked at her questioningly. She drew her glove on and said quietly:

"Let's go."

5

When the elevator doors at the Merrivale closed, the big man put his newspaper down from in front of his face and yawned. He got up slowly from the settee in the corner and loafed across the small but sedate lobby. He squeezed himself into a booth at the end of a row of house phones. He dropped a coin in the slot and dialed with a thick forefinger, forming the number with his lips.

After a pause he leaned close to the mouthpiece and said:

"This is Denny. I'm at the Merrivale. Our man just came in. I lost him outside and came here to wait for him to get back."

He had a heavy voice with a burr in it. He listened to the voice at the other end, nodded and hung up without saying anything more. He went out of the booth, crossed to the elevators. On the way he dropped a cigar butt into a glazed jar full of white sand.

In the elevator he said: "Ten," and took his hat off. He had straight black hair that was damp with perspiration, a wide, flat face and small eyes. His clothes were unpressed, but not shabby. He was a studio dick and he worked for Eclipse Films.

He got out at the tenth floor and went along a dim corridor, turned a corner and knocked at a door. There was a sound of steps inside. The door opened. Mallory opened it.

The big man went in, dropped his hat casually on the bed, sat down in an easy chair by the window without being asked.

He said: "Hi, boy. I hear you need some help."

Mallory looked at him for a moment without answering. Then he said slowly, frowningly: "Maybe—for a tail. I asked for Collins. I thought you'd be too easy to spot."

He turned away and went into the bathroom, came out with two glasses. He mixed the drinks on the bureau, handed one. The big man drank, smacked his lips and put his glass down on the sill of the open window. He took a short, chubby cigar out of his vest pocket.

"Collins wasn't around," he said. "And I was just countin' my thumbs. So the big cheese give me the job. Is it footwork?"

"I don't know. Probably not," Mallory said indifferently.

"If it's a tail in a car, I'm okey. I brought my little coupe."

Mallory took his glass and sat down on the side of the bed. He stared at the big man with a faint smile. The big man bit the end off his cigar and spit it out. Then he bent over and picked up the piece, looked at it, tossed it out of the window.

"It's a swell night. A bit warm for so late in the year," he said.

Mallory said slowly: "How well do you know Derek Walden, Denny?"

Denny looked out of the window. There was a sort of haze in the sky and the reflection of a red Neon sign behind a nearby building looked like a fire.

He said: "I don't what you call know him. I've seen him around. I know he's one of the big money guys on the lot."

"Then you won't fall over if I tell you he's dead," Mallory said evenly.

Denny turned around slowly. The cigar, still unlighted, moved up and down in his wide mouth. He looked mildly interested.

Mallory went on: "It's a funny one. A blackmail gang has been working on him, Denny. Looks like it got his goat. He's dead—with a hole in his head and a gun in his hand. It happened this afternoon."

Denny opened his small eyes a little wider. Mallory sipped his drink and rested the glass on his thigh.

"His girl friend found him. She had a key to the apartment in the Kilmarnock. The Jap boy was away and that's all the help he kept. The gal didn't tell anyone. She beat it and called me up. I went over. . . . I didn't tell anybody either."

The big man said very slowly: "For Pete's sake! The cops'll stick it into you and break it off, brother. You can't get away with that stuff."

Mallory stared at him, then turned his head away and stared at a picture on the wall. He said coldly: "I'm doing it—and you're helping me. We've got a job, and a damn' powerful organization behind us. There's a lot of sugar at stake."

"How do you figure?" Denny asked grimly. He didn't look pleased.

"The girl friend doesn't think Walden suicided, Denny. I don't either, and I've got a sort of lead. But it has to be worked fast, because it's as good a lead for the Law as for us. I didn't expect to be able to check it right away, but I got a break."

Denny said: "Uh-huh. Don't make it too clever. I'm a slow thinker."

He struck a match and lit his cigar. His hand shook just a little.

Mallory said: "It's not clever. It's kind of dumb. The gun that killed Walden is a filed gun. But I broke it and the inside number wasn't filed. And Headquarters has the number, in the special permits."

"And you just went in and asked for it and they gave it to you," Denny said grimly. "And when they pick Walden up and trace the gun themselves, they'll just think it was swell of you to beat them to it." He made a harsh noise in his throat.

Mallory said: "Take it easy, boy. The guy that did the checking rates. I don't have to worry about that."

"Like hell you don't! And what would a guy like Walden be doin' with a filed gun? That's a felony rap."

Mallory finished his drink and carried his empty glass over to the bureau. He held the whiskey bottle out. Denny shook his head. He looked very disgusted.

"If he had the gun, he might not have known about that, Denny. And it could be that it wasn't his gun at all. If it was a killer's gun, then the killer was an amateur. A professional wouldn't have that kind of artillery."

The big man said slowly: "Okey, what you get on the rod?"

Mallory sat down on the bed again. He dug a package of cigarettes out of his pocket, lit one, and leaned forward to toss the match through the open window. He said:

"The permit was issued about a year ago to a newshawk on the *Press-Chronicle*, name of Dart Burwand. This Burwand was bumped off last April on the ramp of the Arcade Depot. He was all set to leave town, but he didn't make it. They never cracked the case, but the hunch is that this Burwand was tied to some racket—like the Lingle killing in Chi—and that he tried to shake one of the big boys. The big boy backfired on the idea. Exit Burwand."

The big man was breathing deeply. He had let his cigar go out. Mallory watched him gravely while he talked.

"I got that from Westfalls, on the *Press-Chronicle*," Mallory said. "He's a friend of mine. There's more of it. This gun was given back to Burwand's wife—probably. She still lives here—out on North Kenmore. She might tell me what she did with the gun . . . and she might be tied to some racket herself, Denny. In that case she wouldn't tell me, but after I talk to her she might make some contacts we ought to know about. Get the idea?"

Denny struck another match and held it to the end of his cigar. His voice said thickly:

"What do I do—tail the broad after you put the idea to her, about the gun?"

"Right."

The big man stood up, pretended to yawn. "Can do," he grunted. "But why all the hush-hush about Walden? Why not let the cops work it out? We're just goin' to get ourselves a lot of bad marks at Headquarters."

Mallory said slowly: "It's got to be risked. We don't know what the blackmail crowd had on Walden, and the studio stands to lose too much money if it comes out in the investigation and gets a front-page spread all over the country."

Denny said: "You talk like Walden was spelled Valentino. Hell, the guy's only a director. All they got to do is take his name off a couple unreleased pictures."

"They figure different," Mallory said. "But maybe that's because they haven't talked to you."

Denny said roughly: "Okey. But me, I'd let the girl friend take the damn' rap! All the Law ever wants is a fall guy."

He went around the bed to get his hat, crammed it on his head.

"Swell," he said sourly. "We gotta find out all about it before the cops even know Walden is dead." He gestured with one hand and laughed mirthlessly. "Like they do in the movies."

Mallory put the whiskey bottle away in the bureau drawer and put his hat on. He opened the door and stood aside for Denny to go out. He switched off the lights.

It was ten minutes to nine.

6

The tall blonde looked at Mallory out of greenish eyes with very small pupils. He went in past her quickly, without seeming to move quickly. He pushed the door shut with his elbow.

He said: "I'm a dick—private—Mrs. Burwand. Trying to dig up a little dope you might know about."

The blonde said: "The name is Dalton, Helen Dalton. Forget the Burwand stuff."

Mallory smiled and said: "I'm sorry. I should have known."

The blonde shrugged her shoulders and drifted away from the door. She sat down on the edge of a chair that had a cigarette burn on the arm. The room was a furnished-apartment living-room with a lot of department store bric-a-brac spread around. Two floor lamps burned. There were flounced pillows on the floor, a French doll sprawled against the base of one lamp, and a row of gaudy novels went across the mantel, above the gas fire.

Mallory said politely, swinging his hat: "It's about a gun Dart Burwand used to own. It's showed up on a case I'm working. I'm trying to trace it—from the time you had it."

Helen Dalton scratched the upper part of her left arm. She had half-inch long fingernails. She said curtly:

"I don't have an idea what you're talking about."

Mallory stared at her and leaned against the wall. His voice got an edge.

"Maybe you remember that you used to be married to Dart Burwand and that he got bumped off last April. . . . Or is that too far back?"

The blonde bit one of her knuckles and said: "Smart guy, huh?"

"Not unless I have to be. But don't fall asleep from that last shot in the arm."

Helen Dalton sat up very straight, suddenly. All the vagueness went out of her expression. She spoke between tight lips.

"What's the howl about the gun?"

"It killed a guy, that's all," Mallory said carelessly.

She stared at him. After a moment she said: "I was broke. I hocked it. I never got it out. I had a husband that made sixty bucks a week but didn't spend any of it on me. I never had a dime."

Mallory nodded. "Remember the pawnshop where you left it?" he asked. "Or maybe you still have the ticket."

"No. It was on Main. The street's lined with them. And I don't have the ticket."

Mallory said: "I was afraid of that."

He walked slowly across the room, looked at the titles of some of the books on the mantel. He went on and stood in front of a small, folding desk. There was a photo in a silver frame on the desk—a snapshot. Mallory stared at it for some time. He turned slowly.

"It's too bad about the gun, Helen. A pretty important name was rubbed out with it this afternoon. The number was filed off the outside. If you hocked it, I'd figure some hood bought it from the hockshop guy, except that a hood wouldn't file a gun that way. He'd know there was another number inside. So it wasn't a hood—and the man it was found with wouldn't be likely to get a gun in a hockshop."

The blonde stood up slowly. Red spots burned in her cheeks. Her arms were rigid at her sides and her breath whispered. She said slowly, strainedly:

"You can't maul me around, dick. I don't want any part of any police business—and I've got some good friends to take care of me. Better scram."

Mallory looked back towards the frame on the desk. He said: "Johnny Sutro oughtn't to leave his mug around in a broad's apartment that way. Somebody might think he was cheating."

The blonde walked stiff-legged across the room and slammed the photo into the drawer of the desk. She slammed the drawer shut, and leaned her hips against the desk.

"You're all wet, shamus. That's not anybody called Sutro. Get on out, will you, for gawd's sake?"

Mallory laughed unpleasantly. "Nerts, sister! I saw you at Sutro's house this afternoon. You were so drunk you don't remember."

The blonde made a movement as though she were going to jump at him. Then she stopped, rigid. A key turned in the room door. It opened and a man came in. He stood just inside the door and pushed it shut very slowly. His right hand was in the pocket of a light tweed overcoat. He was dark-skinned, angular, high-shouldered, with a sharp nose and chin.

Mallory looked at him quietly and said: "Good evening, Councilman Sutro."

The man looked past Mallory at the girl. He took no notice of Mallory. The girl said shakily:

"This guy says he's a dick. He's giving me a third about some gun he says I had. Throw him out, will you?"

Sutro said: "A dick, eh?"

He walked past Mallory without looking at him. The blonde backed away from him and fell into a chair. Her face got a pasty look and her eyes were scared. Sutro looked down at her for a moment, then turned around and took a small automatic out of his pocket. He held it loosely, pointed down at the floor.

He said: "I haven't a lot of time."

Mallory said: "I was just going." He moved near the door. Sutro said sharply:

"Let's have the story first."

Mallory said: "Sure."

He moved lithely, without haste, and threw the door wide open. The gun jerked up in Sutro's hand. Mallory said: "Don't be a sap. You're not starting anything here and you know it."

The two men stared at each other. After a moment or two Sutro put the gun back into his pocket and licked his thin lips. Mallory said:

"Miss Dalton had a gun once that killed a man—recently. But she hasn't had it for a long time. That's all I wanted to know."

Sutro nodded slowly. There was a peculiar expression in his eyes.

"Miss Dalton is a friend of my wife's. I wouldn't want her to be bothered," he said coldly.

"That's right. You wouldn't," Mallory said. "But a legitimate dick has a right to ask legitimate questions. I didn't break in here."

Sutro eyed him slowly. "Okey, but take it easy on my friends. I draw water in this town and I could hang a sign on you."

Mallory nodded. He went quietly out of the door and shut it. He listened a moment. There was no sound inside that he could hear. He shrugged and went on down the hall, down three steps and across a small lobby that had no switchboard. Outside the apartment house he looked along the street. It was an apartment house district and there were cars parked up and down the street. He went towards the lights of the taxi that was waiting for him.

Joey, the red-haired driver, was standing on the edge of the curb in front of his hack. He was smoking a cigarette, staring across the street, apparently at a big, dark coupe that was parked with its left side to the curb. As Mallory came up to him he threw his cigarette away and came to meet him.

He spoke quickly: "Listen, boss. I got a look at the guy in that Cad—"

Pale flame broke in bitter streaks from above the door of the coupe. A gun racketed between the buildings that faced each other across the street. Joey fell against Mallory. The coupe jerked into sudden motion. Mallory went down sidewise, on to one knee, with the driver clinging to him. He tried to reach his gun, couldn't make it. The coupe went around the corner with a squeal of rubber, and Joey fell down Mallory's side and rolled over on his back on the sidewalk. He beat his hands up and down on the cement and a hoarse, anguished sound came from deep inside him.

Tires screeched again and Mallory flung up to his feet, swept his hand to his left armpit. He relaxed as a small car skidded to a stop and Denny fell out of it, charged across the intervening space towards him.

Mallory bent over the driver. Light from lanterns beside the entrance to the apartment house showed blood on the front of Joey's whipcord jacket, blood that was seeping out through the material. Joey's eyes opened and shut like the eyes of a dying bird.

Denny said: "No use to follow that bus. Too fast."

"Get to a phone and call an ambulance," Mallory said quickly. "The kid's got a bellyful. . . . Then take a plant on the blonde."

The big man hurried back to his car, jumped into it and tore off around the corner. A window went open somewhere and a man yelled down. Some cars stopped.

Mallory bent down over Joey and muttered:

"Take it easy, old-timer. . . . Easy, boy . . . easy."

7

The homicide lieutenant's name was Weinkassel. He had thin, blond hair, icy blue eyes and a lot of pockmarks. He sat in a swivel-chair with his feet on the edge of a pulled-out drawer and a telephone scooped close to his elbow. The room smelled of dust and cigar butts.

A man named Lonergan, a bulky dick with gray hair and a

gray mustache, stood near an open window, looking out of it morosely.

Weinkassel chewed on a match, stared at Mallory, who was across the desk from him. He said:

"Better talk a bit. The hack-driver can't. You've had some luck in this town and you wouldn't want to run it into the ground."

Lonergan said: "He's hard. He won't talk." He didn't turn around when he said it.

"A little less of your crap would go farther, Lonnie," Weinkassel said in a dead voice.

Mallory smiled faintly and rubbed the palm of his hand against the side of the desk. It made a squeaking sound.

"What would I talk about?" he asked. "It was dark and I didn't get a flash of the man behind the gun. The car was a Cadillac coupe, without lights. I've told you all this already, Lieutenant."

"It don't listen," Weinkassel grumbled. "There's something screwy about it. You gotta have some kind of a hunch who it could be. It's a cinch the gun was for you."

Mallory said: "Why? The hack-driver was hit and I wasn't. Those lads get around a lot. One of them might be in wrong with some tough boys."

"Like you," Lonergan said. He went on staring out of the window.

Weinkassel frowned at Lonergan's back and said patiently: "The car was outside while you was still inside. The hack-driver was outside. If the guy with the gun had wanted him, he didn't have to wait for you to come out."

Mallory spread his hands and shrugged. "You boys think I know who it was?"

"Not exactly. We think you could give us some names to check on, though. Who'd you go to see in them apartments?"

Mallory didn't say anything for a moment. Lonergan turned away from the window, sat on the end of the desk and swung his leg. There was a cynical grin on his flat face.

"Come through, baby," he said cheerfully.

Mallory tilted his chair back and put his hands into his pockets. He stared at Weinkassel speculatively, ignored the gray-haired dick as though he didn't exist.

He said slowly: "I was there on business for a client. You can't make me talk about that."

Weinkassel shrugged and stared at him coldly. Then he took the chewed match out of his mouth, looked at the flattened end of it, tossed it away.

"I might have a hunch your business had something to do with the shootin'," he said grimly. "That way the hush-hush would be out. Wouldn't it?"

"Maybe," Mallory said. "If that's the way it's going to work out. But I ought to have a chance to talk to my client."

Weinkassel said: "Oke. You can have till the morning. Then you put your papers on the desk, see."

Mallory nodded and stood up. "Fair enough, Lieutenant."

"Hush-hush is all a shamus knows," Lonergan said roughly.

Mallory nodded to Weinkassel and went out of the office. He walked down a bleak corridor and up steps to the lobby floor. Outside the City Hall he went down a long flight of concrete steps and across Spring Street to where a blue Packard roadster, not very new, was parked. He got into it and drove around the corner, then through the Second Street tunnel, dropped over a block and drove out west. He watched in the mirror as he drove.

At Alvarado he went into a drug-store and called his hotel. The clerk gave him a number to call. He called it and heard Denny's heavy voice at the other end of the line. Denny said urgently:

"Where you been? I've got that broad out here at my place. She's drunk. Come on out and we'll get her to tell us what you want to know."

Mallory stared out through the glass of the phone booth without seeing anything. After a pause he said slowly:

"The blonde? How come?"

"It's a story, boy. Come on out and I'll give it to you. Fourteen fifty-four South Livesay. Know where that is?"

"I've got a map. I'll find it," Mallory said in the same tone.

Denny told him just how to find it, at some length. At the end of the explanation he said: "Make it fast. She's asleep now, but she might wake up and start yellin' murder."

Mallory said: "Where you live it probably wouldn't matter much. . . . I'll be right out, Denny."

He hung up and went out to his car. He got a pint bottle of bourbon out of the car pocket and took a long drink. Then he started up and drove towards Fox Hills. Twice on the way he stopped and sat still in the car, thinking. But each time he went on again.

8

The road turned off Pico into a scattered subdivision that spread itself out over rolling hills between two golf courses. It followed the edge of one of the golf courses, separated from it by a high wire fence. There were bungalows here and there dotted about the slopes. After a while the road dipped into a hollow and there was a single bungalow in the hollow, right across the street from the golf course.

Mallory drove past it and parked under a giant eucalyptus that etched deep shadow on the moonlit surface of the road. He got out and walked back, turned up a cement path to the bungalow. It was wide and low and had cottage windows across the front. Bushes grew halfway up the screens. There was faint light inside and the sound of a radio, turned low, came through the open windows.

A shadow moved across the screens and the front door came open. Mallory went into a living-room built across the front of the house. One small bulb burned in a lamp and the luminous dial of the radio glowed. A little moonlight came into the room.

Denny had his coat off and his sleeves rolled up on his big arms.

He said: "The broad's still asleep. I'll wake her up when I've told you how I got her here."

Mallory said: "Sure you weren't tailed?"

"Not a chance." Denny spread a big hand.

Mallory sat down in a wicker chair in the corner, between the radio and the end of the line of windows. He put his hat on the floor, pulled out the bottle of bourbon and regarded it with a dissatisfied air.

"Buy us a real drink, Denny. I'm tired as hell. Didn't get any dinner."

Denny said: "I've got some Three-Star Martel. Be right up."

He went out of the room and light went on in the back part of the house. Mallory put the bottle on the floor beside his hat and rubbed two fingers across his forehead. His head ached. After a little while the light went out in the back and Denny came back with two tall glasses.

The brandy tasted clean and hard. Denny sat down in another wicker chair. He looked very big and dark in the half-lit room. He began to talk slowly, in his gruff voice.

"It sounds goofy, but it worked. After the cops stopped milling around I parked in the alley and went in the back way. I knew which apartment the broad had but I hadn't seen her. I thought I'd make some kind of a stall and see how she was makin' out. I knocked on her door, but she wouldn't answer. I could hear her movin' around inside, and in a minute I could hear a telephone bein' dialed. I went back along the hall and tried the service door. It opened and I went in. It fastened with one of them screw bolts that get out of line and don't fasten when you think they do."

Mallory nodded, said: "I get the idea, Denny."

The big man drank out of his glass and rubbed the edge of it up and down on his lower lip. He went on.

"She was phoning to a guy named Gayn Donner. Know him?"

"I've heard of him," Mallory said. "So she has that kind of connections."

"She was callin' him by name and she sounded mad," Denny said. "That's how I knew. Donner has that place on Mariposa Canyon Drive—the Mariposa Club. You hear his band over the air—Hank Munn and his boys."

Mallory said: "I've heard it, Denny."

"Okay. When she hung up I went in on her. She looked snowed, weaved around funny, didn't seem to know much what was going on. I looked around and there was a photo of John Sutro, the Councilman, on a desk there. I used that for a stall. I said that Sutro wanted her to duck out for a while and that I was one of his boys and she was to come along. She fell for it. Screwy. She wanted some liquor. I said I had some in the car. She got her little hat and coat."

Mallory said softly: "It was that easy, huh?"

"Yeah," Denny said. He finished his drink and put the glass somewhere. "I bottle-fed her in the car to keep her quiet and we came out here. She went to sleep and that's that. What do you figure? Tough downtown?"

"Tough enough," Mallory said. "I didn't fool the boys much."

"Anything on the Walden kill?"

Mallory shook his head slowly.

"I guess the Jap didn't get home yet, Denny."

"Want to talk to the broad?"

The radio was playing a waltz. Mallory listened to it for a moment before he answered. Then he said in a tired voice:

"I guess that's what I came out here for."

Denny got up and went out of the room. There was the sound of a door opening and muffled voices.

Mallory took his gun out from under his arm and put it down in the chair beside his leg.

The blonde staggered a little too much as she came in. She stared around, giggled, made vague motions with her long hands. She blinked at Mallory, stood swaying a moment, then slid down into the chair Denny had been sitting in. The big man kept near her and leaned against a library table that stood by the inside wall.

She said drunkenly: "My old pal the dick. Hey, hey, stranger! How about buyin' a lady a drink?"

Mallory stared at her without expression. He said slowly:

"Got any new ideas about that gun? You know, the one we were talking about when Johnny Sutro crashed in. . . . The filed gun. . . . The gun that killed Derek Walden."

Denny stiffened, then made a sudden motion towards his hip. Mallory brought his Colt up and came to his feet with it. Denny looked at it and became still, relaxed. The girl had not moved at all, but the drunkenness dropped away from her like a dead leaf. Her face was suddenly tense and bitter.

Mallory said evenly: "Keep the hands in sight, Denny, and

everything'll be jake. . . . Now suppose you two cheap cross-
ers tell me what I'm here for."

The big man said thickly: "For gawd's sake! What's eatin'
you? You scared me when you said 'Walden' to the girl."

Mallory grinned. "That's all right, Denny. Maybe she never
heard of him. Let's get this ironed out in a hurry. I have an
idea I'm here for trouble."

"You're crazy as hell!" the big man snarled.

Mallory moved the gun slightly. He put his back against
the end wall of the room, leaned over and turned the radio
off with his left hand. Then he spoke bitterly.

"You sold out, Denny. That's easy. You're too big for a tail
and I've spotted you following me around half a dozen times
lately. When you horned in on the deal tonight I was pretty
sure. . . . And when you told me that funny story about how
you got baby out here I was *damn'* sure. . . . Hell's sake, do
you think a guy that's stayed alive as long as I have would
believe that one? Come on, Denny, be a sport and tell me
who you're working for. . . . I might let you take a powder. . . . Who you working for? Donner? Sutro? Or somebody I don't know? And why the plant out here in the
woods?"

The girl shot to her feet suddenly and sprang at him. He
threw her off with his free hand and she sprawled on the
floor. She yelled:

"Get him, you big punk! Get him!"

Denny didn't move. "Shut up, snow-bird!" Mallory
snapped. "Nobody's getting anybody. This is just a talk between friends. Get up on your feet and stop throwin' curves!"

The blonde stood up slowly.

Denny's face had a stony, immovable look in the dimness.
His voice came with a dull rasp. He said:

"I sold out. It was lousy. Okey, that's that. I got fed up
with watchin' a bunch of extra girls trying to pinch each other's lipsticks. . . . You can take a plug at me, if you feel
like it."

He still didn't move. Mallory nodded slowly and said again:
"Who is it, Denny? Who you working for?"

Denny said: "I don't know. I call a number, get orders and
report that way. I get dough in the mail. I tried to break the

twist here, but no luck. . . . I don't think you're on the spot and I don't know a damn' thing about that shootin' in the street. . . . I think I'm a ——!"

Mallory stared at him. He said slowly: "You wouldn't be stalling—to keep me here—would you, Denny?"

The big man raised his hand slowly. The room suddenly seemed to get very still. A car had stopped outside. The faint throbbing of its motor died.

A red spotlight hit the top of the screens.

It was blinding. Mallory slid down on one knee, shifted his position sidewise very quickly, silently. Denny's harsh voice in the silence said:

"Cops, for gawd's sake!"

The red light dissolved the wire mesh of the screens into a rosy glow, threw a great splash of vivid color on the oiled finish of the inside wall. The girl made a choked sound and her face was a red mask for an instant before she sank down out of the fan of light. Mallory looked into the light, his head low behind the sill of the end window. The leaves of the bushes were black spearpoints in the red glare.

Steps sounded on the walk.

A harsh voice rasped: "Everybody out! Mitts in the air!"

There was a sound of movement inside the house. Mallory swung his gun—uselessly. A switch clicked and a porch light went on. For a moment, before they dodged back, two men in blue police uniforms showed up in the cone of the porch light. One of them held a sub-machine-gun and the other a long Luger with a special magazine fitted to it.

There was a grating sound. Denny was at the door, opening the peep panel. A gun came up in his hand and crashed.

Something heavy clattered on the cement and a man swayed forward into the light, swayed back again. His hands were against his middle. A stiff-vizored cap fell down and rolled on the walk.

Mallory hit the floor low down against the baseboard as the machine-gun cut loose. He ground his face into the wood of the floor. The girl screamed behind him.

The chopper raked the room swiftly from end to end and the air filled with plaster and splinters. A wall mirror crashed down. A sharp stench of powder fought with the sour smell of the plaster dust. This seemed to go on for a very long time. Something fell across Mallory's legs. He kept his eyes shut and his face pressed against the floor.

The stuttering and crashing stopped. The rain of plaster inside the walls kept on. A voice yelled:

"How d'you like it, pals?"

Another voice far back snapped angrily:

"Come on—let's go!"

Steps sounded again, and a dragging sound. More steps. The motor of the car roared into life. A door slammed heavily. Tires screeched on the gravel of the road and the song of the motor swelled and died swiftly.

Mallory got up on his feet. His ears boomed and his nostrils were dry. He got his gun off the floor, unclipped a thin flash from an inside pocket, snapped it on. It probed weakly through the dusty air. The blonde lay on her back with her eyes wide open and her mouth twisted into a sort of grin. She was sobbing. Mallory bent over her. There didn't seem to be a mark on her.

He went on down the room. He found his hat untouched beside a chair that had half the top shot off. The bottle of bourbon lay beside the hat. He picked them both up. The man with the chopper had raked the room waist high, back and forth, without lowering it far enough. Mallory went on farther, came to the door.

Denny was on his knees in front of the door. He was swaying backwards and forwards and holding one of his hands in the other. Blood dribbled between his thick fingers.

Mallory got the door open and went out. There was a smear of blood and a litter of shells on the walk. There was nobody in sight. He stood there with the blood beating in his face, like little hammers. The skin around his nose prickled.

He drank some whiskey out of the bottle and turned and went back into the house. Denny was up on his feet now. He had a handkerchief out and was tying it around his bloody hand. He looked dazed, drunk. He swayed on his feet. Mallory put the beam of the flash on his face.

He said: "Hurt much?"

"No. Clipped on the hand," the big man said thickly. His fingers were clumsy on the handkerchief.

"The blonde's scared blind," Mallory said. "It's your party, boy. Nice pals you have. They meant to get all three of us. You rattled 'em when you took a pot out of the peep-hole. I guess I owe you something for that, Denny. . . . The gunner wasn't so good."

Denny said: "Where you goin'?"

"Where d'you think?"

Denny looked at him. "Sutro's your man," he said slowly. "I'm through—washed up. They can all go to hell."

Mallory went through the door again, down the path to the street. He got into his car and drove away without lights. When he had turned corners and gone some distance he switched the lights on and got out and dusted himself off.

9

Black and silver curtains opened in an inverted V against a haze of cigarette and cigar smoke. The brasses of the dance band shot brief flashes of color through the haze. There was a smell of food and liquor and perfume and face powder. The dance-floor was an empty splash of amber light and looked slightly larger than a screen star's bath-mat.

Then the band started up and the lights went down, and a headwaiter came up the carpeted steps tapping a gold pencil against the satin stripe on his trousers. He had narrow, lifeless eyes and blond-white hair sleeked back off a bony forehead.

Mallory said: "I'd like to see Mister Donner."

The headwaiter tapped his teeth with his gold pencil. "I'm afraid he's busy. What name?"

"Mallory. Tell him I'm a special friend of Johnny Sutro's."

The headwaiter said: "I'll try."

He went across to a panel that had a row of buttons on it and a small one-piece phone. He took it off the hook and put it to his ear, staring at Mallory across the cup with the impersonal stare of a stuffed animal.

Mallory said: "I'll be in the lobby."

He went back through the curtains and prowled over to the

Men's Room. Inside he got out the bottle of bourbon and
drank what was left of it, tilting his head back and standing
splay-legged in the middle of the tiled floor. A wizened negro
in a white jacket fluttered at him, said anxiously:

"No drinkin' in here, boss."

Mallory threw the empty bottle into a receptacle for towels. He took a clean towel off the glass shelf, wiped his lips
with it, put a dime down on the edge of the basin and went
out.

There was a space between an inner and an outer door. He
leaned against the outer door and took a small automatic
about four inches long out of his vest pocket. He held it with
three fingers against the inside of his hat and went on out,
swinging the hat gently beside his body.

After a while a tall Filipino with silky black hair came into
the lobby and looked around. Mallory went towards him. The
headwaiter looked out through the curtains and nodded at
the Filipino.

The Filipino spoke to Mallory: "This way, boss."

They went down a long, quiet corridor. The sound of the
dance band died away behind them. Some deserted green-
topped tables showed through an open door. The corridor
turned into another that was at right angles, and at the end of
this one some light came out through a doorway.

The Filipino paused in mid-stride and made a graceful,
complicated movement, at the end of which he had a big,
black automatic in his hand. He prodded it politely into
Mallory's ribs.

"Got to frisk you, boss. House rules."

Mallory stood still and held his arms out from his sides.
The Filipino took Mallory's Colt away from him and dropped
it into his pocket. He patted the rest of Mallory's pockets,
stepped back and holstered his own cannon.

Mallory lowered his arms and let his hat fall on the floor
and the little automatic that had been inside the hat peered
neatly at the Filipino's belly. The Filipino looked down at it
with a shocked grin.

Mallory said: "That was fun, spig. Let me do it."

He got his Colt back where it belonged, took the big automatic from under the Filipino's arm, slipped the magazine

out of it and ejected the shell that was in the chamber. He gave the empty gun back to the Filipino.

"You can still use it for a sap. If you stay in front of me, your boss don't have to know that's all it's good for."

The Filipino licked his lips. Mallory felt him for another gun, and they went on along the corridor, went in at the door that was partly open. The Filipino went first.

It was a big room with walls paneled in diagonal strips of wood. A yellow Chinese rug on the floor, plenty of good furniture, countersunk doors that told of soundproofing and no windows. There were several gilt gratings high up and a built-in ventilator fan made a faint, soothing murmur. Four men were in the room. Nobody said anything.

Mallory sat down on a leather divan and stared at Ricchio, the smooth boy who had walked him out of Walden's apartment. Ricchio was tied to a high-backed chair. His arms were pulled around behind it and fastened together at the wrists. His eyes were mad and his face was a welter of blood and bruises. He had been pistol whipped. The sandy-haired man, Noddy, who had been with him at the Kilmarnock sat on a sort of stool in the corner, smoking.

John Sutro was rocking slowly in a red leather rocker, staring down at the floor. He did not look up when Mallory came into the room.

The fourth man sat behind a desk that looked as if it had cost a lot of money. He had soft brown hair parted in the middle and brushed back and down; thin lips and reddish-brown eyes that had hot lights in them. He watched Mallory while he sat down and looked around. Then he spoke, glancing at Ricchio.

"The punk got a little out of hand. We've been telling him about it. I guess you're not sorry."

Mallory laughed shortly, without mirth. "All right as far as it goes, Donner. How about the other one? I don't see any marks on him."

"Noddy's all right. He worked under orders," Donner said evenly. He picked up a long-handled file and began to file one of his nails. "You and I have things to talk about. That's why you got in here. You look all right to me—if you don't try to cover too much ground with your private dick racket."

Mallory's eyes widened a little. He said: "I'm listening, Donner."

Sutro lifted his eyes and stared at the back of Donner's head. Donner went on talking in a smooth, indifferent tone.

"I know all about the play at Derek Walden's place and I know about the shooting on Kenmore. If I'd thought Ricchio would go that crazy, I'd have stopped him before. As it is, I figure it's up to me to straighten things out. . . . And when we get through here Mister Ricchio will go downtown and speak his piece.

"Here's how it happened. Ricchio used to work for Walden when the Hollywood crowd went in for bodyguards. Walden bought his liquor in Ensenada—still does, for all I know— and brought it in himself. Nobody bothered him. Ricchio saw a chance to bring in some white goods under good cover. Walden caught him at it. He didn't want a scandal, so he just showed Ricchio the gate. Ricchio took advantage of that by trying to shake Walden down, on the theory that he wasn't clean enough to stand the working over the Feds would give him. Walden didn't shake fast enough to suit Ricchio, so he went hog-wild and decided on a strong-arm play. You and your driver messed it up and Ricchio went gunning for you."

Donner put down his file and smiled. Mallory shrugged and glanced at the Filipino, who was standing by the wall, at the end of the divan.

Mallory said: "I don't have your organization, Donner, but I get around. I think that's a smooth story and it would have got by—with a little cooperation downtown. But it don't fit the facts as they are now."

Donner raised his eyebrows. Sutro began to swing the tip of his polished shoe up and down in front of his knee.

Mallory said: "How does Mister Sutro fit into all this?"

Sutro stared at him and stopped rocking. He made a swift, impatient movement. Donner smiled. "He's a friend of Walden's. Walden talked to him a little and Sutro knows Ricchio worked for me. But being a councilman he didn't want to tell Walden everything he knew."

Mallory said very grimly: "I'll tell you what's wrong with your story, Donner. There's not enough fear in it. Walden was too scared to help me even when I was working for him. . . . And this afternoon somebody was so scared of him that he got shot."

Donner leaned forward and his eyes got small and tight. His hands balled into fists on the desk before him.

"Walden is—dead?" he almost whispered.

Mallory nodded. "Shot in the right temple . . . with a .32. It looks like suicide. It isn't."

Sutro put his hand up quickly and covered his face. The sandy-haired man got rigid on his stool in the corner.

Mallory said: "Want to hear a good honest guess, Donner? . . . We'll call it a guess. . . . Walden was in the dope-smuggling racket himself—and not all by his lonesome. But after Repeal he wanted to quit. The coast guards wouldn't have to spend so much time watching liquor ships, and dope-smuggling up the coast wasn't going to be gravy any more. And Walden got sweet on a gal that had good eyes and could add up to ten. So he wanted to walk out on the dope racket."

Donner moistened his lips and said: "What dope racket?"

Mallory eyed him. "You wouldn't know about anything like that, would you, Donner? Hell, no, that's something for the bad boys to play with. And the bad boys didn't like the idea of Walden quitting that way. He was drinking too much—and he might start to broadcast to his girl friend. They wanted him to quit the way he did—on the receiving end of a gun."

Donner turned his head slowly and stared at the bound man on the high-backed chair. He said very softly: "Ricchio."

Then he got up and walked around his desk. Sutro took his hand down from his face and watched with his lips shaking.

Donner stood in front of Ricchio. He put his hand out against Ricchio's head and jarred it back against the chair. Ricchio moaned. Donner smiled down at him.

"I must be slowing up. *You* killed Walden, you ——! You went back and croaked him. You forgot to tell us about that part, baby."

Ricchio opened his mouth and spit a stream of blood against Donner's hand and wrist. Donner's face twitched and he stepped back and away, holding the hand straight out in front of him. He took out a handkerchief and wiped it off carefully, dropped the handkerchief on the floor.

"Lend me your gun, Noddy," he said quietly, going towards the sandy-haired man.

Sutro jerked and his mouth fell open. His eyes looked sick. The tall Filipino flicked his empty automatic into his hand as if he had forgotten it was empty. Noddy took a blunt revolver from under his right arm, held it out to Donner.

Donner took it from him and went back to Ricchio. He raised the gun.

Mallory said: "Ricchio didn't kill Walden."

The Filipino took a quick step forward and slashed at him with his big automatic. The gun hit Mallory on the point of the shoulder, and a wave of pain billowed down his arm. He rolled away and snapped his Colt into his hand. The Filipino swung at him again, missed.

Mallory slid to his feet, side-stepped and laid the barrel of the Colt along the side of the Filipino's head, with all his strength. The Filipino grunted, sat down on the floor, and the whites showed all around his eyes. He fell over slowly, clawing at the divan.

There was no expression on Donner's face and he held his blunt revolver perfectly still. His long upper lip was beaded with sweat.

Mallory said: "Ricchio didn't kill Walden. Walden was killed with a filed gun and the gun was planted in his hand. Ricchio wouldn't go within a block of a filed gun."

Sutro's face was ghastly. The sandy-haired man had got down off his stool and stood with his right hand swinging at his side.

"Who did? Tell me more," Donner said evenly.

"The filed gun traces to a broad named Helen Dalton or Burwand," Mallory said. "It was her gun. She told me she had hocked it long ago. I didn't believe her. She's a good friend of Sutro's and Sutro was so bothered by my going to see her that he pulled a gat on me himself. Why do you suppose Sutro was bothered, Donner, and how do you suppose he knew I was likely to go see the broad?"

Donner said: "Go ahead and tell me." He looked at Sutro very quietly.

Mallory took a step closer to Donner and held his Colt down at his side, not threateningly.

"I'll tell you how and why. I've been tailed ever since I started to work for Walden—tailed by a clumsy ox of a studio dick I could spot a mile off. He was bought, Donner. The guy that killed Walden bought him. He figured the studio dick had a chance to get next to me, and I let him do just that—to give him rope and spot his game. His boss was Sutro. Sutro killed Walden—with his own hand. It was that kind of a job. An amateur job—a smart-aleck kill. The thing that made it smart was the thing that gave it away—the suicide plant, with a filed gun the killer thought couldn't be traced because he didn't know most guns have numbers inside."

Donner swung the blunt revolver until it pointed midway between the sandy-haired man and Sutro. He didn't say anything. His eyes were thoughtful and interested.

Mallory shifted his weight a little, on to the balls of his feet. The Filipino on the floor put a hand along the divan and his nails scratched on the leather.

"There's more of it, Donner, but what the hell! Sutro was Walden's pal, and he could get close to him, close enough to stick a gun to his head and let go. A shot wouldn't be heard on the penthouse floor of the Kilmarnock, one little shot from a .32. So Sutro put the gun in Walden's hand and went on his way. But he forgot that Walden was left-handed and he didn't know the gun could be traced. When it was—and his bought man wised him up—and I tapped the girl—he hired himself a chopper squad and angled all three of us out to a house in Palms to button our mouths for good. . . . Only the chopper squad, like everything else in this play, didn't do its stuff so good."

Donner nodded slowly. He looked at a spot in the middle of Sutro's stomach and lined his gun on it.

"Tell us about it, Johnny," he said softly. "Tell us how you got clever in your old age—"

The sandy-haired man moved suddenly. He dodged down behind the desk and as he went down his right hand swept for his other gun. It roared from behind the desk. The bullet came through the kneehole and pinged into the wall with a sound of striking metal behind the paneling.

Mallory jerked up his Colt and fired twice into the desk. A few splinters flew. The sandy-haired man yelled behind the desk and came up fast with his gun flaming in his hand. Donner staggered. His gun spoke twice, very quickly. The sandy-haired man yelled again, and blood jumped straight out from one of his cheeks. He went down behind the desk and stayed quiet.

Donner backed until he touched the wall. Sutro stood up and put his hands in front of his stomach and tried to scream.

Donner said: "Okey, Johnny. Your turn."

Then Donner coughed suddenly and slid down the wall with a dry rustle of cloth. He bent forward and dropped his gun and put his hands on the floor and went on coughing. His face got gray.

Sutro stood rigid, his hands in front of his stomach and bent back at the wrists, the fingers curved claw-like. There was no light behind his eyes. They were dead eyes. After a moment his knees buckled and he fell down on the floor on his back.

Donner went on coughing quietly.

Mallory crossed swiftly to the door of the room, listened at it, opened it and looked out. He shut it again quickly.

"Soundproof—and how!" he muttered.

He went back to the desk and lifted the telephone off the prongs. He put his Colt down and dialed, waited, said into the phone:

"Captain Cathcart. . . . Got to talk to him. . . . Sure, it's important . . . very important."

He waited, drumming on the desk, staring hard-eyed around the room. He jerked a little as a sleepy voice came over the wire.

"Mallory, Chief. I'm at the Casa Mariposa, in Gayn Donner's private office. There's been a little trouble, but nobody hurt bad. . . . I've got Derek Walden's killer for you . . . Johnny Sutro did it. . . . Yeah, the Councilman. . . . Make it fast, Chief. . . . I wouldn't want to get in a fight with the help, you know . . ."

He hung up and picked his Colt off the top of the desk, held it on the flat of his hand and stared across at Sutro.

"Get up off the floor, Johnny," he said wearily. "Get up and tell a poor dumb dick how to cover this one up—smart guy!"

10

The light above the big oak table at Headquarters was too bright. Mallory ran a finger along the wood, looked at it, wiped it off on his sleeve. He cupped his chin in his lean hands and stared at the wall above the roll-top desk that was beyond the table. He was alone in the room.

The loudspeaker on the wall droned: "Calling Car 71W in 72's district . . . at Third and Berendo . . . at the drug-store . . . meet a man . . ."

The door opened and Captain Cathcart came in, shut the door carefully behind him. He was a big, battered man with a wide, moist face, a stained mustache, gnarled hands.

He sat down between the oak table and the roll-top desk and fingered a cold pipe that lay in the ashtray.

Mallory raised his head from between his hands. Cathcart said:

"Sutro's dead."

Mallory stared, said nothing.

"His wife did it. He wanted to stop by his house a minute. The boys watched him good but they didn't watch her. She slipped him the dose before they could move."

Cathcart opened and shut his mouth twice. He had strong, dirty teeth.

"She never said a damn' word. Brought a little gun around from behind her and fed him three slugs. One, two, three. Win, place, show. Just like that. Then she turned the gun around in her hand as nice as you could think of and handed it to the boys. . . . What in hell she do that for?"

Mallory said: "Get a confession?"

Cathcart stared at him and put the cold pipe in his mouth. He sucked on it noisily. "From him? Yeah—not on paper, though. . . . What you suppose she done that for?"

"She knew about the blonde," Mallory said. "She thought it was her last chance. Maybe she knew about his rackets."

The captain nodded slowly. "Sure," he said. "That's it. She figured it was her last chance. And why wouldn't she bop the ——? If the D.A.'s smart, he'll let her take a manslaughter plea. That'd be about fifteen months at Tehachapi. A rest cure."

Mallory moved in his chair. He frowned.

Cathcart went on: "It's a break for all of us. No dirt your way, no dirt on the administration. If she hadn't done it, it would have been a kick in the pants all round. She ought to get a pension."

"She ought to get a contract from Eclipse Films," Mallory said. "When I got to Sutro I figured I was licked on the publicity angle. I might have gunned Sutro myself—if he hadn't been so yellow—and if he hadn't been a councilman."

"Nix on that, baby. Leave that stuff to the law," Cathcart growled. "Here's how it looks. I don't figure we can get Walden on the book as a suicide. The filed gun is against it and we got to wait for the autopsy and the gun-shark's report. And a paraffin test of the hand ought to show he didn't fire the gun at all. On the other hand, the case is closed on Walden and Sutro and what has to come out ought not to hurt too bad. Am I right?"

Mallory took out a cigarette and rolled it between his fingers. He lit it slowly and waved the match until it went out.

"Walden was no lily," he said. "It's the dope angle that would raise hell—but that's cold. I guess we're jake, except for a few loose ends."

"Hell with the loose ends," Cathcart grinned. "Nobody's getting away with any fix that I can see. That sidekick of yours, Denny, will fade in a hurry and if I ever get my paws on the Dalton frail, I'll send her to Mendocino for the cure. We might get something on Donner—after the hospital gets through with him. We've got to put the rap on those hoods, for the stick-up and the taxi-driver, whichever of 'em did that, but they won't talk. They still got a future to think about, and the taxi-driver ain't so bad hurt. That leaves the chopper squad." Cathcart yawned. "Those boys must be from Frisco. We don't run to choppers around here much."

Mallory sagged in his chair. "You wouldn't have a drink, would you, Chief?" he said dully.

Cathcart stared at him. "There's just one thing," he said grimly. "I want you to stay told about that. It was okey for you to break that gun—if you didn't spoil the prints. And I guess it was okey for you not to tell me, seein' the jam you were in. But I'll be damned if it's okey for you to beat our time by chiselin' on our own records."

Mallory smiled thoughtfully at him. "You're right all the way, Chief," he said humbly. "It was the job—and that's all a guy can say."

Cathcart rubbed his cheeks vigorously. His frown went away and he grinned. Then he bent over and pulled out a drawer and brought up a quart bottle of rye. He put it on the desk and pressed a buzzer. A very large uniformed torso came part way into the room.

"Hey, Tiny!" Cathcart boomed. "Loan me that corkscrew you swiped out of my desk." The torso disappeared and came back.

"What'll we drink to?" the captain asked a couple of minutes later.

Mallory said: "Let's just drink."

Finger Man

I GOT AWAY from the Grand Jury a little after four, and then sneaked up the back stairs to Fenweather's office. Fenweather, the D.A., was a man with severe, chiseled features and the gray temples women love. He played with a pen on his desk and said:

"I think they believed you. They might even indict Manny Tinnen for the Shannon kill this afternoon. If they do, then is the time you begin to watch your step."

I rolled a cigarette around in my fingers and finally put it in my mouth. "Don't put any men on me, Mr. Fenweather. I know the alleys in this town pretty well, and your men couldn't stay close enough to do me any good."

He looked towards one of the windows. "How well do you know Frank Dorr?" he asked, with his eyes away from me.

"I know he's a big politico, a fixer you have to see if you want to open a gambling hell or a bawdy house—or if you want to sell honest merchandise to the city."

"Right." Fenweather spoke sharply, and brought his head around towards me. Then he lowered his voice. "Having the goods on Tinnen was a surprise to a lot of people. If Frank Dorr had an interest in getting rid of Shannon who was the head of the Board where Dorr's supposed to get his contracts, it's close enough to make him take chances. And I'm told he and Manny Tinnen had dealings. I'd sort of keep an eye on him, if I were you."

I grinned. "I'm just one guy," I said. "Frank Dorr covers a lot of territory. But I'll do what I can."

Fenweather stood up and held his hand across the desk. He said: "I'll be out of town for a couple of days. I'm leaving tonight, if this indictment comes through. Be careful—and if anything should happen to go wrong, see Bernie Ohls, my chief investigator."

I said: "Sure."

We shook hands and I went out past a tired-looking girl who gave me a tired smile and wound one of her lax curls up on the back of her neck as she looked at me. I got back to my office soon after four-thirty. I stopped outside the door of the little reception room for a moment, looking at it. Then I opened it and went in, and of course there wasn't anybody there.

There was nothing there but an old red davenport, two odd chairs, a bit of carpet, and a library table with a few old magazines on it. The reception room was left open for visitors to come in and sit down and wait—if I had any visitors and they felt like waiting.

I went across and unlocked the door into my private office.

Lou Harger was sitting in the wooden chair on the side of the desk away from the window. He had bright yellow gloves clamped on the crook of a cane, a green snap-brim hat set too far back on his head. Very smooth black hair showed under the hat and grew too low on the nape of his neck.

"Hello. I've been waiting," he said, and smiled languidly.

"'Lo, Lou. How did you get in here?"

"The door must have been unlocked. Or maybe I had a key that fitted. Do you mind?"

I went around the desk and sat down in the swivel chair. I put my hat down on the desk, picked a bulldog pipe out of an ash tray and began to fill it up.

"It's all right as long as it's you," I said. "I just thought I had a better lock."

He smiled with his full red lips. He was a very good-looking boy. He said:

"Are you still doing business, or will you spend the next month in a hotel room drinking liquor with a couple of Headquarters boys?"

"I'm still doing business—if there's any business for me to do."

I lit my pipe, leaned back and stared at his clear olive skin, straight, dark eyebrows.

He put his cane on top of the desk and clasped his yellow gloves on the glass. He moved his lips in and out.

"I have a little something for you. Not a hell of a lot. But there's carfare in it."

I waited.

"I'm making a little play at Las Olindas tonight," he said. "At Canales' place."

"The white smoke?"

"Uh-huh. I think I'm going to be lucky—and I'd like to have a guy with a rod."

I took a fresh pack of cigarettes out of a top drawer and slid them across the desk. Lou picked them up and began to break the pack open.

I said: "What kind of a play?"

He got a cigarette halfway out and stared down at it. There was a little something in his manner I didn't like.

"I've been closed up for a month now. I wasn't makin' the kind of money it takes to stay open in this town. The Headquarters boys have been putting the pressure on since repeal. They have bad dreams when they see themselves trying to live on their pay."

I said: "It doesn't cost any more to operate here than anywhere else. And here you pay it all to one organization. That's something."

Lou Harger jabbed the cigarette in his mouth. "Yeah—Frank Dorr," he snarled. "That fat, blood-suckin' ——!"

I didn't say anything. I was way past the age when it's fun to swear at people you can't hurt. I watched Lou light his cigarette with my desk lighter. He went on, through a puff of smoke:

"It's a laugh, in a way. Canales bought a new wheel—from some grafters in the sheriff's office. I know Pina, Canales' head croupier, pretty well. The wheel is one they took away from me. It's got bugs—and I know the bugs."

"And Canales don't . . . That sounds just like Canales," I said.

Lou didn't look at me. "He gets a nice crowd down there," he said. "He has a small dance floor and a five-piece Mexican band to help the customers relax. They dance a bit and then go back for another trimming, instead of going away disgusted."

I said: "What do *you* do?"

"I guess you might call it a system," he said softly, and looked at me under his long lashes.

I looked away from him, looked around the room. It had a rust-red carpet, five green filing-cases in a row under an advertising calendar, an old costumer in the corner, a few

walnut chairs, net curtains over the windows. The fringe of
the curtains was dirty from blowing about in the draft. There
was a bar of late sunlight across my desk and it showed up the
dust.

"I get it like this," I said. "You think you have that roulette
wheel tamed and you expect to win enough money so that
Canales will be mad at you. You'd like to have some protection along—me. I think it's screwy."

"It's not screwy at all," Lou said. "Any roulette wheel has a
tendency to work in a certain rhythm. If you know the wheel
very well indeed—"

I smiled and shrugged. "Okey, I wouldn't know about
that. I don't know enough roulette. It sounds to me like
you're being a sucker for your own racket, but I could be
wrong. And that's not the point anyway."

"What is?" Lou asked thinly.

"I'm not much stuck on bodyguarding—but maybe that's
not the point either. I take it I'm supposed to think this play
is on the level. Suppose I don't, and walk out on you, and
you get in a box? Or suppose I think everything is aces, but
Canales don't agree with me and gets nasty."

"That's why I need a guy with a rod," Lou said, without
moving a muscle except to speak.

I said evenly: "If I'm tough enough for the job—and I
didn't know I was—that still isn't what worries me."

"Forget it," Lou said. "It breaks me up enough to know
you're worried."

I smiled a little more and watched his yellow gloves moving
around on top of the desk, moving too much. I said slowly:
"You're the last guy in the world to be getting expense
money that way just now. I'm the last guy to be standing
behind you while you do it. That's all."

Lou said: "Yeah." He knocked some ash off his cigarette
down on the glass top, bent his head to blow it off. He went
on, as if it was a new subject: "Miss Glenn is going with me.
She's a tall red-head, a swell looker. She used to model. She's
nice people in any kind of a spot and she'll keep Canales from
breathing on my neck. So we'll make out. I just thought I'd
tell you."

I was silent for a minute, then I said:

"You know damn' well I just got through telling the Grand Jury it was Manny Tinnen I saw lean out of that car and cut the ropes on Art Shannon's wrists after they pushed him on to the roadway, filled with lead."

Lou smiled faintly at me. "That'll make it easier for the grafters on the big time; the fellows who take the contracts and don't appear in the business. They say Shannon was square and kept the Board in line. It was a nasty bump-off."

I shook my head. I didn't want to talk about that. I said: "Canales has a noseful of junk a lot of the time. And maybe he doesn't go for red-heads."

Lou stood up slowly and lifted his cane off the desk. He stared at the tip of one yellow finger. He had an almost sleepy expression. Then he moved towards the door, swinging his cane.

"Well, I'll be seein' you some time," he drawled.

I let him get his hand on the knob before I said: "Don't go away sore, Lou. I'll drop down to Las Olindas, if you have to have me. But I don't want any money for it, and for —— sake don't pay any more attention to me than you have to."

He licked his lips softly and didn't quite look at me. "Thanks, keed. I'll be careful as hell."

He went out then and his yellow glove disappeared around the edge of the door.

I sat still for about five minutes and then my pipe got too hot. I put it down, looked at my strap-watch, and got up to switch on a small radio in the corner beyond the end of the desk. When the A.C. hum died down the last tinkle of a chime came out of the horn, then a voice was saying:

"KLI now brings you its regular early evening broadcast of local news releases. An event of importance this afternoon was the indictment returned late today against Maynard J. Tinnen by the Grand Jury. Tinnen is a well-known City Hall lobbyist and man about town. The indictment, a shock to his many friends, was based almost entirely on the testimony—"

My telephone rang sharply and a girl's cool voice said in my ear: "One moment, please. Mr. Fenweather is calling you."

He came on at once. "Indictment returned. Take care of the boy."

I said I was just getting it over the radio. We talked a short moment and then he hung up, after saying he had to leave at once to catch a plane.

I leaned back in my chair again and listened to the radio without exactly hearing it. I was thinking what a damn' fool Lou Harger was and that there wasn't anything I could do to change that.

2

It was about ten o'clock when the little yellow-sashed orchestra got tired of messing around with a rhumba that nobody was dancing to. The marimba player dropped his sticks and got a cigarette into his mouth almost with the same movement. The boys sitting down reached for glasses under their chairs.

It was a good crowd for a Tuesday. The big, old-fashioned room had been a ballroom in the days when Las Olindas was thirty miles by water from San Angelo, and that was the only way anyone went to it. It was still a beautiful room, with damask panels and crystal chandeliers.

I leaned sidewise against the bar, which was on the same side of the room as the orchestra stand. I was turning a small glass of Bacardi around on the top of the bar. All the business was at the center one of the three roulette tables.

The bartender leaned beside me, on his side of the bar.

"The flame top gal must be pickin' them," he said.

I nodded without looking at him. "She's playing with fistfuls now," I said. "Not even counting it."

The red-haired girl was tall. I could see the burnished copper of her hair between the heads of the people behind her. I could see Lou Harger's sleek head beside hers. Everybody seemed to be playing standing up.

"I saw an old horseface crack a bank once in Havana," the barkeep said.

"Havana?" I repeated politely.

"Even a working stiff can get around, mister. You don't play?"

"Not on Tuesdays. I had some trouble on a Tuesday once."

"Yeah? Do you like that stuff straight, or would I smooth it out for you?"

"I like it straight as well as I like it at all," I said. I drank a little of the Bacardi. "What's the limit over there?"

"I wouldn't know, mister. How the boss feels, I guess."

Two men in dinner clothes came across the room, leaned against the bar and asked for Scotch and soda. One of them was excited. He mopped his face with a white silk handkerchief.

The other one said: "She's got 'em worried. Eight wins, two stand-offs, on the red. . . . That's roulette, boy, roulette."

The roulette tables were in a row near the far wall. A low railing of gilt metal joined their ends and the players were outside the railing.

Some kind of a confused wrangle started at the center table. Half a dozen people at the two end tables grabbed their chips up and moved across.

Then a clear, very polite voice, with a slightly foreign accent, spoke out: "If you will just be patient, madame . . . Mr. Canales will be here in a minute."

I went across, squeezed near the railing. Two croupiers stood near me with their heads together and their eyes looking sidewise. One moved a rake slowly back and forth beside the idle wheel. They were staring at the red-haired girl.

She wore a high-cut black evening gown. She had fine white shoulders, was something less than beautiful and more than pretty. She was leaning on the edge of the table, in front of the wheel. Her long eyelashes were twitching. There was a big pile of money and chips in front of her.

She spoke monotonously, as if she had said the same thing several times already.

"What kind of cheap outfit is this anyway? Get busy and spin that wheel! You take it away fast enough, but you don't like to dish it out."

The croupier in charge smiled a cold, even smile. He was tall, dark, disinterested. "The table can't cover your bet," he said with calm precision. "Mr. Canales, perhaps—" He shrugged neat shoulders.

The girl said: "It's your money, highpockets. Don't you want it back?"

Lou Harger licked his lips beside her, put a hand on her arm, stared at the pile of money with hot eyes. He said gently:

"Wait for Canales . . ."

"To hell with Canales! I'm hot—and I want to stay that way."

A door opened in the paneling, beyond the end table nearest to me. A very slight, very pale man came into the room. He had straight, lusterless black hair, a high bony forehead, flat, impenetrable eyes. He had a thin mustache that was trimmed in two sharp lines almost at right angles to each other. They came down below the corners of his mouth a full inch. The effect was Oriental. His skin had a thick, glistening pallor.

He slid behind the croupiers, stopped at a corner of the center table, glanced at the red-haired girl and touched the ends of his mustache with two fingers, the nails of which had a purplish tint.

He smiled suddenly, and the instant after it was as though he had never smiled in his life. He spoke in a dull, ironic voice.

"If you're not playing any more, you must let me send a couple of my boys home with you. I'd hate to see any of that money get in the wrong pockets."

The red-haired girl looked at him, not very pleasantly.

"I have my own escort, Canales. And I'm not leaving—unless you're throwing me out."

Canales said: "No? What would you like to do?"

"Bet the wad—dark meat!"

The crowd noise became a deathly silence. There wasn't a whisper of any kind of sound. Harger's face slowly got ivory-white.

Canales' face was without expression. He lifted a hand, delicately, gravely, slipped a large wallet from his dinner jacket and tossed it in front of the tall croupier.

"Ten grand," he said in a voice that was a dull rustle of sound. "That's my limit—always."

The tall croupier picked the wallet up, spread it, drew out two flat packets of crisp bills, riffled them, refolded the wallet and passed it along the edge of the table to Canales.

Canales did not move to take it. Nobody moved, except the croupier.

The girl said: "Put it on the red."

The croupier leaned across the table and very carefully stacked her money and chips. He placed her bet for her on the red diamond. He placed his hand along the curve of the wheel.

"If no one objects," Canales said, without looking at anyone, "this is just the two of us."

Heads moved. Nobody spoke. The croupier spun the wheel and sent the ball skimming in the groove with a light flirt of his left wrist. Then he drew his hands back and placed them in full view on the edge of the table, on top of it.

The red-haired girl's eyes shone and her lips slowly parted.

The ball drifted along the groove, dipped past one of the bright metal diamonds, slid down the flank of the wheel and chattered along the tines beside the numbers. Movement went out of it suddenly, with a dry click. It fell next the double-zero, in red twenty-seven. The wheel was motionless.

The croupier took up his rake and slowly pushed the two packets of bills across, added them to the stake, pushed the whole thing off the field of play.

Canales put his wallet back in his breast pocket, turned and walked slowly back to the door, went through it.

I took my cramped fingers off the top of the railing, and a lot of people broke for the bar.

3

When Lou came up I was sitting at a little tile-top table in a corner, fooling with some more of the Bacardi. The little orchestra was playing a thin, brittle tango and one couple was maneuvering self-consciously on the dance-floor.

Lou had a cream-colored overcoat on, with the collar turned up around a lot of white silk scarf. He had a fine-drawn, glistening expression. He had white pigskin gloves this time and he put one of them down on the table and leaned at me.

"Over twenty-two thousand," he said softly. "Boy, what a take!"

I said: "Very nice money, Lou. What kind of car are you driving?"

"See anything wrong with it?"

"The play?" I shrugged, fiddled with my glass. "I'm not wised up on roulette, Lou . . . I saw plenty wrong with your broad's manners."

"She's not a broad," Lou said. His voice got a little worried.

"Okey. She made Canales look like a million. What kind of a car?"

"Buick sedan. Nile green, with two spotlights and those little fender lights on rods." His voice was still worried.

I said: "Take it kind of slow through town. Give me a chance to get in the parade."

He moved his glove and went away. The red-haired girl was not in sight anywhere. I looked down at the watch on my wrist. When I looked up again Canales was standing across the table. His eyes looked at me lifelessly above his trick mustache.

"You don't like my place," he said.

"On the contrary."

"You don't come here to play." He was telling me, not asking me.

"Is it compulsory?" I asked dryly.

A very faint smile drifted across his face. He leaned a little down and said:

"I think you are a dick. A smart dick."

"Just a shamus," I said. "And not so smart. Don't let my long upper lip fool you. It runs in the family."

Canales wrapped his fingers around the top of a chair, squeezed on it. "Don't come here again—for anything." He spoke very softly, almost dreamily. "I don't like—pigeons."

I took the cigarette out of my mouth and looked it over before I looked at him. I said:

"I heard you insulted a while back. You took it nicely . . . So we won't count this one."

He had a queer expression for an instant. Then he turned and slid away with a little sway of the shoulders. He put his feet down flat and turned them out a good deal as he walked. His walk, like his face, was a little negroid.

I got up and went out through the big white double doors

into a dim lobby, got my hat and coat and put them on. I went out through another pair of double doors on to a wide veranda with scroll work along the edge of its roof. There was sea fog in the air and the windblown Monterey cypresses in front of the house dripped with it. The grounds sloped gently into the dark for a long distance. Fog hid the ocean.

I had parked my car out on the street, on the other side of the house. I drew my hat down and walked soundlessly on the damp moss that covered the driveway, rounded a corner of the porch, and stopped rigidly.

A man just in front of me was holding a gun—but he didn't see me. He was holding the gun down at his side, pressed against the material of his overcoat, and his big hand made it look quite small. The dim light that reflected from the barrel seemed to come out of the fog, to be part of the fog. He was a big man, and he stood very still, poised on the balls of his feet.

I lifted my right hand very slowly and opened the top two buttons of my coat, reached inside and drew out a long thin .32 with a six and one-half inch barrel. I eased it into my overcoat pocket.

The man in front of me moved, reached his left hand up to his face. He drew on a cigarette cupped inside his hand and the glow put brief light on a heavy chin, wide, dark nostrils, and a square, aggressive nose, the nose of a fighting man.

Then he dropped the cigarette and stepped on it and a quick, light step made faint noise behind me. I was far too late turning.

Something swished and I went out like a light.

4

When I came to I was cold and wet and had a headache a yard wide. There was a soft bruise behind my right ear that wasn't bleeding. I had been put down with a sap.

I got up off my back and saw that I was a few yards from the driveway, between two trees that were wet with fog. There was some mud on the backs of my shoes. I had been dragged off the path, but not very far.

I went through my pockets. My gun was gone, of course, but that was all — that and the idea that this excursion was all fun.

I nosed around through the fog, didn't find anything or see anyone, gave up bothering about that, and went along the blank side of the house to a curving line of palm trees and an old type arc light that hissed and flickered over the entrance to a sort of lane where I had stuck the 1925 Marmon touring car I still used for transportation. I got into it after wiping the seat off with a towel, teased the motor alive, and choked it along to a big empty street with disused car tracks in the middle.

I went from there to De Cazens Boulevard, which was the main drag of Las Olindas and was called after the man who built Canales' place, long ago. After a while there was town, buildings, dead-looking stores, a service station with a night-bell, and at last a drug-store which was still open.

A dolled-up sedan was parked in front of the drug-store and I parked behind that, got out, and saw that a hatless man was sitting at the counter, talking to a clerk in a blue smock. They seemed to have the world to themselves. I started to go in, then I stopped and took another look at the dolled-up sedan.

It was a Buick and of a color that could have been Nile-green in daylight. It had two spotlights and two little egg-shaped amber lights stuck up on thin nickel rods clamped to the front fenders. The window by the driver's seat was down. I went back to the Marmon and got a flash, reached in and twisted the license holder of the Buick around, put the light on it quickly, then off again.

It was registered to Louis N. Harger.

I got rid of the flash and went into the drug-store. There was a liquor display at one side, and the clerk in the blue smock sold me a pint of Canadian Club, which I took over to the counter and opened. There were ten seats at the counter, but I sat down on the one next to the hatless man. He began to look me over, in the mirror, very carefully.

I got a cup of black coffee two-thirds full and added plenty of the rye. I drank it down and waited for a minute, to let it warm me up. Then I looked the hatless man over.

He was about twenty-eight, a little thin on top, had a healthy red face, fairly honest eyes, dirty hands and looked as if he wasn't making much money. He wore a gray whipcord jacket with metal buttons on it, pants that didn't match.

I said carelessly, in a low voice: "That your bus outside?"

He sat very still. His mouth got small and tight and he had trouble pulling his eyes away from mine, in the mirror.

"My brother's," he said, after a moment.

I said: "Care for a drink? . . . Your brother is an old friend of mine."

He nodded slowly, gulped, moved his hand slowly, but finally got the bottle and curdled his coffee with it. He drank the whole thing down. Then I watched him dig up a crumpled pack of cigarettes, spear his mouth with one, strike a match on the counter, after missing twice on his thumb nail, and inhale with a lot of very poor nonchalance that he knew wasn't going over.

I leaned close to him and said evenly: "This doesn't *have* to be trouble."

He said: "Yeah . . . Wh-what's the beef?"

The clerk sidled towards us. I asked for more coffee. When I got it I stared at the clerk until he went and stood in front of the display window with his back to me. I laced my second cup of coffee and drank some of it. I looked at the clerk's back and said: "The guy the car belongs to doesn't have a brother."

He held himself tightly, but turned towards me. "You think it's a hot car?"

"No."

"You don't think it's a hot car?"

I said: "No. I just want the story."

"You a dick?"

"Uh-huh—but it isn't a shakedown, if that's what worries you."

He drew hard on his cigarette and moved his spoon around in his empty cup.

"I can lose my job over this," he said slowly. "But I needed a hundred bucks. I'm a hack driver."

"I guessed that," I said.

He looked surprised, turned his head and stared at me.

"Have another drink and let's get on with it," I said. "Car thieves don't park them on the main drag and then sit around in drug-stores."

The clerk came back from the window and hovered near us, busying himself with rubbing a rag on the coffee urn. A heavy silence fell. The clerk put the rag down, went along to the back of the store, behind the partition, and began to whistle aggressively.

The man beside me took some more of the whiskey and drank it, nodding his head wisely at me. "Listen—I brought a fare out and was supposed to wait for him. A guy and a jane come up alongside me in the Buick and the guy offers me a hundred bucks to let him wear my cap and drive my hack into town. I'm to hang around here an hour, then take his heap to the Carillon hotel on Towne Boulevard. My cab will be there for me. He gives me the hundred bucks."

"What was *his* story?" I asked.

"He said they'd been to a gambling joint and had some luck for a change. They're afraid of hold-ups on the way in. They figure there's always spotters watchin' the play."

I took one of his cigarettes and straightened it out in my fingers. "It's a story I can't hurt much," I said. "Could I see your cards?"

He gave them to me. His name was Tom Sneyd and he was a driver for the Green Top Cab Company. I corked my pint, slipped it into my side pocket, and danced a half dollar on the counter.

The clerk came along and made change. He was almost shaking with curiosity.

"Come on, Tom," I said in front of him. "Let's go get that cab. I don't think you should wait around here any longer."

We went out, and I let the Buick lead me away from the straggling lights of Las Olindas, through a series of small beach towns with little houses built on sandlots close to the ocean, and bigger ones built on the slopes of the hills behind. A window was lit here and there. The tires sang on the moist concrete and the little amber lights on the Buick's fenders peeped back at me from the curves.

At West Cimarron we turned inland, chugged on through

Canal City, and met the San Angelo Cut. It took us almost an hour to get to 5640 Towne Boulevard, which is the number of the Hotel Carillon. It is a big, rambling slate-roofed building with a basement garage and a forecourt fountain on which they play a pale green light in the evening.

Green Top Cab No. 469 was parked across the street, on the dark side. I couldn't see where anybody had been shooting into it. Tom Sneyd found his cap in the driver's compartment, climbed eagerly under the wheel.

"Does that fix me up? Can I go now?" His voice was strident with relief.

I told him it was all right with me, and gave him my card. It was twelve minutes past one as he took the corner. I climbed into the Buick and tooled it down the ramp to the garage and left it with a colored boy who was dusting cars in slow motion. I went around to the lobby.

The clerk was an ascetic-looking young man who was reading a volume of "California Appellate Decisions" under the switchboard light. He said Lou was not in and had not been in since eleven, when he came on duty. After a short argument about the lateness of the hour and the importance of my visit, he rang Lou's apartment, but there wasn't any answer.

I went out and sat in my Marmon for a few minutes, smoked a cigarette, imbibed a little from my pint of Canadian Club. Then I went back into the Carillon and shut myself in a pay-booth. I dialed the *Telegram*, asked for the City Desk, got a man named Von Ballin.

He yelped at me when I told him who I was. "You still walking around? That ought to be a story. I thought Manny Tinnen's friends would have had you laid away in old lavender by this time."

I said: "Can that and listen to this. Do you know a man named Lou Harger? He's a gambler. Had a place that was raided and closed up a month ago."

Von Ballin said he didn't know Lou personally, but knew who he was.

"Who around your rag would know him real well?"

He thought a moment. "There's a lad named Jerry Cross

here," he said, "that's supposed to be an expert on night life. What did you want to know?"

"Where he would go to celebrate," I said. Then I told him some of the story, not too much. I left out the part where I got sapped and the part about the taxi. "He hasn't shown at his hotel," I ended. "I ought to get a line on him."

"Well, if you're a friend of his—"

"Of his—not of his crowd," I said sharply.

Von Ballin stopped to yell at somebody to take a call, then said to me softly, close to the phone:

"Come through, boy. Come through."

"All right. But I'm talking to you, not to your sheet. I got sapped and lost my gun outside Canales' joint. Lou and his girl switched his car for a taxi they picked up. Then they dropped out of sight. I don't like it too well. Lou wasn't drunk enough to chase around town with that much dough in his pockets. And if he was, the girl wouldn't let him. She had the practical eye."

"I'll see what I can do," Von Ballin said. "But it don't sound promising. I'll give you a buzz."

I told him I lived at the Merritt Plaza, in case he had forgotten, went out and got into the Marmon again. I drove home and put hot towels on my head for fifteen minutes, then sat around in my pajamas and drank hot whiskey and lemon and called the Carillon every once in a while. At two-thirty Von Ballin called me and said no luck. Lou hadn't been pinched, he wasn't in any of the Receiving Hospitals, and he hadn't shown at any of the clubs Jerry Cross could think of.

At three I called the Carillon for the last time. Then I put my light out and went to sleep.

In the morning it was the same way. I tried to trace the red-haired girl a little. There were twenty-eight people named Glenn in the phone book, and three women among them. One didn't answer, the other two assured me they didn't have red hair. One offered to show me.

I shaved, showered, had breakfast, walked three blocks down the hill to the Condor Building.

Miss Glenn was sitting in my little reception room.

5

I unlocked the other door and she went in and sat in the chair where Lou had sat the afternoon before. I opened some windows, locked the outer door of the reception room, and struck a match for the unlighted cigarette she held in her ungloved and ringless left hand.

She was dressed in a blouse and plaid skirt with a loose coat over them, and a close-fitting hat that was far enough out of style to suggest a run of bad luck. But it hid almost all of her hair. Her skin was without make-up and she looked about thirty and had the set face of exhaustion.

She held her cigarette with a hand that was almost too steady, a hand on guard. I sat down and waited for her to talk.

She stared at the wall over my head and didn't say anything. After a little while I packed my pipe and smoked for a minute. Then I got up and went across to the door that opened into the hallway and picked up a couple of letters that had been pushed through the slot.

I sat down at the desk again, looked them over, read one of them twice, as if I had been alone. While I was doing this I didn't look at her directly or speak to her, but I kept an eye on her all the same. She looked like a lady who was getting nerved for something.

Finally she moved. She opened up a big black patent-leather bag and took out a fat manila envelope, pulled a rubber band off it and sat holding the envelope between the palms of her hands, with her head tilted way back and the cigarette dribbling gray smoke from the corner of her mouth.

She said slowly: "Lou said if I ever got caught in the rain, you were the boy to see. It's raining hard where I am."

I stared at the manila envelope. "Lou is a pretty good friend of mine," I said. "I'd do anything in reason for him. Some things not in reason—like last night. That doesn't mean Lou and I always play the same games."

She dropped her cigarette into the glass bowl of the ash tray and left it to smoke. A dark flame burned suddenly in her eyes, then went out.

"Lou is dead." Her voice was quite toneless.

I reached over with a pencil and stabbed at the hot end of the cigarette until it stopped smoking.

She went on: "A couple of Canales' boys got him in my apartment—with one shot from a small gun that looked like my gun. Mine was gone when I looked for it afterwards. I spent the night there with him, dead. . . . I had to."

She broke quite suddenly. Her eyes turned up in her head and her head came down and hit the desk. She lay still, with the manila envelope in front of her lax hands.

I jerked a drawer open and brought up a bottle and a glass, poured a stiff one and stepped around with it, heaved her up in her chair. I pushed the edge of the glass hard against her mouth—hard enough to hurt. She struggled and swallowed. Some of it ran down her chin, but life came back into her eyes.

I left the whiskey in front of her and sat down again. The flap of the envelope had come open enough for me to see currency inside, bales of currency.

She began to talk to me in a dreamy sort of voice.

"We got all big bills from the cashier, but it makes quite a package at that. There's twenty-two thousand even in the envelope. I kept out a few odd hundreds.

"Lou was worried. He figured it would be pretty easy for Canales to catch up with us. You might be right behind and not be able to do very much about it."

I said: "Canales lost the money in full view of everybody there. It was good advertising—even if it hurt."

She went on exactly as though I had not spoken. "Going through the town we spotted a cab driver sitting in his parked cab and Lou had a brain wave. He offered the boy a C note to let him drive the cab into San Angelo and bring the Buick to the hotel after a while. The boy took us up and we went over on another street and made the switch. We were sorry about ditching you, but Lou said you wouldn't mind. And we might get a chance to flag you.

"Lou didn't go into his hotel. We took another cab over to my place. I live at the Hobart Arms, eight hundred block on South Minter. It's a place where you don't have to answer questions at the desk. We went up to my apartment and put the lights on and two guys with masks came around the half-wall between the living-room and the dinette. One was small and thin and the other one was a big slob with a chin that stuck out under his mask like a shelf. Lou made a wrong motion and the big one shot him just the once. The gun just made a flat crack, not very loud, and Lou fell down on the floor and never moved."

I said: "It might be the ones that made a sucker out of me. I haven't told you about that yet."

She didn't seem to hear that either. Her face was white and composed, but as expressionless as plaster. "Maybe I'd better have another finger of the hooch," she said.

I poured us a couple of drinks, and we drank them. She went on.

"They went through us, but we didn't have the money. We had stopped at an all-night drug-store and had it weighed and mailed it at a branch post office. They went through the apartment, but of course we had just come in and hadn't had time to hide anything. The big one slammed me down with his fist, and when I woke up again they were gone and I was alone with Lou dead on the floor."

She pointed to a mark on the angle of her jaw. There was something there, but it didn't show much. I moved around in my chair a little and said:

"They passed you on the way in. Smart boys would have looked a taxi over on that road. How did they know where to go?"

"I thought that out during the night," Miss Glenn said. "Canales knows where I live. He followed me home once and tried to get me to ask him up."

"Yeah," I said, "but why did they go to your place and how did they get in?"

"That's not hard. There's a ledge just below the windows and a man could edge along it to the fire escape. They probably had other boys covering Lou's hotel. We thought of that chance, but we didn't think about my place being known to them."

"Tell me the rest of it," I said.

"The money was mailed to me," Miss Glenn explained. "Lou was a swell boy, but a girl has to protect herself. That's why I had to stay there last night with Lou dead on the floor. Until the mail came. Then I came over here."

I got up and looked out of the window. A fat girl was pounding a typewriter across the court. I could hear the clack of it. I sat down again, stared at my thumb.

"Did they plant the gun?" I asked.

"Not unless it's under him. I didn't look there."

"They let you off too easy. Maybe it wasn't Canales at all. Did Lou open his heart to you much?"

She shook her head quietly. Her eyes were slate-blue now, and thoughtful, without the blank stare.

"All right," I said. "Just what did you think of having me do about it all?"

She narrowed her eyes a little, then put a hand out and pushed the bulging envelope slowly across the desk.

"I'm no baby and I'm in a jam. But I'm not going to the cleaners just the same. Half of this money is mine, and I want it with a clean getaway. One-half net. If I'd called the law last night, there'd have been a way figured to chisel me out of it . . . I think Lou would like you to have his half, if you want to play with me."

I said: "It's big money to flash at a private dick, Miss Glenn," and smiled wearily. "You're a little worse off for not calling cops last night. But there's an answer to anything they might say. I think I'd better go over there and see what's broken, if anything."

She leaned forward quickly and said: "Will you take care of the money? . . . Dare you?"

"Sure. I'll pop downstairs and put it in a safe-deposit box. You can hold one of the keys—and we'll talk split later on. I think it would be a swell idea if Canales knew he had to see me, and still sweller if you hid out in a little hotel where I have a friend—at least until I nose around a bit."

She nodded. I put my hat on and put the envelope inside my belt. I went out, telling her there was a gun in the top left-hand drawer, if she felt nervous.

When I got back she didn't seem to have moved. But she said she had phoned Canales' place and left a message for him she thought he would understand.

We went by rather devious ways to the Lorraine, at Brant and Avenue C. Nobody shot at us going over, and as far as I could see we were not trailed.

I shook hands with Jim Dolan, the day clerk at the Lorraine, with a twenty folded in my hand. He put his hand in his pocket and said he would be glad to see that "Miss Thompson" was not bothered.

I left. There was nothing in the noon paper about Lou Harger of the Hobart Arms.

6

The Hobart Arms was just another apartment house, in a block lined with them. It was six stories high and had a buff front. A lot of cars were parked at both curbs all along the block. I drove through slowly and looked things over. The neighborhood didn't have the look of having been excited about anything in the immediate past. It was peaceful and sunny, and the parked cars had a settled look, as if they were right at home.

I circled into an alley with a high board fence on each side and a lot of flimsy garages cutting it. I parked beside one that had a For Rent sign and went between two garbage cans into the concrete yard of the Hobart Arms, along the side to the street. A man was putting golf clubs into the back of a coupé. In the lobby a Filipino was dragging a vacuum cleaner over the rug and a dark Jewess was writing at the switchboard.

I used the automatic elevator and prowled along an upper corridor to the last door on the left. I knocked, waited, knocked again, went in with Miss Glenn's key.

Nobody was dead on the floor.

I looked at myself in the mirror that was the back of a pull-down bed, went across and looked out of a window. There was a ledge below that had once been a coping. It ran along to the fire escape. A blind man could have walked in. I didn't notice anything like footmarks in the dust on it.

There was nothing in the dinette or kitchen except what belonged there. The bedroom had a cheerful carpet and painted gray walls. There was a lot of junk in the corner, around a wastebasket, and a broken comb on the dresser held a few strands of red hair. The closets were empty except for some gin bottles.

I went back to the living-room, looked behind the wall bed, stood around for a minute, left the apartment.

The Filipino in the lobby had made about three yards with the vacuum cleaner. I leaned on the counter beside the switchboard.

"Miss Glenn?"

The dark Jewess said: "Five-two-four," and made a check mark on the laundry list.

"She's not in. Has she been in lately?"

She glanced up at me, very briefly. "I haven't noticed. What is it— a bill?"

I said I was just a friend, thanked her and went away. That established the fact that there had been no excitement in Miss Glenn's apartment. I went back to the alley and the Marmon.

I hadn't believed it quite the way Miss Glenn told it anyhow.

I crossed Cordova, drove a block and stopped beside a forgotten drug-store that slept behind two giant pepper trees and a dusty, cluttered window. It had a single pay-booth in the corner. An old man shuffled towards me wistfully, then went away when he saw what I wanted, lowered a pair of steel spectacles on to the end of his nose and sat down again with his newspaper.

I dropped my nickel, dialed, and a girl's voice said: *"Tele-grayam!"* with a tinny drawl. I asked for Von Ballin.

When I got him and he knew who it was I could hear him clearing his throat. Then his voice came close to the phone and said very distinctly:

"I've got something for you, but it's bad. I'm sorry as all hell. Your friend Harger is in the morgue. We got the flash about ten minutes ago."

I leaned against the wall of the booth and felt my eyes getting haggard. I said: "What else did you get?"

"Couple of radio cops picked him up in somebody's front yard or something, in West Cimarron. He was shot through the heart. It happened last night, but for some reason they only just put out the identification."

I said: "West Cimarron, huh? . . . Well, that takes care of that. I'll be in to see you."

I thanked him and hung up, stood for a moment looking out through the glass at a middle-aged gray-haired man who had come into the store and was pawing over the magazine rack.

Then I dropped another nickel and dialed the Lorraine, asked for the clerk.

I said: "Get your girl to put me on to the red-head, will you, Jim?"

I got a cigarette out and lit it, puffed smoke at the glass of the door. The smoke flattened out against the glass and swirled about in the close air. Then the line clicked and the operator's voice said:

"Sorry, your party does not answer."

"Give me Jim again," I said. Then, when he answered, "Can you take time to run up and find out why she doesn't answer the phone? Maybe she's just being cagey."

Jim said: "You bet. I'll shoot right up with a key."

Sweat was coming out all over me. I put the receiver down on a little shelf and jerked the booth door open. The gray-haired man looked up quickly from the magazines, then scowled and looked at his watch. Smoke poured out of the booth. After a moment I kicked the door shut and picked up the receiver again.

Jim's voice seemed to come to me from a long way off. "She's not here. Maybe she went for a walk."

I said: "Yeah—or maybe it was a ride."

I pronged the receiver and pushed on out of the booth. The gray-haired stranger slammed a magazine down so hard that it fell to the floor. He stooped to pick it up as I went past him. Then he straightened up just behind me and said quietly, but very firmly:

"Keep the hands down, and quiet. Walk on out to your heap. This is business."

Out of the corner of my eye I could see the old man peeking short-sightedly at us. But there wasn't anything for him to see, even if he could see that far. Something prodded my back. It might have been a finger, but I didn't think it was.

We went out of the store very peacefully.

A long gray car had stopped close behind the Marmon. Its rear door was open and a man with a square face and a crooked mouth was standing with one foot out on the running-board. His right hand was behind him, inside the car.

My man's voice said: "Get in your car and drive west. Take this first corner and go about twenty-five, not more."

The narrow street was sunny and quiet and the pepper trees whispered. Traffic threshed by on Cordova a short block away. I shrugged, opened the door of my car and got under the wheel. The gray-haired man got in very quickly beside me, watching my hands. He swung his right hand around, with a snub-nosed gun in it.

"Careful getting your keys out, buddy."

I was careful. As I stepped on the starter a car door slammed behind, there were rapid steps, and someone got into the back seat of the Marmon. I let in the clutch and drove around the corner. In the mirror I could see the gray car making the turn behind. Then it dropped back a little.

I drove west on a street that paralleled Cordova and when we had gone a block and a half a hand came down over my shoulder from behind and took my gun away from me. The gray-haired man rested his short revolver on his leg and felt me over carefully with his free hand. He leaned back satisfied.

"Okey. Drop over to the main drag and snap it up," he said. "But that don't mean trying to sideswipe a prowl car, if you lamp one . . . Or if you think it does, try it and see."

I made the two turns, speeded up to thirty-five and held it there. We went through some nice residential districts, and then the landscape began to thin out. When it was quite thin the gray car behind dropped back, turned towards town and disappeared.

"What's the snatch for?" I asked.

The gray-haired man laughed and rubbed his broad red chin. "Just business. The big boy wants to talk to you."

"Canales?"

"Canales—hell! I said the *big boy*."

I watched traffic, what there was of it that far out, and didn't speak for a few minutes. Then I said:

"Why didn't you pull it in the apartment, or in the alley?"

"Wanted to make sure you wasn't covered."

"Who's this big boy?"

"Skip that—till we get you there. Anything else?"

"Yes. Can I smoke?"

He held the wheel while I lit up. The man in the back seat hadn't said a word at any time. After a while the gray-haired man made me pull up and move over, and he drove.

"I used to own one of these, six years ago, when I was poor," he said jovially.

I couldn't think of a really good answer to that, so I just let smoke seep down into my lungs and wondered why, if Lou had been killed in West Cimarron, the killers didn't get the money. And if he really had been killed at Miss Glenn's apartment, why somebody had taken the trouble to carry him back to West Cimarron.

7

In twenty minutes we were in the foothills. We went over a hogback, drifted down a long white concrete ribbon, crossed a bridge, went halfway up the next slope and turned off on a gravel road that disappeared around a shoulder of scrub oak and manzanita. Plumes of pampas grass flared on the side of the hill, like jets of water. The wheels crunched on the gravel and skidded on the curves.

We came to a mountain cabin with a wide porch and cemented boulder foundations. The windmill of a generator turned slowly on the crest of a spur a hundred feet behind the cabin. A mountain blue jay flashed across the road, zoomed, banked sharply, and fell out of sight like a stone.

The gray-haired man tooled the car up to the porch, beside a tan colored Lincoln coupé, switched off the ignition and set the Marmon's long parking brake. He took the keys out, folded them carefully in their leather case, put the case away in his pocket.

The man in the back seat got out and held the door beside me open. He had a gun in his hand. I got out. The gray-haired man got out. We all went into the house.

There was a big room with walls of knotted pine, beautifully polished. We went across it walking on Indian rugs and the gray-haired man knocked carefully on a door.

A voice shouted: "What is it?"

The gray-haired man put his face against the door and said: "Beasley—and the guy you wanted to talk to."

The voice inside said to come on in. Beasley opened the door, pushed me through it and shut it behind me.

It was another big room with knotted pine walls and Indian rugs on the floor. A driftwood fire hissed and puffed on a stone hearth.

The man who sat behind a flat desk was Frank Dorr, the politico.

He was the kind of man who liked to have a desk in front of him, and shove his fat stomach against it, and fiddle with things on it, and look very wise. He had a fat, muddy face, a thin fringe of white hair that stuck up a little, small sharp eyes, small and very delicate hands.

What I could see of him was dressed in a slovenly gray suit, and there was a large black Persian cat on the desk in front of him. He was scratching the cat's head with one of his little neat hands and the cat was leaning against his hand. Its bushy tail flowed over the edge of the desk and fell straight down.

He said: "Sit down," without looking away from the cat.

I sat down in a leather chair with a very low seat. Dorr said: "How do you like it up here? Kind of nice, ain't it? This is Toby, my girl-friend. Only girl-friend I got. Ain't you, Toby?"

I said: "I like it up here—but I don't like the way I got here."

Dorr raised his head a few inches and looked at me with his mouth slightly open. He had beautiful teeth, but they hadn't grown in his mouth. He said:

"I'm a busy man, brother. It was simpler than arguing. Have a drink?"

"Sure I'll have a drink," I said.

He squeezed the cat's head gently between his two palms, then pushed it away from him and put both hands down on the arms of his chair. He shoved hard and his face got a little red and he finally got up on his feet. He waddled across to a built-in cabinet and took out a squat decanter of whiskey and two gold-veined glasses.

"No ice today," he said, waddling back to the desk. "Have to drink it straight."

He poured two drinks, gestured, and I went over and got mine. He sat down again. I sat down with my drink. Dorr lit a long brown cigar, pushed the box two inches in my direction, leaned back and stared at me with complete relaxation.

"You're the guy that fingered Manny Tinnen," he said. "It won't do."

I sipped my whiskey. It was good enough to sip.

"Life gets complicated at times," Dorr went on, in the same even, relaxed voice. "Politics—even when it's a lot of fun—is tough on the nerves. You know me. I'm tough, and I get what I want. There ain't a hell of a lot I want any more, but what I want—I want bad. And I ain't so damn' particular how I get it."

"You have that reputation," I said politely.

Dorr's eyes twinkled. He looked around for the cat, dragged it towards him by the tail, pushed it down on its side and began to rub its stomach. The cat seemed to like it.

Dorr looked at me and said very softly: "You bumped Lou Harger."

"What makes you think so?" I asked, without any particular emphasis.

"You bumped Harger. Maybe he needed the bump—but you gave it to him. He was shot once through the heart, with a .32. You wear a .32 and you're known to be a fancy shot with it. You were with Harger at Las Olindas last night and saw him win a lot of money. You were supposed to be acting as bodyguard for him, but you got a better idea. You caught up with him and that girl in West Cimarron, slipped Harger the dose and got the money."

I finished my whiskey, got up and poured myself some more of it.

"You made a deal with the girl," Dorr said, "but the deal didn't stick. She got a cute idea. But that don't matter, because the police got your gun along with Harger. And you got the dough."

I said: "Is there a tag out for me?"

"Not till I give the word . . . And the gun hasn't been turned in . . . I got a lot of friends, you know."

I said slowly: "I got sapped outside Canales' place. It served me right. My gun was taken from me. I never caught up with Harger, never saw him again. The girl came to me this morning with the money in an envelope and a story that Harger had been killed in her apartment. That's how I have the money—for safekeeping. I wasn't sure about the girl's story, but her bringing the money carried a lot of weight. And Harger was a friend of mine. I started out to investigate."

"You should have let the cops do that," Dorr said with a grin.

"There was a chance the girl was being framed. Besides there was a possibility I might make a few dollars—legitimately. It has been done, even in San Angelo."

Dorr stuck a finger towards the cat's face and the cat bit it, with an absent expression. Then it pulled away from him, sat down on a corner of the desk and began to lick one toe.

"Twenty-two grand, and the jane passed it over to you to keep," Dorr said. "Ain't that just like a jane?"

I stared at the amber fluid in my glass, shook it round gently.

"You got the dough," Dorr said. "Harger was killed with your gun. The girl's gone—but I could bring her back. I think she'd make a good witness, if we needed one."

"Was the play at Las Olindas crooked?" I asked.

Dorr finished his drink and curled his lips around his cigar again. "Sure," he said carelessly. "The croupier—a guy named Pina—was in on it. The wheel was wired for the double-zero. The old crap. Copper button in the floor, copper button on Pina's shoe sole, wires up his leg, batteries in his hip pockets. The old crap."

I said: "Canales didn't act as if he knew about it."

Dorr chuckled. "He knew the wheel was wired. He didn't know his head croupier was playin' on the other team."

"I'd hate to be Pina," I said.

Dorr made a negligent motion with his cigar. "He's taken care of . . . The play was careful and quiet. They didn't make any fancy long shots, just even money bets, and they didn't win all the time. They couldn't. No wired wheel is that good."

I shrugged, moved around in my chair. "You know a hell of a lot about it," I said. "Was all this just to get me set for a squeeze?"

He grinned softly. "Hell, no! Some of it just happened— the way the best plants do." He waved his cigar again, and a pale gray tendril of smoke curled past his cunning little eyes. There was a muffled sound of talk in the outside room. "I got connections I got to please—even if I don't like all their capers," he added simply.

"Like Manny Tinnen?" I said. "He was around City Hall a lot, knew too much. Okey, Mister Dorr. Just what do you figure on having me do for you? Commit suicide?"

He laughed. His fat shoulders shook cheerfully. He put one of his small hands out with the palm towards me. "I wouldn't think of that," he said dryly, "and the other way's better business. The way public opinion is about the Shannon kill. I ain't sure that louse of a D.A. wouldn't convict Tinnen without you—if he could sell the folks the idea you'd been knocked off to button your mouth."

I got up out of my chair, went over and leaned on the desk, leaned across it towards Dorr.

He said: "No funny business!" a little sharply and breath-lessly. His hand went to a drawer and got it half open. His movements with his hands were very quick by contrast with the movements of his body.

I smiled down at the hand and he took it away from the drawer. I saw a gun just inside the drawer.

I said: "I've already talked to the Grand Jury."

Dorr leaned back and smiled at me. "Guys make mistakes," he said. "Even smart private dicks . . . You could have a change of heart—and put it in writing."

I said very softly: "No. I'd be under a perjury rap—which I couldn't beat. I'd rather be under a murder rap—which I can beat. Especially as Fenweather will *want* me to beat it. He won't want to spoil me as a witness. The Tinnen case is too important to him."

Dorr said evenly: "Then you'll have to try and beat it, brother. And after you get through beating it there'll still be enough mud on your neck so no jury'll convict Manny on your say-so alone."

I put my hand out slowly and scratched the cat's ear. "What about the twenty-two grand?"

"It *could* be all yours, if you want to play. After all, it ain't my money . . . If Manny gets clear, I might add a little something that *is* my money."

I tickled the cat under its chin. It began to purr. I picked it up and held it gently in my arms.

"Who did kill Lou Harger, Dorr?" I asked, not looking at him.

He shook his head. I looked at him, smiling. "Swell cat you have," I said.

Dorr licked his lips. "I think the little —— likes you," he grinned. He looked pleased at the idea.

I nodded — and threw the cat in his face.

He yelped, but his hands came up to catch the cat. The cat twisted neatly in the air and landed with both front paws working. One of them split Dorr's cheek like a banana peel. He yelled very loudly.

I had the gun out of the drawer and the muzzle of it into the back of Dorr's neck when Beasley and the square-faced man dodged in.

For an instant there was a sort of tableau. Then the cat tore itself loose from Dorr's arms, shot to the floor and went under the desk. Beasley raised his snub-nosed gun, but he didn't look as if he was certain what he meant to do with it.

I shoved the muzzle of mine hard into Dorr's neck and said: "Frankie gets it first, boys . . . And that's not a gag."

Dorr grunted in front of me. "Take it easy," he growled to his hoods. He took a handkerchief from his breast pocket and began to dab at his split and bleeding cheek with it. The man with the crooked mouth began to sidle along the wall.

I said: "Don't get the idea I'm enjoying this, but I'm not foolin' either. You heels stay put."

The man with the crooked mouth stopped sidling and gave me a nasty leer. He kept his hands low.

Dorr half-turned his head and tried to talk over his shoulder to me. I couldn't see enough of his face to get any expression, but he didn't seem scared. He said:

"This won't get you anything. I could have you knocked off easy enough, if that was what I wanted. Now where are you? You can't shoot anybody without getting in a worse jam than if you did what I asked you to. It looks like a stalemate to me."

I thought that over for a moment while Beasley looked at me quite pleasantly, as though it was all just routine to him. There was nothing pleasant about the other man. I listened hard, but the rest of the house seemed to be quite silent.

Dorr edged forward from the gun and said: "Well?"

I said: "I'm going out. I have a gun and it looks like a gun that I could hit somebody with, if I have to. I don't want to very much, and if you'll have Beasley throw my keys over and the other one turn back the gun he took from me, I'll forget all about the snatch."

Dorr moved his arms in the lazy beginning of a shrug. "Then what?"

"Figure out your deal a little closer," I said. "If you get enough protection behind me, I might throw in with you . . . And if you're as tough as you think you are, a few hours won't cut any ice one way or the other."

"It's an idea," Dorr said and chuckled. Then to Beasley: "Keep your rod to yourself and give him his keys. Also his gun—the one you got today."

Beasley sighed and very carefully inserted a hand into his pants. He tossed my leather keycase across the room near the end of the desk. The man with the twisted mouth put his hand up, edged it inside his side-pocket and I eased down behind Dorr's back, while he did it. He came out with my gun, let it fall to the floor and kicked it away from him.

I came out from behind Dorr's back, got my keys and the gun up off the floor, moved sidewise towards the door of the room. Dorr watched me with an empty stare that meant nothing. Beasley followed me around with his body and stepped away from the door as I neared it. The other man had trouble holding himself quiet.

I got to the door and reversed a key that was in it. Dorr said dreamily:

"You're just like one of those rubber balls on the end of an elastic. The farther you get away, the suddener you'll bounce back."

I said: "The elastic might be a little rotten," and went through the door, turned the key in it and braced myself for shots that didn't come. As a bluff, mine was thinner than the gold on a week-end wedding ring. It worked because Dorr let it, and that was all.

I got out of the house, got the Marmon started and wrangled it around and sent it skidding past the shoulder of the hill and so on down to the highway. There was no sound of anything coming after me.

When I reached the concrete highway bridge it was a little past two o'clock, and I drove with one hand for a while and wiped the sweat off the back of my neck.

8

The morgue was at the end of a long and bright and silent corridor that branched off from behind the main lobby of the County Building. The corridor ended in two doors and a blank wall faced with marble. One door had "Inquest Room" lettered on a glass panel behind which there was no light. The other opened into a small, cheerful office.

A man with gander-blue eyes and rust-colored hair parted in the exact center of his head was pawing over some printed forms at a table. He looked up, looked me over, and then suddenly smiled.

I said: "Hello, Landon . . . Remember the Shelby case?"

The bright blue eyes twinkled. He got up and came around the table with his hand out. "Sure. What can we do—" He broke off suddenly and snapped his fingers. "Hell! You're the guy that put the bee on that hot rod."

I tossed a butt through the open door into the corridor. "That's not why I'm here," I said. "Anyhow not this time. There's a fellow named Louis Harger . . . picked up shot last night or this morning, in West Cimarron, as I get it. Could I take a look-see?"

"They can't stop you," Landon said.

He led the way through a door on the far side of his office into a place that was all white paint and white enamel and glass and bright light. Against one wall was a double tier of large bins with glass windows in them. Through the peep-holes showed bundles in white sheeting, and, further back, frosted pipes.

A body covered with a sheet lay on a table that was high at the head and sloped down to the foot. Landon pulled the sheet down casually from a man's dead, placid, yellowish face. Long black hair lay loosely on a small pillow, with the dankness of water still in it. The eyes were half open and stared incuriously at the ceiling.

I stepped close, looked at the face. Landon pulled the sheet on down and rapped his knuckles on a chest that rang hollowly, like a board. There was a bullet hole over the heart.

"Nice clean shot," he said.

I turned away quickly, got a cigarette out and rolled it around in my fingers. I stared at the floor.

"Who identified him?"

"Stuff in his pockets," Landon said. "We're checking his prints, of course. You know him?"

I said: "Yes."

Landon scratched the base of his chin softly with his thumbnail. We walked back into the office and Landon went behind his table and sat down.

He thumbed over some papers, separated one from the pile and studied it for a moment.

He said: "A sheriff's radio car found him at twelve thirty-five a.m., on the side of the old road out of West Cimarron, a quarter of a mile from where the cut-off starts. That isn't traveled much, but the prowl car takes a slant down it now and then looking for petting parties."

I said: "Can you say how long he had been dead?"

"Not very long. He was still warm, and the nights are cool along there."

I put my unlighted cigarette in my mouth and moved it up and down with my lips. "And I bet you took a steel-jacketed .32 out of him," I said.

"How did you know that?" Landon asked quickly.

"I just guess. It's that sort of hole."

He stared at me with bright, interested eyes. I thanked him, said I'd be seeing him, went through the door and lit my cigarette in the corridor. I walked back to the elevators and got into one, rode to the seventh floor, then went along another corridor exactly like the one below except that it didn't lead to the morgue. It led to some small, bare offices that were used by the District Attorney's investigators. Halfway along I opened a door and went into one of them.

Bernie Ohls was sitting humped loosely at a desk placed against the wall. He was the chief investigator Fenweather had told me to see, if I got into any kind of a jam. He was a medium-sized blond man with white eyebrows and an outthrust, very deeply cleft chin. There was another desk against the other wall, a couple of hard chairs, a brass spittoon on a rubber mat and very little else.

Ohls nodded casually at me, got out of his chair and fixed the door latch. Then he got a flat tin of little cigars out of his desk, lit one of them, pushed the tin along the desk and stared at me along his nose. I sat down in one of the straight chairs and tilted it back.

Ohls said: "Well?"

"It's Lou Harger," I said. "I thought maybe it wasn't."

"The hell you did. I could have told you it was Harger."

Somebody tried the handle of the door, then knocked. Ohls paid no attention. Whoever it was went away.

I said slowly: "He was killed between eleven-thirty and twelve thirty-five. There was just time for the job to be done where he was found. There wasn't time for it to be done the way the girl said. There wasn't time for me to do it."

Ohls said: "Yeah. Maybe you could prove that. And then maybe you could prove a friend of yours didn't do it with your gun."

I said: "A friend of mine wouldn't be likely to do it with my gun—if he was a friend of mine."

Ohls grunted, smiled sourly at me sidewise. He said: "Most anyone would think that. That's why he might have done it."

I let the legs of my chair settle to the floor. I stared at him.

"Would I come and tell you about the money and the gun—everything that ties me to it?"

Ohls said expressionlessly: "You would—if you knew damn' well somebody else had already told it for you."

I said: "Dorr wouldn't lose much time."

I pinched my cigarette out and flipped it towards the brass cuspidor. Then I stood up.

"Okey. There's no tag out for me yet—so I'll go over and tell my story."

Ohls said: "Sit down a minute."

I sat down. He took his little cigar out of his mouth and flung it away from him with a savage gesture. It rolled along the brown linoleum and smoked in the corner. He put his arms down on the desk and drummed with the fingers of both hands. His lower lip came forward and pressed his upper lip back against his teeth.

"Dorr probably knows you're here now," he said. "The only reason you ain't in the tank upstairs is they're not sure but it would be better to knock you off and take a chance. If Fenweather loses the election, I'll be all washed up—if I mess around with you."

I said: "If he convicts Manny Tinnen, he won't lose the election."

Ohls took another of the little cigars out of the box and lit it. He picked his hat off the desk, fingered it a moment, put it on.

"Why'd the red-head give you that song and dance about the bump in her apartment, the stiff on the floor—all that hot comedy?"

"They wanted me to go over there. They figured I'd go to see if a gun was planted—maybe just to check up on her. That got me away from the busy part of town. They could tell better if the D.A. had any boys watching my blind side."

"That's just a guess," Ohls said sourly.

I said: "Sure."

Ohls swung his thick legs around, planted his feet hard and leaned his hands on his knees. The little cigar twitched in the corner of his mouth.

"I'd like to get to know some of these guys that let loose of twenty-two grand just to color up a fairy tale," he said nastily.

I stood up again and went past him towards the door.

Ohls said: "What's the hurry?"

I turned around and shrugged, looked at him blankly. "You don't act very interested," I said.

He climbed to his feet, said wearily:

"The hack driver's most likely a dirty little crook. But it might just be Dorr's lads don't know he rates in this. Let's go get him while his memory's fresh."

9

The Green Top Garage was on Deviveras, three blocks east of Main. I pulled the Marmon up in front of a fire-plug and got out. Ohls slumped in the seat and growled:

"I'll stay here. Maybe I can spot a tail."

I went into a huge echoing garage, in the inner gloom of which a few brand new paint jobs were splashes of sudden color. There was a small, dirty, glass-walled office in the corner and a short man sat there with a derby hat on the back of his head and a red tie under his stubbled chin. He was whittling tobacco into the palm of his hand.

I said: "You the dispatcher?"

"Yeah."

"I'm looking for one of your drivers," I said. "Name of Tom Sneyd."

He put down the knife and the plug and began to grind the cut tobacco between his two palms. "What's the beef?" he asked cautiously.

"No beef. I'm a friend of his."

"More friends, huh? . . . He works nights, mister . . . So he's home I guess. Seventeen twenty-three Renfrew. That's over by Gray Lake."

I said: "Thanks. Phone?"

"No phone."

I pulled a folded city map from an inside pocket and unfolded part of it on the table in front of his nose. He looked annoyed.

"There's a big one on the wall," he growled, and began to pack a short pipe with his tobacco.

"I'm used to this one," I said. I bent over the spread map, looking for Renfrew Street. Then I stopped and looked suddenly at the face of the man in the derby. "You remembered that address damn' quick," I said.

He put his pipe in his mouth, bit hard on it, and pushed two thick fingers into the pocket of his open vest.

"Couple other muggs was askin' for it a while back."

I folded the map very quickly and shoved it back into my pocket as I went through the door. I jumped across the sidewalk, slid under the wheel, and plunged at the starter.

"We're headed," I told Bernie Ohls. "Two guys got the kid's address there a while back. It might be — "

Ohls grabbed the side of the car and swore as we took the corner on squealing tires. I bent forward over the wheel and drove hard. There was a red light at Central. I swerved into a corner service station, went through the pumps, popped out on Central and jostled through some traffic to make a right turn east again.

A colored traffic cop blew a whistle at me and then stared hard as if trying to read the license number. I kept on going.

Warehouses, a produce market, a big gas tank, more warehouses, railroad tracks, and two bridges dropped behind us. I beat three traffic signals by a hair and went right through a fourth. Six blocks on I got the siren from a motor-cycle cop. Ohls passed me a bronze star and I flashed it out of the car, twisting it so the sun caught it. The siren stopped. The motor-cycle kept right behind us for another dozen blocks, then sheered off.

Gray Lake is an artificial reservoir in a cut between two groups of hills, on the east fringe of San Angelo. Narrow but expensively paved streets wind around in the hills, describing elaborate curves along their flanks for the benefit of a few cheap and scattered bungalows.

We plunged up into the hills, reading street signs on the run. The gray silk of the lake dropped away from us and the exhaust of the old Marmon roared between crumbling banks that shed dirt down on the unused sidewalks. Mongrel dogs quartered in the wild grass among the gopher holes.

Renfrew was almost at the top. Where it began there was a small neat bungalow in front of which a child in a diaper and nothing else fumbled around in a wire pen on a patch of lawn. Then there was a stretch without houses. Then there were two houses, then the road dropped, slipped in and out of sharp turns, went between banks high enough to put the whole street in shadow.

Then a gun roared around a bend ahead of us.

Ohls sat up sharply, said: "Oh-oh! That's no rabbit gun," slipped his service pistol out and unlatched the door on his side.

We came out of the turn and saw two more houses on the down side of the hill, with a couple of steep lots between them. A long gray car was slewed across the street in the space between the two houses. Its left front tire was flat and both its front doors were wide open, like the spread ears of an elephant.

A small, dark-faced man was kneeling on both knees in the street beside the open right-hand door. His right arm hung loose from his shoulder and there was blood on the hand that belonged to it. With his other hand he was trying to pick up an automatic from the concrete in front of him.

I skidded the Marmon to a fast stop and Ohls tumbled out. "Drop that, you!" he yelled.

The man with the limp arm snarled, relaxed, fell back against the running board, and a shot came from behind the car and snapped in the air not very far from my ear. I was out on the road by that time. The gray car was angled enough towards the houses so that I couldn't see any part of its left side except the open door. The shot seemed to come from about there. Ohls put two slugs into the door. I dropped, looked under the car and saw a pair of feet. I shot at them and missed.

About that time there was a thin but very sharp crack from the corner of the nearest house and a small puff of smoke drifted up from some bushes on the edge of the bank. Glass broke in the gray car. The gun behind it roared and plaster jumped out of the corner of the house wall, above the bushes. Then I saw the upper part of a man's body in the bushes. He was lying downhill on his stomach and he had a light rifle to his shoulder.

He was Tom Sneyd, the taxi driver.

Ohls grunted and charged the gray car. He fired twice more into the door, then dodged down behind the hood. More explosions occurred behind the car. I kicked the wounded man's gun out of his way, slid past him and sneaked a look over the gas tank. But the man behind had had too many angles to figure.

He was a big man in a brown suit and he made a clatter running hard for the lip of the hill between the two bunga-lows. Ohls' gun roared. The man whirled and snapshot with-out stopping. Ohls was in the open now. I saw his hat jerk off his head. I saw him stand squarely on well-spread feet, steady his pistol as if he was on the police range.

But the big man was already sagging. My bullet had drilled through his neck. Ohls fired at him very carefully as he fell and the sixth and last slug from his gun caught the man in the chest and twisted him around. The side of his head slapped the curb with a sickening crunch.

We walked towards him from opposite ends of the car. Ohls leaned down, heaved the man over on his back. His face in death had a loose, amiable expression, in spite of the blood all over his neck. Ohls began to go through his pockets.

I looked back to see what the other one was doing. He wasn't doing anything but sitting on the running board hold-ing his right arm against his side and grimacing with pain.

Tom Sneyd scrambled up the bank and came towards us.

Ohls said: "It's a guy named Poke Andrews. I've seen him around the poolrooms." He stood up and brushed off his knee. He had some odds and ends in his left hand. "Yeah, Poke Andrews. Gun work by the day, hour or week. I guess there was a livin' in it—for a while."

"It's not the guy that sapped me," I said. "But it's the guy I was looking at when I got sapped. And if the red-head was giving out any truth at all this morning, it's likely the guy that shot Lou Harger."

Ohls nodded, went over and got his hat. There was a hole in the brim. "I wouldn't be surprised at all," he said, putting the hat on calmly.

Tom Sneyd stood in front of us with his little rifle held rigidly across his chest. He was hatless and coatless, and had sneakers on his feet. His eyes were bright and mad, and he was beginning to shake.

"I knew I'd get them babies!" he crowed. "I knew I'd fix them ——'s!" Then he stopped talking and his face began to change color. It got green. He leaned down slowly, dropped his rifle, put both his hands on his bent knees.

Ohls said: "You better go lay down somewhere, Buddy. If I'm any judge of color, you're goin' to shoot your cookies."

10

Tom Sneyd was lying on his back on a day bed in the front room of his little bungalow. There was a wet towel across his forehead. A little girl with honey-colored hair was sitting beside him, holding his hand. A young woman with hair a couple of shades darker than the little girl's sat in the corner and looked at Tom Sneyd with tired ecstasy.

It was very hot when we came in. All the windows were shut and all the blinds down. Ohls opened a couple of front windows and sat down beside them, looked out towards the gray car. The dark Mexican was anchored to its steering wheel by his good wrist.

"It was what they said about my little girl," Tom Sneyd said from under the towel. "That's what sent me screwy. They said they'd come back and get her, if I didn't play with them."

Ohls said: "Okey, Tom. Let's have it from the start." He put one of his little cigars in his mouth, looked at Tom Sneyd doubtfully, and didn't light it.

I sat in a very hard Windsor chair and looked down at the cheap, new carpet.

"I was readin' a mag, waiting for time to eat and go to work," Tom Sneyd said carefully. "The little girl opened the door. They come in with guns on us, got us all in here and shut the windows. They pulled down all the blinds but one and the Mex sat by that and kept looking out. He never said a word. The big guy sat on the bed here and made me tell him all about last night—twice. Then he said I was to forget I'd met anybody or come into town with anybody. The rest was okey."

Ohls nodded and said: "What time did you first see this man here?"

"I didn't notice," Tom Sneyd said. "Say eleven-thirty, quarter of twelve. I checked in to the office at one-fifteen, right after I got my hack at the Carillon. It took us a good hour to make town from the beach. We was in the drug-store talkin' say fifteen minutes, maybe longer."

"That figures back to around midnight when you met him," Ohls said.

Tom Sneyd shook his head and the towel fell down over his face. He pushed it back up again.

"Well, no," Tom Sneyd said. "The guy in the drug-store told me he closed up at twelve. He wasn't closing up when we left."

Ohls turned his head and looked at me without expression. He looked back at Tom Sneyd. "Tell us the rest about the two gunnies," he said.

"The big guy said most likely I wouldn't have to talk to anybody about it. If I did and talked right, they'd be back with some dough. If I talked wrong, they'd be back for my little girl."

"Go on," Ohls said. "They're full of crap."

"They went away. When I saw them go on up the street I got screwy. Renfrew is just a pocket — one of them graft jobs. It goes on around the hill half a mile, then stops. There's no way to get off it. So they had to come back this way . . . I got my .22, which is all the gun I have, and hid in the bushes. I got the tire with the second shot. I guess they thought it was a blowout. I missed with the next and that put 'em wise. They got guns loose. I got the Mex then, and the big guy ducked behind the car . . . That's all there was to it. Then you come along."

Ohls flexed his thick, hard fingers and smiled grimly at the girl in the corner. "Who lives in the next house, Tom?"

"A man named Grandy, a motorman on the interurban. He lives all alone. He's at work now."

"I didn't guess he was home," Ohls grinned. He got up and went over and patted the little girl on the head. "You'll have to come down and make a statement, Tom."

"Sure." Tom Sneyd's voice was tired, listless. "I guess I lose my job, too, for rentin' out the hack last night."

"I ain't so sure about that," Ohls said softly. "Not if your boss likes guys with a few guts to run his hacks."

He patted the little girl on the head again, went towards the door and opened it. I nodded at Tom Sneyd and followed Ohls out of the house. Ohls said quietly:

"He don't know about the kill yet. No need to spring it in front of the kid."

We went over to the gray car. We had got some sacks out of the basement and spread them over the late Andrews, weighted them down with stones. Ohls glanced that way and said absently:

"I got to get to where there's a phone pretty quick."

He leaned on the door of the car and looked in at the Mexican. The Mexican sat with his head back and his eyes half closed and a drawn expression on his brown face. His left wrist was shackled to the spider of the wheel.

"What's your name?" Ohls snapped at him.

"Luis Cadena," the Mexican said it in a soft voice, without opening his eyes any wider.

"Which one of you heels scratched the guy at West Cimarron last night?"

"No understand, señor," the Mexican said purringly.

"Don't go dumb on me, spig," Ohls said dispassionately. "It gets me sore." He leaned on the window and rolled his little cigar around in his mouth.

The Mexican looked faintly amused and at the same time very tired. The blood on his right hand had dried black.

Ohls said: "Andrews scratched the guy in a taxi at West Cimarron. There was a girl along. We got the girl. You have a lousy chance to prove you weren't in on it."

Light flickered and died behind the Mexican's half-open eyes. He smiled with a glint of small white teeth.

Ohls said: "What did he do with the gun?"

"No understand, señor."

Ohls said: "He's tough. When they get tough it scares me."

He walked away from the car and scuffed some loose dirt from the sidewalk beside the sacks that draped the dead man. His toe gradually uncovered the contractor's stencil in the cement. He read it out loud:

"Dorr Paving and Construction Company, San Angelo. It's a wonder the fat —— wouldn't stay in his own racket."

I stood beside Ohls and looked down the hill between the two houses. Sudden flashes of light darted from the windshields of cars going along the boulevard that fringed Gray Lake, far below.

Ohls said: "Well?"

I said: "The killers knew about the taxi—maybe—and the girl friend reached town with the swag. So it wasn't Canales' job. Canales isn't the boy to let anybody play around with twenty-two grand of his money. The red-head was in on the kill, and it was done for a reason."

Ohls grinned. "Sure. It was done so you could be framed for it."

I said: "It's a shame how little account some folks take of human life—or twenty-two grand. Harger was knocked off so I could be framed and the dough was passed to me to make the frame tighter."

"Maybe they thought you'd highball," Ohls grunted. "That would sew you up right."

I rolled a cigarette around in my fingers. "That would have been a little too dumb, even for me. What do we do now? Wait till the moon comes up so we can sing—or go down the hill and tell some little white lies?"

Ohls spat on one of Poke Andrews' sacks. He said gruffly: "This is county land here. I could take all this mess over to the sub-station at Solano and keep it hush-hush for a while. The hackdriver would be tickled to death to keep it under the hat. And I've gone far enough so I'd like to get the Mex in the goldfish room with me personal."

"I'd like it that way too," I said. "I guess you can't hold it down there for long, but you might hold it down long enough for me to see a fat boy about a cat."

11

It was late afternoon when I got back to the hotel. The clerk handed me a slip which read: "Please phone F. D. as soon as possible."

I went upstairs and drank some liquor that was in the bottom of a bottle. Then I phoned down for another pint, scraped my chin, changed clothes and looked up Frank Dorr's number in the book. He lived in a beautiful old house on Greenview Park Crescent.

I made myself a tall smooth one with a tinkle and sat down in an easy chair with the phone at my elbow. I got a maid

first. Then I got a man who spoke Mister Dorr's name as
though he thought it might blow up in his mouth. After him
I got a voice with a lot of silk in it. Then I got a long silence
and at the end of the silence I got Frank Dorr himself. He
sounded glad to hear from me.

He said: "I've been thinking about our talk this morning,
and I have a better idea. Drop out and see me . . . . And you
might bring that money along. You just have time to get it
out of the bank."

I said: "Yeah. The safe-deposit closes at six. But it's not
your money."

I heard him chuckle. "Don't be foolish. It's all marked, and
I wouldn't want to have to accuse you of stealing it."

I thought that over, and didn't believe it—about the currency being marked. I took a drink out of my glass and said:

"I *might* be willing to turn it over to the party I got it
from—in your presence."

He said: "Well—I told you that party left town. But I'll see
what I can do. No tricks, please."

I said of course no tricks, and hung up. I finished my drink,
called Von Ballin of the *Telegram*. He said the sheriff's people
didn't seem to have any ideas about Lou Harger—or give a
damn. He was a little sore that I still wouldn't let him use my
story. I could tell from the way he talked that he hadn't got
the doings over near Gray Lake.

I called Ohls, couldn't reach him.

I mixed myself another drink, swallowed half of it and began to feel it too much. I put my hat on, changed my mind
about the other half of my drink, went down to my car. The
early evening traffic was thick with householders riding home
to dinner. I wasn't sure whether two cars tailed me or just
one. At any rate nobody tried to catch up and throw a pine-
apple in my lap.

The house was a square two-storied place of old red brick,
with beautiful grounds and a red brick wall with a white stone
coping around them. A shiny black limousine was parked
under the porte-cochère at the side. I followed a red-flagged
walk up over two terraces, and a pale wisp of a man in a
cutaway coat let me into a wide, silent hall with dark old furniture and a glimpse of garden at the end. He led me along

that and along another hall at right angles and ushered me softly into a paneled study that was dimly lit against the gathering dusk. He went away, leaving me alone.

The end of the room was mostly open French windows through which a brass-colored sky showed behind a line of quiet trees. In front of the trees a sprinkler swung slowly on a patch of velvety lawn that was already dark. There were large dim oils on the walls, a huge black desk with books across one end, a lot of deep lounging chairs, a heavy soft rug that went from wall to wall. There was a faint smell of good cigars and beyond that somewhere a smell of garden flowers and moist earth.

The door opened and a youngish man in nose-glasses came in, gave me a slight formal nod, looked around vaguely, and said that Mr. Dorr would be there in a moment. He went out again, and I lit a cigarette.

In a little while the door opened again and Beasley came in, walked past me with a grin and sat down just inside the windows. Then Dorr came in and behind him Miss Glenn.

Dorr had his black cat in his arms and two lovely red scratches, shiny with collodion, down his right cheek. Miss Glenn had on the same clothes I had seen on her in the morning. She looked dark and drawn and spiritless, and she went by me as though she had never seen me before.

Dorr squeezed himself into the high-backed chair behind the desk and put the cat down in front of him. The cat strolled over to one corner of the desk and began to lick its chest with a long, sweeping, businesslike motion.

Dorr said: "Well, well. Here we are," and chuckled pleasantly.

The man in the cutaway came in with a tray of cocktails, passed them around, put the tray with the shaker down on a low table beside Miss Glenn. He went out again, closing the door as if he was afraid he might crack it.

We all drank and looked very solemn.

I said: "We're all here but two. I guess we have a quorum."

Dorr said: "What's that?" sharply and put his head on one side.

I said: "Lou Harger's in the morgue and Canales is dodging cops. Otherwise we're all here. All the interested parties."

Miss Glenn made an abrupt movement, then relaxed suddenly and picked at the arm of her chair.

Dorr took two swallows of his cocktail, put the glass aside and folded his small neat hands on the desk. His face looked a little sinister.

"The money," he said coldly. "I'll take charge of it now."

I said: "Not now or any other time. I didn't bring it."

Dorr stared at me and his face got a little red. I looked at Beasley. Beasley had a cigarette in his mouth and his hands in his pockets and the back of his head against the back of his chair. He looked half asleep.

Dorr said softly, meditatively: "Holding out, huh?"

"Yes," I said grimly. "While I have it I'm fairly safe. You overplayed your hand when you let me get my paws on it. I'd be a fool not to hold what advantage it gives me."

Dorr said: "Safe?" with a gently sinister intonation.

I laughed. "Not safe from a frame," I said. "But the last one didn't click so well . . . Not safe from being gun-walked again. But that's going to be harder next time too . . . But fairly safe from being shot in the back and having you sue my estate for the dough."

Dorr stroked the cat and looked at me under his eyebrows.

"Let's get a couple of more important things straightened out," I said. "Who takes the rap for Lou Harger?"

"What makes you so sure *you* don't?" Dorr asked nastily.

"My alibi's been polished up. I didn't know how good it was until I knew how close Lou's death could be timed. I'm clear now . . . regardless of who turns in what gun with what fairy tale . . . And the lads that were sent to scotch my alibi ran into some trouble."

Dorr said: "That so?" without any apparent emotion.

"A thug named Andrews and a Mexican calling himself Luis Cadena. I daresay you've heard of them."

"I don't know such people," Dorr said sharply.

"Then it won't upset you to hear Andrews got very dead, and the law has Cadena."

"Certainly not," Dorr said. "They were from Canales. Canales had Harger killed."

I said: "So that's your new idea. I think it's lousy."

I leaned over and slipped my empty glass under my chair.

Miss Glenn turned her head towards me and spoke very gravely, as if it was very important to the future of the race for me to believe what she said.

"Of course — *of course* Canales had Lou killed . . . At least, the men he sent after us killed Lou."

I nodded politely. "What for? A packet of money they didn't get? They wouldn't have killed him. They'd have brought him in, brought both of you in. *You* arranged for that kill, and the taxi stunt was to sidetrack me, not to fool Canales' boys."

She put her hand out quickly. Her eyes were shimmering. I went ahead.

"I wasn't very bright, but I didn't figure on anything so flossy. Who the hell would? Canales had no motive to gun Lou, unless it got back the money he had been gypped out of. Supposing he could know that quick he *had* been gypped."

Dorr was licking his lips and quivering his chins and looking from one of us to the other with his small tight eyes. Miss Glenn said drearily:

"Lou knew all about the play. He planned it with the croupier, Pina. Pina wanted some getaway money, wanted to move on to Havana. Of course Canales would have got wise, but not so soon, if I hadn't got noisy and tough. *I* got Lou killed — but not the way you mean."

I dropped an inch of ash off a cigarette I had forgotten all about. "All right," I said grimly. "Canales takes the rap . . . and I suppose you two chiselers think that's all I care about . . . Where was Lou going to be when Canales was *supposed* to find out he'd been gypped?"

"He was going to be gone," Miss Glenn said tonelessly. "A damn' long way off. And I was going to be gone with him."

I said: "Nerts! You seem to forget *I* know *why* Lou was killed."

Beasley sat up in his chair and moved his right hand rather delicately towards his left shoulder. "This wise guy bother you, chief?"

Dorr said: "Not yet. Let him rant."

I moved so that I faced a little more towards Beasley. The

sky had gone dark outside and the sprinkler had been turned off. A damp feeling came slowly into the room. Dorr opened a cedarwood box and put a long brown cigar in his mouth, bit the end off with a dry snap of his false teeth. There was the harsh noise of a match striking, then the slow, rather labored puffing of his breath in the cigar.

He said slowly, through a cloud of smoke: "Let's forget all this and make a deal about that money. . . . Manny Tinnen hung himself in his cell this afternoon."

Miss Glenn stood up suddenly, pushing her arms straight down at her sides. Then she sank slowly down into the chair again, sat motionless. I said: "Did he have any help?" Then I made a sudden, sharp movement—and stopped.

Beasley jerked a swift glance at me, but I wasn't looking at Beasley. There was a shadow outside one of the windows—a lighter shadow than the dark lawn and darker trees. There was a hollow, bitter, coughing plop; a thin spray of whitish smoke in the window.

Beasley jerked, rose half-way to his feet, then fell on his face with one arm doubled under him.

Canales stepped through the windows, past Beasley's body, came three steps further, and stood silent, with a long, black, small-calibered gun in his hand and the larger tube of a silencer flaring from the end of it.

"Be very still," he said. "I am a fair shot—even with this elephant gun."

His face was so white that it was almost luminous. His dark eyes were all smoke-gray iris, without pupils.

"Sound carries well at night, out of open windows," he said tonelessly.

Dorr put both his hands down on the desk and began to pat it. The black cat put its body very low, drifted down over the end of the desk and went under a chair. Miss Glenn turned her head towards Canales very slowly, as if some kind of mechanism moved it.

Canales said: "Perhaps you have a buzzer on that desk. If the door of the room opens, I shoot. It will give me a lot of pleasure to see blood come out of your fat neck."

I moved the fingers of my right hand two inches on the

arm of my chair. The silenced gun swayed towards me and I stopped moving my fingers. Canales smiled very briefly under his angular mustache.

"You are a smart dick," he said. "I thought I had you right. But there are things about you I like."

I didn't say anything. Canales looked back at Dorr. He said very precisely:

"I have been bled by your organization for a long time. But this is something else again. Last night I was cheated out of some money. But that is trivial too. I am wanted for the murder of this Harger. A man named Cadena has been made to confess that I hired him . . . That is just a little too much fix."

Dorr swayed gently over his desk, put his elbows down hard on it, held his face in his small hands and began to shake. His cigar was smoking on the floor.

Canales said: "I would like to get my money back, and I would like to get clear of this rap—but most of all I would like you to say something—so I can shoot you with your mouth open and see blood come out of it."

Beasley's body stirred on the carpet. His hands groped a little. Dorr's eyes were agony trying not to look at him. Canales was rapt and blind in his act by this time. I moved my fingers a little more on the arm of my chair. But I had a long way to go.

Canales said: "Pina has talked to me. I saw to that. You killed Harger. Because he was a secret witness against Manny Tinnen. The D.A. kept the secret, and the dick here kept it. But Harger could not keep it himself. He told his broad— and the broad told you . . . So the killing was arranged, in a way to throw suspicion with a motive on me. First on this dick, and if that wouldn't hold, on me."

There was silence. I wanted to say something, but I couldn't get anything out. I didn't think anybody but Canales would ever again say anything.

Canales said: "You fixed Pina to let Harger and his girl win my money. It was not hard—because I don't play my wheels crooked."

Dorr had stopped shaking. His face lifted, stone-white, and turned towards Canales, slowly, like the face of a man about to have an epileptic fit. Beasley was up on one elbow. His eyes were almost shut but a gun was laboring upwards in his hand.

Canales leaned forward and began to smile. His trigger finger whitened at the exact moment when Beasley's gun began to pulse and roar.

Canales arched his back until his body was a rigid curve. He fell stiffly forward, hit the edge of the desk and slid along it to the floor, without lifting his hands.

Beasley dropped his gun and fell down on his face again. His body got soft and his fingers moved fitfully, then were still.

I got motion into my legs, stood up and went to kick Canales' gun under the desk—senselessly. Doing this I saw that Canales had fired at least once, because Frank Dorr had no right eye.

He sat still and quiet with his chin on his chest and a nice touch of melancholy on the good side of his face.

The door of the room came open and the secretary with the nose-glasses slid in pop-eyed. He staggered back against the door, closing it again. I could hear his rapid breathing across the room.

He gasped: "Is—is anything wrong?"

I thought that very funny, even then. Then I realized that he might be short-sighted and from where he stood Frank Dorr looked natural enough. The rest of it could have been just routine to Dorr's help.

I said: "Yes—but we'll take care of it. Stay out of here."

He said: "Yes, sir," and went out again. That surprised me so much that my mouth fell open. I went down the room and bent over the gray-haired Beasley. He was unconscious, but had a fair pulse. He was bleeding from the side, slowly.

Miss Glenn was standing up and looked almost as dopy as Canales had looked. She was talking to me quickly, in a brittle, very distinct voice:

"I didn't know Lou was to be killed, but I couldn't have done anything about it anyway. They burned me with a branding iron—just for a sample of what I'd get. Look!"

I looked. She tore her dress down in front and there was a hideous red burn on her chest almost between her two breasts.

I said: "Okey, sister. That's nasty medicine. But we've got to have some law here now and an ambulance for Beasley."

I pushed past her towards the telephone, shook her hand off my arm when she grabbed at me. She went on talking to my back in a thin, desperate voice.

"I thought they'd just hold Lou out of the way until after the trial. But they dragged him out of the cab and shot him without a word. Then the little one drove the taxi into town and the big one brought me up into the hills to a shack. Dorr was there. He told me how you had to be framed. He promised me the money, if I went through with it, and torture till I died, if I let them down."

It occurred to me that I was turning my back too much to people. I swung around, got the telephone in my hand, still on the hook, and put my gun down on the desk.

"Listen! Give me a break," she said wildly. "Dorr framed it all with Pina, the croupier. Pina was one of the gang that got Shannon where they could fix him. I didn't—"

I said: "Sure—that's all right. Take it easy."

The room, the whole house seemed very still, as if a lot of people were hunched outside the door, listening.

"It wasn't a bad idea," I said, as if I had all the time in the world. "Lou was just a white chip to Frank Dorr. The play he figured put us both out as witnesses. But it was too elaborate, took in too many people. That sort always blows up in your face."

"Lou was getting out of the state," she said, clutching at her dress. "He was scared. He thought the roulette trick was some kind of a pay-off to him."

I said: "Yeah," lifted the phone and asked for police headquarters.

The room door came open again then and the secretary barged in with a gun. A uniformed chauffeur was behind him with another gun.

I said very loudly into the phone: "This is Frank Dorr's house. There's been a killing . . ."

The secretary and the chauffeur dodged out again. I heard running in the hall. I clicked the phone, called the *Telegram* office and got Von Ballin. When I got through giving him the flash Miss Glenn was gone out of the window into the dark garden.

I didn't go after her. I didn't mind very much if she got away.

I tried to get Ohls, but they said he was still down at Solano. And by that time the night was full of sirens. . . .

I had a little trouble, but not too much. Fenweather pulled too much weight. Not all of the story came out, but enough so that the City Hall boys in the two-hundred-dollar suits had their left elbows in front of their faces for some time.

Pina was picked up in Salt Lake City. He broke and implicated four others of Manny Tinnen's gang. Two of them were killed resisting arrest, and the other two got life without parole.

Miss Glenn made a clean getaway and was never heard of again. I think that's about all, except that I had to turn the twenty-two grand over to the Public Administrator. He allowed me two hundred dollars fee and nine dollars and twenty cents mileage. Sometimes I wonder what he did with the rest of it.

Nevada Gas

Hugo Candless stood in the middle of the squash court bending his big body at the waist, holding the little black ball delicately between left thumb and forefinger. He dropped it near the service line and flicked at it with the long-handled racket.

The black ball hit the front wall a little less than halfway up, floated back in a high, lazy curve, skimmed just below the white ceiling and the lights behind wire protectors. It slid languidly down the back wall, never touching it enough to bounce out.

George Dial made a careless swing at it, whanged the end of his racket against the cement back wall. The ball fell dead.

He said: "That's the story, chief. 21–14. You're just too good for me."

George Dial was tall, dark, handsome, Hollywoodish. He was brown and lean, and had a hard, outdoor look. Everything about him was hard except his full, soft lips and his large, cow-like eyes.

"Yeah. I always was too good for you," Hugo Candless chortled.

He leaned far back from his thick waist and laughed with his mouth wide open. Sweat glistened on his chest and belly. He was naked except for blue shorts, white wool socks and heavy sneakers with crepe soles. He had gray hair and a broad moon face with a small nose and mouth, sharp twinkly eyes.

"Want another lickin'?" he asked.

"Not unless I have to."

Hugo Candless scowled. "Oke," he said shortly. He stuck his racket under his arm and got an oilskin pouch out of his shorts, took a cigarette and a match from it. He lit the cigarette with a flourish and threw the match into the middle of the court, where somebody else would have to pick it up.

He threw the door of the squash court open and paraded down the corridor to the locker room with his chest out. Dial walked behind him silently; catlike, soft-footed, with a lithe grace. They went to the showers.

Candless sang in the showers, covered his big soft body with thick suds, showered dead cold after the hot, and liked it. He rubbed himself dry with immense leisure, took another towel and stalked out of the shower room yelling for the shine attendant to bring ice and ginger ale.

A negro in a stiff white coat came hurrying with a tray. Candless signed the check with a flourish, unlocked his big double locker and planked a bottle of Johnny Walker on the round green table that stood in the locker aisle.

The attendant mixed drinks carefully, two of them, said:

"Yes, suh, Mista Candless," and went away palming a quarter.

George Dial, already fully dressed in smart gray flannels, came around the corner and lifted one of the drinks.

"Through for the day, chief?" He looked at the ceiling light through his drink, with tight eyes.

"Guess so," Candless said largely. "Guess I'll go home and give the little woman a treat." He gave Dial a swift, sidewise glance from his little eyes.

"Mind if I don't ride home with you?" Dial asked carelessly.

"With me it's okey. It's tough on Naomi," Candless said unpleasantly.

Dial made a soft sound with his lips, shrugged, said:

"You like to burn people up, don't you, chief?"

Candless didn't answer, didn't look at him. Dial stood silent with his drink and watched the big man put on monogrammed satin underclothes, purple socks with gray clocks, a monogrammed silk shirt, a suit of tiny black and white checks that made him look as big as a barn.

By the time he got to his purple tie he was yelling for the shine to come and mix another drink.

Dial refused the second drink, nodded, went away softly along the matting between the tall green lockers.

Candless finished dressing, drank his second highball, locked his liquor away and put a fat brown cigar in his mouth. He had the negro light the cigar for him. He went off with a strut and several loud greetings here and there.

It seemed very quiet in the locker room after he went out. There were a few snickers.

It was raining outside the Delmar Club. The liveried door-man helped Hugo Candless on with his belted white slicker and went out for his car. When he had it in front of the canopy he held an umbrella over Hugo across the strip of wooden matting to the curb. The car was a royal blue Lincoln limousine, with buff striping. The license number was 5A6.

The chauffeur, in a black slicker turned up high around his ears, didn't look around. The doorman opened the door and Hugo Candless got in and sank heavily on the back seat.

"'Night, Sam. Tell him to go on home."

The doorman touched his cap, shut the door, and relayed the orders to the driver, who nodded without turning his head. The car moved off in the rain.

The rain came down slantingly and at the intersections sudden gusts blew it rattling against the glass of the limousine. The street corners were clotted with people trying to get across Sunset without being splashed. Hugo Candless grinned out at them, pityingly.

The car went out Sunset, through Sherman, then swung towards the hills. It began to go very fast. It was on a boulevard where traffic was thin now.

It was very hot in the car. The windows were all shut and the glass partition behind the driver's seat was shut all the way across. The smoke of Hugo's cigar was heavy and choking in the tonneau of the limousine.

Candless scowled and reached out to lower a window. The window lever didn't work. He tried the other side. That didn't work either. He began to get mad. He grabbed for the little telephone dingus to bawl his driver out. There wasn't any little telephone dingus.

The car turned sharply and began to go up a long straight hill with eucalyptus trees on one side and no houses. Candless felt something cold touch his spine, all the way up and down his spine. He bent forward and banged on the glass with his fist. The driver didn't turn his head. The car went very fast up the long dark hill road.

Hugo Candless grabbed viciously for the door handle. The doors didn't have any handles—either side. A sick, incredulous grin broke over Hugo's broad moon face.

The driver bent over to the right and reached for something with his gloved right hand. There was a sudden sharp hissing noise. Hugo Candless began to smell the odor of almonds.

Very faint at first—very faint, and rather pleasant. The hissing noise went on. The smell of almonds got bitter and harsh and very deadly. Hugo Candless dropped his cigar and banged with all his strength on the glass of the nearest window. The glass didn't break.

The car was up in the hills now, beyond even the infrequent street lights of the residential sections.

Candless dropped back on the seat and lifted his foot to kick hard at the glass partition in front of him. The kick was never finished. His eyes no longer saw. His face twisted into a snarl and his head went back against the cushions, crushed down against his thick shoulders. His soft white felt hat was shapeless on his big square skull.

The driver looked back quickly, showing a lean, hawklike face for a brief instant. Then he bent to his right again and the hissing noise stopped.

He pulled over to the side of the deserted road, stopped the car, switched off all the lights. The rain made a dull noise pounding on the roof.

The driver got out in the rain and opened the rear door of the car, then backed away from it quickly, holding his nose.

He stood a little way off for a while and looked up and down the road.

In the back of the limousine Hugo Candless didn't move.

2

Francine Ley sat in a low red chair beside a small table on which there was an alabaster bowl. Smoke from the cigarette she had just discarded into the bowl floated up and made patterns in the still, warm air. Her hands were clasped behind her head and her smoke-blue eyes were lazy, inviting. She had dark auburn hair set in loose waves. There were bluish shadows in the troughs of the waves.

George Dial leaned over and kissed her on the lips, hard.

His own lips were hot when he kissed her, and he shivered. The girl didn't move. She smiled up at him lazily when he straightened again.

In a thick, clogged voice Dial said: "Listen, Francy. When do you ditch this gambler and let me set you up?"

Francine Ley shrugged, without taking her hands from behind her head. "He's a square gambler, George," she drawled. "That's something nowadays and you don't have enough money."

"I can get it."

"How?" Her voice was low and husky. It moved George Dial like a 'cello.

"From Candless. I've got plenty on that bird."

"As for instance?" Francine Ley suggested lazily.

Dial grinned softly down at her. He widened his eyes in a deliberately innocent expression. Francine Ley thought the whites of his eyes were tinged ever so faintly with some color that was not white.

Dial flourished an unlighted cigarette. "Plenty—like he sold out a tough boy from Reno last year. The tough boy's half brother was under a murder rap here and Candless took twenty-five grand to get him off. He made a deal with the D.A. on another case and let the tough boy's brother go up."

"And what did the tough boy do about all that?" Francine Ley asked gently.

"Nothing—yet. He thinks it was on the up and up, I guess. You can't always win."

"But he might do plenty, if he knew," Francine Ley said, nodding. "Who was the tough boy, Georgie?"

Dial lowered his voice and leaned down over her again. "I'm a sap to tell you that. A man named Zapparty. I've never met him."

"And never want to—if you've got sense, Georgie. No, thanks. I'm not walking myself into any jam like that with you."

Dial smiled lightly, showing even teeth in a dark, smooth face. "Leave it to me, Francy. Just forget the whole thing except how I'm nuts about you."

"Buy us a drink," the girl said.

The room was a living-room in a hotel apartment. It was all

red and white, with embassy decorations, too stiff. The white walls had red designs painted on them, the white Venetian blinds were framed in white box drapes, there was a half round red rug with a white border in front of the gas fire. There was a kidney-shaped white desk against one wall, between the windows.

Dial went over to the desk and poured Scotch into two glasses, added ice and charged water, carried the glasses back across the room to where a thin wisp of smoke still plumed upward from the alabaster bowl.

"Ditch that gambler," Dial said, handing her a glass. "He's the one will get you in a jam."

She sipped the drink, nodded. Dial took the glass out of her hand, sipped from the same place on the rim, leaned over holding both glasses and kissed her on the lips again.

There were red curtains over a door to a short hallway. They were parted a few inches and a man's face appeared in the opening, cool gray eyes stared in thoughtfully at the kiss. The curtains fell together again without sound.

After a moment a door shut loudly and steps came along the hallway. Johnny De Ruse came through the curtains into the room. By that time Dial was lighting his cigarette.

Johnny De Ruse was tall, lean, quiet, dressed in dark clothes dashingly cut. His cool gray eyes had fine laughter wrinkles at the corners. His thin mouth was delicate but not soft, and his long chin had a cleft in it.

Dial stared at him, made a vague motion with his hand. De Ruse walked over to the desk without speaking, poured some whiskey into a glass and drank it straight.

He stood a moment with his back to the room, tapping on the edge of the desk. Then he turned around, smiled faintly, said: "'Lo, people," in a gentle, rather drawling voice and went out of the room through an inner door.

He was in a big over-decorated bedroom with twin beds. He went to a closet and got a tan calfskin suitcase out of it, opened it on the nearest bed. He began to rob the drawers of a highboy and put things in the suitcase, arranging them carefully, without haste. He whistled quietly through his teeth while he was doing it.

When the suitcase was packed he snapped it shut and lit a

cigarette. He stood for a moment in the middle of the room, without moving. His gray eyes looked at the wall without seeing it.

After a little while he went back into the closet and came out with a small gun in a soft leather harness with two short straps. He pulled up the left leg of his trousers and strapped the holster on his leg. Then he picked up the suitcase and went back to the living-room.

Francine Ley's eyes narrowed swiftly when she saw the suit-case.

"Going some place?" she asked in her low, husky voice.

"Uh-huh. Where's Dial?"

"He had to leave."

"That's too bad," De Ruse said softly. He put the suitcase down on the floor and stood beside it, moving his cool gray eyes over the girl's face, up and down her slim body, from her ankles to her auburn head. "That's too bad," he said. "I like to see him around. I'm kind of dull for you."

"Maybe you are, Johnny."

He bent to the suitcase, but straightened without touching it and said casually:

"Remember Mops Parisi? I saw him in town today."

Her eyes widened and then almost shut. Her teeth clicked lightly. The line of her jawbone stood out very distinctly for a moment.

De Ruse kept moving his glance up and down her face and body.

"Going to do anything about it?" she asked.

"I thought of taking a trip," De Ruse said. "I'm not so scrappy as I was once."

"A powder," Francine Ley said softly. "Where do we go?"

"Not a powder—a trip," De Ruse said tonelessly. "And not we—*me*. I'm going alone."

She sat still, watching his face, not moving a muscle.

De Ruse reached inside his coat and got out a long wallet that opened like a book. He tossed a tight sheaf of bills into the girl's lap, put the wallet away. She didn't touch the bills.

"That'll hold you for longer than you'll need to find a new playmate," he said, without expression. "I wouldn't say I won't send you more, if you need it."

She stood up slowly and the sheaf of bills slid down her skirt to the floor. She held her arms straight down at the sides, the hands clenched so that the tendons on the backs of them were sharp. Her eyes were as dull as slate.

"That means we're through, Johnny?"

He lifted his suitcase. She stepped in front of him swiftly, with two long steps. She put a hand against his coat. He stood quite still, smiling gently with his eyes, but not with his lips. The perfume of shalimar twitched at his nostrils.

"You know what you are, Johnny?" Her husky voice was almost a lisp.

He waited.

"A pigeon, Johnny. A pigeon."

He nodded slightly. "Check. I called copper on Mops Parisi. I don't like the snatch racket, baby. I'd call copper on it any day. I might even get myself hurt blocking it. That's old stuff. Through?"

"You called copper on Mops Parisi and you don't think he knows it, but maybe he does. So you're running away from him. . . . That's a laugh, Johnny. I'm kidding you. That's not why you're leaving me."

"Maybe I'm just tired of you, baby."

She put her head back and laughed sharply, almost with a wild note. De Ruse didn't budge.

"You're not a tough boy, Johnny. You're soft. George Dial is harder than you are. Gawd, how soft you are, Johnny!"

She stepped back, staring at his face. Some flicker of almost unbearable emotion came and went in her eyes.

"You're such a handsome pup, Johnny. Gawd, but you're handsome. It's too bad you're soft."

De Ruse said gently, without moving: "Not soft, baby— just a bit sentimental. I like to clock the ponies and play seven-card stud and mess around with little red cubes with white spots on them. I like games of chance, including women. But when I lose I don't get sore and I don't chisel. I just move on to the next table. Be seein' you."

He stooped, hefted the suitcase, and walked around her. He went across the room and through the red curtains without looking back. The outer door made a gentle sound closing.

Francine Ley stared with stiff eyes at the floor.

3

Standing under the scalloped glass canopy of the side entrance to the Chatterton, De Ruse looked up and down Irolo, towards the flashing lights of Wilshire and towards the dark quiet end of the side street.

The rain fell softly, slantingly. A light drop blew in under the canopy and hit the red end of his cigarette with a sputter. He hefted the suitcase and went along Irolo towards his sedan. It was parked almost at the next corner, a shiny black Packard with a little discreet chromium here and there.

He stopped and opened the door and a gun came up swiftly from inside the car. The gun prodded against his chest. A voice said sharply:

"Hold it! The mitts high, sweets!"

De Ruse saw the man dimly inside the car. A lean hawklike face on which some reflected light fell without making it distinct. He felt a gun hard against his chest, hurting his breastbone. Quick steps came up behind him and another gun prodded his back.

"Satisfied?" another voice inquired.

De Ruse dropped the suitcase, lifted his hands and put them against the top of the car.

"Okey," he said wearily. "What is it—a heist?"

A snarling laugh came from the man in the car. A hand smacked De Ruse's hips from behind.

"Back up—slow!"

De Ruse backed up, holding his hands very high in the air.

"Not so high, punk," the man behind said dangerously. "Just shoulder high."

De Ruse lowered them. The man in the car got out, straightened. He put his gun against De Ruse's chest again, put out a long arm and unbuttoned De Ruse's overcoat. De Ruse leaned backwards. The hand belonging to the long arm explored his pockets, his armpits. A .38 in a spring-holster ceased to make weight under his arm.

"Got one, Chuck. Anything your side?"

"Nothin' on the hip."

The man in front stepped away and picked up the suitcase.

"March, sweets. We'll ride in our heap."

They went farther along Irolo. A big Lincoln limousine loomed up, a blue car with a lighter stripe. The hawk-faced man opened the rear door.

"In."

De Ruse got in listlessly, spitting his cigarette end into the wet darkness, as he stooped under the roof of the car. A faint smell assailed his nose, a smell that might have been overripe peaches or almonds. He got into the car.

"In beside him, Chuck."

"Listen. Let's all ride up front. I can handle—"

"Nix. In beside him, Chuck," the hawk-faced one snapped.

Chuck growled, got into the back seat beside De Ruse. The other man slammed the door hard. His lean face showed through the closed window in a sardonic grin. Then he went around to the driver's seat and started the car, tooled it away from the curb.

De Ruse wrinkled his nose, sniffing at the queer smell.

They spun at the corner, went east on Eighth to Normandie, north on Normandie across Wilshire, across other streets, up over a steep hill and down the other side to Melrose. The big Lincoln slid through the light rain without a whisper. Chuck sat in the corner, held his gun on his knee, scowled. Street lights showed a square, arrogant red face, a face that was not at ease.

The back of the driver's head was motionless beyond the glass partition. They passed Sunset and Hollywood, turned east on Franklin, swung north to Los Feliz and down Los Feliz towards the river bed.

Cars coming up the hill threw sudden brief glares of white light into the interior of the Lincoln. De Ruse tensed, waited. At the next pair of lights that shot squarely into the car he bent over swiftly and jerked up the left leg of his trousers. He was back against the cushions before the blinding light was gone.

Chuck hadn't moved, hadn't noticed movement.

Down at the bottom of the hill, at the intersection of Riverside Drive, a whole phalanx of cars surged towards them as a light changed. De Ruse waited, timed the impact of the headlights. His body stooped briefly, his hand swooped down, snatched the small gun from the leg-holster.

He leaned back once more, the gun against the bulk of his left thigh, concealed behind it from where Chuck sat.

The Lincoln shot over on to Riverside and passed the entrance to Griffith Park.

"Where we going, punk?" De Ruse asked casually.

"Save it," Chuck snarled. "You'll find out."

"Not a stick-up, huh?"

"Save it," Chuck snarled again.

"Mops Parisi's boys?" De Ruse asked thinly, slowly.

The red-faced gunman jerked, lifted the gun off his knee. "I said—save it!"

De Ruse said: "Sorry, punk."

He turned the gun over his thigh, lined it swiftly, squeezed the trigger left-handed. The gun made a small flat sound— almost an unimportant sound.

Chuck yelled and his hand jerked wildly. The gun kicked out of it and fell on the floor of the car. His left hand raced for his right shoulder.

De Ruse shifted the little Mauser to his right hand and put it deep into Chuck's side.

"Steady, boy, steady. Keep your hands out of trouble. Now—kick that cannon over this way—fast!"

Chuck kicked the big automatic along the floor of the car. De Ruse reached down for it swiftly, got it. The lean-faced driver jerked a look back and the car swerved, then straightened again.

De Ruse hefted the big gun. The Mauser was too light for a sap. He slammed Chuck hard on the side of the head. Chuck groaned, sagged forward, clawing.

"The gas!" he bleated. "The gas! He'll turn on the gas!"

De Ruse hit him again, harder. Chuck was a tumbled heap on the floor of the car.

The Lincoln swung off Riverside, over a short bridge and a bridle path, down a narrow dirt road that split a golf course. It went into darkness and among trees. It went fast, rocketed from side to side, as if the driver wanted it to do just that.

De Ruse steadied himself, felt for the door handle. There wasn't any door handle. His lips curled and he smashed at a window with the gun. The heavy glass was like a wall of stone.

The hawk-faced man leaned over and there was a hissing sound. Then there was a sudden sharp increase of intensity of the smell of almonds.

De Ruse tore a handkerchief out of his pocket and pressed it to his nose. The driver had straightened again now and was driving hunched over, trying to keep his head down.

De Ruse held the muzzle of the big gun close to the glass partition behind the driver's head, who ducked sidewise. He squeezed lead four times quickly, shutting his eyes and turning his head away, like a nervous woman.

No glass flew. When he looked again there was a jagged round hole in the glass and the windshield in a line with it was starred but not broken.

He slammed the gun at the edges of the hole and managed to knock a piece of glass loose. He was getting the gas now, through the handkerchief. His head felt like a balloon. His vision waved and wandered.

The hawk-faced driver, crouched, wrenched the door open at his side, swung the wheel of the car the opposite way and jumped clear.

The car tore over a low embankment, looped a little and smacked sidewise against a tree. The body twisted enough for one of the rear doors to spring open.

De Ruse went through the door in a headlong dive. Soft earth smacked him, knocked some of the wind out of him. Then his lungs breathed clean air. He rolled up on his stomach and elbows, kept his head down, his gun-hand up.

The hawk-faced man was on his knees a dozen yards away. De Ruse watched him drag a gun out of his pocket and lift it.

Chuck's gun pulsed and roared in De Ruse's hand until it was empty.

The hawk-faced man folded down slowly and his body merged with the dark shadows and the wet ground. Cars went by distantly on Riverside Drive. Rain dripped off the trees. The Griffith Park beacon turned in the thick sky. The rest was darkness and silence.

De Ruse took a deep breath and got up on his feet. He dropped the empty gun, took a small flash out of his overcoat pocket and pulled his overcoat up against his nose and mouth, pressing the thick cloth hard against his face. He went

to the car, switched off the lights and threw the beam of the
flash into the driver's compartment. He leaned in quickly and
turned a petcock on a copper cylinder like a fire-extinguisher.
The hissing noise of the gas stopped.

He went over to the hawk-faced man. He was dead. There
was some loose money, currency and silver in his pockets,
cigarettes, a folder of matches from the Club Egypt, no wallet,
a couple of extra clips of cartridges, De Ruse's .38. De Ruse
put the last back where it belonged and straightened from the
sprawled body.

He looked across the darkness of the Los Angeles river bed
towards the lights of Glendale. In the middle distance a green
Neon sign far from any other light winked on and off: Club
Egypt.

De Ruse smiled quietly to himself, and went back to the
Lincoln. He dragged Chuck's body out on to the wet
ground. Chuck's red face was blue now, under the beam of
the small flash. His open eyes held an empty stare. His chest
didn't move. De Ruse put the flash down and went through
some more pockets.

He found the usual things a man carries, including a wallet
showing a driver's license issued to Charles LeGrand, Hotel
Metropole, Los Angeles. He found more Club Egypt matches
and a tabbed hotel key marked 809, Hotel Metropole.

He put the key in his pocket, slammed the sprung door of
the Lincoln, got in under the wheel. The motor caught. He
backed the car away from the tree with a wrench of broken
fender metal, swung it around slowly over the soft earth and
got it back again on the road.

When he reached Riverside again he turned the lights on
and drove back to Hollywood. He put the car under some
pepper trees in front of a big brick apartment house on Kenmore half a block north of Hollywood Boulevard, locked the
ignition and lifted out his suitcase.

Light from the entrance of the apartment house rested on
the front license plate as he walked away. He wondered why
gunmen would use a car with plate numbers reading 5A6,
almost a privilege number.

In a drug-store he phoned for a taxi. The taxi took him
back to the Chatterton.

4

The apartment was empty. The smell of shalimar and cigarette smoke lingered on the warm air, as if someone had been there not long before. De Ruse pushed into the bedroom, looked at clothes in two closets, articles on a dresser, then went back to the red and white living-room and mixed himself a stiff highball.

He put the night latch on the outside door and carried his drink into the bedroom, stripped off his muddy clothes and put on another suit of somber material but dandified cut. He sipped his drink while he knotted a black four-in-hand in the opening of a soft white linen shirt.

He swabbed the barrel of the little Mauser, reassembled it, and added a shell to the small clip, slipped the gun back into the leg-holster. Then he washed his hands and took his drink to the telephone.

The first number he called was the *Chronicle*. He asked for the City Room, Werner.

A drawly voice dripped over the wire: "Werner talkin'. Go ahead. Kid me."

De Ruse said: "This is John De Ruse, Claude. Look up California License 5A6 on your list for me."

"Must be a bloody politician," the drawly voice said, and went away.

De Ruse sat motionless, looking at a fluted white pillar in the corner. It had a red and white bowl of red and white artificial roses on top of it. He wrinkled his nose at it disgustedly.

Werner's voice came back on the wire: "1930 Lincoln limousine registered to Hugo Candless, Casa de Oro Apartments, 2942 Clearwater Street, West Hollywood."

De Ruse said in a tone that meant nothing: "That's the mouthpiece, isn't it?"

"Yeah. The big lip. Mister Take the Witness." Werner's voice came down lower. "Speaking to you, Johnny, and not for publication—a big crooked tub of guts that's not even smart; just been around long enough to know who's for sale. . . . Story in it?"

"Hell, no," De Ruse said softly. "He just sideswiped me and didn't stop."

He hung up and finished his drink, stood up to mix another. Then he swept a telephone directory on to the white desk and looked up the number of the Casa de Oro. He dialed it. A switchboard operator told him Mr. Hugo Candless was out of town.

"Give me his apartment," De Ruse said.

A woman's cool voice answered the phone. "Yes. This is Mrs. Hugo Candless speaking. What is it, please?"

De Ruse said: "I'm a client of Mr. Candless, very anxious to get hold of him. Can you help me?"

"I'm very sorry," the cool, almost lazy voice told him. "My husband was called out of town quite suddenly. I don't even know where he went, though I expect to hear from him later this evening. He left his club—"

"What club was that?" De Ruse asked casually.

"The Delmar Club. I say he left there without coming home. If there is any message—"

De Ruse said: "Thank you, Mrs. Candless. Perhaps I may call you again later."

He hung up, smiled slowly and grimly, sipped his fresh drink and looked up the number of the Hotel Metropole. He called it and asked for "Mister Charles LeGrand in Room 809."

"Six-o-nine," the operator said casually. "I'll connect you." A moment later: "There is no answer."

De Ruse thanked her, took the tabbed key out of his pocket, looked at the number on it. The number was 809.

5

Sam, the doorman at the Delmar Club, leaned against the buff stone of the entrance and watched the traffic swish by on Sunset Boulevard. The headlights hurt his eyes. He was tired and he wanted to go home. He wanted a smoke and a big slug of gin. He wished the rain would stop. It was dead inside the club when it rained.

He straightened away from the wall and walked the length of the sidewalk canopy a couple of times, slapping together his big black hands in big white gloves. He tried to whistle the *Skaters' Waltz*, couldn't get within a block of the tune, whistled *Low Down Lady* instead. That didn't have any tune.

De Ruse came around the corner from Hudson Street and stood beside him near the wall.

"Hugo Candless inside?" he asked, not looking at Sam.

Sam clicked his teeth disapprovingly. "He ain't."

"Been in?"

"Ask at the desk 'side, please, mistah."

De Ruse took gloved hands out of his pocket and began to roll a five-dollar bill around his left forefinger.

"What do they know that you don't know?"

Sam grinned slowly, watched the bill being wound tightly around the gloved finger.

"That's a fac', boss. Yeah—he was in. Comes most every day."

"What time he leave?"

"He leave 'bout six-thirty, Ah reckon."

"Drive his blue Lincoln limousine?"

"Shuah. Only he don't drive it hisself. What for you ask?"

"It was raining then," De Ruse said calmly. "Raining pretty hard. Maybe it wasn't the Lincoln."

"'Twas, too, the Lincoln," Sam protested. "Ain't I tucked him in? He never rides nothin' else."

"License 5A6?" De Ruse bored on relentlessly.

"That's it," Sam chortled. "Just like a councilman's number that number is."

"Know the driver?"

"Shuah —" Sam began, and then stopped cold. He raked a black jaw with a white finger the size of a banana. "Well, Ah'll be a big black slob if he ain't got hisself a new driver again. I ain't *know* that man, sure 'nough."

De Ruse poked the rolled bill into Sam's big white paw. Sam grabbed it but his large eyes suddenly got suspicious.

"Say, for what you ask all of them questions, mistah man?"

De Ruse said: "I paid my way, didn't I?"

He went back around the corner to Hudson and got into his black Packard sedan. He drove it out on to Sunset, then west on Sunset almost to Beverly Hills, then turned towards the foothills and began to peer at the signs on street corners. Clearwater Street ran along the flank of a hill and had a view of the entire city. The Casa de Oro, at the corner of Parkinson, was a tricky block of high-class bungalow apartments surrounded by an adobe wall with red tiles on top. It had a lobby in a separate building, a big private garage on Parkinson, opposite one length of the wall.

De Ruse parked across the street from the garage and sat looking through the wide window into a glassed-in office where an attendant in spotless white coveralls sat with his feet on the desk, reading a magazine. From time to time the man took his eyes off the magazine and spit over his shoulder at an invisible cuspidor.

De Ruse got out of the Packard, crossed the street farther up, came back and slipped into the garage without the attendant seeing him.

The cars were in four rows. Two rows backed against the white walls, two against each other in the middle. There were plenty of vacant stalls, but plenty of cars had gone to bed also. They were mostly big, expensive closed models, with two or three flashy open jobs.

There was only one limousine. It had License No. 5A6.

It was a well-kept car, bright and shiny; royal blue with a buff trimming. De Ruse took a glove off and rested his hand on the radiator shell. Quite cold. He felt the tires, looked at his fingers. A little fine dry dust adhered to the skin. There was no mud in the treads, just bone-dry dust.

He went back along the row of dark car bodies and leaned in the open door of the little office. After a moment the attendant looked up, almost with a start.

"Seen the Candless chauffeur around?" De Ruse asked him.

The man shook his head and spat deftly into a copper spittoon.

"Not since I come on—three o'clock."

"Didn't he go down to the club for the old man?"

"Nope. I guess not. The big hack ain't been out. He always takes that."

"Where does he hang his hat?"

"Who? Mattick? They got servants' quarters in back of the jungle. But I think I heard him say he parks at some hotel. Let's see—" A brow got furrowed.

"The Metropole?" De Ruse suggested.

The garage man thought it over while De Ruse stared at the point of his chin.

"Yeah. I think that's it. I ain't just positive though. Mattick don't open up much."

De Ruse thanked him and crossed the street and got into the Packard again. He drove downtown.

It was twenty-five minutes past nine when he got to the corner of Seventh and Spring, where the Metropole was.

It was an old hotel that had once been exclusive and was now steering a shaky course between a receivership and a bad name at Headquarters. It had too much oily dark wood paneling, too many chipped gilt mirrors. Too much smoke hung below its low beamed lobby ceiling and too many grifters bummed around in its worn leather rockers.

The blonde who looked after the big horseshoe cigar counter wasn't young any more and her eyes were cynical from standing off cheap dates. De Ruse leaned on the glass and pushed his hat back on his crisp black hair.

"Camels, honey," he said in his low-pitched gambler's voice.

The girl smacked the pack in front of him, rang up fifteen cents and slipped the dime change under his elbow, with a faint smile. Her eyes said they liked him. She leaned opposite him and put her head near enough so that he could smell the perfume in her hair.

"Tell me something," De Ruse said.

"What?" she asked softly.

"Find out who lives in eight-o-nine, without telling any answers to the clerk."

The blonde looked disappointed. "Why don't you ask him yourself, mister?"

"I'm too shy," De Ruse said.

"Yes you are!"

She went to her telephone and talked into it with languid grace, came back to De Ruse.

"Name of Mattick. Mean anything?"

"Guess not," De Ruse said. "Thanks a lot. How do you like it in this nice hotel?"

"Who said it was a nice hotel?"

De Ruse smiled, touched his hat, strolled away. Her eyes

looked after him sadly. She leaned her sharp elbows on the counter and cupped her chin in her hands to stare after him.

De Ruse crossed the lobby and went up three steps and got into an open-cage elevator that started with a lurch.

"Eight," he said, and leaned against the cage with his hands in his pockets.

Eight was as high as the Metropole went. De Ruse followed a long corridor that smelled of varnish. A turn at the end brought him face to face with 809. He knocked on the dark wood panel. Nobody answered. He bent over, looked through an empty keyhole, knocked again.

Then he took the tabbed key out of his pocket and unlocked the door and went in.

Windows were shut in two walls. The air reeked of whiskey. Lights were on in the ceiling. There was a wide brass bed, a dark bureau, a couple of brown leather rockers, a stiff-looking desk with a flat brown quart of Four Roses on it, nearly empty, without a cap. De Ruse sniffed it and set his hips against the edge of the desk, let his eyes prowl the room.

His glance traversed from the dark bureau across the bed and the wall with the door in it to another door behind which light showed. He crossed to that and opened it.

The man lay on his face, on the yellowish brown woodstone floor of the bathroom. Blood on the floor looked sticky and black. Two soggy patches on the back of the man's head were the points from which rivulets of dark red had run down the side of his neck to the floor. The blood had stopped flowing a long time ago.

De Ruse slipped a glove off and stooped to hold two fingers against the place where a jugular vein would beat. He shook his head and put his hand back into his glove.

He left the bathroom, shut the door and went to open one of the windows. He leaned out, breathing clean rain-wet air, looking down along slants of thin rain into the dark slit of an alley.

After a little while he shut the window again, switched off the light in the bathroom, took a "Do Not Disturb" sign out of the top bureau drawer, doused the ceiling lights, and went out.

He hung the sign on the knob and went back along the corridor to the elevators and left the Hotel Metropole.

6

Francine Ley hummed low down in her throat as she went along the silent corridor of the Chatterton. She hummed unsteadily without knowing what she was humming, and her left hand with its cherry-red fingernails held a green velvet cape from slipping down off her shoulders. There was a wrapped bottle under her other arm.

She unlocked the door, pushed it open and stopped, with a quick frown. She stood still, remembering, trying to remember. She was still a little tight.

She had left the lights on; that was it. They were off now. Could be the maid service, of course. She went on in, fumbled through the red curtains into the living-room.

The glow from the heater prowled across the red and white rug and touched shiny black things with a ruddy glow. The shiny black things were shoes. They didn't move.

Francine Ley said: "Oh—oh," in a sick voice. The hand holding the cape almost tore into her neck with its long, beautifully molded nails.

Something clicked and light glowed in a lamp beside an easy chair. De Ruse sat in the chair, looking at her woodenly.

He had his coat and hat on. His eyes were shrouded, far away, filled with a remote brooding.

He said: "Been out, Francy?"

She sat down slowly on the edge of a half round settee, put the bottle down beside her.

"I got tight," she said. "Thought I'd better eat. Then I thought I'd get tight again." She patted the bottle.

De Ruse said: "I think your friend Dial's boss has been snatched." He said it casually, as if it was of no importance to him.

Francine Ley opened her mouth slowly and as she opened it all the prettiness went out of her face. Her face became a blank haggard mask on which rouge burned violently. Her mouth looked as if it wanted to scream.

After a little while it closed again and her face got pretty again and her voice, from far off, said:

"Would it do any good to say I don't know what you're talking about?"

De Ruse didn't change his wooden expression. He said:

"When I went down to the street from here a couple of hoods jumped me. One of them was stashed in the car. Of course they could have spotted me somewhere else—followed me here."

"They did," Francine Ley said breathlessly. "They did, Johnny."

His long chin moved an inch. "They piled me into a big Lincoln, a limousine. It was quite a car. It had heavy glass that didn't break easily and no door handles and it was all shut up tight. In the front seat it had a tank of Nevada gas, cyanide, which the guy driving could turn into the back part without getting it himself. They took me out Griffith Parkway, towards the Club Egypt. That's that joint on county land, near the airport." He paused, rubbed the end of one eyebrow, went on: "They overlooked the Mauser I sometimes wear on my leg. The driver crashed the car and I got loose."

He spread his hands and looked down at them. A faint metallic smile showed at the corners of his lips.

Francine Ley said: "I didn't have anything to do with it, Johnny." Her voice was as dead as the summer before last.

De Ruse said: "The guy that rode in the car before I did probably didn't have a gun. He was Hugo Candless. The car was a ringer for his car—same model, same paint job, same plates—but it wasn't his car. Somebody took a lot of trouble. Candless left the Delmar Club in the wrong car about six-thirty. His wife says he's out of town. I talked to her an hour ago. His car hasn't been out of the garage since noon. . . . Maybe his wife knows he's snatched by now, maybe not."

Francine Ley's nails clawed at her skirt. Her lips shook.

De Ruse went on calmly, tonelessly: "Somebody gunned the Candless chauffeur in a downtown hotel tonight or this afternoon. The cops haven't found it yet. Somebody took a lot of trouble, Francy. You wouldn't want to be in on that kind of a set-up, would you, precious?"

Francine Ley bent her head forward and stared at the floor. She said thickly:

"I need a drink. What I had is dying in me. I feel awful."

De Ruse stood up and went to the white desk. He drained a bottle into a glass and brought it across to her. He stood in front of her, holding the glass out of her reach.

"I only get tough once in a while, baby, but when I get tough I'm not so easy to stop, if I say it myself. If you know anything about all this, now would be a good time to spill it."

He handed her the glass. She gulped the whiskey and a little more light came into her smoke-blue eyes. She said slowly:

"I don't know anything about it, Johnny. Not in the way you mean. But George Dial made me a love nest proposition tonight and he told me he could get money out of Candless by threatening to spill a dirty trick Candless played on some tough boy from Reno."

"Damn clever, these greasers," De Ruse said. "Reno's my town, baby. I know all the tough boys in Reno. Who was it?"

"Somebody named Zapparty."

De Ruse said very softly: "Zapparty is the name of the man who runs the Club Egypt."

Francine Ley stood up suddenly and grabbed his arm. "Stay out of it, Johnny! For —— sake, can't you stay out of it for just this once?"

De Ruse shook his head, smiled delicately, lingeringly at her. Then he lifted her hand off his arm and stepped back.

"I had a ride in their gas car, baby, and I didn't like it. I smelled their Nevada gas. I left my lead in somebody's gun punk. That makes me call copper or get jammed up with the law. If somebody's snatched and I call copper, there'll be another kidnap victim bumped off, more likely than not. Zapparty's a tough boy from Reno and that could tie in with what Dial told you, and if Mops Parisi is playing with Zapparty, that could make a reason to pull me into it. Parisi loathes my guts."

"You don't have to be a one-man riot squad, Johnny," Francine Ley said desperately.

He kept on smiling, with tight lips and solemn eyes. "There'll be two of us, baby. Get yourself a long coat. It's still raining a little."

She goggled at him. Her outstretched hand, the one that had been on his arm, spread its fingers stiffly, bent back from the palm, straining back. Her voice was hollow with fear.

"Me, Johnny? . . . Oh, please, not. . . ."

De Ruse said gently: "Get the coat, honey. Make yourself look nice. It might be the last time we'll go out together."

She staggered past him. He touched her arm softly, held it a moment, said almost in a whisper:

"*You* didn't put the finger on me, did you, Francy?"

She looked back stonily at the pain in his eyes, made a hoarse sound under her breath and jerked her arm loose, went quickly into the bedroom.

After a moment the pain went out of De Ruse's eyes and the metallic smile came back to the corners of his lips.

7

De Ruse half closed his eyes and watched the croupier's fingers as they slid back across the table and rested on the edge. They were round, plump, tapering fingers, graceful fingers. De Ruse raised his head and looked at the croupier's face. He was a baldheaded man of no particular age, with quiet blue eyes. He had no hair on his head at all, not a single hair.

De Ruse looked down at the croupier's hands again. The right hand turned a little on the edge of the table. The buttons on the sleeve of the croupier's brown velvet coat—cut like a dinner coat—rested on the edge of the table. De Ruse smiled his thin metallic smile.

He had three blue chips on the red. On that play the ball stopped at Black 2. The croupier paid off two of the four other men who were playing.

De Ruse pushed five blue chips forward and settled them on the red diamond. Then he turned his head to the left and watched a huskily built blond young man put three red chips on the zero.

De Ruse licked his lips and turned his head farther, looked towards the side of the rather small room. Francine Ley was sitting on a couch backed to the wall, with her head leaning against it.

"I think I've got it, baby," De Ruse said to her. "I think I've got it."

Francine Ley blinked and lifted her head away from the wall. She reached for a drink on a low round table in front of her.

She sipped the drink, looked at the floor, didn't answer.

De Ruse looked back at the blond man. The three other men had made bets. The croupier looked impatient and at the same time watchful.

De Ruse said: "How come you always hit zero when I hit red, and double zero when I hit black?"

The blond young man smiled, shrugged, said nothing.

De Ruse put his hand down on the layout and said very softly:

"I asked you a question, mister."

"Maybe I'm Jesse Livermore," the blond young man grunted. "I like to sell short."

"What is this—slow motion?" one of the other men snapped.

"Make your plays, please, gentlemen," the croupier said.

De Ruse looked at him, said: "Let it go."

The croupier spun the wheel left-handed, flicked the ball with the same hand the opposite way. His right hand rested on the edge of the table.

The ball stopped at Black 28, next to zero. The blond man laughed. "Close," he said. "Close."

De Ruse checked his chips, stacked them carefully. "I'm down six grand," he said. "It's a little raw, but I guess there's money in it. Who runs this clip joint?"

The croupier smiled slowly and stared straight into De Ruse's eyes. He asked quietly:

"Did you say clip joint?"

De Ruse nodded. He didn't bother to answer.

"I thought you said clip joint," the croupier said, and moved one foot, put weight on it.

Three of the men who had been playing picked their chips up quickly and went over to a small bar in the corner of the room. They ordered drinks and leaned their backs against the wall by the bar, watching De Ruse and the croupier. The blond man stayed put and smiled sarcastically at De Ruse.

"Tsk. Tsk," he said thoughtfully. "Your manners."

Francine Ley finished her drink and leaned her head back against the wall again. Her eyes came down and watched De Ruse furtively, under the long lashes.

A paneled door opened after a moment and a very big man with a black mustache and very rough black eyebrows came in. The croupier moved his eyes to him, then to De Ruse, pointing with his glance.

"Yes, I thought you said clip joint," he repeated tonelessly.

The big man drifted to De Ruse's elbow, touched him with his own elbow.

"Out," he said impassively.

The blond man grinned and put his hands in the pockets of his dark gray suit. The big man didn't look at him.

De Ruse glanced across the layout at the croupier and said: "I'll take back my six grand and call it a day."

"Out," the big man said wearily, jabbing his elbow into De Ruse's side.

The baldheaded croupier smiled politely.

"You," the big man said to De Ruse, "ain't goin' to get tough, are you?"

De Ruse looked at him with sarcastic surprise. "Well, well, the bouncer," he said softly. "Take him, Nicky."

The blond man took his right hand out of his pocket and swung it. The sap looked black and shiny under the bright lights. It hit the big man on the back of the head with a soft thud. The big man clawed at De Ruse, who stepped away from him quickly and took a gun out from under his arm. The big man clawed at the edge of the roulette table and fell heavily on the floor.

Francine Ley stood up and made a strangled sound in her throat.

The blond man skipped sidewise, whirled and looked at the bartender. The bartender put his hands on top of the bar. The three men who had been playing roulette looked very interested, but they didn't move.

De Ruse said: "The middle button on his right sleeve, Nicky. I think it's copper."

"Yeah." The blond man drifted around the end of the table putting the sap back in his pocket. He went close to the croupier and took hold of the middle of three buttons on his right cuff, jerked it hard. At the second jerk it came away and a thin wire followed it out of the sleeve.

"Correct," the blond man said casually, let the croupier's arm drop.

"I'll take my six grand now," De Ruse said. "Then we'll go talk to your boss."

The croupier nodded slowly and reached for the rack of chips beside the roulette table.

The big man on the floor didn't move. The blond man put his right hand behind his hip and took a .45 automatic out from inside his waistband at the back.

He swung it in his hand, smiling pleasantly around the room.

8

They went along a balcony that looked down over the dining-room and the dance-floor. The lisp of hot jazz came up to them from the lithe, swaying bodies of a high yaller band. With the lisp of jazz came the smell of food and cigarette smoke and perspiration. The balcony was high and the scene down below had a patterned look, like an overhead camera shot.

The baldheaded croupier opened a door in the corner of the balcony and went through without looking back. The blond man De Ruse had called Nicky went after him. Then De Ruse and Francine Ley.

There was a short hall with a frosted light in the ceiling. The door at the end of that looked like painted metal. The croupier put a plump finger on the small push button at the side, rang it in a certain way. There was a buzzing noise like the sound of an electric door release. The croupier pushed on the door and opened it.

Inside was a cheerful room, half den and half office. There was a grate fire and a green leather davenport at right angles to it, facing the door. A man sitting on the davenport put a newspaper down and looked up and his face suddenly got livid. He was a small man with a tight round head, a tight round dark face. He had little lightless black eyes like buttons of jet.

There was a big flat desk in the middle of the room and a very tall man stood at the end of it with a cocktail shaker in his hands. His head turned slowly and he looked over his shoulder at the four people who came into the room while his hands continued to agitate the cocktail shaker in gentle rhythm. He had a cavernous face with sunken eyes, loose grayish skin, and close cropped reddish hair without shine or parting. A thin criss-cross scar like a German *mensur* scar showed on his left cheek.

The tall man put the cocktail shaker down and turned his body around and stared at the croupier. The man on the davenport didn't move. There was a crouched tensity in his not moving.

The croupier said: "I think it's a stick-up. But I couldn't help myself. They sapped Big George."

The blond man smiled gaily and took his .45 out of his pocket. He pointed it at the floor.

"He thinks it's a stick-up," he said. "Wouldn't that positively slay you?"

De Ruse shut the heavy door. Francine Ley moved away from him, towards the side of the room away from the fire. He didn't look at her. The man on the davenport looked at her, looked at everybody.

De Ruse said quietly: "The tall one is Zapparty. The little one is Mops Parisi."

The blond man stepped to one side, leaving the croupier alone in the middle of the room. The .45 covered the man on the davenport.

"Sure, I'm Zapparty," the tall man said. He looked at De Ruse curiously for a moment.

Then he turned his back and picked the cocktail shaker up again, took out the plug and filled a shallow glass. He drained the glass, wiped his lips with a sheer lawn handkerchief and tucked the handkerchief back into his breast pocket very carefully, so that three points showed.

De Ruse smiled his thin metallic smile and touched one end of his left eyebrow with his forefinger. His right hand was in his jacket pocket.

"Nicky and I put on a little act," he said. "That was so the boys outside would have something to talk about if the going got too noisy when we came in to see you."

"It sounds interesting," Zapparty agreed. "What did you want to see me about?"

"About that gas car you take people for rides in," De Ruse said.

The man on the davenport made a very sudden movement and his hand jumped off his leg as if something had stung it. The blond man said:

"No . . . or yes, if you'd rather, Mister Parisi. It's all a matter of taste."

Parisi became motionless again. His hand dropped back to his short thick thigh.

Zapparty widened his deep eyes a little. "Gas car?" His tone was of mild puzzlement.

De Ruse went forward into the middle of the room near the croupier. He stood balanced on the balls of his feet. His gray eyes had a sleepy glitter but his face was drawn and tired, not young.

He said: "Maybe somebody just tossed it in your lap, Zapparty, but I don't think so. I'm talking about the blue Lincoln, License 5A6, with the tank of Nevada gas in front. You know, Zapparty, the stuff they use on killers in our State."

Zapparty swallowed and his large Adam's apple moved in and out. He puffed his lips, then drew them back against his teeth, then puffed them again.

The man on the davenport laughed out loud, seemed to be enjoying himself.

A voice that came from no one in the room said sharply:

"Just drop the gat, blondie. The rest of you grab air."

De Ruse looked up towards an opened panel in the wall beyond the desk. A gun showed in the opening, and a hand, but no body or face. Light from the room lit up the hand and the gun.

The gun seemed to point directly at Francine Ley. De Ruse said: "Okey," quickly, and lifted his hands, empty.

The blond man said: "That'll be Big George—all rested and ready to go." He opened his hand and let the .45 thud to the floor in front of him.

Parisi stood up very swiftly from the davenport and took a gun from under his arm. Zapparty took a revolver out of the desk drawer, leveled it. He spoke towards the panel:

"Get out, and stay out."

The panel clicked shut. Zapparty jerked his head at the baldheaded croupier, who had not seemed to move a muscle since he came into the room.

"Back on the job, Louie. Keep the chin up."

The croupier nodded and turned and went out of the room, closing the door carefully behind him.

Francine Ley laughed foolishly. Her hand went up and pulled the collar of her wrap close around her throat, as if it was cold in the room. But there were no windows and it was very warm, from the fire.

Parisi made a whistling sound with his lips and teeth and went quickly to De Ruse and stuck the gun he was holding in De Ruse's face, pushing his head back. He felt in De Ruse's pockets with his left hand, took the Colt, felt under his arms, circled around him, touched his hips, came to the front again.

He stepped back a little and hit De Ruse on the cheek with the flat of one gun. De Ruse stood perfectly still except that his head jerked a little when the hard metal hit his face.

Parisi hit him again in the same place. Blood began to run down De Ruse's cheek from the cheekbone, lazily. His head sagged a little and his knees gave way. He went down slowly, leaned with his left hand on the floor, shaking his head. His body was crouched, his legs doubled under him. His right hand dangled loosely beside his left foot.

Zapparty said: "All right, Mops. Don't get blood-hungry. We want words out of these people."

Francine Ley laughed again, rather foolishly. She swayed along the wall, holding one hand up against it.

Parisi breathed hard and backed away from De Ruse with a happy smile on his round swart face.

"I been waitin' a long time for this," he said.

When he was about six feet from De Ruse something small and darkly glistening seemed to slide out of the left leg of De Ruse's trousers into his hand. There was a sharp, snapping explosion, a tiny orange-green flame down on the floor.

Parisi's head jerked back. A round hole appeared under his chin. It got large and red almost instantly. His hands opened laxly and the two guns fell out of them. His body began to sway. He fell heavily.

Zapparty said: "Holy ——!" and jerked up his revolver.

Francine Ley screamed flatly and hurled herself at him— clawing, kicking, shrilling.

The revolver went off twice with a heavy crash. Two slugs plunked into a wall. Plaster rattled.

Francine Ley slid down to the floor, on her hands and knees. A long slim leg sprawled out from under her dress.

The blond man, down on one knee with his .45 in his hand again, rasped:

"She got the ——'s gun!"

Zapparty stood with his hands empty, a terrible expression on his face. There was a long red scratch on the back of his right hand. His revolver lay on the floor beside Francine Ley. His horrified eyes looked down at it unbelievingly.

Parisi coughed once on the floor and after that was still.

De Ruse got up on his feet. The little Mauser looked like a toy in his hand. His voice seemed to come from far away, saying:

"Watch that panel, Nicky. . . ."

There was no sound outside the room, no sound anywhere. Zapparty stood at the end of the desk, frozen, ghastly.

De Ruse bent down and touched Francine Ley's shoulder. "All right, baby?"

She drew her legs under her and got up, stood looking down at Parisi. Her body shook with a nervous chill.

"I'm sorry, baby," De Ruse said softly beside her. "I guess I had a wrong idea about you."

He took a handkerchief out of his pocket and moistened it with his lips, then rubbed his left cheek lightly and looked at blood on the handkerchief.

Nicky said: "I guess Big George went to sleep again. I was a sap not to blast at him."

De Ruse nodded a little, and said:

"Yeah. The whole play was lousy. Where's your hat and coat, Mister Zapparty? We'd like to have you go riding with us."

9

In the shadows under the pepper trees De Ruse said:

"There it is, Nicky. Over there. Nobody's bothered it. Better take a look around."

The blond man got out from under the wheel of the Packard and went off under the trees. He stood a little while on the same side of the street as the Packard, then he slipped across to where the big Lincoln was parked in front of the brick apartment house on North Kenmore.

De Ruse leaned forward across the back of the front seat and pinched Francine Ley's cheek. "You're going home now, baby—with this bus. I'll see you later."

"Johnny"—she clutched at his arm—"what are you going to do? For —— sake, can't you stop having fun for tonight?"

"Not yet, baby. Mister Zapparty wants to tell us things. I figure a little ride in that gas car will pep him up. Anyway I need it for evidence."

He looked sidewise at Zapparty in the corner of the back seat. Zapparty made a harsh sound in his throat and stared in front of him with a shadowed face.

Nicky came back across the road, stood with one foot on the running-board.

"No keys," he said. "Got 'em?"

De Ruse said: "Sure." He took keys out of his pocket and handed them to Nicky. Nicky went around to Zapparty's side of the car and opened the door.

"Out, mister."

Zapparty got out stiffly, stood in the soft, slanting rain, his mouth working. De Ruse got out after him.

"Take it away, baby."

Francine Ley slid along the seat under the steering wheel of the Packard and pushed the starter. The motor caught with a soft whirr.

"So long, baby," De Ruse said gently. "Get my slippers warmed for me. And do me a big favor, honey. Don't phone anyone."

The Packard went off along the dark street, under the big pepper trees. De Ruse watched it turn a corner. He prodded Zapparty with his elbow.

"Let's go. You're going to ride in the back of your gas car. We can't feed you much gas on account of the hole in the glass, but you'll like the smell of it. We'll go off in the country somewhere. We've got all night to play with you."

"I guess you know this is a snatch," Zapparty said harshly.

"Don't I love to think it," De Ruse purred.

They went across the street, three men walking together without haste. Nicky opened the good rear door of the Lincoln. Zapparty got into it. Nicky banged the door shut, got under the wheel and fitted the ignition key in the lock. De Ruse got in beside him and sat with his legs straddling the tank of gas.

The whole car still smelled of the gas.

Nicky started the car, turned it in the middle of the block and drove north to Franklin, back over Los Feliz towards Glendale. After a little while Zapparty leaned forward and banged on the glass. De Ruse put his ear to the hole in the glass behind Nicky's head.

Zapparty's harsh voice said: "Stone house—Castle Road—in the La Crescenta flood area."

"Jeeze, but he's a softy," Nicky grunted, his eyes on the road ahead.

De Ruse nodded, said thoughtfully: "There's more to it than that. With Parisi dead he'd clam up unless he figured he had an out."

Nicky said: "Me, I'd rather take a beating and keep my chin buttoned. Light me a pill, Johnny."

De Ruse lit two cigarettes and passed one to the blond man. He glanced back at Zapparty's long body in the corner of the car. Passing light touched up his taut face, made the shadows on it look very deep.

The big car slid noiselessly through Glendale and up the grade towards Montrose. From Montrose over to the Sunland highway and across that into the almost deserted flood area of La Crescenta.

They found Castle Road and followed it towards the mountains. In a few minutes they came to the stone house.

It stood back from the road, across a wide space which might once have been lawn but which was now packed sand, small stones and a few large boulders. The road made a square turn just before they came to it. Beyond it the road ended in a clean edge of concrete chewed off by the flood of New Year's Day, 1934.

Beyond this edge was the main wash of the flood. Bushes grew in it and there were many huge stones. On the very edge a tree grew with half its roots in the air, eight feet above the bed of the wash.

Nicky stopped the car and turned off the lights and took a big nickeled flash out of the car pocket. He handed it to De Ruse.

De Ruse got out of the car and stood for a moment with his hand on the open door, holding the flash. He took a gun out of his overcoat pocket and held it down at his side.

"Looks like a stall," he said. "I don't think there's anything stirring here."

He glanced in at Zapparty, smiled sharply and walked off across the ridges of sand, towards the house. The front door stood half open, wedged that way by sand. De Ruse went towards the corner of the house, keeping out of line with the door as well as he could. He went along the side wall, looking at boarded up windows behind which there was no trace of light.

At the back of the house was what had been a chicken house. A piece of rusted junk in a squashed garage was all that remained of the family sedan. The back door was nailed up like the windows. De Ruse stood silent in the rain, wondering why the front door was open. Then he remembered that there had been another flood a few months before, not such a bad one. There might have been enough water to break open the door on the side towards the mountains.

Two stucco houses, both abandoned, loomed on the adjoining lots. Farther away from the wash, on a bit of higher ground, there was a lighted window. It was the only light anywhere in the range of De Ruse's vision.

He went back to the front of the house and slipped through the open door, stood inside it and listened. After quite a long time he snapped the flash on.

The house didn't smell like a house. It smelled like out of doors. There was nothing in the front room but sand, a few pieces of smashed furniture, some marks on the walls, above the dark line of the flood water, where pictures had hung.

De Ruse went through a short hall into a kitchen that had a hole in the floor where the sink had been and a rusty gas stove stuck in the hole. From the kitchen he went into a bedroom. He had not heard any whisper of sound in the house so far.

The bedroom was square and dark. A carpet stiff with old mud was plastered to the floor. There was a metal bed with a rusted spring, and a waterstained mattress over part of the spring.

Feet stuck out from under the bed.

They were large feet in walnut brown brogues, with purple socks above them. The socks had gray clocks down the sides. Above the socks were trousers of black and white check.

De Ruse stood very still and played the flash down on the feet. He made a soft sucking sound with his lips. He stood like that for a couple of minutes, without moving at all. Then he stood the flash on the floor, on its end, so that the light it shot against the ceiling was reflected down to make dim light all over the room.

He took hold of the mattress and pulled it off the bed. He reached down and touched one of the hands of the man who was under the bed. The hand was ice cold. He took hold of the ankles and pulled, but the man was large and heavy.

It was easier to move the bed from over him.

10

Zapparty leaned his head back against the upholstery and shut his eyes and turned his head away a little. His eyes were shut very tight and he tried to turn his head far enough so that the light from the big flash wouldn't shine through his eyelids.

Nicky held the flash close to his face and snapped it on, off again, on, off again, monotonously, in a kind of rhythm.

De Ruse stood with one foot on the running board by the open door and looked off through the rain. On the edge of the murky horizon an airplane beacon flashed weakly.

Nicky said carelessly: "You never know what'll get a guy. I

saw one break once because a cop held his fingernail against the dimple in his chin."

De Ruse laughed under his breath. "This one is tough," he said. "You'll have to think of something better than a flashlight."

Nicky snapped the flash on, off, on, off. "I could," he said. "But I don't want to get my hands dirty."

After a little while Zapparty raised his hands in front of him and let them fall slowly and began to talk. He talked in a low monotonous voice, keeping his eyes shut against the flash.

"Parisi worked the snatch. I didn't know anything about it until it was done. Parisi muscled in on me about a month ago, with a couple of tough boys to back him up. He had found out somehow that Candless beat me out of twenty-five grand to defend my half brother on a murder rap, then sold the kid out. I didn't tell Parisi that. I didn't know he knew until tonight.

"He came into the club about seven or a little after and said: 'We've got a friend of yours, Hugo Candless. It's a hundred grand job, a quick turnover. All you have to do is help spread the payoff across the tables here, get it mixed up with a bunch of other money. You have to do that because we give you a cut—and because the caper is right up your alley, if anything goes sour.' That's about all. Parisi sat around then and chewed his fingers and waited for his boys. He got pretty jumpy when they didn't show. He went out once to make a phone call from a beer parlor."

De Ruse drew on a cigarette he held cupped inside a hand.

He said: "Who fingered the job, and how did you know Candless was up here?"

Zapparty said: "Mops told me. But I didn't know he was dead."

Nicky laughed and snapped the flash several times quickly.

De Ruse said: "Hold it steady for a minute."

Nicky held the beam steady on Zapparty's white face. Zapparty moved his lips in and out. He opened his eyes once. They were blind eyes, like the eyes of a dead fish.

Nicky said: "It's damn cold up here. What do we do with his nobs?"

De Ruse said: "We'll take him into the house and tie him to

Candless. They can keep each other warm. We'll come up again in the morning and see if he's got any fresh ideas."

Zapparty shuddered. The gleam of something like a tear showed in the corner of his nearest eye. After a moment of silence he said:

"Okey. I planned the whole thing. The gas car was my idea. I didn't want the money. I wanted Candless, and I wanted him dead. My kid brother was hanged in Quentin a week ago Friday."

There was a little silence. Nicky said something under his breath. De Ruse didn't move or make a sound.

Zapparty went on: "Mattick, the Candless driver, was in on it. He hated Candless. He was supposed to drive the ringer car to make everything look good and then take a powder. But he lapped up too much corn getting set for the job and Parisi got leery of him, had him knocked off. Another boy drove the car. It was raining and that helped."

De Ruse said: "Better—but still not all of it, Zapparty."

Zapparty shrugged quickly, slightly opened his eyes against the flash, almost grinned.

"What the hell do you want? Jam on both sides?"

De Ruse said: "I want a finger put on the bird that had me grabbed. . . . Let it go. I'll do it myself."

He took his foot off the running-board and snapped his butt away into the darkness. He slammed the car door shut, got in the front, Nicky put the flash away and slid around under the wheel, started the engine.

De Ruse said: "Somewhere where I can phone for a cab, Nicky. Then you take this riding for another hour and then call Francy. I'll have a word for you there."

The blond man shook his head slowly from side to side. "You're a good pal, Johnny, and I like you. But this has gone far enough this way. I'm taking it down to Headquarters. Don't forget I've got a private dick license under my old shirts at home."

De Ruse said: "Give me an hour, Nicky. Just an hour."

The car slid down the hill and crossed the Sunland Highway, started down another hill towards Montrose. After a while Nicky said:

"Check."

II

It was twelve minutes past one by the stamping clock on the end of the desk in the lobby of the Casa de Oro. The lobby was antique Spanish, with black and red Indian rugs, nail-studded chairs with leather cushions and leather tassels on the corners of the cushions; the gray-green olivewood doors were fitted with clumsy wrought-iron strap hinges.

A thin, dapper clerk with a waxed blond mustache and a blond pompadour leaned on the desk and looked at the clock and yawned, tapping his teeth with the backs of his bright fingernails.

The door opened from the street and De Ruse came in. He took off his hat and shook it, put it on again and yanked the brim down. His eyes looked slowly around the deserted lobby and he went to the desk, slapped a gloved palm on it.

"What's the number of the Hugo Candless bungalow?" he asked.

The clerk looked annoyed. He glanced at the clock, at De Ruse's face, back at the clock. He smiled superciliously, spoke with a slight accent.

"Twelve C. Do you wish to be announced—at this hour?"

De Ruse said: "No."

He turned away from the desk and went towards a large door with a diamond of glass in it. It looked like the door of a very high-class privy.

As he put his hand out to the door a bell rang sharply behind him.

De Ruse looked back over his shoulder, turned and went back to the desk. The clerk took his hand away from the bell, rather quickly.

His voice was cold, sarcastic, insolent, saying:

"It's not that kind of apartment house, if you please."

Two patches above De Ruse's cheek bones got a dusky red. He leaned across the counter and took hold of the braided lapel of the clerk's jacket, pulled the man's chest against the edge of the desk.

"What was that crack, nance?"

The clerk paled but managed to bang his bell again with a flailing hand.

A pudgy man in a baggy suit and a seal-brown toupee came around the corner of the desk, put out a plump finger and said: "Hey."

De Ruse let the clerk go. He looked expressionlessly at cigar ash on the front of the pudgy man's coat.

The pudgy man said: "I'm the house man. You gotta see me if you want to get tough."

De Ruse said: "You speak my language. Come over in the corner."

They went over in the corner and sat down beside a palm. The pudgy man yawned amiably and lifted the edge of his toupee and scratched under it.

"I'm Kuvalick," he said. "Times I could bop that Swiss myself. What's the beef?"

De Ruse said: "Are you a guy that can stay clammed?"

"No. I like to talk. It's all the fun I get around this dude ranch." Kuvalick got half of a cigar out of a pocket and burned his nose lighting it.

De Ruse said: "This is one time you stay clammed."

He reached inside his coat, got his wallet out, took out two tens. He rolled them around his forefinger, then slipped them off in a tube and tucked the tube into the outside pocket of the pudgy man's coat.

Kuvalick blinked, but didn't say anything.

De Ruse said: "There's a man in the Candless apartment named George Dial. His car's outside, and that's where he would be. I want to see him and I don't want to send a name in. You can take me in and stay with me."

The pudgy man said cautiously: "It's kind of late. Maybe he's in bed."

"If he is, he's in the wrong bed," De Ruse said. "He ought to get up."

The pudgy man stood up. "I don't like what I'm thinkin', but I like your tens," he said. "I'll go in and see if they're up. You stay put."

De Ruse nodded. Kuvalick went along the wall and slipped through a door in the corner. The clumsy square butt of a hip holster showed under the back of his coat as he walked. The clerk looked after him, then looked contemptuously towards De Ruse and got out a nail file.

Ten minutes went by, fifteen. Kuvalick didn't come back. De Ruse stood up suddenly, scowled and marched towards the door in the corner. The clerk at the desk stiffened, and his eyes went to the telephone on the desk, but he didn't touch it.

De Ruse went through the door and found himself under a roofed gallery. Rain dripped softly off the slanting tiles of the roof. He went along a patio the middle of which was an oblong pool framed in a mosaic of gayly colored tiles. At the end of that other patios branched off. There was a window light at the far end of the one to the left. He went towards it, at a venture, and when he came close to it made out the number 12C on the door.

He went up two flat steps and punched a bell that rang in the distance. Nothing happened. In a little while he rang again, then tried the door. It was locked. Somewhere inside he thought he heard a faint muffled thumping sound.

He stood in the rain a moment, then went around the corner of the bungalow, down a narrow, very wet passage to the back. He tried the service door; locked also. De Ruse swore, took his gun out from under his arm, held his hat against the glass panel of the service door and smashed the pane with the butt of the gun. Glass fell tinkling lightly inside.

He put his gun away, straightened his hat on his head and reached in through the broken pane to unlock the door.

The kitchen was large and bright with black and yellow tiling, looked as if it was used mostly for mixing drinks. Two bottles of Haig and Haig, a bottle of Hennessey, three or four kinds of fancy cordial bottles stood on the tiled drain board. A short hall with a closed door led to the living-room. There was a grand piano in the corner with a lamp lit beside it. Another lamp on a low table with drinks and glasses. A wood fire was dying down on the hearth.

The thumping noise got louder.

De Ruse went across the living-room and through a door framed in a valance into another hallway, thence into a beautifully paneled bedroom. The thumping noise came from a closet. De Ruse opened the door of the closet and saw a man.

He was sitting on the floor with his back in a forest of

dresses on hangers. A towel was tied around his face. Another held his ankles together. His wrists were tied behind him. He was a very bald man, as bald as the croupier at the Club Egypt.

De Ruse stared down at him harshly, then suddenly grinned, bent and cut him loose.

The man spit a washcloth out of his mouth, swore hoarsely and dived into the clothes at the back of the closet. He came up with something furry clutched in his hand, straightened it out, and put it on his hairless head.

That made him Kuvalick, the house dick.

He got up still swearing and backed away from De Ruse, with a stiff alert grin on his fat face. His right hand shot to his hip holster.

De Ruse spread his hands, said: "Tell it," and sat down in a small chintz-covered slipper chair.

Kuvalick stared at him quietly for a moment, then took his hand away from his gun.

"There's lights," he said, "so I push the buzzer. A tall dark guy opens. I seen him around here a lot. That's Dial. I say to him there's a guy outside in the lobby wants to see him hush-hush, won't give a name."

"That made you a sap," De Ruse commented dryly.

"Not yet, but soon," Kuvalick grinned, and spit a shred of cloth out of his mouth. "I describe you. *That* makes me a sap. He smiled kind of funny and asks me to come in a minute. I go in past him and he shuts the door and sticks a gun in my kidney. He says: 'Did you say he wore all dark clothes?' I say: 'Yes. And what's that gat for?' He says: 'Does he have gray eyes and sort of crinkly black hair and is he hard around the teeth?' I say: 'Yes, you —— —— and what's the gat for?'

"He says: 'For this,' and lets me have it on the back of the head. I go down, groggy, but not out. Then the Candless broad comes out from a doorway and they tie me up and shove me in the closet and that's that. I hear them fussin' around for a little while and then I hear silence. That's all until you ring the bell."

De Ruse smiled lazily, pleasantly. His whole body was lax in the chair. His manner had become indolent and unhurried.

"They faded," he said softly. "They got tipped off. I don't think that was very bright."

Kuvalick said: "I'm an old Wells Fargo dick and I can stand a shock. What they been up to?"

"What kind of woman is Mrs. Candless?"

"Dark, a looker. Sex hungry, as the fellow says. Kind of worn and tight. They get a new chauffeur every three months. There's a couple guys in the Casa she likes too. I guess there's this gigolo that bopped me."

De Ruse looked at his watch, nodded, leaned forward to get up. "I guess it's about time for some law. Got any friends downtown you'd like to give a snatch story to?"

A voice said: "Not quite yet."

George Dial came quickly into the room from the hallway and stood quietly inside it with a long, thin, silenced automatic in his hand. His eyes were bright and mad, but his lemon-colored finger was very steady on the trigger of the small gun.

"We didn't fade," he said. "We weren't quite ready. But it might not have been a bad idea—for you two."

Kuvalick's pudgy hand swept for his hip-holster.

The small automatic with the black tube on it made two flat dull sounds.

A puff of dust jumped from the front of Kuvalick's coat. His hands jerked sharply away from his sides and his small eyes snapped very wide open, like seeds bursting from a pod. He fell heavily on his side against the wall, lay quite still on his left side, with his eyes half open and his back against the wall. His toupee was tipped over rakishly.

De Ruse looked at him swiftly, looked back at Dial. No emotion showed in his face, not even excitement.

He said: "You're a crazy fool, Dial. That kills your last chance. You could have bluffed it out. But that's not your only mistake."

Dial said calmly: "No. I see that now. I shouldn't have sent the boys after you. I did that just for the hell of it. That comes of not being a professional."

De Ruse nodded slightly, looked at Dial almost with friendliness. "Just for the fun of it—who tipped you off the game had gone smash?"

"Francy—and she took her damn' time about it," Dial said savagely. "I'm leaving, so I won't be able to thank her for a while."

"Not ever," De Ruse said. "You won't get out of the State. You won't ever touch a nickel of the big boy's money. Not you or your sidekicks or your woman. The cops are getting the story—right now."

Dial said: "We'll get clear. We have enough to tour on, Johnny. So long."

Dial's face tightened and his hand jerked up, with the gun in it. De Ruse half-closed his eyes, braced himself for the shock. The little gun didn't go off. There was a rustle behind Dial and a tall dark woman in a gray fur coat slid into the room. A small hat was balanced on dark hair knotted on the nape of her neck. She was pretty, in a thin, haggard sort of way. The lip rouge on her mouth was as black as soot; there was no color in her cheeks.

She had a cool lazy voice that didn't match with her taut expression. "Who is Francy?" she asked coldly.

De Ruse opened his eyes wide and his body got stiff in the chair and his right hand began to slide up towards his chest.

"Francy is my girl friend," he said. "Mister Dial has been trying to get her away from me. But that's all right. He's a handsome lad and ought to be able to pick lots."

The tall woman's face suddenly became dark and wild and furious. She grabbed fiercely at Dial's arm, the one that held the gun.

De Ruse snatched for his shoulder-holster, got his .38 loose. But it wasn't his gun that went off. It wasn't the silenced automatic in Dial's hand. It was a huge frontier Colt with an eight-inch barrel and a boom like an exploding bomb. It went off from the floor, from beside Kuvalick's right hip, where Kuvalick's plump hand held it.

It went off just once. Dial was thrown back against the wall as if by a giant hand. His head crashed against the wall and instantly his darkly handsome face was a mask of blood.

He fell laxly down the wall and the little automatic with the black tube on it fell in front of him. The dark woman dived for it, down on her hands and knees in front of Dial's sprawled body.

She got it, began to bring it up. Her face was convulsed, her lips were drawn back over thin wolfish teeth that shimmered.

Kuvalick's voice said: "I'm a tough guy. I used to be a Wells Fargo dick."

His great cannon slammed again. A shrill scream was torn from the woman's lips. Her body was flung against Dial's. Her eyes opened and shut, opened and shut. Her face got white and vacant.

"Shoulder shot. She's okay," Kuvalick said, and got up on his feet. He jerked open his coat and patted his chest.

"Bullet proof vest," he said proudly. "But I thought I'd better lie quiet for a while or he'd popped me in the face."

12

Francine Ley yawned and stretched out a long green pajama-clad leg and looked at a slim green slipper on her bare foot. She yawned again, got up and walked nervously across the room to the kidney-shaped desk. She poured a drink, drank it quickly, with a sharp nervous shudder. Her face was drawn and tired, her eyes hollow; there were dark smudges under her eyes.

She looked at the tiny watch on her wrist. It was almost four o'clock in the morning. Still with her wrist up she whirled at a sound, put her back to the desk and began to breathe very quickly, pantingly.

De Ruse came in through the red curtains. He stopped and looked at her without expression, then slowly took off his hat and overcoat and dropped them on a chair. He took off his suit coat and his tan shoulder-harness and walked over to the drinks.

He sniffed at a glass, filled it a third full of whiskey, put it down in a gulp.

"So you had to tip the louse off," he said somberly, looking down into the empty glass he held.

Francine Ley shivered, turned her head away from him.

"You're all right, Johnny?" she asked softly, tiredly.

"You had to phone the louse," De Ruse said in exactly the

same tone. "You knew damn' well he was mixed up in it. You'd rather he got loose, even if he cooled me off doing it."

Francine Ley said: "Yes. I had to phone him. What happened?"

De Ruse didn't speak, didn't look at her. He put the glass down slowly and poured more whiskey into it, added charged water, looked around for some ice. Not finding any he began to sip the drink with his eyes on the white top of the desk.

Francine Ley said: "There isn't a guy in the world that doesn't rate a start on you, Johnny. It wouldn't do him any good, but he'd have to have it, if I knew him."

De Ruse said slowly: "That's swell. Only I'm not quite that good. I'd be a stiff right now except for a comic hotel dick that wears a Buntline Special and a bullet-proof vest to work."

After a little while Francine Ley said: "Do you want me to blow?"

De Ruse looked at her quickly, looked away again. He put his glass down and walked away from the desk. Over his shoulder he said:

"Not so long as you keep on telling me the truth."

He sat down in a deep chair and leaned his elbows on the arms of it, cupped his face in his hands. Francine Ley watched him for a moment, then went over and sat on an arm of the chair. She pulled his head back gently until it was against the back of the chair. She began to stroke his forehead.

De Ruse closed his eyes. His body became loose and relaxed. His voice began to sound sleepy.

"You saved my life over at the Club Egypt maybe. I guess that gave you the right to let Handsome have a shot at me."

Francine Ley stroked his head, without speaking.

"Handsome is dead," De Ruse went on. "The peeper shot his face off."

Francine Ley's hand stopped. In a moment it began again, stroking his head.

"The Candless frau was in on it. Seems she's a hot number. She wanted Hugo's dough, and she wanted all the men in the world except Hugo. Thank —— *she* didn't get bumped. She talked plenty. So did Zapparty."

"Yes, honey," Francine Ley said quietly.

De Ruse yawned. "Candless is dead. He was dead before we started. They never wanted him anything else but dead. Parisi didn't care one way or the other, as long as he got paid."

Francine Ley said: "Yes, honey."

"Tell you the rest in the morning," De Ruse said thickly. "I guess Nicky and I are all square with the law. . . . Let's go to Reno, get married. . . . I'm sick of this tomcat life. . . . Get me 'nother drink, baby."

Francine Ley didn't move except to draw her fingers softly and soothingly across his forehead and back over his temples. De Ruse moved lower in the chair. His head rolled to one side.

"Yes, honey."

"Don't call me honey," De Ruse said thickly. "Just call me pigeon."

When he was quite asleep she got off the arm of the chair and went and sat down near him. She sat very still and watched him, her face cupped in her long delicate hands with the cherry-colored nails.

Spanish Blood

BIG JOHN MASTERS was large, fat, oily. He had sleek blue jowls and very thick fingers on which the knuckles were dimples. His brown hair was combed straight back from his forehead and he wore a wine-colored suit with patch pockets, a wine-colored tie, a tan silk shirt. There was a lot of red and gold band around the thick brown cigar between his lips.

He wrinkled his nose, peeped at his hole card again, tried not to grin. He said:

"Hit me again, Dave—and don't hit me with the City Hall."

A four and a deuce showed. Dave Aage looked at them solemnly across the table, looked down at his own hand. He was very tall and thin, with a long bony face and hair the color of wet sand. He held the deck flat on the palm of his hand, turned the top card slowly, and flicked it across the table. It was a queen of spades.

Big John Masters opened his mouth wide, waved his cigar about, chuckled.

"Pay me, Dave. For once a lady was right." He turned his hole card with a flourish. A five.

Dave Aage smiled politely, didn't move. A muted telephone bell rang close to him, behind long silk drapes that bordered the very high lancet windows. He took a cigarette out of his mouth and laid it carefully on the edge of a tray on a tabouret beside the card table, reached behind the curtain for the phone.

He spoke into the cup with a cool, almost whispering voice, then listened for a long time. Nothing changed in his greenish eyes, no flicker of emotion showed on his narrow face. Masters squirmed, bit hard on his cigar.

After a long time Aage said, "Okey, you'll hear from us." He pronged the instrument and put it back behind the curtain.

He picked his cigarette up, pulled the lobe of his ear. Masters swore. "What's eating you, for ——'s sake? Gimme ten bucks."

Aage said softly: "I have a lady too, John. Also an ace." He turned his hole card over, showed the queen of hearts beside the ace. "Blackjack." He reached lazily for the two five-dollar bills that lay at Masters' elbow, added them to a loose pile of currency beside the deck.

Masters tore his cigar out of his mouth, slammed it to shapelessness on the edge of the table. After a moment he grinned. He had a hard, sharp grin.

"I'm a sucker to play any games at all with you, you damned highbinder!"

Aage smiled dryly and leaned back. He reached for a drink, sipped it, put it down, spoke around his cigarette. All his movements were slow, thoughtful, almost absent-minded. He said:

"Are we a couple of smart guys, John?"

"Yeah. We own the town. But it don't help my blackjack game any."

"It's just two months to election, isn't it, John?"

Masters scowled at him, fished in his pocket for a fresh cigar, jammed it into his mouth.

"So what?"

"Suppose something happened to our toughest opposition. Right now. Would that be a good idea, or not?"

"Huh?" Masters raised eyebrows so thick that his whole face seemed to have to work to push them up. He thought for a moment, sourly. "It would be lousy—if they didn't catch the guy pronto. Hell, the voters would figure we hired it done."

"You're talking about murder, John," Aage said patiently. "I didn't say anything about murder."

Masters lowered his eyebrows and pulled at a coarse black hair that grew out of his nose.

"Well, spit it out for ——'s sake! What's eatin' you?"

Aage smiled, blew a smoke ring, watched it float off and come apart in frail wisps.

"I just had a phone call," he said very softly. "Donegan Marr is dead."

Masters moved slowly. His whole body moved slowly to-wards the card table, leaned far over it. When his body couldn't go any farther his chin came out until his jaw muscles stood out like thick wires.

"Huh?" he said thickly. "Huh?"

Aage nodded, calm as ice. "But you were right about murder, John. It *was* murder. Just half an hour ago, or so. In his office. They don't know who did it—yet."

Masters shrugged heavily and leaned back. He looked around him with a stupid expression. Very suddenly he began to laugh. His laughter bellowed and roared around the little turret-like room where the two men sat, overflowed into an enormous living-room beyond, echoed back and forth through a maze of heavy dark furniture, enough standing lamps to light a boulevard, a double row of oil paintings in massive gold frames.

Aage sat silent. He rubbed his cigarette out slowly in the tray until there was nothing of the fire left but a thick dark smudge. He dusted his bony fingers together and waited.

Masters stopped laughing as abruptly as he had begun. The room was very still. Masters looked tired. He mopped his big face.

"We got to do something, Dave," he said quietly. "I almost forgot. We got to break this fast. It's dynamite."

Aage reached behind the curtain again and brought the phone out, pushed it across the table over the scattered cards.

"Well—we know how, don't we?" he said calmly.

A cunning light shone in Big John Masters' muddy brown eyes. He licked his lips, reached a big hand for the phone.

"Yeah," he said purringly, "we do, Dave. We do at that, by ——!"

He dialed with a thick finger that would hardly go into the holes.

2

Donegan Marr's face looked cool, neat, poised, even then. He was dressed in soft gray flannels and his hair was the same soft gray color as his suit, brushed back from a ruddy, youngish face. The skin was pale on the frontal bones where the hair would fall when he stood up. The rest of the skin was tanned.

He was lying back in a padded blue office chair. A cigar had gone out in a tray with a bronze greyhound on its rim. His left hand dangled beside the chair and his right hand held a gun loosely on the desk top. The polished nails glittered in sunlight from the big closed window behind him.

Blood had soaked the left side of his vest, made the gray flannel almost black. He was quite dead, had been dead for some time.

A tall man, very brown and slender and silent, leaned against a brown mahogany filing cabinet and looked fixedly at the dead man. His hands were in the pockets of a neat blue serge suit. There was a straw hat on the back of his head. But there was nothing casual about his eyes or his tight, straight mouth.

A big sandy-haired man was groping around on the blue rug. He said thickly, stooped over: "No shells, Sam."

The dark man didn't move, didn't answer. The other stood up, yawned, looked at the man in the chair.

"Hell! This one will stink. Two months to election. Boy, is this a smack in the puss for somebody."

The dark man said slowly: "We went to school together. We used to be buddies. We carried the torch for the same girl. He won, but we stayed good friends, all three of us. He was always a great kid . . . Maybe a shade too smart."

The sandy-haired man walked around the room without touching anything. He bent over and sniffed at the gun on the desk, shook his head, said: "Not used—this one." He wrinkled his nose, sniffed at the air. "Air-conditioned. The three top floors. Sound-proofed too. High grade stuff. They tell me this whole building is electric-welded. Not a rivet in it. Ever hear that, Sam?"

The dark man shook his head slowly.

"Wonder where the help was," the sandy-haired man went on. "A big shot like him would have more than one girl."

The dark man shook his head again. "That's all, I guess. She was out to lunch. He was a lone wolf, Pete. Sharp as a weasel. In a few more years he'd have taken the town over."

The sandy-haired man was behind the desk now, almost leaning over the dead man's shoulder. He was looking down at a leather-backed appointment pad with buff leaves. He said slowly: "Somebody named Imlay was due here at twelve-fifteen. Only date on the pad."

He glanced at a cheap watch on his wrist. "One-thirty. Long gone. Who's Imlay? . . . Say, wait a minute! There's an assistant D.A. named Imlay. He's running for judge on the Masters-Aage ticket. D'you figure — "

There was a sharp knock on the door. The office was so long that the two men had to think a moment before they placed which of the three doors it was. Then the sandy-haired man went towards the most distant of them, saying over his shoulder:

"M.E.'s man maybe. Leak this to your favorite newshawk and you're out a job. Am I right?"

The dark man didn't answer. He moved slowly to the desk, leaned forward a little, spoke softly to the dead man.

"Good-by, Donny. Just let it all go. I'll take care of it. I'll take care of Belle."

The door at the end of the office opened and a brisk man with a bag came in, trotted down the blue carpet and put his bag on the desk. The sandy-haired man shut the door against a bulge of faces. He strolled back to the desk.

The brisk man cocked his head on one side, examining the corpse. "Two of them," he muttered. "Look like about .32's — hard slugs. Close to the heart but not touching. He must have died pretty soon. Maybe a minute or two."

The dark man made a disgusted sound and walked to the window, stood with his back to the room, looking out, at the tops of high buildings and a warm blue sky. The sandy-haired man watched the examiner lift a dead eyelid. He said: "Wish the powder guy would get here. I wanta use the phone. This Imlay — "

The dark man turned his head slightly, with a dull smile. "Use it. This isn't going to be any mystery."

"Oh I don't know," the M.E.'s man said, flexing a wrist, then holding the back of his hand against the skin of the dead man's face. "Might not be so damn' political as you think, Delaguerra. He's a good-looking stiff."

The sandy-haired man took hold of the phone gingerly,

with a handkerchief, laid the receiver down, dialed, picked the receiver up with the handkerchief and put it to his ear.

After a moment he snapped his chin down, said: "Pete Marcus. Wake the Inspector." He yawned, waited again, then spoke in a different tone: "Marcus and Delaguerra, Inspector, from Donegan Marr's office. No print or camera men here yet . . . Huh? . . . Holding off till the Commissioner gets here? . . . Okey . . . Yeah, he's here."

The dark man turned. The man at the phone gestured at him. "Take it, Spanish."

Sam Delaguerra took the phone, ignoring the careful handkerchief, listened. His face got hard. He said quietly: "Sure I knew him—but I didn't sleep with him . . . Nobody's here but his secretary, a girl. She phoned the alarm in. There's a name on a pad—Imlay, a twelve-fifteen appointment. No, we haven't touched anything yet . . . No . . . Okey, right away."

He hung up so slowly that the click of the instrument was barely audible. His hand stayed on it, then fell suddenly and heavily to his side. His voice was thick.

"I'm called off it, Pete. You're to hold it down until Commissioner Drew gets here. Nobody gets in. White, black or Cherokee Indian."

"What you called in for?" the sandy-haired man yelped angrily.

"Don't know. It's an order," Delaguerra said tonelessly.

The M.E.'s man stopped writing on a form pad to look curiously at Delaguerra, with a sharp, sidelong look.

Delaguerra crossed the office and went through the communicating door. There was a smaller office outside, partly partitioned off for a waiting-room, with a group of leather chairs and a table with magazines. Inside a counter was a typewriter desk, a safe, some filing cabinets. A small dark girl sat at the desk with her head down on a wadded handkerchief. Her hat was crooked on her head. Her shoulders jerked and her thick sobs were like panting.

Delaguerra patted her shoulder. She looked up at him with a tear-bloated face, a twisted mouth. He smiled down at her questioning face, said gently:

"Did you call Mrs. Marr yet?"

She nodded, speechless, shaken with rough sobs. He patted her shoulder again, stood a moment beside her, then went on out, with his mouth tight and a hard, dark glitter in his black eyes.

3

The big English house stood a long way back from the narrow, winding ribbon of concrete that was called De Neve Lane. The lawn had rather long grass with a curving path of stepping stones half hidden in it. There was a gable over the front door and ivy on the wall. Trees grew all around the house, close to it, made it a little dark and remote.

All the houses in De Neve Lane had that same calculated air of neglect. But the tall green hedge that hid the driveway and the garages was trimmed as carefully as a French poodle, and there was nothing dark or mysterious about the mass of yellow and flame-colored gladioli that flared at the opposite end of the lawn.

Delaguerra got out of a tan-colored Cadillac touring car that had no top. It was an old model, heavy and dirty. A taut canvas formed a deck over the back part of the car. He wore a white linen cap and dark glasses and had changed his blue serge for a gray cloth outing suit with a jerkin-style zipper jacket.

He didn't look very much like a cop. He hadn't looked very much like a cop in Donegan Marr's office. He walked slowly up the path of stepping stones, touched a brass knocker on the front door of the house, then didn't knock with it. He pushed a bell at the side, almost hidden by the ivy.

There was a long wait. It was very warm, very silent. Bees droned over the warm bright grass. There was the distant whirring of a lawnmower.

The door opened slowly and a black face looked out at him, a long, sad black face with tear streaks on its lavender face powder. The black face almost smiled, said haltingly:

"Hello there, Mistah Sam. It's sure good to see you."

Delaguerra took his cap off, swung the dark glasses at his side. He said: "Hello, Minnie. I'm sorry. I've got to see Mrs. Marr."

"Sure. Come right in, Mistah Sam."

The maid stood aside and he went into a shadowy hall with a tile floor. "No reporters yet?"

The girl shook her head slowly. Her warm brown eyes were stunned, doped with shock.

"Ain't been nobody yet . . . She ain't been in long. She ain't said a word. She just stand there in that there sun room that ain't got no sun."

Delaguerra nodded, said: "Don't talk to anybody, Minnie. They're trying to keep this quiet for a while, out of the papers."

"Ah sure won't, Mistah Sam. Not me. Not nohow."

Delaguerra smiled at her, walked noiselessly on crepe soles along the tiled hall to the back of the house, turned into another hall just like it at right angles. He knocked at a door. There was no answer. He turned the knob and went into a long narrow room that was dim in spite of many windows. Trees grew close to the windows, pressing their leaves against the glass. Some of the windows were masked by long cretonne drapes.

The tall girl in the middle of the room didn't look at him. She stood motionless, rigid. She stared at the windows. Her hands were tightly clenched at her sides.

She had red-brown hair that seemed to gather all the light there was and make a soft halo around her coldly beautiful face. She wore a sportily cut blue velvet ensemble with patch pockets. A white handkerchief with a blue border stuck out of the breast pocket, arranged carefully in points, like a foppish man's handkerchief.

Delaguerra waited, letting his eyes get used to the dimness. After a while the girl spoke through the silence, in a low, husky voice.

"Well . . . they got him, Sam. They got him at last. Was he so much hated?"

Delaguerra said softly: "He was in a tough racket, Belle. I guess he played it as clean as he could, but he couldn't help but make enemies."

She turned her head slowly and looked at him. Lights shifted in her hair. Gold glinted in it. Her eyes were vividly, startlingly blue. Her voice faltered a little, saying:

"Who killed him, Sam? Have they any ideas?"

Delaguerra nodded slowly, sat down in a wicker chair, swung his cap and glasses between his knees.

"Yeah. We think we know who did it. A man named Imlay, an assistant in the D.A.'s office."

"My God!" the girl breathed. "What's this rotten city coming to?"

Delaguerra went on tonelessly: "It was like this—if you're sure you want to know . . . yet."

"I do, Sam. His eyes stare at me from the wall, wherever I look. Asking me to do something. He was pretty swell to me, Sam. We had our troubles, of course, but . . . they didn't mean anything."

Delaguerra said: "This Imlay is running for judge with the backing of the Masters-Aage group. He's in the gay forties and it seems he's been playing house with a night-club number called Stella La Motte. Somehow, someway, photos were taken of them together, very drunk and undressed. Donny got the photos, Belle. They were found in his desk. According to his desk pad he had a date with Imlay at twelve-fifteen. We figure they had a row and Imlay beat him to the punch."

"You found those photos, Sam?" the girl asked, very quietly.

He shook his head, smiled crookedly. "No. If I had, I guess I might have ditched them. Commissioner Drew found them—after I was pulled off the investigation."

Her head jerked at him. Her vivid blue eyes got wide. "Pulled off the investigation? You—Donny's friend?"

"Yeah. Don't take it too big. I'm a cop, Belle. After all I take orders."

She didn't speak, didn't look at him any more. After a little while he said: "I'd like to have the keys to your cabin at Puma Lake. I'm detailed to go up there and look around, see if there's any evidence. Donny had conferences there."

Something changed in the girl's face. It got almost contemptuous. Her voice was empty. "I'll get them. But you won't find anything there. If you're helping them to find dirt on Donny—so they can clear this Imlay person. . . ."

He smiled a little, shook his head slowly. His eyes were very deep, very sad.

"That's crazy talk, kid. I'd turn my badge in before I did that."

"I see." She walked past him to the door, went out of the room. He sat quite still while she was gone, looked at the wall with an empty stare. There was a hurt look on his face. He swore very softly, under his breath.

The girl came back, walked up to him and held her hand out. Something tinkled into his palm.

"The keys, copper."

Delaguerra stood up, dropped the keys into a pocket. His face got wooden. Belle Marr went over to a table and her nails scratched harshly on a cloisonné box, getting a cigarette out of it. With her back turned she said:

"I don't think you'll have any luck, as I said. It's too bad you've only got blackmailing on him so far."

Delaguerra breathed out slowly, stood a moment, then turned away. "Okey," he said softly. His voice was quite off-hand now, as if it was a nice day, as if nobody had been killed.

At the door he turned again. "I'll see you when I get back, Belle. Maybe you'll feel better."

She didn't answer, didn't move. She held the unlighted cigarette rigidly in front of her mouth, close to it. After a moment Delaguerra went on: "You ought to know how I feel about it. Donny and I were like brothers once. I—I heard you were not getting on so well with him . . . I'm glad as all hell that was wrong. But don't let yourself get too hard, Belle. There's nothing to be hard about—with me."

He waited a few seconds, staring at her back. When she still didn't move or speak he went on out.

4

A narrow rocky road dropped down from the highway and ran along the flank of the hill above the lake. The tops of cabins showed here and there among the pines. An open shed was cut into the side of the hill. Delaguerra put his dusty Cadillac under it and climbed down a narrow path towards the water.

The lake was deep blue but very low. Two or three canoes drifted about on it and the chugging of an outboard motor sounded in the distance, around a bend. He went along between thick walls of undergrowth, walking on pine needles, turned around a stump and crossed a small rustic bridge to the Marr cabin.

It was built of half-round logs and had a wide porch on the lake side. It looked very lonely and empty. The spring that ran under the bridge curved around beside the house and one end of the porch dropped down sheer to the big flat stones through which the water trickled. The stones would be covered when the water was high, in the spring.

Delaguerra went up wooden steps and took the keys out of his pocket, unlocked the heavy front door, then stood on the porch a little while and lit a cigarette before he went in. It was very still, very pleasant, very cool and clear after the heat of the city. A mountain bluejay sat on a stump and pecked at its wings. Somebody far out on the lake fooled with a ukulele. He went into the cabin.

He looked at some dusty antlers, a big rough table spattered with magazines, an old-fashioned battery-type radio, a box-shaped phonograph with a disheveled pile of records beside it. There were tall glasses that hadn't been washed and a half-bottle of Scotch beside them, on a table near the big stone fireplace. A car went along the road up above and stopped somewhere not far off. Delaguerra frowned around, said: "Stall," under his breath, with a defeated feeling. There wasn't any sense in it. A man like Donegan Marr wouldn't leave anything that mattered in a mountain cabin.

He looked into a couple of bedrooms, one just a shakedown with a couple of cots, one better furnished, with a made-up bed, and a pair of women's gaudy pajamas tossed across it. They didn't look quite like Belle Marr's.

At the back there was a small kitchen with a gasoline stove and a wood stove. He opened the back door with another key and stepped out on a small porch flush with the ground, near a big pile of cordwood and a double-bitted axe on a chopping block.

Then he saw the flies.

A wooden walk went down the side of the house to a woodshed under it. A beam of sunlight had slipped through the trees and lay across the walk. In the sunlight there a clotted mass of flies festered on something brownish, sticky. The flies didn't want to move. Delaguerra bent down, then put his hand down and touched the sticky place, sniffed at his finger. His face got shocked and stiff.

There was another smaller patch of the brownish stuff farther on, in the shade, outside the door of the shed. He took the keys out of his pocket very quickly and found the one that unlocked the big padlock of the woodshed. He yanked the door open.

There was a big loose pile of cordwood inside. Not split wood—cordwood. Not stacked, just thrown in anyhow. Delaguerra began to toss the big rough pieces to one side.

After he had thrown a lot of it aside he was able to reach down and take hold of two cold stiff ankles in lisle socks and drag the dead man out into the light.

He was a slender man, neither tall nor short, in a well-cut basket weave suit. His small neat shoes were polished, a little dust over the polish. He didn't have any face, much. It was broken to pulp by a terrific smash. The top of his head was split open and brains and blood were mixed in the thin grayish-brown hair.

Delaguerra straightened quickly and went back into the house to where the half-bottle of Scotch stood on the table in the living-room. He uncorked it, drank from the neck, waited a moment, drank again.

He said: "Phew!" out loud, and shivered as the whiskey whipped at his nerves.

He went back to the woodshed, leaned down again as an automobile motor started up somewhere. He stiffened. The motor swelled in sound, then the sound faded and there was silence again. Delaguerra shrugged, went through the dead man's pockets. They were empty. One of them, with cleaner's marks on it probably, had been cut away. The tailor's label had been cut from the inside pocket of the coat, leaving ragged stitches.

The man was stiff. He might have been dead twenty-four hours, not more. The blood on his face had coagulated thickly but had not dried completely.

Delaguerra squatted beside him for a little while, looking at the bright glitter of Puma Lake, the distant flash of a paddle from a canoe. Then he went back into the woodshed and pawed around for a heavy block of wood with a great deal of blood on it, didn't find one. He went back into the house and out on the front porch, went to the end of the porch, stared down the drop, then at the big flat stones in the spring.

"Yeah," he said softly.

There were flies clotted on two of the stones, a lot of flies. He hadn't noticed them before. The drop was about thirty feet, enough to smash a man's head open if he landed just right.

He sat down in one of the big rockers and smoked for several minutes without moving. His face was stiff with thought, his black eyes withdrawn and remote. There was a tight, hard smile, ever so faintly sardonic, at the corners of his mouth.

At the end of that he went silently back through the house and dragged the dead man into the woodshed again, covered him up loosely with the wood. He locked the woodshed, locked the house up, went back along the narrow, steep path to the road above and to his car.

It was past six o'clock, but the sun was still bright as he drove off.

5

An old store counter served as bar in the roadside beerstube. Three low stools stood against it. Delaguerra sat on the end one near the door, looked at the foamy inside of an empty beer glass. The bartender was a dark kid in overalls, with shy eyes and lank hair. He stuttered. He said:

"Sh-should I d-draw you another g-glass, mister?"

Delaguerra shook his head, stood up off the stool. "Racket beer, sonny," he said sadly. "Tasteless as a roadhouse blonde."

"P-portola B-brew, mister. Supposed to be the b-best."

"Uh-huh. The worst. You use it, or you don't have a license. So long, sonny."

He went across to the screen door, looked out at the sunny highway on which the shadows were getting quite long. Beyond the concrete there was a graveled space edged by a white fence of four-by-fours. There were two cars parked there: Delaguerra's old Cadillac and a dusty hard-bitten Ford. A tall, thin man in khaki whipcord stood beside the Cadillac, looking at it.

Delaguerra got a bulldog pipe out, filled it half full from a zipper pouch, lit it with slow care and flicked the match into the corner. Then he stiffened a little, looking out through the screen.

The tall, thin man was unsnapping the canvas that covered the back part of Delaguerra's car. He rolled part of it back, stood peering down into the space underneath.

Delaguerra opened the screen door softly and walked in long, loose strides across the concrete of the highway. His crepe soles made sound on the gravel beyond, but the thin man didn't turn. Delaguerra came up beside him.

"Thought I noticed you behind me," he said dully. "What's the grift?"

The man turned without any haste. He had a long, sour face, eyes the color of seaweed. His coat was open, pushed back by a hand on a left hip. That showed a gun worn butt to the front in a belt holster, cavalry style.

He looked Delaguerra up and down with a faint crooked smile.

"This your crate?"

"What do you think?"

The thin man pulled his coat back farther and showed a bronze badge on his pocket.

"I think I'm a Toluca County game warden, mister. I think this ain't deer-hunting time and it ain't ever deer-hunting time for does."

Delaguerra lowered his eyes very slowly, looked into the back of his car, bending over to see past the canvas. The body of a young deer lay there on some junk, beside a rifle. The soft eyes of the dead animal, unglazed by death, seemed to look at him with a gentle reproach. There was dried blood on the doe's slender neck.

Delaguerra straightened, said gently: "That's damn' cute."

"Got a hunting license?"

"I don't hunt," Delaguerra said.

"Wouldn't help much. I see you got a rifle."

"I'm a cop."

"Oh—cop, huh? Would you have a badge?"

"I would."

Delaguerra reached into his breast pocket, got the badge out, rubbed it on his sleeve, held it in the palm of his hand. The thin game warden stared down at it, licking his lips.

"Detective lieutenant, huh? City police." His face got distant and lazy. "Okey, Lieutenant. We'll ride about ten miles downgrade in your heap. I'll thumb a ride back to mine."

Delaguerra put the badge away, knocked his pipe out carefully, stamped the embers into the gravel. He replaced the canvas loosely.

"Pinched?" he asked gravely.

"Pinched, Lieutenant."

"Let's go."

He got in under the wheel of the Cadillac. The thin warden went around the other side, got in beside him. Delaguerra started the car, backed around and started off down the smooth concrete of the highway. The valley was a deep haze in the distance. Beyond the haze other peaks were enormous on the skyline. Delaguerra coasted the big car easily, without haste. The two men stared straight before them without speaking.

After a long time Delaguerra said: "I didn't know they had deer at Puma Lake. That's as far as I've been."

"There's a reservation by there, Lieutenant," the warden said calmly. He stared through the dusty windshield. "Part of the Toluca County Forest—or wouldn't you know that?"

Delaguerra said: "I guess I wouldn't know it. I never shot a deer in my life. Police work hasn't made me that tough."

The warden grinned, said nothing. The highway went through a saddle, then the drop was on the right side of the highway. Little canyons began to open out into the hills on the left. Some of them had rough roads in them, half over-grown, with wheel tracks.

Delaguerra swung the big car hard and suddenly to the left, shot it into a cleared space of reddish earth and dry grass, slammed the brake on. The car skidded, swayed, ground to a lurching stop.

The warden was flung violently to the right, then forward against the windshield. He cursed, jerked up straight and threw his right hand across his body at the holstered gun.

Delaguerra took hold of a thin, hard wrist and twisted it sharply towards the man's body. The warden's face whitened behind the tan. His left hand fumbled at the holster, then relaxed. He spoke in a tight, hurt voice:

"Makin' it worse, copper. I got a phone tip at Salt Springs. Described your car, said where it was. Said there was a doe carcass in it. I—"

Delaguerra loosed the wrist, snapped the belt holster open and jerked the Colt out of it. He tossed the gun from the car.

"Get out, County! Thumb that ride you spoke of. What's the matter—can't you live on your salary any more? You planted it yourself, back at Puma Lake, you —— damn' chiseler!"

The warden got out slowly, stood on the ground with his face blank, his jaw loose and slack.

"Tough guy," he muttered. "You'll be sorry for this, copper. I'll swear a complaint."

Delaguerra slid across the seat, got out of the right-hand door. He stood close to the warden, said very slowly:

"Maybe I'm wrong, mister. Maybe you did get a call. Maybe you did."

He swung the doe's body out of the car, laid it down on the ground, watching the warden. The thin man didn't move, didn't try to get near his gun lying on the grass a dozen feet away. His seaweed eyes were dull, very cold.

Delaguerra got back into the Cadillac, snapped the brake off, started the engine. He backed to the highway. The warden still didn't make a move.

The Cadillac leaped forward, shot down the grade, out of sight. When it was quite gone the warden picked his gun up and holstered it, dragged the doe behind some bushes, and started to walk back along the highway towards the crest of the grade.

6

The girl at the desk in the Kenworthy said: "This man called you three times, Lieutenant, but he wouldn't give a number. A lady called twice. Wouldn't leave name or number."

Delaguerra took three slips of paper from her, read the name "Joey Chill" on them and the various times. He picked up a couple of letters, touched his cap to the desk girl and got into the automatic elevator. He got off at four, walked down a narrow, quiet corridor, unlocked a door. Without switching on any lights he went across to a big French window, opened it wide, stood there looking at the thick dark sky, the flash of neon lights, the stabbing beams of headlamps on Ortega Boulevard, two blocks over.

He lit a cigarette and smoked half of it without moving. His face in the dark was very long, very troubled. Finally he left the window and went into a small bedroom, switched on a table lamp and undressed to the skin. He got under the shower, toweled himself, put on clean linen and went into the kitchenette to mix a drink. He sipped that and smoked another cigarette while he finished dressing. The telephone in the living room rang as he was strapping on his holster.

It was Belle Marr. Her voice was blurred and throaty, as if she had been crying for hours.

"I'm so glad to get you, Sam. I—I didn't mean the way I talked. I was shocked and confused, absolutely wild inside. You knew that, didn't you, Sam?"

"Sure, kid," Delaguerra said. "Think nothing of it. Anyway you were right. I just got back from Puma Lake and I think I was just sent up there to get rid of me."

"You're all I have now, Sam. You won't let them hurt you, will you?"

"Who?"

"You know. I'm no fool, Sam. I know this was all a plot, a vile political plot to get rid of him."

Delaguerra held the phone very tight. His mouth felt stiff and hard. For a moment he couldn't speak. Then he said:

"It might be just what it looks like, Belle. A quarrel over those pictures. After all Donny had a right to tell a guy like that to get off the ticket. That wasn't blackmail . . . And he had a gun in his hand, you know."

"Come out and see me when you can, Sam." Her voice lingered with a spent emotion, a note of wistfulness.

He drummed on the desk, hesitated again, said: "Sure . . . When was anybody at Puma Lake last, at the cabin?"

"I don't know. I haven't been there in a year. He went . . . alone. Perhaps he met people there. I don't know."

He said something vaguely, after a moment said good-by and hung up. He stared at the wall over the writing desk. There was a fresh light in his eyes, a hard glint. His whole face was tight, not doubtful any more.

He went back to the bedroom for his coat and straw hat. On the way out he picked up the three telephone slips with the name "Joey Chill" on them, tore them into small pieces and burned the pieces in an ashtray.

7

Pete Marcus, the big, sandy-haired dick, sat sidewise at a small littered desk in a bare office in which there were two such desks, faced to opposite walls. The other desk was neat and tidy, had a green blotter with an onyx pen set, a small brass calendar and an abalone shell for an ashtray.

A round straw cushion that looked something like a target was propped on end in a straight chair by the window. Pete Marcus had a handful of bank pens in his left hand and he was flipping them at the cushion, like a Mexican knife thrower. He was doing it absently, without much skill.

The door opened and Delaguerra came in. He shut the door and leaned against it, looking woodenly at Marcus. The sandy-haired man creaked his chair around and tilted it back against the desk, scratched his chin with a broad thumbnail.

"Hi, Spanish. Nice trip? The Chief's yappin' for you."

Delaguerra grunted, stuck a cigarette between his smooth brown lips.

"Were you in Marr's office when those photos were found, Pete?"

"Yeah, but I didn't find them. The Commish did. Why?"

"Did you see him find them?"

Marcus stared a moment, then said quietly, guardedly: "He found them all right, Sam. He didn't plant them—if that's what you mean."

Delaguerra nodded, shrugged. "Anything on the slugs?"

"Yeah. Not .32's—.25's. A damn' vest-pocket rod. Copper-nickel slugs. An automatic, though, and we didn't find any shells."

"Imlay remembered those," Delaguerra said evenly, "but he left without the photos he killed for."

Marcus lowered his feet to the floor and leaned forward, looking up past his tawny eyebrows.

"That could be. They give him a motive, but with the gun in Marr's hand they kind of knock a premeditation angle."

"Good headwork, Pete." Delaguerra walked over to the small window, stood looking out of it. After a moment Marcus said dully:

"You don't see me doin' any work, do you, Spanish?"

Delaguerra turned slowly, went over and stood close to Marcus, looking down at him.

"Don't be sore, kid. You're my partner and I'm tagged as Marr's line into Headquarters. You're getting some of that. You're sitting still and I was hiked up to Puma Lake for no good reason except to have a deer carcass planted in the back of my car and have a game warden nick me with it."

Marcus stood up very slowly, knotting his fists at his sides. His heavy gray eyes opened very wide. His big nose was white at the nostrils.

"—— ——!" he said, throatily. "Nobody here'd go *that* far, Sam."

Delaguerra shook his head. "I don't think so either. But they could take a hint to send me up there. And somebody outside the department could do the rest."

Pete Marcus sat down again. He picked up one of the pointed bank pens and flipped it viciously at the round straw cushion. The point stuck, quivered, broke, and the pen rattled to the floor.

"Listen," he said thickly, not looking up, "this is a job to me. That's all it is. A living. I don't have any ideals about this police work like you have. Say the word and I'll heave the —— damn' badge in the old boy's puss."

Delaguerra bent down, punched him in the ribs. "Skip it, copper. I've got ideas. Go on home and get drunk."

He opened the door and went out quickly, walked along a marble-faced corridor to a place where it widened into an alcove with three doors. The middle one said: "Chief of Detectives. Enter." Delaguerra went into a small reception-room with a plain railing across it. A police stenographer behind the railing looked up, then jerked his head at an inner door. Delaguerra opened a gate in the railing and knocked at the inner door, then went in.

Two men were in the big office. Chief of Detectives Tod McKim sat behind a heavy desk, looked at Delaguerra hardeyed as he came in. He was a big, loose man who had gone saggy. He had a long, petulantly melancholy face. One of his eyes was not quite straight in his head.

The man who sat in a round-backed chair at the end of the desk was dandyishly dressed, wore spats. A pearl-gray hat and gray gloves and an ebony cane lay beside him on another chair. He had a shock of soft white hair and a handsome dissipated face kept pink by constant massaging. He smiled at Delaguerra, looked vaguely amused and ironical, smoked a cigarette in a long amber holder.

Delaguerra sat down opposite McKim. Then he looked at the white-haired man briefly and said: "Good evening, Commissioner."

Commissioner Drew nodded offhandedly, didn't speak.

McKim leaned forward and clasped blunt, nail-chewed fingers on the shiny desk top. He said quietly:

"Took your time reporting back. Find anything?"

Delaguerra stared at him, a level expressionless stare.

"I wasn't meant to—except maybe a doe carcass in the back of my car."

Nothing changed in McKim's face. Not a muscle of it moved. Drew dragged a pink and polished fingernail across the front of his throat and made a tearing sound with his tongue and teeth.

"That's no crack to be makin' at your boss, lad."

Delaguerra kept on looking at McKim, waited. McKim spoke slowly, sadly:

"You've got a good record, Delaguerra. Your grandfather

was one of the best sheriffs this county ever had. You've blown a lot of dirt on it today. You're charged with violating game laws, interfering with a Toluca County officer in the performance of his duty, and resisting arrest. Got anything to say to all that?"

Delaguerra said tonelessly: "Is there a tag out for me?"

McKim shook his head very slowly. "It's a department charge. There's no formal complaint. Lack of evidence, I guess." He smiled dryly, without humor.

Delaguerra said quietly: "In that case I guess you'll want my badge."

McKim nodded, silent. Drew said: "You're a little quick on the trigger. Just a shade fast on the snap-up."

Delaguerra took his badge out, rubbed it on his sleeve, looked at it, pushed it across the smooth wood of the desk.

"Okey, Chief," he said very softly. "My blood is Spanish, pure Spanish. Not nigger-Mex and not Yaqui-Mex. My grandfather would have handled a situation like this with fewer words and more powder smoke, but that doesn't mean I think it's funny. I've been deliberately framed into this spot because I was a close friend of Donegan Marr once. You know and I know that never counted for anything on the job. The Commissioner and his political backers may not feel so sure."

Drew stood up suddenly. "By God, you'll not talk like that to me," he yelped.

Delaguerra smiled slowly. He said nothing, didn't look towards Drew at all. Drew sat down again, scowling, breathing hard.

After a moment McKim scooped the badge into the middle drawer of his desk and got to his feet.

"You're suspended for a board, Delaguerra. Keep in touch with me." He went out of the room quickly, by the inner door, without looking back.

Delaguerra pushed his chair back and straightened his hat on his head. Drew cleared his throat, assumed a conciliatory smile and said:

"Maybe I was a little hasty myself. The Irish in me. Have no hard feelings. The lesson you're learning is something we've all had to learn. Might I give you a word of advice?"

Delaguerra stood up, smiled at him, a small dry smile that moved the corners of his mouth and left the rest of his face wooden.

"I know what it is, Commissioner. Lay off the Marr case."

Drew laughed, good-humored again. "Not exactly. There isn't any Marr case. Imlay has admitted the shooting through his attorney, claiming self-defense. He's to surrender in the morning. No, my advice was something else. Go back to Toluca County and tell the warden you're sorry. I think that's all that's needed. You might try it and see."

Delaguerra moved quietly to the corridor and opened it. Then he looked back, with a sudden flashing grin that showed all his white teeth.

"I know a crook when I see one, Commissioner. He's been paid for his trouble already."

He went out. Drew watched the door close shut with a faint whoosh, a dry click. His face was stiff with rage. His pink skin had turned a doughy gray. His hand shook furiously, holding the amber holder, and ash fell on the knee of his immaculate knife-edged trousers.

"By God," he said rigidly, in the silence, "you may be a damn' smooth Spaniard. You may be smooth as plate glass—but you're a hell of a lot easier to poke a hole through!"

He rose, awkward with anger, brushed the ashes from his trousers carefully and reached a hand out for hat and cane. The manicured fingers of the hand were trembling.

8

Newton Street, between Third and Fourth, was a block of cheap clothing stores, pawnshops, arcades of slot machines, mean hotels in front of which furtive-eyed men slid words delicately along their cigarettes, without moving their lips. Midway of the block a jutting wooden sign on a canopy said: "Stoll's Billiard Parlors." Steps went down from the sidewalk edge. Delaguerra went down the steps.

It was almost dark in the front of the poolroom. The tables were sheeted, the cues racked in rigid lines. But there was light far at the back, hard white light against which clustered heads and shoulders were silhouetted. There was noise, wrangling, shouting of odds. Delaguerra went towards the light.

Suddenly, as if at a signal, the noise stopped and out of the silence came the sharp click of balls, the dull thud of cue ball against cushion after cushion, the final click of a three-bank carom. Then the noise flared up again.

Delaguerra stopped beside a sheeted table and got a ten-dollar bill from his wallet, got a small gummed label from a pocket in the wallet. He wrote on it: "Where is Joe?" pasted it to the bill, folded the bill in four. He went on to the fringe of the crowd and inched his way through until he was close to the table.

A tall, pale man with an impassive face and neatly parted brown hair was chalking a cue, studying the set-up on the table. He leaned over, bridged with strong white fingers. The betting ring noise dropped like a stone. The tall man made a smooth, effortless three-cushion shot.

A chubby-faced man on a high stool intoned: "Forty for Chill. Eight's the break."

The tall man chalked his cue again, looked around idly. His eyes passed over Delaguerra without sign. Delaguerra stepped closer to him, said:

"Back yourself, Max? Five spot against the next shot."

The tall man nodded. "Take it."

Delaguerra put the folded bill on the edge of the table. A youth in a striped shirt reached for it. Max Chill blocked him off without seeming to, tucked the bill in a pocket of his vest, said tonelessly: "Five bet," and bent to make another shot.

It was a clean criss-cross at the top of the table, a hairline shot. There was a lot of applause. The tall man handed his cue to his helper in the striped shirt, said:

"Time out. I got to go a place."

He went back through the shadows, through a door marked: "Men." Delaguerra lit a cigarette, looked around at the usual Newton Street riff-raff. Max Chill's opponent, another tall, pale, impassive man, stood beside the marker and talked to him without looking at him. Near them, alone and supercilious, a very good-looking Filipino in a smart tan suit was puffing at a chocolate-colored cigarette.

Max Chill came back to the table, reached for his cue, chalked it. He reached a hand into his vest, said lazily: "Owe you five, buddy," passed a folded bill to Delaguerra.

He made three caroms in a row, almost without stopping. The marker said: "Forty-four for Chill. Twelve's the break."

Two men detached themselves from the edge of the crowd, started towards the entrance. Delaguerra fell in behind them, followed them among the sheeted tables to the foot of the steps. He stopped there, unfolded the bill in his hand, read the address scribbled on the label under his question. He crumpled the bill in his hand, started it towards his pocket.

Something hard poked into his back. A twangy voice like a plucked banjo string said:

"Help a guy out, huh?"

Delaguerra's nostrils quivered, got sharp. He looked up the steps at the legs of the two men ahead, at the reflected glare of street lights.

"Okey," the twangy voice said grimly.

Delaguerra dropped sidewise, twisting in the air. He shot a snakelike arm back. His hand grabbed an ankle as he fell. A swept gun missed his head, cracked the point of his shoulder and sent a dart of pain down his left arm. There was hard, hot breathing. Something without force slammed his straw hat. There was a thin tearing snarl close to him. He rolled, twisted the ankle, tucked a knee under him and lunged up. He was on his feet, catlike, lithe. He threw the ankle away from him, hard.

The Filipino in the tan suit hit the floor with his back. A gun wobbled up. Delaguerra kicked it out of a small brown hand and it skidded under a table. The Filipino lay still on his back, his head straining up, his snap-brim hat still glued to his oily hair.

At the back of the poolroom the three-cushion match went on peacefully. If anyone noticed the scuffling sound, at least no one moved to investigate. Delaguerra jerked a thonged blackjack from his hip pocket, bent over. The Filipino's tight brown face cringed.

"Got lots to learn. On the feet, baby."

Delaguerra's voice was chilled but casual. The dark man scrambled up, lifted his arms, then his left hand snaked for his right shoulder. The blackjack knocked it down, with a careless flip of Delaguerra's wrist. The brown man screamed thinly, like a hungry kitten.

Delaguerra shrugged. His mouth moved in a sardonic grin. "Stick-up, huh? Okey, yellowpuss, some other time. I'm busy now. Dust!"

The Filipino slid back among the tables, crouched down. Delaguerra shifted the blackjack to his left hand, shot his right to a gun butt. He stood for a moment like that, watching the Filipino's eyes. Then he turned and went quickly up the steps, out of sight.

The brown man darted forward along the wall, crept under the table for his gun.

9

Joey Chill, who jerked the door open, held a short, worn gun without a foresight. He was a small man, hardbitten, with a tight, worried face. He needed a shave and a clean shirt. A harsh animal smell came out of the room behind him.

He lowered the gun, grinned sourly, stepped back into the room.

"Okey, copper. Took your sweet time gettin' here."

Delaguerra went in and shut the door. He pushed his straw hat far back on his wiry hair, and looked at Joey Chill without any expression. He said: "Am I supposed to remember the address of every punk in town? I had to get it from Max."

The small man growled something and went and lay down on the bed, shoved his gun under the pillow. He clasped his hands behind his head and blinked at the ceiling.

"Got a C note on you, copper?"

Delaguerra jerked a straight chair in front of the bed and straddled it. He got his bulldog pipe out, filled it slowly, looking with distaste at the shut window, the chipped enamel of the bed frame, the dirty, tumbled bedclothes, the washbowl in the corner with two smeared towels hung over it, the bare dresser with half a bottle of gin planked on top of the Gideon Bible.

"Holed up?" he inquired, without much interest.

"I'm hot, copper. I mean I'm hot. I got something, see. It's worth a C note."

Delaguerra put his pouch away slowly, indifferently, held a lighted match to his pipe, puffed with exasperating leisure. The small man on the bed fidgeted, watching him with side-long looks. Delaguerra said slowly:

"You're a good stoolie, Joey. I'll always say that for you. But a hundred bucks is important money to a copper."

"Worth it, guy. If you like the Marr killing well enough to want to break it right."

Delaguerra's eyes got steady and very cold. His teeth clamped on the pipe stem. He spoke very quietly, very grimly.

"I'll listen, Joey. I'll pay if it's worth it. It better be right, though."

The small man rolled over on his elbow. "Know who the girl was with Imlay in those pajama-pajama snaps?"

"Know her name," Delaguerra said evenly. "I haven't seen the pictures."

"Stella La Motte's a hoofer name. Real name Stella Chill. My kid sister."

Delaguerra folded his arms on the back of the chair. "That's nice," he said. "Go on."

"She framed him, copper. Framed him for a few bindles of heroin from a slant-eyed Flip."

"Flip?" Delaguerra spoke the word swiftly, harshly. His face was tense now.

"Yeah, a little brown brother. A looker, a neat dresser, a snow peddler. A —— damn' dodo. Name, Toribo. They call him the Caliente Kid. He had a place across the hall from Stella. He got to feedin' her the stuff. Then he works her into the frame. She puts heavy drops in Imlay's liquor and he passes out. She lets the Flip in to shoot pictures with a Minny camera. Cute, huh? . . . And then, just like a broad, she gets sorry and spills the whole thing to Max and me."

Delaguerra nodded, silent, almost rigid.

The little man grinned sharply, showed his small teeth. "What do I do? I take a plant on the Flip. I live in his shadow, copper. And after a while I tail him bang into Dave Aage's skyline apartment in the Vendome. . . . I guess that rates a yard."

Delaguerra nodded slowly, shook a little ash into the palm of his hand and blew it off. "Who else knows this?"

"Max. He'll back me up, if you handle him right. Only he don't want any part of it. He don't play those games. He gave Stella dough to leave town and signed off. Because those boys are tough."

"Max couldn't know where you followed the Filipino to, Joey."

The small man sat up sharply, swung his feet to the floor. His face got sullen.

"I'm not kidding you, copper. I never have."

Delaguerra said quietly: "I believe you, Joey. I'd like more proof, though. What do you make of it?"

The little man snorted. "Hell, it sticks up so hard it hurts. Either the Flip's working for Masters and Aage before or he makes a deal with them after he gets the snaps. Then Marr gets the pictures and it's a cinch he don't get them unless they say so and he don't know they had them. Imlay was running for judge, on their ticket. Okey, he's their punk, but he's still a punk. It happens he's a guy who drinks and has a nasty temper. That's known."

Delaguerra's eyes glistened a little. The rest of his face was like carved wood. The pipe in his mouth was as motionless as though set in cement.

Joey Chill went on, with his sharp little grin: "So they deal the big one. They get the pictures to Marr without Marr's knowing where they came from. Then Imlay gets tipped off who has them, what they are, that Marr is set to put the squeeze on him. What would a guy like Imlay do? He'd go hunting, copper—and Big John Masters and his sidekick would eat the ducks."

"Or the venison," Delaguerra said absently.

"Huh? Well, does it rate?"

Delaguerra reached for his wallet, shook the money out of it, counted some bills on his knee. He rolled them into a tight wad and flipped them on to the bed.

"I'd like a line to Stella pretty well, Joey. How about it?"

The small man stuffed the money in his shirt pocket, shook his head. "No can do. You might try Max again. I think she's left town, and me, I'm doin' that too, now I've got the scratch. Because those boys are tough like I said—and maybe I didn't tail so good . . . Because some mugg's been tailin' me." He stood up, yawned, added: "Snort of gin?"

Delaguerra shook his head, watched the little man go over to the dresser and lift the gin bottle, pour a big dose into a thick glass. He drained the glass, started to put it down.

Glass tinkled at the window. There was a sound like the loose slap of a glove. A small piece of the window glass dropped to the bare stained wood beyond the carpet, almost at Joey Chill's feet.

The little man stood quite motionless for two or three seconds. Then the glass fell from his hand, bounced and rolled against the wall. Then his legs gave. He went down on his side, slowly, rolled slowly over on his back.

Blood began to move sluggishly down his cheek from a hole over his left eye. It moved faster. The hole got large and red. Joey Chill's eyes looked blankly at the ceiling, as if those things no longer concerned him at all.

Delaguerra slipped quietly down out of the chair to his hands and knees. He crawled along the side of the bed, over to the wall by the window, reached out from there and groped inside Joey Chill's shirt. He held fingers against his heart for a little while, took them away, shook his head. He squatted down low, took his hat off, and pushed his head up very carefully until he could see over a lower corner of the window.

He looked at the high blank wall of a storage warehouse, across an alley. There were scattered windows in it, high up, none of them lighted. Delaguerra pulled his head down again, said quietly, under his breath:

"Silenced rifle, maybe. And very sweet shooting."

His hand went forward again, diffidently, took the little roll of bills from Joey Chill's shirt. He went back along the wall to the door, still crouched, reached up and got the key from the door, opened it, straightened and stepped through quickly, locked the door from the outside.

He went along a dirty corridor and down four flights of steps to a narrow lobby. The lobby was empty. There was a desk and a bell on it, no one behind it. Delaguerra stood behind the plate-glass street door and looked across the street at a frame rooming house where a couple of old men rocked on the porch, smoking. They looked very peaceful. He watched them for a couple of minutes.

He went out, searched both sides of the block quickly with sharp glances, walked along beside parked cars to the next corner. Two blocks over he picked up a cab and rode back to Stoll's Billiard Parlors on Newton Street.

Lights were lit all over the poolroom now. Balls clicked and spun, players weaved in and out of a thick haze of cigarette smoke. Delaguerra looked around, then went to where a chubby-faced man sat on a high stool beside a cash register.

"You Stoll?"

The chubby-faced man nodded.

"Where did Max Chill get to?"

"Long gone, brother. They only played a hundred up. Home, I guess."

"Where's home?"

The chubby-faced man gave him a swift, flickering glance that passed like a finger of light.

"I wouldn't know."

Delaguerra lifted a hand to the pocket where he carried his badge. He dropped it again—tried not to drop it too quickly. The chubby-faced man grinned.

"Flattie, eh? Okey, he lives at the Mansfield, three blocks west on Grand."

10

Ceferino Toribo, the good-looking Filipino in the well-cut tan suit, gathered two dimes and three pennies off the counter in the telegraph office, smiled at the bored blonde who was waiting on him.

"That goes out right away, Sugar?"

She glanced at the message acidly. "Hotel Mansfield? Be there in twenty minutes—and save the sugar."

"Okey, Sugar."

Toribo dawdled elegantly out of the office. The blonde spiked the message with a jab, said over her shoulder: "Guy must be nuts. Sending a wire to a hotel three blocks away."

Ceferino Toribo strolled along Spring Street, trailing smoke over his neat shoulder from a chocolate-colored cigarette. At Fourth he turned west, went three blocks more, turned into the side entrance of the Mansfield, by the barbershop. He went up some marble steps to a mezzanine, along the back of a writing-room and up carpeted steps to the third floor. He passed the elevators and swaggered down a long corridor to the end, looking at the numbers on doors.

He came back halfway to the elevators, sat down in an open space where there were a pair of windows on the court, a glass-topped table and chairs. He lit a fresh cigarette from his stub, leaned back and listened to the elevators.

He leaned forward sharply whenever one stopped at that floor, listening for steps. The steps came in something over ten minutes. He stood up and went to the corner of the wall where the widened out space began. He took a long thin gun out from under his right arm, transferred it to his right hand, held it down against the wall beside his leg.

A squat, pockmarked Filipino in bellhop's uniform came along the corridor, carrying a small tray. Toribo made a hissing noise, lifted the gun. The squat Filipino whirled. His mouth opened and his eyes bulged at the gun.

Toribo said: "What room, punk?"

The squat Filipino smiled very nervously, placatingly. He came close, showed Toribo a yellow envelope on his tray. The figures 338 were penciled on the window of the envelope.

"Put it down," Toribo said calmly.

The squat Filipino put the telegram on the table. He kept his eyes on the gun.

"Beat it," Toribo said. "You put it under the door, see?"

The squat Filipino ducked his round black head, smiled nervously again, and went away very quickly towards the elevators.

Toribo put the gun in his jacket pocket, took out a folded white paper. He opened it very carefully, shook glistening white powder from it on to the hollow place formed between his left thumb and forefinger when he spread his hand. He sniffed the powder sharply up his nose, took out a flame-colored silk handkerchief and wiped his nose.

He stood still for a little while. His eyes got the dullness of slate and the skin on his brown face seemed to tighten over his high cheekbones. He breathed audibly between his teeth.

He picked the yellow envelope up and went along the corridor to the end, stopped in front of the last door, knocked.

A voice called out. He put his lips close to the door, spoke in a high-pitched, very deferential voice.

"Mail for you, sar."

Bedsprings creaked. Steps came across the floor inside. A key turned and the door opened. Toribo had his thin gun out again by this time. As the door opened he stepped swiftly into the opening, sidewise, with a graceful sway of his hips. He put the muzzle of the thin gun against Max Chill's abdomen.

"Back up!" he snarled, and his voice now had the metallic twang of a plucked banjo string.

Max Chill backed away from the gun. He backed across the room to the bed, sat down on the bed when his legs struck the side of it. Springs creaked and a newspaper rustled. Max Chill's pale face under the neatly parted brown hair had no expression at all.

Toribo shut the door softly, snapped the lock. When the door latch snapped, Max Chill's face suddenly became a sick face. His lips began to shake, kept on shaking.

Toribo said mockingly, in his twangy voice: "You talk to the cops, huh? *Adios.*"

The thin gun jumped in his hand, kept on jumping. A little pale smoke lisped from the muzzle. The noise the gun made was no louder than a hammer striking a nail or knuckles rapping sharply on wood. It made that noise seven times.

Max Chill lay down on the bed very slowly. His feet stayed on the floor. His eyes went blank, and his lips parted and a pinkish froth seethed on them. Blood showed in several places on the front of his loose shirt. He lay quite still on his back and looked at the ceiling with his feet touching the floor and the pink froth bubbling on his blue lips.

Toribo moved the gun to his left hand and put it away under his arm. He sidled over to the bed and stood beside it, looking down at Max Chill. After a while the pink froth stopped bubbling and Max Chill's face became the quiet, empty face of a dead man.

Toribo went back to the door, opened it, started to back

out, his eyes still on the bed. There was a stir of movement behind him.

He started to whirl, snatching a hand up. Something looped at his head. The floor tilted queerly before his eyes, rushed up at his face. He didn't know when it struck his face.

Delaguerra kicked the Filipino's legs into the room, out of the way of the door. He shut the door, locked it, walked stiffly over to the bed, swinging a thonged sap at his side. He stood beside the bed for quite a long time. At last he said under his breath:

"They clean up. Yeah—they clean up."

He went back to the Filipino, rolled him over and went through his pockets. There was a well-lined wallet without any identification, a gold lighter set with garnets, a gold cigarette case, keys, a gold pencil and knife, the flame-colored handkerchief, loose money, two guns and spare clips for them, and five bindles of heroin powder in the ticket pocket of the tan jacket.

He left it thrown around on the floor, stood up. The Filipino breathed heavily, with his eyes shut, a muscle twitching in one cheek. Delaguerra took a coil of thin wire out of his pocket and wired the brown man's wrists behind him. He dragged him over to the bed, sat him up against the leg, looped a strand of the wire around his neck and around the bed post. He tied the flame-colored handkerchief to the looped wire.

He went into the bathroom and got a glass of water and threw it into the Filipino's face as hard as he could throw it.

Toribo jerked, gagged sharply as the wire caught his neck. His eyes jumped open. He opened his mouth to yell.

Delaguerra jerked the wire taut against the brown throat. The yell was cut off as though by a switch. There was a strained anguished gurgle. Toribo's mouth drooled.

Delaguerra let the wire go slack again and put his head down close to the Filipino's head. He spoke to him gently, with a dry, very deadly gentleness.

"You want to talk to me, spig. Maybe not right away, maybe not even soon. But after a while you want to talk to me."

The Filipino's eyes rolled yellowly. He spat. Then his lips came together, tight.

Delaguerra smiled a faint, grim smile. "Tough boy," he said softly. He jerked the handkerchief back, held it tight and hard, biting into the brown throat above the adam's apple.

The Filipino's legs began to jump on the floor. His body moved in sudden lunges. The brown of his face became a thick congested purple. His eyes bulged, shot with blood.

Delaguerra let the wire go loose again.

The Filipino gasped air into his lungs. His head sagged, then jerked back against the bed post. He shook with a chill.

"*Si* . . . I talk," he breathed.

11

When the bell rang Ironhead Toomey very carefully put a black ten down on a red jack. Then he licked his lips and put all the cards down and looked around towards the front door of the bungalow, through the dining-room arch. He stood up slowly, a big brute of a man with loose gray hair and a big nose.

In the living-room beyond the arch a thin blond girl was lying on a davenport, reading a magazine under a lamp with a torn red shade. She was pretty, but too pale, and her thin, high-arched eyebrows gave her face a startled look. She put the magazine down and swung her feet to the floor and looked at Ironhead Toomey with sharp, sudden fear in her eyes.

Toomey jerked his thumb silently. The girl stood up and went very quickly through the arch and through a swing door into the kitchen. She shut the swing door slowly, so that it made no noise.

The bell rang again, longer. Toomey shoved his white-socked feet into carpet slippers, hung a pair of glasses on his big nose, took a revolver off a chair beside him. He picked a crumpled newspaper off the floor and arranged it loosely in front of the gun, which he held in his left hand. He strolled unhurriedly to the front door.

He was yawning as he opened it, peering with sleepy eyes through the glasses at the tall man who stood on the porch.

"Okey," he said wearily. "Talk it up."

Delaguerra said: "I'm a police officer. I want to see Stella La Motte."

Ironhead Toomey put an arm like a Yule log across the door frame and leaned solidly against it. His expression remained bored.

"Wrong dump, copper. No broads here."

Delaguerra said: "I'll come in and look."

Toomey said cheerfully: "You will—like hell."

Delaguerra jerked a gun out of his pocket very smoothly and swiftly, smashed it at Toomey's left wrist. The newspaper and the big revolver fell down on the floor of the porch. Toomey's face got a less bored expression.

"Old gag," Delaguerra snapped. "Let's go in."

Toomey shook his left wrist, took his other arm off the door frame and swung hard at Delaguerra's jaw. Delaguerra moved his head about four inches. He frowned, made a disapproving noise with his tongue and lips.

Toomey dived at him. Delaguerra sidestepped and chopped the gun at a big gray head. Toomey landed on his stomach, half in the house and half out on the porch. He grunted, planted his hands firmly and started to get up again, as if nothing had hit him.

Delaguerra kicked Toomey's gun out of the way. A swing door inside the house made a light sound. Toomey was up on one knee and one hand as Delaguerra looked towards the noise. He took a swing at Delaguerra's stomach, hit him. Delaguerra grunted and hit Toomey on the head again, hard. Toomey shook his head, growled: "Sappin' me is a waste of time, bo."

He dived sidewise, got hold of Delaguerra's leg, jerked the leg off the floor. Delaguerra sat down on the boards of the porch, jammed in the doorway. His head hit the side of the doorway, dazed him.

The thin blonde rushed through the arch with a small automatic in her hand. She pointed it at Delaguerra, said furiously: "Reach, damn you!"

Delaguerra shook his head, started to say something, then caught his breath as Toomey twisted his foot. Toomey set his teeth hard and twisted the foot as if he was all alone in the world with it and it was his foot and he could do what he liked with it.

Delaguerra's head jerked back again and his face got white. His mouth twisted into a harsh grimace of pain. He heaved up, grabbed Toomey's hair with his left hand, dragged the big head up and over until his chin came up, straining. Delaguerra smashed the barrel of his Colt on the skin.

Toomey became limp, an inert mass, fell across his legs and pinned him to the floor. Delaguerra couldn't move. He was propped on the floor on his right hand, trying to keep from being pushed flat by Toomey's weight. He couldn't get his right hand with the gun in it, off the floor. The blonde was closer to him now, wild-eyed, white-faced with rage.

Delaguerra said in a spent voice: "Don't be a fool, Stella. Joey—"

The blonde's face was unnatural. Her eyes were unnatural, with small pupils, a queer flat glitter in them.

"Cops!" she almost screamed. "Cops! God, how I hate cops!"

The gun in her hand crashed, flamed. The echoes of it filled the room, went out of the open front door, died against the highboard fence across the street.

A sharp blow like the blow of a club hit the left side of Delaguerra's head. Pain filled his head. Light flared—blinding white light that filled the world. Then it was dark. He fell soundlessly, into bottomless darkness.

12

Light came back as a red fog in front of his eyes. Hard, bitter pain racked the side of his head, his whole face, ground in his teeth. His tongue was hot and thick when he tried to move it. He tried to move his hands. They were far away from him, not his hands at all.

Then he opened his eyes and the red fog went away and he was looking at a face. It was a big face, very close to him, a huge face. It was fat and had sleek blue jowls and there was a cigar with a bright band in a grinning, thick-lipped mouth. The face chuckled. Delaguerra closed his eyes again and the pain washed over him, submerged him. He passed out.

Seconds, or years, passed. He was looking at the face again. He heard a thick voice.

"Well, he's with us again. A pretty tough lad at that."

The face came closer, the end of the cigar glowed cherry red. Then he was coughing rackingly, gagging on smoke. The side of his head seemed to burst open. He felt fresh blood slide down his cheekbone, tickling the skin, then slide over stiff dried blood that had already caked on his face.

"That fixes him up swell," the thick voice said.

Another voice with a touch of brogue to it said something gentle and obscene. The big face whirled towards the sound, snarling.

Delaguerra came wide awake then. He saw the room clearly, saw the four people in it. The big face was the face of Big John Masters.

The thin blond girl was hunched on one end of the davenport, staring at the floor with a doped expression, her arms stiff at her sides, her hands out of sight in the cushions.

Dave Aage had his long lank body propped against a wall beside a curtained window. His wedge-shaped face looked bored. Commissioner Drew was on the other end of the davenport, under the frayed lamp. The light made silver in his hair. His blue eyes were very bright, very intent.

There was a shiny gun in Big John Masters' hand. Delaguerra blinked at it, started to get up. A hard hand jerked at his chest, jarred him back. A wave of nausea went over him. The thick voice said harshly:

"Hold it, pussyfoot. You've had your fun. This is our party."

Delaguerra licked his lips, said: "Give me a drink of water."

Dave Aage stood away from the wall and went through the dining-room arch. He came back with a glass, held it to Delaguerra's mouth. Delaguerra drank.

Masters said: "We like your guts, copper. But you don't use them right. It seems you're a guy that can't take a hint. That's too bad. That makes you through. Get me?"

The blonde turned her head and looked at Delaguerra with heavy eyes, looked away again. Aage went back to his wall. Drew began to stroke the side of his face with quick nervous fingers, as if Delaguerra's bloody head made his own face hurt. Delaguerra said slowly:

"Killing me will just hang you a little higher, Masters. A sucker on the big time is still a sucker. You've had two men killed already for no reason at all. You don't even know what you're trying to cover."

The big man swore harshly, jerked the shiny gun up, then lowered it slowly, with a heavy leer. Aage said indolently:

"Take it easy, John. Let him speak his piece."

Delaguerra said in the same slow, careless voice: "The lady over there is the sister of the two men you've had killed. She told them her story, about framing Imlay, who got the pictures, how they got to Donegan Marr. Your little Filipino hood has done some singing. I get the general idea all right. You couldn't be sure Imlay would kill Marr. Maybe Marr would get Imlay. It would work out all right either way. Only, if Imlay did kill Marr, the case had to be broken fast. That's where you slipped. You started to cover up before you really knew what happened."

Masters said harshly: "Crummy, copper, crummy. You're wasting my time."

The blonde turned her head towards Delaguerra, towards Masters' back. There was hard green hate in her eyes now. Delaguerra shrugged very slightly, went on:

"It was routine stuff for you to put killers on the Chill brothers. It was routine stuff to get me off the investigation, get me framed and suspended because you figured I was on Marr's payroll. But it wasn't routine when you couldn't find Imlay—and that crowded you."

Masters' hard black eyes got wide and empty. His thick neck swelled. Aage came away from the wall a few feet and stood rigidly. After a moment Masters snapped his teeth, spoke very quietly:

"That's a honey, copper. Tell us about that one."

Delaguerra touched his smeared face with the tips of two fingers, looked at the fingers. His eyes were depthless, ancient.

"Imlay is dead, Masters. He was dead before Marr was killed."

The room was very still. Nobody moved in it. The four people Delaguerra looked at were frozen with shock. After a long time Masters drew in a harsh breath and blew it out and almost whispered:

"Tell it, copper. Tell it fast, or by —— I'll—"

Delaguerra's voice cut in on him coldly, without any emotion at all: "Imlay went to see Marr all right. Why wouldn't he? He didn't know he was double-crossed. Only he went to see him last night, not today. He rode up to the cabin at Puma Lake with him, to talk things over in a friendly way. That was the gag, anyhow. Then, up there, they had their fight and Imlay got killed, got dumped off the end of the porch, got his head smashed open on some rocks. He's dead as last Christmas, in the woodshed of Marr's cabin . . . Okey, Marr hid him and came back to town. Then today he got a phone call, mentioning the name Imlay, making a date for twelve-fifteen. What would Marr do? Stall, of course, send his office girl off to lunch, put a gun where he could reach it in a hurry. He was all set for trouble then. Only the visitor fooled him and he didn't use the gun."

Masters said gruffly: "Hell, man, you're just cracking wise. You couldn't know all those things."

He looked back at Drew. Drew was gray-faced, taut. Aage came a little farther away from the wall and stood close to Drew. The blond girl didn't move a muscle.

Delaguerra said wearily: "Sure, I'm guessing, but I'm guessing to fit the facts. It had to be like that. Marr was no slouch with a gun and he was on edge, all set. Why didn't he get a shot in? Because it was a woman that called on him."

He lifted an arm, pointed at the blonde. "There's your killer. She loved Imlay even though she framed him. She's a junkie and junkies are like that. She got sad and sorry and she went after Marr herself. Ask her!"

The blonde stood up in a smooth lunge. Her right hand jerked up from the cushions with a small automatic in it, the one she had shot Delaguerra with. Her green eyes were pale and empty and staring. Masters whirled around, flailed at her arm with the shiny revolver.

She shot him twice, pointblank, without a flicker of hesitation. Blood spurted from the side of his thick neck, down the front of his coat. He staggered, dropped the shiny revolver, almost at Delaguerra's feet. He fell outwards towards the wall behind Delaguerra's chair, one arm groping out for the wall. His hand hit the wall and trailed down it as he fell. He crashed heavily, didn't move again.

Delaguerra had the shiny revolver almost in his hand.

Drew was on his feet yelling. The girl turned slowly towards Aage, seemed to ignore Delaguerra. Aage jerked a Luger from under his arm and knocked Drew out of the way with his arm. The small automatic and the Luger roared at the same time. The small gun missed. The girl was flung down on the davenport, her left hand clutching at her breast. She rolled her eyes, tried to lift the gun again. Then she fell sidewise on the cushions and her left hand went lax, dropped away from her breast. The front of her dress was a sudden welter of blood. Her eyes opened and shut, opened and stayed open.

Aage swung the Luger towards Delaguerra. His eyebrows were twisted up into a sharp grin of intense strain. His smoothly combed, sand-colored hair flowed down his bony scalp as tightly as though it were painted on it.

Delaguerra shot him four times, so rapidly that the explosions were like the rattle of a machine-gun.

In the instant of time before he fell Aage's face became the thin, empty face of an old man, his eyes the vacant eyes of an idiot. Then his long body jackknifed to the floor, the Luger still in his hand. One leg doubled under him as if there was no bone in it.

Powder smell was sharp on the air. The air was stunned by the sound of guns. Delaguerra got to his feet slowly, motioned to Drew with the shiny revolver.

"Your party, Commissioner. Is this anything like what you wanted?"

Drew nodded slowly, white-faced, quivering. He swallowed, moved slowly across the floor, past Aage's sprawled body. He looked down at the girl on the davenport, shook his head. He went over to Masters, went down on one knee, touched him. He stood up again.

"All dead, I think," he muttered.

Delaguerra said: "That's swell. What happened to the big boy, the bruiser?"

"They sent him away. I—I don't think they meant to kill you, Delaguerra."

Delaguerra nodded a little. His face began to soften, the rigid lines began to go out of it. The side that was not a blood-stained mask began to look human again. He sopped at his face with a handkerchief. It came away bright red with blood. He threw it away and lightly fingered his matted hair into place. Some of it was caught in the dried blood.

"The hell they didn't," he said.

The house was very still. There was no noise outside. Drew listened, sniffed, went to the front door and looked out. The street outside was dark, silent. He came back close to Delaguerra. Very slowly a smile worked itself on to his face.

"It's a hell of a note," he said, "when a commissioner of police has to be his own undercover man—and a square cop has to be framed off the force to help him."

Delaguerra looked at him without expression. "You want to play it that way?"

Drew spoke calmly now. The pink was back in his face. "For the good of the department, man, and the city—and ourselves, it's the only way to play it."

Delaguerra looked him straight in the eyes.

"I like it that way too," he said in a dead voice. "If it gets played—*exactly* that way."

13

Marcus braked the car to a stop and grinned admiringly at the big tree-shaded house.

"Pretty nice," he said. "I could go for a long rest there myself."

Delaguerra got out of the car slowly, as if he was stiff and very tired. He was hatless, carried his straw under his arm. Part of the left side of his head was shaved and the shaved part covered by a thick pad of gauze and tape, over the stitches. A wick of wiry black hair stuck up over one edge of the bandage, with a ludicrous effect.

He said: "Yeah—but I'm not staying here, sap. Wait for me."

He went along the path of stones that wound through the grass. Trees speared long shadows across the lawn, through the morning sunlight. The house was very still, with drawn blinds, a dark wreath on the brass knocker. Delaguerra didn't go up to the door. He turned off along another path under the windows and went along the side of the house past the gladioli beds.

There were more trees at the back, more lawn, more flowers, more sun and shadow. There was a pond with water-lilies in it and a big stone bullfrog. Beyond was a half circle of lawn chairs around an iron table with a tile top. In one of the chairs Belle Marr sat.

She wore a black-and white dress, loose and casual, and there was a wide-brimmed garden hat on her chestnut hair. She sat very still, looking into the distance across the lawn. Her face was white. The makeup glared on it.

She turned her head slowly, smiled a dull smile, motioned to a chair beside her. Delaguerra didn't sit down. He took his straw from under his arm, snapped a finger at the brim, said:

"The case is closed. There'll be inquests, investigations, threats, a lot of people shouting their mouths off to horn in on the publicity, that sort of thing. The papers will play it big for a while. But underneath, on the record, it's closed. You can begin to try to forget it."

The girl looked at him suddenly, widened her vivid blue eyes, looked away again, over the grass.

"Is your head very bad, Sam?" she asked softly.

Delaguerra said: "No. It's fine. . . . What I mean is the La Motte girl shot Masters—and she shot Donny. Aage shot her. I shot Aage. All dead, ring around the rosy. Just how Imlay got killed we'll not know ever, I guess. I can't see that it matters now."

Without looking up at him Belle Marr said quietly: "But how did you know it was Imlay up at the cabin? The paper said—" She broke off, shuddered suddenly.

He stared woodenly at the hat he was holding. "I didn't. I thought a woman shot Donny. It looked like a good hunch that was Imlay up at the lake. It fitted his description."

"How did you know it was a woman . . . that killed Donny?" Her voice had a lingering, half-whispered stillness.

"I just knew."

He walked away a few steps, stood looking at the trees. He turned slowly, came back, stood beside her chair again. His face was very weary.

"We had great times together—the three of us. You and Donny and I. Life seems to do nasty things to people. It's all gone now—all the good part."

Her voice was still a whisper saying: "Maybe not all gone, Sam. We must see a lot of each other, from now on."

A vague smile moved the corners of his lips, went away again. "It's my first frame-up," he said quietly. "I hope it will be my last."

Belle Marr's head jerked a little. Her hands took hold of the arms of the chair, looked white against the varnished wood. Her whole body seemed to get rigid.

After a moment Delaguerra reached in his pocket and something gold glittered in his hand. He looked down at it dully.

"Got the badge back," he said. "It's not quite as clean as it was. Clean as most, I suppose. I'll try to keep it that way." He put it back in his pocket.

Very slowly the girl stood up in front of him. She lifted her chin, stared at him with a long level stare. Her face was a mask of white plaster behind the rouge.

She said: "My God, Sam—I begin to understand."

Delaguerra didn't look at her face. He looked past her shoulder at some vague spot in the distance. He spoke vaguely, distantly.

"Sure. . . . I thought it was a woman because it was a small gun such as a woman would use. But not only on that account. After I went up to the cabin I knew Donny was primed for trouble and it wouldn't be that easy for a man to get the drop on him. But it was a perfect set-up for Imlay to have done it. Masters and Aage assumed he'd done it and had a lawyer phone in admitting he did it and promising to surrender him in the morning. So it was natural for anyone who didn't know Imlay was dead to fall in line. Besides, no cop would expect a woman to pick up her shells.

"After I got Joey Chill's story I thought it might be the La Motte girl. But I didn't think so when I said it in front of her. That was dirty. It got her killed, in a way. Though I wouldn't give much for her chances anyway, with that bunch."

Belle Marr was still staring at him. The breeze blew a wisp of her hair and that was the only thing about her that moved.

He brought his eyes back from the distance, looked at her gravely for a brief moment, looked away again. He took a small bunch of keys out of his pocket, tossed them down on the table.

"Three things were tough to figure until I got completely wise. The writing on the pad, the gun in Donny's hand, the missing shells. Then I tumbled to it. He didn't die right away. He had guts and he used them to the last flicker — to protect somebody. The writing on the pad was a bit shaky. He wrote it afterwards, when he was alone, dying. He had been think-ing of Imlay and writing the name helped mess the trail. Then he got the gun out of his desk to die with it in his hand. That left the shells. I got that too, after a while.

"The shots were fired close, across the desk, and there were books on one end of the desk. The shells fell there, stayed on the desk where he could get them. He couldn't have got them off the floor. There's a key to the office on your ring. I went there last night, late. I found the shells in a humidor with his cigars. Nobody looked for them there. You only find what you expect to find, after all."

He stopped talking and rubbed the side of his face. After a moment he added: "Donny did the best he could — and then he died. It was a swell job — and I'm letting him get away with it."

Belle Marr opened her mouth slowly. A kind of babble came out of it first, then words, clear words.

"It wasn't just women, Sam. It was the kind of women he had." She shivered. "I'll go downtown now and give myself up."

Delaguerra said: "No. I told you I was letting him get away with it. Downtown they like it the way it is. It's swell politics. It gets the city out from under the Masters-Aage mob. It puts Drew on top for a little while, but he's too weak to last. So that doesn't matter. . . . You're not going to do anything about any of it. You're going to do what Donny used his last strength to show he wanted. You're staying out. Good-by."

He looked at her white shattered face once more, very quickly. Then he swung around, walked away over the lawn, past the pool with the lily pads and the stone bullfrog along the side of the house and out to the car.

Pete Marcus swung the door open. Delaguerra got in and sat down and put his head far back against the seat, slumped down in the car and closed his eyes. He said flatly:

"Take it easy, Pete. My head hurts like hell."

Marcus started the car and turned in to the street, drove slowly back along De Neve Lane towards town. The tree-shaded house disappeared behind them. The tall trees finally hid it.

When they were a long way from it Delaguerra opened his eyes again.

Guns at Cyrano's

TED MALVERN liked the rain; liked the feel of it, the sound of it, the smell of it. He got out of his LaSalle coupé and stood for a while by the side entrance to the Carondelet, the high collar of his blue suede ulster tickling his ears, his hands in his pockets and a limp cigarette sputtering between his lips. Then he went in past the barber shop and the drug-store and the perfume shop with its rows of delicately lighted bottles, ranged like the ensemble in the finale of a Broadway musical.

He rounded a gold-veined pillar and got into an elevator with a cushioned floor.

"'Lo, Albert. A swell rain. Nine."

The slim tired looking kid in pale blue and silver held a white gloved hand against the closing doors, said:

"Jeeze, you think I don't know your floor, Mister Malvern?"

He shot the car up to nine without looking at his signal light, whooshed the doors open, then leaned suddenly against the cage and closed his eyes.

Malvern stopped on his way out, flicked a sharp glance from bright brown eyes. "What's the matter, Albert? Sick?"

The boy worked a pale smile on his face. "I'm workin' double shift. Corky's sick. He's got boils. I guess maybe I didn't eat enough."

The tall, brown-eyed man fished a crumpled five-spot out of his pocket, snapped it under the boy's nose. The boy's eyes bulged. He heaved upright.

"Jeeze, Mister Malvern. I didn't mean—"

"Skip it, Albert. What's a fin between pals? Eat some extra meals on me."

He got out of the car and started along the corridor. Softly, under his breath, he said:

"Sucker. . . ."

The running man almost knocked him off his feet. He rounded the turn fast, lurched past Malvern's shoulder, ran for the elevator.

"Down!" He slammed through the closing doors.

Malvern saw a white set face under a pulled-down hat that was wet with rain; two empty black eyes set very close. Eyes in which there was a peculiar stare he had seen before. A load of dope.

The car dropped like lead. Malvern looked at the place where it had been for a long moment, then he went on down the corridor and around the turn.

He saw the girl lying half in and half out of the open door of 914.

She lay on her side, in a sheen of steel gray lounging pajamas, her cheek pressed into the nap of the hall carpet, her head a mass of thick corn blond hair, waved with glassy precision. Not a hair looked out of place. She was young, very pretty, and she didn't look dead.

Malvern slid down beside her, touched her cheek. It was warm. He lifted the hair softly away from her head and saw the bruise.

"Sapped." His lips pressed back against his teeth.

He picked her up in his arms, carried her through a short hallway to the living-room of a suite, put her down on a big velour davenport in front of some gas logs.

She lay motionless, her eyes shut, her face bluish behind the makeup. He shut the outer door and looked through the apartment, then went back to the hallway and picked up something that gleamed white against the baseboard. It was a bone-handled .22 automatic, seven-shot. He sniffed it, dropped it into his pocket and went back to the girl.

He took a big hammered silver flask out of his inside breast pocket and unscrewed the top, opened her mouth with his fingers and poured whiskey against her small white teeth. She gagged and her head jerked out of his hand. Her eyes opened. They were deep blue, with a tint of purple. Light came into them and the light was brittle.

He lit a cigarette and stood looking down at her. She moved a little more. After awhile she whispered:

"I like your whiskey. Could I have a little more?"

He got a glass from the bathroom, poured whiskey into it. She sat up very slowly, touched her head, groaned. Then she took the glass out of his hand and put the liquor down with a practised flip of the wrist.

"I still like it," she said. "Who are you?"

She had a deep soft voice. He liked the sound of it. He said:

"Ted Malvern. I live down the hall in 937."

"I—I got a dizzy spell, I guess."

"Uh-huh. You got sapped, angel." His bright eyes looked at her probingly. There was a smile tucked to the corners of his lips.

Her eyes got wider. A glaze came over them, the glaze of a protective enamel.

He said: "I saw the guy. He was snowed to the hairline. And here's your gun."

He took it out of his pocket, held it on the flat of his hand.

"I suppose that makes me think up a bedtime story," the girl said slowly.

"Not for me. If you're in a jam, I might help you. It all depends."

"Depends on what?" Her voice was colder, sharper.

"On what the racket is," he said softly. He broke the magazine from the small gun, glanced at the top cartridge. "Copper-nickel, eh? You know your ammunition, angel."

"Do you have to call me angel?"

"I don't know your name."

He grinned at her, then walked over to a desk in front of the windows, put the gun down on it. There was a leather photo frame on the desk, with two photos side by side. He looked at them casually at first, then his gaze tightened. A handsome dark woman and a thin blondish cold-eyed man whose high stiff collar, large knotted tie and narrow lapels dated the photo back many years. He stared at the man.

The girl was talking behind him. "I'm Jean Adrian. I do a number at Cyrano's, in the floor show."

Malvern still stared at the photo. "I know Benny Cyrano pretty well," he said absently. "These your parents?"

He turned and looked at her. She lifted her head slowly. Something that might have been fear showed in her deep blue eyes.

"Yes. They've been dead for years," she said dully. "Next question?"

He went quickly back to the davenport and stood in front of her. "Okey," he said thinly. "I'm nosey. So what? This is my town. My dad used to run it. Old Marcus Malvern, the People's Friend. This is my hotel. I own a piece of it. That snowed-up hoodlum looked like a life-taker to me. Why wouldn't I want to help out?"

The blond girl stared at him lazily. "I still like your whiskey," she said. "Could I — "

"Take it from the neck, angel. You get it down faster," he grunted.

She stood up suddenly and her face got a little white. "You talk to me as if I was a crook," she snapped. "Here it is, if you have to know. A boy friend of mine has been getting threats. He's a fighter, and they want him to drop a fight. Now they're trying to get at him through me. Does that satisfy you a little?"

Malvern picked his hat off a chair, took the cigarette end out of his mouth and rubbed it out in a tray. He nodded quietly, said in a changed voice:

"I beg your pardon." He started towards the door.

The giggle came when he was halfway there. The girl said behind him softly:

"You have a nasty temper. And you've forgotten your flask."

He went back and picked the flask up. Then he bent suddenly, put a hand under the girl's chin and kissed her on the lips.

"To hell with you, angel. I like you," he said softly.

He went back to the hallway and out. The girl touched her lips with one finger, rubbed it slowly back and forth. There was a shy smile on her face.

2

Tony Acosta, the bell captain, was slim and dark and slight as a girl, with small delicate hands and velvety eyes and a hard little mouth. He stood in the doorway and said:

"Seventh row was the best I could get, Mister Malvern. This Deacon Werra ain't bad and Duke Targo's the next light heavy champ."

Malvern said: "Come in and have a drink, Tony." He went over to the window, stood looking out at the rain. "If they buy it for him," he added over his shoulder.

"Well—just a short one, Mister Malvern."

The dark boy mixed a highball carefully at a tray on an imitation Sheraton desk. He held the bottle against the light and gauged his drink carefully, tinkled ice gently with a long spoon, sipped, smiled, showing small white teeth.

"Targo's a lu, Mister Malvern. He's fast, clever, got a sock in both mitts, plenty guts, don't ever take a step back."

"He has to hold up the bums they feed him," Malvern drawled.

"Well, they ain't fed him no lion meat yet," Tony said.

The rain beat against the glass. The thick drops flattened out and washed down the pane in tiny waves.

Malvern said: "He's a bum. A bum with color and looks, but still a bum."

Tony sighed deeply. "I wisht I was goin'. It's my night off, too."

Malvern turned slowly and went over to the desk, mixed a drink. Two dusky spots showed in his cheeks and his voice was tired, drawling.

"So that's it. What's stopping you?"

"I got a headache."

"You're broke again," Malvern almost snarled.

The dark boy looked sidewise under his long lashes, said nothing.

Malvern clenched his left hand, unclenched it slowly. His eyes were sullen.

"Just ask Ted," he sighed. "Good old Ted. He leaks dough. He's soft. Just ask Ted. Okey, Tony, take the ducat back and get a pair together."

He reached into his pocket, held a bill out. The dark boy looked hurt.

"Jeeze, Mister Malvern, I wouldn't have you think—"

"Skip it! What's a fight ticket between pals? Get a couple and take your girl. To hell with this Targo."

Tony Acosta took the bill. He watched the older man carefully for a moment. Then his voice was very soft, saying:

"I'd rather go with you, Mister Malvern. Targo knocks

them over, and not only in the ring. He's got a peachy blonde right on this floor. Miss Adrian, in 914."

Malvern stiffened. He put his glass down slowly, turned it on the top of the desk. His voice got a little hoarse.

"He's still a bum, Tony. Okey, I'll meet you for dinner, in front of your hotel at seven."

"Jeeze, that's swell, Mister Malvern."

Tony Acosta went out softly, closed the outer door without a sound.

Malvern stood by the desk, his finger tips stroking the top of it, his eyes on the floor. He stood like that for a long time.

"Ted Malvern, the All-American sucker," he said grimly, out loud. "A guy that plays with the help and carries the torch for stray broads. Yeah."

He finished his drink, looked at his wrist-watch, put on his hat and the blue suede raincoat, went out. Down the corridor in front of 914 he stopped, lifted his hand to knock, then dropped it without touching the door.

He went slowly on to the elevators and rode down to the street and his car.

The *Tribune* office was at Fourth and Spring, Malvern parked around the corner, went in at the employees' entrance and rode to the fourth floor in a rickety elevator operated by an old man with a dead cigar in his mouth and a rolled magazine which he held six inches from his nose while he ran the elevator.

On the fourth floor big double doors were lettered City Room. Another old man sat outside them at a small desk with a call box.

Malvern tapped on the desk, said: "Adams. Ted Malvern calling."

The old man made noises into the box, released a key, pointed with his chin.

Malvern went through the doors, past a horseshoe copy desk, then past a row of small desks at which typewriters were being banged. At the far end a lanky red-haired man was doing nothing, with his feet on a pulled out drawer, the back of his neck on the back of a dangerously tilted swivel chair and a big pipe in his mouth pointed straight at the ceiling.

When Malvern stood beside him he moved his eyes down without moving any other part of his body and said around the pipe:

"Greetings, Teddy. How's the idle rich?"

Malvern said: "How's a glance at your clips on a guy named Courtway? State Senator John Myerson Courtway, to be precise."

Adams put his feet on the floor. He raised himself erect by pulling on the edge of his desk. He brought his pipe down level, took it out of his mouth and spit into a waste basket. He said:

"That old icicle? When was he ever news? Sure." He stood up wearily, added: "Come along, Uncle," and started along the end of the room.

They went along another row of desks, past a fat girl in smudged makeup who was typing and laughing at what she was writing.

They went through a door into a big room that was mostly six-foot tiers of filing cases with an occasional alcove in which there was a small table and a chair.

Adams prowled the filing cases, jerked one out and set a folder on a table.

"Park yourself. What's the graft?"

Malvern leaned on the table on an elbow, scuffed through a thick wad of cuttings. They were monotonous, political in nature, not front page. Senator Courtway said this and that on this and that matter of public interest, addressed this and that meeting, went to or returned from this and that place. It all seemed very dull.

He looked at a few halftone cuts of a thin, white-haired man with a blank, composed face, deep set dark eyes in which there was no light or warmth. After a while he said:

"Got a print I could sneeze? A real one, I mean."

Adams sighed, stretched himself, disappeared down the line of file walls. He came back with a shiny narrow black and white photograph, tossed it down on the table.

"You can keep it," he said. "We got dozens. The guy lives forever. Shall I have it autographed for you?"

Malvern looked at the photo with narrow eyes, for a long time. "It's right," he said slowly. "Was Courtway ever married?"

"Not since I left off my diapers," Adams growled. "Probably not ever. Say, what'n hell's the mystery?"

Malvern smiled slowly at him. He reached his flask out, set it on the table beside the folder. Adams' face brightened swiftly and his long arm reached.

"Then he never had a kid," Malvern said.

Adams leered over the flask. "Well—not for publication, I guess. If I'm any judge of a mug, not at all." He drank deeply, wiped his lips, drank again.

"And that," Malvern said, "is very funny indeed. Have three more drinks—and forget you ever saw me."

3

The fat man put his face close to Malvern's face. He said with a wheeze:

"You think it's fixed, neighbor?"

"Yeah. For Werra."

"How much says so?"

"Count your poke."

"I got five yards that want to grow."

"Take it," Malvern said tonelessly, and kept on looking at the back of a corn-blond head in a ringside seat. A white wrap with white fur was below the glassily waved hair. He couldn't see the face. He didn't have to.

The fat man blinked his eyes and got a thick wallet carefully out of a pocket inside his vest. He held it on the edge of his knee, counted out ten fifty-dollar bills, rolled them up, edged the wallet back against his ribs.

"You're on, sucker," he wheezed. "Let's see your dough."

Malvern brought his eyes back, reached out a flat pack of new hundreds, riffled them. He slipped five from under the printed band, held them out.

"Boy, this is from home," the fat man said. He put his face close to Malvern's face again. "I'm Skeets O'Neal. No little powders, huh?"

Malvern smiled very slowly and pushed his money into the

fat man's hand. "You hold it, Skeets. I'm Ted Malvern. Old Marcus Malvern's son. I can shoot faster than you can run—and fix it afterwards."

The fat man took a long hard breath and leaned back in his seat. Tony Acosta stared soft-eyed at the money in the fat man's pudgy tight hand. He licked his lips and turned a small embarrassed smile on Malvern.

"Gee, that's lost dough, Mister Malvern," he whispered. "Unless—unless you got something inside."

"Enough to be worth a five-yard plunge," Malvern growled.

The buzzer sounded for the sixth.

The first five had been anybody's fight. The big blond boy, Duke Targo, wasn't trying. The dark one, Deacon Werra, a powerful, loose-limbed Polack with bad teeth and only two cauliflower ears, had the physique but didn't know anything but rough clinching and a giant swing that started in the basement and never connected. He had been good enough to hold Targo off so far. The fans razzed Targo a good deal.

When the stool swung back out of the ring Targo hitched at his black and silver trunks, smiled with a small tight smile at the girl in the white wrap. He was very good-looking, without a mark on him. There was blood on his left shoulder from Werra's nose.

The bell rang and Werra charged across the ring, slid off Targo's shoulder, got a left hook in. Targo got more of the hook than was in it. He piled back into the ropes, bounced out, clinched.

Malvern smiled quietly in the darkness.

The referee broke them easily. Targo broke clean. Werra tried for an uppercut and missed. They sparred for a minute. There was waltz music from the gallery. Then Werra started a swing from his shoetops. Targo seemed to wait for it, to wait for it to hit him. There was a queer strained smile on his face. The girl in the white wrap stood up suddenly.

Werra's swing grazed Targo's jaw. It barely staggered him. Targo lashed a long right that caught Werra over the eye. A left hook smashed into Werra's jaw, then a right cross almost to the same spot.

The dark boy went down on his hands and knees, slipped

slowly all the way to the floor, lay with both his gloves under him. There were catcalls as he was counted out.

The fat man struggled to his feet, grinning hugely. He said: "How you like it, pal? Still think it was a set piece?"

"It came unstuck," Malvern said in a voice as toneless as a police radio.

The fat man said: "So long, pal. Come around lots." He kicked Malvern's ankle climbing over him.

Malvern sat motionless, watched the auditorium empty. The fighters and their handlers had gone down the stairs under the ring. The girl in the white wrap had disappeared in the crowd. The lights went out and the barnlike structure looked cheap, sordid.

Tony Acosta fidgeted, watching a man in striped overalls picking up papers between the seats.

Malvern stood up suddenly, said: "I'm going to talk to that bum, Tony. Wait outside in the car for me."

He went swiftly up the slope to the lobby, through the remnants of the gallery crowd to a gray door marked: "No Admittance." He went through that and down a ramp to another door marked the same way. A special cop in faded and unbuttoned khaki stood in front of it, with a bottle of beer in one hand and a hamburger in the other.

Malvern flashed a police card and the cop lurched out of the way without looking at the card. He hiccoughed peacefully as Malvern went through the door, then along a narrow passage with numbered doors lining it. There was noise behind the doors. The fourth door on the left had a scribbled card with the name "Duke Targo" fastened to the panel by a thumbtack.

Malvern opened it into the heavy sound of a shower going, out of sight.

In a narrow and utterly bare room a man in a white sweater was sitting on the end of a rubbing table that had clothes scattered on it. Malvern recognized him as Targo's chief second.

He said: "Where's the Duke?"

The sweatered man jerked a thumb towards the shower noise. Then a man came around the door and lurched very close to Malvern. He was tall and had curly brown hair with hard gray color in it. He had a big drink in his hand. His face had the flat glitter of extreme drunkenness. His hair was damp, his eyes bloodshot. His lips curled and uncurled in rapid smiles without meaning. He said thickly: "Scramola umpchay."

Malvern shut the door calmly and leaned against it and started to get his cigarette case from his vest pocket, inside his open blue raincoat. He didn't look at the curly haired man at all.

The curly haired man lunged his free right hand up suddenly, snapped it under his coat, out again. A blue steel gun shone dully against his light suit. The glass in his left hand slopped liquor.

"None of that!" he snarled.

Malvern brought the cigarette case out very slowly, showed it in his hand, opened it and put a cigarette between his lips. The blue gun was very close to him, not very steady. The hand holding the glass shook in a sort of jerky rhythm.

Malvern said loosely: "Yeah. You *ought* to be looking for trouble."

The sweatered man got off the rubbing table. Then he stood very still and looked at the gun. The curly haired man said:

"We like trouble. Frisk him, Mike."

The sweatered man said: "I don't want any part of it, Shenvair. For Pete's sake, take it easy. You're lit like a ferry boat."

Malvern said: "It's okey to frisk me. I'm not rodded."

"Nix," the sweatered man said. "This guy is the Duke's bodyguard. Deal me out."

The curly haired man said: "Sure, I'm drunk," and giggled.

"You're a friend of the Duke?" the sweatered man asked.

"I've got some information for him," Malvern said.

"About what?"

Malvern didn't say anything. "Okey," the sweatered man said. He shrugged bitterly.

"Know what, Mike?" the curly haired man said suddenly and violently. "I think this —— wants my job. Hell, yes. He looks like a bum. You ain't a shamus, are you, mister?" He punched Malvern with the muzzle of the gun.

"Yeah," Malvern said. "And keep your iron next your own belly."

The curly haired man turned his head a little and grinned back over his shoulder.

"What d'you know about that, Mike? He's a shamus. Sure he wants my job. Sure he does."

"Put the heater up, you fool," the sweatered man said disgustedly.

The curly haired man turned a little more. "I'm his protection, ain't I?" he complained.

Malvern knocked the gun aside almost casually, with the hand that held his cigarette case. The curly haired man snapped his head around again. Malvern slid close to him, sank a stiff punch in his stomach, holding the gun away with his forearm. The curly haired man gagged, sprayed liquor down the front of Malvern's raincoat. His glass shattered on the floor. The blue gun left his hand and went over in a corner. The sweatered man went after it.

The noise of the shower had stopped unnoticed and the blond fighter came out toweling himself vigorously. He stared open-mouthed at the tableau.

Malvern said: "I don't need this any more."

He heaved the curly haired man away from him and laced his jaw with a hard right as he went back. The curly haired man staggered across the room, hit the wall, slid down it and sat on the floor.

The sweatered man snatched the gun up and stood rigid, watching Malvern.

Malvern got out a handkerchief and wiped the front of his coat, while Targo shut his large well-shaped mouth slowly and began to move the towel back and forth across his chest. After a moment he said:

"Just who the hell may you be?"

Malvern said: "I used to be a private dick. Malvern's the name. I think you need help."

Targo's face got a little redder than the shower had left it. "Why?"

"I heard you were supposed to throw it, and I think you

tried to. But Werra was too lousy. You couldn't help yourself. That means you're in a jam."

Targo said very slowly: "People get their teeth kicked in for saying things like that."

The room was very still for a moment. The drunk sat up on the floor and blinked, tried to get his feet under him, and gave it up.

Malvern added quietly: "Benny Cyrano is a friend of mine. He's your backer, isn't he?"

The sweatered man laughed harshly. Then he broke the gun and slid the shells out of it, dropped the gun on the floor. He went to the door, went out, slammed the door shut.

Targo looked at the shut door, looked back at Malvern. He said very slowly:

"What did you hear?"

"Your friend Jean Adrian lives in my hotel, on my floor. She got sapped by a hood this afternoon. I happened by and saw the hood running away, picked her up. She told me a little of what it was all about."

Targo had put on his underwear and socks and shoes. He reached into a locker for a black satin shirt, put that on. He said:

"She didn't tell me."

"She wouldn't—before the fight."

Targo nodded slightly. Then he said: "If you know Benny, you may be all right. I've been getting threats. Maybe it's a lot of birdseed and maybe it's some Spring Street punter's idea of how to make himself a little easy dough. I fought my fight the way I wanted to. Now you can take the air, mister."

He put on high-waisted black trousers and knotted a white tie on his black shirt. He got a white serge coat trimmed with black braid out of the locker, put that on. A black and white handkerchief flared from the pocket in three points.

Malvern stared at the clothes, moved a little towards the door and looked down at the drunk.

"Okey," he said. "I see you've got a bodyguard. It was just an idea I had. Excuse it, please."

He went out, closed the door gently, and went back up the ramp to the lobby, out to the street. He walked through the rain around the corner of the building to a big graveled parking lot.

The lights of a car blinked at him and his coupé slid along the wet gravel and pulled up. Tony Acosta was at the wheel.

Malvern got in at the right side and said: "Let's go out to Cyrano's, and have a drink, Tony."

"Jeeze, that's swell. Miss Adrian's in the floor show there. You know, the blonde I told you about."

Malvern said: "Yeah. I saw Targo. I kind of liked him—but I didn't like his clothes."

4

Gus Neishacker was a two hundred pound fashion plate with very red cheeks and thin, exquisitely penciled eyebrows— eyebrows from a Chinese vase. There was a red carnation in the lapel of his wide-shouldered dinner jacket and he kept sniffing at it while he watched the headwaiter seat a party of guests. When Malvern and Tony Acosta came through the foyer arch he flashed a sudden smile and went to them with his hand out.

"How's a boy, Ted? Party?"

Malvern said: "Just the two of us. Meet Mister Acosta. Gus Neishacker, Cyrano's floor manager."

Gus Neishacker shook hands with Tony without looking at him. He said: "Let's see, the last time you dropped in—"

"She left town," Malvern said. "We'll sit near the ring but not too near. We don't dance together."

Gus Neishacker jerked a menu from under the headwaiter's arm and led the way down five crimson steps, along the tables that skirted the oval dance floor.

They sat down. Malvern ordered rye highballs and Denver sandwiches. Neishacker gave the order to a waiter, pulled a chair out and sat down at the table. He took a pencil out and made triangles on the inside of a match cover.

"See the fights?" he asked carelessly.

"Was that what they were?"

Gus Neishacker smiled indulgently. "Benny talked to the Duke. He says you're wise." He looked suddenly at Tony Acosta.

"Tony's all right," Malvern said.

"Yeah. Well do us a favor, will you? See it stops right here. Benny likes this boy. He wouldn't let him get hurt. He'd put protection all around him—*real* protection—if he thought that threat stuff was anything but some pool-hall bum's idea of a very funny joke. Benny never backs but one boxfighter at a time, and he picks them damn' careful."

Malvern lit a cigarette, blew smoke from a corner of his mouth, said quietly: "It's none of my business, but I'm telling you it's screwy. I have a nose for that sort of thing."

Gus Neishacker stared at him a minute, then shrugged. He said: "I hope you're wrong," stood up quickly and walked away among the tables. He bent to smile here and there, and speak to a customer.

Tony Acosta's velvet eyes shone. He said: "Jeeze, Mister Malvern, you think it's rough stuff?"

Malvern nodded, didn't say anything. The waiter put their drinks and sandwiches on the table, went away. The band on the stage at the end of the oval floor blared out a long chord and a slick, grinning M.C. slid out on the stage and put his lips to a small open mike.

The floor show began. A line of half naked girls ran out under a rain of colored lights. They coiled and uncoiled in a long sinuous line, their bare legs flashing, their navels little dimples of darkness in soft white, very nude flesh.

A hard-boiled red-head sang a hard-boiled song in a voice that could have been used to split firewood. The girls came back in black tights and silk hats, did the same dance with a slightly different exposure.

The music softened and a tall high yaller torch singer drooped under an amber light and sang of something very far away and unhappy, in a voice like old ivory.

Malvern sipped his drink, poked at his sandwich in the dim light. Tony Acosta's hard young face was a small tense blur beside him.

The torch singer went away and there was a little pause and then suddenly all the lights in the place went out except the lights over the music racks of the band and the little pale amber lights at the entrances to the radiating aisles of booths beyond the tables.

There were squeals in the thick darkness. A single white spot winked on, high up under the roof, settled on a runway beside the stage. Faces were chalk white in the reflected glare. There was the red glow of a cigarette tip here and there. Four tall black men moved in the light, carrying a white mummy case on their shoulders. They came slowly, in rhythm, down the runway. They wore white Egyptian headdresses and loin-cloths of white leather and white sandals laced to the knees. The black smoothness of their limbs was like black marble in the moonlight.

They reached the middle of the dance-floor and slowly upended the mummy case until the cover tipped forward and fell and was caught. Then slowly, very slowly, a swathed white figure tipped forward and fell—slowly, like the last leaf from a dead tree. It tipped in the air, seemed to hover, then plunged towards the floor under a shattering roll of drums.

The light went off, went on. The swathed figure was up-right on the floor, spinning, and one of the blacks was spin-ning the opposite way, winding the white shroud around his body. Then the shroud fell away and a girl was all tinsel and smooth white limbs under the hard light and her body shot through the air glittering and was caught and passed around swiftly among the four black men, like a baseball handled by a fast infield.

Then the music changed to a waltz and she danced among the black men slowly and gracefully, as though among four ebony pillars, very close to them but never touching them.

The act ended. The applause rose and fell in thick waves. The light went out and it was dark again, and then all the lights went up and the girl and the four black men were gone.

"Keeno," Tony Acosta breathed. "Oh, keeno. That was Miss Adrian, wasn't it?"

Malvern said slowly: "Yeah. A little daring." He lit another cigarette, looked around. "There's another black and white number, Tony. The Duke himself, in person."

Duke Targo stood applauding violently at the entrance to one of the radiating booth aisles. There was a loose grin on his face. He looked as if he might have had a few drinks.

An arm came down over Malvern's shoulder. A hand planted itself in the ashtray at his elbow. He smelled Scotch in heavy gusts. He turned his head slowly, looked up at the liquor-shiny face of Shenvair, Duke Targo's drunken body-guard.

"Smokes and a white gal," Shenvair said thickly. "Lousy. Crummy. Godawful crummy."

Malvern smiled slowly, moved his chair a little. Tony Acosta stared at Shenvair round-eyed, his little mouth a thin line.

"Blackface, Mister Shenvair. Not real smokes. I liked it."

"And who the hell cares what you like?" Shenvair wanted to know.

Malvern smiled delicately, laid his cigarette down on the edge of a plate. He turned his chair a little more.

"Still think I want your job, Shenvair?"

"Yeah. I owe you a smack in the puss too." He took his hand out of the ashtray, wiped it off on the tablecloth. He doubled it into a fist. "Like it now?"

A waiter caught him by the arm, spun him around.

"You lost your table, sir? This way."

Shenvair patted the waiter on the shoulder, tried to put an arm around his neck. "Swell, let's go nibble a drink. I don't like these people."

They went away, disappeared among the tables.

Malvern said: "To hell with this place, Tony," and stared moodily towards the band stage. Then his eyes became intent.

A girl with corn-blond hair, in a white wrap with a white fur collar, appeared at the edge of the shell, went behind it, reappeared nearer. She came along the edge of the booths to the place where Targo had been standing. She slipped in between the booths there, disappeared.

Malvern said: "Yeah. To hell with this place. Let's go, Tony," in a low angry voice. Then very softly, in a tensed tone: "No—wait a minute. I see another guy I don't like."

The man was on the far side of the dance-floor, which was empty at the moment. He was following its curve around, past the tables that fringed it. He looked a little different without his hat. But he had the same flat white expressionless face, the same close-set eyes. He was youngish, not more than thirty, but already having trouble with his bald spot. The slight bulge of a gun under his left arm was barely noticeable.

He was the man who had run away from Jean Adrian's apartment in the Carondelet.

He reached the aisle into which Targo had gone, into which a moment before Jean Adrian had gone. He went into it.

Malvern said sharply: "Wait here, Tony." He kicked his chair back and stood up.

Somebody rabbit-punched him from behind. He swiveled, close to Shenvair's grinning sweaty face.

"Back again, pal," the curly heared man chortled, and hit him on the jaw.

It was a short jab, well placed for a drunk. It caught Malvern off balance, staggered him. Tony Acosta came to his feet snarling, catlike. Malvern was still rocking when Shenvair let go with the other fist. That was too slow, too wide. Malvern slid inside it, uppercut the curly haired man's nose savagely, got a handful of blood before he could get his hand away. He put most of it back on Shenvair's face.

Shenvair wobbled, staggered back a step and sat down on the floor, hard. He clapped a hand to his nose.

"Keep an eye on this bird, Tony," Malvern growled swiftly.

Shenvair took hold of the nearest tablecloth and yanked it. It came off the table. Silver and glasses and china followed it to the floor. A man swore and a woman squealed. A waiter ran towards them with a livid, furious face.

Malvern almost didn't hear the two shots.

They were small and flat, close together, a small caliber gun. The rushing waiter stopped dead, and a deeply etched white line appeared around his mouth as instantly as though the lash of a whip had cut it there.

A dark woman with a sharp nose opened her mouth to yell and no sound came from her. There was that instant when nobody makes a sound, when it almost seems as if there will never again be any sound—after the sound of a gun. Then Malvern was running.

He bumped into people who stood up and craned their necks. He reached the entrance to the aisle into which the white-faced man had gone. The booths had high walls and swing doors not so high. Heads stuck out over the doors, but no one was in the aisle yet. Malvern charged up a shallow carpeted slope, at the far end of which booth doors stood wide open.

Legs in dark cloth showed past the doors, slack on the floor, the knees sagged. The toes of black shoes were pointed into the booth.

Malvern shook an arm off, reached the place.

The man lay across the end of a table, his stomach and one side of his face on the white cloth, his left hand dropped between the table and the padded seat. His right hand on top of the table didn't quite hold a big black gun, a .45 with a cut barrel. The bald spot on his head glistened under the light, and the oily metal of the gun glistened beside it.

Blood leaked from under his chest, vivid scarlet on the white cloth, seeping into it as into blotting paper.

Duke Targo was standing up, deep in the booth. His left arm in the white serge coat was braced on the end of the table. Jean Adrian was sitting down at his side. Targo looked at Malvern blankly, as if he had never seen him before. He pushed his big right hand forward.

A small white-handled automatic lay on his palm.

"I shot him," he said thickly. "He pulled a gun on us and I shot him."

Jean Adrian was scrubbing her hands together on a scrap of handkerchief. Her face was strained, cold, not scared. Her eyes were dark.

"I shot him," Targo said. He threw the small gun down on the cloth. It bounced, almost hit the fallen man's head. "Let's—let's get out of here."

Malvern put a hand against the side of the sprawled man's neck, held it there a second or two, took it away.

"He's dead," he said. "When a citizen drops a redhot—that's news."

Jean Adrian was staring at him stiff-eyed. He flashed a smile at her, put a hand against Targo's chest, pushed him back.

"Sit down, Targo. You're not going any place."

Targo said: "Well—okey. I shot him, see."

"That's all right," Malvern said. "Just relax."

People were close behind him now, crowding him. He leaned back against the press of bodies and kept on smiling at the girl's white face.

5

Benny Cyrano was shaped like two eggs, a little one that was his head on top of a big one that was his body. His small dapper legs and feet in patent leather shoes were pushed into the kneehole of a dark sheenless desk. He held a corner of a handkerchief tightly between his teeth and pulled against it with his left hand and held his right hand out pudgily in front of him, pushing against the air. He was saying in a voice muffled by the handkerchief:

"Now wait a minute, boys. Now wait a minute."

There was a striped built-in sofa in one corner of the office, and Duke Targo sat in the middle of it, between two Headquarters dicks. He had a dark bruise over one cheekbone, his thick blond hair was tousled and his black satin shirt looked as if somebody had tried to swing him by it.

One of the dicks, the gray-haired one, had a split lip. The young one with hair as blond as Targo's had a black eye. They both looked mad, but the blond one looked madder.

Malvern straddled a chair against the wall and looked sleepily at Jean Adrian, near him in a leather rocker. She was twisting a handkerchief in her hands, rubbing her palms with it. She had been doing this for a long time, as if she had forgotten she was doing it. Her small firm mouth was angry.

Gus Neishacker leaned against the closed door smoking.

"Now wait a minute, boys," Cyrano said. "If you didn't get tough with him, he wouldn't fight back. He's a good boy—the best I ever had. Give him a break."

Blood dribbled from one corner of Targo's mouth, in a fine thread down to his jutting chin. It gathered there and glistened. His face was empty, expressionless.

Malvern said coldly: "You wouldn't want the boys to stop playing blackjack pinochle, would you, Benny?"

The blond dick snarled: "You still got that private dick license, Malvern?"

"It's lying around somewhere, I guess," Malvern said.

"Maybe we could take it away from you," the blond dick snarled.

"Maybe you could do a fan dance, copper. You might be all kinds of a smart guy for all I'd know."

The blond dick started to get up. The older one said: "Leave him be. Give him six feet. If he steps over that, we'll take the screws out of him."

Malvern and Gus Neishacker grinned at each other. Cyrano made helpless gestures in the air. The girl looked at Malvern under her lashes. Targo opened his mouth and spat blood straight before him on the blue carpet.

Something pushed against the door and Neishacker stepped to one side, opened it a crack, then opened it wide. McChesney came in.

McChesney was a lieutenant of detectives, tall, sandy haired, fortyish, with pale eyes and a narrow suspicious face. He shut the door and turned the key in it, went slowly over and stood in front of Targo.

"Plenty dead," he said. "One under the heart, one in it. Nice snap shooting. In any league."

"When you've got to deliver you've got to deliver," Targo said dully.

"Make him?" the gray-haired dick asked his partner, moving away along the sofa.

McChesney nodded. "Torchy Plant. A gun for hire. I haven't seen him around for all of two years. Tough as an ingrowing toenail with his right load. A bindle punk."

"He'd have to be that to throw his party in here," the gray-haired dick said.

McChesney's long face was serious, not hard. "Got a permit for the gun, Targo?"

Targo said: "Yes. Benny got me one two weeks ago. I been getting a lot of threats."

"Listen, Lieutenant," Cyrano chirped, "some gamblers try to scare him into a dive, see? He wins nine straight fights by knockouts so they get a swell price. I told him he should take one at that maybe."

"I almost did," Targo said sullenly.

"So they sent the redhot to him," Cyrano said.

McChesney said: "I wouldn't say no. How'd you beat his draw, Targo? Where was your gun?"

"On my hip."

"Show me."

Targo put his hand back into his right hip pocket and

jerked a handkerchief out quickly, stuck his finger through it like a gun barrel.

"That handkerchief in the pocket?" McChesney asked. "With the gun?"

Targo's big reddish face clouded a little. He nodded.

McChesney leaned forward casually and twitched the handkerchief from his hand. He sniffed at it, unwrapped it, sniffed at it again, folded it and put it away in his own pocket. His face said nothing.

"What did he say, Targo?"

"He said: 'I got a message for you, punk, and this is it.' Then he went for the gat and it stuck a little in the clip. I got mine out first."

McChesney smiled faintly and leaned far back, teetering on his heels. His faint smile seemed to slide off the end of his long nose. He looked Targo up and down.

"Yeah," he said softly. "I'd call it damn' nice shooting with a .22. But you're fast for a big guy. . . . Who got these threats?"

"I did," Targo said. "Over the phone."

"Know the voice?"

"It might have been this same guy. I'm not just positive."

McChesney walked stiff-legged to the other end of the office, stood a moment looking at a hand-tinted sporting print. He came back slowly, drifted over to the door.

"A guy like that don't mean a lot," he said quietly, "but we got to do our job. The two of you will have to come downtown and make statements. Let's go."

He went out. The two dicks stood up, with Duke Targo between them. The gray-haired one snapped:

"You goin' to act nice, bo?"

Targo sneered: "If I get to wash my face."

They went out. The blond dick waited for Jean Adrian to pass in front of him. He swung the door, snarled back at Malvern:

"As for you—nuts!"

Malvern said softly: "I like them. It's the squirrel in me, copper."

Gus Neishacker laughed, then shut the door and went to the desk.

"I'm shaking like Benny's third chin," he said. "Let's all have a shot of cognac."

He poured three glasses a third full, took one over to the striped sofa and spread his long legs out on it, leaned his head back and sipped the brandy.

Malvern stood up and downed his drink. He got a cigarette out and rolled it around in his fingers, staring at Cyrano's smooth white face with an up-from-under look.

"How much would you say changed hands on that fight tonight?" he asked softly. "Bets."

Cyrano blinked, massaged his lips with a fat hand. "A few grand. It was just a regular weekly show. It don't listen, does it?"

Malvern put the cigarette in his mouth and leaned over the desk to strike a match. He said:

"If it does, murder's getting awfully cheap in this town."

Cyrano didn't say anything. Gus Neishacker sipped the last of his brandy and carefully put the empty glass down on a round cork table beside the sofa. He stared at the ceiling, silently.

After a moment Malvern nodded at the two men, crossed the room and went out, closed the door behind him. He went along a corridor off which dressing-rooms opened, dark now. A curtained archway let him out at the back of the stage.

In the foyer the headwaiter was standing at the glass doors, looking out at the rain and the back of a uniformed policeman. Malvern went into the empty cloak room, found his hat and coat, put them on, came out to stand beside the headwaiter.

He said: "I guess you didn't notice what happened to the kid I was with?"

The headwaiter shook his head and reached forward to unlock the door.

"There was four hundred people here—and three hundred scrammed before the Law checked in. I'm sorry."

Malvern nodded and went out into the rain. The uniformed man glanced at him casually. He went along the street to where the car had been left. It wasn't there. He looked up and down the street, stood for a few moments in the rain, then walked towards Melrose.

After a little while he found a taxi.

6

The ramp of the Carondelet garage curved down into semi-darkness and chilled air. The dark bulks of stalled cars looked ominous against the white washed walls, and the single drop-light in the small office had the relentless glitter of the death house.

A big negro in stained coveralls came out rubbing his eyes, then his face split in an enormous grin.

"Hello, there, Mistuh Malvu'n. You kinda restless to-night?"

Malvern said: "I get a little wild when it rains. I bet my heap isn't here."

"No, it ain't Mistuh Malvu'n. I been all around wipin' off and yours ain't here aytall."

Malvern said woodenly: "I lent it to a pal. He probably wrecked it. . . ."

He flicked a half-dollar through the air and went back up the ramp to the side street. He turned towards the back of the hotel, came to an alley-like street one side of which was the rear wall of the Carondelet. The other side had two frame houses and a four-story brick building. Hotel Blaine was lettered on a round milky globe over the door.

Malvern went up three cement steps and tried the door. It was locked. He looked through the glass panel into a small dim empty lobby. He got out two passkeys; the second one moved the lock a little. He pulled the door hard towards him, tried the first one again. That snicked the bolt back far enough for the loosely fitted door to open.

He went in and looked at an empty counter with a sign: "Manager" beside a plunger bell. There was an oblong of empty numbered pigeon holes on the wall. Malvern went around the counter and fished a leather register out of a space under the top. He read names back three pages, found the boyish scrawl: "Tony Acosta," and a room number in another writing.

He put the register away and went past the automatic elevator and upstairs to the fourth floor.

The hallway was very silent. There was weak light from a

ceiling fixture. The last door but one on the left-hand side had a crack of light showing around its transom. That was the door—411. He put his hand out to knock, then withdrew it without touching the door.

The door-knob was heavily smeared with something that looked like blood.

Malvern's eyes looked down and saw what was almost a pool of blood on the stained wood before the door, beyond the edge of the runner.

His hand suddenly felt clammy inside his glove. He took the glove off, held the hand stiff, clawlike for a moment, then shook it slowly. His eyes had a sharp strained light in them.

He got a handkerchief out, grasped the door-knob inside it, turned it slowly. The door was unlocked. He went in.

He looked across the room and said very softly: "Tony . . . oh, Tony."

Then he shut the door behind him and turned a key in it, still with the handkerchief.

There was light from the bowl that hung on three brass chains from the middle of the ceiling. It shone on a made-up bed, some painted, light colored furniture, a dull green carpet, a square writing desk of eucalyptus wood.

Tony Acosta sat at the desk. His head was slumped forward on his left arm. Under the chair on which he sat, between the legs of the chair and his feet, there was a glistening brownish pool.

Malvern walked across the room so rigidly that his ankles ached after the second step. He reached the desk, touched Tony Acosta's shoulder.

"Tony," he said thickly, in a low, meaningless voice. "My God, Tony!"

Tony didn't move. Malvern went around to his side. A blood-soaked bath towel glared against the boy's stomach, across his pressed-together thighs. His right hand was crouched against the front edge of the desk, as if he was trying to push himself up. Almost under his face there was a scrawled envelope.

Malvern pulled the envelope towards him slowly, lifted it like a thing of weight, read the wandering scrawl of words.

"Tailed him . . . woptown . . . 28 Court Street . . . over garage . . . shot me . . . think I got . . . him . . . your car. . ."

The line trailed over the edge of the paper, became a blot there. The pen was on the floor. There was a bloody thumb print on the envelope.

Malvern folded it meticulously to protect the print, put the envelope in his wallet. He lifted Tony's head, turned it a little towards him. The neck was still warm; it was beginning to stiffen. Tony's soft dark eyes were open and they held the quiet brightness of a cat's eyes. They had that effect the eyes of the new dead have of almost, but not quite, looking at you.

Malvern lowered the head gently on the outstretched left arm. He stood laxly, his head on one side, his eyes almost sleepy. Then his head jerked straight and his eyes hardened.

He stripped off his raincoat and the suitcoat underneath, rolled his sleeves up, wet a face towel in the basin in the corner of the room and went to the door. He wiped the knobs off, bent down and wiped up the smeared blood from the floor outside.

He rinsed the towel and hung it up to dry, wiped his hands carefully, put his coat on again. He used his handkerchief to open the transom, to reverse the key and lock the door from the outside. He threw the key in over the top of the transom, heard it tinkle inside.

He went downstairs and out of the Hotel Blaine. It still rained. He walked to the corner, looked along a tree-shaded block. His car was a dozen yards from the intersection, parked carefully, the lights off, the keys in the ignition. He drew them out, felt the seat under the wheel. It was wet, sticky. Malvern wiped his hand off, ran the windows up and locked the car. He left it where it was.

Going back to the Carondelet he didn't meet anybody. The hard slanting rain still pounded down into the empty streets.

7

There was a thin thread of light under the door of 914. Malvern knocked lightly, looking up and down the hall, moved his gloved finger softly on the panel while he waited. He waited a long time. Then a voice spoke wearily behind the wood of the door.

"Yes? What is it?"

"Ted Malvern, angel. I have to see you. It's strictly business."

The door clicked, opened. He looked at a tired white face, dark eyes that were slatelike, not violet-blue. There were smudges under them as though mascara had been rubbed into the skin. The girl's strong little hand twitched on the edge of the door.

"You," she said wearily. "It would be you. Yes. . . . Well, I've simply got to have a shower. I smell of policemen."

"Fifteen minutes?" Malvern asked casually, but his eyes were very sharp on her face.

She shrugged slowly, then nodded. The closing door seemed to jump at him. He went along to his own rooms, threw off his hat and coat, poured whiskey into a glass and went into the bathroom to get ice water from the small tap over the basin.

He drank slowly, looking out of the windows at the dark breadth of the boulevard. A car slid by now and then, two beams of white light attached to nothing, emanating from nowhere.

He finished the drink, stripped to the skin, went under a shower. He dressed in fresh clothes, refilled his big flask and put it in his inner pocket, took a snubnosed automatic out of a suit-case and held it in his hand for a minute staring at it. Then he put it back in the suit-case, lit a cigarette and smoked it through.

He got a dry hat and a tweed coat and went back to 914.

The door was almost insidiously ajar. He slipped in with a light knock, shut the door, went on into the living-room and looked at Jean Adrian.

She was sitting on the davenport, with a freshly scrubbed look, in loose plum-colored pajamas and a Chinese coat. A tendril of damp hair drooped over one temple. Her small even features had the cameo-like clearness that tiredness gives to the very young.

Malvern said: "Drink?"

She gestured emptily. "I suppose so."

He got glasses, mixed whiskey and ice water, went to the davenport with them.

"Are they keeping Targo on ice?"

She moved her chin an eighth of an inch, staring into her glass.

"He cut loose again, knocked two cops halfway through the wall. They love that boy."

Malvern said: "He has a lot to learn about cops. In the morning the cameras will be all set for him. I can think of some nice headlines, such as: "Wellknown Fighter too Fast for Gunmen. Duke Targo Puts Crimp in Underworld Hot Rod.""

The girl sipped her drink. "I'm tired," she said. "And my foot itches. Let's talk about what makes this your business."

"Sure." He flipped his cigarette case open, held it under her chin. Her hand fumbled at it and while it still fumbled he said: "When you light that tell me why you shot him."

Jean Adrian put the cigarette between her lips, bent her head to the match, inhaled and threw her head back. Color awakened slowly in her eyes and a small smile curved the line of her pressed lips. She didn't answer.

Malvern watched her for a minute, turning his glass in his hands. Then he stared at the floor, said:

"It was your gun—the gun I picked up here in the afternoon. Targo said he drew it from his hip pocket, the slowest draw in the world. Yet he's supposed to have shot twice, accurately enough to kill a man, while the man wasn't even getting his gun loose from a shoulder-holster. That's hooey. But you, with the gun in a bag in your lap, and knowing the hood, might just have managed it. He would have been watching Targo."

The girl said emptily: "You're a private dick, I hear. You're the son of a boss politician. They talked about you downtown. They act a little afraid of you, of people you might know. Who sicked you on to me?"

Malvern said: "They're not afraid of me, angel. They just talked like that to see how you'd react, if I was involved, so on. They don't know what it's all about."

"They were told plainly enough what it was all about."

Malvern shook his head. "A cop never believes what he gets without a struggle. He's too used to cooked-up stories. I think McChesney's wise you did the shooting. He knows by now if that handkerchief of Targo's had been in a pocket with a gun."

Her limp fingers discarded her cigarette half-smoked. A curtain eddied at the window and loose flakes of ash crawled around in the ashtray. She said slowly:

"All right. I shot him. Do you think I'd hesitate after this afternoon?"

Malvern rubbed the lobe of his ear. "I'm playing this too light," he said softly. "You don't know what's in my heart. Something has happened, something nasty. Do you think the hood meant to kill Targo?"

"I thought so— or I wouldn't have shot a man."

"I think maybe it was just a scare. Like the other one. After all a night-club is a poor place for a get-away."

She said sharply: "They don't do many low tackles on forty-fives. He'd have got away all right. Of course he meant to kill somebody. And of course I didn't mean Duke to front for me. He just grabbed the gun out of my hand and slammed into his act. What did it matter? I knew it would all come out in the end."

She poked absently at the still burning cigarette in the tray, kept her eyes down. After a moment she said, almost in a whisper: "Is that all you wanted to know?"

Malvern let his eyes crawl sidewise, without moving his head, until he could just see the firm curve of her cheek, the strong line of her throat. He said thickly:

"Shenvair was in on it. The fellow I was with at Cyrano's followed Shenvair to a hideout. Shenvair shot him. He's dead. He's dead, angel—just a young kid that worked here in the hotel. Tony, the bell captain. The cops don't know that yet."

The muffled clang of elevator doors was heavy through the silence. A horn tooted dismally out in the rain on the boulevard. The girl sagged forward suddenly, then sidewise, fell across Malvern's knees. Her body was half-turned and she lay almost on her back across his thighs, her eyelids flickering. The small blue veins in them stood out rigid in the soft skin.

He put his arms around her slowly, loosely, then they tightened, lifted her. He brought her face close to his own face. He kissed her on the side of the mouth.

Her eyes opened, stared blankly, unfocused. He kissed her again, tightly, then pushed her upright on the davenport.

He said quietly: "That wasn't just an act, was it?"

She leaped to her feet, spun around. Her voice was low, tense and angry.

"There's something horrible about you! Something—satanic. You come here and tell me another man has been killed—and then you kiss me. It isn't real."

Malvern said dully: "There's something horrible about any man that goes suddenly gaga over another man's woman."

"I'm not his woman!" she snapped. "I don't even like him—and I don't like you."

Malvern shrugged. They stared at each other with bleak hostile eyes. The girl clicked her teeth shut, then said almost violently:

"Get out! I can't talk to you any more. I can't stand you around. Will you get out?"

Malvern said: "Why not?" He stood up, went over and got his hat and coat.

The girl sobbed once sharply, then she went in light quick strides across the room to the windows, became motionless with her back to him.

Malvern looked at her back, went over near her and stood looking at the soft hair low down on her neck. He said:

"Why the hell don't you let me help? I know there's something wrong. I wouldn't hurt you."

The girl spoke to the curtain in front of her face, savagely:

"Get out! I don't want your help. Go away and stay away. I won't be seeing you—ever."

Malvern said slowly: "I think you've got to have help. Whether you like it or not. That man in the photo frame on the desk there—I think I know who he is. And I don't think he's dead."

The girl turned. Her face now was as white as paper. Her eyes strained at his eyes. She breathed thickly, harshly. After what seemed a long time she said:

"I'm caught. Caught. There's nothing you can do about it."

Malvern lifted a hand and drew his fingers slowly down her cheek, down the angle of her tight jaw. His eyes held a hard brown glitter, his lips a smile. It was cunning, almost a dishonest smile.

He said: "I'm wrong, angel. I don't know him at all. Good night."

He went back across the room, through the little hallway, opened the door. When the door opened the girl clutched at the curtain and rubbed her face against it slowly.

Malvern didn't shut the door. He stood quite still halfway through it, looking at two men who stood there with guns.

They stood close to the door, as if they had been about to knock. One was thick, dark saturnine. The other one was an albino with sharp red eyes, a narrow head that showed shining snow-white hair under a rain-spattered dark hat. He had the thin sharp teeth and the drawn-back grin of a rat.

Malvern started to close the door behind him. The albino said: "Hold it, rube. The door, I mean. We're goin' in."

The other man slid forward and pressed his left hand up and down Malvern's body carefully. He stepped away, said:

"No gat, but a swell flask under his arm."

The albino gestured with his gun. "Back up, rube. We want the broad, too."

Malvern said tonelessly: "It doesn't take a gun, Critz. I know you and I know your boss. If he wants to see me, I'll be glad to talk to him."

He turned and went back into the room with the two gunmen behind him.

Jean Adrian hadn't moved. She stood by the window still, the curtain against her cheek, her eyes closed, as if she hadn't heard the voices at the door at all.

Then she heard them come in and her eyes snapped open. She turned slowly, stared past Malvern at the two gunmen. The albino walked to the middle of the room, looked around it without speaking, went on into the bedroom and bathroom. Doors opened and shut. He came back on quiet catlike feet, pulled his overcoat open and pushed his hat back on his head.

"Get dressed, sister. We have to go for a ride in the rain. Okey?"

The girl stared at Malvern now. He shrugged, smiled a little, spread his hands.

"That's how it is, angel. Might as well fall in line."

The lines of her face got thin and contemptuous. She said slowly: "You—you—." Her voice trailed off into a sibilant, meaningless mutter. She went across the room stiffly and out of it into the bedroom.

The albino slipped a cigarette between his sharp lips, chuckled with a wet, gurgling sound, as if his mouth was full of saliva.

"She don't seem to like you, rube."

Malvern frowned. He walked slowly to the writing desk, leaned his hips against it, stared at the floor.

"She thinks I sold her out," he said dully.

"Maybe you did, rube," the albino drawled.

Malvern said: "Better watch her. She's neat with a gun."

His hands, reaching casually behind him on the desk, tapped the top of it lightly, then without apparent change of movement folded the leather photo frame down on its side and edged it under the blotter.

8

There was a padded arm rest in the middle of the rear seat of the car, and Malvern leaned an elbow on it, cupped his chin in his hand, stared through the half-misted windows at the rain. It was thick white spray in the headlights, and the noise of it on the top of the car was like drum-fire very far off.

Jean Adrian sat on the other side of the arm rest, in the corner. She wore a black hat and a gray coat with tufts of silky hair on it, longer than caracul and not so curly. She didn't look at Malvern or speak to him.

The albino sat on the right of the thick dark man, who drove. They went through the silent streets, past blurred houses, blurred trees, the blurred shine of street lights. There were neon signs behind thick curtains of mist. There was no sky.

Then they climbed and a feeble arc light strung over an

intersection threw light on a sign post, and Malvern read the name "Court Street."

He said softly: "This is woptown, Critz. The big guy can't be so dough-heavy as he used to be."

Light flickered from the albino's eyes as he glanced back. "You should know, rube."

The car slowed in front of a big frame house with a trellised porch, walls finished in round shingles, blind, lightless windows. Across the street a stencil sign on a brick building built sheer to the sidewalk said: "Paolo Perrugini Funeral Parlors."

The car swung out to make a wide turn into a gravel driveway. Lights splashed into an open garage. They went in, slid to a stop beside a big shiny undertaker's ambulance.

The albino snapped: "All out!"

Malvern said: "I see our next trip is all arranged for."

"Funny guy," the albino snarled. "A wise monkey."

"Uh-huh. I just have nice scaffold manners," Malvern drawled.

The dark man cut the motor and snapped on a big flash, then cut the lights, got out of the car. He shot the beam of the flash up a narrow flight of wooden steps in the corner. The albino said:

"Up you go, rube. Push the girl ahead of you. I'm behind with my rod."

Jean Adrian got out of the car past Malvern, without looking at him. She went up the steps stiffly, and the three men made a procession behind her.

There was a door at the top. The girl opened it and hard white light came out at them. They went into a bare attic with exposed studding, a square window in front and rear, shut tight, the glass painted black. A bright bulb hung on a drop cord over a kitchen table and a big man sat at the table with a saucer of cigarette butts at his elbow. Two of them still smoked.

A thin loose-lipped man sat on a bed with a Luger beside his left hand. There was a worn carpet on the floor, a few sticks of furniture, a half-open clapboard door in the corner through which a toilet seat showed, and one end of a big old-fashioned bathtub standing up from the floor on iron legs.

The man at the kitchen table was large but not handsome. He had carroty hair and eyebrows a shade darker, a square aggressive face, a strong jaw. His thick lips held his cigarette brutally. His clothes looked as if they had cost a great deal of money and had been slept in.

He glanced carelessly at Jean Adrian, said around the cigarette:

"Park the body, sister. Hi, Malvern. Gimme that rod, Lefty, and you boys drop down below again."

The girl went quietly across the attic and sat down in a straight wooden chair. The man on the bed stood up, put the Luger at the big man's elbow on the kitchen table. The three gunmen went down the stairs, leaving the door open.

The big man touched the Luger, stared at Malvern, said sarcastically:

"I'm Doll Conant. Maybe you remember me."

Malvern stood loosely by the kitchen table, with his legs spread wide, his hands in his overcoat pockets, his head tilted back. His half-closed eyes were sleepy, very cold.

He said: "Yeah. I helped my dad hang the only rap on you that ever stuck."

"It didn't stick, mugg. Not with the Court of Appeals."

"Maybe this one will," Malvern said carelessly. "Kidnapping is apt to be a sticky rap in this State."

Conant grinned without opening his lips. His expression was grimly good-humored. He said:

"Let's not barber. We got business to do and you know better than that last crack. Sit down—or rather take a look at Exhibit One first. In the bathtub behind you. Yeah, take a look at that. Then we can get down to tacks."

Malvern turned, went across to the clapboard door, pushed through it. There was a bulb sticking out of the wall, with a key-switch. He snapped it on, bent over the tub.

For a moment his body was quite rigid and his breath was held rigidly. Then he let it out very slowly, and reached his left hand back and pushed the door almost shut. He bent farther over the big iron tub.

It was long enough for a man to stretch out in, and a man was stretched out in it, on his back. He was fully dressed even to a hat, although his hat didn't look as if he had put it on himself. He had thick, gray-brown curly hair. There was blood on his face and there was a gouged, red-rimmed hole at the inner corner of his left eye.

He was Shenvair and he was long since dead.

Malvern sucked in his breath and straightened slowly, then suddenly bent forward still further until he could see into the space between the tub and the wall. Something blue and metallic glistened down there in the dust. A blue steel gun. A gun like Shenvair's gun.

Malvern glanced back quickly. The not quite shut door showed him a part of the attic, the top of the stairs, one of Doll Conant's feet square and placid on the carpet, under the kitchen table. He reached his arm out slowly down behind the tub, gathered the gun up. The four exposed chambers had steeljacketed bullets in them.

Malvern opened his coat, slipped the gun down inside the waistband of his trousers, tightened his belt, and buttoned his coat again. He went out of the bathroom, shut the clapboard door carefully.

Doll Conant gestured at a chair across the table from him: "Sit down."

Malvern glanced at Jean Adrian. She was staring at him with a kind of rigid curiosity, her eyes dark and colorless in a stone white face under the black hat.

He gestured at her, smiled faintly. "It's Mister Shenvair, angel. He met with an accident. He's—dead."

The girl stared at him without any expression at all. Then she shuddered once, violently. She stared at him again, made no sound of any kind.

Malvern sat down in the chair across the table from Conant.

Conant eyed him, added a smoking stub to the collection in the white saucer, lit a fresh cigarette, streaking the match the whole length of the kitchen table.

He puffed, said casually: "Yeah, he's dead. You shot him."

Malvern shook his head very slightly, smiled. "No."

"Skip the baby eyes, feller. You shot him. Perrugini, the wop undertaker across the street, owns this place, rents it out now and then to a right boy for a quick dust. Incidentally, he's a friend of mine, does me a lot of good among the other wops. He rented it to Shenvair. Didn't know him, but Shenvair got a right ticket into him. He heard shooting over here tonight, took a look out of his window, saw a guy make it to a car. He saw the license number on the car. Your car."

Malvern shook his head again. "But I didn't shoot him, Conant."

"Try and prove it. . . . The wop ran over and found Shenvair halfway up the stairs, dead. He dragged him up and stuck him in the bathtub. Some crazy idea about the blood, I suppose. Then he went through him, found a police card, a private dick license, and that scared him. He got me on the phone and when I got the name, I came steaming."

Conant stopped talking, eyed Malvern steadily. Malvern said very softly:

"You hear about the shooting at Cyrano's tonight?"

Conant nodded.

Malvern went on:

"I was there, with a kid friend of mine from the hotel. Just before the shooting this Shenvair threw a punch at me. The kid followed Shenvair here and they shot at each other. Shenvair was drunk and scared and I'll bet he shot first. I didn't even know the kid had a gun. Shenvair shot him through the stomach. He got home, died there. He left me a note. I have the note."

After a moment Conant said:

"You killed Shenvair, or hired that boy to do it. Here's why. He tried to copper his bet on your blackmail racket. He sold out to Courtway."

Malvern looked startled. He snapped his head around to look at Jean Adrian. She was leaning forward, staring at him with color in her cheeks, a shine in her eyes. She said very softly:

"I'm sorry—angel. I had you wrong."

Malvern smiled a little, turned back to Conant. He said:

"She thought I was the one that sold out. Who's Courtway? Your bird dog, the State Senator?"

Conant's face turned a little white. He laid his cigarette down very carefully in the saucer, leaned across the table and hit Malvern in the mouth with his fist. Malvern went over backwards in the rickety chair. His head struck the floor.

Jean Adrian stood up quickly and her teeth made a sharp clicking sound. Then she didn't move.

Malvern rolled over on his side and got up and set the chair upright. He got a handkerchief out, patted his mouth, looked at the handkerchief.

Steps clattered on the stairs and the albino poked his narrow head into the room, poked a gun still farther in.

"Need any help, Boss?"

Without looking at him Conant said: "Get out—and shut that door—and stay out!"

The door was shut. The albino's steps died down the stairs. Malvern put his left hand on the back of the chair and moved it slowly back and forth. His right hand still held the handkerchief. His lips were getting puffed and darkish. His eyes looked at the Luger by Conant's elbow.

Conant picked up his cigarette and put it in his mouth. He said:

"Maybe you think I'm going to neck this blackmail racket. I'm not, brother. I'm going to kill it—so it'll stay killed. You're going to spill your guts. I have three boys downstairs who need exercise. Get busy and talk."

Malvern said: "Yeah—but your three boys are downstairs." He slipped the handkerchief inside his coat. His hand came out with the blued gun in it. He said: "Take that Luger by the barrel and push it across the table so I can reach it."

Conant didn't move. His eyes narrowed to slits. His hard mouth jerked the cigarette in it once. He didn't touch the Luger. After a moment he said:

"Guess you know what will happen to you now."

Malvern shook his head slightly. He said: "Maybe I'm not particular about that. If it does happen, I promise you *you* won't know anything about it."

Conant stared at him, didn't move. He stared at him for quite a long time, stared at the blue gun. "Where did you get it? Didn't the heels frisk you?"

Malvern said: "They did. This is Shenvair's gun. Your wop friend must have kicked it behind the bathtub. Careless."

Conant reached two thick fingers forward and turned the Luger around and pushed it to the far edge of the table. He nodded and said tonelessly:

"I lose this hand. I ought to have thought of that. That makes me do the talking."

Jean Adrian came quickly across the room and stood at the end of the table. Malvern reached forward across the chair and took the Luger in his left hand and slipped it down into his overcoat pocket, kept his hand on it. He rested the hand holding the blue gun on the top of the chair.

Jean Adrian said: "Who is this man?"

"Doll Conant, a local bigtimer. Senator John Myerson Courtway is his pipe line into the State Senate. And Senator Courtway, angel, is the man in your photo frame on your desk. The man you said was your father, that you said was dead."

The girl said very quietly: "He *is* my father. I knew he wasn't dead. I'm blackmailing him—for a hundred grand. Shenvair and Targo and I. He never married my mother, so I'm illegitimate. But I'm still his child. I have rights and he won't recognize them. He treated my mother abominably, left her without a nickel. He had detectives watch me for years. Shenvair was one of them. He recognized my photos when I came here and met Targo. He remembered. He went up to San Francisco and got a copy of my birth certificate. I have it here."

She fumbled at her bag, felt around in it, opened a small zipper pocket in the lining. Her hand came out with a folded paper. She tossed it on the table.

Conant stared at her, reached a hand for the paper, spread it out and studied it. He said slowly:

"This doesn't prove anything."

Malvern took his left hand out of his pocket and reached for the paper. Conant pushed it towards him.

It was a certified copy of a birth certificate, dated originally in 1912. It recorded the birth of a girl child, Adriana Gianni Myerson, to John and Antonina Gianni Myerson. Malvern dropped the paper again.

He said: "Adriana Gianni—Jean Adrian. Was that the tip-off, Conant?"

Conant shook his head. "Shenvair got cold feet. He tipped Courtway. He was scared. That's why he had this hideout lined up. I thought that was why he got killed. Targo couldn't have done it, because Targo's still in the can. Maybe I had you wrong, Malvern."

Malvern stared at him woodenly, didn't say anything. Jean Adrian said:

"It's my fault. I'm the one that's to blame. It was pretty rotten. I see that now. I want to see him and tell him I'm sorry and that he'll never hear from me again. I want to make him promise he won't do anything to Duke Targo. May I?"

Malvern said: "You can do anything you want to, angel. I have two guns that say so. But why did you wait so long? And why didn't you go at him through the courts? You're in show business. The publicity would have made you—even if he beat you out."

The girl bit her lip, said in a low voice: "My mother never really knew who he was, never knew his last name even. He was John Myerson to her. I didn't know until I came here and happened to see a picture in the local paper. He had changed, but I knew the face. And of course the first part of his name—"

Conant said sneeringly: "You didn't go at him openly because you knew damn well you weren't his kid. That your mother just wished you on to him like any cheap broad who sees herself out of a swell meal ticket. Courtway says he can prove it, and that he's going to prove it and put you where you belong. And believe me, sister, he's just the stiff-necked kind of sap who would kill himself in public life raking up a twenty-year-old scandal to do that little thing."

The big man spit his cigarette stub out viciously, added: "It cost me money to put him where he is and I aim to keep him there. That's why I'm in it. No dice, sister. I'm putting the pressure on. You're going to take a lot of air and keep on taking it. As for your two-gun friend—maybe he didn't know, but he knows now and that ties him up in the same package."

Conant banged on the table top, leaned back, looking calmly at the blue gun in Malvern's hand.

Malvern stared into the big man's eyes, said very softly: "That hood at Cyrano's tonight—he wasn't your idea of putting on the pressure by any chance, Conant, was he?"

Conant grinned harshly, shook his head. The door at the

top of the stairs opened a little, silently. Malvern didn't see it. He was staring at Conant. Jean Adrian saw it.

Her eyes widened and she stepped back with a startled exclamation, that jerked Malvern's eyes to her.

The albino stepped softly through the door with a gun leveled.

His red eyes glistened, his mouth was drawn wide in a snarling grin. He said:

"The door's kind of thin, Boss. I listened. Okey? . . . Shed the heater, rube, or I blow you both in half."

Malvern turned slightly and opened his right hand and let the blue gun bounce on the thin carpet. He shrugged, spread his hands out wide, didn't look at Jean Adrian.

The albino stepped clear of the door, came slowly forward and put his gun against Malvern's back.

Conant stood up, came around the table, took the Luger out of Malvern's coat pocket and hefted it. Without a word or a change of expression he slammed it against the side of Malvern's jaw.

Malvern sagged drunkenly, then went down on the floor on his side.

Jean Adrian screamed, clawed at Conant. He threw her off, changed the gun to his left hand and slapped the side of her face with a hard palm.

"Pipe down, sister. You've had all your fun."

The albino went to the head of the stairs and called down it. The two other gunmen came up into the room, stood grinning.

Malvern didn't move on the floor. After a little while Conant lit another cigarette and rattled a knuckle on the table top beside the birth certificate. He said gruffly:

"She wants to see the old man. Okey, she can see him. We'll all go see him. There's still something in this that stinks." He raised his eyes, looked at the stocky man. "You and Lefty go downtown and spring Targo, get him out to the Senator's place as soon as you can. Step on it."

The two hoods went back down the stairs.

Conant looked down at Malvern, kicked him in the ribs lightly, kept on kicking them until Malvern opened his eyes and stirred.

9

The car waited at the top of a hill, before a pair of tall wrought iron gates, inside which there was a lodge. A door of the lodge stood open and yellow light framed a big man in an overcoat and a pulled down hat. He came forward slowly into the rain, his hands down in his pockets.

The rain slithered about his feet and the albino leaned against the uprights of the gate, clicking his teeth. The big man said:

"What yuh want? I can see yuh."

"Shake it up, rube. Mister Conant wants to call on your boss."

The man inside spat into the wet darkness. "So what? Know what time it is?"

Conant opened the car door suddenly and went over to the gates. The rain made noise between the car and the voices.

Malvern turned his head slowly and patted Jean Adrian's hand. She pushed his hand away from her quickly.

Her voice said softly: "You fool—oh, you fool!"

Malvern sighed. "I'm having a swell time, angel. A swell time."

The man inside the gates took out keys on a long chain, unlocked the gates and pushed them back until they clicked on the chocks. Conant and the albino came back to the car.

Conant stood in the rain with a heel hooked on the running board. Malvern took his big flask out of his pocket, felt it over to see if it was dented, then unscrewed the top. He held it out towards the girl, said:

"Have a little bottle courage."

She didn't answer him, didn't move. He drank from the flask, put it away, looked past Conant's broad back at acres of dripping trees, a cluster of lighted windows that seemed to hang in the sky.

A car came up the hill stabbing the wet dark with its headlights, pulled behind the sedan and stopped. Conant went over to it, put his head into it and said something. The car backed, turned into the driveway, and its lights splashed on retaining walls, disappeared, reappeared at the top of the drive as a hard white oval against a stone porte-cochère.

Conant got into the sedan and the albino swung it into the driveway after the other car. At the top in a cement parking circle ringed with cypresses, they all got out.

At the top of steps a big door was open and a man in a bathrobe stood in it. Targo, between two men who leaned hard against him, was halfway up the steps. He was bareheaded and without an overcoat. His big body in the white coat looked enormous between the two gunmen.

The rest of the party went up the steps and into the house and followed the bathrobed butler down a hall lined with portraits of somebody's ancestors, through a stiff oval foyer to another hall and into a paneled study with soft lights and heavy drapes and deep leather chairs.

A man stood behind a big dark desk that was set in an alcove made by low, outjutting bookcases. He was enormously tall and thin. His white hair was so thick and fine that no single hair was visible in it. He had a small straight bitter mouth, black eyes without depth in a white lined face. He stooped a little and a blue corduroy bathrobe faced with satin was wrapped around his almost freakish thinness.

The butler shut the door and Conant opened it again and jerked his chin at the two men who had come in with Targo. They went out. The albino stepped behind Targo and pushed him down into a chair. Targo looked dazed, stupid. There was a smear of dirt on one side of his face and his eyes had a drugged look.

The girl went over to him quickly, said: "Oh, Duke—are you all right, Duke?"

Targo blinked at her, half-grinned. "So you had to rat, huh? Skip it. I'm fine." His voice had an unnatural sound.

Jean Adrian went away from him and sat down and hunched herself together as if she was cold.

The tall man stared coldly at everyone in the room in turn, then said lifelessly: "Are these the blackmailers—and was it necessary to bring them here in the middle of the night?"

Conant shook himself out of his coat, threw it on the floor behind a lamp. He lit a fresh cigarette and stood spread-legged in the middle of the room, a big, rough, rugged man very sure of himself. He said:

"The girl wanted to see you and tell you she was sorry and

wants to play ball. The guy in the ice cream coat is Targo, the fighter. He got himself in a shooting scrape at a night spot and acted so wild downtown they fed him sleep tablets to quiet him. The other guy is Ted Malvern, old Marcus Malvern's boy. I don't figure him yet."

Malvern said dryly: "I'm a private detective, Senator. I'm here in the interests of my client, Miss Adrian." He laughed.

The girl looked at him suddenly, then looked at the floor.

Conant said gruffly, "Shenvair, the one you know about, got himself bumped off. Not by us. That's still to straighten out."

The tall man nodded coldly. He sat down at his desk and picked up a white quill pen, tickled one ear with it.

"And what is your idea of the way to handle this matter, Conant?" he asked thinly.

Conant shrugged. "I'm a rough boy, but I'd handle this one legal. Talk to the D.A., toss them in a coop on suspicion of extortion. Cook up a story for the papers, then give it time to cool. Then dump these birds across the State line and tell them not to come back—or else."

Senator Courtway moved the quill around to his other ear. "They could attack me again, from a distance," he said icily. "I'm in favor of a showdown, put them where they belong."

"You can't try them, Courtway. It would kill you politically."

"I'm tired of public life, Conant. I'll be glad to retire." The tall thin man curved his mouth into a faint smile.

"The hell you are," Conant growled. He jerked his head around, snapped: "Come here, sister."

Jean Adrian stood up, came slowly across the room, stood in front of the desk.

"Make her?" Conant snarled.

Courtway stared at the girl's set face for a long time, without a trace of expression. He put his quill down on the desk, opened a drawer and took out a photograph. He looked from the photo to the girl, back to the photo, said tonelessly:

"This was taken a number of years ago, but there's a very strong resemblance. I don't think I'd hesitate to say its the same face."

He put the photo down on the desk and with the same

unhurried motion took an automatic out of the drawer and put it down on the desk beside the photo.

Conant stared at the gun. His mouth twisted. He said thickly: "You won't need that, Senator. Listen, your showdown idea is all wrong. I'll get detailed confessions from these people and we'll hold them. If they ever act up again, it'll be time enough then to crack down with the big one."

Malvern smiled a little and walked across the carpet until he was near the end of the desk. He said: "I'd like to see that photograph," and leaned over suddenly and took it.

Courtway's thin hand dropped to the gun, then relaxed. He leaned back in his chair and stared at Malvern.

Malvern stared at the photograph, lowered it, said softly to Jean Adrian: "Go sit down."

She turned and went back to her chair, dropped into it wearily.

Malvern said: "I like your showdown idea, Senator. It's clean and straightforward and a wholesome change in policy for Mr. Conant. But it won't work." He snicked a fingernail at the photo. "This has a superficial resemblance, no more. I don't think it's the same girl at all myself. Her ears are differently shaped and lower on her head. Her eyes are closer together than Miss Adrian's eyes, the line of her jaw is longer. Those things don't change. So what have you got? An extortion letter. Maybe, but you can't tie it to anyone or you'd have done it already. The girl's name. Just coincidence. What else?"

Conant's face was granite hard, his mouth bitter. His voice shook a little, saying: "And how about that certificate the gal took out of her purse, wise guy?"

Malvern smiled faintly, rubbed the side of his jaw with his fingertips. "I thought you got that from Shenvair?" he said slyly. "And Shenvair is dead."

Conant's face was a mask of fury. He balled his fist, took a jerky step forward. "Why you —— damn' louse—"

Jean Adrian was leaning forward staring round-eyed, at Malvern. Targo was staring at him, with a loose grin, pale hard eyes. Courtway was staring at him. There was no expression of any kind on Courtway's face. He sat cold, relaxed, distant.

Conant laughed suddenly, snapped his fingers. "Okey, toot your horn," he grunted.

Malvern said slowly: "I'll tell you another reason why there'll be no showdown. That shooting at Cyrano's. Those threats to make Targo drop an unimportant fight. That hood that went to Miss Adrian's hotel room and sapped her, left her lying on her doorway. Can't you use your big noodle at all? Can't you tie all that in, Conant? *I* can."

Courtway leaned forward suddenly and placed his hand on his gun, folded it around the butt. His black eyes were holes in a white frozen face.

Conant didn't move, didn't speak.

Malvern went on: "Why did Targo get those threats, and after he didn't drop the fight, why did a gun go to see him at Cyrano's, a night-club a very bad place for that kind of play? Because at Cyrano's he was with the girl, and Cyrano was his backer, and if anything happened at Cyrano's the law would get the threat story before they had time to think of anything else. That's why. The threats were a build-up for a killing. When the shooting came off Targo was to be with the girl, so the hood could get the girl and it would look as if Targo was the one he was after.

"He would have tried for Targo, too, of course, but above all he would have got the girl. Because she was the dynamite behind this shakedown, without her it meant nothing, and with her it could always be made over into a legitimate paternity suit, if it didn't work the other way. You know about her and about Targo, because Shenvair got cold feet and sold out. And Shenvair knew about the hood—because when the hood showed, and I saw him—and Shenvair knew I knew him, because he had heard me tell Targo about him—then Shenvair tried to pick a drunken fight with me and keep me from trying to interfere."

Malvern stopped, rubbed the side of his head again, very slowly, very gently. He watched Conant with an up from under look.

Conant said slowly, very harshly: "I don't play those games, buddy. Believe it or not—I don't."

Malvern said: "Listen. The hood could have killed the girl at the hotel with his sap. He didn't, because Targo wasn't there and the fight hadn't been fought, and the build-up would have been all wasted. He went there to have a close look at her, without makeup. And she was scared about something, and had a gun with her. So he sapped her down and ran away. That visit was just a finger.

Conant said again: "I don't play those games, buddy." Then he took the Luger out of his pocket and held it down at his side.

Malvern shrugged, turned his head to stare at Senator Courtway.

"No, but *he* does," he said softly. "He had the motive, and the play wouldn't look like him. He cooked it up with Shenvair—and if it went wrong, as it did, Shenvair would have breezed and if the law got wise, big tough Doll Conant is the boy whose nose would be in the mud."

Courtway smiled a little and said in an utterly dead voice:

"The young man is very ingenious, but surely—"

Targo stood up. His face was a stiff mask. His lips moved slowly and he said:

"It sounds pretty good to me. I think I'll twist your —— damn' neck, Mister Courtway."

The albino snarled, "Sit down, punk," and lifted his gun.

Targo turned slightly and slammed the albino on the jaw. He went over backwards, smashed his head against the wall. The gun sailed along the floor from his limp hand.

Targo started across the room.

Conant looked at him sidewise and didn't move. Targo went past him, almost touching him. Conant didn't move a muscle. His big face was blank, his eyes narrowed to a faint glitter between the heavy lids.

Nobody moved but Targo. Then Courtway lifted his gun and his finger whitened on the trigger and the gun roared.

Malvern moved across the room very swiftly and stood in front of Jean Adrian, between her and the rest of the room.

Targo looked down at his hands. His face twisted into a silly smile. He sat down on the floor and pressed both his hands against his chest.

Courtway lifted his gun again and then Conant moved. The Luger jerked up, flamed twice. Blood flowed down Courtway's hand. His gun fell behind his desk. His long body seemed to swoop down after the gun. It jackknifed until only his shoulders showed humped above the line of the desk.

Conant said: "Stand up and take it, you —— —— double-crossing swine!"

There was a shot behind the desk. Courtway's shoulders went down out of sight.

After a moment Conant went around behind the desk, stooped, straightened.

"He ate one," he said very calmly. "Through the mouth. . . . And I lose me a nice clean senator."

Targo took his hands from his chest and fell over sidewise on the floor and lay still.

The door of the room slammed open. The butler stood in it, tousle-headed, his mouth gaping. He tried to say something, saw the gun in Conant's hand, saw Targo slumped on the floor. He didn't say anything.

The albino was getting to his feet, rubbing his chin, feeling his teeth, shaking his head. He went slowly along the wall and gathered up his gun.

Conant snarled at him: "Swell gut you turned out to be. Get on the phone. Get Malloy, the night captain—and snap it up!"

Malvern turned, put his hand down and lifted Jean Adrian's cold chin.

"It's getting light, angel. And I think the rain has stopped," he said slowly. He pulled his inevitable flask out. "Let's take a drink—to Mister Targo."

The girl shook her head, covered her face with her hands.

After a long time there were sirens.

10

The slim, tired-looking kid in the pale blue and silver of the Carondelet held his white glove in front of the closing doors and said:

"Corky's boils is better, but he didn't come to work, Mister Malvern. Tony the bell captain ain't showed this morning neither. Pretty soft for some guys."

Malvern stood close to Jean Adrian in the corner of the car. They were alone in it. He said:

"That's what you think."

The boy turned red. Malvern moved over and patted his shoulder, said: "Don't mind me, son. I've been up all night with a sick friend. Here, buy yourself a second breakfast."

"Jeeze, Mister Malvern, I didn't mean—"

The doors opened at nine and they went down the corridor to 914. Malvern took the key and opened the door, put the key on the inside, held the door, said:

"Get some sleep and wake up with your fist in your eye. Take my flask and get a mild toot on. Do you good."

The girl went in through the door, said over her shoulder: "I don't want liquor. Come in a minute. There's something I want to tell you."

He shut the door and followed her in. A bright bar of sunlight lay across the carpet all the way to the davenport. He lit a cigarette and stared at it.

Jean Adrian sat down and jerked her hat off and rumpled her hair. She was silent a moment, then she said slowly, carefully:

"It was swell of you to go to all that trouble for me. I don't know why you should do it."

Malvern said: "I can think of a couple of reasons, but they didn't keep Targo from getting killed, and that was my fault in a way. Then in another way it wasn't. I didn't ask him to twist Senator Courtway's neck."

The girl said: "You think you're hard-boiled but you're just a big slob that argues himself into a jam for the first tramp he finds in trouble. Forget it. Forget Targo and forget me. Neither of us was worth any part of your time. I wanted to tell you that because I'll be going away as soon as they let me, and I won't be seeing you any more. This is good-by."

Malvern nodded, stared at the sun on the carpet. The girl went on:

"It's a little hard to tell. I'm not looking for sympathy when I say I'm a tramp. I've smothered in too many hall bedrooms, stripped in too many filthy dressing-rooms, missed too many meals, told too many lies to be anything else. That's why I wouldn't want to have anything to do with you, ever."

Malvern said: "I like the way you tell it. Go on."

She looked at him quickly, looked away again. "I'm not the

Gianni girl. You guessed that. But I knew her. We did a cheap
sister act together when they still did sister acts. Ada and Jean
Adrian. We made up our names from hers. That flopped, and
we went in a road show and that flopped too. In New
Orleans. The going was a little too rough for her. She swallowed bichloride. I kept her photos because I knew her story.
And looking at that thin cold guy and thinking what he could
have done for her I got to hate him. She was his kid all right.
Don't ever think she wasn't. I even wrote letters to him, asking for help for her, just a little help, signing her name. But
they didn't get any answer. I got to hate him so much I
wanted to do something to him, after she took the bichloride.
So I came out here when I got a stake."

She stopped talking and laced her fingers together tightly,
then pulled them apart violently, as if she wanted to hurt herself. She went on:

"I met Targo through Cyrano and Shenvair through him.
Shenvair knew the photos. He'd worked once for an agency
in Frisco that was hired to watch Ada. You know all the rest
of it."

Malvern said:

"It sounds pretty good. I wondered why the touch wasn't
made sooner. Do you want me to think you didn't want his
money?"

"No. I'd have taken his money all right. But that wasn't
what I wanted most. I said I was a tramp."

Malvern smiled very faintly and said: "You don't know a lot
about tramps, angel. You made an illegitimate pass and you
got caught. That's that, but the money wouldn't have done
you any good. It would have been dirty money. I know."

She looked up at him, stared at him. He touched the side
of his face and winced and said: "I know because that's the
kind of money mine is. My dad made it out of crooked sew-
erage and paving contracts, out of gambling concessions, appointment pay-offs, even vice, I daresay. He made it every
rotten way there is to make money in city politics. And when
it was made and there was nothing left to do but sit and look
at it, he died and left it to me. It hasn't brought me any fun
either. I always hope it's going to, but it never does. Because
I'm his pup, his blood, reared in the same gutter. I'm worse

than a tramp, angel. I'm a guy that lives on crooked dough and doesn't even do his own stealing."

He stopped, flicked ash on the carpet, straightened his hat on his head.

"Think that over, and don't run too far, because I have all the time in the world and it wouldn't do you any good. It would be so much more fun to run away together."

He went a little way towards the door, stood looking down at the sunlight on the carpet, looked back at her quickly and then went on out.

When the door shut she stood up and went into the bedroom and lay down on the bed just as she was, with her coat on. She stared at the ceiling. After a long time she smiled. In the middle of the smile she fell asleep.

Pick-Up on Noon Street

THE MAN and the girl walked slowly, close together, past a dim stencil sign that said: Surprise Hotel. The man wore a purple suit, a Panama hat over his shiny, slicked-down hair. He walked splay-footed, soundlessly.

The girl wore a green hat and a short skirt and sheer stockings, four-and-a-half inch French heels. She smelled of Midnight Narcissus.

At the corner the man leaned close, said something in the girl's ear. She jerked away from him, giggled.

"You gotta buy liquor if you take *me* home, Smiler."

"Next time, baby. I'm fresh outa dough."

The girl's voice got hard. "Then I tells you goodbye in the next block, handsome."

"Like hell, baby," the man answered.

The arc at the intersection threw light on them. They walked across the street far apart. At the other side the man caught the girl's arm. She twisted away from him.

"Listen, you cheap grifter!" she shrilled. "Keep your paws down, see! Tinhorns are dust to me. Dangle!"

"How much liquor you gotta have, baby?"

"Plenty."

"Me bein' on the nut, where do I collect it?"

"You got hands, ain't you?" the girl sneered. Her voice dropped the shrillness. She leaned close to him again. "Maybe you got a gun, big boy. Got a gun?"

"Yeah. And no shells for it."

"The goldbricks over on Central don't know that."

"Don't be that way," the man in the purple suit snarled. Then he snapped his fingers and stiffened. "Wait a minute. I got me a idea."

He stopped and looked back along the street toward the dim stencil hotel sign. The girl slapped a glove across his chin caressingly. The glove smelled to him of the perfume, Midnight Narcissus.

The man snapped his fingers again, grinned widely in the

dim light. "If that drunk is still holed up in Doc's place—I collect. Wait for me, huh?"

"Maybe, at home. If you ain't gone too long."

"Where's home, baby?"

The girl stared at him. A half-smile moved along her full lips, died at the corners of them. The breeze picked a sheet of newspaper out of the gutter and tossed it against the man's leg. He kicked at it savagely.

"Calliope Apartments, Four-B, Two-Forty-Six East Forty-Eight. How soon you be there?"

The man stepped very close to her, reached back and tapped his hip. His voice was low, chilling.

"You wait for me, baby."

She caught her breath, nodded. "Okey, handsome. I'll wait."

The man went back along the cracked sidewalk, across the intersection, along to where the stencil sign hung out over the street. He went through a glass door into a narrow lobby with a row of brown wooden chairs pushed against the plaster wall. There was just space to walk past them to the desk. A bald-headed colored man lounged behind the desk, fingering a large green pin in his tie.

The Negro in the purple suit leaned across the counter and his teeth flashed in a quick, hard smile. He was very young, with a thin, sharp jaw, a narrow bony forehead, the flat brilliant eyes of the gangster. He said softly: "That pug with the husky voice still here? The guy that banked the crap game last night."

The bald-headed clerk looked at the flies on the ceiling fixture. "Didn't see him go out, Smiler."

"Ain't what I asked you, Doc."

"Yeah. He still here."

"Still drunk?"

"Guess so. Hasn't been out."

"Three-forty-nine, ain't it?"

"You been there, ain't you? What you wanta know for?"

"He cleaned me down to my lucky piece. I gotta make a touch."

The bald-headed man looked nervous. The Smiler stared softly at the green stone in the man's tie pin.

"Get rolling, Smiler. Nobody gets bent around here. We ain't no Central Avenue flop."

The Smiler said very softly: "He's my pal, Doc. He'll lend me twenty. You touch half."

He put his hand out palm up. The clerk stared at the hand for a long moment. Then he nodded sourly, went behind a ground-glass screen, came back slowly, looking toward the street door.

His hand went out and hovered over the palm. The palm closed over a passkey, dropped inside the cheap purple suit.

The sudden flashing grin on the Smiler's face had an icy edge to it.

"Careful, Doc—while I'm up above."

The clerk said: "Step on it. Some of the customers get home early." He glanced at the green electric clock on the wall. It was seven-fifteen. "And the walls ain't any too thick," he added.

The thin youth gave him another flashing grin, nodded, went delicately back along the lobby to the shadowy staircase. There was no elevator in the Surprise Hotel.

At one minute past seven Pete Anglich, narcotic squad under-cover man, rolled over on the hard bed and looked at the cheap strap watch on his left wrist. There were heavy shadows under his eyes, a thick dark stubble on his broad chin. He swung his bare feet to the floor and stood up in cheap cotton pajamas, flexed his muscles, stretched, bent over stiff-kneed and touched the floor in front of his toes with a grunt.

He walked across to a chipped bureau, drank from a quart bottle of cheap rye whiskey, grimaced, pushed the cork into the neck of the bottle, and rammed it down hard with the heel of his hand.

"Boy, have I got a hangover," he grumbled huskily.

He stared at his face in the bureau mirror, at the stubble on his chin, the thick white scar on his throat close to the wind-pipe. His voice was husky because the bullet that had made the scar had done something to his vocal chords. It was a smooth huskiness, like the voice of a blues singer.

He stripped his pajamas off and stood naked in the middle

of the room, his toes fumbling the rough edge of a big rip in the carpet. His body was very broad, and that made him look a little shorter than he was. His shoulders sloped, his nose was a little thick, the skin over his cheekbones looked like leather. He had short, curly, black hair, utterly steady eyes, the small set mouth of a quick thinker.

He went into a dim, dirty bathroom, stepped into the tub and turned the shower on. The water was warmish, but not hot. He stood under it and soaped himself, rubbed his whole body over, kneaded his muscles, rinsed off.

He jerked a dirty towel off the rack and started to rub a glow into his skin.

A faint noise behind the loosely closed bathroom door stopped him. He held his breath, listened, heard the noise again, a creak of boarding, a click, a rustle of cloth. Pete Anglich reached for the door and pulled it open slowly.

The Negro in the purple suit and Panama hat stood beside the bureau, with Pete Anglich's coat in his hand. On the bureau in front of him were two guns. One of them was Pete Anglich's old worn Colt. The room door was shut and a key with a tag lay on the carpet near it, as though it had fallen out of the door, or been pushed out from the other side.

The Smiler let the coat fall to the floor and held a wallet in his left hand. His right hand lifted the Colt. He grinned.

"Okey, white boy. Just go on dryin' yourself off after your shower," he said.

Pete Anglich toweled himself. He rubbed himself dry, stood naked with the wet towel in his left hand.

The Smiler had the billfold empty on the bureau, was counting the money with his left hand. His right still clutched the Colt.

"Eighty-seven bucks. Nice money. Some of it's mine from the crap game, but I'm lifting it all, pal. Take it easy. I'm friends with the management here."

"Gimme a break, Smiler," Pete Anglich said hoarsely. "That's every dollar I got in the world. Leave a few bucks, huh?" He made his voice thick, coarse, heavy as though with liquor.

The Smiler gleamed his teeth, shook his narrow head. "Can't do it, pal. Got me a date and I need the kale."

Pete Anglich took a loose step forward and stopped, grinning sheepishly. The muzzle of his own gun had jerked at him.

The Smiler sidled over to the bottle of rye and lifted it.

"I can use this, too. My baby's got a throat for liquor. Sure has. What's in your pants is yours, pal. Fair enough?"

Pete Anglich jumped sideways, about four feet. The Smiler's face convulsed. The gun jerked around and the bottle of rye slid out of his left hand, slammed down on his foot. He yelped, kicked out savagely, and his toe caught in the torn place in the carpet.

Pete Anglich flipped the wet end of the bathtowel straight at the Smiler's eyes.

The Smiler reeled and yelled with pain. Then Pete Anglich held the Smiler's gun wrist in his hard left hand. He twisted up, around. His hand started to slide down over the Smiler's hand, over the gun. The gun turned inward and touched the Smiler's side.

A hard knee kicked viciously at Pete Anglich's abdomen. He gagged, and his finger tightened convulsively on the Smiler's trigger finger.

The shot was dull, muffled against the purple cloth of the suit. The Smiler's eyes rolled whitely and his narrow jaw fell slack.

Pete Anglich let him down on the floor and stood panting, bent over, his face greenish. He groped for the fallen bottle of rye, got the cork out, got some of the fiery liquid down his throat.

The greenish look went away from his face. His breathing slowed. He wiped sweat off his forehead with the back of his hand.

He felt the Smiler's pulse. The Smiler didn't have any pulse. He was dead. Pete Anglich loosened the gun from his hand, went over to the door and glanced out into the hallway. Empty. There was a passkey in the outside of the lock. He removed it, locked the door from the inside.

He put his underclothes and socks and shoes on, his worn

blue serge suit, knotted a black tie around the crumpled shirt collar, went back to the dead man and took a roll of bills from his pocket. He packed a few odds and ends of clothes and toilet articles in a cheap fiber suitcase, stood it by the door.

He pushed a torn scrap of sheet through his revolver barrel with a pencil, replaced the used cartridge, crushed the empty shell with his heel on the bathroom floor and then flushed it down the toilet.

He locked the door from the outside and walked down the stairs to the lobby.

The bald-headed clerk's eyes jumped at him, then dropped. The skin of his face turned gray. Pete Anglich leaned on the counter and opened his hand to let two keys tinkle on the scarred wood. The clerk stared at the keys, shuddered.

Pete Anglich said in his slow, husky voice: "Hear any funny noises?"

The clerk shook his head, gulped.

"Creep joint, eh?" Pete Anglich said.

The clerk moved his head painfully, twisted his neck in his collar. His bald head winked darkly under the ceiling light.

"Too bad," Pete Anglich said. "What name did I register under last night?"

"You ain't registered," the clerk whispered.

"Maybe I wasn't here even," Pete Anglich said softly.

"Never saw you before, mister."

"You're not seeing me now. You never will see me—to know me—will you, Doc?"

The clerk moved his neck and tried to smile.

Pete Anglich drew his wallet out and shook three dollar bills from it.

"I'm a guy that likes to pay his way," he said slowly. "This pays for Room 349—till way in the morning, kind of late. The lad you gave the passkey to looks like a heavy sleeper." He paused, steadied his cool eyes on the clerk's face, added thoughtfully: "Unless, of course, he's got friends who would like to move him out."

Bubbles showed on the clerk's lips. He stuttered: "He ain't—ain't—"

"Yeah," Pete Anglich said. "What would you expect?"

He went across to the street door, carrying his suitcase,

stepped out under the stencil sign, stood a moment looking toward the hard white glare of Central Avenue.

Then he walked the other way. The street was very dark, very quiet. There were four blocks of frame houses before he came to Noon Street. It was all a Negro quarter.

He met only one person on the way, a brown girl in a green hat, very sheer stockings, and four-and-a-half-inch heels, who smoked a cigarette under a dusty palm tree and stared back toward the Surprise Hotel.

2

The lunch wagon was an old buffet car without wheels, set end to the street in a space between a machine shop and a rooming house. The name Bella Donna was lettered in faded gold on the sides. Pete Anglich went up the two iron steps at the end, into a smell of fry grease.

The Negro cook's fat white back was to him. At the far end of the low counter a white girl in a cheap brown felt hat and a shabby polo coat with a high turned-up collar was sipping coffee, her cheek propped in her left hand. There was nobody else in the car.

Pete Anglich put his suitcase down and sat on a stool near the door, saying: "Hi, Mopsy!"

The fat cook turned a shiny black face over his white shoulder. The face split in a grin. A thick bluish tongue came out and wiggled between the cook's thick lips.

"How's a boy? W'at you eat?"

"Scramble two light, coffee, toast, no spuds."

"Dat ain't no food for a he-guy," Mopsy complained.

"I been drunk," Pete Anglich said.

The girl at the end of the counter looked at him sharply, looked at the cheap alarm clock on the shelf, at the watch on her gloved wrist. She drooped, stared into her coffee cup again.

The fat cook broke eggs into a pan, added milk, stirred them around. "You want a shot, boy?"

Pete Anglich shook his head.

"I'm driving the wagon, Mopsy."

The cook grinned. He reached a brown bottle from under

the counter, and poured a big drink into a water glass, set the glass down beside Pete Anglich.

Pete Anglich reached suddenly for the glass, jerked it to his lips, drank the liquor down.

"Guess I'll drive the wagon some other time." He put the glass down empty.

The girl stood up, came along the stools, put a dime on the counter. The fat cook punched his cash register, put down a nickel change. Pete Anglich stared casually at the girl. A shabby, innocent-eyed girl, brown hair curling on her neck, eyebrows plucked clean as a bone and startled arches painted above the place where they had been.

"Not lost, are you, lady?" he asked in his softly husky voice.

The girl had fumbled her bag open to put the nickel away. She started violently, stepped back and dropped the bag. It spilled its contents on the floor. She stared down at it, wide-eyed.

Pete Anglich went down on one knee and pushed things into the bag. A cheap nickel compact, cigarettes, a purple matchfolder lettered in gold: The Juggernaut Club. Two colored handkerchiefs, a crumpled dollar bill and some silver and pennies.

He stood up with the closed bag in his hand, held it out to the girl.

"Sorry," he said softly. "I guess I startled you."

Her breath made a rushing sound. She caught the bag out of his hand, ran out of the car, and was gone.

The fat cook looked after her. "That doll don't belong in Tough Town," he said slowly.

He dished up the eggs and toast, poured coffee in a thick cup, put them down in front of Pete Anglich.

Pete Anglich touched the food, said absently: "Alone, and matches from the Juggernaut. Trimmer Waltz's spot. You know what happens to girls like that when he gets hold of them."

The cook licked his lips, reached under the counter for the whiskey bottle. He poured himself a drink, added about the same amount of water to the bottle, put it back under the counter.

"I ain't never been a tough guy, and don' want to start,"

he said slowly. "But I'se all tired of white boys like dat guy. Some day he gonna get cut."

Pete Anglich kicked his suitcase.

"Yeah. Keep the keister for me, Mopsy."

He went out.

Two or three cars flicked by in the crisp fall night, but the sidewalks were dark and empty. A colored night watchman moved slowly along the street, trying the doors of a small row of dingy stores. There were frame houses across the street, and a couple of them were noisy.

Pete Anglich went on past the intersection. Three blocks from the lunch wagon he saw the girl again.

She was pressed against a wall, motionless. A little beyond her, dim yellow light came from the stairway of a walk-up apartment house. Beyond that a small parking lot with billboards across most of its front. Faint light from somewhere touched her hat, her shabby polo coat with the turned-up collar, one side of her face. He knew it was the same girl.

He stepped into a doorway, watched her. Light flashed on her upraised arm, on something bright, a wrist watch. Somewhere not far off a clock struck eight, slow, pealing notes.

Lights stabbed into the street from the corner behind. A big car swung slowly into view and as it swung its headlights dimmed. It crept along the block, a dark shininess of glass and polished paint.

Pete Anglich grinned sharply in his doorway. A custombuilt Duesenberg, six blocks from Central Avenue! He stiffened at the sharp sound of running steps, clicking high heels.

The girl was running toward him along the sidewalk. The car was not near enough for its dimmed lights to pick her up. Pete Anglich stepped out of the doorway, grabbed her arm, dragged her back into the doorway. A gun snaked from under his coat.

The girl panted at his side.

The Duesenberg passed the doorway slowly. No shots came from it. The uniformed driver didn't slow down.

"I can't do it. I'm scared," the girl gasped in Pete Anglich's ear. Then she broke away from him and ran farther along the sidewalk, away from the car.

Pete Anglich looked after the Duesenberg. It was opposite

the row of billboards that screened the parking lot. It was barely crawling now. Something sailed from its left front window, fell with a dry slap on the sidewalk. The car picked up speed soundlessly, purred off into the darkness. A block away its head lights flashed up full again.

Nothing moved. The thing that had been thrown out of the car lay on the inner edge of the sidewalk, almost under one of the billboards.

Then the girl was coming back again, a step at a time, haltingly. Pete Anglich watched her come, without moving. When she was level with him he said softly: "What's the racket? Could a fellow help?"

She spun around with a choked sound, as though she had forgotten all about him. Her head moved in the darkness at his side. There was a swift shine as her eyes moved. There was a pale flicker across her chin. Her voice was low, hurried, scared.

"You're the man from the lunch wagon. I saw you."

"Open up. What is it—a pay-off?"

Her head moved again in the darkness at his side, up and down.

"What's in the package?" Pete Anglich growled. "Money?"

Her words came in a rush. "Would you get it for me? Oh, would you, please? I'd be so grateful. I'd—"

He laughed. His laugh had a low growling sound. "Get it for *you*, baby? I use money in my business, too. Come on, what's the racket? Spill."

She jerked away from him, but he didn't let go of her arm. He slid the gun out of sight under his coat, held her with both hands. Her voice sobbed as she whispered: "He'll kill me, if I don't get it."

Very sharply, coldly, Pete Anglich said, "Who will? Trimmer Waltz?"

She started violently, almost tore out of his grasp. Not quite. Steps shuffled on the sidewalk. Two dark forms showed in front of the billboards, didn't pause to pick anything up. The steps came near, cigarette tips glowed.

A voice said softly: "'Lo there, sweets. Yo' want to change yo'r boy frien', honey?"

The girl shrank behind Pete Anglich. One of the Negroes laughed gently, waved the red end of his cigarette.

"Hell, it's a white gal," the other one said quickly. "Le's dust."

They went on, chuckling. At the corner they turned, were gone.

"There you are," Pete Anglich growled. "Shows you where you are." His voice was hard, angry. "Oh, hell, stay here and I'll get your damn pay-off for you."

He left the girl and went lightly along close to the front of the apartment house. At the edge of the billboards he stopped, probed the darkness with his eyes, saw the package. It was wrapped in dark material, not large but large enough to see. He bent down and looked under the billboards. He didn't see anything behind them.

He went on four steps, leaned down and picked up the package, felt cloth and two thick rubber bands. He stood quite still, listening.

Distant traffic hummed on a main street. A light burned across the street in a rooming house, behind a glass-paneled door. A window was open and dark above it.

A woman's voice screamed shrilly behind him.

He stiffened, whirled, and the light hit him between the eyes. It came from the dark window across the street, a blinding white shaft that impaled him against the billboard.

His face leered in it, his eyes blinked. He didn't move any more.

Shoes dropped on cement and a smaller spot stabbed at him sideways from the end of the billboards. Behind the spot a casual voice spoke: "Don't shift an eyelash, bud. You're all wrapped up in law."

Men with revolvers out closed in on him from both ends of the line of billboards. Heels clicked far off on concrete. Then it was silent for a moment. Then a car with a red spotlight swung around the corner and bore down on the group of men with Pete Anglich in their midst.

The man with the casual voice said: "I'm Angus, detective-lieutenant. I'll take the packet, if you don't mind. And if you'll just keep your hands together a minute—"

The handcuffs clicked dryly on Pete Anglich's wrists.

He listened hard for the sound of the heels far off, running away. But there was too much noise around him now.

Doors opened and dark people began to boil out of the houses.

3

John Vidaury was six feet two inches in height and had the most perfect profile in Hollywood. He was dark, winsome, romantic, with an interesting touch of gray at his temples. His shoulders were wide, his hips narrow. He had the waist of an English guards officer, and his dinner clothes fit him so beautifully that it hurt.

So he looked at Pete Anglich as if he was about to apologize for not knowing him. Pete Anglich looked at his handcuffs, at his worn shoes on the thick rug, at the tall chiming clock against the wall. There was a flush on his face and his eyes were bright.

In a smooth, clear, modulated voice Vidaury said, "No, I've never seen him before." He smiled at Pete Anglich.

Angus, the plainclothes lieutenant, leaned against one end of a carved library table and snapped a finger against the brim of his hat. Two other detectives stood near a side wall. A fourth sat at a small desk with a stenographer's notebook in front of him.

Angus said, "Oh, we just thought you might know him. We can't get much of anything out of him."

Vidaury raised his eyebrows, smiled very faintly. "Really I'm surprised at that." He went around collecting glasses, and took them over to a tray, started to mix more drinks.

"It happens," Angus said.

"I thought you had ways," Vidaury said delicately, pouring Scotch into the glasses.

Angus looked at a fingernail. "When I say he won't tell us anything, Mr. Vidaury, I mean anything that counts. He says his name is Pete Anglich, that he used to be a fighter, but hasn't fought for several years. Up to about a year ago he was a private detective, but has no work now. He won some money in a crap game and got drunk, and was just wandering about. That's how he happened to be on Noon Street. He saw the package tossed out of your car and picked it up. We can vag him, but that's about all."

"It could happen that way," Vidaury said softly. He carried the glasses two at a time to the four detectives, lifted his own, and nodded slightly before he drank. He drank gracefully, with a superb elegance of movement. "No, I don't know him," he said again. "Frankly, he doesn't look like an acid-thrower to me." He waved a hand. "So I'm afraid bringing him here—"

Pete Anglich lifted his head suddenly, stared at Vidaury. His voice sneered.

"It's a great compliment, Vidaury. They don't often use up the time of four coppers taking prisoners around to call on people."

Vidaury smiled amiably. "That's Hollywood," he smiled. "After all, one had a reputation."

"Had," Pete Anglich said. "Your last picture was a pain where you don't tell the ladies."

Angus stiffened. Vidaury's face went white. He put his glass down slowly, let his hand fall to his side. He walked springily across the rug and stood in front of Pete Anglich.

"That's your opinion," he said harshly, "but I warn you—"

Pete Anglich scowled at him. "Listen, big shot. You put a grand on the line because some punk promised to throw acid at you if you didn't. I picked up the grand, but I didn't get any of your nice, new money. So you got it back. You get ten grand worth of publicity and it won't cost you a nickel. I call that pretty swell."

Angus said sharply, "That's enough from you, mug."

"Yeah?" Pete Anglich sneered. "I thought you wanted me to talk. Well, I'm talking, and I hate pikers, see?"

Vidaury breathed hard. Very suddenly he balled his fist and swung at Pete Anglich's jaw. Pete Anglich's head rolled under the blow, and his eyes blinked shut, then wide open. He shook himself and said coolly: "Elbow up and thumb down, Vidaury. You break a hand hitting a guy that way."

Vidaury stepped back and shook his head, looked at his thumb. His face lost its whiteness. His smile stole back.

"I'm sorry," he said contritely. "I am very sorry. I'm not used to being insulted. As I don't know this man, perhaps you'd better take him away, Lieutenant. Handcuffed, too. Not very sporting, was it?"

"Tell that to your polo ponies," Pete Anglich said. "I don't bruise so easy."

Angus walked over to him, tapped his shoulder. "Up on the dogs, bo. Let's drift. You're not used to nice people, are you?"

"No. I like bums," Pete Anglich said.

He stood up slowly, scuffed at the pile of the carpet.

The two dicks against the wall fell in beside him, and they walked away down the huge room, under an arch. Angus and the other man came behind. They waited in the small private lobby for the elevator to come up.

"What was the idea?" Angus snapped. "Getting gashouse with him?"

Pete Anglich laughed. "Jumpy," he said. "Just jumpy."

The elevator came up and they rode down to the huge, silent lobby of the Chester Towers. Two house detectives lounged at the end of the marble desk, two clerks stood alert behind it.

Pete Anglich lifted his manacled hands in the fighter's salute. "What, no newshawks yet?" he jeered. "Vidaury won't like hush-hush on this.

"Keep goin', smartie," one of the dicks snapped, jerking his arm.

They went down a corridor and out of a side entrance to a narrow street that dropped almost sheer to treetops. Beyond the treetops the lights of the city were a vast golden carpet, stitched with brilliant splashes of red and green and blue and purple.

Two starters whirred. Pete Anglich was pushed into the back seat of the first car. Angus and another man got in on either side of him. The cars drifted down the hill, turned east on Fountain, slid quietly through the evening for mile after mile. Fountain met Sunset, and the cars dropped downtown toward the tall, white tower of the City Hall. At the plaza the first car swung over to Los Angeles Street and went south. The other car went on.

After a while Pete Anglich dropped the corners of his mouth and looked sideways at Angus.

"Where you taking me? This isn't the way to headquarters."

Angus' dark, austere face turned toward him slowly. After a moment the big detective leaned back and yawned at the night. He didn't answer.

The car slid along Los Angeles to Fifth, east to San Pedro, south again for block after block, quiet blocks and loud blocks, blocks where silent men sat on shaky front porches and blocks where noisy young toughs of both colors snarled and wisecracked at one another in front of cheap restaurants and drugstores and beer parlors full of slot machines.

At Santa Barbara the police car turned east again, drifted slowly along the curb to Noon Street. It stopped at the corner above the lunch wagon. Pete Anglich's face tightened again, but he didn't say anything.

"Okey," Angus drawled. "Take the nippers off."

The dick on Pete Anglich's other side dug a key out of his vest, unlocked the handcuffs, jangled them pleasantly before he put them away on his hip. Angus swung the door open and stepped out of the car.

"Out," he said over his shoulder.

Pete Anglich got out. Angus walked a little way from the street light, stopped, beckoned. His hand moved under his coat, came out with a gun. He said softly: "Had to play it this way. Otherwise we'd tip the town. Pearson's the only one that knows you. Any ideas?"

Pete Anglich took his gun, shook his head slowly, slid the gun under his own coat, keeping his body between it and the car at the curb behind.

"The stake-out was spotted, I guess," he said slowly. "There was a girl hanging around there, but maybe that just happened, too."

Angus stared at him silently for a moment, then nodded and went back to the car. The door slammed shut, and the car drifted off down the street and picked up speed.

Pete Anglich walked along Santa Barbara to Central, south on Central. After a while a bright sign glared at him in violet letters—Juggernaut Club. He went up broad carpeted stairs toward noise and dance music.

4

The girl had to go sideways to get between the close-set tables around the small dance floor. Her hips touched the back of a man's shoulder and he reached out and grabbed her hand, grinning. She smiled mechanically, pulled her hand away and came on.

She looked better in the bronze metal-cloth dress with bare arms and the brown hair curling low on her neck; better than in the shabby polo coat and cheap felt hat, better even than in skyscraper heels, bare legs and thighs, the irreducible minimum above the waistline, and a dull gold opera hat tipped rakishly over one ear.

Her face looked haggard, small, pretty, shallow. Her eyes had a wide stare. The dance band made a sharp racket over the clatter of dishes, the thick hum of talk, the shuffling feet on the dance floor. The girl came slowly up to Pete Anglich's table, pulled the other chair out and sat down.

She propped her chin on the backs of her hands, put her elbows on the tablecloth, stared at him.

"Hello there," she said in a voice that shook a little.

Pete Anglich pushed a pack of cigarettes across the table, watched her shake one loose and get it between her lips. He struck a match. She had to take it out of his hand to light her cigarette.

"Drink?"

"I'll say."

He signaled the fuzzy-haired, almond-eyed waiter, ordered a couple of sidecars. The waiter went away. Pete Anglich leaned back on his chair and looked at one of his blunt fingertips.

The girl said very softly: "I got your note, mister."

"Like it?" His voice was stiffly casual. He didn't look at her.

She laughed off key. "We've got to please the customers."

Pete Anglich looked past her shoulder at the corner of the band shell. A man stood there smoking, beside a small microphone. He was heavily built, old for an m.c., with slick gray hair and a big nose and the thickened complexion of a steady drinker. He was smiling at everything and everybody. Pete Anglich looked at him a little while, watching the direction of his glances. He said stiffly, in the same casual voice, "But you'd be here anyway."

The girl stiffened, then slumped. "You don't have to insult me, mister."

He looked at her slowly, with an empty up-from-under look. "You're down and out, knee-deep in nothing, baby. I've been that way often enough to know the symptoms. Besides, you got me in plenty jam tonight. I owe you a couple insults."

The fuzzy-haired waiter came back and slid a tray on the cloth, wiped the bottoms of two glasses with a dirty towel, set them out. He went away again.

The girl put her hand around a glass, lifted it quickly and took a long drink. She shivered a little as she put the glass down. Her face was white.

"Wisecrack or something," she said rapidly. "Don't just sit there. I'm watched."

Pete Anglich touched his fresh drink, smiled very deliberately toward the corner of the band shell.

"Yeah, I can imagine. Tell me about that pick-up on Noon Street."

She reached out quickly and touched his arm. Her sharp nails dug into it. "Not here," she breathed. "I don't know how you found me and I don't care. You looked like the kind of Joe that would help a girl out. I was scared stiff. But don't talk about it here. I'll do anything you want, go anywhere you want. Only not here."

Pete Anglich took his arm from under her hand, leaned back again. His eyes were cold, but his mouth was kind.

"I get it. Trimmer's wishes. Was he tailing the job?"

She nodded quickly. "I hadn't gone three blocks before he picked me up. He thought it was a swell gag, what I did, but he won't think so when he sees you here. That makes you wise."

Pete Anglich sipped his drink. "He is coming this way," he said, coolly.

The gray-haired m.c. was moving among the tables, bowing

and talking, but edging toward the one where Pete Anglich sat with the girl. The girl was staring into a big gilt mirror behind Pete Anglich's head. Her face was suddenly distorted, shattered with terror. Her lips were shaking uncontrollably.

Trimmer Waltz idled casually up to the table, leaned a hand down on it. He poked his big-veined nose at Pete Anglich. There was a soft, flat grin on his face.

"Hi, Pete. Haven't seen you around since they buried McKinley. How's tricks?"

"Not bad, not good," Pete Anglich said huskily. "I been on a drunk."

Trimmer Waltz broadened his smile, turned it on the girl. She looked at him quickly, looked away, picking at the table-cloth.

Waltz's voice was soft, cooing. "Know the little lady before—or just pick her out of the line-up?"

Pete Anglich shrugged, looked bored. "Just wanted somebody to share a drink with, Trimmer. Sent her a note. Okey?"

"Sure. Perfect." Waltz picked one of the glasses up, sniffed at it. He shook his head sadly. "Wish we could serve better stuff. At four bits a throw it can't be done. How about tipping a few out of a right bottle, back in my den?"

"Both of us?" Pete Anglich asked gently.

"Both of you is right. In about five minutes. I got to circulate a little first."

He pinched the girl's cheek, went on, with a loose swing of his tailored shoulders.

The girl said slowly, thickly, hopelessly, "So Pete's your name. You must want to die young, Pete. Mine's Token Ware. Silly name, isn't it?"

"I like it," Pete Anglich said softly.

The girl stared at a point below the white scar on Pete Anglich's throat. Her eyes slowly filled with tears.

Trimmer Waltz drifted among the tables, speaking to a customer here and there. He edged over to the far wall, came along it to the band shell, stood there ranging the house with his eyes until he was looking directly at Pete Anglich. He jerked his head, stepped back through a pair of thick curtains.

Pete Anglich pushed his chair back and stood up. "Let's go," he said.

Token Ware crushed a cigarette out in a glass tray with jerky fingers, finished the drink in her glass, stood up. They went back between the tables, along the edge of the dance floor, over to the side of the band shell.

The curtains opened on to a dim hallway with doors on both sides. A shabby red carpet masked the floor. The walls were chipped, the doors cracked.

"The one at the end on the left," Token Ware whispered.

They came to it. Pete Anglich knocked. Trimmer Waltz's voice called out to come in. Pete Anglich stood a moment looking at the door, then turned his head and looked at the girl with his eyes hard and narrow. He pushed the door open, gestured at her. They went in.

The room was not very light. A small oblong reading lamp on the desk shed glow on polished wood, but less on the shabby red carpet, and the long heavy red drapes across the outer wall. The air was close, with a thick, sweetish smell of liquor.

Trimmer Waltz sat behind the desk with his hands touching a tray that contained a cut-glass decanter, some gold-veined glasses, an ice bucket and a siphon of charged water.

He smiled, rubbed one side of his big nose.

"Park yourselves, folks. Liqueur Scotch at six-ninety a fifth. That's what it costs me—wholesale."

Pete Anglich shut the door, looked slowly around the room, at the floor-length window drapes, at the unlighted ceiling light. He unbuttoned the top button of his coat with a slow, easy movement.

"Hot in here," he said softly. "Any windows behind those drapes?"

The girl sat in a round chair on the opposite side of the desk from Waltz. He smiled at her very gently.

"Good idea," Waltz said. "Open one up, will you?"

Pete Anglich went past the end of the desk, toward the curtains. As he got beyond Waltz, his hand went up under his coat and touched the butt of his gun. He moved softly toward the red drapes. The tips of wide, square-toed black shoes just barely showed under the curtains, in the shadow between the curtains and the wall.

Pete Anglich reached the curtains, put his left hand out and jerked them open.

The shoes on the floor against the wall were empty. Waltz laughed dryly behind Pete Anglich. Then a thick, cold voice said: "Put 'em high, boy."

The girl made a strangled sound, not quite a scream. Pete Anglich dropped his hands and turned slowly and looked. The Negro was enormous in stature, gorilla-like, and wore a baggy checked suit that made him even more enormous. He had come soundlessly on shoeless feet out of a closet door, and his right hand almost covered a huge black gun.

Trimmer Waltz held a gun too, a Savage. The two men stared quietly at Pete Anglich. Pete Anglich put his hands up in the air, his eyes blank, his small mouth set hard.

The Negro in the checked suit came toward him in long, loose strides, pressed the gun against his chest, then reached under his coat. His hand came out with Pete Anglich's gun. He dropped it behind him on the floor. He shifted his own gun casually and hit Pete Anglich on the side of the jaw with the flat of it.

Pete Anglich staggered and the salt taste of blood came under his tongue. He blinked, said thickly: "I'll remember you a long time, big boy."

The Negro grinned. "Not so long, pal. Not so long."

He hit Pete Anglich again with the gun, then suddenly he jammed it into a side pocket and his two big hands shot out, clamped themselves on Pete Anglich's throat.

"When they's tough I likes to squeeze 'em," he said almost softly.

Thumbs that felt as big and hard as doorknobs pressed into the arteries on Pete Anglich's neck. The face before him and above him grew enormous, an enormous shadowy face with a wide grin in the middle of it. It waved in lessening light, an unreal, a fantastic face.

Pete Anglich hit the face, with puny blows, the blows of a toy balloon. His fists didn't feel anything as they hit the face. The big man twisted him around and put a knee into his back, and bent him down over the knee.

There was no sound for a while except the thunder of blood threshing in Pete Anglich's head. Then, far away, he seemed to hear a girl scream thinly. From still farther away the voice of Trimmer Waltz muttered: "Easy now, Rufe. Easy."

A vast blackness shot with hot red filled Pete Anglich's world. The darkness grew silent. Nothing moved in it now, not even blood.

The Negro lowered Pete Anglich's limp body to the floor, stepped back and rubbed his hands together.

"Yeah, I likes to squeeze 'em," he said.

5

The Negro in the checked suit sat on the side of the daybed and picked languidly at a five stringed banjo. His large face was solemn and peaceful, a little sad. He plucked the banjo strings slowly, with his bare fingers, his head on one side, a crumpled cigarette-end sticking barely past his lips at one corner of his mouth.

Low down in his throat he was making a kind of droning sound. He was singing.

A cheap electric clock on the mantel said 11.35. It was a small living room with bright, overstuffed furniture, a red floor lamp with a cluster of French dolls at its base, a gay carpet with large diamond shapes in it, two curtained windows with a mirror between them.

A door at the back was ajar. A door near it opening into the hall was shut.

Pete Anglich lay on his back on the floor, with his mouth open and his arms outflung. His breath was a thick snore. His eyes were shut, and his face in the reddish glow of the lamp looked flushed and feverish.

The Negro put the banjo down out of his immense hands, stood up and yawned and stretched. He walked across the room and looked at a calendar over the mantel.

"This ain't August," he said disgustedly.

He tore a leaf from the calendar, rolled it into a ball and threw it at Pete Anglich's face. It hit the unconscious man's cheek. He didn't stir. The Negro spit the cigarette-end into his palm, held his palm out flat, and flicked a fingernail at it, sent it sailing in the same direction as the paper ball.

He loafed a few steps and leaned down, fingering a bruise on Pete Anglich's temple. He pressed the bruise, grinning softly. Pete Anglich didn't move.

The Negro straightened and kicked the unconscious man in the ribs, thoughtfully, over and over again, not very hard. Pete Anglich moved a little, gurgled, and rolled his head to one side. The Negro looked pleased, left him, went back to the daybed. He carried his banjo over to the hall door and leaned it against the wall. There was a gun lying on a newspaper on a small table. He went through a partly open inner door and came back with a pint bottle of gin, half full. He rubbed the bottle over carefully with a handkerchief, set it on the mantel.

"About time now, pal," he mused out loud. "When you wake up, maybe you don't feel so good. Maybe need a shot . . . Hey, I gotta better hunch."

He reached for the bottle again, went down on one big knee, poured gin over Pete Anglich's mouth and chin, slopped it loosely on the front of his shirt. He stood the bottle on the floor, after wiping it off again, and flicked the glass stopper under the daybed.

"Grab it, white boy," he said softly. "Prints don't never hurt."

He got the newspaper with the gun on it, slid the gun off on the carpet, and moved it with his foot until it lay just out of reach of Pete Anglich's outflung hand.

He studied the layout carefully from the door, nodded, picked his banjo up. He opened the door, peeped out, then looked back.

"So long, pal," he said softly. "Time for me to breeze. You ain't got a lot of future comin', but what you got you get sudden."

He shut the door, went along the hallway to stairs and down the stairs. Radios made faint sound behind shut doors. The entrance lobby of the apartment house was empty. The Negro in the checked suit slipped into a pay booth in the dark corner of the lobby, dropped his nickel and dialed.

A heavy voice said: "Police department."

The Negro put his lips close to the transmitter and got a whine into his voice.

"This the cops? Say, there's been a shootin' scrape in the Calliope Apartments, Two-Forty-Six East Forty-Eight, Apartment Four–B. Got it? . . . Well, do somethin' about it, flatfoot!"

He hung up quickly, giggling, ran down the front steps of the apartment house and jumped into a small, dirty sedan. He kicked it to life and drove toward Central Avenue. He was a block from Central Avenue when the red eye of a prowl car swung around from Central on to East Forty-Eight Street.

The Negro in the sedan chuckled and went on his way. He was singing down in his throat when the prowl car whirred past him.

The instant the door latch clicked Pete Anglich opened his eyes halfway. He turned his head slowly, and a grin of pain came on his face and stayed on it, but he kept on turning his head until he could see the emptiness of one end of the room and the middle. He tipped his head far back on the floor, saw the rest of the room.

He rolled toward the gun and took hold of it. It was his own gun. He sat up and snapped the gate open mechanically. His face stiffened out of the grin. One shell in the gun had been fired. The barrel smelled of powder fumes.

He came to his feet and crept toward the slightly open inner door, keeping his head low. When he reached the door he bent still lower, and slowly pushed the door wide open. Nothing happened. He looked into a bedroom with twin beds, made up and covered with rose damask with a gold design in it.

Somebody lay on one of the beds. A woman. She didn't move. The hard, tight grin came back on Pete Anglich's face. He rose straight up and walked softly on the balls of his feet over to the side of the bed. A door beyond was open on a bathroom, but no sound came from it. Pete Anglich looked down at the colored girl on the bed.

He caught his breath and let it out slowly. The girl was dead. Her eyes were half open, uninterested, her hands lazy at her sides. Her legs were twisted a little and bare skin showed above one sheer stocking, below the short skirt. A green hat lay on the floor. She had four-and-a-half-inch French heels. There was a scent of Midnight Narcissus in the room. He remembered the girl outside the Surprise Hotel.

She was quite dead, dead long enough for the blood to have clotted over the powder-scorched hole below her left breast.

Pete Anglich went back to the living room, grabbed up the gin bottle, and emptied it without stopping or choking. He stood a moment, breathing hard, thinking. The gun hung slack in his left hand. His small, tight mouth hardly showed at all.

He worked his fingers around on the glass of the gin bottle, tossed it empty on top of the daybed, slid his gun into the underarm holster, went to the door and stepped quietly into the hall.

The hall was long and dim and yawning with chill air. A single bracket light loomed yellowly at the top of the stairs. A screen door led to a balcony over the front porch of the building. There was a gray splash of cold moonlight on one corner of the screen.

Pete Anglich went softly down the stairs to the front hall, put his hand out to the knob of the glass door.

A red spot hit the front of the door. It sifted a hard red glare through the glass and the sleazy curtain that masked it.

Pete Anglich slid down the door, below the panel, hunched along the wall to the side. His eyes ranged the place swiftly, held on the dark telephone booth.

"Man trap," he said softly, and dodged over to the booth, into it. He crouched and almost shut the door.

Steps slammed on the porch and the front door squeaked open. The steps hammered into the hallway, stopped.

A heavy voice said: "All quiet, huh? Maybe a phony."

Another voice said: "Four–B. Let's give it the dust, any-way."

The steps went along the lower hall, came back. They sounded on the stairs going up. They drummed in the upper hall.

Pete Anglich pushed the door of the booth back, slid over

to the front door, crouched and squinted against the red glare.

The prowl car at the curb was a dark bulk. Its headlights burned along the cracked sidewalk. He couldn't see into it. He sighed, opened the door and walked quickly, but not too quickly, down the wooden steps from the porch.

The prowl car was empty, with both front doors hanging open. Shadowy forms were converging cautiously from across the street. Pete Anglich marched straight to the prowl car and got into it. He shut the doors quietly, stepped on the starter, threw the car in gear.

He drove off past the gathering crowd of neighbors. At the first corner he turned and switched off the red spot. Then he drove fast, wound in and out of blocks, away from Central, after a while turned back toward it.

When he was near its lights and chatter and traffic he pulled over to the side of the dusty tree-lined street, left the prowl car standing.

He walked towards Central.

6

Trimmer Waltz cradled the phone with his left hand. He put his right index finger along the edge of his upper lip, pushed the lip out of the way, and rubbed his finger slowly along his teeth and gums. His shallow, colorless eyes looked across the desk at the big Negro in the checked suit.

"Lovely," he said in a dead voice. "Lovely. He got away before the law jumped him. A very swell job, Rufe."

The Negro took a cigar stub out of his mouth and crushed it between a huge flat thumb and a huge flat forefinger.

"Hell, he was out cold," he snarled. "The prowlies passed me before I got to Central. Hell, he *can't* get away."

"That was him talking," Waltz said lifelessly. He opened the top drawer of his desk and laid his heavy Savage in front of him.

The Negro looked at the Savage. His eyes got dull and lightless, like obsidian. His lips puckered and gouged at each other.

"That gal's been cuttin' corners on me with three, four other guys," he grumbled. "I owed her the slug. Oky-doke. That's jake. Now, I go out and collect me the smart monkey."

He started to get up. Waltz barely touched the butt of his gun with two fingers. He shook his head, and the Negro sat down again. Waltz spoke.

"He got away, Rufe. And you called the buttons to find a dead woman. Unless they get him with the gun on him—one chance in a thousand—there's no way to tie it to him. That makes you the fall guy. You live there."

The Negro grinned and kept his dull eyes on the Savage.

He said: "That makes me get cold feet. And my feet are big enough to get plenty cold. Guess I take me a powder, huh?"

Waltz sighed. He said thoughtfully: "Yeah, I guess you leave town for a while. From Glendale. The 'Frisco late train will be about right."

The Negro looked sulky. "Nix on 'Frisco, boss. I put my thumbs on a frail there. She croaked. Nix on 'Frisco, boss."

"You've got ideas, Rufe," Waltz said calmly. He rubbed the side of his veined nose with one finger, then slicked his gray hair back with his palm. "I see them in your big brown eyes. Forget it. I'll take care of you. Get the car in the alley. We'll figure the angles on the way to Glendale."

The Negro blinked and wiped cigar ash off his chin with his huge hand.

"And better leave your big shiny gun here," Waltz added. "It needs a rest."

Rufe reached back and slowly drew his gun from a hip pocket. He pushed it across the polished wood of the desk with one finger. There was a faint, sleepy smile at the back of his eyes.

"Okey, boss," he said, almost dreamily.

He went across to the door, opened it, and went out. Waltz stood up and stepped over to the closet, put on a dark felt hat and a lightweight overcoat, a pair of dark gloves. He dropped the Savage into his left-hand pocket, Rufe's gun into the right. He went out of the room down the hall toward the sound of the dance band.

At the end he parted the curtains just enough to peer through. The orchestra was playing a waltz. There was a good crowd, a quiet crowd for Central Avenue. Waltz sighed, watched the dancers for a moment, let the curtains fall together again.

He went back along the hall past his office to a door at the end that gave on stairs. Another door at the bottom of the stairs opened on a dark alley behind the building.

Waltz closed the door gently, stood in the darkness against the wall. The sound of an idling motor came to him, the light clatter of loose tappets. The alley was blind at one end, at the other turned at right angles toward the front of the building. Some of the light from Central Avenue splashed on a brick wall at the end of the cross alley, beyond the waiting car, a small sedan that looked battered and dirty even in the darkness.

Waltz reached his right hand into his overcoat pocket, took out Rufe's gun and held it down in the cloth of his overcoat. He walked to the sedan soundlessly, went around to the right-hand door, opened it to get in.

Two huge hands came out of the car and took hold of his throat. Hard hands, hands with enormous strength in them. Waltz made a faint gurgling sound before his head was bent back and his almost blind eyes were groping at the sky.

Then his right hand moved, moved like a hand that had nothing to do with his stiff, straining body, his tortured neck, his bulging blind eyes. It moved forward cautiously, delicately, until the muzzle of the gun it held pressed against something soft. It explored the something soft carefully, without haste, seemed to be making sure just what it was.

Trimmer Waltz didn't see, he hardly felt. He didn't breathe. But his hand obeyed his brain like a detached force beyond the reach of Rufe's terrible hands. Waltz's finger squeezed the trigger.

The hands fell slack on his throat, dropped away. He staggered back, almost fell across the alley, hit the far wall with his shoulder. He straightened slowly, gasping deep down in his tortured lungs. He began to shake.

He hardly noticed the big gorilla's body fall out of the car and slam the concrete at his feet. It lay at his feet, limp, enormous, but no longer menacing. No longer important.

Waltz dropped the gun on the sprawled body. He rubbed his throat gently for a little while. His breathing was deep, racking, noisy. He searched the inside of his mouth with his tongue, tasted blood. His eyes looked up wearily at the indigo slit of the night sky above the alley.

After a while he said huskily, "I thought of that, Rufe . . . You see, I thought of that."

He laughed, shuddered, adjusted his coat collar, went around the sprawled body to the car and reached in to switch the motor off. He started back along the alley to the rear door of the Juggernaut Club.

A man stepped out of the shadows at the back of the car. Waltz's left hand flashed to his overcoat pocket. Shiny metal blinked at him. He let his hand fall loosely at his side.

Pete Anglich said, "Thought that call would bring you out, Trimmer. Thought you might come this way. Nice going."

After a moment Waltz said thickly: "He choked me. It was self-defense."

"Sure. There's two of us with sore necks. Mine's a pip."

"What do you want, Pete?"

"You tried to frame me for bumping off a girl."

Waltz laughed suddenly, almost crazily. He said quietly: "When I'm crowded I get nasty, Pete. You should know that. Better lay off little Token Ware."

Pete Anglich moved his gun so that the light flickered on the barrel. He came up to Waltz, pushed the gun against his stomach.

"Rufe's dead," he said softly. "Very convenient. Where's the girl?"

"What's it to you?"

"Don't be a bunny. I'm wise. You tried to pick some jack off John Vidaury. I stepped in front of Token. I want to know the rest of it."

Waltz stood very still with the gun pressing his stomach. His fingers twisted in the gloves.

"Okay," he said dully. "How much to button your lip— and keep it buttoned?"

"Couple of centuries. Rufe lifted my poke."

"What does it buy me?" Waltz asked slowly.

"Not a damn thing. I want the girl, too."

Waltz said very gently: "Five C's. But not the girl. Five C's is heavy dough for a Central Avenue punk. Be smart and take it, and forget the rest."

The gun went away from his stomach. Pete Anglich circled him deftly, patted pockets, took the Savage, made a gesture with his left hand, holding it.

"Sold," he said grudgingly. "What's a girl between pals? Feed it to me."

"Have to go up to the office," Waltz said.

Pete Anglich laughed shortly. "Better play ball, Trimmer. Lead on."

They went back along the upstairs hall. The dance band beyond the distant curtains was wailing a Duke Ellington lament, a forlorn monotone of stifled brasses, bitter violins, softly clicking gourds. Waltz opened his office door, snapped the light on, went across to his desk and sat down. He tilted his hat back, smiled, opened a drawer with a key.

Pete Anglich watched him, reached back to turn the key in the door, went along the wall to the closet and looked into it, went behind Waltz to the curtains that masked the windows. He still had his gun out.

He came back to the end of the desk. Waltz was pushing a loose sheaf of bills away from him.

Pete Anglich ignored the money, leaned down over the end of the desk.

"Keep that and give me the girl, Trimmer."

Waltz shook his head, kept on smiling.

"The Vidaury squeeze was a grand, Trimmer—or started with a grand. Noon Street is almost in your alley. Do you have to scare women into doing your dirty work? I think you wanted something on the girl, so you could make her say uncle."

Waltz narrowed his eyes a little, pointed to the sheaf of bills.

Pete Anglich said slowly: "A shabby, lonesome, scared kid. Probably lives in a cheap furnished room. No friends, or she wouldn't be working in your joint. Nobody would wonder about her, except me. You wouldn't have put her in a house, would you, Trimmer?"

"Take your money and beat it," Waltz said thinly. "You know what happens to rats in this district."

"Sure, they run night clubs," Pete Anglich said gently.

He put his gun down, started to reach for the money. His fist doubled, swept upward casually. His elbow went up with the punch, the fist turned, landed almost delicately on the angle of Waltz's jaw.

Waltz became a loose bag of clothes. His mouth fell open. His hat fell off the back of his head. Pete Anglich stared at him, grumbled: "Lot of good that does me."

The room was very still. The dance band sounded faintly, like a turned-down radio. Pete Anglich moved behind Waltz and reached down under his coat into his breast pocket. He took a wallet out, shook out money, a driver's license, a police pistol permit, several insurance cards.

He put the stuff back, stared morosely at the desk, rubbed a thumbnail on his jaw. There was a shiny buff memo pad in front of him. Impressions of writing showed on the top blank sheet. He held it sideways against the light, then picked up a pencil and began to make light loose strokes across the paper. Writing came out dimly. When the sheet was shaded all over Pete Anglich read: 4623 Noon Street. Ask for Reno.

He tore the sheet off, folded it into a pocket, picked his gun up and crossed to the door. He reversed the key, locked the room from the outside, went back to the stairs and down them to the alley.

The body of the Negro lay as it had fallen, between the small sedan and the dark wall. The alley was empty. Pete Anglich stooped, searched the dead man's pockets, came up with a roll of money. He counted the money in the dim light of a match, separated eighty-seven dollars from what there was, and started to put the few remaining bills back. A piece of torn paper fluttered to the pavement. One side only was torn, jaggedly.

Pete Anglich crouched beside the car, struck another match, looked at a half-sheet from a buff memo pad on which was written, beginning with the tear: ———t. Ask for Reno.

He clicked his teeth and let the match fall. "Better," he said softly.

He got into the car, started it and drove out of the alley.

7

The number was on a front-door transom, faintly lit from behind, the only light the house showed. It was a big frame house, in the block above where the stake-out had been. The windows in front were closely curtained. Noise came from behind them, voices and laughter, the high-pitched whine of a colored girl's singing. Cars were parked along the curb, on both sides of the street.

A tall thin Negro in dark clothes and gold nose-glasses opened the door. There was another door behind him, shut. He stood in a dark box between the two doors.

Pete Anglich said: "Reno?"

The tall Negro nodded, said nothing.

"I've come for the girl Rufe left, the white girl."

The tall Negro stood a moment quite motionless, looking over Pete Anglich's head. When he spoke, his voice was a lazy rustle of sound that seemed to come from somewhere else.

"Come in and shut the do'."

Pete Anglich stepped into the house, shut the outer door behind him. The tall Negro opened the inner door. It was thick, heavy. When he opened it sound and light jumped at them. A purplish light. He went through the inner door, into a hallway.

The purplish light came through a broad arch from a long living room. It had heavy velour drapes, davenports and deep chairs, a glass bar in the corner, and a white-coated Negro behind the bar. Four couples lounged about the room drinking; slim, slick-haired Negro sheiks and girls with bare arms, sheer silk legs, plucked eyebrows. The soft, purplish light made the scene unreal.

Reno stared vaguely past Pete Anglich's shoulder, dropped his heavy-lidded eyes, said wearily: "You says which?"

The Negroes beyond the arch were quiet, staring. The barman stooped and put his hands down under the bar.

Pete Anglich put his hand into his pocket slowly, brought out a crumpled piece of paper.

"This any help?"

Reno took the paper, studied it. He reached languidly into

his vest and brought out another piece of the same color. He fitted the pieces together. His head went back and he looked at the ceiling.

"Who send you?"

"Trimmer."

"I don' like it," the tall Negro said. "He done write my name. I don' like that. That ain't sma't. Apa't from that I guess I check you."

He turned and started up a long, straight flight of stairs. Pete Anglich followed him. One of the Negro youths in the living room snickered loudly.

Reno stopped suddenly, turned and went back down the steps, through the arch. He went up to the snickerer.

"This is business," he said exhaustedly. "Ain't no white folks comin' heah. Git me?"

The boy who had laughed said, "Okey, Reno," and lifted a tall, misted glass.

Reno came up the stairs again, talking to himself. Along the upper hall were many closed doors. There was faint pink light from flame-colored wall lamps. At the end Reno took a key out and unlocked the door.

He stood aside. "Git her out," he said tersely. "I don' handle no white cargo heah."

Pete Anglich stepped past him into a bedroom. An orange floor lamp glowed in the far corner near a flounced, gaudy bed. The windows were shut, the air heavy, sickish.

Token Ware lay on her side on the bed, with her face to the wall, sobbing quietly.

Pete Anglich stepped to the side of the bed, touched her. She whirled, cringed. Her head jerked around at him, her eyes dilated, her mouth half open as if to yell.

"Hello, there," he said quietly, very gently. "I've been looking all over for you."

The girl stared back at him. Slowly all the fear went out of her face.

8

The *News* photographer held the flashbulb holder high up in his left hand, leaned down over his camera. "Now, the smile,

Mr. Vidaury," he said. "The sad one—that one that makes
'em pant."

Vidaury turned in the chair and set his profile. He smiled at
the girl in the red hat, then turned his face to the camera with
the smile still on.

The bulb flared and the shutter clicked.

"Not bad, Mr. Vidaury. I've seen you do better."

"I've been under a great strain," Vidaury said gently.

"I'll say. Acid in the face is no fun," the photographer said.

The girl in the red hat tittered, then coughed, behind a
gauntleted glove with red stitching on the back.

The photographer packed his stuff together. He was an
oldish man in shiny blue serge, with sad eyes. He shook his
gray head and straightened his hat.

"No, acid in the puss is no fun," he said. "Well, I hope our
boys can see you in the morning, Mr. Vidaury."

"Delighted," Vidaury said wearily. "Just tell them to ring
me from the lobby before they come up. And have a drink on
your way out."

"I'm crazy," the photographer said. "I don't drink."

He hoisted his camera bag over his shoulder and trudged
down the room. A small Jap in a white coat appeared from
nowhere and let him out, then went away.

"Acid in the puss," the girl in the red hat said. "Ha, ha, ha!
That's positively excruciating, if a nice girl may say so. Can I
have a drink?"

"Nobody's stopping you," Vidaury growled.

"Nobody ever did, sweets."

She walked sinuously over to a table with a square Chinese
tray on it. She mixed a stiff one. Vidaury said half absently:
"That should be all till morning. The *Bulletin*, the *Press-
Tribune*, the three wire services, the *News*. Not bad."

"I'd call it a perfect score," the girl in the red hat said.

Vidaury scowled at her. "But nobody caught," he said
softly, "except an innocent passer-by. *You* wouldn't know
anything about this squeeze, would you, Irma?"

Her smile was lazy, but cold. "Me take you for a measly
grand? Be your forty years plus, Johnny. I'm a home-run hit-
ter, always."

Vidaury stood up and crossed the room to a carved wood

cabinet, unlocked a small drawer and took a large ball of crystal out of it. He went back to his chair, sat down, and leaned forward, holding the ball in his palms and staring into it, almost vacantly.

The girl in the red hat watched him over the rim of her glass. Her eyes widened, got a little glassy.

"Hell! He's gone psychic on the folks," she breathed. She put her glass down with a sharp slap on the tray, drifted over to his side and leaned down. Her voice was cooing, edged. "Ever hear of senile decay, Johnny? It happens to exceptionally wicked men in their forties. They get ga-ga over flowers and toys, cut out paper dolls and play with glass balls . . . Can it, for God's sake, Johnny! You're not a punk yet."

Vidaury stared fixedly into the crystal ball. He breathed slowly, deeply.

The girl in the red hat leaned still closer to him. "Let's go riding, Johnny," she cooed. "I like the night air. It makes me remember my tonsils."

"I don't want to go riding," Vidaury said vaguely. "I—I feel something. Something imminent."

The girl bent suddenly and knocked the ball out of his hands. It thudded heavily on the floor, rolled sluggishly in the deep nap of the rug.

Vidaury shot to his feet, his face convulsed.

"I want to go riding, handsome," the girl said coolly. "It's a nice night, and you've got a nice car. So I want to go riding."

Vidaury stared at her with hate in his eyes. Slowly he smiled. The hate went away. He reached out and touched her lips with two fingers.

"Of course we'll go riding, baby," he said softly.

He got the ball, locked it up in the cabinet, went through an inner door. The girl in the red hat opened a bag and touched her lips with rouge, pursed them, made a face at herself in the mirror of her compact, found a rough wool coat in beige braided with red, and shrugged into it carefully, tossed a scarflike collar end over her shoulder.

Vidaury came back with a hat and coat on, a fringed muffler hanging down his coat.

They went down the room.

"Let's sneak out the back way," he said at the door. "In case any more newshawks are hanging around."

"Why, Johnny!" the girl in the red hat raised mocking eyebrows. "People saw me come in, saw me here. Surely you wouldn't want them to think your girl friend stayed the night?"

"Hell!" Vidaury said violently and wrenched the door open.

The telephone bell jangled back in the room. Vidaury swore again, took his hand from the door and stood waiting while the little Jap in the white jacket came in and answered the phone.

The boy put the phone down, smiled deprecatingly and gestured with his hands.

"You take, prease? I not understand."

Vidaury walked back and lifted the instrument. He said, "Yes? This is John Vidaury." He listened.

Slowly his fingers tightened on the phone. His whole face tightened, got white. He said slowly, thickly: "Hold the line a minute."

He put the phone down on its side, put his hand down on the table and leaned on it. The girl in the red hat came up behind him.

"Bad news, handsome? You look like a washed egg."

Vidaury turned his head slowly and stared at her. "Get the hell out of here," he said tonelessly.

She laughed. He straightened, took a single long step and slapped her across the mouth, hard.

"I said, get the hell out of here," he repeated in an utterly dead voice.

She stopped laughing and touched her lips with fingers in the gauntleted glove. Her eyes were round, but not shocked.

"Why, Johnny. You sweep me right off my feet," she said wonderingly. "You're simply terrific. Of course I'll go."

She turned quickly, with a light toss of her head, went back along the room to the door, waved her hand, and went out.

Vidaury was not looking at her when she waved. He lifted the phone as soon as the door clicked shut after her, said into it grimly: "Get over here, Waltz—and get over here quick!"

He dropped the phone on its cradle, stood a moment

blank-eyed. He went back through the inner door, reappeared in a moment without his hat and overcoat. He held a thick, short automatic in his hand. He slipped it nose-down into the inside breast pocket of his dinner jacket, lifted the phone again slowly, said into it coldly and firmly: "If a Mr. Anglich calls to see me, send him up. Anglich." He spelled the name out, put the phone down carefully, and sat down in the easy chair beside it.

He folded his arms and waited.

9

The white-jacketed Japanese boy opened the door, bobbed his head, smiled, hissed politely: "Ah, you come inside, prease. Quite so, prease."

Pete Anglich patted Token Ware's shoulder, pushed her through the door into the long, vivid room. She looked shabby and forlorn against the background of handsome furnishings. Her eyes were reddened from crying, her mouth was smeared.

The door shut behind them and the little Japanese stole away.

They went down the stretch of thick, noiseless carpet, past quiet brooding lamps, bookcases sunk into the wall, shelves of alabaster and ivory, and porcelain and jade knickknacks, a huge mirror framed in blue glass, and surrounded by a frieze of lovingly autographed photos, low tables with lounging chairs, high tables with flowers, more books, more chairs, more rugs—and Vidaury sitting remotely with a glass in his hand, staring at them coldly.

He moved his hand carelessly, looked the girl up and down.

"Ah, yes, the man the police had here. Of course. Something I can do for you? I heard they made a mistake."

Pete Anglich turned a chair a little, pushed Token Ware into it. She sat down slowly, stiffly, licked her lips and stared at Vidaury with a frozen fascination.

A touch of polite distaste curled Vidaury's lips. His eyes were watchful.

Pete Anglich sat down. He drew a stick of gum out of his

pocket, unwrapped it, slid it between his teeth. He looked worn, battered, tired. There were dark bruises on the side of his face and on his neck. He still needed a shave.

He said slowly, "This is Miss Ware. The girl that was supposed to get your dough."

Vidaury stiffened. A hand holding a cigarette began to tap restlessly on the arm of his chair. He stared at the girl, but didn't say anything. She half smiled at him, then flushed.

Pete Anglich said: "I hang around Noon Street. I know the sharpshooters, know what kind of folks belong there and what kind don't. I saw this little girl in a lunchwagon on Noon Street this evening. She looked uneasy and she was watching the clock. She didn't belong. When she left I followed her."

Vidaury nodded slightly. A gray tip of ash fell off the end of his cigarette. He looked down at it vaguely, nodded again.

"She went up Noon Street," Pete Anglich said. "A bad street for a white girl. I found her hiding in a doorway. Then a big Duesenberg slid around the corner and doused lights, and your money was thrown out on the sidewalk. She was scared. She asked me to get it. I got it."

Vidaury said smoothly, not looking at the girl: "She doesn't look like a crook. Have you told the police about her? I suppose not, or you wouldn't be here."

Pete Anglich shook his head, ground the gum around in his jaws. "Tell the law? A couple of times nix. This is velvet for us. We want our cut."

Vidaury started violently, then he was very still. His hand stopped beating the chair arm. His face got cold and white and grim. Then he reached up inside his dinner jacket and quietly took the short automatic out, held it on his knees. He leaned forward a little and smiled.

"Blackmailers," he said gravely, "are always rather interesting. How much would your cut be—and what have you got to sell?"

Pete Anglich looked thoughtfully at the gun. His jaws moved easily, crunching the gum. His eyes were unworried.

"Silence," he said gravely. "Just silence."

Vidaury made a sharp sudden gesture with the gun. "Talk," he said. "And talk fast. I don't like silence."

Pete Anglich nodded, said: "The acid-throwing threats were just a dream. You didn't get any. The extortion attempt was a phony. A publicity stunt. That's all." He leaned back in his chair.

Vidaury looked down the room past Pete Anglich's shoulder. He started to smile, then his face got wooden.

Trimmer Waltz had slid into the room through an open side door. He had his big Savage in his hand. He came slowly along the carpet without sound. Pete Anglich and the girl didn't see him.

Pete Anglich said, "Phony all the way through. Just a build-up. Guessing? Sure I am, but look a minute, see how soft it was played first—and how tough it was played afterward, after I showed in it. The girl works for Trimmer Waltz at the Juggernaut. She's down and out, and she scares easily. So Waltz sends her on a caper like that. Why? Because she's supposed to be nabbed. The stake-out's all arranged. If she squawks about Waltz, he laughs it off, points to the fact that the plant was almost in his alley, that it was a small stake at best, and his joint's doing all right. He points to the fact that a dumb girl goes to get it, and would he, a smart guy, pull anything like that? Certainly not.

"The cops will half believe him, and you'll make a big gesture and refuse to prosecute the girl. If she doesn't spill, you'll refuse to prosecute anyway, and you'll get your publicity just the same, either way. You need it bad, because you're slipping, and you'll get it, and all it will cost you is what you pay Waltz—or that's what you think. Is that crazy? Is that too far for a Hollywood heel to stretch? Then tell me why no Feds were on the case. Because those lads would keep on digging until they found the mouse, and then you'd be up for obstructing justice. That's why. The local law don't give a damn. They're so used to movie build-ups they just yawn and turn over and go to sleep again."

Waltz was halfway down the room now. Vidaury didn't look at him. He looked at the girl, smiled at her faintly.

"Now, see how tough it was played after I got into it," Pete Anglich said. "I went to the Juggernaut and talked to the girl. Waltz got us into his office and a big ape that works for him damn near strangled me. When I came to I was in an apartment and a dead girl was there, and she was shot, and a bullet was gone from my gun. The gun was on the floor beside me, and I stank of gin, and a prowl car was booming around the corner. And Miss Ware here was locked up in a whore house on Noon Street.

"Why all that hard stuff? Because Waltz had a perfectly swell blackmail racket lined up for you, and he'd have bled you whiter than an angel's wing. As long as you had a dollar, half of it would have been his. And you'd have paid it and liked it, Vidaury. You'd have had publicity, and you'd have had protection, but how you'd have paid for it!"

Waltz was close now, almost too close. Vidaury stood up suddenly. The short gun jerked at Pete Anglich's chest. Vidaury's voice was thin, an old man's voice. He said drearily: "Take him, Waltz. I'm too jittery for this sort of thing."

Pete Anglich didn't even turn. His face became the face of a wooden Indian.

Waltz put his gun into Pete Anglich's back. He stood there half smiling, with the gun against Pete Anglich's back, looking across his shoulder at Vidaury.

"Dumb, Pete," he said dryly. "You had enough evening already. You ought to have stayed away from here—but I figured you couldn't pass it up."

Vidaury moved a little to one side, spread his legs, flattened his feet to the floor. There was a queer, greenish tint to his handsome face, a sick glitter in his deep eyes.

Token Ware stared at Waltz. Her eyes glittered with panic, the lids straining away from the eyeballs, showing the whites all around the iris.

Waltz said, "I can't do anything here, Vidaury. I'd rather not walk him out alone, either. Get your hat and coat."

Vidaury nodded very slightly. His head just barely moved. His eyes were still sick.

"What about the girl?" he asked whisperingly.

Waltz grinned, shook his head, pressed the gun hard into Pete Anglich's back.

Vidaury moved a little more to the side, spread his feet again. The thick gun was very steady in his hand, but not pointed at anything in particular.

He closed his eyes, held them shut a brief instant, then

opened them wide. He said slowly, carefully: "It looked all right as it was planned. Things just as far-fetched, just as unscrupulous, have been done before in Hollywood, often. I just didn't expect it to lead to hurting people, to killing. I'm—I'm just not enough of a heel to go on with it, Waltz. Not any further. You'd better put your gun up and leave."

Waltz shook his head; smiled a peculiar strained smile. He stepped back from Pete Anglich and held the Savage a little to one side.

"The cards are dealt," he said coldly. "You'll play 'em. Get going."

Vidaury sighed, sagged a little. Suddenly he was a lonely, forlorn man, no longer young.

"No," he said softly. "I'm through. The last flicker of a not-so-good reputation. It's my show, after all. Always the ham, but still my show. Put the gun up, Waltz. Take the air."

Waltz's face got cold and hard and expressionless. His eyes became the expressionless eyes of the killer. He moved the Savage a little more.

"Get—your—hat, Vidaury," he said very clearly.

"Sorry," Vidaury said, and fired.

Waltz's gun flamed at the same instant, the two explosions blended. Vidaury staggered to his left and half turned, then straightened his body again.

He looked steadily at Waltz. "Beginner's luck," he said, and waited.

Pete Anglich had his Colt out now, but he didn't need it. Waltz fell slowly on his side. His cheek and the side of his big-veined nose pressed the nap of the rug. He moved his left arm a little, tried to throw it over his back. He gurgled, then was still.

Pete Anglich kicked the Savage away from Waltz's sprawled body.

Vidaury asked draggingly: "Is he dead?"

Pete Anglich grunted, didn't answer. He looked at the girl. She was standing up with her back against the telephone table, the back of her hand to her mouth in the conventional attitude of startled horror. So conventional it looked silly.

Pete Anglich looked at Vidaury. He said sourly: "Beginner's luck—yeah. But suppose you'd missed him? He was bluffing.

Just wanted you in a little deeper, so you wouldn't squawk. As a matter of fact, I'm his alibi on a kill."

Vidaury said: "Sorry . . . I'm sorry." He sat down suddenly, leaned his head back and closed his eyes.

"God, but he's handsome!" Token Ware said reverently. "And brave."

Vidaury put his hand to his left shoulder, pressed it hard against his body. Blood oozed slowly between his fingers. Token Ware let out a stifled screech.

Pete Anglich looked down the room. The little Jap in the white coat had crept into the end of it, stood silently, a small huddled figure against the wall. Pete Anglich looked at Vidaury again. Very slowly, as though unwillingly, he said: "Miss Ware has folks in 'Frisco. You can send her home, with a little present. That's natural—and open. She turned Waltz up to me. That's how I came into it. I told him you were wise and he came here to shut you up. Tough-guy stuff. The coppers will laugh at it, but they'll laugh in their cuffs. After all, they're getting publicity too. The phony angle is out. Check?"

Vidaury opened his eyes, said faintly, "You're—you're very decent about it. I won't forget." His head lolled.

"He's fainted," the girl cried.

"So he has," Pete Anglich said. "Give him a nice big kiss and he'll snap out of it . . . And you'll have something to remember all your life."

He ground his teeth, went to the phone, and lifted it.

Goldfish

I wasn't doing any work that day, just catching up on my foot-dangling. A warm gusty breeze was blowing in at the office window and the soot from the Mansion House Hotel oil-burners across the alley was rolling across the glass top of my desk in tiny particles, like pollen drifting over a vacant lot.

I was just thinking about going to lunch when Kathy Horne came in.

She was a tall, seedy, sad-eyed blonde who had once been a policewoman and had lost her job when she married a cheap little check-bouncer named Johnny Horne, to reform him. She hadn't reformed him, but she was waiting for him to come out so she could try again. In the meantime she ran the cigar counter at the Mansion House, and watched the grifters go by in a haze of nickel cigar smoke. And once in a while lent one of them ten dollars to get out of town. She was just that soft. She sat down and opened her big shiny bag and got out a package of cigarettes and lit one with my desk lighter. She blew a plume of smoke, wrinkled her nose at it.

"Did you ever hear of the Leander pearls?" she asked. "Gosh, that blue serge shines. You must have money in the bank, the clothes you wear."

"No," I said, "to both your ideas. I never heard of the Leander pearls and don't have any money in the bank."

"Then you'd like to make yourself a cut of twenty-five grand maybe."

I lit one of her cigarettes. She got up and shut the window, saying: "I get enough of that hotel smell on the job."

She sat down again, went on:

"It's nineteen years ago. They had the guy in Leavenworth fifteen and it's four since they let him out. A big lumberman from up north named Sol Leander bought them for his wife—the pearls, I mean—just two of them. They cost two hundred grand."

"It must have taken a hand truck to move them," I said.

"I see you don't know a lot about pearls," Kathy Horne said. "It's not just size. Anyhow they're worth more today

326

and the twenty-five grand reward the Reliance people put out is still good."

"I get it," I said. "Somebody copped them off."

"Now you're getting yourself some oxygen." She dropped her cigarette into a tray and let it smoke, as ladies will. I put it out for her. "That's what the guy was in Leavenworth for, only they never proved he got the pearls. It was a mail-car job. He got himself hidden in the car somehow and up in Wyoming he shot the clerk, cleaned out the registered mail and dropped off. He got to B.C. before he was nailed. But they didn't get any of the stuff—not then. All they got was him. He got life."

"If it's going to be a long story, let's have a drink."

"I never drink until sundown. That way you don't get to be a heel."

"Tough on the Eskimos," I said. "In the summertime anyway."

She watched me get my little flat bottle out. Then she went on:

"His name was Sype—Wally Sype. He did it alone. And he wouldn't squawk about the stuff, not a peep. Then after fifteen long years they offered him a pardon, if he would loosen up with the loot. He gave up everything but the pearls."

"Where did he have it?" I asked. "In his hat?"

"Listen, this isn't just a bunch of gag lines. I've got a lead to those marbles."

I shut my mouth with my hand and looked solemn.

"He said he never had the pearls and they must have halfway believed him because they gave him the pardon. Yet the pearls were in the load, registered mail, and they were never seen again."

My throat began to feel a little thick. I didn't say anything. Kathy Horne went on:

"One time in Leavenworth, just one time in all those years, Wally Sype wrapped himself around a can of white shellac and got as tight as a fat lady's girdle. His cell mate was a little man they called Peeler Mardo. He was doing twenty-seven months for splitting twenty dollar bills. Sype told him he had the pearls buried somewhere in Idaho."

I leaned forward a little.

"Beginning to get to you, eh?" she said. "Well get this. Peeler Mardo is rooming at my house and he's a coke hound and he talks in his sleep."

I leaned back again. "Good grief," I said. "And I was practically spending the reward money."

She stared at me coldly. Then her face softened. "All right," she said a little hopelessly. "I know it sounds screwy. All those years gone by and all the smart heads that must have worked on the case, postal men and private agencies and all. And then a cokehead to turn it up. But he's a nice little runt and somehow I believe him. He knows where Sype is."

I said: "Did he talk all this in his sleep?"

"Of course not. But you know me. An old policewoman's got ears. Maybe I was nosey, but I guessed he was an ex-con and I worried about him using the stuff so much. He's the only roomer I've got now and I'd kind of go in by his door and listen to him talking to himself. That way I got enough to brace him. He told me the rest. He wants help to collect."

I leaned forward again. "Where's Sype?"

Kathy Horne smiled, and shook her head. "That's the one thing he wouldn't tell, that and the name Sype is using now. But it's somewhere up North, in or near Olympia, Washington. Peeler saw him up there and found out about him and he says Sype didn't see *him*."

"What's Peeler doing down here?" I asked.

"Here's where they put the Leavenworth rap on him. You know an old con always goes back to look at the piece of sidewalk he slipped on. But he doesn't have any friends here now."

I lit another cigarette and had another little drink.

"Sype has been out four years, you say. Peeler did twenty-seven months. What's he been doing with all the time since?"

Kathy Horne widened her china blue eyes pityingly. "Maybe you think there's only one jailhouse he could get into."

"Okey," I said. "Will he talk to me? I guess he wants help to deal with the insurance people, in case there are any pearls and Sype will put them right in Peeler's hand and so on. Is that it?"

Kathy Horne sighed. "Yes, he'll talk to you. He's aching to.

He's scared about something. Will you go out now, before he gets junked up for the evening?"

"Sure—if that's what you want."

She took a flat key out of her bag and wrote an address on my pad. She stood up slowly.

"It's a double house. My side's separate. There's a door in between, with the key on my side. That's just in case he won't come to the door."

"Okey," I said. I blew smoke at the ceiling and stared at her.

She went towards the door, stopped, came back. She looked down at the floor.

"I don't rate much in it," she said. "Maybe not anything. But if I could have a grand or two waiting for Johnny when he came out, maybe—"

"Maybe you could hold him straight," I said. "It's a dream, Kathy. It's all a dream. But if it isn't, you cut an even third."

She caught her breath and glared at me to keep from crying. She went towards the door, stopped and came back again.

"That isn't all," she said. "It's the old guy—Sype. He did fifteen years. He paid. Paid hard. Doesn't it make you feel kind of mean?"

I shook my head. "He stole them, didn't he? He killed a man. What does he do for a living?"

"His wife has money," Kathy Horne said. "He just plays around with goldfish."

"Goldfish?" I said. "To hell with him."

She went on out.

2

The last time I had been in the Gray Lake district I had helped a D.A.'s man named Bernie Ohls shoot a gunman named Poke Andrews. But that was higher up the hill, farther away from the lake. This house was on the second level, in a loop the street made rounding a spur of the hill. It stood by itself high up, with a cracked retaining wall in front and several vacant lots behind.

Being originally a double house it had two front doors

and two sets of front steps. One of the doors had a sign tacked over the grating that masked the peep window: Ring 1432.

I parked my car and went up right-angled steps, passed between two lines of pinks, went up more steps to the side with the sign. That should be the roomer's side. I rang the bell. Nobody answered it, so I went across to the other door. Nobody answered that one either.

While I was waiting a gray Dodge coupe whished around the curve and a small neat girl in blue looked up at me for a second. I didn't see who else was in the car. I didn't pay much attention. I didn't know it was important.

I took out Kathy Horne's key and let myself into a closed living-room that smelled of cedar oil. There was just enough furniture to get by, net curtains, a quiet shaft of sunlight under the drapes in front. There was a tiny breakfast room, a kitchen, a bedroom in the back that was obviously Kathy's, a bathroom, another bedroom in front that seemed to be used as a sewing-room. It was this room that had the door cut through to the other side of the house.

I unlocked it and stepped, as it were, through a mirror. Everything was backwards, except the furniture. The living-room on that side had twin beds, didn't have the look of being lived in.

I went towards the back of the house, past the second bathroom, knocked at the shut door that corresponded to Kathy's bedroom.

No answer. I tried the knob and went in. The little man on the bed was probably Peeler Mardo. I noticed his feet first, because although he had on trousers and a shirt, his feet were bare and hung over the end of the bed. They were tied there by a rope around the ankles.

They had been burned raw on the soles. There was a smell of scorched flesh in spite of the open window. Also a smell of scorched wood. An electric iron on a desk was still connected. I went over and shut it off.

I went back to Kathy Horne's kitchen and found a pint of Brooklyn Scotch in the cooler. I used some of it and breathed deeply for a little while and looked out over the vacant lots.

There was a narrow cement walk behind the house and green wooden steps down to the street.

I went back to Peeler Mardo's room. The coat of a brown suit with a red pin stripe hung over a chair with the pockets turned out and what had been in them on the floor.

He was wearing the trousers of the suit, and their pockets were turned out also. Some keys and change and a handkerchief lay on the bed beside him, and a metal box like a woman's compact, from which some glistening white powder had spilled. Cocaine.

He was a little man, not more than five feet four, with thin brown hair and large ears. His eyes had no particular color. They were just eyes, and very wide open, and quite dead. His arms were pulled out from him and tied at the wrists by a rope that went under the bed.

I looked him over for bullet or knife wounds, didn't find any. There wasn't a mark on him except his feet. Shock or heart failure or a combination of the two must have done the trick. He was still warm. The gag in his mouth was both warm and wet.

I wiped off everything I had touched, looked out of Kathy's front window for a while before I left the house.

It was three-thirty when I walked into the lobby of the Mansion House, over to the cigar counter in the corner. I leaned on the glass and asked for Camels.

Kathy Horne flicked the pack at me, dropped the change into my outside breast pocket, and gave me her customer's smile.

"Well? You didn't take long," she said, and looked sidewise along her eyes at a drunk who was trying to light a cigar with the old-fashioned flint and steel lighter.

"It's heavy," I told her. "Get set."

She turned away quickly and flipped a pack of paper matches along the glass to the drunk. He fumbled for them, dropped both matches and cigar, scooped them angrily off the floor and went off looking back over his shoulder, as if he expected a kick.

Kathy looked past my head, her eyes cool and empty.

"I'm set," she whispered.

"You cut a full half," I said. "Peeler's out. He's been bumped off—in his bed."

Her eyes twitched. Two fingers curled on the glass near my elbow. A white line showed around her mouth. That was all.

"Listen," I said. "Don't say anything until I'm through. He died of shock. Somebody burned his feet with a cheap electric iron. Not yours, I looked. I'd say he died rather quickly and couldn't have said much. The gag was still in his mouth. When I went out there, frankly, I thought it was all hooey. Now I'm not so sure. If he gave up his dope, we're through, and so is Sype, unless I can find him first. Those workers didn't have any inhibitions at all. If he didn't give up, there's still time."

Her head turned, her set eyes looked towards the revolving door of the lobby entrance. White patches glared in her cheeks.

"What do I do?" she breathed.

I poked at a box of wrapped cigars, dropped her key into it. Her long fingers got it out smoothly, hid it.

"When you get home you find him. You don't know a thing. Leave the pearls out, leave me out. When they check his prints they'll know he had a record and they'll just figure it was something caught up with him."

I broke my cigarettes open and lit one, watched her for a moment. She didn't move an inch.

"Can you face it down?" I asked. "If you can't, now's the time to speak."

"Of course." Her eyebrows arched. "Do I look like a torturer?"

"You married a crook," I said grimly.

She flushed, which was what I wanted. "He isn't! He's just a damn fool! Nobody thinks any the worse of me, not even the boys down at Headquarters."

"All right. I like it that way. It's not our murder, after all. And if we talk now, you can say good-by to any share in any reward—even if one is ever paid."

"Darn tootin'," Kathy Horne said pertly. "Oh, the poor little runt," she almost sobbed.

I patted her arm, grinned as heartily as I could and left the Mansion House.

3

The Reliance Indemnity Company had offices in the Graas Building, three small rooms that looked like nothing at all. They were a big enough outfit to be as shabby as they liked.

The resident manager was named Lutin, a middle-aged bald-headed man with quiet eyes, dainty fingers that caressed a dappled cigar. He sat behind a large, well-dusted desk and stared peacefully at my chin.

"Carmady, eh? I've heard of you." He touched my card with a shiny little finger. "What's on your mind?"

I rolled a cigarette around in my fingers and lowered my voice. "Remember the Leander pearls?"

His smile was slow, a little bored. "I'm not likely to forget them. They cost this company one hundred and fifty thousand dollars. I was a cocky young adjuster then."

I said: "I've got an idea. It may be all haywire. It very likely is. But I'd like to try it out. Is your twenty-five grand reward still good?"

He chuckled. "Twenty grand, Carmady. We spent the difference ourselves. You're wasting time."

"It's my time. Twenty it is then. How much co-operation can I get?"

"What kind of co-operation?"

"Can I have a letter identifying me to your other branches? In case I have to go out of the State. In case I need kind words from some local law."

"Which way out of the State?"

I smiled at him. He tapped his cigar on the edge of a tray and smiled back. Neither of our smiles was honest.

"No letter," he said. "New York wouldn't stand for it. We have our own tie-up. But all the co-operation you can use, under the hat. And the twenty grand, if you click. Of course you won't."

I lit my cigarette and leaned back, puffed smoke at the ceiling.

"No? Why not? You never got those marbles. They existed, didn't they?"

"Darn' right they existed. And if they still do, they belong to us. But two hundred grand doesn't get buried for twenty years—and then get dug up."

"All right. It's still my own time."

He knocked a little ash off his cigar and looked down his eyes at me. "I like your front," he said, "even if you are crazy. But we're a large organization. Suppose I have you covered from now on. What then?"

"I lose. I'll know I'm covered. I'm too long in the game to miss that. I'll quit, give up what I know to the law, and go home."

"Why would you do that?"

I leaned forward over the desk again. "Because," I said slowly, "the guy that had the lead got bumped off today."

"Oh—oh." Lutin rubbed his nose.

"I didn't bump him off," I added.

We didn't talk any more for a little while. Then Lutin said: "You don't want any letter. You wouldn't even carry it. And after your telling me that, you know damn' well I won't dare give it to you."

I stood up, grinned, started for the door. He got up himself, very fast, ran around the desk and put his small neat hand on my arm.

"Listen, I know you're crazy, but if you do get anything, bring it in through our boys. We need the advertising."

"What the hell do you think I live on?" I growled.

"Twenty-five grand."

"I thought it was twenty."

"Twenty-five. And you're still crazy. Sype never had those pearls. If he had, he'd have made some kind of terms with us many years ago."

"Okey," I said. "You've had plenty of time to make up your mind."

We shook hands, grinned at each other like a couple of wise boys who know they're not kidding anybody, but won't give up trying.

It was a quarter to five when I got back to the office. I had a couple of short drinks and stuffed a pipe and sat down to interview my brains. The phone rang.

A woman's voice said: "Carmady?" It was a small, tight, cold voice. I didn't know it.

"Yeah."

"Better see Rush Madder. Know him?"

"No," I lied. "Why should I see him?"

There was sudden tinkling, icy-cold laugh on the wire. "On account of a guy had sore feet," the voice said.

The phone clicked. I put my end of it aside, struck a match and stared at the wall until the flame burned my fingers.

Rush Madder was a shyster in the Quorn Building. An ambulance chaser, a small time fixer, an alibi builder-upper, anything that smelled a little and paid a little more. I hadn't heard of him in connection with any big operations like burning people's feet.

4

It was getting toward quitting time on lower Spring Street. Taxis were dawdling close to the curb, stenographers were getting an early start home, street cars were clogging up, and traffic cops were preventing people from making perfectly legal right turns.

The Quorn Building was a narrow front, the color of dried mustard, with a large case of false teeth in the entrance. The directory held the names of painless dentists, people who teach you how to become a letter-carrier, just names, and numbers without any names. Rush Madder, Attorney-at-Law, was in Room 619.

I got out of a jolting open cage elevator, looked at a dirty spittoon on a dirty rubber mat, walked down a corridor that smelled of butts, and tried the knob below the frosted glass panel of 619. The door was locked. I knocked.

A shadow came against the glass and the door was pulled back with a squeak. I was looking at a thick-set man with a soft round chin, heavy black eyebrows, an oily complexion and a Charlie Chan mustache that made his face look fatter than it was.

He put out a couple of nicotined fingers. "Well, well, the old dog-catcher himself. The eye that never forgets. Carmady is the name, I believe?"

I stepped inside and waited for the door to squeak shut. A bare carpetless room paved in brown linoleum, a flat desk and a rolltop at right angles to it, a big green safe that looked as fireproof as a delicatessen bag, two filing cases, three chairs, a built-in closet and washbowl in the corner by the door.

"Well, well, sit down," Madder said. "Glad to see you." He fussed around behind his desk and adjusted a burst-out seat cushion, sat on it. "Nice of you to drop around. Business?"

I sat down and put a cigarette between my teeth and looked at him. I didn't say a word. I watched him start to sweat. It started up in his hair. Then he grabbed a pencil and made marks on his blotter. Then he looked at me with a quick darting glance, down at his blotter again. He talked—to the blotter.

"Any ideas?" he asked softly.

"About what?"

He didn't look at me. "About how we could do a little business together. Say, in stones."

"Who was the wren?" I asked.

"Huh? What wren?" He still didn't look at me.

"The one that phoned me."

"Did somebody phone you?"

I reached for his telephone, which was the old-fashioned gallows type. I lifted off the receiver and started to dial the number of Police Headquarters, very slowly. I knew he would know that number about as well as he knew his hat.

He reached over and pushed the hook down. "Now, listen," he complained. "You're too fast. What you calling copper for?"

I said slowly: "They want to talk to you. On account of you know a broad that knows a man had sore feet."

"Does it have to be that way?" His collar was too tight now. He yanked at it.

"Not from my side. But if you think I'm going to sit here and let you play with my reflexes, it does."

Madder opened a flat tin of cigarettes and pushed one past his lips with a sound like somebody gutting a fish. His hand shook.

"All right," he said thickly. "All right. Don't get sore."

"Just stop trying to count clouds with me," I growled. "Talk sense. If you've got a job for me, it's probably too dirty for me to touch. But I'll at least listen."

He nodded. He was comfortable now. He knew I was bluffing. He puffed a pale swirl of smoke and watched it float up.

"That's all right," he said evenly. "I play dumb myself once in a while. The thing is we're wise. Carol saw you go to the house and leave it again. No law came."

"Carol?"

"Carol Donovan. Friend of mine. She called you up."

I nodded. "Go ahead."

He didn't say anything. He just sat there and looked at me owlishly.

I grinned and leaned across the desk a little and said: "Here's what's bothering you. You don't know why I went to the house or why, having gone, I didn't yell police. That's easy. I thought it was a secret."

"We're just kidding each other," Madder said sourly.

"All right," I said. "Let's talk about pearls. Does that make it any easier?"

His eyes shone. He wanted to let himself get excited, but he didn't. He kept his voice down, said coolly:

"Carol picked him up one night, the little guy. A crazy little number, full of snow, but way back in his noodle an idea. He'd talk about pearls, about an old guy up in the northwest of Canada that swiped them a long time ago and still had them. Only he wouldn't say who the old guy was or where he was. Foxy about that. Holding out. I wouldn't know why."

"He wanted to get his feet burned," I said.

Madder's lips shook and another fine sweat showed in his hair.

"I didn't do that," he said thickly.

"You or Carol, what's the odds? The little guy died. They can make murder out of it. You didn't find out what you wanted to know. That's why *I'm* here. You think I have information you didn't get. Forget it. If I knew enough, I wouldn't be here, and if you knew enough, you wouldn't want me here. Check?"

He grinned, very slowly, as if it hurt him. He struggled up in his chair and dragged a deep drawer out from the side of his desk, put a nicely molded brown bottle up on the desk, and two striped glasses. He whispered: "Two-way split. You and me. I'm cutting Carol out. She's too damn' rough, Carmady. I've seen hard women, but she's the bluing on armor plate. And you'd never think it to look at her, would you?"

"Have I seen her?"

"I guess so. She says you did."

"Oh, the girl in the Dodge."

He nodded, and poured two good-sized drinks, put the bottle down and stood up. "Water? I like it in mine."

"No," I said, "but why cut me in? I don't know any more than you mentioned. Or very little. Certainly not as much as you must know to go that far."

He leered across the glasses. "I know where I can get fifty grand for the Leander pearls, twice what you could get. I can give you yours and still have mine. You've got the front I need to work in the open. How about the water?"

"No water," I said.

He went across to the built-in wash place and ran the water and came back with his glass half full. He sat down again, grinned, lifted it.

We drank.

5

So far I had only made four mistakes. The first was mixing in at all, even for Kathy Horne's sake. The second was staying mixed after I found Peeler Mardo dead. The third was letting Rush Madder see I knew what he was talking about. The fourth, the whiskey, was the worst.

It tasted funny even on the way down. Then there was that sudden moment of sharp lucidity when I knew, exactly as though I had seen it, that he had switched his drink for a harmless one cached in the closet.

I sat still for a moment, with the empty glass at my fingers' ends, gathering my strength. Madder's face began to get large and moony and vague. A fat smile jerked in and out under his Charlie Chan mustache as he watched me.

I reached back into my hip pocket and pulled out a loosely wadded handkerchief. The small safe inside it didn't seem to show. At least Madder didn't move, after his first grab under the coat.

I stood up and swayed forward drunkenly and smacked him square on the top of the head.

He gagged. He started to get up. I tapped him on the jaw. He became limp and his hand sweeping down from under his coat knocked his glass over on the desk top. I straightened it, stood silent, listening, struggling with a rising wave of nauseous stupor.

I went over to a communicating door and tried the knob. It was locked. I was staggering by now. I dragged an office chair to the entrance door and propped the back of it under the knob. I leaned against the door panting, gritting my teeth, cursing myself. I got handcuffs out and started back towards Madder.

A very pretty black-haired, gray-eyed girl stepped out of the clothes closet and poked a .32 at me.

She wore a blue suit cut with a lot of snap. An inverted saucer of a hat came down in a hard line across her forehead. Shiny black hair showed at the sides. Her eyes were slate-gray, cold, and yet lighthearted. Her face was fresh and young and delicate and as hard as a chisel.

"All right, Carmady. Lie down and sleep it off. You're through."

I stumbled towards her waving my sap. She shook her head. When her face moved it got large before my eyes. Its outlines changed and wobbled. The gun in her hand looked like anything from a tunnel to a toothpick.

"Don't be a goof, Carmady," she said. "A few hours sleep for you, a few hours start for us. Don't make me shoot. I would."

"Damn you," I mumbled. "I believe you would."

"Right as rain, toots. I'm a lady that wants her own way. That's fine. Sit down."

The floor rose up and bumped me. I sat on it as on a raft in a rough sea. I braced myself on flat hands. I could hardly feel the floor. My hands were numb. My whole body was numb.

I tried to stare her down. "Ha-a! L-lady K-killer!" I giggled.

She threw a chilly laugh at me which I only just barely heard. Drums were beating in my head now, war drums from a far off jungle. Waves of light were moving, and dark shadows and a rustle as of a wind in treetops. I didn't want to lie down. I lay down.

The girl's voice came from very far off, an elfin voice.

"Two-way split, eh? He doesn't like my method, eh? Bless his big soft heart. We'll see about him."

Vaguely as I floated off I seemed to feel a dull jar that might have been a shot. I hoped she had shot Madder, but she hadn't. She had merely helped me on my way out—with my own sap.

When I came around again it was night. Something clacked overhead with a heavy sound. Through the open window beyond the desk yellow light splashed on the high side walls of a building. The thing clacked again and the light went off. An advertising sign on the roof.

I got up off the floor like a man climbing out of thick mud. I waded over to the washbowl, sloshed water on my face, felt the top of my head and winced, waded back to the door and found the light switch.

Strewn papers lay around the desk, broken pencils, envelopes, an empty brown whiskey bottle, cigarette ends and ashes. The debris of hastily emptied drawers. I didn't bother going through any of it. I left the office, rode down to the street in the shuddering elevator, slid into a bar and had a brandy, then got my car and drove on home.

I changed clothes, packed a bag, had some whiskey and answered the telephone. It was about nine-thirty.

Kathy Horne's voice said: "So you're not gone yet. I hoped you wouldn't be."

"Alone?" I asked, still thick in the voice.

"Yes, but I haven't been. The house has been full of coppers for hours. They were very nice, considering. Old grudge of some kind, they figured."

"And the line is likely tapped now," I growled. "Where was I supposed to be going?"

"Well—you know. Your girl told me."

"Little dark girl? Very cool? Name of Carol Donovan?"

"She had your card. Why, wasn't it—"

"I don't have any girl," I said simply. "And I bet that just very casually, without thinking at all, a name slipped past your lips—the name of a town up north. Did it?"

"Ye-es," Kathy Horne admitted weakly.

I caught the night plane north.

It was a nice trip except that I had a sore head and a raging thirst for ice water.

6

The Snoqualmie Hotel in Olympia was on Capitol Way, fronting on the usual square city block of park. I left by the coffee shop door and walked down a hill to where the last, loneliest reach of Puget Sound died and decomposed against a line of disused wharves. Corded firewood filled the foreground and old men pottered about in the middle of the stacks, or sat on boxes with pipes in their mouths and signs behind their heads reading: "Firewood and Split Kindling. Free Delivery."

Behind them a low cliff rose and the vast pines of the north loomed against a gray-blue sky.

Two of the old men sat on boxes about twenty feet apart, ignoring each other. I drifted near one of them. He wore corduroy pants and what had been a red and black mackinaw. His felt hat showed the sweat of twenty summers. One of his hands clutched a short black pipe, and with the grimed fingers of the other he slowly, carefully, ecstatically jerked at a long curling hair that grew out of his nose.

I set a box on end, sat down, filled my own pipe, lit it, puffed a cloud of smoke. I waved a hand at the water and said:

"You'd never think that ever met the Pacific Ocean."

He looked at me.

I said: "Dead end—quiet, restful, like your town. I like a town like this."

He went on looking at me.

"I'll bet," I said, "that a man that's been around a town like this knows everybody in it and in the country near it."

He said: "How much you bet?"

I took a silver dollar out of my pocket. They still had a few up there. The old man looked it over, nodded, suddenly yanked the long hair out of his nose and held it up against the light.

"You'd lose," he said.

I put the dollar down on my knee. "Know anybody around here that keeps a lot of goldfish?" I asked.

He stared at the dollar. The other old man near by was wearing overalls and shoes without any laces. He stared at the dollar. They both spat at the same instant. The first old man turned his head and yelled at the top of his voice:

"Know anybody keeps goldfish?"

The other old man jumped up off his box and seized a big ax, set a log on end and whanged the ax down on it, splitting it evenly. He looked at the first old man triumphantly and screamed:

"I ain't neither."

The first old man said: "Leetle deef." He got up slowly and went over to a shack built of old boards of uneven lengths. He went into it, banged the door.

The second old man threw his ax down pettishly, spat in the direction of the closed door and went off among the stacks of cordwood.

The door of the shack opened, the man in the mackinaw poked his head out of it.

"Sewer crabs is all," he said, and slammed the door again.

I put my dollar in my pocket and went back up the hill. I figured it would take too long to learn their language.

Capitol Way ran north and south. A dull green street car shuttled past on the way to a place called Tumwater. In the distance I could see the government buildings. Northward the street passed two hotels and some stores and branched right and left. Right went to Tacoma and Seattle. Left went over a bridge and out on to the Olympic Peninsula.

Beyond this right and left turn the street suddenly became old and shabby, with broken asphalt paving, a Chinese restaurant, a boarded up movie house, a pawnbroker's establishment. A sign jutting over the dirty sidewalk said: "Smoke Shop," and in small letters underneath, as if it hoped nobody was looking, "Pool."

I went in past a rack of gaudy magazines and a cigar show-

case that had flies inside it. There was a long wooden counter
on the left, a few slot machines, a single pool table. Three
kids fiddled with the slot machines and a tall thin man with a
long nose and no chin played pool all by himself, with a dead
cigar in his face.

I sat on a stool and a hard-eyed bald-headed man behind
the counter got up from a chair, wiped his hands on a thick
gray apron, showed me a gold tooth.

"A little rye," I said. "Know anybody that keeps goldfish?"

"Yeah," he said. "No."

He poured something behind the counter and shoved a
thick glass across.

"Two bits."

I sniffed the stuff, wrinkled my nose. "Was it the rye the
'yeah' was for?"

The bald-headed man held up a large bottle with a label
that said something about: "Cream of Dixie Straight Rye
Whiskey Guaranteed at Least Four Months Old."

"Okey," I said. "I see it just moved in."

I poured some water in it and drank it. It tasted like a
cholera culture. I put a quarter on the counter. The barman
showed me a gold tooth on the other side of his face and
took hold of the counter with two hard hands and pushed his
chin at me.

"What was that crack?" he asked, almost gently.

"I just moved in," I said. "I'm looking for some goldfish
for the front window. Goldfish."

The barman said very slowly: "Do I look like a guy would
know a guy would have goldfish?" His face was a little white.

The long-nosed man who had been playing himself a round
of pool racked his cue and strolled over to the counter beside
me and threw a nickel on it.

"Draw me a coke before you get too nervous yourself," he
told the barman.

The barman pried himself loose from the counter with a
good deal of effort. I looked down to see if his fingers had
made any dents in the wood. He drew a coke, stirred it with a
swizzle-stick, dumped it on the bar top, took a deep breath
and let it out through his nose, grunted and went away towards a door marked: "Toilet."

The long-nosed man lifted his coke and looked into the smeared mirror behind the bar. The left side of his mouth twitched briefly. A dim voice came from it, saying: "How's Peeler?"

I pressed my thumb and forefinger together, put them to my nose, sniffed, shook my head sadly.

"Hitting it high, huh?"

"Yeah," I said. "I didn't catch the name."

"Call me Sunset. I'm always movin' west. Think he'll stay clammed?"

"He'll stay clammed," I said.

"What's your handle?"

"Dodge Willis, El Paso," I said.

"Got a room somewhere?"

"Hotel."

He put his glass down empty. "Let's dangle."

7

We went up to my room and sat down and looked at each other over a couple of glasses of Scotch and ginger ale. Sunset studied me with his close-set expressionless eyes, a little at a time, but very thoroughly in the end, adding it all up.

I sipped my drink and waited. At last he said in his lipless "stir" voice:

"How come Peeler didn't come hisself?"

"For the same reason he didn't stay when he was here."

"Meaning which?"

"Figure it out for yourself," I said.

He nodded, just as though I had said something with a meaning. Then:

"What's the top price?"

"Twenty-five grand."

"Nuts." Sunset was emphatic, even rude.

I leaned back and lit a cigarette, puffed smoke at the open window and watched the breeze pick it up and tear it to pieces.

"Listen," Sunset complained. "I don't know you from last Sunday's sports section. You may be all to the silk. I just don't know."

"Why'd you brace me?" I asked.

"You had the word, didn't you?"

This was where I took the dive. I grinned at him. "Yeah. Goldfish was the password. The Smoke Shop was the place."

His lack of expression told me I was right. It was one of those breaks you dream of, but don't handle right even in dreams.

"Well, what's the next angle?" Sunset inquired, sucking a piece of ice out of his glass and chewing on it.

I laughed. "Okey, Sunset. I'm satisfied you're cagey. We could go on like this for weeks. Let's put our cards on the table. Where is the old guy?"

Sunset tightened his lips, moistened them, tightened them again. He set his glass down very slowly and his right hand hung lax on his thigh. I knew I had made a mistake, that Peeler knew where the old guy was, exactly. Therefore I should know.

Nothing in Sunset's voice showed I had made a mistake. He said crossly: "You mean why don't I put my cards on the table and you just sit back and look 'em over. Nix."

"Then how do you like this?" I growled. "Peeler's dead."

One eyebrow twitched, and one corner of his mouth. His eyes got a little blanker than before, if possible. His voice rasped lightly, like a finger on dry leather.

"How come?"

"Competition you two didn't know about." I leaned back, smiled.

The gun made a soft metallic blur in the sunshine. I hardly saw where it came from. Then the muzzle was round and dark and empty looking at me.

"You're kidding the wrong guy," Sunset said lifelessly. "I ain't no soft spot for chiselers to lie on."

I folded my arms, taking care that my right hand was outside, in view.

"I would be—if I was kidding. I'm not. Peeler played with a girl and she milked him—up to a point. He didn't tell her where to find the old fellow. So she and her top man went to see Peeler where he lived. They used a hot iron on his feet. He died of the shock."

Sunset looked unimpressed. "I got a lot of room in my ears yet," he said.

"So have I," I snarled, suddenly pretending anger. "Just what the hell have you said that means anything—except that you know Peeler?"

He spun his gun on his trigger finger, watching it spin. "Old man Sype's at Westport," he said casually. "That mean anything to you?"

"Yeah. Has he got the marbles?"

"How the hell would I know?" He steadied the gun again, dropped it to his thigh. It wasn't pointing at me now. "Where's this competish you mentioned?"

"I hope I ditched them," I said. "I'm not too sure. Can I put my hands down and take a drink?"

"Yeah, go ahead. How did you cut in?"

"Peeler roomed with the wife of a friend of mine who's in stir. A straight girl, one you can trust. He let her in and she passed it to me—afterwards."

"After the bump? How many cuts your side? My half is set."

I took my drink, shoved the empty glass away. "The hell it is."

The gun lifted an inch, dropped again. "How many altogether?" he snapped.

"Three, now Peeler's out. If we can hold off the competition."

"The feet-toasters? No trouble about that. What they look like?"

"Man named Rush Madder, a shyster down south, fifty, fat, thin down-curving mustache, dark hair thin on top, five-nine, a hundred and eighty, not much guts. The girl, Carol Donovan, black hair, long bob, gray eyes, pretty, small features, twenty-five to eight, five-two, hundred twenty, last seen wearing blue, hard as they come. The real iron in the combination."

Sunset nodded indifferently and put his gun away. "We'll soften her, if she pokes her snoot in," he said. "I've got a heap at the house. Let's take the air Westport way and look it over. You might be able to ease in on the goldfish angle. They say he's nuts about them. I'll stay under cover. He's too stir-wise for me. I smell of the bucket."

"Swell," I said heartily. "I'm an old goldfish fancier myself."

Sunset reached for the bottle, poured two fingers of Scotch and put it down. He stood up, twitched his collar straight, then shot his chinless jaw forward as far as it would go.

"But don't make no error, bo. It's goin' to take pressure. It's goin' to mean a run out in the deep woods and some thumb-twisting. Snatch stuff, likely."

"That's okey," I said. "The insurance people are behind us."

Sunset jerked down the points of his vest and rubbed the back of his thin neck. I put my hat on, locked the Scotch in the bag by the chair I'd been sitting in, went over and shut the window.

We started towards the door. Knuckles rattled on it just as I reached for the knob. I gestured Sunset back along the wall. I stared at the door for a moment and then I opened it up.

The two guns came forward almost on the same level, one small—a .32, one a big Smith and Wesson. They couldn't come into the room abreast, so the girl came in first.

"Okey, hot shot," she said dryly. "Ceiling zero. See if you can reach it."

8

I backed slowly into the room. The two visitors bored in on me, either side. I tripped over my bag and fell backwards, hit the floor and rolled on my side groaning.

Sunset said casually: "H'ist 'em, folks. Pretty now!"

Two heads jerked away from looking down at me and then I had my gun loose, down at my side. I kept on groaning.

There was a silence. I didn't hear any guns fall. The door of the room was still wide open and Sunset was flattened against the wall more or less behind it.

The girl said between her teeth: "Cover the shamus, Rush—and shut the door. Skinny can't shoot here. Nobody can." Then, in a whisper I barely caught, she added: "Slam it!"

Rush Madder waddled backwards across the room keeping

the Smith and Wesson pointed my way. His back was to Sunset and the thought of that made his eyes roll. I could have shot him easily enough, but it wasn't the play. Sunset stood with his feet spread and his tongue showing. Something that could have been a smile wrinkled his flat eyes.

He stared at the girl and she stared at him. Their guns stared at each other.

Rush Madder reached the door, grabbed the edge of it and gave it a hard swing. I knew exactly what was going to happen. As the door slammed the .32 was going to go off. It wouldn't be heard if it went off at the right instant. The explosion would be lost in the slamming of the door.

I reached out and took hold of Carol Donovan's ankle and jerked it hard.

The door slammed. Her gun went off and chipped the ceiling.

She whirled on me kicking. Sunset said in his tight but somehow penetrating drawl:

"If this is it, this is it. Let's go!" The hammer clicked back on his Colt.

Something in his voice steadied Carol Donovan. She relaxed, let her automatic fall to her side and stepped away from me with a vicious look back.

Madder turned the key in the door and leaned against the wood, breathing noisily. His hat had tipped over one ear and the ends of two strips of adhesive showed under the brim.

Nobody moved while I had these thoughts. There was no sound of feet outside in the hall, no alarm. I got up on my knees, slid my gun out of sight, rose on my feet and went over to the window. Nobody down on the sidewalk was staring up at the upper floors of the Snoqualmie Hotel.

I sat on the broad old-fashioned sill and looked faintly embarrassed, as though the minister had said a bad word.

The girl snapped at me: "Is this lug your partner?"

I didn't answer. Her face flushed slowly and her eyes burned. Madder put a hand out and fussed:

"Now listen, Carol, now listen here. This sort of act ain't the way—"

"Shut up!"

"Yeah," Madder said in a clogged voice. "Sure."

Sunset looked the girl over lazily for the third or fourth time. His gun hand rested easily against his hipbone and his whole attitude was of complete relaxation. Having seen him pull his gun once I hoped the girl wasn't fooled.

He said slowly: "We've heard about you two. What's your offer? I wouldn't listen even, only I can't stand a shooting rap."

The girl said: "There's enough in it for four." Madder nodded his big head vigorously, almost managed a smile.

Sunset glanced at me. I nodded. "Four it is," he sighed. "But that's the top. We'll go to my place and gargle. I don't like it here."

"We must look simple," the girl said nastily.

"Kill-simple," Sunset drawled. "I've met lots of them. That's why we're going to talk it over. It's not a shooting play."

Carol Donovan slipped a suede bag from under her left arm and tucked her .32 into it. She smiled. She was pretty when she smiled.

"My ante is in," she said quietly. "I'll play. Where is the place?"

"Out Water Street. We'll go in a hack."

"Lead on, sport."

We went out of the room and down in the elevator, four friendly people walking out through a lobby full of antlers and stuffed birds and pressed wildflowers in glass frames. The taxi went out Capitol Way, past the square, past a big red apartment house that was too big for the town except when the Legislature was sitting. Along car tracks past the distant Capitol buildings and the high closed gates of the governor's mansion.

Oak trees bordered the sidewalks. A few largish residences showed behind garden walls. The taxi shot past them and veered on to a road that led towards the tip of the Sound. In a short while a house showed in a narrow clearing between tall trees. Water glistened far back behind the tree trunks. The house had a roofed porch, a small lawn rotten with weeds and overgrown bushes. There was a shed at the end of a dirt driveway and an antique touring car squatted under the shed.

We got out and I paid the taxi. All four of us carefully watched it out of sight. Then Sunset said:

"My place is upstairs. There's a schoolteacher lives down below. She ain't home. Let's go up and gargle."

We crossed the lawn to the porch and Sunset threw a door open, pointed up narrow steps.

"Ladies first. Lead on, beautiful. Nobody locks a door in this town."

The girl gave him a cool glance and passed him to go up the stairs. I went next, then Madder, Sunset last.

The single room that made up most of the second floor was dark from the trees, had a dormer window, a wide daybed pushed back under the slope of the roof, a table, some wicker chairs, a small radio and a round black stove in the middle of the floor.

Sunset drifted into a kitchenette and came back with a square bottle and some glasses. He poured drinks, lifted one and left the others on the table.

We helped ourselves and sat down.

Sunset put his drink down in a lump, leaned over to put his glass on the floor and came up with his Colt out.

I heard Madder's gulp in the sudden cold silence. The girl's mouth twitched as if she were going to laugh. Then she leaned forward, holding her glass on top of her bag with her left hand.

Sunset slowly drew his lips into a thin straight line. He said slowly and carefully: "Feet-burners, huh? Burned my pal's feet, huh?"

Madder choked, started to spread his fat hands. The Colt flicked at him. He put his hands on his knees and clutched his kneecaps.

"And suckers at that," Sunset went on tiredly. "Burn a guy's feet to make him sing and then walk right into the parlor of one of his pals. You couldn't tie that with Christmas ribbon."

Madder said jerkily: "All r-right. W-what's the p-pay-off?" The girl smiled slightly but she didn't say anything.

Sunset grinned. "Rope," he said softly. "A lot of rope tied in hard knots, with water on it. Then me and my pal trundle off to catch fireflies—pearls to you—and when we come back—" he stopped, drew his left hand across the front of his throat. "Like the idea?" he glanced at me.

"Yeah, but don't make a song about it," I said. "Where's the rope?"

"Bureau," Sunset answered, and pointed with one ear at the corner.

I started in that direction, by way of the walls. Madder made a sudden thin whimpering noise and his eyes turned up in his head and he fell straight forward off the chair on his face, in a dead faint.

That jarred Sunset. He hadn't expected anything so foolish. His right hand jerked around until the Colt was pointing down at Madder's back.

The girl slipped her hand under her bag. The bag lifted an inch. The gun that was caught there in a trick clip—the gun that Sunset thought was inside the bag—spat and flamed briefly.

Sunset coughed. His Colt boomed and a piece of wood detached itself from the back of the chair Madder had been sitting in. Sunset dropped the Colt and put his chin down on his chest and tried to look at the ceiling. His long legs slid out in front of him and his heels made a rasping sound on the floor. He sat like that, limp, his chin on his chest, his eyes looking upward. Dead as a pickled walnut.

I kicked Miss Donovan's chair out from under her and she banged down on her side in a swirl of silken legs. Her hat went crooked on her head. She yelped. I stood on her hand and then shifted suddenly and kicked her gun clear across the attic. I sent her bag after it—with her other gun inside it. She screamed at me.

"Get up," I snarled.

She got up slowly, backed away from me biting her lip, savage-eyed, suddenly a nasty-faced little brat at bay. She kept on backing until the wall stopped her. Her eyes glittered in a ghastly face.

I glanced down at Madder, went over to a closed door. A bathroom was behind it. I reversed a key and gestured at the girl.

"In."

She walked stiff-legged across the floor and passed in front of me, almost touching me.

"Listen a minute, shamus—"

I pushed her through the door and slammed it and turned the key. It was all right with me if she wanted to jump out of the window. I had seen the windows from below.

I went across to Sunset, felt him, felt the small hard lump of keys on a ring in his pocket, and got them out without quite knocking him off his chair. I didn't look for anything else.

There were car keys on the ring.

I looked at Madder again, noticed that his fingers were as white as snow. I went down the narrow dark stairs to the porch, around to the side of the house and got into the old touring car under the shed. One of the keys on the ring fitted its ignition lock.

The car took a beating before it started up and let me back it down the dirt driveway to the curb. Nothing moved in the house that I saw or heard. The tall pines behind and beside the house stirred their upper branches listlessly and a cold heartless sunlight sneaked through them intermittently as they moved.

I drove back to Capitol Way and downtown again as fast as I dared, past the square and the Snoqualmie Hotel and over the bridge towards the Pacific Ocean and Westport.

9

An hour's fast driving through thinned-out timberland, interrupted by three stops for water and punctuated by the cough of a head gasket leak, brought me within sound of surf. The broad white road, striped with yellow down the center, swept around the flank of a hill, a distant cluster of buildings loomed up in front of the shine of the ocean, and the road forked. The left fork was signposted: "Westport—9 Miles," and didn't go towards the buildings. It crossed a rusty cantilever bridge and plunged into a region of wind-distorted apple orchards.

Twenty minutes more and I chugged into Westport, a sandy spit of land with scattered frame houses dotted over

rising ground behind it. The end of the spit was a long narrow pier, and the end of the pier a cluster of sailing boats with
half-lowered sails flapping against their single masts. And
beyond them a buoyed channel and a long irregular line
where the water creamed on a hidden sandbar.

Beyond the sandbar the Pacific rolled over to Japan. This
was the last outpost of the coast, the farthest west a man
could go and still be on the mainland of the United States. A
swell place for an ex-convict to hide out with a couple of
somebody else's pearls the size of new potatoes—if he didn't
have any enemies.

I pulled up in front of a cottage that had a sign in the yard:
"Luncheons, Teas, Dinners." A small rabbit-faced man with
freckles was waving a garden rake at two black chickens. The
chickens appeared to be sassing him back. He turned when
the engine of Sunset's car coughed itself still.

I got out, went through a wicket gate, pointed to the sign.
"Luncheon ready?"

He threw the rake at the chickens, wiped his hands on his
trousers and leered. "The wife put that up," he confided to
me in a thin, impish voice. "Ham and eggs is what it means."

"Ham and eggs get along with me," I said.

We went into the house. There were three tables covered
with patterned oilcloth, some chromos on the walls, a full-
rigged ship in a bottle on the mantel. I sat down. The host
went away through a swing door and somebody yelled at him
and a sizzling noise was heard from the kitchen. He came
back and leaned over my shoulder, put some cutlery and a
paper napkin on the oilcloth.

"Too early for apple brandy, ain't it?" he whispered.

I told him how wrong he was. He went away again and
came back with glasses and a quart of clear amber fluid. He
sat down with me and poured. A rich baritone voice in the
kitchen was singing "Chloe," over the sizzling.

We clinked glasses and drank and waited for the heat to
crawl up our spines.

"Stranger, ain't you?" the little man asked.

I said I was.

"From Seattle maybe? That's a nice piece of goods you got
on."

"Seattle," I agreed.

"We don't git many strangers," he said, looking at my left ear. "Ain't on the way to nowheres. Now before repeal—" he stopped, shifted his sharp, woodpecker gaze to my other ear.

"Ah, before repeal," I said with a large gesture, and drank knowingly.

He leaned over and breathed on my chin. "Hell, you could load up in any fish stall on the pier. The stuff come in under catches of crabs and oysters. Hell, Westport was lousy with it. They give the kids cases of Scotch to play with. There wasn't a car in this town, that slept in a garage, mister. The garages was all full to the roof of Canadian hooch. Hell, they had a coast-guard cutter off the pier watchin' the boats unload one day every week. Friday. Always the same day." He winked.

I puffed a cigarette and the sizzling noise and the baritone rendering of "Chloe" went on in the kitchen.

"But hell, you wouldn't be in the liquor business," he said.

"Hell, no. I'm a goldfish buyer," I said.

"Okey," he said sulkily.

I poured us another round of the apple-brandy. "This bottle is on me," I said. "And I'm taking a couple more with me."

He brightened up. "What did you say the name was?"

"Carmady. You think I'm kidding you about the goldfish. I'm not."

"Hell, there ain't a livin' in them little fellers, is there?"

I held my sleeve out. "You said it was a nice piece of goods. Sure there's a living out of the fancy brands. New brands, new types all the time. My information is there's an old guy down here somewhere that has a real collection. Maybe would sell it. Some he's bred himself."

I poured us another round of the apple brandy. A large woman with a mustache kicked the swing door open a foot and yelled: "Pick up the ham and eggs!"

My host scuttled across and came back with my food. I ate. He watched me minutely. After a time he suddenly smacked his skinny leg under the table.

"Old Wallace," he chuckled. "Sure, you come to see old

Wallace. Hell, we don't know him right well. He don't act neighborly."

He turned around in his chair and pointed out through the sleazy curtains at a distant hill. On top of the hill was a yellow and white house that shone in the sun.

"Hell, that's where he lives. He's got a mess of them. Goldfish, huh? Hell, you could bend me with an eye dropper."

That ended my interest in the little man. I gobbled my food, paid off for it and for three quarts of apple brandy at a dollar a quart, shook hands and went back out to the touring car.

There didn't seem to be any hurry. Rush Madder would come out of his faint, and he would turn the girl loose. But they didn't know anything about Westport. Sunset hadn't mentioned the name in their presence. They didn't know it when they reached Olympia, or they would have gone there at once. And if they had listened outside my room at the hotel, they would have known I wasn't alone. They hadn't acted as if they knew that when they charged in.

I had lots of time. I drove down to the pier and looked it over. It looked tough. There were fishstalls, drinking dives, a tiny honkytonk for the fishermen, a pool room, an arcade of slot machines and smutty peep shows. Bait fish squirmed and darted in big wooden tanks down in the water along the piles. There were loungers and they looked like trouble for anyone that tried to interfere with them. I didn't see any law enforcement around.

I drove back up the hill to the yellow and white house. It stood very much alone, four blocks from the next nearest dwelling. There were flowers in front, a trimmed green lawn, a rock garden. A woman in a brown and white print dress was popping at aphids with a spray-gun.

I let my heap stall itself, got out and took my hat off.

"Mister Wallace live here?"

She had a handsome face, quiet, firm-looking. She nodded.

"Would you like to see him?" She had a quiet firm voice, a good accent.

It didn't sound like the voice of a train-robber's wife.

I gave her my name, said I'd been hearing about his fish down in the town. I was interested in fancy goldfish.

She put the spray gun down and went into the house. Bees

buzzed around my head, large fuzzy bees that wouldn't mind the cold wind off the sea. Far off like background music the surf pounded on the sandbars. The northern sunshine seemed bleak to me, had no heat in the core of it.

The woman came out of the house and held the door open.

"He's at the top of the stairs," she said, "if you'd like to go up."

I went past a couple of rustic rockers and into the house of the man who had stolen the Leander pearls.

10

Fish tanks were all around the big room, two tiers of them on braced shelves, big oblong tanks with metal frames, some with lights over them and some with lights down in them. Water grasses were festooned in careless patterns behind the algae-coated glass and the water held a ghostly greenish light and through the greenish light moved fish of all the colors of the rainbow.

There were long slim fish like golden darts and Japanese Veiltails with fantastic trailing tails, and X-ray fish as transparent as colored glass, tiny guppies half an inch long, calico popeyes spotted like a bride's apron, and big lumbering Chinese Moors with telescope eyes, froglike faces and unnecessary fins, waddling through the green water like fat men going to lunch.

Most of the light came from a big sloping skylight. Under the skylight at a bare wooden table a tall gaunt man stood with a squirming red fish in his left hand, and in his right hand a safety razor blade backed with adhesive tape.

He looked at me from under wide gray eyebrows. His eyes were sunken, colorless, opaque. I went over beside him and looked down at the fish he was holding.

"Fungus?" I asked.

He nodded slowly. "White fungus." He put the fish down on the table and carefully spread its dorsal fin. The fin was ragged and split and the ragged edges had a mossy white color.

"White fungus," he said, "ain't so bad. I'll trim this feller up and he'll be right as rain. What can I do for you, Mister?"

I rolled a cigarette around in my fingers and smiled at him.

"Like people," I said. "The fish, I mean. They get things wrong with them."

He held the fish against the wood and trimmed off the ragged part of the fin. He spread the tail and trimmed that. The fish had stopped squirming.

"Some you can cure," he said, "and some you can't. You can't cure swimming-bladder disease, for instance." He glanced up at me. "This don't hurt him, 'case you think it does," he said. "You can shock a fish to death but you can't hurt it like a person."

He put the razor blade down and dipped a cotton swab in some purplish liquid, painted the cut places. Then he dipped a finger in a jar of white vaseline and smeared that over. He dropped the fish in a small tank off to one side of the room. The fish swam around peacefully, quite content.

The gaunt man wiped his hands, sat down at the edge of a bench and stared at me with lifeless eyes. He had been good-looking once, a long time ago.

"You interested in fish?" he asked. His voice had the quiet careful murmur of the cell block and the exercise yard.

I shook my head. "Not particularly. That was just an excuse. I came a long way to see you, Mister Sype."

He moistened his lips and went on staring at me. When his voice came again it was tired and soft.

"Wallace is the name, Mister."

I puffed a smoke ring and poked my finger through it. "For my job it's got to be Sype."

He leaned forward and dropped his hands between his spread bony knees, clasped them together. Big gnarled hands that had done a lot of hard work in their time. His head tipped up at me and his dead eyes were cold under the shaggy brows. But his voice stayed soft.

"Haven't seen a dick in a year. To talk to. What's your lay?"

"Guess," I said.

His voice got still softer. "Listen, dick. I've got a nice home here, quiet. Nobody bothers me any more. Nobody's got a right to. I got a pardon straight from the White House. I've got the fish to play with and a man gets fond of anything he takes care of. I don't owe the world a nickel. I paid up. My wife's got enough dough for us to live on. All I want is to be let alone, dick." He stopped talking, shook his head once. "You can't burn me up—not any more."

I didn't say anything. I smiled a little and watched him.

"Nobody can touch me," he said. "I got a pardon straight from the President's study. I just want to be let alone."

I shook my head and kept on smiling at him. "That's the one thing you can never have—until you give in."

"Listen," he said softly. "You may be new on this case. It's kind of fresh to you. You want to make a rep for yourself. But me, I've had almost twenty years of it, and so have a lot of other people, some of 'em pretty smart people too. *They* know I don't have nothing that don't belong to me. Never did have. Somebody else got it."

"The mail clerk," I said. "Sure."

"Listen," he said, still softly. "I did my time. I know all the angles. I know they ain't going to stop wondering—long as anybody's alive that remembers. I know they're going to send some punk out once in a while to kind of stir it up. That's okey. No hard feelings. Now what do I do to get you to go home again?"

I shook my head and stared past his shoulder at the fish drifting in their big silent tanks. I felt tired. The quiet of the house made ghosts in my brain, ghosts of a lot of years ago. A train pounding through the darkness, a stick-up hidden in a mail car, a gun flash, a dead clerk on the floor, a silent drop off at some water tank, a man who had kept a secret for nineteen years—almost kept it.

"You made one mistake," I said slowly. "Remember a fellow named Peeler Mardo?"

He lifted his head. I could see him searching in his memory. The name didn't seem to mean anything to him.

"A fellow you knew in Leavenworth," I said. "A little runt that was in there for splitting twenty-dollar bills and putting phoney backs on them."

"Yeah," he said. "I remember."

"You told him you had the pearls," I said.

I could see he didn't believe me. "I must have been kidding him," he said slowly, emptily.

"Maybe. But here's the point. He didn't think so. He was up in this country a while ago with a pal, a guy who called himself Sunset. They saw you somewhere and Peeler recognized you. He got to thinking how he could make himself some jack. But he was a coke hound and he talked in his sleep. A girl got wise and then another girl and a shyster. Peeler got his feet burned and he's dead."

Sype stared at me unblinkingly. The lines at the corners of his mouth deepened.

I waved my cigarette and went on:

"We don't know how much he told, but the shyster and a girl are in Olympia. Sunset's in Olympia, only he's dead. They killed him. I don't know if they know where you are or not. But they will sometime, or others like them. You can wear the cops down, if they can't find the pearls and you don't try to sell them. You can wear the insurance company down and even the postal men."

Sype didn't move a muscle. His big knotty hands clenched between his knees didn't move. His dead eyes just stared.

"But you can't wear the chiselers down," I said. "They'll never lay off. There'll always be a couple or three with time enough and money enough and meanness enough to bear down. They'll find out what they want to know some way. They'll snatch your wife or take you out in the woods and give you the works. And you'll have to come through . . . Now I've got a decent, square proposition."

"Which bunch are you?" Sype asked suddenly. "I thought you smelled of dick, but I ain't so sure now."

"Insurance," I said. "Here's the deal. Twenty-five grand reward in all. Five grand to the girl that passed me the info. She got it on the square and she's entitled to that cut. Ten grand to me. I've done all the work and looked into all the guns. Ten grand to you, through me. You couldn't get a nickel direct. Is there anything in it? How does it look?"

"It looks fine," he said gently. "Except for one thing. I don't have no pearls, dick."

I scowled at him. That was my wad. I didn't have any

more. I straightened away from the wall and dropped a cigarette end on the wood floor, crushed it out. I turned to go.

He stood up and put a hand out. "Wait a minute," he said gravely, "and I'll prove it to you."

He went across the floor in front of me and out of the room. I stared at the fish and chewed my lip. I heard the sound of a car engine somewhere, not very close. I heard a drawer open and shut, apparently in a near-by room.

Sype came back into the fish room. He had a shiny Colt .45 in his gaunt fist. It looked as long as a man's forearm.

He pointed it at me and said: "I got pearls in this, six of them. Lead pearls. I can comb a fly's whiskers at sixty yards. You ain't no dick. Now get up and blow—and tell your red-hot friends I'm ready to shoot their teeth out any day of the week and twice on Sunday."

I didn't move. There was a madness in the man's dead eyes. I didn't dare move.

"That's grandstand stuff," I said slowly. "I can prove I'm a dick. You're an ex-con and it's felony just having that rod. Put it down and talk sense."

The car I had heard seemed to be stopping outside the house. Brakes whined on drums. Feet clattered, up a walk, up steps. Sudden sharp voices, a caught exclamation.

Sype backed across the room until he was between the table and a big twenty or thirty gallon tank. He grinned at me, the wide clear grin of a fighter at bay.

"I see your friends kind of caught up with you," he drawled. "Take your gat out and drop it on the floor while you still got time—and breath."

I didn't move. I looked at the wiry hair above his eyes. I looked into his eyes. I knew if I moved—even to do what he told me—he would shoot.

Steps came up the stairs. They were clogged, shuffling steps, with a hint of struggle in them.

Three people came into the room.

11

Mrs. Sype came in first, stiff-legged, her eyes glazed, her arms bent rigidly at the elbows and the hands clawing straight forward at nothing, feeling for something that wasn't there. There was a gun in her back, one of Carol Donovan's small .32's, held efficiently in Carol Donovan's small ruthless hand.

Madder came last. He was drunk, brave from the bottle, flushed and savage. He threw the Smith and Wesson down on me and leered.

Carol Donovan pushed Mrs. Sype aside. The older woman stumbled over into the corner and sank down on her knees, blank-eyed.

Sype stared at the Donovan girl. He was rattled because she was a girl and young and pretty. He hadn't been used to the type. Seeing her took the fire out of him. If men had come in he would have shot them to pieces.

The small dark white-faced girl faced him coldly, said in her tight chilled voice:

"All right, Dad. Shed the heater. Make it smooth now."

Sype leaned down slowly, not taking his eyes off her. He put his enormous frontier Colt on the floor.

"Kick it away from you, Dad."

Sype kicked it. The gun skidded across the bare boards, over towards the center of the room.

"That's the way, old-timer. You hold on him, Rush, while I unrod the dick."

The two guns swiveled and the hard gray eyes were looking at me now. Madder went a little way towards Sype and pointed his Smith and Wesson at Sype's chest.

The girl smiled, not a nice smile. "Bright boy, eh? You sure stick your neck out all the time, don't you? Made a beef, shamus. Didn't frisk your skinny pal. He had a little map in one shoe."

"I didn't need one," I said smoothly, and grinned at her.

I tried to make the grin appealing, because Mrs. Sype was moving her knees on the floor, and every move took her nearer to Sype's Colt.

"But you're all washed up now, you and your big smile. Hoist the mitts while I get your iron. Up, Mister."

She was a girl, about five feet two inches tall, and weighed around a hundred and twenty. Just a girl. I was five-eleven and a half, weighed one-ninety-five. I put my hands up and hit her on the jaw.

That was crazy, but I had all I could stand of the Donovan-Madder act, the Donovan-Madder guns, the Donovan-Madder tough talk. I hit her on the jaw.

She went back a yard and her popgun went off. A slug burned my ribs. She started to fall. Slowly, like a slow motion picture, she fell. There was something silly about it.

Mrs. Sype got the Colt and shot her in the back.

Madder whirled and the instant he turned Sype rushed him. Madder jumped back and yelled and covered Sype again. Sype stopped cold and the wide crazy grin came back on his gaunt face.

The slug from the Colt knocked the girl forward as though a door had whipped in a high wind. A flurry of blue cloth, something thumped my chest—her head. I saw her face for a moment as she bounced back, a strange face that I had never seen before.

Then she was a huddled thing on the floor at my feet, small, deadly, extinct, with redness coming out from under her, and the tall quiet woman behind her with the smoking Colt held in both hands.

Madder shot Sype twice. Sype plunged forward still grinning and hit the end of the table. The purplish liquid he had used on the sick fish sprayed up over him. Madder shot him again as he was falling.

I jerked my Luger out and shot Madder in the most painful place I could think of that wasn't likely to be fatal—the back of the knee. He went down exactly as if he had tripped over a hidden wire. I had cuffs on him before he even started to groan.

I kicked guns here and there and went over to Mrs. Sype and took the big Colt out of her hands.

It was very still in the room for a little while. Eddies of smoke drifted towards the skylight, filmy gray, pale in the afternoon sun. I heard the surf booming in the distance. Then I heard a whistling sound close at hand.

It was Sype trying to say something. His wife crawled across to him, still on her knees, huddled beside him. There was blood on his lips and bubbles. He blinked hard, trying to clear his head. He smiled up at her. His whistling voice said very faintly:

"The Moors, Hattie—the Moors."

Then his neck went loose and the smile melted off his face. His head rolled to one side on the bare floor.

Mrs. Sype touched him, then got very slowly to her feet and looked at me, calm, dry-eyed.

She said in a low clear voice: "Will you help me carry him to the bed? I don't like him here with these people."

I said: "Sure. What was that he said?"

"I don't know. Some nonsense about his fish, I think."

I lifted Sype's shoulders and she took his feet and we carried him into the bedroom and put him on the bed. She folded his hands on his chest and shut his eyes. She went over and pulled the blinds down.

"That's all, thank you," she said, not looking at me. "The telephone is downstairs."

She sat down in a chair beside the bed and put her head down on the coverlet near Sype's arm.

I went out of the room and shut the door.

12

Madder's leg was bleeding slowly, not dangerously. He stared at me with fear-crazed eyes while I tied a tight handkerchief above his knee. I figured he had a cut tendon and maybe a chipped kneecap. He might walk a little lame when they came to hang him.

I went downstairs and stood on the porch looking at the two cars in front, then down the hill towards the pier. Nobody could have told where the shots came from, unless he happened to be passing. Quite likely nobody had even noticed them. There was probably shooting in the woods around there a good deal.

I went back into the house and looked at the crank telephone on the living-room wall, but didn't touch it yet. Something was bothering me. I lit a cigarette and stared out of the window and a ghost voice said in my ears: "The Moors, Hattie. The Moors."

I went back upstairs into the fish room. Madder was groaning now, thick panting groans. What did I care about a torturer like Madder?

The girl was quite dead. None of the tanks was hit. The fish swam peacefully in their green water, slow and peaceful and easy. They didn't care about Madder either.

The tank with the black Chinese Moors in it was over in the corner, about ten gallon size. There were just four of them, big fellows, about four inches body length, coal black all over. Two of them were sucking oxygen on top of the water and two were waddling sluggishly on the bottom. They had thick deep bodies with a lot of spreading tail and high dorsal fins and their bulging telescope eyes that made them look like frogs when they were head towards you.

I watched them fumbling around in the green stuff that was growing in the tank. A couple of red pond snails were window-cleaning. The two on the bottom looked thicker and more sluggish than the two on the top. I wondered why.

There was a long-handled strainer made of woven string lying between two of the tanks. I got it and fished down in the tank, trapped one of the big Moors and lifted it out. I turned it over in the net, looked at its faintly silver belly. I saw something that looked like a suture. I felt the place. There was a hard lump under it.

I pulled the other one off the bottom. Same suture, same hard round lump. I got one of the two that had been sucking air on top. No suture, no hard round lump. It was harder to catch too.

I put it back in the tank. My business was with the other two. I like goldfish as well as the next man, but business is business and crime is crime. I took my coat off and rolled my sleeves up and picked the razor blade backed with adhesive off the table.

It was a very messy job. It took about five minutes. Then they lay in the palm of my hand, three-quarters of an inch in diameter, heavy, perfectly round, milky white and shimmering with that inner light no other jewel has. The Leander pearls.

I washed them off, wrapped them in my handkerchief, rolled down my sleeves and put my coat back on. I looked at Madder, at his little pain and fear-tortured eyes, the sweat on his face. I didn't care anything about Madder. He was a killer, a torturer.

I went out of the fish room. The bedroom door was still shut. I went down below and cranked the wall telephone.

"This is the Wallace place at Westport," I said. "There's been an accident. We need a doctor and we'll have to have the police. What can you do?"

The girl said: "I'll try and get you a doctor, Mr. Wallace. It may take a little time though. There's a town marshal at Westport. Will he do?"

"I suppose so," I said and thanked her and hung up. There were points about a country telephone after all.

I lit another cigarette and sat down in one of the rustic rockers on the porch. In a little while there were steps and Mrs. Sype came out of the house. She stood a moment looking off down the hills, then she sat down in the other rocker beside me. Her dry eyes looked at me steadily.

"You're a detective, I suppose," she said slowly, diffidently.

"Yes, I represent the company that insured the Leander pearls."

She looked off into the distance. "I thought he would have peace here," she said. "That nobody would bother him any more. That this place would be a sort of sanctuary."

"He ought not to have tried to keep the pearls."

She turned her head, quickly this time. She looked blank now, then she looked scared.

I reached down in my pocket and got out the wadded handkerchief, opened it up on the palm of my hand. They lay there together on the white linen, two hundred grand worth of murder.

"He could have had his sanctuary," I said. "Nobody wanted to take it away from him. But he wasn't satisfied with that."

She looked slowly, lingeringly at the pearls. Then her lips twitched. Her voice got hoarse.

"Poor Wally," she said. "So you did find them. You're pretty clever, you know. He killed dozens of fish before he learned how to do that trick." She looked up into my face. A little wonder showed at the back of her eyes.

She said: "I always hated the idea. Do you remember the old Bible theory of the scapegoat?"

I shook my head, no.

"The animal on which the sins of a man were laid and then it was driven off into the wilderness. The fish were his scapegoat."

She smiled at me. I didn't smile back.

She said, still smiling faintly: "You see, he once had the pearls, the real ones, and suffering seemed to him to make them his. But he couldn't have had any profit from them, even if he had found them again. It seems some landmark changed, while he was in prison, and he never could find the spot in Idaho where they were buried."

An icy finger was moving slowly up and down my spine. I opened my mouth and something I supposed might be my voice said:

"Huh?"

She reached a finger out and touched one of the pearls. I was still holding them out, as if my hand was a shelf nailed to the wall.

"So he got these," she said. "In Seattle. They're hollow, filled with white wax. I forget what they call the process. They look very fine. Of course I never saw any really valuable pearls."

"What did he get them for?" I croaked.

"Don't you see? They were his sin. He had to hide them in the wilderness, this wilderness. He hid them in the fish. And do you know—" she leaned towards me again and her eyes shone. She said very slowly, very earnestly:

"Sometimes I think that in the very end, just the last year or so, he actually believed they were the real pearls he was hiding. Does all this mean anything to you?"

I looked down at my pearls. My hand and the handkerchief closed over them slowly.

I said: "I'm a plain man, Mrs. Sype. I guess the scapegoat idea is a bit over my head. I'd say he was just trying to kid himself a bit—like any heavy loser."

She smiled again. She was handsome when she smiled. Then she shrugged quite lightly.

"Of course, you would see it that way. But me—" she spread her hands. "Oh, well, it doesn't matter much now. May I have them for a keepsake?"

"Have them?"

"The—the phoney pearls. Surely you don't—"

I stood up. An old Ford roadster without a top was chugging up the hill. A man in it had a big star on his vest. The chatter of the motor was like the chatter of some old angry bald-headed ape in the zoo.

Mrs. Sype was standing beside me, with her hand half out, a thin, beseeching look on her face.

I grinned at her with sudden ferocity.

"Yeah, you were pretty good in there for a while," I said. "I damn' near fell for it. And was I cold down the back, lady! But you helped. 'Phoney' was a shade out of character for you. Your work with the Colt was fast and kind of ruthless. Most of all Sype's last words queered it. 'The Moors, Hattie—the Moors.' He wouldn't have bothered with that if the stones had been ringers. And he wasn't sappy enough to kid himself all the way."

For a moment her face didn't change at all. Then it did. Something horrible showed in her eyes. She put her lips out and spit at me. Then she slammed into the house.

I tucked twenty-five thousand dollars into my vest pocket. Twelve thousand five hundred for me and twelve thousand five hundred for Kathy Horne. I could see her eyes when I brought her the check, and when she put it in the bank, to wait for Johnny to get paroled from Quentin.

The Ford had pulled up behind the other cars. The man driving spit over the side, yanked his emergency brake on, got out without using the door. He was a big fellow in shirt sleeves.

I went down the steps to meet him.

Red Wind

THERE WAS a desert wind blowing that night. It was one of those hot dry Santa Anas that come down through the mountain passes and curl your hair and make your nerves jump and your skin itch. On nights like that every booze party ends in a fight. Meek little wives feel the edge of the carving knife and study their husbands' necks. Anything can happen. You can even get a full glass of beer at a cocktail lounge.

I was getting one in a flossy new place across the street from the apartment house where I lived. It had been open about a week and it wasn't doing any business. The kid behind the bar was in his early twenties and looked as if he had never had a drink in his life.

There was only one other customer, a souse on a bar stool with his back to the door. He had a pile of dimes stacked neatly in front of him, about two dollars' worth. He was drinking straight rye in small glasses and he was all by himself in a world of his own.

I sat farther along the bar and got my glass of beer and said: "You sure cut the clouds off them, buddy. I will say that for you."

"We just opened up," the kid said. "We got to build up trade. Been in before, haven't you, mister?"

"Uh-huh."

"Live around here?"

"In the Berglund Apartments across the street," I said. "And the name is John Dalmas."

"Thanks, mister. Mine's Lew Petrolle." He leaned close to me across the polished dark bar. "Know that guy?"

"No."

"He ought to go home, kind of. I ought to call a taxi and send him home. He's doing his next week's drinking too soon."

"A night like this," I said. "Let him alone."

"It's not good for him," the kid said, scowling at me.

"Rye!" the drunk croaked, without looking up. He snapped

his fingers so as not to disturb his piles of dimes by banging on the bar.

The kid looked at me and shrugged. "Should I?"

"Whose stomach is it? Not mine."

The kid poured him another straight rye and I think he doctored it with water down behind the bar because when he came up with it he looked as guilty as if he'd kicked his grandmother. The drunk paid no attention. He lifted two dimes off his pile with the exact care of a crack surgeon operating on a brain tumor.

The kid came back and put more beer in my glass. Outside the wind howled. Every once in a while it blew the stained-glass swing-door open a few inches. It was a heavy door.

The kid said: "I don't like drunks in the first place and in the second place I don't like them getting drunk in here, and in the third place I don't like them in the first place."

"Warner Brothers could use that," I said.

"They did."

Just then we had another customer. A car squeaked to a stop outside and the swinging door came open. A fellow came in who looked a little in a hurry. He held the door and ranged the place quickly with flat, shiny, dark eyes. He was well set up, dark, good-looking in a narrow-faced, tight-lipped way. His clothes were dark and a white handkerchief peeped coyly from his pocket and he looked cool as well as under a tension of some sort. I guessed it was the hot wind. I felt a bit the same myself only not cool.

He looked at the drunk's back. The drunk was playing checkers with his empty glasses. The new customer looked at me, then he looked along the line of half-booths at the other side of the place. They were all empty. He came on in— down past where the drunk sat swaying and muttering to himself—and spoke to the bar kid.

"Seen a lady in here, buddy? Tall, pretty, brown hair, in a print bolero jacket over a blue crepe silk dress. Wearing a wide-brimmed straw hat with a velvet band." He had a tight voice I didn't like.

"No, sir. Nobody like that's been in," the bar kid said.

"Thanks. Straight Scotch. Make it fast, will you?"

The kid gave it to him and the fellow paid and put the

drink down in a gulp and started to go out. He took three or four steps and stopped, facing the drunk. The drunk was grinning. He swept a gun from somewhere so fast that it was just a blur coming out. He held it steady and he didn't look any drunker than I was. The tall dark guy stood quite still and then his head jerked back a little and then he was still again.

A car tore by outside. The drunk's gun was a .22 target automatic, with a large front sight. It made a couple of hard snaps and a little smoke curled—very little.

"So long, Waldo," the drunk said.

Then he put the gun on the barman and me.

The dark guy took a week to fall down. He stumbled, caught himself, waved one arm, stumbled again. His hat fell off, and then he hit the floor with his face. After he hit it he might have been poured concrete for all the fuss he made.

The drunk slid down off the stool and scooped his dimes into a pocket and slid towards the door. He turned sideways, holding the gun across his body. I didn't have a gun. I hadn't thought I needed one to buy a glass of beer. The kid behind the bar didn't move or make the slightest sound.

The drunk felt the door lightly with his shoulder, keeping his eyes on us, then pushed through it backwards. When it was wide a hard gust of air slammed in and lifted the hair of the man on the floor. The drunk said: "Poor Waldo. I bet I made his nose bleed."

The door swung shut. I started to rush it—from long practice in doing the wrong thing. In this case it didn't matter. The car outside let out a roar and when I got onto the sidewalk it was flicking a red smear of tail-light around the nearby corner. I got its license number the way I got my first million.

There were people and cars up and down the block as usual. Nobody acted as if a gun had gone off. The wind was making enough noise to make the hard quick rap of .22 ammunition sound like a slammed door, even if anyone heard it. I went back into the cocktail bar.

The kid hadn't moved, even yet. He just stood with his hands flat on the bar, leaning over a little and looking down at the dark guy's back. The dark guy hadn't moved either. I bent down and felt his neck artery. He wouldn't move—ever.

The kid's face had as much expression as a cut of round

steak and was about the same color. His eyes were more angry than shocked.

I lit a cigarette and blew smoke at the ceiling and said shortly: "Get on the phone."

"Maybe he's not dead," the kid said.

"When they use a .22 that means they don't make mistakes. Where's the phone?"

"I don't have one. I got enough expenses without that. Boy, can I kick eight hundred bucks in the face!"

"You own this place?"

"I did till this happened."

He pulled his white coat off and his apron and came around the inner end of the bar. "I'm locking the door," he said, taking keys out.

He went out, swung the door to and jiggled the lock from the outside until the bolt clicked into place. I bent down and rolled Waldo over. At first I couldn't even see where the shots went in. Then I could. A couple of tiny holes in his coat, over his heart. There was a little blood on his shirt.

The drunk was everything you could ask—as a killer.

The prowl-car boys came in about eight minutes. The kid, Lew Petrolle, was back behind the bar by then. He had his white coat on again and he was counting the money in the register and putting it in his pocket and making notes in a little book.

I sat at the edge of one of the half-booths and smoked cigarettes and watched Waldo's face get deader and deader. I wondered who the girl in the print coat was, why Waldo had left the engine of his car running outside, why he was in a hurry, whether the drunk had been waiting for him or just happened to be there.

The prowl-car boys came in perspiring. They were the usual large size and one of them had a flower stuck under his cap and his cap on a bit crooked. When he saw the dead man he got rid of the flower and leaned down to feel Waldo's pulse.

"Seems to be dead," he said, and rolled him around a little more. "Oh yeah, I see where they went in. Nice clean work. You two see him get it?"

I said yes. The kid behind the bar said nothing. I told them about it, that the killer seemed to have left in Waldo's car.

The cop yanked Waldo's wallet out, went through it rapidly and whistled. "Plenty jack and no driver's license." He put the wallet away. "O.K., we didn't touch him, see? Just a chance we could find did he have a car and put it on the air."

"The hell you didn't touch him," Lew Petrolle said.

The cop gave him one of these looks. "O.K., pal," he said softly. "We touched him."

The kid picked up a clean highball glass and began to polish it. He polished it all the rest of the time we were there.

In another minute a homicide fast-wagon sirened up and screeched to a stop outside the door and four men came in, two dicks, a photographer and a laboratory man. I didn't know either of the dicks. You can be in the detecting business a long time and not know all the men on a big city force.

One of them was a short, smooth, dark, quiet, smiling man, with curly black hair and soft intelligent eyes. The other was big, raw-boned, long-jawed, with a veined nose and glassy eyes. He looked like a heavy drinker. He looked tough, but he looked as if he thought he was a little tougher than he was. He shooed me into the last booth against the wall and his partner got the kid up front and the bluecoats went out. The fingerprint man and photographer set about their work.

A medical examiner came, stayed just long enough to get sore because there was no phone for him to call the morgue wagon.

The short dick emptied Waldo's pockets and then emptied his wallet and dumped everything into a large handkerchief on a booth table. I saw a lot of currency, keys, cigarettes, another handkerchief, very little else.

The big dick pushed me back into the end of the half-booth. "Give," he said. "I'm Copernik, Detective-Lieutenant."

I put my wallet in front of him. He looked at it, went through it, tossed it back, made a note in a book.

"John Dalmas, huh? A shamus. You here on business?"

"Drinking business," I said. "I live just across the street in the Berglund."

"Know this kid up front?"

"I've been in here once since he opened up."

"See anything funny about him now?"

"No."

"Takes it too light for a young fellow, don't he? Never mind answering. Just tell the story."

I told it—three times. Once for him to get the outline, once for him to get the details and once for him to see if I had it too pat. At the end he said: "This dame interests me. And the killer called the guy Waldo, yet didn't seem to be anyways sure he would be in. I mean, if Waldo wasn't sure the dame would be here, nobody, could be sure Waldo would be here."

"That's pretty deep," I said.

He studied me. I wasn't smiling. "Sounds like a grudge job, don't it? Don't sound planned. No getaway except by accident. A guy don't leave his car unlocked much in this town. And the killer works in front of two good witnesses. I don't like that."

"I don't like being a witness," I said. "The pay's too low."

He grinned. His teeth had a freckled look. "Was the killer drunk really?"

"With that shooting? No."

"Me too. Well, it's a simple job. The guy will have a record and he's left plenty prints. Even if we don't have his mug here we'll make him in hours. He had something on Waldo, but he wasn't meeting Waldo tonight. Waldo just dropped in to ask about a dame he had a date with and had missed connections on. It's a hot night and this wind would kill a girl's face. She'd be apt to drop in somewhere to wait. So the killer feeds Waldo two in the right place and scrams and don't worry about you boys at all. It's that simple."

"Yeah," I said.

"It's so simple it stinks," Copernik said.

He took his felt hat off and tousled up his ratty blond hair and leaned his head on his hands. He had a long mean horse face. He got a handkerchief out and mopped it, and the back of his neck and the back of his hands. He got a comb out and combed his hair—he looked worse with it combed—and put his hat back on.

"I was just thinking," I said.

"Yeah? What?"

"This Waldo knew just how the girl was dressed. So he must already have been with her tonight."

"So what? Maybe he had to go to the can. And when he came back she's gone. Maybe she changed her mind about him."

"That's right," I said.

But that wasn't what I was thinking at all. I was thinking that Waldo had described the girl's clothes in a way the ordinary man wouldn't know how to describe them. Printed bolero jacket over blue crepe silk dress. I didn't even know what a bolero jacket was. And I might have said blue dress or even blue silk dress, but never blue crepe silk dress.

After a while two men came with a basket. Lew Petrolle was still polishing his glass and talking to the short dark dick.

We all went down to headquarters.

Lew Petrolle was all right when they checked on him. His father had a grape ranch near Antioch in Contra Costa County. He had given Lew a thousand dollars to go into business and Lew had opened the cocktail bar, neon sign and all, on eight hundred flat.

They let him go and told him to keep the bar closed until they were sure they didn't want to do any more printing. He shook hands all around and grinned and said he guessed the killing would be good for business after all, because nobody believed a newspaper account of anything and people would come to him for the story and buy drinks while he was telling it.

"There's a guy won't ever do any worrying," Copernik said, when he was gone. "Over anybody else."

"Poor Waldo," I said. "The prints any good?"

"Kind of smudged," Copernik said sourly. "But we'll get a classification and teletype it to Washington some time tonight. If it don't click, you'll be in for a day on the steel picture-racks downstairs."

I shook hands with him and his partner, whose name was Ybarra, and left. They didn't know who Waldo was yet either. Nothing in his pockets told.

2

I got back to my street about 9 P.M. I looked up and down the block before I went into the Berglund. The cocktail bar was farther down on the other side, dark, with a nose or two against the glass, but no real crowd. People had seen the law and the morgue wagon, but they didn't know what had happened. Except the boys playing pinball games in the drugstore on the corner. They know everything, except how to hold a job.

The wind was still blowing, oven-hot, swirling dust and torn paper up against the walls.

I went into the lobby of the apartment house and rode the automatic elevator up to the fourth floor. I unwound the doors and stepped out and there was a tall girl standing there waiting for the car.

She had brown wavy hair under a wide-brimmed straw hat with a velvet band and loose bow. She had wide blue eyes and eyelashes that didn't quite reach her chin. She wore a blue dress that might have been crepe silk, simple in lines but not missing any curves. Over it she wore what might have been a print bolero jacket.

I said: "Is that a bolero jacket?"

She gave me a distant glance and made a motion as if to brush a cobweb out of the way.

"Yes. Would you mind—I'm rather in a hurry. I'd like——"

I didn't move. I blocked her off from the elevator. We stared at each other and she flushed very slowly.

"Better not go out on the street in those clothes," I said.

"Why, how dare you——"

The elevator clanked and started down again. I didn't know what she was going to say. Her voice lacked the edgy twang of a beer-parlor frill. It had a soft light sound, like spring rain.

"It's not a make," I said. "You're in trouble. If they come to this floor in the elevator, you have just that much time to get off the hall. First take off the hat and jacket—and snap it up!"

She didn't move. Her face seemed to whiten a little behind the not-too-heavy make-up.

"Cops," I said, "are looking for you. In those clothes. Give me the chance and I'll tell you why."

She turned her head swiftly and looked back along the corridor. With her looks I didn't blame her for trying one more bluff.

"You're impertinent, whoever you are. I'm Mrs. Leroy in Apartment Thirty-one. I can assure you——"

"That you're on the wrong floor," I said. "This is the fourth." The elevator had stopped down below. The sound of doors being wrenched open came up the shaft.

"Off!" I rapped. "Now!"

She switched her hat off and slipped out of the bolero jacket, fast. I grabbed them and wadded them into a mess under my arm. I took her elbow and turned her and we were going down the hall.

"I live in Forty-two. The front one across from yours, just a floor up. Take your choice. Once again—I'm not on the make."

She smoothed her hair with that quick gesture, like a bird preening itself. Ten thousand years of practice behind it.

"Mine," she said, and tucked her bag under her arm and strode down the hall fast. The elevator stopped at the floor below. She stopped when it stopped. She turned and faced me.

"The stairs are back by the elevator shaft," I said gently.

"I don't have an apartment," she said.

"I didn't think you had."

"Are they searching for me?"

"Yes, but they won't start gouging the block stone by stone before tomorrow. And then only if they don't make Waldo."

She stared at me. "Waldo?"

"Oh, you don't know Waldo," I said.

She shook her head slowly. The elevator started down in the shaft again. Panic flicked in her blue eyes like a ripple on water.

"No," she said breathlessly, "but take me out of this hall."

We were almost at my door. I jammed the key in and shook the lock around and heaved the door inward. I reached in far enough to switch lights on. She went in past me like a wave. Sandalwood floated on the air, very faint.

I shut the door, threw my hat into a chair and watched her stroll over to a card table on which I had a chess problem set out that I couldn't solve. Once inside, with the door locked, her panic had left her.

"So you're a chess-player," she said, in that guarded tone, as if she had come to look at my etchings. I wished she had.

We both stood still then and listened to the distant clang of elevator doors and then steps—going the other way.

I grinned, but with strain, not pleasure, went out into the kitchenette and started to fumble with a couple of glasses and then realized I still had her hat and bolero jacket under my arm. I went into the dressing-room behind the wall bed and stuffed them into a drawer, went back out to the kitchenette, dug out some extra fine Scotch and made a couple of high-balls.

When I went in with the drinks she had a gun in her hand. It was a small automatic with a pearl grip. It jumped up at me and her eyes were full of horror.

I stopped, with a glass in each hand, and said: "Maybe this hot wind has got you crazy too. I'm a private detective. I'll prove it if you let me."

She nodded slightly and her face was white. I went over slowly and put a glass down beside her, and went back and set mine down and got a card out that had no bent corners. She was sitting down, smoothing one blue knee with her left hand, and holding the gun on the other. I put the card down beside her drink and sat with mine.

"Never let a guy get that close to you," I said. "Not if you mean business. And your safety catch is on."

She flashed her eyes down, shivered, and put the gun back in her bag. She drank half the drink without stopping, put the glass down hard and picked the card up.

"I don't give many people that liquor," I said. "I can't afford to."

Her lips curled. "I supposed you would want money."

"Huh?"

She didn't say anything. Her hand was close to her bag again.

"Don't forget the safety catch," I said. Her hand stopped. I went on: "This fellow I called Waldo is quite tall, say five-eleven, slim, dark, brown eyes with a lot of glitter. Nose and mouth too thin. Dark suit, white handkerchief showing, and in a hurry to find you. Am I getting anywhere?"

She took her glass again. "So that's Waldo," she said. "Well, what about him?" Her voice seemed to have a slight liquor edge now.

"Well, a funny thing. There's a cocktail bar across the street . . . Say, where have you been all evening?"

"Sitting in my car," she said coldly, "most of the time."

"Didn't you see a fuss across the street up the block?"

Her eyes tried to say no and missed. Her lips said: "I knew there was some kind of disturbance. I saw policemen and red searchlights. I supposed someone had been hurt."

"Someone was. And this Waldo was looking for you before that. In the cocktail bar. He described you and your clothes."

Her eyes were set like rivets now and had the same amount of expression. Her mouth began to tremble and kept on trembling.

"I was in there," I said, "talking to the kid that runs it. There was nobody in there but a drunk on a stool and the kid and myself. The drunk wasn't paying any attention to anything. Then Waldo came in and asked about you and we said no, we hadn't seen you and he started to leave."

I sipped my drink. I like an effect as well as the next fellow. Her eyes ate me.

"Just started to leave. Then this drunk that wasn't paying any attention to anyone called him Waldo and took a gun out. He shot him twice——" I snapped my fingers twice— "like that. Dead."

She fooled me. She laughed in my face. "So my husband hired you to spy on me," she said. "I might have known the whole thing was an act. You and your Waldo."

I gawked at her.

"I never thought of him as jealous," she snapped. "Not of a man who had been our chauffeur anyhow. A little about Stan, of course—that's natural. But Joseph Choate——"

I made motions in the air. "Lady, one of us has this book open at the wrong page," I grunted. "I don't know anybody named Stan or Joseph Choate. So help me, I didn't even know you had a chauffeur. People around here don't run to them. As for husbands—yeah, we do have a husband once in a while. Not often enough."

She shook her head slowly and her hand stayed near her bag and her blue eyes had glitters in them.

"Not good enough, Mr. Dalmas. No, not nearly good enough. I know you private detectives. You're all rotten. You tricked me into your apartment, if it is your apartment. More likely it's the apartment of some horrible man who will swear anything for a few dollars. Now you're trying to scare me. So you can blackmail me—as well as get money from my husband. All right," she said breathlessly, "how much do I have to pay?"

I put my empty glass aside and leaned back. "Pardon me if I light a cigarette," I said. "My nerves are frayed."

I lit it while she watched me grimly, no fear—or not enough fear for any real guilt to be under it. "So Joseph Choate is his name," I said. "The guy that killed him in the cocktail bar called him Waldo."

She smiled a bit disgustedly, but almost tolerantly. "Don't stall. How much?"

"Why were you trying to meet this Joseph Choate?"

"I was going to buy something he stole from me, of course. Something I happen to value. Something that's valuable in the ordinary way too. It cost fifteen thousand dollars. The man I loved gave it to me. He's dead. There! He's dead! He died in a burning plane. Now, go back and tell my husband that, you slimy little rat!"

"Hey, I weigh a hundred and ninety stripped," I yelled.

"You're still slimy," she yelled back. "And don't bother about telling my husband. I'll tell him myself. He probably knows anyway."

I grinned. "That's smart. Just what was I supposed to find out?"

She grabbed her glass and finished what was left of her drink. "So he thinks I'm meeting Joseph," she sneered. "Well, I was. But not to make love. Not with a chauffeur. Not with a bum I picked off the front step and gave a job to. I don't have to dig down that far, if I want to play around."

"Lady," I said, "you don't indeed."

"Now I'm going," she said. "You just try and stop me." She snatched the pearl-handled gun out of her bag.

I grinned and kept on grinning. I didn't move.

"Why you nasty little string of nothing," she stormed. "How do I know you're a private detective at all? You might be a crook. This card you gave me doesn't mean anything. Anybody can have cards printed."

"Sure," I said. "And I suppose I'm smart enough to live here two years because you were going to move in today so I could blackmail you for not meeting a man named Joseph Choate who was bumped off across the street under the name of Waldo. Have you got the money to buy this something that cost fifteen grand?"

"Oh! You think you'll hold me up, I suppose!"

"Oh!" I mimicked her, "I'm a stick-up artist now, am I? Lady, will you please either put that gun away or take the safety catch off? It hurts my professional feelings to see a nice gun made a monkey of that way."

"You're a full portion of what I don't like," she said. "Get out of my way."

I didn't move. She didn't move. We were both sitting down—and not even close to each other.

"Let me in on one secret before you go," I pleaded. "What in hell did you take the apartment down on the floor below for? Just to meet a guy down on the street?"

"Stop being silly," she snapped. "I didn't. I lied. It's his apartment."

"Joseph Choate's?"

She nodded sharply.

"Does my description of Waldo sound like Joseph Choate?"

She nodded sharply again.

"All right. That's one fact learned at last. Don't you realize Waldo described your clothes before he was shot—when he was looking for you—that the description was passed on to the police—that the police don't know who Waldo is—and are looking for somebody in those clothes to help tell them? Don't you get that much?"

The gun suddenly started to shake in her hand. She looked down at it, sort of vacantly, slowly put it back in her bag.

"I'm a fool," she whispered, "to be even talking to you." She stared at me for a long time, then pulled in a deep breath. "He told me where he was staying. He didn't seem afraid. I guess blackmailers are like that. He was to meet me on the street, but I was late. It was full of police when I got here. So I went back and sat in my car for a while. Then I came up to Joseph's apartment and knocked. Then I went back to my car and waited again. I came up here three times in all. The last time I walked up a flight to take the elevator. I had already been seen twice on the third floor. I met you. That's all."

"You said something about a husband," I grunted. "Where is he?"

"He's at a meeting."

"Oh, a meeting," I said nastily.

"My husband's a very important man. He has lots of meetings. He's a hydro-electric engineer. He's been all over the world. I'd have you know——"

"Skip it," I said. "I'll take him to lunch some day and have him tell me himself. Whatever Joseph had on you is dead stock now. Like Joseph."

She believed it at last. I hadn't thought she ever would somehow. "He's really dead?" she whispered. "Really?"

"He's dead," I said. "Dead, dead, dead. Lady, he's dead."

Her face fell apart like a bride's piecrust. Her mouth wasn't large, but I could have got my fist into it at that moment. In the silence the elevator stopped at my floor.

"Scream," I rapped, "and I'll give you two black eyes."

It didn't sound nice, but it worked. It jarred her out of it. Her mouth shut like a trap.

I heard steps coming down the hall. We all have hunches. I put my finger to my lips. She didn't move now. Her face had a frozen look. Her big blue eyes were as black as the shadows below them. The hot wind boomed against the shut windows. Windows have to be shut when a Santa Ana blows, heat or no heat.

The steps that came down the hall were the casual ordinary steps of one man. But they stopped outside my door, and somebody knocked.

I pointed to the dressing-room behind the wall bed. She stood up without a sound, her bag clenched against her side.

I pointed again, to her glass. She lifted it swiftly, slid across the carpet, through the door, drew the door quietly shut after her.

I didn't know just what I was going to all this trouble for. The knocking sounded again. The backs of my hands were wet. I creaked my chair and stood up and made a loud yawning sound. Then I went over and opened the door—without a gun. That was a mistake.

3

I didn't know him at first. Perhaps for the opposite reason Waldo hadn't seemed to know him. He'd had a hat on all the time over at the cocktail bar and he didn't have one on now. His hair ended completely and exactly where his hat would start. Above that line was hard white sweatless skin almost as glaring as scar tissue. He wasn't just twenty years older. He was a different man.

But I knew the gun he was holding, the .22 target automatic with the big front sight. And I knew his eyes. Bright, brittle, shallow eyes like the eyes of a lizard.

He was alone. He put the gun against my face very lightly and said between his teeth: "Yeah, me. Let's go on in."

I backed in just far enough and stopped. Just the way he would want me to, so he could shut the door without moving much. I knew from his eyes that he would want me to do just that.

I wasn't scared. I was paralyzed.

When he had the door shut he backed me some more, slowly, until there was something against the back of my legs. His eyes looked into mine.

"That's a card table," he said. "Some goon here plays chess. You?"

I swallowed. "I don't exactly play it. I just fool around."

"That means two," he said with a kind of hoarse softness, as if some cop had hit him across the windpipe with a blackjack once, in a third-degree session.

"It's a problem," I said. "Not a game. Look at the pieces."

"I wouldn't know."

"Well, I'm alone," I said, and my voice shook just enough.

"It don't make any difference," he said. "I'm washed up anyway. Some nose puts the but on me tomorrow, next week, what the hell? I just didn't like your map, pal. And that smug-faced pansy in the barcoat that played left tackle for Fordham or something. To hell with guys like you guys."

I didn't speak or move. The big front sight raked my cheek lightly, almost caressingly. The man smiled.

"It's kind of good business too," he said. "Just in case. An old con like me don't make good prints—not even when he's lit. And if I don't make good prints all I got against me is two witnesses. The hell with it. You're slammin' off, pal. I guess you know that."

"What did Waldo do to you?" I tried to make it sound as if I wanted to know, instead of just not wanting to shake too hard.

"Stooled on a bank job in Michigan and got me four years. Got himself a nolle prosse. Four years in Michigan ain't no summer cruise. They make you be good in them lifer states."

"How'd you know he'd come in there?" I croaked.

"I didn't. Oh yeah, I was lookin' for him. I was wanting to see him all right. I got a flash of him on the street night before last but I lost him. Up to then I wasn't lookin' for him. Then I was. A cute guy, Waldo. How is he?"

"Dead," I said.

"I'm still good," he chuckled. "Drunk or sober. Well, that don't make no doughnuts for me now. They make me down-town yet?"

I didn't answer him quick enough. He jabbed the gun into my throat and I choked and almost grabbed for it by instinct.

"Naw," he cautioned me softly. "Naw. You ain't that dumb."

I put my hands back, down at my sides, open, the palms towards him. He would want them that way. He hadn't touched me, except with the gun. He didn't seem to care whether I might have one too. He wouldn't—if he just meant the one thing.

He didn't seem to care very much about anything, coming back on that block. Perhaps the hot wind did something to him. It was booming against my shut windows like the surf under a pier.

"They got prints," I said. "I don't know how good."

"They'll be good enough—but not for teletype work. Take 'em airmail time to Washington and back to check 'em right. Tell me why I come here, pal."

"You heard the kid and me talking in the bar. I told him my name, where I lived."

"That's how, pal. I said why." He smiled at me. It was a lousy smile to be the last one you might see.

"Skip it," I said. "The hangman won't ask you to guess why he's there."

"Say, you're tough at that. After you, I visit that kid. I tailed him home from headquarters, but I figure you're the guy to put the bee on first. I tail him home from the city hall, in the rent car Waldo had. From headquarters, pal. Them funny dicks. You can sit in their laps and they don't know you. Start runnin' for a street car and they open up with machine guns and bump two pedestrians, a hacker asleep in his cab, and an old scrubwoman on the second floor workin' a mop. And they miss the guy they're after. Them funny lousy dicks."

He twisted the gun muzzle in my neck. His eyes looked madder than before.

"I got time," he said. "Waldo's rent car don't get a report right away. And they don't make Waldo very soon. I know Waldo. Smart he was. A smooth boy, Waldo."

"I'm going to vomit," I said, "if you don't take that gun out of my throat."

He smiled and moved the gun down to my heart. "This about right? Say when."

I must have spoken louder than I meant to. The door of the dressing-room by the wall bed showed a crack of darkness. Then an inch. Then four inches. I saw eyes, but I didn't look at them. I stared hard into the baldheaded man's eyes. Very hard. I didn't want him to take his eyes off mine.

"Scared?" he asked softly.

I leaned against his gun and began to shake. I thought he would enjoy seeing me shake. The girl came out through the door. She had her gun in her hand again. I was sorry as hell for her. She'd try to make the door—or scream. Either way it would be curtains—for both of us.

"Well, don't take all night about it," I bleated. My voice sounded far away, like a voice on a radio, on the other side of a street.

"I like this, pal," he smiled. "I'm like that."

The girl floated in the air, somewhere behind him. Nothing was ever more soundless than the way she moved. It wouldn't do any good, though. He wouldn't fool around with her at all. I had known him all my life but I had been looking into his eyes for only five minutes.

"Suppose, I yell," I said.

"Yeah. Suppose you yell. Go ahead and yell," he said, with his killer's smile.

She didn't go near the door. She was right behind him.

"Well—here's where I yell," I said.

As if that was the cue she jabbed the little gun hard into his short ribs, without a single sound.

He had to react. It was like a knee reflex. His mouth snapped open and both his arms jumped out from his sides and he arched his back just a little. The gun was pointing at my right eye.

I sank and kneed him with all my strength, in the groin.

His chin came down and I hit it. I hit it as if I was driving the last spike on the first transcontinental railroad. I can still feel it when I flex my knuckles.

His gun raked the side of my face but it didn't go off. He was already limp. He writhed down gasping, his left side against the floor. I kicked his right shoulder hard. The gun jumped away from him, skidded on the carpet, under a chair. I heard the chessmen tinkling on the floor behind me somewhere.

The girl stood over him, looking down. Then her wide dark horrified eyes came up and fastened on mine.

"That buys me," I said. "Anything I have is yours—now and forever."

She didn't hear me. Her eyes were strained open so hard that the whites showed under the vivid blue iris. She backed quickly to the door with her little gun up, felt behind her for the knob and twisted it. She pulled the door open and slipped out.

The door shut.

She was bareheaded and without her bolero jacket.

She had only the gun, and the safety catch on that was still set so that she couldn't fire it.

It was silent in the room then, in spite of the wind. Then I heard him gasping on the floor. His face had a greenish pallor. I moved behind him and pawed him for more guns, and didn't find any. I got a pair of store cuffs out of my desk and pulled his arms in front of him and snapped them on his wrists. They would hold if he didn't shake them too hard.

His eyes measured me for a coffin, in spite of their suffering. He lay in the middle of the floor, still on his left side, a twisted, wizened, bald-headed little guy with drawn-back lips and teeth spotted with cheap silver fillings. His mouth looked like a black pit and his breath came in little waves, choked, stopped, came on again, limping.

"I'm sorry, guy," I grunted. "What could I do?"

That—to this sort of killer.

I went into the dressing-room and opened the drawer of the chest. Her hat and jacket lay there on my shirts. I put them underneath, at the back, and smoothed the shirts over them. Then I went out to the kitchenette and poured a stiff jolt of whiskey and put it down and stood a moment listening to the hot wind howl against the window glass. A garage door banged, and a power-line wire with too much play between the insulators thumped the side of the building with a sound like somebody beating a carpet.

The drink worked on me. I went back into the living-room and opened a window. The guy on the floor hadn't smelled her sandalwood, but somebody else might.

I shut the window again, wiped the palms of my hands and used the phone to dial headquarters.

Copernik was still there. His smart-aleck voice said: "Yeah? Dalmas? Don't tell me. I bet you got an idea."

"Make that killer yet?"

"We're not saying, Dalmas. Sorry as all hell and so on. You know how it is."

"O.K. I don't care who he is. Just come and get him off the floor of my apartment."

"Holy ——!" Then his voice hushed and went down low. "Wait a minute, now. Wait a minute." A long way off I seemed to hear a door shut. Then his voice again. "Shoot," he said softly.

"Handcuffed," I said. "All yours. I had to knee him, but he'll be all right. He came here to eliminate a witness."

Another pause. The voice was full of honey. "Now listen, boy, who else is in this with you?"

"Who else? Nobody. Just me."

"Keep it that way, boy. All quiet. O.K.?"

"Think I want all the bums in the neighborhood in here sightseeing?"

"Take it easy, boy. Easy. Just sit tight and sit still. I'm practically there. No touch nothing. Get me?"

"Yeah." I gave him the address and apartment number again to save him time.

I could see his big bony face glisten. I got the .22 target gun from under the chair and sat holding it until feet hit the hallway outside my door and knuckles did a quiet tattoo on the door panel.

Copernik was alone. He filled the doorway quickly, pushed me back into the room with a tight grin and shut the door. He stood with his back to it, his hand under the left side of his coat. A big hard bony man with flat cruel eyes.

He lowered them slowly and looked at the man on the floor. The lad's neck was twitching a little. His eyes moved in short stabs—sick eyes.

"Sure it's the guy?" Copernik's voice was hoarse.

"Positive. Where's Ybarra?"

"Oh, he was busy." He didn't look at me when he said that. "Those your cuffs?"

"Yeah."

"Key."

I tossed it to him. He went down swiftly on one knee beside the killer and took my cuffs off his wrists, tossed them to one side. He got his own off his hip, twisted the bald man's hands behind him and snapped the cuffs on.

"All right, you ——" the killer said tonelessly.

Copernik grinned and balled his fist and hit the handcuffed man in the mouth a terrific blow. His head snapped back almost enough to break his neck. Blood dribbled from the lower corner of his mouth.

"Get a towel," Copernik ordered.

I got a hand towel and gave it to him. He stuffed it between the handcuffed man's teeth, viciously, stood up and rubbed his bony fingers through his ratty blond hair.

"All right. Tell it."

I told it—leaving the girl out completely. It sounded a little funny. Copernik watched me, said nothing. He rubbed the side of his veined nose. Then he got his comb out and worked on his hair just as he had done earlier in the evening, in the cocktail bar.

I went over and gave him the gun. He looked at it casually, dropped it into his side pocket. His eyes had something in them and his face moved in a hard bright grin.

I bent down and began picking up my chessmen and dropping them into the box. I put the box on the mantel, straightened out a leg of the card table, played around for a while. All the time Copernik watched me. I wanted him to think something out.

At last he came out with it. "This guy uses a twenty-two," he said. "He uses it because he's good enough to get by with that much gun. That mean's he's good. He knocks at your door, pokes that gat in your belly, walks you back into the room, says he's here to close your mouth for keeps—and yet you take him. You not having any gun. You take him alone. You're kind of good yourself, pal."

"Listen," I said, and looked at the floor. I picked up another chessman and twisted it between my fingers. "I was doing a chess problem," I said. "Trying to forget things."

"You got something on your mind, pal," Copernik said softly. "You wouldn't try to fool an old copper, would you, boy?"

"It's a swell pinch and I'm giving it to you," I said. "What the hell more do you want?"

The man on the floor made a vague sound behind the towel. His bald head glistened with sweat.

"What's the matter, pal? You been up to something?" Copernik almost whispered.

I looked at him quickly, looked away again. "All right," I said. "You know damn well I couldn't take him alone. He had the gun on me and he shoots where he looks."

Copernik closed one eye and squinted at me amiably with the other. "Go on, pal. I kind of thought of that too."

I shuffled around a little more, to make it look good. I said slowly: "There was a kid here who pulled a job over in Boyle Heights, a heist job, and didn't take. A two-bit service station stickup. I know his family. He's not really bad. He was here trying to beg train money off me. When the knock came he sneaked in—there."

I pointed at the wall bed and the door beside. Copernik's head swiveled slowly, swiveled back. His eyes winked again. "And this kid had a gun," he said.

I nodded. "And he got behind him. That takes guts, Copernik. You've got to give the kid a break. You've got to let him stay out of it."

"Tag out for this kid?" Copernik asked softly.

"Not yet, he says. He's scared there will be."

Copernik smiled. "I'm a homicide man," he said. "What you have done, pal?"

I pointed down at the gagged and handcuffed man on the floor. "You took him, didn't you?" I said gently.

Copernik kept on smiling. A big whitish tongue came out and massaged his thick lower lip. "How'd I do it?" he whispered.

"Get the slugs out of Waldo?"

"Sure. Long twenty-twos. One smashed on a rib, one good."

"You're a careful guy. You don't miss any angles. You don't know anything about me. You dropped in on me to see what guns I had."

Copernik got up and went down on one knee again beside the killer. "Can you hear me, guy?" he asked with his face close to the face of the man on the floor.

The man made some vague sound. Copernik stood up and yawned. "Who the hell cares what he says? Go on, pal."

"You wouldn't expect to find I had anything, but you wanted to look around my place. And while you were mousing around in there"—I pointed to the dressing-room—"and me not saying anything, being a little sore, maybe, a knock came on the door. So he came in. So after a while you sneaked out and took him."

"Ah." Copernik grinned widely, with as many teeth as a horse. "You're on, pal. I socked him and I kneed him and I took him. You didn't have no gun and the guy swiveled on me pretty sharp and I left-hooked him down the backstairs. O.K.?"

"O.K.," I said.

"You'll tell it like that downtown?"

"Yeah," I said.

"I'll protect you, pal. Treat me right and I'll always play ball. Forget about that kid. Let me know if he needs a break."

He came over and held out his hand. I shook it. It was as clammy as a dead fish. Clammy hands and the people who own them make me sick.

"There's just one thing," I said. "This partner of yours— Ybarra. Won't he be a bit sore you didn't bring him along on this?"

Copernik tousled his hair and wiped his hatband with a large yellowish silk handkerchief.

"That guinea?" he sneered. "To hell with him!" He came close to me and breathed in my face. "No mistakes, pal— about that story of ours."

His breath was bad. It would be.

4

There were just five of us in the chief-of-detective's office when Copernik laid it before them. A stenographer, the chief, Copernik, myself, Ybarra. Ybarra sat on a chair tilted against the side wall. His hat was down over his eyes but their softness loomed underneath, and the small still smile hung at the corners of the cleancut Latin lips. He didn't look directly at Copernik. Copernik didn't look at him at all.

Outside in the corridor there had been photos of Copernik shaking hands with me, Copernik with his hat on straight and his gun in his hand and a stern, purposeful look on his face.

They said they knew who Waldo was, but they wouldn't tell me. I didn't believe they knew, because the chief-of-detectives had a morgue photo of Waldo on his desk. A beautiful job, his hair combed, his tie straight, the light hitting his eyes just right to make them glisten. Nobody would have known it was a photo of a dead man with two bullet holes in his heart. He looked like a dance-hall sheik making up his mind whether to take the blonde or the redhead.

It was about midnight when I got home. The apartment-house door was locked and while I was fumbling for my keys a low voice spoke to me out of the darkness.

All it said was: "Please!" but I knew it. I turned and looked at a dark Cadillac coupe parked just off the loading zone. It had no lights. Light from the street touched the brightness of a woman's eyes.

I went over there. "You're a darn fool," I said.

She said: "Get in."

I climbed in and she started the car and drove it a block and a half along Franklin and turned down Kingsley Drive. The hot wind still burned and blustered. A radio lilted from an open, sheltered, side window of an apartment house. There were a lot of parked cars but she found a vacant space behind a small brand-new Packard cabriolet that had the dealer's sticker on the windshield glass. After she'd jockeyed us up to the curb she leaned back in the corner with her gloved hands on the wheel.

She was all in black now, or dark brown, with a small foolish hat. I smelled the sandalwood in her perfume.

"I wasn't very nice to you, was I?" she said.

"All you did was save my life."

"What happened?"

"I called the law and fed a few lies to a cop I don't like and gave him all the credit for the pinch and that was that. That guy you took away from me was the man who killed Waldo."

"You mean—you didn't tell them about me?"

"Lady," I said again, "all you did was save my life. What else do you want done? I'm ready, willing, and I'll try to be able."

She didn't say anything, or move.

"Nobody learned who you are from me," I said. "Incidentally, I don't know myself."

"I'm Mrs. Frank C. Barsaly, Two-twelve Fremont Place. Olympia Two-four-five-nine-six. Is that what you wanted?"

"Thanks," I mumbled, and rolled a dry unlit cigarette around in my fingers. "Why did you come back?" Then I snapped the fingers of my left hand. "The hat and jacket," I said. "I'll go up and get them."

"It's more than that," she said. "I want my pearls."

I might have jumped a little. It seemed as if there had been enough without pearls.

A car tore by down the street going twice as fast as it should. A thin bitter cloud of dust lifted in the street lights and whirled and vanished. The girl ran the window up quickly against it.

"All right," I said. "Tell me about the pearls. We have had a murder and a mystery woman and a mad killer and a heroic rescue and a police detective framed into making a false report. Now we will have pearls. All right—feed it to me."

"I was to buy them for five thousand dollars. From the man you call Waldo and I call Joseph Choate. He should have had them."

"No pearls," I said. "I saw what came out of his pockets. A lot of money but no pearls."

"Could they be hidden in his apartment?"

"Yes," I said. "So far as I know he could have had them hidden anywhere in California except in his pockets. How's Mr. Barsaly this hot night?"

"He's still downtown at his meeting. Otherwise I couldn't have come."

"Well, you could have brought him," I said. "He could have sat in the rumble seat."

"Oh, I don't know," she said. "Frank weighs two hundred pounds and he's pretty solid. I don't think he would like to sit in the rumble seat, Mr. Dalmas."

"What the hell are we talking about, anyway?"

She didn't answer. Her gloved hands tapped lightly, provokingly on the rim of the slender wheel. I threw the unlit cigarette out the window, turned a little and took hold of her.

I was shaking when I let go of her. She pulled as far away from me as she could against the side of the car and rubbed the back of her glove against her mouth. I sat quite still.

We didn't speak for some time. Then she said very slowly: "I meant you to do that. But I wasn't always that way. It's only been since Stan Phillips was killed in his plane. If it hadn't been for that, I'd be Mrs. Phillips now. Stan gave me the pearls. They cost fifteen thousand dollars, he said once. White pearls, forty-one of them, the largest about a third of an inch across. I don't know how many grains. I never had them appraised or showed them to a jeweler, so I don't know those things. But I loved them on Stan's account. I loved Stan. The way you do just the one time. Can you understand?"

"What's your first name?" I asked.

"Lola."

"Go on talking, Lola." I got another dry cigarette out of my pocket and fumbled it between my fingers just to give them something to do.

"They had a simple silver clasp in the shape of a two-bladed propeller. There was one small diamond where the boss would be. That was because I told Frank they were store pearls I had bought myself. He didn't know the difference. It's not so easy to tell, I dare say. You see — Frank is pretty jealous."

In the darkness she came closer to me and her side touched my side. But I didn't move this time. The wind howled and the trees shook. I kept on rolling the cigarette around in my fingers.

"I suppose you've read that story," she said. "About the wife and the real pearls and her telling her husband — "

"I've read it," I said.

"I hired Joseph. My husband was in Argentina at the time. I was pretty lonely."

"*You* should be lonely," I said.

"Joseph and I went driving a good deal. Sometimes we had a drink or two together. But that's all. I don't go around — "

"You told him about the pearls," I snarled. "And when your two hundred pounds of beef came back from Argentina and kicked him out — he took the pearls, because he knew they were real. And then offered them back to you for five grand."

"Yes," she said simply. "Of course I didn't want to go to the police. And of course in the circumstance Joseph wasn't afraid of my knowing where he lived."

"Poor Waldo," I said. "I feel kind of sorry for him. It was a hell of a time to run into an old friend that had a down on you."

I struck a match on my shoe sole and lit the cigarette. The tobacco was so dry from the hot wind that it burned like grass. The girl sat quietly beside me, her hands on the wheel again.

"Hell with women—these fliers," I said. "And you're still in love with him, or think you are. Where did you keep the pearls?"

"In a Russian malachite jewelry box on my dressing-table. With some other costume jewelry. I had to, if I ever wanted to wear them."

"And they were worth fifteen grand. And you think Joseph might have hidden them in his apartment. Thirty-one, wasn't it?"

"Yes," she said. "I guess it's a lot to ask."

I opened the door and got out of the car. "I've been paid," I said. "I'll go look. The doors in my apartment house are not very obstinate. The cops will find out where Waldo lived when they publish his photo, but not tonight, I guess."

"It's awfully sweet of you," she said. "Shall I wait here?"

I stood with a foot on the running-board, leaning in, looking at her. I didn't answer her question. I just stood there looking in at the shine of her eyes. Then I shut the car door and walked up the street towards Franklin.

Even with the wind shriveling my face I could still smell the sandalwood in her hair. And feel her lips.

I unlocked the Berglund door, walked through the silent lobby to the elevator, and rode up to 3. Then I soft-footed along the silent corridor and peered down at the sill of Apartment 31. No light. I rapped—the old light, confidential tattoo of the bootlegger with the big smile and the extra-deep hip pockets. No answer. I took the piece of thick hard celluloid that pretended to be a window over the driver's license in my wallet, and eased it between the lock and the jamb, leaning hard on the knob, pushing it toward the hinges. The edge of the celluloid caught the slope of the spring lock and snapped it back with a small brittle sound, like an icicle breaking. The door yielded and I went into near darkness. Street light filtered in and touched a high spot here and there.

I shut the door and snapped the light on and just stood. There was a queer smell in the air. I made it in a moment —the smell of dark-cured tobacco. I prowled over to a smoking-stand by the window and looked down at four brown butts—Mexican or South American cigarettes.

Upstairs, on my floor, feet hit the carpet and somebody went into a bathroom. I heard the toilet flush. I went into the bathroom of Apartment 31. A little rubbish, nothing, no place to hide anything. The kitchenette was a longer job, but I only half searched. I knew there were no pearls in that apartment. I knew Waldo had been on his way out and that he was in a hurry and that something was riding him when he turned and took two bullets from an old friend.

I went back to the living-room and swung the wall bed and looked past its mirror side into the dressing-room for signs of still current occupancy. Swinging the bed farther I was no longer looking for pearls. I was looking at a man.

He was small, middle-aged, iron-gray at the temples, with a very dark skin, dressed in a fawn-colored suit with a wine-colored tie. His neat little brown hands hung limply down by his sides. His small feet, in pointed polished shoes, pointed almost at the floor.

He was hanging by a belt around his neck from the metal top of the bed. His tongue stuck out farther than I thought it possible for a tongue to stick out.

He swung a little and I didn't like that, so I pulled the bed down and he nestled quietly between the two clamped pillows. I didn't touch him yet. I didn't have to touch him to know that he would be cold as ice.

I went around him into the dressing-room and used my handkerchief on drawer-knobs. The place was stripped clean except for the light litter of a man living alone.

I came out of there and began on the man. No wallet. Waldo would have taken that and ditched it. A flat box of cigarettes, half full, stamped in gold: *"Louis Tapia y Cia, Calle de Paysand, 19, Montevideo."* Matches from the Spezzia Club. An under-arm holster of dark grained leather and in it a 9 millimeter Mauser.

The Mauser made him a professional, so I didn't feel so badly. But not a very good professional, or bare hands would not have finished him, with the Mauser—a gun you can blast through a wall with—undrawn in his shoulder holster.

I made a little sense of it, not much. Four of the brown cigarettes had been smoked, so there had been either waiting or discussion. Somewhere along the line Waldo had got the little man by the throat and held him in just the right way to make him pass out in a matter of seconds. The Mauser had been less useful to him than a toothpick. Then Waldo had hung him up by the strap, probably dead already. That would account for haste, for cleaning out the apartment, for Waldo's anxiety about the girl. It would account for the car left unlocked outside the cocktail bar.

That is, it would account for these things if Waldo had killed him, if this was really Waldo's apartment—if I wasn't just being kidded.

I examined some more pockets. In the left trouser one I found a gold penknife, some silver. In the left hip pocket a handkerchief, folded, scented. On the right hip another, unfolded but clean. In the right leg pocket four or five tissue handkerchiefs. A clean little guy. He didn't like to blow his nose on his handkerchief. Under these there was a small new keytainer holding four new keys—car keys. Stamped in gold on the keytainer was: *Compliments of R. K. Vogelsang, Inc. "The Packard House."*

I put everything as I had found it, swung the bed back, used my handkerchief on knobs and other projections, and flat surfaces, killed the light and poked my nose out the door. The hall was empty. I went down to the street and around the corner to Kingsley Drive. The Cadillac hadn't moved.

I opened the car door and leaned on it. She didn't seem to have moved, either. It was hard to see any expression on her face. Hard to see anything but her eyes and chin, but not hard to smell the sandalwood.

"That perfume," I said, "would drive a deacon nuts . . . no pearls."

"Well—thanks for trying," she said in a low, soft, vibrant voice. "I guess I can stand it. Shall I . . . Do we . . . Or . . . ?"

"You go on home now," I said. "And whatever happens

you never saw me before. Whatever happens. Just as you may never see me again."

"I'd hate—"

"Good luck, Lola." I shut the car door and stepped back.

The lights blazed on, the motor turned over. Against the wind at the corner the big coupe made a slow contemptuous turn and was gone. I stood there by the vacant space at the curb where it had been.

It was quite dark there now. Windows had become blanks in the apartment where the radio sounded. I stood looking at the back of a Packard cabriolet which seemed to be brand new. I had seen it before—before I went upstairs, in the same place, in front of Lola's car. Parked, dark, silent, with a blue sticker pasted to the right-hand corner of the shiny windshield.

And in my mind I was looking at something else, a set of brand-new car keys in a keytainer stamped, *"The Packard House,"* upstairs, in a dead man's pocket.

I went up to the front of the cabriolet and put a small pocket flash on the blue slip. It was the same dealer all right. Written in ink below his name and slogan was a name and address—*Eugenie Kolchenko, 5315 Arvieda Street, West Los Angeles.*

It was crazy. I went back up to Apartment 31, jimmied the door as I had done before, stepped in behind the wall bed and took the keytainer from the trousers pocket of the neat brown dangling corpse. I was back down on the street beside the cabriolet in five minutes. The keys fitted.

5

It was a small house, near a canyon rim out beyond Sawtelle, with a circle of writhing eucalyptus trees in front of it. Beyond that, on the other side of the street, one of those parties was going on where they come out and smash bottles on the sidewalk with a whoop like Yale making a touchdown against Princeton.

There was a wire fence at my number and some rose-trees, and a flagged walk and a garage that was wide open and had no car in it. There was no car in front of the house either. I rang the bell. There was a long wait, then the door opened rather suddenly.

I wasn't the man she had been expecting. I could see it in her glittering kohl-rimmed eyes. Then I couldn't see anything in them. She just stood and looked at me, a long, lean, hungry brunette, with rouged cheekbones, thick black hair parted in the middle, a mouth made for three-decker sandwiches, coral-and-gold pajamas, sandals—and gilded toenails. Under her ear lobes a couple of miniature temple bells gonged lightly in the breeze. She made a slow disdainful motion with a cigarette in a holder as long as a baseball bat.

"We-el, what ees it, little man? You want sometheeng? You are lost from the bee-ootiful party across the street, hein?"

"Ha, ha," I said. "Quite a party, isn't it? No. I just brought your car home. Lost it, didn't you?"

Across the street somebody had delirium tremens in the front yard and a mixed quartet tore what was left of the night into small strips and did what they could to make the strips miserable. While this was going on the exotic brunette didn't move more than one eyelash.

She wasn't beautiful, she wasn't even pretty, but she looked as if things would happen where she was.

"You have said what?" she got out, at last, in a voice as silky as a burnt crust of toast.

"Your car." I pointed over my shoulder and kept my eyes on her. She was the type that uses a knife.

The long cigarette holder dropped very slowly to her side and the cigarette fell out of it. I stamped it out, and that put me in the hall. She backed away from me and I shut the door.

The hall was like the long hall of a railroad flat. Lamps glowed pinkly in iron brackets. There was a bead curtain at the end, a tiger skin on the floor. The place went with her.

"You're Miss Kolchenko?" I asked, not getting any more action.

"Ye-es. I am Mees Kolchenko. What thee 'ell you want?"

She was looking at me now as if I had come to wash the windows, but at an inconvenient time.

I got a card out with my left hand, held it out to her. She

read it in my hand, moving her head just enough. "A detective?" she breathed.

"Yeah."

She said something in a spitting language. Then in English: "Come in! Thees damn wind dry up my skeen like so much teessue paper."

"We're in," I said. "I just shut the door. Snap out of it, Nazimova. Who was he? The little guy?"

Beyond the bead curtain a man coughed. She jumped as if she had been stuck with an oyster fork. Then she tried to smile. It wasn't very successful.

"A reward," she said softly. "You weel wait 'ere? Ten dollars it is fair to pay, no?"

"No," I said.

I reached a finger towards her slowly and added: "He's dead."

She jumped about three feet and let out a yell.

A chair creaked harshly. Feet pounded beyond the bead curtain, a large hand plunged into view and snatched it aside, and a big hard-looking blond man was with us. He had a purple robe over his pajamas. His right hand held something in his robe pocket. He stood quite still as soon as he was through the curtain, his feet planted solidly, his jaw out, his colorless eyes like gray ice. He looked like a man who would be hard to take out on an off-tackle play.

"What's the matter, honey?" He had a solid, burring voice, with just the right sappy tone to belong to a guy who would go for a woman with gilded toenails.

"I came about Miss Kolchenko's car," I said.

"Well, you could take your hat off," he said. "Just for a light workout."

I took it off and apologized.

"O.K.," he said, and kept his right hand shoved down hard in the purple pocket. "So you came about Miss Kolchenko's car. Take it from there."

I pushed past the woman and went closer to him. She shrank back against the wall and flattened her palms against it. Camille in a high-school play. The long holder lay empty at her toes.

When I was six feet from the big man he said easily: "I

can hear you from there. Just take it easy. I've got a gun in this pocket and I've had to learn to use one. Now about the car?"

"The man who borrowed it couldn't bring it," I said, and pushed the card I was still holding towards his face. He barely glanced at it. He looked back at me.

"So what?" he said.

"Are you always this tough?" I asked, "or only when you have your pajamas on?"

"So why couldn't he bring it himself?" he asked. "And skip the mushy talk."

The dark woman made a stuffed sound at my elbow.

"It's all right, honeybunch," the man said. "I'll handle this. Go on in."

She slid past both of us and flicked through the bead curtain.

I waited a little while. The big man didn't move a muscle. He didn't look any more bothered than a toad in the sun.

"He couldn't bring it because somebody bumped him off," I said. "Let's see you handle that."

"Yeah?" he said. "Did you bring him with you to prove it?"

"No," I said. "But if you put your tie and crush hat on, I'll take you down and show you."

"Who the hell did you say you were, now?"

"I didn't say. I thought maybe you could read." I held the card at him some more.

"Oh, that's right," he said. "John Dalmas, Private Investigator. Well, well. So I should go with you to look at who, why?"

"Maybe he stole the car," I said.

The big man nodded. "That's a thought. Maybe he did. Who?"

"The little brown guy who had the keys to it in his pocket, and had it parked around the corner from the Berglund Apartments."

He thought that over, without any apparent embarrassment. "You've got something there," he said. "Not much. But a little. I guess this must be the night of the Police Smoker. So you're doing all their work for them."

"Huh?"

"The card says private detective to me," he said. "Have you got some cops outside that were too shy to come in?"

"No, I'm alone."

He grinned. The grin showed white ridges in his tanned skin. "So you find somebody dead and take some keys and find a car and come riding out here—all alone. No cops. Am I right?"

"Correct."

He sighed. "Let's go inside," he said. He yanked the bead curtain aside and made an opening for me to go through. "It might be you have an idea I ought to hear."

I went past him and he turned, keeping his heavy pocket towards me. I hadn't noticed until I got quite close that there were beads of sweat on his face. It might have been the hot wind, but I didn't think so.

We were in the living-room of the house.

We sat down and looked at each other across a dark floor, on which a few Navajo rugs and a few dark Turkish rugs made a decorating combination with some well-used overstuffed furniture. There was a fireplace, a small baby grand, a Chinese screen, a tall Chinese lantern on a teakwood pedestal, and gold net curtains against lattice windows. The windows to the south were open. A fruit tree with a whitewashed trunk whipped about outside the screen, adding its bit to the noise from across the street.

The big man eased back into a brocaded chair and put his slippered feet on a footstool. He kept his right hand where it had been since I met him—on his gun.

The brunette hung around in the shadows and a bottle gurgled and her temple bells gonged in her ears.

"It's all right, honeybunch," the man said. "It's all under control. Somebody bumped somebody off and this lad thinks we're interested. Just sit down and relax."

The girl tilted her head and poured half a tumbler of whiskey down her throat. She sighed, said, "Goddam," in a casual voice, and curled up on a davenport. It took all of the davenport. She had plenty of legs. Her gilded toenails winked at me from the shadowy corner where she kept herself quiet from then on.

I got a cigarette out without being shot at, lit it and went into my story. It wasn't all true, but some of it was. I told them about the Berglund Apartments and that I had lived there and that Waldo was living there in Apartment 31 on the floor below mine and that I had been keeping an eye on him for business reasons.

"Waldo what?" the blond man put in. "And what business reasons?"

"Mister," I said, "have you no secrets?" He reddened slightly.

I told him about the cocktail lounge across the street from the Berglund and what had happened there. I didn't tell him about the printed bolero jacket or the girl who had worn it. I left her out of the story altogether.

"It was an undercover job—from my angle," I said. "If you know what I mean." He reddened again, bit his teeth. I went on: "I got back from the city hall without telling anybody I knew Waldo. In due time, when I decided they couldn't find out where he lived that night, I took the liberty of examining his apartment."

"Looking for what?" the big man said thickly.

"For some letters. I might mention in passing there was nothing there at all—except a dead man. Strangled and hanging by a belt to the top of the wall bed—well out of sight. A small man, about forty-five, Mexican or South American, well-dressed in a fawn-colored—"

"That's enough," the big man said. "I'll bite, Dalmas. Was it a blackmail job you were on?"

"Yeah. The funny part was this little brown man had plenty of gun under his arm."

"He wouldn't have five hundred bucks in twenties in his pocket, of course? Or are you saying?"

"He wouldn't. But Waldo had over seven hundred in currency when he was killed in the cocktail bar."

"Looks like I underrated this Waldo," the big man said calmly. "He took my guy and his payoff money, gun and all. Waldo have a gun?"

"Not on him."

"Get us a drink, honeybunch," the big man said. "Yes, I certainly did sell this Waldo person shorter than a bargain-counter shirt."

The brunette unwound her legs and made two drinks with soda and ice. She took herself another gill without trimmings, wound herself back on the davenport. Her big glittering black eyes watched me solemnly.

"Well, here's how," the big man said, lifting his glass in salute. "I haven't murdered anybody, but I've got a divorce suit on my hands from now on. You haven't murdered anybody, the way you tell it, but you laid an egg down at police headquarters. What the hell! Life's a lot of trouble, anyway you look at it. I've still got honeybunch, here. She's a white Russian I met in Shanghai. She's safe as a vault and she looks as if she would cut your throat for a nickel. That's what I like about her. You get the glamor without the risk."

"You talk damn foolish," the girl spit at him.

"You look O.K. to me," the big man went on ignoring her. "That is, for a keyhole peeper. Is there an out?"

"Yeah. But it will cost a little money."

"I expected that. How much?"

"Say another five hundred."

"Goddam, thees hot wind make me dry like the ashes of love," the Russian girl said bitterly.

"Five hundred might do," the blond man said. "What do I get for it?"

"If I swing it—you get left out of the story. If I don't— you don't pay."

He thought it over. His face looked lined and tired now. The small beads of sweat twinkled in his short blond hair.

"This murder will make you talk," he grumbled. "The second one, I mean. And I don't have what I was going to buy. And if it's a hush, I'd rather buy it direct."

"Who was the little brown man?" I asked.

"Name's Leon Valesanos, a Uruguayan. Another of my importations. I'm in a business that takes me a lot of places. He was working in the Spezzia Club in Chiseltown—you know, the strip of Sunset next to Beverly Hills. Working on roulette, I think. I gave him the five hundred to go down to this—this Waldo—and buy back some bills for stuff Miss Kolchenko had charged to my account and delivered here. That wasn't bright, was it? I had them in my brief case and this Waldo got a chance to steal them. What's your hunch about what happened?"

I sipped my drink and looked at him down my nose. "Your Uruguayan pal probably talked cut and Waldo didn't listen good. Then the little guy thought maybe that Mauser might help his argument—and Waldo was too quick for him. I wouldn't say Waldo was a killer—not by intention. A blackmailer seldom is. Maybe he lost his temper and maybe he just held on to the little guy's neck too long. Then he had to take it on the lam. But he had another date, with more money coming up. And he worked the neighborhood looking for the party. And accidentally he ran into a pal who was hostile enough and drunk enough to blow him down."

"There's a hell of a lot of coincidence in all this business," the big man said.

"It's the hot wind," I grinned. "Everybody's screwy tonight."

"For the five hundred you guarantee nothing? If I don't get my cover-up, you don't get your dough. Is that it?"

"That's it," I said, smiling at him.

"Screwy is right," he said, and drained his highball. "I'm taking you up on it."

"There are just two things," I said softly, leaning forward in my chair. "Waldo had a getaway car parked outside the cocktail bar where he was killed, unlocked with the motor running. The killer took it. There's always the chance of a kickback from that direction. You see, all Waldo's stuff must have been in that car."

"Including my bills and your letters."

"Yeah. But the police are reasonable about things like that—unless you're good for a lot of publicity. If you're not, I think I can eat some stale dog downtown and get by. If you are—that's the second thing. What did you say your name was?"

The answer was a long time coming. When it came I didn't get as much kick out of it as I thought I would. All at once it was too logical.

"Frank C. Barsaly," he said.

After a while the Russian girl called me a taxi. When I left the party across the street was still doing all that a party could do. I noticed the walls of the house were still standing. That seemed a pity.

6

When I unlocked the glass entrance door of the Berglund I smelled policeman. I looked at my wrist watch. It was nearly 3 A.M. In the dark corner of the lobby a man dozed in a chair with a newspaper over his face. Large feet stretched out before him. A corner of the paper lifted an inch, dropped again. The man made no other movement.

I went on along the hall to the elevator and rode up to my floor. I soft-footed along the hallway, unlocked my door, pushed it wide and reached in for the light-switch.

A chain-switch tinkled and light glared from a standing-lamp by the easy chair, beyond the card table on which my chessmen were still scattered.

Copernik sat there with a stiff unpleasant grin on his face. The short dark man, Ybarra, sat across the room from him, on my left, silent, half-smiling as usual.

Copernik showed more of his big yellow horse teeth and said: "Hi. Long time no see. Been out with the girls?"

I shut the door and took my hat off and wiped the back of my neck slowly, over and over again. Copernik went on grinning. Ybarra looked at nothing with his soft dark eyes.

"Take a seat, pal," Copernik drawled. "Make yourself to home. We got pow-wow to make. Boy, do I hate this night sleuthing. Did you know you were all out of hooch?"

"I could have guessed it," I said. I leaned against the wall.

Copernik kept on grinning. "I always did hate private dicks," he said, "but I never had a chance to twist one like I got tonight."

He reached down lazily beside his chair and picked up a printed bolero jacket, tossed it on the card table. He reached down again and put a wide-brimmed hat beside it.

"I bet you look cuter than all hell with these on," he said.

I took hold of a straight chair, twisted it around and straddled it, leaned my folded arms on the chair and looked at Copernik.

He got up very slowly—with an elaborate slowness, walked across the room and stood in front of me smoothing his coat down. Then he lifted his open right hand and hit me across the face with it—hard. It stung but I didn't move.

Ybarra looked at the wall, looked at the floor, looked at nothing.

"Shame on you, pal," Copernik said lazily. "The way you was taking care of this nice exclusive merchandise. Wadded down behind your old shirts. You punk peepers always did make me sick."

He stood there over me for a moment. I didn't move or speak. I looked into his glazed drinker's eyes. He doubled a fist at his side, then shrugged and turned and went back to the chair.

"O.K.," he said. "The rest will keep. Where did you get these things?"

"They belong to a lady."

"Do tell. They belong to a lady. Ain't you the lighthearted ——! I'll tell you what lady they belong to. They belong to the lady a guy named Waldo asked about in a bar across the street—about two minutes before he got shot kind of dead. Or would that have slipped your mind?"

I didn't say anything.

"You was curious about her yourself," Copernik sneered on. "But you were smart, pal. You fooled me."

"That wouldn't make me smart," I said.

His face twisted suddenly and he started to get up. Ybarra laughed, suddenly and softly, almost under his breath. Copernik's eyes swung on him, hung there. Then he faced me again, blank-eyed.

"The guinea likes you," he said. "He thinks you're good."

The smile left Ybarra's face, but no expression took its place. No expression at all.

Copernik said: "You knew who the dame was all the time. You knew who Waldo was and where he lived. Right across the hall a floor below you. You knew this Waldo person had bumped a guy off and started to lam, only this broad came into his plans somewhere and he was anxious to meet up with her before he went away. Only he never got the chance. A heist guy from back East named Al Tessilore took care of that by taking care of Waldo. So you met the gal and hid her clothes and sent her on her way and kept your trap glued. That's the way guys like you make your beans. Am I right?"

"Yeah," I said. "Except that I only knew these things very recently. Who was Waldo?"

Copernik bared his teeth at me. Red spots burned high on his sallow cheeks. Ybarra, looking down at the floor, said very softly: "Waldo Ratigan. We got him from Washington by teletype. He was a two-bit porch-climber with a few small terms on him. He drove a car in a bank stickup job in Detroit. He turned the gang in later and got a nolle prosse. One of the gang was this Al Tessilore. He hasn't talked a word, but we think the meeting across the street was purely accidental."

Ybarra spoke in the soft quiet modulated voice of a man for whom sounds have a meaning. I said: "Thanks, Ybarra. Can I smoke—or would Copernik kick it out of my mouth?"

Ybarra smiled suddenly. "You may smoke, sure," he said.

"The guinea likes you all right," Copernik jeered. "You never know what a guinea will like, do you?"

I lit a cigarette. Ybarra looked at Copernik and said very softly: "The word guinea—you overwork it. I don't like it so well applied to me."

"The hell with what you like, guinea."

Ybarra smiled a little more. "You are making a mistake," he said. He took a pocket nailfile out and began to use it, looking down.

Copernik blared: "I smelled something rotten on you from the start, Dalmas. So when we make these two mugs, Ybarra and me think we'll drift over and dabble a few more words with you. I bring one of Waldo's morgue photos—nice work, the light just right in his eyes, his tie all straight and a white handkerchief showing just right in his pocket. Nice work. So on the way up, just as a matter of routine, we rout out the manager here and let him lamp it. And he knows the guy. He's here as A. B. Hummel, Apartment Thirty-one. So we go in there and find a stiff. Then we go round and round with that. Nobody knows him yet, but he's got some swell finger bruises under that strap and I hear they fit Waldo's fingers very nicely."

"That's something," I said. "I thought maybe I murdered him."

Copernik stared at me for a long time. His face had

stopped grinning and was just a hard brutal face now. "Yeah.
We got something else even," he said. "We got Waldo's getaway car—and what Waldo had in it to take with him."

I blew cigarette smoke jerkily. The wind pounded the shut
windows. The air in the room was foul.

"Oh we're bright boys," Copernik sneered. "We never figured you with that much guts. Take a look at this."

He plunged his bony hand into his coat pocket and drew
something up slowly over the edge of the card table, drew it
along the green top and left it there stretched out, gleaming.
A string of white pearls with a clasp like a two-bladed propeller. They shimmered softly in the thick smoky air.

Lola Barsaly's pearls. The pearls the flier had given her. The
guy who was dead, the guy she still loved.

I stared at them, but I didn't move. After a long moment
Copernik said almost gravely: "Nice, ain't they? Would you
feel like telling us a story about now, Mis-ter Dalmas?"

I stood up and pushed the chair from under me, walked
slowly across the room and stood looking down at the pearls.
The largest was perhaps a third of an inch across. They were
pure white, iridescent, with a mellow softness. I lifted them
slowly off the card table from beside her clothes. They felt
heavy, smooth, fine.

"Nice," I said. "A lot of the trouble was about these. Yeah,
I'll talk now. They must be worth a lot of money."

Ybarra laughed behind me. It was a very gentle laugh.
"About a hundred dollars," he said. "They're good phonies
—but they're phoney."

I lifted the pearls again. Copernik's glassy eyes gloated at
me. "How do you tell?" I asked.

"I know pearls," Ybarra said. "These are good stuff, the
kind women very often have made on purpose, as a kind of
insurance. But they are slick like glass. Real pearls are gritty
between the edges of the teeth. Try."

I put two or three of them between my teeth and moved
my teeth back and forth, then sideways. Not quite biting
them. The beads were hard and slick.

"Yes. They are very good," Ybarra said. "Several even have
little waves and flat spots, as real pearls might have."

"Would they cost fifteen grand—if they were real?" I asked.

"Si. Probably. That's hard to say. It depends on a lot of things."

"This Waldo wasn't so bad," I said.

Copernik stood up quickly, but I didn't see him swing. I was still looking down at the pearls. His fist caught me on the side of the face, against the molars. I tasted blood at once. I staggered back and made it look like a worse blow than it was.

"Sit down and talk, you —— !" Copernik almost whispered.

I sat down and used a handkerchief to pat my cheek. I licked at the cut inside my mouth. Then I got up again and went over and picked up the cigarette he had knocked out of my mouth. I crushed it out in a tray and sat down again.

Ybarra filed at his nails and held one up against the lamp. There were beads of sweat on Copernik's eyebrows, at the inner ends.

"You found the beads in Waldo's car," I said, looking at Ybarra. "Find any papers?"

He shook his head without looking up.

"I'd believe *you*," I said. "Here it is. I never saw Waldo until he stepped into the cocktail bar tonight and asked about the girl. I knew nothing I didn't tell. When I got home and stepped out of the elevator this girl, in the printed bolero jacket and the wide hat and the blue silk crepe dress—all as he had described them—was waiting for the elevator, here, on my floor. And she looked like a nice girl."

Copernik laughed jeeringly. It didn't make any difference to me. I had him cold. All he had to do was know that. He was going to know it now, very soon.

"I knew what she was up against as a police witness," I said. "And I suspected there was something else to it. But I didn't suspect for a minute that there was anything wrong with her. She was just a nice girl in a jam—and she didn't even know she was in a jam. I got her in here. She pulled a gun on me. But she didn't mean to use it."

Copernik sat up very suddenly and he began to lick his lips.

His face had a stony look now. A look like wet gray stone. He didn't make a sound.

"Waldo had been her chauffeur," I went on. "His name then was Joseph Choate. Her name is Mrs. Frank C. Barsaly. Her husband is a big hydro-electric engineer. Some guy gave her the pearls once and she told her husband they were just store pearls. Waldo got wise somehow there was a romance behind them and when Barsaly came home from South America and fired him, because he was too good-looking, he lifted the pearls."

Ybarra lifted his head suddenly and his teeth flashed. "You mean he didn't know they were phoney?"

"I thought he fenced the real ones and had imitations fixed up," I said.

Ybarra nodded. "It's possible."

"He lifted something else," I said. "Some stuff from Barsaly's briefcase that showed he was keeping a woman—out in Brentwood. He was blackmailing wife and husband both, without either knowing about the other. Get it so far?"

"I get it," Copernik said harshly, between his tight lips. His face was still wet gray stone. "Get the hell on with it."

"Waldo wasn't afraid of them," I said. "He didn't conceal where he lived. That was foolish, but it saved a lot of finagling, if he was willing to risk it. The girl came down here tonight with five grand to buy back her pearls. She never met Waldo. She came up here to look for him and walked up a floor before she went back down. A woman's idea of being cagey. So I met her. So I brought her in here. So she was in that dressing-room when Al Tessilore visited me to rub out a witness." I pointed to the dressing-room door. "So she came out with her little gun and stuck it in his back and saved my life," I said.

Copernik didn't move. There was something horrible in his face now. Ybarra slipped his nailfile into a small leather case and slowly tucked it into his pocket.

"Is that all?" he asked gently.

I nodded. "Except that she told me where Waldo's apartment was and I went in there and looked for the pearls. I found the dead man. In his pocket I found new car keys in a case from a Packard agency. And down on the street I found the Packard and took it to where it came from. Barsaly's kept woman. Barsaly had sent a friend from the Spezzia Club down to buy something and he had tried to buy it with his gun instead of the money Barsaly gave him. And Waldo beat him to the punch."

"Is that all?" Ybarra asked softly.

"That's all," I said, licking the torn place on the inside of my cheek.

Ybarra said slowly: "What do you want?"

Copernik's face convulsed and he slapped his long hard thigh. "This guy is good," he jeered. "He falls for a stray broad and breaks every law in the book and you ask him what does he want? I'll give him what he wants, guinea!"

Ybarra turned his head slowly and looked at him. "I don't think you will," he said. "I think you'll give him a clean bill of health and anything else he wants. He's giving you a lesson in police work."

Copernik didn't move or make a sound for a long minute. None of us moved. Then Copernik leaned forward and his coat fell open. The butt of his service gun looked out of its underarm holster.

"So what do you want?" he asked me.

"What's on the card table there. The jacket and hat and the phoney pearls. And some names kept away from the papers. Is that too much?"

"Yeah—it's too much," Copernik said almost gently. He swayed sideways and his gun jumped neatly into his hand. He rested his forearm on his thigh and pointed the gun at my stomach.

"I like better that you get a slug in the guts resisting arrest," he said. "I like that better, because of a report I made out on Al Tessilore's arrest and how I made the pinch. Because of some photos of me that are in the morning sheets going out about now. I like it better that you don't live long enough to laugh about that, baby."

My mouth felt suddenly hot and dry. Far off I heard the wind booming. It seemed like the sound of guns.

Ybarra moved his feet on the floor and said coldly: "You've got a couple of cases all solved, policeman. All you do for it is leave some junk here and keep some names from the papers. Which means from the D.A. If he gets them anyway, too bad for you."

Copernik said: "I like the other way." The blue gun in his hand was like a rock. "And God help you, if you don't back me up on it."

Ybarra said: "If the woman is brought out into the open, you'll be a liar on a police report and a chiseler on your own partner. In a week they won't even speak your name at headquarters. The taste of it would make them sick."

The hammer clicked back on Copernik's gun and I watched his big bony finger slide in farther around the trigger. The back of my neck was as wet as a dog's nose.

Ybarra stood up. The gun jumped at him. He said: "We'll see how yellow a guinea is. I'm telling you to put that gun up, Sam."

He started to move. He moved four even steps. Copernik was a man without a breath of movement, a stone man.

Ybarra took one more step and quite suddenly the gun began to shake.

Ybarra said evenly: "Put it up, Sam. If you keep your head everything lies the way it is. If you don't—you're gone."

He took one more step. Copernik's mouth opened wide and made a gasping sound and then he sagged in the chair as if he had been hit on the head. His eyelids drooped.

Ybarra jerked the gun out of his hand with a movement so quick it was no movement at all. He stepped back quickly, held the gun low at his side.

"It's the hot wind, Sam. Let's forget it," he said in the same even, almost dainty voice.

Copernik's shoulders sagged lower and he put his face in his hands. "O.K.," he said between his fingers.

Ybarra went softly across the room and opened the door. He looked at me with lazy, half-closed eyes. "I'd do a lot for a woman who saved my life, too," he said. "I'm eating this dish, but as a cop you can't expect me to like it."

I said: "The little man in the bed is called Leon Valesanos. He was a croupier at the Spezzia Club."

"Thanks," Ybarra said. "Let's go, Sam."

Copernik got up heavily and walked across the room and

out of the open door and out of my sight. Ybarra stepped
through the door after him and started to close it.

I said: "Wait a minute."

He turned his head slowly, his left hand on the door, the
blue gun hanging down close to his right side.

"I'm not in this for money," I said. "The Barsalys live at
Two-twelve Fremont Place. You can take the pearls to her. If
Barsaly's name stays out of the paper, I get five C's. It goes to
the Police Fund. I'm not so damn smart as you think. It just
happened that way—and you had a heel for a partner."

Ybarra looked across the room at the pearls on the card
table. His eyes glistened. "You take them," he said. "The five
hundred's O.K. I think the fund has it coming."

He shut the door quietly and in a moment I heard the
elevator doors clang.

7

I opened a window and stuck my head out into the wind and
watched the squad car tool off down the block. The wind
blew in hard and I let it blow. A picture fell off the wall and
two chessmen rolled off the card table. The material of Lola
Barsaly's bolero jacket lifted and shook.

I went out to the kitchenette and drank some Scotch and
went back into the living-room and called her—late as it was.

She answered the phone herself, very quickly, with no sleep
in her voice.

"Dalmas," I said. "O.K. your end?"

"Yes . . . yes," she said. "I'm alone."

"I found something," I said. "Or rather the police did. But
your dark boy gypped you. I have a string of pearls. They're
not real. He sold the real ones, I guess, and made you up a
string of ringers, with your clasp."

She was silent for a long time. Then, a little faintly: "The
police found them?"

"In Waldo's car. But they're not telling. We have a deal.
Look at the papers in the morning and you'll be able to figure
out why."

"There doesn't seem to be anything more to say," she said.
"Can I have the clasp?"

"Yes. Can you meet me tomorrow at four in the Club Esquire bar?"

"You're rather sweet," she said in a dragged out voice. "I can. Frank is still at his meeting."

"Those meetings—they take it out of a guy," I said. We said good-bye.

I called a West Los Angeles number. He was still there, with the Russian girl.

"You can send me a check for five hundred in the morning," I told him. "Made out to the Police Fund, if you want to. Because that's where it's going."

Copernik made the third page of the morning papers with two photos and a nice half-column. The little brown man in Apartment 31 didn't make the paper at all. The Apartment House Association has a good lobby too.

I went out after breakfast and the wind was all gone. It was soft, cool, a little foggy. The sky was close and comfortable and gray. I rode down to the boulevard and picked out the best jewellry store on it and laid a string of pearls on a black velvet mat under a daylight-blue lamp. A man in a wing collar and striped trousers looked down at them languidly.

"How good?" I asked.

"I'm sorry, sir. We don't make appraisals. I can give you the name of an appraiser."

"Don't kid me," I said. "They're Dutch."

He focussed the light a little and leaned down and toyed with a few inches of the string.

"I want a string just like them, fitted to that clasp, and in a hurry," I added.

"How, like them?" He didn't look up. "And they're not Dutch. They're Bohemian."

"O.K., can you duplicate them?"

He shook his head and pushed the velvet pad away as if it soiled him. "In three months, perhaps. We don't blow glass like that in this country. If you wanted them matched—three months at least. And this house would not do that sort of thing at all."

"It must be swell to be that snooty," I said. I put a card

under his black sleeve. "Give me a name that will—and not in three months—and maybe not exactly like them."

He shrugged, went away with the card, came back in five minutes and handed it back to me. There was something written on the back.

The old Levantine had a shop on Melrose, a junk shop with everything in the window from a folding baby carriage to a French horn, from a mother-of-pearl lorgnette in a faded plush case to one of those .44 Special Single Action Six-shooters they still make for Western peace officers whose grandfathers were tough.

The old Levantine wore a skull cap and two pairs of glasses and a full beard. He studied my pearls, shook his head sadly, and said: "For twenty dollars, almost so good. Not so good, you understand. Not so good glass."

"How like will they look?"

He spread his firm strong hands. "I am telling you the truth," he said. "They would not fool a baby."

"Make them up," I said. "With this clasp. And I want the others back too, of course."

"Yah. Two o'clock," he said.

Leon Valesanos, the little brown man from Uruguay, made the afternoon papers. He had been found hanging in an un-named apartment. The police were investigating.

At four o'clock I walked into the long cool bar of the Club Esquire and prowled along the row of booths until I found one where a woman sat alone. She wore a hat like a shallow soup plate with a very wide edge, a brown tailor-made suit with a severe mannish shirt and tie.

I sat down beside her and slipped a parcel along the seat. "You don't open that," I said. "In fact you can slip it into the incinerator as is, if you want to."

She looked at me with dark tired eyes. Her fingers twisted a thin glass that smelled of peppermint. "Thanks." Her face was very pale.

I ordered a highball and the waiter went away. "Read the papers?"

"Yes."

"You understand now about this fellow Copernik who stole

your act? That's why they won't change the story or bring you into it."

"It doesn't matter now," she said. "Thank you, all the same. Please—please, show them to me."

I pulled a string of pearls out of the loosely wrapped tissue paper in my pocket and slid them across to her. The silver propeller clasp winked in the light of the wall bracket. The little diamond winked. The pearls were as dull as white soap. They didn't even match in size.

"You were right," she said tonelessly. "They are not my pearls."

The waiter came with my drink and she put her bag on them deftly. When he was gone she fingered them slowly once more, dropped them into the bag and gave me a dry mirthless smile.

"As you said—I'll keep the clasp."

I said slowly: "You don't know anything about me. You saved my life last night and we had a moment, but it was just a moment. You still don't know anything about me. There's a detective downtown named Ybarra, a Mexican of the nice sort, who was on the job when the pearls were found in Waldo's suitcase. That's in case you would like to make sure—"

She said: "Don't be silly. It's all finished. It was a memory. I'm too young to nurse memories. It may be all for the best. I loved Stan Phillips—but he's gone—long gone."

I stared at her, didn't say anything.

She added quietly: "This morning my husband told me something I hadn't known. We are to separate. So I have very little to laugh about today."

"I'm sorry," I said lamely. "There's nothing to say. I may see you sometime. Maybe not. I don't move much in your circle. Good luck."

I stood up. We looked at each other for a moment. "You haven't touched your drink," she said.

"You drink it. That peppermint stuff will just make you sick."

I stood there a moment with a hand hard on the table.

"If anybody ever bothers you," I said, "let me know."

I went out of the bar without looking back at her, got into

my car and drove west on Sunset and down all the way to the Coast Highway. Everywhere along the way gardens were full of withered and blackened leaves and flowers which the hot wind had burned.

But the ocean looked cool and languid and just the same as ever. I drove on almost to Malibu and then parked and went and sat on a big rock that was inside somebody's wire fence. It was about half-tide and coming in. The air smelled of kelp. I watched the water for a while and then I pulled a string of Bohemian glass imitation pearls out of my pocket and cut the knot at one end and slipped the pearls off one by one.

When I had them all loose in my left hand I held them like that for a while and thought. There wasn't really anything to think about. I was sure.

"To the memory of Mr. Stan Phillips," I said out loud. "Just another four-flusher."

I flipped her pearls out into the water one by one, at the floating seagulls.

They made little splashes and the seagulls rose off the water and swooped at the splashes.

The King in Yellow

GEORGE MILLAR, night auditor at the Carlton Hotel, was a dapper wiry little man, with a soft deep voice like a torch-singer's. He kept it low, but his eyes were sharp and angry, as he said into the PBX mouthpiece: "I'm very sorry. It won't happen again. I'll send up at once."

He tore off the head-piece, dropped it on the keys of the switchboard and marched swiftly from behind the pebbled screen and out into the entrance lobby. It was past one and the Carlton was two-thirds residential. In the main lobby, down three shallow steps, lamps were dimmed and the night porter had finished tidying up. The place was deserted—a wide space of dim furniture, rich carpet. Faintly in the distance a radio sounded. Millar went down the steps and walked quickly towards the sound, turned through an archway and looked at a man stretched out on a pale-green davenport and what looked like all the loose cushions in the hotel. He lay on his side, dreamy-eyed and listened to the radio two yards away from him.

Millar barked: "Hey, you! Are you the house dick here or the house cat?"

Steve Grayce turned his head slowly and looked at Millar. He was a long black-haired man, about twenty-eight, with deep-set silent eyes and a rather gentle mouth. He jerked a thumb at the radio and smiled. "King Leopardi, George. Hear that trumpet tone. Smooth as an angel's wing, boy."

"Swell! Go on back upstairs and get him out of the corridor!"

Steve Grayce looked shocked. "What—again? I thought I had those birds put to bed long ago." He swung his feet to the floor and stood up. He was at least a foot taller than Millar.

"Well, Eight-sixteen says no. Eight-sixteen says he's out in the hall with two of his stooges. He's dressed in yellow satin shorts and a trombone and he and his pals are putting on a jam session. And one of those hustlers Quillan registered in

Eight-eleven is out there truckin' for them. Now get on to it, Steve—and this time make it stick."

Steve Grayce smiled wryly. He said: "Leopardi doesn't belong here anyway. Can I use chloroform or just my blackjack?"

He stepped long legs over the pale-green carpet, through the arch and across the main lobby to the single elevator that was open and lighted. He slid the doors shut and ran it up to Eight, stopped it roughly and stepped out into the corridor.

The noise hit him like a sudden wind. The walls echoed with it. Half a dozen doors were open and angry guests in night robes stood in them peering.

"It's O.K. folks," Steve Grayce said rapidly. "This is absolutely the last act. Just relax."

He rounded a corner and the hot music almost took him off his feet. Three men were lined up against the wall, near an open door from which light streamed. The middle one, the one with the trombone, was six feet tall, powerful and graceful, with a hairline mustache. His face was flushed and his eyes had an alcoholic glitter. He wore yellow satin shorts with large initials embroidered in black on the left leg—nothing more. His torso was tanned and naked.

The two with him were in pajamas, the usual halfway-good-looking band boys, both drunk, but not staggering drunk. One jittered madly on a clarinet and the other on a tenor saxophone.

Back and forth in front of them, strutting, trucking, preening herself like a magpie, arching her arms and her eyebrows, bending her fingers back until the carmine nails almost touched her arms, a metallic blonde swayed and went to town on the music. Her voice was a throaty screech, without melody, as false as her eyebrows and as sharp as her nails. She wore high-heeled slippers and black pajamas with a long purple sash.

Steve Grayce stopped dead and made a sharp downward motion with his hand. "Wrap it up!" he snapped. "Can it. Put it on ice. Take it away and bury it. The show's out. Scram, now—scram!"

King Leopardi took the trombone from his lips and bellowed: "Fanfare to a house dick!"

The three drunks blew a stuttering note that shook the walls. The girl laughed foolishly and kicked out. Her slipper caught Steve Grayce in the chest. He picked it out of the air, jumped towards the girl and took hold of her wrist.

"Tough, eh?" he grinned. "I'll take you first."

"Get him!" Leopardi yelled. "Sock him low! Dance the gum-heel on his neck!"

Steve swept the girl off her feet, tucked her under his arm and ran. He carried her as easily as a parcel. She tried to kick his legs. He laughed and shot a glance through a lighted doorway. A man's brown brogues lay under a bureau. He went on past that to a second lighted doorway, slammed through and kicked the door shut, turned far enough to twist the tabbed key in the lock. Almost at once a fist hit the door. He paid no attention to it.

He pushed the girl along the short passage past the bathroom, and let her go. She reeled away from him and put her back to the bureau, panting, her eyes furious. A lock of damp gold-dipped hair swung down over one eye. She shook her head violently and bared her teeth.

"How would you like to get vagged, sister?"

"Go to hell!" she spit out. "The King's a friend of mine, see? You better keep your paws off me, copper."

"You run the circuit with the boys?"

She spat at him again.

"How'd you know they'd be here?"

Another girl was sprawled across the bed, her head to the wall, tousled black hair over a white face. There was a tear in the leg of her pajamas. She lay limp and groaned.

Steve said harshly: "Oh, oh, the torn-pajama act. It flops here, sister, it flops hard. Now listen, you kids. You can go to bed and stay till morning or you can take the bounce. Make up your minds."

The black-haired girl groaned. The blonde said: "You get out of my room, you damned gum-heel!"

She reached behind her and threw a hand mirror. Steve ducked. The mirror slammed against the wall and fell without breaking. The black-haired girl rolled over on the bed and said wearily: "Oh lay off. I'm sick."

She lay with her eyes closed, the lids fluttering.

The blonde swiveled her hips across the room to a desk by the window, poured herself a full half-glass of Scotch in a water glass and gurgled it down before Steve could get to her. She choked violently, dropped the glass and went down on her hands and knees.

Steve said grimly: "That's the one that kicks you in the face, sister."

The girl crouched, shaking her head. She gagged once, lifted the carmine nails to paw at her mouth. She tried to get up, and her foot skidded out from under her and she fell down on her side and went fast asleep.

Steve sighed, went over and shut the window and fastened it. He rolled the black-haired girl over and straightened her on the bed and got the bedclothes from under her, tucked a pillow under her head. He picked the blonde bodily off the floor and dumped her on the bed and covered both girls to the chin. He opened the transom, switched off the ceiling-light and unlocked the door. He relocked it from the outside, with a master-key on a chain.

"Hotel business," he said under his breath. "Phooey."

The corridor was empty now. One lighted door still stood open. Its number was 815, two doors from the room the girls were in. Trombone music came from it softly—but not softly enough for 1:25 A.M.

Steve Grayce turned into the room, crowded the door shut with his shoulder and went along past the bathroom. King Leopardi was alone in the room.

The bandleader was sprawled out in an easy chair, with a tall misted glass at his elbow. He swung the trombone in a tight circle as he played it and the lights danced in the horn.

Steve lit a cigarette, blew a plume of smoke and stared through it at Leopardi with a queer, half-admiring, half-contemptuous expression.

He said softly: "Lights out, yellow pants. You play a sweet trumpet and your trombone don't hurt either. But we can't use it here. I already told you that once. Lay off. Put that thing away."

Leopardi smiled nastily and blew a stuttering raspberry that sounded like a devil laughing.

"Says you," he sneered. "Leopardi does what he likes,

where he likes, when he likes. Nobody's stopped him yet, gum-shoe. Take the air."

Steve hunched his shoulders and went close to the tall dark man. He said patiently: "Put that bazooka down, big-stuff. People are trying to sleep. They're funny that way. You're a great guy on a bandshell. Everywhere else you're just a guy with a lot of jack and a personal reputation that stinks from here to Miami and back. I've got a job to do and I'm doing it. Blow that thing again and I'll wrap it around your neck."

Leopardi lowered the trombone and took a long drink from the glass at his elbow. His eyes glinted nastily. He lifted the trombone to his lips again, filled his lungs with air and blew a blast that rocked the walls. Then he stood up very suddenly and smoothly and smashed the instrument down on Steve's head.

"I never did like house-peepers," he sneered. "They smell like public toilets."

Steve took a short step back and shook his head. He leered, slid forward on one foot and smacked Leopardi open-handed. The blow looked light, but Leopardi reeled all the way across the room and sprawled at the foot of the bed, sitting on the floor, his right arm draped in an open suitcase.

For a moment neither man moved. Then Steve kicked the trombone away from him and squashed his cigarette in a glass tray. His black eyes were empty but his mouth grinned whitely.

"If you want trouble," he said, "I come from where they make it."

Leopardi smiled, thinly, tautly, and his right hand came up out of the suitcase with a gun in it. His thumb snicked the safety catch. He held the gun steady, pointing.

"Make some with this," he said, and fired.

The bitter roar of the gun seemed a tremendous sound in the closed room. The bureau mirror splintered and glass flew. A sliver cut Steve's cheek like a razor blade. Blood oozed in a small narrow line on his skin.

He left his feet in a dive. His right shoulder crashed against Leopardi's bare chest and his left hand brushed the gun away from him, under the bed. He rolled swiftly to his right and came up on his knees spinning.

He said thickly, harshly: "You picked the wrong gee, brother."

He swarmed on Leopardi and dragged him to his feet by his hair, by main strength. Leopardi yelled and hit him twice on the jaw and Steve grinned and kept his left hand twisted in the bandleader's long sleek black hair. He turned his hand and the head twisted with it and Leopardi's third punch landed on Steve's shoulder. Steve took hold of the wrist behind the punch and twisted that and the bandleader went down on his knees yowling. Steve lifted him by the hair again, let go of his wrist and punched him three times in the stomach, short terrific jabs. He let go of the hair then as he sank the fourth punch almost to his wrist.

Leopardi sagged blindly to his knees and vomited.

Steve stepped away from him and went into the bathroom and got a towel off the rack. He threw it at Leopardi, jerked the open suitcase onto the bed and started throwing things into it.

Leopardi wiped his face and got to his feet still gagging. He swayed, braced himself on the end of the bureau. He was white as a sheet.

Steve Grayce said: "Get dressed, Leopardi. Or go out the way you are. It's all one to me."

Leopardi stumbled into the bathroom, pawing the wall like a blind man.

2

Millar stood very still behind the desk as the elevator opened. His face was white and scared and his cropped black mustache was a smudge across his upper lip. Leopardi came out of the elevator first, a muffler around his neck, a lightweight coat tossed over his arm, a hat tilted on his head. He walked stiffly, bent forward a little, his eyes vacant. His face had a greenish pallor.

Steve Grayce stepped out behind him carrying a suitcase, and Carl, the night porter, came last with two more suitcases and two instrument cases in black leather. Steve marched over to the desk and said harshly: "Mr. Leopardi's bill—if any. He's checking out."

Millar goggled at him across the marble desk. "I—I don't think, Steve—"

"O.K. I thought not."

Leopardi smiled very thinly and unpleasantly and walked out through the brass-edged swing doors the porter held open for him. There were two nighthawk cabs in the line. One of them came to life and pulled up to the canopy and the porter loaded Leopardi's stuff into it. Leopardi got into the cab and leaned forward to put his head to the open window. He said slowly and thickly: "I'm sorry for you, gum-heel. I mean sorry."

Steve Grayce stepped back and looked at him woodenly. The cab moved off down the street, rounded a corner and was gone. Steve turned on his heel, took a quarter from his pocket and tossed it up in the air. He slapped it into the night porter's hand.

"From the King," he said. "Keep it to show your grand-children."

He went back into the hotel, got into the elevator without looking at Millar, shot it up to Eight again and went along the corridor, master-keyed his way into Leopardi's room. He relocked it from the inside, pulled the bed out from the wall and went in behind it. He got a .32 automatic off the carpet, put it in his pocket and prowled the floor with his eyes look-ing for the ejected shell. He found it against the wastebasket, reached to pick it up, and stayed bent over, staring into the basket. His mouth tightened. He picked up the shell and dropped it absently into his pocket, then reached a questing finger into the basket and lifted out a torn scrap of paper on which a piece of newsprint had been pasted. Then he picked up the basket, pushed the bed back against the wall and dumped the contents of the basket out on it.

From the trash of torn papers and matches he separated a number of pieces with newsprint pasted to them. He went over to the desk with them and sat down. A few minutes later he had the torn scraps put together like a jigsaw puzzle and could read the message that had been made by cutting words and letters from magazines and pasting them on a sheet.

Ten grand by Thursday night, Leopardi. Day after you open at the Club Shalotte. Or else—curtains. From Her Brother.

Steve Grayce said: "Huh." He scooped the torn pieces into a hotel envelope, put that in his inside breast pocket and lit a cigarette. "The guy had guts," he said. "I'll grant him that—and his trumpet."

He locked the room, listened a moment in the now silent corridor, then went along to the room occupied by the two girls. He knocked softly and put his ear to the panel. A chair squeaked and feet came towards the door.

"What is it?" The girl's voice was cool, wide awake. It was not the blonde's voice.

"The house man. Can I speak to you a minute?"

"You're speaking to me."

"Without the door between, lady."

"You've got the passkey. Help yourself." The steps went away. He unlocked the door with his master-key, stepped quietly inside, and shut it. There was a dim light in a lamp with a shirred shade on the desk. On the bed the blonde snored heavily, one hand clutched in her brilliant metallic hair. The black-haired girl sat in the chair by the window, her legs crossed at right angles like a man's and stared at Steve emptily.

He went close to her and pointed to the long tear in her pajama leg. He said softly: "You're not sick. You were not drunk. That tear was done a long time ago. What's the racket? A shakedown on the King?"

The girl stared at him coolly, puffed at a cigarette and said nothing.

"He checked out," Steve said. "Nothing doing in that direction now, sister." He watched her like a hawk, his black eyes hard and steady on her face.

"Aw, you house dicks make me sick!" the girl said with sudden anger. She surged to her feet and went past him into the bathroom, shut and locked the door.

Steve shrugged and felt the pulse of the girl asleep in the bed—a thumpy, draggy pulse, a liquor pulse.

"Poor damn hustlers," he said under his breath.

He looked at a large purple bag that lay on the bureau, lifted it idly and let it fall. His face stiffened again. The bag made a heavy sound on the glass top, as if there were a lump of lead inside it. He snapped it open quickly and plunged a hand in. His fingers touched the cold metal of a gun. He opened the bag wide and stared down into it at a small .25 automatic. A scrap of white paper caught his eye. He fished it out and held it to the light—a rent receipt with a name and address. He stuffed it into his pocket, closed the bag and was standing by the window when the girl came out of the bathroom.

"Hell, are you still haunting me?" she snapped. "You know what happens to hotel dicks that master-key their way into ladies' bedrooms at night?"

Steve said loosely: "Yeah. They get in trouble. They might even get shot at."

The girl's face became set, but her eyes crawled sideways and looked at the purple bag. Steve looked at her. "Know Leopardi in Frisco?" he asked. "He hasn't played here in two years. Then he was just a trumpet player in Vane Utigore's band—a cheap outfit."

The girl curled her lip, went past him and sat down by the window again. Her face was white, stiff. She said dully: "Blossom did. That's Blossom on the bed."

"Know he was coming to this hotel tonight?"

"What makes it your business?"

"I can't figure him coming here at all," Steve said. "This is a quiet place. So I can't figure anybody coming here to put the bite on him."

"Go somewhere else and figure. I need sleep."

Steve said: "Good night, sweetheart—and keep your door locked."

A thin man with thin blond hair and thin face was standing by the desk, tapping on the marble with thin fingers. Millar was still behind the desk and he still looked white and scared. The thin man wore a dark gray suit with a scarf inside the collar of the coat. He had a look of having just got up. He turned sea-green eyes slowly on Steve as he got out of the elevator, waited for him to come up to the desk and throw a tabbed key on it.

Steve said: "Leopardi's key, George. There's a busted mirror in his room and the carpet has his dinner on it—mostly Scotch." He turned to the thin man. "You want to see me, Mr. Peters?"

"What happened, Grayce?" The thin man had a tight voice that expected to be lied to.

"Leopardi and two of his boys were on Eight, the rest of the gang on Five. The bunch on Five went to bed. A couple of obvious hustlers managed to get themselves registered just two rooms from Leopardi. They managed to contact him and everybody was having a lot of nice noisy fun out in the hall. I could only stop it by getting a little tough."

"There's blood on your cheek," Peters said coldly. "Wipe it off."

Steve scratched at his cheek with a handkerchief. The thin thread of blood had dried. "I got the girls tucked away in their room," he said. "The two stooges took the hint and holed up, but Leopardi still thought the guests wanted to hear trombone music. I threatened to wrap it around his neck and he beaned me with it. I slapped him open-handed and he pulled a gun and took a shot at me. Here's the gun."

He took the .32 automatic out of his pocket and laid it on the desk. He put the used shell beside it. "So I beat some sense into him and threw him out," he added.

Peters tapped on the marble. "Your usual tact seems to have been well in evidence."

Steve stared at him. "He shot at me," he repeated quietly. "With a gun. This gun. I'm tender to bullets. He missed, but suppose he hadn't? I like my stomach the way it is, with just one way in and one way out."

Peters narrowed his tawny eyebrows. He said very politely: "We have you down on the payroll here as a night clerk, because we don't like the name house detective. But neither night clerks nor house detectives put guests out of the hotel without consulting me. Not ever, Mr. Grayce."

Steve said: "The guy shot at me, pal. With a gun. Catch on? I don't have to take that without a kickback, do I?" His face was a little white.

Peters said: "Another point for your consideration. The controlling interest in this hotel is owned by Mr. Halsey G.

Walters. Mr. Walters also owns the Club Shalotte, where King Leopardi is opening on Wednesday night. And that, Mr. Grayce, is why Leopardi was good enough to give us his business. Can you think of anything else I should like to say to you?"

"Yeah. I'm canned," Steve said mirthlessly.

"Very correct, Mr. Grayce. Good-night, Mr. Grayce."

The thin blond man moved to the elevator and the night porter took him up.

Steve looked at Millar.

"Jumbo Walters, huh?" he said softly. "A tough, smart guy. Much too smart to think this dump and the Club Shalotte belong to the same sort of customers. Did Peters write Leopardi to come here?"

"I guess he did, Steve." Millar's voice was low and gloomy.

"Then why wasn't he put in a tower suite with a private balcony to dance on, at eighteen bucks a day? Why was he put on a medium-priced transient floor? And why did Quillan let those girls get so close to him?"

Millar pulled at his black mustache. "Tight with money—as well as with Scotch, I suppose. As to the girls, I don't know."

Steve slapped the counter open-handed. "Well, I'm canned, for not letting a drunken heel make a parlor house and a shooting gallery out of the eighth floor. Nuts! Well, I'll miss the joint at that."

"I'll miss you too, Steve," Millar said gently. "But not for a week. I take a week off starting tomorrow. My brother has a cabin at Crestline."

"Didn't know you had a brother," Steve said absently. He opened and closed his fist on the marble desk-top.

"He doesn't come into town much. A big guy. Used to be a fighter."

Steve nodded and straightened from the counter. "Well, I might as well finish out the night," he said. "On my back. Put this gun away somewhere, George."

He grinned coldly and walked away, down the steps into the dim main lobby and across to the room where the radio was. He punched the pillows into shape on the pale green davenport, then suddenly reached into his pocket and took out the scrap of white paper he had lifted from the black-haired girl's purple hand-bag. It was a receipt for a week's rent, to a Miss Marilyn Delorme, Apt. 211, Ridgeland Apartments, 118 Court Street.

He tucked it into his wallet and stood staring at the silent radio. "Steve, I think you got another job," he said under his breath. "Something about this set-up smells."

He slipped into a closetlike phone booth in the corner of the room, dropped a nickel and dialed an all-night radio station. He had to dial four times before he got a clear line to the Owl Program announcer.

"How's to play King Leopardi's record of *Solitude* again?" he asked him.

"Got a lot of requests piled up. Played it twice already. Who's calling?"

"Steve Grayce, night man at the Carlton Hotel."

"Oh, a sober guy on his job. For you, pal, anything."

Steve went back to the davenport, snapped the radio on and lay down on his back, with his hands clasped behind his head.

Ten minutes later the high, piercingly sweet trumpet notes of King Leopardi came softly from the radio, muted almost to a whisper, and sustaining E in Alt for an almost incredible period of time.

"Shucks," Steve grumbled, when the record ended. "A guy that can play like that—maybe I was too tough with him."

3

Court Street was old town, wop town, crook town, arty town. It lay across the top of Bunker Hill and you could find anything there from down-at-heels ex-Greenwich-villagers to crooks on the lam, from ladies of anybody's evening to County Relief clients brawling with haggard landladies in grand old houses with scrolled porches, parquetry floors, and immense sweeping banisters of white oak, mahogany and Circassian walnut.

It had been a nice place once, had Bunker Hill, and from the days of its niceness there still remained the funny little funicular railway, called the Angel's Flight, which crawled up and down a yellow clay bank from Hill Street. It was afternoon when

Steve Grayce got off the car at the top, its only passenger. He walked along in the sun, a tall, wide-shouldered, rangy-looking man in a well-cut blue suit.

He turned west at Court and began to read the numbers. The one he wanted was two from the corner, across the street from a red brick funeral parlor with a sign in gold over it— *Paolo Perrugini Funeral Home*. A swarthy iron-gray Italian in a cutaway coat stood in front of the curtained door of the red brick building, smoking a cigar and waiting for somebody to die.

118 was a three-storied frame apartment house. It had a glass door, well masked by a dirty net curtain, a hall runner eighteen inches wide, dim doors with numbers painted on them with dim paint, a staircase halfway back. Brass stair rods glittered in the dimness of the hallway.

Steve Grayce went up the stairs and prowled back to the front. Apartment 211, Miss Marilyn Delorme, was on the right, a front apartment. He tapped lightly on the wood, waited, tapped again. Nothing moved beyond the silent door, or in the hallway. Behind another door across the hall somebody coughed and kept on coughing.

Standing there in the half-light Steve Grayce wondered why he had come. Miss Delorme had carried a gun. Leopardi had received some kind of a threat letter and torn it up and thrown it away. Miss Delorme had checked out of the Carlton about an hour after Steve told her Leopardi was gone. Even at that—

He took out a leather keyholder and studied the lock of the door. It looked as if it would listen to reason. He tried a pick on it, snicked the bolt back and stepped softly into the room. He shut the door, but the pick wouldn't lock it.

The room was dim with drawn shades across two front windows. The air smelled of face powder. There was light-painted furniture, a pull-down double bed which was pulled down but had been made up. There was a magazine on it, a glass tray full of cigarette butts, a pint bottle half full of whiskey, and a glass on a chair beside the bed. Two pillows had been used for a back rest and were still crushed in the middle.

On the dresser there was a composition toilet set, neither

cheap nor expensive, a comb with black hair in it, a tray of manicuring stuff, plenty of spilled powder—in the bathroom, nothing. In a closet behind the bed a lot of clothes and two suitcases. The shoes were all one size.

Steve stood beside the bed and pinched his chin. "Blossom, the spitting blonde, doesn't live here," he said under his breath. "Just Marilyn the torn-pants brunette."

He went back to the dresser and pulled drawers out. In the bottom drawer, under the piece of wall paper that lined it, he found a box of .25 copper-nickel automatic shells. He poked at the butts in the ash tray. All had lipstick on them. He pinched his chin again, then feathered the air with the palm of his hand, like an oarsman with a scull.

"Bunk," he said softly. "Wasting your time, Stevie."

He walked over to the door and reached for the knob, then turned back to the bed and lifted it by the footrail.

Miss Marilyn Delorme was in.

She lay on her side on the floor under the bed, long legs scissored out as if in running. One mule was on, one off. Garters and skin showed at the tops of her stockings, and a blue rose on something pink. She wore a square-necked, beige-sleeved dress that was not too clean. Her neck above the dress was blotched with purple bruises.

Her face was a dark plum color, her eyes had the faint stale glitter of death, and her mouth was open so far that it foreshortened her face. She was colder than ice, and still quite limp. She had been dead two or three hours at least, six hours at most.

The purple bag was beside her, gaping like her mouth. Steve didn't touch any of the stuff that had been emptied out on the floor. There was no gun and there were no papers.

He let the bed down over her again, then made the rounds of the apartment, wiping everything he had touched and a lot of things he couldn't remember whether he had touched or not.

He listened at the door and stepped out. The hall was still empty. The man behind the opposite door still coughed. Steve went down the stairs, looked at the mailboxes and went back along the lower hall to a door.

Behind this door a chair creaked monotonously. He knocked and a woman's sharp voice called out. Steve opened the door with his handkerchief and stepped in.

In the middle of the room a woman rocked in an old Boston rocker, her body in the slack boneless attitude of exhaustion. She had a mud-colored face, stringy hair, gray cotton stockings—everything a Bunker Hill landlady should have. She looked at Steve with the interested eye of a dead goldfish.

"Are you the manager?"

The woman stopped rocking, screamed, "Hi, Jake! Company!" at the top of her voice, and started rocking again.

An icebox door thudded shut behind a partly open inner door and a very big man came into the room carrying a can of beer. He had a doughy mooncalf face, a tuft of fuzz on top of an otherwise bald head, a thick brutal neck and chin, and brown pig eyes about as expressionless as the woman's. He needed a shave—had needed one the day before—and his collarless shirt gaped over a big hard hairy chest. He wore scarlet suspenders with large gilt buckles on them.

He held the can of beer out to the woman. She clawed it out of his hand and said bitterly: "I'm so tired I ain't got no sense."

The man said: "Yah. You ain't done the halls so good at that."

The woman snarled: "I done 'em as good as I aim to." She sucked the beer thirstily.

Steve looked at the man and said: "Manager?"

"Yah. 'S me. Jake Stoyanoff. Two hun'erd eighty-six stripped, and still plenty tough."

Steve said: "Who lives in Two-eleven?"

The big man leaned forward a little from the waist and snapped his suspenders. Nothing changed in his eyes. The skin along his big jaw may have tightened a little. "A dame," he said.

"Alone?"

"Go on—ask me," the big man said. He stuck his hand out and lifted a cigar off the edge of a stained-wood table. The cigar was burning unevenly and it smelled as if somebody had set fire to the doormat. He pushed it into his mouth with a hard, thrusting motion, as if he expected his mouth wouldn't want it to go in.

"I'm asking you," Steve said.

"Ask me out in the kitchen," the big man drawled.

He turned and held the door open. Steve went past him.

The big man kicked the door shut against the squeak of the rocking chair, opened up the icebox and got out two cans of beer. He opened them and handed one to Steve.

"Dick?"

Steve drank some of the beer, put the can down on the sink, got a brand-new card out of his wallet—a business card printed that morning. He handed it to the man.

The man read it, put it down on the sink, picked it up and read it again. "One of them guys," he growled over his beer. "What's she pulled this time?"

Steve shrugged and said: "I guess it's the usual. The torn-pajama act. Only there's a kickback this time."

"How come? You handling it, huh? Must be a nice cozy one."

Steve nodded. The big man blew smoke from his mouth. "Go ahead and handle it," he said.

"You don't mind a pinch here?"

The big man laughed heartily. "Nuts to you, brother," he said pleasantly enough. "You're a private dick. So it's a hush. O.K. Go out and hush it. And if it *was* a pinch—that bothers me like a quart of milk. Go into your act. Take all the room you want. Cops don't bother Jake Stoyanoff."

Steve stared at the man. He didn't say anything. The big man talked it up some more, seemed to get more interested. "Besides," he went on, making motions with the cigar, "I'm softhearted. I never turn up a dame. I never put a frill in the middle." He finished his beer and threw the can in a basket under the sink, and pushed his hand out in front of him, revolving the large thumb slowly against the next two fingers. "Unless there's some of that," he added.

Steve said softly: "You've got big hands. You could have done it."

"Huh?" His small brown leathery eyes got silent and stared.

Steve said: "Yeah. You might be clean as an angel's wing.

But with those hands the cops'd go round and round with you just the same."

The big man moved a little to his left, away from the sink. He let his right hand hang down at his side, loosely. His mouth got so tight that the cigar almost touched his nose.

"What's the beef, huh?" he barked. "What you shovin' at me, guy? What—"

"Cut it," Steve drawled. "She's been croaked. Strangled. Upstairs, on the floor under her bed. About midmorning, I'd say. Big hands did it—hands like yours."

The big man did a nice job of getting the gun off his hip. It arrived so suddenly that it seemed to have grown in his hand and been there all the time.

Steve frowned at the gun and didn't move. The big man looked him over. "You're tough," he said. "I been in the ring long enough to size up a guy's meat. You're plenty hard, boy. But you ain't as hard as lead. Talk it up fast."

"I knocked at her door. No answer. The lock was a push-over. I went in. I almost missed her because the bed was pulled down and she had been sitting on it, reading a maga-zine. There was no sign of struggle. I lifted the bed just be-fore I left—and there she was. Very dead, Mr. Stoyanoff. Put the gat away. Cops don't bother you, you said a minute ago."

The big man whispered: "Yes and no. They don't make me happy neither. I get a bump once'n a while. Mostly a Dutch. You said something about my hands, mister."

Steve shook his head. "That was a gag," he said. "Her neck has nail marks. You bite your nails down close. You're clean."

The big man didn't look at his fingers. He was very pale. There was sweat on his lower lip, in the black stubble of his beard. He was still leaning forward, still motionless, when there was a knocking beyond the kitchen door, the door from the living room to the hallway. The creaking chair stopped and the woman's sharp voice screamed: "Hi, Jake! Company!"

The big man cocked his head. "That old slut wouldn't climb off'n her fanny if the house caught fire," he said thickly.

He stepped to the door and slipped through it, locking it behind him.

Steve ranged the kitchen swiftly with his eyes. There was a small high window beyond the sink, a trap low down for a garbage pail and parcels, but no other door. He reached for his card Stoyanoff had left lying on the drainboard and slipped it back into his pocket. Then he took a short-barreled Detective Special out of his left breast pocket where he wore it nose down, as in a holster.

He had got that far when the shots roared beyond the wall—muffled a little, but still loud—four of them blended in a blast of sound.

Steve stepped back and hit the kitchen door with his leg out straight. It held and jarred him to the top of his head and in his hip joint. He swore, took the whole width of the kitchen and slammed into it with his left shoulder. It gave this time. He pitched into the living room. The mud-faced woman sat leaning forward in her rocker, her head to one side and a lock of mousy hair smeared down over her bony forehead.

"Backfire, huh?" she said stupidly. "Sounded kinda close. Musta been in the alley."

Steve jumped across the room, yanked the outer door open and plunged out into the hall.

The big man was still on his feet, a dozen feet down the hallway, in the direction of a screen door that opened flush on an alley. He was clawing at the wall. His gun lay at his feet. His left knee buckled and he went down on it.

A door was flung open and a hard-looking woman peered out, and instantly slammed her door shut again. A radio suddenly gained in volume beyond her door.

The big man got up off his left knee and the leg shook violently inside his trousers. He went down on both knees and got the gun into his hand and began to crawl towards the screen door. Then, suddenly he went down flat on his face and tried to crawl that way, grinding his face into the narrow hall runner.

Then he stopped crawling and stopped moving altogether. His body went limp and the hand holding the gun opened and the gun rolled out of it.

Steve hit the screen door and was out in the alley. A gray

sedan was speeding towards the far end of it. He stopped, steadied himself and brought his gun up level, and the sedan whisked out of sight around the corner.

A man boiled out of another apartment house across the alley. Steve ran on, gesticulating back at him and pointing ahead. As he ran he slipped the gun back into his pocket. When he reached the end of the alley, the gray sedan was out of sight. Steve skidded around the wall onto the sidewalk, slowed to a walk and then stopped.

Half a block down a man finished parking a car, got out and went across the sidewalk to a lunchroom. Steve watched him go in, then straightened his hat and walked along the wall to the lunchroom.

He went in, sat at the counter and ordered coffee. In a little while there were sirens.

Steve drank his coffee, asked for another cup and drank that. He lit a cigarette and walked down the long hill to Fifth, across to Hill, back to the foot of the Angel's Flight, and got his convertible out of a parking lot.

He drove out west, beyond Vermont, to the small hotel where he had taken a room that morning.

4

Bill Dockery, floor manager of the Club Shalotte, teetered on his heels and yawned in the unlighted entrance to the dining-room. It was a dead hour for business, late cocktail time, too early for dinner, and much too early for the real business of the club, which was high-class gambling.

Dockery was a handsome mug in a midnight-blue dinner jacket and a maroon carnation. He had a two-inch forehead under black lacquer hair, good features a little on the heavy side, alert brown eyes and very long curly eyelashes which he liked to let down over his eyes, to fool troublesome drunks into taking a swing at him.

The entrance door of the foyer was opened by the uni-formed doorman and Steve Grayce came in.

Dockery said, "Ho, hum," tapped his teeth and leaned his weight forward. He walked across the lobby slowly to meet the guest. Steve stood just inside the doors and ranged his

eyes over the high foyer walled with milky glass, lighted softly
from behind. Molded in the glass were etchings of sailing-
ships, beasts of the jungle, Siamese pagodas, temples of Yuca-
tan. The doors were square frames of chromium, like photo
frames. The Club Shalotte had all the class there was, and the
mutter of voices from the bar lounge on the left was not
noisy. The faint Spanish music behind the voices was delicate
as a carved fan.

Dockery came up and leaned his sleek head forward an
inch. "May I help you?"

"King Leopardi around?"

Dockery leaned back again. He looked less interested. "The
bandleader? He opens tomorrow night."

"I thought he might be around—rehearsing or something."

"Friend of his?"

"I know him. I'm not job-hunting, and I'm not a song-
plugger if that's what you mean."

Dockery teetered on his heels. He was tone deaf and Leopardi meant no more to him than a bag of peanuts. He half
smiled. "He was in the bar lounge a while ago." He pointed
with his square rock-like chin. Steve Grayce went into the bar
lounge.

It was about a third full, warm and comfortable and not
too dark nor too light. The little Spanish orchestra was in an
archway, playing with muted strings small seductive melodies
that were more like memories than sounds. There was no
dance floor. There was a long bar with comfortable seats, and
there were small round composition-top tables, not too close
together. A wall seat ran around three sides of the room.
Waiters flitted among the tables like moths.

Steve Grayce saw Leopardi in the far corner, with a girl.
There was an empty table on each side of him. The girl was a
knockout.

She looked tall and her hair was the color of a brush fire
seen through a dust cloud. On it, at the ultimate rakish angle,
she wore a black velvet double-pointed beret with two artificial butterflies made of polka-dotted feathers and fastened on
with tall silver pins. Her dress was burgundy-red wool and the
blue fox draped over one shoulder was at least a foot wide.

Her eyes were large, smoke-blue, and looked bored. She slowly turned a small glass on the tabletop with a gloved left hand.

Leopardi faced her, leaning forward, talking. His shoulders looked very big in a shaggy, cream-colored sports coat. Above the neck of it his hair made a point on his brown neck. He laughed across the table as Steve came up, and his laugh had a confident, sneering sound.

Steve stopped, then moved behind the next table. The movement caught Leopardi's eye. His head turned, he looked annoyed, and then his eyes got very wide and brilliant and his whole body turned slowly, like a mechanical toy.

Leopardi put both his rather small well-shaped hands down on the table, on either side of a highball glass. He smiled. Then he pushed his chair back and stood up. He put one finger up and touched his hair-line mustache, with theatrical delicacy. Then he said drawlingly, but distinctly: "You —— — – ——!"

A man at a near-by table turned his head and scowled. A waiter who had started to come over stopped in his tracks, then faded back among the tables. The girl looked at Steve Grayce and then leaned back against the cushion of the wall seat and moistened the end of one bare finger on her right hand and smoothed a chestnut eyebrow.

Steve stood quite still. There was a sudden high flush on his cheekbones. He said softly: "You left something at the hotel last night. I think you ought to do something about it. Here."

He reached a folded paper out of his pocket and held it out. Leopardi took it, still smiling, opened it and read it. It was a sheet of yellow paper with torn pieces of white paper pasted on it. Leopardi crumpled the sheet and let it drop at his feet.

He took a smooth step toward Steve and repeated more loudly: "You —— — – ——!"

The man who had first looked around stood up sharply and turned. He said clearly: "I don't like that sort of language in front of my wife."

Without even looking at the man Leopardi said: "To hell with you and your wife."

The man's face got a dusky red. The woman with him stood up and grabbed a bag and a coat and walked away. After a moment's indecision the man followed her. Everybody in the place was staring now. The waiter who had faded back among the tables went through the doorway into the entrance foyer, walking very quickly.

Leopardi took another, longer step and slammed Steve Grayce on the jaw. Steve rolled with the punch and stepped back and put his hand down on another table and upset a glass. He turned to apologize to the couple at the table. Leopardi jumped forward very fast and hit him behind the ear.

Dockery came through the doorway, split two waiters like a banana skin and started down the room showing all his teeth.

Steve gagged a little and ducked away. He turned and said thickly: "Wait a minute, you fool—that isn't all of it— there's—"

Leopardi closed in fast and smashed him full on the mouth. Blood oozed from Steve's lip and crawled down the line at the corner of his mouth and glistened on his chin. The girl with the red hair reached for her bag, white-faced with anger, and started to get up from behind her table.

Leopardi turned abruptly on his heel and walked away. Dockery put out a hand to stop him. Leopardi brushed it aside and went on, went out of the lounge.

The tall red-haired girl put her bag down on the table again and dropped her handkerchief on the floor. She looked at Steve quietly, spoke quietly. "Wipe the blood off your chin before it drips on your shirt." She had a soft, husky voice with a trill in it.

Dockery came up harsh-faced, took Steve by the arm and put weight on the arm. "All right, you! Let's go!"

Steve stood quite still, his feet planted, staring at the girl. He dabbed at his mouth with a handkerchief. He half smiled. Dockery couldn't move him an inch. Dockery dropped his hand, signaled two waiters and they jumped behind Steve, but didn't touch him.

Steve felt his lip carefully and looked at the blood on his handkerchief. He turned to the people at the table behind him and said: "I'm terribly sorry. I lost my balance."

The girl whose drink he had spilled was mopping her dress with a small fringed napkin. She smiled up at him and said: "It wasn't your fault."

The two waiters suddenly grabbed Steve's arms from behind. Dockery shook his head and they let go again. Dockery said tightly: "You hit him?"

"No."

"You say anything to make him hit you?"

"No."

The girl at the corner table bent down to get her fallen handkerchief. It took her quite a time. She finally got it and slid into the corner behind the table again. She spoke coldly.

"Quite right, Bill. It was just some more of the King's sweet way with his public."

Dockery said "Huh?" and swiveled his head on his thick hard neck. Then he grinned and looked back at Steve.

Steve said grimly: "He gave me three good punches, one from behind, without a return. You look pretty hard. See can you do it."

Dockery measured him with his eyes. He said evenly: "You win. I couldn't . . . Beat it!" he added sharply to the waiters. They went away. Dockery sniffed his carnation, and said quietly: "We don't go for brawls in here." He smiled at the girl again and went away, saying a word here and there at the tables. He went out through the foyer doors.

Steve tapped his lip, put his handkerchief in his pocket and stood searching the floor with his eyes.

The red-haired girl said calmly: "I think I have what you want—in my handkerchief. Won't you sit down?"

Her voice had a remembered quality, as if he had heard it before.

He sat down opposite her, in the chair where Leopardi had been sitting.

The red-haired girl said: "The drink's on me. I was with him."

Steve said, "Coke with a dash of bitters," to the waiter.

The waiter said: "Madame?"

"Brandy and soda. Light on the brandy, please." The waiter bowed and drifted away. The girl said amusedly:

"Coke with a dash of bitters. That's what I love about Hollywood. You meet so many neurotics."

Steve stared into her eyes and said softly: "I'm an occasional drinker, the kind of guy who goes out for a beer and wakes up in Singapore with a full beard."

"I don't believe a word of it. Have you known the King long?"

"I met him last night. I didn't get along with him."

"I sort of noticed that." She laughed. She had a rich low laugh, too.

"Give me that paper, lady."

"Oh, one of these impatient men. Plenty of time." The handkerchief with the crumpled yellow sheet inside it was clasped tightly in her gloved hand. Her middle right finger played with an eyebrow. "You're not in pictures, are you?"

"Hell, no."

"Same here. Me, I'm too tall. The beautiful men have to wear stilts in order to clasp me to their bosoms."

The waiter set the drinks down in front of them, made a few grace notes in the air with his napkin and went away.

Steve said quietly, stubbornly: "Give me that paper, lady."

"I don't like that 'lady' stuff. It sounds like cop to me."

"I don't know your name."

"I don't know yours. Where did you meet Leopardi?"

Steve sighed. The music from the little Spanish orchestra had a melancholy minor sound now and the muffled clicking of gourds dominated it.

Steve listened to it with his head on one side. He said: "The E string is a half-tone flat. Rather cute effect."

The girl stared at him with new interest. "I'd never have noticed that," she said. "And I'm supposed to be a pretty good singer. But you haven't answered my question."

He said slowly: "Last night I was house dick at the Carlton Hotel. They called me night clerk, but house dick was what I was. Leopardi stayed there and cut up too rough. I threw him out and got canned."

The girl said: "Ah. I begin to get the idea. He was being the King and you were being—if I might guess—a pretty tough order of house detective."

"Something like that. Now will you please—"

"You still haven't told me your name."

He reached for his wallet, took one of the brand-new cards out of it and passed it across the table. He sipped his drink while she read it.

"A nice name," she said slowly. "But not a very good address. And *Private Investigator* is bad. It should have been *Investigations*, very small, in the lower left-hand corner."

"They'll be small enough," Steve grinned. "Now will you please—"

She reached suddenly across the table and dropped the crumpled ball of paper in his hand.

"Of course I haven't read it—and of course I'd like to. You do give me that much credit, I hope"—she looked at the card again, and added—"Steve. Yes, and your office should be in a Georgian or very modernistic building in the Sunset Eighties. Suite Something-or-other. And your clothes should be very jazzy. Very jazzy indeed, Steve. To be inconspicuous in this town is to be a busted flush."

He grinned at her. His deep-set black eyes had lights in them. She put the card away in her bag, gave her fur piece a yank, and drank about half of her drink. "I have to go." She signaled the waiter and paid the check. The waiter went away and she stood up.

Steve said sharply: "Sit down."

She stared at him wonderingly. Then she sat down again and leaned against the wall, still staring at him. Steve leaned across the table, asked: "How well do *you* know Leopardi?"

"Off and on for years. If it's any of your business. Don't go masterful on me, for God's sake. I loathe masterful men. I once sang for him, but not for long. You can't just sing for Leopardi—if you get what I mean."

"You were having a drink with him."

She nodded slightly and shrugged. "He opens here tomorrow night. He was trying to talk me into singing for him again. I said no, but I may have to, for a week or two anyway. The man who owns the Club Shalotte also owns my contract—and the radio station where I work a good deal."

"Jumbo Walters," Steve said. "They say he's tough but

square. I never met him, but I'd like to. After all I've got a living to get. Here."

He reached back across the table and dropped the crumpled paper. "The name was—"

"Dolores Chiozza."

Steve repeated it lingeringly. "I like it. I like your singing too. I've heard a lot of it. You don't oversell a song, like most of these high-money torchers." His eyes glistened.

The girl spread the paper on the table and read it slowly, without expression. Then she said quietly: "Who tore it up?"

"Leopardi, I guess. The pieces were in his wastebasket last night. I put them together, after he was gone. The guy has guts—or else he gets these things so often they don't register any more."

"Or else he thought it was a gag." She looked across the table levelly, then folded the paper and handed it back.

"Maybe. But if he's the kind of guy I hear he is—one of them is going to be on the level and the guy behind it is going to do more than just shake him down."

Dolores Chiozza said: "He's the kind of guy you hear he is."

"It wouldn't be hard for a woman to get to him then—would it—a woman with a gun?"

She went on staring at him. "No. And everybody would give her a big hand, if you ask me. If I were you, I'd just forget the whole thing. If he wants protection—Walters can throw more around him than the police. If he doesn't—who cares? I don't. I'm damn sure I don't."

"You're kind of tough yourself, Miss Chiozza—over some things."

She said nothing. Her face was a little white and more than a little hard.

Steve finished his drink, pushed his chair back and reached for his hat. He stood up. "Thank you very much for the drink, Miss Chiozza. Now that I've met you I'll look forward all the more to hearing you sing again."

"You're damn formal all of a sudden," she said.

He grinned. "So long, Dolores."

"So long, Steve. Good luck—in the sleuth racket. If I hear of anything—"

He turned and walked among the tables out of the bar lounge.

5

In the crisp fall evening the lights of Hollywood and Los Angeles winked at him. Searchlight beams probed the cloudless sky as if searching for bombing-planes.

Steve got his convertible out of the parking lot and drove it east along Sunset. At Sunset and Fairfax he bought an evening paper and pulled over to the curb to look through it. There was nothing in the paper about 118 Court Street.

He drove on and ate dinner at the little coffee shop beside his hotel and went to a movie. When he came out he bought a Home Edition of the *Tribune*, a morning sheet. They were in that—both of them.

Police thought Jake Stoyanoff might have strangled the girl, but she had not been attacked. She was described as a stenographer, unemployed at the moment. There was no picture of her. There was a picture of Stoyanoff that looked like a touched-up police photo. Police were looking for a man who had been talking to Stoyanoff just before he was shot. Several people said he was a tall man in a dark suit. That was all the description the police got—or gave out.

Steve grinned sourly, stopped at the coffee shop for a good-night cup of coffee and then went up to his room. It was a few minutes to eleven o'clock. As he unlocked his door the telephone started to ring.

He shut the door and stood in the darkness remembering where the phone was. Then he walked straight to it, catlike in the dark room, sat in an easy chair and reached the phone up from the lower shelf of a small table. He held the one-piece to his ear and said: "Hello."

"Is this Steve?" It was a rich, husky voice, low, vibrant. It held a note of strain.

"Yeah, this is Steve. I can hear you. I know who you are."

There was a faint dry laugh. "You'll make a detective after all. And it seems I'm to give you your first case. Will you come over to my place at once? It's Twenty-four-twelve Renfrew—North, there isn't any South—just half a block below

Fountain. It's a sort of bungalow court. My house is the last in line, at the back."

Steve said: "Yes. Sure. What's the matter?"

There was a pause. A horn blared in the street outside the hotel. A wave of white light went across the ceiling from some car rounding the corner uphill. The low voice said very slowly: "Leopardi. I can't get rid of him. He's—he's passed out in my bedroom." Then a tinny laugh that didn't go with the voice at all.

Steve held the phone so tight his hand ached. His teeth clicked in the darkness. He said flatly, in a dull, brittle voice: "Yeah. It'll cost you twenty bucks."

"Of course. Hurry, please."

He hung up, sat there in the dark room breathing hard. He pushed his hat back on his head, then yanked it forward again with a vicious jerk and laughed out loud. "Hell," he said. "*That* kind of a dame."

2412 Renfrew was not strictly a bungalow court. It was a staggered row of six bungalows, all facing the same way, but so arranged that no two of their front entrances overlooked each other. There was a brick wall at the back and beyond the brick wall a church. There was a long smooth lawn, moon-silvered.

The door was up two steps, with lanterns on each side and an ironwork grill over the peep hole. This opened to his knock and a girl's face looked out, a small oval face with a Cupid's-bow mouth, arched and plucked eyebrows, wavy brown hair. The eyes were like two fresh and shiny chestnuts.

Steve dropped a cigarette and put his foot on it. "Miss Chiozza. She's expecting me. Steve Grayce."

"Miss Chiozza has retired, sir," the girl said with a half-insolent twist to her lips.

"Break it up, kid. You heard me, I'm expected."

The wicket slammed shut. He waited, scowling back along the narrow moonlit lawn towards the street. O.K. So it was like that—well, twenty bucks was worth a ride in the moon-light anyway.

The lock clicked and the door opened wide. Steve went past the maid into a warm cheerful room, old-fashioned with chintz. The lamps were neither old nor new and there were

enough of them—in the right places. There was a hearth behind a paneled copper screen, a davenport close to it, a bartop radio in the corner.

The maid said stiffly: "I'm sorry, sir. Miss Chiozza forgot
to tell me. Please to have a chair." The voice was soft, and it
might be cagey. The girl went off down the room—short
skirts, sheer silk stockings, and four-inch spike heels.

Steve sat down and held his hat on his knee and scowled at
the wall. A swing door creaked shut. He got a cigarette out
and rolled it between his fingers and then deliberately
squeezed it to a shapeless flatness of white paper and ragged
tobacco. He threw it away from him, at the fire screen.

Dolores Chiozza came towards him. She wore green velvet
lounging pajamas with a long gold-fringed sash. She spun the
end of the sash as if she might be going to throw a loop with
it. She smiled a slight artificial smile. Her face had a clean
scrubbed look and her eyelids were bluish and they twitched.

Steve stood up and watched the green morocco slippers
peep out under the pajamas as she walked. When she was
close to him he lifted his eyes to her face and said dully:
"Hello."

She looked at him very steadily, then spoke in a high, carrying voice. "I know it's late, but I knew you were used to
being up all night. So I thought what we had to talk over—
Won't you sit down?"

She turned her head very slightly, seemed to be listening
for something.

Steve said: "I never go to bed before two. Quite all right."

She went over and pushed a bell beside the hearth. After a
moment the maid came through the arch.

"Bring some ice cubes, Agatha. Then go along home. It's
getting pretty late."

"Yes'm." The girl disappeared.

There was a silence then that almost howled till the tall girl
took a cigarette absently out of a box, put it between her lips
and Steve struck a match clumsily on his shoe. She pushed the
end of the cigarette into the flame and her smoke-blue eyes
were very steady on his black ones. She shook her head very
slightly.

The maid came back with a copper ice bucket. She pulled a low Indian-brass tray-table between them before the davenport, put the ice bucket on it, then a siphon, glasses and spoons, and a triangular bottle that looked like good Scotch had come in it except that it was covered with silver filigree work and fitted with a stopper.

Dolores Chiozza said, "Will you mix a drink?" in a formal voice.

He mixed two drinks, stirred them, handed her one. She sipped it, shook her head. "Too light," she said. He put more whiskey in it and handed it back. She said, "Better," and leaned back against the corner of the davenport.

The maid came into the room again. She had a small rakish red hat on her wavy brown hair and was wearing a gray coat trimmed with nice fur. She carried a black brocade bag that could have cleaned out a fair-sized icebox. She said: "Good night, Miss Dolores."

"Good night, Agatha."

The girl went out the front door, closed it softly. Her heels clicked down the walk. A car door opened and shut distantly and a motor started. Its sound soon dwindled away. It was a very quiet neighborhood.

Steve put his drink down on the brass tray and looked levelly at the tall girl, said harshly: "That means she's out of the way?"

"Yes. She goes home in her own car. She drives me home from the studio in mine—when I go to the studio, which I did tonight. I don't like to drive a car myself."

"Well, what are you waiting for?"

The red-haired girl looked steadily at the paneled fire screen and the unlit log fire behind it. A muscle twitched in her cheek.

After a moment she said: "Funny that I called you instead of Walters. He'd have protected me better than you can. Only he wouldn't have believed me. I thought perhaps you would. I didn't invite Leopardi here. So far as I know—we two are the only people in the world who know he's here."

Something in her voice jerked Steve upright.

She took a small crisp handkerchief from the breast pocket

of the green velvet pajama-suit, dropped it on the floor, picked it up swiftly and pressed it against her mouth. Suddenly, without making a sound, she began to shake like a leaf.

Steve said swiftly: "What the hell—I can handle that heel in my hip pocket. I did last night—and last night he had a gun and took a shot at me."

Her head turned. Her eyes were very wide and staring. "But it couldn't have been my gun," she said in a dead voice.

"Huh? Of course not—what—?"

"It's my gun tonight," she said and stared at him. "You said a woman could get to him with a gun very easily."

He just stared at her. His face was white now and he made a vague sound in his throat.

"He's not drunk, Steve," she said gently. "He's dead. In yellow pajamas—in my bed. With my gun in his hand. You didn't think he was just drunk—did you, Steve?"

He stood up in a swift lunge, then became absolutely motionless, staring down at her. He moved his tongue on his lips and after a long time he formed words with it. "Let's go look at him," he said in a hushed voice.

6

The room was at the back of the house to the left. The girl took a key out of her pocket and unlocked the door. There was a low light on a table, and the venetian blinds were drawn. Steve went in past her silently, on cat feet.

Leopardi lay squarely in the middle of the bed, a large smooth silent man, waxy and artificial in death. Even his mustache looked phoney. His half-open eyes, sightless as marbles, looked as if they had never seen. He lay on his back, on the sheet, and the bedclothes were thrown over the foot of the bed.

The King wore yellow silk pajamas, the slip-on kind, with a turned collar. They were loose and thin. Over his breast they were dark with blood that had seeped into the silk as if into blotting-paper. There was a little blood on his bare brown neck.

Steve stared at him and said tonelessly: "The King in Yellow. I read a book with that title once. He liked yellow, I guess. I packed some of his stuff last night. And he wasn't yellow either. Guys like him usually are—or are they?"

The girl went over to the corner and sat down in a slipper chair and looked at the floor. It was a nice room, as modernistic as the living room was casual. It had a chenille rug, café-au-lait color, severely angled furniture in inlaid wood, and a trick dresser with a mirror for a top, a kneehole and drawers like a desk. It had a box mirror above and a semi-cylindrical frosted wall-light set above the mirror. In the corner there was a glass table with a crystal greyhound on top of it, and a lamp with the deepest drum shade Steve had ever seen.

He stopped looking at all this and looked at Leopardi again. He pulled the King's pajamas up gently and examined the wound. It was directly over the heart and the skin was scorched and mottled there. There was not so very much blood. He had died in a fraction of a second.

A small Mauser automatic lay cuddled in his right hand, on top of the bed's second pillow.

"That's artistic," Steve said and pointed. "Yeah, that's a nice touch. Typical contact wound, I guess. He even pulled his pajama shirt up. I've heard they do that. A Mauser Seven Sixty-Three about. Sure it's your gun?"

"Yes." She kept on looking at the floor. "It was in a desk in the living room—not loaded. But there were shells. I don't know why. Somebody gave it to me once. I didn't even know how to load it."

Steve smiled. Her eyes lifted suddenly and she saw the smile and shuddered. "I don't expect anybody to believe that," she said. "We may as well call the police, I suppose."

Steve nodded absently, put a cigarette in his mouth and flipped it up and down with his lips that were still puffy from Leopardi's punch. He lit a match on his thumbnail, puffed a small plume of smoke and said quietly: "No cops. Not yet. Just tell it."

The red-haired girl said: "I sing at KFQC, you know. Three nights a week—on a quarter-hour automobile program. This was one of the nights. Agatha and I got home— oh, close to half-past ten. At the door I remembered there was no fizzwater in the house, so I sent her back to the liquor store three blocks away, and came in alone. There was a queer

smell in the house. I don't know what it was. As if several
men had been in here, somehow. When I came in the bedroom—he was exactly as he is now. I saw the gun and I went
and looked and then I knew I was sunk. I didn't know what
to do. Even if the police cleared me, everywhere I went from
now on—"

Steve said sharply: "He got in here—how?"

"I don't know."

"Go on," he said.

"I locked the door. Then I undressed—with that on my
bed. I went into the bathroom to shower and collect my
brains, if any. I locked the door when I left the room and
took the key. Agatha was back then, but I don't think she saw
me. Well, I took the shower and it braced me up a bit. Then I
had a drink and then I came in here and called you."

She stopped and moistened the end of a finger and
smoothed the end of her left eyebrow with it. "That's all,
Steve—absolutely all."

"Domestic help can be pretty nosey. This Agatha's nosier
than most—or I miss my guess." He walked over to the door
and looked at the lock. "I bet there are three or four keys in
the house that knock this over." He went to the windows and
felt the catches, looked down at the screens through the glass.
He said over his shoulder, casually: "Was the King in love
with you?"

Her voice was sharp, almost angry. "He never was in love
with any woman. A couple of years back in San Francisco,
when I was with his band for a while, there was some slapsilly
publicity about us. Nothing to it. It's been revived here in the
hand-outs to the press, to build up his opening. I was telling
him this afternoon I wouldn't stand for it, that I wouldn't be
linked with him in anybody's mind. His private life was filthy.
It reeked. Everybody in the business knows that. And it's not
a business where daisies grow very often."

Steve said: "Yours was the only bedroom he couldn't
make."

The girl flushed to the roots of her dusky red hair.

"That sounds lousy," he said. "But I have to figure the
angles. That's about true, isn't it?"

"Yes—I suppose so. I wouldn't say the only one."

"Go on out in the other room and buy yourself a drink."

She stood up and looked at him squarely across the bed. "I didn't kill him, Steve. I didn't let him into this house tonight. I didn't know he was coming here, or had any reason to come here. Believe that or not. But something about this is wrong. Leopardi was the last man in the world to take his lovely life himself."

Steve said: "He didn't, angel. Go buy that drink. He was murdered. The whole thing is a frame—to get a cover-up from Jumbo Walters. Go on out."

He stood silent, motionless, until sounds he heard from the living room told him she was out there. Then he took out his handkerchief and loosened the gun from Leopardi's right hand and wiped it over carefully on the outside, broke out the magazine and wiped that off, spilled out all the shells and wiped every one, ejected the one in the breech and wiped that. He reloaded the gun and put it back in Leopardi's dead hand and closed his fingers around it and pushed his index finger against the trigger. Then he let the hand fall naturally back on the bed.

He pawed through the bedclothes and found an ejected shell and wiped that off, put it back where he had found it. He put the handkerchief to his nose, sniffed it wryly, went around the bed to a clothes closet and opened the door.

"Careless of your clothes, boy," he said softly.

The rough cream-colored coat hung in there, on a hook, over dark gray slacks with a lizard-skin belt. A yellow satin shirt and a wine-colored tie dangled alongside. A handkerchief to match the tie flowed loosely four inches from the breast pocket of the coat. On the floor lay a pair of gazelle-leather nutmeg-brown sports shoes, and socks without garters. And there were yellow satin shorts with heavy black initials on them lying close by.

Steve felt carefully in the gray slacks and got out a leather keyholder. He left the room, went along the cross-hall and into the kitchen. It had a solid door, a good spring lock with a key stuck in it. He took it out and tried keys from the bunch in the keyholder, found none that fitted, put the other key back and went into the living room. He opened the front door, went outside and shut it again without looking at the girl huddled in a corner of the davenport. He tried keys in the lock, finally found the right one. He let himself back into the house, returned to the bedroom and put the keyholder in the pocket of the gray slacks again. Then he went to the living room.

The girl was still huddled motionless, staring at him.

He put his back to the mantel and puffed at a cigarette. "Agatha with you all the time at the studio?"

She nodded. "I suppose so. So he had a key. That was what you were doing, wasn't it?"

"Yes. Had Agatha long?"

"About a year."

"She steal from you? Small stuff, I mean?"

Dolores Chiozza shrugged wearily. "What does it matter? Most of them do. A little face cream or powder, a handkerchief, a pair of stockings once in a while. Yes, I think she stole from me. They look on that sort of thing as more or less legitimate."

"Not the nice ones, angel."

"Well—the hours were a little trying. I work at night, often get home very late. She's a dresser as well as a maid."

"Anything else about her? She use cocaine or weed. Hit the bottle? Ever have laughing fits?"

"I don't think so. What has she got to do with it, Steve?"

"Lady, she sold somebody a key to your apartment. That's obvious. You didn't give him one, the landlord wouldn't give him one, but Agatha had one. Check?"

Her eyes had a stricken look. Her mouth trembled a little, not much. A drink was untasted at her elbow. Steve bent over and drank some of it.

She said slowly: "We're wasting time, Steve. We have to call the police. There's nothing anybody can do. I'm done for as a nice person, even if not as a lady at large. They'll think it was a lovers' quarrel and I shot him and that's that. If I could convince them I didn't, then he shot himself in my bed, and I'm still ruined. So I might as well make up my mind to face the music."

Steve said softly: "Watch this. My mother used to do it."

He put a finger to his mouth, bent down and touched her

lips at the same spot with the same finger. He smiled, said: "We'll go to Walters—or you will. He'll pick his cops and the ones he picks won't go screaming through the night with reporters sitting in their laps. They'll sneak in quiet, like process servers. Walters can handle this. That was what was counted on. Me, I'm going to collect Agatha. Because I want a description of the guy she sold that key to—and I want it fast. And by the way, you owe me twenty bucks for coming over here. Don't let that slip your memory."

The tall girl stood up, smiling. "You're a kick, you are," she said. "What makes you so sure he was murdered?"

"He's not wearing his own pajamas. His have his initials on them. I packed his stuff last night—before I threw him out of the Carlton. Get dressed, angel—and get me Agatha's address."

He went into the bedroom and pulled a sheet over Leopardi's body, held it a moment above the still waxed face before letting it fall.

"So long, guy," he said gently. "You were a louse—but you sure had music in you."

It was a small frame house on Brighton Avenue near Jefferson, in a block of small frame houses, all old-fashioned, with front porches. This one had a narrow concrete walk which the moon made whiter than it was.

Steve mounted the steps and looked at the light-edged shade of the wide front window. He knocked. There were shuffling steps and a woman opened the door and looked at him through the hooked screen—a dumpy elderly woman with frizzled gray hair. Her body was shapeless in a wrapper and her feet slithered in loose slippers. A man with a polished bald head and milky eyes sat in a wicker chair beside a table. He held his hands in his lap and twisted the knuckles aimlessly. He didn't look toward the door.

Steve said: "I'm from Miss Chiozza. Are you Agatha's mother?"

The woman said dully: "I reckon. But she ain't home, mister." The man in the chair got a handkerchief from somewhere and blew his nose. He snickered darkly.

Steve said: "Miss Chiozza's not feeling so well tonight. She was hoping Agatha would come back and stay the night with her."

The milky-eyed man snickered again, sharply. The woman said: "We dunno where she is. She don't come home. Pa'n me waits up for her to come home. She stays out till we're sick."

The old man snapped in a reedy voice: "She'll stay out till the cops get her one of these times."

"Pa's half blind," the woman said. "Makes him kinda mean. Won't you step in?"

Steve shook his head and turned his hat around in his hands like a bashful cowpuncher in a horse opera. "I've got to find her," he said. "Where would she go?"

"Out drinkin' liquor with cheap spenders," Pa cackled. "Pantywaists with silk handkerchiefs 'stead of neckties. If I had eyes, I'd strap her till she dropped." He grabbed the arms of his chair and the muscles knotted on the backs of his hands. Then he began to cry. Tears welled from his milky eyes and started through the white stubble on his cheeks. The woman went across and took the handkerchief out of his fist and wiped his face with it. Then she blew her nose on it and came back to the door.

"Might be anywhere," she said to Steve. "This is a big town, mister. I dunno where at to say."

Steve said dully: "I'll call back. If she comes in, will you hang onto her. What's your phone number?"

"What's the phone number, Pa?" the woman called back over her shoulder.

"I ain't sayin'," Pa snorted.

The woman said: "I remember now. South Two-four-five-four. Call any time. Pa'n me ain't got nothing to do."

Steve thanked her and went back down the white walk to the street and along the walk half a block to where he had left his car. He glanced idly across the way and started to get into his car, then stopped moving suddenly with his hand gripping the car door. He let go of that, took three steps sideways and stood looking across the street tight-mouthed.

All the houses in the block were much the same, but the one opposite had a FOR RENT placard stuck in the front window and a real-estate sign spiked into the small patch of front lawn. The house itself looked neglected, utterly empty, but in its little driveway stood a small neat black coupe.

Steve said under his breath: "Hunch. Play it up, Stevie."

He walked almost delicately across the wide dusty street, his hand touching the hard metal of the gun in his pocket, and came up behind the little car, stood and listened. He moved silently along its left side, glanced back across the street, then looked in the car's open left-front window.

The girl sat almost as if driving, except that her head was tipped a little too much into the corner. The little red hat was still on her head, the gray coat, trimmed with fur, still around her body. In the reflected moonlight her mouth was strained open. Her tongue stuck out. And her chestnut eyes stared at the roof of the car.

Steve didn't touch her. He didn't have to touch her or look any closer to know there would be heavy bruises on her neck.

"Tough on women, these guys," he muttered.

The girl's big black brocade bag lay on the seat beside her, gaping open like her mouth—like Miss Marilyn Delorme's mouth, and Miss Marilyn Delorme's purple bag.

"Yeah—tough on women."

He backed away till he stood under a small palm tree by the entrance to the driveway. The street was as empty and deserted as a closed theater. He crossed silently to his car, got into it and drove away.

Nothing to it. A girl coming home alone late at night, stuck up and strangled a few doors from her own home by some tough guy. Very simple. The first prowl car that cruised that block—if the boys were half awake—would take a look the minute they spotted the FOR RENT sign. Steve tramped hard on the throttle and went away from there.

At Washington and Figueroa he went into an all-night drugstore and pulled shut the door of the phone booth at the back. He dropped his nickel and dialed the number of police headquarters.

He asked for the desk and said: "Write this down, will you, sergeant? Brighton Avenue, thirty-two-hundred block, west side, in driveway of empty house. Got that much?"

"Yeah. So what?"

"Car with dead woman in it," Steve said, and hung up.

7

Quillan, head day clerk and assistant manager of the Carlton Hotel, was on night duty, because Millar, the night auditor, was off for a week. It was half-past one and things were dead and Quillan was bored. He had done everything there was to do long ago, because he had been a hotel man for twenty years and there was nothing to it.

The night porter had finished cleaning up and was in his room beside the elevator bank. One elevator was lighted and open, as usual. The main lobby had been tidied up and the lights had been properly dimmed. Everything was exactly as usual.

Quillan was a rather short, rather thickset man with clear bright toadlike eyes that seemed to hold a friendly expression without really having any expression at all. He had pale sandy hair and not much of it. His pale hands were clasped in front of him on the marble top of the desk. He was just the right height to put his weight on the desk without looking as if he were sprawling. He was looking at the wall across the entrance lobby, but he wasn't seeing it. He was half asleep, even though his eyes were wide open, and if the night porter struck a match behind his door, Quillan would know it and bang on his bell.

The brass-trimmed swing-doors at the street entrance pushed open and Steve Grayce came in, a summer-weight coat turned up around his neck, his hat yanked low and a cigarette wisping smoke at the corner of his mouth. He looked very casual, very alert, and very much at ease. He strolled over to the desk and rapped on it.

"Wake up!" he snorted.

Quillan moved his eyes an inch and said: "All outside rooms with bath. But positively no parties on the eighth floor. Hiyah, Steve. So you finally got the axe. And for the wrong thing. That's life."

Steve said: "O.K. O.K. Have you got a new night man here?"

"Don't need one, Steve. Never did, in my opinion."

"You'll need one as long as old hotel men like you register floozies on the same corridor with people like Leopardi."

Quillan half closed his eyes and then opened them to where they had been before. He said indifferently: "Not me, pal. But anybody can make a mistake. Millar's really an accountant—not a desk man."

Steve leaned back and his face became very still. The smoke almost hung at the tip of his cigarette. His eyes were like black glass now. He smiled a little dishonestly.

"And why was Leopardi put in a four-dollar room on Eight instead of in a tower suite at eighteen per?"

Quillan smiled back at him. "I didn't register Leopardi, old sock. There were reservations in. I supposed they were what he wanted. Some guys don't spend. Any other questions, Mr. Grayce?"

"Yeah. Was Eight-fourteen empty last night?"

"It was on change, so it was empty. Something about the plumbing. Proceed."

"Who marked it on change?"

Quillan's bright fathomless eyes turned and became curiously fixed. He didn't answer.

Steve said: "Here's why. Leopardi was in Eight-fifteen and the two girls in Eight-eleven. Just Eight-thirteen between. A lad with a passkey could have gone into Eight-thirteen and turned both the bolt locks on the communicating doors. Then, if the folks in the two other rooms had done the same thing on their side, they'd have a suite set up."

"So what?" Quillan asked. "We got chiseled out of four bucks, eh? Well, it happens, in better hotels than this." His eyes looked sleepy now.

Steve said: "Millar could have done that. But hell, it doesn't make sense. Millar's not that kind of a guy. Risk a job for a buck tip—phooey. Millar's no dollar pimp."

Quillan said: "All right, policeman. Tell me what's really on your mind."

"One of the girls in Eight-eleven had a gun. Leopardi got a threat letter yesterday—I don't know where or how. It didn't faze him, though. He tore it up. That's how I know. I collected the pieces from his basket. I suppose Leopardi's boys all checked out of here."

"Of course. They went to the Normandy."

"Call the Normandy and ask to speak to Leopardi. If he's there, he'll still be at the bottle. Probably with a gang."

"Why?" Quillan asked gently.

"Because you're a nice guy. If Leopardi answers—just hang up." Steve paused and pinched his chin hard. "If he went out, try to find out where."

Quillan straightened, gave Steve another long quiet look and went behind the pebbled-glass screen. Steve stood very still, listening, one hand clenched at his side, the other tapping noiselessly on the marble desk.

In about three minutes Quillan came back and leaned on the desk again and said: "Not there. Party going on in his suite—they sold him a big one—and sounds loud. I talked to a guy who was fairly sober. He said Leopardi got a call around ten—some girl. He went out preening himself, as the fellow says. Hinting about a very juicy date. The guy was just lit enough to hand me all this."

Steve said: "You're a real pal. I hate not to tell you the rest. Well, I liked working here. Not much work at that."

He started towards the entrance doors again. Quillan let him get his hand on the brass handle before he called out. Steve turned and came back slowly.

Quillan said: "I heard Leopardi took a shot at you. I don't think it was noticed. It wasn't reported down here. And I don't think Peters fully realized that until he saw the mirror in Eight-fifteen. If you care to come back, Steve—"

Steve shook his head. "Thanks for the thought."

"And hearing about that shot," Quillan added, "made me remember something. Two years ago a girl shot herself in Eight-fifteen."

Steve straightened his back so sharply that he almost jumped. "What girl?" he almost yelled.

Quillan looked surprised. "I don't know. I don't remember her real name. Some girl who had been kicked around all she could stand and wanted to die in a clean bed—alone."

Steve reached across and took hold of Quillan's arm. "The hotel files," he rasped. "The clippings, whatever there was in the papers will be in them. I want to see those clippings."

Quillan stared at him for a long moment. Then he said:

"Whatever game you're playing, kid—you're playing it damn close to your vest. I will say that for you. And me bored stiff with a night to kill."

He reached along the desk and thumped the call bell. The door of the night porter's room opened and the porter came across the entrance lobby. He nodded and smiled at Steve.

Quillan said: "Take the board, Carl. I'll be in Mr. Peters' office for a little while."

He went to the safe and got keys out of it.

8

The cabin was high up on the side of the mountain, against a thick growth of digger pine, oak and incense cedar. It was solidly built, with a stone chimney, shingled all over and heavily braced against the slope of the hill. By daylight the roof was green and the sides dark reddish brown and the window frames and draw-curtains red. In the uncanny brightness of an all-night mid-October moon in the mountains, it stood out sharply in every detail, except color.

It was at the end of a road, a quarter of a mile from any other cabin. Steve rounded the bend towards it without lights, at five in the morning. He stopped his car at once, when he was sure it was the right cabin, got out and walked soundlessly along the side of the gravel road, on a carpet of wild iris.

On the road level there was a rough pineboard garage, and from this a path went up to the cabin porch. The garage was unlocked. Steve swung the door open carefully, groped in past the dark bulk of a car and felt the top of the radiator. It was still warmish. He got a small flash out of his pocket and played it over the car. A gray sedan, dusty, the gas gauge low. He snapped the flash off, shut the garage door carefully and slipped into place the piece of wood that served for a hasp. Then he climbed the path to the house.

There was light behind the drawn red curtains. The porch was high and juniper logs were piled on it, with the bark still on them. The front door had a thumb latch and a rustic door handle above.

He went up, neither too softly nor too noisily, lifted his

hand, sighed deep in his throat, and knocked. His hand touched the butt of the gun in the inside pocket of his coat, once, then came away empty.

A chair creaked and steps padded across the floor and a voice called out softly: "What is it?" Millar's voice.

Steve put his lips close to the wood and said: "This is Steve, George. You up already?"

The key turned, and the door opened. George Millar, the dapper night auditor of the Carlton Hotel, didn't look dapper now. He was dressed in old trousers and a thick blue sweater with a roll collar. His feet were in ribbed wool socks and fleece-lined slippers. His clipped black mustache was a curved smudge across his pale face. Two electric bulbs burned in their sockets in a low beam across the room, below the slope of the high roof. A table lamp was lit and its shade was tilted to throw light on a big Morris chair with a leather seat and back-cushion. A fire burned lazily in a heap of soft ash on the big open hearth.

Millar said in his low, husky voice: "Hell's sake, Steve. Glad to see you. How'd you find us anyway? Come on in, guy."

Steve stepped through the door and Millar locked it. "City habit," he said grinning. "Nobody locks anything in the mountains. Have a chair. Warm your toes. Cold out at this time of night."

Steve said: "Yeah. Plenty cold."

He sat down in the Morris chair and put his hat and coat on the end of the solid wood table behind it. He leaned forward and held his hands out to the fire.

Millar said: "How the hell did you find us, Steve? I didn't know—"

Steve didn't look at him. He said quietly: "Not so easy at that. You told me last night your brother had a cabin up here—remember? So I had nothing to do, so I thought I'd drive up and bum some breakfast. The guy in the inn at Crestline didn't know who had cabins where. His trade is with people passing through. I rang up a garage man and he didn't know any Millar cabin. Then I saw a light come on down the street in a coal-and-wood yard and a little guy who is forest ranger and deputy sheriff and wood-and-gas dealer and half a dozen other things was getting his car out to go down to San Bernardino for some tank gas. A very smart little guy. The minute I said your brother had been a fighter he wised up. So here I am."

Millar pawed at his mustache. Bedsprings creaked at the back of the cabin somewhere. "Sure, he still goes under his fighting name—Gaff Talley. I'll get him up and we'll have some coffee. I guess you and me are both in the same boat. Used to working at night and can't sleep. I haven't been to bed at all."

Steve looked at him slowly and looked away. A burly voice behind them said: "Gaff is up. Who's your pal, George?"

Steve stood up casually and turned. He looked at the man's hands first. He couldn't help himself. They were large hands, well kept as to cleanliness, but coarse and ugly. One knuckle had been broken badly. He was a big man with reddish hair. He wore a sloppy bathrobe over outing-flannel pajamas. He had a leathery expressionless face, scarred over the cheekbones. There were fine white scars over his eyebrows and at the corners of his mouth. His nose was spread and thick. His whole face looked as if it had caught a lot of gloves. His eyes alone looked vaguely like Millar's eyes.

Millar said: "Steve Grayce. Night man at the hotel—until last night." His grin was a little vague.

Gaff Talley came over and shook hands. "Glad to meet you," he said. "I'll get some duds on and we'll scrape a breakfast off the shelves. I slept enough. George ain't slept any, the poor sap."

He went back across the room towards the door through which he'd come. He stopped there and leaned on an old phonograph, put his big hand down behind a pile of records in paper envelopes. He stayed just like that, without moving.

Millar said: "Any luck on a job, Steve? Or did you try yet?"

"Yeah. In a way. I guess I'm a sap, but I'm going to have a shot at the private agency racket. Not much in it unless I can land some publicity." He shrugged. Then he said very quietly: "King Leopardi's been bumped off."

Millar's mouth snapped wide open. He stayed like that for almost a minute—perfectly still, with his mouth open. Gaff

Talley leaned against the wall and stared without showing anything in his face. Millar finally said: "Bumped off? Where? Don't tell me—"

"Not in the hotel, George. Too bad, wasn't it? In a girl's apartment. Nice girl too. She didn't entice him there. The old suicide gag—only it won't work. And the girl is my client."

Millar didn't move. Neither did the big man. Steve leaned his shoulders against the stone mantel. He said softly: "I went out to the Club Shalotte this afternoon to apologize to Leopardi. Silly idea, because I didn't owe him an apology. There was a girl there in the bar lounge with him. He took three socks at me and left. The girl didn't like that. We got rather clubby. Had a drink together. Then late tonight—last night—she called me up and said Leopardi was over at her place and he was drunk and she couldn't get rid of him. I went there. Only he wasn't drunk. He was dead, in her bed, in yellow pajamas."

The big man lifted his left hand and roughed back his hair. Millar leaned slowly against the edge of the table, as if he were afraid the edge might be sharp enough to cut him. His mouth twitched under the clipped black mustache.

He said huskily: "That's lousy."

The big man said: "Well, for cryin' into a milk bottle."

Steve said: "Only they weren't Leopardi's pajamas. He had initials on them—big black initials. And his were satin, not silk. And although he had a gun in his hand—this girl's gun by the way—*he* didn't shoot himself in the heart. The cops will determine that. Maybe you birds never heard of the Lund test, with paraffin wax, to find out who did or didn't fire a gun recently. The kill ought to have been pulled in the hotel last night, in Room Eight-fifteen. I spoiled that by heaving him out on his neck before that black-haired girl in Eight-eleven could get to him. Didn't I, George?"

Millar said: "I guess you did—if I know what you're talking about."

Steve said slowly: "I think you know what I'm talking about, George. It would have been a kind of poetic justice if King Leopardi had been knocked off in Room Eight-fifteen. Because that was the room where a girl shot herself two years ago. A girl who registered as Mary Smith—but whose usual name was Eve Talley. And whose real name was Eve Millar."

The big man leaned heavily on the victrola and said thickly: "Maybe I ain't woke up yet. That sounds like it might grow up to be a dirty crack. We had a sister named Eve that shot herself in the Carlton. So what?"

Steve smiled a little crookedly. He said: "Listen, George. You told me Quillan registered those girls in Eight-eleven. *You* did. You told me Leopardi registered on Eight, instead of in a good suite, because he was tight. He wasn't tight. He just didn't care where he was put, as long as female company was handy. And you saw to that. You planned the whole thing, George. You even got Peters to write Leopardi at the Raleigh in Frisco and ask him to use the Carlton when he came down—because the same man owned it who owned the Club Shalotte. As if a guy like Jumbo Walters would care where a bandleader registered."

Millar's face was dead white, expressionless. His voice cracked. "Steve—for God's sake, Steve, what are you talking about? How the hell could I—"

"Sorry, kid. I liked working with you. I liked you a lot. I guess I still like you. But I don't like people who strangle women—or people who smear women in order to cover up a revenge murder."

His hand shot up—and stopped. The big man said: "Take it easy—and look at this one."

Gaff's hand had come up from behind the pile of records. A Colt .45 was in it. He said between his teeth: "I always thought house dicks were just a bunch of cheap grafters. I guess I missed out on you. You got a few brains. Hell, I bet you even run out to One-eighteen Court Street. Right?"

Steve let his hand fall empty and looked straight at the big Colt. "Right. I saw the girl—dead—with your fingers marked into her neck. They can measure those, fella. Killing Dolores Chiozza's maid the same way was a mistake. They'll match up the two sets of marks, find out that your black-haired gun girl was at the Carlton last night, and piece the whole story together. With the information they get at the hotel they can't miss. I give you two weeks, if you beat it quick. And I mean quick."

Millar licked his dry lips and said softly: "There's no hurry, Steve. No hurry at all. Our job is done. Maybe not the best way, maybe not the nicest way, but it wasn't a nice job. And Leopardi was the worst kind of a louse. We loved our sister, and he made a tramp out of her. She was a wide-eyed kid that fell for a flashy greaseball, and the greaseball went up in the world and threw her out on her ear for a red-headed torcher who was more his kind. He threw her out and broke her heart and she killed herself."

Steve said harshly: "Yeah—and what were you doing all that time—manicuring your nails?"

"We weren't around when it happened. It took us a little time to find out the why of it."

Steve said: "So that was worth killing four people for, was it? And as for Dolores Chiozza, she wouldn't have wiped her feet on Leopardi—then, or any time since. But you had to put her in the middle too, with your rotten little revenge murder. You make me sick, George. Tell your big tough brother to get on with his murder party."

The big man grinned and said: "Nuff talk, George. See has he a gat—and don't get behind him or in front of him. This beanshooter goes on through."

Steve stared at the big man's .45. His face was hard as white bone. There was a thin cold sneer on his lips and his eyes were cold and dark.

Millar moved softly in his fleece-lined slippers. He came around the end of the table and went close to Steve's side and reached out a hand to tap his pockets. He stepped back and pointed: "In there."

Steve said softly: "I must be nuts. I could have taken you then, George."

Gaff Talley barked: "Stand away from him."

He walked solidly across the room and put the big Colt against Steve's stomach hard. He reached up with his left hand and worked the Detective Special from the inside breast pocket. His eyes were sharp on Steve's eyes. He held Steve's gun out behind him. "Take this, George."

Millar took the gun and went over beyond the big table again and stood at the far corner of it. Gaff Talley backed away from Steve.

"You're through, wise guy," he said. "You got to know that. There's only two ways outa these mountains and we gotta have time. And maybe you didn't tell nobody. See?"

Steve stood like a rock, his face white, a twisted half-smile working at the corners of his lips. He stared hard at the big man's gun and his stare was faintly puzzled.

Millar said: "Does it have to be that way, Gaff?" His voice was a croak now, without tone, without its usual pleasant huskiness.

Steve turned his head a little and looked at Millar. "Sure it has, George. You're just a couple of cheap hoodlums after all. A couple of nasty-minded sadists playing at being revengers of wronged girlhood. Hillbilly stuff. And right this minute you're practically cold meat—cold, rotten meat."

Gaff Talley laughed and cocked the big revolver with his thumb. "Say your prayers, guy," he jeered.

Steve said grimly: "What makes you think you're going to bump me off with that thing? No shells in it, strangler. Better try to take me the way you handle women—with your hands."

The big man's eyes flicked down, clouded. Then he roared with laughter. "Geez, the dust on that one must be a foot thick," he chuckled. "Watch."

He pointed the big gun at the floor and squeezed the trigger. The firing-pin clicked dryly—on an empty chamber. The big man's face convulsed.

For a short moment nobody moved. Then Gaff turned slowly on the balls of his feet and looked at his brother. He said almost gently: "You, George?"

Millar licked his lips and gulped. He had to move his mouth in and out before he could speak.

"Me, Gaff. I was standing by the window when Steve got out of his car down the road, I saw him go into the garage. I knew the car would still be warm. There's been enough killing, Gaff. Too much. So I took the shells out of your gun."

Millar's thumb moved back the hammer on the Detective Special. Gaff's eyes bulged. He stared fascinated at the snub-nosed gun. Then he lunged violently towards it, flailing with the empty Colt. Millar braced himself and stood very still and said dimly, like an old man: "Goodbye, Gaff."

The gun jumped three times in his small neat hand. Smoke curled lazily from its muzzle. A piece of burned log fell over in the fireplace.

Gaff Talley smiled queerly and stopped and stood perfectly still. The gun dropped at his feet. He put his big heavy hands against his stomach, said slowly, thickly: "'S all right, kid. 'S all right, I guess . . . I guess I . . ."

His voice trailed off and his legs began to twist under him. Steve took three long quick silent steps, and slammed Millar hard on the angle of the jaw. The big man was still fall-ing—as slowly as a tree falls.

Millar spun across the room and crashed against the end wall and a blue-and-white plate fell off the plate-molding and broke. The gun sailed from his fingers. Steve dived for it and came up with it. Millar crouched and watched his brother.

Gaff Talley bent his head to the floor and braced his hands and then lay down quietly, on his stomach, like a man who was very tired. He made no sound of any kind.

Daylight showed at the windows, around the red glass-curtains. The piece of broken log smoked against the side of the hearth and the rest of the fire was a heap of soft gray ash with a glow at its heart.

Steve said dully: "You saved my life, George—or at least you saved a lot of shooting. I took the chance because what I wanted was evidence. Step over there to the desk and write it all out and sign it."

Millar said: "Is he dead?"

"He's dead, George. You killed him. Write that too."

Millar said quietly: "It's funny. I wanted to finish Leopardi myself, with my own hands, when he was at the top, when he had the farthest to fall. Just finish him and then take what came. But Gaff was the guy who wanted it done cute. Gaff, the tough mug who never had any education and never dodged a punch in his life, wanted to do it smart and figure angles. Well, maybe that's why he owned property, like that apartment house on Court Street that Jake Stoyanoff man-aged for him. I don't know how he got to Dolores Chiozza's maid. It doesn't matter much, does it?"

Steve said: "Go and write it. You were the one called Leo-pardi up and pretended to be the girl, huh?"

Millar said: "Yes. I'll write it all down, Steve. I'll sign it and then you'll let me go—just for an hour. Won't you, Steve? Just an hour's start. That's not much to ask of an old friend, is it, Steve?"

Millar smiled. It was a small, frail, ghostly smile. Steve bent beside the big sprawled man and felt his neck artery. He looked up, said: "Quite dead . . . Yes, you get an hour's start, George—if you write it all out."

Millar walked softly over to a tall oak highboy desk, studded with tarnished brass nails. He opened the flap and sat down and reached for a pen. He unscrewed the top from a bottle of ink and began to write in his neat, clear accountant's handwriting.

Steve Grayce sat down in front of the fire and lit a cigarette and stared at the ashes. He held the gun with his left hand on his knee. Outside the cabin, birds began to sing. Inside there was no sound but the scratching pen.

9

The sun was well up when Steve left the cabin, locked it up, walked down the steep path and along the narrow gravel road to his car. The garage was empty now. The gray sedan was gone. Smoke from another cabin floated lazily above the pines and oaks half a mile away. He started his car, drove it around a bend, past two old box-cars that had been converted into cabins, then on to a main road with a stripe down the middle and so up the hill to Crestline.

He parked on the main street before the Rim-of-the-World Inn, had a cup of coffee at the counter, then shut himself in a phone booth at the back of the empty lounge. He had the long distance operator get Jumbo Walters' number in Los Angeles, then called the owner of the Club Shalotte.

A voice said silkily: "This is Mr. Walters' residence."

"Steve Grayce. Put him on, if you please."

"One moment, please." A click, another voice, not so smooth and much harder. "Yeah?"

"Steve Grayce. I want to speak to Mr. Walters."

"Sorry. I don't seem to know you. It's a little early, amigo. What's your business?"

"Did he go to Miss Chiozza's place?"

"Oh." A pause. "The shamus. I get it. Hold the line, pal."

Another voice now—lazy, with the faintest color of Irish in it. "You can talk, son. This is Walters."

"I'm Steve Grayce. I'm the man—"

"I know all about that, son. The lady is O.K., by the way. I think she's asleep upstairs. Go on."

"I'm at Crestline—top of the Arrowhead grade. Two men murdered Leopardi. One was George Millar, night auditor at the Carlton Hotel. The other his brother, an ex-fighter named Gaff Talley. Talley's dead—shot by his brother. Millar got away—but he left me a full confession signed, detailed, complete."

Walters said slowly: "You're a fast worker, son—unless you're just plain crazy. Better come in here fast. Why did they do it?"

"They had a sister."

Walters repeated quietly: "They had a sister . . . What about this fellow that got away? We don't want some hick sheriff or publicity-hungry county attorney to get ideas—"

Steve broke in quietly: "I don't think you'll have to worry about that, Mr. Walters. I think I know where he's gone."

He ate breakfast at the inn, not because he was hungry, but because he was weak. He got into his car again and started down the long smooth grade from Crestline to San Bernardino, a broad paved boulevard skirting the edge of a sheer drop into the deep valley. There were places where the road went close to the edge, white guard-fences alongside.

Two miles below Crestline was the place. The road made a sharp turn around a shoulder of the mountain. Cars were parked on the gravel off the pavement—several private cars, an official car, and a wrecking car. The white fence was broken through and men stood around the broken place looking down.

Eight hundred feet below, what was left of a gray sedan lay silent and crumpled in the morning sunshine.

Pearls Are a Nuisance

I<small>T IS QUITE TRUE</small> that I wasn't doing anything that morning except looking at a blank sheet of paper in my typewriter and thinking about writing a letter. It is also quite true that I don't have a great deal to do any morning. But that is no reason why I should have to go out hunting for old Mrs. Penruddock's pearl necklace. I don't happen to be a policeman.

It was Ellen Macintosh who called me up, which made a difference, of course. "How are you, darling?" she asked. "Busy?"

"Yes and no," I said. "Mostly no. I am very well. What is it now?"

"I don't think you love me, Walter. And anyway you ought to get some work to do. You have too much money. Somebody has stolen Mrs. Penruddock's pearls and I want you to find them."

"Possibly you think you have the police department on the line," I said coldly. "This is the residence of Walter Gage. Mr. Gage talking."

"Well, you can tell Mr. Gage from Miss Ellen Macintosh," she said, "that if he is not out here in half an hour, he will receive a small parcel by registered mail containing one diamond engagement ring."

"And a lot of good it did me," I said. "That old crow will live for another fifty years."

But she had already hung up so I put my hat on and went down and drove off in the Packard. It was a nice late April morning, if you care for that sort of thing. Mrs. Penruddock lived on a wide quiet street in Carondelet Park. The house had probably looked exactly the same for the last fifty years, but that didn't make me any better pleased that Ellen Macintosh might live in it another fifty years, unless old Mrs. Penruddock died and didn't need a nurse any more. Mr. Penruddock had died a few years before, leaving no will, a thoroughly tangled-up estate, and a list of pensioners as long as a star boarder's arm.

I rang the front doorbell and the door was opened, not very soon, by a little old woman with a maid's apron and a strangled knot of gray hair on the top of her head. She looked at me as if she had never seen me before and didn't want to see me now.

"Miss Ellen Macintosh, please," I said. "Mr. Walter Gage calling."

She sniffed, turned without a word and we went back into the musty recesses of the house and came to a glassed-in porch full of wicker furniture and the smell of Egyptian tombs. She went away, with another sniff.

In a moment the door opened again and Ellen Macintosh came in. Maybe you don't like tall girls with honey-colored hair and skin like the first strawberry peach the grocer sneaks out of the box for himself. If you don't, I'm sorry for you.

"Darling, so you did come," she said. "That was nice of you, Walter. Now sit down and I'll tell you all about it."

We sat down.

"Mrs. Penruddock's pearl necklace has been stolen, Walter."

"You told me that over the telephone. My temperature is still normal."

"If you will excuse a professional guess," she said, "it is probably subnormal—permanently. The pearls are a string of forty-nine matched pink ones which Mr. Penruddock gave to Mrs. Penruddock for her golden wedding present. She hardly ever wore them lately, except perhaps on Christmas or when she had a couple of very old friends in to dinner and was well enough to sit up. And every Thanksgiving she gives a dinner to all the pensioners and friends and old employees Mr. Penruddock left on her hands, and she wore them then."

"You are getting your verb tenses a little mixed," I said, "but the general idea is clear. Go on."

"Well, Walter," Ellen said, with what some people call an arch look, "the pearls have been stolen. Yes, I know that is the third time I told you that, but there's a strange mystery about it. They were kept in a leather case in an old safe which was open half the time and which I should judge a strong man could open with his fingers even when it was locked. I had to go there for a paper this morning and I looked in at the pearls just to say hello—"

"I hope your idea in hanging on to Mrs. Penruddock has not been that she might leave you that necklace," I said stiffly. "Pearls are all very well for old people and fat blondes, but for tall willowy—"

"Oh shut up, darling," Ellen broke in. "I should certainly not have been waiting for these pearls—because they were false."

I swallowed hard and stared at her. "Well," I said, with a leer, "I have heard that old Penruddock pulled some cross-eyed rabbits out of the hat occasionally, but giving his own wife a string of phoney pearls on her golden wedding gets my money."

"Oh, don't be such a fool, Walter! They were real enough then. The fact is Mrs. Penruddock sold them and had imitations made. One of her old friends, Mr. Lansing Gallemore of the Gallemore Jewelry Company, handled it all for her very quietly, because of course she didn't want anyone to know. And that is why the police have not been called in. You *will* find them for her, won't you, Walter?"

"How? And what did she sell them for?"

"Because Mr. Penruddock died suddenly without making any provision for all these people he had been supporting. Then the depression came, and there was hardly any money at all. Only just enough to carry on the household and pay the servants, all of whom have been with Mrs. Penruddock so long that she would rather starve than let any of them go."

"That's different," I said. "I take my hat off to her. But how the dickens am I going to find them, and what does it matter anyway—if they were false?"

"Well, the pearls—the imitations, I mean—cost two hundred dollars and were specially made in Bohemia and it took several months and the way things are over there now she might never be able to get another set of really good imitations. And she is terrified somebody will find out they were false, or that the thief will blackmail her, when he finds out they were false. You see, darling, I know who stole them."

I said, "Huh?" a word I very seldom use as I do not think it part of the vocabulary of a gentleman.

"The chauffeur we had here a few months, Walter—a horrid big brute named Henry Eichelberger. He left suddenly the day before yesterday, for no reason at all. Nobody ever leaves Mrs. Penruddock. Her last chauffeur was a very old man and he died. But Henry Eichelberger left without a word and I'm sure he had stolen the pearls. He tried to kiss me once, Walter."

"Oh, he did," I said in a different voice. "Tried to kiss you, eh? Where is this big slab of meat, darling? Have you any idea at all? It seems hardly likely he would be hanging around on the street corner for me to punch his nose for him."

Ellen lowered her long silky eyelashes at me—and when she does that I go limp as a scrubwoman's back hair.

"He didn't run away. He must have known the pearls were false and that he was safe enough to blackmail Mrs. Penruddock. I called up the agency he came from and he has been back there and registered again for employment. But they said it was against their rules to give his address."

"Why couldn't somebody else have taken the pearls? A burglar, for instance?"

"There is no one else. The servants are beyond suspicion and the house is locked up as tight as an icebox every night and there were no signs of anybody having broken in. Besides Henry Eichelberger knew where the pearls were kept, because he saw me putting them away after the last time she wore them—which was when she had two very dear friends in to dinner on the occasion of the anniversary of Mr. Penruddock's death."

"That must have been a pretty wild party," I said. "All right, I'll go down to the agency and make them give me his address. Where is it?"

"It is called the Ada Twomey Domestic Employment Agency, and it is in the two-hundred block on East Second, a very unpleasant neighborhood."

"Not half as unpleasant as my neighborhood will be to Henry Eichelberger," I said. "So he tried to kiss you, eh?"

"The pearls, Walter," Ellen said gently, "are the important thing. I do hope he hasn't already found out they are false and thrown them in the ocean."

"If he has, I'll make him dive for them."

"He is six feet three and very big and strong, Walter," Ellen said coyly. "But not handsome like you, of course."

"Just my size," I said. "I am six three and a half. It will be a pleasure. Good-bye, darling."

She took hold of my sleeve. "There is just one thing, Walter. I don't mind a little fighting because it is manly. But you mustn't cause a disturbance that would bring the police in, you know. And although you are very big and strong and played right tackle at college, you are a little weak about one thing. Will you promise me not to drink any whiskey?"

"This Eichelberger," I said, "is all the drink I want."

2

The Ada Twomey Domestic Employment Agency on East Second Street proved to be all that the name and location implied. The odor of the anteroom, in which I was compelled to wait for a short time, was not at all pleasant. The agency was presided over by a hard-faced middle-aged woman who said that Henry Eichelberger was registered with them for employment as a chauffeur, and that she could arrange to have him call upon me, or could bring him there to the office for an interview. But when I placed a ten-dollar bill on her desk and indicated that it was merely an earnest of good faith, without prejudice to any commission which might become due to her agency, she relented and gave me his address, which was out west on Santa Monica Boulevard, near the part of the city which used to be called Sherman.

I drove out there without delay, for fear that Henry Eichelberger might telephone in and be informed that I was coming. The address proved to be a seedy hotel, conveniently close to the interurban car tracks and having its entrance adjoining a Chinese laundry. The hotel was upstairs, the steps being covered—in places—with strips of decayed rubber matting to which were screwed irregular fragments of unpolished brass. The smell of the Chinese laundry ceased about halfway up the stairs and was replaced by a smell of kerosene, cigar butts, slept-in air and greasy paper bags. There was a register at the head of the stairs on a wooden shelf. The last entry was in pencil, three weeks previous as to date, and had been written by someone with a very unsteady hand. I deduced from this that the management was not overparticular.

There was a bell besides the book and a sign reading— *Manager*. I rang the bell and waited. Presently a door opened down the hall and feet shuffled towards me without haste. A man appeared wearing frayed leather slippers and trousers of a nameless color, which had the two top buttons unlatched to permit more freedom to the suburbs of his extensive stomach. He also wore red suspenders, his shirt was darkened under the arms, and elsewhere, and his face badly needed a thorough laundering and trimming.

He said, "Full-up, bud," and sneered.

I said: "I am not looking for a room. I am looking for one Eichelberger, who, I am informed lives here, but who, I observe, has not registered in your book. And this, as of course you know, is contrary to the law."

"A wise guy," the fat man sneered again. "Down the hall, bud. Two-eighteen." He waved a thumb the color and almost the size of a burnt baked potato.

"Have the kindness to show me the way," I said.

"Geez, the lootenant-governor," he said, and began to shake his stomach. His small eyes disappeared in folds of yellow fat. "O.K., bud. Follow on."

We went into the gloomy depths of the back hall and came to a wooden door at the end with a closed wooden transom above it. The fat man smote the door with a fat hand. Nothing happened.

"Out," he said.

"Have the kindness to unlock the door," I said. "I wish to go in and wait for Eichelberger."

"In a pig's valise," the fat man said nastily. "Who the hell you think you are, bum?"

This angered me. He was a fair-sized man, about six feet tall, but too full of the memories of beer. I looked up and down the dark hall. The place seemed utterly deserted.

I hit the fat man in the stomach.

He sat down on the floor and belched and his right kneecap came into sharp contact with his jaw. He coughed and tears welled up in his eyes.

"Cripes, bud," he whined. "You got twenty years on me. That ain't fair."

"Open the door," I said. "I have no time to argue with you."

"A buck," he said, wiping his eyes on his shirt. "Two bucks and no tip-off."

I took two dollars out of my pocket and helped the man to his feet. He folded the two dollars and produced an ordinary passkey which I could have purchased for five cents.

"Brother, you sock," he said. "Where you learn it? Most big guys are muscle-bound." He unlocked the door.

"If you hear any noises later on," I said, "ignore them. If there is any damage, it will be paid for generously."

He nodded and I went into the room. He locked the door behind me and his steps receded. There was silence.

The room was small, mean and tawdry. It contained a brown chest of drawers with a small mirror hanging over it, a straight wooden chair, a wooden rocking chair, a single bed of chipped enamel, with a much mended cotton counterpane. The curtains at the single window had fly marks on them and the green shade was without a slat at the bottom. There was a wash bowl in the corner with two paper-thin towels hanging beside it. There was, of course, no bathroom, and there was no closet. A piece of dark figured material hanging from a shelf made a substitute for the latter. Behind this I found a gray business suit of the largest size made, which would be my size, if I wore ready made clothes, which I do not. There was a pair of black brogues on the floor, size number ten at least. There was also a cheap fiber suitcase, which of course I searched, as it was not locked.

I also searched the bureau and was surprised to find that everything in it was neat and clean and decent. But there was not much in it. Particularly there were no pearls in it. I searched in all other likely and unlikely places in the room but I found nothing of interest.

I sat on the side of the bed and lit a cigarette and waited. It was now apparent to me that either Henry Eichelberger was a very great fool or entirely innocent. The room and the open trail he had left behind him did not suggest a man dealing in operations like stealing pearl necklaces.

I had smoked four cigarettes, more than I usually smoke in an entire day, when approaching steps sounded. They were light quick steps but not at all clandestine. A key was thrust into the door and turned and the door swung carelessly open. A man stepped through it and looked at me.

I am six feet three inches in height and weigh over two hundred pounds. This man was tall, but he seemed lighter. He wore a blue serge suit of the kind which is called 'neat' for lack of anything better to say about it. He had thick wiry blond hair, a neck like a Prussian corporal in a cartoon, very wide shoulders and large hard hands, and he had a face that had taken much battering in its time. His small greenish eyes glinted at me with what I then took to be evil humor. I saw at once that he was not a man to trifle with, but I was not afraid of him. I was his equal in size and strength, and, I had small doubt, his superior in intelligence.

I stood up off the bed calmly and said: "I am looking for one Eichelberger."

"How you get in here, bud?" It was a cheerful voice, rather heavy, but not unpleasant to the ear.

"The explanation of that can wait," I said stiffly. "I am looking for one Eichelberger. Are you he?"

"Haw," the man said. "A gut-buster. A comedian. Wait'll I loosen my belt." He took a couple of steps farther into the room and I took the same number towards him.

"My name is Walter Gage," I said. "Are you Eichelberger?"

"Gimme a nickel," he said, "and I'll tell you."

I ignored that. "I am the fiancé of Miss Ellen Macintosh," I told him coldly. "I am informed that you tried to kiss her."

He took another step towards me and I another towards him. "Whaddaya mean—tried?" he sneered.

I led sharply with my right and it landed flush on his chin. It seemed to me a good solid punch, but it scarcely moved him. I then put two hard left jabs into his neck and landed a second hard right at the side of his rather wide nose. He snorted and hit me in the solar plexus.

I bent over and took hold of the room with both hands and spun it. When I had it nicely spinning I gave it a full swing and hit myself on the back of the head with the floor. This made me lose my balance temporarily and while I was thinking about how to regain it a wet towel began to slap at my face and I opened my eyes. The face of Henry Eichelberger was close to mine and bore a certain appearance of solicitude.

"Bud," his voice said, "your stomach is as weak as a Chinaman's tea."

"Brandy!" I croaked. "What happened?"

"You tripped on a little bitty tear in the carpet, bud. You really got to have liquor?"

"Brandy," I croaked again, and closed my eyes.

"I hope it don't get me started," his voice said.

A door opened and closed. I lay motionless and tried to avoid being sick at my stomach. The time passed slowly, in a long gray veil. Then the door of the room opened and closed once more and a moment later something hard was being pressed against my lips. I opened my mouth and whiskey poured down my throat. I coughed, but the fiery liquid coursed through my veins and strengthened me at once. I sat up.

"Thank you, Henry," I said. "May I call you Henry?"

"No tax on it, bud."

I got to my feet and stood before him. He stared at me curiously. "You look O.K.," he said. "Why'n't you told me you was sick?"

"Damn you, Eichelberger!" I said and hit with all my strength on the side of his jaw. He shook his head and his eyes seemed annoyed. I delivered three more punches to his face and jaw while he was still shaking his head.

"So you wanta play for keeps!" he yelled and took hold of the bed and threw it at me.

I dodged the corner of the bed, but in doing so I moved a little too quickly and lost my balance and pushed my head about four inches into the baseboard under the window.

A wet towel began to slap at my face. I opened my eyes.

"Listen, kid. You got two strikes and no balls on you. Maybe you oughta try a lighter bat."

"Brandy," I croaked.

"You'll take rye." He pressed a glass against my lips and I drank thirstily. Then I climbed to my feet again.

The bed, to my astonishment, had not moved. I sat down

on it and Henry Eichelberger sat down beside me and patted my shoulder.

"You and me could get along," he said. "I never kissed your girl, although I ain't saying I wouldn't like to. Is that all is worrying at you?"

He poured himself half a waterglassful of the whiskey out of the pint bottle which he had gone out to buy. He swallowed the liquor thoughtfully.

"No, there is another matter," I said.

"Shoot. But no more haymakers. Promise?"

I promised him rather reluctantly. "Why did you leave the employ of Mrs. Penruddock?" I asked him.

He looked at me from under his shaggy blond eyebrows. Then he looked at the bottle he was holding in his hand. "Would you call me a looker?" he asked.

"Well, Henry—"

"Don't pansy up on me," he snarled.

"No, Henry, I should not call you very handsome. But unquestionably you are virile."

He poured another half-waterglassful of whiskey and handed it to me. "Your turn," he said. I drank it down without fully realizing what I was doing. When I had stopped coughing Henry took the glass out of my hand and refilled it. He took his own drink moodily. The bottle was now nearly empty.

"Suppose you fell for a dame with all the looks this side of heaven. With a map like mine. A guy like me, a guy from the stockyards that played himself a lot of very tough left end at a cow college and left his looks and education on the scoreboard. A guy that has fought everything but whales and freight hogs—engines to you—and licked 'em all, but naturally had to take a sock now and then. Then I get a job where I see this lovely all the time and every day and know it's no dice. What would you do, pal? Me, I just quit the job."

"Henry, I'd like to shake your hand," I said.

He shook hands with me listlessly. "So I ask for my time," he said. "What else would I do?" He held the bottle up and looked at it against the light. "Bo, you made an error when you had me get this. When I start drinking it's a world cruise. You got plenty dough?"

"Certainly," I said. "If whiskey is what you want, Henry, whiskey it what you shall have. I have a very nice apartment on Franklin Avenue in Hollywood and while I cast no aspersions on your own humble and of course quite temporary abode, I now suggest we repair to my apartment, which is a good deal larger and gives one more room to extend one's elbow." I waved my hand airily.

"Say, you're drunk," Henry said, with admiration in his small green eyes.

"I am not yet drunk, Henry, although I do in fact feel the effect of that whiskey and very pleasantly. You must not mind my way of talking which is a personal matter, like your own clipped and concise method of speech. But before we depart there is one other rather insignificant detail I wish to discuss with you. I am empowered to arrange for the return of Mrs. Penruddock's pearls. I understand there is some possibility that you may have stolen them."

"Son, you take some awful chances," Henry said softly.

"This is a business matter, Henry, and plain talk is the best way to settle it. The pearls are only false pearls, so we should very easily be able to come to an agreement. I mean you no ill will, Henry, and I am obliged to you for procuring the whiskey, but business is business. Will you take fifty dollars and return the pearls and no questions asked?"

Henry laughed shortly and mirthlessly, but he seemed to have no animosity in his voice when he said: "So you think I stole some marbles and am sitting around here waiting for a flock of dicks to swarm me?"

"No police have been told, Henry, and you may not have known the pearls were false. Pass the liquor, Henry."

He poured me most of what was left in the bottle, and I drank it down with the greatest good humor. I threw the glass at the mirror, but unfortunately missed. The glass, which was of heavy and cheap construction, fell on the floor and did not break. Henry Eichelberger laughed heartily.

"What are you laughing at, Henry?"

"Nothing," he said. "I was just thinking what a sucker some guy is finding out he is—about them marbles."

"You mean you did not steal the pearls, Henry?"

He laughed again, a little gloomily. "Yeah," he said,

"meaning no. I oughta sock you, but what the hell? Any guy can get a bum idea. No, I didn't steal no pearls, bud. If they was ringers, I wouldn't be bothered, and if they was what they looked like the one time I saw them on the old lady's neck, I wouldn't decidedly be holed up in no cheap flop in L.A. waiting for a couple carloads of johns to put the sneeze on me."

I reached for his hand again and shook it.

"That is all I required to know," I said happily. "Now I am at peace. We shall now go to my apartment and consider ways and means to recover these pearls. You and I together should make a team that can conquer any opposition, Henry."

"You ain't kidding me, huh?"

I stood up and put my hat on—upside down. "No, Henry. I am making you an offer of employment which I understand you need, and all the whiskey you can drink. Let us go. Can you drive a car in your condition?"

"Hell, I ain't drunk," Henry said, looking surprised.

We left the room and walked down the dark hallway. The fat manager very suddenly appeared from some nebulous shade and stood in front of us rubbing his stomach and looking at me with small greedy expectant eyes. "Everything oke?" he inquired, chewing on a time-darkened toothpick.

"Give him a buck," Henry said.

"What for, Henry?"

"Oh, I dunno. Just give him a buck."

I withdrew a dollar bill from my pocket and gave it to the fat man.

"Thanks, pal," Henry said. He chucked the fat man under the Adam's apple, and removed the dollar bill deftly from between his fingers. "That pays for the hooch," he added. "I hate to have to bum dough."

We went down the stairs arm in arm, leaving the manager trying to cough the toothpick up from his oesophagus.

3

At five o'clock that afternoon I awoke from slumber and found that I was lying on my bed in my apartment in the Chateau Moraine, on Franklin Avenue near Ivar Street, in

Hollywood. I turned my head, which ached, and saw that Henry Eichelberger was lying beside me in his undershirt and trousers. I then perceived that I also was as lightly attired. On the table nearby there stood an almost full bottle of Old Plantation rye whiskey, the full quart size, and on the floor lay an entirely empty bottle of the same excellent brand. There were garments lying here and there on the floor, and a cigarette had burned a hole in the brocaded arm of one of my easy chairs.

I felt myself over carefully. My stomach was stiff and sore and my jaw seemed a little swollen on one side. Otherwise I was none the worse for wear. A sharp pain darted through my temples as I stood up off the bed, but I ignored it and walked steadily to the bottle on the table and raised it to my lips. After a steady draught of the fiery liquid I suddenly felt much better. A hearty and cheerful mood came over me and I was ready for any adventure. I went back to the bed and shook Henry firmly by the shoulder.

"Wake up, Henry," I said. "The sunset hour is nigh. The robins are calling and the squirrels are scolding and the morning glories furl themselves in sleep."

Like all men of action Henry Eichelberger came awake with his fist doubled. "What was that crack?" he snarled. "Oh, yeah. Hi, Walter. How you feel?"

"I feel splendid. Are you rested?"

"Sure." He swung his shoeless feet to the floor and rumpled his thick blond hair with his fingers. "We was going swell until you passed out," he said. "So I had me a nap. I never drink solo. You O.K.?"

"Yes, Henry, I feel very well indeed. And we have work to do."

"Swell." He went to the whiskey bottle and quaffed from it freely. He rubbed his stomach with the flat of his hand. His green eyes shone peacefully. "I'm a sick man," he said, "and I got to take my medicine." He put the bottle down on the table and surveyed the apartment. "Geez," he said, "we thrown it into us so fast I ain't hardly looked at the dump. You got a nice little place here, Walter. Geez, a white typewriter and a white telephone. What's the matter, kid—you just been confirmed?"

"Just a foolish fancy, Henry," I said, waving an airy hand.

Henry went over and looked at the typewriter and the telephone side by side on my writing desk, and the silver-mounted desk set, each piece chased with my initials.

"Well fixed, huh?" Henry said, turning his green gaze on me.

"Tolerably so, Henry," I said modestly.

"Well, what next pal? You got any ideas or do we just drink some?"

"Yes, Henry, I do have an idea. With a man like you to help me I think it can be put into practise. I feel that we must, as they say, tap the grapevine. When a string of pearls is stolen, all the underworld knows it at once. Pearls are hard to sell, Henry, inasmuch as they cannot be cut and can be identified by experts, I have read. The underworld will be seething with activity. It should not be too difficult for us to find someone who would send a message to the proper quarter that we are willing to pay a reasonable sum for their return."

"You talk nice—for a drunk guy," Henry said, reaching for the bottle. "But ain't you forgot these marbles are phoneys?"

"For sentimental reasons I am quite willing to pay for their return, just the same."

Henry drank some whiskey, appeared to enjoy the flavor of it and drank some more. He waved the bottle at me politely.

"That's O.K.—as far as it goes," he said. "But this underworld that's doing all this here seething you spoke of, ain't going to seethe a hell of a lot over a string of glass beads. Or am I screwy?"

"I was thinking, Henry, that the underworld probably has a sense of humor and the laugh that would go around would be quite emphatic."

"There's an idea in that," Henry said. "Here's some mug finds out lady Penruddock has a string of oyster fruit worth oodles of kale, and he does hisself a neat little box job and trots down to the fence. And the fence gives him the belly laugh. I would say something like that could get around the poolrooms and start a little idle chatter. So far, so nutty. But this box man is going to dump them beads in a hurry, because he has a three-to-ten on him even if they are only worth a nickel plus sales tax. Breaking and entering is the rap, Walter."

"However, Henry," I said, "there is another element in the situation. If this thief is very stupid, it will not, of course, have much weight. But if he is even moderately intelligent, it will. Mrs. Penruddock is a very proud woman and lives in a very exclusive section of the city. If it should become known that she wore imitation pearls, and above all, if it should be even hinted in the public press that these were the very pearls her own husband had given her for her golden wedding present—well, I am sure you see the point, Henry."

"Box guys ain't too bright," he said and rubbed his stony chin. Then he lifted his right thumb and bit it thoughtfully. He looked at the windows, at the corner of the room, at the floor. He looked at me from the corners of his eyes.

"Blackmail, huh?" he said. "Maybe. But crooks don't mix their rackets much. Still, the guy might pass the word along. There's a chance, Walter. I wouldn't care to hock my gold fillings to buy me a piece of it, but there's a chance. How much you figure to put out?"

"A hundred dollars should be ample, but I am willing to go as high as two hundred, which is the actual cost of the imitations."

Henry shook his head and patronized the bottle. "Nope. The guy wouldn't uncover hisself for that kind of money. Wouldn't be worth the chance he takes. He'd dump the marbles and keep his nose clean."

"We can at least try, Henry."

"Yeah, but where? And we're getting low on liquor. Maybe I better put my shoes on and run out, huh?"

At that very moment, as if in answer to my unspoken prayer, a soft dull thump sounded on the door of my apartment. I opened it and picked up the final edition of the evening paper. I closed the door again and carried the paper back across the room, opening it up as I went. I touched it with my right forefinger and smiled confidently at Henry Eichelberger.

"Here. I will wager you a full quart of Old Plantation that the answer will be on the crime page of this paper."

"There ain't any crime page," Henry chortled. "This is Los Angeles. I'll fade you."

I opened the paper to page three with some trepidation, for, although I had already seen the item I was looking for in an early edition of the paper while waiting in Ada Twomey's Domestic Employment Agency, I was not certain it would appear intact in the later editions. But my faith was rewarded. It had not been removed, but appeared midway of column three exactly as before. The paragraph, which was quite short, was headed: LOU GANDESI QUESTIONED IN GEM THEFTS.

"Listen to this, Henry," I said, and began to read.

"Acting on an anonymous tip police late last night picked up Louis G. (Lou) Gandesi, proprietor of a well known Spring Street tavern, and quizzed him intensively concerning the recent wave of dinner-party hold-ups in an exclusive western section of this city, hold-ups during which, it is alleged, more than two hundred thousand dollars worth of valuable jewels have been torn at gun's point from women guests in fashionable homes. Gandesi was released at a late hour and refused to make any statement to reporters. 'I never kibitz the cops,' he said modestly. Captain William Norgaard, of the Central Robbery Detail, announced himself as satisfied that Gandesi had no connection with the robberies, and that the tip was merely an act of personal spite."

I folded the paper and threw it on the bed.

"You win, bo," Henry said, and handed me the bottle. I took a long drink and returned it to him. "Now what? Brace this Gandesi and take him through the hoops?"

"He may be a dangerous man, Henry. Do you think we are equal to it?"

Henry snorted contemptuously. "Yah, a Spring Street punk. Some fat slob with a phoney ruby on his mitt. Lead me to him. We'll turn the slob inside out and drain his liver. But we're just about fresh out of liquor. All we got is maybe a pint." He examined the bottle against the light.

"We have had enough for the moment, Henry."

"We ain't drunk, are we? I only had seven drinks since I got here, maybe nine."

"Certainly we are not drunk, Henry, but you take very

large drinks, and we have a difficult evening before us. I think we should now get shaved and dressed, and I further think that we should wear dinner clothes. I have an extra suit which will fit you admirably, as we are almost exactly the same size. It is certainly a remarkable omen that two such large men should be associated in the same enterprise. Evening clothes impress these low characters, Henry."

"Swell," Henry said. "They'll think we're mugs workin' for some big shot. This Gandesi will be scared enough to swallow his necktie."

We decided to do as I had suggested and I laid out clothes for Henry, and while he was bathing and shaving I telephoned to Ellen Macintosh.

"Oh, Walter, I am so glad you called up," she cried. "Have you found anything?"

"Not yet, darling," I said. "But we have an idea. Henry and I are just about to put it into execution."

"Henry, Walter? Henry who?"

"Why, Henry Eichelberger, of course, darling. Have you forgotten him so soon? Henry and I are warm friends and we—"

She interrupted me coldly. "Are you drinking, Walter?" she demanded in a very distant voice.

"Certainly not, darling. Henry is a teetotaler."

She sniffed sharply. I could hear the sound distinctly over the telephone. "But didn't Henry take the pearls?" she asked, after quite a long pause.

"Henry, angel? Of course not. Henry left because he was in love with you."

"Oh, Walter. That ape? I'm sure you're drinking terribly. I don't ever want to speak to you again. Good-bye." And she hung the phone up very sharply so that a painful sensation made itself felt in my ear.

I sat down in a chair with a bottle of Old Plantation in my hand wondering what I had said that could be construed as offensive or indiscreet. As I was unable to think of anything, I consoled myself with the bottle until Henry came out of the bathroom looking extremely personable in one of my pleated shirts and a wing collar and black bow tie.

It was dark when we left the apartment and I, at least, was

full of hope and confidence, although a little depressed by the way Ellen Macintosh had spoken to me over the telephone.

4

Mr. Gandesi's establishment was not difficult to find, inasmuch as the first taxicab driver Henry yelled at on Spring Street directed us to it. It was called the Blue Lagoon and its interior was bathed in an unpleasant blue light. Henry and I entered it steadily, since we had consumed a partly solid meal at Mandy's Caribbean Grotto before starting out to find Mr. Gandesi. Henry looked almost handsome in my second-best dinner suit, with a fringed white scarf hanging over his shoulder, a lightweight black felt hat on the back of his head (which was only a little larger than mine), and a bottle of whiskey in each of the side pockets of the summer overcoat he was wearing.

The bar of the Blue Lagoon was crowded, but Henry and I went on back to the small dim dining-room behind it. A man in a dirty dinner suit came up to us and Henry asked him for Gandesi, and he pointed out another man who sat alone at a small table in the far corner of the room. We went that way.

The man who sat alone at the table was shaped like two eggs, a robin's egg, which was his head, on top of a hen's egg, which was his body. He sat with a small glass of red wine in front of him and slowly twisted a large green stone on his finger. He did not look up. There were no other chairs at the table, so Henry leaned on it with both elbows.

"You Gandesi?" he said.

The man did not look up even then. He moved his thick black eyebrows together and said in an absent voice: "Si. Yes."

"We got to talk to you in private," Henry told him. "Where we won't be disturbed."

Gandesi looked up now and there was extreme boredom in his flat black almond-shaped eyes. "So?" he asked and shrugged. "Eet ees about what?"

"About some pearls," Henry said. "Forty-nine on the string, matched and pink."

"You sell—or you buy?" Gandesi inquired and his chin began to shake up and down as if with amusement.

"Buy," Henry said.

The man at the table crooked his finger quietly and a very large waiter appeared at his side. "Ees dronk," he said lifelessly. "Put dees men out."

The waiter took hold of Henry's shoulder. Henry reached up carelessly and took hold of the waiter's hand and twisted it. The waiter's face in that bluish light turned some color I could not describe, but which was not at all healthy. He let out a low moan. Henry dropped the hand and said to me: "Put a C-note on the table."

I took my wallet out and extracted from it one of the two hundred-dollar bills I had taken the precaution to obtain from the cashier at the Chateau Moraine. Gandesi stared at the bill and made a gesture to the large waiter, who went away rubbing his hand and holding it tight against his chest.

"What for?" Gandesi asked.

"Five minutes of your time alone."

"Ees very fonny. O.K., I bite." Gandesi took the bill and folded it neatly and put it in his vest pocket. Then he put both hands on the table and pushed himself heavily to his feet. He started to waddle away without looking at us.

Henry and I followed him among the crowded tables to the far side of the dining-room and through a door in the wainscoting and then down a narrow dim hallway. At the end of this Gandesi opened a door into a lighted room and stood holding it for us, with a grave smile on his olive face. I went in first.

As Henry passed in front of Gandesi into the room the latter, with surprising agility, took a small shiny black leather club from his clothes and hit Henry on the head with it very hard. Henry sprawled forward on his hands and knees. Gandesi shut the door of the room very quickly for a man of his build and leaned against it with the small club in his left hand. Now, very suddenly, in his right hand appeared a short but heavy black revolver.

"Ees very fonny," he said politely and chuckled to himself.

Exactly what happened then I did not see clearly. Henry

was at one instant on his hands and knees with his back to Gandesi. In the next, or possibly even in the same instant, something swirled like a big fish in water and Gandesi grunted. I then saw that Henry's hard blond head was buried in Gandesi's stomach and that Henry's large hands held both of Gandesi's hairy wrists. Then Henry straightened his body to its full height and Gandesi was high up in the air balanced on top of Henry's head, his mouth strained wide open and his face a dark purple color. Then Henry shook himself, as it seemed, quite lightly, and Gandesi landed on his back on the floor with a terrible thud and lay gasping. Then a key turned in the door and Henry stood with his back to it, holding both the club and the revolver in his left hand, and solicitously feeling the pockets which contained our supply of whiskey. All this happened with such rapidity that I leaned against the side wall and felt a little sick at my stomach.

"A gut-buster," Henry drawled. "A comedian. Wait'll I loosen my belt."

Gandesi rolled over and got to his feet very slowly and painfully and stood swaying and passing his hand up and down his face. His clothes were covered with dust.

"This here's a sap," Henry said, showing me the small black club. "He hit me with it, didn't he?"

"Why, Henry, don't you know?" I inquired.

"I just wanted to be sure," Henry said. "You don't do that to the Eichelbergers."

"O.K., what you boys want?" Gandesi asked abruptly, with no trace whatever of his Italian accent.

"I told you what we wanted, dough-face."

"I don't think I know you boys," Gandesi said and lowered his body with care into a wooden chair beside a shabby office desk. He mopped his face and neck and felt himself in various places.

"You got the wrong idea, Gandesi. A lady living in Carondelet Park lost a forty-nine-bead pearl necklace a couple days back. A box job, but a pushover. Our outfit's carrying a little insurance on those marbles. And I'll take that C-note."

He walked over to Gandesi and Gandesi quickly reached the folded bill from his pocket and handed it to him. Henry gave me the bill and I put it back in my wallet.

"I don't think I hear about it," Gandesi said carefully.

"You hit me with a sap," Henry said. "Listen kind of hard."

Gandesi shook his head and then winced. "I don't back no petermen," he said, "nor no heist guys. You got me wrong."

"Listen hard," Henry said in a low voice. "You might hear something." He swung the small black club lightly in front of his body with two fingers of his right hand. The slightly too-small hat was still on the back of his head, although a little crumpled.

"Henry," I said, "you seem to be doing all the work this evening. Do you think that is quite fair?"

"O.K., work him over," Henry said. "These fat guys bruise something lovely."

By this time Gandesi had become a more natural color and was gazing at us steadily. "Insurance guys, huh?" he inquired dubiously.

"You said it, dough-face."

"You try Melachrino?" Gandesi asked.

"Haw," Henry began raucously, "a gut-buster. A——" but I interrupted him sharply.

"One moment, Henry," I said. Then turning to Gandesi, "Is this Melachrino a person?" I asked him.

Gandesi's eyes rounded in surprise. "Sure—is a guy. You don't know him, huh?" A look of dark suspicion was born in his sloe-black eyes, but vanished almost as soon as it appeared.

"Phone him," Henry said, pointing to the instrument which stood on the shabby office desk.

"Phone is bad," Gandesi objected thoughtfully.

"So is sap poison," Henry said.

Gandesi sighed and turned his thick body in the chair and drew the telephone towards him. He dialed a number with an inky nail and listened. After an interval he said: "Joe? . . . Lou. Couple insurance guys tryin' to deal on a Carondelet Park job. . . . Yeah. . . . No, marbles. . . . You ain't heard a whisper, huh? . . . O.K., Joe."

Gandesi replaced the phone and swung around in the chair again. He studied us with sleepy eyes. "No soap. What insurance outfit you boys work for?"

"Give him a card," Henry said to me.

I took my wallet out once more and withdrew one of my

cards from it. It was an engraved calling card and contained nothing but my name. So I used my pocket pencil to write, *Chateau Moraine Apartments, Franklin near Ivar,* below the name. I showed the card to Henry and then gave it to Gandesi.

Gandesi read the card and quietly bit his finger. His face brightened suddenly. "You boys better see Jack Lawler," he said.

Henry stared at him closely. Gandesi's eyes were now bright and unblinking and guileless.

"Who's he?" Henry asked.

"Runs the Penguin Club. Out on the Strip—Eighty-six Forty-four Sunset or some number like that. He can find out, if any guy can."

"Thanks," Henry said quietly. He glanced at me. "You believe him?"

"Well, Henry," I said, "I don't really think he would be above telling us an untruth."

"Haw!" Gandesi began suddenly. "A gut-buster! A—"

"Can it!" Henry snarled. "That's my line. Straight goods, is it, Gandesi? About this Jack Lawler?"

Gandesi nodded vigorously. "Straight goods, absolute. Jack Lawler got a finger in everything high class that's touched. But he ain't easy to see."

"Don't worry none about that. Thanks, Gandesi."

Henry tossed the black club into the corner of the room and broke open the breech of the revolver he had been holding all this time in his left hand. He ejected the shells and then bent down and slid the gun along the floor until it disappeared under the desk. He tossed the cartridges idly in his hand for a moment and then let them spill on the floor.

"So long, Gandesi," he said coldly. "And keep that schnozzle of yours clean, if you don't want to be looking for it under the bed."

He opened the door then and we both went out quickly and left the Blue Lagoon without interference from any of the employees.

5

My car was parked a short distance away down the block. We entered it and Henry leaned his arms on the wheel and stared moodily through the windshield.

"Well, what you think, Walter?" he inquired at length.

"If you ask my opinion, Henry, I think Mr. Gandesi told us a cock-and-bull story merely to get rid of us. Furthermore I do not believe he thought we were insurance agents."

"Me too, and an extra helping," Henry said. "I don't figure there's any such guy as this Melachrino or this Jack Lawler and this Gandesi called up some dead number and had himself a phoney chin with it. I oughta go back there and pull his arms and legs off. The hell with the fat slob."

"We had the best idea we could think of, Henry, and we executed it to the best of our ability. I now suggest that we return to my apartment and try to think of something else."

"And get drunk," Henry said, starting the car and guiding it away from the curb.

"We could perhaps have a small allowance of liquor, Henry."

"Yah!" Henry snorted. "A stall. I oughta go back there and wreck the joint."

He stopped at the intersection, although no traffic signal was in operation at the time, and raised a bottle of whiskey to his lips. He was in the act of drinking when a car came up behind us and collided with our car, but not very severely. Henry choked and lowered his bottle, spilling some of the liquor on his garments.

"This town's getting too crowded," he snarled. "A guy can't take hisself a drink without some smart monkey bumps his elbow."

Whoever it was in the car behind us blew a horn with some insistence, inasmuch as our car had not yet moved forward. Henry wrenched the door open and got out and went back. I heard voices of considerable loudness, the louder being Henry's voice. He came back after a moment and got into the car and drove on.

"I oughta have pulled his mush off," he said, "but I went soft." He drove rapidly the rest of the way to Hollywood and the Chateau Moraine and we went up to my apartment and sat down with large glasses in our hands.

"We got better than a quart and a half of hooch," Henry said, looking at the two bottles which he had placed on the table beside others which had long since been emptied. "That oughta be good for an idea."

"If it isn't enough, Henry, there is an abundant further supply where it came from." I drained my glass cheerfully.

"You seem a right guy," Henry said. "What makes you always talk so funny?"

"I cannot seem to change my speech, Henry. My father and mother were both severe purists in the New England tradition, and the vernacular has never come naturally to my lips, even while I was in college."

Henry made an attempt to digest this remark, but I could see that it lay somewhat heavily on his stomach.

We talked for a time concerning Gandesi and the doubtful quality of his advice, and thus passed perhaps half an hour. Then rather suddenly the white telephone on my desk began to ring. I hurried over to it, hoping that it was Ellen Macintosh and that she had recovered from her ill humor. But it proved to be a male voice and a strange one to me. It spoke crisply, with an unpleasant metallic quality of tone.

"You Walter Gage?"

"This is Mr. Gage speaking."

"Well, *Mister* Gage, I understand you're in the market for some jewelry."

I held the phone very tightly and turned my body and made grimaces at Henry over the top of the instrument. But he was moodily pouring himself another large portion of Old Plantation.

"That is so," I said into the telephone, trying to keep my voice steady, although my excitement was almost too much for me. "If by jewelry you mean pearls."

"Forty-nine in a rope, brother. And five grand is the price."

"Why that is entirely absurd," I gasped. "Five thousand dollars for those—"

The voice broke in on me rudely. "You heard me, brother. Five grand. Just hold up the hand and count the fingers. No more, no less. Think it over. I'll call you later."

The phone clicked drily and I replaced my instrument shakily in its cradle. I was trembling. I walked back to my chair and sat down and wiped my face with my handkerchief.

"Henry," I said in a low tense voice, "it worked. But how strangely."

Henry put his empty glass down on the floor. It was the first time that I had ever seen him put an empty glass down and leave it empty. He stared at me closely with his tight unblinking green eyes.

"Yeah?" he said gently. "What worked, kid?" He licked his lips slowly with the tip of his tongue.

"What we accomplished down at Gandesi's place, Henry. A man just called me on the telephone and asked me if I was in the market for pearls."

"Geez." Henry pursed his lips and whistled gently. "That damn dago had something after all."

"But the price is five thousand dollars, Henry. That seems beyond reasonable explanation."

"Huh?" Henry's eyes seemed to bulge as if they were about to depart from their orbits. "Five grand for them ringers? The guy's nuts. They cost two C's, you said. Bugs completely is what the guy is. Five grand? Why, for five grand I could buy me enough hot ice to cover Mae West's hips."

I could see that Henry seemed puzzled. He refilled our glasses silently and we stared at each other over them. "Well, what the heck can you do with that, Walter?" he asked after a long silence.

"Henry," I said firmly, "there is only one thing to do. It is true that Ellen Macintosh spoke to me in confidence, and as she did not have Mrs. Penruddock's express permission to tell me about the pearls, I suppose I should respect that confidence. But Ellen is now angry with me and does not wish to speak to me, for the reason that I am drinking whiskey in considerable quantities, although my speech and brain are still reasonably clear. This last is a very strange development and I think, in spite of everything, some close friend of the family should be consulted. Preferably of course, a man, someone of large business experience, and in addition to that a man who understands about jewels. There *is* such a man, Henry, and tomorrow morning I shall call upon him."

"Geez," Henry said. "You coulda said all that in nine words, bo. Who is this guy?"

"His name is Mr. Lansing Gallemore, and he is president of the Gallemore Jewelry Company on Seventh Street. He is a very old friend of Mrs. Penruddock—Ellen has often mentioned him—and is, in fact, the very man who procured for her the imitation pearls."

"But this guy will tip the bulls," Henry objected.

"I do not think so, Henry. I do not think he will do anything to embarrass Mrs. Penruddock in any way."

Henry shrugged. "Phonies are phonies," he said. "You can't make nothing else outa them. Not even no president of no jewelry store can't."

"Nevertheless, there must be a reason why so large a sum is demanded, Henry. The only reason that occurs to me is blackmail and, frankly, that is a little too much for me to handle alone, because I do not know enough about the background of the Penruddock family."

"Oke," Henry said, sighing. "If that's your hunch, you better follow it, Walter. And I better breeze on home and flop so as to be in good shape for the rough work, if any."

"You would not care to pass the night here, Henry?"

"Thanks, pal, but I'm O.K. back at the hotel. I'll just take this spare bottle of the tiger sweat to put me to sleep. I might happen to get a call from the agency in the A.M. and would have to brush my teeth and go after it. And I guess I better change my duds back to where I can mix with the common people."

So saying he went into the bathroom and in a short time emerged wearing his own blue serge suit. I urged him to take my car, but he said it would not be safe in his neighborhood. He did, however, consent to use the topcoat he had been wearing and, placing in it carefully the unopened quart of whiskey, he shook me warmly by the hand.

"One moment, Henry," I said and took out my wallet. I extended a twenty-dollar bill to him.

"What's that in favor of?" he growled.

"You are temporarily out of employment, Henry, and you have done a noble piece of work this evening, puzzling as are the results. You should be rewarded and I can well afford this small token."

"Well, thanks, pal," Henry said. "But it's just a loan." His voice was gruff with emotion. "Should I give you a buzz in the A.M.?"

"By all means. And there is one thing more that has occurred to me. Would it not be advisable for you to change your hotel? Suppose, through no fault of mine, the police learn of this theft. Would they not at least suspect you?"

"Hell, they'd bounce me up and down for hours," Henry said. "But what'll it get them? I ain't no ripe peach."

"It is for you to decide, of course, Henry."

"Yeah. Good-night, pal, and don't have no nightmares."

He left me then and I felt suddenly very depressed and lonely. Henry's company had been very stimulating to me, in spite of his rough way of talking. He was very much of a man. I poured myself a rather large drink of whiskey from the remaining bottle and drank it quickly but gloomily.

The effect was such that I had an overmastering desire to speak to Ellen Macintosh at all costs. I went to the telephone and called her number. After a long wait a sleepy maid answered. But Ellen, upon hearing my name, refused to come to the telephone. That depressed me still further and I finished the rest of the whiskey almost without noticing what I was doing. I then lay down on the bed and fell into fitful slumber.

6

The busy ringing of the telephone awoke me and I saw that the morning sunlight was streaming into the room. It was nine o'clock and all the lamps were still burning. I arose feeling a little stiff and dissipated, for I was still wearing my dinner suit. But I am a healthy man with very steady nerves and I did not feel as badly as I expected. I went to the telephone and answered it.

Henry's voice said: "How you feel, pal? I got a hangover like twelve Swedes."

"Not too badly, Henry."

"I got a call from the agency about a job. I better go down and take a gander at it. Should I drop around later?"

"Yes, Henry, by all means do that. By eleven o'clock I should be back from the errand about which I spoke to you last night."

"Any more calls from you know?"

"Not yet, Henry."

"Check. Abyssinia." He hung up and I took a cold shower and shaved and dressed. I donned a quiet brown business suit and had some coffee sent up from the coffee-shop downstairs. I also had the waiter remove the empty bottles from my apartment and gave him a dollar for his trouble. After drinking two cups of black coffee I felt my own man once more and drove downtown to the Gallemore Jewelry Company's large and brilliant store on West Seventh Street.

It was another bright, golden morning and it seemed that somehow things should adjust themselves on so pleasant a day.

Mr. Lansing Gallemore proved to be a little difficult to see, so that I was compelled to tell his secretary that it was a matter concerning Mrs. Penruddock and of a confidential nature. Upon this message being carried in to him I was at once ushered into a long paneled office, at the far end of which Mr. Gallemore stood behind a massive desk. He extended a thin pink hand to me.

"Mr. Gage? I don't believe we have met, have we?"

"No, Mr. Gallemore, I do not believe we have. I am the fiancé—or was until last night—of Miss Ellen Macintosh, who, as you probably know, is Mrs. Penruddock's nurse. I am come to you upon a very delicate matter and it is necessary that I ask for your confidence before I speak."

He was a man of perhaps seventy-five years of age, and very thin and tall and correct and well preserved. He had cold blue eyes but a warming smile. He was attired youthfully enough in a gray flannel suit with a red carnation at his lapel.

"That is something I make it a rule never to promise, Mr. Gage," he said. "I think it is almost always a very unfair request. But if you assure me the matter concerns Mrs. Penruddock and is really of a delicate and confidential nature, I will make an exception."

"It is indeed, Mr. Gallemore," I said, and thereupon told him the entire story, concealing nothing, not even the fact that I had consumed far too much whiskey the day before.

He stared at me curiously at the end of my story. His finely-shaped hand picked up an old-fashioned white quill pen and he slowly tickled his right ear with the feather of it.

"Mr. Gage," he said, "can't you guess why they ask five thousand dollars for that string of pearls?"

"If you permit me to guess, in a matter of so personal a nature, I could perhaps hazard an explanation, Mr. Gallemore."

He moved the white feather around to his left ear and nodded. "Go ahead, son."

"The pearls are in fact real, Mr. Gallemore. You are a very old friend of Mrs. Penruddock—perhaps even a childhood sweetheart. When she gave you her pearls, her golden wedding present, to sell because she was in sore need of money for a generous purpose, you did not sell them, Mr. Gallemore. You only pretended to sell them. You gave her twenty thousand dollars of your own money, and you returned the real pearls to her, pretending that they were an imitation made in Czechoslovakia."

"Son, you think a lot smarter than you talk," Mr. Gallemore said. He arose and walked to a window, pulled aside a fine net curtain and looked down on the bustle of Seventh Street. He came back to his desk and seated himself and smiled a little wistfully.

"You are almost embarrassingly correct, Mr. Gage," he said, and sighed. "Mrs. Penruddock is a very proud woman, or I should simply have offered her the twenty thousand dollars as an unsecured loan. I happened to be the co-administrator of Mr. Penruddock's estate and I knew that in the condition of the financial market at that time it would be out of the question to raise enough cash, without damaging the corpus of the estate beyond reason, to care for all those relatives and pensioners. So Mrs. Penruddock sold her pearls—as she thought—but she insisted that no one should know about it. And I did what you have guessed. It was unimportant. I could afford the gesture. I have never married, Gage, and I am rated a wealthy man. As a matter of fact, at that time, the pearls would not have fetched more than half of what I gave her, or of what they should bring today."

I lowered my eyes for fear this kindly old gentleman might be troubled by my direct gaze.

"So I think we had better raise that five thousand, son," Mr. Gallemore at once added in a brisk voice. "The price is pretty low, although stolen pearls are a great deal more difficult to deal in than cut stones. If I should care to trust you that far on your face, do you think you could handle the assignment?"

"Mr. Gallemore," I said firmly but quietly, "I am a total stranger to you and I am only flesh and blood. But I promise you by the memories of my dead and revered parents that there will be no cowardice."

"Well, there is a good deal of the flesh and blood, son," Mr. Gallemore said kindly. "And I am not afraid of your stealing the money, because possibly I know a little more about Miss Ellen Macintosh and her boy friend than you might suspect. Furthermore, the pearls are insured, in my name, of course, and the insurance company should really handle this affair. But you and your funny friend seem to have got along very nicely so far, and I believe in playing out a hand. This Henry must be quite a man."

"I have grown very attached to him, in spite of his uncouth ways," I said.

Mr. Gallemore played with his white quill pen a little longer and then he brought out a large checkbook and wrote a check, which he carefully blotted and passed across the desk.

"If you get the pearls, I'll see that the insurance people refund this to me," he said. "If they like my business, there will be no difficulty about that. The bank is down at the corner and I will be waiting for their call. They won't cash the check without telephoning me, probably. Be careful, son, and don't get hurt."

He shook hands with me once more and I hesitated. "Mr. Gallemore, you are placing a greater trust in me than any man ever has," I said. "With the exception, of course, of my own father."

"I am acting like a damn fool," he said with a peculiar

smile. "It is so long since I heard anyone talk the way Jane Austen writes that it is making a sucker out of me."

"Thank you, sir. I know my language is a bit stilted. Dare I ask you to do me a small favor, sir?"

"What is it, Gage?"

"To telephone Miss Ellen Macintosh, from whom I am now a little estranged, and tell her that I am not drinking today, and that you have entrusted me with a very delicate mission."

He laughed aloud. "I'll be glad to, Walter. And as I know she can be trusted, I'll give her an idea of what's going on."

I left him then and went down to the bank with the check, and the teller, after looking at me suspiciously, then absenting himself from his cage for a long time, finally counted out the money in hundred-dollar bills with the reluctance one might have expected, if it had been his own money.

I placed the flat packet of bills in my pocket and said: "Now give me a roll of quarters, please."

"A roll of quarters, sir?" His eyebrows lifted.

"Exactly. I use them for tips. And naturally I should prefer to carry them home in the wrapping."

"Oh, I see. Ten dollars, please."

I took the fat hard roll of coins and dropped it into my pocket and drove back to Hollywood.

Henry was waiting for me in the lobby of the Chateau Moraine, twirling his hat between his rough hard hands. His face looked a little more deeply lined than it had the day before and I noticed that his breath smelled of whiskey. We went up to my apartment and he turned to me eagerly.

"Any luck, pal?"

"Henry," I said, "before we proceed further into this day I wish it clearly understood that I am not drinking. I see that already you have been at the bottle."

"Just a pick-up, Walter," he said a little contritely. "That job I went out for was gone before I got there. What's the good word?"

I sat down and lit a cigarette and stared at him evenly. "Well, Henry, I don't really know whether I should tell you or not. But it seems a little petty not to do so after all you did last night to Gandesi." I hesitated a moment longer while Henry stared at me and pinched the muscles of his left arm. "The pearls are real, Henry. And I have instructions to proceed with the business and I have five thousand dollars in cash in my pocket at this moment."

I told him briefly what had happened.

He was more amazed than words could tell. "Cripes!" he exclaimed, his mouth hanging wide open. "You mean you got the five grand from this Gallemore—just like that?"

"Precisely that, Henry."

"Kid," he said earnestly, "you got something with that daisy pan and that fluff talk that a lot of guys would give important dough to cop. Five grand—out of a business guy—just like that. Why, I'll be a monkey's uncle. I'll be a snake's daddy. I'll be a mickey finn at a woman's-club lunch."

At that exact moment, as if my entrance to the building had been observed, the telephone rang again and I sprang to answer it.

It was one of the voices I was awaiting, but not the one I wanted to hear with the greater longing. "How's it looking to you this morning, Gage?"

"It is looking better," I said. "If I can have any assurance of honorable treatment, I am prepared to go through with it."

"You mean you got the dough?"

"In my pocket at this exact moment."

The voice seemed to exhale a slow breath. "You'll get your marbles O.K.—if we get the price, Gage. We're in this business for a long time and we don't welsh. If we did, it would soon get around and nobody would play with us any more."

"Yes, I can readily understand that," I said. "Proceed with your instructions," I added coldly.

"Listen close, Gage. Tonight at eight sharp you be in Pacific Palisades. Know where that is?"

"Certainly. It is a small residential section west of the polo fields on Sunset Boulevard."

"Right. Sunset goes slap through it. There's one drugstore there—open till nine. Be there waiting a call at eight sharp tonight. Alone. And I mean alone, Gage. No cops and no strong-arm guys. It's rough country down there and we got a way to get you to where we want you and know if you're alone. Get all this?"

"I am not entirely an idiot," I retorted.

"No dummy packages, Gage. The dough will be checked. No guns. You'll be searched and there's enough of us to cover you from all angles. We know your car. No funny business, no smart work, no slip-up and nobody hurt. That's the way we do business. How's the dough fixed?"

"One-hundred-dollar bills," I said. "And only a few of them are new."

"Attaboy. Eight o'clock then. Be smart, Gage."

The phone clicked in my ear and I hung up. It rang again almost instantly. This time it was the *one* voice.

"Oh, Walter," Ellen cried, "I was so mean to you! Please forgive me, Walter. Mr. Gallemore has told me everything and I'm so frightened."

"There is nothing of which to be frightened," I told her warmly. "Does Mrs. Penruddock know, darling?"

"No, darling. Mr. Gallemore told me not to tell her. I am phoning from a store down on Sixth Street. Oh, Walter, I really am frightened. Will Henry go with you?"

"I am afraid not, darling. The arrangements are all made and they will not permit it. I must go alone."

"Oh, Walter! I'm terrified. I can't bear the suspense."

"There is nothing to fear," I assured her. "It is a simple business transaction. And I am not exactly a midget."

"But, Walter—oh, I *will* try to be brave, Walter. Will you promise me just one teensy-weensy little thing?"

"Not a drop, darling," I said firmly. "Not a single solitary drop."

"Oh, Walter!"

There was a little more of that sort of thing, very pleasant to me in the circumstances, although possibly not of great interest to others. We finally parted with my promise to telephone Ellen as soon as the meeting between the crooks and myself had been consummated.

I turned from the telephone to find Henry drinking deeply from a bottle he had taken from his hip pocket.

"Henry!" I cried sharply.

He looked at me over the bottle with a shaggy determined

look. "Listen pal," he said in a low hard voice. "I got enough of your end of the talk to figure the set-up. Some place out in the tall weeds and you go alone and they feed you the old sap poison and take your dough and leave you lying—with the marbles still in their kitty. Nothing doing, pal. I said—nothing doing!" He almost shouted the last words.

"Henry, it is my duty and I must do it," I said quietly.

"Haw!" Henry snorted. "I say no. You're a nut, but you're a sweet guy on the side. I say no. Henry Eichelberger of the Wisconsin Eichelbergers—in fact, I might just as leave say of the Milwaukee Eichelbergers—says no. And he says it with both hands working." He drank again from his bottle.

"You certainly will not help matters by becoming intoxicated," I told him rather bitterly.

He lowered the bottle and looked at me with amazement written all over his rugged features. "Drunk, Walter?" he boomed. "Did I hear you say drunk? An Eichelberger drunk? Listen, son. We ain't got a lot of time now. It would take maybe three months. Some day when you got three months and maybe five thousand gallons of whiskey and a funnel, I would be glad to take my own time and show you what an Eichelberger looks like when drunk. You wouldn't believe it. Son, there wouldn't be nothing left of this town but a few sprung girders and a lot of busted bricks, in the middle of which—Geez, I'll get talking English myself if I hang around you much longer—in the middle of which, peaceful, with no human life nearer than maybe fifty miles. Henry Eichelberger will be on his back smiling at the sun. Drunk, Walter. Not stinking drunk, not even country-club drunk. But you could use the word drunk and I wouldn't take no offense."

He sat down and drank again. I stared moodily at the floor. There was nothing for me to say.

"But that," Henry said, "is some other time. Right now I am just taking my medicine. I ain't myself without a slight touch of delirium tremens, as the guy says. I was brought up on it. And I'm going with you, Walter. Where is this place at?"

"It's down near the beach, Henry, and you are not going with me. If you must get drunk—get drunk, but you are not going with me."

"You got a big car, Walter. I'll hide in back on the floor under a rug. It's a cinch."

"No, Henry."

"Walter, you are a sweet guy," Henry said, "and I am going with you into this frame. Have a smell from the barrel, Walter. You look to me kind of frail."

We argued for an hour and my head ached and I began to feel very nervous and tired. It was then that I made what might have been a fatal mistake. I succumbed to Henry's blandishments and took a small portion of whiskey, purely for medicinal purposes. This made me feel so much more relaxed that I took another and larger portion. I had had no food except coffee that morning and only a very light dinner the evening before. At the end of another hour Henry had been out for two more bottles of whiskey and I was as bright as a bird. All difficulties had now disappeared and I had agreed heartily that Henry should lie in the back of my car hidden by a rug and accompany me to the rendezvous.

We passed the time very pleasantly until two o'clock, at which hour I began to feel sleepy and lay down on the bed, and fell into a deep slumber.

7

When I awoke again it was almost dark. I rose from the bed with panic in my heart, and also a sharp shoot of pain through my temples. It was only six-thirty, however. I was alone in the apartment and lengthening shadows were stealing across the floor. The display of empty whiskey bottles on the table was very disgusting. Henry Eichelberger was nowhere to be seen. With an instinctive pang, of which I was almost immediately ashamed, I hurried to my jacket hanging on the back of a chair and plunged my hand into the inner breast pocket. The packet of bills was there intact. After a brief hesitation, and with a feeling of secret guilt, I drew them out and slowly counted them over. Not a bill was missing. I replaced the money and tried to smile at myself for this lack of trust, and then switched on a light and went into the bathroom to take alternate hot and cold showers until my brain was once more comparatively clear.

I had done this and was dressing in fresh linen when a key turned in the lock and Henry Eichelberger entered with two wrapped bottles under his arm. He looked at me with what I thought was genuine affection.

"A guy that can sleep it off like you is a real champ, Walter," he said admiringly. "I snuck your keys so as not to wake you. I had to get some eats and some more hooch. I done a little solo drinking, which as I told you is against my principles, but this is a big day. However, we take it easy from now on as to the hooch. We can't afford no jitters till it's all over."

He had unwrapped a bottle while he was speaking and poured me a small drink. I drank it gratefully and immediately felt a warm glow in my veins.

"I bet you looked in your poke for that deck of mazuma," Henry said, grinning at me.

I felt myself reddening, but I said nothing. "O.K., pal, you done right. What the heck do you know about Henry Eichelberger anyways? I done something else." He reached behind him and drew a short automatic from his hip pocket. "If these boys wanta play rough," he said, "I got me five bucks worth of iron that don't mind playin' rough a little itself. And the Eichelbergers ain't missed a whole lot of the guys they shot at."

"I don't like that, Henry," I said severely. "That is contrary to the agreement."

"Nuts to the agreement," Henry said. "The boys get their dough and no cops. I'm out to see that they hand over them marbles and don't pull any fast footwork."

I saw there was no use arguing with him, so I completed my dressing and prepared to leave the apartment. We each took one more drink and then Henry put a full bottle in his pocket and we left.

On the way down the hall to the elevator he explained in a low voice: "I got a hack out front to tail you, just in case these boys got the same idea. You might circle a few quiet blocks so as I can find out. More like they don't pick you up till down close to the beach."

"All this must be costing you a great deal of money, Henry," I told him, and while we were waiting for the elevator to come up I took another twenty-dollar bill from my wallet and offered it to him. He took the money reluctantly, but finally folded it and placed it in his pocket.

I did as Henry had suggested, driving up and down a number of the hilly streets north of Hollywood Boulevard, and presently I heard the unmistakable hoot of a taxicab horn behind me. I pulled over to the side of the road. Henry got out of the cab and paid off the driver and got into my car beside me.

"All clear," he said. "No tail. I'll just keep kind of slumped down and you better stop somewhere for some groceries on account of if we have to get rough with these mugs, a full head of steam will help."

So I drove westward and dropped down to Sunset Boulevard and presently stopped at a crowded drive-in restaurant where we sat at the counter and ate a light meal of omelette and black coffee. We then proceeded on our way. When we reached Beverly Hills, Henry again made me wind in and out through a number of residential streets where he observed very carefully through the rear window of the car.

Fully satisfied at last we drove back to Sunset, and without incident onwards through Bel-Air and the fringes of Westwood, almost as far as the Riviera Polo field. At this point, down in the hollow, there is a canyon called Mandeville Canyon, a very quiet place. Henry had me drive up this for a short distance. We then stopped and had a little whiskey from his bottle and he climbed into the back of the car and curled his big body up on the floor, with the rug over him and his automatic pistol and his bottle down on the floor conveniently to his hand. That done I once more resumed my journey.

Pacific Palisades is a district whose inhabitants seem to retire rather early. When I reached what might be called the business center nothing was open but the drugstore beside the bank. I parked the car, with Henry remaining silent under the rug in the back, except for a slight gurgling noise I noticed as I stood on the dark sidewalk. Then I went into the drugstore and saw by its clock that it was now fifteen minutes to eight. I bought a package of cigarettes and lit one and took up my position near the open telephone booth.

The druggist, a heavy-set red-faced man of uncertain age,

had a small radio up very loud and was listening to some
foolish serial. I asked him to turn it down, as I was expecting
an important telephone call. This he did, but not with any
good grace, and immediately retired to the back part of his
store whence I saw him looking out at me malignantly
through a small glass window.

At precisely one minute to eight by the drugstore clock the
phone rang sharply in the booth. I hastened into it and pulled
the door tight shut. I lifted the receiver, trembling a little in
spite of myself.

It was the same cool metallic voice. "Gage?"

"This is Mr. Gage."

"You done just what I told you?"

"Yes," I said. "I have the money in my pocket and I am
entirely alone." I did not like the feeling of lying so brazenly,
even to a thief, but I steeled myself to it.

"Listen, then. Go back about three hundred feet the way
you come. Beside the firehouse there's a service station,
closed up, painted green and red and white. Beside that,
going south, is a dirt road. Follow it three quarters of a mile
and you come to a white fence of four-by-fours built almost
across the road. You can just squeeze your car by at the left
side. Dim your lights and get through there and keep going
down the little hill into a hollow with sage all around. Park
there, cut your lights, and wait. Get it?"

"Perfectly," I said coldly, "and it shall be done exactly that
way."

"And listen, pal. There ain't a house in half a mile, and
there ain't any folks around at all. You got ten minutes to get
there. You're watched right this minute. You get there fast
and you get there alone—or you got a trip for biscuits. And
don't light no matches or pills nor use no flashlights. On your
way."

The phone went dead and I left the booth. I was scarcely
outside the drugstore before the druggist rushed at his radio
and turned it up to a booming blare. I got into my car and
turned it and drove back along Sunset Boulevard, as directed.
Henry was as still as the grave on the floor behind me.

I was now very nervous and Henry had all the liquor which

we had brought with us. I reached the firehouse in no time at all and through its front window I could see four firemen playing cards. I turned to the right down the dirt road past the red-and-green-and-white service station and almost at once the night was so still, in spite of the quiet sound of my car, that I could hear the crickets and treefrogs chirping and trilling in all directions, and from some near-by watery spot came the hoarse croak of a solitary bullfrog.

The road dipped and rose again and far off there was a yellow window. Then ahead of me, ghostly in the blackness of the moonless night, appeared the dim white barrier across the road. I noted the gap at the side and then dimmed my head-lamps and steered carefully through it and so on down a rough short hill into an oval-shaped hollow space surrounded by low brush and plentifully littered with empty bottles and cans and pieces of paper. It was entirely deserted, however, at this dark hour. I stopped my car and shut off the ignition and the lights, and sat there motionless, hands on the wheel.

Behind me I heard no murmur of sound from Henry. I waited possibly five minutes, although it seemed much longer, but nothing happened. It was very still, very lonely, and I did not feel happy.

Finally there was a faint sound of movement behind me and I looked back to see the pale blur of Henry's face peering at me from under the rug.

His voice whispered huskily. "Anything stirring, Walter?"

I shook my head at him vigorously and he once more pulled the rug over his face. I heard a faint sound of gurgling.

Fully fifteen minutes passed before I dared to move again. By this time the tensity of waiting had made me stiff. I there-fore boldly unlatched the door of the car and stepped out upon the rough ground. Nothing happened. I walked slowly back and forth with my hands in my pockets. More and more time dragged by. More than half an hour had now elapsed and I became impatient. I went to the rear window of the car and spoke softly into the interior.

"Henry, I fear we have been victimized in a very cheap way. I fear very much that this is nothing but a low practical joke on the part of Mr. Gandesi in retaliation for the way you handled him last night. There is no one here and only one possible way of arriving. It looks to me like a very unlikely place for the sort of meeting we have been expecting."

"The —— — ——!" Henry whispered back, and the gurgling sound was repeated in the darkness of the car. Then there was movement and his face appeared free of the rug. The door opened against my body. Henry's head emerged. He looked in all directions his eyes could command. "Sit down on the running board," he whispered. "I'm getting out. If they got a bead on us from them bushes, they'll only see one head."

I did what Henry suggested and turned my collar up high and pulled my hat down over my eyes. As noiselessly as a shadow Henry stepped out of the car and shut the door without sound and stood before me ranging the limited horizon with his eyes. I could see the dim reflection of light on the gun in his hand. We remained thus for ten more minutes.

Henry then got angry and threw discretion to the winds. "Suckered!" he snarled. "You know what happened, Walter?"

"No, Henry. I do not."

"It was just a tryout, that's what it was. Somewhere along the line these dirty-so-and-so's checked on you to see did you play ball, and then again they checked on you at that drugstore back there. I bet you a pair of solid platinum bicycle wheels that was a long-distance call you caught back there."

"Yes, Henry, now that you mention it, I am sure it was," I said sadly.

"There you are, kid. The bums ain't even left town. They are sitting back there beside their plush-lined spittoons giving you the big razzoo. And tomorrow this guy calls you again on the phone and says O.K. so far, but they had to be careful, and they will try again tonight maybe out in San Fernando Valley and the price will be upped to ten grand, on account of their extra trouble. I oughta go back there and twist that Gandesi so he would be lookin' up his left pants leg."

"Well, Henry," I said, "after all, I did not do exactly what they told me to, because you insisted on coming with me. And perhaps they are more clever than you think. So I think

the best thing now is to go back to town and hope there will
be a chance tomorrow to try again. And you must promise
me faithfully not to interfere."

"Nuts!" Henry said angrily. "Without me along they
would take you the way the cat took the canary. You are a
sweet guy, Walter, but you don't know as many answers as
Baby Leroy. These guys are thieves and they have a string of
marbles that might probably bring them twenty grand with
careful handling. They are out for a quick touch, but they will
squeeze all they can just the same. I oughta go back to that
fat wop Gandesi right now. I could do things to that slob that
ain't been invented yet."

"Now, Henry, don't get violent," I said.

"Haw," Henry snarled. "Them guys give me an ache in the
back of my lap." He raised his bottle to his lips with his left
hand and drank thirstily. His voice came down a few tones
and sounded more peaceful. "Better dip the bill, Walter. The
party's a flop."

"Perhaps you are right, Henry," I sighed. "I will admit that
my stomach has been trembling like an autumn leaf for all of
half an hour."

So I stood up boldly beside him and poured a liberal portion of the fiery liquid down my throat. At once my courage
revived. I handed the bottle back to Henry and he placed it
carefully down on the running board. He stood beside me
dancing the short automatic pistol up and down on the broad
palm of his hand.

"I don't need no tools to handle that bunch. The hell with
it." And with a sweep of his arm he hurled the pistol off
among the bushes, where it fell to the ground with a muffled
thud. He walked away from the car and stood with his arms
akimbo, looking up at the sky.

I moved over beside him and watched his averted face, in
sofar as I was able to see it in that dim light. A strange melancholy came over me. In the brief time I had known Henry I
had grown very fond of him.

"Well, Henry," I said at last, "what is the next move?"

"Beat it on home, I guess," he said slowly and mournfully.
"And get good and drunk." He doubled his hands into fists
and shook them slowly. Then he turned to face me. "Yeah,"

he said. "Nothing else to do. Beat it on home, kid, is all that is left to us."

"Not quiet yet, Henry," I said softly.

I took my right hand out of my pocket. I have large hands. In my right hand nestled the roll of wrapped quarters which I had obtained at the bank that morning. My hand made a large fist around them.

"Good night, Henry," I said quietly, and swung my fist with all the weight of my arm and body. "You had two strikes on me, Henry," I said. "The big one is still left."

But Henry was not listening to me. My fist with the wrapped weight of metal inside it had caught him fairly and squarely on the point of his jaw. His legs became boneless and he pitched straight forward, brushing my sleeve as he fell. I stepped quickly out of his way.

Henry Eichelberger lay motionless on the ground, as limp as a rubber glove.

I looked down at him a little sadly, waiting for him to stir, but he did not move a muscle. He lay inert, completely unconscious. I dropped the roll of quarters back into my pocket, bent over him, searched him thoroughly, moving him around like a sack of meal, but it was a long time before I found the pearls. They were twined around his ankle inside his left sock.

"Well, Henry," I said, speaking to him for the last time, although he could not hear me, "you are a gentleman, even if you are a thief. You could have taken the money a dozen times this afternoon and given me nothing. You could have taken it a little while ago when you had the gun in your hand, but even that repelled you. You threw the gun away and we were man to man, far from help, far from interference. And even then you hesitated, Henry. In fact, Henry, I think for a successful thief you hesitated just a little too long. But as a man of sporting feelings I can only think the more highly of you. Good-bye, Henry, and good luck."

I took my wallet out and withdrew a one-hundred-dollar bill and placed it carefully in the pocket where I had seen Henry put his money. Then I went back to the car and took a drink out of the whiskey bottle and corked it firmly and laid it beside him, convenient to his right hand.

I felt sure that when he awakened he would need it.

8

It was past ten o'clock when I returned home to my apartment, but I at once went to the telephone and called Ellen Macintosh. "Darling!" I cried. "I have the pearls."

I caught the sound of her indrawn breath over the wire. "Oh darling," she said tensely and excitedly, "and you are not hurt? They did not hurt you, darling? They just took the money and let you go?"

"There was no 'they,' darling." I said proudly. "I still have Mr. Gallemore's money intact. There was only Henry."

"Henry!" she cried in a very strange voice. "But I thought— Come over here at once, Walter Gage, and tell me—"

"I have whiskey on my breath, Ellen."

"Darling! I'm sure you needed it. Come at once."

So once more I went down to the street and hurried to Carondelet Park and in no time at all was at the Penruddock residence. Ellen came out on the porch to meet me and we talked there quietly in the dark, holding hands, for the household had gone to bed. As simply as I could I told her my story.

"But, darling," she said at last, "how did you know it was Henry? I thought Henry was your friend. And this other voice on the telephone—"

"Henry *was* my friend," I said a little sadly, "and that is what destroyed him. As to the voice on the telephone, that was a small matter and easily arranged. Henry was away from me a number of times to arrange it. There was just one small point that gave me thought. After I gave Gandesi my private card with the name of my apartment house scribbled upon it, it was necessary for Henry to communicate to his confederate that we had seen Gandesi and given him my name and address. For of course when I had this foolish, or perhaps not so very foolish idea of visiting some well known underworld character in order to send a message that we would buy back the pearls, this was Henry's opportunity to make me think the telephone messages came as a result of our talking to Gandesi, and telling him our difficulty. But since the first call came to me at my apartment before Henry had had a chance to inform his confederate of our meeting with Gandesi, it was obvious that a trick had been employed.

"Then I recalled that a car had bumped into us from behind and Henry had gone back to abuse the driver. And of course the bumping was deliberate, and Henry had made the opportunity for it on purpose, and his confederate was in the car. So Henry, while pretending to shout at him, was able to convey the necessary information."

"But, Walter," Ellen said, having listened to this explanation a little impatiently, "that is a very small matter. What I really want to know is how you decided that Henry had the pearls at all."

"But you told me he had them," I said. "You were quite sure of it. Henry is a very durable character. It would be just like him to hide the pearls somewhere, having no fear of what the police might do to him, and get another position and then after perhaps quite a long time, retrieve the pearls and quietly leave this part of the country."

Ellen shook her head impatiently in the darkness of the porch. "Walter," she said sharply, "you are hiding something. You could not have been sure and you would not have hit Henry in that brutal way, unless you had been sure. I know you well enough to know that."

"Well, darling," I said modestly, "there was indeed another small indication, one of those foolish trifles which the cleverest men overlook. As you know, I do not use the regular apartment-house telephone, not wishing to be annoyed by solicitors and such people. The phone which I use is a private line and its number is unlisted. But the calls I received from Henry's confederate came over that phone, and Henry had been in my apartment a great deal, and I had been careful not to give Mr. Gandesi that number, because of course I did not expect anything from Mr. Gandesi, as I was perfectly sure from the beginning that Henry had the pearls, if only I could get him to bring them out of hiding."

"Oh, darling," Ellen cried, and threw her arms around me. "How brave you are, and I really think that you are actually clever in your own peculiar way. Do you believe that Henry was in love with me?"

But that was a subject in which I had no interest whatever. I left the pearls in Ellen's keeping and late as the hour now was I drove at once to the residence of Mr. Lansing Gallemore and told him my story and gave him back his money.

A few months later I was happy to receive a letter postmarked in Honolulu and written on a very inferior brand of paper.

Well, pal, that Sunday punch of yours was the money and I did not think you had it in you, altho of course I was not set for it. But it was a pip and made me think of you for a week every time I brushed my teeth. It was too bad I had to scram because you are a sweet guy altho a little on the goofy side and I'd like to be getting plastered with you right now instead of wiping oil valves where I am at which is not where this letter is mailed by several thousand miles. There is just two things I would like you to know and they are both kosher. I did fall hard for that tall blond and this was the main reason I took my time from the old lady. Glomming the pearls was just one of those screwy ideas a guy can get when he is dizzy with a dame. It was a crime the way they left them marbles lying around in that bread box and I worked for a Frenchy once in Djibouty and got to know pearls enough to tell them from snowballs. But when it came to the clinch down there in that brush with us two alone and no holds barred I just was too soft to go through with the deal. Tell that blond you got a loop on I was asking for her.

Yrs as ever,

Henry Eichelberger (Alias)

P.S. What do you know, that punk that did the phone work on you tried to take me for a fifty cut on that C-note you tucked in my vest. I had to twist the sucker plenty.

Yrs, H. E. (Alias)

Trouble Is My Business

A NNA HALSEY was about two hundred and forty pounds of middle-aged putty-faced woman in a black tailor-made suit. Her eyes were shiny black shoe-buttons, her cheeks were as soft as suet and about the same color. She was sitting behind a black glass desk that looked like Napoleon's tomb and she was smoking a cigarette in a black holder that was not quite as long as a rolled umbrella. She said: "I need a man."

I watched her shake ash from the cigarette to the shiny top of the desk where flakes of it curled and crawled in the draft from an open window.

"I need a man good-looking enough to pick up a dame who has a sense of class, but he's got to be tough enough to swap punches with a power shovel. I need a guy who can act like a bar lizard and backchat like Fred Allen, only better, and get hit on the head with a beer truck and think some cutie in the leg-line topped him with a breadstick."

"It's a cinch," I said. "You need the New York Yankees, Robert Donat, and the Yacht Club Boys."

"You might do," Anna said, "cleaned up a little. Twenty bucks a day and ex's. I haven't brokered a job in years, but this one is out of my line. I'm in the smooth-angles of the detecting business and I make money without getting my can knocked off. Let's see how Gladys likes you."

She reversed the cigarette holder and tipped a key on a large black-and-chromium annunciator box. "Come in and empty Anna's ash tray, honey."

We waited.

The door opened and a tall blonde dressed better than the Duchess of Windsor strolled in.

She swayed elegantly across the room, emptied Anna's ash tray, patted her fat cheek, gave me a smooth rippling glance and went out again.

"I think she blushed," Anna said when the door closed. "I guess you still have it."

"She blushed—and I have a dinner date with Darryl Zanuck," I said. "Quit horsing around. What's the story?"

"It's to smear a girl. A redheaded number with bedroom eyes. She's shill for a gambler and she's got her hooks into a rich man's pup."

"What do I do to her?"

Anna sighed. "It's kind of a mean job, Johnny, I guess. If she's got a record of any sort, you dig it up and toss it in her face. If she hasn't, which is more likely as she comes from good people, it's kind of up to you. You get an idea once in a while, don't you?"

"I can't remember the last one I had. What gambler and what rich man?"

"Marty Estel."

I started to get up from my chair, then remembered that business had been bad for a month and that I needed the money.

I sat down again.

"You might get into trouble, of course," Anna said. "I never heard of Marty bumping anybody off in the public square at high noon, but he don't play with cigar coupons."

"Trouble is my business," I said. "Twenty-five a day and a guarantee of two-fifty, if I pull the job."

"I gotta make a little something for myself," Anna whined.

"O.K. There's plenty of coolie labor around town. Nice to have seen you looking so well. So long, Anna."

I stood up this time. My life wasn't worth much, but it was worth that much. Marty Estel was supposed to be pretty tough people, with the right helpers and the right protection behind him. His place was out in West Hollywood, on the Strip. He wouldn't pull anything crude, but if he pulled at all, something would pop.

"Sit down, it's a deal," Anna sneered. "I'm a poor old broken-down woman trying to run a high-class detective agency on nothing but fat and bad health, so take my last nickel and laugh at me."

"Who's the girl?" I had sat down again.

"Her name is Harriet Huntress—a swell name for the part too. She lives in the El Milano, nineteen-hundred block on North Sycamore, very high-class. Father went broke back in thirty-one and jumped out of his office window. Mother dead. Kid sister in boarding school back in Connecticut. That might make an angle."

"Who dug up all this?"

"The client got a bunch of photostats of notes the pup had given to Marty. Fifty grand worth. The pup—he's an adopted son to the old man—denied the notes, as kids will. So the client had the photostats experted by a guy named Arbogast, who pretends to be good at that sort of thing. He said O.K. and dug around a bit, but he's too fat to do leg-work, like me, and he's off the case now."

"But I could talk to him?"

"I don't know why not." Anna nodded several of her chins.

"This client—does he have a name?"

"Son, you have a treat coming. You can meet him in person—right now."

She tipped the key of her call-box again. "Have Mr. Jeeter come in, honey."

"That Gladys," I said, "does she have a steady?"

"You lay off Gladys!" Anna almost screamed at me. "She's worth eighteen grand a year in divorce business to me. Any guy that lays a finger on her, Johnny Dalmas, is practically cremated."

"She's got to fall some day," I said. "Why couldn't I catch her?"

The opening door stopped that.

I hadn't seen him in the paneled reception room, so he must have been waiting in a private office. He hadn't enjoyed it. He came in quickly, shut the door quickly, and yanked a thin octagonal platinum watch from his vest and glared at it. He was a tall white-blond type in pin-striped flannel of youthful cut. There was a small pink rosebud in his lapel. He had a keen frozen face, a little pouchy under the eyes, a little thick in the lips. He carried an ebony cane with a silver knob, wore spats and looked a smart sixty, but I gave him close to ten years more. I didn't like him.

"Twenty-six minutes, Miss Halsey," he said icily. "My time happens to be valuable. By regarding it as valuable I have managed to make a great deal of money."

"Well, we're trying to save you some of the money," Anna drawled. She didn't like him either. "Sorry to keep you waiting, Mr. Jeeter, but you wanted to see the operative I selected and I had to send for him."

"He doesn't look the type to me," Mr. Jeeter said, giving me a nasty glance. "I think more of a gentleman—"

"You're not the Jeeter of *Tobacco Road*, are you?" I asked him.

He came slowly towards me and half lifted the stick. His icy eyes tore at me like claws. "So you insult me," he said. "Me—a man in my position."

"Now wait a minute," Anna began.

"Wait a minute nothing," I said. "This party said I was not a gentleman. Maybe that's O.K. for a man in his position, whatever it is—but a man in my position doesn't take a dirty crack from anybody. He can't afford to. Unless, of course, it wasn't intended."

Mr. Jeeter stiffened and glared at me. He took his watch out again and looked at it. "Twenty-eight minutes," he said. "I apologize, young man. I had no desire to be rude."

"That's swell," I said. "I knew you weren't the Jeeter in *Tobacco Road* all along."

That almost started him again, but he let it go. He wasn't sure how I meant it.

"A question or two while we are together," I said. "Are you willing to give this Huntress girl a little money—for expenses?"

"Not one cent," he barked. "Why should I?"

"It's got to be a sort of custom. Suppose she married him. What would he have?"

"At the moment a thousand dollars a month from a trust fund established by his mother, my late wife." He dipped his head. "When he is twenty-eight years old, far too much money."

"You can't blame the girl for trying," I said. "Not these days. How about Marty Estel? Any settlement there?"

He crumpled his gray gloves with a purple-veined hand. "The debt is uncollectible. It is a gambling debt."

Anna sighed wearily and flicked ash around on her desk.

"Sure," I said. "But gamblers can't afford to let people welsh on them. After all, if your son had won, Marty would have paid *him*."

"I'm not interested in that," the tall thin man said coldly.

"Yeah, but think of Marty sitting there with fifty grand in notes. Not worth a nickel. How will he sleep nights?"

Mr. Jeeter looked thoughtful. "You mean there is danger of violence?" he suggested, almost suavely.

"That's hard to say. He runs an exclusive place, gets a good movie crowd. He has his own reputation to think of. But he's in a racket and he knows people. Things can happen—a long way off from where Marty is. And Marty is no bathmat. He gets up and walks."

Mr. Jeeter looked at his watch again and it annoyed him. He slammed it back into his vest. "All that is your affair," he snapped. "The district attorney is a personal friend of mine. If this matter seems to be beyond your powers—"

"Yeah," I told him. "But you came slumming down our street just the same. Even if the D.A. is in your vest pocket—along with that watch."

He put his hat on, drew on one glove, tapped the edge of his shoe with his stick, walked to the door and opened it.

"I ask results and I pay for them," he said coldly. "I pay promptly. I even pay generously sometimes, although I am not considered a generous man. I think we all understand one another."

He almost winked then and went on out. The door closed softly against the cushion of air in the door-closer. I looked at Anna and grinned.

"Sweet, isn't he?" she said. "I'd like eight of him for my cocktail set."

I gouged twenty dollars out of her—for expenses.

2

The Arbogast I wanted was John D. Arbogast and he had an office on Sunset near Ivar. I called him up from a phone booth. The voice that answered was fat. It wheezed softly, like the voice of a man who had just won a pie-eating contest.

"Mr. John D. Arbogast?"

"Yeah."

"This is John Dalmas, a private detective working on a case you did some experting on. Party named Jeeter."

"Yeah?"

"Can I come up and talk to you about it—after I eat lunch?"

"Yeah." He hung up. I decided he was not a talkative man.

I had lunch and drove out there. It was east of Ivar, an old two-story building faced with brick which had been painted recently. The street floor was stores and a restaurant. The building entrance was the foot of a wide straight stairway to the second floor. On the directory at the bottom I read— *John D. Arbogast, Suite 212.* I went up the stairs and found myself in a wide straight hall that ran parallel with the street. A man in a smock was standing in an open doorway down to my right. He wore a round mirror strapped to his forehead and pushed back and his face had a puzzled expression. He went back to his office and shut the door.

I went the other way, about half the distance along the hall. A door on the side away from Sunset was lettered—*John D. Arbogast, Examiner of Questioned Documents. Private Investigator. Enter.* The door opened without resistance onto a small windowless anteroom with a couple of easy chairs, some magazines, two chromium smoking-stands. There were two floor lamps and a ceiling fixture, all lighted. A door on the other side of the cheap but thick and new rug was lettered —*John D. Arbogast, Examiner of Questioned Documents. Private.*

A buzzer had rung when I opened the outer door and gone on ringing until it closed. Nothing happened. Nobody was in the waiting-room. The inner door didn't open. I went over and listened at the panel—no sound of conversation inside. I knocked. That didn't buy me anything either. I tried the knob. It turned, so I opened the door and went in.

This room had two north windows, both curtained at the sides and both shut tight. There was dust on the sills. There was a desk, two filing-cases, a carpet which was just a carpet, and walls which were just walls. To the left another door with a glass panel was lettered: *John D. Arbogast. Laboratory. Private.*

I had an idea I might be able to remember the name.

The room in which I stood was small. It seemed almost too small even for the pudgy hand that rested on the edge of the desk, motionless, holding a fat pencil like a carpenter's pencil. The hand had a wrist, hairless as a plate. A buttoned shirt-cuff, not too clean, came down out of a coat-sleeve. The rest of the sleeve dropped over the far edge of the desk out of sight. The desk was less than six feet long, so he couldn't have been a very tall man. The hand and the ends of the sleeves were all I saw of him from where I stood. I went quietly back through the anteroom and fixed its door so that it couldn't be opened from the outside and put out the three lights and went back to the private office. I went around an end of the desk.

He was fat all right, enormously fat, fatter by far than Anna Halsey. His face, what I could see of it, looked about the size of a basket ball. It had a pleasant pinkness, even now. He was kneeling on the floor. He had his large head against the sharp inner corner of the kneehole of the desk, and his left hand was flat on the floor with a piece of yellow paper under it. The fingers were outspread as much as such fat fingers could be, and the yellow paper showed between. He looked as if he were pushing hard on the floor, but he wasn't really. What was holding him up was his own fat. His body was folded down against his enormous thighs, and the thickness and fatness of them held him that way, kneeling, poised solid. It would have taken a couple of good blocking backs to knock him over. That wasn't a very nice idea at the moment, but I had it just the same. I took time out and wiped the back of my neck, although it was not a warm day.

His hair was gray and clipped short and his neck had as many folds as a concertina. His feet were small, as the feet of fat men often are, and they were in black shiny shoes which were sideways on the carpet and close together and neat and nasty. He wore a dark suit that needed cleaning. I leaned down and buried my fingers in the bottomless fat of his neck. He had an artery in there somewhere, probably, but I couldn't find it and he didn't need it anymore anyway. Between his bloated knees on the carpet a dark stain had spread and spread—

I knelt in another place and lifted the pudgy fingers that were holding down the piece of yellow paper. They were cool, but not cold, and soft and a little sticky. The paper was from a scratch pad. It would have been very nice if it had had a message on it, but it hadn't. There were vague meaningless marks, not words, not even letters. He had tried to write something after he was shot—perhaps even thought he *was* writing something—but all he managed was some hen scratches.

He had slumped down then, still holding the paper, pinned it to the floor with his fat hand, held on to the fat pencil with his other hand, wedged his torso against his huge thighs, and so died. John D. Arbogast. Examiner of Questioned Documents. Private. Very damned private. He had said "yeah" to me three times over the phone.

And here he was.

I wiped doorknobs with my handkerchief, put off the lights in the anteroom, left the outer door so that it was locked from the outside, left the hallway, left the building and left the neighborhood. So far as I could tell nobody saw me go. So far as I could tell.

3

The El Milano was, as Anna had told me, in the 1900 block on North Sycamore. It was most of the block. I parked fairly near the ornamental forecourt and went along to the pale blue neon sign over the entrance to the basement garage. I walked down a railed ramp into a bright space of glistening cars and cold air. A trim light-colored Negro in a spotless coverall suit with blue cuffs came out of a glass office. His black hair was as smooth as a bandleader's.

"Busy?" I asked him.

"Yes and no, sir."

"I've got a car outside that needs a dusting. About five bucks worth of dusting."

It didn't work. He wasn't the type. His chestnut eyes became thoughtful and remote. "That is a good deal of dusting, sir. May I ask if anything else would be included?"

"A little. Is Miss Harriet Huntress's car in?"

He looked. I saw him look along the glistening row at a canary-yellow convertible which was about as inconspicuous as a privy on the front lawn.

"Yes, sir. It is in."

"I'd like her apartment number and a way to get up there without going through the lobby. I'm a private detective." I showed him a buzzer. He looked at the buzzer. It failed to amuse him.

He smiled the faintest smile I ever saw. "Five dollars is nice money, sir, to a working man. It falls a little short of being nice enough to make me risk my position. About from here to Chicago short, sir. I suggest that you save your five dollars, sir, and try the customary mode of entry."

"You're quite a guy," I said. "What are you going to be when you grow up—a five-foot shelf?"

"I am already grown up, sir. I am thirty-four years old, married happily, and have two children. Good-afternoon, sir."

He turned on his heel. "Well, goodbye," I said. "And pardon my whiskey breath. I just got in from Butte."

I went back up along the ramp and wandered along the street to where I should have gone in the first place. I might have known that five bucks and a buzzer wouldn't buy me anything in a place like the El Milano.

The Negro was probably telephoning the office right now.

The building was a huge white stucco affair, Moorish in style, with great fretted lanterns in the forecourt and huge date palms. The entrance was at the inside corner of an L, up marble steps, through an arch framed in California or dishpan mosaic.

A doorman opened the door for me and I went in. The lobby was not quite as big as the Yankee Stadium. It was floored with a pale blue carpet with sponge rubber underneath. It was so soft it made me want to lie down and roll. I waded over to the desk and put an elbow on it and was stared at by a pale thin clerk with one of those mustaches that get stuck under your fingernail. He toyed with it and looked past my shoulder at an Ali Baba oil jar big enough to keep a tiger in.

"Miss Huntress in?"

"Who shall I announce?"

"Mr. Marty Estel."

That didn't take any better than my play in the garage. He leaned on something with his left foot. A blue-and-gilt door opened at the end of the desk and a large sandy-haired man with cigar ash on his vest came out and leaned absently on the end of the desk and stared at the Ali Baba oil jar, as if trying to make up his mind whether it was a spittoon.

The clerk raised his voice. "You are Mr. Marty Estel?"

"From him."

"Isn't that a little different? And what is your name, sir, if one may ask?"

"One may ask," I said. "One may not be told. Such are my orders. Sorry to be stubborn and all that rot."

He didn't like my manner. He didn't like anything about me. "I'm afraid I can't announce you," he said coldly. "Mr. Hawkins, might I have your advice on a matter?"

The sandy-haired man took his eyes off the oil jar and slid along the desk until he was within blackjack range of me.

"Yes, Mr. Gregory?" he yawned.

"Nuts to both of you," I said. "And that includes your lady friends."

Hawkins grinned. "Come into my office, bo. We'll kind of see if we can get you straightened out."

I followed him into the doghole he had come out of. It was large enough for a pint-sized desk, two chairs, a knee-high cuspidor, and an open box of cigars. He placed his rear end against the desk and grinned at me sociably.

"Didn't play it very smooth, did you, bo? I'm the house man here. Spill it."

"Some days I feel like playing it smooth," I said, "and some days I feel like playing it like a waffle-iron." I got my wallet out and showed him the buzzer and the small photostat of my license behind a celluloid window.

"One of the boys, huh?" He nodded. "You ought to of asked for me in the first place."

"Sure. Only I never heard of you. I want to see this Huntress frail. She doesn't know me, but I have business with her, and it's not noisy business."

He made a yard and a half sideways and cocked his cigar in

the other corner of his mouth. He looked at my right eyebrow. "What's the gag? Why try to apple-polish the dinge
downstairs? You gettin' any expense money?"

"Could be."

"I'm nice people," he said. "But I gotta protect the
guests."

"You're almost out of cigars," I said, looking at the ninety
or so in the box. I lifted a couple, smelled them, tucked a
folded ten-dollar bill below them and put them back.

"That's cute," he said. "You and me could get along. What
you want done?"

"Tell her I'm from Marty Estel. She'll see me."

"It's the job if I get a kickback."

"You won't. I've got important people behind me."

"How far behind?"

I started to reach for my ten, but he pushed my hand
away. "I'll take a chance," he said. He reached for his
phone and asked for Suite 814 and began to hum. His
humming sounded like a cow being sick. He leaned forward
suddenly and his face became a honeyed smile. His voice
dripped.

"Miss Huntress? This is Hawkins, the house man. Hawkins.
Yeah . . . Hawkins. Sure, you meet a lot of people, Miss
Huntress. Say, there's a gentleman in my office wanting to see
you with a message from Mr. Estel. We can't let him up without your say so, because he don't want to give us no
name. . . . Yeah, Hawkins, the house detective, Miss Huntress. Yeah, he says you don't know him personal, but he looks
O.K. to me . . . O.K. Thanks a lot, Miss Huntress. Serve
him right up."

He put the phone down and patted it gently.

"All you needed was some background music," I said.

"You can ride up," he said dreamily. He reached absently
into his cigar box and removed the folded bill. "A darb," he
said softly. "Every time I think of that dame I have to go out
and walk around the block. Let's go."

We went out to the lobby again and Hawkins took me to
the elevator and highsigned me in.

As the elevator doors closed I saw him on his way to the
entrance, probably for his walk around the block.

The elevator had a carpeted floor and mirrors and indirect lighting. It rose as softly as the mercury in a thermometer. The doors whispered open, I wandered over the moss they used for a hall carpet and came to a door marked *814*. I pushed a little button beside it, chimes rang inside and the door opened.

She wore a street dress of pale green wool and a small cockeyed hat that hung on her ear like a butterfly. Her eyes were wide-set and there was thinking room between them. Their color was lapis-lazuli blue and the color of her hair was dusky red, like a fire under control but still dangerous. She was too tall to be cute. She wore plenty of make-up in the right places and the cigarette she was poking at me had a built-on mouthpiece about three inches long. She didn't look hard, but she looked as if she had heard all the answers and remembered the ones she thought she might be able to use sometime.

She looked me over coolly. "Well, what's the message, brown-eyes?"

"I'd have to come in," I said. "I never could talk on my feet."

She laughed disinterestedly and I slid past the end of her cigarette into a long rather narrow room with plenty of nice furniture, plenty of windows, plenty of drapes, plenty of everything. A fire blazed behind a screen, a big log on top of a gas teaser. There was a silk Oriental rug in front of a nice rose davenport in front of the nice fire, and beside that there was Scotch and swish on a tabouret, ice in a bucket, everything to make a man feel at home.

"You'd better have a drink," she said. "You probably can't talk without a glass in your hand."

I sat down and reached for the Scotch. The girl sat in a deep chair and crossed her knees. I thought of Hawkins walking around the block. I could see a little something in his point of view.

"So you're from Marty Estel," she said, refusing a drink.

"Never met him."

"I had an idea to that effect. What's the racket, bum? Marty will love to hear how you used his name."

"I'm shaking in my shoes. What made you let me up?"

"Curiosity. I've been expecting lads like you any day. I never dodge trouble. Some kind of a dick, aren't you?"

I lit a cigarette and nodded. "Private. I have a little deal to propose."

"Propose it." She yawned.

"How much will you take to lay off young Jeeter?"

She yawned again. "You interest me—so little I could hardly tell you."

"Don't scare me to death. Honest, how much are you asking? Or is that an insult?"

She smiled. She had a nice smile. She had lovely teeth. "I'm a bad girl now," she said. "I don't have to ask. They bring it to me, tied up with ribbon."

"The old man's a little tough. They say he draws a lot of water."

"Water doesn't cost much."

I nodded and drank some more of my drink. It was good Scotch. In fact it was perfect. "His idea is you get nothing. You get smeared. You get put in the middle. I can't see it that way."

"But you're working for him."

"Sounds funny, doesn't it? There's probably a smart way to play this, but I just can't think of it at the moment. How much would you take—or would you?"

"How about fifty grand?"

"Fifty grand for you and another fifty for Marty?"

She laughed. "Now, you ought to know Marty wouldn't like me to mix in his business. I was just thinking of my end."

She crossed her legs the other way. I put another lump of ice in my drink.

"I was thinking of five hundred," I said.

"Five hundred what?" She looked puzzled.

"Dollars—not Rolls-Royces."

She laughed heartily. "You amuse me. I ought to tell you to go to hell, but I like brown eyes. Warm brown eyes with flecks of gold in them."

"You're throwing it away. I don't have a nickel."

She smiled and fitted a fresh cigarette between her lips. I went over to light it for her. Her eyes came up and looked into mine. Hers had sparks in them.

"Maybe I have a nickel already," she said softly.

"Maybe that's why he hired the fat boy—so you couldn't make him dance." I sat down again.

"Who hired what fat boy?"

"Old Jeeter hired a fat boy named Arbogast. He was on the case before me. Didn't you know? He got bumped off this afternoon."

I said it quite casually for the shock effect, but she didn't move. The provocative smile didn't leave the corners of her lips. Her eyes didn't change. She made a dim sound with her breath.

"Does it have to have something to do with me?" she asked quietly.

"I don't know. I don't know who murdered him. It was done in his office, around noon or a little later. It may not have anything to do with the Jeeter case. But it happened pretty pat—just after I had been put on the job and before I got a chance to talk to him."

She nodded. "I see. And you think Marty does things like that. And of course you told the police?"

"Of course I did not."

"You're giving away a little weight there, brother."

"Yeah. But let's get together on a price and it had better be low. Because whatever the cops do to me they'll do plenty to Marty Estel and you when they get the story—if they get it."

"A little spot of blackmail," the girl said coolly. "I think I might call it that. Don't go too far with me, brown-eyes. By the way, do I know your name?"

"John Dalmas."

"Then listen, John. I was in the Social Register once. My family were nice people. Old man Jeeter ruined my father—all proper and legitimate, the way that kind of heel ruins people—but he ruined him, and my father committed sui cide, and my mother died and I've got a kid sister back East in school and perhaps I'm not too damn particular how I get the money to take care of her. And maybe I'm going to take care of old Jeeter one of these days, too—even if I have to marry his son to do it."

"Stepson, adopted son," I said. "No relation at all."

"It'll hurt him just as hard, brother. And the boy will have plenty of the long green in a couple of years. I could do worse—even if he does drink too much."

"You wouldn't say that in front of him, lady."

"No? Take a look behind you, gumshoe. You ought to have the wax taken out of your ears."

I stood up and turned fast. He stood about four feet from me. He had come out of some door and sneaked across the carpet and I had been too busy being clever with nothing on the ball to hear him. He was big, blond, dressed in a rough sporty suit, with a scarf and open neck shirt. He was red-faced and his eyes glittered and they were not focusing any too well. He was a bit drunk for that early in the day.

"Beat it while you can still walk," he sneered at me. "I heard it. Harry can say anything she likes about me. I like it. Dangle, before I knock your teeth down your throat!"

The girl laughed behind me. I didn't like that. I took a step towards the big blond boy. His eyes blinked. Big as he was, he was a pushover.

"Ruin him, baby," the girl said coldly behind my back. "I love to see these hard numbers bend at the knees."

I looked back at her with a leer. That was a mistake. He was wild, probably, but he could still hit a wall that didn't jump. He hit me while I was looking back over my shoulder. It hurts to be hit that way. He hit me plenty hard, on the back end of the jawbone.

I went over sideways, tried to spread my legs, and slid on the silk rug. I did a nose dive somewhere or other and my head was not as hard as the piece of furniture it smashed into.

For a brief blurred moment I saw his red face sneering down at me in triumph. I think I was a little sorry for him—even then.

Darkness folded down and I went out.

4

When I came to, the light from the windows across the room was hitting me square in the eyes. The back of my head ached. I felt it and it was sticky. I moved around slowly, like a cat in a strange house, got up on my knees and reached for the bottle of Scotch on the tabouret at the end of the davenport. By some miracle I hadn't knocked it over. Falling I had hit my head on the clawlike leg of a chair. That had hurt me a lot more than young Jeeter's haymaker. I could feel the sore place on my jaw all right, but it wasn't important enough to write in my diary.

I got up on my feet, took a swig of the Scotch and looked around. There wasn't anything to see. The room was empty. It was full of silence and the memory of a nice perfume. One of those perfumes you don't notice until they are almost gone, like the last leaf on a tree. I felt my head again, touched the sticky place with my handkerchief, decided it wasn't worth yelling about, and took another drink.

I sat down with the bottle on my knees, listening to traffic noise somewhere, far off. It was a nice room. Miss Harriet Huntress was a nice girl. She knew a few wrong numbers, but who didn't? I should criticize a little thing like that. I took another drink. The level in the bottle was a lot lower now. It was smooth and you hardly noticed it going down. It didn't take half your tonsils with it, like some of the stuff I had to drink. I took some more. My head felt all right now. I felt fine. I felt like singing the *Prologue to Pagliacci*. Yes, she was a nice girl. If she was paying her own rent, she was doing right well. I was for her. She was swell. I used some more of her Scotch.

The bottle was still half full. I shook it gently, stuffed it in my overcoat pocket, put my hat somewhere on my head and left. I made the elevator without hitting the walls on either side of the corridor, floated downstairs, strolled out into the lobby.

Hawkins, the house dick, was leaning on the end of the desk again, staring at the Ali Baba oil jar. The same clerk was nuzzling at the same itsy-bitsy mustache. I smiled at him. He smiled back. Hawkins smiled at me. I smiled back. Everybody was swell.

I made the front door the first time and gave the doorman two bits and floated down the steps and along the walk to the street and my car. The swift California twilight was falling. It was a lovely night. Venus in the west was as bright as a street lamp, as bright as life, as bright as Miss Huntress's eyes, as bright as a bottle of Scotch. That reminded me. I got the square bottle out and tapped it with discretion, corked it, and tucked it away again. There was still enough to get home on.

I crashed five red lights on the way back but my luck was in and nobody pinched me. I parked more or less in front of my apartment house and more or less near the curb. I rode to my floor in the elevator, had a little trouble opening the doors and helped myself out with my bottle. I got the key into my door and unlocked it and stepped inside and found the light switch. I took a little more of my medicine before exhausting myself any further. Then I started for the kitchen to get some ice and ginger ale for a real drink.

I thought there was a funny smell in the apartment—nothing I could put a name to offhand—a sort of medicinal smell. I hadn't put it there and it hadn't been there when I went out. But I felt too well to argue about it. I started for the kitchen, got about halfway there.

They came out at me, almost side by side, from the dressing-room beside the wall bed—two of them—with guns. The tall one was grinning. He had his hat low on his forehead and he had a wedge-shaped face that ended in a point, like the bottom half of the ace of diamonds. He had dark moist eyes and a nose so bloodless that it might have been made of white wax. His gun was a Colt Woodsman with a long barrel and the front sight filed off. That meant he thought he was good.

The other was a little terrier-like punk with bristly reddish hair and no hat and watery blank eyes and bat ears and small feet in dirty white sneakers. He had an automatic that looked too heavy for him to hold up, but he seemed to like holding it. He breathed open-mouthed and noisily and the smell I had noticed came from him in waves—menthol.

"Reach, you ——," he said.

I put my hands up. There was nothing else to do.

The little one circled around to the side and came at me from the side. "Tell us we can't get away with it," he sneered.

"You can't get away with it," I said.

The tall one kept on grinning loosely and his nose kept on looking as if it was made of white wax. The little one spat on my carpet. "Yah!" He came close to me, leering, and made a pass at my chin with the big gun.

I dodged. Ordinarily that would have been just something which, in the circumstances, I had to take and like. But I was feeling better than ordinary. I was a world-beater. I took them in sets, guns and all. I took the little man around the throat and jerked him hard against my stomach and put a hand over his little gun-hand and knocked the gun to the floor. It was easy. Nothing was bad about it but his breath. Blobs of saliva came out on his lips. He spit curses.

The tall man stood and leered and didn't shoot. He didn't move. His eyes looked a little anxious, I thought, but I was too busy to make sure. I went down behind the little punk, still holding him, and got hold of his gun. That was wrong. I ought to have pulled my own.

I threw him away from me and he reeled against a chair and fell down and began to kick the chair savagely. The tall man laughed.

"It ain't got any firing pin in it," he said.

"Listen," I told him earnestly, "I'm half full of good Scotch and ready to go places and get things done. Don't waste much of my time. What do you boys want?"

"It still ain't got any firing pin in it," Waxnose said. "Try and see. I don't never let Frisky carry a loaded rod. He's too impulsive. You got a nice arm action there, pal. I will say that for you."

Frisky sat up on the floor and spat on the carpet again and laughed. I pointed the muzzle of the big automatic at the floor and squeezed the trigger. It clicked dryly, but from the balance it felt as if it had cartridges in it.

"We don't mean no harm," Waxnose said. "Not this trip. Maybe next trip. Who knows? Maybe you're a guy that will take a hint. Lay off the Jeeter kid is the word. See?"

"No."

"You won't do it?"

"No, I don't see. Who's the Jeeter kid?"

Waxnose was not amused. He waved his long .22 gently. "You oughta get your memory fixed, pal, about the same time you get your door fixed. A pushover that was. Frisky just blew it in with his breath."

"I can understand that," I said.

"Gimme my gat," Frisky yelped. He was up off the floor again, but this time he rushed his partner instead of me.

"Lay off, dummy," the tall one said. "We just got a message for a guy. We don't blast him. Not today."

"Says you!" Frisky snarled and tried to grab the .22 out of Waxnose's hand. Waxnose threw him to one side without trouble but the interlude allowed me to switch the big automatic to my left hand and jerk out my Luger. I showed it to Waxnose. He nodded, but did not seem impressed.

"He ain't got no parents," he said sadly. "I just let him run around with me. Don't pay him no attention unless he bites you. We'll be on our way now. You get the idea. Lay off the Jeeter kid."

"You're looking at a Luger," I said. "Who is the Jeeter kid? And maybe we'll have some cops before you leave."

He smiled wearily. "Mister, I pack this small-bore because I can shoot. If you think you can take me, go to it."

"O.K.," I said. "Do you know anybody named Arbogast?"

"I meet such a lot of people," he said, with another weary smile. "Maybe yes, maybe no. So long, pal. Be pure."

He strolled over to the door, moving a little sideways, so that he had me covered all the time, and I had him covered, and it was just a case of who shot first and straightest, or whether it was worth while to shoot at all, or whether I could hit anything with so much nice warm Scotch in me. I let him go. He didn't look like a killer to me, but I could have been wrong.

The little man rushed me again while I wasn't thinking about him. He clawed his big automatic out of my left hand, skipped over to the door, spat on the carpet again, and slipped out. Waxnose backed after him—long sharp face, white nose, pointed chin, weary expression. I wouldn't forget him.

He closed the door softly and I stood there, foolish, holding my gun. I heard the elevator come up and go down again and stop. I still stood there. Marty Estel wouldn't be very likely to hire a couple of comics like that to throw a scare into anybody. I thought about that, but thinking got me nowhere. I remembered the half-bottle of Scotch I had left and went into executive session with it.

An hour and a half later I felt fine, but I still didn't have any ideas. I just felt sleepy.

The jarring of the telephone bell woke me. I had dozed off in the chair, which was a bad mistake, because I woke up with two flannel blankets in my mouth, a splitting headache, a bruise on the back of my head and another on my jaw, neither of them larger than a Yakima apple, but sore for all that. I felt terrible. I felt like an amputated leg.

I crawled over to the telephone and humped myself in a chair beside it and answered it. The voice dripped icicles.

"Mr. Dalmas? This is Mr. Jeeter. I believe we met this morning. I'm afraid I was a little stiff with you."

"I'm a little stiff myself. Your son poked me in the jaw. I mean your stepson, or your adopted son—or whatever he is."

"He is both my stepson and my adopted son. Indeed?" He sounded interested. "And where did you meet him?"

"In Miss Huntress's apartment."

"Oh I see." There had been a sudden thaw. The icicles had melted. "Very interesting. What did Miss Huntress have to say?"

"She liked it. She liked him poking me in the jaw."

"I see. And why did he do that?"

"She had him hid out. He overheard some of our talk. He didn't like it."

"I see. I have been thinking that perhaps some consideration—not large, of course—should be granted to her for her cooperation. That is, if we can secure it."

"Fifty grand is the price."

"I'm afraid I don't—"

"Don't kid me," I snarled. "Fifty thousand dollars. Fifty grand. I offered her five hundred—just for a gag."

"You seem to treat this whole business in a spirit of considerable levity," he snarled back. "I am not accustomed to that sort of thing and I don't like it."

I yawned. I didn't give a damn if school kept or not. "Listen, Mr. Jeeter, I'm a great guy to horse around, but I have my mind on the job just the same. And there are some very unusual angles to this case. For instance a couple of gunmen just stuck me up in my apartment here and told me to lay off the Jeeter case. I don't see why it should get so tough."

"Good heavens!" He sounded shocked. "I think you had better come out to my house at once and we will discuss matters. I'll send my car for you. Can you come right away?"

"Yeah. But I can drive myself. I—"

"No. I'm sending my car and chauffeur. His name is George; you may rely upon him absolutely. He should be there in about twenty minutes."

"O.K.," I said. "That just gives me time to drink my dinner. Have him park around the corner on Kenmore, facing towards Franklin." I hung up.

When I'd had a hot-and-cold shower and put on some clean clothes I felt more respectable. I had a couple of drinks, small ones for a change, and put a light overcoat on and went down to the street.

The car was there already. I could see it half a block down the side street. It looked like a new market opening. It had a couple of headlamps like the one on the front end of a streamliner, two amber foglights hooked to the front fender, and a couple of sidelights as big as ordinary headlights. I came up beside it and stopped and a man stepped out of the shadows, tossing a cigarette over his shoulder with a neat flip of the wrist. He was tall, broad, dark, wore a peaked cap, a Russian tunic with a Sam Browne belt, shiny leggings and breeches that flared like an English staff major's whipcords.

"Mr. Dalmas?" He touched the peak of his cap with a gloved forefinger.

"Yeah," I said. "At ease. Don't tell me that's old man Jeeter's car."

"One of them." It was a cool voice that could get fresh.

He opened the rear door and I got in and sank down into the cushions and George slid under the wheel and started the big car. It moved away from the curb and around the corner with as much noise as a bill makes in a wallet. We went west. We seemed to be drifting with the current, but we passed everything. We slid through the heart of Hollywood, the west end of it, down to the Strip and along the glitter of that to the cool quiet of Beverly Hills where the bridle path divides the boulevard.

We gave Beverly Hills the swift and climbed along the foothills, saw the distant lights of the university buildings and swung north into Bel-Air. We began to slide up long narrow streets with high walls and no sidewalks and big gates. Lights on mansions glowed politely through the early night. Nothing stirred. There was no sound but the soft purr of the tires on concrete. We swung left again and I caught a sign which read Calvello Drive. Halfway up this George started to swing the car wide to make a left turn in at a pair of twelve-foot wrought-iron gates. Then something happened.

A pair of lights flared suddenly just beyond the gates and a horn screeched and a motor raced. A car charged at us fast. George straightened out with a flick of the wrist, braked the car and slipped off his right glove, all in one motion.

The car came on, the lights swaying. "Damn drunk," George swore over his shoulder.

It could be. Drunks in cars go all kinds of places to drink. It could be. I slid down onto the floor of the car and yanked the Luger from under my arm and reached up to open the catch. I opened the door a little and held it that way, looking out over the sill. The headlights hit me in the face and I ducked, then came up again as the beam passed.

The other car jammed to a stop. Its door slammed open and a figure jumped out of it, waving a gun and shouting. I heard the voice and knew.

"Reach, you ——!" Frisky screamed at us.

George put his left hand on the wheel and I opened my door a little more. The little man in the street was bouncing up and down and yelling. Out of the small dark car from which he had jumped came no sound except the noise of its motor.

"This is a heist!" Frisky yelled. "Out of there and line up, you —— — ——!"

I kicked my door open and started to get out, the Luger down at my side.

"You asked for it!" the little man yelled.

I dropped—fast! The gun in his hand belched flame. Somebody must have put a firing pin in it. Glass smashed behind my head. Out of the corner of my eye, which oughtn't to have had any corners at that particular moment, I saw George make a movement as smooth as a ripple of water. I brought the Luger up and started to squeeze the trigger, but a shot crashed beside me—George.

I held my fire. It wasn't needed now.

The dark car lurched forward and started down the hill furiously. It roared into the distance while the little man out in the middle of the pavement was still reeling grotesquely in the light reflected from the walls.

There was something dark on his face that spread. His gun bounded along the concrete. His little legs buckled and he plunged sideways and rolled and then, very suddenly, became still.

George said, "Yah!" and sniffed at the muzzle of his revolver.

"Nice shooting." I got out of the car, stood there looking at the little man—a crumpled nothing. The dirty white of his sneakers gleamed a little in the side glare of the car's lights.

George got out beside me. "Why me, brother?"

"I didn't fire. I was watching that pretty hip draw of yours. It was sweeter than honey."

"Thanks, pal. They were after Mister Gerald, of course. I usually ferry him home from the club about this time, full of liquor and bridge losses."

We went over to the little man and looked down at him. He wasn't anything to see. He was just a little man who was dead, with a big slug in his face and blood on him.

"Turn some of those damn lights off," I growled. "And let's get away from here fast."

"The house is just across the street." George sounded as casual as if he had just shot a nickel in a slot machine instead of a man.

"The Jeeters are out of this, if you like your job. You ought to know that. We'll go back to my place and start all over."

"I get it," he snapped, and jumped back into the big car. He cut the foglights and the sidelights and I got in beside him in the front seat.

We straightened out and started up the hill, over the brow.

I looked back at the broken window. It was the small one at the extreme back of the car and it wasn't shatterproof. A large piece was gone from it. They could fit that, if they got around to it, and make some evidence. I didn't think it would matter, but it might.

At the crest of the hill a large limousine passed us going down. Its dome light was on and in the interior, as in a lighted showcase, an elderly couple sat stiffly, taking the royal salute. The man was in evening clothes, with a white scarf and a crush hat. The woman was in furs and diamonds.

George passed them casually, gunned the car and we made a fast right turn into a dark street. "There's a couple of good dinners all shot to hell," he drawled. "And I bet they don't even report it."

"Yeah. Let's get back home and have a drink," I said. "I never really got to like killing people."

5

We sat with some of Miss Harriet Huntress's Scotch in our glasses and looked at each other across the rims. George looked nice with his cap off. His head was clustered over with wavy dark-brown hair and his teeth were very white and clean. He sipped his drink and nibbled a cigarette at the same time. His snappy black eyes had a cool glitter in them.

"Yale?" I asked.

"Dartmouth, if it's any of your business."

"Everything's my business. What's a college education worth these days?"

"Three squares and a uniform," he drawled.

"What kind of guy is young Jeeter?"

"Big blond bruiser, plays a fair game of golf, thinks he's hell with the women, drinks heavy but hasn't sicked up on the rugs so far."

"What kind of guy is old Jeeter?"

"He'd probably give you a dime—if he didn't have a nickel with him."

"*Tsk, tsk,* you're talking about your boss."

George grinned. "He's so tight his head squeaks when he takes his hat off. I always took chances. Maybe that's why I'm just somebody's driver. This is good Scotch."

I made another drink, which finished the bottle. I sat down again.

"You think those two gunnies were stashed out for Mister Gerald?"

"Why not? I usually drive him home about that time. Didn't today. He had a bad hangover and didn't go out until late. You're a dick, you know what it's all about, don't you?"

"Who told you I was a dick?"

"Nobody but a dick ever asked so goddam many questions."

I shook my head. "Uh-uh. I've asked you just six questions. Your boss has a lot of confidence in you. He must have told you."

The dark man nodded, grinned faintly and sipped. "The whole set-up is pretty obvious," he said. "When the car started to swing for the turn into the driveway these boys went to work. I don't figure they meant to kill anybody, somehow. It was just a scare. Only that little guy was nuts."

I looked at George's eyebrows. They were nice black eyebrows, with a gloss on them like horsehair.

I said: "It doesn't sound like Marty Estel to pick that sort of helpers."

"Sure. Maybe that's why he picked that sort of helpers."

"You're smart. You and I can get along. But shooting that little punk makes it tougher. What will you do about that?"

"Nothing."

"O.K. If they get to you and tie it to your gun, if you still have the gun, which you probably won't, I suppose it will be passed off as an attempted stick-up. There's just one thing."

"What?" George finished his second drink, laid the glass aside, lit a fresh cigarette and smiled.

"It's pretty hard to tell a car from in front—at night. Even with all those lights. It might have been a visitor."

He shrugged and nodded. "But if it's a scare, that would do just as well. Because the family would hear about it and the old man would guess whose boys they were—and why."

"Hell, you really are smart," I said admiringly, and the phone rang.

It was an English-butler voice, very clipped and precise, and it said that if I was Mr. John Dalmas, Mr. Jeeter would like to speak to me. He came on at once, with plenty of frost.

"I must say that you take your time about obeying orders," he barked. "Or hasn't that chauffeur of mine—"

"Yeah, he got here, Mr. Jeeter," I said. "But we ran into a little trouble. George will tell you."

"Young man, when I want something done—"

"Listen, Mr. Jeeter, I've had a hard day. Your son punched me on the jaw and I fell and cut my head open. When I staggered back to my apartment, more dead than alive, I was stuck up by a couple of hard guys with guns who told me to lay off the Jeeter case. I'm doing my best but I'm feeling a little frail, so don't scare me."

"Young man—"

"Listen," I told him earnestly, "if you want to call all the plays in this game, you can carry the ball yourself. Or you can save yourself a lot of money and hire an order-taker. I have to do things my way. Any cops visit you tonight?"

"Cops?" he echoed in a sour voice. "You mean policemen?"

"By all means—I mean policemen."

"And why should I see any policemen?" he almost snarled.

"There was a stiff in front of your gates half an hour ago. Stiff meaning dead man. He's quite small. You could sweep him up in a dustpan, if he bothers you."

"My God! Are you serious?"

"Yes. What's more he took a shot at George and me. He recognized the car. He must have been all set for your son, Mr. Jeeter."

A silence with barbs on it. "I thought you said a dead man," Mr. Jeeter's voice said very coldly. "Now you say he shot at you."

"That was while he wasn't dead," I said. "George will tell you. George—"

"You come out here at once!" he yelled at me over the phone. "At once, do you hear? At once!"

"George will tell you," I said softly and hung up—in his face.

George looked at me coldly. He stood up and put his cap on. "O.K., pal," he said. "Maybe some day I can put you on to a soft thing." He started for the door.

"It had to be that way. It's up to him. He'll have to decide."

"Nuts," George said, looking back over his shoulder. "Save your breath, shamus. Anything you say to me is just so much noise in the wrong place."

He opened the door, went out, shut it, and I sat there still holding the telephone, with my mouth open and nothing in it but my tongue and a bad taste on that.

I went out to the kitchen and shook the Scotch bottle, but it was still empty. I opened some rye and swallowed a drink and it tasted sour. Something was bothering me. I had a feeling it was going to bother me a lot more before I was through.

They must have missed George by a whisker. I heard the elevator come up again almost as soon as it had stopped going down. Solid steps grew louder along the hallway. A fist hit the door. I went over and opened it.

One was in brown, one in blue, both large, hefty and bored.

The one in brown pushed his hat back on his head with a freckled hand and said: "You John Dalmas?"

"Me," I said.

They rode me back into the room without seeming to. The one in blue shut the door. The one in brown palmed a shield and let me catch a glint of the gold and enamel.

"Finlayson, Detective-Lieutenant working out of Central Homicide," he said. "This is Sebold, my partner. We're a couple of swell guys not to get funny with. We hear you're kind of sharp with a gun."

Sebold took his hat off and dusted his salt-and-pepper hair back with the flat of his hand. He drifted noiselessly out to the kitchen.

Finlayson sat down on the edge of a chair and flicked his chin with a thumbnail as square as an ice cube and yellow as a mustard plaster. He was older than Sebold, but not so good-looking. He had the frowsy expression of a veteran cop who hadn't got very far.

I sat down. I said: "How do you mean, sharp with a gun?"

"Shooting people is how I mean."

I lit a cigarette. Sebold came out of the kitchen and went into the dressing-room behind the wall-bed.

"We understand you're a private-license guy," Finlayson said heavily.

"That's right."

"Give." He held his hand out. I gave him my wallet. He chewed it over and handed it back. "Carry a gun?"

I nodded. He held out his hand for it. Sebold came out of the dressing-room. Finlayson sniffed at the Luger, snapped the magazine out, cleared the breech and held the gun so that a little light shone up through the magazine opening into the breech end of the barrel. He looked down the muzzle, squinting. He handed the gun to Sebold. Sebold did the same thing.

"Don't think so," Sebold said. "Clean, but not that clean. Couldn't have been cleaned within the hour. A little dust."

"Right."

Finlayson picked the ejected shell off the carpet, pressed it into the magazine and snapped the magazine back in place. He handed me the gun. I put it back under my arm.

"Been out anywhere tonight?" he asked tersely.

"Don't tell me the plot," I said. "I'm just a bit-player."

"Smart guy," Sebold said dispassionately. He dusted his hair again and opened a desk drawer. "Funny stuff. Good for a column. I like 'em that way—with my blackjack."

Finlayson sighed. "Been out tonight, shamus?"

"Sure. In and out all the time. Why?"

He ignored the question. "Where you been?"

"Out to dinner. Business call or two."

"Where at?"

"I'm sorry, boys. Every business has its private files."

"Had company, too," Sebold said, picking up George's glass and sniffing it. "Recent—within the hour."

"You're not that good," I told him sourly.

"Had a ride in a big Caddy?" Finlayson bored on, taking a deep breath. "Over West L.A. direction?"

"Had a ride in a Chrysler—over Vine Street direction."

"Maybe we better just take him down," Sebold said, looking at his fingernails.

"Maybe you better skip the gang-buster stuff and tell me what's stuck in your nose. I get along with cops—except when they act as if the law is only for citizens."

Finlayson studied me. Nothing I had said made an impression on him. Nothing Sebold said made any impression on him. He had an idea and he was holding it like a sick baby.

"You know a little rat named Frisky Lavon?" he sighed. "Used to be a dummy-chucker, then found out he could bug his way outa raps. Been doing that for say twelve years. Totes a gun and acts simple. But he quit acting tonight at seven-thirty about. Quit cold—with a slug in his head."

"Never heard of him," I said.

"You bumped anybody off tonight?"

"I'd have to look at my notebook."

Sebold leaned forward politely. "Would you care for a smack in the kisser?" he inquired.

Finlayson held his hand out sharply. "Cut it, Ben. Cut it. Listen, Dalmas. Maybe we're going at this wrong. We're not talking about murder. Could have been legitimate. This Frisky Lavon got froze off tonight on Calvello Drive in Bel-Air. Out in the middle of the street. Nobody seen or heard anything. So we kind of want to know."

"All right," I growled. "What makes it my business? And keep that piano tuner out of my hair. He has a nice suit and his nails are clean, but he bears down on his shield too hard."

"Nuts to you," Sebold said.

"We got a funny phone call," Finlayson said. "Which is where you come in. We ain't just throwing our weight around. And we want a forty-five. They ain't sure what kind yet."

"He's smart. He threw it under the bar at Levy's," Sebold sneered.

"I never had a forty-five," I said. "A guy who needs that much gun ought to use a pick."

Finlayson scowled at me and counted his thumbs. Then he took a deep breath and suddenly went human on me. "Sure, I'm just a dumb flatheel," he said. "Anybody could pull my ears off and I wouldn't even notice it. Let's all quit horsing around and talk sense.

"This Frisky was found dead after a no-name phone call to West L.A. police. Found dead outside a big house belonging to a man named Jeeter who owns a string of investment companies. He wouldn't use a guy like Frisky for a penwiper, so there's nothing in that. The servants there didn't hear nothing, nor the servants at any of the four houses on the block. Frisky is lying in the street and somebody run over his foot, but what killed him was a forty-five slug smack in his face. West L.A. ain't hardly started the routine when some guy calls up Central and says to tell Homicide if they want to know who got Frisky Lavon, ask a private eye named John Dalmas, complete with address and everything, then a quick hang-up.

"O.K. The guy on the board gives me the dope and I don't know Frisky from a hole in my sock, but I ask Identification and sure enough they have him and just about the time I'm looking it over the flash comes from West L.A. and the description seems to check pretty close. So we get together and it's the same guy all right and the chief of detectives has us drop around here. So we drop around."

"So here you are," I said. "Will you have a drink?"

"Can we search the joint, if we do?"

"Sure. It's a good lead—that phone call, I mean—if you put in about six months on it."

"We already got that idea," Finlayson growled. "A hundred guys could have chilled this little wart, and two-three of them maybe could have thought it was a smart rib to pin it on you. Them two-three is what interests us."

I shook my head.

"No ideas at all, huh?"

"Just for wisecracks," Sebold said.

Finlayson lumbered to his feet. "Well, we gotta look around."

"Maybe we had ought to have brought a search warrant," Sebold said, tickling his upper lip with the end of his tongue.

"I don't *have* to fight this guy, do I?" I asked Finlayson. "I mean, is it all right if I leave him his gag lines and just keep my temper?"

Finlayson looked at the ceiling and said dryly: "His wife left him day before yesterday. He's just trying to compensate, as the fellow says."

Sebold turned white and twisted his knuckles savagely. Then he laughed shortly and got to his feet.

They went at it. Ten minutes of opening and shutting drawers and looking at the backs of shelves and under seat cushions and letting the bed down and peering into the electric refrigerator and the garbage pail fed them up.

They came back and sat down again. "Just a nut," Finlayson said wearily. "Some guy that picked your name outa the directory maybe. Could be anything."

"Now I'll get that drink."

"I don't drink," Sebold snarled.

Finlayson crossed his hands on his stomach. "That don't mean any liquor gets poured in the flowerpot, son."

I got three drinks and put two of them beside Finlayson. He drank half of one of them and looked at the ceiling. "I got another killing, too," he said thoughtfully. "A guy in your racket, Dalmas. A fat guy on Sunset. Name of Arbogast. Ever hear of him?"

"I thought he was a handwriting expert," I said.

"You're talking about police business," Sebold told his partner coldly.

"Sure. Police business that's already in the morning paper. This Arbogast was shot three times with a twenty-two. Target gun. You know any crooks that pack that kind of heat?"

I held my glass tightly and took a long slow swallow. I hadn't thought Waxnose looked dangerous enough, but you never knew.

"I did," I said slowly. "A killer named Al Tessilore. But he's in Folsom. He used a Colt Woodsman."

Finlayson finished the first drink, used the second in about the same time, and stood up. Sebold stood up, still mad.

Finlayson opened the door. "Come on, Ben." They went out.

I heard their steps along the hall, the clang of the elevator once more. A car started just below in the street and growled off into the night.

"Clowns like that don't kill," I said out loud. But it looked as if they did.

I waited fifteen minutes before I went out again. The phone rang while I was waiting, but I didn't answer it.

I drove towards the El Milano and circled around enough to make sure I wasn't followed.

6

The lobby hadn't changed any. The blue carpet still tickled my ankles while I ambled over to the desk, the same pale clerk was handing a key to a couple of horse-faced females in tweeds, and when he saw me he put his weight on his left foot again and the door at the end of the desk popped open and out popped the fat and erotic Hawkins, with what looked like the same cigar stub in his face.

He hustled over and gave me a big warm smile this time, took hold of my arm. "Just the guy I was hoping to see," he chuckled. "Let's us go upstairs a minute."

"What's the matter?"

"Matter?" His smile became broad as the door to a two-car garage. "Nothing ain't the matter. This way."

He pushed me into the elevator and said "Eight" in a fat cheerful voice and up we sailed and out we got and slid along the corridor. Hawkins had a hard hand and knew where to hold an arm. I was interested enough to let him get away with it. He pushed the buzzer beside Miss Huntress's door and Big Ben chimed inside and the door opened and I was looking at a deadpan in a derby hat and a dinner coat. He had his right hand in the side pocket of the coat, and under the derby a pair of scarred eyebrows and under the eyebrows a pair of eyes that had as much expression as the cap on a gas tank.

The mouth moved enough to say: "Yeah?"

"Company for the boss," Hawkins said expansively.

"What company?"

"Let me play too," I said. "Limited liability company. Gimme the apple."

"Huh?" The eyebrows went this way and that and the jaw came out. "Nobody ain't kiddin' nobody, I hope."

"Now, now, gents—" Hawkins began.

A voice behind the derby-hatted man interrupted him. "What's the matter, Beef?"

"He's in a stew," I said.

"Listen, mug—"

"Now, now, gents—" as before.

"Ain't nothing the matter," Beef said, throwing his voice over his shoulder as if it were a coil of rope. "The hotel dick got a guy up here and he says he's company."

"Show the company in, Beef." I liked this voice. It was smooth, quiet, and you could have cut your name in it with a thirty-pound sledge and a cold chisel.

"Lift the dogs," Beef said, and stood to one side.

We went in. I went first, then Hawkins, then Beef wheeled neatly behind us like a door. We went in so close together that we must have looked like a three-decker sandwich.

Miss Huntress was not in the room. The log in the fireplace had almost stopped smoldering. There was still that smell of sandalwood on the air. With it cigarette smoke blended.

A man stood at the end of the davenport, both hands in the pockets of a blue camel's hair coat with the collar high to a black snapbrim hat. A loose scarf hung outside his coat. He stood motionless, the cigarette in his mouth lisping smoke. He was tall, black-haired, suave, dangerous. He said nothing.

Hawkins ambled over to him. "This is the guy I was telling you about, Mr. Estel," the fat man burbled. "Come in earlier today and said he was from you. Kinda fooled me."

"Give him a ten, Beef."

The derby hat took its left hand from somewhere and there was a bill in it. It pushed the bill at Hawkins. Hawkins took the bill, blushing.

"This ain't necessary, Mr. Estel. Thanks a lot just the same."

"Scram."

"Huh?" Hawkins looked shocked.

"You heard him," Beef said truculently. "Want your fanny out the door first, huh?"

Hawkins drew himself up. "I gotta protect the tenants. You gentlemen know how it is. A man in a job like this."

"Yeah. Scram," Estel said without moving his lips.

Hawkins turned and went out quickly, softly. The door clicked gently shut behind him. Beef looked back at it, then moved behind me.

"See if he's rodded, Beef."

The derby hat saw if I was rodded. He took the Luger and went away from me. Estel looked casually at the Luger, back at me. His eyes held an expression of indifferent dislike.

"Name's John Dalmas, eh? A private dick."

"So what?" I said.

"Somebody is goin' to get somebody's face pushed into somebody's floor," Beef said coldly.

"Aw, keep that crap for the boiler-room," I told him. "I'm sick of hard guys for this evening. I said 'so what,' and 'so what' is what I said."

Marty Estel looked mildly amused. "Hell, keep your shirt in. I've got to look after my friends, don't I? You know who I am. O.K., I know what you talked to Miss Huntress about. And I know something about you that you don't know I know."

"All right," I said. "This fat slob Hawkins collected ten from me for letting me up here this afternoon—knowing perfectly well who I was—and he has just collected ten from your iron man for slipping me the nasty. Give me back my gun and tell me what makes my business your business."

"Plenty. First off, Harriet's not home. We're waiting for her on account of a thing that happened. I can't wait any longer. Got to go to work at the club. So what did you come after this time?"

"Looking for the Jeeter boy. Somebody shot at his car tonight. From now on he needs somebody to walk behind him."

"You think I play games like that?" Estel asked me coldly.

I walked over to a cabinet and opened it and found a bottle of Scotch. I twisted the cap off, lifted a glass from the tabouret and poured some out. I tasted it. It tasted all right.

I looked around for ice, but there wasn't any. It had all melted long since in the bucket.

"I asked you a question," Estel said gravely.

"I heard it. I'm making my mind up. The answer is, I wouldn't have thought it—no. But it happened. I was there.

I was in the car—instead of young Jeeter. His father had sent for me to come to the house to talk things over."

"What things?"

I didn't bother to look surprised. "You hold fifty grand of the boy's paper. That looks bad for you, if anything happens to him."

"I don't figure it that way. Because that way I would lose my dough. The old man won't pay—granted. But I wait a couple of years and I collect from the kid. He gets his estate out of trust when he's twenty-eight. Right now he gets a grand a month and he can't even will anything, because it's still in trust. Savvy?"

"So you wouldn't knock him off," I said, using my Scotch. "But you might throw a scare into him."

Estel frowned. He discarded his cigarette into a tray and watched it smoke a moment before he picked it up again and snubbed it out. He shook his head.

"If you're going to bodyguard him, it would almost pay me to stand part of your salary, wouldn't it? Almost. A man in my racket can't take care of everything. He's of age and it's his business who he runs around with. For instance, women. Any reason why a nice girl shouldn't cut herself a piece of five million bucks?"

I said: "I think it's a swell idea. What was it you knew about me that I didn't know you knew?"

He smiled, faintly. "What was it you were waiting to tell Miss Huntress—the thing that happened?"

He smiled faintly again.

"Listen, Dalmas, there are lots of ways to play any game. I play mine on the house percentage, because that's all I need to win. What makes me get tough?"

I rolled a fresh cigarette around in my fingers and tried to roll it around my glass with two fingers. "Who said you were tough? I always heard the nicest things about you."

Marty Estel nodded and looked faintly amused. "I have sources of information," he said quietly. "When I have fifty grand invested in a guy, I'm apt to find out a little about him. Jeeter hired a man named Arbogast to do a little work. Arbogast was killed in his office today—with a twenty-two. That could have nothing to do with Jeeter's business. But there was a tail on you when you went there and you didn't give it to the law. Does that make you and me friends?"

I licked the edge of my glass, nodded. "It seems it does."

"From now on just forget about bothering Harriet, see?"

"O.K."

"So we understand each other real good, now."

"Yeah."

"Well, I'll be going. Give the guy back his Luger, Beef."

The derby hat came over and smacked my gun into my hand hard enough to break a bone.

"Staying?" Estel asked, moving towards the door.

"I guess I'll wait a little while. Until Hawkins comes up to touch me for another ten."

Estel grinned. Beef walked in front of him wooden-faced to the door and opened it. Estel went out. The door closed. The room was silent. I sniffed at the dying perfume of sandalwood and stood motionless, looking around.

Somebody was nuts. I was nuts. Everybody was nuts. None of it fitted together worth a nickel. Marty Estel, as he said, had no good motive for murdering anybody, because that would be the surest way to kill his chances to collect his money. Even if he had a motive for murdering anybody, Wax-nose and Frisky didn't seem like the team he would select for the job. I was in bad with the police, I had spent ten dollars of my twenty expense money, and I didn't have enough lever-age anywhere to lift a dime off a cigar counter.

I finished my drink, put the glass down, walked up and down the room, smoked a third cigarette, looked at my watch, shrugged and felt disgusted. The inner doors of the suite were closed. I went across to the one out of which young Jeeter must have sneaked that afternoon. Opening it I looked into a bedroom done in ivory and ashes of roses. There was a big double bed with no footboard, covered with figured brocade. Toilet articles glistened on a built-in dressing table with a panel-light. The light was lit. A small lamp on a table beside the door was lit also. A door near the dressing table showed the cool green of bathroom tiles.

I went over and looked in there. Chromium, a glass stall shower, monogrammed towels on a rack, a glass shelf for per-fume and bath salts at the foot of the tub, everything nice and

refined. Miss Huntress did herself well. I hoped she was paying her own rent. It didn't make any difference to me—I just
liked it that way.

I went back towards the living-room, stopped in the doorway to take another pleasant look around, and noticed something I ought to have noticed the instant I stepped into the
room. I noticed the sharp tang of cordite on the air, almost,
but not quite gone. And then I noticed something else.

The bed had been moved over until its head overlapped the
edge of a closet door which was not quite closed. The weight
of the bed was holding it from opening. I went over there to
find out why it wanted to open. I went slowly and about
halfway there I noticed that I was holding a gun in my hand.

I leaned against the closet door. It didn't move. I threw
more weight against it. It still didn't move. Braced against it I
pushed the bed away with my foot, gave ground slowly.

A weight pushed against me hard. I had gone back a foot
or so before anything else happened. Then it happened suddenly. He came out—sideways, in a sort of roll. I put some
more weight back on the door and held him like that a moment, looking at him.

He was still big, still blond, still dressed in rough sporty
material, with scarf and open-necked shirt. But his face wasn't
red any more.

I gave ground again and he rolled down the back of the
door, turning a little like a swimmer in the surf, thumped the
floor and lay there, almost on his back, still looking at me.
Light from the bedside lamp glittered on his head. There was
a scorched and soggy stain on the rough coat—about where
his heart would be. So he wouldn't get that five million after
all. And nobody would get anything and Marty Estel
wouldn't get his fifty grand. Because young Mister Gerald
was dead.

I looked back into the closet where he had been. Its door
hung wide open now. There were clothes on racks, feminine
clothes, nice clothes. He had been backed in among them,
probably with his hands in the air and a gun against his chest.
And then he had been shot dead, and whoever did it hadn't
been quite quick enough or quite strong enough to get the

door shut. Or had been scared and had just yanked the bed over against the door and left it that way.

Something glittered down on the floor. I picked it up. A small automatic, .25 caliber, a woman's purse gun with a beautifully engraved butt inlaid with silver and ivory. I put the gun in my pocket. That seemed a funny thing to do, too.

I didn't touch him. He was as dead as John D. Arbogast and looked a whole lot deader. I left the door open and listened, walked quickly back across the room and into the living-room and shut the bedroom door, smearing the knob as I did it.

A lock was being tinkled at with a key. Hawkins was back again, to see what delayed me. He was letting himself in with his passkey.

I was pouring a drink when he came in.

He came well into the room, stopped with his feet planted and surveyed me coldly.

"I seen Estel and his boy leave," he said. "I didn't see you leave. So I come up. I gotta—"

"You gotta protect the guests," I said.

"Yeah. I gotta protect the guests. You can't stay up here, pal. Not without the lady of the house is home."

"But Marty Estel and his hard boy can."

He came a little closer to me. He had a mean look in his eye. He had always had it, probably, but I noticed it more now.

"You don't want to make nothing of that, do you?" he asked me.

"No. Every man to his own chisel. Have a drink."

"That ain't your liquor."

"Miss Huntress gave me a bottle. We're pals. Marty Estel and I are pals. Everybody is pals. Don't you want to be pals?"

"You ain't trying to kid me, are you?"

"Have a drink and forget it."

I found a glass and poured him one. He took it.

"It's the job if anybody smells it on me," he said.

"Uh-huh."

He drank slowly, rolling it around on his tongue. "Good Scotch."

"Won't be the first time you tasted it, will it?"

He started to get hard again, then relaxed. "Hell, I guess you're just a kidder." He finished the drink, put the glass down, patted his lips with a large and very crumpled handkerchief and sighed.

"O.K.," he said. "But we'll have to leave now."

"All set. I guess she won't be home for a while. You see them go out?"

"Her and the boy friend. Yeah, long time ago."

I nodded. We went towards the door and Hawkins saw me out. He saw me downstairs and off the premises. But he didn't see what was in Miss Huntress's bedroom. I wondered if he would go back up. If he did, the Scotch bottle would probably stop him.

I got into my car and drove off home—to talk to Anna Halsey on the phone. There wasn't any case any more—for us.

7

I parked close to the curb this time. I wasn't feeling gay any more. I rode up in the elevator and unlocked my door and clicked the light on.

Waxnose sat in my best chair, an unlit hand-rolled brown cigarette between his fingers, his bony knees crossed, and his long Woodsman resting solidly on his leg. He was smiling. It wasn't the nicest smile I ever saw.

"Hi, pal," he drawled. "You still ain't had that door fixed. Kind of shut it, huh?" His voice, for all the drawl, was deadly.

I shut the door, stood looking across the room at him.

"So you killed my pal," he said.

He stood up slowly, came across the room slowly and leaned the .22 against my throat. His smiling thin-lipped mouth seemed as expressionless, for all its smile, as his wax-white nose. He reached quietly under my coat and took the Luger. I might as well leave it home from now on. Everybody in town seemed to be able to take it away from me.

He stepped back across the room and sat down again in the chair. "Steady does it," he said almost gently. "Park the body, friend. No false moves. No moves at all. You and me are at the jumping-off place. The clock's tickin' and we're waiting to go."

I sat down and stared at him. A curious bird. I moistened my dry lips. "You told me his gun had no firing pin," I said.

"Yeah. He fooled me on that, the little so-and-so. And I told you to lay off the Jeeter kid. That's cold now. It's Frisky I'm thinking about. Crazy, ain't it? Me bothering about a dimwit like that, packin' him around with me, and letting him get hisself bumped off." He sighed and added simply, "He was my kid brother."

"I didn't kill him," I said.

He smiled a little more. He had never stopped smiling. The corners of his mouth just tucked in a little deeper.

"Yeah?"

He slid the safety catch off the Luger, laid it carefully on the arm of the chair at his right, and reached into his pocket. What he brought out made me as cold as an ice bucket.

It was a metal tube, dark and rough-looking, about four inches long and drilled with a lot of small holes. He held his Woodsman in his left hand and began to screw the tube casually on the end of it.

"Silencer," he said. "They're the bunk, I guess you smart guys think. This one ain't the bunk—not for three shots. I oughta know. I made it myself."

I moistened my lips again. "It'll work for one shot," I said. "Then it jams your action. That one looks like cast-iron. It will probably blow your hand off."

He smiled his waxy smile, screwed it on, slowly, lovingly, gave it a last hard turn and sat back relaxed. "Not this baby. She's packed with steel wool and that's good for three shots, like I said. Then you got to repack it. And there ain't enough back pressure to jam the action on this gun. You feel good? I'd like you to feel good."

"I feel swell, you sadistic —— — – ——," I said.

"I'm having you lie down on the bed after a while. You won't feel nothing. I'm kind of fussy about my killings. Frisky didn't feel nothing, I guess. You got him neat."

"You don't see good," I sneered. "The chauffeur got him with a Smith & Wesson forty-four. I didn't even fire."

"Uh-huh."

"O.K., you don't believe me," I said. "What did you kill Arbogast for? There was nothing fussy about that killing. He was just shot at his desk, three times with a twenty-two and he fell down on the floor. What did he ever do to your filthy little brother?"

He jerked the gun up, but his smile held. "You got guts," he said. "Who is this here Arbogast?"

I told him. I told him slowly and carefully, in detail. I told him a lot of things. And he began in some vague way to look worried. His eyes flickered at me, away, back again, restlessly, like a humming-bird.

"I don't know any party named Arbogast, pal," he said slowly. "Never heard of him. And I ain't shot any fat guys today."

"You killed him," I said. "And you killed young Jeeter—in the girl's apartment at the El Milano. He's lying there dead right now. You're working for Marty Estel. He's going to be awfully damn sorry about that kill. Go ahead and make it three in a row."

His face froze. The smile went away at last. His whole face looked waxy now. He opened his mouth and breathed through it, and his breath made a restless worrying sound. I could see the faint glitter of sweat on his forehead, and I could feel the cold from the evaporation of sweat on mine.

Waxnose said very gently: "I ain't killed anybody at all, friend. Not anybody. I wasn't hired to kill people. Until Frisky stopped that slug I didn't have no such ideas. That's straight."

I tried not to stare at the metal tube on the end of the Woodsman.

A flame flickered at the back of his eyes, a small, weak, smoky flame. It seemed to grow larger and clearer. He looked down at the floor between his feet. I looked around at the light-switch, but it was too far away. He looked up again. Very slowly he began to unscrew the silencer. He had it loose in his hand. He dropped it back into his pocket, stood up, holding the two guns, one in each hand. Then he had another idea. He sat down again, took all the shells out of the Luger quickly and threw it on the floor after them.

He came towards me softly across the room. "I guess this is your lucky day," he said. "I got to go a place and see a guy."

"I knew all along it was my lucky day. I've been feeling so good."

He moved delicately around me to the door and opened it a foot and started through the narrow opening, smiling again.

"I gotta see a guy," he said very gently, and his tongue moved along his lips.

"Not yet," I said, and jumped.

His gun hand was at the edge of the door, almost beyond the edge. I hit the door hard and he couldn't bring it in quickly enough. He couldn't get out of the way. I pinned him in the doorway, and used all the strength I had. It was a crazy thing. He had given me a break and all I had to do was to stand still and let him go. But I had a guy to see too—and I wanted to see him first.

Waxnose leered at me. He grunted. He fought with his hand beyond the door edge. I shifted and hit his jaw with all I had. It was enough. He went limp. I hit him again. His head bounced against the wood. I heard a light thud beyond the door edge. I hit him a third time. I never hit anything any harder.

I took my weight back from the door then and he slid towards me, blank-eyed, rubber-kneed and I caught him and twisted his empty hands behind him and let him fall. I stood over him panting. I went to the door. His Woodsman lay almost on the sill. I picked it up, dropped it into my pocket—not the pocket that held Miss Huntress's gun. He hadn't even found that.

There he lay on the floor. He was thin, he had no weight, but I panted just the same. In a little while his eyes flickered open and looked up at me.

"Greedy guy," he whispered wearily. "Why did I ever leave Saint Looey?"

I snapped handcuffs on his wrists and pulled him by the shoulders into the dressing room and tied his ankles with a piece of rope. I left him lying on his back, a little sideways, his nose as white as ever, his eyes empty now, his lips moving a little as if he were talking to himself. A funny lad, not all bad, but not so pure I had to weep over him either.

I put my Luger together and left with my three guns. There was nobody outside the apartment house.

8

The Jeeter mansion was on a nine- or ten-acre knoll, a big colonial pile with fat white columns and dormer windows and magnolias and a four-car garage. There was a circular parking space at the top of the driveway with two cars parked in it—one was the big dreadnaught in which I'd ridden and the other a canary-yellow sports convertible I had seen before.

I rang a bell the size of a silver dollar. The door opened and a tall narrow cold-eyed bird in dark clothes looked out at me.

"Mr. Jeeter home? Mr. Jeeter, Senior?"

"May I arsk who is calling?" The accent was a little too thick, like cut Scotch.

"John Dalmas. I'm working for him. Maybe I had ought to of gone to the servant's entrance."

He hitched a finger at a wing collar and looked at me without pleasure. "Aw, possibly. You may step in. I shall inform Mr. Jeeter. I believe he is engaged at the moment. Kindly wait 'ere in the 'all."

"The act stinks," I said. "English butlers aren't dropping their h's this year."

"Smart guy, huh?" he snarled, in a voice from not any farther across the Atlantic than Hoboken. "Wait here." He slid away.

I sat down in a carved chair and felt thirsty. After a while the butler came catfooting back along the hall and jerked his chin at me unpleasantly.

We went along a mile of hallway. At the end it broadened without any doors into a huge sunroom. On the far side of the sunroom the butler opened a wide door and I stepped past him into an oval room with a black-and-silver oval rug, a black marble table in the middle of the rug, stiff high-backed carved chairs against the walls, a huge oval mirror with a rounded surface that made me look like a pygmy with water on the brain, and in the room three people.

By the door opposite where I came in, George the chauffeur stood stiffly in his neat dark uniform, with his peaked cap in his hand. In the least uncomfortable of the chairs sat Miss Harriet Huntress holding a glass in which there was half a drink. And around the silver margin of the oval rug, Mr. Jeeter, Senior, was trying his legs out in a brisk canter, still under wraps, but mad inside. His face was red and the veins on his nose were distended. His hands were in the pockets of a velvet smoking jacket. He wore a pleated shirt with a black pearl in the bosom, a batwing black tie and one of his patent-leather oxfords was unlaced.

He whirled and yelled at the butler behind me: "Get out and keep those doors shut! And I'm not at home to anybody, understand? Nobody!"

The butler closed the doors. Presumably, he went away. I didn't hear him go.

George gave me a cool one-sided smile and Miss Huntress gave me a bland stare over her glass. "You made a nice come back," she said demurely.

"You took a chance leaving me alone in your apartment," I told her. "I might have sneaked some of your perfume."

"Well, what do you want?" Jeeter yelled at me. "A nice sort of detective you turned out to be. I put you on a confidential job and you walk right in on Miss Huntress and explain the whole thing to her."

"It worked, didn't it?"

He stared. They all stared. "How do you know that?" he barked.

"I know a nice girl when I see one. She's here telling you she had an idea she got not to like, and for you to quit worrying about it. Where's Mister Gerald?"

Old Man Jeeter stopped and gave me a hard level stare. "I still regard you as incompetent," he said. "My son is missing."

"I'm not working for you. I'm working for Anna Halsey. Any complaints you have to make should be addressed to her. Do I pour my own drink or do you have a flunky in a purple suit to do it? And what do you mean, your son is missing?"

"Should I give him the heave, sir?" George asked quietly.

Jeeter waved his hand at a decanter and siphon and glasses on the black marble table and started around the rug again. "Don't be silly," he snapped at George.

George flushed a little, high on his cheekbones. His mouth looked tough.

I mixed myself a drink and sat down with it and tasted it and asked again: "What do you mean your son is missing, Mr. Jeeter?"

"I'm paying you good money," he started to yell at me, still mad.

"When?"

He stopped dead in his canter and looked at me again. Miss Huntress laughed lightly. George scowled.

"What do you suppose I mean—my son is missing?" he snapped. "I should have thought that would be clear enough even to you. Nobody knows where he is. Miss Huntress doesn't know. I don't know. No one at any of the places where he might be knows."

"But I'm smarter than they are," I said. "*I* know."

Nobody moved for a long minute. Jeeter stared at me fish-eyed. George stared at me. The girl stared at me. She looked puzzled. The other two just stared.

I looked at her. "Where did you go when you went out, if you're telling?"

Her dark blue eyes were water-clear. "There's no secret about it. We went out together—in a taxi. Gerald had had his driving license suspended for a month. Too many tickets. We went down towards the beach and I had a change of heart, as you guessed. I decided I was just being a chiseler after all. I didn't want Gerald's money really. What I wanted was revenge. On Mr. Jeeter here for ruining my father. Done all legally of course, but done just the same. But I got myself in a spot where I couldn't have my revenge and not look like a cheap chiseler. So I told Gerald to find some other girl to play with. He was sore and we quarreled. I stopped the taxi and got out in Beverly Hills. He went on. I don't know where. Later I went back to the El Milano and got my car out of the garage and came here. To tell Mr. Jeeter to forget the whole thing and not bother to sick sleuths on to me."

"You say you went with him in a taxi," I said. "Why wasn't George driving him, if he couldn't drive himself?"

I stared at her, but I wasn't talking to her. Jeeter answered me, frostily. "George drove me home from the office, of course. At that time Gerald had already gone out. Is there anything important about that?"

I turned to him. "Yeah. There's going to be. Mister Gerald is at the El Milano. Hawkins the house dick told me. He went back there to wait for Miss Huntress and Hawkins let him into her apartment. Hawkins will do you those little favors— for ten bucks. He may be there still and he may not."

I kept on watching them. It was hard to watch all three of them. But they didn't move. They just looked at me.

"Well—I'm glad to hear it," Old Man Jeeter said. "I was afraid he was off somewhere getting drunk."

"No. He's not off anywhere getting drunk," I said. "By the way, among these places you called to see if he was there, you didn't call the El Milano?"

George nodded. "Yes, I did. They said he wasn't there. Looks like this house peeper tipped the phone girl off not to say anything."

"He wouldn't have to do that. She'd just ring the apartment and he wouldn't answer—naturally." I watched old man Jeeter hard then, with a lot of interest. It was going to be hard for him to take that up, but he was going to have to do it.

He did. He licked his lips first. "Why—naturally, if I may ask?" he said coldly.

I put my glass down on the marble table and stood against the wall, with my hands hanging free. I still tried to watch them—all three of them.

"Let's go back over this thing a little," I said. "We're all wise to the situation. I know George is, although he shouldn't be, being just a servant. I know Miss Huntress is. And of course *you* are, Mr. Jeeter. So let's see what we have got. We have a lot of things that don't add up, but I'm smart. I'm going to add them up anyhow. First-off a handful of photostats of notes from Marty Estel. Gerald denies having given these and Mr. Jeeter won't pay them, but he has a handwriting man named Arbogast check the signatures, to see if they look genuine. They do. They are. This Arbogast may have done other things. I don't know. I couldn't ask him. When I went to see him, he was dead—shot three times—as I've since heard—with a twenty-two. No, I didn't tell the police, Mr. Jeeter."

The tall silver-haired man looked horribly shocked. His lean body shook like a bullrush. "Dead?" he whispered. "Murdered?"

I looked at George. George didn't move a muscle. I looked at the girl. She sat quietly, waiting, tight-lipped.

I said: "There's only one reason to suppose his killing had anything to do with Mr. Jeeter's affairs. He was shot with a twenty-two—and there is a man in this case who wears a twenty-two."

I still had their attention. And their silence.

"Why he was shot I haven't the faintest idea. He was not a dangerous man to Miss Huntress or Marty Estel. He was too fat to get around much. My guess is he was a little too smart. He got a simple case of signature identification and he went on from there to find out more than he should. And after he had found out more than he should—he guessed more than he ought—and maybe he even tried a little blackmail. And somebody rubbed him out this afternoon with a twenty-two. O.K., I can stand it. I never knew him.

"So I went over to see Miss Huntress and after a lot of finaygling around with this itchy-handed house dick I got to see her and we had a chat, and then Mister Gerald stepped neatly out of hiding and bopped me a nice one on the chin and over I went and hit my head on a chair leg. And when I came out of that the joint was empty. So I went on home.

"And home I found the man with the twenty-two and with him a dimwit called Frisky Lavon, with a bad breath and a very large gun, neither of which matters now as he was shot dead in front of your house tonight, Mr. Jeeter—shot trying to stick up your car. The cops know about that one—they came to see me about it—because the other guy, the one that packs the twenty-two, is the little dimwit's brother and he thought I shot Dimwit and tried to put the bee on me. But it didn't work. That's two killings.

"We now come to the third and most important. I went back to the El Milano because it no longer seemed a good idea for Mister Gerald to be running around casually. He seemed to have a few enemies. It even seemed that he was supposed to be in the car this evening when Frisky Lavon shot at it—but of course that was just a plant."

Old Jeeter drew his white eyebrows together in an expression of puzzlement. George didn't look puzzled. He didn't look anything. He was as wooden-faced as a cigar-store Indian. The girl looked a little white now, a little tense. I plowed on.

"Back at the El Milano I found that Hawkins had let Marty Estel and his bodyguard into Miss Huntress's apartment to wait for her. Marty had something to tell her—that Arbogast had been killed. That made it a good idea for her to lay off young Jeeter for a while—until the cops quieted down anyhow. A thoughtful guy, Marty. A much more thoughtful guy than you would suppose. For instance, he knew about Arbogast and he knew Mr. Jeeter went to Anna Halsey's office this morning and he knew somehow—Anna might have told him herself, I wouldn't put it past her—that I was working on the case now. So he had me tailed to Arbogast's place and away, and he found out later from his cop friends that Arbogast had been murdered, and he knew I hadn't given it out. So he had me there and that made us pals. He went away after telling me this and once more I was left alone in Miss Huntress's apartment. But this time for no reason at all I poked around. And I found young Mister Gerald, in the bedroom, in a closet."

I stepped quickly over to the girl and reached into my pocket and took out the small fancy .25 automatic and laid it down on her knee.

"Ever see this before?"

Her voice had a curious tight sound, but her dark blue eyes looked at me levelly.

"Yes. It's mine."

"You kept it where?"

"In the drawer of a small table beside the bed."

"Sure about that?"

She thought. Neither of the two men stirred.

George began to twitch the corner of his mouth. She shook her head suddenly, sideways.

"No. I have an idea now I took it out to show somebody—because I don't know much about guns—and left it lying on the mantel in the living-room. In fact, I'm almost sure I did. It was Gerald I showed it to."

"So he might have reached for it there, if anybody tried to make a wrong play at him?"

She nodded, troubled. "What do you mean—he's in the closet?" she asked in a small quick voice.

"You know. Everybody in this room knows what I mean. They know that I showed you that gun for a purpose." I stepped away from her and faced George and his boss. "He's dead, of course. Shot through the heart—probably with this gun. It was left there with him. That's why it would be left."

The old man took a step and stopped and braced himself against the table. I wasn't sure whether he had turned white or whether he had been white already. He stared stonily at the girl. He said very slowly, between his teeth: "You damned murderess!"

"Couldn't it have been suicide?" I sneered.

He turned his head enough to look at me. I could see that the idea interested him. He half nodded.

"No," I said. "It couldn't have been suicide."

He didn't like that so well. His face congested with blood and the veins on his nose thickened. The girl touched the gun lying on her knee, then put her hand loosely around the butt. I saw her thumb slide very gently towards the safety catch. She didn't know much about guns, but she knew that much.

"It couldn't be suicide," I said again, very slowly. "As an isolated event—maybe. But not with all the other stuff that's been happening. Arbogast, the stick-up down on Calvello Drive outside this house, the thugs planted in my apartment, the job with the twenty-two."

I reached into my pocket again and pulled out Waxnose's Woodsman. I held it carelessly on the flat of my left hand. "And curiously enough, I don't think it was *this* twenty-two—although this happens to be the gunman's twenty-two. Yeah, I have the gunman, too. He's tied up in my apartment.

He came back to knock me off, but I talked him out of it. I'm a swell talker."

"Except that you overdo it," the girl said coolly, and lifted the gun a little.

"It's obvious who killed him, Miss Huntress," I said. "It's simply a matter of motive and opportunity. Marty Estel didn't, and didn't have it done. That would spoil his chances to get his fifty grand. Frisky Lavon's pal didn't, regardless of who he was working for, and I don't think he was working for Marty Estel. He couldn't have got into the El Milano to do the job, and certainly not into Miss Huntress's apartment. Whoever did it had something to gain by it and an opportunity to get to the place where it was done. Well, who had something to gain? Gerald had five million coming to him in two years out of a trust. He couldn't will it until he got it. So if he died, his natural heir got it. Who's his natural heir? You'd be surprised. Did you know that in the state of California and some others, but not in all, a man can by his own act become a natural heir? Just by adopting somebody who has money and no heirs!"

George moved then. His movement was once more as smooth as a ripple of water. The Smith & Wesson gleamed dully in his hand, but he didn't fire it. The small automatic in the girl's hand cracked. Blood spurted from George's brown hard hand. The Smith & Wesson dropped to the floor. He cursed. She didn't know much about guns—not very much.

"Of course!" she said grimly. "George could get into the apartment without any trouble, if Gerald was there. He would go in through the garage, a chauffeur in uniform, ride up in the elevator and knock at the door. And when Gerald opened it, George would back him in with that Smith & Wesson. But how did he know Gerald was there?"

I said: "He must have followed your taxi. We don't know where he has been all evening since he left me. He had a car with him. The cops will find out. How much was in it for you, George?"

George held his right wrist with his left hand, held it tightly, and his face was twisted, savage. He said nothing.

"George would back him in with the Smith & Wesson,"

the girl said wearily. "Then he would see my gun on the mantelpiece. That would be better. He would use that. He would back Gerald into the bedroom, away from the corridor, into the closet, and there, quietly, calmly, he would kill him and drop the gun on the floor."

"Nice people these college boys. Was it Dartmouth or Dannemora, George? George killed Arbogast, too. He killed him with a twenty-two because he knew that Frisky Lavon's brother had a twenty-two, and he knew that because he had hired Frisky and his brother to put over a big scare on Gerald—so that when he was murdered it would look as if Marty Estel had had it done. That was why I was brought out here tonight in the Jeeter car—so that the two thugs who had been warned and planted could pull their act and maybe knock me off, if I got too tough. Only George likes to kill people. He made a neat shot at Frisky. He hit him in the face. It was so good a shot I think he meant it to be a miss. How about it, George?"

Silence.

I looked at old Jeeter at last. I had been expecting him to pull a gun himself, but he hadn't. He just stood there, openmouthed, appalled, leaning against the black marble table, shaking.

"My God!" he whispered. "My God!"

"You don't have one—except money. You—"

A door squeaked behind me. I whirled, but I needn't have bothered. A hard voice, about as English as Amos and Andy, said: "Put 'em up, bud."

The butler, the very English butler, stood there in the doorway, a gun in his hand, tight-lipped. The girl turned her wrist and shot him just kind of casually, in the shoulder or something. He squealed like a stuck pig.

"Go away, you're intruding," she said coldly.

He ran. We heard his steps running.

"He's going to fall," she said.

I was wearing my Luger in my right hand now, a little late in the season, as usual. I came around with it. Old Man Jeeter was holding on to the table, his face gray as a paving block. His knees were giving. George stood cynically, holding a handkerchief around his bleeding wrist, watching him.

"Let him fall," I said. "Down is where he belongs."

He fell. His head twisted. His mouth went slack. He hit the carpet on his side and rolled a little and his knees came up. His mouth drooled a little. His skin turned violet.

"Go call the law, angel," I said. "I'll watch them now."

"All right," she said standing up. "But you certainly need a lot of help in your private-detecting business, Mr. Dalmas."

9

A shiny black bug with a pink head crawled slowly along the top of the scarred old desk. It wobbled as it crawled, like an old lady with too many parcels. At the edge it marched straight off into the air, fell on its back on the dirty brown linoleum, waved a few thin worn legs in the air and then played dead. A minute of that and it put the legs out again, struggled over on its face and trundled off, wobbling towards the corner of the room.

I had been in there for a solid hour, alone. There was the scarred desk in the middle, another against the wall, a brass spittoon on a mat, a police loudspeaker box on the wall, three squashed flies, a smell of cold cigars and old clothes. There were two hard armchairs with felt pads and two hard straight chairs without pads. The electric light fixture had been dusted about Coolidge's first term.

The door opened with a jerk and Finlayson and Sebold came in. Sebold looked as spruce and nasty as ever, but Finlayson looked older, more worn, mousier. He held a sheaf of papers in his hand. He sat down across the desk from me and gave me a hard bleak stare.

The loudspeaker on the wall put out a bulletin about a middle-aged Negro running south on San Pedro from 11th after a holdup. He was wearing a gray suit and felt hat. "Approach carefully. This suspect is armed with a thirty-two caliber revolver. That is all." (When they caught him he had an ammonia gun, brown pants, a torn blue sweater, no hat, was sixteen years old, had thirty-five cents in his pocket, and was a Mexican.)

"Guys like you get in a lot of trouble," Finlayson said sourly. Sebold sat down against the wall and tilted his hat over his eyes and yawned and looked at his new stainless-steel wrist watch.

"Trouble is my business," I said. "How else would I make a nickel?"

"We oughta throw you in the can for all this cover-up stuff. How much you making on this one?"

"I was working for Anna Halsey who was working for old man Jeeter. I guess I made a bad debt."

Sebold smiled his blackjack smile at me. Finlayson lit a cigar and licked at a tear on the side of it and pasted it down, but it leaked smoke just the same when he drew on it. He pushed papers across the desk at me.

"Sign three copies."

I signed three copies.

He took them back, yawned and rumpled his old gray head. "The old man's had a stroke," he said. "No dice there. Probably won't know what time it is when he comes out. This George Hasterman, this chauffeur guy, he just laughs at us. Too bad he got pinked. I'd like to wrastle him a bit."

"He's tough," I said.

"Yeah. O.K., you can beat it for now."

I got up and nodded to them and went to the door. "Well, good night, boys."

Neither of them spoke to me.

I went out, along the corridor and down in the night elevator to the City Hall lobby. I went out the Spring Street side and down the long flight of empty steps and the wind blew cold. I lit a cigarette at the bottom. My car was still out at the Jeeter place. I lifted a foot to start walking to a taxi half a block down across the street. A voice spoke sharply from a parked car.

"Come here a minute."

It was a man's voice, tight, hard. It was Marty Estel's voice. It came from a big sedan with two men in the front seat. I went over there. The rear window was down and Marty Estel leaned a gloved hand on it.

"Get in." He pushed the door open. I got in. I was too tired to argue. "Take it away, Skin."

The car drove west through dark, almost quiet streets, almost clean streets. The night air was not pure but it was cool. We went up over a hill and began to pick up speed.

"What they get?" Estel asked coolly.

"They didn't tell me. They didn't break the chauffeur yet."

"You can't convict a couple million bucks of murder in this man's town." The driver called Skin laughed without turning his head. "Maybe I don't even touch my fifty grand now . . . . She likes you."

"Uh-huh. So what?"

"Lay off her."

"What will it get me?"

"It's what it'll get you if you don't."

"Yeah, sure," I said. "Go to hell, will you please. I'm tired." I shut my eyes and leaned in the corner of the car and just like that went to sleep. I can do that sometimes, after a strain.

A hand shaking my shoulder woke me. The car had stopped. I looked out at the front of my apartment house.

"Home," Marty Estel said. "And remember. Lay off her."

"Why the ride home? Just to tell me that?"

"She asked me to look out for you. That's why you're loose. She likes you. I like her. See? You don't want any more trouble."

"Trouble—" I started to say, and stopped. I was tired of that gag for that night. "Thanks for the ride, and apart from that, nuts to you." I turned away and went into the apartment house and up.

The doorlock was still loose but nobody waited for me this time. They had taken Waxnose away long since. I left the door open and threw the windows up and I was still sniffing at policemen's cigar butts when the phone rang. It was her voice, cool, a little hard, not touched by anything, almost amused. Well, she'd been through enough to make her that way, probably.

"Hello, brown-eyes. Make it home all right?"

"Your pal Marty brought me home. He told me to lay off you. Thanks with all my heart, if I have any, but don't call me up any more."

"A little scared, Mr. Dalmas?"

"No. Wait for me to call you," I said. "Good night, angel."

"Good night, brown-eyes."

The phone clicked. I put it away and shut the door and pulled the bed down. I undressed and lay on it for a while in the cold air.

Then I got up and had a drink and a shower and went to sleep.

They broke George at last, but not enough. He said there had been a fight over the girl and young Jeeter had grabbed the gun off the mantel and George had fought with him and it had gone off. All of which, of course, looked possible—in the papers. They never pinned the Arbogast killing on him or on anybody. They never found the gun that did it, but it was not Waxnose's gun. Waxnose disappeared—I never heard where. They didn't touch old man Jeeter, because he never came out of his stroke, except to lie on his back and have nurses and tell people how he hadn't lost a nickel in the depression.

Marty Estel called me up four times to tell me to lay off Harriet Huntress. I felt kind of sorry for the poor guy. He had it bad. I went out with her twice and sat with her twice more at home, drinking her Scotch. It was nice, but I didn't have the money, the clothes, the time or the manners. Then she stopped being at the El Milano and I heard she had gone to New York.

I was glad when she left—even though she didn't bother to tell me good-bye.

I'll Be Waiting

AT ONE O'CLOCK in the morning, Carl, the night porter, turned down the last of three table lamps in the main lobby of the Windermere Hotel. The blue carpet darkened a shade or two and the walls drew back into remoteness. The chairs filled with shadowy loungers. In the corners were memories like cobwebs.

Tony Reseck yawned. He put his head on one side and listened to the frail, twittery music from the radio room beyond a dim arch at the far side of the lobby. He frowned. That should be his radio room after one A.M. Nobody should be in it. That red-haired girl was spoiling his nights.

The frown passed and a miniature of a smile quirked at the corners of his lips. He sat relaxed, a short, pale, paunchy, middle-aged man with long, delicate fingers clasped on the elk's tooth on his watch chain; the long delicate fingers of a sleight-of-hand artist, fingers with shiny, molded nails and tapering first joints, fingers a little spatulate at the ends. Hand some fingers. Tony Reseck rubbed them gently together and there was peace in his quiet, sea-gray eyes.

The frown came back on his face. The music annoyed him. He got up with a curious litheness, all in one piece, without moving his clasped hands from the watch chain. At one moment he was leaning back relaxed, and the next he was standing balanced on his feet, perfectly still, so that the movement of rising seemed to be a thing imperfectly perceived, an error of vision.

He walked with small, polished shoes delicately across the blue carpet and under the arch. The music was louder. It contained the hot, acid blare, the frenetic, jittering runs of a jam session. It was too loud. The red-haired girl sat there and stared silently at the fretted part of the big radio cabinet as though she could see the band with its fixed professional grin and the sweat running down its back. She was curled up with her feet under her on a davenport which seemed to contain most of the cushions in the room. She was tucked among them carefully, like a corsage in the florist's tissue paper.

She didn't turn her head. She leaned there, one hand in a small fist on her peach-colored knee. She was wearing lounging pajamas of heavy ribbed silk embroidered with black lotus buds.

"You like Goodman, Miss Cressy?" Tony Reseck asked.

The girl moved her eyes slowly. The light in there was dim, but the violet of her eyes almost hurt. They were large, deep eyes without a trace of thought in them. Her face was classical and without expression.

She said nothing.

Tony smiled and moved his fingers at his sides, one by one, feeling them move. "You like Goodman, Miss Cressy?" he repeated gently.

"Not to cry over," the girl said tonelessly.

Tony rocked back on his heels and looked at her eyes. Large, deep, empty eyes. Or were they? He reached down and muted the radio.

"Don't get me wrong," the girl said. "Goodman makes money, and a lad that makes legitimate money these days is a lad you have to respect. But this jitterbug music gives me the backdrop of a beer flat. I like something with roses in it."

"Maybe you like Mozart," Tony said.

"Go on, kid me," the girl said.

"I wasn't kidding you, Miss Cressy. I think Mozart was the greatest man that ever lived—and Toscanini is his prophet."

"I thought you were the house dick." She put her head back on a pillow and stared at him through her lashes. "Make me some of that Mozart," she added.

"It's too late," Tony sighed. "You can't get it now."

She gave him another long lucid glance. "Got the eye on me, haven't you, flatfoot?" She laughed a little, almost under her breath. "What did I do wrong?"

Tony smiled his toy smile. "Nothing, Miss Cressy. Nothing at all. But you need some fresh air. You've been five days in this hotel and you haven't been outdoors. And you have a tower room."

She laughed again. "Make me a story about it. I'm bored."

"There was a girl here once had your suite. She stayed in the hotel a whole week, like you. Without going out at all, I mean. She didn't speak to anybody hardly. What do you think she did then?"

The girl eyed him gravely. "She jumped her bill."

He put his long delicate hand out and turned it slowly, fluttering the fingers, with an effect almost like a lazy wave breaking. "Unh-uh. She sent down for her bill and paid it. Then she told the hop to be back in half an hour for her suitcases. Then she went out on her balcony."

The girl leaned forward a little, her eyes still grave, one hand capping her peach-colored knee. "What did you say your name was?"

"Tony Reseck."

"Sounds like a hunky."

"Yeah," Tony said. "Polish."

"Go on, Tony."

"All the tower suites have private balconies, Miss Cressy. The walls of them are too low, for fourteen stories above the street. It was a dark night, that night, high clouds." He dropped his hand with a final gesture, a farewell gesture. "Nobody saw her jump. But when she hit, it was like a big gun going off."

"You're making it up, Tony." Her voice was a clean dry whisper of sound.

He smiled his toy smile. His quiet sea-gray eyes seemed almost to be smoothing the long waves of her hair. "Eve Cressy," he said musingly. "A name waiting for lights to be in."

"Waiting for a tall dark guy that's no good, Tony. You wouldn't care why. I was married to him once. I might be married to him again. You can make a lot of mistakes in just one lifetime." The hand on her knee opened slowly until the fingers were strained back as far as they would go. Then they closed quickly and tightly, and even in that dim light the knuckles shone like little polished bones. "I played him a low trick once. I put him in a bad place—without meaning to. You wouldn't care about that either. It's just that I owe him something."

He leaned over softly and turned the knob on the radio. A waltz formed itself dimly on the warm air. A tinsel waltz, but a waltz. He turned the volume up. The music gushed from the loud-speaker in a swirl of shadowed melody. Since Vienna died, all waltzes are shadowed.

The girl put her head on one side and hummed three or four bars and stopped with a sudden tightening of her mouth. "Eve Cressy," she said. "It was in lights once. At a bum night club. A dive. They raided it and the lights went out."

He smiled at her almost mockingly. "It was no dive while you were there, Miss Cressy. . . . That's the waltz the orchestra always played when the old porter walked up and down in front of the hotel entrance, all swelled up with his medals on his chest. The Last Laugh. Emil Jannings. You wouldn't remember that one, Miss Cressy."

"Spring, Beautiful Spring," she said. "No, I never saw it."

He walked three steps away from her and turned. "I have to go upstairs and palm doorknobs. I hope I didn't bother you. You ought to go to bed now. It's pretty late."

The tinsel waltz stopped and a voice began to talk. The girl spoke through the voice, "You really thought something like that—about the balcony?"

He nodded. "I might have," he said softly. "I don't any more."

"No chance, Tony." Her smile was a dim lost leaf. "Come and talk to me some more. Redheads don't jump, Tony. They hang on—and wither."

He looked at her gravely for a moment and then moved away over the carpet. The porter was standing in the archway that led to the main lobby. Tony hadn't looked that way yet, but he knew somebody was there. He always knew if anybody was close to him. He could hear the grass grow, like the donkey in The Blue Bird.

The porter jerked his chin at him urgently. His broad face above the uniform collar looked sweaty and excited. Tony stepped up close to him and they went together through the arch and out to the middle of the dim lobby.

"Trouble?" Tony asked wearily.

"There's a guy outside to see you, Tony. He won't come in. I'm doing a wipe-off on the plate glass of the doors and he comes up beside me, a tall guy. 'Get Tony,' he says, out of the side of his mouth."

Tony said: "Uh-huh," and looked at the porter's pale blue eyes. "Who was it?"

"Al, he said to say he was."

Tony's face became as expressionless as dough. "Okey." He started to move off.

The porter caught his sleeve. "Listen, Tony. You got any enemies?"

Tony laughed politely, his face still like dough.

"Listen, Tony." The porter held his sleeve tightly. "There's a big black car down the block, the other way from the hacks. There's a guy standing beside it with his foot on the running board. This guy that spoke to me, he wears a dark-colored, wrap-around overcoat with a high collar turned up against his ears. His hat's way low. You can't hardly see his face. He says, 'Get Tony,' out of the side of his mouth. You ain't got any enemies, have you, Tony?"

"Only the finance company," Tony said. "Beat it."

He walked slowly and a little stiffly across the blue carpet, up the three shallow steps to the entrance lobby with the three elevators on one side and the desk on the other. Only one elevator was working. Beside the open doors, his arms folded, the night operator stood silent in a neat blue uniform with silver facings. A lean, dark Mexican named Gomez. A new boy, breaking in on the night shift.

The other side was the desk, rose marble, with the night clerk leaning on it delicately. A small neat man with a wispy reddish mustache and cheeks so rosy they looked rouged. He stared at Tony and poked a nail at his mustache.

Tony pointed a stiff index finger at him, folded the other three fingers tight to his palm, and flicked his thumb up and down on the stiff finger. The clerk touched the other side of his mustache and looked bored.

Tony went on past the closed and darkened newsstand and the side entrance to the drugstore, out to the brassbound plate-glass doors. He stopped just inside them and took a deep, hard breath. He squared his shoulders, pushed the doors open and stepped out into the cold, damp, night air.

The street was dark, silent. The rumble of traffic on Wilshire, two blocks away, had no body, no meaning. To the left were two taxis. Their drivers leaned against a fender, side by side, smoking. Tony walked the other way. The big dark car was a third of a block from the hotel entrance. Its lights were dimmed and it was only when he was almost up to it that he heard the gentle sound of its engine turning over.

A tall figure detached itself from the body of the car and strolled toward him, both hands in the pockets of the dark overcoat with the high collar. From the man's mouth a cigarette tip glowed faintly, a rusty pearl.

They stopped two feet from each other.

The tall man said: "Hi, Tony. Long time no see."

"Hello, Al. How's it going?"

"Can't complain." The tall man started to take his right hand out of his overcoat pocket, then stopped and laughed quietly. "I forgot. Guess you don't want to shake hands."

"That don't mean anything," Tony said. "Shaking hands. Monkeys can shake hands. What's on your mind, Al?"

"Still the funny little fat guy, eh, Tony?"

"I guess." Tony winked his eyes tight. His throat felt tight.

"You like your job back there?"

"It's a job."

Al laughed his quiet laugh again. "You take it slow, Tony. I'll take it fast. So it's a job and you want to hold it. Oke. There's a girl named Eve Cressy flopping in your quiet hotel. Get her out. Fast and right now."

"What's the trouble?"

The tall man looked up and down the street. A man behind in the car coughed lightly. "She's hooked with a wrong number. Nothing against her personal, but she'll lead trouble to you. Get her out, Tony. You got maybe an hour."

"Sure," Tony said aimlessly, without meaning.

Al took his hand out of his pocket and stretched it against Tony's chest. He gave him a light lazy push. "I wouldn't be telling you just for the hell of it, little fat brother. Get her out of there."

"Okey," Tony said, without any tone in his voice.

The tall man took back his hand and reached for the car door. He opened it and started to slip in like a lean black shadow.

Then he stopped and said something to the men in the car

and got out again. He came back to where Tony stood silent, his pale eyes catching a little dim light from the street.

"Listen, Tony. You always kept your nose clean. You're a good brother, Tony."

Tony didn't speak.

Al leaned toward him, a long urgent shadow, the high collar almost touching his ears. "It's trouble business, Tony. The boys won't like it, but I'm telling you just the same. This Cressy was married to a lad named Johnny Ralls. Ralls is out of Quentin two, three days, or a week. He did a three-spot for manslaughter. The girl put him there. He ran down an old man one night when he was drunk, and she was with him. He wouldn't stop. She told him to go in and tell it, or else. He didn't go in. So the Johns come for him."

Tony said, "That's too bad."

"It's kosher, kid. It's my business to know. This Ralls flapped his mouth in stir about how the girl would be waiting for him when he got out, all set to forgive and forget, and he was going straight to her."

Tony said: "What's he to you?" His voice had a dry, stiff crackle, like thick paper.

Al laughed. "The trouble boys want to see him. He ran a table at a spot on the Strip and figured out a scheme. He and another guy took the house for fifty grand. The other lad coughed up, but we still need Johnny's twenty-five. The trouble boys don't get paid to forget."

Tony looked up and down the dark street. One of the taxi drivers flicked a cigarette stub in a long arc over the top of one of the cabs. Tony watched it fall and spark on the pavement. He listened to the quiet sound of the big car's motor.

"I don't want any part of it," he said. "I'll get her out."

Al backed away from him, nodding. "Wise kid. How's mom these days?"

"Okey," Tony said.

"Tell her I was asking for her."

"Asking for her isn't anything," Tony said.

Al turned quickly and got into the car. The car curved lazily in the middle of the block and drifted back toward the corner. Its lights went up and sprayed on a wall. It turned a corner and was gone. The lingering smell of its exhaust drifted past Tony's nose. He turned and walked back to the hotel, and into it. He went along to the radio room.

The radio still muttered, but the girl was gone from the davenport in front of it. The pressed cushions were hollowed out by her body. Tony reached down and touched them. He thought they were still warm. He turned the radio off and stood there, turning a thumb slowly in front of his body, his hand flat against his stomach. Then he went back through the lobby toward the elevator bank and stood beside a majolica jar of white sand. The clerk fussed behind a pebbled-glass screen at one end of the desk. The air was dead.

The elevator bank was dark. Tony looked at the indicator of the middle car and saw that it was at 14.

"Gone to bed," he said under his breath.

The door of the porter's room beside the elevators opened and the little Mexican night operator came out in street clothes. He looked at Tony with a quiet sidewise look out of eyes the color of dried-out chestnuts.

"Good night, boss."

"Yeah," Tony said absently.

He took a thin dappled cigar out of his vest pocket and smelled it. He examined it slowly, turning it around in his neat fingers. There was a small tear along the side. He frowned at that and put the cigar away.

There was a distant sound and the hand on the indicator began to steal around the bronze dial. Light glittered up in the shaft and the straight line of the car floor dissolved the darkness below. The car stopped and the doors opened, and Carl came out of it.

His eyes caught Tony's with a kind of jump and he walked over to him, his head on one side, a thin shine along his pink upper lip.

"Listen, Tony."

Tony took his arm in a hard swift hand and turned him. He pushed him quickly, yet somehow casually, down the steps to the dim main lobby and steered him into a corner. He let go of the arm. His throat tightened again, for no reason he could think of.

"Well?" he said darkly. "Listen to what?"

The porter reached into a pocket and hauled out a dollar bill. "He gimme this," he said loosely. His glittering eyes looked past Tony's shoulder at nothing. They winked rapidly. "Ice and ginger ale."

"Don't stall," Tony growled.

"Guy in 14B," the porter said.

"Lemme smell your breath."

The porter leaned toward him obediently.

"Liquor," Tony said harshly.

"He gimme a drink."

Tony looked down at the dollar bill. "Nobody's in 14B. Not on my list," he said.

"Yeah. There is." The porter licked his lips and his eyes opened and shut several times. "Tall dark guy."

"All right," Tony said crossly. "All right. There's a tall dark guy in 14B and he gave you a buck and a drink. Then what?"

"Gat under his arm," Carl said, and blinked.

Tony smiled, but his eyes had taken on the lifeless glitter of thick ice. "You take Miss Cressy up to her room?"

Carl shook his head. "Gomez. I saw her go up."

"Get away from me," Tony said between his teeth. "And don't accept any more drinks from the guests."

He didn't move until Carl had gone back into his cubbyhole by the elevators and shut the door. Then he moved silently up the three steps and stood in front of the desk, looking at the veined rose marble, the onyx pen set, the fresh registration card in its leather frame. He lifted a hand and smacked it down hard on the marble. The clerk popped out from behind the glass screen like a chipmunk coming out of its hole.

Tony took a flimsy out of his breast pocket and spread it on the desk. "No 14B on this," he said in a bitter voice.

The clerk wisped politely at his mustache. "So sorry. You must have been out to supper when he checked in."

"Who?"

"Registered as James Watterson, San Diego." The clerk yawned.

"Ask for anybody?"

The clerk stopped in the middle of the yawn and looked at

the top of Tony's head. "Why, yes. He asked for a swing band. Why?"

"Smart, fast and funny," Tony said. "If you like 'em that way." He wrote on his flimsy and stuffed it back into his pocket. "I'm going upstairs and palm doorknobs. There's four tower rooms you ain't rented yet. Get up on your toes, son. You're slipping."

"I make out," the clerk drawled, and completed his yawn. "Hurry back, pop. I don't know how I'll get through the time."

"You could shave that pink fuzz off your lip," Tony said, and went across to the elevators.

He opened up a dark one and lit the dome light and shot the car up to fourteen. He darkened it again, stepped out and closed the doors. This lobby was smaller than any other, except the one immediately below it. It had a single blue-paneled door in each of the walls other than the elevator wall. On each door was a gold number and letter with a gold wreath around it. Tony walked over to 14A and put his ear to the panel. He heard nothing. Eve Cressy might be in bed asleep, or in the bathroom, or out on the balcony. Or she might be sitting there in the room, a few feet from the door, looking at the wall. Well, he wouldn't expect to be able to hear her sit and look at the wall. He went over to 14B and put his ear to that panel. This was different. There was a sound in there. A man coughed. It sounded somehow like a solitary cough. There were no voices. Tony pressed the small nacre button beside the door.

Steps came without hurry. A thickened voice spoke through the panel. Tony made no answer, no sound. The thickened voice repeated the question. Lightly, maliciously, Tony pressed the bell again.

Mr. James Watterson, of San Diego, should now open the door and give forth noise. He didn't. A silence fell beyond that door that was like the silence of a glacier. Once more Tony put his ear to the wood. Silence utterly.

He got out a master key on a chain and pushed it delicately into the lock of the door. He turned it, pushed the door inward three inches and withdrew the key. Then he waited.

"All right," the voice said harshly. "Come in and get it."

Tony pushed the door wide and stood there, framed against the light from the lobby. The man was tall, black-haired, angular and white-faced. He held a gun. He held it as though he knew about guns.

"Step right in," he drawled.

Tony went in through the door and pushed it shut with his shoulder. He kept his hands a little out from his sides, the clever fingers curled and slack. He smiled his quiet little smile.

"Mr. Watterson?"

"And after that what?"

"I'm the house detective here."

"It slays me."

The tall, white-faced, somehow handsome and somehow not handsome man backed slowly into the room. It was a large room with a low balcony around two sides of it. French doors opened out on the little, private, open-air balcony that each of the tower rooms had. There was a grate set for a log fire behind a paneled screen in front of a cheerful davenport. A tall misted glass stood on a hotel tray beside a deep, cozy chair. The man backed toward this and stood in front of it. The large, glistening gun drooped and pointed at the floor.

"It slays me," he said. "I'm in the dump an hour and the house copper gives me the buzz. Okey, sweetheart, look in the closet and bathroom. But she just left."

"You didn't see her yet," Tony said.

The man's bleached face filled with unexpected lines. His thickened voice edged toward a snarl. "Yeah? Who didn't I see yet?"

"A girl named Eve Cressy."

The man swallowed. He put his gun down on the table beside the tray. He let himself down into the chair backwards, stiffly, like a man with a touch of lumbago. Then he leaned forward and put his hands on his kneecaps and smiled brightly between his teeth. "So she got here, huh? I didn't ask about her yet. I'm a careful guy. I didn't ask yet."

"She's been here five days," Tony said. "Waiting for you. She hasn't left the hotel a minute."

The man's mouth worked a little. His smile had a knowing tilt to it. "I got delayed a little up north," he said smoothly.

"You know how it is. Visiting old friends. You seem to know a lot about my business, copper."

"That's right, Mr. Ralls."

The man lunged to his feet and his hand snapped at the gun. He stood leaning over, holding it on the table, staring. "Dames talk too much," he said with a muffled sound in his voice, as though he held something soft between his teeth and talked through it.

"Not dames, Mr. Ralls."

"Huh?" The gun slithered on the hard wood of the table. "Talk it up, copper. My mind reader just quit."

"Not dames. Guys. Guys with guns."

The glacier silence fell between them again. The man straightened his body slowly. His face was washed clean of expression, but his eyes were haunted. Tony leaned in front of him, a shortish plump man with a quiet, pale, friendly face and eyes as simple as forest water.

"They never run out of gas—those boys," Johnny Ralls said, and licked at his lip. "Early and late, they work. The old firm never sleeps."

"You know who they are?" Tony said softly.

"I could maybe give nine guesses. And twelve of them would be right."

"The trouble boys," Tony said, and smiled a brittle smile.

"Where is she?" Johnny Ralls asked harshly.

"Right next door to you."

The man walked to the wall and left his gun lying on the table. He stood in front of the wall, studying it. He reached up and gripped the grillwork of the balcony railing. When he dropped his hand and turned, his face had lost some of its lines. His eyes had a quieter glint. He moved back to Tony and stood over him.

"I've got a stake," he said. "Eve sent me some dough and I built it up with a touch I made up north. Case dough, what I mean. The trouble boys talk about twenty-five grand." He smiled crookedly. "Five C's I can count. I'd have a lot of fun making them believe that, I would."

"What did you do with it?" Tony asked indifferently.

"I never had it, copper. Leave that lay. I'm the only guy in the world that believes it. It was a little deal I got suckered on."

"I'll believe it," Tony said.

"They don't kill often. But they can be awful tough."

"Mugs," Tony said with a sudden bitter contempt. "Guys with guns. Just mugs."

Johnny Ralls reached for his glass and drained it empty. The ice cubes tinkled softly as he put it down. He picked his gun up, danced it on his palm, then tucked it, nose down, into an inner breast pocket. He stared at the carpet.

"How come you're telling me this, copper?"

"I thought maybe you'd give her a break."

"And if I wouldn't?"

"I kind of think you will," Tony said.

Johnny Ralls nodded quietly. "Can I get out of here?"

"You could take the service elevator to the garage. You could rent a car. I can give you a card to the garage-man."

"You're a funny little guy," Johnny Ralls said.

Tony took out a worn ostrich-skin billfold and scribbled on a printed card. Johnny Ralls read it, and stood holding it, tapping it against a thumbnail.

"I could take her with me," he said, his eyes narrow.

"You could take a ride in a basket too," Tony said. "She's been here five days, I told you. She's been spotted. A guy I know called me up and told me to get her out of here. Told me what it was all about. So I'm getting you out instead."

"They'll love that," Johnny Ralls said. "They'll send you violets."

"I'll weep about it on my day off."

Johnny Ralls turned his hand over and stared at the palm. "I could see her, anyway. Before I blow. Next door to here, you said?"

Tony turned on his heel and started for the door. He said over his shoulder, "Don't waste a lot of time, handsome. I might change my mind."

The man said, almost gently: "You might be spotting me right now, for all I know."

Tony didn't turn his head. "That's a chance you have to take."

He went on to the door and passed out of the room. He shut it carefully, silently, looked once at the door of 14A and got into his dark elevator. He rode it down to the linen-room floor and got out to remove the basket that held the service elevator open at that floor. The door slid quietly shut. He held it so that it made no noise. Down the corridor, light came from the open door of the housekeeper's office. Tony got back into his elevator and went on down to the lobby.

The little clerk was out of sight behind his pebbled-glass screen, auditing accounts. Tony went through the main lobby and turned into the radio room. The radio was on again, soft. She was there, curled on the davenport again. The speaker hummed to her, a vague sound so low that what it said was as wordless as the murmur of trees. She turned her head slowly and smiled at him.

"Finished palming doorknobs? I couldn't sleep worth a nickel. So I came down again. Okey?"

He smiled and nodded. He sat down in a green chair and patted the plump brocade arms of it. "Sure, Miss Cressy."

"Waiting is the hardest kind of work, isn't it? I wish you'd talk to that radio. It sounds like a pretzel being bent."

Tony fiddled with it, got nothing he liked, set it back where it had been.

"Beer-parlor drunks are all the customers now."

She smiled at him again.

"I don't bother you being here, Miss Cressy?"

"I like it. You're a sweet little guy, Tony."

He looked stiffly at the floor and a ripple touched his spine. He waited for it to go away. It went slowly. Then he sat back, relaxed again, his neat fingers clasped on his elk's tooth. He listened. Not to the radio—to far-off, uncertain things, menacing things. And perhaps to just the safe whir of wheels going away into a strange night.

"Nobody's all bad," he said out loud.

The girl looked at him lazily. "I've met two or three I was wrong on, then."

He nodded. "Yeah," he admitted judiciously. "I guess there's some that are."

The girl yawned and her deep violet eyes half closed. She

nestled back into the cushions. "Sit there a while, Tony. Maybe I could nap."

"Sure. Not a thing for me to do. Don't know why they pay me."

She slept quickly and with complete stillness, like a child. Tony hardly breathed for ten minutes. He just watched her, his mouth a little open. There was a quiet fascination in his limpid eyes, as if he was looking at an altar.

Then he stood up with infinite care and padded away under the arch to the entrance lobby and the desk. He stood at the desk listening for a little while. He heard a pen rustling out of sight. He went around the corner to the row of house phones in little glass cubbyholes. He lifted one and asked the night operator for the garage.

It rang three or four times and then a boyish voice answered: "Windermere Hotel. Garage speaking."

"This is Tony Reseck. That guy Watterson I gave a card to. He leave?"

"Sure, Tony. Half an hour almost. Is it your charge?"

"Yeah," Tony said. "My party. Thanks. Be seein' you."

He hung up and scratched his neck. He went back to the desk and slapped a hand on it. The clerk wafted himself around the screen with his greeter's smile in place. It dropped when he saw Tony.

"Can't a guy catch up on his work?" he grumbled.

"What's the professional rate on 14B?"

The clerk stared morosely. "There's no professional rate in the tower."

"Make one. The fellow left already. Was there only an hour."

"Well, well," the clerk said airily. "So the personality didn't click tonight. We get a skip-out."

"Will five bucks satisfy you?"

"Friend of yours?"

"No. Just a drunk with delusions of grandeur and no dough."

"Guess we'll have to let it ride, Tony. How did he get out?"

"I took him down the service elevator. You was asleep. Will five bucks satisfy you?"

"Why?"

The worn ostrich-skin wallet came out and a weedy five slipped across the marble. "All I could shake him for," Tony said loosely.

The clerk took the five and looked puzzled. "You're the boss," he said, and shrugged. The phone shrilled on the desk and he reached for it. He listened and then pushed it toward Tony. "For you."

Tony took the phone and cuddled it close to his chest. He put his mouth close to the transmitter. The voice was strange to him. It had a metallic sound. Its syllables were meticulously anonymous.

"Tony? Tony Reseck?"

"Talking."

"A message from Al. Shoot?"

Tony looked at the clerk. "Be a pal," he said over the mouthpiece. The clerk flicked a narrow smile at him and went away. "Shoot," Tony said into the phone.

"We had a little business with a guy in your place. Picked him up scramming. Al had a hunch you'd run him out. Tailed him and took him to the curb. Not so good. Backfire."

Tony held the phone very tight and his temples chilled with the evaporation of moisture. "Go on," he said. "I guess there's more."

"A little. The guy stopped the big one. Cold. Al—Al said to tell you good-by."

Tony leaned hard against the desk. His mouth made a sound that was not speech.

"Get it?" The metallic voice sounded impatient, a little bored. "This guy had him a rod. He used it. Al won't be phoning anybody any more."

Tony lurched at the phone, and the base of it shook on the rose marble. His mouth was a hard dry knot.

The voice said: "That's as far as we go, bud. G'night." The phone clicked dryly, like a pebble hitting a wall.

Tony put the phone down in its cradle very carefully, so as not to make any sound. He looked at the clenched palm of his left hand. He took a handkerchief out and rubbed the palm softly and straightened the fingers out with his other hand. Then he wiped his forehead. The clerk came around the screen again and looked at him with glinting eyes.

"I'm off Friday. How about lending me that phone number?"

Tony nodded at the clerk and smiled a minute frail smile. He put his handkerchief away and patted the pocket he had put it in. He turned and walked away from the desk, across the entrance lobby, down the three shallow steps, along the shadowy reaches of the main lobby, and so in through the arch to the radio room once more. He walked softly, like a man moving in a room where somebody is very sick. He reached the chair he had sat in before and lowered himself into it inch by inch. The girl slept on, motionless, in that curled-up looseness achieved by some women and all cats. Her breath made no slightest sound against the vague murmur of the radio.

Tony Reseck leaned back in the chair and clasped his hands on his elk's tooth and quietly closed his eyes.

THE BIG SLEEP

I<small>T WAS</small> about eleven o'clock in the morning, mid October, with the sun not shining and a look of hard wet rain in the clearness of the foothills. I was wearing my powder-blue suit, with dark blue shirt, tie and display handkerchief, black brogues, black wool socks with dark blue clocks on them. I was neat, clean, shaved and sober, and I didn't care who knew it. I was everything the well-dressed private detective ought to be. I was calling on four million dollars.

The main hallway of the Sternwood place was two stories high. Over the entrance doors, which would have let in a troop of Indian elephants, there was a broad stained-glass panel showing a knight in dark armor rescuing a lady who was tied to a tree and didn't have any clothes on but some very long and convenient hair. The knight had pushed the vizor of his helmet back to be sociable, and he was fiddling with the knots on the ropes that tied the lady to the tree and not getting anywhere. I stood there and thought that if I lived in the house, I would sooner or later have to climb up there and help him. He didn't seem to be really trying.

There were French doors at the back of the hall, beyond them a wide sweep of emerald grass to a white garage, in front of which a slim dark young chauffeur in shiny black leggings was dusting a maroon Packard convertible. Beyond the garage were some decorative trees trimmed as carefully as poodle dogs. Beyond them a large greenhouse with a domed roof. Then more trees and beyond everything the solid, uneven, comfortable line of the foothills.

On the east side of the hall a free staircase, tile-paved, rose to a gallery with a wrought-iron railing and another piece of stained-glass romance. Large hard chairs with rounded red plush seats were backed into the vacant spaces of the wall round about. They didn't look as if anybody had ever sat in them. In the middle of the west wall there was a big empty fireplace with a brass screen in four hinged panels, and over the fireplace a marble mantel with cupids at the corners. Above the mantel there was a large oil portrait, and above the portrait two bullet-torn or moth-eaten cavalry pennants crossed in a glass frame. The portrait was a stiffly posed job of an officer in full regimentals of about the time of the Mexican war. The officer had a neat black imperial, black mustachios, hot hard coal-black eyes, and the general look of a man it would pay to get along with. I thought this might be General Sternwood's grandfather. It could hardly be the General himself, even though I had heard he was pretty far gone in years to have a couple of daughters still in the dangerous twenties.

I was still staring at the hot black eyes when a door opened far back under the stairs. It wasn't the butler coming back. It was a girl.

She was twenty or so, small and delicately put together, but she looked durable. She wore pale blue slacks and they looked well on her. She walked as if she were floating. Her hair was a fine tawny wave cut much shorter than the current fashion of pageboy tresses curled in at the bottom. Her eyes were slate-gray, and had almost no expression when they looked at me. She came over near me and smiled with her mouth and she had little sharp predatory teeth, as white as fresh orange pith and as shiny as porcelain. They glistened between her thin too taut lips. Her face lacked color and didn't look too healthy.

"Tall, aren't you?" she said.

"I didn't mean to be."

Her eyes rounded. She was puzzled. She was thinking. I could see, even on that short acquaintance, that thinking was always going to be a bother to her.

"Handsome too," she said. "And I bet you know it."

I grunted.

"What's your name?"

"Reilly," I said. "Doghouse Reilly."

"That's a funny name." She bit her lip and turned her head a little and looked at me along her eyes. Then she lowered her lashes until they almost cuddled her cheeks and slowly raised them again, like a theater curtain. I was to get to know that trick. That was supposed to make me roll over on my back with all four paws in the air.

"Are you a prizefighter?" she asked, when I didn't.

"Not exactly. I'm a sleuth."

"A—a—" She tossed her head angrily, and the rich color

of it glistened in the rather dim light of the big hall. "You're making fun of me."

"Uh-uh."

"What?"

"Get on with you," I said. "You heard me."

"You didn't say anything. You're just a big tease." She put a thumb up and bit it. It was a curiously shaped thumb, thin and narrow like an extra finger, with no curve in the first joint. She bit it and sucked it slowly, turning it around in her mouth like a baby with a comforter.

"You're awfully tall," she said. Then she giggled with secret merriment. Then she turned her body slowly and lithely, without lifting her feet. Her hands dropped limp at her sides. She tilted herself towards me on her toes. She fell straight back into my arms. I had to catch her or let her crack her head on the tessellated floor. I caught her under her arms and she went rubber legged on me instantly. I had to hold her close to hold her up. When her head was against my chest she screwed it around and giggled at me.

"You're cute," she giggled. "I'm cute too."

I didn't say anything. So the butler chose that convenient moment to come back through the French doors and see me holding her.

It didn't seem to bother him. He was a tall, thin, silver man, sixty or close to it or a little past it. He had blue eyes as remote as eyes could be. His skin was smooth and bright and he moved like a man with very sound muscles. He walked slowly across the floor towards us and the girl jerked away from me. She flashed across the room to the foot of the stairs and went up them like a deer. She was gone before I could draw a long breath and let it out.

The butler said tonelessly: "The General will see you now, Mr. Marlowe."

I pushed my lower jaw up off my chest and nodded at him. "Who was that?"

"Miss Carmen Sternwood, sir."

"You ought to wean her. She looks old enough."

He looked at me with grave politeness and repeated what he had said.

2

We went out at the French doors and along a smooth red-flagged path that skirted the far side of the lawn from the garage. The boyish-looking chauffeur had a big black and chromium sedan out now and was dusting that. The path took us along to the side of the greenhouse and the butler opened a door for me and stood aside. It opened into a sort of vestibule that was about as warm as a slow oven. He came in after me, shut the outer door, opened an inner door and we went through that. Then it was really hot. The air was thick, wet, steamy and larded with the cloying smell of tropical orchids in bloom. The glass walls and roof were heavily misted and big drops of moisture splashed down on the plants. The light had an unreal greenish color, like light filtered through an aquarium tank. The plants filled the place, a forest of them, with nasty meaty leaves and stalks like the newly washed fingers of dead men. They smelled as overpowering as boiling alcohol under a blanket.

The butler did his best to get me through without being smacked in the face by the sodden leaves, and after a while we came to a clearing in the middle of the jungle, under the domed roof. Here, in a space of hexagonal flags, an old red Turkish rug was laid down and on the rug was a wheel chair, and in the wheel chair an old and obviously dying man watched us come with black eyes from which all fire had died long ago, but which still had the coal-black directness of the eyes in the portrait that hung above the mantel in the hall. The rest of his face was a leaden mask, with the bloodless lips and the sharp nose and the sunken temples and the outward-turning earlobes of approaching dissolution. His long narrow body was wrapped—in that heat—in a traveling rug and a faded red bathrobe. His thin clawlike hands were folded loosely on the rug, purple-nailed. A few locks of dry white hair clung to his scalp, like wild flowers fighting for life on a bare rock.

The butler stood in front of him and said: "This is Mr. Marlowe, General."

The old man didn't move or speak, or even nod. He just

looked at me lifelessly. The butler pushed a damp wicker chair against the backs of my legs and I sat down. He took my hat with a deft scoop.

Then the old man dragged his voice up from the bottom of a well and said: "Brandy, Norris. How do you like your brandy, sir?"

"Any way at all," I said.

The butler went away among the abominable plants. The General spoke again, slowly, using his strength as carefully as an out-of-work showgirl uses her last good pair of stockings.

"I used to like mine with champagne. The champagne as cold as Valley Forge and about a third of a glass of brandy beneath it. You may take your coat off, sir. It's too hot in here for a man with blood in his veins."

I stood up and peeled off my coat and got a handkerchief out and mopped my face and neck and the backs of my wrists. St. Louis in August had nothing on that place. I sat down again and felt automatically for a cigarette and then stopped. The old man caught the gesture and smiled faintly.

"You may smoke, sir. I like the smell of tobacco."

I lit the cigarette and blew a lungful at him and he sniffed at it like a terrier at a rathole. The faint smile pulled at the shadowed corners of his mouth.

"A nice state of affairs when a man has to indulge his vices by proxy," he said dryly. "You are looking at a very dull survival of a rather gaudy life, a cripple paralyzed in both legs and with only half of his lower belly. There's very little that I can eat and my sleep is so close to waking that it is hardly worth the name. I seem to exist largely on heat, like a newborn spider, and the orchids are an excuse for the heat. Do you like orchids?"

"Not particularly," I said.

The General half-closed his eyes. "They are nasty things. Their flesh is too much like the flesh of men. And their perfume has the rotten sweetness of a prostitute."

I stared at him with my mouth open. The soft wet heat was like a pall around us. The old man nodded, as if his neck was afraid of the weight of his head. Then the butler came pushing back through the jungle with a teawagon, mixed me a brandy and soda, swathed the copper ice bucket with a damp napkin, and went away softly among the orchids. A door opened and shut behind the jungle.

I sipped the drink. The old man licked his lips watching me, over and over again, drawing one lip slowly across the other with a funereal absorption, like an undertaker dry-washing his hands.

"Tell me about yourself, Mr. Marlowe. I suppose I have a right to ask?"

"Sure, but there's very little to tell. I'm thirty-three years old, went to college once and can still speak English if there's any demand for it. There isn't much in my trade. I worked for Mr. Wilde, the District Attorney, as an investigator once. His chief investigator, a man named Bernie Ohls, called me and told me you wanted to see me. I'm unmarried because I don't like policemen's wives."

"And a little bit of a cynic," the old man smiled. "You didn't like working for Wilde?"

"I was fired. For insubordination. I test very high on insubordination, General."

"I always did myself, sir. I'm glad to hear it. What do you know about my family?"

"I'm told you are a widower and have two young daughters, both pretty and both wild. One of them has been married three times, the last time to an ex-bootlegger who went in the trade by the name of Rusty Regan. That's all I heard, General."

"Did any of it strike you as peculiar?"

"The Rusty Regan part, maybe. But I always got along with bootleggers myself."

He smiled his faint economical smile. "It seems I do too. I'm very fond of Rusty. A big curly-headed Irishman from Clonmel, with sad eyes and a smile as wide as Wilshire Boulevard. The first time I saw him I thought he might be what you are probably thinking he was, an adventurer who happened to get himself wrapped up in some velvet."

"You must have liked him," I said. "You learned to talk the language."

He put his thin bloodless hands under the edge of the rug. I put my cigarette stub out and finished my drink.

"He was the breath of life to me—while he lasted. He

spent hours with me, sweating like a pig, drinking brandy by the quart and telling me stories of the Irish revolution. He had been an officer in the I.R.A. He wasn't even legally in the United States. It was a ridiculous marriage of course, and it probably didn't last a month, as a marriage. I'm telling you the family secrets, Mr. Marlowe."

"They're still secrets," I said. "What happened to him?"

The old man looked at me woodenly. "He went away, a month ago. Abruptly, without a word to anyone. Without saying good-by to me. That hurt a little, but he had been raised in a rough school. I'll hear from him one of these days. Meantime I am being blackmailed again."

I said: "Again?"

He brought his hands from under the rug with a brown envelope in them. "I should have been very sorry for anybody who tried to blackmail me while Rusty was around. A few months before he came—that is to say about nine or ten months ago—I paid a man named Joe Brody five thousand dollars to let my younger daughter Carmen alone."

"Ah," I said.

He moved his thin white eyebrows. "That means what?"

"Nothing," I said.

He went on staring at me, half frowning. Then he said: "Take this envelope and examine it. And help yourself to the brandy."

I took the envelope off his knees and sat down with it again. I wiped off the palms of my hands and turned it around. It was addressed to General Guy Sternwood, 3765 Alta Brea Crescent, West Hollywood, California. The address was in ink, in the slanted printing engineers use. The envelope was slit. I opened it up and took out a brown card and three slips of stiff paper. The card was of thin brown linen, printed in gold: "Mr. Arthur Gwynn Geiger." No address. Very small in the lower left-hand corner: "Rare Books and De Luxe Editions." I turned the card over. More of the slanted printing on the back. "Dear Sir: In spite of the legal uncollectibility of the enclosed, which frankly represent gambling debts, I assume you might wish them honored. Respectfully, A. G. Geiger."

I looked at the slips of stiffish white paper. They were

promissory notes filled out in ink, dated on several dates early in the month before, September. "On Demand I promise to pay to Arthur Gwynn Geiger or Order the sum of One Thousand Dollars ($1000.00) without interest. Value Received. Carmen Sternwood."

The written part was in a sprawling moronic handwriting with a lot of fat curlicues and circles for dots. I mixed myself another drink and sipped it and put the exhibit aside.

"Your conclusions?" the General asked.

"I haven't any yet. Who is this Arthur Gwynn Geiger?"

"I haven't the faintest idea."

"What does Carmen say?"

"I haven't asked her. I don't intend to. If I did, she would suck her thumb and look coy."

I said: "I met her in the hall. She did that to me. Then she tried to sit in my lap."

Nothing changed in his expression. His clasped hands rested peacefully on the edge of the rug, and the heat, which made me feel like a New England boiled dinner, didn't seem to make him even warm.

"Do I have to be polite?" I asked. "Or can I just be natural?"

"I haven't noticed that you suffer from many inhibitions, Mr. Marlowe."

"Do the two girls run around together?"

"I think not. I think they go their separate and slightly divergent roads to perdition. Vivian is spoiled, exacting, smart and quite ruthless. Carmen is a child who likes to pull wings off flies. Neither of them has any more moral sense than a cat. Neither have I. No Sternwood ever had. Proceed."

"They're well educated, I suppose. They know what they're doing."

"Vivian went to good schools of the snob type and to college. Carmen went to half a dozen schools of greater and greater liberality, and ended up where she started. I presume they both had, and still have, all the usual vices. If I sound a little sinister as a parent, Mr. Marlowe, it is because my hold on life is too slight to include any Victorian hypocrisy." He leaned his head back and closed his eyes, then opened them again suddenly. "I need not add that a man who indulges in parenthood for the first time at the age of fifty-four deserves all he gets."

I sipped my drink and nodded. The pulse in his lean gray throat throbbed visibly and yet so slowly that it was hardly a pulse at all. An old man two thirds dead and still determined to believe he could take it.

"Your conclusions?" he snapped suddenly.

"I'd pay him."

"Why?"

"It's a question of a little money against a lot of annoyance. There has to be something behind it. But nobody's going to break your heart, if it hasn't been done already. And it would take an awful lot of chiselers an awful lot of time to rob you of enough so that you'd even notice it."

"I have pride, sir," he said coldly.

"Somebody's counting on that. It's the easiest way to fool them. That or the police. Geiger can collect on these notes, unless you can show fraud. Instead of that he makes you a present of them and admits they are gambling debts, which gives you a defense, even if he had kept the notes. If he's a crook, he knows his onions, and if he's an honest man doing a little loan business on the side, he ought to have his money. Who was this Joe Brody you paid the five thousand dollars to?"

"Some kind of gambler. I hardly recall. Norris would know. My butler."

"Your daughters have money in their own right, General?"

"Vivian has, but not a great deal. Carmen is still a minor under her mother's will. I give them both generous allowances."

I said: "I can take this Geiger off your back, General, if that's what you want. Whoever he is and whatever he has. It may cost you a little money, besides what you pay me. And of course it won't get you anything. Sugaring them never does. You're already listed on their book of nice names."

"I see." He shrugged his wide sharp shoulders in the faded red bathrobe. "A moment ago you said pay him. Now you say it won't get me anything."

"I mean it might be cheaper and easier to stand for a certain amount of squeeze. That's all."

"I'm afraid I'm rather an impatient man, Mr. Marlowe. What are your charges?"

"I get twenty-five a day and expenses—when I'm lucky."

"I see. It seems reasonable enough for removing morbid growths from people's backs. Quite a delicate operation. You realize that, I hope. You'll make your operation as little of a shock to the patient as possible? There might be several of them, Mr. Marlowe."

I finished my second drink and wiped my lips and my face. The heat didn't get any less hot with the brandy in me. The General blinked at me and plucked at the edge of his rug.

"Can I make deal with this guy, if I think he's within hooting distance of being on the level?"

"Yes. The matter is now in your hands. I never do things by halves."

"I'll take him out," I said. "He'll think a bridge fell on him."

"I'm sure you will. And now I must excuse myself. I am tired." He reached out and touched the bell on the arm of his chair. The cord was plugged into a black cable that wound along the side of the deep dark green boxes in which the orchids grew and festered. He closed his eyes, opened them again in a brief bright stare, and settled back among his cushions. The lids dropped again and he didn't pay any more attention to me.

I stood up and lifted my coat off the back of the damp wicker chair and went off with it among the orchids, opened the two doors and stood outside in the brisk October air getting myself some oxygen. The chauffeur over by the garage had gone away. The butler came along the red path with smooth light steps and his back as straight as an ironing board. I shrugged into my coat and watched him come.

He stopped about two feet from me and said gravely: "Mrs. Regan would like to see you before you leave, sir. And in the matter of money the General has instructed me to give you a check for whatever seems desirable."

"Instructed you how?"

He looked puzzled, then he smiled. "Ah, I see, sir. You are, of course, a detective. By the way he rang his bell."

"You write his checks?"

"I have that privilege."

"That ought to save you from a pauper's grave. No money now, thanks. What does Mrs. Regan want to see me about?"

His blue eyes gave me a smooth level look. "She has a misconception of the purpose of your visit, sir."

"Who told her anything about my visit?"

"Her windows command the greenhouse. She saw us go in. I was obliged to tell her who you were."

"I don't like that," I said.

His blue eyes frosted. "Are you attempting to tell me my duties, sir?"

"No. But I'm having a lot of fun trying to guess what they are."

We stared at each other for a moment. He gave me a blue glare and turned away.

3

This room was too big, the ceiling was too high, the doors were too tall, and the white carpet that went from wall to wall looked like a fresh fall of snow at Lake Arrowhead. There were full-length mirrors and crystal doodads all over the place. The ivory furniture had chromium on it, and the enormous ivory drapes lay tumbled on the white carpet a yard from the windows. The white made the ivory look dirty and the ivory made the white look bled out. The windows stared towards the darkening foothills. It was going to rain soon. There was pressure in the air already.

I sat down on the edge of a deep soft chair and looked at Mrs. Regan. She was worth a stare. She was trouble. She was stretched out on a modernistic chaise-longue with her slippers off, so I stared at her legs in the sheerest silk stockings. They seemed to be arranged to stare at. They were visible to the knee and one of them well beyond. The knees were dimpled, not bony and sharp. The calves were beautiful, the ankles long and slim and with enough melodic line for a tone poem. She was tall and rangy and strong-looking. Her head was against an ivory satin cushion. Her hair was black and wiry and parted in the middle and she had the hot black eyes of the portrait in the hall. She had a good mouth and a good chin. There was a sulky droop to her lips and the lower lip was full.

She had a drink. She took a swallow from it and gave me a cool level stare over the rim of the glass.

"So you're a private detective," she said. "I didn't know they really existed, except in books. Or else they were greasy little men snooping around hotels."

There was nothing in that for me, so I let it drift with the current. She put her glass down on the flat arm of the chaise-longue and flashed an emerald and touched her hair. She said slowly: "How did you like Dad?"

"I liked him," I said.

"He liked Rusty. I suppose you know who Rusty is?"

"Uh-huh."

"Rusty was earthy and vulgar at times, but he was very real. And he was a lot of fun for Dad. Rusty shouldn't have gone off like that. Dad feels very badly about it, although he won't say so. Or did he?"

"He said something about it."

"You're not much of a gusher, are you, Mr. Marlowe? But he wants to find him, doesn't he?"

I stared at her politely through a pause. "Yes and no," I said.

"That's hardly an answer. Do you think you can find him?"

"I didn't say I was going to try. Why not try the Missing Persons Bureau? They have the organization. It's not a one-man job."

"Oh, Dad wouldn't hear of the police being brought into it." She looked at me smoothly across her glass again, emptied it, and rang a bell. A maid came into the room by a side door. She was a middle-aged woman with a long yellow gentle face, a long nose, no chin, large wet eyes. She looked like a nice old horse that had been turned out to pasture after long service. Mrs. Regan waved the empty glass at her and she mixed another drink and handed it to her and left the room, without a word, without a glance in my direction.

When the door shut Mrs. Regan said: "Well, how will you go about it then?"

"How and when did he skip out?"

"Didn't Dad tell you?"

I grinned at her with my head on one side. She flushed. Her hot black eyes looked mad. "I don't see what there is to be cagey about," she snapped. "And I don't like your manners."

"I'm not crazy about yours," I said. "I didn't ask to see you. You sent for me. I don't mind your ritzing me or drinking your lunch out of a Scotch bottle. I don't mind your showing me your legs. They're very swell legs and it's a pleasure to make their acquaintance. I don't mind if you don't like my manners. They're pretty bad. I grieve over them during the long winter evenings. But don't waste your time trying to cross-examine me."

She slammed her glass down so hard that it slopped over on an ivory cushion. She swung her legs to the floor and stood up with her eyes sparking fire and her nostrils wide. Her mouth was open and her bright teeth glared at me. Her knuckles were white.

"People don't talk like that to me," she said thickly.

I sat there and grinned at her. Very slowly she closed her mouth and looked down at the spilled liquor. She sat down on the edge of the chaise-longue and cupped her chin in one hand.

"My God, you big dark handsome brute! I ought to throw a Buick at you."

I snicked a match on my thumbnail and for once it lit. I puffed smoke into the air and waited.

"I loathe masterful men," she said. "I simply loathe them."

"Just what is it you're afraid of, Mrs. Regan?"

Her eyes whitened. Then they darkened until they seemed to be all pupil. Her nostrils looked pinched.

"That wasn't what he wanted with you at all," she said in a strained voice that still had shreds of anger clinging to it. "About Rusty. Was it?"

"Better ask him."

She flared up again. "Get out! Damn you, get out!"

I stood up. "Sit down!" she snapped. I sat down. I flicked a finger at my palm and waited.

"Please," she said. "Please. You could find Rusty—if Dad wanted you to."

That didn't work either. I nodded and asked: "When did he go?"

"One afternoon a month back. He just drove away in his car without saying a word. They found the car in a private garage somewhere."

"They?"

She got cunning. Her whole body seemed to go lax. Then she smiled at me winningly. "He didn't tell you then." Her voice was almost gleeful, as if she had outsmarted me. Maybe she had.

"He told me about Mr. Regan, yes. That's not what he wanted to see me about. Is that what you've been trying to get me to say?"

"I'm sure I don't care what you say."

I stood up again. "Then I'll be running along." She didn't speak. I went over to the tall white door I had come in at. When I looked back she had her lip between her teeth and was worrying it like a puppy at the fringe of a rug.

I went out, down the tile staircase to the hall, and the butler drifted out of somewhere with my hat in his hand. I put it on while he opened the door for me.

"You made a mistake," I said. "Mrs. Regan didn't want to see me."

He inclined his silver head and said politely: "I'm sorry, sir. I make many mistakes." He closed the door against my back.

I stood on the step breathing my cigarette smoke and looking down a succession of terraces with flowerbeds and trimmed trees to the high iron fence with gilt spears that hemmed in the estate. A winding driveway dropped down between retaining walls to the open iron gates. Beyond the fence the hill sloped for several miles. On this lower level faint and far off I could just barely see some of the old wooden derricks of the oilfield from which the Sternwoods had made their money. Most of the field was public park now, cleaned up and donated to the city by General Sternwood. But a little of it was still producing in groups of wells pumping five or six barrels a day. The Sternwoods, having moved up the hill, could no longer smell the stale sump water or the oil, but they could still look out of their front windows and see what had made them rich. If they wanted to. I didn't suppose they would want to.

I walked down a brick path from terrace to terrace, followed along inside the fence and so out of the gates to where I had left my car under a pepper tree on the street. Thunder was crackling in the foothills now and the sky above them was purple-black. It was going to rain hard. The air had the damp foretaste of rain. I put the top up on my convertible before I started downtown.

She had lovely legs. I would say that for her. They were a couple of pretty smooth citizens, she and her father. He was probably just trying me out; the job he had given me was a lawyer's job. Even if Mr. Arthur Gwynn Geiger, *Rare Books and De Luxe Editions*, turned out to be a blackmailer, it was still a lawyer's job. Unless there was a lot more to it than met the eye. At a casual glance I thought I might have a lot of fun finding out.

I drove down to the Hollywood public library and did a little superficial research in a stuffy volume called Famous First Editions. Half an hour of it made me need my lunch.

4

A. G. Geiger's place was a store frontage on the north side of the boulevard near Las Palmas. The entrance door was set far back in the middle and there was a copper trim on the windows, which were backed with Chinese screens, so I couldn't see into the store. There was a lot of oriental junk in the windows. I didn't know whether it was any good, not being a collector of antiques, except unpaid bills. The entrance door was plate glass, but I couldn't see much through that either, because the store was very dim. A building entrance adjoined it on one side and on the other was a glittering credit jewelry establishment. The jeweler stood in his entrance, teetering on his heels and looking bored, a tall handsome white-haired Jew in lean dark clothes, with about nine carats of diamond on his right hand. A faint knowing smile curved his lips when I turned into Geiger's store. I let the door close softly behind me and walked on a thick blue rug that paved the floor from wall to wall. There were blue leather easy chairs with smoke stands beside them. A few sets of tooled leather bindings were set out on narrow polished tables, between book ends. There were more tooled bindings in glass cases on the walls. Nice-looking merchandise, the kind a rich promoter would buy by the yard and have somebody paste his bookplate in. At the back there was a grained wood partition with a door in the middle of it, shut. In the corner made by the partition and one wall a woman sat behind a small desk with a carved wooden lantern on it.

She got up slowly and swayed towards me in a tight black dress that didn't reflect any light. She had long thighs and she walked with a certain something I hadn't often seen in bookstores. She was an ash blonde with greenish eyes, beaded lashes, hair waved smoothly back from ears in which large jet buttons glittered. Her fingernails were silvered. In spite of her get-up she looked as if she would have a hall bedroom accent.

She approached me with enough sex appeal to stampede a business men's lunch and tilted her head to finger a stray, but not very stray, tendril of softly glowing hair. Her smile was tentative, but could be persuaded to be nice.

"Was it something?" she enquired.

I had my horn-rimmed sunglasses on. I put my voice high and let a bird twitter in it. "Would you happen to have a Ben Hur 1860?"

She didn't say: "Huh?" but she wanted to. She smiled bleakly. "A first edition?"

"Third," I said. "The one with the erratum on page 116."

"I'm afraid not—at the moment."

"How about a Chevalier Audubon 1840—the full set, of course?"

"Er—not at the moment," she purred harshly. Her smile was now hanging by its teeth and eyebrows and wondering what it would hit when it dropped.

"You *do* sell books?" I said in my polite falsetto.

She looked me over. No smile now. Eyes medium to hard.

Pose very straight and stiff. She waved silver fingernails at the glassed-in shelves. "What do they look like—grapefruit?" she enquired tartly.

"Oh, that sort of thing hardly interests me, you know. Probably has duplicate sets of steel engravings, tuppence colored and a penny plain. The usual vulgarity. No. I'm sorry. No."

"I see." She tried to jack the smile back up on her face. She was as sore as an alderman with the mumps. "Perhaps Mr. Geiger—but he's not in at the moment." Her eyes studied me carefully. She knew as much about rare books as I knew about handling a flea circus.

"He might be in later?"

"I'm afraid not until late."

"Too bad," I said. "Ah, too bad. I'll sit down and smoke a cigarette in one of these charming chairs. I have rather a blank afternoon. Nothing to think about but my trigonometry lesson."

"Yes," she said. "Ye-es, of course."

I stretched out in one and lit a cigarette with the round nickel lighter on the smoking stand. She still stood, holding her lower lip with her teeth, her eyes vaguely troubled. She nodded at last, turned slowly and walked back to her little desk in the corner. From behind the lamp she stared at me. I crossed my ankles and yawned. Her silver nails went out to the cradle phone on the desk, didn't touch it, dropped and began to tap on the desk.

Silence for about five minutes. The door opened and a tall hungry-looking bird with a cane and a big nose came in neatly, shut the door behind him against the pressure of the door closer, marched over to the corner and placed a wrapped parcel on the desk. He took a pin-seal wallet with gold corners from his pocket and showed the blonde something. She pressed a button on the desk. The tall bird went to the door in the paneled partition and opened it barely enough to slip through.

I finished my cigarette and lit another. The minutes dragged by. Horns tooted and grunted on the boulevard. A big red interurban car grumbled past. A traffic light gonged. The blonde leaned on her elbow and cupped a hand over her eyes and stared at me behind it. The partition door opened and the tall bird with the cane slid out. He had another wrapped parcel, the shape of a large book. He went over to the desk and paid money. He left as he had come, walking on the balls of his feet, breathing with his mouth open, giving me a sharp side glance as he passed.

I got to my feet, tipped my hat to the blonde and went out after him. He walked west, swinging his cane in a small tight arc just above his right shoe. He was easy to follow. His coat was cut from a rather loud piece of horse robe with shoulders so wide that his neck stuck up out of it like a celery stalk and his head wobbled on it as he walked. We went a block and a half. At the Highland Avenue traffic signal I pulled up beside him and let him see me. He gave me a casual, then a suddenly sharpened side glance, and quickly turned away. We crossed Highland with the green light and made another block. He stretched his long legs and had twenty yards on me at the corner. He turned right. A hundred feet up the hill he stopped and hooked his cane over his arm and fumbled a leather cigarette case out of an inner pocket. He put a cigarette in his mouth, dropped his match, looked back when he picked it up, saw me watching him from the corner, and straightened up as if somebody had booted him from behind. He almost raised dust going up the block, walking with long gawky strides and jabbing his cane into the sidewalk. He turned left again. He had at least half a block on me when I reached the place where he had turned. He had me wheezing. This was a narrow tree-lined street with a retaining wall on one side and three bungalow courts on the other.

He was gone. I loafed along the block peering this way and that. At the second bungalow court I saw something. It was called "The La Baba," a quiet dim place with a double row of tree-shaded bungalows. The central walk was lined with Italian cypresses trimmed short and chunky, something the shape of the oil jars in Ali Baba and the Forty Thieves. Behind the third jar a loud-patterned sleeve edge moved.

I leaned against a pepper tree in the parkway and waited. The thunder in the foothills was rumbling again. The glare of lightning was reflected on piled-up black clouds off to the south. A few tentative raindrops splashed down on the sidewalk and made spots as large as nickels. The air was as still as the air in General Sternwood's orchid house.

The sleeve behind the tree showed again, then a big nose and one eye and some sandy hair without a hat on it. The eye stared at me. It disappeared. Its mate reappeared like a woodpecker on the other side of the tree. Five minutes went by. It got him. His type are half nerves. I heard a match strike and then whistling started. Then a dim shadow slipped along the grass to the next tree. Then he was out on the walk coming straight towards me, swinging the cane and whistling. A sour whistle with jitters in it. I stared vaguely up at the dark sky. He passed within ten feet of me and didn't give me a glance. He was safe now. He had ditched it.

I watched him out of sight and went up the central walk of the La Baba and parted the branches of the third cypress. I drew out a wrapped book and put it under my arm and went away from there. Nobody yelled at me.

5

Back on the boulevard I went into a drugstore phone booth and looked up Mr. Arthur Gwynn Geiger's residence. He lived on Laverne Terrace, a hillside street off Laurel Canyon Boulevard. I dropped my nickel and dialed his number just for fun. Nobody answered. I turned to the classified section and noted a couple of bookstores within blocks of where I was.

The first I came to was on the north side, a large lower floor devoted to stationery and office supplies, a mass of books on the mezzanine. It didn't look the right place. I crossed the street and walked two blocks east to the other one. This was more like it, a narrowed cluttered little shop stacked with books from floor to ceiling and four or five browsers taking their time putting thumb marks on the new jackets. Nobody paid any attention to them. I shoved on back into the store, passed through a partition and found a small dark woman reading a law book at a desk.

I flipped my wallet open on her desk and let her look at the buzzer pinned to the flap. She looked at it, took her glasses off and leaned back in her chair. I put the wallet away. She had the fine-drawn face of an intelligent Jewess. She stared at me and said nothing.

I said: "Would you do me a favor, a very small favor?"

"I don't know. What is it?" She had a smoothly husky voice.

"You know Geiger's store across the street, two blocks west?"

"I think I may have passed it."

"It's a bookstore," I said. "Not your kind of bookstore. You know darn well."

She curled her lip slightly and said nothing. "You know Geiger by sight?" I asked.

"I'm sorry. I don't know Mr. Geiger."

"Then you couldn't tell me what he looks like?"

Her lip curled some more. "Why should I?"

"No reason at all. If you don't want to, I can't make you."

She looked out through the partition door and leaned back again. "That was a sheriff's star, wasn't it?"

"Honorary deputy. Doesn't mean a thing. It's worth a dime cigar."

"I see." She reached for a pack of cigarettes and shook one loose and reached for it with her lips. I held a match for her. She thanked me, leaned back again and regarded me through smoke. She said carefully:

"You wish to know what he looks like and you don't want to interview him?"

"He's not there," I said.

"I presume he will be. After all, it's his store."

"I don't want to interview him just yet," I said.

She looked out through the open doorway again. I said: "Know anything about rare books?"

"You could try me."

"Would you have a Ben Hur, 1860, Third Edition, the one with the duplicated line on page 116?"

She pushed her yellow law book to one side and reached a fat volume up on the desk, leafed it through, found her page, and studied it. "Nobody would," she said without looking up. "There isn't one."

"Right."

"What in the world are you driving at?"

"The girl in Geiger's store didn't know that."

She looked up. "I see. You interest me. Rather vaguely."

"I'm a private dick on a case. Perhaps I ask too much. It didn't seem much to me somehow."

She blew a soft gray smoke ring and poked her finger through. It came to pieces in frail wisps. She spoke smoothly, indifferently. "In his early forties, I should judge. Medium height, fattish. Would weigh about a hundred and sixty pounds. Fat face, Charlie Chan moustache, thick soft neck. Soft all over. Well dressed, goes without a hat, affects a knowledge of antiques and hasn't any. Oh yes. His left eye is glass."

"You'd make a good cop," I said.

She put the reference book back on an open shelf at the end of her desk, and opened the law book in front of her again. "I hope not," she said. She put her glasses on.

I thanked her and left. The rain had started. I ran for it, with the wrapped book under my arm. My car was on a side street pointing at the boulevard almost opposite Geiger's store. I was well sprinkled before I got there. I tumbled into the car and ran both windows up and wiped my parcel off with my handkerchief. Then I opened it up.

I knew about what it would be, of course. A heavy book, well bound, handsomely printed in handset type on fine paper. Larded with full-page arty photographs. Photos and letterpress were alike of an indescribable filth. The book was not new. Dates were stamped on the front endpaper, in and out dates. A rent book. A lending library of elaborate smut.

I rewrapped the book and locked it up behind the seat. A racket like that, out in the open on the boulevard, seemed to mean plenty of protection. I sat there and poisoned myself with cigarette smoke and listened to the rain and thought about it.

6

Rain filled the gutters and splashed knee-high off the sidewalk. Big cops in slickers that shone like gun barrels had a lot of fun carrying giggling girls across the bad places. The rain drummed hard on the roof of the car and the burbank top began to leak. A pool of water formed on the floorboards for me to keep my feet in. It was too early in the fall for that kind of rain. I struggled into a trench coat and made a dash for the nearest drugstore and bought myself a pint of whiskey. Back in the car I used enough of it to keep warm and interested. I was long overparked, but the cops were too busy carrying girls and blowing whistles to bother about that.

In spite of the rain, or perhaps even because of it, there was business done at Geiger's. Very nice cars stopped in front and very nice-looking people went in and out with wrapped parcels. They were not all men.

He showed about four o'clock. A cream-colored coupe stopped in front of the store and I caught a glimpse of the fat face and the Charlie Chan moustache as he dodged out of it and into the store. He was hatless and wore a belted green leather raincoat. I couldn't see his glass eye at that distance. A tall and very good-looking kid in a jerkin came out of the store and rode the coupe off around the corner and came back walking, his glistening black hair plastered with rain.

Another hour went by. It got dark and the rain-clouded lights of the stores were soaked up by the black street. Streetcar bells jangled crossly. At around five-fifteen the tall boy in the jerkin came out of Geiger's with an umbrella and went after the cream-colored coupe. When he had it in front Geiger came out and the tall boy held the umbrella over Geiger's bare head. He folded it, shook it off and handed it into the car. He dashed back into the store. I started my motor.

The coupe went west on the boulevard, which forced me to make a left turn and a lot of enemies, including a motorman who stuck his head out into the rain to bawl me out. I was two blocks behind the coupe before I got in the groove. I hoped Geiger was on his way home. I caught sight of him two or three times and then made him turning north into

Laurel Canyon Drive. Halfway up the grade he turned left and took a curving ribbon of wet concrete which was called Laverne Terrace. It was a narrow street with a high bank on one side and a scattering of cabin-like houses built down the slope on the other side, so that their roofs were not very much above road level. Their front windows were masked by hedges and shrubs. Sodden trees dripped all over the landscape.

Geiger had his lights on and I hadn't. I speeded up and passed him on a curve, picked a number off a house as I went by and turned at the end of the block. He had already stopped. His car lights were tilted in at the garage of a small house with a square box hedge so arranged that it masked the front door completely. I watched him come out of the garage with his umbrella up and go in through the hedge. He didn't act as if he expected anybody to be tailing him. Light went on in the house. I drifted down to the next house above it, which seemed empty but had no signs out. I parked, aired out the convertible, had a drink from my bottle, and sat. I didn't know what I was waiting for, but something told me to wait. Another army of sluggish minutes dragged by.

Two cars came up the hill and went over the crest. It seemed to be a very quiet street. At a little after six more bright lights bobbed through the driving rain. It was pitch black by then. A car dragged to a stop in front of Geiger's house. The filaments of its lights glowed dimly and died. The door opened and a woman got out. A small slim woman in a vagabond hat and a transparent raincoat. She went in through the box maze. A bell rang faintly, light through the rain, a closing door, silence.

I reached a flash out of my car pocket and went downgrade and looked at the car. It was a Packard convertible, maroon or dark brown. The left window was down. I felt for the license holder and poked light at it. The registration read: Carmen Sternwood, 3765 Alta Brea Crescent, West Hollywood. I went back to my car again and sat and sat. The top dripped on my knees and my stomach burned from the whiskey. No more cars came up the hill. No lights went on in the house before which I was parked. It seemed like a nice neighborhood to have bad habits in.

At seven-twenty a single flash of hard white light shot out of Geiger's house like a wave of summer lightning. As the darkness folded back on it and ate it up a thin tinkling scream echoed out and lost itself among the rain-drenched trees. I was out of the car and on my way before the echoes died.

There was no fear in the scream. It had a sound of half-pleasurable shock, an accent of drunkenness, an overtone of pure idiocy. It was a nasty sound. It made me think of men in white and barred windows and hard narrow cots with leather wrist and ankle straps fastened to them. The Geiger hideaway was perfectly silent again when I hit the gap in the hedge and dodged around the angle that masked the front door. There was an iron ring in a lion's mouth for a knocker. I reached for it, I had hold of it. At that exact instant, as if somebody had been waiting for the cue, three shots boomed in the house. There was a sound that might have been a long harsh sigh. Then a soft messy thump. And then rapid footsteps in the house—going away.

The door fronted on a narrow run, like a footbridge over a gully, that filled the gap between the house wall and the edge of the bank. There was no porch, no solid ground, no way to get around to the back. The back entrance was at the top of a flight of wooden steps that rose from the alley-like street below. I knew this because I heard a clatter of feet on the steps, going down. Then I heard the sudden roar of a starting car. It faded swiftly into the distance. I thought the sound was echoed by another car, but I wasn't sure. The house in front of me was as silent as a vault. There wasn't any hurry. What was in there was in there.

I straddled the fence at the side of the runway and leaned far out to the draped but unscreened French window and tried to look in at the crack where the drapes came together. I saw lamplight on a wall and one end of a bookcase. I got back on the runway and took all of it and some of the hedge and gave the front door the heavy shoulder. This was foolish. About the only part of a California house you can't put your foot through is the front door. All it did was hurt my shoulder and make me mad. I climbed over the railing again and kicked the French window in, used my hat for a glove and pulled out most of the lower small pane of glass. I could now reach in and draw a bolt that fastened the window to the sill. The rest was easy. There was no top bolt. The catch gave. I climbed in and pulled the drapes off my face.

Neither of the two people in the room paid any attention to the way I came in, although only one of them was dead.

7

It was a wide room, the whole width of the house. It had a low beamed ceiling and brown plaster walls decked out with strips of Chinese embroidery and Chinese and Japanese prints in grained wood frames. There were low bookshelves, there was a thick pinkish Chinese rug in which a gopher could have spent a week without showing his nose above the nap. There were floor cushions, bits of odd silk tossed around, as if whoever lived there had to have a piece he could reach out and thumb. There was a broad low divan of old rose tapestry. It had a wad of clothes on it, including lilac-colored silk underwear. There was a big carved lamp on a pedestal, two other standing lamps with jade-green shades and long tassels. There was a black desk with carved gargoyles at the corners and behind it a yellow satin cushion on a polished black chair with carved arms and back. The room contained an odd assortment of odors, of which the most emphatic at the moment seemed to be the pungent aftermath of cordite and the sickish aroma of ether.

On a sort of low dais at one end of the room there was a high-backed teakwood chair in which Miss Carmen Sternwood was sitting on a fringed orange shawl. She was sitting very straight, with her hands on the arms of the chair, her knees close together, her body stiffly erect in the pose of an Egyptian goddess, her chin level, her small bright teeth shining between her parted lips. Her eyes were wide open. The dark slate color of the iris had devoured the pupil. They were mad eyes. She seemed to be unconscious, but she didn't have the pose of unconsciousness. She looked as if, in her mind, she was doing something very important and making a fine job of it. Out of her mouth came a tinny chuckling noise which didn't change her expression or even move her lips.

She was wearing a pair of long jade earrings. They were nice earrings and had probably cost a couple of hundred dollars. She wasn't wearing anything else.

She had a beautiful body, small, lithe, compact, firm, rounded. Her skin in the lamplight had the shimmering luster of a pearl. Her legs didn't quite have the raffish grace of Mrs. Regan's legs, but they were very nice. I looked her over without either embarrassment or ruttishness. As a naked girl she was not there in that room at all. She was just a dope. To me she was always just a dope.

I stopped looking at her and looked at Geiger. He was on his back on the floor, beyond the fringe of the Chinese rug, in front of a thing that looked like a totem pole. It had a profile like an eagle and its wide round eye was a camera lens. The lens was aimed at the naked girl in the chair. There was a blackened flash bulb clipped to the side of the totem pole. Geiger was wearing Chinese slippers with thick felt soles, and his legs were in black satin pajamas and the upper part of him wore a Chinese embroidered coat, the front of which was mostly blood. His glass eye shone brightly up at me and was by far the most lifelike thing about him. At a glance none of the three shots I heard had missed. He was very dead.

The flash bulb was the sheet lightning I had seen. The crazy scream was the doped and naked girl's reaction to it. The three shots had been somebody else's idea of how the proceedings might be given a new twist. The idea of the lad who had gone down the back steps and slammed into a car and raced away. I could see merit in his point of view.

A couple of fragile gold-veined glasses rested on a red lacquer tray on the end of the black desk, beside a potbellied flagon of brown liquid. I took the stopper out and sniffed at it. It smelled of ether and something else, possibly laudanum. I had never tried the mixture but it seemed to go pretty well with the Geiger menage.

I listened to the rain hitting the roof and the north windows. Beyond was no other sound, no cars, no siren, just the rain beating. I went over to the divan and peeled off my trench coat and pawed through the girl's clothes. There was a pale green rough wool dress of the pull-on type, with half sleeves. I thought I might be able to handle it. I decided to pass up her underclothes, not from feelings of delicacy, but because I couldn't see myself putting her pants on and snapping her brassiere. I took the dress over to the teak chair on the dais. Miss Sternwood smelled of ether also, at a distance of several feet. The tinny chuckling noise was still coming from her and a little froth oozed down her chin. I slapped her face. She blinked and stopped chuckling. I slapped her again.

"Come on," I said brightly. "Let's be nice. Let's get dressed."

She peered at me, her slaty eyes as empty as holes in a mask. "Gugugoterell," she said.

I slapped her around a little more. She didn't mind the slaps. They didn't bring her out of it. I set to work with the dress. She didn't mind that either. She let me hold her arms up and she spread her fingers out wide, as if that was cute. I got her hands through the sleeves, pulled the dress down over her back, and stood her up. She fell into my arms giggling. I set her back in the chair and got her stockings and shoes on her.

"Let's take a little walk," I said. "Let's take a nice little walk."

We took a little walk. Part of the time her earrings banged against my chest and part of the time we did the splits in unison, like adagio dancers. We walked over to Geiger's body and back. I had her look at him. She thought he was cute. She giggled and tried to tell me so, but she just bubbled. I walked her over to the divan and spread her out on it. She hiccuped twice, giggled a little and went to sleep. I stuffed her belongings into my pockets and went over behind the totem pole thing. The camera was there all right, set inside it, but there was no plateholder in the camera. I looked around on the floor, thinking he might have got it out before he was shot. No plateholder. I took hold of his limp chilling hand and rolled him a little. No plateholder. I didn't like this development.

I went into a hall at the back of the room and investigated

the house. There was a bathroom on the right and a locked door, a kitchen at the back. The kitchen window had been jimmied. The screen was gone and the place where the hook had pulled out showed on the sill. The back door was unlocked. I left it unlocked and looked into a bedroom on the left side of the hall. It was neat, fussy, womanish. The bed had a flounced cover. There was perfume on the triple-mirrored dressing table, beside a handkerchief, some loose money, a man's brushes, a keyholder. A man's clothes were in the closet and a man's slippers under the flounced edge of the bed cover. Mr. Geiger's room. I took the keyholder back to the living room and went through the desk. There was a locked steel box in the deep drawer. I used one of the keys on it. There was nothing in it but a blue leather book with an index and a lot of writing in code, in the same slanting printing that had written to General Sternwood. I put the notebook in my pocket, wiped the steel box where I had touched it, locked the desk up, pocketed the keys, turned the gas logs off in the fireplace, wrapped myself in my coat and tried to rouse Miss Sternwood. It couldn't be done. I crammed her vagabond hat on her head and swathed her in her coat and carried her out to her car. I went back and put all the lights out and shut the front door, dug her keys out of her bag and started the Packard. We went off down the hill without lights. It was less than ten minutes' drive to Alta Brea Crescent. Carmen spent them snoring and breathing ether in my face. I couldn't keep her head off my shoulder. It was all I could do to keep it out of my lap.

8

There was dim light behind narrow leaded panes in the side door of the Sternwood mansion. I stopped the Packard under the porte-cochere and emptied my pockets out on the seat. The girl snored in the corner, her hat tilted rakishly over her nose, her hands hanging limp in the folds of the raincoat. I got out and rang the bell. Steps came slowly, as if from a long dreary distance. The door opened and the straight, silvery butler looked out at me. The light from the hall made a halo of his hair.

He said: "Good evening, sir," politely and looked past me at the Packard. His eyes came back to look at my eyes.

"Is Mrs. Regan in?"

"No, sir."

"The General is asleep, I hope?"

"Yes. The evening is his best time for sleeping."

"How about Mrs. Regan's maid?"

"Mathilda? She's here, sir."

"Better get her down here. The job needs the woman's touch. Take a look in the car and you'll see why."

He took a look in the car. He came back. "I see," he said. "I'll get Mathilda."

"Mathilda will do right by her," I said.

"We all try to do right by her," he said.

"I guess you'll have had practice," I said.

He let that one go. "Well, good-night," I said. "I'm leaving it in your hands."

"Very good, sir. May I call you a cab?"

"Positively," I said, "not. As a matter of fact I'm not here. You're just seeing things."

He smiled then. He gave me a duck of his head and I turned and walked down the driveway and out of the gates.

Ten blocks of that, winding down curved rain-swept streets, under the steady drip of trees, past lighted windows in big houses in ghostly enormous grounds, vague clusters of eaves and gables and lighted windows high on the hillside, remote and inaccessible, like witch houses in a forest. I came out at a service station glaring with wasted light, where a bored attendant in a white cap and a dark blue windbreaker sat hunched on a stool, inside the steamed glass, reading a paper. I started in, then kept going. I was as wet as I could get already. And on a night like that you can grow a beard waiting for a taxi. And taxi drivers remember.

I made it back to Geiger's house in something over half an hour of nimble walking. There was nobody there, no car on the street except my own car in front of the next house. It looked as dismal as a lost dog. I dug my bottle of rye out of it and poured half of what was left down my throat and got inside to light a cigarette. I smoked half of it, threw it away, got out again and went down to Geiger's. I unlocked the door and stepped into the still warm darkness and stood there, dripping quietly on the floor and listening to the rain. I groped to a lamp and lit it.

The first thing I noticed was that a couple of strips of embroidered silk were gone from the wall. I hadn't counted them, but the spaces of brown plaster stood out naked and obvious. I went a little farther and put another lamp on. I looked at the totem pole. At its foot, beyond the margin of the Chinese rug, on the bare floor another rug had been spread. It hadn't been there before. Geiger's body had. Geiger's body was gone.

That froze me. I pulled my lips back against my teeth and leered at the glass eye in the totem pole. I went through the house again. Everything was exactly as it had been. Geiger wasn't in his flounced bed or under it or in his closet. He wasn't in the kitchen or the bathroom. That left the locked door on the right of the hall. One of Geiger's keys fitted the lock. The room inside was interesting, but Geiger wasn't in it. It was interesting because it was so different from Geiger's room. It was a hard bare masculine bedroom with a polished wood floor, a couple of small throw rugs in an Indian design, two straight chairs, a bureau in dark grained wood with a man's toilet set and two black candles in foot-high brass candlesticks. The bed was narrow and looked hard and had a maroon batik cover. The room felt cold. I locked it up again, wiped the knob off with my handkerchief, and went back to the totem pole. I knelt down and squinted along the nap of the rug to the front door. I thought I could see two parallel grooves pointing that way, as though heels had dragged. Whoever had done it had meant business. Dead men are heavier than broken hearts.

It wasn't the law. They would have been there still, just about getting warmed up with their pieces of string and chalk and their cameras and dusting powders and their nickel cigars. They would have been very much there. It wasn't the killer. He had left too fast. He must have seen the girl. He couldn't be sure she was too batty to see him. He would be on his way to distant places. I couldn't guess the answer, but it was all right with me if somebody wanted Geiger missing instead of just murdered. It gave me a chance to find out if I could tell it leaving Carmen Sternwood out. I locked up again, choked my car to life and rode off home to a shower, dry clothes and a late dinner. After that I sat around in the apartment and drank too much hot toddy trying to crack the code in Geiger's blue indexed notebook. All I could be sure of was that it was a list of names and addresses, probably of the customers. There were over four hundred of them. That made it a nice racket, not to mention any blackmail angles, and there were probably plenty of those. Any name on the list might be a prospect as the killer. I didn't envy the police their job when it was handed to them.

I went to bed full of whiskey and frustration and dreamed about a man in a bloody Chinese coat who chased a naked girl with long jade earrings while I ran after them and tried to take a photograph with an empty camera.

9

The next morning was bright, clear and sunny. I woke up with a motorman's glove in my mouth, drank two cups of coffee and went through the morning papers. I didn't find any reference to Mr. Arthur Gwynn Geiger in either of them. I was shaking the wrinkles out of my damp suit when the phone rang. It was Bernie Ohls, the D.A.'s chief investigator, who had given me the lead to General Sternwood.

"Well, how's the boy?" he began. He sounded like a man who had slept well and didn't owe too much money.

"I've got a hangover," I said.

"Tsk, tsk." He laughed absently and then his voice became a shade too casual, a cagey cop voice. "Seen General Sternwood yet?"

"Uh-huh."

"Done anything for him?"

"Too much rain," I answered, if that was an answer.

"They seem to be a family things happen to. A big Buick belonging to one of them is washing about in the surf off Lido fish pier."

I held the telephone tight enough to crack it. I also held my breath.

"Yeah," Ohls said cheerfully. "A nice new Buick sedan all messed up with sand and sea water. . . . Oh, I almost forgot. There's a guy inside it."

I let my breath out so slowly that it hung on my lip. "Regan?" I asked.

"Huh? Who? Oh, you mean the ex-legger the eldest girl picked up and went and married. I never saw him. What would he be doing down there?"

"Quit stalling. What would anybody be doing down there?"

"I don't know, pal. I'm dropping down to look see. Want to go along?"

"Yes."

"Snap it up," he said. "I'll be in my hutch."

Shaved, dressed and lightly breakfasted I was at the Hall of Justice in less than an hour. I rode up to the seventh floor and went along to the group of small offices used by the D.A.'s men. Ohls' was no larger than the others, but he had it to himself. There was nothing on his desk but a blotter, a cheap pen set, his hat and one of his feet. He was a medium-sized blondish man with stiff white eyebrows, calm eyes and well-kept teeth. He looked like anybody you would pass on the street. I happened to know he had killed nine men — three of them when he was covered, or somebody thought he was.

He stood up and pocketed a flat tin of toy cigars called Entractes, jiggled the one in his mouth up and down and looked at me carefully along his nose, with his head thrown back.

"It's not Regan," he said. "I checked. Regan's a big guy, as tall as you and a shade heavier. This is a young kid."

I didn't say anything.

"What made Regan skip out?" Ohls asked. "You interested in that?"

"I don't think so," I said.

"When a guy out of the liquor traffic marries into a rich family and then waves good-by to a pretty dame and a couple million legitimate bucks — that's enough to make even me think. I guess you thought that was a secret."

"Uh-huh."

"Okey, keep buttoned, kid. No hard feelings." He came around the desk tapping his pockets and reaching for his hat.

"I'm not looking for Regan," I said.

He fixed the lock on his door and we went down to the official parking lot and got into a small blue sedan. We drove out Sunset, using the siren once in a while to beat a signal. It was a crisp morning, with just enough snap in the air to make life seem simple and sweet, if you didn't have too much on your mind. I had.

It was thirty miles to Lido on the coast highway, the first ten of them through traffic. Ohls made the run in three quarters of an hour. At the end of that time we skidded to a stop in front of a faded stucco arch and I took my feet out of the floorboards and we got out. A long pier railed with white two by fours stretched seaward from the arch. A knot of people leaned out at the far end and a motorcycle officer stood under the arch keeping another group of people from going out on the pier. Cars were parked on both sides of the highway, the usual ghouls, of both sexes. Ohls showed the motorcycle officer his badge and we went out on the pier, into a loud fish smell which one night's hard rain hadn't even dented.

"There she is — on the power barge," Ohls said, pointing with one of his toy cigars.

A low black barge with a wheelhouse like a tug's was crouched against the pilings at the end of the pier. Something that glistened in the morning sunlight was on its deck, with hoist chains still around it, a large black and chromium car. The arm of the hoist had been swung back into position and lowered to deck level. Men stood around the car. We went down slippery steps to the deck.

Ohls said hello to a deputy in green khaki and a man in plain clothes. The barge crew of three men leaned against the front of the wheelhouse and chewed tobacco. One of them was rubbing at his wet hair with a dirty bath-towel. That would be the man who had gone down into the water to put the chains on.

We looked the car over. The front bumper was bent, one headlight smashed, the other bent up but the glass still unbroken. The radiator shell had a big dent in it, and the paint and nickel were scratched up all over the car. The upholstery was sodden and black. None of the tires seemed to be damaged.

The driver was still draped around the steering post with his head at an unnatural angle to his shoulders. He was a slim dark-haired kid who had been good-looking not so long ago. Now his face was bluish white and his eyes were a faint dull gleam under the lowered lids and his open mouth had sand in it. On the left side of his forehead there was a dull bruise that stood out against the whiteness of the skin.

Ohls backed away, made a noise in his throat and put a match to his little cigar. "What's the story?"

The uniformed man pointed up at the rubbernecks on the end of the pier. One of them was fingering a place where the white two-by-fours had been broken through in a wide space. The splintered wood showed yellow and clean, like fresh-cut pine.

"Went through there. Must have hit pretty hard. The rain stopped early down here, around nine p.m. The broken wood's dry inside. That puts it after the rain stopped. She fell in plenty of water not to be banged up worse, not more than half tide or she'd have drifted farther, and not more than half tide going out or she'd have crowded the piles. That makes it around ten last night. Maybe nine-thirty, not earlier. She shows under the water when the boys come down to fish this morning, so we get the barge to hoist her out and we find the dead guy."

The plainclothesman scuffed at the deck with the toe of his shoe. Ohls looked sideways along his eyes at me, and twitched his little cigar like a cigarette.

"Drunk?" he asked, of nobody in particular.

The man who had been toweling his head went over to the rail and cleared his throat in a loud hawk that made everybody look at him. "Got some sand," he said, and spat. "Not as much as the boy friend got—but some."

The uniformed man said: "Could have been drunk. Showing off all alone in the rain. Drunks will do anything."

"Drunk, hell," the plainclothesman said. "The hand throttle's set halfway down and the guy's been sapped on the side of the head. Ask me and I'll call it murder."

Ohls looked at the man with the towel. "What do you think, buddy?"

The man with the towel looked flattered. He grinned. "I say suicide, Mac. None of my business, but you ask me, I say suicide. First off the guy plowed an awful straight furrow down that pier. You can read his tread marks all the way nearly. That puts it after the rain like the Sheriff said. Then he hit the pier hard and clean or he don't go through and land right side up. More likely turned over a couple of times. So he had plenty of speed and hit the rail square. That's more than half-throttle. He could have done that with his hand falling and he could have hurt his head falling too."

Ohls said: "You got eyes, buddy. Frisked him?" he asked the deputy. The deputy looked at me, then at the crew against the wheelhouse. "Okey, save that," Ohls said.

A small man with glasses and a tired face and a black bag came down the steps from the pier. He picked out a fairly clean spot on the deck and put the bag down. Then he took his hat off and rubbed the back of his neck and stared out to sea, as if he didn't know where he was or what he had come for.

Ohls said: "There's your customer, Doc. Dove off the pier last night. Around nine to ten. That's all we know."

The small man looked in at the dead man morosely. He fingered the head, peered at the bruise on the temple, moved the head around with both hands, felt the man's ribs. He lifted a lax dead hand and stared at the fingernails. He let it fall and watched it fall. He stepped back and opened his bag and took out a printed pad of D.O.A. forms and began to write over a carbon.

"Broken neck's the apparent cause of death," he said, writing. "Which means there won't be much water in him. Which means he's due to start getting stiff pretty quick now he's out in the air. Better get him out of the car before he does. You won't like doing it after."

Ohls nodded. "How long dead, Doc?"

"I wouldn't know."

Ohls looked at him sharply and took the little cigar out of his mouth and looked at that sharply. "Pleased to know you, Doc. A coroner's man that can't guess within five minutes has me beat."

The little man grinned sourly and put his pad in his bag and clipped his pencil back on his vest. "If he ate dinner last night, I'll tell you—if I know what time he ate it. But not within five minutes."

"How would he get that bruise—falling?"

The little man looked at the bruise again. "I don't think so. That blow came from something covered. And it had already bled subcutaneously while he was alive."

"Blackjack, huh?"

"Very likely."

The little M.E.'s man nodded, picked his bag off the deck and went back up the steps to the pier. An ambulance was backing into position outside the stucco arch. Ohls looked at me and said: "Let's go. Hardly worth the ride, was it?"

We went back along the pier and got into Ohls' sedan again. He wrestled it around on the highway and drove back towards town along a three-lane highway washed clean by the rain, past low rolling hills of yellow-white sand terraced with pink moss. Seaward a few gulls wheeled and swooped over something in the surf and far out a white yacht looked as if it was hanging in the sky.

Ohls cocked his chin at me and said: "Know him?"

"Sure. The Sternwood chauffeur. I saw him dusting that very car out there yesterday."

"I don't want to crowd you, Marlowe. Just tell me, did the job have anything to do with him?"

"No. I don't even know his name."

"Owen Taylor. How do I know? Funny about that. About a year or so back we had him in the cooler on a Mann Act rap. It seems he run Sternwood's hotcha daughter, the young one, off to Yuma. The sister ran after them and brought them back and had Owen heaved into the icebox. Then next day she comes down to the D.A. and gets him to beg the kid off with the U.S. 'cutor. She says the kid meant to marry her sister and wanted to, only the sister can't see it. All *she* wanted was to kick a few high ones off the bar and have herself a party. So we let the kid go and then darned if they don't have him come back to work. And a little later we get the routine report on his prints from Washington, and he's got a prior back in Indiana, attempted hold-up six years ago. He got off with a six months in the county jail, the very one Dillinger bust out of. We hand that to the Sternwoods and they keep him on just the same. What do you think of that?"

"They seem to be a screwy family," I said. "Do they know about last night?"

"No. I gotta go up against them now."

"Leave the old man out of it, if you can."

"Why?"

"He has enough troubles and he's sick."

"You mean Regan?"

I scowled. "I don't know anything about Regan, I told you. I'm not looking for Regan. Regan hasn't bothered anybody that I know of."

Ohls said: "Oh," and stared thoughtfully out to sea and the sedan nearly went off the road. For the rest of the drive back to town he hardly spoke. He dropped me off in Hollywood near the Chinese Theater and turned back west to Alta Brea Crescent. I ate lunch at a counter and looked at an afternoon paper and couldn't find anything about Geiger in it.

After lunch I walked east on the boulevard to have another look at Geiger's store.

10

The lean black-eyed credit jeweler was standing in his entrance in the same position as the afternoon before. He gave me the same knowing look as I turned in. The store looked just the same. The same lamp glowed on the small desk in the

corner and the same ash blonde in the same black suede-like
dress got up from behind it and came towards me with the
same tentative smile on her face.

"Was it—?" she said and stopped. Her silver nails twitched
at her side. There was an overtone of strain in her smile. It
wasn't a smile at all. It was a grimace. She just thought it was
a smile.

"Back again," I chirped airily, and waved a cigarette. "Mr.
Geiger in today?"

"I'm—I'm afraid not. No—I'm afraid not. Let me see—
you wanted . . . ?"

I took my dark glasses off and tapped them delicately on
the inside of my left wrist. If you can weigh a hundred and
ninety pounds and look like a fairy, I was doing my best.

"That was just a stall about those first editions," I whispered. "I have to be careful. I've got something he'll want.
Something he's wanted for a long time."

The silver fingernails touched the blond hair over one small
jet-buttoned ear. "Oh, a salesman," she said. "Well—you
might come in tomorrow. I think he'll be here tomorrow."

"Drop the veil," I said. "I'm in the business too."

Her eyes narrowed until they were a faint greenish glitter,
like a forest pool far back in the shadow of trees. Her fingers
clawed at her palm. She stared at me and chopped off a
breath.

"Is he sick? I could go up to the house," I said impatiently.
"I haven't got forever."

"You—a—you—a—" her throat jammed. I thought she
was going to fall on her nose. Her whole body shivered and
her face fell apart like a bride's pie crust. She put it together
again slowly, as if lifting a great weight, by sheer will power.
The smile came back, with a couple of corners badly bent.

"No," she breathed. "No. He's out of town. That—
wouldn't be any use. Can't you—come in—tomorrow?"

I had my mouth open to say something when the partition
door opened a foot. The tall dark handsome boy in the jerkin
looked out, pale-faced and tight-lipped, saw me, shut the
door quickly again, but not before I had seen on the floor
behind him a lot of wooden boxes lined with newspapers and
packed loosely with books. A man in very new overalls was

fussing with them. Some of Geiger's stock was being moved out.

When the door shut I put my dark glasses on again and touched my hat. "Tomorrow, then. I'd like to give you a card, but you know how it is."

"Ye-es. I know how it is." She shivered a little more and made a faint sucking noise between her bright lips. I went out of the store and west on the boulevard to the corner and north on the street to the alley which ran behind the stores. A small black truck with wire sides and no lettering on it was backed up to Geiger's place. The man in the very new overalls was just heaving a box up on the tailboard. I went back to the boulevard and along the block next to Geiger's and found a taxi standing at a fireplug. A fresh-faced kid was reading a horror magazine behind the wheel. I leaned in and showed him a dollar: "Tail job?"

He looked me over. "Cop?"

"Private."

He grinned. "My meat, Jack." He tucked the magazine over his rear view mirror and I got into the cab. We went around the block and pulled up across from Geiger's alley, beside another fireplug.

There were about a dozen boxes on the truck when the man in overalls closed the screened doors and hooked the tailboard up and got in behind the wheel.

"Take him," I told my driver.

The man in overalls gunned his motor, shot a glance up and down the alley and ran away fast in the other direction. He turned left out of the alley. We did the same. I caught a glimpse of the truck turning east on Franklin and told my driver to close in a little. He didn't or couldn't do it. I saw the truck two blocks away when we got to Franklin. We had it in sight to Vine and across Vine and all the way to Western. We saw it twice after Western. There was a lot of traffic and the fresh-faced kid tailed from too far back. I was telling him about that without mincing words when the truck, now far ahead, turned north again. The street at which it turned was called Brittany Place. When we got to Brittany Place the truck had vanished.

The fresh-faced kid made comforting sounds at me

through the panel and we went up the hill at four miles an hour looking for the truck behind bushes. Two blocks up, Brittany Place swung to the east and met Randall Place in a tongue of land on which there was a white apartment house with its front on Randall Place and its basement garage opening on Brittany. We were going past that and the fresh-faced kid was telling me the truck couldn't be far away when I looked through the arched entrance of the garage and saw it back in the dimness with its rear doors open again.

We went around to the front of the apartment house and I got out. There was nobody in the lobby, no switchboard. A wooden desk was pushed back against the wall beside a panel of gilt mailboxes. I looked the names over. A man named Joseph Brody had Apartment 405. A man named Joe Brody had received five thousand dollars from General Sternwood to stop playing with Carmen and find some other little girl to play with. It could be the same Joe Brody. I felt like giving odds on it.

I went around an elbow of wall to the foot of tiled stairs and the shaft of the automatic elevator. The top of the elevator was level with the floor. There was a door beside the shaft lettered "Garage." I opened it and went down narrow steps to the basement. The automatic elevator was propped open and the man in new overalls was grunting hard as he stacked heavy boxes in it. I stood beside him and lit a cigarette and watched him. He didn't like my watching him.

After a while I said: "Watch the weight, bud. She's only tested for half a ton. Where's the stuff going?"

"Brody, four-o-five," he grunted. "Manager?"

"Yeah. Looks like a nice lot of loot."

He glared at me with pale white rimmed eyes. "Books," he snarled. "A hundred pounds a box, easy, and me with a seventy-five pound back."

"Well, watch the weight," I said.

He got into the elevator with six boxes and shut the doors. I went back up the steps to the lobby and out to the street and the cab took me downtown again to my office building. I gave the fresh-faced kid too much money and he gave me a dog-eared business card which for once I didn't drop into the majolica jar of sand beside the elevator bank.

I had a room and a half on the seventh floor at the back. The half room was an office split in two to make reception rooms. Mine had my name on it and nothing else, and that only on the reception room. I always left this unlocked, in case I had a client, and the client cared to sit down and wait.

I had a client.

II

She wore brownish speckled tweeds, a mannish shirt and tie, hand-carved walking shoes. Her stockings were just as sheer as the day before, but she wasn't showing as much of her legs. Her black hair was glossy under a brown Robin Hood hat that might have cost fifty dollars and looked as if you could have made it with one hand out of a desk blotter.

"Well, you *do* get up," she said, wrinkling her nose at the faded red settee, the two odd semi-easy chairs, the net curtains that needed laundering and the boy's size library table with the venerable magazines on it to give the place a professional touch. "I was beginning to think perhaps you worked in bed, like Marcel Proust."

"Who's he?" I put a cigarette in my mouth and stared at her. She looked a little pale and strained, but she looked like a girl who could function under a strain.

"A French writer, a connoisseur in degenerates. You wouldn't know him."

"Tut, tut," I said. "Come into my boudoir."

She stood up and said: "We didn't get along very well yesterday. Perhaps I was rude."

"We were both rude," I said. I unlocked the communicating door and held it for her. We went into the rest of my suite, which contained a rust-red carpet, not very young, five green filing cases, three of them full of California climate, an advertising calendar showing the Quints rolling around on a sky-blue floor, in pink dresses, with seal-brown hair and sharp black eyes as large as mammoth prunes. There were three near-walnut chairs, the usual desk with the usual blotter, pen set, ashtray and telephone, and the usual squeaky swivel chair behind it.

"You don't put on much of a front," she said, sitting down at the customer's side of the desk.

I went over to the mail slot and picked up six envelopes, two letters and four pieces of advertising matter. I hung my hat on the telephone and sat down.

"Neither do the Pinkertons," I said. "You can't make much money at this trade, if you're honest. If you have a front, you're making money—or expect to."

"Oh—are you honest?" she asked and opened her bag. She picked a cigarette out of a French enamel case, lit it with a pocket lighter, dropped case and lighter back into the bag and left the bag open.

"Painfully."

"How did you ever get into this slimy kind of business then?"

"How did you come to marry a bootlegger?"

"My God, let's not start quarreling again. I've been trying to get you on the phone all morning. Here and at your apartment."

"About Owen?"

Her face tightened sharply. Her voice was soft. "Poor Owen," she said. "So you know about that."

"A D.A.'s man took me down to Lido. He thought I might know something about it. But he knew much more than I did. He knew Owen wanted to marry your sister—once."

She puffed silently at her cigarette and considered me with steady black eyes. "Perhaps it wouldn't have been a bad idea," she said quietly. "He was in love with her. We don't find much of that in our circle."

"He had a police record."

She shrugged. She said negligently: "He didn't know the right people. That's all a police record means in this rotten crime-ridden country."

"I wouldn't go that far."

She peeled her right glove off and bit her index finger at the first joint, looking at me with steady eyes. "I didn't come to see you about Owen. Do you feel yet that you can tell me what my father wanted to see you about?"

"Not without his permission."

"Was it about Carmen?"

"I can't even say that." I finished filling a pipe and put a match to it. She watched the smoke for a moment. Then her hand went into her open bag and came out with a thick white envelope. She tossed it across the desk.

"You'd better look at it anyway," she said.

I picked it up. The address was typewritten to Mrs. Vivian Regan, 3765 Alta Brea Crescent, West Hollywood. Delivery had been by messenger service and the office stamp showed 8.35 a.m. as the time out. I opened the envelope and drew out the shiny 4¼ by 3¼ photo that was all there was inside.

It was Carmen sitting in Geiger's high-backed teakwood chair on the dais, in her earrings and her birthday suit. Her eyes looked even a little crazier than as I remembered them. The back of the photo was blank. I put it back in the envelope.

"How much do they want?" I asked.

"Five thousand—for the negative and the rest of the prints. The deal has to be closed tonight, or they give the stuff to some scandal sheet."

"The demand came how?"

"A woman telephoned me, about half an hour after this thing was delivered."

"There's nothing in the scandal sheet angle. Juries convict without leaving the box on that stuff nowadays. What else is there?"

"Does there have to be something else?"

"Yes "

She stared at me, a little puzzled. "There is. The woman said there was a police jam connected with it and I'd better lay it on the line fast, or I'd be talking to my little sister through a wire screen."

"Better," I said. "What kind of jam?"

"I don't know."

"Where is Carmen now?"

"She's at home. She was sick last night. She's still in bed, I think."

"Did she go out last night?"

"No. I was out, but the servants say she wasn't. I was down at Las Olindas, playing roulette at Eddie Mars' Cypress Club. I lost my shirt."

"So you like roulette. You would."

She crossed her legs and lit another cigarette. "Yes. I like roulette. All the Sternwoods like losing games, like roulette and marrying men that walk out on them and riding steeplechases at fifty-eight years old and being rolled on by a jumper and crippled for life. The Sternwoods have money. All it has bought them is a rain check."

"What was Owen doing last night with your car?"

"Nobody knows. He took it without permission. We always let him take a car on his night off, but last night wasn't his night off." She made a wry mouth. "Do you think—?"

"He knew about this nude photo? How would I be able to say? I don't rule him out. Can you get five thousand in cash right away?"

"Not unless I tell Dad—or borrow it. I could probably borrow it from Eddie Mars. He ought to be generous with me, heaven knows."

"Better try that. You may need it in a hurry."

She leaned back and hung an arm over the back of the chair. "How about telling the police?"

"It's a good idea. But you won't do it."

"Won't I?"

"No. You have to protect your father and your sister. You don't know what the police might turn up. It might be something they couldn't sit on. Though they usually try in blackmail cases."

"Can you do anything?"

"I think I can. But I can't tell you why or how."

"I like you," she said suddenly. "You believe in miracles. Would you have a drink in the office?"

I unlocked my deep drawer and got out my office bottle and two pony glasses. I filled them and we drank. She snapped her bag shut and pushed her chair back.

"I'll get the five grand," she said. "I've been a good customer of Eddie Mars. There's another reason why he should be nice to me, which you may not know." She gave me one of those smiles the lips have forgotten before they reach the eyes. "Eddie's blonde wife is the lady Rusty ran away with."

I didn't say anything. She stared tightly at me and added: "That doesn't interest you?"

"It ought to make it easier to find him—if I was looking for him. You don't think he's in this mess, do you?"

She pushed her empty glass at me. "Give me another drink. You're the hardest guy to get anything out of. You don't even move your ears."

I filled the little glass. "You've got all you wanted out of me—a pretty good idea I'm not looking for your husband."

She put the drink down very quickly. It made her gasp—or gave her an opportunity to gasp. She let a breath out slowly.

"Rusty was no crook. If he had been, it wouldn't have been for nickels. He carried fifteen thousand dollars, in bills. He called it his mad money. He had it when I married him and he had it when he left me. No—Rusty's not in on any cheap blackmail racket."

She reached for the envelope and stood up. "I'll keep in touch with you," I said. "If you want to leave me a message, the phone girl at my apartment house will take care of it."

We walked over to the door. Tapping the white envelope against her knuckles, she said: "You still feel you can't tell me what Dad—"

"I'd have to see him first."

She took the photo out and stood looking at it, just inside the door. "She has a beautiful little body, hasn't she?"

"Uh-huh."

She leaned a little towards me. "You ought to see mine," she said gravely.

"Can it be arranged?"

She laughed suddenly and sharply and went halfway through the door, then turned her head to say coolly: "You're as cold-blooded a beast as I ever met, Marlowe. Or can I call you Phil?"

"Sure."

"You can call me Vivian."

"Thanks, Mrs. Regan."

"Oh, go to hell, Marlowe." She went on out and didn't look back.

I let the door shut and stood with my hand on it, staring at the hand. My face felt a little hot. I went back to the desk and put the whiskey away and rinsed out the two pony glasses and put them away.

I took my hat off the phone and called the D.A.'s office and asked for Bernie Ohls.

He was back in his cubbyhole. "Well, I let the old man alone," he said. "The butler said he or one of the girls would tell him. This Owen Taylor lived over the garage and I went through his stuff. Parents at Dubuque, Iowa. I wired the Chief of Police there to find out what they want done. The Sternwood family will pay for it."

"Suicide?" I asked.

"No can tell. He didn't leave any notes. He had no leave to take the car. Everybody was home last night but Mrs. Regan. She was down at Las Olindas with a playboy named Larry Cobb. I checked on that. I know a lad on one of the tables."

"You ought to stop some of that flash gambling," I said.

"With the syndicate we got in this county? Be your age, Marlowe. That sap mark on the boy's head bothers me. Sure you can't help me on this?"

I liked his putting it that way. It let me say no without actually lying. We said good-by and I left the office, bought all three afternoon papers and rode a taxi down to the Hall of Justice to get my car out of the lot. There was nothing in any of the papers about Geiger. I took another look at his blue notebook, but the code was just as stubborn as it had been the night before.

12

The trees on the upper side of Laverne Terrace had fresh green leaves after the rain. In the cool afternoon sunlight I could see the steep drop of the hill and the flight of steps down which the killer had run after his three shots in the darkness. Two small houses fronted on the street below. They might or might not have heard the shots.

There was no activity in front of Geiger's house or anywhere along the block. The box hedge looked green and peaceful and the shingles on the roof were still damp. I drove past slowly, gnawing at an idea. I hadn't looked in the garage the night before. Once Geiger's body slipped away I hadn't really wanted to find it. It would force my hand. But dragging him to the garage, to his own car and driving that off into one of the hundred odd lonely canyons around Los Angeles would be a good way to dispose of him for days or even for weeks. That supposed two things: a key to his car and two in the party. It would narrow the sector of search quite a lot, especially as I had had his personal keys in my pocket when it happened.

I didn't get a chance to look at the garage. The doors were shut and padlocked and something moved behind the hedge as I drew level. A woman in a green and white check coat and a small button of a hat on soft blond hair stepped out of the maze and stood looking wild-eyed at my car, as if she hadn't heard it come up the hill. Then she turned swiftly and dodged back out of sight. It was Carmen Sternwood, of course.

I went on up the street and parked and walked back. In the daylight it seemed an exposed and dangerous thing to do. I went in through the hedge. She stood there straight and silent against the locked front door. One hand went slowly up to her teeth and her teeth bit at her funny thumb. There were purple smears under her eyes and her face was gnawed white by nerves.

She half smiled at me. She said: "Hello," in a thin, brittle voice. "Wha—what—?" That tailed off and she went back to the thumb.

"Remember me?" I said. "Doghouse Reilly, the man that grew too tall. Remember?"

She nodded and a quick jerky smile played across her face.

"Let's go in," I said. "I've got a key. Swell, huh?"

"Wha—wha—?"

I pushed her to one side and put the key in the door and opened it and pushed her in through it. I shut the door again and stood there sniffing. The place was horrible by daylight.

The Chinese junk on the walls, the rug, the fussy lamps, the teakwood stuff, the sticky riot of colors, the totem pole, the flagon of ether and laudanum—all this in the daytime had a stealthy nastiness, like a fag party.

The girl and I stood looking at each other. She tried to keep a cute little smile on her face but her face was too tired to be bothered. It kept going blank on her. The smile would wash off like water off sand and her pale skin had a harsh granular texture under the stunned and stupid blankness of her eyes. A whitish tongue licked at the corners of her mouth. A pretty, spoiled and not very bright little girl who had gone very, very wrong, and nobody was doing anything about it. To hell with the rich. They made me sick. I rolled a cigarette in my fingers and pushed some books out of the way and sat on the end of the black desk. I lit my cigarette, puffed a plume of smoke and watched the thumb and tooth act for a while in silence. Carmen stood in front of me, like a bad girl in the principal's office.

"What are you doing here?" I asked her finally.

She picked at the cloth of her coat and didn't answer.

"How much do you remember of last night?"

She answered that—with a foxy glitter rising at the back of her eyes. "Remember what? I was sick last night. I was home." Her voice was a cautious throaty sound that just reached my ears.

"Like hell you were."

Her eyes flicked up and down very swiftly.

"Before you went home," I said. "Before I took you home. Here. In that chair—" I pointed to it—"on that orange shawl. You remember all right."

A slow flush crept up her throat. That was something. She could blush. A glint of white showed under the clogged gray irises. She chewed hard on her thumb.

"You—were the one?" she breathed.

"Me. How much of it stays with you?"

She said vaguely: "Are you the police?"

"No. I'm a friend of your father's."

"You're not the police?"

"No."

She let out a thin sigh. "Wha—what do you want?"

"Who killed him?"

Her shoulders jerked, but nothing more moved in her face. "Who else — knows?"

"About Geiger? I don't know. Not the police, or they'd be camping here. Maybe Joe Brody."

It was a stab in the dark but it got a yelp out of her. "Joe Brody! Him!"

Then we were both silent. I dragged at my cigarette and she ate her thumb.

"Don't get clever, for God's sake," I urged her. "This is a spot for a little old-fashioned simplicity. Did Brody kill him?"

"Kill who?"

"Oh, Christ," I said.

She looked hurt. Her chin came down an inch. "Yes," she said solemnly. "Joe did it."

"Why?"

"I don't know." She shook her head, persuading herself that she didn't know.

"Seen much of him lately?"

Her hands went down and made small white knots. "Just once or twice. I hate him."

"Then you know where he lives."

"Yes."

"And you don't like him any more?"

"I hate him!"

"Then you'd like him for the spot."

A little blank again. I was going too fast for her. It was hard not to. "Are you willing to tell the police it was Joe Brody?" I probed.

Sudden panic flamed all over her face. "If I can kill the nude photo angle, of course," I added soothingly.

She giggled. That gave me a nasty feeling. If she had screeched or wept or even nosedived to the floor in a dead faint, that would have been all right. She just giggled. It was suddenly a lot of fun. She had had her photo taken as Isis and somebody had swiped it and somebody had bumped Geiger off in front of her and she was drunker than a Legion convention, and it was suddenly a lot of nice clean fun. So she giggled. Very cute. The giggles got louder and ran around the corners of the room like rats behind the wainscoting. She started to go hysterical. I slid off the desk and stepped up close to her and gave her a smack on the side of the face.

"Just like last night," I said. "We're a scream together. Reilly and Sternwood, two stooges in search of a comedian."

The giggles stopped dead, but she didn't mind the slap any more than last night. Probably all her boy friends got around to slapping her sooner or later. I could understand how they might. I sat down on the end of the black desk again.

"Your name isn't Reilly," she said seriously. "It's Philip Marlowe. You're a private detective. Viv told me. She showed me your card." She smoothed the cheek I had slapped. She smiled at me, as if I was nice to be with.

"Well, you do remember," I said. "And you came back to look for that photo and you couldn't get into the house. Didn't you?"

Her chin ducked down and up. She worked the smile. I was having the eye put on me. I was being brought into camp. I was going to yell "Yippee!" in a minute and ask her to go to Yuma.

"The photo's gone," I said. "I looked last night, before I took you home. Probably Brody took it with him. You're not kidding me about Brody?"

She shook her head earnestly.

"It's a pushover," I said. "You don't have to give it another thought. Don't tell a soul you were here, last night or today. Not even Vivian. Just forget you were here. Leave it to Reilly."

"Your name isn't—" she began, and then stopped and shook her head vigorously in agreement with what I had said or with what she had just thought of. Her eyes became narrow and almost black and as shallow as enamel on a cafeteria tray. She had had an idea. "I have to go home now," she said, as if we had been having a cup of tea.

"Sure."

I didn't move. She gave me another cute glance and went on towards the front door. She had her hand on the knob when we both heard a car coming. She looked at me with questions in her eyes. I shrugged. The car stopped, right in front of the house. Terror twisted her face. There were steps and the bell rang. Carmen stared back at me over her shoulder, her hand clutching the door knob, almost drooling with fear. The bell kept on ringing. Then the ringing stopped. A key tickled at the door and Carmen jumped away from it and stood frozen. The door swung open. A man stepped through it briskly and stopped dead, staring at us quietly, with complete composure.

13

He was a gray man, all gray, except for his polished black shoes and two scarlet diamonds in his gray satin tie that looked like the diamonds on roulette layouts. His shirt was gray and his double-breasted suit of soft, beautifully cut flannel. Seeing Carmen he took a gray hat off and his hair underneath it was gray and as fine as if it had been sifted through gauze. His thick gray eyebrows had that indefinably sporty look. He had a long chin, a nose with a hook to it, thoughtful gray eyes that had a slanted look because the fold of skin over his upper lid came down over the corner of the lid itself.

He stood there politely, one hand touching the door at his back, the other holding the gray hat and flapping it gently against his thigh. He looked hard, not the hardness of the tough guy. More like the hardness of a well-weathered horseman. But he was no horseman. He was Eddie Mars.

He pushed the door shut behind him and put that hand in the lap-seamed pocket of his coat and left the thumb outside to glisten in the rather dim light of the room. He smiled at Carmen. He had a nice easy smile. She licked her lips and stared at him. The fear went out of her face. She smiled back.

"Excuse the casual entrance," he said. "The bell didn't seem to rouse anybody. Is Mr. Geiger around?"

I said: "No. We don't know just where he is. We found the door a little open. We stepped inside."

He nodded and touched his long chin with the brim of his hat. "You're friends of his, of course?"

"Just business acquaintances. We dropped by for a book."

"A book, eh?" He said that quickly and brightly and, I thought, a little slyly, as if he knew all about Geiger's books. Then he looked at Carmen again and shrugged.

I moved towards the door. "We'll trot along now," I said. I took hold of her arm. She was staring at Eddie Mars. She liked him.

"Any message—if Geiger comes back?" Eddie Mars asked gently.

"We won't bother you."

"That's too bad," he said, with too much meaning. His gray eyes twinkled and then hardened as I went past him to open the door. He added in a casual tone: "The girl can dust. I'd like to talk to you a little, soldier."

I let go of her arm. I gave him a blank stare. "Kidder, eh?" he said nicely. "Don't waste it. I've got two boys outside in a car that always do just what I want them to."

Carmen made a sound at my side and bolted through the door. Her steps faded rapidly downhill. I hadn't seen her car, so she must have left it down below. I started to say: "What the hell—!"

"Oh, skip it," Eddie Mars sighed. "There's something wrong around here. I'm going to find out what it is. If you want to pick lead out of your belly, get in my way."

"Well, well," I said, "a tough guy."

"Only when necessary, soldier." He wasn't looking at me any more. He was walking around the room, frowning, not paying any attention to me. I looked out above the broken pane of the front window. The top of a car showed over the hedge. Its motor idled.

Eddie Mars found the purple flagon and the two gold-veined glasses on the desk. He sniffed at one of the glasses, then at the flagon. A disgusted smile wrinkled his lips. "The lousy pimp," he said tonelessly.

He looked at a couple of books, grunted, went on around the desk and stood in front of the little totem pole with the camera eye. He studied it, dropped his glance to the floor in front of it. He moved the small rug with his foot, then bent swiftly, his body tense. He went down on the floor with one gray knee. The desk hid him from me partly. There was a sharp exclamation and he came up again. His arm flashed under his coat and a black Luger appeared in his hand. He held it in long brown fingers, not pointing it at me, not pointing it at anything.

"Blood," he said. "Blood on the floor there, under the rug. Quite a lot of blood."

"Is that so?" I said, looking interested.

He slid into the chair behind the desk and hooked the mulberry-colored phone towards him and shifted the Luger to his left hand. He frowned sharply at the telephone, bringing his thick gray eyebrows close together and making a hard crease in the weathered skin at the top of his hooked nose. "I think we'll have some law," he said.

I went over and kicked at the rug that lay where Geiger had lain. "It's old blood," I said. "Dried blood."

"Just the same we'll have some law."

"Why not?" I said.

His eyes went narrow. The veneer had flaked off him, leaving a well-dressed hard boy with a Luger. He didn't like my agreeing with him.

"Just who the hell are you, soldier?"

"Marlowe is the name. I'm a sleuth."

"Never heard of you. Who's the girl?"

"Client. Geiger was trying to throw a loop on her with some blackmail. We came to talk it over. He wasn't here. The door being open we walked in to wait. Or did I tell you that?"

"Convenient," he said. "The door being open. When you didn't have a key."

"Yes. How come *you* had a key?"

"Is that any of your business, soldier?"

"I could make it my business."

He smiled tightly and pushed his hat back on his gray hair. "And I could make your business my business."

"You wouldn't like it. The pay's too small."

"All right, bright eyes. I own this house. Geiger is my tenant. Now what do you think of that?"

"You know such lovely people."

"I take them as they come. They come all kinds." He glanced down at the Luger, shrugged and tucked it back under his arm. "Got any good ideas, soldier?"

"Lots of them. Somebody gunned Geiger. Somebody got gunned by Geiger, who ran away. Or it was two other fellows. Or Geiger was running a cult and made blood sacrifices in front of that totem pole. Or he had chicken for dinner and liked to kill his chickens in the front parlor."

The gray man scowled at me.

"I give up," I said. "Better call your friends downtown."

"I don't get it," he snapped. "I don't get your game here."

"Go ahead, call the buttons. You'll get a big reaction from it."

He thought that over without moving. His lips went back against his teeth. "I don't get that, either," he said tightly.

"Maybe it just isn't your day. I know you, Mr. Mars. The Cypress Club at Las Olindas. Flash gambling for flash people. The local law in your pocket and a well-greased line into L.A. In other words, protection. Geiger was in a racket that needed that too. Perhaps you spared him a little now and then, seeing he's your tenant."

His mouth became a hard white grimace. "Geiger was in what racket?"

"The smut book racket."

He stared at me for a long level minute. "Somebody got to him," he said softly. "You know something about it. He didn't show at the store today. They don't know where he is. He didn't answer the phone here. I came up to see about it. I find blood on the floor, under a rug. And you and a girl here."

"A little weak," I said. "But maybe you can sell the story to a willing buyer. You missed a little something, though. Somebody moved his books out of the store today—the nice books he rented out."

He snapped his fingers sharply and said: "I should have thought of that, soldier. You seem to get around. How do you figure it?"

"I think Geiger was rubbed. I think that is his blood. And the books being moved out gives a motive for hiding the body for a while. Somebody is taking over the racket and wants a little time to organize."

"They can't get away with it," Eddie Mars said grimly.

"Who says so? You and a couple of gunmen in your car outside? This is a big town now, Eddie. Some very tough people have checked in here lately. The penalty of growth."

"You talk too damned much," Eddie Mars said. He bared his teeth and whistled twice, sharply. A car door slammed outside and running steps came through the hedge. Mars flicked the Luger out again and pointed it at my chest. "Open the door."

The knob rattled and a voice called out. I didn't move. The muzzle of the Luger looked like the mouth of the Second Street tunnel, but I didn't move. Not being bullet proof is an idea I had had to get used to.

"Open it yourself, Eddie. Who the hell are you to give me orders? Be nice and I might help you out."

He came to his feet rigidly and moved around the end of the desk and over to the door. He opened it without taking his eyes off me. Two men tumbled into the room, reaching busily under their arms. One was an obvious pug, a good-looking pale-faced boy with a bad nose and one ear like a club steak. The other man was slim, blond, deadpan, with close-set eyes and no color in them.

Eddie Mars said: "See if this bird is wearing any iron."

The blond flicked a short-barreled gun out and stood pointing it at me. The pug sidled over flatfooted and felt my pockets with care. I turned around for him like a bored beauty modeling an evening gown.

"No gun," he said in a burry voice.

"Find out who he is."

The pug slipped a hand into my breast pocket and drew out my wallet. He flipped it open and studied the contents. "Name's Philip Marlowe, Eddie. Lives at the Hobart Arms on Franklin. Private license, deputy's badge and all. A shamus." He slipped the wallet back in my pocket, slapped my face lightly and turned away.

"Beat it," Eddie Mars said.

The two gunmen went out again and closed the door. There was the sound of them getting back into the car. They started its motor and kept it idling once more.

"All right. Talk," Eddie Mars snapped. The peaks of his eyebrows made sharp angles against his forehead.

"I'm not ready to give out. Killing Geiger to grab his racket would be a dumb trick and I'm not sure it happened that way, assuming he has been killed. But I'm sure that whoever got the books knows what's what, and I'm sure that the blonde lady down at his store is scared batty about something or other. And I have a guess who got the books."

"Who?"

"That's the part I'm not ready to give out. I've got a client, you know."

He wrinkled his nose. "That—" he chopped it off quickly.

"I expected you would know the girl," I said.

"Who got the books, soldier?"

"Not ready to talk, Eddie. Why should I?"

He put the Luger down on the desk and slapped it with his open palm. "This," he said. "And I might make it worth your while."

"That's the spirit. Leave the gun out of it. I can always hear the sound of money. How much are you clinking at me?"

"For doing what?"

"What did you want done?"

He slammed the desk hard. "Listen, soldier. I ask you a question and you ask me another. We're not getting anywhere. I want to know where Geiger is, for my own personal reasons. I didn't like his racket and I didn't protect him. I happen to own this house. I'm not so crazy about that right now. I can believe that whatever you know about all this is under glass, or there would be a flock of johns squeaking sole leather around this dump. You haven't got anything to sell. My guess is you need a little protection yourself. So cough up."

It was a good guess, but I wasn't going to let him know it. I lit a cigarette and blew the match out and flicked it at the glass eye of the totem pole. "You're right," I said. "If anything has happened to Geiger, I'll have to give what I have to the law. Which puts it in the public domain and doesn't leave me anything to sell. So with your permission I'll just drift."

His face whitened under the tan. He looked mean, fast and tough for a moment. He made a movement to lift the gun. I added casually: "By the way, how is Mrs. Mars these days?"

I thought for a moment I had kidded him a little too far. His hand jerked at the gun, shaking. His face was stretched out by hard muscles. "Beat it," he said quite softly. "I don't give a damn where you go or what you do when you get there. Only take a word of advice, soldier. Leave me out of your plans or you'll wish your name was Murphy and you lived in Limerick."

"Well, that's not so far from Clonmel," I said. "I hear you had a pal came from there."

He leaned down on the desk, frozen-eyed, unmoving. I went over to the door and opened it and looked back at him. His eyes had followed me, but his lean gray body had not moved. There was hate in his eyes. I went out and through the hedge and up the hill to my car and got into it. I turned it around and drove up over the crest. Nobody shot at me. After a few blocks I turned off, cut the motor and sat for a few moments. Nobody followed me either. I drove back into Hollywood.

14

It was ten minutes to five when I parked near the lobby entrance of the apartment house on Randall Place. A few windows were lit and radios were bleating at the dusk. I rode the automatic elevator up to the fourth floor and went along a wide hall carpeted in green and paneled in ivory. A cool breeze blew down the hall from the open screened door to the fire escape.

There was a small ivory pushbutton beside the door marked "405." I pushed it and waited what seemed a long time. Then the door opened noiselessly about a foot. There was a steady, furtive air in the way it opened. The man was long-legged, long-waisted, high-shouldered and he had dark brown eyes in a brown expressionless face that had learned to control its expressions long ago. Hair like steel wool grew far back on his head and gave him a great deal of domed brown forehead that might at a careless glance have seemed a dwelling place for brains. His somber eyes probed at me impersonally. His long thin brown fingers held the edge of the door. He said nothing.

I said: "Geiger?"

Nothing in the man's face changed that I could see. He brought a cigarette from behind the door and tucked it between his lips and drew a little smoke from it. The smoke came towards me in a lazy, contemptuous puff and behind it words in a cool, unhurried voice that had no more inflection than the voice of a faro dealer.

"You said what?"

"Geiger. Arthur Gwynn Geiger. The guy that has the books."

The man considered that without any haste. He glanced down at the tip of his cigarette. His other hand, the one that had been holding the door, dropped out of sight. His shoulder had a look as though his hidden hand might be making motions.

"Don't know anybody by that name," he said. "Does he live around here?"

I smiled. He didn't like the smile. His eyes got nasty. I said: "You're Joe Brody?"

The brown face hardened. "So what? Got a grift, brother —or just amusing yourself?"

"So you're Joe Brody," I said. "And you don't know anybody named Geiger. That's very funny."

"Yeah? You got a funny sense of humor maybe. Take it away and play on it somewhere else."

I leaned against the door and gave him a dreamy smile. "You got the books, Joe. I got the sucker list. We ought to talk things over."

He didn't shift his eyes from my face. There was a faint sound in the room behind him, as though a metal curtain ring clicked lightly on a metal rod. He glanced sideways into the room. He opened the door wider.

"Why not—if you think you've got something?" he said coolly. He stood aside from the door. I went past him into the room.

It was a cheerful room with good furniture and not too much of it. French windows in the end wall opened on a stone porch and looked across the dusk at the foothills. Near the windows a closed door in the west wall and near the entrance door another door in the same wall. This last had a plush curtain drawn across it on a thin brass rod below the lintel.

That left the east wall, in which there were no doors. There was a davenport backed against the middle of it, so I sat down on the davenport. Brody shut the door and walked crab-fashion to a tall oak desk studded with square nails. A cedarwood box with gilt hinges lay on the lowered leaf of the desk. He carried the box to an easy chair midway between the other two doors and sat down. I dropped my hat on the davenport and waited.

"Well, I'm listening," Brody said. He opened the cigar box and dropped his cigarette stub into a dish at his side. He put a long thin cigar in his mouth. "Cigar?" He tossed one at me through the air.

I reached for it. Brody took a gun out of the cigar box and pointed it at my nose. I looked at the gun. It was a black Police .38. I had no argument against it at the moment.

"Neat, huh?" Brody said. "Just kind of stand up a minute. Come forward just about two yards. You might grab a little air while you're doing that." His voice was the elaborately casual voice of the tough guy in pictures. Pictures have made them all like that.

"Tsk, tsk," I said, not moving at all. "Such a lot of guns around town and so few brains. You're the second guy I've met within hours who seems to think a gat in the hand means a world by the tail. Put it down and don't be silly, Joe."

His eyebrows came together and he pushed his chin at me. His eyes were mean.

"The other guy's name is Eddie Mars," I said. "Ever hear of him?"

"No." Brody kept the gun pointed at me.

"If he ever gets wise to where you were last night in the rain, he'll wipe you off the way a check raiser wipes a check."

"What would I be to Eddie Mars?" Brody asked coldly. But he lowered the gun to his knee.

"Not even a memory," I said.

We stared at each other. I didn't look at the pointed black slipper that showed under the plush curtain on the doorway to my left.

Brody said quietly: "Don't get me wrong. I'm not a tough guy—just careful. I don't know hell's first whisper about you. You might be a lifetaker for all I know."

"You're not careful enough," I said. "That play with Geiger's books was terrible."

He drew a long slow breath and let it out silently. Then he leaned back and crossed his long legs and held the Colt on his knee.

"Don't kid yourself I won't use this heat, if I have to," he said. "What's your story?"

"Have your friend with the pointed slippers come on in. She gets tired holding her breath."

Brody called out without moving his eyes off my stomach. "Come on in, Agnes."

The curtain swung aside and the green-eyed, thigh-swinging ash blonde from Geiger's store joined us in the room. She looked at me with a kind of mangled hatred. Her nostrils were pinched and her eyes had darkened a couple of shades. She looked very unhappy.

"I knew damn well you were trouble," she snapped at me. "I told Joe to watch his step."

"It's not his step, it's the back of his lap he ought to watch," I said.

"I suppose that's funny," the blonde squealed.

"It has been," I said. "But it probably isn't any more."

"Save the gags," Brody advised me. "Joe's watchin' his step plenty. Put some light on so I can see to pop this guy, if it works out that way."

The blonde snicked on a light in a big square standing lamp. She sank down into a chair beside the lamp and sat stiffly, as if her girdle was too tight. I put my cigar in my mouth and bit the end off. Brody's Colt took a close interest in me while I got matches out and lit the cigar. I tasted the smoke and said:

"The sucker list I spoke of is in code. I haven't cracked it yet, but there are about five hundred names. You got twelve boxes of books that I know of. You should have at least five hundred books. There'll be a bunch more out on loan, but say five hundred is the full crop, just to be cautious. If it's a good active list and you could run it even fifty per cent down the line, that would be one hundred and twenty-five thousand rentals. Your girl friend knows all about that. I'm only guessing. Put the average rental as low as you like, but it won't be less than a dollar. That merchandise costs money. At a dollar a rental you take one hundred and twenty-five grand and you still have your capital. I mean, you still have Geiger's capital. That's enough to spot a guy for."

The blonde yelped: "You're crazy, you goddam egg-headed—!"

Brody put his teeth sideways at her and snarled: "Pipe down, for Chrissake. Pipe down!"

She subsided into an outraged mixture of slow anguish and bottled fury. Her silvery nails scraped on her knees.

"It's no racket for bums," I told Brody almost affection-ately. "It takes a smooth worker like you, Joe. You've got to get confidence and keep it. People who spend their money for second-hand sex jags are as nervous as dowagers who can't find the rest room. Personally I think the blackmail angles are a big mistake. I'm for shedding all that and sticking to legiti-mate sales and rentals."

Brody's dark brown stare moved up and down my face. His Colt went on hungering for my vital organs. "You're a funny guy," he said tonelessly. "Who has this lovely racket?"

"*You* have," I said. "Almost."

The blonde choked and clawed her ear. Brody didn't say anything. He just looked at me.

"What?" the blonde yelped. "You sit there and try to tell us Mr. Geiger ran that kind of business right down on the main drag? You're nuts!"

I leered at her politely. "Sure I do. Everybody knows the racket exists. Hollywood's made to order for it. If a thing like that has to exist, then right out on the street is where all practical coppers want it to exist. For the same reason they favor red light districts. They know where to flush the game when they want to."

"My God," the blonde wailed. "You let this cheese-head sit

there and insult me, Joe? You with a gun in your hand and him holding nothing but a cigar and his thumb?"

"I like it," Brody said. "The guy's got good ideas. Shut your trap and keep it shut, or I'll slap it shut for you with this." He flicked the gun around in an increasingly negligent manner.

The blonde gasped and turned her face to the wall. Brody looked at me and said cunningly: "*How* have I got that lovely racket?"

"You shot Geiger to get it. Last night in the rain. It was dandy shooting weather. The trouble is he wasn't alone when you whiffed him. Either you didn't notice that, which seems unlikely, or you got the wind up and lammed. But you had nerve enough to take the plate out of his camera and you had nerve enough to come back later on and hide his corpse, so you could tidy up on the books before the law knew it had a murder to investigate."

"Yah," Brody said contemptuously. The Colt wobbled on his knee. His brown face was as hard as a piece of carved wood. "You take chances, mister. It's kind of goddamned lucky for you I *didn't* bop Geiger."

"You can step off for it just the same," I told him cheerfully. "You're made to order for the rap."

Brody's voice rustled. "Think you got me framed for it?"

"Positive."

"How come?"

"There's somebody who'll tell it that way. I told you there was a witness. Don't go simple on me, Joe."

He exploded then. "That goddamned little hot pants!" he yelled. "She would, god damn her! She would—just that!"

I leaned back and grinned at him. "Swell. I thought you had those nude photos of her."

He didn't say anything. The blonde didn't say anything. I let them chew on it. Brody's face cleared slowly, with a sort of grayish relief. He put his Colt down on the end table beside his chair but kept his right hand close to it. He knocked ash from his cigar on the carpet and stared at me with eyes that were a tight shine between narrowed lids.

"I guess you think I'm dumb," Brody said.

"Just average, for a grifter. Get the pictures."

"What pictures?"

I shook my head. "Wrong play, Joe. Innocence gets you nowhere. You were either there last night, or you got the nude photo from somebody that was there. You know *she* was there, because you had your girl friend threaten Mrs. Regan with a police rap. The only ways you could know enough to do that would be by seeing what happened or by holding the photo and knowing where and when it was taken. Cough up and be sensible."

"I'd have to have a little dough," Brody said. He turned his head a little to look at the green-eyed blonde. Not now green-eyed and only superficially a blonde. She was as limp as a fresh-killed rabbit.

"No dough," I said.

He scowled bitterly. "How'd you get to me?"

I flicked my wallet out and let him look at my buzzer. "I was working on Geiger—for a client. I was outside last night, in the rain. I heard the shots. I crashed in. I didn't see the killer. I saw everything else."

"And kept your lip buttoned," Brody sneered.

I put my wallet away. "Yes," I admitted. "Up till now. Do I get the photos or not?"

"About these books," Brody said. "I don't get that."

"I tailed them here from Geiger's store. I have a witness."

"That punk kid?"

"What punk kid?"

He scowled again. The kid that works at the store. He skipped out after the truck left. Agnes don't even know where he flops."

"That helps," I said, grinning at him. "That angle worried me a little. Either of you ever been in Geiger's house—before last night?"

"Not even last night," Brody said sharply. "So she says I gunned him, eh?"

"With the photos in hand I might be able to convince her she was wrong. There was a little drinking being done."

Brody sighed. "She hates my guts. I bounced her out. I got paid, sure, but I'd of had to do it anyway. She's too screwy for a simple guy like me." He cleared his throat. "How about a little dough? I'm down to nickels. Agnes and me gotta move on."

"Not from my client."

"Listen—"

"Get the pictures, Brody."

"Oh, hell," he said. "You win." He stood up and slipped the Colt into his side pocket. His left hand went up inside his coat. He was holding it there, his face twisted with disgust, when the door buzzer rang and kept on ringing.

15

He didn't like that. His lower lip went in under his teeth, and his eyebrows drew down sharply at the corners. His whole face became sharp and foxy and mean.

The buzzer kept up its song. I didn't like it either. If the visitors should happen to be Eddie Mars and his boys, I might get chilled off just for being there. If it was the police, I was caught with nothing to give them but a smile and a promise. And if it was some of Brody's friends—supposing he had any—they might turn out to be tougher than he was.

The blonde didn't like it. She stood up in a surge and chipped at the air with one hand. Nerve tension made her face old and ugly.

Watching me, Brody jerked a small drawer in the desk and picked a bone-handled automatic out of it. He held it at the blonde. She slid over to him and took it, shaking.

"Sit down next to him," Brody snapped. "Hold it on him low down, away from the door. If he gets funny use your own judgment. We ain't licked yet, baby."

"Oh, Joe," the blonde wailed. She came over and sat next to me on the davenport and pointed the gun at my leg artery. I didn't like the jerky look in her eyes.

The door buzzer stopped humming and a quick impatient rapping on the wood followed it. Brody put his hand in his pocket, on his gun, and walked over to the door and opened it with his left hand. Carmen Sternwood pushed him back into the room by putting a little revolver against his lean brown lips.

Brody backed away from her with his mouth working and an expression of panic on his face. Carmen shut the door behind her and looked neither at me nor at Agnes. She stalked Brody carefully, her tongue sticking out a little between her teeth. Brody took both hands out of his pockets and gestured placatingly at her. His eyebrows designed themselves into an odd assortment of curves and angles. Agnes turned the gun away from me and swung it at Carmen. I shot my hand out and closed my fingers down hard over her hand and jammed my thumb on the safety catch. It was already on. I kept it on. There was a short silent tussle, to which neither Brody nor Carmen paid any attention whatever. I had the gun. Agnes breathed deeply and shivered the whole length of her body. Carmen's face had a bony scraped look and her breath hissed. Her voice said without tone:

"I want my pictures, Joe."

Brody swallowed and tried to grin. "Sure, kid, sure." He said it in a small flat voice that was as much like the voice he had used to me as a scooter is like a ten-ton truck.

Carmen said: "You shot Arthur Geiger. I saw you. I want my pictures." Brody turned green.

"Hey, wait a minute, Carmen," I yelped.

Blonde Agnes came to life with a rush. She ducked her head and sank her teeth in my right hand. I made more noises and shook her off.

"Listen, kid," Brody whined. "Listen a minute—"

The blonde spat at me and threw herself on my leg and tried to bite that. I cracked her on the head with the gun, not very hard, and tried to stand up. She rolled down my legs and wrapped her arms around them. I fell back on the davenport. The blonde was strong with the madness of love or fear, or a mixture of both, or maybe she was just strong.

Brody grabbed for the little revolver that was so close to his face. He missed. The gun made a sharp rapping noise that was not very loud. The bullet broke glass in a folded-back French window. Brody groaned horribly and fell down on the floor and jerked Carmen's feet from under her. She landed in a heap and the little revolver went skidding off into a corner. Brody jumped up on his knees and reached for his pocket.

I hit Agnes on the head with less delicacy than before, kicked her off my feet, and stood up. Brody flicked his eyes at me. I showed him the automatic. He stopped trying to get his hand into his pocket.

"Christ!" he whined. "Don't let her kill me!"

I began to laugh. I laughed like an idiot, without control. Blonde Agnes was sitting up on the floor with her hands flat on the carpet and her mouth wide open and a wick of metallic blond hair down over her right eye. Carmen was crawling on her hands and knees, still hissing. The metal of her little revolver glistened against the baseboard over in the corner. She crawled towards it relentlessly.

I waved my share of the guns at Brody and said: "Stay put. You're all right."

I stepped past the crawling girl and picked the gun up. She looked up at me and began to giggle. I put her gun in my pocket and patted her on the back. "Get up, angel. You look like a Pekinese."

I went over to Brody and put the automatic against his midriff and reached his Colt out of his side pocket. I now had all the guns that had been exposed to view. I stuffed them into my pockets and held my hand out to him.

"Give."

He nodded, licking his lips, his eyes still scared. He took a fat envelope out of his breast pocket and gave it to me. There was a developed plate in the envelope and five glossy prints.

"Sure these are all?"

He nodded again. I put the envelope in my own breast pocket and turned away. Agnes was back on the davenport, straightening her hair. Her eyes ate Carmen with a green distillation of hate. Carmen was up on her feet too, coming towards me with her hand out, still giggling and hissing. There was a little froth at the corners of her mouth. Her small white teeth glinted close to her lips.

"Can I have them now?" she asked me with a coy smile.

"I'll take care of them for you. Go on home."

"Home?"

I went to the door and looked out. The cool night breeze was blowing peacefully down the hall. No excited neighbors hung out of doorways. A small gun had gone off and broken a pane of glass, but noises like that don't mean much any more. I held the door open and jerked my head at Carmen. She came towards me, smiling uncertainly.

"Go on home and wait for me," I said soothingly.

She put her thumb up. Then she nodded and slipped past me into the hall. She touched my cheek with her fingers as she went by. "You'll take care of Carmen, won't you?" she cooed.

"Check."

"You're cute."

"What you see is nothing," I said. "I've got a Bali dancing girl tattooed on my right thigh."

Her eyes rounded. She said: "Naughty," and wagged a finger at me. Then she whispered: "Can I have my gun?"

"Not now. Later. I'll bring it to you."

She grabbed me suddenly around the neck and kissed me on the mouth. "I like you," she said. "Carmen likes you a lot." She ran off down the hall as gay as a thrush, waved at me from the stairs and ran down the stairs out of my sight.

I went back into Brody's apartment.

16

I went over to the folded-back French window and looked at the small broken pane in the upper part of it. The bullet from Carmen's gun had smashed the glass like a blow. It had not made a hole. There was a small hole in the plaster which a keen eye would find quickly enough. I pulled the drapes over the broken pane and took Carmen's gun out of my pocket. It was a Banker's Special, .22 caliber, hollow point cartridges. It had a pearl grip, and a small round silver plate set into the butt was engraved: "Carmen from Owen." She made saps of all of them.

I put the gun back in my pocket and sat down close to Brody and stared into his bleak brown eyes. A minute passed.

The blonde adjusted her face by the aid of a pocket mirror. Brody fumbled around with a cigarette and jerked: "Satisfied?"

"So far. Why did you put the bite on Mrs. Regan instead of the old man?"

"Tapped the old man once. About six, seven months ago. I figure maybe he gets sore enough to call in some law."

"What made you think Mrs. Regan wouldn't tell him about it?"

He considered that with some care, smoking his cigarette and keeping his eyes on my face. Finally he said: "How well you know her?"

"I've met her twice. You must know her a lot better to take a chance on that squeeze with the photo."

"She skates around plenty. I figure maybe she has a couple of soft spots she don't want the old man to know about. I figure she can raise five grand easy."

"A little weak," I said. "But pass it. You're broke, eh?"

"I been shaking two nickels together for a month, trying to get them to mate."

"What you do for a living?"

"Insurance. I got desk room in Puss Walgreen's office, Fulwider Building, Western and Santa Monica."

"When you open up, you open up. The books here in your apartment?"

He snapped his teeth and waved a brown hand. Confidence was oozing back into his manner. "Hell, no. In storage."

"You had a man bring them here and then you had a storage outfit come and take them away again right afterwards?"

"Sure. I don't want them moved direct from Geiger's place, do I?"

"You're smart," I said admiringly. "Anything incriminating in the joint right now?"

He looked worried again. He shook his head sharply.

"That's fine," I told him. I looked across at Agnes. She had finished fixing her face and was staring at the wall, blank-eyed, hardly listening. Her face had the drowsiness which strain and shock induce, after their first incidence.

Brody flicked his eyes warily. "Well?"

"How'd you come by the photo?"

He scowled. "Listen, you got what you came after, got it plenty cheap. You done a nice neat job. Now go peddle it to your top man. I'm clean. I don't know nothing about any photo, do I, Agnes?"

The blonde opened her eyes and looked at him with vague but uncomplimentary speculation. "A half smart guy," she said with a tired sniff. "That's all I ever draw. Never once a guy that's smart all the way around the course. Never once."

I grinned at her. "Did I hurt your head much?"

"You and every other man I ever met."

I looked back at Brody. He was pinching his cigarette between his fingers, with a sort of twitch. His hand seemed to be shaking a little. His brown poker face was still smooth.

"We've got to agree on a story," I said. "For instance, Carmen wasn't here. That's very important. She wasn't here. That was a vision you saw."

"Huh!" Brody sneered. "If you say so, pal, and if—" he put his hand out palm up and cupped the fingers and rolled the thumb gently against the index and middle fingers.

I nodded. "We'll see. There might be a small contribution. You won't count it in grands, though. Now where did you get the picture?"

"A guy slipped it to me."

"Uh-huh. A guy you just passed in the street. You wouldn't know him again. You never saw him before."

Brody yawned. "It dropped out of his pocket," he leered.

"Uh-huh. Got an alibi for last night, poker pan?"

"Sure. I was right here. Agnes was with me. Okey, Agnes?"

"I'm beginning to feel sorry for you again," I said.

His eyes flicked wide and his mouth hung loose, the cigarette balanced on his lower lip.

"You think you're smart and you're so goddamned dumb," I told him. "Even if you don't dance off up in Quentin, you have such a bleak long lonely time ahead of you."

His cigarette jerked and dropped ash on his vest.

"Thinking about how smart you are," I said.

"Take the air," he growled suddenly. "Dust. I got enough chinning with you. Beat it."

"Okey." I stood up and went over to the tall oak desk and took his two guns out of my pockets, laid them side by side on the blotter so that the barrels were exactly parallel. I reached my hat off the floor beside the davenport and started for the door.

Brody yelped: "Hey!"

I turned and waited. His cigarette was jiggling like a doll on a coiled spring. "Everything's smooth, ain't it?" he asked.

"Why, sure. This is a free country. You don't have to stay out of jail, if you don't want to. That is, if you're a citizen. Are you a citizen?"

He just stared at me, jiggling the cigarette. The blonde Agnes turned her head slowly and stared at me along the same level. Their glances contained almost the exact same blend of foxiness, doubt and frustrated anger. Agnes reached her silvery nails up abruptly and yanked a hair out of her head and broke it between her fingers, with a bitter jerk.

Brody said tightly: "You're not going to any cops, brother. Not if it's the Sternwoods you're working for. I've got too much stuff on that family. You got your pictures and you got your hush. Go and peddle your papers."

"Make your mind up," I said. "You told me to dust, I was on my way out, you hollered at me and I stopped, and now I'm on my way out again. Is that what you want?"

"You ain't got anything on me," Brody said.

"Just a couple of murders. Small change in your circle."

He didn't jump more than an inch, but it looked like a foot. The white cornea showed all around the tobacco-colored iris of his eyes. The brown skin of his face took on a greenish tinge in the lamplight.

Blonde Agnes let out a low animal wail and buried her head in a cushion on the end of the davenport. I stood there and admired the long line of her thighs.

Brody moistened his lips slowly and said: "Sit down, pal. Maybe I have a little more for you. What's that crack about two murders mean?"

I leaned against the door. "Where were you last night about seven-thirty, Joe?"

His mouth drooped sulkily and he stared down at the floor. "I was watching a guy, a guy who had a nice racket I figured he needed a partner in. Geiger. I was watching him now and then to see had he any tough connections. I figure he has friends or he don't work the racket as open as he does. But they don't go to his house. Only dames."

"You didn't watch hard enough," I said. "Go on."

"I'm there last night on the street below Geiger's house. It's raining hard and I'm buttoned up in my coupe and I don't see anything. There's a car in front of Geiger's and another car a little way up the hill. That's why I stay down below. There's a big Buick parked down where I am and after a while I go over and take a gander into it. It's registered to Vivian Regan. Nothing happens, so I scram. That's all." He waved his cigarette. His eyes crawled up and down my face.

"Could be," I said. "Know where that Buick is now?"

"Why would I?"

"In the Sheriff's garage. It was lifted out of twelve feet of water off Lido fish pier this a.m. There was a dead man in it. He had been sapped and the car pointed out the pier and the hand throttle pulled down."

Brody was breathing hard. One of his feet tapped restlessly. "Jesus, guy, you can't pin that one on me," he said thickly.

"Why not? This Buick was down back of Geiger's according to you. Well, Mrs. Regan didn't have it out. Her chauffeur, a lad named Owen Taylor, had it out. He went over to Geiger's place to have words with him, because Owen Taylor was sweet on Carmen, and he didn't like the kind of games Geiger was playing with her. He let himself in the back way with a jimmy and a gun and he caught Geiger taking a photo of Carmen without any clothes on. So his gun went off, as guns will, and Geiger fell down dead and Owen ran away, but not without the photo negative Geiger had just taken. So you ran after him and took the photo from him. How else would you have got hold of it?"

Brody licked his lips. "Yeah," he said. "But that don't make me knock him off. Sure, I heard the shots and saw this killer come slamming down the back steps into the Buick and off. I took out after him. He hit the bottom of the canyon and went west on Sunset. Beyond Beverly Hills he skidded off the road and had to stop and I came up and played copper. He had a gun but his nerve was bad and I sapped him down. So I went through his clothes and found out who he was and I lifted the plateholder, just out of curiosity. I was wondering what it was all about and getting my neck wet when he came out of it all of a sudden and knocked me off the car. He was out of sight when I picked myself up. That's the last I saw of him."

"How did you know it was Geiger he shot?" I asked gruffly.

Brody shrugged. "I figure it was, but I can be wrong. When I had the plate developed and saw what was on it, I was pretty damn sure. And when Geiger didn't come down to the store this morning and didn't answer his phone I was plenty sure. So I figure it's a good time to move his books out and make a quick touch on the Sternwoods for travel money and blow for a while."

I nodded. "That seems reasonable. Maybe you didn't murder anybody at that. Where did you hide Geiger's body?"

He jumped his eyebrows. Then he grinned. "Nix, nix. Skip it. You think I'd go back there and handle him, not knowing when a couple carloads of law would come tearing around the corner? Nix."

"Somebody hid the body," I said.

Brody shrugged. The grin stayed on his face. He didn't believe me. While he was still not believing me the door buzzer started to ring again. Brody stood up sharply, hard-eyed. He glanced over at his guns on the desk.

"So she's back again," he growled.

"If she is, she doesn't have her gun," I comforted him. "Don't you have any other friends?"

"Just about one," he growled. "I got enough of this puss in the corner game." He marched to the desk and took the Colt. He held it down at his side and went to the door. He put his left hand to the knob and twisted it and opened the door a foot and leaned into the opening, holding the gun tight against his thigh.

A voice said: "Brody?"

Brody said something I didn't hear. The two quick reports were muffled. The gun must have been pressed tight against Brody's body. He tilted forward against the door and the weight of his body pushed it shut with a bang. He slid down the wood. His feet pushed the carpet away behind him. His left hand dropped off the knob and the arm slapped the floor with a thud. His head was wedged against the door. He didn't move. The Colt clung to his right hand.

I jumped across the room and rolled him enough to get the door open and crowd through. A woman peered out of a door almost opposite. Her face was full of fright and she pointed along the hall with a clawlike hand.

I raced down the hall and heard thumping feet going down the tile steps and went down after the sound. At the lobby level the front door was closing itself quietly and running feet slapped the sidewalk outside. I made the door before it was shut, clawed it open again and charged out.

A tall hatless figure in a leather jerkin was running diagonally across the street between the parked cars. The figure turned and flame spurted from it. Two heavy hammers hit the stucco wall beside me. The figure ran on, dodged between two cars, vanished.

A man came up beside me and barked: "What happened?"

"Shooting going on," I said.

"Jesus!" He scuttled into the apartment house.

I walked quickly down the sidewalk to my car and got in and started it. I pulled out from the curb and drove down the hill, not fast. No other car started up on the other side of the street. I thought I heard steps, but I wasn't sure about that. I rode down the hill a block and a half, turned at the intersection and started back up. The sound of a muted whistling came to me faintly along the sidewalk. Then steps. I double parked and slid out between two cars and went down low. I took Carmen's little revolver out of my pocket.

The sound of the steps grew louder, and the whistling went on cheerfully. In a moment the jerkin showed. I stepped out between the two cars and said: "Got a match, buddy?"

The boy spun towards me and his right hand darted up to go inside the jerkin. His eyes were a wet shine in the glow of the round electroliers. Moist dark eyes shaped like almonds, and a pallid handsome face with wavy black hair growing low on the forehead in two points. A very handsome boy indeed, the boy from Geiger's store.

He stood there looking at me silently, his right hand on the edge of the jerkin, but not inside it yet. I held the little revolver down at my side.

"You must have thought a lot of that queen," I said.

"Go —— yourself," the boy said softly, motionless between the parked cars and the five-foot retaining wall on the inside of the sidewalk.

A siren wailed distantly coming up the long hill. The boy's head jerked towards the sound. I stepped in close and put my gun into his jerkin.

"Me or the cops?" I asked him.

His head rolled a little sideways as if I had slapped his face. "Who are you?" he snarled.

"Friend of Geiger's."

"Get away from me, you son of a bitch."

"This is a small gun, kid. I'll give it to you through the navel and it will take three months to get you well enough to walk. But you'll get well. So you can walk to the nice new gas chamber up in Quentin."

He said: "Go —— yourself." His hand moved inside the jerkin. I pressed harder on his stomach. He let out a long soft sigh, took his hand away from the jerkin and let it fall limp at his side. His wide shoulders sagged. "What you want?" he whispered.

I reached inside the jerkin and plucked out the automatic. "Get into my car, kid."

He stepped past me and I crowded him from behind. He got into the car.

"Under the wheel, kid. You drive."

He slid under the wheel and I got into the car beside him. I said: "Let the prowl car pass up the hill. They'll think we moved over when we heard the siren. Then turn her down hill and we'll go home."

I put Carmen's gun away and leaned the automatic against the boy's ribs. I looked back through the window. The whine of the siren was very loud now. Two red lights swelled in the middle of the street. They grew larger and blended into one and the car rushed by in a wild flurry of sound.

"Let's go," I said.

The boy swung the car and started off down the hill.

"Let's go home," I said. "To Laverne Terrace."

His smooth lips twitched. He swung the car west on Franklin. "You're a simple-minded lad. What's your name?"

"Carol Lundgren," he said lifelessly.

"You shot the wrong guy, Carol. Joe Brody didn't kill your queen."

He spoke three words to me and kept on driving.

17

A moon half gone from the full glowed through a ring of mist among the high branches of the eucalyptus trees on Laverne Terrace. A radio sounded loudly from a house low down the hill. The boy swung the car over to the box hedge in front of Geiger's house, killed the motor and sat looking straight before him with both hands on the wheel. No light showed through Geiger's hedge.

I said: "Anybody home, son?"

"You ought to know."

"How would I know?"

"Go —— yourself."

"That's how people get false teeth."

He showed me his in a tight grin. Then he kicked the door open and got out. I scuttled out after him. He stood with his fists on his hips, looking silently at the house above the top of the hedge.

"All right," I said. "You have a key. Let's go on in."

"Who said I had a key?"

"Don't kid me, son. The fag gave you one. You've got a nice clean manly little room in there. He shooed you out and locked it up when he had lady visitors. He was like Caesar, a husband to women and a wife to men. Think I can't figure people like him and you out?"

I still held his automatic more or less pointed at him, but he swung on me just the same. It caught me flush on the chin. I backstepped fast enough to keep from falling, but I took plenty of the punch. It was meant to be a hard one, but a pansy has no iron in his bones, whatever he looks like.

I threw the gun down at the kid's feet and said: "Maybe you need this."

He stooped for it like a flash. There was nothing slow

about his movements. I sank a fist in the side of his neck. He toppled over sideways, clawing for the gun and not reaching it. I picked it up again and threw it in the car. The boy came up on all fours, leering with his eyes too wide open. He coughed and shook his head.

"You don't want to fight," I told him. "You're giving away too much weight."

He wanted to fight. He shot at me like a plane from a catapult, reaching for my knees in a diving tackle. I side-stepped and reached for his neck and took it into chancery. He scraped the dirt hard and got his feet under him enough to use his hands on me where it hurt. I twisted him around and heaved him a little higher. I took hold of my right wrist with my left hand and turned my right hipbone into him and for a moment it was a balance of weights. We seemed to hang there in the misty moonlight, two grotesque creatures whose feet scraped on the road and whose breath panted with effort.

I had my right forearm against his windpipe now and all the strength of both arms in it. His feet began a frenetic shuffle and he wasn't panting any more. He was ironbound. His left foot sprawled off to one side and the knee went slack. I held on half a minute longer. He sagged on my arm, an enormous weight I could hardly hold up. Then I let go. He sprawled at my feet, out cold. I went to the car and got a pair of handcuffs out of the glove compartment and twisted his wrists behind him and snapped them on. I lifted him by the armpits and managed to drag him in behind the hedge, out of sight from the street. I went back to the car and moved it a hundred feet up the hill and locked it.

He was still out when I got back. I unlocked the door, dragged him into the house, shut the door. He was beginning to gasp now. I switched a lamp on. His eyes fluttered open and focused on me slowly.

I bent down, keeping out of the way of his knees and said: "Keep quiet or you'll get the same and more of it. Just lie quiet and hold your breath. Hold it until you can't hold it any longer and then tell yourself that you have to breathe, that you're black in the face, that your eyeballs are popping out, and that you're going to breathe right now, but that you're sitting strapped in the chair in the clean little gas chamber up in San Quentin and when you take that breath you're fighting with all your soul not to take, it won't be air you'll get, it will be cyanide fumes. And that's what they call humane execution in our state now."

"Go —— yourself," he said with a soft stricken sigh.

"You're going to cop a plea, brother, don't ever think you're not. And you're going to say just what we want you to say and nothing we don't want you to say."

"Go —— yourself."

"Say that again and I'll put a pillow under your head."

His mouth twitched. I left him lying on the floor with his wrists shackled behind him and his cheek pressed into the rug and an animal brightness in his visible eye. I put on another lamp and stepped into the hallway at the back of the living room. Geiger's bedroom didn't seem to have been touched. I opened the door, not locked now, of the bedroom across the hall from it. There was a dim flickering light in the room and a smell of sandalwood. Two cones of incense ash stood side by side on a small brass tray on the bureau. The light came from the two tall black candles in the foot-high candlesticks. They were standing on straight-backed chairs, one on either side of the bed.

Geiger lay on the bed. The two missing strips of Chinese tapestry made a St. Andrew's Cross over the middle of his body, hiding the blood-smeared front of his Chinese coat. Below the cross his black-pajama'd legs lay stiff and straight. His feet were in the slippers with thick white felt soles. Above the cross his arms were crossed at the wrists and his hands lay flat against his shoulders, palms down, fingers close together and stretched out evenly. His mouth was closed and his Charlie Chan moustache was as unreal as a toupee. His broad nose was pinched and white. His eyes were almost closed, but not entirely. The faint glitter of his glass eye caught the light and winked at me.

I didn't touch him. I didn't go very near him. He would be as cold as ice and as stiff as a board.

The black candles guttered in the draft from the open door. Drops of black wax crawled down their sides. The air of the room was poisonous and unreal. I went out and shut the door again and went back to the living room. The boy hadn't moved. I stood still, listening for sirens. It was all a question of how soon Agnes talked and what she said. If she talked about Geiger, the police would be there any minute. But she might not talk for hours. She might even have got away.

I looked down at the boy. "Want to sit up, son?"

He closed his eye and pretended to go to sleep. I went over to the desk and scooped up the mulberry-colored phone and dialed Bernie Ohls' office. He had left to go home at six o'clock. I dialed the number of his home. He was there.

"This is Marlowe," I said. "Did your boys find a revolver on Owen Taylor this morning?"

I could hear him clearing his throat and then I could hear him trying to keep the surprise out of his voice. "That would come under the heading of police business," he said.

"If they did, it had three empty shells in it."

"How the hell did you know that?" Ohls asked quietly.

"Come over to 7244 Laverne Terrace, off Laurel Canyon Boulevard. I'll show you where the slugs went."

"Just like that, huh?"

"Just like that."

Ohls said: "Look out the window and you'll see me coming round the corner. I thought you acted a little cagey on that one."

"Cagey is no word for it," I said.

18

Ohls stood looking down at the boy. The boy sat on the couch leaning sideways against the wall. Ohls looked at him silently, his pale eyebrows bristling and stiff and round like the little vegetable brushes the Fuller Brush man gives away.

He asked the boy: "Do you admit shooting Brody?"

The boy said his favorite three words in a muffled voice.

Ohls sighed and looked at me. I said: "He doesn't have to admit that. I have his gun."

Ohls said: "I wish to Christ I had a dollar for every time I've had that said to me. What's funny about it?"

"It's not meant to be funny," I said.

"Well, that's something," Ohls said. He turned away. "I've called Wilde. We'll go over and see him and take this punk. He can ride with me and you can follow on behind in case he tries to kick me in the face."

"How do you like what's in the bedroom?"

"I like it fine," Ohls said. "I'm kind of glad that Taylor kid went off the pier. I'd hate to have to help send him to the deathhouse for rubbing that skunk."

I went back into the small bedroom and blew out the black candles and let them smoke. When I got back to the living room Ohls had the boy up on his feet. The boy stood glaring at him with sharp black eyes in a face as hard and white as cold mutton fat.

"Let's go," Ohls said and took him by the arm as if he didn't like touching him. I put the lamps out and followed them out of the house. We got into our cars and I followed Ohls' twin tail-lights down the long curving hill. I hoped this would be my last trip to Laverne Terrace.

Taggart Wilde, the District Attorney, lived at the corner of Fourth and Lafayette Park, in a white frame house the size of a carbarn, with a red sandstone porte-cochere built on to one side and a couple of acres of soft rolling lawn in front. It was one of those solid old-fashioned houses which it used to be the thing to move bodily to new locations as the city grew westward. Wilde came of an old Los Angeles family and had probably been born in the house when it was on West Adams or Figueroa or St. James Park.

There were two cars in the driveway already, a big private sedan and a police car with a uniformed chauffeur who leaned smoking against his rear fender and admired the moon. Ohls went over and spoke to him and the chauffeur looked in at the boy in Ohls' car.

We went up to the house and rang the bell. A slick-haired blond man opened the door and led us down the hall and through a huge sunken living room crowded with heavy dark furniture and along another hall on the far side of it. He knocked at a door and stepped inside, then held the door wide and we went into a paneled study with an open French door at the end and a view of dark garden and mysterious trees. A smell of wet earth and flowers came in at the window. There were large dim oils on the walls, easy chairs, books, a smell of good cigar smoke which blended with the smell of wet earth and flowers.

Taggart Wilde sat behind a desk, a middle-aged plump man with clear blue eyes that managed to have a friendly expression without really having any expression at all. He had a cup of black coffee in front of him and he held a dappled thin cigar between the neat careful fingers of his left hand. Another man sat at the corner of the desk in a blue leather chair, a cold-eyed hatchet-faced man, as lean as a rake and as hard as the manager of a loan office. His neat well-kept face looked as if it had been shaved within the hour. He wore a well-pressed brown suit and there was a black pearl in his tie. He had the long nervous fingers of a man with a quick brain. He looked ready for a fight.

Ohls pulled a chair up and sat down and said: "Evening, Cronjager. Meet Phil Marlowe, a private eye who's in a jam." Ohls grinned.

Cronjager looked at me without nodding. He looked me over as if he was looking at a photograph. Then he nodded his chin about an inch. Wilde said: "Sit down, Marlowe. I'll try to handle Captain Cronjager, but you know how it is. This is a big city now."

I sat down and lit a cigarette. Ohls looked at Cronjager and asked: "What did you get on the Randall Place killing?"

The hatchet-faced man pulled one of his fingers until the knuckle cracked. He spoke without looking up. "A stiff, two slugs in him. Two guns that hadn't been fired. Down on the street we got a blonde trying to start a car that didn't belong to her. Hers was right next to it, the same model. She acted rattled so the boys brought her in and she spilled. She was in there when this guy Brody got it. Claims she didn't see the killer."

"That all?" Ohls asked.

Cronjager raised his eyebrows a little. "Only happened about an hour ago. What did you expect—moving pictures of the killing?"

"Maybe a description of the killer," Ohls said.

"A tall guy in a leather jerkin—if you call that a description."

"He's outside in my heap," Ohls said. "Handcuffed. Marlowe put the arm on him for you. Here's his gun." Ohls took the boy's automatic out of his pocket and laid it on a corner of Wilde's desk. Cronjager looked at the gun but didn't reach for it.

Wilde chuckled. He was leaning back and puffing his dappled cigar without letting go of it. He bent forward to sip from his coffee cup. He took a silk handkerchief from the breast pocket of the dinner jacket he was wearing and touched his lips with it and tucked it away again.

"There's a couple more deaths involved," Ohls said, pinching the soft flesh at the end of his chin.

Cronjager stiffened visibly. His surly eyes became points of steely light.

Ohls said: "You heard about a car being lifted out of the Pacific Ocean off Lido pier this a.m. with a dead guy in it?"

Cronjager said: "No," and kept on looking nasty.

"The dead guy in the car was chauffeur to a rich family," Ohls said. "The family was being blackmailed on account of one of the daughters. Mr. Wilde recommended Marlowe to the family, through me. Marlowe played it kind of close to the vest."

"I love private dicks that play murders close to the vest," Cronjager snarled. "You don't have to be so goddamned coy about it."

"Yeah," Ohls said. "I don't have to be so goddamned coy about it. It's not so goddamned often I get a chance to be coy with a city copper. I spend most of my time telling them where to put their feet so they won't break an ankle."

Cronjager whitened around the corners of his sharp nose. His breath made a soft hissing sound in the quiet room. He said very quietly: "You haven't had to tell any of *my* men where to put their feet, smart guy."

"We'll see about that," Ohls said. "This chauffeur I spoke of that's drowned off Lido shot a guy last night in your territory. A guy named Geiger who ran a dirty book racket in a store on Hollywood Boulevard. Geiger was living with the punk I got outside in my car. I mean living with him, if you get the idea."

Cronjager was staring at him levelly now. "That sounds like it might grow up to be a dirty story," he said.

"It's my experience most police stories are," Ohls growled and turned to me, his eyebrows bristling. "You're on the air, Marlowe. Give it to him."

I gave it to him.

I left out two things, not knowing just why, at the moment, I left out one of them. I left out Carmen's visit to Brody's apartment and Eddie Mars' visit to Geiger's in the afternoon. I told the rest of it just as it happened.

Cronjager never took his eyes off my face and no expression of any kind crossed his as I talked. At the end of it he was perfectly silent for a long minute. Wilde was silent, sipping his coffee, puffing gently at his dappled cigar. Ohls stared at one of his thumbs.

Cronjager leaned slowly back in his chair and crossed one ankle over his knee and rubbed the ankle bone with his thin nervous hand. His lean face wore a harsh frown. He said with deadly politeness:

"So all you did was not report a murder that happened last night and then spend today foxing around so that this kid of Geiger's could commit a second murder this evening."

"That's all," I said. "I was in a pretty tough spot. I guess I did wrong, but I wanted to protect my client and I hadn't any reason to think the boy would go gunning for Brody."

"That kind of thinking is police business, Marlowe. If Geiger's death had been reported last night, the books could never have been moved from the store to Brody's apartment. The kid wouldn't have been led to Brody and wouldn't have killed him. Say Brody was living on borrowed time. His kind usually are. But a life is a life."

"Right," I said. "Tell that to your coppers next time they shoot down some scared petty larceny crook running away up an alley with a stolen spare."

Wilde put both his hands down on his desk with a solid smack. "That's enough of that," he snapped. "What makes you so sure, Marlowe, that this Taylor boy shot Geiger? Even if the gun that killed Geiger was found on Taylor's body or in the car, it doesn't absolutely follow that he was the killer. The gun might have been planted—say by Brody, the actual killer."

"It's physically possible," I said, "but morally impossible. It assumes too much coincidence and too much that's out of character for Brody and his girl, and out of character for what he was trying to do. I talked to Brody for a long time. He was a crook, but not a killer type. He had two guns, but he wasn't wearing either of them. He was trying to find a way to cut in on Geiger's racket, which naturally he knew all about from the girl. He says he was watching Geiger off and on to see if he had any tough backers. I believe him. To suppose he killed Geiger in order to get his books, then scrammed with the nude photo Geiger had just taken of Carmen Sternwood, then planted the gun on Owen Taylor and pushed Taylor into the ocean off Lido, is to suppose a hell of a lot too much. Taylor had the motive, jealous rage, and the opportunity to kill Geiger. He was out in one of the family cars without permission. He killed Geiger right in front of the girl, which Brody would never have done, even if he had been a killer. I can't see anybody with a purely commercial interest in Geiger doing that. But Taylor would have done it. The nude photo business was just what would have made him do it."

Wilde chuckled and looked along his eyes at Cronjager. Cronjager cleared his throat with a snort. Wilde asked: "What's this business about hiding the body? I don't see the point of that."

I said: "The kid hasn't told us, but he must have done it. Brody wouldn't have gone into the house after Geiger was shot. The boy must have got home when I was away taking Carmen to her house. He was afraid of the police, of course, being what he is, and he probably thought it a good idea to have the body hidden until he had removed his effects from the house. He dragged it out of the front door, judging by the marks on the rug, and very likely put it in the garage. Then he packed up what ever belongings he had there and took them away. And later on, sometime in the night and before the body stiffened, he had a revulsion of feeling and thought he hadn't treated his dead friend very nicely. So he went back and laid him out on the bed. That's all guessing, of course."

Wilde nodded. "Then this morning he goes down to the store as if nothing had happened and keeps his eyes open. And when Brody moved the books out he found out where they were going and assumed that whoever got them had killed Geiger just for that purpose. He may even have known more about Brody and the girl than they suspected. What do you think, Ohls?"

Ohls said: "We'll find out—but that doesn't help Cronjager's troubles. What's eating him is all this happened last night and he's only just been rung in on it."

Cronjager said sourly: "I think I can find some way to deal with that angle too." He looked at me sharply and immediately looked away again.

Wilde waved his cigar and said: "Let's see the exhibits, Marlowe."

I emptied my pockets and put the catch on his desk: the three notes and Geiger's card to General Sternwood, Carmen's photos, and the blue notebook with the code list of names and addresses. I had already given Geiger's keys to Ohls.

Wilde looked at what I gave him, puffing gently at his cigar. Ohls lit one of his own toy cigars and blew smoke peacefully at the ceiling. Cronjager leaned on the desk and looked at what I had given Wilde.

Wilde tapped the three notes signed by Carmen and said: "I guess these were just a come-on. If General Sternwood paid them, it would be through fear of something worse. Then Geiger would have tightened the screws. Do you know what he was afraid of?" He was looking at me.

I shook my head.

"Have you told your story complete in all relevant details?"

"I left out a couple of personal matters. I intend to keep on leaving them out, Mr. Wilde."

Cronjager said: "Hah!" and snorted with deep feeling.

"Why?" Wilde asked quietly.

"Because my client is entitled to that protection, short of anything but a Grand Jury. I have a license to operate as a private detective. I suppose that word 'private' has some meaning. The Hollywood Division has two murders on its hands, both solved. They have both killers. They have the motive, the instrument in each case. The blackmail angle has got to be suppressed, as far as the names of the parties are concerned."

"Why?" Wilde asked again.

"That's okey," Cronjager said dryly. "We're glad to stooge for a shamus of his standing."

I said: "I'll show you." I got up and went back out of the house to my car and got the book from Geiger's store out of it. The uniformed police driver was standing beside Ohls' car. The boy was inside it, leaning back sideways in the corner.

"Has he said anything?" I asked.

"He made a suggestion," the copper said and spat. "I'm letting it ride."

I went back into the house, put the book on Wilde's desk and opened up the wrappings. Cronjager was using a telephone on the end of the desk. He hung up and sat down as I came in.

Wilde looked through the book, wooden-faced, closed it and pushed it towards Cronjager. Cronjager opened it, looked at a page or two, shut it quickly. A couple of red spots the size of half dollars showed on his cheekbones.

I said: "Look at the stamped dates on the front endpaper."

Cronjager opened the book again and looked at them. "Well?"

"If necessary," I said, "I'll testify under oath that that book came from Geiger's store. The blonde, Agnes, will admit what kind of business the store did. It's obvious to anybody with eyes that that store is just a front for something. But the Hollywood police allowed it to operate, for their own reasons. I dare say the Grand Jury would like to know what those reasons are."

Wilde grinned. He said: "Grand Juries do ask those embarrassing questions sometimes—in a rather vain effort to find out just why cities are run as they are run."

Cronjager stood up suddenly and put his hat on. "I'm one against three here," he snapped. "I'm a homicide man. If this Geiger was running indecent literature, that's no skin off my nose. But I'm ready to admit it won't help my division any to have it washed over in the papers. What do you birds want?"

Wilde looked at Ohls. Ohls said calmly: "I want to turn a prisoner over to you. Let's go."

He stood up. Cronjager looked at him fiercely and stalked out of the room. Ohls went after him. The door closed again. Wilde tapped on his desk and stared at me with his clear blue eyes.

"You ought to understand how any copper would feel about a cover-up like this," he said. "You'll have to make statements of all of it—at least for the files. I think it may be possible to keep the two killings separate and to keep General Sternwood's name out of both of them. Do you know why I'm not tearing your ear off?"

"No. I expected to get both ears torn off."

"What are you getting for it all?"

"Twenty-five dollars a day and expenses."

"That would make fifty dollars and a little gasoline so far."

"About that."

He put his head on one side and rubbed the back of his left little finger along the lower edge of his chin.

"And for that amount of money you're willing to get yourself in Dutch with half the law enforcement of this county?"

"I don't like it," I said. "But what the hell am I to do? I'm on a case. I'm selling what I have to sell to make a living. What little guts and intelligence the Lord gave me and a willingness to get pushed around in order to protect a client. It's against my principles to tell as much as I've told tonight, without consulting the General. As for the cover-up, I've been in police business myself, as you know. They come a dime a dozen in any big city. Cops get very large and emphatic when an outsider tries to hide anything, but they do the same things themselves every other day, to oblige their friends or anybody with a little pull. And I'm not through. I'm still on the case. I'd do the same thing again, if I had to."

"Providing Cronjager doesn't get your license," Wilde grinned. "You said you held back a couple of personal matters. Of what import?"

"I'm still on the case," I said, and stared straight into his eyes.

Wilde smiled at me. He had the frank daring smile of an Irishman. "Let me tell you something, son. My father was a close friend of old Sternwood. I've done all my office permits—and maybe a good deal more—to save the old man from grief. But in the long run it can't be done. Those girls of his are bound certain to hook up with something that can't be hushed, especially that little blonde brat. They ought not to be running around loose. I blame the old man for that. I guess he doesn't realize what the world is today. And there's another thing I might mention while we're talking man to man and I don't have to growl at you. I'll bet a dollar to a Canadian dime that the General's afraid his son-in-law, the ex-bootlegger, is mixed up in this somewhere, and what he really hoped you would find out is that he isn't. What do you think of that?"

"Regan didn't sound like a blackmailer, what I heard of him. He had a soft spot where he was and he walked out on it."

Wilde snorted. "The softness of that spot neither you nor I could judge. If he was a certain sort of man, it would not have been so very soft. Did the General tell you he was looking for Regan?"

"He told me he wished he knew where he was and that he was all right. He liked Regan and was hurt the way he bounced off without telling the old man good-by."

Wilde leaned back and frowned. "I see," he said in a changed voice. His hand moved the stuff on his desk around, laid Geiger's blue notebook to one side and pushed the other exhibits towards me. "You may as well take these," he said. "I've no further use for them."

19

It was close to eleven when I put my car away and walked around to the front of the Hobart Arms. The plate-glass door was put on the lock at ten, so I had to get my keys out. Inside, in the square barren lobby, a man put a green evening paper down beside a potted palm and flicked a cigarette butt into the tub the palm grew in. He stood up and waved his hat at me and said: "The boss wants to talk to you. You sure keep your friends waiting, pal."

I stood still and looked at his flattened nose and club steak ear.

"What about?"

"What do you care? Just keep your nose clean and everything will be jake." His hand hovered near the upper buttonhole of his open coat.

"I smell of policemen," I said. "I'm too tired to talk, too tired to eat, too tired to think. But if you think I'm not too tired to take orders from Eddie Mars—try getting your gat out before I shoot your good ear off."

"Nuts. You ain't got no gun." He stared at me levelly. His dark wiry brows closed in together and his mouth made a downward curve.

"That was then," I told him. "I'm not always naked."

He waved his left hand. "Okey. You win. I wasn't told to blast anybody. You'll hear from him."

"Too late will be too soon," I said, and turned slowly as he passed me on his way to the door. He opened it and went out without looking back. I grinned at my own foolishness, went along to the elevator and upstairs to the apartment. I took Carmen's little gun out of my pocket and laughed at it. Then I cleaned it thoroughly, oiled it, wrapped it in a piece of canton flannel and locked it up. I made myself a drink and was drinking it when the phone rang. I sat down beside the table on which it stood.

"So you're tough tonight," Eddie Mars' voice said.

"Big, fast, tough and full of prickles. What can I do for you?"

"Cops over there—you know where. You keep me out of it?"

"Why should I?"

"I'm nice to be nice to, soldier. I'm not nice not to be nice to."

"Listen hard and you'll hear my teeth chattering."

He laughed dryly. "Did you—or did you?"

"I did. I'm damned if I know why. I guess it was just complicated enough without you."

"Thanks, soldier. Who gunned him?"

"Read it in the paper tomorrow—maybe."

"I want to know now."

"Do you get everything you want?"

"No. Is that an answer, soldier?"

"Somebody you never heard of gunned him. Let it go at that."

"If that's on the level, someday I may be able to do you a favor."

"Hang up and let me go to bed."

He laughed again. "You're looking for Rusty Regan, aren't you?"

"A lot of people seem to think I am, but I'm not."

"If you were, I could give you an idea. Drop in and see me down at the beach. Any time. Glad to see you."

"Maybe."

"Be seeing you then." The phone clicked and I sat holding it with a savage patience. Then I dialed the Sternwoods' number and heard it ring four or five times and then the butler's suave voice saying: "General Sternwood's residence."

"This is Marlowe. Remember me? I met you about a hundred years ago—or was it yesterday?"

"Yes, Mr. Marlowe. I remember, of course."

"Is Mrs. Regan home?"

"Yes, I believe so. Would you— "

I cut in on him with a sudden change of mind. "No. You give her the message. Tell her I have the pictures, all of them, and that everything is all right."

"Yes . . . yes. . . ." The voice seemed to shake a little. "You have the pictures—all of them—and everything is all right. . . . Yes, sir. I may say—thank you very much, sir."

The phone rang back in five minutes. I had finished my drink and it made me feel as if I could eat the dinner I had forgotten all about; I went out leaving the telephone ringing. It was ringing when I came back. It rang at intervals until half-past twelve. At that time I put my lights out and opened the windows up and muffled the phone bell with a piece of paper and went to bed. I had a bellyful of the Sternwood family.

I read all three of the morning papers over my eggs and

bacon the next morning. Their accounts of the affair came as close to the truth as newspaper stories usually come—as close as Mars is to Saturn. None of the three connected Owen Taylor, driver of the Lido Pier Suicide Car, with the Laurel Canyon Exotic Bungalow Slaying. None of them mentioned the Sternwoods, Bernie Ohls or me. Owen Taylor was "chauffeur to a wealthy family." Captain Cronjager of the Hollywood Division got all the credit for solving the two slayings in his district, which were supposed to arise out of a dispute over the proceeds from a wire service maintained by one Geiger in the back of the bookstore on Hollywood Boulevard. Brody had shot Geiger and Carol Lundgren had shot Brody in revenge. Police were holding Carol Lundgren in custody. He had confessed. He had a bad record—probably in high school. Police were also holding one Agnes Lozelle, Geiger's secretary, as a material witness.

It was a nice write-up. It gave the impression that Geiger had been killed the night before, that Brody had been killed about an hour later, and that Captain Cronjager had solved both murders while lighting a cigarette. The suicide of Taylor made Page One of Section II. There was a photo of the sedan on the deck of the power lighter, with the license plate blacked out, and something covered with a cloth lying on the deck beside the running board. Owen Taylor had been despondent and in poor health. His family lived in Dubuque, and his body would be shipped there. There would be no inquest.

20

Captain Gregory of the Missing Persons Bureau laid my card down on his wide flat desk and arranged it so that its edges exactly paralleled the edges of the desk. He studied it with his head on one side, grunted, swung around in his swivel chair and looked out of his window at the barred top floor of the Hall of Justice half a block away. He was a burly man with tired eyes and the slow deliberate movements of a night watchman. His voice was toneless, flat and uninterested.

"Private dick, eh?" he said, not looking at me at all, but looking out of his window. Smoke wisped from the blackened bowl of a briar that hung on his eye tooth. "What can I do for you?"

"I'm working for General Guy Sternwood, 3765 Alta Brea Crescent, West Hollywood."

Captain Gregory blew a little smoke from the corner of his mouth without removing the pipe. "On what?"

"Not exactly on what you're working on, but I'm interested. I thought you could help me."

"Help you on what?"

"General Sternwood's a rich man," I said. "He's an old friend of the D.A.'s father. If he wants to hire a full-time boy to run errands for him, that's no reflection on the police. It's just a luxury he is able to afford himself."

"What makes you think I'm doing anything for him?"

I didn't answer that. He swung around slowly and heavily in his swivel chair and put his large feet flat on the bare linoleum that covered his floor. His office had the musty smell of years of routine. He stared at me bleakly.

"I don't want to waste your time, Captain," I said and pushed my chair back—about four inches.

He didn't move. He kept on staring at me out of his washed-out tired eyes. "You know the D.A.?"

"I've met him. I worked for him once. I know Bernie Ohls, his chief investigator, pretty well."

Captain Gregory reached for a phone and mumbled into it: "Get me Ohls at the D.A.'s office."

He sat holding the phone down on its cradle. Moments passed. Smoke drifted from his pipe. His eyes were heavy and motionless like his hand. The bell tinkled and he reached for my card with his left hand. "Ohls? . . . Al Gregory at headquarters. A guy named Philip Marlowe is in my office. His card says he's a private investigator. He wants information from me. . . . Yeah? What does he look like? . . . Okey, thanks."

He dropped the phone and took his pipe out of his mouth and tamped the tobacco with the brass cap of a heavy pencil.

He did it carefully and solemnly, as if that was as important as anything he would have to do that day. He leaned back and stared at me some more.

"What you want?"

"An idea of what progress you're making, if any."

He thought that over. "Regan?" he asked finally.

"Sure."

"Know him?"

"I never saw him. I hear he's a good-looking Irishman in his late thirties, that he was once in the liquor racket, that he married General Sternwood's older daughter and that they didn't click. I'm told he disappeared about a month back."

"Sternwood oughta think himself lucky instead of hiring private talent to beat around in the tall grass."

"The General took a big fancy to him. Such things happen. The old man is crippled and lonely. Regan used to sit around with him and keep him company."

"What you think you can do that we can't do?"

"Nothing at all, in so far as finding Regan goes. But there's a rather mysterious blackmail angle. I want to make sure Regan isn't involved. Knowing where he is or isn't might help."

"Brother, I'd like to help you, but I don't know where he is. He pulled down the curtain and that's that."

"Pretty hard to do against your organization, isn't it, Captain?"

"Yeah—but it can be done—for a while." He touched a bell button on the side of his desk. A middle-aged woman put her head in at a side door. "Get me the file on Terence Regan, Abba."

The door closed. Captain Gregory and I looked at each other in some more heavy silence. The door opened again and the woman put a tabbed green file on his desk. Captain Gregory nodded her out, put a pair of heavy horn-rimmed glasses on his veined nose and turned the papers in the file over slowly. I rolled a cigarette around in my fingers.

"He blew on the 16th of September," he said. "The only thing important about that is it was the chauffeur's day off and nobody saw Regan take his car out. It was late afternoon, though. We found the car four days later in a garage belonging to a ritzy bungalow court place near the Sunset Towers. A garage man reported it to the stolen car detail, said it didn't belong there. The place is called the Casa de Oro. There's an angle to that I'll tell you about in a minute. We couldn't find out anything about who put the car in there. We print the car but don't find any prints that are on file anywhere. The car in that garage don't jibe with foul play, although there's a reason to suspect foul play. It jibes with something else I'll tell you about in a minute."

I said: "That jibes with Eddie Mars' wife being on the missing list."

He looked annoyed. "Yeah. We investigate the tenants and find she's living there. Left about the time Regan did, within two days anyway. A guy who sounds a bit like Regan had been seen with her, but we don't get a positive identification. It's goddamned funny in this police racket how an old woman can look out of a window and see a guy running and pick him out of a line-up six months later, but we can show hotel help a clear photo and they just can't be sure."

"That's one of the qualifications for good hotel help," I said.

"Yeah. Eddie Mars and his wife didn't live together, but they were friendly, Eddie says. Here's some of the possibilities. First off Regan carried fifteen grand, packed it in his clothes all the time. Real money, they tell me. Not just a top card and a bunch of hay. That's a lot of jack but this Regan might be the boy to have it around so he could take it out and look at it when somebody was looking at him. Then again maybe he wouldn't give a damn. His wife says he never made a nickel off of old man Sternwood except room and board and a Packard 120 his wife gave him. Tie that for an ex-legger in the rich gravy."

"It beats me," I said.

"Well, here we are with a guy who ducks out and has fifteen grand in his pants and folks know it. Well, that's money. I might duck out myself, if I had fifteen grand, and me with two kids in high school. So the first thought is somebody rolls him for it and rolls him too hard, so they have to take him out in the desert and plant him among the cactuses. But I don't like that too well. Regan carried a gat and had plenty of experience using it, and not just in a greasy-faced liquor mob. I understand he commanded a whole brigade in the Irish troubles back in 1922 or whenever it was. A guy like that wouldn't be white meat to a heister. Then, his car being in that garage makes whoever rolled him know he was sweet on Eddie Mars' wife, which he was, I guess, but it ain't something every poolroom bum would know."

"Got a photo?" I asked.

"Him, not her. That's funny too. There's a lot of funny angles to this case. Here." He pushed a shiny print across the desk and I looked at an Irish face that was more sad than merry and more reserved than brash. Not the face of a tough guy and not the face of a man who could be pushed around much by anybody. Straight dark brows with strong bone under them. A forehead wide rather than high, a mat of dark clustering hair, a thin short nose, a wide mouth. A chin that had strong lines but was small for the mouth. A face that looked a little taut, the face of a man who would move fast and play for keeps. I passed the print back. I would know that face, if I saw it.

Captain Gregory knocked his pipe out and refilled it and tamped the tobacco down with his thumb. He lit it, blew smoke and began to talk again.

"Well, there could be people who would know he was sweet on Eddie Mars' frau. Besides Eddie himself. For a wonder *he* knew it. But he don't seem to give a damn. We check him pretty thoroughly around that time. Of course Eddie wouldn't have knocked him off out of jealousy. The set-up would point to him too obvious."

"It depends how smart he is," I said. "He might try the double bluff."

Captain Gregory shook his head. "If he's smart enough to get by in his racket, he's too smart for that. I get your idea. He pulls the dumb play because he thinks we wouldn't expect him to pull the dumb play. From a police angle that's wrong. Because he'd have us in his hair so much it would interfere with his business. *You* might think a dumb play would be smart. I might think so. The rank and file wouldn't. They'd make his life miserable. I've ruled it out. If I'm wrong, you can prove it on me and I'll eat my chair cushion. Till then I'm leaving Eddie in the clear. Jealousy is a bad motive for his type. Top-flight racketeers have business brains. They learn to do things that are good policy and let their personal feelings take care of themselves. I'm leaving that out."

"What are you leaving in?"

"The dame and Regan himself. Nobody else. She was a blonde then, but she won't be now. We don't find her car, so they probably left in it. They had a long start on us—fourteen days. Except for that car of Regan's I don't figure we'd have got the case at all. Of course I'm used to them that way, especially in good-class families. And of course everything I've done has had to be under the hat."

He leaned back and thumped the arms of his chair with the heels of his large heavy hands.

"I don't see nothing to do but wait," he said. "We've got readers out, but it's too soon to look for results. Regan had fifteen grand we know of. The girl had some, maybe a lot in rocks. But they'll run out of dough some day. Regan will cash a check, drop a marker, write a letter. They're in a strange town and they've got new names, but they've got the same old appetites. They got to get back in the fiscal system."

"What did the girl do before she married Eddie Mars?"

"Torcher."

"Can't you get any old professional photos?"

"No. Eddie must of had some, but he won't loosen up. He wants her let alone. I can't make him. He's got friends in town, or he wouldn't be what he is." He grunted. "Any of this do you any good?"

I said: "You'll never find either of them. The Pacific Ocean is too close."

"What I said about my chair cushion still goes. We'll find him. It may take time. It could take a year or two."

"General Sternwood may not live that long," I said.

"We've done all we could, brother. If he wants to put out a reward and spend some money, we might get results. The city don't give me the kind of money it takes." His large eyes peered at me and his scratchy eyebrows moved. "You serious about thinking Eddie put them both down?"

I laughed. "No. I was just kidding. I think what you think, Captain. That Regan ran away with a woman who meant more to him than a rich wife he didn't get along with. Besides, she isn't rich yet."

"You met her, I suppose?"

"Yes. She'd make a jazzy week-end, but she'd be wearing for a steady diet."

He grunted and I thanked him for his time and information and left. A gray Plymouth sedan tailed me away from the City Hall. I gave it a chance to catch up with me on a quiet street. It refused the offer, so I shook it off and went about my business.

21

I didn't go near the Sternwood family. I went back to the office and sat in my swivel chair and tried to catch up on my foot-dangling. There was a gusty wind blowing in at the windows and the soot from the oil burners of the hotel next door was down-drafted into the room and rolling across the top of the desk like tumbleweed drifting across a vacant lot. I was thinking about going out to lunch and that life was pretty flat and that it would probably be just as flat if I took a drink and that taking a drink all alone at that time of day wouldn't be any fun anyway. I was thinking this when Norris called up. In his carefully polite manner he said that General Sternwood was not feeling very well and that certain items in the newspaper had been read to him and he assumed that my investigation was now completed.

"Yes, as regards Geiger," I said. "I didn't shoot him, you know."

"The General didn't suppose you did, Mr. Marlowe."

"Does the General know anything about those photographs Mrs. Regan was worrying about?"

"No, sir. Decidedly not."

"Did you know what the General gave me?"

"Yes, sir. Three notes and a card, I believe."

"Right. I'll return them. As to the photos I think I'd better just destroy them."

"Very good, sir. Mrs. Regan tried to reach you a number of times last night—"

"I was out getting drunk," I said.

"Yes. Very necessary, sir, I'm sure. The General has instructed me to send you a check for five hundred dollars. Will that be satisfactory?"

"More than generous," I said.

"And I presume we may now consider the incident closed?"

"Oh sure. Tight as a vault with a busted time lock."

"Thank you, sir. I am sure we all appreciate it. When the General is feeling a little better—possibly tomorrow—he would like to thank you in person."

"Fine," I said. "I'll come out and drink some more of his brandy, maybe with champagne."

"I shall see that some is properly iced," the old boy said, almost with a smirk in his voice.

That was that. We said good-by and hung up. The coffee shop smell from next door came in at the windows with the soot but failed to make me hungry. So I got out my office bottle and took the drink and let my self-respect ride its own race.

I counted it up on my fingers. Rusty Regan had run away from a lot of money and a handsome wife to go wandering with a vague blonde who was more or less married to a racketeer named Eddie Mars. He had gone suddenly without good-bys and there might be any number of reasons for that. The General had been too proud, or, at the first interview he gave me, too careful, to tell me the Missing Persons Bureau had the matter in hand. The Missing Persons people were dead on their feet on it and evidently didn't think it worth bothering over. Regan had done what he had done and that was his business. I agreed with Captain Gregory that Eddie Mars would have been very unlikely to involve himself in a double murder just because another man had gone to town with the blonde he was not even living with. It might have annoyed him, but business is business, and you have to hold your teeth clamped around Hollywood to keep from chewing on stray blondes. If there had been a lot of money involved, that would be different. But fifteen grand wouldn't be a lot of money to Eddie Mars. He was no two-bit chiseler like Brody.

Geiger was dead and Carmen would have to find some other shady character to drink exotic blends of hooch with. I didn't suppose she would have any trouble. All she would have to do would be to stand on the corner for five minutes and look coy. I hoped that the next grifter who dropped the hook on her would play her a little more smoothly, a little more for the long haul rather than the quick touch.

Mrs. Regan knew Eddie Mars well enough to borrow money from him. That was natural, if she played roulette and was a good loser. Any gambling house owner would lend a good client money in a pinch. Apart from this they had an added bond of interest in Regan. He was her husband and he had gone off with Eddie Mars' wife.

Carol Lundgren, the boy killer with the limited vocabulary, was out of circulation for a long, long time, even if they didn't strap him in a chair over a bucket of acid. They wouldn't, because he would take a plea and save the county money. They all do when they don't have the price of a big lawyer. Agnes Lozelle was in custody as a material witness. They wouldn't need her for that, if Carol took a plea, and if he pleaded guilty on arraignment, they would turn her loose. They wouldn't want to open up any angles on Geiger's business, apart from which they had nothing on her.

That left me. I had concealed a murder and suppressed evidence for twenty-four hours, but I was still at large and had a five-hundred-dollar check coming. The smart thing for me to do was to take another drink and forget the whole mess.

That being the obviously smart thing to do, I called Eddie Mars and told him I was coming down to Las Olindas that evening to talk to him. That was how smart I was.

I got down there about nine, under a hard high October moon that lost itself in the top layers of a beach fog. The Cypress Club was at the far end of the town, a rambling frame mansion that had once been the summer residence of a rich man named De Cazens, and later had been a hotel. It was now a big dark outwardly shabby place in a thick grove of wind-twisted Monterey cypresses, which gave it its name. It had enormous scrolled porches, turrets all over the place, stained-glass trims around the big windows, big empty stables at the back, a general air of nostalgic decay. Eddie Mars had left the outside much as he had found it, instead of making it over to look like an MGM set. I left my car on a street with sputtering arc lights and walked into the grounds along a damp gravel path to the main entrance. A doorman in a double-breasted guards coat let me into a huge dim silent lobby from which a white oak staircase curved majestically up to the darkness of an upper floor. I checked my hat and coat and waited, listening to music and confused voices behind heavy double doors. They seemed a long way off, and not quite of the same world as the building itself. Then the slim pasty-faced blond man who had been with Eddie Mars and the pug at Geiger's place came through a door under the staircase, smiled at me bleakly and took me back with him along a carpeted hall to the boss's office.

This was a square room with a deep old bay window and a stone fireplace in which a fire of juniper logs burned lazily. It was wainscoted in walnut and had a frieze of faded damask above the paneling. The ceiling was high and remote. There was a smell of cold sea.

Eddie Mars' dark sheenless desk didn't belong in the room, but neither did anything made after 1900. His carpet had a Florida suntan. There was a bartop radio in the corner and a Sèvres china tea set on a copper tray beside a samovar. I wondered who that was for. There was a door in the corner that had a time lock on it.

Eddie Mars grinned at me sociably and shook hands and moved his chin at the vault. "I'm a pushover for a heist mob here except for that thing," he said cheerfully. "The local johns drop in every morning and watch me open it. I have an arrangement with them."

"You hinted you had something for me," I said. "What is it?"

"What's your hurry? Have a drink and sit down."

"No hurry at all. You and I haven't anything to talk about but business.'

"You'll have the drink and like it," he said. He mixed a couple and put mine down beside a red leather chair and stood crosslegged against the desk himself, one hand in the side pocket of his midnight-blue dinner jacket, the thumb outside and the nail glistening. In dinner clothes he looked a little harder than in gray flannel, but he still looked like a horseman. We drank and nodded at each other.

"Ever been here before?" he asked.

"During prohibition. I don't get any kick out of gambling."

"Not with money," he smiled. "You ought to look in tonight. One of your friends is outside betting the wheels. I hear she's doing pretty well. Vivian Regan."

I sipped my drink and took one of his monogrammed cigarettes.

"I kind of liked the way you handled that yesterday," he said. "You made me sore at the time but I could see afterwards how right you were. You and I ought to get along. How much do I owe you?"

"For doing what?"

"Still careful, eh? I have my pipe line into headquarters, or I wouldn't be here. I get them the way they happen, not the way you read them in the papers." He showed me his large white teeth.

"How much have you got?" I asked.

"You're not talking money?"

"Information was the way I understood it."

"Information about what?"

"You have a short memory. Regan."

"Oh, that." He waved his glistening nails in the quiet light from one of those bronze lamps that shoot a beam at the ceiling. "I hear you got the information already. I felt I owed you a fee. I'm used to paying for nice treatment."

"I didn't drive down here to make a touch. I get paid for what I do. Not much by your standards, but I make out. One customer at a time is a good rule. You didn't bump Regan off, did you?"

"No. Did you think I did?"

"I wouldn't put it past you."

He laughed. "You're kidding."

I laughed. "Sure, I'm kidding. I never saw Regan, but I saw his photo. You haven't got the men for the work. And while we're on that subject don't send me any more gun punks with orders. I might get hysterical and blow one down."

He looked through his glass at the fire, set it down on the end of the desk and wiped his lips with a sheer lawn handkerchief.

"You talk a good game," he said. "But I dare say you can break a hundred and ten. You're not really interested in Regan, are you?"

"No, not professionally. I haven't been asked to be. But I know somebody who would like to know where he is."

"She doesn't give a damn," he said.

"I mean her father."

He wiped his lips again and looked at the handkerchief almost as if he expected to find blood on it. He drew his thick gray eyebrows close together and fingered the side of his weatherbeaten nose.

"Geiger was trying to blackmail the General," I said. "The General wouldn't say so, but I figure he was at least half scared Regan might be behind it."

Eddie Mars laughed. "Uh-uh. Geiger worked that one on everybody. It was strictly his own idea. He'd get notes from people that looked legal—were legal, I dare say, except that he wouldn't have dared sue on them. He'd present the notes, with a nice flourish, leaving himself empty-handed. If he drew an ace, he had a prospect that scared and he went to work. If he didn't draw an ace, he just dropped the whole thing."

"Clever guy," I said. "He dropped it all right. Dropped it and fell on it. How come *you* know all this?"

He shrugged impatiently. "I wish to Christ I didn't know half the stuff that's brought to me. Knowing other people's business is the worst investment a man can make in my circle. Then if it was just Geiger you were after, you're washed up on that angle."

"Washed up and paid off."

"I'm sorry about that. I wish old Sternwood would hire himself a soldier like you on a straight salary, to keep those girls of his home at least a few nights a week."

"Why?"

His mouth looked sulky. "They're plain trouble. Take the dark one. She's a pain in the neck around here. If she loses, she plunges and I end up with a fistful of paper which nobody will discount at any price. She has no money of her own except an allowance and what's in the old man's will is a secret. If she wins, she takes my money home with her."

"You get it back the next night," I said.

"I get some of it back. But over a period of time I'm loser."

He looked earnestly at me, as if that was important to me. I wondered why he thought it necessary to tell me at all. I yawned and finished my drink.

"I'm going out and look the joint over," I said.

"Yes, do." He pointed to a door near the vault door. "That leads to a door behind the tables."

"I'd rather go in the way the suckers enter."

"Okey. As you please. We're friends, aren't we, soldier?"

"Sure." I stood up and we shook hands.

"Maybe I can do you a real favor some day," he said. "You got it all from Gregory this time."

"So you own a piece of him too."

"Oh not that bad. We're just friends."

I stared at him for a moment, then went over to the door I had come in at. I looked back at him when I had it open.

"You don't have anybody tailing me around in a gray Plymouth sedan, do you?"

His eyes widened sharply. He looked jarred. "Hell, no. Why should I?"

"I couldn't imagine," I said, and went on out. I thought his surprise looked genuine enough to be believed. I thought he even looked a little worried. I couldn't think of any reason for that.

22

It was about ten-thirty when the little yellow-sashed Mexican orchestra got tired of playing a low-voiced, prettied-up rhumba that nobody was dancing to. The gourd player rubbed his finger tips together as if they were sore and got a cigarette into his mouth almost with the same movement.

The other four, with a timed simultaneous stoop, reached under their chairs for glasses from which they sipped, smacking their lips and flashing their eyes. Tequila, their manner said. It was probably mineral water. The pretense was as wasted as the music. Nobody was looking at them.

The room had been a ballroom once and Eddie Mars had changed it only as much as his business compelled him. No chromium glitter, no indirect lighting from behind angular cornices, no fused glass pictures, or chairs in violent leather and polished metal tubing, none of the pseudo-modernistic circus of the typical Hollywood night trap. The light was from heavy crystal chandeliers and the rose-damask panels of the wall were still the same rose damask, a little faded by time and darkened by dust, that had been matched long ago against the parquetry floor, of which only a small glass-smooth space in front of the little Mexican orchestra showed bare. The rest was covered by a heavy old-rose carpeting that must have cost plenty. The parquetry was made of a dozen kinds of hardwood, from Burma teak through half a dozen shades of oak and ruddy wood that looked like mahogany, and fading out to the hard pale wild lilac of the California hills, all laid in elaborate patterns, with the accuracy of a transit.

It was still a beautiful room and now there was roulette in it instead of measured, old-fashioned dancing. There were three tables close to the far wall. A low bronze railing joined them and made a fence around the croupiers. All three tables were working, but the crowd was at the middle one. I could see Vivian Regan's black head close to it, from across the room where I was leaning against the bar and turning a small glass of bacardi around on the mahogany.

The bartender leaned beside me watching the cluster of well-dressed people at the middle table. "She's pickin' 'em tonight, right on the nose," he said. "That tall blackheaded frail."

"Who is she?"

"I wouldn't know her name. She comes here a lot though."

"The hell you wouldn't know her name."

"I just work here, mister," he said without any animosity. "She's all alone too. The guy was with her passed out. They took him out to his car."

"I'll take her home," I said.

"The hell you will. Well, I wish you luck anyways. Should I gentle up that bacardi or do you like it the way it is?"

"I like it the way it is as well as I like it at all," I said.

"Me, I'd just as leave drink croup medicine," he said.

The crowd parted and two men in evening clothes pushed their way out and I saw the back of her neck and her bare shoulders in the opening. She wore a low-cut dress of dull green velvet. It looked too dressy for the occasion. The crowd closed and hid all but her black head. The two men came across the room and leaned against the bar and asked for Scotch and soda. One of them was flushed and excited. He was mopping his face with a black-bordered handkerchief. The double satin stripes down the side of his trousers were wide enough for tire tracks.

"Boy, I never saw such a run," he said in a jittery voice. "Eight wins and two stand-offs in a row on that red. That's roulette, boy, that's roulette."

"It gives me the itch," the other one said. "She's betting a grand at a crack. She can't lose." They put their beaks in their drinks, gurgled swiftly and went back.

"So wise the little men are," the barkeep drawled. "A grand a crack, huh. I saw an old horseface in Havana once—"

The noise swelled over at the middle table and a chiseled foreign voice rose above it saying: "If you will just be patient a moment, madam. The table cannot cover your bet. Mr. Mars will be here in a moment."

I left my bacardi and padded across the carpet. The little orchestra started to play a tango, rather loud. No one was dancing or intending to dance. I moved through a scattering of people in dinner clothes and full evening dress and sports clothes and business suits to the end table at the left. It had gone dead. Two croupiers stood behind it with their heads together and their eyes sideways. One moved a rake back and forth aimlessly over the empty layout. They were both staring at Vivian Regan.

Her long lashes twitched and her face looked unnaturally white. She was at the middle table, exactly opposite the wheel. There was a disordered pile of money and chips in front of her. It looked like a lot of money. She spoke to the croupier with a cool, insolent, ill-tempered drawl.

"What kind of a cheap outfit is this, I'd like to know. Get busy and spin that wheel, highpockets. I want one more play and I'm playing table stakes. You take it away fast enough I've noticed, but when it comes to dishing it out you start to whine."

The croupier smiled a cold polite smile that had looked at thousands of boors and millions of fools. His tall dark disinterested manner was flawless. He said gravely: "The table cannot cover your bet, madam. You have over sixteen thousand dollars there."

"It's your money," the girl jeered. "Don't you want it back?"

A man beside her tried to tell her something. She turned swiftly and spat something at him and he faded back into the crowd red-faced. A door opened in the paneling at the far end of the enclosed place made by the bronze railing. Eddie Mars came through the door with a set indifferent smile on his face, his hands thrust into the pockets of his dinner jacket, both thumbnails glistening outside. He seemed to like that pose. He strolled behind the croupiers and stopped at the corner of the middle table. He spoke with lazy calm, less politely than the croupier.

"Something the matter, Mrs. Regan?"

She turned her face to him with a sort of lunge. I saw the curve of her cheek stiffen, as if with an almost unbearable inner tautness. She didn't answer him.

Eddie Mars said gravely: "If you're not playing any more, you must let me send someone home with you."

The girl flushed. Her cheekbones stood out white in her face. Then she laughed off-key. She said bitterly:

"One more play, Eddie. Everything I have on the red. I like red. It's the color of blood."

Eddie Mars smiled faintly, then nodded and reached into his inner breast pocket. He drew out a large pin-seal wallet with gold corners and tossed it carelessly along the table to the croupier. "Cover her bet in even thousands," he said, "if no one objects to this turn of the wheel being just for the lady."

No one objected. Vivian Regan leaned down and pushed all her winnings savagely with both hands on to the large red diamond on the layout.

The croupier leaned over the table without haste. He counted and stacked her money and chips, placed all but a few chips and bills in a neat pile and pushed the rest back off the layout with his rake. He opened Eddie Mars' wallet and drew out two flat packets of thousand-dollar bills. He broke one, counted six bills out, added them to the unbroken packet, put the four loose bills in the wallet and laid it aside as carelessly as if it had been a packet of matches. Eddie Mars didn't touch the wallet. Nobody moved except the croupier. He spun the wheel lefthanded and sent the ivory ball skittering along the upper edge with a casual flirt of his wrist. Then he drew his hands back and folded his arms.

Vivian's lips parted slowly until her teeth caught the light and glittered like knives. The ball drifted lazily down the slope of the wheel and bounced on the chromium ridges above the numbers. After a long time and then very suddenly motion left it with a dry click. The wheel slowed, carrying the ball around with it. The croupier didn't unfold his arms until the wheel had entirely ceased to revolve.

"The red wins," he said formally, without interest. The little ivory ball lay in Red 25, the third number from the Double Zero. Vivian Regan put her head back and laughed triumphantly.

The croupier lifted his rake and slowly pushed the stack of thousand-dollar bills across the layout, added them to the stake, pushed everything slowly out of the field of play.

Eddie Mars smiled, put his wallet back in his pocket, turned on his heel and left the room through the door in the paneling.

A dozen people let their breath out at the same time and broke for the bar. I broke with them and got to the far end of the room before Vivian had gathered up her winnings and turned away from the table. I went out into the large quiet lobby, got my hat and coat from the check girl, dropped a quarter in her tray and went out on the porch. The doorman loomed up beside me and said: "Can I get your car for you, sir?"

I said: "I'm just going for a walk."

The scrollwork along the edge of the porch roof was wet with the fog. The fog dripped from the Monterey cypresses that shadowed off into nothing towards the cliff above the ocean. You could see a scant dozen feet in any direction. I went down the porch steps and drifted off through the trees, following an indistinct path until I could hear the wash of the surf licking at the fog, low down at the bottom of the cliff. There wasn't a gleam of light anywhere. I could see a dozen trees clearly at one time, another dozen dimly, then nothing at all but the fog. I circled to the left and drifted back towards the gravel path that went around to the stables where they parked the cars. When I could make out the outlines of the house I stopped. A little in front of me I had heard a man cough.

My steps hadn't made any sound on the soft moist turf. The man coughed again, then stifled the cough with a hand-kerchief or a sleeve. While he was still doing that I moved forward closer to him. I made him out, a vague shadow close to the path. Something made me step behind a tree and crouch down. The man turned his head. His face should have been a white blur when he did that. It wasn't. It remained dark. There was a mask over it.

I waited, behind the tree.

23

Light steps, the steps of a woman, came along the invisible pathway and the man in front of me moved forward and seemed to lean against the fog. I couldn't see the woman, then I could see her indistinctly. The arrogant carriage of her head seemed familiar. The man stepped out very quickly. The two figures blended in the fog, seemed to be part of the fog. There was dead silence for a moment. The man said:

"This is a gun, lady. Gentle now. Sound carries in the fog. Just hand me the bag."

The girl didn't make a sound. I moved forward a step. Quite suddenly I could see the foggy fuzz on the man's hat brim. The girl stood motionless. Then her breathing began to make a rasping sound, like a small file on soft wood.

"Yell," the man said, "and I'll cut you in half."

She didn't yell. She didn't move. There was a movement from him, and a dry chuckle. "It better be in here," he said. A catch clicked and a fumbling sound came to me. The man turned and came towards my tree. When he had taken three or four steps he chuckled again. The chuckle was something out of my own memories. I reached a pipe out of my pocket and held it like a gun.

I called out softly: "Hi, Lanny."

The man stopped dead and started to bring his hand up. I said: "No. I told you never to do that, Lanny. You're covered."

Nothing moved. The girl back on the path didn't move. I didn't move. Lanny didn't move.

"Put the bag down between your feet, kid," I told him. "Slow and easy."

He bent down. I jumped out and reached him still bent over. He straightened up against me breathing hard. His hands were empty.

"Tell me I can't get away with it," I said. I leaned against him and took the gun out of his overcoat pocket. "Somebody's always giving me guns," I told him. "I'm weighted down with them till I walk all crooked. Beat it."

Our breaths met and mingled, our eyes were like the eyes of two tomcats on a wall. I stepped back.

"On your way, Lanny. No hard feelings. You keep it quiet and I keep it quiet. Okey?"

"Okey," he said thickly.

The fog swallowed him. The faint sound of his steps and then nothing. I picked the bag up and felt in it and went towards the path. She still stood there motionless, a gray fur coat held tight around her throat with an ungloved hand on which a ring made a faint glitter. She wore no hat. Her dark parted hair was part of the darkness of the night. Her eyes too.

"Nice work, Marlowe. Are you my bodyguard now?" Her voice had a harsh note.

"Looks that way. Here's the bag."

She took it. I said: "Have you a car with you?"

She laughed. "I came with a man. What are you doing here?"

"Eddie Mars wanted to see me."

"I didn't know you knew him. Why?"

"I don't mind telling you. He thought I was looking for somebody he thought had run away with his wife."

"Were you?"

"No."

"Then what did you come for?"

"To find out why he thought I was looking for somebody he thought had run away with his wife."

"Did you find out?"

"No."

"You leak information like a radio announcer," she said. "I suppose it's none of my business—even if the man was my husband. I thought you weren't interested in that."

"People keep throwing it at me."

She clicked her teeth in annoyance. The incident of the masked man with the gun seemed to have made no impression on her at all. "Well, take me to the garage," she said. "I have to look in at my escort."

We walked along the path and around a corner of the building and there was light ahead, then around another corner and came to a bright enclosed stable yard lit with two floodlights. It was still paved with brick and still sloped down to a grating in the middle. Cars glistened and a man in a brown smock got up off a stool and came forward.

"Is my boy friend still blotto?" Vivian asked him carelessly.

"I'm afraid he is, miss. I put a rug over him and run the windows up. He's okey, I guess. Just kind of resting."

We went over to a big Cadillac and the man in the smock pulled the rear door open. On the wide back seat, loosely arranged, covered to the chin with a plaid robe, a man lay snoring with his mouth open. He seemed to be a big blond man who would hold a lot of liquor.

"Meet Mr. Larry Cobb," Vivian said. "Mister Cobb—Mister Marlowe."

I grunted.

"Mr. Cobb was my escort," she said. "Such a nice escort,

Mr. Cobb. So attentive. You should see him sober. *I* should see him sober. Somebody should see him sober. I mean, just for the record. So it could become a part of history, that brief flashing moment, soon buried in time, but never forgotten—when Larry Cobb was sober."

"Yeah," I said.

"I've even thought of marrying him," she went on in a high strained voice, as if the shock of the stick-up was just beginning to get to her. "At odd times when nothing pleasant would come into my mind. We all have those spells. Lots of money, you know. A yacht, a place on Long Island, a place at Newport, a place at Bermuda, places dotted here and there all over the world probably—just a good Scotch bottle apart. And to Mr. Cobb a bottle of Scotch is not very far."

"Yeah," I said. "Does he have a driver to take him home?"

"Don't say 'yeah.' It's common." She looked at me with arched eyebrows. The man in the smock was chewing his lower lip hard. "Oh, undoubtedly a whole platoon of drivers. They probably do squads right in front of the garage every morning, buttons shining, harness gleaming, white gloves immaculate—a sort of West Point elegance about them."

"Well, where the hell is this driver?" I asked.

"He drove hisself tonight," the man in the smock said, almost apologetically. "I could call his home and have somebody come down for him."

Vivian turned around and smiled at him as if he had just presented her with a diamond tiara. "That would be lovely," she said. "Would you do that? I really wouldn't want Mr. Cobb to die like that—with his mouth open. Someone might think he had died of thirst."

The man in the smock said: "Not if they sniffed him, miss."

She opened her bag and grabbed a handful of paper money and pushed it at him. "You'll take care of him, I'm sure."

"Jeeze," the man said, pop-eyed. "I sure will, miss."

"Regan is the name," she said sweetly. "Mrs. Regan. You'll probably see me again. Haven't been here long, have you?"

"No'm." His hands were doing frantic things with the fistful of money he was holding.

"You'll get to love it here," she said. She took hold of my arm. "Let's ride in your car, Marlowe."

"It's outside on the street."

"Quite all right with me, Marlowe. I love a nice walk in the fog. You meet such interesting people."

"Oh nuts," I said.

She held on to my arm and began to shake. She held me hard all the way to the car. She had stopped shaking by the time we reached it. I drove down a curving lane of trees on the blind side of the house. The lane opened on De Cazens Boulevard, the main drag of Las Olindas. We passed under the ancient sputtering arc lights and after a while there was a town, buildings, dead-looking stores, a service station with a light over a night bell, and at last a drugstore that was still open.

"You better have a drink," I said.

She moved her chin, a point of paleness in the corner of the seat. I turned diagonally into the curb and parked. "A little black coffee and a smattering of rye would go well," I said.

"I could get as drunk as two sailors and love it."

I held the door for her and she got out close to me, brushing my cheek with her hair. We went into the drugstore. I bought a pint of rye at the liquor counter and carried it over to the stools and set it down on the cracked marble counter.

"Two coffees," I said. "Black, strong and made this year."

"You can't drink liquor in here," the clerk said. He had a washed-out blue smock, was thin on top as to hair, had fairly honest eyes and his chin would never hit a wall before he saw it.

Vivian Regan reached into her bag for a pack of cigarettes and shook a couple loose just like a man. She held them towards me.

"It's against the law to drink liquor in here," the clerk said.

I lit the cigarettes and didn't pay any attention to him. He drew two cups of coffee from a tarnished nickel urn and set them in front of us. He looked at the bottle of rye, muttered under his breath and said wearily: "Okey, I'll watch the street while you pour it."

He went and stood at the display window with his back to us and his ears hanging out.

"My heart's in my mouth doing this," I said, and unscrewed the top of the whiskey bottle and loaded the coffee.

"The law enforcement in this town is terrific. All through prohibition Eddie Mars' place was a night club and they had two uniformed men in the lobby every night—to see that the guests didn't bring their own liquor instead of buying it from the house."

The clerk turned suddenly and walked back behind the counter and went in behind the little glass window of the prescription room.

We sipped our loaded coffee. I looked at Vivian's face in the mirror back of the coffee urn. It was taut, pale, beautiful and wild. Her lips were red and harsh.

"You have wicked eyes," I said. "What's Eddie Mars got on you?"

She looked at me in the mirror. "I took plenty away from him tonight at roulette—starting with five grand I borrowed from him yesterday and didn't have to use."

"That might make him sore. You think he sent that loogan after you?"

"What's a loogan?"

"A guy with a gun."

"Are you a loogan?"

"Sure," I laughed. "But strictly speaking a loogan is on the wrong side of the fence."

"I often wonder if there is a wrong side."

"We're losing the subject. What has Eddie Mars got on you?"

"You mean a hold on me of some sort?"

"Yes."

Her lip curled. "Wittier, please, Marlowe. Much wittier."

"How's the General? I don't pretend to be witty."

"Not too well. He didn't get up today. You could at least stop questioning me."

"I remember a time when I thought the same about you. How much does the General know?"

"He probably knows everything."

"Norris would tell him?"

"No. Wilde, the District Attorney, was out to see him. Did you burn those pictures?"

"Sure. You worry about your little sister, don't you—from time to time."

"I think she's all I do worry about. I worry about Dad in a way, to keep things from him."

"He hasn't many illusions," I said, "but I suppose he still has pride."

"We're his blood. That's the hell of it." She stared at me in the mirror with deep, distant eyes. "I don't want him to die despising his own blood. It was always wild blood, but it wasn't always rotten blood."

"Is it now?"

"I guess you think so."

"Not yours. You're just playing the part."

She looked down. I sipped some more coffee and lit another cigarette for us. "So you shoot people," she said quietly. "You're a killer."

"Me? How?"

"The papers and the police fixed it up nicely. But I don't believe everything I read."

"Oh, you think I accounted for Geiger—or Brody—or both of them."

She didn't say anything. "I didn't have to," I said. "I might have, I suppose, and got away with it. Neither of them would have hesitated to throw lead at me."

"That makes you just a killer at heart, like all cops."

"Oh, nuts."

"One of those dark deadly quiet men who have no more feelings than a butcher has for slaughtered meat. I knew it the first time I saw you."

"You've got enough shady friends to know different."

"They're all soft compared to you."

"Thanks, lady. You're no English muffin yourself."

"Let's get out of this rotten little town."

I paid the check, put the bottle of rye in my pocket, and we left. The clerk still didn't like me.

We drove away from Las Olindas through a series of little dank beach towns with shack-like houses built down on the sand close to the rumble of the surf and larger houses built back on the slopes behind. A yellow window shone here and there, but most of the houses were dark. A smell of kelp came in off the water and lay on the fog. The tires sang on the moist concrete of the boulevard. The world was a wet emptiness.

We were close to Del Rey before she spoke to me for the first time since we left the drugstore. Her voice had a muffled sound, as if something was throbbing deep under it.

"Drive down by the Del Rey beach club. I want to look at the water. It's the next street on the left."

There was a winking yellow light at the intersection. I turned the car and slid down a slope with a high bluff on one side, interurban tracks to the right, a low straggle of lights far off beyond the tracks, and then very far off a glitter of pier lights and a haze in the sky over a city. That way the fog was almost gone. The road crossed the tracks where they turned to run under the bluff, then reached a paved strip of water-front highway that bordered an open and uncluttered beach. Cars were parked along the sidewalk, facing out to sea, dark. The lights of the beach club were a few hundred yards away.

I braked the car against the curb and switched the head-lights off and sat with my hands on the wheel. Under the thinning fog the surf curled and creamed, almost without sound, like a thought trying to form itself on the edge of consciousness.

"Move closer," she said almost thickly.

I moved out from under the wheel into the middle of the seat. She turned her body a little away from me as if to peer out of the window. Then she let herself fall backwards, with-out a sound, into my arms. Her head almost struck the wheel. Her eyes were closed, her face was dim. Then I saw that her eyes opened and flickered, the shine of them visible even in the darkness.

"Hold me close, you beast," she said.

I put my arms around her loosely at first. Her hair had a harsh feeling against my face. I tightened my arms and lifted her up. I brought her face slowly up to my face. Her eyelids were flickering rapidly, like moth wings.

I kissed her tightly and quickly. Then a long slow clinging kiss. Her lips opened under mine. Her body began to shake in my arms.

"Killer," she said softly, her breath going into my mouth.

I strained her against me until the shivering of her body was almost shaking mine. I kept on kissing her. After a long time she pulled her head away enough to say: "Where do you live?"

"Hobart Arms. Franklin near Kenmore."

"I've never seen it."

"Want to?"

"Yes," she breathed.

"What has Eddie Mars got on you?"

Her body stiffened in my arms and her breath made a harsh sound. Her head pulled back until her eyes, wide open, ringed with white, were staring at me.

"So that's the way it is," she said in a soft dull voice.

"That's the way it is. Kissing is nice, but your father didn't hire me to sleep with you."

"You son of a bitch," she said calmly, without moving.

I laughed in her face. "Don't think I'm an icicle," I said. "I'm not blind or without senses. I have warm blood like the next guy. You're easy to take—too damned easy. What has Eddie Mars got on you?"

"If you say that again, I'll scream."

"Go ahead and scream."

She jerked away and pulled herself upright, far back in the corner of the car.

"Men have been shot for little things like that, Marlowe."

"Men have been shot for practically nothing. The first time we met I told you I was a detective. Get it through your lovely head. I work at it, lady. I don't play at it."

She fumbled in her bag and got a handkerchief out and bit on it, her head turned away from me. The tearing sound of the handkerchief came to me. She tore it with her teeth, slowly, time after time.

"What makes you think he has anything on me?" she whispered, her voice muffled by the handkerchief.

"He lets you win a lot of money and sends a gunpoke around to take it back for him. You're not more than mildly surprised. You didn't even thank me for saving it for you. I think the whole thing was just some kind of an act. If I wanted to flatter myself, I'd say it was at least partly for my benefit."

"You think he can win or lose as he pleases."

"Sure. On even money bets, four times out of five."

"Do I have to tell you I loathe your guts, Mister Detective?"

"You don't owe me anything. I'm paid off."

She tossed the shredded handkerchief out of the car window. "You have a lovely way with women."

"I liked kissing you."

"You kept your head beautifully. That's so flattering. Should I congratulate you, or my father?"

"I liked kissing you."

Her voice became an icy drawl. "Take me away from here, if you will be so kind. I'm quite sure I'd like to go home."

"You won't be a sister to me?"

"If I had a razor, I'd cut your throat—just to see what ran out of it."

"Caterpillar blood," I said.

I started the car and turned it and drove back across the interurban tracks to the highway and so on into town and up to West Hollywood. She didn't speak to me. She hardly moved all the way back. I drove through the gates and up the sunken driveway to the porte-cochere of the big house. She jerked the car door open and was out of it before it had quite stopped. She didn't speak even then. I watched her back as she stood against the door after ringing the bell. The door opened and Norris looked out. She pushed past him quickly and was gone. The door banged shut and I was sitting there looking at it.

I turned back down the driveway and home.

24

The apartment house lobby was empty this time. No gunman waiting under the potted palm to give me orders. I took the automatic elevator up to my floor and walked along the hallway to the tune of a muted radio behind a door. I needed a drink and was in a hurry to get one. I didn't switch the light on inside the door. I made straight for the kitchenette and brought up short in three or four feet. Something was wrong.

Something on the air, a scent. The shades were down at the windows and the street light leaking in at the sides made a dim light in the room. I stood still and listened. The scent on the air was a perfume, a heavy cloying perfume.

There was no sound, no sound at all. Then my eyes adjusted themselves more to the darkness and I saw there was something across the floor in front of me that shouldn't have been there. I backed, reached the wall switch with my thumb and flicked the light on.

The bed was down. Something in it giggled. A blond head was pressed into my pillow. Two bare arms curved up and the hands belonging to them were clasped on top of the blond head. Carmen Sternwood lay on her back, in my bed, giggling at me. The tawny wave of her hair was spread out on the pillow as if by a careful and artificial hand. Her slaty eyes peered at me and had the effect, as usual, of peering from behind a barrel. She smiled. Her small sharp teeth glinted.

"Cute, aren't I?" she said.

I said harshly: "Cute as a Filipino on Saturday night."

I went over to a floor lamp and pulled the switch, went back to put off the ceiling light, and went across the room again to the chessboard on a card table under the lamp. There was a problem laid out on the board, a six-mover. I couldn't solve it, like a lot of my problems. I reached down and moved a knight, then pulled my hat and coat off and threw them somewhere. All this time the soft giggling went on from the bed, that sound that made me think of rats behind a wainscoting in an old house.

"I bet you can't even guess how I got in."

I dug a cigarette out and looked at her with bleak eyes. "I bet I can. You came through the keyhole, just like Peter Pan."

"Who's he?"

"Oh, a fellow I used to know around the poolroom."

She giggled. "You're cute, aren't you?" she said.

I began to say: "About that thumb—" but she was ahead of me. I didn't have to remind her. She took her right hand from behind her head and started sucking the thumb and eyeing me with very round and naughty eyes.

"I'm all undressed," she said, after I had smoked and stared at her for a minute.

"By God," I said, "it was right at the back of my mind. I was groping for it. I almost had it, when you spoke. In another minute I'd have said 'I bet you're all undressed.' I always wear my rubbers in bed myself, in case I wake up with a bad conscience and have to sneak away from it."

"You're cute." She rolled her head a little, kittenishly. Then she took her left hand from under her head and took hold of the covers, paused dramatically, and swept them aside. She was undressed all right. She lay there on the bed in the lamplight, as naked and glistening as a pearl. The Sternwood girls were giving me both barrels that night.

I pulled a shred of tobacco off the edge of my lower lip.

"That's nice," I said. "But I've already seen it all. Remember? I'm the guy that keeps finding you without any clothes on."

She giggled some more and covered herself up again. "Well, how *did* you get in?" I asked her.

"The manager let me in. I showed him your card. I'd stolen it from Vivian. I told him you told me to come here and wait for you. I was—I was mysterious." She glowed with delight.

"Neat," I said. "Managers are like that. Now I know how you got in tell me how you're going to go out."

She giggled. "Not going—not for a long time. . . . I like it here. You're cute."

"Listen," I pointed my cigarette at her. "Don't make me dress you again. I'm tired. I appreciate all you're offering me. It's just more than I could possibly take. Doghouse Reilly never let a pal down that way. I'm your friend. I won't let you down—in spite of yourself. You and I have to keep on being friends, and this isn't the way to do it. Now will you dress like a nice little girl?"

She shook her head from side to side.

"Listen," I plowed on, "you don't really care anything about me. You're just showing how naughty you can be. But you don't have to show me. I knew it already. I'm the guy that found—"

"Put the light out," she giggled.

I threw my cigarette on the floor and stamped on it. I took

a handkerchief out and wiped the palms of my hands. I tried it once more.

"It isn't on account of the neighbors," I told her. "They don't really care a lot. There's a lot of stray broads in any apartment house and one more won't make the building rock. It's a question of professional pride. You know—professional pride. I'm working for your father. He's a sick man, very frail, very helpless. He sort of trusts me not to pull any stunts. Won't you please get dressed, Carmen?"

"Your name isn't Doghouse Reilly," she said. "It's Philip Marlowe. You can't fool me."

I looked down at the chessboard. The move with the knight was wrong. I put it back where I had moved it from. Knights had no meaning in this game. It wasn't a game for knights.

I looked at her again. She lay still now, her face pale against the pillow, her eyes large and dark and empty as rain barrels in a drought. One of her small five-fingered thumbless hands picked at the cover restlessly. There was a vague glimmer of doubt starting to get born in her somewhere. She didn't know about it yet. It's so hard for women—even nice women—to realize that their bodies are not irresistible.

I said: "I'm going out in the kitchen and mix a drink. Want one?"

"Uh-huh." Dark silent mystified eyes stared at me solemnly, the doubt growing larger in them, creeping into them noiselessly, like a cat in long grass stalking a young blackbird.

"If you're dressed when I get back, you'll get the drink. Okey?"

Her teeth parted and a faint hissing noise came out of her mouth. She didn't answer me. I went out to the kitchenette and got out some Scotch and fizzwater and mixed a couple of highballs. I didn't have anything really exciting to drink, like nitroglycerin or distilled tiger's breath. She hadn't moved when I got back with the glasses. The hissing had stopped. Her eyes were dead again. Her lips started to smile at me. Then she sat up suddenly and threw all the covers off her body and reached.

"Gimme."

"When you're dressed. Not *until* you're dressed."

I put the two glasses down on the card table and sat down myself and lit another cigarette. "Go ahead. I won't watch you."

I looked away. Then I was aware of the hissing noise very sudden and sharp. It startled me into looking at her again. She sat there naked, propped on her hands, her mouth open a little, her face like scraped bone. The hissing noise came tearing out of her mouth as if she had nothing to do with it. There was something behind her eyes, blank as they were, that I had never seen in a woman's eyes.

Then her lips moved very slowly and carefully, as if they were artificial lips and had to be manipulated with springs.

She called me a filthy name.

I didn't mind that. I didn't mind what she called me, what anybody called me. But this was the room I had to live in. It was all I had in the way of a home. In it was everything that was mine, that had any association for me, any past, anything that took the place of a family. Not much; a few books, pictures, radio, chessmen, old letters, stuff like that. Nothing. Such as they were they had all my memories.

I couldn't stand her in that room any longer. What she called me only reminded me of that.

I said carefully: "I'll give you three minutes to get dressed and out of here. If you're not out by then, I'll throw you out—by force. Just the way you are, naked. And I'll throw your clothes after you into the hall. Now—get started."

Her teeth chattered and the hissing noise was sharp and animal. She swung her feet to the floor and reached for her clothes on a chair beside the bed. She dressed. I watched her. She dressed with stiff awkward fingers—for a woman—but quickly at that. She was dressed in a little over two minutes. I timed it.

She stood there beside the bed, holding a green bag tight against a fur-trimmed coat. She wore a rakish green hat crooked on her head. She stood there for a moment and hissed at me, her face still like scraped bone, her eyes still empty and yet full of some jungle emotion. Then she walked quickly to the door and opened it and went out, without speaking, without looking back. I heard the elevator lurch into motion and move in the shaft.

I walked to the windows and pulled the shades up and opened the windows wide. The night air came drifting in with a kind of stale sweetness that still remembered automobile exhausts and the streets of the city. I reached for my drink and drank it slowly. The apartment house door closed itself down below me. Steps tinkled on the quiet sidewalk. A car started up not far away. It rushed off into the night with a rough clashing of gears. I went back to the bed and looked down at it. The imprint of her head was still in the pillow, of her small corrupt body still on the sheets.

I put my empty glass down and tore the bed to pieces savagely.

25

It was raining again the next morning, a slanting gray rain like a swung curtain of crystal beads. I got up feeling sluggish and tired and stood looking out of the windows, with a dark harsh taste of Sternwoods still in my mouth. I was as empty of life as a scarecrow's pockets. I went out to the kitchenette and drank two cups of black coffee. You can have a hangover from other things than alcohol. I had one from women. Women made me sick.

I shaved and showered and dressed and got my raincoat out and went downstairs and looked out of the front door. Across the street, a hundred feet up, a gray Plymouth sedan was parked. It was the same one that had tried to trail me around the day before, the same one that I had asked Eddie Mars about. There might be a cop in it, if a cop had that much time on his hands and wanted to waste it following me around. Or it might be a smoothie in the detective business trying to get a noseful of somebody else's case in order to chisel a way into it. Or it might be the Bishop of Bermuda disapproving of my night life.

I went out back and got my convertible from the garage and drove it around front past the gray Plymouth. There was

a small man in it, alone. He started up after me. He worked
better in the rain. He stayed close enough so that I couldn't
make a short block and leave that before he entered it, and he
stayed back far enough so that other cars were between us
most of the time. I drove down to the boulevard and parked
in the lot next to my building and came out of there with my
raincoat collar up and my hat brim low and the raindrops
tapping icily at my face in between. The Plymouth was across
the way at a fireplug. I walked down to the intersection and
crossed with the green light and walked back, close to the
edge of the sidewalk and the parked cars. The Plymouth
hadn't moved. Nobody got out of it. I reached it and jerked
open the door on the curb side.

A small bright-eyed man was pressed back into the corner
behind the wheel. I stood and looked in at him, the rain
thumping my back. His eyes blinked behind the swirling
smoke of a cigarette. His hands tapped restlessly on the thin
wheel.

I said: "Can't you make your mind up?"

He swallowed and the cigarette bobbed between his lips. "I
don't think I know you," he said, in a tight little voice.

"Marlowe's the name. The guy you've been trying to follow around for a couple of days."

"I ain't following anybody, doc."

"This jaloppy is. Maybe you can't control it. Have it your
own way. I'm now going to eat breakfast in the coffee shop
across the street, orange juice, bacon and eggs, toast, honey,
three or four cups of coffee and a toothpick. I am then going
up to my office, which is on the seventh floor of the building
right opposite you. If you have anything that's worrying you
beyond endurance, drop up and chew it over. I'll only be
oiling my machine gun."

I left him blinking and walked away. Twenty minutes later I
was airing the scrubwoman's Soirée d'Amour out of my office
and opening up a thick rough envelope addressed in a fine
old-fashioned pointed handwriting. The envelope contained a
brief formal note and a large mauve check for five hundred
dollars, payable to Philip Marlowe and signed, Guy de Brisay
Sternwood, by Vincent Norris. That made it a nice morning.
I was making out a bank slip when the buzzer told me some-

body had entered my two by four reception room. It was the little man from the Plymouth.

"Fine," I said. "Come in and shed your coat."

He slid past me carefully as I held the door, as carefully as though he feared I might plant a kick in his minute buttocks. We sat down and faced each other across the desk. He was a very small man, not more than five feet three and would hardly weigh as much as a butcher's thumb. He had tight brilliant eyes that wanted to look hard, and looked as hard as oysters on the half shell. He wore a double-breasted dark gray suit that was too wide in the shoulders and had too much lapel. Over this, open, an Irish tweed coat with some badly worn spots. A lot of foulard tie bulged out and was rain-spotted above his crossed lapels.

"Maybe you know me," he said. "I'm Harry Jones."

I said I didn't know him. I pushed a flat tin of cigarettes at him. His small neat fingers speared one like a trout taking the fly. He lit it with the desk lighter and waved his hand.

"I been around," he said. "Know the boys and such. Used to do a little liquor-running down from Hueneme Point. A tough racket, brother. Riding the scout car with a gun in your lap and a wad on your hip that would choke a coal shute. Plenty of times we paid off four sets of law before we hit Beverly Hills. A tough racket."

"Terrible," I said.

He leaned back and blew smoke at the ceiling from the small tight corner of his small tight mouth.

"Maybe you don't believe me," he said.

"Maybe I don't," I said. "And maybe I do. And then again maybe I haven't bothered to make my mind up. Just what is the build-up supposed to do to me?"

"Nothing," he said tartly.

"You've been following me around for a couple of days," I said. "Like a fellow trying to pick up a girl and lacking the last inch of nerve. Maybe you're selling insurance. Maybe you knew a fellow called Joe Brody. That's a lot of maybes, but I have a lot on hand in my business."

His eyes bulged and his lower lip almost fell in his lap. "Christ, how'd you know that?" he snapped.

"I'm psychic. Shake your business up and pour it. I haven't got all day."

The brightness of his eyes almost disappeared between the suddenly narrowed lids. There was silence. The rain pounded down on the flat tarred roof over the Mansion House lobby below my windows. His eyes opened a little, shined again, and his voice was full of thought.

"I was trying to get a line on you, sure," he said. "I've got something to sell—cheap, for a couple of C notes. How'd you tie me to Joe?"

I opened a letter and read it. It offered me a six months' correspondence course in fingerprinting at a special professional discount. I dropped it into the waste basket and looked at the little man again. "Don't mind me. I was just guessing. You're not a cop. You don't belong to Eddie Mars' outfit. I asked him last night. I couldn't think of anybody else but Joe Brody's friends who would be that much interested in me."

"Jesus," he said and licked his lower lip. His face had turned white as paper when I mentioned Eddie Mars. His mouth drooped open and his cigarette hung to the corner of it by some magic, as if it had grown there. "Aw, you're kidding me," he said at last, with the sort of smile the operating room sees.

"All right. I'm kidding you." I opened another letter. This one wanted to send me a daily newsletter from Washington, all inside stuff, straight from the cookhouse. "I suppose Agnes is loose," I added.

"Yeah. She sent me. You interested?"

"Well—she's a blonde."

"Nuts. You made a crack when you were up there that night—the night Joe got squibbed off. Something about Brody must have known something good about the Sternwoods or he wouldn't have taken the chance on that picture he sent them."

"Uh-huh. So he had? What was it?"

"That's what the two hundred bucks pays for."

I dropped some more fan mail into the basket and lit myself a fresh cigarette.

"We gotta get out of town," he said. "Agnes is a nice girl.

You can't hold that stuff on her. It's not so easy for a dame to get by these days."

"She's too big for you," I said. "She'll roll on you and smother you."

"That's kind of a dirty crack, brother," he said with something that was near enough to dignity to make me stare at him.

I said: "You're right. I've been meeting the wrong kind of people lately. Let's cut out the gabble and get down to cases. What have you got for the money?"

"Would you pay it?"

"If it does what?"

"If it helps you find Rusty Regan."

"I'm not looking for Rusty Regan."

"Says you. Want to hear it or not?"

"Go ahead and chirp. I'll pay for anything I use. Two C notes buys a lot of information in my circle."

"Eddie Mars had Regan bumped off," he said calmly, and leaned back as if he had just been made a vice-president.

I waved a hand in the direction of the door. "I wouldn't even argue with you," I said. "I wouldn't waste the oxygen. On your way, small size."

He leaned across the desk, white lines at the corners of his mouth. He snubbed his cigarette out carefully, over and over again, without looking at it. From behind a communicating door came the sound of a typewriter clacking monotonously to the bell, to the shift, line after line.

"I'm not kidding," he said.

"Beat it. Don't bother me. I have work to do."

"No you don't," he said sharply. "I ain't that easy. I came here to speak my piece and I'm speaking it. I knew Rusty myself. Not well, well enough to say 'How's a boy?' and he'd answer me or he wouldn't, according to how he felt. A nice guy though. I always liked him. He was sweet on a singer named Mona Grant. Then she changed her name to Mars. Rusty got sore and married a rich dame that hung around the joints like she couldn't sleep well at home. You know all about her, tall, dark, enough looks for a Derby winner, but the type would put a lot of pressure on a guy. High-strung.

Rusty wouldn't get along with her. But Jesus, he'd get along with her old man's dough, wouldn't he? That's what you think. This Regan was a cockeyed sort of buzzard. He had long-range eyes. He was looking over into the next valley all the time. He wasn't scarcely around where he was. I don't think he gave a damn about dough. And coming from me, brother, that's a compliment."

The little man wasn't so dumb after all. A three for a quarter grifter wouldn't even think such thoughts, much less know how to express them.

I said: "So he ran away."

"He started to run away, maybe. With this girl Mona. She wasn't living with Eddie Mars, didn't like his rackets. Especially the side lines, like blackmail, bent cars, hideouts for hot boys from the east, and so on. The talk was Regan told Eddie one night, right out in the open, that if he ever messed Mona up in any criminal rap, he'd be around to see him."

"Most of this is on the record, Harry," I said. "You can't expect money for that."

"I'm coming to what isn't. So Regan blew. I used to see him every afternoon in Vardi's drinking Irish whiskey and staring at the wall. He don't talk much any more. He'd give me a bet now and then, which was what I was there for, to pick up bets for Puss Walgreen."

"I thought he was in the insurance business."

"That's what it says on the door. I guess he'd sell you insurance at that, if you tramped on him. Well, about the middle of September I don't see Regan any more. I don't notice it right away. You know how it is. A guy's there and you see him and then he ain't there and you don't not see him until something makes you think of it. What makes me think about it is I hear a guy say laughing that Eddie Mars' woman lammed out with Rusty Regan and Mars is acting like he was best man, instead of being sore. So I tell Joe Brody and Joe was smart."

"Like hell he was," I said.

"Not copper smart, but still smart. He's out for the dough. He gets to figuring could he get a line somehow on the two lovebirds he could maybe collect twice—once from Eddie Mars and once from Regan's wife. Joe knew the family a little."

"Five grand worth," I said. "He nicked them for that a while back."

"Yeah?" Harry Jones looked mildly surprised. "Agnes ought to of told me that. There's a frail for you. Always holding out. Well, Joe and me watch the papers and we don't see anything, so we know old Sternwood has a blanket on it. Then one day I see Lash Canino in Vardi's. Know him?"

I shook my head.

"There's a boy that is tough like some guys think they are tough. He does a job for Eddie Mars when Mars needs him—trouble-shooting. He'd bump a guy off between drinks. When Mars don't need him he don't go near him. And he don't stay in L.A. Well it might be something and it might not. Maybe they got a line on Regan and Mars has just been sitting back with a smile on his puss, waiting for the chance. Then again it might be something else entirely. Anyway I tell Joe and Joe gets on Canino's tail. He can tail. Me, I'm no good at it. I'm giving that one away. No charge. And Joe tails Canino out to the Sternwood place and Canino parks outside the estate and a car come up beside him with a girl in it. They talk for a while and Joe thinks the girl passes something over, like maybe dough. The girl beats it. It's Regan's wife. Okey, she knows Canino and Canino knows Mars. So Joe figures Canino knows something about Regan and is trying to squeeze a little on the side for himself. Canino blows and Joe loses him. End of Act One."

"What does this Canino look like?"

"Short, heavy set, brown hair, brown eyes, and always wears brown clothes and a brown hat. Even wears a brown suede raincoat. Drives a brown coupe. Everything brown for Mr. Canino."

"Let's have Act Two," I said.

"Without some dough that's all."

"I don't see two hundred bucks in it. Mrs. Regan married an ex-bootlegger out of the joints. She'd know other people of his sort. She knows Eddie Mars well. If she thought anything had happened to Regan, Eddie would be the very man she'd go to, and Canino might be the man Eddie would pick to handle the assignment. Is that all you have?"

"Would you give the two hundred to know where Eddie's wife is?" the little man asked calmly.

He had all my attention now. I almost cracked the arms of my chair leaning on them.

"Even if she was alone?" Harry Jones added in a soft, rather sinister tone. "Even if she never run away with Regan at all, and was being kept now about forty miles from L.A. in a hideout—so the law would keep on thinking she had dusted with him? Would you pay two hundred bucks for that, shamus?"

I licked my lips. They tasted dry and salty. "I think I would," I said. "Where?"

"Agnes found her," he said grimly. "Just by a lucky break. Saw her out riding and managed to tail her home. Agnes will tell you where that is—when she's holding the money in her hand."

I made a hard face at him. "You could tell the coppers for nothing, Harry. They have some good wreckers down at Central these days. If they killed you trying, they still have Agnes."

"Let 'em try," he said. "I ain't so brittle."

"Agnes must have something I didn't notice."

"She's a grifter, shamus. I'm a grifter. We're all grifters. So we sell each other out for a nickel. Okey. See can you make me." He reached for another of my cigarettes, placed it neatly between his lips and lit it with a match the way I do myself, missing twice on his thumbnail and then using his foot. He puffed evenly and stared at me level-eyed, a funny little hard guy I could have thrown from home plate to second base. A small man in a big man's world. There was something I liked about him.

"I haven't pulled anything in here," he said steadily. "I come in talking two C's. That's still the price. I come because I thought I'd get a take it or leave it, one right gee to an-other. Now you're waving cops at me. You oughta be ashamed of yourself."

I said: "You'll get the two hundred—for that information. I have to get the money myself first."

He stood up and nodded and pulled his worn little Irish tweed coat tight around his chest. "That's okey. After dark is better anyway. It's a leery job—buckin' guys like Eddie Mars. But a guy has to eat. The book's been pretty dull lately. I think the big boys have told Puss Walgreen to move on. Suppose you come over there to the office, Fulwider Building, Western and Santa Monica, four-twenty-eight at the back. You bring the money, I'll take you to Agnes."

"Can't you tell me yourself? I've seen Agnes."

"I promised her," he said simply. He buttoned his overcoat, cocked his hat jauntily, nodded again and strolled to the door. He went out. His steps died along the hall.

I went down to the bank and deposited my five-hundred-dollar check and drew out two hundred in currency. I went upstairs again and sat in my chair thinking about Harry Jones and his story. It seemed a little too pat. It had the austere simplicity of fiction rather than the tangled woof of fact. Captain Gregory ought to have been able to find Mona Mars, if she was that close to his beat. Supposing, that is, he had tried.

I thought about it most of the day. Nobody came into the office. Nobody called me on the phone. It kept on raining.

26

At seven the rain had stopped for a breathing spell, but the gutters were still flooded. On Santa Monica the water was level with the sidewalk and a thin film of it washed over the top of the curbing. A traffic cop in shining black rubber from boots to cap sloshed through the flood on his way from the shelter of a sodden awning. My rubber heels slithered on the sidewalk as I turned into the narrow lobby of the Fulwider Building. A single drop light burned far back, beyond an open, once gilt elevator. There was a tarnished and well-missed spittoon on a gnawed rubber mat. A case of false teeth hung on the mustard-colored wall like a fuse box in a screen porch. I shook the rain off my hat and looked at the building directory beside the case of teeth. Numbers with names and numbers without names. Plenty of vacancies or plenty of tenants who wished to remain anonymous. Painless dentists, shyster detective agencies, small sick businesses that had crawled there to die, mail order schools that would teach you how to become a railroad clerk or a radio technician or a screen writer—if the postal inspectors didn't catch up with them first. A nasty building. A building in which the smell of stale cigar butts would be the cleanest odor.

An old man dozed in the elevator, on a ramshackle stool, with a burst-out cushion under him. His mouth was open, his veined temples glistened in the weak light. He wore a blue uniform coat that fitted him the way a stall fits a horse. Under that gray trousers with frayed cuffs, white cotton socks and black kid shoes, one of which was slit across a bunion. On the stool he slept miserably, waiting for a customer. I went past him softly, the clandestine air of the building prompting me, found the fire door and pulled it open. The fire stairs hadn't been swept in a month. Bums had slept on them, eaten on them, left crusts and fragments of greasy newspaper, matches, a gutted imitation-leather pocketbook. In a shadowy angle against the scribbled wall a pouched ring of pale rubber had fallen and had not been disturbed. A very nice building.

I came out at the fourth floor sniffing for air. The hallway had the same dirty spittoon and frayed mat, the same mustard walls, the same memories of low tide. I went down the line and turned a corner. The name: "L. D. Walgreen—Insurance," showed on a dark pebbled glass door, on a second dark door, on a third behind which there was a light. One of the dark doors said: "Entrance."

A glass transom was open above the lighted door. Through it the sharp birdlike voice of Harry Jones spoke, saying:

"Canino? . . . Yeah, I've seen you around somewhere. Sure."

I froze. The other voice spoke. It had a heavy purr, like a small dynamo behind a brick wall. It said: "I thought you would." There was a vaguely sinister note in that voice.

A chair scraped on linoleum, steps sounded, the transom above me squeaked shut. A shadow melted from behind the pebbled glass.

I went back to the first of the three doors marked with the name Walgreen. I tried it cautiously. It was locked. It moved in a loose frame, an old door fitted many years past, made of half-seasoned wood and shrunken now. I reached my wallet out and slipped the thick hard window of celluloid from over my driver's license. A burglar's tool the law had forgotten to proscribe. I put my gloves on, leaned softly and lovingly against the door and pushed the knob hard away from the frame. I pushed the celluloid plate into the wide crack and felt for the slope of the spring lock. There was a dry click, like a small icicle breaking. I hung there motionless, like a lazy fish in the water. Nothing happened inside. I turned the knob and pushed the door back into darkness. I shut it behind me as carefully as I had opened it.

The lighted oblong of an uncurtained window faced me, cut by the angle of a desk. On the desk a hooded typewriter took form, then the metal knob of a communicating door. This was unlocked. I passed into the second of the three offices. Rain rattled suddenly against the closed window. Under its noise I crossed the room. A tight fan of light spread from an inch opening of the door into the lighted office. Everything very convenient. I walked like a cat on a mantel and reached the hinged side of the door, put an eye to the crack and saw nothing but light against the angle of the wood.

The purring voice was now saying quite pleasantly: "Sure, a guy could sit on his fanny and crab what another guy done if he knows what it's all about. So you go to see this peeper. Well, that was your mistake. Eddie don't like it. The peeper told Eddie some guy in a gray Plymouth was tailing him. Eddie naturally wants to know who and why, see."

Harry Jones laughed lightly. "What makes it his business?"

"That don't get you no place."

"You know why I went to the peeper. I already told you. Account of Joe Brody's girl. She has to blow and she's shatting on her uppers. She figures the peeper can get her some dough. I don't have any."

The purring voice said gently: "Dough for what? Peepers don't give that stuff out to punks."

"He could raise it. He knows rich people." Harry Jones laughed, a brave little laugh.

"Don't fuss with me, little man." The purring voice had an edge, like sand in the bearings.

"Okey, okey. You know the dope on Brody's bump-off. That screwy kid done it all right, but the night it happened this Marlowe was right there in the room."

"That's known, little man. He told it to the law."

"Yeah—here's what isn't. Brody was trying to peddle a nudist photo of the young Sternwood girl. Marlowe got wise to him. While they were arguing about it the young Sternwood girl dropped around herself—with a gat. She took a shot at Brody. She lets one fly and breaks a window. Only the peeper didn't tell the coppers about that. And Agnes didn't neither. She figures it's railroad fare for her not to."

"This ain't got anything to do with Eddie?"

"Show me how."

"Where's this Agnes at?"

"Nothing doing."

"You'll tell me, little man. Here, or in the back room where the boys pitch dimes against the wall."

"She's my girl now, Canino. I don't put my girl in the middle for anybody."

A silence followed. I listened to the rain lashing the windows. The smell of cigarette smoke came through the crack of the door. I wanted to cough. I bit hard on a handkerchief.

The purring voice said, still gentle: "From what I hear this blonde broad was just a shill for Geiger. I'll talk it over with Eddie. How much you tap the peeper for?"

"Two centuries."

"Get it?"

Harry Jones laughed again. "I'm seeing him tomorrow. I have hopes."

"Where's Agnes?"

"Listen—"

"Where's Agnes?"

Silence.

"Look at it, little man."

I didn't move. I wasn't wearing a gun. I didn't have to see through the crack of the door to know that a gun was what the purring voice was inviting Harry Jones to look at. But I didn't think Mr. Canino would do anything with his gun beyond showing it. I waited.

"I'm looking at it," Harry Jones said, his voice squeezed

tight as if it could hardly get past his teeth. "And I don't see anything I didn't see before. Go ahead and blast and see what it gets you."

"A Chicago overcoat is what it would get *you*, little man."

Silence.

"Where's Agnes?"

Harry Jones sighed. "Okey," he said wearily. "She's in an apartment house at 28 Court Street, up on Bunker Hill. Apartment 301. I guess I'm yellow all right. Why should I front for that twist?"

"No reason. You got good sense. You and me'll go out and talk to her. All I want is to find out is she dummying up on you, kid. If it's the way you say it is, everything is jakeloo. You can put the bite on the peeper and be on your way. No hard feelings?"

"No," Harry Jones said. "No hard feelings, Canino."

"Fine. Let's dip the bill. Got a glass?" The purring voice was now as false as an usherette's eyelashes and as slippery as a watermelon seed. A drawer was pulled open. Something jarred on wood. A chair squeaked. A scuffing sound on the floor. "This is bond stuff," the purring voice said.

There was a gurgling sound. "Moths in your ermine, as the ladies say."

Harry Jones said softly: "Success."

I heard a short sharp cough. Then a violent retching. There was a small thud on the floor, as if a thick glass had fallen. My fingers curled against my raincoat.

The purring voice said gently: "You ain't sick from just one drink, are you, pal?"

Harry Jones didn't answer. There was labored breathing for a short moment. Then thick silence folded down. Then a chair scraped.

"So long, little man," said Mr. Canino.

Steps, a click, the wedge of light died at my feet, a door opened and closed quietly. The steps faded, leisurely and assured.

I stirred around the edge of the door and pulled it wide and looked into blackness relieved by the dim shine of a window. The corner of a desk glittered faintly. A hunched shape took form in a chair behind it. In the close air there was a heavy clogged smell, almost a perfume. I went across to the corridor door and listened. I heard the distant clang of the elevator.

I found the light switch and light glowed in a dusty glass bowl hanging from the ceiling by three brass chains. Harry Jones looked at me across the desk, his eyes wide open, his face frozen in a tight spasm, the skin bluish. His small dark head was tilted to one side. He sat upright against the back of the chair.

A street-car bell clanged at an almost infinite distance and the sound came buffeted by innumerable walls. A brown half pint of whiskey stood on the desk with the cap off. Harry Jones' glass glinted against a castor of the desk. The second glass was gone.

I breathed shallowly, from the top of my lungs, and bent above the bottle. Behind the charred smell of the bourbon another odor lurked, faintly, the odor of bitter almonds. Harry Jones dying had vomited on his coat. That made it cyanide.

I walked around him carefully and lifted a phone book from a hook on the wooden frame of the window. I let it fall again, reached the telephone as far as it would go from the little dead man. I dialed information. The voice answered.

"Can you give me the phone number of Apartment 301, 28 Court Street?"

"One moment, please." The voice came to me borne on the smell of bitter almonds. A silence. "The number is Wentworth 2528. It is listed under Glendower Apartments."

I thanked the voice and dialed the number. The bell rang three times, then the line opened. A radio blared along the wire and was muted. A burly male voice said: "Hello."

"Is Agnes there?"

"No Agnes here, buddy. What number you want?"

"Wentworth two-five-two-eight."

"Right number, wrong gal. Ain't that a shame?" The voice cackled.

I hung up and reached for the phone book again and looked up the Wentworth Apartments. I dialed the manager's number. I had a blurred vision of Mr. Canino driving fast through rain to another appointment with death.

"Glendower Apartments. Mr. Schiff speaking."

"This is Wallis, Police Identification Bureau. Is there a girl named Agnes Lozelle registered in your place?"

"Who did you say you were?"

I told him again.

"If you give me your number, I'll—"

"Cut the comedy," I said sharply, "I'm in a hurry. Is there or isn't there?"

"No. There isn't." The voice was as stiff as a breadstick.

"Is there a tall blonde with green eyes registered in the flop?"

"Say, this isn't any flop—"

"Oh, can it, *can it!*" I rapped at him in a police voice. "You want me to send the vice squad over there and shake the joint down? I know all about Bunker Hill apartment houses, mister. Especially the ones that have phone numbers listed for each apartment."

"Hey, take it easy, officer. I'll co-operate. There's a couple of blondes here, sure. Where isn't there? I hadn't noticed their eyes much. Would yours be alone?"

"Alone, or with a little chap about five feet three, a hundred and ten, sharp black eyes, wears double-breasted dark gray suit and Irish tweed overcoat, gray hat. My information is Apartment 301, but all I get there is the big razzoo."

"Oh, she ain't there. There's a couple of car salesmen living in three-o-one."

"Thanks, I'll drop around."

"Make it quiet, won't you? Come to my place, direct?"

"Much obliged, Mr. Schiff." I hung up.

I wiped sweat off my face. I walked to the far corner of the office and stood with my face to the wall, patted it with a hand. I turned around slowly and looked across at little Harry Jones grimacing in his chair.

"Well, you fooled him, Harry," I said out loud, in a voice that sounded queer to me. "You lied to him and you drank your cyanide like a little gentleman. You died like a poisoned rat, Harry, but you're no rat to me."

I had to search him. It was a nasty job. His pockets yielded nothing about Agnes, nothing that I wanted at all. I didn't think they would, but I had to be sure. Mr. Canino might be back. Mr. Canino would be the kind of self-confident gentle-man who would not mind returning to the scene of his crime.

I put the light out and started to open the door. The phone bell rang jarringly down on the baseboard. I listened to it, my jaw muscles drawn into a knot, aching. Then I shut the door and put the light on again and went across to it.

"Yeah?"

A woman's voice. Her voice. "Is Harry around?"

"Not for a minute, Agnes."

She waited a while on that. Then she said slowly: "Who's talking?"

"Marlowe, the guy that's trouble to you."

"Where is he?" sharply.

"I came over to give him two hundred bucks in return for certain information. The offer holds. I have the money. Where are you?"

"Didn't he tell you?"

"No."

"Perhaps you'd better ask him. Where is he?"

"I can't ask him. Do you know a man named Canino?"

Her gasp came as clearly as though she had been beside me.

"Do you want the two C's or not?" I asked.

"I—I want it pretty bad, mister."

"All right then. Tell me where to bring it."

"I—I—" Her voice trailed off and came back with a panic rush. "Where's Harry?"

"Got scared and blew. Meet me somewhere—anywhere at all—I have the money."

"I don't believe you—about Harry. It's a trap."

"Oh stuff. I could have had Harry hauled in long ago. There isn't anything to make a trap for. Canino got a line on Harry somehow and he blew. I want quiet, you want quiet, Harry wants quiet." Harry already had it. Nobody could take it away from him. "You don't think I'd stooge for Eddie Mars, do you, angel?"

"No-o, I guess not. Not that. I'll meet you in half an hour. Beside Bullocks Wilshire, the east entrance to the parking lot."

"Right," I said.

I dropped the phone in its cradle. The wave of almond odor flooded me again, and the sour smell of vomit. The little dead man sat silent in his chair, beyond fear, beyond change.

I left the office. Nothing moved in the dingy corridor. No pebbled glass door had light behind it. I went down the fire stairs to the second floor and from there looked down at the lighted roof of the elevator cage. I pressed the button. Slowly the car lurched into motion. I ran down the stairs again. The car was above me when I walked out of the building.

It was raining hard again. I walked into it with the heavy drops slapping my face. When one of them touched my tongue I knew that my mouth was open and the ache at the side of my jaws told me it was open wide and strained back, mimicking the rictus of death carved upon the face of Harry Jones.

27

"Give me the money."

The motor of the gray Plymouth throbbed under her voice and the rain pounded above it. The violet light at the top of Bullocks green-tinged tower was far above us, serene and withdrawn from the dark, dripping city. Her black-gloved hand reached out and I put the bills in it. She bent over to count them under the dim light of the dash. A bag clicked open, clicked shut. She let a spent breath die on her lips. She leaned towards me.

"I'm leaving, copper. I'm on my way. This is a get-away stake and God how I need it. What happened to Harry?"

"I told you he ran away. Canino got wise to him somehow. Forget Harry. I've paid and I want my information."

"You'll get it. Joe and I were out riding Foothill Boulevard Sunday before last. It was late and the lights coming up and the usual mess of cars. We passed a brown coupe and I saw the girl who was driving it. There was a man beside her, a dark short man. The girl was a blonde. I'd seen her before.

She was Eddie Mars' wife. The guy was Canino. You wouldn't forget either of them, if you ever saw them. Joe tailed the coupe from in front. He was good at that. Canino, the watchdog, was taking her out for air. A mile or so east of Realito a road turns towards the foothills. That's orange country to the south but to the north it's as bare as hell's back yard and smack up against the hills there's a cyanide plant where they make the stuff for fumigation. Just off the highway there's a small garage and paintshop run by a gee named Art Huck. Hot car drop, likely. There's a frame house beyond this, and beyond the house nothing but the foothills and the bare stone outcrop and the cyanide plant a couple of miles on. That's the place where she's holed up. They turned off on this road and Joe swung around and went back and we saw the car turn off the road where the frame house was. We sat there half an hour looking through the cars going by. Nobody came back out. When it was quite dark Joe sneaked up there and took a look. He said there were lights in the house and a radio was going and just the one car out in front, the coupe. So we beat it."

She stopped talking and I listened to the swish of tires on Wilshire. I said: "They might have shifted quarters since then but that's what you have to sell—that's what you have to sell. Sure you knew her?"

"If you ever see her, you won't make a mistake the second time. Good-by, copper, and wish me luck. I got a raw deal."

"Like hell you did," I said, and walked away across the street to my own car.

The gray Plymouth moved forward, gathered speed, and darted around the corner on to Sunset Place. The sound of its motor died, and with it blonde Agnes wiped herself off the slate for good, so far as I was concerned. Three men dead, Geiger, Brody and Harry Jones, and the woman went riding off in the rain with my two hundred in her bag and not a mark on her. I kicked my starter and drove on downtown to eat. I ate a good dinner. Forty miles in the rain is a hike, and I hoped to make it a round trip.

I drove north across the river, on into Pasadena, through Pasadena and almost at once I was in orange groves. The tumbling rain was solid white spray in the headlights. The windshield wiper could hardly keep the glass clear enough to see through. But not even the drenched darkness could hide the flawless lines of the orange trees wheeling away like endless spokes into the night.

Cars passed with a tearing hiss and a wave of dirty spray. The highway jerked through a little town that was all packing houses and sheds, and railway sidings nuzzling them. The groves thinned out and dropped away to the south and the road climbed and it was cold and to the north the black foothills crouched closer and sent a bitter wind whipping down their flanks. Then faintly out of the dark two yellow vapor lights glowed high up in the air and a neon sign between them said: "Welcome to Realito."

Frame houses were spaced far back from a wide main street, then a sudden knot of stores, the lights of a drugstore behind fogged glass, the fly-cluster of cars in front of the movie theater, a dark bank on a corner with a clock sticking out over the sidewalk and a group of people standing in the rain looking at its windows, as if they were some kind of a show. I went on. Empty fields closed in again.

Fate stage-managed the whole thing. Beyond Realito, just about a mile beyond, the highway took a curve and the rain fooled me and I went too close to the shoulder. My right front tire let go with an angry hiss. Before I could stop the right rear went with it. I jammed the car to a stop, half on the pavement, half on the shoulder, got out and flashed a spotlight around. I had two flats and one spare. The flat butt of a heavy galvanized tack stared at me from the front tire. The edge of the pavement was littered with them. They had been swept off, but not far enough off.

I snapped the flash off and stood there breathing rain and looking up a side road at a yellow light. It seemed to come from a skylight. The skylight could belong to a garage, the garage could be run by a man named Art Huck, and there could be a frame house next door to it. I tucked my chin down in my collar and started towards it, then went back to unstrap the license holder from the steering post and put it in my pocket. I leaned lower under the wheel. Behind a weighted flap, directly under my right leg as I sat in the car, there was a hidden compartment. There were two guns in it. One belonged to Eddie Mars' boy Lanny and one belonged to me. I took Lanny's. It would have had more practice than mine. I stuck it nose down in an inside pocket and started up the side road.

The garage was a hundred yards from the highway. It showed the highway a blank side wall. I played the flash on it quickly. "Art Huck—Auto Repairs and Painting." I chuckled, then Harry Jones' face rose up in front of me, and I stopped chuckling. The garage doors were shut, but there was an edge of light under them and a thread of light where the halves met. I went on past. The frame house was there, light in two front windows, shades down. It was set well back from the road, behind a thin clump of trees. A car stood on the gravel drive in front. It was dark, indistinct, but it would be a brown coupe and it would belong to Mr. Canino. It squatted there peacefully in front of the narrow wooden porch.

He would let her take it out for a spin once in a while, and sit beside her, probably with a gun handy. The girl Rusty Regan ought to have married, that Eddie Mars couldn't keep, the girl that hadn't run away with Regan. Nice Mr. Canino.

I trudged back to the garage and banged on the wooden door with the butt of my flash. There was a hung instant of silence, as heavy as thunder. The light inside went out. I stood there grinning and licking the rain off my lip. I clicked the spot on the middle of the doors. I grinned at the circle of white. I was where I wanted to be.

A voice spoke through the door, a surly voice: "What you want?"

"Open up. I've got two flats back on the highway and only one spare. I need help."

"Sorry, mister. We're closed up. Realito's a mile west. Better try there."

I didn't like that. I kicked the door hard. I kept on kicking it. Another voice made itself heard, a purring voice, like a small dynamo behind a wall. I liked this voice. It said: "A wise guy, huh? Open up, Art."

A bolt squealed and half of the door bent inward. My flash burned briefly on a gaunt face. Then something that glittered swept down and knocked the flash out of my hand. A gun had peaked at me. I dropped low where the flash burned on the wet ground and picked it up.

The surly voice said: "Kill that spot, bo. Folks get hurt that way."

I snapped the flash off and straightened. Light went on inside the garage, outlined a tall man in coveralls. He backed away from the open door and kept a gun leveled at me.

"Step inside and shut the door, stranger. We'll see what we can do."

I stepped inside, and shut the door behind my back. I looked at the gaunt man, but not at the other man who was shadowy over by a workbench, silent. The breath of the garage was sweet and sinister with the smell of hot pyroxylin paint.

"Ain't you got no sense?" the gaunt man chided me. "A bank job was pulled at Realito this noon."

"Pardon," I said, remembering the people staring at the bank in the rain. "I didn't pull it. I'm a stranger here."

"Well, there was," he said morosely. "Some say it was a couple of punk kids and they got 'em cornered back here in the hills."

"It's a nice night for hiding," I said. "I suppose they threw tacks out. I got some of them. I thought you just needed the business."

"You didn't ever get socked in the kisser, did you?" the gaunt man asked me briefly.

"Not by anybody your weight."

The purring voice from over in the shadows said: "Cut out the heavy menace, Art. This guy's in a jam. You run a garage, don't you?"

"Thanks," I said, and didn't look at him even then.

"Okey, okey," the man in the coveralls grumbled. He tucked his gun through a flap in his clothes and bit a knuckle, staring at me moodily over it. The smell of the pyroxylin paint was as sickening as ether. Over in the corner, under a drop light, there was a big new-looking sedan with a paint gun lying on its fender.

I looked at the man by the workbench now. He was short and thick-bodied with strong shoulders. He had a cool face and cool dark eyes. He wore a belted brown suede raincoat that was heavily spotted with rain. His brown hat was tilted rakishly. He leaned his back against the workbench and looked me over without haste, without interest, as if he was looking at a slab of cold meat. Perhaps he thought of people that way.

He moved his dark eyes up and down slowly and then glanced at his fingernails one by one, holding them up against the light and studying them with care, as Hollywood has taught it should be done. He spoke around a cigarette.

"Got two flats, huh? That's tough. They swept them tacks, I thought."

"I skidded a little on the curve."

"Stranger in town you said?"

"Traveling through. On the way to L.A. How far is it?"

"Forty miles. Seems longer this weather. Where from, stranger?"

"Santa Rosa."

"Come the long way, eh? Tahoe and Lone Pine?"

"Not Tahoe. Reno and Carson City."

"Still the long way." A fleeting smile curved his lips.

"Any law against it?" I asked him.

"Huh? No, sure not. Guess you think we're nosey. Just on account of that heist back there. Take a jack and get his flats, Art."

"I'm busy," the gaunt man growled. "I've got work to do. I got this spray job. And it's raining, you might have noticed."

The man in brown said pleasantly: "Too damp for a good spray job, Art. Get moving."

I said: "They're front and rear, on the right side. You could use the spare for one spot, if you're busy."

"Take two jacks, Art," the brown man said.

"Now, listen—" Art began to bluster.

The brown man moved his eyes, looked at Art with a soft quiet-eyed stare, lowered them again almost shyly. He didn't speak. Art rocked as if a gust of wind had hit him. He stamped over to the corner and put a rubber coat over his coveralls, a sou'wester on his head. He grabbed a socket wrench and a hand jack and wheeled a dolly jack over to the doors.

He went out silently, leaving the door yawning. The rain blustered in. The man in brown strolled over and shut it and strolled back to the workbench and put his hips exactly where they had been before. I could have taken him then. We were alone. He didn't know who I was. He looked at me lightly and threw his cigarette on the cement floor and stamped on it without looking down.

"I bet you could use a drink," he said. "Wet the inside and even up." He reached a bottle from the workbench behind him and set it on the edge and set two glasses beside it. He poured a stiff jolt into each and held one out.

Walking like a dummy I went over and took it. The memory of the rain was still cold on my face. The smell of hot paint drugged the close air of the garage.

"That Art," the brown man said. "He's like all mechanics. Always got his face in a job he ought to have done last week. Business trip?"

I sniffed my drink delicately. It had the right smell. I watched him drink some of his before I swallowed mine. I rolled it around on my tongue. There was no cyanide in it. I emptied the little glass and put it down beside him and moved away.

"Partly," I said. I walked over to the half-painted sedan with the big metal paint gun lying along its fender. The rain hit the flat roof hard. Art was out in it, cursing.

The brown man looked at the big car. "Just a panel job, to start with," he said casually, his purring voice still softer from the drink. "But the guy had dough and his driver needed a few bucks. You know the racket."

I said: "There's only one that's older." My lips felt dry. I didn't want to talk. I lit a cigarette. I wanted my tires fixed. The minutes passed on tiptoe. The brown man and I were two strangers chance-met, looking at each other across a little dead man named Harry Jones. Only the brown man didn't know that yet.

Feet crunched outside and the door was pushed open. The light hit pencils of rain and made silver wires of them. Art trundled two muddy flats in sullenly, kicked the door shut, let one of the flats fall over on its side. He looked at me savagely.

"You sure pick spots for a jack to stand on," he snarled.

The brown man laughed and took a rolled cylinder of nickels out of his pocket and tossed it up and down on the palm of his hand.

"Don't crab so much," he said dryly. "Fix those flats."

"I'm fixin' them, ain't I?"

"Well, don't make a song about it."

"Yah!" Art peeled his rubber coat and sou'wester off and threw them away from him. He heaved one tire up on a spreader and tore the rim loose viciously. He had the tube out and cold-patched in nothing flat. Still scowling, he strode over to the wall beside me and grabbed an air hose, put enough air into the tube to give it body and let the nozzle of the air hose smack against the whitewashed wall.

I stood watching the roll of wrapped coins dance in Canino's hand. The moment of crouched intensity had left me. I turned my head and watched the gaunt mechanic beside me toss the air-stiffened tube up and catch it with his hands wide, one on each side of the tube. He looked it over sourly, glanced at a big galvanized tub of dirty water in the corner and grunted.

The teamwork must have been very nice. I saw no signal, no glance of meaning, no gesture that might have a special import. The gaunt man had the stiffened tube high in the air, staring at it. He half turned his body, took one long quick step, and slammed it down over my head and shoulders, a perfect ringer.

He jumped behind me and leaned hard on the rubber. His weight dragged on my chest, pinned my upper arms tight to my sides. I could move my hands, but I couldn't reach the gun in my pocket.

The brown man came almost dancing towards me across the floor. His hand tightened over the roll of nickels. He came up to me without sound, without expression. I bent forward and tried to heave Art off his feet.

The fist with the weighted tube inside it went through my spread hands like a stone through a cloud of dust. I had the stunned moment of shock when the lights danced and the visible world went out of focus but was still there. He hit me again. There was no sensation in my head. The bright glare got brighter. There was nothing but hard aching white light. Then there was darkness in which something red wriggled like a germ under a microscope. Then there was nothing bright or wriggling, just darkness and emptiness and a rushing wind and a falling as of great trees.

28

It seemed there was a woman and she was sitting near a lamp, which was where she belonged, in a good light. Another light shone hard on my face, so I closed my eyes again and tried to look at her through the lashes. She was so platinumed that her hair shone like a silver fruit bowl. She wore a green knitted dress with a broad white collar turned over it. There was a sharp-angled glossy bag at her feet. She was smoking and a glass of amber fluid was tall and pale at her elbow.

I moved my head a little, carefully. It hurt, but not more than I expected. I was trussed like a turkey ready for the oven. Handcuffs held my wrists behind me and a rope went from them to my ankles and then over the end of the brown davenport on which I was sprawled. The rope dropped out of sight over the davenport. I moved enough to make sure it was tied down.

I stopped these furtive movements and opened my eyes again and said: "Hello."

The woman withdrew her gaze from some distant mountain peak. Her small firm chin turned slowly. Her eyes were the blue of mountain lakes. Overhead the rain still pounded, with a remote sound, as if it was somebody else's rain.

"How do you feel?" It was a smooth silvery voice that matched her hair. It had a tiny tinkle in it, like bells in a doll's house. I thought that was silly as soon as I thought of it.

"Great," I said. "Somebody built a filling station on my jaw."

"What did you expect, Mr. Marlowe—orchids?"

"Just a plain pine box," I said. "Don't bother with bronze or silver handles. And don't scatter my ashes over the blue

Pacific. I like the worms better. Did you know that worms are of both sexes and that any worm can love any other worm?"

"You're a little light-headed," she said, with a grave stare.

"Would you mind moving this light?"

She got up and went behind the davenport. The light went off. The dimness was a benison.

"I don't think you're so dangerous," she said. She was tall rather than short, but no bean-pole. She was slim, but not a dried crust. She went back to her chair.

"So you know my name."

"You slept well. They had plenty of time to go through your pockets. They did everything but embalm you. So you're a detective."

"Is that all they have on me?"

She was silent. Smoke floated dimly from the cigarette. She moved it in the air. Her hand was small and had shape, not the usual bony garden tool you see on women nowadays.

"What time is it?" I asked.

She looked sideways at her wrist, beyond the spiral of smoke, at the edge of the grave luster of the lamplight. "Ten-seventeen. You have a date?"

"I wouldn't be surprised. Is this the house next to Art Huck's garage?"

"Yes."

"What are the boys doing—digging a grave?"

"They had to go somewhere."

"You mean they left you here alone?"

Her head turned slowly again. She smiled. "You don't look dangerous."

"I thought they were keeping you a prisoner."

It didn't seem to startle her. It even slightly amused her. "What made you think that?"

"I know who you are."

Her very blue eyes flashed so sharply that I could almost see the sweep of their glance, like the sweep of a sword. Her mouth tightened. But her voice didn't change.

"Then I'm afraid you're in a bad spot. And I hate killing."

"And you Eddie Mars' wife? Shame on you."

She didn't like that. She glared at me. I grinned. "Unless

you can unlock these bracelets, which I'd advise you not to do, you might spare me a little of that drink you're neglecting."

She brought the glass over. Bubbles rose in it like false hopes. She bent over me. Her breath was as delicate as the eyes of a fawn. I gulped from the glass. She took it away from my mouth and watched some of the liquid run down my neck.

She bent over me again. Blood began to move around in me, like a prospective tenant looking over a house.

"Your face looks like a collision mat," she said.

"Make the most of it. It won't last long even this good."

She swung her head sharply and listened. For an instant her face was pale. The sounds were only the rain drifting against the walls. She went back across the room and stood with her side to me, bent forward a little, looking down at the floor.

"Why did you come here and stick your neck out?" she asked quietly. "Eddie wasn't doing you any harm. You know perfectly well that if I hadn't hid out here, the police would have been certain Eddie murdered Rusty Regan."

"He did," I said.

She didn't move, didn't change position an inch. Her breath made a harsh quick sound. I looked around the room. Two doors, both in the same wall, one half open. A carpet of red and tan squares, blue curtains at the windows, a wallpaper with bright green pine trees on it. The furniture looked as if it had come from one of those places that advertise on bus benches. Gay, but full of resistance.

She said softly: "Eddie didn't do anything to him. I haven't seen Rusty in months. Eddie's not that sort of man."

"You left his bed and board. You were living alone. People at the place where you lived identified Regan's photo."

"That's a lie," she said coldly.

I tried to remember whether Captain Gregory had said that or not. My head was too fuzzy. I couldn't be sure.

"And it's none of your business," she added.

"The whole thing is my business. I'm hired to find out."

"Eddie's not that sort of man."

"Oh, you like racketeers."

"As long as people will gamble there will be places for them to gamble."

"That's just protective thinking. Once outside the law

you're all the way outside. You think he's just a gambler. I think he's a pornographer, a blackmailer, a hot car broker, a killer by remote control, and a suborner of crooked cops. He's whatever looks good to him, whatever has the cabbage pinned to it. Don't try to sell me on any high-souled racketeers. They don't come in that pattern."

"He's not a killer." Her nostrils flared.

"Not personally. He has Canino. Canino killed a man tonight, a harmless little guy who was trying to help somebody out. I almost saw him killed."

She laughed wearily.

"All right," I growled. "Don't believe it. If Eddie is such a nice guy, I'd like to get to talk to him without Canino around. You know what Canino will do—beat my teeth out and then kick me in the stomach for mumbling."

She put her head back and stood there thoughtful and withdrawn, thinking something out.

"I thought platinum hair was out of style," I bored on, just to keep sound alive in the room, just to keep from listening.

"It's a wig, silly. While mine grows out." She reached up and yanked it off. Her own hair was clipped short all over, like a boy's. She put the wig back on.

"Who did that to you?"

She looked surprised. "I had it done. Why?"

"Yes. Why?"

"Why, to show Eddie I was willing to do what he wanted me to do—hide out. That he didn't need to have me guarded. I wouldn't let him down. I love him."

"Good grief," I groaned. "And you have me right here in the room with you."

She turned a hand over and stared at it. Then abruptly she walked out of the room. She came back with a kitchen knife. She bent and sawed at my rope.

"Canino has the key to the handcuffs," she breathed. "I can't do anything about those."

She stepped back, breathing rapidly. She had cut the rope at every knot.

"You're a kick," she said. "Kidding with every breath—the spot you're in."

"I thought Eddie wasn't a killer."

She turned away quickly and went back to her chair by the lamp and sat down and put her face in her hands. I swung my feet to the floor and stood up. I tottered around, stiff-legged. The nerve on the left side of my face was jumping in all its branches. I took a step. I could still walk. I could run, if I had to.

"I guess you mean me to go," I said.

She nodded without lifting her head.

"You'd better go with me—if you want to keep on living."

"Don't waste time. He'll be back any minute."

"Light a cigarette for me."

I stood beside her, touching her knees. She came to her feet with a sudden lurch. Our eyes were only inches apart.

"Hello, Silver-Wig," I said softly.

She stepped back, around the chair, and swept a package of cigarettes up off the table. She jabbed one loose and pushed it roughly into my mouth. Her hand was shaking. She snapped a small green leather lighter and held it to the cigarette. I drew in the smoke, staring into her lake-blue eyes. While she was still close to me I said:

"A little bird named Harry Jones led me to you. A little bird that used to hop in and out of cocktail bars picking up horse bets for crumbs. Picking up information too. This little bird picked up an idea about Canino. One way and another he and his friends found out where you were. He came to me to sell the information because he knew—how he knew is a long story—that I was working for General Sternwood. I got his information, but Canino got the little bird. He's a dead little bird now, with his feathers ruffled and his neck limp and a pearl of blood on his beak. Canino killed him. But Eddie Mars wouldn't do that, would he, Silver-Wig? He never killed anybody. He just hires it done."

"Get out," she said harshly. "Get out of here quick."

Her hand clutched in midair on the green lighter. The fingers strained. The knuckles were as white as snow.

"But Canino doesn't know I know that," I said. "About the little bird. All he knows is I'm nosing around."

Then she laughed. It was almost a racking laugh. It shook her as the wind shakes a tree. I thought there was puzzlement in it, not exactly surprise, but as if a new idea had been added to something already known and it didn't fit. Then I thought that was too much to get out of a laugh.

"It's very funny," she said breathlessly. "Very funny, because, you see—I still love him. Women—" She began to laugh again.

I listened hard, my head throbbing. Just the rain still. "Let's go," I said. "Fast."

She took two steps back and her face set hard. "Get out, you! Get out! You can walk to Realito. You can make it—and you can keep your mouth shut—for an hour or two at least. You owe me that much."

"Let's go," I said. "Got a gun, Silver-Wig?"

"You know I'm not going. You know that. Please, please get out of here quickly."

I stepped up close to her, almost pressing against her. "You're going to stay here after turning me loose? Wait for that killer to come back so you can say so sorry? A man who kills like swatting a fly. Not much. You're going with me, Silver-Wig."

"No."

"Suppose," I said thinly, "your handsome husband *did* kill Regan? Or suppose Canino did, without Eddie's knowing it. Just suppose. How long will *you* last, after turning me loose?"

"I'm not afraid of Canino. I'm still his boss's wife."

"Eddie's a handful of mush," I snarled. "Canino would take him with a teaspoon. He'll take him the way the cat took the canary. A handful of mush. The only time a girl like you goes for a wrong gee is when he's a handful of mush."

"Get out!" she almost spit at me.

"Okey." I turned away from her and moved out through the half-open door into a dark hallway. Then she rushed after me and pushed past to the front door and opened it. She peered out into the wet blackness and listened. She motioned me forward.

"Good-by," she said under her breath. "Good luck in everything but one thing. Eddie didn't kill Rusty Regan. You'll find him alive and well somewhere, when he wants to be found."

I leaned against her and pressed her against the wall with

my body. I pushed my mouth against her face. I talked to her that way.

"There's no hurry. All this was arranged in advance, rehearsed to the last detail, timed to the split second. Just like a radio program. No hurry at all. Kiss me, Silver-Wig."

Her face under my mouth was like ice. She put her hands up and took hold of my head and kissed me hard on the lips. Her lips were like ice, too.

I went out through the door and it closed behind me, without sound, and the rain blew in under the porch, not as cold as her lips.

29

The garage next door was dark. I crossed the gravel drive and a patch of sodden lawn. The road ran with small rivulets of water. It gurgled down a ditch on the far side. I had no hat. That must have fallen in the garage. Canino hadn't bothered to give it back to me. He hadn't thought I would need it any more. I imagined him driving back jauntily through the rain, alone, having left the gaunt and sulky Art and the probably stolen sedan in a safe place. She loved Eddie Mars and she was hiding to protect him. So he would find her there when he came back, calm beside the light and the untasted drink, and me tied up on the davenport. He would carry her stuff out to the car and go through the house carefully to make sure nothing incriminating was left. He would tell her to go out and wait. She wouldn't hear a shot. A blackjack is just as effective at short range. He would tell her he had left me tied up and I would get loose after a while. He would think she was that dumb. Nice Mr. Canino.

The raincoat was open in front and I couldn't button it, being handcuffed. The skirts flapped against my legs like the wings of a large and tired bird. I came to the highway. Cars went by in a wide swirl of water illuminated by headlights. The tearing noise of their tires died swiftly. I found my convertible where I had left it, both tires fixed and mounted, so it could be driven away, if necessary. They thought of every-thing. I got into it and leaned down sideways under the wheel and fumbled aside the flap of leather that covered the pocket. I got the other gun, stuffed it up under my coat and started back. The world was small, shut in, black. A private world for Canino and me.

Halfway there the headlights nearly caught me. They turned swiftly off the highway and I slid down the bank into the wet ditch and flopped there breathing water. The car hummed by without slowing. I lifted my head, heard the rasp of its tires as it left the road and took the gravel of the drive-way. The motor died, the lights died, a door slammed. I didn't hear the house door shut, but a fringe of light trickled through the clump of trees, as though a shade had been moved aside from a window, or the light had been put on in the hall.

I came back to the soggy grass plot and sloshed across it. The car was between me and the house, the gun was down at my side, pulled as far around as I could get it, without pulling my left arm out by the roots. The car was dark, empty, warm. Water gurgled pleasantly in the radiator. I peered in at the door. The keys hung on the dash. Canino was very sure of himself. I went around the car and walked carefully across the gravel to the window and listened. I couldn't hear any voices, any sound but the swift bong-bong of the raindrops hitting the metal elbows at the bottom of the rain gutters.

I kept on listening. No loud voices, everything quiet and refined. He would be purring at her and she would be telling him she had let me go and I had promised to let them get away. He wouldn't believe me, as I wouldn't believe him. So he wouldn't be in there long. He would be on his way and take her with him. All I had to do was wait for him to come out.

I couldn't do it. I shifted the gun to my left hand and leaned down to scoop up a handful of gravel. I tossed it against the screen of the window. It was a feeble effort. Very little of it reached the glass above the screen, but the loose rattle of that little was like a dam bursting.

I ran back to the car and got on the running board behind

it. The house had already gone dark. That was all. I dropped quietly on the running board and waited. No soap. Canino was too cagey.

I straightened up and got into the car backwards, fumbled around for the ignition key and turned it. I reached with my foot, but the starter button had to be on the dash. I found it at last, pulled it and the starter ground. The warm motor caught at once. It purred softly, contentedly. I got out of the car again and crouched down by the rear wheels.

I was shivering now but I knew Canino wouldn't like that last effect. He needed that car badly. A darkened window slid down inch by inch, only some shifting of light on the glass showing it moved. Flame spouted from it abruptly, the blended roar of three swift shots. Glass starred in the coupe. I yelled with agony. The yell went off into a wailing groan. The groan became a wet gurgle, choked with blood. I let the gurgle die sickeningly, on a choked gasp. It was nice work. I liked it. Canino liked it very much. I heard him laugh. It was a large booming laugh, not at all like the purr of his speaking voice.

Then silence for a little while, except for the rain and the quietly throbbing motor of the car. Then the house door crawled open, a deeper blackness in the black night. A figure showed in it cautiously, something white around the neck. It was her collar. She came out on the porch stiffly, a wooden woman. I caught the pale shine of her silver wig. Canino came crouched methodically behind her. It was so deadly it was almost funny.

She came down the steps. Now I could see the white stiffness of her face. She started towards the car. A bulwark of defense for Canino, in case I could still spit in his eye. Her voice spoke through the lisp of the rain, saying slowly, without any tone: "I can't see a thing, Lash. The windows are misted."

He grunted something and the girl's body jerked hard, as though he had jammed a gun into her back. She came on again and drew near the lightless car. I could see him behind her now, his hat, a side of his face, the bulk of his shoulder. The girl stopped rigid and screamed. A beautiful thin tearing scream that rocked me like a left hook.

"I can see him!" she screamed. "Through the window. Behind the wheel, Lash!"

He fell for it like a bucket of lead. He knocked her roughly to one side and jumped forward, throwing his hand up. Three more spurts of flame cut the darkness. More glass scarred. One bullet went on through and smacked into a tree on my side. A ricochet whined off into the distance. But the motor went quietly on.

He was low down, crouched against the gloom, his face a grayness without form that seemed to come back slowly after the glare of the shots. If it was a revolver he had, it might be empty. It might not. He had fired six times, but he might have reloaded inside the house. I hoped he had. I didn't want him with an empty gun. But it might be an automatic.

I said: "Finished?"

He whirled at me. Perhaps it would have been nice to allow him another shot or two, just like a gentleman of the old school. But his gun was still up and I couldn't wait any longer. Not long enough to be a gentleman of the old school. I shot him four times, the Colt straining against my ribs. The gun jumped out of his hand as if it had been kicked. He reached both his hands for his stomach. I could hear them smack hard against his body. He fell like that, straight forward, holding himself together with his broad hands. He fell face down in the wet gravel. And after that there wasn't a sound from him.

Silver-Wig didn't make a sound either. She stood rigid, with the rain swirling at her. I walked around Canino and kicked his gun, without any purpose. Then I walked after it and bent over sideways and picked it up. That put me close beside her. She spoke moodily, as if she was talking to herself.

"I—I was afraid you'd come back."

I said: "We had a date. I told you it was all arranged." I began to laugh like a loon.

Then she was bending down over him, touching him. And after a little while she stood up with a small key on a thin chain.

She said bitterly: "Did you have to kill him?"

I stopped laughing as suddenly as I had started. She went behind me and unlocked the handcuffs.

"Yes," she said softly. "I suppose you did."

30

This was another day and the sun was shining again.

Captain Gregory of the Missing Persons Bureau looked heavily out of his office window at the barred upper floor of the Hall of Justice, white and clean after the rain. Then he turned ponderously in his swivel chair and tamped his pipe with a heat-scarred thumb and stared at me bleakly.

"So you got yourself in another jam."

"Oh, you heard about it."

"Brother, I sit here all day on my fanny and I don't look as if I had a brain in my head. But you'd be surprised what I hear. Shooting this Canino was all right I guess, but I don't figure the homicide boys pinned any medals on you."

"There's been a lot of killing going on around me," I said. "I haven't been getting my share of it."

He smiled patiently. "Who told you this girl out there was Eddie Mars' wife?"

I told him. He listened carefully and yawned. He tapped his gold-studded mouth with a palm like a tray. "I guess you figure I ought to of found her."

"That's a fair deduction."

"Maybe I knew," he said. "Maybe I thought if Eddie and his woman wanted to play a little game like that, it would be smart—or as smart as I ever get—to let them think they were getting away with it. And then again maybe you think I was letting Eddie get away with it for more personal reasons." He held his big hand out and revolved the thumb against the index and second fingers.

"No," I said. "I didn't really think that. Not even when Eddie seemed to know all about our talk here the other day."

He raised his eyebrows as if raising them was an effort, a trick he was out of practice on. It furrowed his whole forehead and when it smoothed out it was full of white lines that turned reddish as I watched them.

"I'm a copper," he said. "Just a plain ordinary copper. Reasonably honest. As honest as you could expect a man to be in a world where it's out of style. That's mainly why I asked you to come in this morning. I'd like you to believe that. Being a copper I like to see the law win. I'd like to see the flashy well-dressed muggs like Eddie Mars spoiling their manicures in the rock quarry at Folsom, alongside of the poor little slum-bred hard guys that got knocked over on their first caper and never had a break since. That's what I'd like. You and me both lived too long to think I'm likely to see it happen. Not in this town, not in any town half this size, in any part of this wide, green and beautiful U.S.A. We just don't run our country that way."

I didn't say anything. He blew smoke with a backward jerk of his head, looked at the mouthpiece of his pipe and went on:

"But that don't mean I think Eddie Mars bumped off Regan or had any reason to or would have done it if he had. I just figured maybe he knows something about it, and maybe sooner or later something will sneak out into the open. Hiding his wife out at Realito was childish, but it's the kind of childishness a smart monkey thinks is smart. I had him in here last night, after the D.A. got through with him. He admitted the whole thing. He said he knew Canino as a reliable protection guy and that's what he had him for. He didn't know anything about his hobbies or want to. He didn't know Harry Jones. He didn't know Joe Brody. He did know Geiger, of course, but claims he didn't know about his racket. I guess you heard all that."

"Yes."

"You played it smart down there at Realito, brother. Not trying to cover up. We keep a file on unidentified bullets nowadays. Someday you might use that gun again. Then you'd be over a barrel."

"I played it smart," I said, and leered at him.

He knocked his pipe out and stared down at it broodingly. "What happened to the girl?" he asked, not looking up.

"I don't know. They didn't hold her. We made statements, three sets of them, for Wilde, for the Sheriff's office, for the Homicide Bureau. They turned her loose. I haven't seen her since. I don't expect to."

"Kind of a nice girl, they say. Wouldn't be one to play dirty games."

"Kind of a nice girl," I said.

Captain Gregory sighed and rumpled his mousy hair.

"There's just one more thing," he said almost gently. "You look like a nice guy, but you play too rough. If you really want to help the Sternwood family—leave 'em alone."

"I think you're right, Captain."

"How you feel?"

"Swell," I said. "I was standing on various pieces of carpet most of the night, being balled out. Before that I got soaked to the skin and beaten up. I'm in perfect condition."

"What the hell did you expect, brother?"

"Nothing else." I stood up and grinned at him and started for the door. When I had almost reached it he cleared his throat suddenly and said in a harsh voice: "I'm wasting my breath, huh? You still think you can find Regan."

I turned around and looked him straight in the eyes. "No, I don't think I can find Regan. I'm not even going to try. Does that suit you?"

He nodded slowly. Then he shrugged. "I don't know what the hell I even said that for. Good luck, Marlowe. Drop around any time."

"Thanks, Captain."

I went down out of the City Hall and got my car from the parking lot and drove home to the Hobart Arms. I lay down on the bed with my coat off and stared at the ceiling and listened to the traffic sounds on the street outside and watched the sun move slowly across a corner of the ceiling. I tried to go to sleep, but sleep didn't come. I got up and took a drink, although it was the wrong time of day, and lay down again. I still couldn't go to sleep. My brain ticked like a clock. I sat up on the side of the bed and stuffed a pipe and said out loud:

"That old buzzard knows something."

The pipe tasted as bitter as lye. I put it aside and lay down again. My mind drifted through waves of false memory, in which I seemed to do the same thing over and over again, go to the same places, meet the same people, say the same words to them, over and over again, and yet each time it seemed real, like something actually happening, and for the first time. I was driving hard along the highway through the rain, with Silver-Wig in the corner of the car, saying nothing, so that by the time we reached Los Angeles we seemed to be utter strangers again. I was getting out at an all night drugstore and phoning Bernie Ohls that I had killed a man at Realito and was on my way over to Wilde's house with Eddie Mars' wife, who had seen me do it. I was pushing the car along the silent, rain-polished streets to Lafayette Park and up under the porte-cochere of Wilde's big frame house and the porch light was already on, Ohls having telephoned ahead that I was coming. I was in Wilde's study and he was behind his desk in a flowered dressing-gown and a tight hard face and a dappled cigar moved in his fingers and up to the bitter smile on his lips. Ohls was there and a slim gray scholarly man from the Sheriff's office who looked and talked more like a professor of economics than a cop. I was telling the story and they were listening quietly and Silver-Wig sat in a shadow with her hands folded in her lap, looking at nobody. There was a lot of telephoning. There were two men from the Homicide Bureau who looked at me as if I was some kind of strange beast escaped from a traveling circus. I was driving again, with one of them beside me, to the Fulwider Building. We were there in the room where Harry Jones was still in the chair behind the desk, the twisted stiffness of his dead face and the sour-sweet smell in the room. There was a medical examiner, very young and husky, with red bristles on his neck. There was a fingerprint man fussing around and I was telling him not to forget the latch of the transom. (He found Canino's thumb print on it, the only print the brown man had left to back up my story.)

I was back again at Wilde's house, signing a typewritten statement his secretary had run off in another room. Then the door opened and Eddie Mars came in and an abrupt smile flashed to his face when he saw Silver-Wig, and he said: "Hello, sugar," and she didn't look at him or answer him. Eddie Mars fresh and cheerful, in a dark business suit, with a fringed white scarf hanging outside his tweed overcoat. Then they were gone, everybody was gone out of the room but myself and Wilde, and Wilde was saying in a cold, angry voice: "This is the last time, Marlowe. The next fast one you pull I'll throw you to the lions, no matter whose heart it breaks."

It was like that, over and over again, lying on the bed and watching the patch of sunlight slide down the corner of the wall. Then the phone rang, and it was Norris, the Sternwood butler, with his usual untouchable voice.

"Mr. Marlowe? I telephoned your office without success, so I took the liberty of trying to reach you at home."

"I was out most of the night," I said. "I haven't been down."

"Yes, sir. The General would like to see you this morning, Mr. Marlowe, if it's convenient."

"Half an hour or so," I said. "How is he?"

"He's in bed, sir, but not doing badly."

"Wait till he sees me," I said, and hung up.

I shaved, changed clothes and started for the door. Then I went back and got Carmen's little pearl-handled revolver and dropped it into my pocket. The sunlight was so bright that it danced. I got to the Sternwood place in twenty minutes and drove up under the arch at the side door. It was eleven-fifteen. The birds in the ornamental trees were crazy with song after the rain, the terraced lawns were as green as the Irish flag, and the whole estate looked as though it had been made about ten minutes before. I rang the bell. It was five days since I had rung it for the first time. It felt like a year.

A maid opened the door and led me along a side hall to the main hallway and left me there, saying Mr. Norris would be down in a moment. The main hallway looked just the same. The portrait over the mantel had the same hot black eyes and the knight in the stained-glass window still wasn't getting anywhere untying the naked damsel from the tree.

In a few minutes Norris appeared, and he hadn't changed either. His acid blue eyes were as remote as ever, his grayish-pink skin looked healthy and rested, and he moved as if he was twenty years younger than he really was. I was the one who felt the weight of the years.

We went up the tiled staircase and turned the opposite way from Vivian's room. With each step the house seemed to grow larger and more silent. We reached a massive old door that looked as if it had come out of a church. Norris opened it softly and looked in. Then he stood aside and I went in past him across what seemed to be about a quarter of a mile of carpet to a huge canopied bed like the one Henry the Eighth died in.

General Sternwood was propped up on pillows. His blood-less hands were clasped on top of the sheet. They looked gray against it. His black eyes were still full of fight and the rest of his face still looked like the face of a corpse.

"Sit down, Mr. Marlowe." His voice sounded weary and a little stiff.

I pulled a chair close to him and sat down. All the windows were shut tight. The room was sunless at that hour. Awnings cut off what glare there might be from the sky. The air had the faint sweetish smell of old age.

He stared at me silently for a long minute. He moved a hand, as if to prove to himself that he could still move it, then folded it back over the other. He said lifelessly:

"I didn't ask you to look for my son-in-law, Mr. Marlowe."

"You wanted me too, though."

"I didn't ask you to. You assume a great deal. I usually ask for what I want."

I didn't say anything.

"You have been paid," he went on coldly. "The money is of no consequence one way or the other. I merely feel that you have, no doubt unintentionally, betrayed a trust."

He closed his eyes on that. I said: "Is that all you wanted to see me about?"

He opened his eyes again, very slowly, as though the lids were made of lead. "I suppose you are angry at that remark," he said.

I shook my head. "You have an advantage over me, General. It's an advantage I wouldn't want to take away from you, not a hair of it. It's not much, considering what you have to put up with. You can say anything you like to me and I wouldn't think of getting angry. I'd like to offer you your money back. It may mean nothing to you. It might mean something to me."

"What does it mean to you?"

"It means I have refused payment for an unsatisfactory job. That's all."

"Do you do many unsatisfactory jobs?"

"A few. Everyone does."

"Why did you go to see Captain Gregory?"

I leaned back and hung an arm over the back of the chair. I studied his face. It told me nothing. I didn't know the answer to his question—no satisfactory answer.

I said: "I was convinced you put those Geiger notes up to me chiefly as a test, and that you were a little afraid Regan might somehow be involved in an attempt to blackmail you. I didn't know anything about Regan then. It wasn't until I talked to Captain Gregory that I realized Regan wasn't that sort of guy in all probability."

"That is scarcely answering my question."

I nodded. "No. That is scarcely answering your question. I guess I just don't like to admit that I played a hunch. The morning I was here, after I left you out in the orchid house, Mrs. Regan sent for me. She seemed to assume I was hired to look for her husband and she didn't seem to like it. She let drop however that 'they' had found his car in a certain garage. The 'they' could only be the police. Consequently the police must know something about it. If they did, the Missing Persons Bureau would be the department that would have the case. I didn't know whether you had reported it, of course, or somebody else, or whether they had found the car through somebody reporting it abandoned in a garage. But I know cops, and I knew that if they got that much, they would get a little more—especially as your driver happened to have a police record. I didn't know how much more they would get. That started me thinking about the Missing Persons Bureau. What convinced me was something in Mr. Wilde's manner the night we had the conference over at his house about Geiger and so on. We were alone for a minute and he asked me whether you had told me you were looking for Regan. I said you had told me you wished you knew where he was and that he was all right. Wilde pulled his lip in and looked funny. I knew just as plainly as though he had said it that by 'looking for Regan' he meant using the machinery of the law to look for him. Even then I tried to go up against Captain Gregory in such a way that I wouldn't tell him anything he didn't know already."

"And you allowed Captain Gregory to think I had employed you to find Rusty?"

"Yeah. I guess I did—when I was sure he had the case."

He closed his eyes. They twitched a little. He spoke with them closed. "And do you consider that ethical?"

"Yes," I said. "I do."

The eyes opened again. The piercing blackness of them was startling coming suddenly out of that dead face. "Perhaps I don't understand," he said.

"Maybe you don't. The head of a Missing Persons Bureau isn't a talker. He wouldn't be in that office if he was. This one is a very smart cagey guy who tries, with a lot of success at first, to give the impression he's a middle-aged hack fed up with his job. The game I play is not spillikins. There's always a large element of bluff connected with it. Whatever I might say to a cop, he would be apt to discount it. And to *that* cop it wouldn't make much difference what I said. When you hire a boy in my line of work it isn't like hiring a window-washer and showing him eight windows and saying: 'Wash those and you're through.' *You* don't know what I have to go through or over or under to do your job for you. I do it my way. I do my best to protect you and I may break a few rules, but I break them in your favor. The client comes first, unless he's crooked. Even then all I do is hand the job back to him and keep my mouth shut. After all you didn't tell me *not* to go to Captain Gregory."

"That would have been rather difficult," he said with a faint smile.

"Well, what have I done wrong? Your man Norris seemed to think when Geiger was eliminated the case was over. I don't see it that way. Geiger's method of approach puzzled me and still does. I'm not Sherlock Holmes or Philo Vance. I don't expect to go over ground the police have covered and pick up a broken pen point and build a case from it. If you think there is anybody in the detective business making a living doing that sort of thing, you don't know much about cops. It's not things like that they overlook, if they overlook anything. I'm not saying they often overlook anything when they're really allowed to work. But if they do, it's apt to be something looser and vaguer, like a man of Geiger's type sending you his evidence of debt and asking you to pay like a gentleman—Geiger, a man in a shady racket, in a vulnerable position, protected by a racketeer and having at least some negative protection from some of the police. Why did he do that? Because he wanted to find out if there was anything putting pressure on you. If there was, you would pay him. If not, you would ignore him and wait for his next move. But there was something putting a pressure on you. Regan. You were afraid he was not what he had appeared to be, that he had stayed around and been nice to you just long enough to find out how to play games with your bank account."

He started to say something but I interrupted him. "Even at that it wasn't your money you cared about. It wasn't even your daughters. You've more or less written them off. It's that you're still too proud to be played for a sucker—and you really liked Regan."

There was a silence. Then the General said quietly: "You talk too damn much, Marlowe. Am I to understand you are still trying to solve that puzzle?"

"No. I've quit. I've been warned off. The boys think I play too rough. That's why I thought I should give you back your money—because it isn't a completed job by my standards."

He smiled. "Quit, nothing," he said. "I'll pay you another thousand dollars to find Rusty. He doesn't have to come back. I don't even have to know where he is. A man has a right to live his own life. I don't blame him for walking out on my daughter, nor even for going so abruptly. It was probably a sudden impulse. I want to know that he is all right wherever he is. I want to know it from him directly, and if he should happen to need money, I should want him to have that also. Am I clear?"

I said: "Yes, General."

He rested a little while, lax on the bed, his eyes closed and dark-lidded, his mouth tight and bloodless. He was used up. He was pretty nearly licked. He opened his eyes again and tried to grin at me.

"I guess I'm a sentimental old goat," he said. "And no soldier at all. I took a fancy to that boy. He seemed pretty clean to me. I must be a little too vain about my judgment of character. Find him for me, Marlowe. Just find him."

"I'll try," I said. "You'd better rest now. I've talked your arm off."

I got up quickly and walked across the wide floor and out. He had his eyes shut again before I opened the door. His hands lay limp on the sheet. He looked a lot more like a dead man than most dead men look. I shut the door quietly and went back along the upper hall and down the stairs.

31

The butler appeared with my hat. I put it on and said: "What do you think of him?"

"He's not as weak as he looks, sir."

"If he was, he'd be ready for burial. What did this Regan fellow have that bored into him so?"

The butler looked at me levelly and yet with a queer lack of expression. "Youth, sir," he said. "And the soldier's eye."

"Like yours," I said.

"If I may say so, sir, not unlike yours."

"Thanks. How are the ladies this morning?"

He shrugged politely.

"Just what I thought," I said, and he opened the door for me.

I stood outside on the step and looked down the vistas of grassed terraces and trimmed trees and flowerbeds to the tall metal railing at the bottom of the gardens. I saw Carmen about halfway down, sitting on a stone bench, with her head between her hands, looking forlorn and alone.

I went down the red brick steps that led from terrace to terrace. I was quite close before she heard me. She jumped up and whirled like a cat. She wore the light blue slacks she had worn the first time I saw her. Her blond hair was the same loose tawny wave. Her face was white. Red spots flared in her cheeks as she looked at me. Her eyes were slaty.

"Bored?" I said.

She smiled slowly, rather shyly, then nodded quickly. Then she whispered: "You're not mad at me?"

"I thought you were mad at me."

She put her thumb up and giggled. "I'm not." When she giggled I didn't like her any more. I looked around. A target hung on a tree about thirty feet away, with some darts sticking to it. There were three or four more on the stone bench where she had been sitting.

"For people with money you and your sister don't seem to have much fun," I said.

She looked at me under her long lashes. This was the look that was supposed to make me roll over on my back. I said: "You like throwing those darts?"

"Uh-huh."

"That reminds me of something." I looked back towards the house. By moving about three feet I made a tree hide me from it. I took her little pearl-handled gun out of my pocket. "I brought you back your artillery. I cleaned it and loaded it up. Take my tip—don't shoot it at people, unless you get to be a better shot. Remember?"

Her face went paler and her thin thumb dropped. She looked at me, then at the gun I was holding. There was a fascination in her eyes. "Yes," she said, and nodded. Then suddenly: "Teach me to shoot."

"Huh?"

"Teach me how to shoot. I'd like that."

"Here? It's against the law."

She came close to me and took the gun out of my hand, cuddled her hand around the butt. Then she tucked it quickly inside her slacks, almost with a furtive movement, and looked around.

"I know where," she said in a secret voice. "Down by some of the old wells." She pointed off down the hill. "Teach me?"

I looked into her slaty blue eyes. I might as well have looked at a couple of bottle-tops. "All right. Give me back the gun until I see if the place looks all right."

She smiled and made a mouth, then handed it back with a secret naughty air, as if she was giving me a key to her room. We walked up the steps and around to my car. The gardens seemed deserted. The sunshine was as empty as a headwaiter's smile. We got into the car and I drove down the sunken driveway and out through the gates.

"Where's Vivian?" I asked.

"Not up yet." She giggled.

I drove on down the hill through the quiet opulent streets with their faces washed by the rain, bore east to La Brea, then south. We reached the place she meant in about ten minutes.

"In there." She leaned out of the window and pointed.

It was a narrow dirt road, not much more than a track, like the entrance to some foothill ranch. A wide five-barred gate was folded back against a stump and looked as if it hadn't been shut in years. The road was fringed with tall eucalyptus trees and deeply rutted. Trucks had used it. It was empty and sunny now, but not yet dusty. The rain had been too hard and too recent. I followed the ruts along and the noise of city traffic grew curiously and quickly faint, as if this were not in the city at all, but far away in a daydream land. Then the oil-stained, motionless walking-beam of a squat wooden derrick stuck up over a branch. I could see the rusty old steel cable that connected this walking-beam with half a dozen others. The beams didn't move, probably hadn't moved for a year. The wells were no longer pumping. There was a pile of rusted pipe, a loading platform that sagged at one end, half a dozen empty oil drums lying in a ragged pile. There was the stagnant, oil-scummed water of an old sump iridescent in the sunlight.

"Are they going to make a park of all this?" I asked.

She dipped her chin down and gleamed at me.

"It's about time. The smell of that sump would poison a herd of goats. This the place you had in mind?"

"Uh-huh. Like it?"

"It's beautiful." I pulled up beside the loading platform. We got out. I listened. The hum of the traffic was a distant web of sound, like the buzzing of bees. The place was as lonely as a churchyard. Even after the rain the tall eucalyptus trees still looked dusty. They always look dusty. A branch broken off by the wind had fallen over the edge of the sump and the flat leathery leaves dangled in the water.

I walked around the sump and looked into the pump-house. There was some junk in it, nothing that looked like recent activity. Outside a big wooden bull wheel was tilted against the wall. It looked like a good place all right.

I went back to the car. The girl stood beside it preening her hair and holding it out in the sun. "Gimme," she said, and held her hand out.

I took the gun out and put it in her palm. I bent down and picked up a rusty can.

"Take it easy now," I said. "It's loaded in all five. I'll go over and set this can in that square opening in the middle of that big wooden wheel. See?" I pointed. She ducked her head, delighted. "That's about thirty feet. Don't start shooting until I get back beside you. Okey?"

"Okey," she giggled.

I went back around the sump and set the can up in the middle of the bull wheel. It made a swell target. If she missed the can, which she was certain to do, she would probably hit the wheel. That would stop a small slug completely. However, she wasn't going to hit even that.

I went back towards her around the sump. When I was about ten feet from her, at the edge of the sump, she showed me all her sharp little teeth and brought the gun up and started to hiss.

I stopped dead, the sump water stagnant and stinking at my back.

"Stand there, you son of a bitch," she said.

The gun pointed at my chest. Her hand seemed to be quite steady. The hissing sound grew louder and her face had the scraped bone look. Aged, deteriorated, become animal, and not a nice animal.

I laughed at her. I started to walk towards her. I saw her small finger tighten on the trigger and grow white at the tip. I was about six feet away from her when she started to shoot.

The sound of the gun made a sharp slap, without body, a brittle crack in the sunlight. I didn't see any smoke. I stopped again and grinned at her.

She fired twice more, very quickly. I don't think any of the shots would have missed. There were five in the little gun. She had fired four. I rushed her.

I didn't want the last one in my face, so I swerved to one side. She gave it to me quite carefully, not worried at all. I think I felt the hot breath of the powder blast a little.

I straightened up. "My, but you're cute," I said.

Her hand holding the empty gun began to shake violently.

The gun fell out of it. Her mouth began to shake. Her whole face went to pieces. Then her head screwed up towards her left ear and froth showed on her lips. Her breath made a whining sound. She swayed.

I caught her as she fell. She was already unconscious. I pried her teeth open with both hands and stuffed a wadded handkerchief in between them. It took all my strength to do it. I lifted her up and got her into the car, then went back for the gun and dropped it into my pocket. I climbed in under the wheel, backed the car and drove back the way we had come along the rutted road, out of the gateway, back up the hill and so home.

Carmen lay crumpled in the corner of the car, without motion. I was halfway up the drive to the house before she stirred. Then her eyes suddenly opened wide and wild. She sat up.

"What happened?" she gasped.

"Nothing. Why?"

"Oh, yes it did," she giggled. "I wet myself."

"They always do," I said.

She looked at me with a sudden sick speculation and began to moan.

32

The gentle-eyed, horse-faced maid let me into the long gray and white upstairs sitting room with the ivory drapes tumbled extravagantly on the floor and the white carpet from wall to wall. A screen star's boudoir, a place of charm and seduction, artificial as a wooden leg. It was empty at the moment. The door closed behind me with the unnatural softness of a hospital door. A breakfast table on wheels stood by the chaise-longue. Its silver glittered. There were cigarette ashes in the coffee cup. I sat down and waited.

It seemed a long time before the door opened again and Vivian came in. She was in oyster-white lounging pajamas trimmed with white fur, cut as flowingly as a summer sea frothing on the beach of some small and exclusive island.

She went past me in long smooth strides and sat down on the edge of the chaise-longue. There was a cigarette in her lips, at the corner of her mouth. Her nails today were copper red from quick to tip, without half moons.

"So you're just a brute after all," she said quietly, staring at me. "An utter callous brute. You killed a man last night. Never mind how I heard it. I heard it. And now you have to come out here and frighten my kid sister into a fit."

I didn't say a word. She began to fidget. She moved over to a slipper chair and put her head back against a white cushion that lay along the back of the chair against the wall. She blew pale gray smoke upwards and watched it float towards the ceiling and come apart in wisps that were for a little while distinguishable from the air and then melted and were nothing. Then very slowly she lowered her eyes and gave me a cool hard glance.

"I don't understand you," she said. "I'm thankful as hell one of us kept his head the night before last. It's bad enough to have a bootlegger in my past. Why don't you for Christ's sake say something?"

"How is she?"

"Oh, she's all right, I suppose. Fast asleep. She always goes to sleep. What did you do to her?"

"Not a thing. I came out of the house after seeing your father and she was out in front. She had been throwing darts at a target on a tree. I went down to speak to her because I had something that belonged to her. A little revolver Owen Taylor gave her once. She took it over to Brody's place the other evening, the evening he was killed. I had to take it away from her there. I didn't mention it, so perhaps you didn't know it."

The black Sternwood eyes got large and empty. It was her turn not to say anything.

"She was pleased to get her little gun back and she wanted me to teach her how to shoot and she wanted to show me the old oil wells down the hill where your family made some of its money. So we went down there and the place was pretty creepy, all rusted metal and old wood and silent wells and greasy scummy sumps. Maybe that upset her. I guess you've been there yourself. It was kind of eerie."

"Yes—it is." It was a small breathless voice now.

"So we went in there and I stuck a can up in a bull wheel for her to pop at. She threw a wingding. Looked like a mild epileptic fit to me."

"Yes." The same minute voice. "She has them once in a while. Is that all you wanted to see me about?"

"I guess you still wouldn't tell me what Eddie Mars has on you."

"Nothing at all. And I'm getting a little tired of that question," she said coldly.

"Do you know a man named Canino?"

She drew her fine black brows together in thought. "Vaguely. I seem to remember the name."

"Eddie Mars' trigger man. A tough hombre, they said. I guess he was. Without a little help from a lady I'd be where he is—in the morgue."

"The ladies seem to—" She stopped dead and whitened. "I can't joke about it," she said simply.

"I'm not joking, and if I seem to talk in circles, it just seems that way. It all ties together—everything. Geiger and his cute little blackmail tricks, Brody and his pictures, Eddie Mars and his roulette tables, Canino and the girl Rusty Regan didn't run away with. It all ties together."

"I'm afraid I don't even know what you're talking about."

"Suppose you did—it would be something like this. Geiger got his hooks into your sister, which isn't very difficult, and got some notes from her and tried to blackmail your father with them, in a nice way. Eddie Mars was behind Geiger, protecting him and using him for a cat's-paw. Your father sent for me instead of paying up, which showed he wasn't scared about anything. Eddie Mars wanted to know that. He had something on you and he wanted to know if he had it on the General too. If he had, he could collect a lot of money in a hurry. If not, he would have to wait until you got your share of the family fortune, and in the meantime be satisfied with whatever spare cash he could take away from you across the roulette table. Geiger was killed by Owen Taylor, who was in love with your silly little sister and didn't like the kind of games Geiger played with her. That didn't mean anything to

Eddie. He was playing a deeper game than Geiger knew anything about, or than Brody knew anything about, or anybody except you and Eddie and a tough guy named Canino. Your husband disappeared and Eddie, knowing everybody knew there had been bad blood between him and Regan, hid his wife out at Realito and put Canino to guard her, so that it would look as if she had run away with Regan. He even got Regan's car into the garage of the place where Mona Mars had been living. But that sounds a little silly taken merely as an attempt to divert suspicion that Eddie had killed your husband or had him killed. It isn't so silly, really. He had another motive. He was playing for a million or so. He knew where Regan had gone and why and he didn't want the police to have to find out. He wanted them to have an explanation of the disappearance that would keep them satisfied. Am I boring you?"

"You tire me," she said in a dead, exhausted voice. "God, how you tire me!"

"I'm sorry. I'm not just fooling around trying to be clever. Your father offered me a thousand dollars this morning to find Regan. That's a lot of money to me, but I can't do it."

Her mouth jumped open. Her breath was suddenly strained and harsh. "Give me a cigarette," she said thickly. "Why?" The pulse in her throat had begun to throb.

I gave her a cigarette and lit a match and held it for her. She drew in a lungful of smoke and let it out raggedly and then the cigarette seemed to be forgotten between her fingers. She never drew on it again.

"Well, the Missing Persons Bureau can't find him," I said. "It's not so easy. What they can't do it's not likely that I can do."

"Oh." There was a shade of relief in her voice.

"That's one reason. The Missing Persons people think he just disappeared on purpose, pulled down the curtain, as they call it. They don't think Eddie Mars did away with him."

"Who said anybody did away with him?"

"We're coming to it," I said.

For a brief instant her face seemed to come to pieces, to become merely a set of features without form or control. Her mouth looked like the prelude to a scream. But only for an instant. The Sternwood blood had to be good for something more than her black eyes and her recklessness.

I stood up and took the smoking cigarette from between her fingers and killed it in an ashtray. Then I took Carmen's little gun out of my pocket and laid it carefully, with exaggerated care, on her white satin knee. I balanced it there, and stepped back with my head on one side like a window-dresser getting the effect of a new twist of a scarf around a dummy's neck.

I sat down again. She didn't move. Her eyes came down millimeter by millimeter and looked at the gun.

"It's harmless," I said. "All five chambers empty. She fired them all. She fired them all at me."

The pulse jumped wildly in her throat. Her voice tried to say something and couldn't. She swallowed.

"From a distance of five or six feet," I said. "Cute little thing, isn't she? Too bad I had loaded the gun with blanks." I grinned nastily. "I had a hunch about what she would do—if she got the chance."

She brought her voice back from a long way off. "You're a horrible man," she said. "Horrible."

"Yeah. You're her big sister. What are you going to do about it?"

"You can't prove a word of it."

"Can't prove what?"

"That she fired at you. You said you were down there around the wells with her, alone. You can't prove a word of what you say."

"Oh that," I said. "I wasn't thinking of trying. I was thinking of another time—when the shells in the little gun had bullets in them."

Her eyes were pools of darkness, much emptier than darkness.

"I was thinking of the day Regan disappeared," I said. "Late in the afternoon. When he took her down to those old wells to teach her to shoot and put up a can somewhere and told her to pop at it and stood near her while she shot. And she didn't shoot at the can. She turned the gun and shot him, just the way she tried to shoot me today, and for the same reason."

She moved a little and the gun slid off her knee and fell to the floor. It was one of the loudest sounds I ever heard. Her eyes were riveted on my face. Her voice was a stretched whisper of agony. "Carmen! . . . Merciful God, Carmen! . . . Why?"

"Do I really have to tell you why she shot at me?"

"Yes." Her eyes were still terrible. "I'm—I'm afraid you do."

"Night before last when I got home she was in my apartment. She'd kidded the manager into letting her in to wait for me. She was in my bed—naked. I threw her out on her ear. I guess maybe Regan did the same thing to her sometime. But you can't do that to Carmen."

She drew her lips back and made a half-hearted attempt to lick them. It made her, for a brief instant, look like a frightened child. The lines of her cheeks sharpened and her hand went up slowly like an artificial hand worked by wires and its fingers closed slowly and stiffly around the white fur at her collar. They drew the fur tight against her throat. After that she just sat staring.

"Money," she croaked. "I suppose you want money."

"How much money?" I tried not to sneer.

"Fifteen thousand dollars?"

I nodded. "That would be about right. That would be the established fee. That was what he had in his pockets when she shot him. That would be what Mr. Canino got for disposing of the body when you went to Eddie Mars for help. But that would be small change to what Eddie expects to collect one of these days, wouldn't it?"

"You son of a bitch!" she said.

"Uh-uh. I'm a very smart guy. I haven't a feeling or a scruple in the world. All I have the itch for is money. I am so money greedy that for twenty-five bucks a day and expenses, mostly gasoline and whiskey, I do my thinking myself, what there is of it; I risk my whole future, the hatred of the cops and of Eddie Mars and his pals, I dodge bullets and eat saps, and say thank you very much, if you have any more trouble, I hope you'll think of me, I'll just leave one of my cards in case anything comes up. I do all this for twenty-five bucks a day— and maybe just a little to protect what little pride a broken and sick old man has left in his blood, in the thought that his blood is not poison, and that although his two little girls are a trifle wild, as many nice girls are these days, they are not perverts or killers. And that makes me a son of a bitch. All right. I don't care anything about that. I've been called that by people of all sizes and shapes, including your little sister. She called me worse than that for not getting into bed with her. I got five hundred dollars from your father, which I didn't ask for, but he can afford to give it to me. I can get another thousand for finding Mr. Rusty Regan, if I could find him. Now you offer me fifteen grand. That makes me a big shot. With fifteen grand I could own a home and a new car and four suits of clothes. I might even take a vacation without worrying about losing a case. That's fine. What are you offering it to me for? Can I go on being a son of a bitch, or do I have to become a gentleman, like that lush that passed out in his car the other night?"

She was as silent as a stone woman.

"All right," I went on heavily. "Will you take her away? Somewhere far off from here where they can handle her type, where they will keep guns and knives and fancy drinks away from her? Hell, she might even get herself cured, you know. It's been done."

She got up and walked slowly to the windows. The drapes lay in heavy ivory folds beside her feet. She stood among the folds and looked out, towards the quiet darkish foothills. She stood motionless, almost blending into the drapes. Her hands hung loose at her sides. Utterly motionless hands. She turned and came back along the room and walked past me blindly. When she was behind me she caught her breath sharply and spoke.

"He's in the sump," she said. "A horrible decayed thing. I did it. I did just what you said. I went to Eddie Mars. She came home and told me about it, just like a child. She's not normal. I knew the police would get it all out of her. In a little while she would even brag about it. And if dad knew, he would call them instantly and tell them the whole story. And sometime in that night he would die. It's not his dying—it's what he would be thinking just before he died. Rusty wasn't a bad fellow. I didn't love him. He was all right, I guess. He just didn't mean anything to me, one way or another, alive or dead, compared with keeping it from dad."

"So you let her run around loose," I said, "getting into other jams."

"I was playing for time. Just for time. I played the wrong way, of course. I thought she might even forget it herself. I've heard they do forget what happens in those fits. Maybe she has forgotten it. I knew Eddie Mars would bleed me white, but I didn't care. I had to have help and I could only get it from somebody like him. . . . There have been times when I hardly believed it all myself. And other times when I had to get drunk quickly—whatever time of day it was. Awfully damn quickly."

"You'll take her away," I said. "And do that awfully damn quickly."

She still had her back to me. She said softly now: "What about you?"

"Nothing about me. I'm leaving. I'll give you three days. If you're gone by then—okey. If you're not, out it comes. And don't think I don't mean that."

She turned suddenly. "I don't know what to say to you. I don't know how to begin."

"Yeah. Get her out of here and see that she's watched every minute. Promise?"

"I promise. Eddie—"

"Forget Eddie. I'll go see him after I get some rest. I'll handle Eddie."

"He'll try to kill you."

"Yeah," I said. "His best boy couldn't. I'll take a chance on the others. Does Norris know?"

"He'll never tell."

"I thought he knew."

I went quickly away from her down the room and out and down the tiled staircase to the front hall. I didn't see anybody when I left. I found my hat alone this time. Outside the bright gardens had a haunted look, as though small wild eyes were watching me from behind the bushes, as though the sunshine itself had a mysterious something in its light. I got into my car and drove off down the hill.

What did it matter where you lay once you were dead? In a

dirty sump or in a marble tower on top of a high hill? You were dead, you were sleeping the big sleep, you were not bothered by things like that. Oil and water were the same as wind and air to you. You just slept the big sleep, not caring about the nastiness of how you died or where you fell. Me, I was part of the nastiness now. Far more a part of it than Rusty Regan was. But the old man didn't have to be. He could lie quiet in his canopied bed, with his bloodless hands folded on the sheet, waiting. His heart was a brief, uncertain murmur. His thoughts were as gray as ashes. And in a little while he too, like Rusty Regan, would be sleeping the big sleep.

On the way downtown I stopped at a bar and had a couple of double Scotches. They didn't do me any good. All they did was make me think of Silver-Wig, and I never saw her again.

FAREWELL, MY LOVELY

I

IT WAS one of the mixed blocks over on Central Avenue, the blocks that are not yet all negro. I had just come out of a three-chair barber shop where an agency thought a relief barber named Dimitrios Aleidis might be working. It was a small matter. His wife said she was willing to spend a little money to have him come home.

I never found him, but Mrs. Aleidis never paid me any money either.

It was a warm day, almost the end of March, and I stood outside the barber shop looking up at the jutting neon sign of a second floor dine and dice emporium called Florian's. A man was looking up at the sign too. He was looking up at the dusty windows with a sort of ecstatic fixity of expression, like a hunky immigrant catching his first sight of the Statue of Liberty. He was a big man but not more than six feet five inches tall and not wider than a beer truck. He was about ten feet away from me. His arms hung loose at his sides and a forgotten cigar smoked behind his enormous fingers.

Slim quiet negroes passed up and down the street and stared at him with darting side glances. He was worth looking at. He wore a shaggy borsalino hat, a rough gray sports coat with white golf balls on it for buttons, a brown shirt, a yellow tie, pleated gray flannel slacks and alligator shoes with white explosions on the toes. From his outer breast pocket cascaded a show handkerchief of the same brilliant yellow as his tie. There were a couple of colored feathers tucked into the band of his hat, but he didn't really need them. Even on Central Avenue, not the quietest dressed street in the world, he looked about as inconspicuous as a tarantula on a slice of angel food.

His skin was pale and he needed a shave. He would always need a shave. He had curly black hair and heavy eyebrows that almost met over his thick nose. His ears were small and neat for a man of that size and his eyes had a shine close to tears that gray eyes often seem to have. He stood like a statue, and after a long time he smiled.

He moved slowly across the sidewalk to the double swinging doors which shut off the stairs to the second floor. He pushed them open, cast a cool expressionless glance up and down the street, and moved inside. If he had been a smaller man and more quietly dressed, I might have thought he was going to pull a stick-up. But not in those clothes, and not with that hat, and that frame.

The doors swung back outwards and almost settled to a stop. Before they had entirely stopped moving they opened again, violently, outwards. Something sailed across the sidewalk and landed in the gutter between two parked cars. It landed on its hands and knees and made a high keening noise like a cornered rat. It got up slowly, retrieved a hat and stepped back onto the sidewalk. It was a thin, narrow-shouldered brown youth in a lilac colored suit and a carnation. It had slick black hair. It kept its mouth open and whined for a moment. People stared at it vaguely. Then it settled its hat jauntily, sidled over to the wall and walked silently splay-footed off along the block.

Silence. Traffic resumed. I walked along to the double doors and stood in front of them. They were motionless now. It wasn't any of my business. So I pushed them open and looked in.

A hand I could have sat in came out of the dimness and took hold of my shoulder and squashed it to a pulp. Then the hand moved me through the doors and casually lifted me up a step. The large face looked at me. A deep soft voice said to me, quietly:

"Smokes in here, huh? Tie that for me, pal."

It was dark in there. It was quiet. From up above came vague sounds of humanity, but we were alone on the stairs. The big man stared at me solemnly and went on wrecking my shoulder with his hand.

"A dinge," he said. "I just thrown him out. You seen me throw him out?"

He let go of my shoulder. The bone didn't seem to be broken, but the arm was numb.

"It's that kind of a place," I said, rubbing my shoulder. "What did you expect?"

"Don't say that, pal," the big man purred softly, like four tigers after dinner. "Velma used to work here. Little Velma."

He reached for my shoulder again. I tried to dodge him but he was as fast as a cat. He began to chew my muscles up some more with his iron fingers.

"Yeah," he said. "Little Velma. I ain't seen her in eight years. You say this here is a dinge joint?"

I croaked that it was.

He lifted me up two more steps. I wrenched myself loose and tried for a little elbow room. I wasn't wearing a gun. Looking for Dimitrios Aleidis hadn't seemed to require it. I doubted if it would do me any good. The big man would probably take it away from me and eat it.

"Go on up and see for yourself," I said, trying to keep the agony out of my voice.

He let go of me again. He looked at me with a sort of sadness in his gray eyes. "I'm feelin' good," he said. "I wouldn't want anybody to fuss with me. Let's you and me go on up and maybe nibble a couple."

"They won't serve you. I told you it's a colored joint."

"I ain't seen Velma in eight years," he said in his deep sad voice. "Eight long years since I said goodby. She ain't wrote to me in six. But she'll have a reason. She used to work here. Cute she was. Let's you and me go on up, huh?"

"All right," I yelled. "I'll go up with you. Just lay off carrying me. Let me walk. I'm fine. I'm all grown up. I go to the bathroom alone and everything. Just don't carry me."

"Little Velma used to work here," he said gently. He wasn't listening to me.

We went on up the stairs. He let me walk. My shoulder ached. The back of my neck was wet.

2

Two more swing doors closed off the head of the stairs from whatever was beyond. The big man pushed them open lightly with his thumbs and we went into the room. It was a long narrow room, not very clean, not very bright, not very cheer-ful. In the corner a group of negroes chanted and chattered in the cone of light over a crap table. There was a bar against the right hand wall. The rest of the room was mostly small round tables. There were a few customers, men and women, all negroes.

The chanting at the crap table stopped dead and the light over it jerked out. There was a sudden silence as heavy as a water-logged boat. Eyes looked at us, chestnut colored eyes, set in faces that ranged from gray to deep black. Heads turned slowly and the eyes in them glistened and stared in the dead alien silence of another race.

A large, thick-necked negro was leaning against the end of the bar with pink garters on his shirt sleeves and pink and white suspenders crossing his broad back. He had bouncer written all over him. He put his lifted foot down slowly and turned slowly and stared at us, spreading his feet gently and moving a broad tongue along his lips. He had a battered face that looked as if it had been hit by everything but the bucket of a dragline. It was scarred, flattened, thick-ened, checkered, and welted. It was a face that had nothing to fear. Everything had been done to it that anybody could think of.

The short crinkled hair had a touch of gray. One ear had lost the lobe.

The negro was heavy and wide. He had big heavy legs and they looked a little bowed, which is unusual in a negro. He moved his tongue some more and smiled and moved his body. He came towards us in a loose fighter's crouch. The big man waited for him silently.

The negro with the pink garters on his arms put a massive brown hand against the big man's chest. Large as it was, the hand looked like a stud. The big man didn't move. The bouncer smiled gently.

"No white folks, brother. Jes' fo' the colored people. I'se sorry."

The big man moved his small sad gray eyes and looked around the room. His cheeks flushed a little. "Shine box," he said angrily, under his breath. He raised his voice. "Where's Velma at?" he asked the bouncer.

The bouncer didn't quite laugh. He studied the big man's clothes, his brown shirt and yellow tie, his rough gray coat and the white golf balls on it. He moved his thick head around delicately and studied all this from various angles. He looked down at the alligator shoes. He chuckled lightly. He seemed amused. I felt a little sorry for him. He spoke softly again.

"Velma you says? No Velma heah, brother. No hooch, no gals, no nothing. Jes' the scram, white boy, jes' the scram."

"Velma used to work here," the big man said. He spoke almost dreamily, as if he was all by himself, out in the woods, picking johnny-jump-ups. I got my handkerchief out and wiped the back of my neck again.

The bouncer laughed suddenly. "Shuah," he said, throwing a quick look back over his shoulder at his public. "Velma used to work here. But Velma don't work heah no mo'. She done reti'ed. Haw. Haw."

"Kind of take your goddamned mitt off my shirt," the big man said.

The bouncer frowned. He was not used to being talked to like that. He took his hand off the shirt and doubled it into a fist about the size and color of a large eggplant. He had his job, his reputation for toughness, his public esteem to consider. He considered them for a second and made a mistake. He swung the fist very hard and short with a sudden outward jerk of the elbow and hit the big man on the side of the jaw. A soft sigh went around the room.

It was a good punch. The shoulder dropped and the body swung behind it. There was a lot of weight in that punch and the man who landed it had had plenty of practise. The big man didn't move his head more than an inch. He didn't try to block the punch. He took it, shook himself lightly, made a quiet sound in his throat and took hold of the bouncer by the throat.

The bouncer tried to knee him in the groin. The big man turned him in the air and slid his gaudy shoes apart on the scaly linoleum that covered the floor. He bent the bouncer backwards and shifted his right hand to the bouncer's belt. The belt broke like a piece of butcher's string. The big man put his enormous hand flat against the bouncer's spine and heaved. He threw him clear across the room, spinning and staggering and flailing with his arms. Three men jumped out of the way. The bouncer went over with a table and smacked into the baseboard with a crash that must have been heard in Denver. His legs twitched. Then he lay still.

"Some guys," the big man said, "has got wrong ideas about when to get tough." He turned to me. "Yeah," he said. "Let's you and me nibble one."

We went over to the bar. The customers, by ones and twos and threes, became quiet shadows that drifted soundless across the floor, soundless through the doors at the head of the stairs. Soundless as shadows on grass. They didn't even let the doors swing.

We leaned against the bar. "Whiskey sour," the big man said. "Call yours."

"Whiskey sour," I said.

We had whiskey sours.

The big man licked his whiskey sour impassively down the side of the thick squat glass. He stared solemnly at the barman, a thin, worried-looking negro in a white coat who moved as if his feet hurt him.

"*You* know where Velma is?"

"Velma, you says?" the barman whined. "I ain't seen her 'round heah lately. Not right lately, nossuh."

"How long you been here?"

"Le's see," the barman put his towel down and wrinkled his forehead and started to count on his fingers. "'Bout ten months, I reckon. 'Bout a yeah. Bout—"

"Make your mind up," the big man said.

The barman goggled and his Adam's apple flopped around like a headless chicken.

"How long's this coop been a dinge joint?" the big man demanded gruffly.

"Says which?"

The big man made a fist into which his whiskey sour glass melted almost out of sight.

"Five years anyway," I said. "This fellow wouldn't know anything about a white girl named Velma. Nobody here would."

The big man looked at me as if I had just hatched out. His whiskey sour hadn't seemed to improve his temper.

"Who the hell asked you to stick your face in?" he asked me.

I smiled, I made it a big warm friendly smile. "I'm the fellow that came in with you. Remember?"

He grinned back then, a flat white grin without meaning. "Whiskey sour," he told the barman. "Shake them fleas outa your pants. Service."

The barman scuttled around, rolling the whites of his eyes. I put my back against the bar and looked at the room. It was now empty, save for the barman, the big man and myself, and the bouncer crushed over against the wall. The bouncer was moving. He was moving slowly as if with great pain and effort. He was crawling softly along the baseboard like a fly with one wing. He was moving behind the tables, wearily, a man suddenly old, suddenly disillusioned. I watched him move. The barman put down two more whiskey sours. I turned to the bar. The big man glanced casually over at the crawling bouncer and then paid no further attention to him.

"There ain't nothing left of the joint," he complained. "They was a little stage and band and cute little rooms where a guy could have fun. Velma did some warbling. A redhead she was. Cute as lace pants. We was to of been married when they hung the frame on me."

I took my second whiskey sour. I was beginning to have enough of the adventure. "What frame?" I asked.

"Where you figure I been them eight years I said about?"

"Catching butterflies."

He prodded his chest with a forefinger like a banana. "In the caboose. Malloy is the name. They call me Moose Malloy, on account of I'm large. The Great Bend bank job. Forty grand. Solo job. Ain't that something?"

"You going to spend it now?"

He gave me a sharp look. There was a noise behind us. The bouncer was on his feet again, weaving a little. He had his hand on the knob of a dark door over behind the crap table. He got the door open, half fell through. The door clattered shut. A lock clicked.

"Where's that go?" Moose Malloy demanded.

The barman's eyes floated in his head, focussed with difficulty on the door through which the bouncer had stumbled.

"Tha—tha's Mistah Montgomery's office, suh. He's the boss. He's got his office back there."

"He might know," the big man said. He drank his drink at a gulp. "He better not crack wise neither. Two more of the same."

He crossed the room slowly, lightfooted, without a care in the world. His enormous back hid the door. It was locked. He shook it and a piece of the panel flew off to one side. He went through and shut the door behind him.

There was silence. I looked at the barman. The barman looked at me. His eyes became thoughtful. He polished the counter and sighed and leaned down with his right arm.

I reached across the counter and took hold of the arm. It was thin, brittle. I held it and smiled at him.

"What you got down there, bo?"

He licked his lips. He leaned on my arm, and said nothing. Grayness invaded his shining face.

"This guy is tough," I said. "And he's liable to go mean. Drinks do that to him. He's looking for a girl he used to know. This place used to be a white establishment. Get the idea?"

The barman licked his lips.

"He's been away a long time," I said. "Eight years. He doesn't seem to realize how long that is, although I'd expect him to think it a life time. He thinks the people here should know where his girl is. Get the idea?"

The barman said slowly: "I thought you was with him."

"I couldn't help myself. He asked me a question down below and then dragged me up. I never saw him before. But I didn't feel like being thrown over any houses. What you got down there?"

"Got me a sawed-off," the barman said.

"Tsk. That's illegal," I whispered. "Listen, you and I are together. Got anything else?"

"Got me a gat," the barman said. "In a cigar box. Leggo my arm."

"That's fine," I said. "Now move along a bit. Easy now. Sideways. This isn't the time to pull the artillery."

"Says you," the barman sneered, putting his tired weight against my arm. "Says—"

He stopped. His eyes rolled. His head jerked.

There was a dull flat sound at the back of the place, behind the closed door beyond the crap table. It might have been a slammed door. I didn't think it was. The barman didn't think so either.

The barman froze. His mouth drooled. I listened. No other sound. I started quickly for the end of the counter. I had listened too long.

The door at the back opened with a bang and Moose Malloy came through it with a smooth heavy lunge and stopped dead, his feet planted and a wide pale grin on his face.

A Colt Army .45 looked like a toy pistol in his hand.

"Don't nobody try to fancy pants," he said cozily. "Freeze the mitts on the bar."

The barman and I put our hands on the bar.

Moose Malloy looked the room over with a raking glance. His grin was taut, nailed on. He shifted his feet and moved silently across the room. He looked like a man who could take a bank single-handed—even in those clothes.

He came to the bar. "Rise up, nigger," he said softly. The barman put his hands high in the air. The big man stepped to my back and prowled me over carefully with his left hand. His breath was hot on my neck. It went away.

"Mister Montgomery didn't know where Velma was neither," he said. "He tried to tell me—with this." His hard hand patted the gun. I turned slowly and looked at him. "Yeah," he said. "You'll know me. You ain't forgetting me, pal. Just tell them johns not to get careless is all." He waggled the gun. "Well so long, punks. I gotta catch a street car."

He started towards the head of the stairs.

"You didn't pay for the drinks," I said.

He stopped and looked at me carefully.

"Maybe you got something there," he said, "but I wouldn't squeeze it too hard."

He moved on, slipped through the double doors, and his steps sounded remotely going down the stairs.

The barman stooped. I jumped around behind the counter and jostled him out of the way. A sawed-off shotgun lay under a towel on a shelf under the bar. Beside it was a cigar box. In the cigar box was a .38 automatic. I took both of them. The barman pressed back against the tier of glasses behind the bar.

I went back around the end of the bar and across the room to the gaping door behind the crap table. There was a hall-way behind it, L-shaped, almost lightless. The bouncer lay sprawled on its floor unconscious, with a knife in his hand. I leaned down and pulled the knife loose and threw it down a back stairway. The bouncer breathed stertorously and his hand was limp.

I stepped over him and opened a door marked "Office" in flaked black paint.

There was a small scarred desk close to a partly boarded-up window. The torso of a man was bolt upright in the chair. The chair had a high back which just reached to the nape of the man's neck. His head was folded back over the high back of the chair so that his nose pointed at the boarded-up win-dow. Just folded, like a handkerchief or a hinge.

A drawer of the desk was open at the man's right. Inside it was a newspaper with a smear of oil in the middle. The gun would have come from there. It had probably seemed like a good idea at the time, but the position of Mr. Montgomery's head proved that the idea had been wrong.

There was a telephone on the desk. I laid the sawed-off shotgun down and went over to lock the door before I called the police. I felt safer that way and Mr. Montgomery didn't seem to mind.

When the prowl car boys stamped up the stairs, the bouncer and the barman had disappeared and I had the place to myself.

3

A man named Nulty got the case, a lean-jawed sourpuss with long yellow hands which he kept folded over his kneecaps most of the time he talked to me. He was a detective-lieutenant attached to the 77th Street Division and we talked in a bare room with two small desks against opposite walls and room to move between them, if two people didn't try it at once. Dirty brown linoleum covered the floor and the smell of old cigar butts hung in the air. Nulty's shirt was frayed and his coat sleeves had been turned in at the cuffs. He looked poor enough to be honest, but he didn't look like a man who could deal with Moose Malloy.

He lit half of a cigar and threw the match on the floor, where a lot of company was waiting for it. His voice said bitterly:

"Shines. Another shine killing. That's what I rate after eighteen years in this man's police department. No pix, no space, not even four lines in the want-ad section."

I didn't say anything. He picked my card up and read it again and threw it down.

"Philip Marlowe, Private Investigator. One of those guys, huh? Jesus, you look tough enough. What was you doing all that time?"

"All what time?"

"All the time this Malloy was twisting the neck of this smoke."

"Oh, that happened in another room," I said. "Malloy hadn't promised me he was going to break anybody's neck."

"Ride me," Nulty said bitterly. "Okey, go ahead and ride me. Everybody else does. What's another one matter? Poor old Nulty. Let's go on up and throw a couple of nifties at him. Always good for a laugh, Nulty is."

"I'm not trying to ride anybody," I said. "That's the way it happened—in another room."

"Oh, sure," Nulty said through a fan of rank cigar smoke. "I was down there and saw, didn't I? Don't you pack no rod?"

"Not on that kind of a job."

"What kind of a job?"

"I was looking for a barber who had run away from his wife. She thought he could be persuaded to come home."

"You mean a dinge?"

"No, a Greek."

"Okey," Nulty said and spit into his waste basket. "Okey. You met the big guy how?"

"I told you already. I just happened to be there. He threw

a negro out of the doors of Florian's and I unwisely poked my head in to see what was happening. So he took me upstairs."

"You mean he stuck you up?"

"No, he didn't have the gun then. At least, he didn't show one. He took the gun away from Montgomery, probably. He just picked me up. I'm kind of cute sometimes."

"I wouldn't know," Nulty said. "You seem to pick up awful easy."

"All right," I said. "Why argue? I've seen the guy and you haven't. He could wear you or me for a watch charm. I didn't know he had killed anybody until after he left. I heard a shot, but I got the idea somebody had got scared and shot at Malloy and then Malloy took the gun away from whoever did it."

"And why would you get an idea like that?" Nulty asked almost suavely. "He used a gun to take that bank, didn't he?"

"Consider the kind of clothes he was wearing. He didn't go there to kill anybody; not dressed like that. He went there to look for this girl named Velma that had been his girl before he was pinched for the bank job. She worked there at Florian's or whatever place was there when it was still a white joint. He was pinched there. You'll get him all right."

"Sure," Nulty said. "With that size and them clothes. Easy."

"He might have another suit," I said. "And a car and a hideout and money and friends. But you'll get him."

Nulty spit in the wastebasket again. "I'll get him," he said, "about the time I get my third set of teeth. How many guys is put on it? One. Listen, you know why? No space. One time there was five smokes carved Harlem sunsets on each other down on East Eighty-four. One of them was cold already. There was blood on the furniture, blood on the walls, blood even on the ceiling. I go down and outside the house a guy that works on the *Chronicle*, a newshawk, is coming off the porch and getting into his car. He makes a face at us and says, 'Aw, hell, shines,' and gets in his heap and goes away. Don't even go in the house."

"Maybe he's a parole breaker," I said. "You'd get some co-operation on that. But pick him up nice or he'll knock off a brace of prowlies for you. Then you'll get space."

"And I wouldn't have the case no more neither," Nulty sneered.

The phone rang on his desk. He listened to it and smiled sorrowfully. He hung up and scribbled on a pad and there was a faint gleam in his eyes, a light far back in a dusty corridor.

"Hell, they got him. That was Records. Got his prints, mug and everything. Jesus, that's a little something anyway." He read from his pad. "Jesus, this is a man. Six five and one-half, two hundred sixty-four pounds, without his necktie. Jesus, that's a boy. Well, the hell with him. They got him on the air now. Probably at the end of the hot car list. Ain't nothing to do but just wait." He threw his cigar into a spittoon.

"Try looking for the girl," I said. "Velma. Malloy will be looking for her. That's what started it all. Try Velma."

"You try her," Nulty said. "I ain't been in a joy house in twenty years."

I stood up. "Okey," I said, and started for the door.

"Hey, wait a minute," Nulty said. "I was only kidding. You ain't awful busy, are you?"

I rolled a cigarette around in my fingers and looked at him and waited by the door.

"I mean you got time to sort of take a gander around for this dame. That's a good idea you had there. You might pick something up. You can work under glass."

"What's in it for me?"

He spread his yellow hands sadly. His smile was as cunning as a broken mousetrap. "You been in jams with us boys before. Don't tell me no. I heard different. Next time it ain't doing you any harm to have a pal."

"What good is it going to do me?"

"Listen," Nulty urged. "I'm just a quiet guy. But any guy in the department can do you a lot of good."

"Is this for love—or are you paying anything in money?"

"No money," Nulty said, and wrinkled his sad yellow nose. "But I'm needing a little credit bad. Since the last shake-up, things is really tough. I wouldn't forget it, pal. Not ever."

I looked at my watch. "Okey, if I think of anything, it's yours. And when you get the mug, I'll identify it for you. After lunch." We shook hands and I went down the mud-colored hall and stairway to the front of the building and my car.

It was two hours since Moose Malloy had left Florian's with the Army Colt in his hand. I ate lunch at a drugstore, bought a pint of bourbon, and drove eastward to Central Avenue and north on Central again. The hunch I had was as vague as the heat waves that danced above the sidewalk.

Nothing made it my business except curiosity. But strictly speaking, I hadn't had any business in a month. Even a no-charge job was a change.

4

Florian's was closed up, of course. An obvious plainclothesman sat in front of it in a car, reading a paper with one eye. I didn't know why they bothered. Nobody there knew anything about Moose Malloy. The bouncer and the barman had not been found. Nobody on the block knew anything about them, for talking purposes.

I drove past slowly and parked around the corner and sat looking at a negro hotel which was diagonally across the block from Florian's and beyond the nearest intersection. It was called the Hotel Sans Souci. I got out and walked back across the intersection and went into it. Two rows of hard empty chairs stared at each other across a strip of tan fiber carpet. A desk was back in the dimness and behind the desk a baldheaded man had his eyes shut and his soft brown hands clasped peacefully on the desk in front of him. He dozed, or appeared to. He wore an Ascot tie that looked as if it had been tied about the year 1880. The green stone in his stickpin was not quite as large as an apple. His large loose chin was folded down gently on the tie, and his folded hands were peaceful and clean, with manicured nails, and gray halfmoons in the purple of the nails.

A metal embossed sign at his elbow said: "This Hotel is Under the Protection of The International Consolidated Agencies, Ltd. Inc."

When the peaceful brown man opened one eye at me thoughtfully I pointed at the sign.

"H.P.D. man checking up. Any trouble here?"

H.P.D. means Hotel Protective Department, which is the department of a large agency that looks after check bouncers and people who move out by the back stairs leaving unpaid bills and second hand suitcases full of bricks.

"Trouble, brother," the clerk said in a high sonorous voice, "is something we is fresh out of." He lowered his voice four or five notches and added: "What was the name again?"

"Marlowe. Philip Marlowe—"

"A nice name, brother. Clean and cheerful. You're looking right well today." He lowered his voice again. "But you ain't no H.P.D. man. Ain't seen one in years." He unfolded his hands and pointed languidly at the sign. "I acquired that second-hand, brother, just for the effect."

"Okey," I said. I leaned on the counter and started to spin a half dollar on the bare, scarred wood of the counter.

"Heard what happened over at Florian's this morning?"

"Brother, I forgit." Both his eyes were open now and he was watching the blur of light made by the spinning coin.

"The boss got bumped off," I said. "Man named Montgomery. Somebody broke his neck."

"May the Lawd receive his soul, brother." Down went the voice again. "Cop?"

"Private—on a confidential lay. And I know a man who can keep things confidential when I see one."

He studied me, then closed his eyes and thought. He reopened them cautiously and stared at the spinning coin. He couldn't resist looking at it.

"Who done it?" he asked softly. "Who fixed Sam?"

"A tough guy out of the jailhouse got sore because it wasn't a white joint. It used to be, it seems. Maybe you remember?"

He said nothing. The coin fell over with a light ringing whirr and lay still.

"Call your play," I said. "I'll read you a chapter of the Bible or buy you a drink. Say which."

"Brother, I kind of like to read my Bible in the seclusion of my family." His eyes were bright, toadlike, steady.

"Maybe you've just had lunch," I said.

"Lunch," he said, "is something a man of my shape and disposition aims to do without." Down went the voice. "Come 'round this here side of the desk."

I went around and drew the flat pint of bonded bourbon out of my pocket and put it on the shelf. I went back to the front of the desk. He bent over and examined it. He looked satisfied.

"Brother, this don't buy you nothing at all," he said. "But I is pleased to take a light snifter in your company."

He opened the bottle, put two small glasses on the desk and quietly poured each full to the brim. He lifted one, sniffed it carefully, and poured it down his throat with his little finger lifted.

He tasted it, thought about it, nodded and said: "This come out of the correct bottle, brother. In what manner can I be of service to you? There ain't a crack in the sidewalk 'round here I don't know by its first name. Yessuh, this liquor has been keepin' the right company." He refilled his glass.

I told him what had happened at Florian's and why. He stared at me solemnly and shook his bald head.

"A nice quiet place Sam run too," he said. "Ain't nobody been knifed there in a month."

"When Florian's was a white joint some six or eight years ago or less, what was the name of it?"

"Electric signs come kind of high, brother."

I nodded. "I thought it might have had the same name. Malloy would probably have said something if the name had been changed. But who ran it?"

"I'm a mite surprised at you, brother. The name of that pore sinner was Florian. Mike Florian—"

"And what happened to Mike Florian?"

The negro spread his gentle brown hands. His voice was sonorous and sad. "Daid, brother. Gathered to the Lawd. Nineteen hundred and thirty-four, maybe thirty-five. I ain't precise on that. A wasted life, brother, and a case of pickled kidneys, I heard say. The ungodly man drops like a polled steer, brother, but mercy waits for him up yonder." His voice went down to the business level. "Damn if I know why."

"Who did he leave behind him? Pour another drink."

He corked the bottle firmly and pushed it across the counter. "Two is all, brother—before sundown. I thank you. Your method of approach is soothin' to a man's dignity . . . Left a widow. Name of Jessie."

"What happened to her?"

"The pursuit of knowledge, brother, is the askin' of many questions. I ain't heard. Try the phone book."

There was a booth in the dark corner of the lobby. I went over and shut the door far enough to put the light on. I looked up the name in the chained and battered book. No Florian in it at all. I went back to the desk.

"No soap," I said.

The negro bent regretfully and heaved a city directory up on top of the desk and pushed it towards me. He closed his eyes. He was getting bored. There was a Jessie Florian, Widow, in the book. She lived at 1644 West 54th Place. I wondered what I had been using for brains all my life.

I wrote the address down on a piece of paper and pushed the directory back across the desk. The negro put it back where he had found it, shook hands with me, then folded his hands on the desk exactly where they had been when I came in. His eyes drooped slowly and he appeared to fall asleep.

The incident for him was over. Halfway to the door I shot a glance back at him. His eyes were closed and he breathed softly and regularly, blowing a little with his lips at the end of each breath. His bald head shone.

I went out of the Hotel Sans Souci and crossed the street to my car. It looked too easy. It looked much too easy.

5

1644 West 54th Place was a dried-out brown house with a dried-out brown lawn in front of it. There was a large bare patch around a tough-looking palm tree. On the porch stood one lonely wooden rocker, and the afternoon breeze made the unpruned shoots of last year's poinsettias tap-tap against the cracked stucco wall. A line of stiff yellowish half-washed clothes jittered on a rusty wire in the side yard.

I drove on a quarter block, parked my car across the street and walked back.

The bell didn't work so I rapped on the wooden margin of the screen door. Slow steps shuffled and the door opened and I was looking into dimness at a blowsy woman who was blowing her nose as she opened the door. Her face was gray and puffy. She had weedy hair of that vague color which is neither brown nor blond, that hasn't enough life in it to be ginger, and isn't clean enough to be gray. Her body was thick in a shapeless outing flannel bathrobe many moons past color and design. It was just something around her body. Her toes were large and obvious in a pair of man's slippers of scuffed brown leather.

I said: "Mrs. Florian? Mrs. Jessie Florian?"

"Uh-huh," the voice dragged itself out of her throat like a sick man getting out of bed.

"You are the Mrs. Florian whose husband once ran a place of entertainment on Central Avenue? Mike Florian?"

She thumbed a wick of hair past her large ear. Her eyes glittered with surprise. Her heavy clogged voice said:

"Wha—what? My goodness sakes alive. Mike's been gone these five years. Who did you say you was?"

The screen door was still shut and hooked.

"I'm a detective," I said. "I'd like a little information."

She stared at me a long dreary minute. Then with effort she unhooked the door and turned away from it.

"Come on in then. I ain't had time to get cleaned up yet," she whined. "Cops, huh?"

I stepped through the door and hooked the screen again. A large handsome cabinet radio droned to the left of the door in the corner of the room. It was the only decent piece of furniture the place had. It looked brand new. Everything else was junk—dirty overstuffed pieces, a wooden rocker that matched the one on the porch, a square arch into a dining room with a stained table, finger marks all over the swing door to the kitchen beyond. A couple of frayed lamps with once gaudy shades that were now as gay as superannuated streetwalkers.

The woman sat down in the rocker and flopped her slippers and looked at me. I looked at the radio and sat down on the end of a davenport. She saw me looking at it. A bogus heartiness, as weak as a Chinaman's tea, moved into her face and voice. "All the comp'ny I got," she said. Then she tittered. "Mike ain't done nothing new, has he? I don't get cops calling on me much."

Her titter contained a loose alcoholic overtone. I leaned back against something hard, felt for it and brought up an empty quart gin bottle. The woman tittered again.

"A joke that was," she said. "But I hope to Christ they's enough cheap blondes where he is. He never got enough of them here."

"I was thinking more about a redhead," I said.

"I guess he could use a few of them too." Her eyes, it seemed to me, were not so vague now. "I don't call to mind. Any special redhead?"

"Yes. A girl named Velma. I don't know what last name she used except that it wouldn't be her real one. I'm trying to trace her for her folks. Your place on Central is a colored place now, although they haven't changed the name, and of course the people there never heard of her. So I thought of you."

"Her folks taken their time getting around to it—looking for her," the woman said thoughtfully.

"There's a little money involved. Not much. I guess they have to get her in order to touch it. Money sharpens the memory."

"So does liquor," the woman said. "Kind of hot today, ain't it? You said you was a copper though." Cunning eyes, steady attentive face. The feet in the man's slippers didn't move.

I held up the dead soldier and shook it. Then I threw it to one side and reached back on my hip for the pint of bond bourbon the negro hotel clerk and I had barely tapped. I held it out on my knee. The woman's eyes became fixed in an incredulous stare. Then suspicion climbed all over her face, like a kitten, but not so playfully.

"You ain't no copper," she said softly. "No copper ever bought a drink of that stuff. What's the gag, mister?"

She blew her nose again, on one of the dirtiest handker-chiefs I ever saw. Her eyes stayed on the bottle. Suspicion fought with thirst, and thirst was winning. It always does.

"This Velma was an entertainer, a singer. You wouldn't know her? I don't suppose you went there much."

Seaweed colored eyes stayed on the bottle. A coated tongue coiled on her lips.

"Man, that's liquor," she sighed. "I don't give a damn who you are. Just hold it careful, mister. This ain't no time to drop anything."

She got up and waddled out of the room and came back with two thick smeared glasses.

"No fixin's. Just what you brought is all," she said.

I poured her a slug that would have made me float over a wall. She reached for it hungrily and put it down her throat like an aspirin tablet and looked at the bottle. I poured her another and a smaller one for me. She took it over to her rocker. Her eyes had turned two shades browner already.

"Man, this stuff dies painless with me," she said and sat down. "It never knows what hit it. What was we talkin' about?"

"A redhaired girl named Velma who used to work in your place on Central Avenue."

"Yeah." She used her second drink. I went over and stood the bottle on an end beside her. She reached for it. "Yeah. Who you say you was?"

I took out a card and gave it to her. She read it with her tongue and lips, dropped it on a table beside her and set her empty glass on it.

"Oh, a private guy. You ain't said that, mister." She waggled a finger at me with gay reproach. "But your liquor says you're an all right guy at that. Here's to crime." She poured a third drink for herself and drank it down.

I sat down and rolled a cigarette around in my fingers and waited. She either knew something or she didn't. If she knew something, she either would tell me or she wouldn't. It was that simple.

"Cute little redhead," she said slowly and thickly. "Yeah, I remember her. Song and dance. Nice legs and generous with 'em. She went off somewheres. How would I know what them tramps do?"

"Well, I didn't really think you would know," I said. "But it was natural to come and ask you, Mrs. Florian. Help yourself to the whiskey—I could run out for more when we need it."

"You ain't drinkin'," she said suddenly.

I put my hand around my glass and swallowed what was in it slowly enough to make it seem more than it was.

"Where's her folks at?" she asked suddenly.

"What does that matter?"

"Okey," she sneered. "All cops is the same. Okey, handsome. A guy that buys me a drink is a pal." She reached for the bottle and set up Number 4. "I shouldn't ought to barber with you. But when I like a guy, the ceiling's the limit." She simpered. She was as cute as a washtub. "Hold onto your chair and don't step on no snakes," she said. "I got me an idea."

She got up out of the rocker, sneezed, almost lost the bathrobe, slapped it back against her stomach and stared at me coldly.

"No peekin'," she said, and went out of the room again, hitting the door frame with her shoulder.

I heard her fumbling steps going into the back part of the house.

The poinsettia shoots tap-tapped dully against the front wall. The clothes line creaked vaguely at the side of the house. The ice cream peddler went by ringing his bell. The big new handsome radio in the corner whispered of dancing and love with a deep soft throbbing note like the catch in a torch singer's voice.

Then from the back of the house there were various types of crashing sounds. A chair seemed to fall over backwards, a bureau drawer was pulled out too far and crashed to the floor, there was fumbling and thudding and muttered thick language. Then the slow click of a lock and the squeak of a trunk top going up. More fumbling and banging. A tray landed on the floor. I got up from the davenport and sneaked into the dining room and from that into a short hall. I looked around the edge of an open door.

She was in there swaying in front of the trunk, making

grabs at what was in it, and then throwing her hair back over her forehead with anger. She was drunker than she thought. She leaned down and steadied herself on the trunk and coughed and sighed. Then she went down on her thick knees and plunged both hands into the trunk and groped.

They came up holding something unsteadily. A thick package tied with faded pink tape. Slowly, clumsily, she undid the tape. She slipped an envelope out of the package and leaned down again to thrust the envelope out of sight into the right-hand side of the trunk. She retied the tape with fumbling fingers.

I sneaked back the way I had come and sat down on the davenport. Breathing stertorous noises, the woman came back into the living room and stood swaying in the doorway with the tape-tied package.

She grinned at me triumphantly, tossed the package and it fell somewhere near my feet. She waddled back to the rocker and sat down and reached for the whiskey.

I picked the package off the floor and untied the faded pink tape.

"Look 'em over," the woman grunted. "Photos. Newspaper stills. Not that them tramps ever got in no newspapers except by way of the police blotter. People from the joint they are. They're all the bastard left me—them and his old clothes."

I leafed through the bunch of shiny photographs of men and women in professional poses. The men had sharp foxy faces and racetrack clothes or eccentric clownlike makeup. Hoofers and comics from the filling station circuit. Not many of them would ever get west of Main Street. You would find them in tanktown vaudeville acts, cleaned up, or down in the cheap burlesque houses, as dirty as the law allowed and once in a while just enough dirtier for a raid and a noisy police court trial, and then back in their shows again, grinning, sadistically filthy and as rank as the smell of stale sweat. The women had good legs and displayed their inside curves more than Will Hays would have liked. But their faces were as threadbare as a bookkeeper's office coat. Blondes, brunettes, large cowlike eyes with a peasant dullness in them. Small sharp eyes with urchin greed in them. One or two of the faces obviously vicious. One or two of them might have had red hair. You couldn't tell from the photographs. I looked them over casually, without interest and tied the tape again.

"I wouldn't know any of these," I said. "Why am I looking at them?"

She leered over the bottle her right hand was grappling with unsteadily. "Ain't you looking for Velma?"

"Is she one of these?"

Thick cunning played on her face, had no fun there and went somewhere else. "Ain't you got a photo of her—from her folks?"

"No."

That troubled her. Every girl has a photo somewhere, if it's only in short dresses with a bow in her hair. I should have had it.

"I ain't beginnin' to like you again," the woman said almost quietly.

I stood up with my glass and went over and put it down beside hers on the end table.

"Pour me a drink before you kill the bottle."

She reached for the glass and I turned and walked swiftly through the square arch into the dining room, into the hall, into the cluttered bedroom with the open trunk and the spilled tray. A voice shouted behind me. I plunged ahead down into the right side of the trunk, felt an envelope and brought it up swiftly.

She was out of her chair when I got back to the living room, but she had only taken two or three steps. Her eyes had a peculiar glassiness. A murderous glassiness.

"Sit down," I snarled at her deliberately. "You're not dealing with a simple-minded lug like Moose Malloy this time."

It was a shot more or less in the dark, and it didn't hit anything. She blinked twice and tried to lift her nose with her upper lip. Some dirty teeth showed in a rabbit leer.

"Moose? The Moose? What about him?" she gulped.

"He's loose," I said. "Out of jail. He's wandering, with a forty-five gun in his hand. He killed a nigger over on Central this morning because he wouldn't tell him where Velma was. Now he's looking for the fink that turned him up eight years ago."

A white look smeared the woman's face. She pushed the

bottle against her lips and gurgled at it. Some of the whiskey ran down her chin.

"And the cops are looking for *him*," she said and laughed. "Cops. Yah!"

A lovely old woman. I liked being with her. I liked getting her drunk for my own sordid purposes. I was a swell guy. I enjoyed being me. You find almost anything under your hand in my business, but I was beginning to be a little sick at my stomach.

I opened the envelope my hand was clutching and drew out a glazed still. It was like the others but it was different, much nicer. The girl wore a Pierrot costume from the waist up. Under the white conical hat with a black pompon on the top, her fluffed out hair had a dark tinge that might have been red. The face was in profile but the visible eye seemed to have gaiety in it. I wouldn't say the face was lovely and un-spoiled, I'm not that good at faces. But it was pretty. People had been nice to that face, or nice enough for their circle. Yet it was a very ordinary face and its prettiness was strictly assem-bly line. You would see a dozen faces like it on a city block in the noon hour.

Below the waist the photo was mostly legs and very nice legs at that. It was signed across the lower right hand corner: "Always yours—Velma Valento."

I held it up in front of the Florian woman, out of her reach. She lunged but came short.

"Why hide it?" I asked.

She made no sound except thick breathing. I slipped the photo back into the envelope and the envelope into my pocket.

"Why hide it?" I asked again. "What makes it different from the others? Where is she?"

"She's dead," the woman said. "She was a good kid, but she's dead, copper. Beat it."

The tawny mangled brows worked up and down. Her hand opened and the whiskey bottle slid to the carpet and began to gurgle. I bent to pick it up. She tried to kick me in the face. I stepped away from her.

"And that still doesn't say why you hid it," I told her. "When did she die? How?"

"I am a poor sick old woman," she grunted. "Get away from me, you son of a bitch."

I stood there looking at her, not saying anything, not thinking of anything particular to say. I stepped over to her side after a moment and put the flat bottle, now almost empty, on the table at her side.

She was staring down at the carpet. The radio droned pleasantly in the corner. A car went by outside. A fly buzzed in a window. After a long time she moved one lip over the other and spoke to the floor, a meaningless jumble of words from which nothing emerged. Then she laughed and threw her head back and drooled. Then her right hand reached for the bottle and it rattled against her teeth as she drained it. When it was empty she held it up and shook it and threw it at me. It went off in the corner somewhere, skidding along the carpet and bringing up with a thud against the baseboard.

She leered at me once more, then her eyes closed and she began to snore.

It might have been an act, but I didn't care. Suddenly I had enough of the scene, too much of it, far too much of it.

I picked my hat off the davenport and went over to the door and opened it and went out past the screen. The radio still droned in the corner and the woman still snored gently in her chair. I threw a quick look back at her before I closed the door, then shut it, opened it again silently and looked again.

Her eyes were still shut but something gleamed below the lids. I went down the steps, along the cracked walk to the street.

In the next house a window curtain was drawn aside and a narrow intent face was close to the glass, peering, an old woman's face with white hair and a sharp nose.

Old Nosey checking up on the neighbors. There's always at least one like her to the block. I waved a hand at her. The curtain fell.

I went back to my car and got into it and drove back to the 77th Street Division, and climbed upstairs to Nulty's smelly little cubbyhole of an office on the second floor.

6

Nulty didn't seem to have moved. He sat in his chair in the same attitude of sour patience. But there were two more cigar stubs in his ashtray and the floor was a little thicker in burnt matches.

I sat down at the vacant desk and Nulty turned over a photo that was lying face down on his desk and handed it to me. It was a police mug, front and profile, with a fingerprint classification underneath. It was Malloy all right, taken in a strong light, and looking as if he had no more eyebrows than a French roll.

"That's the boy." I passed it back.

"We got a wire from Oregon State pen on him," Nulty said. "All time served except his copper. Things look better. We got him cornered. A prowl car was talking to a conductor the end of the Seventh Street line. The conductor mentioned a guy that size, looking like that. He got off Third and Alexandria. What he'll do is break into some big house where the folks are away. Lots of 'em there, old-fashioned places too far downtown now and hard to rent. He'll break in one and we got him bottled. What you been doing?"

"Was he wearing a fancy hat and white golf balls on his jacket?"

Nulty frowned and twisted his hands on his kneecaps. "No, a blue suit. Maybe brown."

"Sure it wasn't a sarong?"

"Huh? Oh yeah, funny. Remind me to laugh on my day off."

I said: "That wasn't the Moose. He wouldn't ride a street car. He had money. Look at the clothes he was wearing. He couldn't wear stock sizes. They must have been made to order."

"Okey, ride me," Nulty scowled. "What you been doing?"

"What you ought to have done. This place called Florian's was under the same name when it was a white night trap. I talked to a negro hotelman who knows the neighborhood. The sign was expensive so the shines just went on using it when they took over. The man's name was Mike Florian. He's dead some years, but his widow is still around. She lives at 1644 West 54th Place. Her name is Jessie Florian. She's not in the phone book, but she is in the city directory."

"Well, what do I do—date her up?" Nulty asked.

"I did it for you. I took in a pint of bourbon with me. She's a charming middle-aged lady with a face like a bucket of mud and if she has washed her hair since Coolidge's second term, I'll eat my spare tire, rim and all."

"Skip the wisecracks," Nulty said.

"I asked Mrs. Florian about Velma. You remember, Mr. Nulty, the redhead named Velma that Moose Malloy was looking for? I'm not tiring you, am I, Mr. Nulty?"

"What you sore about?"

"You wouldn't understand. Mrs. Florian said she didn't remember Velma. Her home is very shabby except for a new radio, worth seventy or eighty dollars."

"You ain't told me why that's something I should start screaming about."

"Mrs. Florian—Jessie to me—said her husband left her nothing but his old clothes and a bunch of stills of the gang who worked at his joint from time to time. I plied her with liquor and she is a girl who will take a drink if she has to knock you down to get the bottle. After the third or fourth she went into her modest bedroom and threw things around and dug the bunch of stills out of the bottom of an old trunk. But I was watching her without her knowing it and she slipped one out of the packet and hid it. So after a while I snuck in there and grabbed it."

I reached into my pocket and laid the Pierrot girl on his desk. He lifted it and stared at it and his lips quirked at the corners.

"Cute," he said. "Cute enough. I could of used a piece of that once. Haw, haw. Velma Valento, huh? What happened to this doll?"

"Mrs. Florian says she died—but that hardly explains why she hid the photo."

"It don't do at that. Why did she hide it?"

"She wouldn't tell me. In the end, after I told her about the Moose being out, she seemed to take a dislike to me. That seems impossible, doesn't it?"

"Go on," Nulty said.

"That's all. I've told you the facts and given you the exhibit. If you can't get somewhere on this set-up, nothing I could say would help."

"Where would I get? It's still a shine killing. Wait'll we get the Moose. Hell, it's eight years since he saw the girl unless she visited him in the pen."

"All right," I said. "But don't forget he's looking for her and he's a man who would bear down. By the way, he was in for a bank job. That means a reward. Who got it?"

"I don't know," Nulty said. "Maybe I could find out. Why?"

"Somebody turned him up. Maybe he knows who. That would be another job he would give time to." I stood up. "Well, goodby and good luck."

"You walking out on me?"

I went over to the door. "I have to go home and take a bath and gargle my throat and get my nails manicured."

"You ain't sick, are you?"

"Just dirty," I said. "Very, very dirty."

"Well, what's your hurry? Sit down a minute." He leaned back and hooked his thumbs in his vest, which made him look a little more like a cop, but didn't make him look any more magnetic.

"No hurry," I said. "No hurry at all. There's nothing more I can do. Apparently this Velma is dead, if Mrs. Florian is telling the truth—and I don't at the moment know of any reason why she should lie about it. That was all I was interested in."

"Yeah," Nulty said suspiciously—from force of habit.

"And you have Moose Malloy all sewed up anyway, and that's that. So I'll just run on home now and go about the business of trying to earn a living."

"We might miss out on the Moose," Nulty said. "Guys get away once in a while. Even big guys." His eyes were suspicious also, insofar as they contained any expression at all. "How much she slip you?"

"What?"

"How much this old lady slip you to lay off?"

"Lay off what?"

"Whatever it is you're layin' off from now on." He moved

his thumbs from his armholes and placed them together in front of his vest and pushed them against each other. He smiled.

"Oh, for Christ's sake," I said, and went out of the office, leaving his mouth open.

When I was about a yard from the door, I went back and opened it again quietly and looked in. He was sitting in the same position, pushing his thumbs at each other. But he wasn't smiling any more. He looked worried. His mouth was still open.

He didn't move or look up. I didn't know whether he heard me or not. I shut the door again and went away.

7

They had Rembrandt on the calendar that year, a rather smeary self-portrait due to imperfectly registered color plates. It showed him holding a smeared palette with a dirty thumb and wearing a tam-o'-shanter which wasn't any too clean either. His other hand held a brush poised in the air, as if he might be going to do a little work after a while, if somebody made a down payment. His face was aging, saggy, full of the disgust of life and the thickening effects of liquor. But it had a hard cheerfulness that I liked, and the eyes were as bright as drops of dew.

I was looking at him across my office desk at about four-thirty when the phone rang and I heard a cool, supercilious voice that sounded as if it thought it was pretty good. It said drawlingly, after I had answered:

"You are Philip Marlowe, a private detective?"

"Check."

"Oh—you mean, yes. You have been recommended to me as a man who can be trusted to keep his mouth shut. I should like you to come to my house at seven o'clock this evening. We can discuss a matter. My name is Lindsay Marriott and I live at 4212 Cabrillo Street, Montemar Vista. Do you know where that is?"

"I know where Montemar Vista is, Mr. Marriott."

"Yes. Well, Cabrillo Street is rather hard to find. The streets down here are all laid out in a pattern of interesting but intricate curves. I should suggest that you walk up the steps from the sidewalk cafe. If you do that, Cabrillo is the third street you come to and my house is the only one on the block. At seven then?"

"What is the nature of the employment, Mr. Marriott?"

"I should prefer not to discuss that over the phone."

"Can't you give me some idea? Montemar Vista is quite a distance."

"I shall be glad to pay your expenses, if we don't agree. Are you particular about the nature of the employment?"

"Not as long as it's legitimate."

The voice grew icicles. "I should not have called you, if it were not."

A Harvard boy. Nice use of the subjunctive mood. The end of my foot itched, but my bank account was still trying to crawl under a duck. I put honey into my voice and said: "Many thanks for calling me, Mr. Marriott. I'll be there."

He hung up and that was that. I thought Mr. Rembrandt had a faint sneer on his face. I got the office bottle out of the deep drawer of the desk and took a short drink. That took the sneer out of Mr. Rembrandt in a hurry.

A wedge of sunlight slipped over the edge of the desk and fell noiselessly to the carpet. Traffic lights bong-bonged outside on the boulevard, interurban cars pounded by, a typewriter clacked monotonously in the lawyer's office beyond the party wall. I had just filled and lit a pipe when the telephone rang again.

It was Nulty this time. His voice sounded full of baked potato. "Well, I guess I ain't quite bright at that," he said, when he knew who he was talking to. "I miss one. Malloy went to see that Florian dame."

I held the phone tight enough to crack it. My upper lip suddenly felt a little cold. "Go on. I thought you had him cornered."

"Was some other guy. Malloy ain't around there at all. We get a call from some old window-peeker on West Fifty-four. Two guys was to see the Florian dame. Number one parked the other side of the street and acted kind of cagey. Looked the dump over good before he went in. Was in about an hour. Six feet, dark hair, medium heavy built. Come out quiet."

"He had liquor on his breath too," I said.

"Oh, sure. That was you, wasn't it? Well, Number Two was the Moose. Guy in loud clothes as big as a house. He come in a car too but the old lady don't get the license, can't read the number that far off. This was about a hour after you was there, she says. He goes in fast and is in about five minutes only. Just before he gets back in his car he takes a big gat out and spins the chamber. I guess that's what the old lady saw he done. That's why she calls up. She don't hear no shots though, inside the house."

"That must have been a big disappointment," I said.

"Yeah. A nifty. Remind me to laugh on my day off. The old lady misses one too. The prowl boys go down there and don't get no answer on the door, so they walk in, the front door not being locked. Nobody's dead on the floor. Nobody's home. The Florian dame has skipped out. So they stop by next door and tell the old lady and she's sore as a boil on account of she didn't see the Florian dame go out. So they report back and go on about the job. So about an hour, maybe hour and a half after that, the old lady phones in again and says Mrs. Florian is home again. So they give the call to me and I ask her what makes that important and she hangs up in my face."

Nulty paused to collect a little breath and wait for my comments. I didn't have any. After a moment he went on grumbling.

"What you make of it?"

"Nothing much. The Moose would be likely to go by there, of course. He must have known Mrs. Florian pretty well. Naturally he wouldn't stick around very long. He would be afraid the law might be wise to Mrs. Florian."

"What I figure," Nulty said calmly, "Maybe I should go over and see her—kind of find out where she went to."

"That's a good idea," I said. "If you can get somebody to lift you out of your chair."

"Huh? Oh, another nifty. It don't make a lot of difference any more now though. I guess I won't bother."

"All right," I said. "Let's have it whatever it is."

He chuckled. "We got Malloy all lined up. We really got him this time. We make him at Girard, headed north in a rented hack. He gassed up there and the service station kid recognized him from the description we broadcast a while back. He said everything jibed except Malloy had changed to a dark suit. We got county and state law on it. If he goes on north we get him at the Ventura line, and if he slides over to the Ridge Route, he has to stop at Castaic for his check ticket. If he don't stop, they phone ahead and block the road. We don't want no cops shot up, if we can help it. That sound good?"

"It sounds all right," I said. "If it really is Malloy, and if he does exactly what you expect him to do."

Nulty cleared his throat carefully. "Yeah. What you doing on it—just in case?"

"Nothing. Why should I be doing anything on it?"

"You got along pretty good with that Florian dame. Maybe she would have some more ideas."

"All you need to find out is a full bottle," I said.

"You handled her real nice. Maybe you ought to kind of spend a little more time on her."

"I thought this was a police job."

"Oh sure. Was your idea about the girl though."

"That seems to be out—unless the Florian is lying about it."

"Dames lie about anything—just for practice," Nulty said grimly. "You ain't real busy, huh?"

"I've got a job to do. It came in since I saw you. A job where I get paid. I'm sorry."

"Walking out, huh?"

"I wouldn't put it that way. I just have to work to earn a living."

"Okey, pal. If that's the way you feel about it, okey."

"I don't feel any way about it," I almost yelled. "I just don't have time to stooge for you or any other cop."

"Okey, get sore," Nulty said, and hung up.

I held the dead phone and snarled into it: "Seventeen hundred and fifty cops in this town and they want me to do their leg work for them."

I dropped the phone into its cradle and took another drink from the office bottle.

After a while I went down to the lobby of the building to buy an evening paper. Nulty was right in one thing at least. The Montgomery killing hadn't even made the want-ad section so far.

I left the office again in time for an early dinner.

8

I got down to Montemar Vista as the light began to fade, but there was still a fine sparkle on the water and the surf was breaking far out in long smooth curves. A group of pelicans was flying bomber formation just under the creaming lip of the waves. A lonely yacht was taking in toward the yacht harbor at Bay City. Beyond it the huge emptiness of the Pacific was purple-gray.

Montemar Vista was a few dozen houses of various sizes and shapes hanging by their teeth and eyebrows to a spur of mountain and looking as if a good sneeze would drop them down among the box lunches on the beach.

Above the beach the highway ran under a wide concrete arch which was in fact a pedestrian bridge. From the inner end of this a flight of concrete steps with a thick galvanized handrail on one side ran straight as a ruler up the side of the mountain. Beyond the arch the sidewalk cafe my client had spoken of, was bright and cheerful inside, but the iron-legged tile-topped tables outside under the striped awning were empty save for a single dark woman in slacks who smoked and stared moodily out to sea, with a bottle of beer in front of her. A fox terrier was using one of the iron chairs for a lamppost. She chided the dog absently as I drove past and gave the sidewalk cafe my business to the extent of using its parking space.

I walked back through the arch and started up the steps. It was a nice walk if you liked grunting. There were two hundred and eighty steps up to Cabrillo Street. They were drifted over with windblown sand and the handrail was as cold and wet as a toad's belly.

When I reached the top the sparkle had gone from the water and a seagull with a broken trailing leg was twisting against the offsea breeze. I sat down on the damp cold top step and shook the sand out of my shoes and waited for my pulse to come down into the low hundreds. When I was breathing more or less normally again I shook my shirt loose from my back and went along to the lighted house which was the only one within yelling distance of the steps.

It was a nice little house with a salt-tarnished spiral of staircase going up to the front door and an imitation coachlamp for a porchlight. The garage was underneath and to one side. Its door was lifted up and rolled back and the light of the porchlamp shone obliquely on a huge black battleship of a car with chromium trimmings, a coyote tail tied to the Winged Victory on the radiator cap and engraved initials where the emblem should be. The car had a right-hand drive and looked as if it had cost more than the house.

I went up the spiral steps, looked for a bell, and used a knocker in the shape of a tiger's head. Its clatter was swallowed in the early evening fog. I heard no steps in the house. My damp shirt felt like an icepack on my back. The door opened silently, and I was looking at a tall blond man in a white flannel suit with a violet satin scarf around his neck.

There was a cornflower in the lapel of his white coat and his pale blue eyes looked faded out by comparison. The violet scarf was loose enough to show that he wore no tie and that he had a thick, soft brown neck, like the neck of a strong woman. His features were a little on the heavy side, but handsome, he had an inch more of height than I had, which made him six feet one. His blond hair was arranged, by art or nature, in three precise blond ledges which reminded me of steps, so that I didn't like them. I wouldn't have liked them anyway. Apart from all this he had the general appearance of a lad who would wear a white flannel suit with a violet scarf around his neck and a cornflower in his lapel.

He cleared his throat lightly and looked past my shoulder at the darkening sea. His cool supercilious voice said: "Yes?"

"Seven o'clock," I said. "On the dot."

"Oh yes. Let me see, your name is—" he paused and frowned in the effort of memory. The effect was as phony as the pedigree of a used car. I let him work at it for a minute, then I said:

"Philip Marlowe. The same as it was this afternoon."

He gave me a quick darting frown, as if perhaps something ought to be done about that. Then he stepped back and said coldly:

"Ah yes. Quite so. Come in, Marlowe. My house boy is away this evening."

He opened the door wide with a fingertip, as though opening the door himself dirtied him a little.

I went in past him and smelled perfume. He closed the door. The entrance put us on a low balcony with a metal railing that ran around three sides of a big studio living room. The fourth side contained a big fireplace and two doors. A fire was crackling in the fireplace. The balcony was lined with bookshelves and there were pieces of glazed metallic looking bits of sculpture on pedestals.

We went down three steps to the main part of the living room. The carpet almost tickled my ankles. There was a concert grand piano, closed down. On one corner of it stood a tall silver vase on a strip of peach-colored velvet, and a single yellow rose in the vase. There was plenty of nice soft furniture, a great many floor cushions, some with golden tassels and some just naked. It was a nice room, if you didn't get rough. There was a wide damask covered divan in a shadowy corner, like a casting couch. It was the kind of room where people sit with their feet in their laps and sip absinthe through lumps of sugar and talk with high affected voices and sometimes just squeak. It was a room where anything could happen except work.

Mr. Lindsay Marriott arranged himself in the curve of the grand piano, leaned over to sniff at the yellow rose, then opened a French enamel cigarette case and lit a long brown cigarette with a gold tip. I sat down on a pink chair and hoped I wouldn't leave a mark on it. I lit a Camel, blew smoke through my nose and looked at a piece of black shiny metal on a stand. It showed a full, smooth curve with a shallow fold in it and two protuberances on the curve. I stared at it. Marriott saw me staring at it.

"An interesting bit," he said negligently, "I picked it up just the other day. Asta Dial's *Spirit of Dawn*."

"I thought it was Klopstein's *Two Warts on a Fanny*," I said.

Mr. Lindsay Marriott's face looked as if he had swallowed a bee. He smoothed it out with an effort.

"You have a somewhat peculiar sense of humor," he said.

"Not peculiar," I said. "Just uninhibited."

"Yes," he said very coldly. "Yes—of course. I've no doubt . . . Well, what I wished to see you about is, as a matter of fact, a very slight matter indeed. Hardly worth bringing you down here for. I am meeting a couple of men tonight and paying them some money. I thought I might as well have someone with me. You carry a gun?"

"At times. Yes," I said. I looked at the dimple in his broad, fleshy chin. You could have lost a marble in it.

"I shan't want you to carry that. Nothing of that sort at all. This is a purely business transaction."

"I hardly ever shoot anybody," I said. "A matter of blackmail?"

He frowned. "Certainly not. I'm not in the habit of giving people grounds for blackmail."

"It happens to the nicest people. I might say particularly to the nicest people."

He waved his cigarette. His aquamarine eyes had a faintly thoughtful expression, but his lips smiled. The kind of smile that goes with a silk noose.

He blew some more smoke and tilted his head back. This accentuated the soft firm lines of his throat. His eyes came down slowly and studied me.

"I'm meeting these men—most probably—in a rather lonely place. I don't know where yet. I expect a call giving me the particulars. I have to be ready to leave at once. It won't be very far away from here. That's the understanding."

"You've been making this deal some time?"

"Three or four days, as a matter of fact."

"You left your bodyguard problem until pretty late."

He thought that over. He snicked some dark ash from his

cigarette. "That's true. I had some difficulty making my mind up. It would be better for me to go alone, although nothing has been said definitely about my having someone with me. On the other hand I'm not much of a hero."

"They know you by sight, of course?"

"I—I'm not sure. I shall be carrying a large amount of money and it is not my money. I'm acting for a friend. I shouldn't feel justified in letting it out of my possession, of course."

I snubbed out my cigarette and leaned back in the pink chair and twiddled my thumbs. "How much money—and what for?"

"Well, really—" it was a fairly nice smile now, but I still didn't like it. "I can't go into that."

"You just want me to go along and hold your hat?"

His hand jerked again and some ash fell off on his white cuff. He shook it off and stared down at the place where it had been.

"I'm afraid I don't like your manner," he said, using the edge of his voice.

"I've had complaints about it," I said. "But nothing seems to do any good. Let's look at this job a little. You want a bodyguard, but he can't wear a gun. You want a helper, but he isn't supposed to know what he's supposed to do. You want me to risk my neck without knowing why or what for or what the risk is. What are you offering for all this?"

"I hadn't really got around to thinking about it." His cheekbones were dusky red.

"Do you suppose you could get around to thinking about it?"

He leaned forward gracefully and smiled between his teeth. "How would you like a swift punch on the nose?"

I grinned and stood up and put my hat on. I started across the carpet towards the front door, but not very fast.

His voice snapped at my back. "I'm offering you a hundred dollars for a few hours of your time. If that isn't enough, say so. There's no risk. Some jewels were taken from a friend of mine in a holdup—and I'm buying them back. Sit down and don't be so touchy."

I went back to the pink chair and sat down again.

"All right," I said. "Let's hear about it."

We stared at each other for all of ten seconds. "Have you ever heard of Fei Tsui jade?" he asked slowly, and lit another of his dark cigarettes.

"No."

"It's the only really valuable kind. Other kinds are valuable to some extent for the material, but chiefly for the workmanship on them. Fei Tsui is valuable in itself. All known deposits were exhausted hundreds of years ago. A friend of mine owns a necklace of sixty beads of about six carats each, intricately carved. Worth eighty or ninety thousand dollars. The Chinese government has a very slightly larger one valued at a hundred and twenty-five thousand. My friend's necklace was taken in a holdup a few nights ago. I was present, but quite helpless. I had driven my friend to an evening party and later to the Trocadero and we were on our way back to her home from there. A car brushed the left front fender and stopped, as I thought, to apologize. Instead of that it was a very quick and very neat holdup. Either three or four men, I really saw only two, but I'm sure another stayed in the car behind the wheel, and I thought I saw a glimpse of still a fourth at the rear window. My friend was wearing the jade necklace. They took that and two rings and a bracelet. The one who seemed to be the leader looked the things over without any apparent hurry under a small flashlight. Then he handed one of the rings back and said that would give us an idea what kind of people we were dealing with and to wait for a phone call before reporting to the police or the insurance company. So we obeyed their instructions. There's plenty of that sort of thing going on, of course. You keep the affair to yourself and pay ransom, or you never see your jewels again. If they're fully insured, perhaps you don't mind, but if they happen to be rare pieces, you would rather pay ransom."

I nodded. "And this jade necklace is something that can't be picked up every day."

He slid a finger along the polished surface of the piano with a dreamy expression, as if touching smooth things pleased him.

"Very much so. It's irreplaceable. She shouldn't have worn it out—ever. But she's a reckless sort of woman. The other things were good but ordinary."

"Uh-huh. How much are you paying?"

"Eight thousand dollars. It's dirt cheap. But if my friend couldn't get another like it, these thugs couldn't very easily dispose of it either. It's probably known to every one in the trade, all over the country."

"This friend of yours—does she have a name?"

"I'd prefer not to mention it at the moment."

"What are the arrangements?"

He looked at me along his pale eyes. I thought he seemed a bit scared, but I didn't know him very well. Maybe it was a hangover. The hand that held the dark cigarette couldn't keep still.

"We have been negotiating by telephone for several days—through me. Everything is settled except the time and place of meeting. It is to be sometime tonight. I shall presently be getting a call to tell me of that. It will not be very far away, they say, and I must be prepared to leave at once. I suppose that is so that no plant could be arranged. With the police, I mean."

"Uh-huh. Is the money marked? I suppose it *is* money?"

"Currency, of course. Twenty dollar bills. No, why should it be marked?"

"It can be done so that it takes black light to detect it. No reason—except that the cops like to break up these gangs—if they can get any co-operation. Some of the money might turn up on some lad with a record."

He wrinkled his brow thoughtfully. "I'm afraid I don't know what black light is."

"Ultra-violet. It makes certain metallic inks glisten in the dark. I could get it done for you."

"I'm afraid there isn't time for that now," he said shortly.

"That's one of the things that worries me."

"Why?"

"Why you only called me this afternoon. Why you picked on me. Who told you about me?"

He laughed. His laugh was rather boyish, but not a very young boy. "Well, as a matter of fact I'll have to confess I merely picked your name at random out of the phone book. You see I hadn't intended to have anyone go with me. Then this afternoon I got to thinking why not."

I lit another of my squashed cigarettes and watched his throat muscles. "What's the plan?"

He spread his hands. "Simply to go where I am told, hand over the package of money, and receive back the jade necklace."

"Uh-huh."

"You seem fond of that expression."

"What expression?"

"Uh-huh."

"Where will I be—in the back of the car?"

"I suppose so. It's a big car. You could easily hide in the back of it."

"Listen," I said slowly. "You plan to go out with me hidden in your car to a destination you are to get over the phone some time tonight. You will have eight grand in currency on you and with that you are supposed to buy back a jade necklace worth ten or twelve times that much. What you will probably get will be a package you won't be allowed to open—providing you get anything at all. It's just as likely they will simply take your money, count it over in some other place, and mail you the necklace, if they feel bighearted. There's nothing to prevent them double-crossing you. Certainly nothing I could do would stop them. These are heist guys. They're tough. They might even knock you on the head—not hard—just enough to delay you while they go on their way."

"Well, as a matter of fact, I'm a little afraid of something like that," he said quietly, and his eyes twitched. "I suppose that's really why I wanted somebody with me."

"Did they put a flash on you when they pulled the stickup?"

He shook his head, no.

"No matter. They've had a dozen chances to look you over since. They probably knew all about you before that anyway. These jobs are cased. They're cased the way a dentist cases your tooth for a gold inlay. You go out with this dame much?"

"Well—not infrequently," he said stiffly.

"Married?"

"Look here," he snapped. "Suppose we leave the lady out of this entirely."

"Okey," I said. "But the more I know the fewer cups I break. I ought to walk away from this job, Marriott. I really ought. If the boys want to play ball, you don't need me. If they don't want to play ball, I can't do anything about it."

"All I want is your company," he said quickly.

I shrugged and spread my hands. "Okey—but I drive the car and carry the money—and you do the hiding in the back. We're about the same height. If there's any question, we'll just tell them the truth. Nothing to lose by it."

"No." He bit his lip.

"I'm getting a hundred dollars for doing nothing. If anybody gets conked, it ought to be me."

He frowned and shook his head, but after quite a long time his face cleared slowly and he smiled.

"Very well," he said slowly. "I don't suppose it matters much. We'll be together. Would you care for a spot of brandy?"

"Uh-huh. And you might bring me my hundred bucks. I like to feel money."

He moved away like a dancer, his body almost motionless from the waist up.

The phone rang as he was on his way out. It was in a little alcove off the living room proper, cut into the balcony. It wasn't the call we were thinking about though. He sounded too affectionate.

He danced back after a while with a bottle of Five-Star Martell and five nice crisp twenty-dollar bills. That made it a nice evening—so far.

9

The house was very still. Far off there was a sound which might have been beating surf or cars zooming along a highway, or wind in pine trees. It was the sea, of course, breaking far down below. I sat there and listened to it and thought long, careful thoughts.

The phone rang four times within the next hour and a half. The big one came at eight minutes past ten. Marriott talked briefly, in a very low voice, cradled the instrument without a sound and stood up with a sort of hushed movement. His face looked drawn. He had changed to dark clothes now. He walked silently back into the room and poured himself a stiff drink in a brandy glass. He held it against the light a moment with a queer unhappy smile, swirled it once quickly and tilted his head back to pour it down his throat.

"Well—we're all set, Marlowe. Ready?"

"That's all I've been all evening. Where do we go?"

"A place called Purissima Canyon."

"I never heard of it."

"I'll get a map." He got one and spread it out quickly and the light blinked in his brassy hair as he bent over it. Then he pointed with his finger. The place was one of the many canyons off the foothill boulevard that turns into town from the coast highway north of Bay City. I had a vague idea where it was, but no more. It seemed to be at the end of a street called Camino de la Costa.

"It will be not more than twelve minutes from here," Marriott said quickly. "We'd better get moving. We only have twenty minutes to play with."

He handed me a light colored overcoat which made me a fine target. It fitted pretty well. I wore my own hat. I had a gun under my arm, but I hadn't told him about that.

While I put the coat on, he went on talking in a light nervous voice and dancing on his hands the thick manila envelope with the eight grand in it.

"Purissima Canyon has a sort of level shelf at the inner end of it, they say. This is walled off from the road by a white fence of four-by-fours, but you can just squeeze by. A dirt road winds down into a little hollow and we are to wait there without lights. There are no houses around."

"We?"

"Well, I mean 'I'—theoretically."

"Oh."

He handed me the manila envelope and I opened it up and looked at what was inside. It was money all right, a huge wad of currency. I didn't count it. I snapped the rubber around again and stuffed the packet down inside my overcoat. It almost caved in a rib.

We went to the door and Marriott switched off all the lights. He opened the front door cautiously and peered out at the foggy air. We went out and down the salt-tarnished spiral stairway to the street level and the garage.

It was a little foggy, the way it always is down there at night. I had to start up the windshield wiper for a while.

The big foreign car drove itself, but I held the wheel for the sake of appearances.

For two minutes we figure-eighted back and forth across the face of the mountain and then popped out right beside the sidewalk cafe. I could understand now why Marriott had told me to walk up the steps. I could have driven about in those curving, twisting streets for hours without making any more yardage than an angleworm in a bait can.

On the highway the lights of the streaming cars made an almost solid beam in both directions. The big corn-poppers were rolling north growling as they went and festooned all over with green and yellow overhang lights. Three minutes of that and we turned inland, by a big service station, and wound along the flank of the foothills. It got quiet. There was loneliness and the smell of kelp and the smell of wild sage from the hills. A yellow window hung here and there, all by itself, like the last orange. Cars passed, spraying the pavement with cold white light, then growled off into the darkness again. Wisps of fog chased the stars down the sky.

Marriott leaned forward from the dark rear seat and said:

"Those lights off to the right are the Belvedere Beach Club. The next canyon is Las Pulgas and the next after that Purissima. We turn right at the top of the second rise." His voice was hushed and taut.

I grunted and kept on driving. "Keep your head down," I said over my shoulder. "We may be watched all the way. This car sticks out like spats at an Iowa picnic. Could be the boys don't like your being twins."

We went down into a hollow at the inward end of a canyon and then up on the high ground and after a little while down again and up again. Then Marriott's tight voice said in my ear: "Next street on the right. The house with the square turret. Turn beside that."

"You didn't help them pick this place out, did you?"

"Hardly," he said, and laughed grimly. "I just happen to know these canyons pretty well."

I swung the car to the right past a big corner house with a square white turret topped with round tiles. The headlights sprayed for an instant on a street sign that read: Camino de la Costa. We slid down a broad avenue lined with unfinished electroliers and weed-grown sidewalks. Some realtor's dream had turned into a hangover there. Crickets chirped and bull-frogs whooped in the darkness behind the overgrown side-walks. Marriott's car was that silent.

There was a house to a block, then a house to two blocks, then no houses at all. A vague window or two was still lighted, but the people around there seemed to go to bed with the chickens. Then the paved avenue ended abruptly in a dirt road packed as hard as concrete in dry weather. The dirt road narrowed and dropped slowly downhill between walls of brush. The lights of the Belvedere Beach Club hung in the air to the right and far ahead there was a gleam of moving water. The acrid smell of the sage filled the night. Then a white painted barrier loomed across the dirt road and Marriott spoke at my shoulder again.

"I don't think you can get past it," he said. "The space doesn't look wide enough."

I cut the noiseless motor, dimmed the lights and sat there, listening. Nothing. I switched the lights off altogether and got out of the car. The crickets stopped chirping. For a little while the silence was so complete that I could hear the sound of tires on the highway at the bottom of the cliffs, a mile away. Then one by one the crickets started up again until the night was full of them.

"Sit tight. I'm going down there and have a look see," I whispered into the back of the car.

I touched the gun butt inside my coat and walked forward. There was more room between the brush and the end of the

white barrier than there had seemed to be from the car.
Someone had hacked the brush away and there were car
marks in the dirt. Probably kids going down there to neck on
warm nights. I went on past the barrier. The road dropped
and curved. Below was darkness and a vague far off sea-
sound. And the lights of cars on the highway. I went on. The
road ended in a shallow bowl entirely surrounded by brush. It
was empty. There seemed to be no way into it but the way I
had come. I stood there in the silence and listened.

Minute passed slowly after minute, but I kept on waiting
for some new sound. None came. I seemed to have that hollow entirely to myself.

I looked across to the lighted beach club. From its upper
windows a man with a good night glass could probably cover
this spot fairly well. He could see a car come and go, see who
got out of it, whether there was a group of men or just one.
Sitting in a dark room with a good night glass you can see a
lot more detail than you would think possible.

I turned to go back up the hill. From the base of a bush a
cricket chirped loud enough to make me jump. I went on up
around the curve and past the white barricade. Still nothing.
The black car stood dimly shining against a grayness which
was neither darkness nor light. I went over to it and put a
foot on the running board beside the driver's seat.

"Looks like a tryout," I said under my breath, but loud
enough for Marriott to hear me from the back of the car.
"Just to see if you obey orders."

There was a vague movement behind but he didn't answer.
I went on trying to see something besides bushes.

Whoever it was had a nice easy shot at the back of my head.
Afterwards I thought I might have heard the swish of a sap.
Maybe you always think that—afterwards.

10

"Four minutes," the voice said. "Five, possibly six. They
must have moved quick and quiet. He didn't even let out a
yell."

I opened my eyes and looked fuzzily at a cold star. I was lying on my back. I felt sick.

The voice said: "It could have been a little longer. Maybe even eight minutes altogether. They must have been in the brush, right where the car stopped. The guy scared easily. They must have thrown a small light in his face and he passed out—just from panic. The pansy."

There was silence. I got up on one knee. Pains shot from the back of my head clear to my ankles.

"Then one of them got into the car," the voice said, "and waited for you to come back. The others hid again. They must have figured he would be afraid to come alone. Or something in his voice made them suspicious, when they talked to him on the phone."

I balanced myself woozily on the flat of my hands, listening.

"Yeah, that was about how it was," the voice said.

It was my voice. I was talking to myself, coming out of it. I was trying to figure the thing out subconsciously.

"Shut up, you dimwit," I said, and stopped talking to myself.

Far off the purl of motors, nearer the chirp of crickets, the peculiar long drawn ee-ee-ee of tree frogs. I didn't think I was going to like those sounds any more.

I lifted a hand off the ground and tried to shake the sticky sage ooze off it, then rubbed it on the side of my coat. Nice work, for a hundred dollars. The hand jumped at the inside pocket of the overcoat. No manila envelope, naturally. The hand jumped inside my own suit coat. My wallet was still there. I wondered if my hundred was still in it. Probably not. Something felt heavy against my left ribs. The gun in the shoulder holster.

That was a nice touch. They left me my gun. A nice touch of something or other—like closing a man's eyes after you knife him.

I felt the back of my head. My hat was still on. I took it off, not without discomfort and felt the head underneath. Good old head, I'd had it a long time. It was a little soft now, a little pulpy, and more than a little tender. But a pretty light sapping at that. The hat had helped. I could still use the head. I could use it another year anyway.

I put my right hand back on the ground and took the left off and swivelled it around until I could see my watch. The illuminated dial showed 10.56, as nearly as I could focus on it. The call had come at 10.08. Marriott had talked maybe two minutes. Another four had got us out of the house. Time passes very slowly when you are actually doing something. I mean, you can go through a lot of movements in very few minutes. Is that what I mean? What the hell do I care what I mean? Okey, better men than me have meant less. Okey, what I mean is, that would be 10.15, say. The place was about twelve minutes away. 10.27. I get out, walk down in the hollow, spend at the most eight minutes fooling around and come on back up to get my head treated. 10.35. Give me a minute to fall down and hit the ground with my face. The reason I hit it with my face, I got my chin scraped. It hurts. It feels scraped. That way I know it's scraped. No, I can't see it. I don't have to see it. It's my chin and I know whether it's scraped or not. Maybe you want to make something of it. Okey, shut up and let me think. What with? . . .

The watch showed 10.56 p.m. That meant I had been out for twenty minutes.

Twenty minutes' sleep. Just a nice doze. In that time I had muffed a job and lost eight thousand dollars. Well, why not? In twenty minutes you can sink a battleship, down three or four planes, hold a double execution. You can die, get married, get fired and find a new job, have a tooth pulled, have your tonsils out. In twenty minutes you can even get up in the morning. You can get a glass of water at a night club— maybe.

Twenty minutes' sleep. That's a long time. Especially on a cold night, out in the open. I began to shiver.

I was still on my knees. The smell of the sage was beginning to bother me. The sticky ooze from which wild bees get their honey. Honey was sweet, much too sweet. My stomach took a whirl. I clamped my teeth tight and just managed to keep it down my throat. Cold sweat stood out in lumps on my forehead, but I shivered just the same. I got up on one foot, then on both feet, straightened up, wobbling a little. I felt like an amputated leg.

I turned slowly. The car was gone. The dirt road stretched empty, back up the shallow hill towards the paved street, the end of Camino de la Costa. To the left the barrier of white-painted four-by-fours stood out against the darkness. Beyond the low wall of brush the pale glow in the sky would be the lights of Bay City. And over farther to the right and near by were the lights of the Belvedere Club.

I went over where the car had stood and got a fountain pen flash unclipped from my pocket and poked the little light down at the ground. The soil was red loam, very hard in dry weather, but the weather was not bone dry. There was a little fog in the air, and enough of the moisture had settled on the surface of the ground to show where the car had stood. I could see, very faint, the tread marks of the heavy ten-ply Vogue tires. I put the light on them and bent over and the pain made my head dizzy. I started to follow the tracks. They went straight ahead for a dozen feet, then swung over to the left. They didn't turn. They went towards the gap at the left hand end of the white barricade. Then I lost them.

I went over to the barricade and shone the little light on the brush. Fresh-broken twigs. I went through the gap, on down the curving road. The ground was still softer here. More marks of the heavy tires. I went on down, rounded the curve and was at the edge of the hollow closed in by brush.

It was there all right, the chromium and glossy paint shining a little even in the dark, and the red reflector glass of the tail-lights shining back at the pencil flash. It was there, si-lent, lightless, all the doors shut. I went towards it slowly, gritting my teeth at every step. I opened one of the rear doors and put the beam of the flash inside. Empty. The front was empty too. The ignition was off. The key hung in the lock on a thin chain. No torn upholstery, no scarred glass, no blood, no bodies. Everything neat and orderly. I shut the doors and circled the car slowly, looking for a sign and not finding any.

A sound froze me.

A motor throbbed above the rim of the brush. I didn't jump more than a foot. The flash in my hand went out. A gun slid into my hand all by itself. Then headlight beams tilted up towards the sky, then tilted down again. The motor sounded like a small car. It had that contented sound that comes with moisture in the air.

The lights tilted down still more and got brighter. A car was coming down the curve of the dirt road. It came two-thirds of the way and then stopped. A spotlight clicked on and swung out to the side, held there for a long moment, went out again. The car came on down the hill. I slipped the gun out of my pocket and crouched behind the motor of Marriott's car.

A small coupe of no particular shape or color slid into the hollow and turned so that its headlights raked the sedan from one end to the other. I got my head down in a hurry. The lights swept above me like a sword. The coupe stopped. The motor died. The headlights died. Silence. Then a door opened and a light foot touched the ground. More silence. Even the crickets were silent. Then a beam of light cut the darkness low down, parallel to the ground and only a few inches above it. The beam swept, and there was no way I could get my ankles out of it quickly enough. The beam stopped on my feet. Silence. The beam came up and raked the top of the hood again.

Then a laugh. It was a girl's laugh. Strained, taut as a man-dolin wire. A strange sound in that place. The white beam shot under the car again and settled on my feet.

The voice said, not quite shrilly: "All right, you. Come out of there with your hands up and very damned empty. You're covered."

I didn't move.

The light wavered a little, as though the hand that held it wavered. It swept slowly along the hood once more. The voice stabbed at me again.

"Listen, stranger. I'm holding a ten shot automatic. I can shoot straight. Both your feet are vulnerable. What do you bid?"

"Put it up—or I'll blow it out of your hand!" I snarled. My voice sounded like somebody tearing slats off a chicken coop.

"Oh—a hardboiled gentleman." There was a quaver in the voice, a nice little quaver. Then it hardened again. "Coming

out? I'll count three. Look at the odds I'm giving you—
twelve fat cylinders, maybe sixteen. But your feet will hurt.
And ankle bones take years and years to get well and sometimes they never do really—"

I straightened up slowly and looked into the beam of the
flashlight.

"I talk too much when I'm scared too," I said.

"Don't—don't move another inch! Who are you?"

I moved around the front of the car towards her. When I
was six feet from the slim dark figure behind the flash I
stopped. The flash glared at me steadily.

"You stay right there," the girl snapped angrily, after I had
stopped. "Who are you?"

"Let's see your gun."

She held it forward into the light. It was pointed at my
stomach. It was a little gun, it looked like a small Colt vest
pocket automatic.

"Oh, that," I said. "That toy. It doesn't either hold ten
shots. It holds six. It's just a little bitty gun, a butterfly gun.
They shoot butterflies with them. Shame on you for telling a
deliberate lie like that."

"Are you crazy?"

"Me? I've been sapped by a holdup man. I might be a little
goofy."

"Is that—is that your car?"

"No."

"Who are you?"

"What were you looking at back there with your spotlight?"

"I get it. You ask the answers. He-man stuff. I was looking
at a man."

"Does he have blond hair in waves?"

"Not now," she said quietly. "He might have had—once."

That jarred me. Somehow I hadn't expected it. "I didn't
see him," I said lamely. "I was following the tire marks with a
flashlight down the hill. Is he badly hurt?" I went another
step towards her. The little gun jumped at me and the flash
held steady.

"Take it easy," she said quietly. "Very easy. Your friend is
dead."

I didn't say anything for a moment. Then I said: "All right, let's go look at him."

"Let's stand right here and not move and you tell me who you are and what happened." The voice was crisp. It was not afraid. It meant what it said.

"Marlowe. Philip Marlowe. An investigator. Private."

"That's who you are—if it's true. Prove it."

"I'm going to take my wallet out."

"I don't think so. Just leave your hands where they happen to be. We'll skip the proof for the time being. What's your story?"

"This man may not be dead."

"He's dead all right. With his brains on his face. The story, mister. Make it fast."

"As I said—he may not be dead. We'll go look at him." I moved one foot forward.

"Move and I'll drill you!" she snapped.

I moved the other foot forward. The flash jumped about a little. I think she took a step back.

"You take some awful chances, mister," she said quietly. "All right, go on ahead and I'll follow. You look like a sick man. If it hadn't been for that—"

"You'd have shot me. I've been sapped. It always makes me a little dark under the eyes."

"A nice sense of humor—like a morgue attendant," she almost wailed.

I turned away from the light and immediately it shone on the ground in front of me. I walked past the little coupe, an ordinary little car, clean and shiny under the misty starlight. I went on, up the dirt road, around the curve. The steps were close behind me and the flashlight guided me. There was no sound anywhere now except our steps and the girl's breathing. I didn't hear mine.

II

Halfway up the slope I looked off to the right and saw his foot. She swung the light. Then I saw all of him. I ought to have seen him as I came down, but I had been bent over, peering at the ground with the fountain pen flash, trying to read tire marks by a light the size of a quarter.

"Give me the flash," I said and reached back.

She put it into my hand, without a word. I went down on a knee. The ground felt cold and damp through the cloth.

He lay smeared to the ground, on his back, at the base of a bush, in that bag-of-clothes position that always means the same thing. His face was a face I had never seen before. His hair was dark with blood, the beautiful blond ledges were tangled with blood, and some thick grayish ooze, like primeval slime.

The girl behind me breathed hard, but she didn't speak. I held the light on his face. He had been beaten to a pulp. One of his hands was flung out in a frozen gesture, the fingers curled. His overcoat was half twisted under him, as though he had rolled as he fell. His legs were crossed. There was a trickle as black as dirty oil at the corner of his mouth.

"Hold the flash on him," I said, passing it back to her. "If it doesn't make you sick."

She took it and held it without a word, as steady as an old homicide veteran. I got my fountain pen flash out again and started to go through his pockets, trying not to move him.

"You shouldn't do that," she said tensely. "You shouldn't touch him until the police come."

"That's right," I said. "And the prowl car boys are not supposed to touch him until the K-car men come and they're not supposed to touch him until the coroner's examiner sees him and the photographers have photographed him and the fingerprint man has taken his prints. And do you know how long all that is liable to take out here? A couple of hours."

"All right," she said. "I suppose you're always right. I guess you must be that kind of person. Somebody must have hated him to smash his head in like that."

"I don't suppose it was personal," I growled. "Some people just like to smash heads."

"Seeing that I don't know what it's all about, I couldn't guess," she said tartly.

I went through his clothes. He had loose silver and bills in one trouser pocket, a tooled leather keycase in the other, also a small knife. His left hip pocket yielded a small billfold with more currency, insurance cards, a driver's license, a couple of receipts. In his coat loose match folders, a gold pencil clipped to a pocket, two thin cambric handkerchiefs as fine and white as dry powdered snow. Then the enamel cigarette case from which I had seen him take his brown gold-tipped cigarettes. They were South American, from Montevideo. And in the other inside pocket a second cigarette case I hadn't seen before. It was made of embroidered silk, a dragon on each side, a frame of imitation tortoise-shell so thin it was hardly there at all. I tickled the catch open and looked in at three over-sized Russian cigarettes under the band of elastic. I pinched one. They felt old and dry and loose. They had hollow mouthpieces.

"He smoked the others," I said over my shoulder. "These must have been for a lady friend. He would be a lad who would have a lot of lady friends."

The girl was bent over, breathing on my neck now. "Didn't you know him?"

"I only met him tonight. He hired me for a bodyguard."

"Some bodyguard."

I didn't say anything to that.

"I'm sorry," she almost whispered. "Of course I don't know the circumstances. Do you suppose those could be jujus? Can I look?"

I passed the embroidered case back to her.

"I knew a guy once who smoked jujus," she said. "Three highballs and three sticks of tea and it took a pipe wrench to get him off the chandelier."

"Hold the light steady."

There was a rustling pause. Then she spoke again.

"I'm sorry." She handed the case down again and I slipped it back in his pocket. That seemed to be all. All it proved was that he hadn't been cleaned out.

I stood up and took my wallet out. The five twenties were still in it.

"High class boys," I said. "They only took the large money."

The flash was drooping to the ground. I put my wallet away again, clipped my own small flash to my pocket and reached suddenly for the little gun she was still holding in the same hand with the flashlight. She dropped the flashlight, but I got the gun. She stepped back quickly and I reached down for the light. I put it on her face for a moment, then snapped it off.

"You didn't have to be rough," she said, putting her hands down into the pockets of a long rough coat with flaring shoulders. "I didn't think you killed him."

I liked the cool quiet of her voice. I liked her nerve. We stood in the darkness, face to face, not saying anything for a moment. I could see the brush and light in the sky.

I put the light on her face and she blinked. It was a small neat vibrant face with large eyes. A face with bone under the skin, fine drawn like a Cremona violin. A very nice face.

"Your hair's red," I said. "You look Irish."

"And my name's Riordan. So what? Put that light out. It's not red, it's auburn."

I put it out. "What's your first name?"

"Anne. And don't call me Annie."

"What are you doing around here?"

"Sometimes at night I go riding. Just restless. I live alone. I'm an orphan. I know all this neighborhood like a book. I just happened to be riding along and noticed a light flickering down in the hollow. It seemed a little cold for young love. And they don't use lights, do they?"

"I never did. You take some awful chances, Miss Riordan."

"I think I said the same about you. I had a gun. I wasn't afraid. There's no law against going down there."

"Uh-huh. Only the law of self preservation. Here. It's not my night to be clever. I suppose you have a permit for the gun." I held it out to her, butt first.

She took it and tucked it down into her pocket. "Strange how curious people can be, isn't it? I write a little. Feature articles."

"Any money in it?"

"Very damned little. What were you looking for—in his pockets?"

"Nothing in particular. I'm a great guy to snoop around.

We had eight thousand dollars to buy back some stolen jewelry for a lady. We got hijacked. Why they killed him I don't know. He didn't strike me as a fellow who would put up much of a fight. And I didn't hear a fight. I was down in the hollow when he was jumped. He was in the car, up above. We were supposed to drive down into the hollow but there didn't seem to be room for the car without scratching it up. So I went down there on foot and while I was down there they must have stuck him up. Then one of them got into the car and dry-gulched me. I thought he was still in the car, of course."

"That doesn't make you so terribly dumb," she said.

"There was something wrong with the job from the start. I could feel it. But I needed the money. Now I have to go to the cops and eat dirt. Will you drive me to Montemar Vista? I left my car there. He lived there."

"Sure. But shouldn't somebody stay with him? You could take my car—or I could go call the cops."

I looked at the dial of my watch. The faintly glowing hands said that it was getting towards midnight.

"No."

"Why not?"

"I don't know why not. I just feel it that way. I'll play it alone."

She said nothing. We went back down the hill and got into her little car and she started it and jockeyed it around without lights and drove it back up the hill and eased it past the barrier. A block away she sprang the lights on.

My head ached. We didn't speak until we came level with the first house on the paved part of the street. Then she said:

"You need a drink. Why not go back to my house and have one? You can phone the law from there. They have to come from West Los Angeles anyway. There's nothing up here but a fire station."

"Just keep on going down to the coast. I'll play it solo."

"But why? I'm not afraid of them. My story might help you."

"I don't want any help. I've got to think. I want to be by myself for a while."

"I—okey," she said.

She made a vague sound in her throat and turned on to the boulevard. We came to the service station at the coast highway and turned north to Montemar Vista and the sidewalk cafe there. It was lit up like a luxury liner. The girl pulled over on to the shoulder and I got out and stood holding the door.

I fumbled a card out of my wallet and passed it in to her. "Some day you may need a strong back," I said. "Let me know. But don't call me if it's brain work."

She tapped the card on the wheel and said slowly: "You'll find me in the Bay City phone book. 819 Twenty-fifth Street. Come around and pin a putty medal on me for minding my own business. I think you're still woozy from that crack on the head."

She swung her car swiftly around on the highway and I watched its twin tail-lights fade into the dark.

I walked past the arch and the sidewalk cafe into the parking space and got into my car. A bar was right in front of me and I was shaking again. But it seemed smarter to walk into the West Los Angeles police station the way I did twenty minutes later, as cold as a frog and as green as the back of a new dollar bill.

12

It was an hour and a half later. The body had been taken away, the ground gone over, and I had told my story three or four times. We sat, four of us, in the day captain's room at the West Los Angeles station. The building was quiet except for a drunk in a cell who kept giving the Australian bush call while he waited to go downtown for sunrise court.

A hard white light inside a glass reflector shone down on the flat topped table on which were spread the things that had come from Lindsay Marriott's pockets, things now that seemed as dead and homeless as their owner. The man across the table from me was named Randall and he was from Central Homicide in Los Angeles. He was a thin quiet man of fifty with smooth creamy gray hair, cold eyes, a distant manner. He wore a dark red tie with black spots on it and the spots kept dancing in front of my eyes. Behind him, beyond the cone of light two beefy men lounged like bodyguards, each of them watching one of my ears.

I fumbled a cigarette around in my fingers and lit it and didn't like the taste of it. I sat watching it burn between my fingers. I felt about eighty years old and slipping fast.

Randall said coldly: "The oftener you tell this story the sillier it sounds. This man Marriott had been negotiating for days, no doubt, about this pay-off and then just a few hours before the final meeting he calls up a perfect stranger and hires him to go with him as a bodyguard."

"Not exactly as a bodyguard," I said. "I didn't even tell him I had a gun. Just for company."

"Where did he hear of you?"

"First he said a mutual friend. Then that he just picked my name out of the book."

Randall poked gently among the stuff on the table and detached a white card with an air of touching something not quite clean. He pushed it along the wood.

"He had your card. Your business card."

I glanced at the card. It had come out of his billfold, together with a number of other cards I hadn't bothered to examine back there in the hollow of Purissima Canyon. It was one of my cards all right. It looked rather dirty at that, for a man like Marriott. There was a round smear across one corner.

"Sure," I said. "I hand those out whenever I get a chance. Naturally."

"Marriott let you carry the money," Randall said. "Eight thousand dollars. He was rather a trusting soul."

I drew on my cigarette and blew the smoke towards the ceiling. The light hurt my eyes. The back of my head ached.

"I don't have the eight thousand dollars," I said. "Sorry."

"No. You wouldn't be here, if you had the money. Or would you?" There was a cold sneer on his face now, but it looked artificial.

"I'd do a lot for eight thousand dollars," I said. "But if I wanted to kill a man with a sap, I'd only hit him twice at the most—on the back of the head."

He nodded slightly. One of the dicks behind him spit into the wastebasket.

"That's one of the puzzling features. It looks like an amateur job, but of course it might be meant to look like an amateur job. The money was not Marriott's, was it?"

"I don't know. I got the impression not, but that was just an impression. He wouldn't tell me who the lady in the case was."

"We don't know anything about Marriott—yet," Randall said slowly. "I suppose it's at least possible he meant to steal the eight thousand himself."

"Huh?" I felt surprised. I probably looked surprised. Nothing changed in Randall's smooth face.

"Did you count the money?"

"Of course not. He just gave me a package. There was money in it and it looked like a lot. He said it was eight grand. Why would he want to steal it from me when he already had it before I came on the scene?"

Randall looked at a corner of the ceiling and drew his mouth down at the corners. He shrugged.

"Go back a bit," he said. "Somebody had stuck up Marriott and a lady and taken this jade necklace and stuff and had later offered to sell it back for what seems like a pretty small amount, in view of its supposed value. Marriott was to handle the payoff. He thought of handling it alone and we don't know whether the other parties made a point of that or whether it was mentioned. Usually in cases like that they are rather fussy. But Marriott evidently decided it was all right to have you along. Both of you figured you were dealing with an organized gang and that they would play ball within the limits of their trade. Marriott was scared. That would be natural enough. He wanted company. You were the company. But you are a complete stranger to him, just a name on a card handed to him by some unknown party, said by him to be a mutual friend. Then at the last minute Marriott decides to have you carry the money and do the talking while he hides in the car. You say that was your idea, but he may have been hoping you would suggest it, and if you didn't suggest it, he would have had the idea himself."

"He didn't like the idea at first," I said.

Randall shrugged again. "He pretended not to like the idea—but he gave in. So finally he gets a call and off you go to the place he describes. All this is coming from Marriott. None of it is known to you independently. When you get there, there seems to be nobody about. You are supposed to drive down into that hollow, but it doesn't look to be room enough for the big car. It wasn't, as a matter of fact, because the car was pretty badly scratched on the left side. So you get out and walk down into the hollow, see and hear nothing, wait a few minutes, come back to the car and then somebody in the car socks you on the back of the head. Now suppose Marriott wanted that money and wanted to make you the fall guy—wouldn't he have acted just the way he did?"

"It's a swell theory," I said. "Marriott socked me, took the money, then he got sorry and beat his brains out, after first burying the money under a bush."

Randall looked at me woodenly. "He had an accomplice of course. Both of you were supposed to be knocked out, and the accomplice would beat it with the money. Only the accomplice double-crossed Marriott by killing him. He didn't have to kill you because you didn't know him."

I looked at him with admiration and ground out my cigarette stub in a wooden tray that had once had a glass lining in it but hadn't any more.

"It fits the facts—so far as we know them," Randall said calmly. "It's no sillier than any other theory we could think up at the moment."

"It doesn't fit one fact—that I was socked from the car, does it? That would make me suspect Marriott of having socked me—other things being equal. Although I didn't suspect him after he was killed."

"The way you were socked fits best of all," Randall said. "You didn't tell Marriott you had a gun, but he may have seen the bulge under your arm or at least suspected you had a gun. In that case he would want to hit you when you suspected nothing. And you wouldn't suspect anything from the back of the car."

"Okey," I said. "You win. It's a good theory, always supposing the money was not Marriott's and that he wanted to steal it and that he had an accomplice. So his plan is that we both wake up with bumps on our heads and the money is gone and we say so sorry and I go home and forget all about it. Is that how it ends? I mean is that how he expected it to end? It had to look good to him too, didn't it?"

Randall smiled wryly. "I don't like it myself. I was just trying it out. It fits the facts—as far as I know them, which is not far."

"We don't know enough to even start theorizing," I said. "Why not assume he was telling the truth and that he perhaps recognized one of the stick-up men?"

"You say you heard no struggle, no cry?"

"No. But he could have been grabbed quickly, by the throat. Or he could have been too scared to cry out when they jumped him. Say they were watching from the bushes and saw me go down the hill. I went some distance, you know. A good hundred feet. They go over to look into the car and see Marriott. Somebody sticks a gun in his face and makes him get out—quietly. Then he's sapped down. But something he says, or some way he looks, makes them think he has recognized somebody."

"In the dark?"

"Yes," I said. "It must have been something like that. Some voices stay in your mind. Even in the dark people are recognized."

Randall shook his head. "If this was an organized gang of jewel thieves, they wouldn't kill without a lot of provocation." He stopped suddenly and his eyes got a glazed look. He closed his mouth very slowly, very tight. He had an idea. "Hijack," he said.

I nodded. "I think that's an idea."

"There's another thing," he said. "How did you get here?"

"I drove my car."

"Where was your car?"

"Down at Montemar Vista, in the parking lot by the side-walk cafe."

He looked at me very thoughtfully. The two dicks behind him looked at me suspiciously. The drunk in the cells tried to yodel, but his voice cracked and that discouraged him. He began to cry.

"I walked back to the highway," I said. "I flagged a car. A girl was driving it alone. She stopped and took me down."

"Some girl," Randall said. "It was late at night, on a lonely road, and she stopped."

"Yeah. Some of them will do that. I didn't get to know her, but she seemed nice." I stared at them, knowing they didn't believe me and wondering why I was lying about it.

"It was a small car," I said. "A Chevvy coupe. I didn't get the license number."

"Haw, he didn't get the license number," one of the dicks said and spat into the wastebasket again.

Randall leaned forward and stared at me carefully. "If you're holding anything back with the idea of working on this case yourself to make yourself a little publicity, I'd forget it, Marlowe. I don't like all the points in your story and I'm going to give you the night to think it over. Tomorrow I'll probably ask you for a sworn statement. In the meantime let me give you a tip. This is a murder and a police job and we wouldn't want your help, even if it was good. All we want from you is facts. Get me?"

"Sure. Can I go home now? I don't feel any too well."

"You can go home now." His eyes were icy.

I got up and started towards the door in a dead silence. When I had gone four steps Randall cleared his throat and said carelessly:

"Oh, one small point. Did you notice what kind of cigarettes Marriott smoked?"

I turned. "Yes. Brown ones. South American, in a French enamel case."

He leaned forward and pushed the embroidered silk case out of the pile of junk on the table and then pulled it towards him.

"Ever see this one before?"

"Sure. I was just looking at it."

"I mean, earlier this evening."

"I believe I did," I said. "Lying around somewhere. Why?"

"You didn't search the body?"

"Okey," I said. "Yes, I looked through his pockets. That was in one of them. I'm sorry. Just professional curiosity. I didn't disturb anything. After all he was my client."

Randall took hold of the embroidered case with both hands and opened it. He sat looking into it. It was empty. The three cigarettes were gone.

I bit hard on my teeth and kept the tired look on my face. It was not easy.

"Did you see him smoke a cigarette out of this?"

"No."

Randall nodded coolly. "It's empty as you see. But it was in his pocket just the same. There's a little dust in it. I'm going to have it examined under a microscope. I'm not sure, but I have an idea it's marihuana."

I said: "If he had any of those, I should think he would have smoked a couple tonight. He needed something to cheer him up."

Randall closed the case carefully and pushed it away.

"That's all," he said. "And keep your nose clean."

I went out.

The fog had cleared off outside and the stars were as bright as artificial stars of chromium on a sky of black velvet. I drove fast. I needed a drink badly and the bars were closed.

13

I got up at nine, drank three cups of black coffee, bathed the back of my head with ice-water and read the two morning papers that had been thrown against the apartment door. There was a paragraph and a bit about Moose Malloy, in Part II, but Nulty didn't get his name mentioned. There was nothing about Lindsay Marriott, unless it was on the society page.

I dressed and ate two soft boiled eggs and drank a fourth cup of coffee and looked myself over in the mirror. I still looked a little shadowy under the eyes. I had the door open to leave when the phone rang.

It was Nulty. He sounded mean.

"Marlowe?"

"Yeah. Did you get him?"

"Oh sure. We got him." He stopped to snarl. "On the Ventura line, like I said. Boy, did we have fun! Six foot six, built like a coffer dam, on his way to Frisco to see the Fair. He had five quarts of hooch in the front seat of the rent car, and he was drinking out of another one as he rode along, doing a quiet seventy. All we had to go up against him with was two county cops with guns and blackjacks."

He paused and I turned over a few witty sayings in my mind, but none of them seemed amusing at the moment. Nulty went on:

"So he done exercises with the cops and when they was tired enough to go to sleep, he pulled one side off their car, threw the radio into the ditch, opened a fresh bottle of hooch, and went to sleep hisself. After a while the boys snapped out of it and bounced blackjacks off his head for about ten minutes before he noticed it. When he began to get sore they got handcuffs on him. It was easy. We got him in the icebox now, drunk driving, drunk in auto, assaulting police officer in performance of duty, two counts, malicious damage to official property, attempted escape from custody, assault less than mayhem, disturbing the peace, and parking on a state highway. Fun, ain't it?"

"What's the gag?" I asked. "You didn't tell me all that just to gloat."

"It was the wrong guy," Nulty said savagely. "This bird is named Stoyanoffsky and he lives in Hemet and he just got through working as a sandhog on the San Jack tunnel. Got a wife and four kids. Boy, is she sore. What you doing on Malloy?"

"Nothing. I have a headache."

"Any time you get a little free time —"

"I don't think so," I said. "Thanks just the same. When is the inquest on the nigger coming up?"

"Why bother?" Nulty sneered, and hung up.

I drove down to Hollywood Boulevard and put my car in the parking space beside the building and rode up to my floor. I opened the door of the little reception room which I always left unlocked, in case I had a client and the client wanted to wait.

Miss Anne Riordan looked up from a magazine and smiled at me.

She was wearing a tobacco brown suit with a high-necked

white sweater inside it. Her hair by daylight was pure auburn and on it she wore a hat with a crown the size of a whiskey glass and a brim you could have wrapped the week's laundry in. She wore it at an angle of approximately forty-five degrees, so that the edge of the brim just missed her shoulder. In spite of that it looked smart. Perhaps because of that.

She was about twenty-eight years old. She had a rather narrow forehead of more height than is considered elegant. Her nose was small and inquisitive, her upper lip a shade too long and her mouth more than a shade too wide. Her eyes were gray-blue with flecks of gold in them. She had a nice smile. She looked as if she had slept well. It was a nice face, a face you get to like. Pretty, but not so pretty that you would have to wear brass knuckles every time you took it out.

"I didn't know just what your office hours were," she said. "So I waited. I gather that your secretary is not here today."

"I don't have a secretary."

I went across and unlocked the inner door, then switched on the buzzer that rang on the outer door. "Let's go into my private thinking parlor."

She passed in front of me with a vague scent of very dry sandalwood and stood looking at the five green filing cases, the shabby rust-red rug, the half-dusted furniture, and the not too clean net curtains.

"I should think you would want somebody to answer the phone," she said. "And once in a while to send your curtains to the cleaners."

"I'll send them out come St. Swithin's Day. Have a chair. I might miss a few unimportant jobs. And a lot of leg art. I save money."

"I see," she said demurely, and placed a large suede bag carefully on the corner of the glass-topped desk. She leaned back and took one of my cigarettes. I burned my finger with a paper match lighting it for her.

She blew a fan of smoke and smiled through it. Nice teeth, rather large.

"You probably didn't expect to see me again so soon. How is your head?"

"Poorly. No, I didn't."

"Were the police nice to you?"

"About the way they always are."

"I'm not keeping you from anything important, am I?"

"No."

"All the same I don't think you're very pleased to see me."

I filled a pipe and reached for the packet of paper matches. I lit the pipe carefully. She watched that with approval. Pipe smokers were solid men. She was going to be disappointed in me.

"I tried to leave you out of it," I said. "I don't know why exactly. It's no business of mine any more anyhow. I ate my dirt last night and banged myself to sleep with a bottle and now it's a police case: I've been warned to leave it alone."

"The reason you left me out of it," she said calmly, "was that you didn't think the police would believe just mere idle curiosity took me down into that hollow last night. They would suspect some guilty reason and hammer at me until I was a wreck."

"How do you know I didn't think the same thing?"

"Cops are just people," she said irrelevantly.

"They start out that way, I've heard."

"Oh—cynical this morning." She looked around the office with an idle but raking glance. "Do you do pretty well in here? I mean financially? I mean, do you make a lot of money—with this kind of furniture?"

I grunted.

"Or should I try minding my own business and not asking impertinent questions?"

"Would it work, if you tried it?"

"Now we're both doing it. Tell me, why did you cover up for me last night? Was it on account of I have reddish hair and a beautiful figure?"

I didn't say anything.

"Let's try this one," she said cheerfully. "Would you like to know who that jade necklace belonged to?"

I could feel my face getting stiff. I thought hard but I couldn't remember for sure. And then suddenly I could. I hadn't said a word to her about a jade necklace.

I reached for the matches and relit my pipe. "Not very much," I said. "Why?"

"Because I know."

"Uh-huh."

"What do you do when you get real talkative—wiggle your toes?"

"All right," I growled. "You came here to tell me. Go ahead and tell me."

Her blue eyes widened and for a moment I thought they looked a little moist. She took her lower lip between her teeth and held it that way while she stared down at the desk. Then she shrugged and let go of her lip and smiled at me candidly.

"Oh I know I'm just a damned inquisitive wench. But there's a strain of bloodhound in me. My father was a cop. His name was Cliff Riordan and he was police chief of Bay City for seven years. I suppose that's what's the matter."

"I seem to remember. What happened to him?"

"He was fired. It broke his heart. A mob of gamblers headed by a man named Laird Brunette elected themselves a mayor. So they put Dad in charge of the Bureau of Records and Identification, which in Bay City is about the size of a tea-bag. So Dad quit and pottered around for a couple of years and then died. And Mother died soon after him. So I've been alone for two years."

"I'm sorry," I said.

She ground out her cigarette. It had no lipstick on it. "The only reason I'm boring you with this is that it makes it easy for me to get along with policemen. I suppose I ought to have told you last night. So this morning I found out who had charge of the case and went to see him. He was a little sore at you at first."

"That's all right," I said. "If I had told him the truth on all points, he still wouldn't have believed me. All he will do is chew one of my ears off."

She looked hurt. I got up and opened the other window. The noise of the traffic from the boulevard came in in waves, like nausea. I felt lousy. I opened the deep drawer of the desk and got the office bottle out and poured myself a drink.

Miss Riordan watched me with disapproval. I was no longer a solid man. She didn't say anything. I drank the drink and put the bottle away again and sat down.

"You didn't offer me one," she said coolly.

"Sorry. It's only eleven o'clock or less. I didn't think you looked the type."

Her eyes crinkled at the corners. "Is that a compliment?"

"In my circle, yes."

She thought that over. It didn't mean anything to her. It didn't mean anything to me either when I thought it over. But the drink made me feel a lot better.

She leaned forward and scraped her gloves slowly across the glass of the desk. "You wouldn't want to hire an assistant, would you? Not if it only cost you a kind word now and then?"

"No."

She nodded. "I thought probably you wouldn't. I'd better just give you my information and go on home."

I didn't say anything. I lit my pipe again. It makes you look thoughtful when you are not thinking.

"First of all, it occurred to me that a jade necklace like that would be a museum piece and would be well known," she said.

I held the match in the air, still burning and watching the flame crawl close to my fingers. Then I blew it out softly and dropped it in the tray and said:

"I didn't say anything to you about a jade necklace."

"No, but Lieutenant Randall did."

"Somebody ought to sew buttons on his face."

"He knew my father. I promised not to tell."

"You're telling me."

"You knew already, silly."

Her hand suddenly flew up as if it was going to fly to her mouth, but it only rose halfway and then fell back slowly and her eyes widened. It was a good act, but I knew something else about her that spoiled it.

"You *did* know, didn't you?" She breathed the words, hushedly.

"I thought it was diamonds. A bracelet, a pair of earrings, a pendant, three rings, one of the rings with emeralds too."

"Not funny," she said. "Not even fast."

"Fei Tsui jade. Very rare. Carved beads about six carats apiece, sixty of them. Worth eighty thousand dollars."

"You have such nice brown eyes," she said. "And you think you're tough."

"Well, who does it belong to and how did you find out?"

"I found out very simply. I thought the best jeweler in town would probably know, so I went and asked the manager of Block's. I told him I was a writer and wanted to do an article on rare jade—you know the line."

"So he believed your red hair and your beautiful figure."

She flushed clear to the temples. "Well, he told me anyway. It belongs to a rich lady who lives in Bay City, in an estate on the canyon. Mrs. Lewin Lockridge Grayle. Her husband is an investment banker or something, enormously rich, worth about twenty millions. He used to own a radio station in Beverly Hills, Station KFDK, and Mrs. Grayle used to work there. He married her five years ago. She's a ravishing blonde. Mr. Grayle is elderly, liverish, stays home and takes calomel while Mrs. Grayle goes places and has a good time."

"This manager of Block's," I said. "He's a fellow that gets around."

"Oh, I didn't get all that from him, silly. Just about the necklace. The rest I got from Giddy Gertie Arbogast."

I reached into the deep drawer and brought the office bottle up again.

"You're not going to turn out to be one of those drunken detectives, are you?" she asked anxiously.

"Why not? They always solve their cases and they never even sweat. Get on with the story."

"Giddy Gertie is the society editor of the *Chronicle*. I've known him for years. He weighs two hundred and wears a Hitler mustache. He got out his morgue file on the Grayles. Look."

She reached into her bag and slid a photograph across the desk, a five-by-three glazed still.

It was a blonde. A blonde to make a bishop kick a hole in a stained glass window. She was wearing street clothes that looked black and white, and a hat to match and she was a little haughty, but not too much. Whatever you needed, wherever you happened to be—she had it. About thirty years old.

I poured a fast drink and burned my throat getting it down. "Take it away," I said. "I'll start jumping."

"Why, I got it for you. You'll want to see her, won't you?"

I looked at it again. Then I slid it under the blotter. "How about tonight at eleven?"

"Listen, this isn't just a bunch of gag lines, Mr. Marlowe. I called her up. She'll see you. On business."

"It may start out that way."

She made an impatient gesture, so I stopped fooling around and got my battle-scarred frown back on my face. "What will she see me about?"

"Her necklace, of course. It was like this. I called her up and had a lot of trouble getting to talk to her, of course, but finally I did. Then I gave her the song and dance I had given the nice man at Block's and it didn't take. She sounded as if she had a hangover. She said something about talking to her secretary, but I managed to keep her on the phone and ask her if it was true she had a Fei Tsui jade necklace. After a while she said, yes. I asked if I might see it. She said, what for? I said my piece over again and it didn't take any better than the first time. I could hear her yawning and bawling somebody outside the mouthpiece for putting me on. Then I said I was working for Philip Marlowe. She said 'So what?' Just like that."

"Incredible. But all the society dames talk like tramps nowadays."

"I wouldn't know," Miss Riordan said sweetly. "Probably some of them *are* tramps. So I asked her if she had a phone with no extension and she said what business was it of mine. But the funny thing was she hadn't hung up on me."

"She had the jade on her mind and she didn't know what you were leading up to. And she may have heard from Randall already."

Miss Riordan shook her head. "No. I called him later and he didn't know who owned the necklace until I told him. He was quite surprised that I had found out."

"He'll get used to you," I said. "He'll probably have to. What then?"

"So I said to Mrs. Grayle: 'You'd still like it back, wouldn't you?' Just like that. I didn't know any other way to say it. I had to say something that would jar her a bit. It did. She gave me another number in a hurry. And I called that and I said I'd like to see her. She seemed surprised. So I had to tell her the story. She didn't like it. But she had been wondering why she hadn't heard from Marriott. I guess she thought he had gone south with the money or something. So I'm to see her at two o'clock. Then I'll tell her about you and how nice and discreet you are and how you would be a good man to help her get it back, if there's any chance and so on. She's already interested."

I didn't say anything. I just stared at her. She looked hurt. "What's the matter? Did I do right?"

"Can't you get it through your head that this is a police case now and that I've been warned to stay off it?"

"Mrs. Grayle has a perfect right to employ you, if she wants to."

"To do what?"

She snapped and unsnapped her bag impatiently. "Oh my goodness—a woman like that—with her looks—can't you see—" She stopped and bit her lip. "What kind of man was Marriott?"

"I hardly knew him. I thought he was a bit of a pansy. I didn't like him very well."

"Was he a man who would be attractive to women?"

"Some women. Others would want to spit."

"Well, it looks as if he might have been attractive to Mrs. Grayle. She went out with him."

"She probably goes out with a hundred men. There's very little chance to get the necklace now."

"Why?"

I got up and walked to the end of the office and slapped the wall with the flat of my hand, hard. The clacking typewriter on the other side stopped for a moment, and then went on. I looked down through the open window into the shaft between my building and the Mansion House Hotel. The coffee shop smell was strong enough to build a garage on. I went back to my desk, dropped the bottle of whiskey back into the drawer, shut the drawer and sat down again. I lit my pipe for the eighth or ninth time and looked carefully across the half-dusted glass to Miss Riordan's grave and honest little face.

You could get to like that face a lot. Glamoured up blondes were a dime a dozen, but that was a face that would wear. I smiled at it.

"Listen, Anne. Killing Marriott was a dumb mistake. The gang behind this holdup would never pull anything like that. What must have happened was that some gowed-up runt they took along for a gun-holder lost his head. Marriott made a false move and some punk beat him down and it was done so quickly nothing could be done to prevent it. Here is an organized mob with inside information on jewels and the movements of the women that wear them. They ask moderate returns and they would play ball. But here also is a back alley murder that doesn't fit at all. My idea is that whoever did it is a dead man hours ago, with weights on his ankles, deep in the Pacific Ocean. And either the jade went down with him or else they have some idea of its real value and they have cached it away in a place where it will stay for a long time—maybe for years before they dare bring it out again. Or, if the gang is big enough, it may show up on the other side of the world. The eight thousand they asked seems pretty low if they really knew the value of the jade. But it would be hard to sell. I'm sure of one thing. They never meant to murder anybody."

Anne Riordan was listening to me with her lips slightly parted and a rapt expression on her face, as if she was looking at the Dalai Lhama.

She closed her mouth slowly and nodded once. "You're wonderful," she said softly. "But you're nuts."

She stood up and gathered her bag to her. "Will you go to see her or won't you?"

"Randall can't stop me—if it comes from her."

"All right. I'm going to see another society editor and get some more dope on the Grayles if I can. About her love life. She would have one, wouldn't she?"

The face framed in auburn hair was wistful.

"Who hasn't?" I sneered.

"*I* never had. Not really."

I reached up and shut my mouth with my hand. She gave me a sharp look and moved towards the door.

"You've forgotten something," I said.

She stopped and turned. "What?" She looked all over the top of the desk.

"You know damn well what."

She came back to the desk and leaned across it earnestly. "Why would they kill the man that killed Marriott, if they don't go in for murder?"

"Because he would be the type that would get picked up sometime and would talk—when they took his dope away from him. I mean they wouldn't kill a customer."

"What makes you so sure the killer took dope?"

"I'm not sure. I just said that. Most punks do."

"Oh." She straightened up and nodded and smiled. "I guess you mean these," she said and reached quickly into her bag and laid a small tissue bag package on the desk.

I reached for it, pulled a rubber band off it carefully and opened up the paper. On it lay three long thick Russian cigarettes with paper mouthpieces. I looked at her and didn't say anything.

"I know I shouldn't have taken them," she said almost breathlessly. "But I knew they were jujus. They usually come in plain papers but lately around Bay City they have been putting them out like this. I've seen several. I thought it was kind of mean for the poor man to be found dead with marihuana cigarettes in his pocket."

"You ought to have taken the case too," I said quietly. "There was dust in it. And it being empty was suspicious."

"I couldn't—with you there. I—I almost went back and did. But I didn't quite have the courage. Did it get you in wrong?"

"No," I lied. "Why should it?"

"I'm glad of that," she said wistfully.

"Why didn't you throw them away?"

She thought about it, her bag clutched to her side, her wide-brimmed absurd hat tilted so that it hid one eye.

"I guess it must be because I'm a cop's daughter," she said at last. "You just don't throw away evidence." Her smile was frail and guilty and her cheeks were flushed. I shrugged.

"Well—" the word hung in the air, like smoke in a closed room. Her lips stayed parted after saying it. I let it hang. The flush on her face deepened.

"I'm horribly sorry. I shouldn't have done it."
I passed that too.
She went very quickly to the door and out.

14

I poked at one of the long Russian cigarettes with a finger, then laid them in a neat row, side by side and squeaked my chair. You just don't throw away evidence. So they were evidence. Evidence of what? That a man occasionally smoked a stick of tea, a man who looked as if any touch of the exotic would appeal to him. On the other hand lots of tough guys smoked marihuana, also lots of band musicians and high school kids, and nice girls who had given up trying. American hasheesh. A weed that would grow anywhere. Unlawful to cultivate now. That meant a lot in a country as big as the U.S.A.

I sat there and puffed my pipe and listened to the clacking typewriter behind the wall of my office and the bong-bong of the traffic lights changing on Hollywood Boulevard and spring rustling in the air, like a paper bag blowing along a concrete sidewalk.

They were pretty big cigarettes, but a lot of Russians are, and marihuana is a coarse leaf. Indian hemp. American hasheesh. Evidence. God, what hats the women wear. My head ached. Nuts.

I got my penknife out and opened the small sharp blade, the one I didn't clean my pipe with, and reached for one of them. That's what a police chemist would do. Slit one down the middle and examine the stuff under a microscope, to start with. There might just happen to be something unusual about it. Not very likely, but what the hell, he was paid by the month.

I slit one down the middle. The mouthpiece part was pretty tough to slit. Okey, I was a tough guy, I slit it anyway. See can you stop me.

Out of the mouthpiece shiny segments of rolled thin cardboard partly straightened themselves and had printing on them. I sat up straight and pawed for them. I tried to spread them out on the desk in order, but they slid around on the desk. I grabbed another of the cigarettes and squinted inside the mouthpiece. Then I went to work with the blade of the pocket knife in a different way. I pinched the cigarette down to the place where the mouthpieces began. The paper was thin all the way, you could feel the grain of what was underneath. So I cut the mouthpiece off carefully and then still more carefully cut through the mouthpiece longways, but only just enough. It opened out and there was another card underneath, rolled up, not touched this time.

I spread it out fondly. It was a man's calling card. Thin pale ivory, just off white. Engraved on that were delicately shaded words. In the lower left hand corner a Stillwood Heights telephone number. In the lower right hand corner the legend, "By Appointment Only." In the middle, a little larger, but still discreet: "Jules Amthor." Below, a little smaller: "Psychic Consultant."

I took hold of the third cigarette. This time, with a lot of difficulty, I teased the card out without cutting anything. It was the same. I put it back where it had been.

I looked at my watch, put my pipe in an ashtray, and then had to look at my watch again to see what time it was. I rolled the two cut cigarettes and the cut card in part of the tissue paper, the one that was complete with card inside in another part of the tissue paper and locked both little packages away in my desk.

I sat looking at the card. Jules Amthor, Psychic Consultant, By Appointment Only, Stillwood Heights phone number, no address. Three like that rolled inside three sticks of tea, in a Chinese or Japanese silk cigarette case with an imitation tortoise-shell frame, a trade article that might have cost thirty-five to seventy-five cents in any Oriental store, Hooey Phooey Sing—Long Sing Tung, that kind of place, where a nice-mannered Jap hisses at you, laughing heartily when you say that the Moon of Arabia incense smells like the girls in Frisco Sadie's back parlor.

And all this in the pocket of a man who was very dead, and who had another and genuinely expensive cigarette case containing cigarettes which he actually smoked.

He must have forgotten it. It didn't make sense. Perhaps it hadn't belonged to him at all. Perhaps he had picked it up in a hotel lobby. Forgotten he had it on him. Forgotten to turn it in. Jules Amthor, Psychic Consultant.

The phone rang and I answered it absently. The voice had the cool hardness of a cop who thinks he is good. It was Randall. He didn't bark. He was the icy type.

"So you didn't know who that girl was last night? And she picked you up on the boulevard and you walked over to there. Nice lying, Marlowe."

"Maybe you have a daughter and you wouldn't like news-cameramen jumping out of bushes and popping flashbulbs in her face."

"You lied to me."

"It was a pleasure."

He was silent a moment, as if deciding something. "We'll let that pass," he said. "I've seen her. She came in and told me her story. She's the daughter of a man I knew and respected, as it happens."

"She told you," I said, "and you told her."

"I told her a little," he said coldly. "For a reason. I'm calling you for the same reason. This investigation is going to be undercover. We have a chance to break this jewel gang and we're going to do it."

"Oh, it's a gang murder this morning. Okey."

"By the way, that was marihuana dust in that funny cigarette case—the one with the dragons on it. Sure you didn't see him smoke one out of it?"

"Quite sure. In my presence he smoked only the others. But he wasn't in my presence all the time."

"I see. Well, that's all. Remember what I told you last night. Don't try getting ideas about this case. All we want from you is silence. Otherwise—"

He paused. I yawned into the mouthpiece.

"I heard that," he snapped. "Perhaps you think I'm not in a position to make that stick. I am. One false move out of you and you'll be locked up as a material witness."

"You mean the papers are not to get the case?"

"They'll get the murder—but they won't know what's behind it."

"Neither do you," I said.

"I've warned you twice now," he said. "The third time is out."

"You're doing a lot of talking," I said, "for a guy that holds cards."

I got the phone hung in my face for that. Okey, the hell with him, let him work at it.

I walked around the office a little to cool off, bought myself a short drink, looked at my watch again and didn't see what time it was, and sat down at the desk once more.

Jules Amthor, Psychic Consultant. Consultations By Appointment Only. Give him enough time and pay him enough money and he'll cure anything from a jaded husband to a grasshopper plague. He would be an expert in frustrated love affairs, women who slept alone and didn't like it, wandering boys and girls who didn't write home, sell the property now or hold it for another year, will this part hurt me with my public or make me seem more versatile? Men would sneak in on him too, big strong guys that roared like lions around their offices and were all cold mush under their vests. But mostly it would be women, fat women that panted and thin women that burned, old women that dreamed and young women that thought they might have Electra complexes, women of all sizes, shapes and ages, but with one thing in common—money. No Thursdays at the County Hospital for Mr. Jules Amthor. Cash on the line for his. Rich bitches who had to be dunned for their milk bills would pay him right now.

A fakeloo artist, a hoopla spreader, and a lad who had his card rolled up inside sticks of tea, found on a dead man.

This was going to be good. I reached for the phone and asked the O-operator for the Stillwood Heights number.

15

A woman's voice answered, a dry, husky-sounding foreign voice: "'Allo."

"May I talk to Mr. Amthor?"

"Ah no. I regret. I am ver-ry sor-ry. Amthor never speaks upon the telephone. I am hees secretary. Weel I take the message?"

"What's the address out there? I want to see him."

"Ah, you weesh to consult Amthor professionally? He weel be ver-ry pleased. But he ees ver-ry beesy. When you weesh to see him?"

"Right away. Sometime today."

"Ah," the voice regretted, "that cannot be. The next week per'aps. I weel look at the book."

"Look," I said, "never mind the book. You 'ave the pencil?"

"But certainly I 'ave the pencil. I—"

"Take this down. My name is Philip Marlowe. My address is 615 Cahuenga Building, Hollywood. That's on Hollywood Boulevard near Ivar. My phone number is Glenview 7537." I spelled the hard ones and waited.

"Yes, Meester Marlowe. I 'ave that."

"I want to see Mr. Amthor about a man named Marriott." I spelled that too. "It is very urgent. It is a matter of life and death. I want to see him fast. F-a-s-t—fast. Sudden, in other words. Am I clear?"

"You talk ver-ry strange," the foreign voice said.

"No." I took hold of the phone standard and shook it. "I feel fine. I always talk like that. This is a very queer business. Mr. Amthor will positively want to see me. I'm a private detective. But I don't want to go to the police until I've seen him."

"Ah," the voice got as cool as a cafeteria dinner. "You are of the police, no?"

"Listen," I said. "I am of the police, no. I am a private detective. Confidential. But it is very urgent just the same. You call me back, no? You 'ave the telephone number, yes?"

"Si. I 'ave the telephone number. Meester Marriott—he ees sick?"

"Well, he's not up and around," I said. "So you know him?"

"But no. You say a matter of life and death. Amthor he cure many people—"

"This is one time he flops," I said. "I'll be waiting for a call."

I hung up and lunged for the office bottle. I felt as if I had been through a meat grinder. Ten minutes passed. The phone rang. The voice said:

"Amthor he weel see you at six o'clock."

"That's fine. What's the address?"

"He weel send a car."

"I have a car of my own. Just give me—"

"He weel send a car," the voice said coldly, and the phone clicked in my ear.

I looked at my watch once more. It was more than time for lunch. My stomach burned from the last drink. I wasn't hungry. I lit a cigarette. It tasted like a plumber's handkerchief. I nodded across the office at Mr. Rembrandt, then I reached for my hat and went out. I was halfway to the elevator before the thought hit me. It hit me without any reason or sense, like a dropped brick. I stopped and leaned against the marbled wall and pushed my hat around on my head and suddenly I laughed.

A girl passing me on the way from the elevators back to her work turned and gave me one of those looks which are supposed to make your spine feel like a run in a stocking. I waved my hand at her and went back to my office and grabbed the phone. I called up a man I knew who worked on the Lot Books of a title company.

"Can you find a property by the address alone?" I asked him.

"Sure. We have a cross-index. What is it?"

"1644 West 54th Place. I'd like to know a little something about the condition of the title."

"I'd better call you back. What's that number?"

He called back in about three minutes.

"Get your pencil out," he said. "It's Lot 8 of Block 11 of Caraday's Addition to the Maplewood Tract Number 4. The owner of record, subject to certain things, is Jessie Pierce Florian, widow."

"Yeah. What things?"

"Second half taxes, two ten-year street improvement bonds, one storm drain assessment bond also ten year, none of these delinquents, also a first trust deed of $2600."

"You mean one of those things where they can sell you out on ten minutes' notice?"

"Not quite that quick, but a lot quicker than a mortgage. There's nothing unusual about it except the amount. It's high for that neighborhood, unless it's a new house."

"It's a very old house and in bad repair," I said. "I'd say fifteen hundred would buy the place."

"Then it's distinctly unusual, because the refinancing was done only four years ago."

"Okey, who holds it? Some investment company?"

"No. An individual. Man named Lindsay Marriott, a single man. Okey?"

I forget what I said to him or what thanks I made. They probably sounded like words. I sat there, just staring at the wall.

My stomach suddenly felt fine. I was hungry. I went down to the Mansion House Coffee Shop and ate lunch and got my car out of the parking lot next to my building.

I drove south and east, towards West 54th Place. I didn't carry any liquor with me this time.

16

The block looked just as it had looked the day before. The street was empty except for an ice truck, two Fords in drive-ways, and a swirl of dust going around a corner. I drove slowly past No. 1644 and parked farther along and studied the houses on either side of mine. I walked back and stopped in front of it, looking at the tough palm tree and the drab un-watered scrap of lawn. The house seemed empty, but prob-ably wasn't. It just had that look. The lonely rocker on the front porch stood just where it had stood yesterday. There was a throw-away paper on the walk. I picked it up and slapped it against my leg and then I saw the curtain move next door, in the near front window.

Old Nosey again. I yawned and tilted my hat down. A sharp nose almost flattened itself against the inside of the glass. White hair above it, and eyes that were just eyes from where I stood. I strolled along the sidewalk and the eyes watched me. I turned in towards her house. I climbed the wooden steps and rang the bell.

The door snapped open as if it had been on a spring. She was a tall old bird with a chin like a rabbit. Seen from close her eyes were as sharp as lights on still water. I took my hat off.

"Are you the lady who called the police about Mrs. Florian?"

She stared at me coolly and missed nothing about me, probably not even the mole on my right shoulder blade.

"I ain't sayin' I am, young man, and I ain't sayin' I ain't. Who are you?" It was a high twangy voice, made for talking over an eight party line.

"I'm a detective."

"Land's sakes. Why didn't you say so? What's she done now? I ain't seen a thing and I ain't missed a minute. Henry done all the goin' to the store for me. Ain't been a sound out of there."

She snapped the screen door unhooked and drew me in. The hall smelled of furniture oil. It had a lot of dark furniture that had once been in good style. Stuff with inlaid panels and scollops at the corners. We went into a front room that had cotton lace antimacassars pinned on everything you could stick a pin into.

"Say, didn't I see you before?" she asked suddenly, a note of suspicion crawling around in her voice. "Sure enough I did. You was the man that—"

"That's right. And I'm still a detective. Who's Henry?"

"Oh, he's just a little colored boy that goes errands for me. Well, what you want, young man?" She patted a clean red and white apron and gave me the beady eye. She clicked her store teeth a couple of times for practice.

"Did the officers come here yesterday after they went to Mrs. Florian's house?"

"What officers?"

"The uniformed officers," I said patiently.

"Yes, they was here a minute. They didn't know nothing."

"Describe the big man to me—the one that had a gun and made you call up."

She described him, with complete accuracy. It was Malloy all right.

"What kind of car did he drive?"

"A little car. He couldn't hardly get into it."

"That's all you can say? This man's a murderer!"

Her mouth gaped, but her eyes were pleased. "Land's sakes, I wish I could tell you, young man. But I never knew much about cars. Murder, eh? Folks ain't safe a minute in this town. When I come here twenty-two years ago we didn't lock our doors hardly. Now it's gangsters and crooked police and politicians fightin' each other with machine guns, so I've heard. Scandalous is what it is, young man."

"Yeah. What do you know about Mrs. Florian?"

The small mouth puckered. "She ain't neighborly. Plays her radio loud late nights. Sings. She don't talk to anybody." She leaned forward a little. "I'm not positive, but my opinion is she drinks liquor."

"She have many visitors?"

"She don't have no visitors at all."

"You'd know, of course, Mrs.—"

"Mrs. Morrison. Land's sakes, yes. What else have I got to do but look out of the windows?"

"I bet it's fun. Mrs. Florian has lived here a long time?"

"About ten years, I reckon. Had a husband once. Looked like a bad one to me. He died." She paused and thought. "I guess he died natural," she added. "I never heard different."

"Left her money?"

Her eyes receded and her chin followed them. She sniffed hard. "You been drinkin' liquor," she said coldly.

"I just had a tooth out. The dentist gave it to me."

"I don't hold with it."

"It's bad stuff, except for medicine," I said.

"I don't hold with it for medicine neither."

"I think you're right," I said. "Did he leave her money? Her husband?"

"I wouldn't know." Her mouth was the size of a prune and as smooth. I had lost out.

"Has anybody at all been there since the officers?"

"Ain't seen."

"Thank you very much, Mrs. Morrison. I won't trouble you any more now. You've been very kind and helpful."

I walked out of the room and opened the door. She followed me and cleared her throat and clicked her teeth a couple more times.

"What number should I call?" she asked, relenting a little.

"University 4-5000. Ask for Lieutenant Nulty. What does she live on—relief?"

"This ain't a relief neighborhood," she said coldly.

"I bet that side piece was the admiration of Sioux Falls once," I said, gazing at a carved sideboard that was in the hall because the dining room was too small for it. It had curved ends, thin carved legs, was inlaid all over, and had a painted basket of fruit on the front.

"Mason City," she said softly. "Yessir, we had a nice home once, me and George. Best there was."

I opened the screen door and stepped through it and thanked her again. She was smiling now. Her smile was as sharp as her eyes.

"Gets a registered letter first of every month," she said suddenly.

I turned and waited. She leaned towards me. "I see the mailman go up to the door and get her to sign. First day of every month. Dresses up then and goes out. Don't come home till all hours. Sings half the night. Times I could have called the police it was so loud."

I patted the thin malicious arm.

"You're one in a thousand, Mrs. Morrison," I said. I put my hat on, tipped it to her and left. Halfway down the walk I thought of something and swung back. She was still standing inside the screen door, with the house door open behind her. I went back up on the steps.

"Tomorrow's the first," I said. "First of April. April Fool's Day. Be sure to notice whether she gets her registered letter, will you, Mrs. Morrison?"

The eyes gleamed at me. She began to laugh—a high-pitched old woman's laugh. "April Fool's Day," she tittered. "Maybe she won't get it."

I left her laughing. The sound was like a hen having hiccups.

17

Nobody answered my ring or knock next door. I tried again. The screen door wasn't hooked. I tried the house door. It was unlocked. I stepped inside.

Nothing was changed, not even the smell of gin. There were still no bodies on the floor. A dirty glass stood on the small table beside the chair where Mrs. Florian had sat yesterday. The radio was turned off. I went over to the davenport and felt down behind the cushions. The same dead soldier and another one with him now.

I called out. No answer. Then I thought I heard a long slow unhappy breathing that was half groaning. I went through the arch and sneaked into the little hallway. The bedroom door was partly open and the groaning sound came from behind it. I stuck my head in and looked.

Mrs. Florian was in bed. She was lying flat on her back with a cotton comforter pulled up to her chin. One of the little fluffballs on the comforter was almost in her mouth. Her long yellow face was slack, half dead. Her dirty hair straggled on the pillow. Her eyes opened slowly and looked at me with no expression. The room had a sickening smell of sleep, liquor and dirty clothes. A sixty-nine cent alarm clock ticked on the peeling gray-white paint of the bureau. It ticked loud enough to shake the walls. Above it a mirror showed a distorted view of the woman's face. The trunk from which she had taken the photos was still open.

I said: "Good afternoon, Mrs. Florian. Are you sick?"

She worked her lips together slowly, rubbed one over the other, then slid a tongue out and moistened them and worked her jaws. Her voice came from her mouth sounding like a worn-out phonograph record. Her eyes showed recognition now, but not pleasure.

"You get him?"

"The Moose?"

"Sure."

"Not yet. Soon, I hope."

She screwed her eyes up and then snapped them open as if trying to get rid of a film over them.

"You ought to keep your house locked up," I said. "He might come back."

"You think I'm scared of the Moose, huh?"

"You acted like it when I was talking to you yesterday."

She thought about that. Thinking was weary work. "Got any liquor?"

"No, I didn't bring any today, Mrs. Florian. I was a little low on cash."

"Gin's cheap. It hits."

"I might go out for some in a little while. So you're not afraid of Malloy?"

"Why would I be?"

"Okey, you're not. What *are* you afraid of?"

Light snapped into her eyes, held for a moment, and faded out again. "Aw beat it. You coppers give me an ache in the fanny."

I said nothing. I leaned against the door frame and put a cigarette in my mouth and tried to jerk it up far enough to hit my nose with it. This is harder than it looks.

"Coppers," she said slowly, as if talking to herself, "will never catch that boy. He's good and he's got dough and he's got friends. You're wasting your time, copper."

"Just the routine," I said. "It was practically a self-defense anyway. Where would he be?"

She snickered and wiped her mouth on the cotton comforter.

"Soap now," she said. "Soft stuff. Copper smart. You guys still think it gets you something."

"I liked the Moose," I said.

Interest flickered in her eyes. "You know him?"

"I was with him yesterday—when he killed the nigger over on Central."

She opened her mouth wide and laughed her head off without making any more sound than you would make cracking a breadstick. Tears ran out of her eyes and down her face.

"A big strong guy," I said. "Soft-hearted in spots too. Wanted his Velma pretty bad."

The eyes veiled. "Thought it was her folks was looking for her," she said softly.

"They are. But she's dead, you said. Nothing there. Where did she die?"

"Dalhart, Texas. Got a cold and went to the chest and off she went."

"You were there?"

"Hell, no. I just heard."

"Oh. Who told you, Mrs. Florian?"

"Some hoofer. I forget the name right now. Maybe a good stiff drink might help some. I feel like Death Valley."

"And you look like a dead mule," I thought, but didn't say it out loud. "There's just one more thing," I said, "then I'll maybe run out for some gin. I looked up the title to your house, I don't know just why."

She was rigid under the bedclothes, like a wooden woman. Even her eyelids were frozen half down over the clogged iris of her eyes. Her breath stilled.

"There's a rather large trust deed on it," I said. "Considering the low value of property around here. It's held by a man named Lindsay Marriott."

Her eyes blinked rapidly, but nothing else moved. She stared.

"I used to work for him," she said at last. "I used to be a servant in his family. He kind of takes care of me a little."

I took the unlighted cigarette out of my mouth and looked at it aimlessly and stuck it back in.

"Yesterday afternoon, a few hours after I saw you, Mr. Marriott called me up at my office. He offered me a job."

"What kind of job?" Her voice croaked now, badly.

I shrugged. "I can't tell you that. Confidential. I went to see him last night."

"You're a clever son of a bitch," she said thickly and moved a hand under the bedclothes.

I stared at her and said nothing.

"Copper-smart," she sneered.

I ran a hand up and down the door frame. It felt slimy. Just touching it made me want to take a bath.

"Well, that's all," I said smoothly. "I was just wondering how come. Might be nothing at all. Just a coincidence. It just looked as if it might mean something."

"Copper-smart," she said emptily. "Not a real copper at that. Just a cheap shamus."

"I suppose so," I said. "Well, good-by, Mrs. Florian. By the way, I don't think you'll get a registered letter tomorrow morning."

She threw the bedclothes aside and jerked upright with her eyes blazing. Something glittered in her right hand. A small revolver, a Banker's Special. It was old and worn, but looked business-like.

"Tell it," she snarled. "Tell it fast."

I looked at the gun and the gun looked at me. Not too steadily. The hand behind it began to shake, but the eyes still blazed. Saliva bubbled at the corners of her mouth.

"You and I could work together," I said.

The gun and her jaw dropped at the same time. I was inches from the door. While the gun was still dropping, I slid through it and beyond the opening.

"Think it over," I called back.

There was no sound, no sound of any kind.

I went fast back through the hall and dining room and out of the house. My back felt queer as I went down the walk. The muscles crawled.

Nothing happened. I went along the street and got into my car and drove away from there.

The last day of March and hot enough for summer. I felt like taking my coat off as I drove. In front of the 77th Street Station, two prowl car men were scowling at a bent front fender. I went in through the swing doors and found a uniformed lieutenant behind the railing looking over the charge sheet. I asked him if Nulty was upstairs. He said he thought he was, was I a friend of his. I said yes. He said okey, go on up, so I went up the worn stairs and along the corridor and knocked at the door. The voice yelled and I went in.

He was picking his teeth, sitting in one chair with his feet on the other. He was looking at his left thumb, holding it up in front of his eyes and at arm's length. The thumb looked all right to me, but Nulty's stare was gloomy, as if he thought it wouldn't get well.

He lowered it to his thigh and swung his feet to the floor and looked at me instead of at his thumb. He wore a dark gray suit and a mangled cigar end was waiting on the desk for him to get through with the toothpick.

I turned the felt seat cover that lay on the other chair with its straps not fastened to anything, sat down, and put a cigarette in my face.

"You," Nulty said, and looked at his toothpick, to see if it was chewed enough.

"Any luck?"

"Malloy? I ain't on it any more."

"Who is?"

"Nobody ain't. Why? The guy's lammed. We got him on the teletype and they got readers out. Hell, he'll be in Mexico long gone."

"Well, all he did was kill a negro," I said. "I guess that's only a misdemeanor."

"You still interested? I thought you was workin'?" His pale eyes moved damply over my face.

"I had a job last night, but it didn't last. Have you still got that Pierrot photo?"

He reached around and pawed under his blotter. He held it out. It still looked pretty. I stared at the face.

"This is really mine," I said. "If you don't need it for the file, I'd like to keep it."

"Should be in the file, I guess," Nulty said. "I forgot about it. Okey, keep it under your hat. I passed the file in."

I put the photo in my breast pocket and stood up. "Well, I guess that's all," I said, a little too airily.

"I smell something," Nulty said coldly.

I looked at the piece of rope on the edge of his desk. His eyes followed my look. He threw the toothpick on the floor and stuck the chewed cigar in his mouth.

"Not this either," he said.

"It's a vague hunch. If it grows more solid, I won't forget you."

"Things is tough. I need a break, pal."

"A man who works as hard as you deserves one," I said.

He struck a match on his thumbnail, looked pleased because it caught the first time, and started inhaling smoke from the cigar.

"I'm laughing," Nulty said sadly, as I went out.

The hall was quiet, the whole building was quiet. Down in front the prowl car men were still looking at their bent fender. I drove back to Hollywood.

The phone was ringing as I stepped into the office. I leaned down over the desk and said, "Yes?"

"Am I addressing Mr. Philip Marlowe?"

"Yes, this is Marlowe."

"This is Mrs. Grayle's residence. Mrs. Lewin Lockridge Grayle. Mrs. Grayle would like to see you here as soon as convenient."

"Where?"

"The address is Number 862 Aster Drive, in Bay City. May I say you will arrive within the hour?"

"Are you Mr. Grayle?"

"Certainly not, sir. I am the butler."

"That's me you hear ringing the door bell," I said.

18

It was close to the ocean and you could feel the ocean in the air but you couldn't see water from the front of the place. Aster Drive had a long smooth curve there and the houses on the inland side were just nice houses, but on the canyon side they were great silent estates, with twelve foot walls and wrought iron gates and ornamental hedges; and inside, if you could get inside, a special brand of sunshine, very quiet, put up in noise-proof containers just for the upper classes.

A man in a dark blue Russian tunic and shiny black puttees and flaring breeches stood in the half-open gates. He was a dark, good-looking lad, with plenty of shoulders and shiny smooth hair and the peak on his rakish cap made a soft shadow over his eyes. He had a cigarette in the corner of his mouth and he held his head tilted a little, as if he liked to keep the smoke out of his nose. One hand had a smooth black gauntlet on it and the other was bare. There was a heavy ring on his third finger.

There was no number in sight, but this should be 862. I

stopped my car and leaned out and asked him. It took him a long time to answer. He had to look me over very carefully. Also the car I was driving. He came over to me and as he came he carelessly dropped his ungloved hand towards his hip. It was the kind of carelessness that was meant to be noticed.

He stopped a couple of feet away from my car and looked me over again.

"I'm looking for the Grayle residence," I said.

"This is it. Nobody in."

"I'm expected."

He nodded. His eyes gleamed like water. "Name?"

"Philip Marlowe."

"Wait there." He strolled, without hurry, over to the gates and unlocked an iron door set into one of the massive pillars. There was a telephone inside. He spoke briefly into it, snapped the door shut, and came back to me.

"You have some identification?"

I let him look at the license on the steering post. "That doesn't prove anything," he said. "How do I know it's your car?"

I pulled the key out of the ignition and threw the door open and got out. That put me about a foot from him. He had a nice breath. Haig and Haig at least.

"You've been at the sideboy again," I said.

He smiled. His eyes measured me. I said:

"Listen, I'll talk to the butler over that phone and he'll know my voice. Will that pass me in or do I have to ride on your back?"

"I just work here," he said softly. "If I didn't—" he let the rest hang in the air, and kept on smiling.

"You're a nice lad," I said and patted his shoulder. "Dartmouth or Dannemora?"

"Christ," he said. "Why didn't you say you were a cop?"

We both grinned. He waved his hand and I went in through the half open gate. The drive curved and tall molded hedges of dark green completely screened it from the street and from the house. Through a green gate I saw a Jap gardener at work weeding a huge lawn. He was pulling a piece of weed out of the vast velvet expanse and sneering at it the way

Jap gardeners do. Then the tall hedge closed in again and I didn't see anything more for a hundred feet. Then the hedge ended in a wide circle in which half a dozen cars were parked.

One of them was a small coupe. There were a couple of very nice two-tone Buicks of the latest model, good enough to go for the mail in. There was a black limousine, with dull nickel louvres and hubcaps the size of bicycle wheels. There was a long sport phaeton with the top down. A short very wide all-weather concrete driveway led from these to the side entrance of the house.

Off to the left, beyond the parking space there was a sunken garden with a fountain at each of the four corners. The entrance was barred by a wrought-iron gate with a flying Cupid in the middle. There were busts on light pillars and a stone seat with crouching griffins at each end. There was an oblong pool with stone waterlilies in it and a big stone bull-frog sitting on one of the leaves. Still farther a rose colonnade led to a thing like an altar, hedged in at both sides, yet not so completely but that the sun lay in an arabesque along the steps of the altar. And far over to the left there was a wild garden, not very large, with a sundial in the corner near an angle of wall that was built to look like a ruin. And there were flowers. There were a million flowers.

The house itself was not so much. It was smaller than Buckingham Palace, rather gray for California, and probably had fewer windows than the Chrysler Building.

I sneaked over to the side entrance and pressed a bell and somewhere a set of chimes made a deep mellow sound like church bells.

A man in a striped vest and gilt buttons opened the door, bowed, took my hat and was through for the day. Behind him in dimness, a man in striped knife-edge pants and a black coat and wing collar with gray striped tie leaned his gray head forward about half an inch and said: "Mr. Marlowe? If you will come this way, please—"

We went down a hall. It was a very quiet hall. Not a fly buzzed in it. The floor was covered with Oriental rugs and there were paintings along the walls. We turned a corner and there was more hall. A French window showed a gleam of blue water far off and I remembered almost with a shock that we were near the Pacific Ocean and that this house was on the edge of one of the canyons.

The butler reached a door and opened it against voices and stood aside and I went in. It was a nice room with large chesterfields and lounging chairs done in pale yellow leather arranged around a fireplace in front of which, on the glossy but not slippery floor, lay a rug as thin as silk and as old as Aesop's aunt. A jet of flowers glistened in a corner, another on a low table, the walls were of dull painted parchment, there was comfort, space, coziness, a dash of the very modern and a dash of the very old, and three people sitting in a sudden silence watching me cross the floor.

One of them was Anne Riordan, looking just as I had seen her last, except that she was holding a glass of amber fluid in her hand. One was a tall thin sad-faced man with a stony chin and deep eyes and no color in his face but an unhealthy yellow. He was a good sixty, or rather a bad sixty. He wore a dark business suit, a red carnation, and looked subdued.

The third was the blonde. She was dressed to go out, in a pale greenish blue. I didn't pay much attention to her clothes. They were what the guy designed for her and she would go to the right man. The effect was to make her look very young and to make her lapis lazuli eyes look very blue. Her hair was of the gold of old paintings and had been fussed with just enough but not too much. She had a full set of curves which nobody had been able to improve on. The dress was rather plain except for a clasp of diamonds at the throat. Her hands were not small, but they had shape, and the nails were the usual jarring note—almost magenta. She was giving me one of her smiles. She looked as if she smiled easily, but her eyes had a still look, as if they thought slowly and carefully. And her mouth was sensual.

"So nice of you to come," she said. "This is my husband. Mix Mr. Marlowe a drink, honey."

Mr. Grayle shook hands with me. His hand was cold and a little moist. His eyes were sad. He mixed a Scotch and soda and handed it to me.

Then he sat down in a corner and was silent. I drank half of the drink and grinned at Miss Riordan. She looked at me with a sort of absent expression, as if she had another clue.

"Do you think you can do anything for us?" the blonde asked slowly, looking down into her glass. "If you think you can, I'd be delighted. But the loss is rather small, compared with having any more fuss with gangsters and awful people."

"I don't know very much about it really," I said.

"Oh, I hope you can." She gave me a smile I could feel in my hip pocket.

I drank the other half of my drink. I began to feel rested. Mrs. Grayle rang a bell set into the arm of the leather chesterfield and a footman came in. She half pointed to the tray. He looked around and mixed two drinks. Miss Riordan was still playing cute with the same one and apparently Mr. Grayle didn't drink. The footman went out.

Mrs. Grayle and I held our glasses. Mrs. Grayle crossed her legs, a little carelessly.

"I don't know whether I can do anything," I said. "I doubt it. What is there to go on?"

"I'm sure you can." She gave me another smile. "How far did Lin Marriott take you into his confidence?"

She looked sideways at Miss Riordan. Miss Riordan just couldn't catch the look. She kept right on sitting. She looked sideways the other way. Mrs. Grayle looked at her husband. "Do you have to bother with this, honey?"

Mr. Grayle stood up and said he was very glad to have met me and that he would go and lie down for a while. He didn't feel very well. He hoped I would excuse him. He was so polite I wanted to carry him out of the room just to show my appreciation.

He left. He closed the door softly, as if he was afraid to wake a sleeper. Mrs. Grayle looked at the door for a moment and then put the smile back on her face and looked at me.

"Miss Riordan is in your complete confidence, of course."

"Nobody's in my complete confidence, Mrs. Grayle. She happens to know about this case—what there is to know."

"Yes." She drank a sip or two, then finished her glass at a swallow and set it aside.

"To hell with this polite drinking," she said suddenly. "Let's get together on this. You're a very good-looking man to be in your sort of racket."

"It's a smelly business," I said.

"I didn't quite mean that. Is there any money in it—or is that impertinent?"

"There's not much money in it. There's a lot of grief. But there's a lot of fun too. And there's always a chance of a big case."

"How does one get to be a private detective? You don't mind my sizing you up a little? And push that table over here, will you? So I can reach the drinks."

I got up and pushed the huge silver tray on a stand across the glossy floor to her side. She made two more drinks. I still had half of my second.

"Most of us are ex-cops," I said. "I worked for the D.A. for a while. I got fired."

She smiled nicely. "Not for incompetence, I'm sure."

"No, for talking back. Have you had any more phone calls?"

"Well—" She looked at Anne Riordan. She waited. Her look said things.

Anne Riordan stood up. She carried her glass, still full, over to the tray and set it down. "You probably won't run short," she said. "But if you do—and thanks very much for talking to me, Mrs. Grayle. I won't use anything. You have my word for it."

"Heavens, you're not leaving," Mrs. Grayle said with her smile.

Anne Riordan took her lower lip between her teeth and held it there for a moment as if making up her mind whether to bite it off and spit it out or leave it on a while longer.

"Sorry, afraid I'll have to. I don't work for Mr. Marlowe, you know. Just a friend. Good-by, Mrs. Grayle."

The blonde gleamed at her. "I hope you'll drop in again soon. Any time." She pressed the bell twice. That got the butler. He held the door open.

Miss Riordan went out quickly and the door closed. For quite a while after it closed, Mrs. Grayle stared at it with a faint smile. "It's much better this way, don't you think?" she said after an interval of silence. I nodded. "You're probably wondering how she knows so much if she's just a friend," I said. "She's a curious little girl. Some of it she dug out herself, like who you were and who owned the jade necklace.

Some of it just happened. She came by last night to that dell where Marriott was killed. She was out riding. She happened to see a light and came down there."

"Oh." Mrs. Grayle lifted a glass quickly and made a face. "It's horrible to think of. Poor Lin. He was rather a heel. Most of one's friends are. But to die like that is awful." She shuddered. Her eyes got large and dark.

"So it's all right about Miss Riordan. She won't talk. Her father was chief of police here for a long time," I said.

"Yes. So she told me. You're not drinking."

"I'm doing what *I* call drinking."

"You and I should get along. Did Lin—Mr. Marriott—tell you how the hold-up happened?"

"Between here and the Trocadero somewhere. He didn't say exactly. Three or four men."

She nodded her golden gleaming head. "Yes. You know there was something rather funny about that holdup. They gave me back one of my rings, rather a nice one, too."

"He told me that."

"Then again I hardly ever wore the jade. After all, it's a museum piece, probably not many like it in the world, a very rare type of jade. Yet they snapped at it. I wouldn't expect them to think it had any value much, would you?"

"They'd know you wouldn't wear it otherwise. Who knew about its value?"

She thought. It was nice to watch her thinking. She still had her legs crossed, and still carelessly.

"All sorts of people, I suppose."

"But they didn't know you would be wearing it that night? Who knew that?"

She shrugged her pale blue shoulders. I tried to keep my eyes where they belonged.

"My maid. But she's had a hundred chances. And I trust her—"

"Why?"

"I don't know. I just trust some people. I trust you."

"Did you trust Marriott?"

Her face got a little hard. Her eyes a little watchful. "Not in some things. In others, yes. There are degrees." She had a nice way of talking, cool, half-cynical, and yet not hard-boiled. She rounded her words well.

"All right—besides the maid. The chauffeur?"

She shook her head, no. "Lin drove me that night, in his own car. I don't think George was around at all. Wasn't it Thursday?"

"I wasn't there. Marriott said four or five days before in telling me about it. Thursday would have been an even week from last night."

"Well, it was Thursday." She reached for my glass and her fingers touched mine a little, and were soft to the touch. "George gets Thursday evening off. That's the usual day, you know." She poured a fat slug of mellow-looking Scotch into my glass and squirted in some fizz-water. It was the kind of liquor you think you can drink for ever and all you do is get reckless. She gave herself the same treatment.

"Lin told you my name?" she asked softly, the eyes still watchful.

"He was careful not to."

"Then he probably misled you a little about the time. Let's see what we have. Maid and chauffeur out. Out of consideration as accomplices, I mean."

"They're not out by me."

"Well, at least I'm trying," she laughed. "Then there's Newton, the butler. He might have seen it on my neck that night. But it hangs down rather low and I was wearing a white fox evening wrap; no, I don't think he could have seen it."

"I bet you looked a dream," I said.

"You're not getting a little tight, are you?"

"I've been known to be soberer."

She put her head back and went off into a peal of laughter. I have only known four women in my life who could do that and still look beautiful. She was one of them.

"Newton is okey," I said. "His type don't run with hood-lums. That's just guessing, though. How about the footman?"

She thought and remembered, then shook her head. "He didn't see me."

"Anybody ask you to wear the jade?"

Her eyes instantly got more guarded. "You're not fooling me a damn bit," she said.

She reached for my glass to refill it. I let her have it, even though it still had an inch to go. I studied the lovely lines of her neck.

When she had filled the glasses and we were playing with them again I said, "Let's get the record straight and then I'll tell you something. Describe the evening."

She looked at her wrist watch, drawing a full length sleeve back to do it. "I ought to be—"

"Let him wait."

Her eyes flashed at that. I liked them that way. "There's such a thing as being just a little too frank," she said.

"Not in my business. Describe the evening. Or have me thrown out on my ear. One or the other. Make your lovely mind up."

"You'd better sit over here beside me."

"I've been thinking that a long time," I said. "Ever since you crossed your legs, to be exact."

She pulled her dress down. "These damn things are always up around your neck."

I sat beside her on the yellow leather chesterfield. "Aren't you a pretty fast worker?" she asked quietly.

I didn't answer her.

"Do you do much of this sort of thing?" she asked with a sidelong look.

"Practically none. I'm a Tibetan monk, in my spare time."

"Only you don't have any spare time."

"Let's focus," I said. "Let's get what's left of our minds —or mine—on the problem. How much are you going to pay me?"

"Oh, that's the problem. I thought you were going to get my necklace back. Or try to."

"I have to work in my own way. This way." I took a long drink and it nearly stood me on my head. I swallowed a little air.

"And investigate a murder," I said.

"That has nothing to do with it. I mean that's a police affair, isn't it?"

"Yeah—only the poor guy paid me a hundred bucks to take care of him—and I didn't. Makes me feel guilty. Makes me want to cry. Shall I cry?"

"Have a drink." She poured us some more Scotch. It didn't seem to affect her any more than water affects Boulder Dam.

"Well, where have we got to?" I said, trying to hold my glass so that the whiskey would stay inside it. "No maid, no chauffeur, no butler, no footman. We'll be doing our own laundry next. How did the holdup happen? Your version might have a few details Marriott didn't give me."

She leaned forward and cupped her chin in her hand. She looked serious without looking silly-serious.

"We went to a party in Brentwood Heights. Then Lin suggested we run over to the Troc for a few drinks and a few dances. So we did. They were doing some work on Sunset and it was very dusty. So coming back Lin dropped down to Santa Monica. That took us past a shabby looking hotel called the Hotel Indio, which I happened to notice for some silly meaningless reason. Across the street from it was a beer joint and a car was parked in front of that."

"Only one car—in front of a beer joint?"

"Yes. Only one. It was a very dingy place. Well, this car started up and followed us and of course I thought nothing of that either. There was no reason to. Then before we got to where Santa Monica turns into Arguello Boulevard, Lin said, 'Let's go over the other road' and turned up some curving residential street. Then all of a sudden a car rushed by us and grazed the fender and then pulled over to stop. A man in an overcoat and scarf and hat low on his face came back to apologize. It was a white scarf bunched out and it drew my eyes. It was about all I really saw of him except that he was tall and thin. As soon as he got close—and I remembered afterwards that he didn't walk in our headlights at all—"

"That's natural. Nobody likes to look into headlights. Have a drink. My treat this time."

She was leaning forward, her fine eyebrows—not daubs of paint—drawn together in a frown of thought. I made two drinks. She went on:

"As soon as he got close to the side where Lin was sitting he jerked the scarf up over his nose and a gun was shining at us. 'Stick-up,' he said. 'Be very quiet and everything will be jake.' Then another man came over on the other side."

"In Beverly Hills," I said, "the best policed four square miles in California."

She shrugged. "It happened just the same. They asked for my jewelry and bag. The man with the scarf did. The one on my side never spoke at all. I passed the things across Lin and the man gave me back my bag and one ring. He said to hold off calling the police and insurance people for a while. They would make us a nice smooth easy deal. He said they found it easier to work on a straight percentage. He seemed to have all the time in the world. He said they could work through the insurance people, if they had to, but that meant cutting in a shyster, and they preferred not to. He sounded like a man with some education."

"It might have been Dressed-Up Eddie," I said. "Only he got bumped off in Chicago."

She shrugged. We had a drink. She went on.

"Then they left and we went home and I told Lin to keep quiet about it. The next day I got a call. We have two phones, one with extensions and one in my bedroom with no extensions. The call was on this. It's not listed, of course."

I nodded. "They can buy the number for a few dollars. It's done all the time. Some movie people have to change their numbers every month."

We had a drink.

"I told the man calling to take it up with Lin and he would represent me and if they were not too unreasonable, we might deal. He said okey, and from then on I guess they just stalled long enough to watch us a little. Finally, as you know, we agreed on eight thousand dollars and so forth."

"Could you recognize any of them?"

"Of course not."

"Randall know all this?"

"Of course. Do we have to talk about it any more? It bores me." She gave me the lovely smile.

"Did he make any comment?"

She yawned. "Probably. I forget."

I sat with my empty glass in my hand and thought. She took it away from me and started to fill it again.

I took the refilled glass out of her hand and transferred it to my left and took hold of her left hand with my right. It felt smooth and soft and warm and comforting. It squeezed mine. The muscles in it were strong. She was a well built woman, and no paper flower.

"I think he had an idea," she said. "But he didn't say what it was."

"Anybody would have an idea out of all that," I said.

She turned her head slowly and looked at me. Then she nodded. "You can't miss it, can you?"

"How long have you known him?"

"Oh, years. He used to be an announcer at the station my husband owned. KFDK. That's where I met him. That's where I met my husband too."

"I knew that. But Marriott lived as if he had money. Not riches, but comfortable money."

"He came into some and quit radio business."

"Do you know for a fact he came into money—or was that just something he said?"

She shrugged. She squeezed my hand.

"Or it may not have been very much money and he may have gone through it pretty fast." I squeezed her hand back. "Did he borrow from you?"

"You're a little old-fashioned, aren't you?" She looked down at the hand I was holding.

"I'm still working. And your Scotch is so good it keeps me half-sober. Not that I'd have to be drunk—"

"Yes." She drew her hand out of mine and rubbed it. "You must have quite a clutch—in your spare time. Lin Marriott was a highclass blackmailer, of course. That's obvious. He lived on women."

"He had something on you?"

"Should I tell you?"

"It probably wouldn't be wise."

She laughed. "I will, anyhow. I got a little tight at his house once and passed out. I seldom do. He took some photos of me—with my clothes up to my neck."

"The dirty dog," I said. "Have you got any of them handy?"

She slapped my wrist. She said softly:

"What's your name?"

"Phil. What's yours?"

"Helen. Kiss me."

She fell softly across my lap and I bent down over her face and began to browse on it. She worked her eyelashes and made butterfly kisses on my cheeks. When I got to her mouth it was half open and burning and her tongue was a darting snake between her teeth.

The door opened and Mr. Grayle stepped quietly into the room. I was holding her and didn't have a chance to let go. I lifted my face and looked at him. I felt as cold as Finnegan's feet, the day they buried him.

The blonde in my arms didn't move, didn't even close her lips. She had a half-dreamy, half-sarcastic expression on her face.

Mr. Grayle cleared his throat slightly and said: "I beg your pardon, I'm sure," and went quietly out of the room. There was an infinite sadness in his eyes.

I pushed her away and stood up and got my handkerchief out and mopped my face.

She lay as I had left her, half sideways along the davenport, the skin showing in a generous sweep above one stocking.

"Who was that?" she asked thickly.

"Mr. Grayle."

"Forget him."

I went away from her and sat down in the chair I had sat in when I first came into the room.

After a moment she straightened herself out and sat up and looked at me steadily.

"It's all right. He understands. What the hell can he expect?"

"I guess he knows."

"Well, I tell you it's all right. Isn't that enough? He's a sick man. What the hell—"

"Don't go shrill on me. I don't like shrill women."

She opened a bag lying beside her and took out a small handkerchief and wiped her lips, then looked at her face in a mirror.

"I guess you're right," she said. "Just too much Scotch.

Tonight at the Belvedere Club. Ten o'clock." She wasn't looking at me. Her breath was fast.

"Is that a good place?"

"Laird Brunette owns it. I know him pretty well."

"Right," I said. I was still cold. I felt nasty, as if I had picked a poor man's pocket.

She got a lipstick out and touched her lips very lightly and then looked at me along her eyes. She tossed the mirror. I caught it and looked at my face. I worked at it with my handkerchief and stood up to give her back the mirror.

She was leaning back, showing all her throat, looking at me lazily down her eyes.

"What's the matter?"

"Nothing. Ten o'clock at the Belvedere Club. Don't be too magnificent. All I have is a dinner suit. In the bar?"

She nodded, her eyes still lazy.

I went across the room and out, without looking back. The footman met me in the hall and gave me my hat, looking like the Great Stone Face.

19

I walked down the curving driveway and lost myself in the shadow of the tall trimmed hedges and came to the gates. Another man was holding the fort now, a husky in plainclothes, an obvious bodyguard. He let me out with a nod.

A horn tooted. Miss Riordan's coupe was drawn up behind my car. I went over there and looked in at her. She looked cool and sarcastic.

She sat there with her hands on the wheel, gloved and slim. She smiled.

"I waited. I suppose it was none of my business. What did you think of her?"

"I bet she snaps a mean garter."

"Do you always have to say things like that?" She flushed bitterly. "Sometimes I hate men. Old men, young men, football players, opera tenors, smart millionaires, beautiful men who are gigolos and almost-heels who are—private detectives."

I grinned at her sadly. "I know I talk too smart. It's in the air nowadays. Who told you he was a gigolo?"

"Who?"

"Don't be obtuse. Marriott."

"Oh, it was a cinch guess. I'm sorry. I don't mean to be nasty. I guess you can snap her garter any time you want to, without much of a struggle. But there's one thing you can be sure of—you're a late comer to the show."

The wide curving street dozed peacefully in the sun. A beautifully painted panel truck slid noiselessly to a stop before a house across the street, then backed a little and went up the driveway to a side entrance. On the side of the panel truck was painted the legend: "Bay City Infant Service."

Anne Riordan leaned towards me, her gray-blue eyes hurt and clouded. Her slightly too long upper lip pouted and then pressed back against her teeth. She made a sharp little sound with her breath.

"Probably you'd like me to mind my own business, is that it? And not have ideas you don't have first. I thought I was helping a little."

"I don't need any help. The police don't want any from me. There's nothing I can do for Mrs. Grayle. She has a yarn about a beer parlor where a car started from and followed them, but what does that amount to? It was a crummy dive on Santa Monica. This was a high class mob. There was somebody in it that could even tell Fei Tsui jade when he saw it."

"If he wasn't tipped off."

"There's that too," I said, and fumbled a cigarette out of a package. "Either way there's nothing for me in it."

"Not even about psychics?"

I stared rather blankly. "Psychics?"

"My God," she said softly. "And I thought you were a detective."

"There's a hush on part of this," I said. "I've got to watch my step. This Grayle packs a lot of dough in his pants. And law is where you buy it in this town. Look at the funny way the cops are acting. No build-up, no newspaper handout, no chance for the innocent stranger to step in with the trifling clue that turns out to be all important. Nothing but silence and warnings to me to lay off. I don't like it at all."

"You got most of the lipstick off," Anne Riordan said. "I mentioned psychics. Well, good-by. It was nice to know you—in a way."

She pressed her starter button and jammed her gears in and was gone in a swirl of dust.

I watched her go. When she was gone I looked across the street. The man from the panel truck that said Bay City Infant Service came out of the side door of the house dressed in a uniform so white and stiff and gleaming that it made me feel clean just to look at it. He was carrying a carton of some sort. He got into his panel truck and drove away.

I figured he had just changed a diaper.

I got into my own car and looked at my watch before starting up. It was almost five.

The Scotch, as good enough Scotch will, stayed with me all the way back to Hollywood. I took the red lights as they came.

"There's a nice little girl," I told myself out loud, in the car, "for a guy that's interested in a nice little girl." Nobody said anything. "But I'm not," I said. Nobody said anything to that either. "Ten o'clock at the Belvedere Club," I said. Somebody said: "Phooey."

It sounded like my voice.

It was a quarter to six when I reached my office again. The building was very quiet. The typewriter beyond the party wall was still. I lit a pipe and sat down to wait.

20

The Indian smelled. He smelled clear across the little reception room when the buzzer sounded and I opened the door between to see who it was. He stood just inside the corridor door looking as if he had been cast in bronze. He was a big

man from the waist up and he had a big chest. He looked like
a bum.

He wore a brown suit of which the coat was too small for
his shoulders and his trousers were probably a little tight at
the waist. His hat was at least two sizes too small and had
been perspired in freely by somebody it fitted better than it
fitted him. He wore it about where a house wears a wind
vane. His collar had the snug fit of a horse-collar and was of
about the same shade of dirty brown. A tie dangled outside
his buttoned jacket, a black tie which had been tied with a
pair of pliers in a knot the size of a pea. Around his bare and
magnificent throat, above the dirty collar, he wore a wide
piece of black ribbon, like an old woman trying to freshen up
her neck.

He had a big flat face and a highbridged fleshy nose that
looked as hard as the prow of a cruiser. He had lidless eyes,
drooping jowls, the shoulders of a blacksmith and the short
and apparently awkward legs of a chimpanzee. I found out
later that they were only short.

If he had been cleaned up a little and dressed in a white
nightgown, he would have looked like a very wicked Roman
senator.

His smell was the earthy smell of primitive man, and not
the slimy dirt of cities.

"Huh," he said. "Come quick. Come now."

I backed into my office and wiggled my finger at him and
he followed me making as much noise as a fly makes walking
on the wall. I sat down behind my desk and squeaked my
swivel chair professionally and pointed to the customer's chair
on the other side. He didn't sit down. His small black eyes
were hostile.

"Come where?" I said.

"Huh. Me Second Planting. Me Hollywood Indian."

"Have a chair, Mr. Planting."

He snorted and his nostrils got very wide. They had been
wide enough for mouseholes to start with.

"Name Second Planting. Name no Mister Planting."

"What can I do for you?"

He lifted his voice and began to intone in a deep-chested

sonorous boom. "He say come quick. Great white father say come quick. He say me bring you in fiery chariot. He say—"

"Yeah. Cut out the pig Latin," I said. "I'm no schoolmarm at the snake dances."

"Nuts," the Indian said.

We sneered at each other across the desk for a moment. He sneered better than I did. Then he removed his hat with massive disgust and turned it upside down. He rolled a finger around under the sweatband. That turned the sweatband up into view, and it had not been misnamed. He removed a paper clip from the edge and threw a fold of tissue paper on the desk. He pointed at it angrily, with a well-chewed fingernail. His lank hair had a shelf around it, high up, from the too-tight hat.

I unfolded the piece of tissue paper and found a card inside. The card was no news to me. There had been three exactly like it in the mouthpieces of three Russian-appearing cigarettes.

I played with my pipe, stared at the Indian and tried to ride him with my stare. He looked as nervous as a brick wall.

"Okey, what does he want?"

"He want you come quick. Come now. Come in fiery—"

"Nuts," I said.

The Indian liked that. He closed his mouth slowly and winked an eye solemnly and then almost grinned.

"Also it will cost him a hundred bucks as a retainer," I added, trying to look as if that was a nickel.

"Huh?" Suspicious again. Stick to basic English.

"Hundred dollars," I said. "Iron men. Fish. Bucks to the number of one hundred. Me no money, me no come. Savvy?" I began to count a hundred with both hands.

"Huh. Big shot," the Indian sneered.

He worked under his greasy hatband and threw another fold of tissue paper on the desk. I took it and unwound it. It contained a brand new hundred dollar bill.

The Indian put his hat back on his head without bothering to tuck the hatband back in place. It looked only slightly more comic that way. I sat staring at the hundred dollar bill, with my mouth open.

"Psychic is right," I said at last. "A guy that smart I'm afraid of."

"Not got all day," the Indian remarked, conversationally.

I opened my desk and took out a Colt .38 automatic of the type known as Super Match. I hadn't worn it to visit Mrs. Lewin Lockridge Grayle. I stripped my coat off and strapped the leather harness on and tucked the automatic down inside it and strapped the lower strap and put my coat back on again.

This meant as much to the Indian as if I had scratched my neck.

"Gottum car," he said. "Big car."

"I don't like big cars any more," I said. "I gottum own car."

"You come my car," the Indian said threateningly.

"I come your car," I said.

I locked the desk and office up, switched the buzzer off and went out, leaving the reception room door unlocked as usual.

We went along the hall and down in the elevator. The Indian smelled. Even the elevator operator noticed it.

21

The car was a dark blue seven-passenger sedan, a Packard of the latest model, custom-built. It was the kind of car you wear your rope pearls in. It was parked by a fire-hydrant and a dark foreign-looking chauffeur with a face of carved wood was behind the wheel. The interior was upholstered in quilted gray chenille. The Indian put me in the back. Sitting there alone I felt like a high-class corpse, laid out by an undertaker with a lot of good taste.

The Indian got in beside the chauffeur and the car turned in the middle of the block and a cop across the street said: "Hey," weakly, as if he didn't mean it, and then bent down quickly to tie his shoe.

We went west, dropped over to Sunset and slid fast and noiseless along that. The Indian sat motionless beside the chauffeur. An occasional whiff of his personality drifted back to me. The driver looked as if he was half asleep but he passed the fast boys in the convertible sedans as though they were being towed. They turned on all the green lights for him. Some drivers are like that. He never missed one.

We curved through the bright mile or two of the Strip, past the antique shops with famous screen names on them, past the windows full of point lace and ancient pewter, past the gleaming new nightclubs with famous chefs and equally famous gambling rooms, run by polished graduates of the Purple Gang, past the Georgian-Colonial vogue, now old hat, past the handsome modernistic buildings in which the Hollywood flesh-peddlers never stop talking money, past a drive-in lunch which somehow didn't belong, even though the girls wore white silk blouses and drum majorettes' shakos and nothing below the hips but glazed kid Hessian boots. Past all this and down a wide smooth curve to the bridle path of Beverly Hills and lights to the south, all colors of the spectrum and crystal clear in an evening without fog, past the shadowed mansions up on the hills to the north, past Beverly Hills altogether and up into the twisting foothill boulevard and the sudden cool dusk and the drift of wind from the sea.

It had been a warm afternoon, but the heat was gone. We whipped past a distant cluster of lighted buildings and an endless series of lighted mansions, not too close to the road. We dipped down to skirt a huge green polo field with another equally huge practice field beside it, soared again to the top of a hill and swung mountainward up a steep hillroad of clean concrete that passed orange groves, some rich man's pet because this is not orange country, and then little by little the lighted windows of the millionaires' homes were gone and the road narrowed and this was Stillwood Heights.

The smell of sage drifted up from a canyon and made me think of a dead man and a moonless sky. Straggly stucco houses were molded flat to the side of the hill, like bas-reliefs. Then there were no more houses, just the still dark foothills with an early star or two above them, and the concrete ribbon of road and a sheer drop on one side into a tangle of scrub oak and manzanita where sometimes you can hear the call of the quails if you stop and keep still and wait. On the other side of the road was a raw clay bank at the edge of which a few unbeatable wild flowers hung on like naughty children that won't go to bed.

Then the road twisted into a hairpin turn and the big tires scratched over loose stones, and the car tore less soundlessly up a long driveway lined with the wild geraniums. At the top of this, faintly lighted, lonely as a lighthouse, stood an eyrie, an eagle's nest, an angular building of stucco and glass brick, raw and modernistic and yet not ugly and altogether a swell place for a psychic consultant to hang out his shingle. Nobody would be able to hear any screams.

The car turned beside the house and a light flicked on over a black door set into the heavy wall. The Indian climbed out grunting and opened the rear door of the car. The chauffeur lit a cigarette with an electric lighter and a harsh smell of tobacco came back to me softly in the evening. I got out.

We went over to the black door. It opened of itself, slowly, almost with menace. Beyond it a narrow hallway probed back into the house. Light glowed from the glass brick walls.

The Indian growled, "Huh. You go in, big shot."

"After you, Mr. Planting."

He scowled and went in and the door closed after us as silently and mysteriously as it had opened. At the end of the narrow hallway we squeezed into a little elevator and the Indian closed the door and pressed a button. We rose softly, without sound. Such smelling as the Indian had done before was a mooncast shadow to what he was doing now.

The elevator stopped, the door opened. There was light and I stepped out into a turret room where the day was still trying to be remembered. There were windows all around it. Far off the sea flickered. Darkness prowled slowly on the hills. There were paneled walls where there were no windows, and rugs on the floor with the soft colors of old Persians, and there was a reception desk that looked as if it had been made of carvings stolen from an ancient church. And behind the desk a woman sat and smiled at me, a dry tight withered smile that would turn to powder if you touched it.

She had sleek coiled hair and a dark, thin, wasted Asiatic face. There were heavy colored stones in her ears and heavy rings on her fingers, including a moonstone and an emerald in a silver setting that may have been a real emerald but somehow managed to look as phony as a dime store slave bracelet. And her hands were dry and dark and not young and not fit for rings.

She spoke. The voice was familiar. "Ah, Meester Marlowe, so ver-ry good of you to come. Amthor he weel be so ver-ry pleased."

I laid the hundred dollar bill the Indian had given me down on the desk. I looked behind me. The Indian had gone down again in the elevator.

"Sorry. It was a nice thought, but I can't take this."

"Amthor he—he weesh to employ you, is it not?" She smiled again. Her lips rustled like tissue paper.

"I'd have to find out what the job is first."

She nodded and got up slowly from behind the desk. She swished before me in a tight dress that fitted her like a mermaid's skin and showed that she had a good figure if you like them four sizes bigger below the waist.

"I weel conduct you," she said.

She pressed a button in the panelling and a door slid open noiselessly. There was a milky glow beyond it. I looked back at her smile before I went through. It was older than Egypt now. The door slid silently shut behind me.

There was nobody in the room.

It was octagonal, draped in black velvet from floor to ceiling, with a high remote black ceiling that may have been of velvet too. In the middle of a coal black lustreless rug stood an octagonal white table, just large enough for two pairs of elbows and in the middle of it a milk white globe on a black stand. The light came from this. How, I couldn't see. On either side of the table there was a white octagonal stool which was a smaller edition of the table. Over against one wall there was one more such stool. There were no windows. There was nothing else in the room, nothing at all. On the walls there was not even a light fixture. If there were other doors, I didn't see them. I looked back at the one by which I had come in. I couldn't see that either.

I stood there for perhaps fifteen seconds with the faint obscure feeling of being watched. There was probably a peephole somewhere, but I couldn't spot it. I gave up trying. I listened to my breath. The room was so still that I could hear it going through my nose, softly, like little curtains rustling.

Then an invisible door on the far side of the room slid open and a man stepped through and the door closed behind him. The man walked straight to the table with his head down and sat on one of the octagonal stools and made a sweeping motion with one of the most beautiful hands I have ever seen.

"Please be seated. Opposite me. Do not smoke and do not fidget. Try to relax, completely. Now how may I serve you?"

I sat down, got a cigarette into my mouth and rolled it along my lips without lighting it. I looked him over. He was thin, tall and straight as a steel rod. He had the palest finest white hair I ever saw. It could have been strained through silk gauze. His skin was as fresh as a rose petal. He might have been thirty-five or sixty-five. He was ageless. His hair was brushed straight back from as good a profile as Barrymore ever had. His eyebrows were coal black, like the walls and ceiling and floor. His eyes were deep, far too deep. They were the depthless drugged eyes of the somnambulist. They were like a well I read about once. It was nine hundred years old, in an old castle. You could drop a stone into it and wait. You could listen and wait and then you would give up waiting and laugh and then just as you were ready to turn away a faint, minute splash would come back up to you from the bottom of that well, so tiny, so remote that you could hardly believe a well like that possible.

His eyes were deep like that. And they were also eyes without expression, without soul, eyes that could watch lions tear a man to pieces and never change, that could watch a man impaled and screaming in the hot sun with his eyelids cut off.

He wore a double-breasted black business suit that had been cut by an artist. He stared vaguely at my fingers.

"Please do not fidget," he said. "It breaks the waves, disturbs my concentration."

"It makes the ice melt, the butter run and the cat squawk," I said.

He smiled the faintest smile in the world. "You didn't come here to be impertinent, I'm sure."

"You seem to forget why I did come. By the way, I gave that hundred dollar bill back to your secretary. I came, as you may recall, about some cigarettes. Russian cigarettes filled with marihuana. With your card rolled in the hollow mouthpieces."

"You wish to find out why that happened?"

"Yeah. I ought to be paying you the hundred dollars."

"That will not be necessary. The answer is simple. There are things I do not know. This is one of them."

For a moment I almost believed him. His face was as smooth as an angel's wing.

"Then why send me a hundred dollars—and a tough Indian that stinks—and a car? By the way, does the Indian have to stink? If he's working for you, couldn't you sort of get him to take a bath?"

"He is a natural medium. They are rare—like diamonds, and like diamonds, are sometimes found in dirty places. I understand you are a private detective?"

"Yes."

"I think you are a very stupid person. You look stupid. You are in a stupid business. And you came here on a stupid mission."

"I get it," I said. "I'm stupid. It sank in after a while."

"And I think I need not detain you any longer."

"You're not detaining me," I said. "I'm detaining you. I want to know why those cards were in those cigarettes."

He shrugged the smallest shrug that could be shrugged. "My cards are available to anybody. I do not give my friends marihuana cigarettes. Your question remains stupid."

"I wonder if this would brighten it up any. The cigarettes were in a cheap Chinese or Japanese case of imitation tortoiseshell. Ever see anything like that?"

"No. Not that I recall."

"I can brighten it up a little more. The case was in the pocket of a man named Lindsay Marriott. Ever hear of him?"

He thought. "Yes. I tried at one time to treat him for camera shyness. He was trying to get into pictures. It was a waste of time. Pictures did not want him."

"I can guess that," I said. "He would photograph like Isadora Duncan. I've still got the big one left. Why did you send me the C-note."

"My dear Mr. Marlowe," he said coldly, "I am no fool. I

am in a very sensitive profession. I am a quack. That is to say I do things which the doctors in their small frightened selfish guild cannot accomplish. I am in danger at all times—from people like you. I merely wish to estimate the danger before dealing with it."

"Pretty trivial in my case, huh?"

"It hardly exists," he said politely and made a peculiar motion with his left hand which made my eyes jump at it. Then he put it down very slowly on the white table and looked down at it. Then he raised his depthless eyes again and folded his arms.

"Your hearing—"

"I smell it now," I said. "I wasn't thinking of him."

I turned my head to the left. The Indian was sitting on the third white stool against the black velvet.

He had some kind of a white smock on him over his other clothes. He was sitting without a movement, his eyes closed, his head bent forward a little, as if he had been asleep for an hour. His dark strong face was full of shadows.

I looked back at Amthor. He was smiling his minute smile.

"I bet that makes the dowagers shed their false teeth," I said. "What does he do for real money—sit on your knee and sing French songs?"

He made an impatient gesture. "Get to the point, please."

"Last night Marriott hired me to go with him on an expedition that involved paying some money to some crooks at a spot they picked. I got knocked on the head. When I came out of it Marriott had been murdered."

Nothing changed much in Amthor's face. He didn't scream or run up the walls. But for him the reaction was sharp. He unfolded his arms and refolded them the other way. His mouth looked grim. Then he sat like a stone lion outside the Public Library.

"The cigarettes were found on him," I said.

He looked at me coolly. "But not by the police, I take it. Since the police have not been here."

"Correct."

"The hundred dollars," he said very softly, "was hardly enough."

"That depends what you expect to buy with it."

"You have these cigarettes with you?"

"One of them. But they don't prove anything. As you said, anybody could get your cards. I'm just wondering why they were where they were. Any ideas?"

"How well did you know Mr. Marriott?" he asked softly.

"Not at all. But I had ideas about him. They were so obvious they stuck out."

Amthor tapped lightly on the white table. The Indian still slept with his chin on his huge chest, his heavy-lidded eyes tight shut.

"By the way, did you ever meet a Mrs. Grayle, a wealthy lady who lives in Bay City?"

He nodded absently. "Yes, I treated her centers of speech. She had a very slight impediment."

"You did a sweet job on her," I said. "She talks as good as I do now."

That failed to amuse him. He still tapped on the table. I listened to the taps. Something about them I didn't like. They sounded like a code. He stopped, folded his arms again and leaned back against the air.

"What I like about this job everybody knows everybody," I said. "Mrs. Grayle knew Marriott too."

"How did you find that out?" he asked slowly.

I didn't say anything.

"You will have to tell the police—about those cigarettes," he said.

I shrugged.

"You are wondering why I do not have you thrown out," Amthor said pleasantly. "Second Planting could break your neck like a celery stalk. I am wondering myself. You seem to have some sort of theory. Blackmail I do not pay. It buys nothing—and I have many friends. But naturally there are certain elements which would like to show me in a bad light. Psychiatrists, sex specialists, neurologists, nasty little men with rubber hammers and shelves loaded with the literature of aberrations. And of course they are all—doctors. While I am still a—quack. What is your theory?"

I tried to stare him down, but it couldn't be done. I felt myself licking my lips.

He shrugged lightly. "I can't blame you for wanting to

keep it to yourself. This is a matter that I must give thought to. Perhaps you are a much more intelligent man than I thought. I also make mistakes. In the meantime—" He leaned forward and put a hand on each side of the milky globe.

"I think Marriott was a blackmailer of women," I said. "And finger man for a jewel mob. But who told him what women to cultivate—so that he would know their comings and goings, get intimate with them, make love to them, make them load up with the ice and take them out, and then slip to a phone and tell the boys where to operate?"

"That," Amthor said carefully, "is your picture of Marriott—and of me. I am slightly disgusted."

I leaned forward until my face was not more than a foot from his. "You're in a racket. Dress it up all you please and it's still a racket. And it wasn't just the cards, Amthor. As you say, anybody could get those. It wasn't the marihuana. You wouldn't be in a cheap line like that—not with your chances. But on the back of each card there is a blank space. And on blank spaces, or even on written ones, there is sometimes invisible writing."

He smiled bleakly, but I hardly saw it. His hands moved over the milky bowl.

The light went out. The room was as black as Carry Nation's bonnet.

22

I kicked my stool back and stood up and jerked the gun out of the holster under my arm. But it was no good. My coat was buttoned and I was too slow. I'd have been too slow anyway, if it came to shooting anybody.

There was a soundless rush of air and an earthy smell. In the complete darkness the Indian hit me from behind and pinned my arms to my sides. He started to lift me. I could have got the gun out still and fanned the room with blind shots, but I was a long way from friends. It didn't seem as if there was any point in it.

I let go of the gun and took hold of his wrists. They were greasy and hard to hold. The Indian breathed gutturally and set me down with a jar that lifted the top of my head. He had my wrists now, instead of me having his. He twisted them behind me fast and a knee like a corner stone went into my back. He bent me. I can be bent. I'm not the City Hall. He bent me.

I tried to yell, for no reason at all. Breath panted in my throat and couldn't get out. The Indian threw me sideways and got a body scissors on me as I fell. He had me in a barrel. His hands went to my neck. Sometimes I wake up in the night. I feel them there and I smell the smell of him. I feel the breath fighting and losing and the greasy fingers digging in. Then I get up and take a drink and turn the radio on.

I was just about gone when the light flared on again, blood red, on account of the blood in my eyeballs and at the back of them. A face floated around and a hand pawed me delicately, but the other hands stayed on my throat.

A voice said softly, "Let him breathe—a little."

The fingers slackened. I wrenched loose from them. Something that glinted hit me on the side of the jaw.

The voice said softly: "Get him on his feet."

The Indian got me on my feet. He pulled me back against the wall, holding me by both twisted wrists.

"Amateur," the voice said softly and the shiny thing that was as hard and bitter as death hit me again, across the face. Something warm trickled. I licked at it and tasted iron and salt.

A hand explored my wallet. A hand explored all my pockets. The cigarette in tissue paper came out and was unwrapped. It went somewhere in the haze that was in front of me.

"There were three cigarettes?" the voice said gently, and the shining thing hit my jaw again.

"Three," I gulped.

"Just where did you say the others were?"

"In my desk—at the office."

The shiny thing hit me again. "You are probably lying—but I can find out." Keys shone with funny little red lights in front of me. The voice said: "Choke him a little more."

The iron fingers went into my throat. I was strained back against him, against the smell of him and the hard muscles of his stomach. I reached up and took one of his fingers and tried to twist it.

The voice said softly: "Amazing. He's learning."

The glinting thing swayed through the air again. It smacked my jaw, the thing that had once been my jaw.

"Let him go. He's tame," the voice said.

The heavy strong arms dropped away and I swayed forward and took a step and steadied myself. Amthor stood smiling very slightly, almost dreamily in front of me. He held my gun in his delicate, lovely hand. He held it pointed at my chest.

"I could teach you," he said in his soft voice. "But to what purpose? A dirty little man in a dirty little world. One spot of brightness on you and you would still be that. Is it not so?" He smiled, so beautifully.

I swung at his smile with everything I had left.

It wasn't so bad considering. He reeled and blood came out of both his nostrils. Then he caught himself and straightened up and lifted the gun again.

"Sit down, my child," he said softly. "I have visitors coming. I am so glad you hit me. It helps a great deal."

I felt for the white stool and sat down and put my head down on the white table beside the milky globe which was now shining again softly. I stared at it sideways, my face on the table. The light fascinated me. Nice light, nice soft light.

Behind me and around me there was nothing but silence.

I think I went to sleep, just like that, with a bloody face on the table, and a thin beautiful devil with my gun in his hand watching me and smiling.

23

"All right," the big one said. "You can quit stalling now."

I opened my eyes and sat up.

"Out in the other room, pally."

I stood up, still dreamy. We went somewhere, through a

door. Then I saw where it was—the reception room with the windows all around. It was black dark now outside.

The woman with the wrong rings sat at her desk. A man stood beside her.

"Sit here, pally."

He pushed me down. It was a nice chair, straight but comfortable but I wasn't in the mood for it. The woman behind the desk had a notebook open and was reading out loud from it. A short elderly man with a deadpan expression and a gray mustache was listening to her.

Amthor was standing by a window, with his back to the room, looking out at the placid line of the ocean, far off, beyond the pier lights, beyond the world. He looked at it as if he loved it. He half turned his head to look at me once, and I could see that the blood had been washed off his face, but his nose wasn't the nose I had first met, not by two sizes. That made me grin, cracked lips and all.

"You got fun, pally?"

I looked at what made the sound, what was in front of me and what had helped me get where I was. He was a wind-blown blossom of some two hundred pounds with freckled teeth and the mellow voice of a circus barker. He was tough, fast and he ate red meat. Nobody could push him around. He was the kind of cop who spits on his blackjack every night instead of saying his prayers. But he had humorous eyes.

He stood in front of me splay-legged, holding my open wallet in his hand, making scratches on the leather with his right thumbnail, as if he just liked to spoil things. Little things, if they were all he had. But probably faces would give him more fun.

"Peeper, huh, pally? From the big bad burg, huh? Little spot of blackmail, huh?"

His hat was on the back of his head. He had dusty brown hair darkened by sweat on his forehead. His humorous eyes were flecked with red veins.

My throat felt as though it had been through a mangle. I reached up and felt it. That Indian. He had fingers like pieces of tool steel.

The dark woman stopped reading out of her notebook and

closed it. The elderly smallish man with the gray mustache nodded and came over to stand behind the one who was talking to me.

"Cops?" I asked, rubbing my chin.

"What do *you* think, pally?"

Policeman's humor. The small one had a cast in one eye, and it looked half blind.

"Not L.A.," I said, looking at him. "That eye would retire him in Los Angeles."

The big man handed me my wallet. I looked through it. It had all the money still. All the cards. It had everything that belonged in it. I was surprised.

"Say something, pally," the big one said. "Something that would make us get fond of you."

"Give me back my gun."

He leaned forward a little and thought. I could see him thinking. It hurt his corns. "Oh, you want your gun, pally?" He looked sideways at the one with the gray mustache. "He wants his gun," he told him. He looked at me again. "And what would you want your gun for, pally?"

"I want to shoot an Indian."

"Oh, you want to shoot an Indian, pally."

"Yeah—just one Indian, pop."

He looked at the one with the mustache again. "This guy is very tough," he told him. "He wants to shoot an Indian."

"Listen, Hemingway, don't repeat everything I say," I said.

"I think the guy is nuts," the big one said. "He just called me Hemingway. Do you think he is nuts?"

The one with the mustache bit a cigar and said nothing. The tall beautiful man at the window turned slowly and said softly: "I think possibly he is a little unbalanced."

"I can't think of any reason why he should call me Hemingway," the big one said. "My name ain't Hemingway."

The older man said: "I didn't see a gun."

They looked at Amthor. Amthor said: "It's inside. I have it. I'll give it to you, Mr. Blane."

The big man leaned down from his hips and bent his knees a little and breathed in my face. "What for did you call me Hemingway, pally?"

"There are ladies present.

"He straightened up again. "You see." He looked at the one with the mustache. The one with the mustache nodded and then turned and walked away, across the room. The sliding door opened. He went in and Amthor followed him.

There was silence. The dark woman looked down at the top of her desk and frowned. The big man looked at my right eyebrow and slowly shook his head from side to side, wonderingly.

The door opened again and the man with the mustache came back. He picked a hat up from somewhere and handed it to me. He took my gun out of his pocket and handed it to me. I knew by the weight it was empty. I tucked it under my arm and stood up.

The big man said: "Let's go, pally. Away from here. I think maybe a little air will help you to get straightened out."

"Okey, Hemingway."

"He's doing that again," the big man said sadly. "Calling me Hemingway on account of there are ladies present. Would you think that would be some kind of dirty crack in his book?"

The man with the mustache said, "Hurry up."

The big man took me by the arm and we went over to the little elevator. It came up. We got into it.

24

At the bottom of the shaft we got out and walked along the narrow hallway and out of the black door. It was crisp clear air outside, high enough to be above the drift of foggy spray from the ocean. I breathed deeply.

The big man still had hold of my arm. There was a car standing there, a plain dark sedan, with private plates.

The big man opened the front door and complained: "It ain't really up to your class, pally. But a little air will set you up fine. Would that be all right with you? We wouldn't want to do anything that you wouldn't like us to do, pally."

"Where's the Indian?"

He shook his head a little and pushed me into the car. I got into the right side of the front seat. "Oh, yeah, the Indian," he said. "You got to shoot him with a bow and arrow. That's the law. We got him in the back of the car."

I looked in the back of the car. It was empty.

"Hell, he ain't there," the big one said. "Somebody must of glommed him off. You can't leave nothing in a unlocked car any more."

"Hurry up," the man with the mustache said, and got into the back seat. Hemingway went around and pushed his hard stomach behind the wheel. He started the car. We turned and drifted off down the driveway lined with wild geraniums. A cold wind lifted off the sea. The stars were too far off. They said nothing.

We reached the bottom of the drive and turned out onto the concrete mountain road and drifted without haste along that.

"How come you don't have a car with you, pally?"

"Amthor sent for me."

"Why would that be, pally?"

"It must have been he wanted to see me."

"This guy is good," Hemingway said. "He figures things out." He spit out of the side of the car and made a turn nicely and let the car ride its motor down the hill. "He says you called him up on the phone and tried to put the bite on him. So he figures he better have a look-see what kind of guy he is doing business with—if he is doing business. So he sends his own car."

"On account of he knows he is going to call some cops he knows and I won't need mine to get home with," I said. "Okey, Hemingway."

"Yeah, that again. Okey. Well, he has a dictaphone under his table and his secretary takes it all down and when we come she reads it back to Mister Blane here."

I turned and looked at Mister Blane. He was smoking a cigar, peacefully, as though he had his slippers on. He didn't look at me.

"Like hell she did," I said. "More likely a stock bunch of notes they had all fixed up for a case like that."

"Maybe you would like to tell us why you wanted to see this guy," Hemingway suggested politely.

"You mean while I still have part of my face?"

"Aw, we ain't those kind of boys at all," he said, with a large gesture.

"You know Amthor pretty well, don't you, Hemingway?"

"Mr. Blane kind of knows him. Me, I just do what the orders is."

"Who the hell is Mister Blane?"

"That's the gentleman in the back seat."

"And besides being in the back seat who the hell is he?"

"Why, Jesus, everybody knows Mr. Blane."

"All right," I said, suddenly feeling very weary.

There was a little more silence, more curves, more winding ribbons of concrete, more darkness, and more pain.

The big man said: "Now that we are all between pals and no ladies present we really don't give so much time to why you went back up there, but this Hemingway stuff is what really has me down."

"A gag," I said. "An old, old gag."

"Who is this Hemingway person at all?"

"A guy that keeps saying the same thing over and over until you begin to believe it must be good."

"That must take a hell of a long time," the big man said. "For a private dick you certainly have a wandering kind of mind. Are you still wearing your own teeth?"

"Yeah, with a few plugs in them."

"Well, you certainly have been lucky, pally."

The man in the back seat said: "This is all right. Turn right at the next."

"Check."

Hemingway swung the sedan into a narrow dirt road that edged along the flank of a mountain. We drove along that about a mile. The smell of the sage became overpowering.

"Here," the man in the back seat said.

Hemingway stopped the car and set the brake. He leaned across me and opened the door.

"Well, it's nice to have met you, pally. But don't come back. Anyways not on business. Out."

"I walk home from here?"

The man in the back seat said: "Hurry up."

"Yeah, you walk home from here, pally. Will that be all right with you?"

"Sure, it will give me time to think a few things out. For instance you boys are not L.A. cops. But one of you is a cop, maybe both of you. I'd say you are Bay City cops. I'm wondering why you were out of your territory."

"Ain't that going to be kind of hard to prove, pally?"

"Goodnight, Hemingway."

He didn't answer. Neither of them spoke. I started to get out of the car and put my foot on the running board and leaned forward, still a little dizzy.

The man in the back seat made a sudden flashing movement that I sensed rather than saw. A pool of darkness opened at my feet and was far, far deeper than the blackest night.

I dived into it. It had no bottom.

25

The room was full of smoke.

The smoke hung straight up in the air, in thin lines, straight up and down like a curtain of small clear beads. Two windows seemed to be open in an end wall, but the smoke didn't move. I had never seen the room before. There were bars across the windows.

I was dull, without thought. I felt as if I had slept for a year. But the smoke bothered me. I lay on my back and thought about it. After a long time I took a deep breath that hurt my lungs.

I yelled: "Fire!"

That made me laugh. I didn't know what was funny about it but I began to laugh. I lay there on the bed and laughed. I didn't like the sound of the laugh. It was the laugh of a nut.

The one yell was enough. Steps thumped rapidly outside the room and a key was jammed into a lock and the door swung open. A man jumped in sideways and shut the door after him. His right hand reached towards his hip.

He was a short thick man in a white coat. His eyes had a queer look, black and flat. There were bulbs of gray skin at the outer corners of them.

I turned my head on the hard pillow and yawned.

"Don't count that one, Jack. It slipped out," I said.

He stood there scowling, his right hand hovering towards his right hip. Greenish malignant face and flat black eyes and gray white skin and nose that seemed just a shell.

"Maybe you want some more strait-jacket," he sneered.

"I'm fine, Jack. Just fine. Had a long nap. Dreamed a little, I guess. Where am I?"

"Where you belong."

"Seems like a nice place," I said. "Nice people, nice atmosphere. I guess I'll have me a short nap again."

"Better be just that," he snarled.

He went out. The door shut. The lock clicked. The steps growled into nothing.

He hadn't done the smoke any good. It still hung there in the middle of the room, all across the room. Like a curtain. It didn't dissolve, didn't float off, didn't move. There was air in the room, and I could feel it on my face. But the smoke couldn't feel it. It was a gray web woven by a thousand spiders. I wondered how they had got them to work together.

Cotton flannel pajamas. The kind they have in the County Hospital. No front, not a stitch more than is essential. Coarse, rough material. The neck chafed my throat. My throat was still sore. I began to remember things. I reached up and felt the throat muscles. They were still sore. Just one Indian, pop. Okey, Hemingway. So you want to be a detective? Earn good money. Nine easy lessons. We provide badge. For fifty cents extra we send you a truss.

The throat felt sore but the fingers feeling it didn't feel anything. They might just as well have been a bunch of bananas. I looked at them. They looked like fingers. No good. Mail order fingers. They must have come with the badge and the truss. And the diploma.

It was night. The world outside the windows was a black world. A glass porcelain bowl hung from the middle of the ceiling on three brass chains. There was light in it. It had little colored lumps around the edge, orange and blue alternately. I stared at them. I was tired of the smoke. As I stared they began to open up like little portholes and heads popped out. Tiny heads, but alive, heads like the heads of small dolls, but alive. There was a man in a yachting cap with a Johnnie Walker nose and a fluffy blonde in a picture hat and a thin man with a crooked bow tie. He looked like a waiter in a beachtown flytrap. He opened his lips and sneered: "Would you like your steak rare or medium, sir?"

I closed my eyes tight and winked them hard and when I opened them again it was just a sham porcelain bowl on three brass chains.

But the smoke still hung motionless in the moving air.

I took hold of the corner of a rough sheet and wiped the sweat off my face with the numb fingers the correspondence school had sent me after the nine easy lessons, one half in advance, Box Two Million Four Hundred and Sixty Eight Thousand Nine Hundred and Twenty Four, Cedar City, Iowa. Nuts. Completely nuts.

I sat up on the bed and after a while I could reach the floor with my feet. They were bare and they had pins and needles in them. Notions counter on the left, madam. Extra large safety pins on the right. The feet began to feel the floor. I stood up. Too far up. I crouched over, breathing hard and held the side of the bed and a voice that seemed to come from under the bed said over and over again: "You've got the dt's . . . you've got the dt's . . . you've got the dt's."

I started to walk, wobbling like a drunk. There was a bottle of whiskey on a small white enamel table between the two barred windows. It looked like a good shape. It looked about half full. I walked towards it. There are a lot of nice people in the world, in spite. You can crab over the morning paper and kick the shins of the guy in the next seat at the movies and feel mean and discouraged and sneer at the politicians, but there are a lot of nice people in the world just the same. Take the guy that left that half bottle of whiskey there. He had a heart as big as one of Mae West's hips.

I reached it and put both my still half-numb hands down on it and hauled it up to my mouth, sweating as if I was lifting one end of the Golden Gate Bridge.

I took a long untidy drink. I put the bottle down again, with infinite care. I tried to lick underneath my chin.

The whiskey had a funny taste. While I was realizing that it had a funny taste I saw a washbowl jammed into the corner of the wall. I made it. I just made it. I vomited. Dizzy Dean never threw anything harder.

Time passed—an agony of nausea and staggering and dazedness and clinging to the edge of the bowl and making animal sounds for help.

It passed. I staggered back to the bed and lay down on my back again and lay there panting, watching the smoke. The smoke wasn't quite so clear. Not quite so real. Maybe it was just something back of my eyes. And then quite suddenly it wasn't there at all and the light from the porcelain ceiling fixture etched the room sharply.

I sat up again. There was a heavy wooden chair against the wall near the door. There was another door besides the door the man in the white coat had come in at. A closet door, probably. It might even have my clothes in it. The floor was covered with green and gray linoleum in squares. The walls were painted white. A clean room. The bed on which I sat was a narrow iron hospital bed, lower than they usually are, and there were thick leather straps with buckles attached to the sides, about where a man's wrists and ankles would be.

It was a swell room—to get out of.

I had feeling all over my body now, soreness in my head and throat and in my arm. I couldn't remember about the arm. I rolled up the sleeve of the cotton pajama thing and looked at it fuzzily. It was covered with pin pricks on the skin all the way from the elbow to the shoulder. Around each was a small discolored patch, about the size of a quarter.

Dope. I had been shot full of dope to keep me quiet. Perhaps scopolamine too, to make me talk. Too much dope for the time. I was having the French fits coming out of it. Some do, some don't. It all depends how you are put together. Dope.

That accounted for the smoke and the little heads around the edge of the ceiling light and the voices and the screwy thoughts and the straps and bars and the numb fingers and feet. The whiskey was probably part of somebody's forty-eight hour liquor cure. They had just left it around so that I wouldn't miss anything.

I stood up and almost hit the opposite wall with my stomach. That made me lie down and breathe very gently for quite a long time. I was tingling all over now and sweating. I could feel little drops of sweat form on my forehead and then slide slowly and carefully down the side of my nose to the corner of my mouth. My tongue licked at them foolishly.

I sat up once more and planted my feet on the floor and stood up.

"Okey, Marlowe," I said between my teeth. "You're a tough guy. Six feet of iron man. One hundred and ninety pounds stripped and with your face washed. Hard muscles and no glass jaw. You can take it. You've been sapped down twice, had your throat choked and been beaten half silly on the jaw with a gun barrel. You've been shot full of hop and kept under it until you're as crazy as two waltzing mice. And what does all that amount to? Routine. Now let's see you do something really tough, like putting your pants on."

I lay down on the bed again.

Time passed again. I don't know how long. I had no watch. They don't make that kind of time in watches anyway.

I sat up. This was getting to be stale. I stood up and started to walk. No fun walking. Makes your heart jump like a nervous cat. Better lie down and go back to sleep. Better take it easy for a while. You're in bad shape, pally. Okey, Hemingway, I'm weak. I couldn't knock over a flower vase. I couldn't break a fingernail.

Nothing doing. I'm walking. I'm tough. I'm getting out of here.

I lay down on the bed again.

The fourth time was a little better. I got across the room and back twice. I went over to the washbowl and rinsed it out and leaned on it and drank water out of the palm of my hand. I kept it down. I waited a little and drank more. Much better.

I walked. I walked. I walked.

Half an hour of walking and my knees were shaking but my head was clear. I drank more water, a lot of water. I almost cried into the bowl while I was drinking it.

I walked back to the bed. It was a lovely bed. It was made of rose-leaves. It was the most beautiful bed in the world. They had got it from Carole Lombard. It was too soft for her. It was worth the rest of my life to lie down in it for two minutes. Beautiful soft bed, beautiful sleep, beautiful eyes closing and lashes falling and the gentle sound of breathing and darkness and rest sunk in deep pillows. . . .

I walked.

They built the Pyramids and got tired of them and pulled them down and ground the stone up to make concrete for Boulder Dam and they built that and brought the water to the Sunny Southland and used it to have a flood with.

I walked all through it. I couldn't be bothered.

I stopped walking. I was ready to talk to somebody.

26

The closet door was locked. The heavy chair was too heavy for me. It was meant to be. I stripped the sheets and pad off the bed and dragged the mattress to one side. There was a mesh spring underneath fastened top and bottom by coil springs of black enameled metal about nine inches long. I went to work on one of them. It was the hardest work I ever did. Ten minutes later I had two bleeding fingers and a loose spring. I swung it. It had a nice balance. It was heavy. It had a whip to it.

And when this was all done I looked across at the whiskey bottle and it would have done just as well, and I had forgotten all about it.

I drank some more water. I rested a little, sitting on the side of the bare springs. Then I went over to the door and put my mouth against the hinge side and yelled:

"Fire! Fire! Fire!"

It was a short wait and a pleasant one. He came running hard along the hallway outside and his key jammed viciously into the lock and twisted hard.

The door jumped open. I was flat against the wall on the

opening side. He had the sap out this time, a nice little tool about five inches long, covered with woven brown leather. His eyes popped at the stripped bed and then began to swing around.

I giggled and socked him. I laid the coil spring on the side of his head and he stumbled forward. I followed him down to his knees. I hit him twice more. He made a moaning sound. I took the sap out of his limp hand. He whined.

I used my knee on his face. It hurt my knee. He didn't tell me whether it hurt his face. While he was still groaning I knocked him cold with the sap.

I got the key from the outside of the door and locked it from the inside and went through him. He had more keys. One of them fitted my closet. In it my clothes hung. I went through my pockets. The money was gone from my wallet. I went back to the man with the white coat. He had too much money for his job. I took what I had started with and heaved him on to the bed and strapped him wrist and ankle and stuffed half a yard of sheet into his mouth. He had a smashed nose. I waited long enough to make sure he could breathe through it.

I was sorry for him. A simple hardworking little guy trying to hold his job down and get his weekly pay check. Maybe with a wife and kids. Too bad. And all he had to help him was a sap. It didn't seem fair. I put the doped whiskey down where he could reach it, if his hands hadn't been strapped.

I patted his shoulder. I almost cried over him.

All my clothes, even my gun harness and gun, but no shells in the gun, hung in the closet. I dressed with fumbling fingers, yawning a great deal.

The man on the bed rested. I left him there and locked him in.

Outside was a wide silent hallway with three closed doors. No sounds came from behind any of them. A wine-colored carpet crept down the middle and was as silent as the rest of the house. At the end there was a jog in the hall and then another hall at right angles and the head of a big old-fashioned staircase with white oak bannisters. It curved graciously down into the dim hall below. Two stained glass inner doors ended the lower hall. It was tessellated and thick rugs lay on it. A crack of light seeped past the edge of an almost closed door. But no sound at all.

An old house, built as once they built them and don't build them any more. Standing probably on a quiet street with a rose arbor at the side and plenty of flowers in front. Gracious and cool and quiet in the bright California sun. And inside it who cares, but don't let them scream too loud.

I had my foot out to go down the stairs when I heard a man cough. That jerked me around and I saw there was a half open door along the other hallway at the end. I tiptoed along the runner. I waited, close to the partly open door, but not in it. A wedge of light lay at my feet on the carpet. The man coughed again. It was a deep cough, from a deep chest. It sounded peaceful and at ease. It was none of my business. My business was to get out of there. But any man whose door could be open in that house interested me. He would be a man of position, worth tipping your hat to. I sneaked a little into the wedge of light. A newspaper rustled.

I could see part of a room and it was furnished like a room, not like a cell. There was a dark bureau with a hat on it and some magazines. Windows with lace curtains, a good carpet.

Bed springs creaked heavily. A big guy, like his cough. I reached out fingertips and pushed the door an inch or two. Nothing happened. Nothing ever was slower than my head craning in. I saw the room now, the bed, and the man on it, the ashtray heaped with stubs that overflowed on to a night table and from that to the carpet. A dozen mangled news-papers all over the bed. One of them in a pair of huge hands before a huge face. I saw the hair above the edge of the green paper. Dark, curly—black even—and plenty of it. A line of white skin under it. The paper moved a little more and I didn't breathe and the man on the bed didn't look up.

He needed a shave. He would always need a shave. I had seen him before, over on Central Avenue, in a negro dive called Florian's. I had seen him in a loud suit with white golf balls on the coat and a whiskey sour in his hand. And I had seen him with an Army Colt looking like a toy in his fist, stepping softly through a broken door. I had seen some of his work and it was the kind of work that stays done.

He coughed again and rolled his buttocks on the bed and yawned bitterly and reached sideways for a frayed pack of cigarettes on the night table. One of them went into his mouth. Light flared at the end of his thumb. Smoke came out of his nose.

"Ah," he said, and the paper went up in front of his face again.

I left him there and went back along the side hall. Mr. Moose Malloy seemed to be in very good hands. I went back to the stairs and down.

A voice murmured behind the almost closed door. I waited for the answering voice. None. It was a telephone conversation. I went over close to the door and listened. It was a low voice, a mere murmur. Nothing carried that meant anything. There was finally a dry clicking sound. Silence continued inside the room after that.

This was the time to leave, to go far away. So I pushed the door open and stepped quietly in.

27

It was an office, not small, not large, with a neat professional look. A glass-doored bookcase with heavy books inside. A first aid cabinet on the wall. A white enamel and glass sterilizing cabinet with a lot of hypodermic needles and syringes inside it being cooked. A wide flat desk with a blotter on it, a bronze paper cutter, a pen set, an appointment book, very little else, except the elbows of a man who sat brooding, with his face in his hands.

Between the spread yellow fingers I saw hair the color of wet brown sand, so smooth that it appeared to be painted on his skull. I took three more steps and his eyes must have looked beyond the desk and seen my shoes move. His head came up and he looked at me. Sunken colorless eyes in a parchment-like face. He unclasped his hands and leaned back slowly and looked at me with no expression at all.

Then he spread his hands with a sort of helpless but disapproving gesture and when they came to rest again, one of them was very close to the corner of the desk.

I took two steps more and showed him the blackjack. His index and second finger still moved towards the corner of the desk.

"The buzzer," I said, "won't buy you anything tonight. I put your tough boy to sleep."

His eyes got sleepy. "You have been a very sick man, sir. A very sick man. I can't recommend your being up and about yet."

I said: "The right hand." I snapped the blackjack at it. It coiled into itself like a wounded snake.

I went around the desk grinning without there being anything to grin at. He had a gun in the drawer of course. They always have a gun in the drawer and they always get it too late, if they get it at all. I took it out. It was a .38 automatic, a standard model not as good as mine, but I could use its ammunition. There didn't seem to be any in the drawer. I started to break the magazine out of his.

He moved vaguely, his eyes still sunken and sad.

"Maybe you've got another buzzer under the carpet," I said. "Maybe it rings in the Chief's office down at headquarters. Don't use it. Just for an hour I'm a very tough guy. Anybody comes in that door is walking into a coffin."

"There is no buzzer under the carpet," he said. His voice had the slightest possible foreign accent.

I got his magazine out and my empty one and changed them. I ejected the shell that was in the chamber of his gun and let it lie. I jacked one up into the chamber of mine and went back to the other side of the desk again.

There was a spring lock on the door. I backed towards it and pushed it shut and heard the lock click. There was also a bolt. I turned that.

I went back to the desk and sat in a chair. It took my last ounce of strength.

"Whiskey," I said.

He began to move his hands around.

"Whiskey," I said.

He went to the medicine cabinet and got a flat bottle with a green revenue stamp on it and a glass.

"Two glasses," I said. "I tried your whiskey once. I damn near hit Catalina Island with it."

He brought two small glasses and broke the seal and filled the two glasses.

"You first," I said.

He smiled faintly and raised one of the glasses.

"Your health, sir—what remains of it." He drank. I drank. I reached for the bottle and stood it near me and waited for the heat to get to my heart. My heart began to pound, but it was back up in my chest again, not hanging on a shoelace.

"I had a nightmare," I said. "Silly idea. I dreamed I was tied to a cot and shot full of dope and locked in a barred room. I got very weak. I slept. I had no food. I was a sick man. I was knocked on the head and brought into a place where they did that to me. They took a lot of trouble. I'm not that important."

He said nothing. He watched me. There was a remote speculation in his eyes, as if he wondered how long I would live.

"I woke up and the room was full of smoke," I said. "It was just a hallucination, irritation of the optic nerve or whatever a guy like you would call it. Instead of pink snakes I had smoke. So I yelled and a toughie in a white coat came in and showed me a blackjack. It took me a long time to get ready to take it away from him. I got his keys and my clothes and even took my money out of his pocket. So here I am. All cured. What were you saying?"

"I made no remark," he said.

"Remarks want you to make them," I said. "They have their tongues hanging out waiting to be said. This thing here—" I waved the blackjack lightly, "is a persuader. I had to borrow it from a guy."

"Please give it to me at once," he said with a smile you would get to love. It was like the executioner's smile when he comes to your cell to measure you for the drop. A little friendly, a little paternal, and a little cautious at the same time. You would get to love it if there was any way you could live long enough.

I dropped the blackjack into his palm, his left palm.

"Now the gun, please," he said softly. "You have been a very sick man, Mr. Marlowe. I think I shall have to insist that you go back to bed."

I stared at him.

"I am Dr. Sonderborg," he said, "and I don't want any nonsense."

He laid the blackjack down on the desk in front of him. His smile was as stiff as a frozen fish. His long fingers made movements like dying butterflies.

"The gun, please," he said softly. "I advise strongly—"

"What time is it, warden?"

He looked mildly surprised. I had my wrist watch on now, but it had run down.

"It is almost midnight. Why?"

"What day is it?"

"Why, my dear sir—Sunday evening, of course."

I steadied myself on the desk and tried to think and held the gun close enough to him so that he might try and grab it.

"That's over forty-eight hours. No wonder I had fits. Who brought me here?"

He stared at me and his left hand began to edge towards the gun. He belonged to the Wandering Hand Society. The girls would have had a time with him.

"Don't make me get tough," I whined. "Don't make me lose my beautiful manners and my flawless English. Just tell me how I got here."

He had courage. He grabbed for the gun. It wasn't where he grabbed. I sat back and put it in my lap.

He reddened and grabbed for the whiskey and poured himself another drink and downed it fast. He drew a deep breath and shuddered. He didn't like the taste of liquor. Dopers never do.

"You will be arrested at once, if you leave here," he said sharply. "You were properly committed by an officer of the law—"

"Officers of the law can't do it."

That jarred him, a little. His yellowish face began to work.

"Shake it up and pour it," I said. "Who put me in here, why and how? I'm in a wild mood tonight. I want to go dance in the foam. I hear the banshees calling. I haven't shot a man in a week. Speak out, Dr. Fell. Pluck the antique viol, let the soft music float."

"You are suffering from narcotic poisoning," he said coldly. "You very nearly died. I had to give you digitalis three times. You fought, you screamed, you had to be restrained." His words were coming so fast they were leap-frogging themselves. "If you leave my hospital in this condition, you will get into serious trouble."

"Did you say you were a doctor—a medical doctor?"

"Certainly. I am Dr. Sonderborg, as I told you."

"You don't scream and fight from narcotic poisoning, doc. You just lie in a coma. Try again. And skim it. All I want is the cream. Who put me in your private funny house?"

"But—"

"But me no buts. I'll make a sop of you. I'll drown you in a butt of Malmsey wine. I wish I had a butt of Malmsey wine myself to drown in. Shakespeare. He knew his liquor too. Let's have a little of our medicine." I reached for his glass and poured us a couple more. "Get on with it, Karloff."

"The police put you in here."

"What police?"

"The Bay City police naturally." His restless yellow fingers twisted his glass. "This is Bay City."

"Oh. Did this police have a name?"

"A Sergeant Galbraith, I believe. Not a regular patrol car officer. He and another officer found you wandering outside the house in a dazed condition on Friday night. They brought you in because this place was close. I thought you were an addict who had taken an overdose. But perhaps I was wrong."

"It's a good story. I couldn't prove it wrong. But why keep me here?"

He spread his restless hands. "I have told you again and again that you were a very sick man and still are. What would you expect me to do?"

"I must owe you some money then."

He shrugged. "Naturally. Two hundred dollars."

I pushed my chair back a little. "Dirt cheap. Try and get it."

"If you leave here," he said sharply, "you will be arrested at once."

I leaned back over the desk and breathed in his face. "Not just for going out of here, Karloff. Open that wall safe."

He stood up in a smooth lunge. "This has gone quite far enough."

"You won't open it?"

"I most certainly will not open it."

"This is a gun I'm holding."

He smiled, narrowly and bitterly.

"It's an awful big safe," I said. "New too. This is a fine gun. You won't open it?"

Nothing changed in his face.

"Damn it," I said. "When you have a gun in your hand, people are supposed to do anything you tell them to. It doesn't work, does it?"

He smiled. His smile held a sadistic pleasure. I was slipping back. I was going to collapse.

I staggered at the desk and he waited, his lips parted softly.

I stood leaning there for a long moment, staring into his eyes. Then I grinned. The smile fell off his face like a soiled rag. Sweat stood out on his forehead.

"So long," I said. "I leave you to dirtier hands than mine."

I backed to the door and opened it and went out.

The front doors were unlocked. There was a roofed porch. The garden hummed with flowers. There was a white picket fence and a gate. The house was on a corner. It was a cool, moist night, no moon.

The sign on the corner said Descanso Street. Houses were lighted down the block. I listened for sirens. None came. The other sign said Twenty-third Street. I plowed over to Twenty-fifth Street and started towards the eight-hundred block. No. 819 was Anne Riordan's number. Sanctuary.

I had walked a long time before I realized that I was still holding the gun in my hand. And I had heard no sirens.

I kept on walking. The air did me good, but the whiskey was dying, and it writhed as it died. The block had fir trees along it, and brick houses, and looked like a house on Capitol Hill in Seattle more than Southern California.

There was a light still in No. 819. It had a white porte-cochère, very tiny, pressed against a tall cypress hedge. There were rose bushes in front of the house. I went up the walk. I listened before I pushed the bell. Still no sirens wailing. The bell chimed and after a little while a voice croaked through one of those electrical contraptions that let you talk with your front door locked.

"What is it, please?"

"Marlowe."

Maybe her breath caught, maybe the electrical thing just made that sound being shut off.

The door opened wide and Miss Anne Riordan stood there in a pale green slack suit looking at me. Her eyes went wide and scared. Her face under the glare of the porchlight was suddenly pale.

"My God," she wailed. "You look like Hamlet's father!"

28

The living room had a tan figured rug, white and rose chairs, a black marble fireplace with very tall brass andirons, high bookcases built back into the walls, and rough cream drapes against the lowered venetian blinds.

There was nothing womanish in the room except a full length mirror with a clear sweep of floor in front of it.

I was half-sitting and half-lying in a deep chair with my legs on a footstool. I had had two cups of black coffee, then I had had a drink, then I had had two soft-boiled eggs and a slice of toast broken into them, then some more black coffee with brandy laced in it. I had had all this in the breakfast room, but I couldn't remember what it looked like any more. It was too long ago.

I was in good shape again. I was almost sober and my stomach was bunting towards third base instead of trying for the centerfield flagpole.

Anne Riordan sat opposite me, leaning forward, her neat chin cupped in her neat hand, her eyes dark and shadowy under the fluffed out reddish-brown hair. There was a pencil stuck through her hair. She looked worried. I had told her some of it, but not all. Especially about Moose Malloy I had not told her.

"I thought you were drunk," she said. "I thought you had to be drunk before you came to see me. I thought you had been out with that blonde. I thought—I don't know what I thought."

"I bet you didn't get all this writing," I said, looking around. "Not even if you got paid for what you thought you thought."

"And my dad didn't get it grafting on the cops either," she said. "Like that fat slob they have for chief of police nowadays."

"It's none of my business," I said.

She said: "We had some lots at Del Rey. Just sand lots they suckered him for. And they turned out to be oil lots."

I nodded and drank out of the nice crystal glass I was holding. What was in it had a nice warm taste.

"A fellow could settle down here," I said. "Move right in. Everything set for him."

"If he was that kind of fellow. And anybody wanted him to," she said.

"No butler," I said. "That makes it tough."

She flushed. "But you—you'd rather get your head beaten to a pulp and your arm riddled with dope needles and your chin used for a backboard in a basketball game. God knows there's enough of it."

I didn't say anything. I was too tired.

"At least," she said, "you had the brains to look in those mouthpieces. The way you talked over on Aster Drive I thought you had missed the whole thing."

"Those cards don't mean anything."

Her eyes snapped at me. "You sit there and tell me that after the man had you beaten up by a couple of crooked policemen and thrown in a two-day liquor cure to teach you to mind your own business? Why the thing stands out so far you could break off a yard of it and still have enough left for a baseball bat."

"I ought to have said that one," I said. "Just my style. Crude. What sticks out?"

"That this elegant psychic person is nothing but a high-class mobster. He picks the prospects and milks the minds and then tells the rough boys to go out and get the jewels."

"You really think that?"

She stared at me. I finished my glass and got my weak look on my face again. She ignored it.

"Of course I think it," she said. "And so do you."

"I think it's a little more complicated than that."

Her smile was cozy and acid at the same time. "I beg your pardon. I forgot for the moment you were a detective. It *would* have to be complicated, wouldn't it? I suppose there's a sort of indecency about a simple case."

"It's more complicated than that," I said.

"All right. I'm listening."

"I don't know. I just think so. Can I have one more drink?"

She stood up. "You know, you'll have to taste water sometime, just for the hell of it." She came over and took my glass. "This is going to be the last." She went out of the room and somewhere ice cubes tinkled and I closed my eyes and listened to the small unimportant sounds. I had no business coming here. If they knew as much about me as I suspected, they might come here looking. That would be a mess.

She came back with the glass and her fingers cold from holding the cold glass touched mine and I held them for a moment and then let them go slowly as you let go of a dream when you wake with the sun in your face and you have been in an enchanted valley.

She flushed and went back to her chair and sat down and made a lot of business of arranging herself in it.

She lit a cigarette, watching me drink.

"Amthor's a pretty ruthless sort of lad," I said. "But I don't somehow see him as the brain guy of a jewel mob. Perhaps I'm wrong. If he was and he thought I had something on him, I don't think I'd have got out of that dope hospital alive. But he's a man who has things to fear. He didn't get really tough until I began to babble about invisible writing."

She looked at me evenly. "Was there some?"

I grinned. "If there was, I didn't read it."

"That's a funny way to hide nasty remarks about a person,

don't you think? In the mouthpieces of cigarettes. Suppose they were never found."

"I think the point is that Marriott feared something and that if anything happened to him, the cards *would* be found. The police would go over anything in his pockets with a fine-tooth comb. That's what bothers me. If Amthor's a crook, nothing would have been left to find."

"You mean if Amthor murdered him—or had him murdered? But what Marriott knew about Amthor may not have had any direct connection with the murder."

I leaned back and pressed my back into the chair and finished my drink and made believe I was thinking that over. I nodded.

"But the jewel robbery had a connection with the murder. And we're assuming Amthor had a connection with the jewel robbery."

Her eyes were a little sly. "I bet you feel awful," she said. "Wouldn't you like to go to bed?"

"Here?"

She flushed to the roots of her hair. Her chin stuck out. "That was the idea. I'm not a child. Who the devil cares what I do or when or how?"

I put my glass aside and stood up. "One of my rare moments of delicacy is coming over me," I said. "Will you drive me to a taxi stand, if you're not too tired?"

"You damned sap," she said angrily. "You've been beaten to a pulp and shot full of God knows how many kinds of narcotics and I suppose all you need is a night's sleep to get up bright and early and start out being a detective again."

"I thought I'd sleep a little late."

"You ought to be in a hospital, you damn fool!"

I shuddered. "Listen," I said. "I'm not very clear-headed tonight and I don't think I ought to linger around here too long. I haven't a thing on any of these people that I could prove, but they seem to dislike me. Whatever I might say would be my word against the law, and the law in this town seems to be pretty rotten."

"It's a nice town," she said sharply, a little breathlessly. "You can't judge—"

"Okey, it's a nice town. So is Chicago. You could live there a long time and not see a Tommygun. Sure, it's a nice town. It's probably no crookeder than Los Angeles. But you can only buy a piece of a big city. You can buy a town this size all complete, with the original box and tissue paper. That's the difference. And that makes me want out."

She stood up and pushed her chin at me. "You'll go to bed now and right here. I have a spare bedroom and you can turn right in and—"

"Promise to lock your door?"

She flushed and bit her lip. "Sometimes I think you're a world-beater," she said, "and sometimes I think you're the worst heel I ever met."

"On either count would you run me over to where I can get a taxi?"

"You'll stay here," she snapped. "You're not fit. You're a sick man."

"I'm not too sick to have my brain picked," I said nastily.

She ran out of the room so fast she almost tripped over the two steps from the living room up to the hall. She came back in nothing flat with a long flannel coat on over her slack suit and no hat and her reddish hair looking as mad as her face. She opened a side door and threw it away from her, bounced through it and her steps clattered on the driveway. A garage door made a faint sound lifting. A car door opened and slammed shut again. The starter ground and the motor caught and the lights flared past the open French door of the living room.

I picked my hat out of a chair and switched off a couple of lamps and saw that the French door had a Yale lock. I looked back a moment before I closed the door. It was a nice room. It would be a nice room to wear slippers in.

I shut the door and the little car slid up beside me and I went around behind it to get in.

She drove me all the way home, tight-lipped, angry. She drove like a fury. When I got out in front of my apartment house she said good-night in a frosty voice and swirled the little car in the middle of the street and was gone before I could get my keys out of my pocket.

They locked the lobby door at eleven. I unlocked it and passed into the always musty lobby and along to the stairs and the elevator. I rode up to my floor. Bleak light shone along it. Milk bottles stood in front of service doors. The red fire door loomed at the back. It had an open screen that let in a lazy trickle of air that never quite swept the cooking smell out. I was home in a sleeping world, a world as harmless as a sleeping cat.

I unlocked the door of my apartment and went in and sniffed the smell of it, just standing there, against the door for a little while before I put the light on. A homely smell, a smell of dust and tobacco smoke, the smell of a world where men live, and keep on living.

I undressed and went to bed. I had nightmares and woke out of them sweating. But in the morning I was a well man again.

29

I was sitting on the side of my bed in my pajamas, thinking about getting up, but not yet committed. I didn't feel very well, but I didn't feel as sick as I ought to, not as sick as I would feel if I had a salaried job. My head hurt and felt large and hot and my tongue was dry and had gravel on it and my throat was stiff and my jaw was not untender. But I had had worse mornings.

It was a gray morning with high fog, not yet warm but likely to be. I heaved up off the bed and rubbed the pit of my stomach where it was sore from vomiting. My left foot felt fine. It didn't have an ache in it. So I had to kick the corner of the bed with it.

I was still swearing when there was a sharp tap at the door, the kind of bossy knock that makes you want to open the door two inches, emit the succulent raspberry and slam it again.

I opened it a little wider than two inches. Detective-Lieutenant Randall stood there, in a brown gabardine suit, with a pork pie lightweight felt on his head, very neat and clean and solemn and with a nasty look in his eye.

He pushed the door lightly and I stepped away from it. He came in and closed it and looked around. "I've been looking for you for two days," he said. He didn't look at me. His eyes measured the room.

"I've been sick."

He walked around with a light springy step, his creamy gray hair shining, his hat under his arm now, his hands in his pockets. He wasn't a very big man for a cop. He took one hand out of his pocket and placed the hat carefully on top of some magazines.

"Not here," he said.

"In a hospital."

"Which hospital?"

"A pet hospital."

He jerked as if I had slapped his face. Dull color showed behind his skin.

"A little early in the day, isn't it—for that sort of thing?"

I didn't say anything. I lit a cigarette. I took one draw on it and sat down on the bed again, quickly.

"No cure for lads like you, is there?" he said. "Except to throw you in the sneezer."

"I've been a sick man and I haven't had my morning coffee. You can't expect a very high grade of wit."

"I told you not to work on this case."

"You're not God. You're not even Jesus Christ." I took another drag on the cigarette. Somewhere down inside me felt raw, but I liked it a little better.

"You'd be amazed how much trouble I could make you."

"Probably."

"Do you know why I haven't done it so far?"

"Yeah."

"Why?" He was leaning over a little, sharp as a terrier, with that stony look in his eyes they all get sooner or later.

"You couldn't find me."

He leaned back and rocked on his heels. His face shone a little. "I thought you were going to say something else," he said. "And if you said it, I was going to smack you on the button."

"Twenty million dollars wouldn't scare you. But you might get orders."

He breathed hard, with his mouth a little open. Very slowly he got a package of cigarettes out of his pocket and tore the wrapper. His fingers were trembling a little. He put a cigarette between his lips and went over to my magazine table for a match folder. He lit the cigarette carefully, put the match in the ashtray and not on the floor, and inhaled.

"I gave you some advice over the telephone the other day," he said. "Thursday."

"Friday."

"Yes—Friday. It didn't take. I can understand why. But I didn't know at that time you had been holding out evidence. I was just recommending a line of action that seemed like a good idea in this case."

"What evidence?"

He stared at me silently.

"Will you have some coffee?" I asked. "It might make you human."

"No."

"*I* will." I stood up and started for the kitchenette.

"Sit down," Randall snapped. "I'm far from through."

I kept on going out to the kitchenette, ran some water into the kettle and put it on the stove. I took a drink of cold water from the faucet, then another. I came back with a third glass in my hand to stand in the doorway and look at him. He hadn't moved. The veil of his smoke was almost a solid thing to one side of him. He was looking at the floor.

"Why was it wrong to go to Mrs. Grayle when she sent for me?" I asked.

"I wasn't talking about that."

"Yeah, but you were just before."

"She didn't send for you." His eyes lifted and had the stony look still. And the flush still dyed his sharp cheekbones. "You forced yourself on her and talked about scandal and practically blackmailed yourself into a job."

"Funny. As I remember it, we didn't even talk job. I didn't think there was anything in her story. I mean, anything to get my teeth into. Nowhere to start. And of course I supposed she had already told it to you."

"She had. That beer joint on Santa Monica is a crook hideout. But that doesn't mean anything. I couldn't get a thing there. The hotel across the street smells too. Nobody we want. Cheap punks."

"She tell you I forced myself on her?"

He dropped his eyes a little. "No."

I grinned. "Have some coffee?"

"No."

I went back into the kitchenette and made the coffee and waited for it to drip. Randall followed me out this time and stood in the doorway himself.

"This jewel gang has been working in Hollywood and around for a good ten years to my knowledge," he said. "They went too far this time. They killed a man. I think I know why."

"Well, if it's a gang job and you break it, that will be the first gang murder solved since I lived in the town. And I could name and describe at least a dozen."

"It's nice of you to say that, Marlowe."

"Correct me if I'm wrong."

"Damn it," he said irritably. "You're not wrong. There were a couple solved for the record, but they were just rappers. Some punk took it for the high pillow."

"Yeah. Coffee?"

"If I drink some, will you talk to me decently, man to man, without wise-cracking?"

"I'll try. I don't promise to spill all my ideas."

"I can do without those," he said acidly.

"That's a nice suit you're wearing."

The flush dyed his face again. "This suit cost twenty-seven-fifty," he snapped.

"Oh Christ, a sensitive cop," I said, and went back to the stove.

"That smells good. How do you make it?"

I poured. "French drip. Coarse ground coffee. No filter papers." I got the sugar from the closet and the cream from the refrigerator. We sat down on opposite sides of the nook.

"Was that a gag, about your being sick, in a hospital?"

"No gag. I ran into a little trouble—down in Bay City. They took me in. Not the cooler, a private dope and liquor cure."

His eyes got distant. "Bay City, eh? You like it the hard way, don't you, Marlowe?"

"It's not that I like it the hard way. It's that I get it that way. But nothing like this before. I've been sapped twice, the second time by a police officer or a man who looked like one and claimed to be one. I've been beaten with my own gun and choked by a tough Indian. I've been thrown unconscious into this dope hospital and kept there locked up and part of the time probably strapped down. And I couldn't prove any of it, except that I actually do have quite a nice collection of bruises and my left arm has been needled plenty."

He stared hard at the corner of the table. "In Bay City," he said slowly.

"The name's like a song. A song in a dirty bathtub."

"What were you doing down there?"

"I didn't go down there. These cops took me over the line. I went to see a guy in Stillwood Heights. That's in L.A."

"A man named Jules Amthor," he said quietly. "Why did you swipe those cigarettes?"

I looked into my cup. The damned little fool. "It looked funny, him—Marriott—having that extra case. With reefers in it. It seems they make them up like Russian cigarettes down in Bay City with hollow mouthpieces and the Romanoff arms and everything."

He pushed his empty cup at me and I refilled it. His eyes were going over my face line by line, corpuscle by corpuscle, like Sherlock Holmes with his magnifying glass or Thorndyke with his pocket lens.

"You ought to have told me," he said bitterly. He sipped and wiped his lips with one of those fringed things they give you in apartment houses for napkins. "But you didn't swipe them. The girl told me."

"Aw well, hell," I said. "A guy never gets to do anything in this country any more. Always women."

"She likes you," Randall said, like a polite FBI man in a movie, a little sad, but very manly. "Her old man was as straight a cop as ever lost a job. She had no business taking those things. She likes you."

"She's a nice girl. Not my type."

"You don't like them nice?" He had another cigarette going. The smoke was being fanned away from his face by his hand.

"I like smooth shiny girls, hardboiled and loaded with sin."

"They take you to the cleaners," Randall said indifferently.

"Sure. Where else have I ever been? What do you call this session?"

He smiled his first smile of the day. He probably allowed himself four.

"I'm not getting much out of you," he said.

"I'll give you a theory, but you are probably way ahead of me on it. This Marriott was a blackmailer of women, because Mrs. Grayle just about told me so. But he was something else. He was the finger man for the jewel mob. The society finger, the boy who would cultivate the victims and set the stage. He would cultivate women he could take out, get to know them pretty well. Take this holdup a week from Thursday. It smells. If Marriott hadn't been driving the car, or hadn't taken Mrs. Grayle to the Troc or hadn't gone home the way he did, past that beer parlor, the holdup couldn't have been brought off."

"The chauffeur could have been driving," Randall said reasonably. "But that wouldn't have changed things much. Chauffeurs are not getting themselves pushed in the face with lead bullets by holdup men—for ninety a month. But there couldn't be many stick-ups with Marriott alone with women or things would get talked about."

"The whole point of this kind of racket is that things are not talked about," I said. "In consideration for that the stuff is sold back cheap."

Randall leaned back and shook his head. "You'll have to do better than that to interest me. Women talk about anything. It would get around that this Marriott was a kind of tricky guy to go out with."

"It probably did. That's why they knocked him off."

Randall stared at me woodenly. His spoon was stirring air in an empty cup. I reached over and he waved the pot aside. "Go on with that one," he said.

"They used him up. His usefulness was exhausted. It was about time for him to get talked about a little, as you suggest.

But you don't quit in those rackets and you don't get your time. So this last holdup was just that for him—the last. Look, they really asked very little for the jade considering its value. And Marriott handled the contact. But all the same Marriott was scared. At the last moment he thought he had better not go alone. And he figured a little trick that if anything did happen to him, something on him would point to a man, a man quite ruthless and clever enough to be the brains of that sort of mob, and a man in an unusual position to get information about rich women. It was a childish sort of trick but it did actually work."

Randall shook his head. "A gang would have stripped him, perhaps even have taken the body out to sea and dumped it."

"No. They wanted the job to look amateurish. They wanted to stay in business. They probably have another finger lined up," I said.

Randall still shook his head. "The man these cigarettes pointed to is not the type. He has a good racket of his own. I've inquired. What did you think of him?"

His eyes were too blank, much too blank. I said: "He looked pretty damn deadly to me. And there's no such thing as too much money, is there? And after all his psychic racket is a temporary racket for any one place. He has a vogue and everybody goes to him and after a while the vogue dies down and the business is licking its shoes. That is, if he's a psychic and nothing else. Just like movie stars. Give him five years. He could work it that long. But give him a couple of ways to use the information he must get out of these women and he's going to make a killing."

"I'll look him up more thoroughly," Randall said with the blank look. "But right now I'm more interested in Marriott. Let's go back farther—much farther. To how you got to know him."

"He just called me up. Picked my name out of the phone book. He said so, at any rate."

"He had your card."

I looked surprised. "Sure. I'd forgotten that."

"Did you ever wonder why he picked *your* name—ignoring that matter of your short memory?"

I stared at him across the top of my coffee cup. I was beginning to like him. He had a lot behind his vest besides his shirt.

"So that's what you really came up for?" I said.

He nodded. "The rest, you know, is just talk." He smiled politely at me and waited.

I poured some more coffee.

Randall leaned over sideways and looked along the cream-colored surface of the table. "A little dust," he said absently, then straightened up and looked me in the eye. "Perhaps I ought to go at this in a little different way," he said. "For instance, I think your hunch about Marriott is probably right. There's twenty-three grand in currency in his safe-deposit box—which we had a hell of a time to locate, by the way. There are also some pretty fair bonds and a trust deed to a property on West Fifty-fourth Place."

He picked a spoon up and rapped it lightly on the edge of his saucer and smiled. "That interest you?" he asked mildly. "The number was 1644 West Fifty-fourth Place."

"Yeah," I said thickly.

"Oh, there was quite a bit of jewelry in Marriott's box too—pretty good stuff. But I don't think he stole it. I think it was very likely given to him. That's one up for you. He was afraid to sell it—on account of the association of thought in his own mind."

I nodded. "He'd feel as if it was stolen."

"Yes. Now that trust deed didn't interest me at all at first, but here's how it works. It's what you fellows are up against in police work. We get all the homicide and doubtful death reports from outlying districts. We're supposed to read them the same day. That's a rule, like you shouldn't search without a warrant or frisk a guy for a gun without reasonable grounds. But we break rules. We have to. I didn't get around to some of the reports until this morning. Then I read one about a killing of a negro on Central, last Thursday. By a tough ex-con called Moose Malloy. And there was an identifying witness. And sink my putt, if you weren't the witness."

He smiled, softly, his third smile. "Like it?"

"I'm listening."

"This was only this morning, understand. So I looked at

the name of the man making the report and I knew him,
Nulty. So I knew the case was a flop. Nulty is the kind of
guy—well, were you ever up at Crestline?"

"Yeah."

"Well, up near Crestline there's a place where a bunch of
old box cars have been made into cabins. I have a cabin up
there myself, but not a box car. These box cars were brought
up on trucks, believe it or not, and there they stand without
any wheels. Now Nulty is the kind of guy who would make a
swell brakeman on one of those box cars."

"That's not nice," I said. "A fellow officer."

"So I called Nulty up and he hemmed and hawed around
and spit a few times and then he said you had an idea about
some girl called Velma something or other that Malloy was
sweet on a long time ago and you went to see the widow of
the guy that used to own the dive where the killing happened
when it was a white joint, and where Malloy and the girl both
worked at that time. And her address was 1644 West Fifty-
fourth Place, the place Marriott had the trust deed on."

"Yes?"

"So I just thought that was enough coincidence for one
morning," Randall said. "And here I am. And so far I've been
pretty nice about it."

"The trouble is," I said, "it looks like more than it is. This
Velma girl is dead, according to Mrs. Florian. I have her
photo."

I went into the living room and reached into my suit coat
and my hand was in midair when it began to feel funny and
empty. But they hadn't even taken the photos. I got them out
and took them to the kitchen and tossed the Pierrot girl
down in front of Randall. He studied it carefully.

"Nobody I ever saw," he said. "That another one?"

"No, this is a newspaper still of Mrs. Grayle. Anne Riordan
got it."

He looked at it and nodded. "For twenty million, I'd marry
her myself."

"There's something I ought to tell you," I said. "Last night
I was so damn mad I had crazy ideas about going down there
and trying to bust it alone. This hospital is at Twenty-third
and Descanso in Bay City. It's run by a man named Sonder-

borg who says he's a doctor. He's running a crook hideout on the side. I saw Moose Malloy there last night. In a room."

Randall sat very still, looking at me. "Sure?"

"You couldn't mistake him. He's a big guy, enormous. He doesn't look like anybody you ever saw."

He sat looking at me, without moving. Then very slowly he moved out from under the table and stood up.

"Let's go see this Florian woman."

"How about Malloy?"

He sat down again. "Tell me the whole thing, carefully."

I told him. He listened without taking his eyes off my face. I don't think he even winked. He breathed with his mouth slightly open. His body didn't move. His fingers tapped gently on the edge of the table. When I had finished he said:

"This Dr. Sonderborg—what did he look like?"

"Like a doper, and probably a dope peddler." I described him to Randall as well as I could.

He went quietly into the other room and sat down at the telephone. He dialed his number and spoke quietly for a long time. Then he came back. I had just finished making more coffee and boiling a couple of eggs and making two slices of toast and buttering them. I sat down to eat.

Randall sat down opposite me and leaned his chin in his hand. "I'm having a state narcotics man go down there with a fake complaint and ask to look around. He may get some ideas. He won't get Malloy. Malloy was out of there ten minutes after you left last night. That's one thing you can bet on."

"Why not the Bay City cops?" I put salt on my eggs.

Randall said nothing. When I looked up at him his face was red and uncomfortable.

"For a cop," I said, "you're the most sensitive guy I ever met."

"Hurry up with that eating. We have to go."

"I have to shower and shave and dress after this."

"Couldn't you just go in your pajamas?" he asked acidly.

"So the town is as crooked as all that?" I said.

"It's Laird Brunette's town. They say he put up thirty grand to elect a mayor."

"The fellow that owns the Belvedere Club?"

"And the two gambling boats."

"But it's in our county," I said.

He looked down at his clean, shiny fingernails.

"We'll stop by your office and get those other two reefers," he said. "If they're still there." He snapped his fingers. "If you'll lend me your keys, I'll do it while you get shaved and dressed."

"We'll go together," I said. "I might have some mail."

He nodded and after a moment sat down and lit another cigarette. I shaved and dressed and we left in Randall's car.

I had some mail, but it wasn't worth reading. The two cut up cigarettes in the desk drawer had not been touched. The office had no look of having been searched.

Randall took the two Russian cigarettes and sniffed at the tobacco and put them away in his pocket.

"He got one card from you," he mused. "There couldn't have been anything on the back of that, so he didn't bother about the others. I guess Amthor is not very much afraid—just thought you were trying to pull something. Let's go."

30

Old Nosey poked her nose an inch outside the front door, sniffed carefully as if there might be an early violet blooming, looked up and down the street with a raking glance, and nodded her white head. Randall and I took our hats off. In that neighborhood that probably ranked you with Valentino. She seemed to remember me.

"Good morning, Mrs. Morrison," I said. "Can we step inside a minute? This is Lieutenant Randall from Headquarters."

"Land's sakes, I'm all flustered. I got a big ironing to do," she said.

"We won't keep you a minute."

She stood back from the door and we slipped past her into her hallway with the side piece from Mason City or wherever it was and from that into the neat living room with the lace curtains at the windows. A smell of ironing came from the back of the house. She shut the door in between as carefully as if it was made of short pie crust.

She had a blue and white apron on this morning. Her eyes were just as sharp and her chin hadn't grown any.

She parked herself about a foot from me and pushed her face forward and looked into my eyes.

"She didn't get it."

I looked wise. I nodded my head and looked at Randall and Randall nodded his head. He went to a window and looked at the side of Mrs. Florian's house. He came back softly, holding his pork pie under his arm, debonair as a French count in a college play.

"She didn't get it," I said.

"Nope, she didn't. Saturday was the first. April Fool's Day. He! He!" She stopped and was about to wipe her eyes with her apron when she remembered it was a rubber apron. That soured her a little. Her mouth got the pruny look.

"When the mailman come by and he didn't go up her walk she run out and called to him. He shook his head and went on. She went back in. She slammed the door so hard I figured a window'd break. Like she was mad."

"I swan," I said.

Old Nosey said to Randall sharply: "Let me see your badge, young man. This young man had a whiskey breath on him t'other day. I ain't never rightly trusted him."

Randall took a gold and blue enamel badge out of his pocket and showed it to her.

"Looks like real police all right," she admitted. "Well, ain't nothing happened over Sunday. She went out for liquor. Come back with two square bottles."

"Gin," I said. "That just gives you an idea. Nice folks don't drink gin."

"Nice folks don't drink no liquor at all," Old Nosey said pointedly.

"Yeah," I said. "Come Monday, that being today, and the mailman went by again. This time she was really sore."

"Kind of smart guesser, ain't you, young man? Can't wait for folks to get their mouth open hardly."

"I'm sorry, Mrs. Morrison. This is an important matter to us—"

"This here young man don't seem to have no trouble keepin' his mouth in place."

"He's married," I said. "He's had practice."

Her face turned a shade of violet that reminded me, unpleasantly, of cyanosis. "Get out of my house afore I call the police!" she shouted.

"There is a police officer standing before you, madam," Randall said shortly. "You are in no danger."

"That's right there is," she admitted. The violet tint began to fade from her face. "I don't take to this man."

"You have company, madam. Mrs. Florian didn't get her registered letter today either—is that it?"

"No." Her voice was sharp and short. Her eyes were furtive. She began to talk rapidly, too rapidly. "People was there last night. I didn't even see them. Folks took me to the picture show. Just as we got back—no, just after they driven off—a car went away from next door. Fast without any lights. I didn't see the number."

She gave me a sharp sidelong look from her furtive eyes. I wondered why they were furtive. I wandered to the window and lifted the lace curtain. An official blue-gray uniform was nearing the house. The man wearing it wore a heavy leather bag over his shoulder and had a vizored cap.

I turned away from the window, grinning.

"You're slipping," I told her rudely. "You'll be playing shortstop in a Class C league next year."

"That's not smart," Randall said coldly.

"Take a look out of the window."

He did and his face hardened. He stood quite still looking at Mrs. Morrison. He was waiting for something, a sound like nothing else on earth. It came in a moment.

It was the sound of something being pushed into the front door mail slot. It might have been a handbill, but it wasn't. There were steps going back down the walk, then along the street, and Randall went to the window again. The mailman didn't stop at Mrs. Florian's house. He went on, his blue-gray back even and calm under the heavy leather pouch.

Randall turned his head and asked with deadly politeness: "How many mail deliveries a morning are there in this district, Mrs. Morrison?"

She tried to face it out. "Just the one," she said sharply— "one mornings and one afternoons."

Her eyes darted this way and that. The rabbit chin was trembling on the edge of something. Her hands clutched at the rubber frill that bordered the blue and white apron.

"The morning delivery just went by," Randall said dreamily. "Registered mail comes by the regular mailman?"

"She always got it Special Delivery," the old voice cracked.

"Oh. But on Saturday she ran out and spoke to the mailman when he didn't stop at her house. And you said nothing about Special Delivery."

It was nice to watch him working—on somebody else.

Her mouth opened wide and her teeth had the nice shiny look that comes from standing all night in a glass of solution. Then suddenly she made a squawking noise and threw the apron over her head and ran out of the room.

He watched the door through which she had gone. It was beyond the arch. He smiled. It was a rather tired smile.

"Neat, and not a bit gaudy," I said. "Next time you play the tough part. I don't like being rough with old ladies— even if they are lying gossips."

He went on smiling. "Same old story." He shrugged. "Police work. Phooey. She started with facts, as she knew facts. But they didn't come fast enough or seem exciting enough. So she tried a little lily-gilding."

He turned and we went out into the hall. A faint noise of sobbing came from the back of the house. For some patient man, long dead, that had been the weapon of final defeat, probably. To me it was just an old woman sobbing, but nothing to be pleased about.

We went quietly out of the house, shut the front door quietly and made sure that the screen door didn't bang. Randall put his hat on and sighed. Then he shrugged, spreading his cool well-kept hands out far from his body. There was a thin sound of sobbing still audible, back in the house.

The mailman's back was two houses down the street.

"Police work," Randall said quietly, under his breath, and twisted his mouth.

We walked across the space to the next house. Mrs. Florian hadn't even taken the wash in. It still jittered, stiff and yellowish on the wire line in the side yard. We went up on the steps and rang the bell. No answer. We knocked. No answer.

"It was unlocked last time," I said.

He tried the door, carefully screening the movement with his body. It was locked this time. We went down off the porch and walked around the house on the side away from Old Nosey. The back porch had a hooked screen. Randall knocked on that. Nothing happened. He came back off the two almost paintless wooden steps and went along the disused and overgrown driveway and opened up a wooden garage. The doors creaked. The garage was full of nothing. There were a few battered old-fashioned trunks not worth breaking up for firewood. Rusted gardening tools, old cans, plenty of those, in cartons. On each side of the doors, in the angle of the wall a nice fat black widow spider sat in its casual untidy web. Randall picked up a piece of wood and killed them absently. He shut the garage up again, walked back along the weedy drive to the front and up the steps of the house on the other side from Old Nosey. Nobody answered his ring or knock.

He came back slowly, looking across the street over his shoulder.

"Back door's easiest," he said. "The old hen next door won't do anything about it now. She's done too much lying."

He went up the two back steps and slid a knife blade neatly into the crack of the door and lifted the hook. That put us in the screen porch. It was full of cans and some of the cans were full of flies.

"Jesus, what a way to live!" he said.

The back door was easy. A five-cent skeleton key turned the lock. But there was a bolt.

"This jars me," I said. "I guess she's beat it. She wouldn't lock up like this. She's too sloppy."

"Your hat's older than mine," Randall said. He looked at

the glass panel in the back door. "Lend it to me to push the glass in. Or shall we do a neat job?"

"Kick it in. Who cares around here?"

"Here goes."

He stepped back and lunged at the lock with his leg parallel to the floor. Something cracked idly and the door gave a few inches. We heaved it open and picked a piece of jagged cast metal off the linoleum and laid it politely on the woodstone drainboard, beside about nine empty gin bottles.

Flies buzzed against the closed windows of the kitchen. The place reeked. Randall stood in the middle of the floor, giving it the careful eye.

Then he walked softly through the swing door without touching it except low down with his toe and using that to push it far enough back so that it stayed open. The living room was much as I had remembered it. The radio was off.

"That's a nice radio," Randall said. "Cost money. If it's paid for. Here's something."

He went down on one knee and looked along the carpet. Then he went to the side of the radio and moved a loose cord with his foot. The plug came into view. He bent and studied the knobs on the radio front.

"Yeah," he said. "Smooth and rather large. Pretty smart, that. You don't get prints on a light cord, do you?"

"Shove it in and see if it's turned on."

He reached around and shoved it into the plug in the baseboard. The light went on at once. We waited. The thing hummed for a while and then suddenly a heavy volume of sound began to pour out of the speaker. Randall jumped at the cord and yanked it loose again. The sound was snapped off sharp.

When he straightened his eyes were full of light.

We went swiftly into the bedroom. Mrs. Jessie Pierce Florian lay diagonally across her bed, in a rumpled cotton house dress, with her head close to one end of the footboard. The corner post of the bed was smeared darkly with something the flies liked.

She had been dead long enough.

Randall didn't touch her. He stared down at her for a long time and then looked at me with a wolfish baring of his teeth.

"Brains on her face," he said. "That seems to be the theme song of this case. Only this was done with just a pair of hands. But Jesus what a pair of hands. Look at the neck bruises, the spacing of the finger marks."

"You look at them," I said. I turned away. "Poor old Nulty. It's not just a shine killing any more."

31

A shiny black bug with a pink head and pink spots on it crawled slowly along the polished top of Randall's desk and waved a couple of feelers around, as if testing the breeze for a takeoff. It wobbled a little as it crawled, like an old woman carrying too many parcels. A nameless dick sat at another desk and kept talking into an old-fashioned hushaphone telephone mouthpiece, so that his voice sounded like someone whispering in a tunnel. He talked with his eyes half closed, a big scarred hand on the desk in front of him holding a burning cigarette between the knuckles of the first and second fingers.

The bug reached the end of Randall's desk and marched straight off into the air. It fell on its back on the floor, waved a few thin worn legs in the air feebly and then played dead. Nobody cared, so it began waving the legs again and finally struggled over on its face. It trundled slowly off into a corner towards nothing, going nowhere.

The police loudspeaker box on the wall put out a bulletin about a holdup on San Pedro south of Forty-fourth. The holdup was a middle-aged man wearing a dark gray suit and gray felt hat. He was last seen running east on Forty-fourth and then dodging between two houses. "Approach carefully," the announcer said. "This suspect is armed with a .32 caliber revolver and has just held up the proprietor of a Greek restaurant at Number 3966 South San Pedro."

A flat click and the announcer went off the air and another one came on and started to read a hot car list, in a slow monotonous voice that repeated everything twice.

The door opened and Randall came in with a sheaf of letter size typewritten sheets. He walked briskly across the room and sat down across the desk from me and pushed some papers at me.

"Sign four copies," he said.

I signed four copies.

The pink bug reached a corner of the room and put feelers out for a good spot to take off from. It seemed a little discouraged. It went along the baseboard towards another corner. I lit a cigarette and the dick at the hushaphone abruptly got up and went out of the office.

Randall leaned back in his chair, looking just the same as ever, just as cool, just as smooth, just as ready to be nasty or nice as the occasion required.

"I'm telling you a few things," he said, "just so you won't go having any more brainstorms. Just so you won't go master-minding all over the landscape any more. Just so maybe for Christ's sake you will let this one lay."

I waited.

"No prints in the dump," he said. "You know which dump I mean. The cord was jerked to turn the radio off, but she turned it up herself probably. That's pretty obvious. Drunks like loud radios. If you have gloves on to do a killing and you turn up the radio to drown shots or something, you can turn it off the same way. But that wasn't the way it was done. And that woman's neck is broken. She was dead before the guy started to smack her head around. Now why did he start to smack her head around?"

"I'm just listening."

Randall frowned. "He probably didn't know he'd broken her neck. He was sore at her," he said. "Deduction." He smiled sourly.

I blew some smoke and waved it away from my face.

"Well, why was he sore at her? There was a grand reward paid the time he was picked up at Florian's for the bank job in Oregon. It was paid to a shyster who is dead since, but the Florians likely got some of it. Malloy may have suspected that. Maybe he actually knew it. And maybe he was just trying to shake it out of her."

I nodded. It sounded worth a nod. Randall went on:

"He took hold of her neck just once and his fingers didn't slip. If we get him, we might be able to prove by the spacing of the marks that his hands did it. Maybe not. The doc figures it happened last night, fairly early. Motion picture time, anyway. So far we don't tie Malloy to the house last night, not by any neighbors. But it certainly looks like Malloy."

"Yeah," I said. "Malloy all right. He probably didn't mean to kill her, though. He's just too strong."

"That won't help him any," Randall said grimly.

"I suppose not. I just make the point that Malloy does not appear to me to be a killer type. Kill if cornered—but not for pleasure or money—and not women."

"Is that an important point?" he asked dryly.

"Maybe you know enough to know what's important. And what isn't. I don't."

He stared at me long enough for a police announcer to have time to put out another bulletin about the holdup of the Greek restaurant on South San Pedro. The suspect was now in custody. It turned out later that he was a fourteen-year-old Mexican armed with a water-pistol. So much for eyewitnesses.

Randall waited until the announcer stopped and went on:

"We got friendly this morning. Let's stay that way. Go home and lie down and have a good rest. You look pretty peaked. Just let me and the police department handle the Marriott killing and find Moose Malloy and so on."

"I got paid on the Marriott business," I said. "I fell down on the job. Mrs. Grayle has hired me. What do you want me to do—retire and live on my fat?"

He stared at me again. "I know. I'm human. They give you guys licenses, which must mean they expect you to do something with them besides hang them on the wall in your office. On the other hand any acting-captain with a grouch can break you."

"Not with the Grayles behind me."

He studied it. He hated to admit I could be even half right. So he frowned and tapped his desk.

"Just so we understand each other," he said after a pause. "If you crab this case, you'll be in a jam. It may be a jam you can wriggle out of this time. I don't know. But little by little you will build up a body of hostility in this department that will make it damn hard for you to do any work."

"Every private dick faces that every day of his life—unless he's just a divorce man."

"You can't work on murders."

"You've said your piece. I heard you say it. I don't expect to go out and accomplish things a big police department can't accomplish. If I have any small private notions, they are just that—small and private."

He leaned slowly across the desk. His thin restless fingers tap-tapped, like the poinsettia shoots tapping against Mrs. Jessie Florian's front wall. His creamy gray hair shone. His cool steady eyes were on mine.

"Let's go on," he said. "With what there is to tell. Amthor's away on a trip. His wife—and secretary—doesn't know or won't say where. The Indian has also disappeared. Will you sign a complaint against these people?"

"No. I couldn't make it stick."

He looked relieved. "The wife says she never heard of you. As to these two Bay City cops, if that's what they were— that's out of my hands. I'd rather not have the thing any more complicated than it is. One thing I feel pretty sure of— Amthor had nothing to do with Marriott's death. The cigarettes with his card in them were just a plant."

"Doc Sonderborg?"

He spread his hands. "The whole shebang skipped. Men from the D.A.'s office went down there on the quiet. No contact with Bay City at all. The house is locked up and empty. They got in, of course. Some hasty attempt had been made to clean up, but there are prints—plenty of them. It will take a week to work out what we have. There's a wall safe they're working on now. Probably had dope in it—and other things. My guess is that Sonderborg will have a record, not local, somewhere else, for abortion, or treating gunshot wounds or altering finger tips or for illegal use of dope. If it comes under Federal statutes, we'll get a lot of help."

"He said he was a medical doctor," I said.

Randall shrugged. "May have been once. May never have been convicted. There's a guy practicing medicine near Palm Springs right now who was indicted as a dope peddler in Hollywood five years ago. He was as guilty as hell—but the protection worked. He got off. Anything else worrying you?"

"What do you know about Brunette—for telling?"

"Brunette's a gambler. He's making plenty. He's making it an easy way."

"All right," I said, and started to get up. "That sounds reasonable. But it doesn't bring us any nearer to this jewel heist gang that killed Marriott."

"I can't tell you everything, Marlowe."

"I don't expect it," I said. "By the way, Jessie Florian told me—the second time I saw her—that she had been a servant in Marriott's family once. That was why he was sending her money. Anything to support that?"

"Yes. Letters in his safety-deposit box from her thanking him and saying the same thing." He looked as if he was going to lose his temper. "*Now* will you for God's sake go home and mind your own business?"

"Nice of him to take such care of the letters, wasn't it?"

He lifted his eyes until their glance rested on the top of my head. Then he lowered the lids until half the iris was covered. He looked at me like that for a long ten seconds. Then he smiled. He was doing an awful lot of smiling that day. Using up a whole week's supply.

"I have a theory about that," he said. "It's crazy, but it's human nature. Marriott was by the circumstances of his life a threatened man. All crooks are gamblers, more or less, and all gamblers are superstitious—more or less. I think Jessie Florian was Marriott's lucky piece. As long as he took care of her, nothing would happen to him."

I turned my head and looked for the pink-headed bug. He had tried two corners of the room now and was moving off disconsolately towards a third. I went over and picked him up in my handkerchief and carried him back to the desk.

"Look," I said. "This room is eighteen floors above ground. And this little bug climbs all the way up here just to make a friend. Me. *My* luck piece." I folded the bug carefully into the soft part of the handkerchief and tucked the handkerchief into my pocket. Randall was pie-eyed. His mouth moved, but nothing came out of it.

"I wonder whose lucky piece Marriott was," I said.

"Not yours, pal." His voice was acid—cold acid.

"Perhaps not yours either." My voice was just a voice. I went out of the room and shut the door.

I rode the express elevator down to the Spring Street entrance and walked out on the front porch of City Hall and down some steps and over to the flower beds. I put the pink bug down carefully behind a bush.

I wondered, in the taxi going home, how long it would take him to make the Homicide Bureau again.

I got my car out of the garage at the back of the apartment house and ate some lunch in Hollywood before I started down to Bay City. It was a beautiful cool sunny afternoon down at the beach. I left Arguello Boulevard at Third Street and drove over to the City Hall.

32

It was a cheap looking building for so prosperous a town. It looked more like something out of the Bible belt. Bums sat unmolested in a long row on the retaining wall that kept the front lawn—now mostly Bermuda grass—from falling into the street. The building was of three stories and had an old belfry at the top, and the bell still hanging in the belfry. They had probably rung it for the volunteer fire brigade back in the good old chaw-and-spit days.

The cracked walk and the front steps led to open double doors in which a knot of obvious city hall fixers hung around waiting for something to happen so they could make something else out of it. They all had the well-fed stomachs, the careful eyes, the nice clothes and the reach-me-down manners. They gave me about four inches to get in.

Inside was a long dark hallway that had been mopped the day McKinley was inaugurated. A wooden sign pointed out the police department Information Desk. A uniformed man dozed behind a pint-sized PBX set into the end of a scarred wooden counter. A plainclothesman with his coat off and his hog's leg looking like a fire plug against his ribs took one eye off his evening paper, bonged a spittoon ten feet away from him, yawned, and said the Chief's office was upstairs at the back.

The second floor was lighter and cleaner, but that didn't mean that it was clean and light. A door on the ocean side, almost at the end of the hall, was lettered: John Wax, Chief of Police. Enter.

Inside there was a low wooden railing and a uniformed man behind it working a typewriter with two fingers and one thumb. He took my card, yawned, said he would see, and managed to drag himself through a mahogany door marked John Wax, Chief of Police. Private. He came back and held the door in the railing for me.

I went on in and shut the door of the inner office. It was cool and large and had windows on three sides. A stained wood desk was set far back like Mussolini's, so that you had to walk across an expanse of blue carpet to get to it, and while you were doing that you would be getting the beady eye.

I walked to the desk. A tilted embossed sign on it read: John Wax, Chief of Police. I figured I might be able to remember the name. I looked at the man behind the desk. No straw was sticking to his hair.

He was a hammered-down heavyweight, with short pink hair and a pink scalp glistening through it. He had small, hungry, heavy-lidded eyes, as restless as fleas. He wore a suit of fawn-colored flannel, a coffee-colored shirt and tie, a diamond ring, a diamond-studded lodge pin in his lapel, and the required three stiff points of handkerchief coming up a little more than the required three inches from his outside breast pocket.

One of his plump hands was holding my card. He read it, turned it over and read the back, which was blank, read the front again, put it down on his desk and laid on it a paperweight in the shape of a bronze monkey, as if he was making sure he wouldn't lose it.

He pushed a pink paw at me. When I gave it back to him, he motioned to a chair.

"Sit down, Mr. Marlowe. I see you are in our business more or less. What can I do for you?"

"A little trouble, Chief. You can straighten it out for me in a minute, if you care to."

"Trouble," he said softly. "A little trouble."

He turned in his chair and crossed his thick legs and gazed thoughtfully towards one of his pairs of windows. That let me see handspun lisle socks and English brogues that looked as if they had been pickled in port wine. Counting what I couldn't see and not counting his wallet he had half a grand on him. I figured his wife had money.

"Trouble," he said, still softly, "is something our little city don't know much about, Mr. Marlowe. Our city is small but very, very clean. I look out of my western windows and I see the Pacific Ocean. Nothing cleaner than that, is there?" He didn't mention the two gambling ships that were hull down on the brass waves just beyond the three-mile limit.

Neither did I. "That's right, Chief," I said.

He threw his chest a couple of inches farther. "I look out of my northern windows and I see the busy bustle of Arguello Boulevard and the lovely California foothills, and in the near foreground one of the nicest little business sections a man could want to know. I look out of my southern windows, which I am looking out of right now, and I see the finest little yacht harbor in the world, for a small yacht harbor. I don't have no eastern windows, but if I did have, I would see a residential section that would make your mouth water. No, sir, trouble is a thing we don't have a lot of on hand in our little town."

"I guess I brought mine with me, Chief. Some of it at least. Do you have a man working for you named Galbraith, a plainclothes sergeant?"

"Why yes, I believe I do," he said, bringing his eyes around. "What about him?"

"Do you have a man working for you that goes like this?" I described the other man, the one who said very little, was short, had a mustache and hit me with a blackjack. "He goes around with Galbraith, very likely. Somebody called him Mister Blane, but that sounded like a phony."

"Quite on the contrary," the fat Chief said as stiffly as a fat man can say anything. "He is my Chief of Detectives. Captain Blane."

"Could I see these two guys in your office?"

He picked my card up and read it again. He laid it down. He waved a soft glistening hand.

"Not without a better reason than you have given me so far," he said suavely.

"I didn't think I could, Chief. Do you happen to know of a man named Jules Amthor? He calls himself a psychic adviser. He lives at the top of a hill in Stillwood Heights."

"No. And Stillwood Heights is not in my territory," the Chief said. His eyes now were the eyes of a man who has other thoughts.

"That's what makes it funny," I said. "You see, I went to call on Mr. Amthor in connection with a client of mine. Mr. Amthor got the idea I was blackmailing him. Probably guys in his line of business get that idea rather easily. He had a tough Indian bodyguard I couldn't handle. So the Indian held me and Amthor beat me up with my own gun. Then he sent for a couple of cops. They happened to be Galbraith and Mister Blane. Could this interest you at all?"

Chief Wax flapped his hands on his desk top very gently. He folded his eyes almost shut, but not quite. The cool gleam of his eyes shone between the thick lids and it shone straight at me. He sat very still, as if listening. Then he opened his eyes and smiled.

"And what happened then?" he inquired, polite as a bouncer at the Stork Club.

"They went through me, took me away in their car, dumped me out on the side of a mountain and socked me with a sap as I got out."

He nodded, as if what I had said was the most natural thing in the world. "And this was in Stillwood Heights," he said softly.

"Yeah."

"You know what I think you are?" He leaned a little over the desk, but not far, on account of his stomach being in the way.

"A liar," I said.

"The door is there," he said, pointing to it with the little finger of his left hand.

I didn't move. I kept on looking at him. When he started

to get mad enough to push his buzzer I said: "Let's not both make the same mistake. You think I'm a small time private dick trying to push ten times his own weight, trying to make a charge against a police officer that, even if it was true, the officer would take damn good care couldn't be proved. Not at all. I'm not making any complaints. I think the mistake was natural. I want to square myself with Amthor and I want your man Galbraith to help me do it. Mister Blane needn't bother. Galbraith will be enough. And I'm not here without backing. I have important people behind me."

"How far behind?" the Chief asked and chuckled wittily.

"How far is 862 Aster Drive, where Mr. Merwin Lockridge Grayle lives?"

His face changed so completely that it was as if another man sat in his chair. "Mrs. Grayle happens to be my client," I said.

"Lock the doors," he said. "You're a younger man than I am. Turn the bolt knobs. We'll make a friendly start on this thing. You have an honest face, Marlowe."

I got up and locked the doors. When I got back to the desk along the blue carpet, the Chief had a nice looking bottle out and two glasses. He tossed a handful of cardamom seeds on his blotter and filled both glasses.

We drank. He cracked a few cardamom seeds and we chewed them silently, looking into each other's eyes.

"That tasted right," he said. He refilled the glasses. It was my turn to crack the cardamom seeds. He swept the shells off his blotter to the floor and smiled and leaned back.

"Now let's have it," he said. "Has this job you are doing for Mrs. Grayle anything to do with Amthor?"

"There's a connection. Better check that I'm telling you the truth, though."

"There's that," he said and reached for his phone. Then he took a small book out of his vest and looked up a number. "Campaign contributors," he said and winked. "The Mayor is very insistent that all courtesies be extended. Yes, here it is." He put the book away and dialed.

He had the same trouble with the butler that I had. It made his ears get red. Finally he got her. His ears stayed red. She must have been pretty sharp with him. "She wants to talk to you," he said and pushed the phone across his broad desk.

"This is Phil," I said, winking naughtily at the Chief.

There was a cool provocative laugh. "What are you doing with that fat slob?"

"There's a little drinking being done."

"Do you have to do it with him?"

"At the moment, yes. Business. I said, is there anything new? I guess you know what I mean."

"No. Are you aware, my good fellow, that you stood me up for an hour the other night? Did I strike you as the kind of girl that lets that sort of thing happen to her?"

"I ran into trouble. How about tonight?"

"Let me see—tonight is—what day of the week is it for heaven's sake?"

"I'd better call you," I said. "I may not be able to make it. This is Friday."

"Liar." The soft husky laugh came again. "It's Monday. Same time, same place—and no fooling this time?"

"I'd better call you."

"You'd better be there."

"I can't be sure. Let me call you."

"Hard to get? I see. Perhaps I'm a fool to bother."

"As a matter of fact you are."

"Why?"

"I'm a poor man, but I pay my own way. And it's not quite as soft a way as you would like."

"Damn you, if you're not there—"

"I said I'd call you."

She sighed. "All men are the same."

"So are all women—after the first nine."

She damned me and hung up. The Chief's eyes popped so far out of his head they looked as if they were on stilts.

He filled both glasses with a shaking hand and pushed one at me.

"So it's like that," he said very thoughtfully.

"Her husband doesn't care," I said, "so don't make a note of it."

He looked hurt as he drank his drink. He cracked the cardamom seeds very slowly, very thoughtfully. We drank to each other's baby blue eyes. Regretfully the Chief put the bottle and glasses out of sight and snapped a switch on his call box.

"Have Galbraith come up, if he's in the building. If not, try and get in touch with him for me."

I got up and unlocked the doors and sat down again. We didn't wait long. The side door was tapped on, the Chief called out, and Hemingway stepped into the room.

He walked solidly over to the desk and stopped at the end of it and looked at Chief Wax with the proper expression of tough humility.

"Meet Mr. Philip Marlowe," the Chief said genially. "A private dick from L.A."

Hemingway turned enough to look at me. If he had ever seen me before, nothing in his face showed it. He put a hand out and I put a hand out and he looked at the Chief again.

"Mr. Marlowe has a rather curious story," the Chief said, cunning, like Richelieu behind the arras. "About a man named Amthor who has a place in Stillwood Heights. He's some sort of crystal-gazer. It seems Marlowe went to see him and you and Blane happened in about the same time and there was an argument of some kind. I forget the details." He looked out of his windows with the expression of a man forgetting details.

"Some mistake," Hemingway said. "I never saw this man before."

"There was a mistake, as a matter of fact," the Chief said dreamily. "Rather trifling, but still a mistake. Mr. Marlowe thinks it of slight importance."

Hemingway looked at me again. His face still looked like a stone face.

"In fact he's not even interested in the mistake," the Chief dreamed on. "But he is interested in going to call on this man Amthor who lives in Stillwood Heights. He would like someone with him. I thought of you. He would like someone who would see that he got a square deal. It seems that Mr. Amthor has a very tough Indian bodyguard and Mr. Marlowe is a little inclined to doubt his ability to handle the situation without help. Do you think you could find out where this Amthor lives?"

"Yeah," Hemingway said. "But Stillwood Heights is over the line, Chief. This just a personal favor to a friend of yours?"

"You might put it that way," the Chief said, looking at his left thumb. "We wouldn't want to do anything not strictly legal, of course."

"Yeah," Hemingway said. "No." He coughed. "When do we go?"

The Chief looked at me benevolently. "Now would be okey," I said. "If it suits Mr. Galbraith."

"I do what I'm told," Hemingway said.

The Chief looked him over, feature by feature. He combed him and brushed him with his eyes. "How is Captain Blane today?" he inquired, munching on a cardamom seed.

"Bad shape. Bust appendix," Hemingway said. "Pretty critical."

The Chief shook his head sadly. Then he got hold of the arms of his chair and dragged himself to his feet. He pushed a pink paw across his desk.

"Galbraith will take good care of you, Marlowe. You can rely on that."

"Well, you've certainly been obliging, Chief," I said. "I certainly don't know how to thank you."

"Pshaw! No thanks necessary. Always glad to oblige a friend of a friend, so to speak." He winked at me. Hemingway studied the wink but he didn't say what he added it up to.

We went out, with the Chief's polite murmurs almost carrying us down the office. The door closed. Hemingway looked up and down the hall and then he looked at me.

"You played that one smart, baby," he said. "You must got something we wasn't told about."

33

The car drifted quietly along a quiet street of homes. Arching pepper trees almost met above it to form a green tunnel. The sun twinkled through their upper branches and their narrow light leaves. A sign at the corner said it was Eighteenth Street.

Hemingway was driving and I sat beside him. He drove very slowly, his face heavy with thought.

"How much you tell him?" he asked, making up his mind.

"I told him you and Blane went over there and took me away and tossed me out of the car and socked me on the back of the head. I didn't tell him the rest."

"Not about Twenty-third and Descanso, huh?"

"No."

"Why not?"

"I thought maybe I could get more co-operation from you if I didn't."

"That's a thought. You really want to go over to Stillwood Heights, or was that just a stall?"

"Just a stall. What I really want is for you to tell me why you put me in that funnyhouse and why I was kept there?"

Hemingway thought. He thought so hard his cheek muscles made little knots under his grayish skin.

"That Blane," he said. "That sawed-off hunk of shin meat. I didn't mean for him to sap you. I didn't mean for you to walk home neither, not really. It was just an act, on account of we are friends with this swami guy and we kind of keep people from bothering him. You'd be surprised what a lot of people would try to bother him."

"Amazed," I said.

He turned his head. His gray eyes were lumps of ice. Then he looked ahead again through the dusty windshield and did some more thinking.

"Them old cops get sap-hungry once in a while," he said. "They just got to crack a head. Jesus, was I scared. You dropped like a sack of cement. I told Blane plenty. Then we run you over to Sonderborg's place on account of it was a little closer and he was a nice guy and would take care of you."

"Does Amthor know you took me there?"

"Hell, no. It was our idea."

"On account of Sonderborg is such a nice guy and he would take care of me. And no kickback. No chance for a doctor to back up a complaint if I made one. Not that a complaint would have much chance in this sweet little town, if I did make it."

"You going to get tough?" Hemingway asked thoughtfully.

"Not me," I said. "And for once in your life neither are you. Because your job is hanging by a thread. You looked in the Chief's eyes and you saw that. I didn't go in there without credentials, not this trip."

"Okey," Hemingway said and spat out of the window. "I didn't have any idea of getting tough in the first place except just the routine big mouth. What next?"

"Is Blane really sick?"

Hemingway nodded, but somehow failed to look sad. "Sure is. Pain in the gut day before yesterday and it bust on him before they could get his appendix out. He's got a chance—but not too good."

"We'd certainly hate to lose him," I said. "A fellow like that is an asset to any police force."

Hemingway chewed that one over and spat it out of the car window.

"Okey, next question," he sighed.

"You told me why you took me to Sonderborg's place. You didn't tell me why he kept me there over forty-eight hours, locked up and shot full of dope."

Hemingway braked the car softly over beside the curb. He put his large hands on the lower part of the wheel side by side and gently rubbed the thumbs together.

"I wouldn't have an idea," he said in a far-off voice.

"I had papers on me showing I had a private license," I said. "Keys, some money, a couple of photographs. If he didn't know you boys pretty well, he might think the crack on the head was just a gag to get into his place and look around. But I figure he knows you boys too well for that. So I'm puzzled."

"Stay puzzled, pally. It's a lot safer."

"So it is," I said. "But there's no satisfaction in it."

"You got the L.A. law behind you on this?"

"On this what?"

"On this thinking about Sonderborg."

"Not exactly."

"That don't mean yes or no."

"I'm not that important," I said. "The L.A. law can come in here any time they feel like it—two thirds of them anyway.

The Sheriff's boys and the D.A.'s boys. I have a friend in the D.A.'s office. I worked there once. His name is Bernie Ohls. He's Chief Investigator."

"You give it to him?"

"No. I haven't spoken to him in a month."

"Thinking about giving it to him?"

"Not if it interferes with a job I'm doing."

"Private job?"

"Yes."

"Okey, what is it you want?"

"What's Sonderborg's real racket?"

Hemingway took his hands off the wheel and spat out of the window. "We're on a nice street here, ain't we? Nice homes, nice gardens, nice climate. You hear a lot about crooked cops, or do you?"

"Once in a while," I said.

"Okey, how many cops do you find living on a street even as good as this, with nice lawns and flowers? I'd know four or five, all vice squad boys. They get all the gravy. Cops like me live in itty-bitty frame houses on the wrong side of town. Want to see where I live?"

"What would it prove?"

"Listen, pally," the big man said seriously. "You got me on a string, but it could break. Cops don't go crooked for money. Not always, not even often. They get caught in the system. They get you where they have you do what is told them or else. And the guy that sits back there in the nice big corner office, with the nice suit and the nice liquor breath he thinks chewing on them seeds makes smell like violets, only it don't—he ain't giving the orders either. You get me?"

"What kind of man is the mayor?"

"What kind of guy is a mayor anywhere? A politician. You think he gives the orders? Nuts. You know what's the matter with this country, baby?"

"Too much frozen capital, I heard."

"A guy can't stay honest if he wants to," Hemingway said. "That's what's the matter with this country. He gets chiseled out of his pants if he does. You gotta play the game dirty or you don't eat. A lot of bastards think all we need is ninety thousand FBI men in clean collars and brief cases. Nuts. The percentage would get them just the way it does the rest of us. You know what I think? I think we gotta make this little world all over again. Now take Moral Rearmament. There you've got something. M.R.A. There you've got something, baby."

"If Bay City is a sample of how it works, I'll take aspirin," I said.

"You could get too smart," Hemingway said softly. "You might not think it, but it could be. You could get so smart you couldn't think about anything but bein' smart. Me, I'm just a dumb cop. I take orders. I got a wife and two kids and I do what the big shots say. Blane could tell you things. Me, I'm ignorant."

"Sure Blane has appendicitis? Sure he didn't just shoot himself in the stomach for meanness?"

"Don't be that way," Hemingway complained and slapped his hands up and down on the wheel. "Try and think nice about people."

"About Blane?"

"He's human—just like the rest of us," Hemingway said. "He's a sinner—but he's human."

"What's Sonderborg's racket?"

"Okey, I was just telling you. Maybe I'm wrong. I had you figured for a guy that could be sold a nice idea."

"You don't know what his racket is," I said.

Hemingway took his handkerchief out and wiped his face with it. "Buddy, I hate to admit it," he said. "But you ought to know damn well that if I knew or Blane knew Sonderborg had a racket, either we wouldn't of dumped you in there or you wouldn't ever have come out, not walking. I'm talking about a real bad racket, naturally. Not fluff stuff like telling old women's fortunes out of a crystal ball."

"I don't think I was meant to come out walking," I said. "There's a drug called scopolamine, truth serum, that some-times makes people talk without their knowing it. It's not sure fire, any more than hypnotism is. But it sometimes works. I think I was being milked in there to find out what I knew. But there are only three ways Sonderborg could have known that there was anything for me to know that might hurt him. Amthor might have told him, or Moose Malloy might have mentioned to him that I went to see Jessie Florian, or he might have thought putting me in there was a police gag."

Hemingway stared at me sadly. "I can't even see your dust," he said. "Who the hell is Moose Malloy?"

"A big hunk that killed a man over on Central Avenue a few days ago. He's on your teletype, if you ever read it. And you probably have a reader of him by now."

"So what?"

"So Sonderborg was hiding him. I saw him there, on a bed reading newspapers, the night I snuck out."

"How'd you get out? Wasn't you locked in?"

"I crocked the orderly with a bed spring. I was lucky."

"This big guy see you?"

"No."

Hemingway kicked the car away from the curb and a solid grin settled on his face. "Let's go collect," he said. "It figures. It figures swell. Sonderborg was hiding hot boys. If they had dough, that is. His set-up was perfect for it. Good money, too."

He kicked the car into motion and whirled around a corner.

"Hell, I thought he sold reefers," he said disgustedly. "With the right protection behind him. But hell, that's a small time racket. A peanut grift."

"Ever hear of the numbers racket? That's a small time racket too—if you're just looking at one piece of it."

Hemingway turned another corner sharply and shook his heavy head. "Right. And pin ball games and bingo houses and horse parlors. But add them all up and give one guy control and it makes sense."

"What guy?"

He went wooden on me again. His mouth shut hard and I could see his teeth were biting at each other inside it. We were on Descanso Street and going east. It was a quiet street even in late afternoon. As we got towards Twenty-third, it became in some vague manner less quiet. Two men were studying a palm tree as if figuring out how to move it. A car was parked near Dr. Sonderborg's place, but nothing showed in it. Halfway down the block a man was reading water meters.

The house was a cheerful spot by daylight. Tea rose begonias made a solid pale mass under the front windows and pansies a blur of color around the base of a white acacia in bloom. A scarlet climbing rose was just opening its buds on a fan-shaped trellis. There was a bed of winter sweet peas and a bronze-green humming bird prodding in them delicately. The house looked like the home of a well-to-do elderly couple who liked to garden. The late afternoon sun on it had a hushed and menacing stillness.

Hemingway slid slowly past the house and a tight little smile tugged at the corners of his mouth. His nose sniffed. He turned the next corner, and looked in his rear view mirror and stepped up the speed of the car.

After three blocks he braked at the side of the street again and turned to give me a hard level stare.

"L.A. law," he said. "One of the guys by the palm tree is called Donnelly. I know him. They got the house covered. So you didn't tell your pal uptown, huh?"

"I said I didn't."

"The Chief'll love this," Hemingway snarled. "They come down here and raid a joint and don't even stop by to say hello."

I said nothing.

"They catch this Moose Malloy?"

I shook my head. "Not so far as I know."

"How the hell far do you know, buddy?" he asked very softly.

"Not far enough. Is there any connection between Amthor and Sonderborg?"

"Not that I know of."

"Who runs this town?"

Silence.

"I heard a gambler named Laird Brunette put up thirty grand to elect the mayor. I heard he owns the Belvedere Club and both the gambling ships out on the water."

"Might be," Hemingway said politely.

"Where can Brunette be found?"

"Why ask me, baby?"

"Where would you make for if you lost your hideout in this town?"

"Mexico."

I laughed. "Okey, will you do me a big favor?"

"Glad to."

"Drive me back downtown."

He started the car away from the curb and tooled it neatly along a shadowed street towards the ocean. The car reached the city hall and slid around into the police parking zone and I got out.

"Come round and see me some time," Hemingway said. "I'll likely be cleaning spittoons."

He put his big hand out. "No hard feelings?"

"M.R.A." I said and shook the hand.

He grinned all over. He called me back when I started to walk away. He looked carefully in all directions and leaned his mouth close to my ear.

"Them gambling ships are supposed to be out beyond city and state jurisdiction," he said. "Panama registry. If it was me that was—" he stopped dead, and his bleak eyes began to worry.

"I get it," I said. "I had the same sort of idea. I don't know why I bothered so much to get you to have it with me. But it wouldn't work—not for just one man."

He nodded, and then he smiled. "M.R.A." he said.

34

I lay on my back on a bed in a waterfront hotel and waited for it to get dark. It was a small front room with a hard bed and a mattress slightly thicker than the cotton blanket that covered it. A spring underneath me was broken and stuck into the left side of my back. I lay there and let it prod me.

The reflection of a red neon light glared on the ceiling. When it made the whole room red it would be dark enough to go out. Outside cars honked along the alley they called the

Speedway. Feet slithered on the sidewalks below my window. There was a murmur and mutter of coming and going in the air. The air that seeped in through the rusted screens smelled of stale frying fat. Far off a voice of the kind that could be heard far off was shouting: "Get hungry, folks. Get hungry. Nice hot doggies here. Get hungry."

It got darker. I thought; and thought in my mind moved with a kind of sluggish stealthiness, as if it was being watched by bitter and sadistic eyes. I thought of dead eyes looking at a moonless sky, with black blood at the corners of the mouths beneath them. I thought of nasty old women beaten to death against the posts of their dirty beds. I thought of a man with bright blond hair who was afraid and didn't quite know what he was afraid of, who was sensitive enough to know that something was wrong, and too vain or too dull to guess what it was that was wrong. I thought of beautiful rich women who could be had. I thought of nice slim curious girls who lived alone and could be had too, in a different way. I thought of cops, tough cops that could be greased and yet were not by any means all bad, like Hemingway. Fat prosperous cops with Chamber of Commerce voices, like Chief Wax. Slim, smart and deadly cops like Randall, who for all their smartness and deadliness were not free to do a clean job in a clean way. I thought of sour old goats like Nulty who had given up trying. I thought of Indians and psychics and dope doctors.

I thought of lots of things. It got darker. The glare of the red neon sign spread farther and farther across the ceiling. I sat up on the bed and put my feet on the floor and rubbed the back of my neck.

I got up on my feet and went over to the bowl in the corner and threw cold water on my face. After a little while I felt a little better, but very little. I needed a drink, I needed a lot of life insurance, I needed a vacation, I needed a home in the country. What I had was a coat, a hat and a gun. I put them on and went out of the room.

There was no elevator. The hallways smelled and the stairs had grimed rails. I went down them, threw the key on the desk and said I was through. A clerk with a wart on his left eyelid nodded and a Mexican bellhop in a frayed uniform coat came forward from behind the dustiest rubber plant in California to take my bags. I didn't have any bags, so being a Mexican, he opened the door for me and smiled politely just the same.

Outside the narrow street fumed, the sidewalks swarmed with fat stomachs. Across the street a bingo parlor was going full blast and beside it a couple of sailors with girls were coming out of a photographer's shop where they had probably been having their photos taken riding on camels. The voice of the hot dog merchant split the dusk like an axe. A big blue bus blared down the street to the little circle where the street car used to turn on a turntable. I walked that way.

After a while there was a faint smell of ocean. Not very much, but as if they had kept this much just to remind people this had once been a clean open beach where the waves came in and creamed and the wind blew and you could smell something besides hot fat and cold sweat.

The little sidewalk car came trundling along the wide concrete walk. I got on it and rode to the end of the line and got off and sat on a bench where it was quiet and cold and there was a big brown heap of kelp almost at my feet. Out to sea they had turned the lights on in the gambling boats. I got back on the sidewalk car the next time it came and rode back almost to where I had left the hotel. If anybody was tailing me, he was doing it without moving. I didn't think there was. In that clean little city there wouldn't be enough crime for the dicks to be very good shadows.

The black piers glittered their length and then disappeared into the dark background of night and water. You could still smell hot fat, but you could smell the ocean too. The hot dog man droned on:

"Get hungry, folks, get hungry. Nice hot doggies. Get hungry."

I spotted him in a white barbecue stand tickling wienies with a long fork. He was doing a good business even that early in the year. I had to wait sometime to get him alone.

"What's the name of the one farthest out?" I asked, pointing with my nose.

"Montecito." He gave me the level steady look.

"Could a guy with reasonable dough have himself a time there?"

"What kind of a time?"

I laughed, sneeringly, very tough.

"Hot doggies," he chanted. "Nice hot doggies, folks." He dropped his voice. "Women?"

"Nix. I was figuring on a room with a nice sea breeze and good food and nobody to bother me. Kind of vacation."

He moved away. "I can't hear a word you say," he said, and then went into his chant.

He did some more business. I didn't know why I bothered with him. He just had that kind of face. A young couple in shorts came up and bought hot dogs and strolled away with the boy's arm around the girl's brassiere and each eating the other's hot dog.

The man slid a yard towards me and eyed me over. "Right now I should be whistling Roses of Picardy," he said, and paused. "That would cost you," he said.

"How much?"

"Fifty. Not less. Unless they want you for something."

"This used to be a good town," I said. "A cool-off town."

"Thought it still was," he drawled. "But why ask me?"

"I haven't an idea," I said. I threw a dollar bill on his counter. "Put it in the baby's bank," I said. "Or whistle Roses of Picardy."

He snapped the bill, folded it longways, folded it across and folded it again. He laid it on the counter and tucked his middle finger behind his thumb and snapped. The folded bill hit me lightly in the chest and fell noiselessly to the ground. I bent and picked it up and turned quickly. But nobody was behind me that looked like a dick.

I leaned against the counter and laid the dollar bill on it again. "People don't throw money at me," I said "They hand it to me. Do you mind?"

He took the bill, unfolded it, spread it out and wiped it off with his apron. He punched his cash-register and dropped the bill into the drawer.

"They say money don't stink," he said. "I sometimes wonder."

I didn't say anything. Some more customers did business with him and went away. The night was cooling fast.

"I wouldn't try the *Royal Crown*," the man said. "That's for good little squirrels, that stick to their nuts. You look like dick to me, but that's your angle. I hope you swim good."

I left him, wondering why I had gone to him in the first place. Play the hunch. Play the hunch and get stung. In a little while you wake up with your mouth full of hunches. You can't order a cup of coffee without shutting your eyes and stabbing the menu. Play the hunch.

I walked around and tried to see if anybody walked behind me in any particular way. Then I sought out a restaurant that didn't smell of frying grease and found one with a purple neon sign and a cocktail bar behind a reed curtain. A male cutie with henna'd hair drooped at a bungalow grand piano and tickled the keys lasciviously and sang Stairway to the Stars in a voice with half the steps missing.

I gobbled a dry martini and hurried back through the reed curtain to the dining room.

The eighty-five cent dinner tasted like a discarded mail bag and was served to me by a waiter who looked as if he would slug me for a quarter, cut my throat for six bits, and bury me at sea in a barrel of concrete for a dollar and a half, plus sales tax.

35

It was a long ride for a quarter. The water taxi, an old launch painted up and glassed in for three-quarters of its length, slid through the anchored yachts and around the wide pile of stone which was the end of the breakwater. The swell hit us without warning and bounced the boat like a cork. But there was plenty of room to be sick that early in the evening. All the company I had was three couples and the man who drove the boat, a tough-looking citizen who sat a little on his left hip on account of having a black leather hip-holster inside his right hip pocket. The three couples began to chew each other's faces as soon as we left the shore.

I stared back at the lights of Bay City and tried not to bear down too hard on my dinner. Scattered points of light drew together and became a jeweled bracelet laid out in the show window of the night. Then the brightness faded and they were a soft orange glow appearing and disappearing over the edge of the swell. It was a long smooth even swell with no whitecaps, and just the right amount of heave to make me glad I hadn't pickled my dinner in bar whiskey. The taxi slid up and down the swell now with a sinister smoothness, like a cobra dancing. There was cold in the air, the wet cold that sailors never get out of their joints. The red neon pencils that outlined the *Royal Crown* faded off to the left and dimmed in the gliding gray ghosts of the sea, then shone out again, as bright as new marbles.

We gave this one a wide berth. It looked nice from a long way off. A faint music came over the water and music over the water can never be anything but lovely. The *Royal Crown* seemed to ride as steady as a pier on its four hausers. Its landing stage was lit up like a theater marquee. Then all this faded into remoteness and another, older, smaller boat began to sneak out of the night towards us. It was not much to look at. A converted seagoing freighter with scummed and rusted plates, the superstructure cut down to the boat deck level, and above that two stumpy masts just high enough for a radio antenna. There was light on the *Montecito* also and music floated across the wet dark sea. The spooning couples took their teeth out of each other's necks and stared at the ship and giggled.

The taxi swept around in a wide curve, careened just enough to give the passengers a thrill, and eased up to the hemp fenders along the stage. The taxi's motor idled and backfired in the fog. A lazy searchlight beam swept a circle about fifty yards out from the ship.

The taximan hooked to the stage and a sloe-eyed lad in a blue mess jacket with bright buttons, a bright smile and a gangster mouth, handed the girls up from the taxi. I was last. The casual neat way he looked me over told me something about him. The casual neat way he bumped my shoulder clip told me more.

"Nix," he said softly. "Nix."

He had a smoothly husky voice, a hard Harry straining himself through a silk handkerchief. He jerked his chin at the taximan. The taximan dropped a short loop over a bitt, turned his wheel a little, and climbed out on the stage. He stepped behind me.

"No gats on the boat, laddy. Sorry and all that rot," Mess-jacket purred.

"I could check it. It's just part of my clothes. I'm a fellow who wants to see Brunette, on business."

He seemed mildly amused. "Never heard of him," he smiled. "On your way, bo."

The taximan hooked a wrist through my right arm.

"I want to see Brunette," I said. My voice sounded weak and frail, like an old lady's voice.

"Let's not argue," the sloe-eyed lad said. "We're not in Bay City now, not even in California, and by some good opinions not even in the U.S.A. Beat it."

"Back in the boat," the taximan growled behind me. "I owe you a quarter. Let's go."

I got back into the boat. Mess-jacket looked at me with his silent sleek smile. I watched it until it was no longer a smile, no longer a face, no longer anything but a dark figure against the landing lights. I watched it and hungered.

The way back seemed longer. I didn't speak to the taximan and he didn't speak to me. As I got off at the wharf he handed me a quarter.

"Some other night," he said wearily, "when we got more room to bounce you."

Half a dozen customers waiting to get in stared at me, hearing him. I went past them, past the door of the little waiting room on the float, towards the shallow steps at the landward end.

A big redheaded roughneck in dirty sneakers and tarry pants and what was left of a torn blue sailor's jersey and a streak of black down the side of his face straightened from the railing and bumped into me casually.

I stopped. He looked too big. He had three inches on me and thirty pounds. But it was getting to be time for me to put my fist into somebody's teeth even if all I got for it was a wooden arm.

The light was dim and mostly behind him. "What's the matter, pardner?" he drawled. "No soap on the hell ship?"

"Go darn your shirt," I told him. "Your belly is sticking out."

"Could be worse," he said. "The gat's kind of bulgy under the light suit at that."

"What pulls your nose into it?"

"Jesus, nothing at all. Just curiosity. No offense, pal."

"Well, get the hell out of my way then."

"Sure. I'm just resting here."

He smiled a slow tired smile. His voice was soft, dreamy, so delicate for a big man that it was startling. It made me think of another soft-voiced big man I had strangely liked.

"You got the wrong approach," he said sadly. "Just call me Red."

"Step aside, Red. The best people make mistakes. I feel one crawling up my back."

He looked thoughtfully this way and that. He had me angled into a corner of the shelter on the float. We seemed to be more or less alone.

"You want on the *Monty?* Can be done. If you got a reason."

People in gay clothes and gay faces went past us and got into the taxi. I waited for them to pass.

"How much is the reason?"

"Fifty bucks. Ten more if you bleed in my boat."

I started around him.

"Twenty-five," he said softly. "Fifteen if you come back with friends."

"I don't have any friends," I said, and walked away. He didn't try to stop me.

I turned right along the cement walk down which the little electric cars come and go, trundling like baby carriages and blowing little horns that wouldn't startle an expectant mother. At the foot of the first pier there was a flaring bingo parlor, jammed full of people already. I went into it and stood against the wall behind the players, where a lot of other people stood and waited for a place to sit down.

I watched a few numbers go up on the electric indicator, listened to the table men call them off, tried to spot the house players and couldn't, and turned to leave.

A large blueness that smelled of tar took shape beside me. "No got the dough—or just tight with it?" the gentle voice asked in my ear.

I looked at him again. He had the eyes you never see, that you only read about. Violet eyes. Almost purple. Eyes like a girl, a lovely girl. His skin was as soft as silk. Lightly reddened, but it would never tan. It was too delicate. He was bigger than Hemingway and younger, by many years. He was not as big as Moose Malloy, but he looked very fast on his feet. His hair was that shade of red that glints with gold. But except for the eyes he had a plain farmer face, with no stagy kind of handsomeness.

"What's your racket?" he asked. "Private eye?"

"Why do I have to tell you?" I snarled.

"I kind of thought that was it," he said. "Twenty-five too high? No expense account?"

"No."

He sighed. "It was a bum idea I had anyway," he said. "They'll tear you to pieces out there."

"I wouldn't be surprised. What's *your* racket?"

"A dollar here, a dollar there. I was on the cops once. They broke me."

"Why tell me?"

He looked surprised. "It's true."

"You must have been leveling."

He smiled faintly.

"Know a man named Brunette?"

The faint smile stayed on his face. Three bingoes were made in a row. They worked fast in there. A tall beak-faced man with sallow sunken cheeks and a wrinkled suit stepped close to us and leaned against the wall and didn't look at us. Red leaned gently towards him and asked: "Is there something we could tell you, pardner?"

The tall beak-faced man grinned and moved away. Red grinned and shook the building leaning against the wall again.

"I've met a man who could take you," I said.

"I wish there was more," he said gravely. "A big guy costs money. Things ain't scaled for him. He costs to feed, to put clothes on, and he can't sleep with his feet in the bed. Here's how it works. You might not think this is a good place to talk, but it is. Any finks drift along I'll know them and the rest of the crowd is watching those numbers and nothing else. I got a boat with an under-water by-pass. That is, I can borrow one. There's a pier down the line without lights. I know a loading port on the *Monty* I can open. I take a load out there once in a while. There ain't many guys below decks."

"They have a searchlight and lookouts," I said.

"We can make it."

I got my wallet out and slipped a twenty and a five against my stomach and folded them small. The purple eyes watched me without seeming to.

"One way?"

I nodded.

"Fifteen was the word."

"The market took a spurt."

A tarry hand swallowed the bills. He moved silently away. He faded into the hot darkness outside the doors. The beak-nosed man materialized at my left side and said quietly:

"I think I know that fellow in sailor clothes. Friend of yours? I think I seen him before."

I straightened away from the wall and walked away from him without speaking, out of the doors, then left, watching a high head that moved along from electrolier to electrolier a hundred feet ahead of me. After a couple of minutes I turned into a space between two concession shacks. The beak-nosed man appeared, strolling with his eyes on the ground. I stepped out to his side.

"Good evening," I said. "May I guess your weight for a quarter?" I leaned against him. There was a gun under the wrinkled coat.

His eyes looked at me without emotion. "Am I goin' to have to pinch you, son? I'm posted along this stretch to maintain law and order."

"Who's dismaintaining it right now?"

"Your friend had a familiar look to me."

"He ought to. He's a cop."

"Aw hell," the beak-nosed man said patiently. "That's where I seen him. Good night to you."

He turned and strolled back the way he had come. The tall

head was out of sight now. It didn't worry me. Nothing about that lad would ever worry me.

I walked on slowly.

36

Beyond the electroliers, beyond the beat and toot of the small sidewalk cars, beyond the smell of hot fat and popcorn and the shrill children and the barkers in the peep shows, beyond everything but the smell of the ocean and the suddenly clear line of the shore and the creaming fall of the waves into the pebbled spume. I walked almost alone now. The noises died behind me, the hot dishonest light became a fumbling glare. Then the lightless finger of a black pier jutted seaward into the dark. This would be the one. I turned to go out on it.

Red stood up from a box against the beginning of the piles and spoke upwards to me. "Right," he said. "You go on out to the seasteps. I gotta go and get her and warm her up."

"Waterfront cop followed me. That guy in the bingo parlor. I had to stop and speak to him."

"Olson. Pickpocket detail. He's good too. Except once in a while he will lift a leather and plant it, to keep up his arrest record. That's being a shade too good, or isn't it?"

"For Bay City I'd say just about right. Let's get going. I'm getting the wind up. I don't want to blow this fog away. It doesn't look much but it would help a lot."

"It'll last enough to fool a searchlight," Red said. "They got Tommyguns on that boat deck. You go on out the pier. I'll be along."

He melted into the dark and I went out the dark boards, slipping on fish-slimed planking. There was a low dirty railing at the far end. A couple leaned in a corner. They went away, the man swearing.

For ten minutes I listened to the water slapping the piles. A night bird whirred in the dark, the faint grayness of a wing cut across my vision and disappeared. A plane droned high in the ceiling. Then far off a motor barked and roared and kept on roaring like half a dozen truck engines. After a while the sound eased and dropped, then suddenly there was no sound at all.

More minutes passed. I went back to the seasteps and moved down them as cautiously as a cat on a wet floor. A dark shape slid out of the night and something thudded. A voice said: "All set. Get in."

I got into the boat and sat beside him under the screen. The boat slid out over the water. There was no sound from its exhaust now but an angry bubbling along both sides of the shell. Once more the lights of Bay City became something distantly luminous beyond the rise and fall of alien waves. Once more the garish lights of the *Royal Crown* slid off to one side, the ship seeming to preen itself like a fashion model on a revolving platform. And once again the ports of the good ship *Montecito* grew out of the black Pacific and the slow steady sweep of the searchlight turned around it like the beam of a lighthouse.

"I'm scared," I said suddenly. "I'm scared stiff."

Red throttled down the beat and let it slide up and down the swell as though the water moved underneath and the boat stayed in the same place. He turned his face and stared at me.

"I'm afraid of death and despair," I said. "Of dark water and drowned men's faces and skulls with empty eyesockets. I'm afraid of dying, of being nothing, of not finding a man named Brunette."

He chuckled. "You had me going for a minute. You sure give yourself a pep talk. Brunette might be any place. On either of the boats, at the club he owns, back east, Reno, in his slippers at home. That all you want?"

"I want a man named Malloy, a huge brute who got out of the Oregon State pen a while back after an eight-year stretch for bank robbery. He was hiding out in Bay City." I told him about it. I told him a great deal more than I intended to. It must have been his eyes.

At the end he thought and then spoke slowly and what he said had wisps of fog clinging to it, like the beads on a mustache. Maybe that made it seem wiser than it was, maybe not.

"Some of it makes sense," he said. "Some not. Some I

wouldn't know about, some I would. If this Sonderborg was running a hideout and peddling reefers and sending boys out to heist jewels off rich ladies with a wild look in their eyes, it stands to reason that he had an in with the city government, but that don't mean they knew everything he did or that every cop on the force knew he had an in. Could be Blane did and Hemingway, as you call him, didn't. Blane's bad, the other guy is just tough cop, neither bad nor good, neither crooked nor honest, full of guts and just dumb enough, like me, to think being on the cops is a sensible way to make a living. This psychic fellow doesn't figure either way. He bought himself a line of protection in the best market, Bay City, and he used it when he had to. You never know what a guy like that is up to and so you never know what he has on his conscience or is afraid of. Could be he's human and fell for a customer once in a while. Them rich dames are easier to make than paper dolls. So my hunch about your stay in Sonderborg's place is simply that Blane knew Sonderborg would be scared when he found out who you were—and the story they told Sonderborg is probably what he told you, that they found you wandering with your head dizzy—and Sonderborg wouldn't know what to do with you and he would be afraid either to let you go or to knock you off, and after long enough Blane would drop around and raise the ante on him. That's all there was to that. It just happened they could use you and they did it. Blane might know about Malloy too. I wouldn't put it past him."

I listened and watched the slow sweep of the searchlight and the coming and going of the water taxi far over to the right.

"I know how these boys figure," Red said. "The trouble with cops is not that they're dumb or crooked or tough, but that they think just being a cop gives them a little something they didn't have before. Maybe it did once, but not any more. They're topped by too many smart minds. That brings us to Brunette. He don't run the town. He couldn't be bothered. He put up big money to elect a mayor so his water taxis wouldn't be bothered. If there was anything in particular he wanted, they would give it to him. Like a while ago one of his friends, a lawyer, was pinched for drunk driving felony and Brunette got the charge reduced to reckless driving. They changed the blotter to do it, and that's a felony too. Which gives you an idea. His racket is gambling and all rackets tie together these days. So he might handle reefers, or touch a percentage from some one of his workers he gave the business to. He might know Sonderborg and he might not. But the jewel heist is out. Figure the work these boys done for eight grand. It's a laugh to think Brunette would have anything to do with that."

"Yeah," I said. "There was a man murdered too — remember?"

"He didn't do that either, nor have it done. If Brunette had that done, you wouldn't have found any body. You never know what might be stitched into a guy's clothes. Why chance it? Look what I'm doing for you for twenty-five bucks. What would Brunette get done with the money *he* has to spend?"

"Would he have a man killed?"

Red thought for a moment. "He might. He probably has. But he's not a tough guy. These racketeers are a new type. We think about them the way we think about old time yeggs or needled-up punks. Big-mouthed police commissioners on the radio yell that they're all yellow rats, that they'll kill women and babies and howl for mercy if they see a police uniform. They ought to know better than to try to sell the public that stuff. There's yellow cops and there's yellow torpedoes — but damn few of either. And as for the top men, like Brunette — they didn't get there by murdering people. They got there by guts and brains — and they don't have the group courage the cops have either. But above all they're business men. What they do is for money. Just like other business men. Sometimes a guy gets badly in the way. Okey. Out. But they think plenty before they do it. What the hell am I giving a lecture for?"

"A man like Brunette wouldn't hide Malloy," I said. "After he had killed two people."

"No. Not unless there was some other reason than money. Want to go back?"

"No."

Red moved his hands on the wheel. The boat picked up speed. "Don't think I *like* these bastards," he said. "I hate their guts."

37

The revolving searchlight was a pale mist-ridden finger that barely skimmed the waves a hundred feet or so beyond the ship. It was probably more for show than anything else. Especially at this time in the evening. Anyone who had plans for hijacking the take on one of these gambling boats would need plenty of help and would pull the job about four in the morning, when the crowd was thinned down to a few bitter gamblers, and the crew were all dull with fatigue. Even then it would be a poor way to make money. It had been tried once.

A taxi curved to the landing stage, unloaded, went back shorewards. Red held his speedboat idling just beyond the sweep of the searchlight. If they lifted it a few feet, just for fun—but they didn't. It passed languidly and the dull water glowed with it and the speedboat slid across the line and closed in fast under the overhang, past the two huge scummy stern hausers. We sidled up to the greasy plates of the hull as coyly as a hotel dick getting set to ease a hustler out of his lobby.

Double iron doors loomed high above us, and they looked too high to reach and too heavy to open even if we could reach them. The speedboat scuffed the *Montecito*'s ancient sides and the swell slapped loosely at the shell under our feet. A big shadow rose in the gloom at my side and a coiled rope slipped upwards through the air, slapped, caught, and the end ran down and splashed in water. Red fished it out with a boathook, pulled it tight and fastened the end to something on the engine cowling. There was just enough fog to make everything seem unreal. The wet air was as cold as the ashes of love.

Red leaned close to me and his breath tickled my ear. "She

rides too high. Come a good blow and she'd wave her screws in the air. We got to climb those plates just the same."

"I can hardly wait," I said, shivering.

He put my hands on the wheel, turned it just as he wanted it, set the throttle, and told me to hold the boat just as she was. There was an iron ladder bolted close to the plates, curving with the hull, its rungs probably as slippery as a greased pole.

Going up it looked as tempting as climbing over the cornice of an office building. Red reached for it, after wiping his hands hard on his pants to get some tar on them. He hauled himself up noiselessly, without even a grunt, and his sneakers caught the metal rungs, and he braced his body out almost at right angles to get more traction.

The searchlight beam swept far outside us now. Light bounced off the water and seemed to make my face as obvious as a flare, but nothing happened. Then there was a dull creak of heavy hinges over my head. A faint ghost of yellowish light trickled out into the fog and died. The outline of one half of the loading port showed. It couldn't have been bolted from inside. I wondered why.

The whisper was a mere sound, without meaning. I left the wheel and started up. It was the hardest journey I ever made. It landed me panting and wheezing in a sour hold littered with packing boxes and barrels and coils of rope and clumps of rusted chain. Rats screamed in dark corners. The yellow light came from a narrow door on the far side.

Red put his lips against my ear. "From here we take a straight walk to the boiler room catwalk. They'll have steam in one auxiliary, because they don't have no Diesels on this piece of cheese. There will be probably one guy below. The crew doubles in brass up on the play decks, table men and spotters and waiters and so on. They all got to sign on as something that sounds like ship. From the boiler room I'll show you a ventilator with no grating in it. It goes to the boat deck and the boat deck is out of bounds. But it's all yours—while you live."

"You must have relatives on board," I said.

"Funnier things have happened. Will you come back fast?"

"I ought to make a good splash from the boat deck," I

said, and got my wallet out. "I think this rates a little more money. Here. Handle the body as if it was your own."

"You don't owe me nothing more, pardner."

"I'm buying the trip back—even if I don't use it. Take the money before I bust out crying and wet your shirt."

"Need a little help up there?"

"All I need is a silver tongue and the one I have is like a lizard's back."

"Put your dough away," Red said. "You paid me for the trip back. I think you're scared." He took hold of my hand. His was strong, hard, warm and slightly sticky. "I *know* you're scared," he whispered.

"I'll get over it," I said. "One way or another."

He turned away from me with a curious look I couldn't read in that light. I followed him among the cases and barrels, over the raised iron sill of the door, into a long dim passage with the ship smell. We came out of this on to a grilled steel platform, slick with oil, and went down a steel ladder that was hard to hold on to. The slow hiss of the oil burners filled the air now and blanketed all other sound. We turned towards the hiss through mountains of silent iron.

Around a corner we looked at a short dirty wop in a purple silk shirt who sat in a wired-together office chair, under a naked hanging light, and read the evening paper with the aid of a black forefinger and steel-rimmed spectacles that had probably belonged to his grandfather.

Red stepped behind him noiselessly. He said gently:

"Hi, Shorty. How's all the bambinos?"

The Italian opened his mouth with a click and threw a hand at the opening of his purple shirt. Red hit him on the angle of the jaw and caught him. He put him down on the floor gently and began to tear the purple shirt into strips.

"This is going to hurt him more than the poke on the button," Red said softly. "But the idea is a guy going up a ventilator ladder makes a lot of racket down below. Up above they won't hear a thing."

He bound and gagged the Italian neatly and folded his glasses and put them in a safe place and we went along to the ventilator that had no grating in it. I looked up and saw nothing but blackness.

"Good-by," I said.

"Maybe you need a little help."

I shook myself like a wet dog. "I need a company of marines. But either I do it alone or I don't do it. So long."

"How long will you be?" His voice still sounded worried.

"An hour or less."

He stared at me and chewed his lip. Then he nodded. "Sometimes a guy has to," he said. "Drop by that bingo parlor, if you get time."

He walked away softly, took four steps, and came back. "That open loading port," he said. "That might buy you something. Use it." He went quickly.

38

Cold air rushed down the ventilator. It seemed a long way to the top. After three minutes that felt like an hour I poked my head out cautiously from the hornlike opening. Canvas-sheeted boats were gray blurs near by. Low voices muttered in the dark. The beam of the searchlight circled slowly. It came from a point still higher, probably a railed platform at the top of one of the stumpy masts. There would be a lad up there with a Tommygun too, perhaps even a light Browning. Cold job, cold comfort when somebody left the loading port unbolted so nicely.

Distantly music throbbed like the phony bass of a cheap radio. Overhead a masthead light and through the higher layers of fog a few bitter stars stared down.

I climbed out of the ventilator, slipped my .38 from the shoulder clip and held it curled against my ribs, hiding it with my sleeve. I walked three silent steps and listened. Nothing happened. The muttering talk had stopped, but not on my account. I placed it now, between two lifeboats. And out of the night and the fog, as it mysteriously does, enough light gathered into one focus to shine on the dark hardness of a machine gun mounted on a high tripod and swung down over the rail. Two men stood near it, motionless, not smoking, and their voices began to mutter again, a quiet whisper that never became words.

I listened to the muttering too long. Another voice spoke clearly behind me.

"Sorry, guests are not allowed on the boat deck."

I turned, not too quickly, and looked at his hands. They were light blurs and empty.

I stepped sideways nodding and the end of a boat hid us. The man followed me gently, his shoes soundless on the damp deck.

"I guess I'm lost," I said.

"I guess you are." He had a youngish voice, not chewed out of marble. "But there's a door at the bottom of the companionway. It has a spring lock on it. It's a good lock. There used to be an open stairway with a chain and a brass sign. We found the livelier element would step over that."

He was talking a long time, either to be nice, or to be waiting. I didn't know which. I said: "Somebody must have left the door open."

The shadowed head nodded. It was lower than mine.

"You can see the spot that puts us in, though. If somebody did leave it open, the boss won't like it a nickel. If somebody didn't, we'd like to know how you got up here. I'm sure you get the idea."

"It seems a simple idea. Let's go down and talk to him about it."

"You come with a party?"

"A very nice party."

"You ought to have stayed with them."

"You know how it is—you turn your head and some other guy is buying her a drink."

He chuckled. Then he moved his chin slightly up and down.

I dropped and did a frogleap sideways and the swish of the blackjack was a long spent sigh in the quiet air. It was getting to be that every blackjack in the neighborhood swung at me automatically. The tall one swore.

I said: "Go ahead and be heroes."

I clicked the safety catch loudly.

Sometimes even a bad scene will rock the house. The tall

one stood rooted, and I could see the blackjack swinging at his wrist. The one I had been talking to thought it over without any hurry.

"This won't buy you a thing," he said gravely. "You'll never get off the boat."

"I thought of that. Then I thought how little you'd care."

It was still a bum scene.

"You want what?" he said quietly.

"I have a loud gun," I said. "But it doesn't have to go off. I want to talk to Brunette."

"He went to San Diego on business."

"I'll talk to his stand-in."

"You're quite a lad," the nice one said. "We'll go down. You'll put the heater up before we go through the door."

"I'll put the heater up when I'm sure I'm going through the door."

He laughed lightly. "Go back to your post, Slim. I'll look into this."

He moved lazily in front of me and the tall one appeared to fade into the dark.

"Follow me, then."

We moved Indian file across the deck. We went down brassbound slippery steps. At the bottom was a thick door. He opened it and looked at the lock. He smiled, nodded, held the door for me and I stepped through, pocketing the gun.

The door closed and clicked behind us. He said:

"Quiet evening, so far."

There was a gilded arch in front of us and beyond it a gaming room, not very crowded. It looked much like any other gaming room. At the far end there was a short glass bar and some stools. In the middle a stairway going down and up this the music swelled and faded. I heard roulette wheels. A man was dealing faro to a single customer. There were not more than sixty people in the room. On the faro table there was a pile of yellowbacks that would start a bank. The player was an elderly white-haired man who looked politely attentive to the dealer, but no more.

Two quiet men in dinner jackets came through the archway sauntering, looking at nothing. That had to be expected.

They strolled towards us and the short slender man with me waited for them. They were well beyond the arch before they let their hands find their side pockets, looking for cigarettes of course.

"From now on we have to have a little organization here," the short man said. "I don't think you'll mind?"

"You're Brunette," I said suddenly.

He shrugged. "Of course."

"You don't look so tough," I said.

"I hope not."

The two men in dinner jackets edged me gently.

"In here," Brunette said. "We can talk at ease."

He opened the door and they took me into dock.

The room was like a cabin and not like a cabin. Two brass lamps swung in gimbels hung above a dark desk that was not wood, possibly plastic. At the end were two bunks in grained wood. The lower of them was made up and on the top one were half a dozen stacks of phonograph record books. A big combination radio-phonograph stood in the corner. There was a red leather chesterfield, a red carpet, smoking stands, a tabouret with cigarettes and a decanter and glasses, a small bar sitting cattycorners at the opposite end from the bunks.

"Sit down," Brunette said and went around the desk. There were a lot of business-like papers on the desk, with columns of figures, done on a bookkeeping machine. He sat in a tall backed director's chair and tilted it a little and looked me over. Then he stood up again and stripped off his overcoat and scarf and tossed them to one side. He sat down again. He picked a pen up and tickled the lobe of one ear with it. He had a cat smile, but I like cats.

He was neither young nor old, neither fat nor thin. Spending a lot of time on or near the ocean had given him a good healthy complexion. His hair was nut-brown and waved naturally and waved still more at sea. His forehead was narrow and brainy and his eyes held a delicate menace. They were yellowish in color. He had nice hands, not babied to the point of insipidity, but well-kept. His dinner clothes were midnight blue, I judged, because they looked so black. I thought his pearl was a little too large, but that might have been jealousy.

He looked at me for quite a long time before he said: "He has a gun."

One of the velvety tough guys leaned against the middle of my spine with something that was probably not a fishing rod. Exploring hands removed the gun and looked for others.

"Anything else?" a voice asked.

Brunette shook his head. "Not now."

One of the gunners slid my automatic across the desk. Brunette put the pen down and picked up a letter opener and pushed the gun around gently on his blotter.

"Well," he said quietly, looking past my shoulder. "Do I have to explain what I want now?"

One of them went out quickly and shut the door. The other was so still he wasn't there. There was a long easy silence, broken by the distant hum of voices and the deep-toned music and somewhere down below a dull almost imperceptible throbbing.

"Drink?"

"Thanks."

The gorilla mixed a couple at the little bar. He didn't try to hide the glasses while he did it. He placed one on each side of the desk, on black glass scooters.

"Cigarette?"

"Thanks."

"Egyptian all right?"

"Sure."

We lit up. We drank. It tasted like good Scotch. The gorilla didn't drink.

"What I want—" I began.

"Excuse me, but that's rather unimportant, isn't it?"

The soft catlike smile and the lazy half-closing of the yellow eyes.

The door opened and the other one came back and with him was Mess-jacket, gangster mouth and all. He took one look at me and his face went oyster-white.

"He didn't get past me," he said swiftly, curling one end of his lips.

"He had a gun," Brunette said, pushing it with the letter opener. "This gun. He even pushed it into my back more or less, on the boat deck."

"Not past me, boss," Mess-jacket said just as swiftly.

Brunette raised his yellow eyes slightly and smiled at me. "Well?"

"Sweep him out," I said. "Squash him somewhere else."

"I can prove it by the taximan," Mess-jacket snarled.

"You've been off the stage since five-thirty?"

"Not a minute, boss."

"That's no answer. An empire can fall in a minute."

"Not a second, boss."

"But he can be had," I said, and laughed.

Mess-jacket took the smooth gliding step of a boxer and his fist lashed like a whip. It almost reached my temple. There was a dull thud. His fist seemed to melt in midair. He slumped sideways and clawed at a corner of the desk, then rolled on his back. It was nice to see somebody else get sapped for a change.

Brunette went on smiling at me.

"I hope you're not doing him an injustice," Brunette said. "There's still the matter of the door to the companionway."

"Accidentally open."

"Could you think of any other idea?"

"Not in such a crowd?"

"I'll talk to you alone," Brunette said, not looking at anyone but me.

The gorilla lifted Mess-jacket by the armpits and dragged him across the cabin and his partner opened an inner door. They went through. The door closed.

"All right," Brunette said. "Who are you and what do you want?"

"I'm a private detective and I want to talk to a man named Moose Malloy."

"Show me you're a private dick."

I showed him. He tossed the wallet back across the desk. His wind-tanned lips continued to smile and the smile was getting stagy.

"I'm investigating a murder," I said. "The murder of a man named Marriott on the bluff near your Belvedere Club last Thursday night. This murder happens to be connected with another murder, of a woman, done by Malloy, an ex-con and bank robber and all-round tough guy."

He nodded. "I'm not asking you yet what it has to do with me. I assume you'll come to that. Suppose you tell me how you got on my boat?"

"I told you."

"It wasn't true," he said gently. "Marlowe is the name? It wasn't true, Marlowe. You know that. The kid down on the stage isn't lying. I pick my men carefully."

"You own a piece of Bay City," I said. "I don't know how big a piece, but enough for what you want. A man named Sonderborg has been running a hideout there. He has been running reefers and stick-ups and hiding hot boys. Naturally, he couldn't do that without connections. I don't think he could do it without you. Malloy was staying with him. Malloy has left. Malloy is about seven feet tall and hard to hide. I think he could hide nicely on a gambling boat."

"You're simple," Brunette said softly. "Supposing I wanted to hide him, why should I take the risk out here?" He sipped his drink. "After all I'm in another business. It's hard enough to keep a good taxi service running without a lot of trouble. The world is full of places a crook can hide. If he has money. Could you think of a better idea?"

"I could, but to hell with it."

"I can't do anything for you. So how did you get on the boat?"

"I don't care to say."

"I'm afraid I'll have to have you made to say, Marlowe." His teeth glinted in the light from the brass ship's lamps. "After all, it can be done."

"If I tell you, will you get word to Malloy?"

"What word?"

I reached for my wallet lying on the desk and drew a card from it and turned it over. I put the wallet away and got a pencil instead. I wrote five words on the back of the card and pushed it across the desk. Brunette took it and read what I had written on it. "It means nothing to me," he said.

"It will mean something to Malloy."

He leaned back and stared at me. "I don't make you out. You risk your hide to come out here and hand me a card to pass on to some thug I don't even know. There's no sense to it."

"There isn't if you don't know him."

"Why didn't you leave your gun ashore and come aboard the usual way?"

"I forgot the first time. Then I knew that toughie in the mess jacket would never let me on. Then I bumped into a fellow who knew another way."

His yellow eyes lighted as with a new flame. He smiled and said nothing.

"This other fellow is no crook but he's been on the beach with his ears open. You have a loading port that has been unbarred on the inside and you have a ventilator shaft out of which the grating has been removed. There's one man to knock over to get to the boat deck. You'd better check your crew list, Brunette."

He moved his lips softly, one over the other. He looked down at the card again. "Nobody named Malloy is on board this boat," he said. "But if you're telling the truth about that loading port, I'll buy."

"Go and look at it."

He still looked down. "If there's any way I can get word to Malloy, I will. I don't know why I bother."

"Take a look at that loading port."

He sat very still for a moment, then leaned forward and pushed the gun across the desk to me.

"The things I do," he mused, as if he was alone. "I run towns, I elect mayors, I corrupt police, I peddle dope, I hide out crooks, I heist old women strangled with pearls. What a lot of time I have." He laughed shortly. "What a lot of time."

I reached for my gun and tucked it back under my arm.

Brunette stood up. "I promise nothing," he said, eyeing me steadily. "But I believe you."

"Of course not."

"You took a long chance to hear so little."

"Yes."

"Well—" he made a meaningless gesture and then put his hand across the desk.

"Shake hands with a chump," he said softly.

I shook hands with him. His hand was small and firm and a little hot.

"You wouldn't tell me how you found out about this loading port?"

"I can't. But the man who told me is no crook."

"I could make you tell," he said, and immediately shook his head. "No. I believed you once. I'll believe you again. Sit still and have another drink."

He pushed a buzzer. The door at the back opened and one of the nice-tough guys came in.

"Stay here. Give him a drink, if he wants it. No rough stuff."

The torpedo sat down and smiled at me calmly. Brunette went quickly out of the office. I smoked. I finished my drink. The torpedo made me another. I finished that, and another cigarette.

Brunette came back and washed his hands over in the corner, then sat down at his desk again. He jerked his head at the torpedo. The torpedo went out silently.

The yellow eyes studied me. "You win, Marlowe. And I have one hundred and sixty-four men on my crew list. Well—" he shrugged. "You can go back by the taxi. Nobody will bother you. As to your message, I have a few contacts. I'll use them. Good night. I probably should say thanks. For the demonstration."

"Good night," I said, and stood up and went out.

There was a new man on the landing stage. I rode to shore on a different taxi. I went along to the bingo parlor and leaned against the wall in the crowd.

Red came along in a few minutes and leaned beside me against the wall.

"Easy, huh?" Red said softly, against the heavy clear voices of the table men calling the numbers.

"Thanks to you. He bought. He's worried."

Red looked this way and that and turned his lips a little more close to my ear. "Get your man?"

"No. But I'm hoping Brunette will find a way to get him a message."

Red turned his head and looked at the tables again. He yawned and straightened away from the wall. The beak-nosed man was in again. Red stepped over to him and said: "Hiya,

Olson," and almost knocked the man off his feet pushing past him.

Olson looked after him sourly and straightened his hat. Then he spat viciously on the floor.

As soon as he had gone, I left the place and went along to the parking lot back towards the tracks where I had left my car.

I drove back to Hollywood and put the car away and went up to the apartment.

I took my shoes off and walked around in my socks feeling the floor with my toes. They would still get numb again once in a while.

Then I sat down on the side of the pulled-down bed and tried to figure time. It couldn't be done. It might take hours or days to find Malloy. He might never be found until the police got him. If they ever did—alive.

39

It was about ten o'clock when I called the Grayle number in Bay City. I thought it would probably be too late to catch her, but it wasn't. I fought my way through a maid and the butler and finally heard her voice on the line. She sounded breezy and well-primed for the evening.

"I promised to call you," I said. "It's a little late, but I've had a lot to do."

"Another stand-up?" Her voice got cool.

"Perhaps not. Does your chauffeur work this late?"

"He works as late as I tell him to."

"How about dropping by to pick me up? I'll be getting squeezed into my commencement suit."

"Nice of you," she drawled. "Should I really bother?" Amthor had certainly done a wonderful job with her centers of speech—if anything had ever been wrong with them.

"I'd show you my etching."

"Just one etching?"

"It's just a single apartment."

"I heard they had such things," she drawled again, then changed her tone. "Don't act so hard to get. You have a lovely build, mister. And don't ever let anyone tell you different. Give me the address again."

I gave it to her and the apartment number. "The lobby door is locked," I said. "But I'll go down and slip the catch."

"That's fine," she said. "I won't have to bring my jimmy."

She hung up, leaving me with a curious feeling of having talked to somebody that didn't exist.

I went down to the lobby and slipped the catch and then took a shower and put my pajamas on and lay down on the bed. I could have slept for a week. I dragged myself up off the bed again and set the catch on the door, which I had forgotten to do, and walked through a deep hard snowdrift out to the kitchenette and laid out glasses and a bottle of liqueur Scotch I had been saving for a really highclass seduction.

I lay down on the bed again. "Pray," I said out loud. "There's nothing left but prayer."

I closed my eyes. The four walls of the room seemed to hold the throb of a boat, the still air seemed to drip with fog and rustle with sea wind. I smelled the rank sour smell of a disused hold. I smelled engine oil and saw a wop in a purple shirt reading under a naked light bulb with his grandfather's spectacles. I climbed and climbed up a ventilator shaft. I climbed the Himalayas and stepped out on top and guys with machine guns were all around me. I talked with a small and somehow very human yellow-eyed man who was a racketeer and probably worse. I thought of the giant with the red hair and the violet eyes, who was probably the nicest man I had ever met.

I stopped thinking. Lights moved behind my closed lids. I was lost in space. I was a gilt-edged sap come back from a vain adventure. I was a hundred dollar package of dynamite that went off with a noise like a pawnbroker looking at a dollar watch. I was a pink-headed bug crawling up the side of the City Hall.

I was asleep.

I woke slowly, unwillingly, and my eyes stared at reflected light on the ceiling from the lamp. Something moved gently in the room.

The movement was furtive and quiet and heavy. I listened to it. Then I turned my head slowly and looked at Moose Malloy. There were shadows and he moved in the shadows, as noiselessly as I had seen him once before. A gun in his hand had a dark oily business-like sheen. His hat was pushed back on his black curly hair and his nose sniffed, like the nose of a hunting dog.

He saw me open my eyes. He came softly over to the side of the bed and stood looking down at me.

"I got your note," he said. "I make the joint clean. I don't make no cops outside. If this is a plant, two guys goes out in baskets."

I rolled a little on the bed and he felt swiftly under the pillows. His face was still wide and pale and his deep-set eyes were still somehow gentle. He was wearing an overcoat to-night. It fitted him where it touched. It was burst out in one shoulder seam, probably just getting it on. It would be the largest size they had, but not large enough for Moose Malloy.

"I hoped you'd drop by," I said. "No copper knows anything about this. I just wanted to see you."

"Go on," he said.

He moved sideways to a table and put the gun down and dragged his overcoat off and sat down in my best easy chair. It creaked, but it held. He leaned back slowly and arranged the gun so that it was close to his right hand. He dug a pack of cigarettes out of his pocket and shook one loose and put it into his mouth without touching it with his fingers. A match flared on a thumbnail. The sharp smell of the smoke drifted across the room.

"You ain't sick or anything?" he said.

"Just resting. I had a hard day."

"Door was open. Expecting someone?"

"A dame."

He stared at me thoughtfully.

"Maybe she won't come," I said. "If she does, I'll stall her."

"What dame?"

"Oh, just a dame. If she comes, I'll get rid of her. I'd rather talk to you."

His very faint smile hardly moved his mouth. He puffed his

cigarette awkwardly, as if it was too small for his fingers to hold with comfort.

"What made you think I was on the *Monty?*" he asked.

"A Bay City cop. It's a long story and too full of guessing."

"Bay City cops after me?"

"Would that bother you?"

He smiled the faint smile again. He shook his head slightly.

"You killed a woman," I said. "Jessie Florian. That was a mistake."

He thought. Then he nodded. "I'd drop that one," he said quietly.

"But that queered it," I said. "I'm not afraid of you. You're no killer. You didn't mean to kill her. The other one—over on Central—you could have squeezed out of. But not out of beating a woman's head on a bedpost until her brains were on her face."

"You take some awful chances, brother," he said softly.

"The way I've been handled," I said, "I don't know the difference any more. You didn't mean to kill her—did you?"

His eyes were restless. His head was cocked in a listening attitude.

"It's about time you learned your own strength," I said.

"It's too late," he said.

"You wanted her to tell you something," I said. "You took hold of her neck and shook her. She was already dead when you were banging her head against the bedpost."

He stared at me.

"I know what you wanted her to tell you," I said.

"Go ahead."

"There was a cop with me when she was found. I had to break clean."

"How clean?"

"Fairly clean," I said. "But not about tonight."

He stared at me. "Okey, how did you know I was on the *Monty?*" He had asked me that before. He seemed to have forgotten.

"I didn't. But the easiest way to get away would be by water. With the set-up they have in Bay City you could get out to one of the gambling boats. From there you could get clean away. With the right help."

"Laird Brunette is a nice guy," he said emptily. "So I've heard. I never even spoke to him."

"He got the message to you."

"Hell, there's a dozen grapevines that might help him to do that, pal. When do we do what you said on the card? I had a hunch you were leveling. I wouldn't take the chance to come here otherwise. Where do we go?"

He killed his cigarette and watched me. His shadow loomed against the wall, the shadow of a giant. He was so big he seemed unreal.

"What made you think I bumped Jessie Florian?" he asked suddenly.

"The spacing of the finger marks on her neck. The fact that you had something to get out of her, and that you are strong enough to kill people without meaning to."

"The johns tied me to it?"

"I don't know."

"What did I want out of her?"

"You thought she might know where Velma was."

He nodded silently and went on staring at me.

"But she didn't," I said. "Velma was too smart for her."

There was a light knocking at the door.

Malloy leaned forward a little and smiled and picked up his gun. Somebody tried the doorknob. Malloy stood up slowly and leaned forward in a crouch and listened. Then he looked back at me from looking at the door.

I sat up on the bed and put my feet on the floor and stood up. Malloy watched me silently, without a motion. I went over to the door.

"Who is it?" I asked with my lips to the panel.

It was her voice all right. "Open up, silly. It's the Duchess of Windsor."

"Just a second."

I looked back at Malloy. He was frowning. I went over close to him and said in a very low voice: "There's no other way out. Go in the dressing room behind the bed and wait. I'll get rid of her."

He listened and thought. His expression was unreadable. He was a man who had now very little to lose. He was a man who would never know fear. It was not built into even that giant frame. He nodded at last and picked up his hat and coat and moved silently around the bed and into the dressing room. The door closed, but did not shut tight.

I looked around for signs of him. Nothing but a cigarette butt that anybody might have smoked. I went to the room door and opened it. Malloy had set the catch again when he came in.

She stood there half smiling, in the highnecked white fox evening cloak she had told me about. Emerald pendants hung from her ears and almost buried themselves in the soft white fur. Her fingers were curled and soft on the small evening bag she carried.

The smile died off her face when she saw me. She looked me up and down. Her eyes were cold now.

"So it's like that," she said grimly. "Pajamas and dressing gown. To show me his lovely little etching. What a fool I am."

I stood aside and held the door. "It's not like that at all. I was getting dressed and a cop dropped in on me. He just left."

"Randall?"

I nodded. A lie with a nod is still a lie, but it's an easy lie. She hesitated a moment, then moved past me with a swirl of scented fur.

I shut the door. She walked slowly across the room, stared blankly at the wall, then turned quickly.

"Let's understand each other," she said. "I'm not this much of a pushover. I don't go for hall bedroom romance. There was a time in my life when I had too much of it. I like things done with an air."

"Will you have a drink before you go?" I was still leaning against the door, across the room from her.

"Am I going?"

"You gave me the impression you didn't like it here."

"I wanted to make a point. I have to be a little vulgar to make it. I'm not one of these promiscuous bitches. I can be had—but not just by reaching. Yes, I'll take a drink."

I went out into the kitchenette and mixed a couple of drinks with hands that were not too steady. I carried them in and handed her one.

There was no sound from the dressing-room, not even a sound of breathing.

She took the glass and tasted it and looked across it at the far wall. "I don't like men to receive me in their pajamas," she said. "It's a funny thing. I liked you. I liked you a lot. But I could get over it. I have often got over such things."

I nodded and drank.

"Most men are just lousy animals," she said. "In fact it's a pretty lousy world, if you ask me."

"Money must help."

"You think it's going to when you haven't always had money. As a matter of fact it just makes new problems." She smiled curiously. "And you forget how hard the old problems were."

She got out a gold cigarette case from her bag and I went over and held a match for her. She blew a vague plume of smoke and watched it with half-shut eyes.

"Sit close to me," she said suddenly.

"Let's talk a little first."

"About what? Oh—my jade?"

"About murder."

Nothing changed in her face. She blew another plume of smoke, this time more carefully, more slowly. "It's a nasty subject. Do we have to?"

I shrugged.

"Lin Marriott was no saint," she said. "But I still don't want to talk about it."

She stared at me coolly for a long moment and then dipped her hand into her open bag for a handkerchief.

"Personally I don't think he was a finger man for a jewel mob, either," I said. "The police pretend that they think that, but they do a lot of pretending. I don't even think he was a blackmailer, in any real sense. Funny, isn't it?"

"Is it?" The voice was very, very cold now.

"Well, not really," I agreed and drank the rest of my drink. "It was awfully nice of you to come here, Mrs. Grayle. But we seem to have hit the wrong mood. I don't even, for example, think Marriott was killed by a gang. I don't think he was going to that canyon to buy a jade necklace. I don't even think a jade necklace was ever stolen. I think he went to that canyon to be murdered, although he thought he went there to help commit a murder. But Marriott was a very bad murderer."

She leaned forward a little and her smile became just a little glassy. Suddenly, without any real change in her, she ceased to be beautiful. She looked merely like a woman who would have been dangerous a hundred years ago, and twenty years ago daring, but who today was just Grade B Hollywood.

She said nothing, but her right hand was tapping the clasp of her bag.

"A very bad murderer," I said. "Like Shakespeare's Second Murderer in that scene in *King Richard III*. The fellow that had certain dregs of conscience, but still wanted the money, and in the end didn't do the job at all because he couldn't make up his mind. Such murderers are very dangerous. They have to be removed—sometimes with blackjacks."

She smiled. "And who was he about to murder, do you suppose?"

"Me."

"That must be very difficult to believe—that anyone would hate you that much. And you said my jade necklace was never stolen at all. Have you any proof of all this?"

"I didn't say I had. I said I thought these things."

"Then why be such a fool as to talk about them?"

"Proof," I said, "is always a relative thing. It's an overwhelming balance of probabilities. And that's a matter of how they strike you. There was a rather weak motive for murdering me—merely that I was trying to trace a former Central Avenue dive singer at the same time that a convict named Moose Malloy got out of jail and started to look for her too. Perhaps I was helping him find her. Obviously, it was possible to find her, or it wouldn't have been worth while to pretend to Marriott that I had to be killed and killed quickly. And obviously he wouldn't have believed it, if it wasn't so. But there was a much stronger motive for murdering Marriott, which he, out of vanity or love or greed or a mixture of all three, didn't evaluate. He was afraid, but not for himself. He was afraid of violence to which he was a part and for which he could be convicted. But on the other hand he was fighting for his meal ticket. So he took the chance."

I stopped. She nodded and said: "Very interesting. If one knows what you are talking about."

"And one does," I said.

We stared at each other. She had her right hand in her bag again now. I had a good idea what it held. But it hadn't started to come out yet. Every event takes time.

"Let's quit kidding," I said. "We're all alone here. Nothing either of us says has the slightest standing against what the other says. We cancel each other out. A girl who started in the gutter became the wife of a multimillionaire. On the way up a shabby old woman recognized her—probably heard her singing at the radio station and recognized the voice and went to see—and this old woman had to be kept quiet. But she was cheap, therefore she only knew a little. But the man who dealt with her and made her monthly payments and owned a trust deed on her home and could throw her into the gutter any time she got funny—that man knew it all. He was expensive. But that didn't matter either, as long as nobody else knew. But some day a tough guy named Moose Malloy was going to get out of jail and start finding things out about his former sweetie. Because the big sap loved her—and still does. That's what makes it funny, tragic-funny. And about that time a private dick starts nosing in also. So the weak link in the chain, Marriott, is no longer a luxury. He has become a menace. They'll get to him and they'll take him apart. He's that kind of lad. He melts under heat. So he was murdered before he could melt. With a blackjack. By you."

All she did was take her hand out of her bag, with a gun in it. All she did was point it at me and smile. All I did was nothing.

But that wasn't all that was done. Moose Malloy stepped out of the dressing room with the Colt .45 still looking like a toy in his big hairy paw.

He didn't look at me at all. He looked at Mrs. Lewin Lockridge Grayle. He leaned forward and his mouth smiled at her and he spoke to her softly.

"I thought I knew the voice," he said. "I listened to that voice for eight years—all I could remember of it. I kind of liked your hair red, though. Hiya, babe. Long time no see."

She turned the gun.

"Get away from me, you son of a bitch," she said.

He stopped dead and dropped the gun to his side. He was still a couple of feet from her. His breath labored.

"I never thought," he said quietly. "It just came to me out of the blue. *You* turned me in to the cops. *You*. Little Velma."

I threw a pillow, but it was too slow. She shot him five times in the stomach. The bullets made no more sound than fingers going into a glove.

Then she turned the gun and shot at me but it was empty. She dived for Malloy's gun on the floor. I didn't miss with the second pillow. I was around the bed and knocked her away before she got the pillow off her face. I picked the Colt up and went away around the bed again with it.

He was still standing, but he was swaying. His mouth was slack and his hands were fumbling at his body. He went slack at the knees and fell sideways on the bed, with his face down. His gasping breath filled the room.

I had the phone in my hand before she moved. Her eyes were a dead gray, like half-frozen water. She rushed for the door and I didn't try to stop her. She left the door wide, so when I had done phoning I went over and shut it. I turned his head a little on the bed, so he wouldn't smother. He was still alive, but after five in the stomach even a Moose Malloy doesn't live very long.

I went back to the phone and called Randall at his home. "Malloy," I said. "In my apartment. Shot five times in the stomach by Mrs. Grayle. I called the Receiving Hospital. She got away."

"So you had to play clever," was all he said and hung up quickly.

I went back to the bed. Malloy was on his knees beside the bed now, trying to get up, a great wad of bedclothes in one hand. His face poured sweat. His eyelids flickered slowly and the lobes of his ears were dark.

He was still on his knees and still trying to get up when the fast wagon got there. It took four men to get him on the stretcher.

"He has a slight chance—if they're .25's," the fast wagon doctor said just before he went out. "All depends what they hit inside. But he has a chance."

"He wouldn't want it," I said.

He didn't. He died in the night.

40

"You ought to have given a dinner party," Anne Riordan said looking at me across her tan figured rug. "Gleaming silver and crystal, bright crisp linen—if they're still using linen in the places where they give dinner parties—candlelight, the women in their best jewels and the men in white ties, the servants hovering discreetly with the wrapped bottles of wine, the cops looking a little uncomfortable in their hired evening clothes, as who the hell wouldn't, the suspects with their brittle smiles and restless hands, and you at the head of the long table telling all about it, little by little, with your charming light smile and a phony English accent like Philo Vance."

"Yeah," I said. "How about a little something to be holding in my hand while you go on being clever?"

She went out to her kitchen and rattled ice and came back with a couple of tall ones and sat down again.

"The liquor bills of your lady friends must be something fierce," she said and sipped.

"And suddenly the butler fainted," I said. "Only it wasn't the butler who did the murder. He just fainted to be cute."

I inhaled some of my drink. "It's not that kind of story," I said. "It's not lithe and clever. It's just dark and full of blood."

"So she got away?"

I nodded. "So far. She never went home. She must have had a little hideout where she could change her clothes and appearance. After all she lived in peril, like the sailors. She was alone when she came to see me. No chauffeur. She came in a small car and she left it a few dozen blocks away."

"They'll catch her—if they really try."

"Don't be like that. Wilde, the D.A. is on the level. I worked for him once. But if they catch her, what then? They're up against twenty million dollars and a lovely face and either Lee Farrell or Rennenkamp. It's going to be awfully hard to prove she killed Marriott. All they have is what looks like a heavy motive and her past life, if they can trace it. She probably has no record, or she wouldn't have played it this way."

"What about Malloy? If you had told me about him before, I'd have known who she was right away. By the way, how did *you* know? Those two photos are not of the same woman."

"No. I doubt if even old lady Florian knew they had been switched on her. She looked kind of surprised when I shoved the photo of Velma—the one that had Velma Valento written on it—in front of her nose. But she may have known. She may have just hid it with the idea of selling it to me later on. Knowing it was harmless, a photo of some other girl Marriott substituted."

"That's just guessing."

"It had to be that way. Just as when Marriott called me up and gave me a song and dance about a jewel ransom payoff it had to be because I had been to see Mrs. Florian asking about Velma. And when Marriott was killed, it had to be because he was the weak link in the chain. Mrs. Florian didn't even know Velma had become Mrs. Lewin Lockridge Grayle. She couldn't have. They bought her too cheap. Grayle says they went to Europe to be married and she was married under her real name. He won't tell where or when. He won't tell what her real name was. He won't tell where she is. I don't think he knows, but the cops don't believe that."

"Why won't he tell?" Anne Riordan cupped her chin on the backs of her laced fingers and stared at me with shadowed eyes.

"He's so crazy about her he doesn't care whose lap she sat in."

"I hope she enjoyed sitting in yours," Anne Riordan said acidly.

"She was playing me. She was a little afraid of me. She didn't want to kill me because it's bad business killing a man who is a sort of cop. But she probably would have tried in the end, just as she would have killed Jessie Florian, if Malloy hadn't saved her the trouble."

"I bet it's fun to be played by handsome blondes," Anne

Riordan said. "Even if there is a little risk. As, I suppose, there usually is."

I didn't say anything.

"I suppose they can't do anything to her for killing Malloy, because he had a gun."

"No. Not with her pull."

The goldflecked eyes studied me solemnly. "Do you think she meant to kill Malloy?"

"She was afraid of him," I said. "She had turned him in eight years ago. He seemed to know that. But he wouldn't have hurt her. He was in love with her too. Yes, I think she meant to kill anybody she had to kill. She had a lot to fight for. But you can't keep that sort of thing up indefinitely. She took a shot at me in my apartment—but the gun was empty then. She ought to have killed me out on the bluff when she killed Marriott."

"He was in love with her," Anne said softly. "I mean Malloy. It didn't matter to him that she hadn't written to him in six years or ever gone to see him while he was in jail. It didn't matter to him that she had turned him in for a reward. He just bought some fine clothes and started to look for her the first thing when he got out. So she pumped five bullets into him, by way of saying hello. He had killed two people himself, but he was in love with her. What a world."

I finished my drink and got the thirsty look on my face again. She ignored it. She said:

"And she had to tell Grayle where she came from and he didn't care. He went away to marry her under another name and sold his radio station to break contact with anybody who might know her and he gave her everything that money can buy and she gave him—what?"

"That's hard to say." I shook the ice cubes at the bottom of my glass. That didn't get me anything either. "I suppose she gave him a sort of pride that he, a rather old man, could have a young and beautiful and dashing wife. He loved her. What the hell are we talking about it for? These things happen all the time. It didn't make any difference what she did or who she played around with or what she had once been. He loved her."

"Like Moose Malloy," Anne said quietly.

"Let's go riding along the water."

"You didn't tell me about Brunette or the cards that were in those reefers or Amthor or Dr. Sonderborg or that little clue that set you on the path of the great solution."

"I gave Mrs. Florian one of my cards. She put a wet glass on it. Such a card was in Marriott's pockets, wet glass mark and all. Marriott was not a messy man. That was a clue, of sorts. Once you suspected anything it was easy to find out other connections, such as that Marriott owned a trust deed on Mrs. Florian's home, just to keep her in line. As for Amthor, he's a bad hat. They picked him up in a New York hotel and they say he's an international con man. Scotland Yard has his prints, also Paris. How the hell they got all that since yesterday or the day before I don't know. These boys work fast when they feel like it. I think Randall has had this thing taped for days and was afraid I'd step on the tapes. But Amthor had nothing to do with killing anybody. Or with Sonderborg. They haven't found Sonderborg yet. They think he has a record too, but they're not sure until they get him. As for Brunette, you can't get anything on a guy like Brunette. They'll have him before the Grand Jury and he'll refuse to say anything, on his constitutional rights. He doesn't have to bother about his reputation. But there's a nice shakeup here in Bay City. The Chief has been canned and half the detectives have been reduced to acting patrolmen, and a very nice guy named Red Norgaard, who helped me get on the *Montecito*, has got his job back. The mayor is doing all this, changing his pants hourly while the crisis lasts."

"Do you have to say things like that?"

"The Shakespearean touch. Let's go riding. After we've had another drink."

"You can have mine," Anne Riordan said, and got up and brought her untouched drink over to me. She stood in front of me holding it, her eyes wide and a little frightened.

"You're so marvelous," she said. "So brave, so determined and you work for so little money. Everybody bats you over the head and chokes you and smacks your jaw and fills you with morphine, but you just keep right on hitting between tackle and end until they're all worn out. What makes you so wonderful?"

"Go on," I growled. "Spill it."

Anne Riordan said thoughtfully: "I'd like to be kissed, damn you!"

41

It took over three months to find Velma. They wouldn't believe Grayle didn't know where she was and hadn't helped her get away. So every cop and newshawk in the country looked in all the places where money might be hiding her. And money wasn't hiding her at all. Although the way she hid was pretty obvious once it was found out.

One night a Baltimore detective with a camera eye as rare as a pink zebra wandered into a night club and listened to the band and looked at a handsome black-haired, black-browed torcher who could sing as if she meant it. Something in her face struck a chord and the chord went on vibrating.

He went back to Headquarters and got out the Wanted file and started through the pile of readers. When he came to the one he wanted he looked at it a long time. Then he straightened his straw hat on his head and went back to the night club and got hold of the manager. They went back to the dressing rooms behind the shell and the manager knocked on one of the doors. It wasn't locked. The dick pushed the manager aside and went in and locked it.

He must have smelled marihuana because she was smoking it, but he didn't pay any attention then. She was sitting in front of a triple mirror, studying the roots of her hair and eyebrows. They were her own eyebrows. The dick stepped across the room smiling and handed her the reader.

She must have looked at the face on the reader almost as long as the dick had down at Headquarters. There was a lot to think about while she was looking at it. The dick sat down and crossed his legs and lit a cigarette. He had a good eye, but he had over-specialized. He didn't know enough about women.

Finally she laughed a little and said: "You're a smart lad,

copper. I thought I had a voice that would be remembered. A friend recognized me by it once, just hearing it on the radio. But I've been singing with this band for a month—twice a week on a network—and nobody gave it a thought."

"I never heard the voice," the dick said and went on smiling.

She said: "I suppose we can't make a deal on this. You know, there's a lot in it, if it's handled right."

"Not with me," the dick said. "Sorry."

"Let's go then," she said and stood up and grabbed up her bag and got her coat from a hanger. She went over to him holding the coat out so he could help her into it. He stood up and held it for her like a gentleman.

She turned and slipped a gun out of her bag and shot him three times through the coat he was holding.

She had two bullets left in the gun when they crashed the door. They got halfway across the room before she used them. She used them both, but the second shot must have been pure reflex. They caught her before she hit the floor, but her head was already hanging by a rag.

"The dick lived until the next day," Randall said, telling me about it. "He talked when he could. That's how we have the dope. I can't understand him being so careless, unless he really was thinking of letting her talk him into a deal of some kind. That would clutter up his mind. But I don't like to think that, of course."

I said I supposed that was so.

"Shot herself clean through the heart—twice," Randall said. "And I've heard experts on the stand say that's impossible, knowing all the time myself that it was. And you know something else?"

"What?"

"She was stupid to shoot that dick. We'd never have convicted her, not with her looks and money and the persecution story these high-priced guys would build up. Poor little girl from a dive climbs to be wife of rich man and the vultures that used to know her won't let her alone. That sort of thing. Hell, Rennenkamp would have half a dozen crummy old burlesque dames in court to sob that they'd blackmailed her for years, and in a way that you couldn't pin anything on them but the jury would go for it. She did a smart thing to run off on her own and leave Grayle out of it, but it would have been smarter to have come home when she was caught."

"Oh you believe now that she left Grayle out of it," I said.

He nodded. I said: "Do you think she had any particular reason for that?"

He stared at me. "I'll go for it, whatever it is."

"She was a killer," I said. "But so was Malloy. And *he* was a long way from being all rat. Maybe that Baltimore dick wasn't so pure as the record shows. Maybe she saw a chance—not to get away—she was tired of dodging by that time—but to give a break to the only man who had ever really given her one."

Randall stared at me with his mouth open and his eyes unconvinced.

"Hell, she didn't have to shoot a cop to do that," he said.

"I'm not saying she was a saint or even a halfway nice girl. Not ever. She wouldn't kill herself until she was cornered. But what she did and the way she did it, kept her from coming back here for trial. Think that over. And who would that trial hurt most? Who would be least able to bear it? And win, lose or draw, who would pay the biggest price for the show? An old man who had loved not wisely, but too well."

Randall said sharply: "That's just sentimental."

"Sure. It sounded like that when I said it. Probably all a mistake anyway. So long. Did my pink bug ever get back up here?"

He didn't know what I was talking about.

I rode down to the street floor and went out on the steps of the City Hall. It was a cool day and very clear. You could see a long way—but not as far as Velma had gone.

THE HIGH WINDOW

I

THE HOUSE was on Dresden Avenue in the Oak Noll section of Pasadena, a big solid cool-looking house with burgundy brick walls, a terra cotta tile roof, and a white stone trim. The front windows were leaded downstairs. Upstairs windows were of the cottage type and had a lot of rococo imitation stonework trimming around them.

From the front wall and its attendant flowering bushes a half acre or so of fine green lawn drifted in a gentle slope down to the street, passing on the way an enormous deodar around which it flowed like a cool green tide around a rock. The sidewalk and the parkway were both very wide and in the parkway were three white acacias that were worth seeing. There was a heavy scent of summer on the morning and everything that grew was perfectly still in the breathless air they get over there on what they call a nice cool day.

All I knew about the people was that they were a Mrs. Elizabeth Bright Murdock and family and that she wanted to hire a nice clean private detective who wouldn't drop cigar ashes on the floor and never carried more than one gun. And I knew she was the widow of an old coot with whiskers named Jasper Murdock who had made a lot of money helping out the community, and got his photograph in the Pasadena paper every year on his anniversary, with the years of his birth and death underneath, and the legend: *His Life Was His Service.*

I left my car on the street and walked over a few dozen stumble stones set into the green lawn, and rang the bell in the brick portico under a peaked roof. A low red brick wall ran along the front of the house the short distance from the door to the edge of the driveway. At the end of the walk, on a concrete block, there was a little painted Negro in white riding breeches and a green jacket and a red cap. He was holding a whip, and there was an iron hitching ring in the block at his feet. He looked a little sad, as if he had been waiting there a long time and was getting discouraged. I went over and patted his head while I was waiting for somebody to come to the door.

After a while a middle-aged sourpuss in a maid's costume opened the front door about eight inches and gave me the beady eye.

"Philip Marlowe," I said. "Calling on Mrs. Murdock. By appointment."

The middle-aged sourpuss ground her teeth, snapped her eyes shut, snapped them open and said in one of those angular hardrock pioneer-type voices: "Which one?"

"Huh?"

"Which Mrs. Murdock?" she almost screamed at me.

"Mrs. Elizabeth Bright Murdock," I said. "I didn't know there was more than one."

"Well, there is," she snapped. "Got a card?"

She still had the door a scant eight inches open. She poked the end of her nose and a thin muscular hand into the opening. I got my wallet out and got one of the cards with just my name on it and put it in the hand. The hand and nose went in and the door slammed in my face.

I thought that maybe I ought to have gone to the back door. I went over and patted the little Negro on the head again.

"Brother," I said, "you and me both."

Time passed, quite a lot of time. I stuck a cigarette in my mouth but didn't light it. The Good Humor man went by in his little blue and white wagon, playing *Turkey in the Straw* on his music box. A large black and gold butterfly fishtailed in and landed on a hydrangea bush almost at my elbow, moved its wings slowly up and down a few times, then took off heavily and staggered away through the motionless hot scented air.

The front door came open again. The sourpuss said: "This way."

I went in. The room beyond was large and square and sunken and cool and had the restful atmosphere of a funeral chapel and something the same smell. Tapestry on the blank roughened stucco walls, iron grilles imitating balconies outside high side windows, heavy carved chairs with plush seats and tapestry backs and tarnished gilt tassels hanging down their sides. At the back a stained-glass window about the size of a tennis court. Curtained french doors underneath it. An old musty, fusty, narrow-minded, clean and bitter room. It didn't look as if anybody ever sat in it or would ever want to. Marble-topped tables with crooked legs, gilt clocks, pieces of small statuary in two colors of marble. A lot of junk that would take a week to dust. A lot of money, and all wasted. Thirty years before, in the wealthy close-mouthed provincial town Pasadena then was, it must have seemed like quite a room.

We left it and went along a hallway and after a while the sourpuss opened a door and motioned me in.

"Mr. Marlowe," she said through the door in a nasty voice, and went away grinding her teeth.

2

It was a small room looking out on the back garden. It had an ugly red and brown carpet and was furnished as an office. It contained what you would expect to find in a small office. A thin fragile-looking blondish girl in shell glasses sat behind a desk with a typewriter on a pulled-out leaf at her left. She had her hands poised on the keys, but she didn't have any paper in the machine. She watched me come into the room with the stiff, half-silly expression of a self-conscious person posing for a snapshot. She had a clear soft voice, asking me to sit down.

"I am Miss Davis. Mrs. Murdock's secretary. She wanted me to ask you for a few references."

"References?"

"Certainly. References. Does that surprise you?"

I put my hat on her desk and the unlighted cigarette on the brim of the hat. "You mean she sent for me without knowing anything about me?"

Her lip trembled and she bit it. I didn't know whether she was scared or annoyed or just having trouble being cool and businesslike. But she didn't look happy.

"She got your name from the manager of a branch of the California-Security Bank. But he doesn't know you personally," she said.

"Get your pencil ready," I said.

She held it up and showed me that it was freshly sharpened and ready to go.

I said: "First off, one of the vice-presidents of that same bank. George S. Leake. He's in the main office. Then State Senator Huston Oglethorpe. He may be in Sacramento, or he may be at his office in the State Building in L.A. Then Sidney Dreyfus, Jr., of Dreyfus, Turner and Swayne, attorneys in the Title-Insurance Building. Got that?"

She wrote fast and easily. She nodded without looking up. The light danced on her blond hair.

"Oliver Fry of the Fry-Krantz Corporation, Oil Well Tools. They're over on East Ninth, in the industrial district. Then, if you would like a couple of cops, Bernard Ohls of the D.A.'s staff, and Detective-Lieutenant Carl Randall of the Central Homicide Bureau. You think maybe that would be enough?"

"Don't laugh at me," she said. "I'm only doing what I'm told."

"Better not call the last two, unless you know what the job is," I said. "I'm not laughing at you. Hot, isn't it?"

"It's not hot for Pasadena," she said, and hoisted her phone book up on the desk and went to work.

While she was looking up the numbers and telephoning hither and yon I looked her over. She was pale with a sort of natural paleness and she looked healthy enough. Her coarse-grained coppery blond hair was not ugly in itself, but it was drawn back so tightly over her narrow head that it almost lost the effect of being hair at all. Her eyebrows were thin and unusually straight and were darker than her hair, almost a chestnut color. Her nostrils had the whitish look of an anaemic person. Her chin was too small, too sharp and looked unstable. She wore no makeup except orange-red on her mouth and not much of that. Her eyes behind the glasses were very large, cobalt blue with big irises and a vague expression. Both lids were tight so that the eyes had a slightly oriental look, or as if the skin of her face was naturally so tight that it stretched her eyes at the corners. The whole face had a sort of off-key neurotic charm that only needed some clever makeup to be striking.

She wore a one-piece linen dress with short sleeves and no ornament of any kind. Her bare arms had down on them, and a few freckles.

I didn't pay much attention to what she said over the telephone. Whatever was said to her she wrote down in shorthand, with deft easy strokes of the pencil. When she was through she hung the phone book back on a hook and stood up and smoothed the linen dress down over her thighs and said:

"If you will just wait a few moments —" and went towards the door.

Halfway there she turned back and pushed a top drawer of her desk shut at the side. She went out. The door closed. There was silence. Outside the window bees buzzed. Far off I heard the whine of a vacuum cleaner. I picked the unlighted cigarette off my hat, put it in my mouth and stood up. I went around the desk and pulled open the drawer she had come back to shut.

It wasn't any of my business. I was just curious. It wasn't any of my business that she had a small Colt automatic in the drawer. I shut it and sat down again.

She was gone about four minutes. She opened the door and stayed at it and said: "Mrs. Murdock will see you now."

We went along some more hallway and she opened half of a double glass door and stood aside. I went in and the door was closed behind me.

It was so dark in there that at first I couldn't see anything but the outdoors light coming through thick bushes and screens. Then I saw that the room was a sort of sun porch that had been allowed to get completely overgrown outside. It was furnished with grass rugs and reed stuff. There was a reed chaise longue over by the window. It had a curved back and enough cushions to stuff an elephant and there was a woman leaning back on it with a wine glass in her hand. I could smell the thick scented alcoholic odor of the wine before I could see her properly. Then my eyes got used to the light and I could see her.

She had a lot of face and chin. She had pewter-colored hair set in a ruthless permanent, a hard beak and large moist eyes with the sympathetic expression of wet stones. There was lace at her throat, but it was the kind of throat that would have looked better in a football sweater. She wore a grayish silk dress. Her thick arms were bare and mottled. There were jet buttons in her ears. There was a low glass-topped table beside her and a bottle of port on the table. She sipped from the glass she was holding and looked at me over it and said nothing.

I stood there. She let me stand while she finished the port in her glass and put the glass down on the table and filled it again. Then she tapped her lips with a handkerchief. Then she spoke. Her voice had a hard baritone quality and sounded as if it didn't want any nonsense.

"Sit down, Mr. Marlowe. Please do not light that cigarette. I'm asthmatic."

I sat down in a reed rocker and tucked the still unlighted cigarette down behind the handkerchief in my outside pocket.

"I've never had any dealing with private detectives, Mr. Marlowe. I don't know anything about them. Your references seem satisfactory. What are your charges?"

"To do what, Mrs. Murdock?"

"It's a very confidential matter, naturally. Nothing to do with the police. If it had to do with the police, I should have called the police."

"I charge twenty-five dollars a day, Mrs. Murdock. And of course expenses."

"It seems high. You must make a great deal of money." She drank some more of her port. I don't like port in hot weather, but it's nice when they let you refuse it.

"No," I said. "It isn't. Of course you can get detective work done at any price—just like legal work. Or dental work. I'm not an organization. I'm just one man and I work at just one case at a time. I take risks, sometimes quite big risks, and I don't work all the time. No, I don't think twenty-five dollars a day is too much."

"I see. And what is the nature of the expenses?"

"Little things that come up here and there. You never know."

"I should prefer to know," she said acidly.

"You'll know," I said. "You'll get it all down in black and white. You'll have a chance to object, if you don't like it."

"And how much retainer would you expect?"

"A hundred dollars would hold me," I said.

"I should hope it would," she said and finished her port and poured the glass full again without even waiting to wipe her lips.

"From people in your position, Mrs. Murdock, I don't necessarily have to have a retainer."

"Mr. Marlowe," she said, "I'm a strong-minded woman. But don't let me scare you. Because if you can be scared by me, you won't be much use to me."

I nodded and let that one drift with the tide.

She laughed suddenly and then she belched. It was a nice light belch, nothing showy, and performed with easy unconcern. "My asthma," she said carelessly. "I drink this wine as medicine. That's why I'm not offering you any."

I swung a leg over my knee. I hoped that wouldn't hurt her asthma.

"Money," she said, "is not really important. A woman in my position is always overcharged and gets to expect it. I hope you will be worth your fee. Here is the situation. Something of considerable value has been stolen from me. I want it back, but I want more than that. I don't want anybody arrested. The thief happens to be a member of my family—by marriage."

She turned the wine glass with her thick fingers and smiled faintly in the dim light of the shadowed room. "My daughter-in-law," she said. "A charming girl—and tough as an oak board."

She looked at me with a sudden gleam in her eyes.

"I have a damn fool of a son," she said. "But I'm very fond of him. About a year ago he made an idiotic marriage, without my consent. This was foolish of him because he is quite incapable of earning a living and he has no money except what I give him, and I am not generous with money. The lady he chose, or who chose him, was a night club singer. Her name, appropriately enough, was Linda Conquest. They have lived here in this house. We didn't quarrel because I don't allow people to quarrel with me in my own house, but there has not been good feeling between us. I have paid their expenses, given each of them a car, made the lady a sufficient but not gaudy allowance for clothes and so on. No doubt she found the life rather dull. No doubt she found my son dull. I find him dull myself. At any rate she moved out, very abruptly, a week or so ago, without leaving a forwarding address or saying good-by."

She coughed, fumbled for a handkerchief, and blew her nose.

"What was taken," she went on, "was a coin. A rare gold coin called a Brasher Doubloon. It was the pride of my husband's collection. I care nothing for such things, but he did. I have kept the collection intact since he died four years ago. It is upstairs, in a locked fireproof room, in a set of fireproof cases. It is insured, but I have not reported the loss yet. I don't want to, if I can help it. I'm quite sure Linda took it. The coin is said to be worth over ten thousand dollars. It's a mint specimen."

"But pretty hard to sell," I said.

"Perhaps. I don't know. I didn't miss the coin until yesterday. I should not have missed it then, as I never go near the collection, except that a man in Los Angeles named Morningstar called up, said he was a dealer, and was the Murdock Brasher, as he called it, for sale? My son happened to take the call. He said he didn't believe it was for sale, it never had been, but that if Mr. Morningstar would call some other time, he could probably talk to me. It was not convenient then, as I was resting. The man said he would do that. My son reported the conversation to Miss Davis, who reported it to me. I had her call the man back. I was faintly curious."

She sipped some more port, flopped her handkerchief about and grunted.

"Why were you curious, Mrs. Murdock?" I asked, just to be saying something.

"If the man was a dealer of any repute, he would know that the coin was not for sale. My husband, Jasper Murdock, provided in his will that no part of his collection might be sold, loaned or hypothecated during my lifetime. Nor removed from this house, except in case of damage to the house necessitating removal, and then only by action of the trustees. My husband—" she smiled grimly— "seemed to feel that I ought to have taken more interest in his little pieces of metal while he was alive."

It was a nice day outside, the sun shining, the flowers blooming, the birds singing. Cars went by on the street with a distant comfortable sound. In the dim room with the hard-faced woman and the winy smell everything seemed a little unreal. I tossed my foot up and down over my knee and waited.

"I spoke to Mr. Morningstar. His full name is Elisha Morningstar and he has offices in the Belfont Building on Ninth Street in downtown Los Angeles. I told him the Murdock collection was not for sale, never had been, and, so far as I was concerned, never would be, and that I was surprised that he didn't know that. He hemmed and hawed and then asked me if he might examine the coin. I said certainly not. He thanked me rather dryly and hung up. He sounded like an old man. So I went upstairs to examine the coin myself, something I had not done in a year. It was gone from its place in one of the locked fireproof cases."

I said nothing. She refilled her glass and played a tattoo with her thick fingers on the arm of the chaise longue. "What I thought then you can probably guess."

I said: "The part about Mr. Morningstar, maybe. Somebody had offered the coin to him for sale and he had known or suspected where it came from. The coin must be very rare."

"What they call a mint specimen is very rare indeed. Yes, I had the same idea."

"How would it be stolen?" I asked.

"By anyone in this house, very easily. The keys are in my bag, and my bag lies around here and there. It would be a very simple matter to get hold of the keys long enough to unlock a door and a cabinet and then return the keys. Difficult for an outsider, but anybody in the house could have stolen it."

"I see. How do you establish that your daughter-in-law took it, Mrs. Murdock?"

"I don't—in a strictly evidential sense. But I'm quite sure of it. The servants are three women who have been here many, many years—long before I married Mr. Murdock, which was only seven years ago. The gardener never comes in the house. I have no chauffeur, because either my son or my secretary drives me. My son didn't take it, first because he is not the kind of fool that steals from his mother, and secondly, if he had taken it, he could easily have prevented me from speaking to the coin dealer, Morningstar. Miss Davis—ridiculous. Just not the type at all. Too mousy. No, Mr. Marlowe, Linda is the sort of lady who might do it just for spite, if nothing else. And you know what these night club people are."

"All sorts of people—like the rest of us," I said. "No signs of a burglar, I suppose? It would take a pretty smooth worker to lift just one valuable coin, so there wouldn't be. Maybe I had better look the room over, though."

She pushed her jaw at me and muscles in her neck made hard lumps. "I have just told you, Mr. Marlowe, that Mrs. Leslie Murdock, my daughter-in-law, took the Brasher Doubloon."

I stared at her and she stared back. Her eyes were as hard as the bricks in her front walk. I shrugged the stare off and said:

"Assuming that is so, Mrs. Murdock, just what do you want done?"

"In the first place I want the coin back. In the second place I want an uncontested divorce for my son. And I don't intend to buy it. I daresay you know how these things are arranged."

She finished the current instalment of port and laughed rudely.

"I may have heard," I said. "You say the lady left no forwarding address. Does that mean you have no idea at all where she went?"

"Exactly that."

"A disappearance then. Your son might have some ideas he hasn't passed along to you. I'll have to see him."

The big gray face hardened into even ruggeder lines. "My son knows nothing. He doesn't even know the doubloon has been stolen. I don't want him to know anything. When the time comes I'll handle him. Until then I want him left alone. He will do exactly what I want him to."

"He hasn't always," I said.

"His marriage," she said nastily, "was a momentary impulse.

Afterwards he tried to act like a gentleman. I have no such scruples."

"It takes three days to have that kind of momentary impulse in California, Mrs. Murdock."

"Young man, do you want this job or don't you?"

"I want it if I'm told the facts and allowed to handle the case as I see fit. I don't want it if you're going to make a lot of rules and regulations for me to trip over."

She laughed harshly. "This is a delicate family matter, Mr. Marlowe. And it must be handled with delicacy."

"If you hire me, you'll get all the delicacy I have. If I don't have enough delicacy, maybe you'd better not hire me. For instance, I take it you don't want your daughter-in-law framed. I'm not delicate enough for that."

She turned the color of a cold boiled beet and opened her mouth to yell. Then she thought better of it, lifted her port glass and tucked away some more of her medicine.

"You'll do," she said dryly, "I wish I had met you two years ago, before he married her."

I didn't know exactly what this last meant, so I let it ride. She bent over sideways and fumbled with the key on a house telephone and growled into it when she was answered.

There were steps and the little copper-blond came tripping into the room with her chin low, as if somebody might be going to take a swing at her.

"Make this man a check for two hundred and fifty dollars," the old dragon snarled at her. "And keep your mouth shut about it."

The little girl flushed all the way to her neck. "You know I never talk about your affairs, Mrs. Murdock," she bleated. "You know I don't. I wouldn't dream of it, I—"

She turned with her head down and ran out of the room. As she closed the door I looked out at her. Her little lip was trembling but her eyes were mad.

"I'll need a photo of the lady and some information," I said when the door was shut again.

"Look in the desk drawer." Her rings flashed in the dimness as her thick gray finger pointed.

I went over and opened the single drawer of the reed desk and took out the photo that lay all alone in the bottom of the drawer, face up, looking at me with cool dark eyes. I sat down again with the photo and looked it over. Dark hair parted loosely in the middle and drawn back loosely over a solid piece of forehead. A wide cool go-to-hell mouth with very kissable lips. Nice nose, not too small, not too large. Good bone all over the face. The expression of the face lacked something. Once the something might have been called breeding, but these days I didn't know what to call it. The face looked too wise and too guarded for its age. Too many passes had been made at it and it had grown a little too smart in dodging them. And behind this expression of wiseness there was the look of simplicity of the little girl who still believes in Santa Claus.

I nodded over the photo and slipped it into my pocket, thinking I was getting too much out of it to get out of a mere photo, and in a very poor light at that.

The door opened and the little girl in the linen dress came in with a three-decker check book and a fountain pen and made a desk of her arm for Mrs. Murdock to sign. She straightened up with a strained smile and Mrs. Murdock made a sharp gesture towards me and the little girl tore the check out and gave it to me. She hovered inside the door, waiting. Nothing was said to her, so she went out softly again and closed the door.

I shook the check dry, folded it and sat holding it. "What can you tell me about Linda?"

"Practically nothing. Before she married my son she shared an apartment with a girl named Lois Magic—charming names these people choose for themselves—who is an entertainer of some sort. They worked at a place called the Idle Valley Club, out Ventura Boulevard way. My son Leslie knows it far too well. I know nothing about Linda's family or origins. She said once she was born in Sioux Falls. I suppose she had parents. I was not interested enough to find out."

Like hell she wasn't. I could see her digging with both hands, digging hard, and getting herself a double handful of gravel.

"You don't know Miss Magic's address?"

"No. I never did know."

"Would your son be likely to know—or Miss Davis?"

"I'll ask my son when he comes in. I don't think so. You can ask Miss Davis. I'm sure she doesn't."

"I see. You don't know of any other friends of Linda's?"

"No."

"It's possible that your son is still in touch with her, Mrs. Murdock—without telling you."

She started to get purple again. I held my hand up and dragged a soothing smile over my face. "After all he has been married to her a year," I said. "He must know something about her."

"You leave my son out of this," she snarled.

I shrugged and made a disappointed sound with my lips. "Very well. She took her car, I suppose. The one you gave her?"

"A steel gray Mercury, 1940 model, a coupé. Miss Davis can give you the license number, if you want that. I don't know whether she took it."

"Would you know what money and clothes and jewels she had with her?"

"Not much money. She might have had a couple of hundred dollars, at most." A fat sneer made deep lines around her nose and mouth. "Unless of course she has found a new friend."

"There's that," I said. "Jewelry?"

"An emerald and diamond ring of no very great value, a platinum Longines watch with rubies in the mounting, a very good cloudy amber necklace which I was foolish enough to give her myself. It has a diamond clasp with twenty-six small diamonds in the shape of a playing card diamond. She had other things, of course. I never paid much attention to them. She dressed well but not strikingly. Thank God for a few small mercies."

She refilled her glass and drank and did some more of her semi-social belching.

"That's all you can tell me, Mrs. Murdock?"

"Isn't it enough?"

"Not nearly enough, but I'll have to be satisfied for the time being. If I find she did not steal the coin, that ends the investigation as far as I'm concerned. Correct?"

"We'll talk it over," she said roughly. "She stole it all right.

And I don't intend to let her get away with it. Paste that in your hat, young man. And I hope you are even half as rough as you like to act, because these night club girls are apt to have some very nasty friends."

I was still holding the folded check by one corner down between my knees. I got my wallet out and put it away and stood up, reaching my hat off the floor.

"I like them nasty," I said. "The nasty ones have very simple minds. I'll report to you when there is anything to report, Mrs. Murdock. I think I'll tackle this coin dealer first. He sounds like a lead."

She let me get to the door before she growled at my back: "You don't like me very well, do you?"

I turned to grin back at her with my hand on the knob. "Does anybody?"

She threw her head back and opened her mouth wide and roared with laughter. In the middle of the laughter I opened the door and went out and shut the door on the rough mannish sound. I went back along the hall and knocked on the secretary's half open door, then pushed it open and looked in.

She had her arms folded on her desk and her face down on the folded arms. She was sobbing. She screwed her head around and looked up at me with tear-stained eyes. I shut the door and went over beside her and put an arm around her thin shoulders.

"Cheer up," I said. "You ought to feel sorry for her. She thinks she's tough and she's breaking her back trying to live up to it."

The little girl jumped erect, away from my arm. "Don't touch me," she said breathlessly. "Please. I never let men touch me. And don't say such awful things about Mrs. Murdock."

Her face was all pink and wet from tears. Without her glasses her eyes were very lovely.

I stuck my long-waiting cigarette into my mouth and lit it.

"I—I didn't mean to be rude," she snuffled. "But she does humiliate me so. And I only want to do my best for her." She snuffled some more and got a man's handkerchief out of her desk and shook it out and wiped her eyes with it. I saw on the hanging down corner the initials L.M. embroidered in purple.

I stared at it and blew cigarette smoke towards the corner of the room, away from her hair. "Is there something you want?" she asked.

"I want the license number of Mrs. Leslie Murdock's car."

"It's 2X1111, a gray Mercury convertible, 1940 model."

"She told me it was a coupé."

"That's Mr. Leslie's car. They're the same make and year and color. Linda didn't take the car."

"Oh. What do you know about a Miss Lois Magic?"

"I only saw her once. She used to share an apartment with Linda. She came here with a Mr.—a Mr. Vannier."

"Who's he?"

She looked down at her desk. "I—she just came with him. I don't know him."

"Okay, what does Miss Lois Magic look like?"

"She's a tall handsome blond. Very—very appealing."

"You mean sexy?"

"Well—" she blushed furiously, "in a nice well-bred sort of way, if you know what I mean."

"I know what you mean," I said, "but I never got anywhere with it."

"I can believe that," she said tartly.

"Know where Miss Magic lives?"

She shook her head, no. She folded the big handkerchief very carefully and put it in the drawer of her desk, the one where the gun was.

"You can swipe another one when that's dirty," I said.

She leaned back in her chair and put her small neat hands on her desk and looked at me levelly.

"I wouldn't carry that tough-guy manner too far, if I were you, Mr. Marlowe. Not with me, at any rate."

"No?"

"No. And I can't answer any more questions without specific instructions. My position here is very confidential."

"I'm not tough," I said. "Just virile."

She picked up a pencil and made a mark on a pad. She smiled faintly up at me, all composure again.

"Perhaps I don't like virile men," she said.

"You're a screwball," I said, "if ever I met one. Good-by."

I went out of her office, shut the door firmly, and walked

back along the empty halls through the big silent sunken funereal living room and out of the front door.

The sun danced on the warm lawn outside. I put my dark glasses on and went over and patted the little Negro on the head again.

"Brother, it's even worse than I expected," I told him.

The stumble-stones were hot through the soles of my shoes. I got into the car and started it and pulled away from the curb.

A small sand-colored coupé pulled away from the curb behind me. I didn't think anything of it. The man driving it wore a dark porkpie type straw hat with a gay print band and dark glasses were over his eyes, as over mine.

I drove back towards the city. A dozen blocks later at a traffic stop, the sand-colored coupé was still behind me. I shrugged and just for the fun of it circled a few blocks. The coupé held its position. I swung into a street lined with immense pepper trees, dragged my heap around in a fast U-turn and stopped against the curbing.

The coupé came carefully around the corner. The blond head under the cocoa straw hat with the tropical print band didn't even turn my way. The coupé sailed on and I drove back to the Arroyo Seco and on towards Hollywood. I looked carefully several times, but I didn't spot the coupé again.

3

I had an office in the Cahuenga Building, sixth floor, two small rooms at the back. One I left open for a patient client to sit in, if I had a patient client. There was a buzzer on the door which I could switch on and off from my private thinking parlor.

I looked into the reception room. It was empty of everything but the smell of dust. I threw up another window, unlocked the communicating door and went into the room beyond. Three hard chairs and a swivel chair, flat desk with a glass top, five green filing cases, three of them full of nothing, a calendar and a framed license bond on the wall, a phone, a washbowl in a stained wood cupboard, a hatrack, a carpet that was just something on the floor, and two open windows with net curtains that puckered in and out like the lips of a toothless old man sleeping.

The same stuff I had had last year, and the year before that. Not beautiful, not gay, but better than a tent on the beach.

I hung my hat and coat on the hatrack, washed my face and hands in cold water, lit a cigarette and hoisted the phone book onto the desk. Elisha Morningstar was listed at 824 Belfont Building, 422 West Ninth Street. I wrote that down and the phone number that went with it and had my hand on the instrument when I remembered that I hadn't switched on the buzzer for the reception room. I reached over the side of the desk and clicked it on and caught it right in stride. Somebody had just opened the door of the outer office.

I turned my pad face down on the desk and went over to see who it was. It was a slim tall self-satisfied looking number in a tropical worsted suit of slate blue, black and white shoes, a dull ivory-colored shirt and a tie and display handkerchief the color of jacaranda bloom. He was holding a long black cigarette-holder in a peeled back white pigskin glove and he was wrinkling his nose at the dead magazines on the library table and the chairs and the rusty floor covering and the general air of not much money being made.

As I opened the communicating door he made a quarter turn and stared at me out of a pair of rather dreamy pale eyes set close to a narrow nose. His skin was sun-flushed, his reddish hair was brushed back hard over a narrow skull, and the thin line of his mustache was much redder than his hair.

He looked me over without haste and without much pleasure. He blew some smoke delicately and spoke through it with a faint sneer.

"You're Marlowe?"

I nodded.

"I'm a little disappointed," he said. "I rather expected something with dirty fingernails."

"Come inside," I said, "and you can be witty sitting down."

I held the door for him and he strolled past me flicking cigarette ash on the floor with the middle nail of his free hand. He sat down on the customer's side of the desk, took off the glove from his right hand and folded this with the other already off and laid them on the desk. He tapped the cigarette end out of the long black holder, prodded the coal with a match until it stopped smoking, fitted another cigarette and lit it with a broad mahogany-colored match. He leaned back in his chair with the smile of a bored aristocrat.

"All set?" I enquired. "Pulse and respiration normal? You wouldn't like a cold towel on your head or anything?"

He didn't curl his lip because it had been curled when he came in. "A private detective," he said. "I never met one. A shifty business, one gathers. Keyhole peeping, raking up scandal, that sort of thing."

"You here on business," I asked him, "or just slumming?"

His smile was as faint as a fat lady at a fireman's ball.

"The name is Murdock. That probably means a little something to you."

"You certainly made nice time over here," I said, and started to fill a pipe.

He watched me fill the pipe. He said slowly: "I understand my mother has employed you on a job of some sort. She has given you a check."

I finished filling the pipe, put a match to it, got it drawing and leaned back to blow smoke over my right shoulder towards the open window. I didn't say anything.

He leaned forward a little more and said earnestly: "I know being cagey is all part of your trade, but I am not guessing. A little worm told me, a simple garden worm, often trodden on, but still somehow surviving—like myself. I happened to be not far behind you. Does that help to clear things up?"

"Yeah," I said. "Supposing it made any difference to me."

"You are hired to find my wife, I gather."

I made a snorting sound and grinned at him over the pipe bowl.

"Marlowe," he said, even more earnestly, "I'll try hard, but I don't think I am going to like you."

"I'm screaming," I said. "With rage and pain."

"And if you will pardon a homely phrase, your tough guy act stinks."

"Coming from you, that's bitter."

He leaned back again and brooded at me with pale eyes. He fussed around in the chair, trying to get comfortable. A lot of people had tried to get comfortable in that chair. I ought to try it myself sometime. Maybe it was losing business for me.

"Why should my mother want Linda found?" he asked slowly. "She hated her guts. I mean my mother hated Linda's guts. Linda was quite decent to my mother. What do you think of her?"

"Your mother?"

"Of course. You haven't met Linda, have you?"

"That secretary of your mother's has her job hanging by a frayed thread. She talks out of turn."

He shook his head sharply. "Mother won't know. Anyhow, Mother couldn't do without Merle. She has to have somebody to bully. She might yell at her or even slap her face, but she couldn't do without her. What did you think of her?"

"Kind of cute—in an old world sort of way."

He frowned. "I mean Mother. Merle's just a simple little girl, I know."

"Your powers of observation startle me," I said.

He looked surprised. He almost forgot to fingernail the ash of his cigarette. But not quite. He was careful not to get any of it in the ashtray, however.

"About my mother," he said patiently.

"A grand old warhorse," I said. "A heart of gold, and the gold buried good and deep."

"But why does she want Linda found? I can't understand it. Spending money on it too. My mother hates to spend money. She thinks money is part of her skin. Why does she want Linda found?"

"Search me," I said. "Who said she did?"

"Why, you implied so. And Merle—"

"Merle's just romantic. She made it up. Hell, she blows her nose in a man's handkerchief. Probably one of yours."

He blushed. "That's silly. Look, Marlowe. Please, be reasonable and give me an idea what it's all about. I haven't much much money, I'm afraid, but would a couple of hundred—"

"I ought to bop you," I said. "Besides I'm not supposed to talk to you. Orders."

"Why, for heaven's sake?"

"Don't ask me things I don't know. I can't tell you the answers. And don't ask me things I do know, because I won't tell you the answers. Where have you been all your life? If a man in my line of work is handed a job, does he go around answering questions about it to anyone that gets curious?"

"There must be a lot of electricity in the air," he said nastily, "for a man in your line of work to turn down two hundred dollars."

There was nothing in that for me either. I picked his broad mahogany match out of the tray and looked at it. It had thin yellow edges and there was white printing on it. ROSEMONT. H. RICHARDS '3—the rest was burnt off. I doubled the match and squeezed the halves together and tossed it in the waste basket.

"I love my wife," he said suddenly and showed me the hard white edges of his teeth. "A corny touch, but it's true."

"The Lombardos are still doing all right."

He kept his lips pulled back from his teeth and talked through them at me. "She doesn't love me. I know of no particular reason why she should. Things have been strained between us. She was used to a fast moving sort of life. With us, well, it has been pretty dull. We haven't quarreled. Linda's the cool type. But she hasn't really had a lot of fun being married to me."

"You're just too modest," I said.

His eyes glinted, but he kept his smooth manner pretty well in place.

"Not good, Marlowe. Not even fresh. Look, you have the air of a decent sort of guy. I know my mother is not putting out two hundred and fifty bucks just to be breezy. Maybe it's not Linda. Maybe it's something else. Maybe—" he stopped and then said this very slowly, watching my eyes, "maybe it's Morny."

"Maybe it is," I said cheerfully.

He picked his gloves up and slapped the desk with them and put them down again. "I'm in a spot there all right," he said. "But I didn't think she knew about it. Morny must have called her up. He promised not to."

This was easy. I said: "How much are you into him for?"

It wasn't so easy. He got suspicious again. "If he called her up, he would have told her. And she would have told you," he said thinly.

"Maybe it isn't Morny," I said, beginning to want a drink very badly. "Maybe the cook is with child by the iceman. But if it was Morny, how much?"

"Twelve thousand," he said, looking down and flushing.

"Threats?"

He nodded.

"Tell him to go fly a kite," I said. "What kind of lad is he? Tough?"

He looked up again, his face being brave. "I suppose he is. I suppose they all are. He used to be a screen heavy. Good looking in a flashy way, a chaser. But don't get any ideas. Linda just worked there, like the waiters and the band. And if you are looking for her, you'll have a hard time finding her."

I sneered at him politely.

"Why would I have a hard time finding her? She's not buried in the back yard, I hope."

He stood up with a flash of anger in his pale eyes. Standing there leaning over the desk a little he whipped his right hand up in a neat enough gesture and brought out a small automatic, about .25 caliber with a walnut grip. It looked like the brother of the one I had seen in the drawer of Merle's desk. The muzzle looked vicious enough pointing at me. I didn't move.

"If anybody tries to push Linda around, he'll have to push me around first," he said tightly.

"That oughtn't to be too hard. Better get more gun—unless you're just thinking of bees."

He put the little gun back in his inside pocket. He gave me a straight hard look and picked his gloves up and started for the door.

"It's a waste of time talking to you," he said. "All you do is crack wise."

I said: "Wait a minute," and got up and went around the

desk. "It might be a good idea for you not to mention this interview to your mother, if only for the little girl's sake."

He nodded. "For the amount of information I got, it doesn't seem worth mentioning."

"That straight goods about your owing Morny twelve grand?"

He looked down, then up, then down again. He said: "Anybody who could get into Alex Morny for twelve grand would have to be a lot smarter than I am."

I was quite close to him. I said: "As a matter of fact I don't even think you are worried about your wife. I think you know where she is. She didn't run away from you at all. She just ran away from your mother."

He lifted his eyes and drew one glove on. He didn't say anything.

"Perhaps she'll get a job," I said. "And make enough money to support you."

He looked down at the floor again, turned his body to the right a little and the gloved fist made a tight unrelaxed arc through the air upwards. I moved my jaw out of the way and caught his wrist and pushed it slowly back against his chest, leaning on it. He slid a foot back on the floor and began to breathe hard. It was a slender wrist. My fingers went around it and met.

We stood there looking into each other's eyes. He was breathing like a drunk, his mouth open and his lips pulled back. Small round spots of bright red flamed on his cheeks. He tried to jerk his wrist away, but I put so much weight on him that he had to take another short step back to brace himself. Our faces were now only inches apart.

"How come your old man didn't leave you some money?" I sneered. "Or did you blow it all?"

He spoke between his teeth, still trying to jerk loose. "If it's any of your rotten business and you mean Jasper Murdock, he wasn't my father. He didn't like me and he didn't leave me a cent. My father was a man named Horace Bright who lost his money in the crash and jumped out of his office window."

"You milk easy," I said, "but you give pretty thin milk. I'm sorry for what I said about your wife supporting you. I just wanted to get your goat."

I dropped his wrist and stepped back. He still breathed hard and heavily. His eyes on mine were very angry, but he kept his voice down.

"Well, you got it. If you're satisfied, I'll be on my way."

"I was doing you a favor," I said. "A gun toter oughtn't to insult so easily. Better ditch it."

"That's my business," he said. "I'm sorry I took a swing at you. It probably wouldn't have hurt much, if it had connected."

"That's all right."

He opened the door and went on out. His steps died along the corridor. Another screwball. I tapped my teeth with a knuckle in time to the sound of his steps as long as I could hear them. Then I went back to the desk, looked at my pad, and lifted the phone.

4

After the bell had rung three times at the other end of the line a light childish sort of girl's voice filtered itself through a hank of gum and said: "Good morning. Mr. Morningstar's office."

"Is the old gentleman in?"

"Who is calling, please?"

"Marlowe."

"Does he know you, Mr. Marlowe?"

"Ask him if he wants to buy any early American gold coins."

"Just a minute, please."

There was a pause suitable to an elderly party in an inner office having his attention called to the fact that somebody on the telephone wanted to talk to him. Then the phone clicked and a man spoke. He had a dry voice. You might even call it parched.

"This is Mr. Morningstar."

"I'm told you called Mrs. Murdock in Pasadena, Mr. Morningstar. About a certain coin."

"About a certain coin," he repeated. "Indeed. Well?"

"My understanding is that you wished to buy the coin in question from the Murdock collection."

"Indeed? And who are you, sir?"

"Philip Marlowe. A private detective. I'm working for Mrs. Murdock."

"Indeed," he said for the third time. He cleared his throat carefully. "And what did you wish to talk to me about, Mr. Marlowe?"

"About this coin."

"But I was informed it was not for sale."

"I still want to talk to you about it. In person."

"Do you mean she has changed her mind about selling?"

"No."

"Then I'm afraid I don't understand what you want, Mr. Marlowe. What have we to talk about?" He sounded sly now.

I took the ace out of my sleeve and played it with a languid grace. "The point is, Mr. Morningstar, that at the time you called up you already knew the coin wasn't for sale."

"Interesting," he said slowly. "How?"

"You're in the business, you couldn't help knowing. It's a matter of public record that the Murdock collection cannot be sold during Mrs. Murdock's lifetime."

"Ah," he said. "Ah." There was a silence. Then, "At three o'clock," he said, not sharp, but quick. "I shall be glad to see you here in my office. You probably know where it is. Will that suit you?"

"I'll be there," I said.

I hung up and lit my pipe again and sat there looking at the wall. My face was stiff with thought, or with something that made my face stiff. I took Linda Murdock's photo out of my pocket, stared at it for a while, decided that the face was pretty commonplace after all, locked the photo away in my desk. I picked Murdock's second match out of my ashtray and looked it over. The lettering on this one read: TOP ROW W. D. WRIGHT '36.

I dropped it back in the tray, wondering what made this important. Maybe it was a clue.

I got Mrs. Murdock's check out of my wallet, endorsed it, made out a deposit slip and a check for cash, got my bank book out of the desk, and folded the lot under a rubber band and put them in my pocket.

Lois Magic was not listed in the phone book.

I got the classified section up on the desk and made a list of the half dozen theatrical agencies that showed in the largest type and called them. They all had bright cheerful voices and wanted to ask a lot of questions, but they either didn't know or didn't care to tell me anything about a Miss Lois Magic, said to be an entertainer.

I threw the list in the waste basket and called Kenny Haste, a crime reporter on the Chronicle.

"What do you know about Alex Morny?" I asked him when we were through cracking wise at each other.

"Runs a plushy night club and gambling joint in Idle Valley, about two miles off the highway back towards the hills. Used to be in pictures. Lousy actor. Seems to have plenty of protection. I never heard of him shooting anybody on the public square at high noon. Or at any other time for that matter. But I wouldn't like to bet on it."

"Dangerous?"

"I'd say he might be, if necessary. All those boys have been to picture shows and know how night club bosses are supposed to act. He has a bodyguard who is quite a character. His name's Eddie Prue, he's about six feet five inches tall and thin as an honest alibi. He has a frozen eye, the result of a war wound."

"Is Morny dangerous to women?"

"Don't be Victorian, old top. Women don't call it danger."

"Do you know a girl named Lois Magic, said to be an entertainer. A tall gaudy blond, I hear."

"No. Sounds as though I might like to."

"Don't be cute. Do you know anybody named Vannier? None of these people are in the phone book."

"Nope. But I could ask Gertie Arbogast, if you want to call back. He knows all the night club aristocrats. And heels."

"Thanks, Kenny. I'll do that. Half an hour?"

He said that would be fine, and we hung up. I locked the office and left.

At the end of the corridor, in the angle of the wall, a youngish blond man in a brown suit and a cocoa-colored straw hat with a brown and yellow tropical print band was reading the evening paper with his back to the wall. As I passed him he yawned and tucked the paper under his arm and straightened up.

He got into the elevator with me. He could hardly keep his eyes open he was so tired. I went out on the street and walked a block to the bank to deposit my check and draw out a little folding money for expenses. From there I went to the Tigertail Lounge and sat in a shallow booth and drank a martini and ate a sandwich. The man in the brown suit posted himself at the end of the bar and drank coca colas and looked bored and piled pennies in front of him, carefully smoothing the edges. He had his dark glasses on again. That made him invisible.

I dragged my sandwich out as long as I could and then strolled back to the telephone booth at the inner end of the bar. The man in the brown suit turned his head quickly and then covered the motion by lifting his glass. I dialed the Chronicle office again.

"Okay," Kenny Haste said. "Gertie Arbogast says Morny married your gaudy blond not very long ago. Lois Magic. He doesn't know Vannier. He says Morny bought a place out beyond Bel-Air, a white house on Stillwood Crescent Drive, about five blocks north of Sunset. Gertie says Morny took it over from a busted flush named Arthur Blake Popham who got caught in a mail fraud rap. Popham's initials are still on the gates. And probably on the toilet paper, Gertie says. He was that kind of a guy. That's all we seem to know."

"Nobody could ask more. Many thanks, Kenny."

I hung up, stepped out of the booth, met the dark glasses above the brown suit under the cocoa straw hat and watched them turn quickly away.

I spun around and went back through a swing door into the kitchen and through that to the alley and along the alley a quarter block to the back of the parking lot where I had put my car.

No sand-colored coupé succeeded in getting behind me as I drove off, in the general direction of Bel-Air.

5

Stillwood Crescent Drive curved leisurely north from Sunset Boulevard, well beyond the Bel-Air Country Club golf course. The road was lined with walled and fenced estates. Some had high walls, some had low walls, some had ornamental iron fences, some were a bit oldfashioned and got along with tall hedges. The street had no sidewalk. Nobody walked in that neighborhood, not even the mailman.

The afternoon was hot, but not hot like Pasadena. There was a drowsy smell of flowers and sun, a swishing of lawn sprinklers gentle behind hedges and walls, the clear ratchety sound of lawn mowers moving delicately over serene and confident lawns.

I drove up the hill slowly, looking for monograms on gates. Arthur Blake Popham was the name. ABP would be the initials. I found them almost at the top, gilt on a black shield, the gates folded back on a black composition driveway.

It was a glaring white house that had the air of being brand new, but the landscaping was well advanced. It was modest enough for the neighborhood, not more than fourteen rooms and probably only one swimming pool. Its wall was low, made of brick with the concrete all oozed out between and set that way and painted over white. On top of the wall a low iron railing painted black. The name A. P. Morny was stencilled on the large silver-colored mailbox at the service entrance.

I parked my crate on the street and walked up the black driveway to a side door of glittering white paint shot with patches of color from the stained glass canopy over it. I hammered on a large brass knocker. Back along the side of the house a chauffeur was washing off a Cadillac.

The door opened and a hard-eyed Filipino in a white coat curled his lip at me. I gave him a card.

"Mrs. Morny," I said.

He shut the door. Time passed, as it always does when I go calling. The swish of water on the Cadillac had a cool sound. The chauffeur was a little runt in breeches and leggings and a sweat-stained shirt. He looked like an overgrown jockey and he made the same kind of hissing noise as he worked on the car that a groom makes rubbing down a horse.

A red-throated hummingbird went into a scarlet bush beside the door, shook the long tubular blooms around a little, and zoomed off so fast he simply disappeared in the air.

The door opened, the Filipino poked my card at me. I didn't take it.

"What you want?"

It was a tight crackling voice, like someone tiptoeing across a lot of eggshells.

"Want to see Mrs. Morny."

"She not at home."

"Didn't you know that when I gave you the card?"

He opened his fingers and let the card flutter to the ground. He grinned, showing me a lot of cut-rate dental work.

"I know when she tell me."

He shut the door in my face, not gently.

I picked the card up and walked along the side of the house to where the chauffeur was squirting water on the Cadillac sedan and rubbing the dirt off with a big sponge. He had red rimmed eyes and a bang of corn-colored hair. A cigarette hung exhausted at the corner of his lower lip.

He gave me the quick side glance of a man who is minding his own business with difficulty. I said:

"Where's the boss?"

The cigarette jiggled in his mouth. The water went on swishing gently on the paint.

"Ask at the house, Jack."

"I done asked. They done shut the door in mah face."

"You're breaking my heart, Jack."

"How about Mrs. Morny?"

"Same answer, Jack. I just work here. Selling something?"

I held my card so that he could read it. It was a business card this time. He put the sponge down on the running board, and the hose on the cement. He stepped around the water to wipe his hands on a towel that hung at the side of the garage doors. He fished a match out of his pants, struck it and tilted his head back to light the dead butt that was stuck in his face.

His foxy little eyes flicked around this way and that and he moved behind the car, with a jerk of the head. I went over near him.

"How's the little old expense account?" he asked in a small careful voice.

"Fat with inactivity."

"For five I could start thinking."

"I wouldn't want to make it that tough for you."

"For ten I could sing like four canaries and a steel guitar."

"I don't like these plushy orchestrations," I said.

He cocked his head sideways. "Talk English, Jack."

"I don't want you to lose your job, son. All I want to know is whether Mrs. Morny is home. Does that rate more than a buck?"

"Don't worry about my job, Jack. I'm solid."

"With Morny—or somebody else?"

"You want that for the same buck?"

"Two bucks."

He eyed me over. "You ain't working for him, are you?"

"Sure."

"You're a liar."

"Sure."

"Gimme the two bucks," he snapped.

I gave him two dollars.

"She's in the backyard with a friend," he said. "A nice friend. You got a friend that don't work and a husband that works, you're all set, see?" He leered.

"You'll be all set in an irrigation ditch one of these days."

"Not me, Jack. I'm wise. I know how to play 'em. I monkeyed around these kind of people all my life."

He rubbed the two dollar bills between his palms, blew on them, folded them longways and wideways and tucked them in the watch pocket of his breeches.

"That was just the soup," he said. "Now for five more—"

A rather large blond cocker spaniel tore around the Cadillac, skidded a little on the wet concrete, took off neatly, hit me in the stomach and thighs with all four paws, licked my face, dropped to the ground, ran around my legs, sat down between them, let his tongue out all the way and started to pant.

I stepped over him and braced myself against the side of the car and got my handkerchief out.

A male voice called: "Here, Heathcliff. Here, Heathcliff." Steps sounded on a hard walk.

"That's Heathcliff," the chauffeur said sourly.

"Heathcliff?"

"Cripes, that's what they call the dog, Jack."

"*Wuthering Heights?*" I asked.

"Now you're double-talking again," he sneered. "Look out —company."

He picked up the sponge and the hose and went back to washing the car. I moved away from him. The cocker spaniel immediately moved between my legs again, almost tripping me.

"Here, Heathcliff," the male voice called out louder, and a man came into view through the opening of a latticed tunnel covered with climbing roses.

Tall, dark, with a clear olive skin, brilliant black eyes, gleaming white teeth. Sideburns. A narrow black mustache. Sideburns too long, much too long. White shirt with embroidered initials on the pocket, white slacks, white shoes. A wrist watch that curved halfway around a lean dark wrist, held on by a gold chain. A yellow scarf around a bronzed slender neck.

He saw the dog squatted between my legs and didn't like it. He snapped long fingers and snapped a clear hard voice:

"Here, Heathcliff. Come here at once!"

The dog breathed hard and didn't move, except to lean a little closer to my right leg.

"Who are you?" the man asked, staring me down.

I held out my card. Olive fingers took the card. The dog quietly backed out from between my legs, edged around the front end of the car, and faded silently into the distance.

"Marlowe," the man said. "Marlowe, eh? What's this? A detective? What do you want?"

"Want to see Mrs. Morny."

He looked me up and down, brilliant black eyes sweeping slowly and the silky fringes of long eyelashes following them.

"Weren't you told she was not in?"

"Yeah, but I didn't believe it. Are you Mr. Morny?"

"No."

"That's Mr. Vannier," the chauffeur said behind my back, in the drawled, over-polite voice of deliberate insolence. "Mr. Vannier's a friend of the family. He comes here quite a lot."

Vannier looked past my shoulder, his eyes furious. The chauffeur came around the car and spit the cigarette stub out of his mouth with casual contempt.

"I told the shamus the boss wasn't here, Mr. Vannier."

"I see."

"I told him Mrs. Morny and you was here. Did I do wrong?"

Vannier said: "You could have minded your own business."

The chauffeur said: "I wonder why the hell I didn't think of that."

Vannier said: "Get out before I break your dirty little neck for you."

The chauffeur eyed him quietly and then went back into the gloom of the garage and started to whistle. Vannier moved his hot angry eyes over to me and snapped:

"You were told Mrs. Morny was not in, but it didn't take. Is that it? In other words the information failed to satisfy you."

"If we have to have other words," I said, "those might do."

"I see. Could you bring yourself to say what point you wish to discuss with Mrs. Morny?"

"I'd prefer to explain that to Mrs. Morny herself."

"The implication is that she doesn't care to see you."

Behind the car the chauffeur said: "Watch his right, Jack. It might have a knife in it."

Vannier's olive skin turned the color of dried seaweed. He turned on his heel and rapped at me in a stifled voice: "Follow me."

He went along the brick path under the tunnel of roses and through a white gate at the end. Beyond was a walled-in garden containing flowerbeds crammed with showy annuals, a badminton court, a nice stretch of greensward, and a small tiled pool glittering angrily in the sun. Beside the pool there was a flagged space set with blue and white garden furniture, low tables with composition tops, reclining chairs with footrests and enormous cushions, and over all a blue and white umbrella as big as a small tent.

A long-limbed languorous type of showgirl blond lay at her ease in one of the chairs, with her feet raised on a padded rest and a tall misted glass at her elbow, near a silver ice bucket and a Scotch bottle. She looked at us lazily as we came over the grass. From thirty feet away she looked like a lot of class. From ten feet away she looked like something made up to be seen from thirty feet away. Her mouth was too wide, her eyes were too blue, her makeup was too vivid, the thin arch of her eyebrows was almost fantastic in its curve and spread, and the mascara was so thick on her eyelashes that they looked like miniature iron railings.

She wore white duck slacks, blue and white open-toed sandals over bare feet and crimson lake toenails, a white silk blouse and a necklace of green stones that were not square cut emeralds. Her hair was as artificial as a night club lobby.

On the chair beside her there was a white straw garden hat with a brim the size of a spare tire and a white satin chin strap. On the brim of the hat lay a pair of green sun glasses with lenses the size of doughnuts.

Vannier marched over to her and snapped out: "You've got to can that nasty little red-eyed driver of yours, but quick. Otherwise I'm liable to break his neck any minute. I can't go near him without getting insulted."

The blond coughed lightly, flicked a handkerchief around without doing anything with it, and said:

"Sit down and rest your sex appeal. Who's your friend?"

Vannier looked for my card, found he was holding it in his hand and threw it on her lap. She picked it up languidly, ran her eyes over it, ran them over me, sighed and tapped her teeth with her fingernails.

"Big, isn't he? Too much for you to handle, I guess."

Vannier looked at me nastily. "All right, get it over with, whatever it is."

"Do I talk to her?" I asked. "Or do I talk to you and have you put it in English?"

The blond laughed. A silvery ripple of laughter that held the unspoiled naturalness of a bubble dance. A small tongue played roguishly along her lips.

Vannier sat down and lit a gold-tipped cigarette and I stood there looking at them.

I said: "I'm looking for a friend of yours, Mrs. Morny. I understand that she shared an apartment with you about a year ago. Her name is Linda Conquest."

Vannier flicked his eyes up, down, up, down. He turned his head and looked across the pool. The cocker spaniel named Heathcliff sat over there looking at us with the white of one eye.

Vannier snapped his fingers. "Here, Heathcliff! Here, Heathcliff! Come here, sir!"

The blond said: "Shut up. The dog hates your guts. Give your vanity a rest, for heaven's sake."

Vannier snapped: "Don't talk like that to me."

The blond giggled and petted his face with her eyes.

I said: "I'm looking for a girl named Linda Conquest, Mrs. Morny."

The blond looked at me and said: "So you said. I was just thinking. I don't think I've seen her in six months. She got married."

"You haven't seen her in six months?"

"That's what I said, big boy. What do you want to know for?"

"Just a private enquiry I'm making."

"About what?"

"About a confidential matter," I said.

"Just think," the blond said brightly. "He's making a private enquiry about a confidential matter. You hear that, Lou? Busting in on total strangers that don't want to see him is quite all right, though, isn't it, Lou? On account of he's making a private enquiry about a confidential matter."

"Then you don't know where she is, Mrs. Morny?"

"Didn't I say so?" Her voice rose a couple of notches.

"No. You said you didn't think you had seen her in six months. Not quite the same thing."

"Who told you I shared an apartment with her?" the blond snapped.

"I never reveal a source of information, Mrs. Morny."

"Sweetheart, you're fussy enough to be a dance director. I should tell you everything, you should tell me nothing."

"The position is quite different," I said. "I'm a hired hand obeying instructions. The lady has no reason to hide out, has she?"

"Who's looking for her?"

"Her folks."

"Guess again. She doesn't have any folks."

"You must know her pretty well, if you know that," I said.

"Maybe I did once. That don't prove I do now."

"Okay," I said. "The answer is you know, but you won't tell."

"The answer," Vannier said suddenly, "is that you're not wanted here and the sooner you get out, the better we like it."

I kept on looking at Mrs. Morny. She winked at me and said to Vannier: "Don't get so hostile, darling. You have a lot of charm, but you have small bones. You're not built for the rough work. That right, big boy?"

I said: "I hadn't thought about it, Mrs. Morny. Do you think Mr. Morny could help me — or would?"

She shook her head. "How would I know? You could try. If he don't like you, he has guys around that can bounce you."

"I think you could tell me yourself, if you wanted to."

"How are you going to make me want to?" Her eyes were inviting.

"With all these people around," I said, "how can I?"

"That's a thought," she said, and sipped from her glass, watching me over it.

Vannier stood up very slowly. His face was white. He put his hand inside his shirt and said slowly, between his teeth: "Get out, mugg. While you can still walk."

I looked at him in surprise. "Where's your refinement?" I asked him. "And don't tell me you wear a gun with your garden clothes."

The blond laughed, showing a fine strong set of teeth. Vannier thrust his hand under his left arm inside the shirt and set his lips. His black eyes were sharp and blank at the same time, like a snake's eyes.

"You heard me," he said, almost softly. "And don't write me off too quick. I'd plug you as soon as I'd strike a match. And fix it afterwards."

I looked at the blond. Her eyes were bright and her mouth looked sensual and eager, watching us.

I turned and walked away across the grass. About halfway across it I looked back at them. Vannier stood in exactly the same position, his hand inside his shirt. The blond's eyes were still wide and her lips parted, but the shadow of the umbrella had dimmed her expression and at that distance it might have been either fear or pleased anticipation.

I went on over the grass, through the white gate and along the brick path under the rose arbor. I reached the end of it, turned, walked quietly back to the gate and took another look at them. I didn't know what there would be to see or what I cared about it when I saw it.

What I saw was Vannier practically sprawled on top of the blond, kissing her.

I shook my head and went back along the walk.

The red-eyed chauffeur was still at work on the Cadillac. He had finished the wash job and was wiping off the glass and nickel with a large chamois. I went around and stood beside him.

"How you come out?" he asked me out of the side of his mouth.

"Badly. They tramped all over me," I said.

He nodded and went on making the hissing noise of a groom rubbing down a horse.

"You better watch your step. The guy's heeled," I said. "Or pretends to be."

The chauffeur laughed shortly. "Under that suit? Nix."

"Who is this guy Vannier? What does he do?"

The chauffeur straightened up, put the chamois over the sill of a window and wiped his hands on the towel that was now stuck in his waistband.

"Women, my guess would be," he said.

"Isn't it a bit dangerous—playing with this particular woman?"

"I'd say it was," he agreed. "Different guys got different ideas of danger. It would scare me."

"Where does he live?"

"Sherman Oaks. She goes over there. She'll go once too often."

"Ever run across a girl named Linda Conquest? Tall, dark, handsome, used to be a singer with a band?"

"For two bucks, Jack, you expect a lot of service."

"I could build it up to five."

He shook his head. "I don't know the party. Not by that name. All kinds of dames come here, mostly pretty flashy. I don't get introduced." He grinned.

I got my wallet out and put three ones in his little damp paw. I added a business card.

"I like small close-built men," I said. "They never seem to be afraid of anything. Come and see me some time."

"I might at that, Jack. Thanks. Linda Conquest, huh? I'll keep my ear flaps off."

"So long," I said. "The name?"

"They call me Shifty. I never knew why."

"So long, Shifty."

"So long. Gat under his arm—in them clothes? Not a chance."

"I don't know," I said. "He made the motion. I'm not hired to gunfight with strangers."

"Hell, that shirt he's wearing only got two buttons at the top. I noticed. Take him a week to pull a rod from under that." But he sounded faintly worried.

"I guess he was just bluffing," I agreed. "If you hear mention of Linda Conquest, I'll be glad to talk business with you."

"Okay, Jack."

I went back along the black driveway. He stood there scratching his chin.

6

I drove along the block looking for a place to park so that I could run up to the office for a moment before going on downtown.

A chauffeur-driven Packard edged out from the curb in front of a cigar store about thirty feet from the entrance to my building. I slid into the space, locked the car and stepped out. It was only then that I noticed the car in front of which I had parked was a familiar-looking sand-colored coupé. It didn't have to be the same one. There were thousands of them. Nobody was in it. Nobody was near it that wore a cocoa straw hat with a brown and yellow band.

I went around to the street side and looked at the steering post. No license holder. I wrote the license plate number down on the back of an envelope, just in case, and went on into my building. He wasn't in the lobby, or in the corridor upstairs.

I went into the office, looked on the floor for mail, didn't find any, bought myself a short drink out of the office bottle and left. I didn't have any time to spare to get downtown before three o'clock.

The sand-colored coupé was still parked, still empty. I got into mine and started up and moved out into the traffic stream.

I was below Sunset on Vine before he picked me up. I kept on going, grinning, and wondering where he had hid. Perhaps in the car parked behind his own. I hadn't thought of that

I drove south to Third and all the way downtown on Third. The sand-colored coupé kept half a block behind me all the way. I moved over to Seventh and Grand, parked near Seventh and Olive, stopped to buy cigarettes I didn't need, and then walked east along Seventh without looking behind me. At Spring I went into the Hotel Metropole, strolled over to the big horseshoe cigar counter to light one of my cigarettes and then sat down in one of the old brown leather chairs in the lobby.

A blond man in a brown suit, dark glasses and the now familiar hat came into the lobby and moved unobtrusively among the potted palms and the stucco arches to the cigar counter. He bought a package of cigarettes and broke it open standing there, using the time to lean his back against the counter and give the lobby the benefit of his eagle eye.

He picked up his change and went over and sat down with his back to a pillar. He tipped his hat down over his dark glasses and seemed to go to sleep with an unlighted cigarette between his lips.

I got up and wandered over and dropped into the chair beside him. I looked at him sideways. He didn't move. Seen at close quarters his face seemed young and pink and plump and the blond beard on his chin was very carelessly shaved. Behind the dark glasses his eyelashes flicked up and down rapidly. A hand on his knee tightened and pulled the cloth into wrinkles. There was a wart on his cheek just below the right eyelid.

I struck a match and held the flame to his cigarette. "Light?"

"Oh—thanks," he said, very surprised. He drew breath in until the cigarette tip glowed. I shook the match out, tossed it into the sand jar at my elbow and waited. He looked at me sideways several times before he spoke.

"Haven't I seen you somewhere before?"

"Over on Dresden Avenue in Pasadena. This morning."

I could see his cheeks get pinker than they had been. He sighed.

"I must be lousy," he said.

"Boy, you stink," I agreed.

"Maybe it's the hat," he said.

"The hat helps," I said. "But you don't really need it."

"It's a pretty tough dollar in this town," he said sadly. "You can't do it on foot, you ruin yourself with taxi fares if you use taxis, and if you use your own car, it's always where you can't get to it fast enough. You have to stay too close."

"But you don't have to climb in a guy's pocket," I said. "Did you want something with me or are you just practising?"

"I figured I'd find out if you were smart enough to be worth talking to."

"I'm very smart," I said. "It would be a shame not to talk to me."

He looked carefully around back of his chair and on both sides of where we were sitting and then drew a small, pigskin wallet out. He handed me a nice fresh card from it. It read: George Anson Phillips. Confidential Investigations. 212 Senger Building, 1924 North Wilcox Avenue, Hollywood. A Glenview telephone number. In the upper left hand corner there was an open eye with an eyebrow arched in surprise and very long eyelashes.

"You can't do that," I said, pointing to the eye. "That's the Pinkerton's. You'll be stealing their business."

"Oh hell," he said, "what little I get wouldn't bother them."

I snapped the card on my fingernail and bit down hard on my teeth and slipped the card into my pocket.

"You want one of mine—or have you completed your file on me?"

"Oh, I know all about you," he said. "I was a deputy at Ventura the time you were working on the Gregson case."

Gregson was a con man from Oklahoma City who was followed all over the United States for two years by one of his victims until he got so jittery that he shot up a service station attendant who mistook him for an acquaintance. It seemed a long time ago to me.

I said: "Go on from there."

"I remembered your name when I saw it on your registration this a.m. So when I lost you on the way into town I just looked you up. I was going to come in and talk, but it would have been a violation of confidence. This way I kind of can't help myself."

Another screwball. That made three in one day, not counting Mrs. Murdock, who might turn out to be a screwball too.

I waited while he took his dark glasses off and polished them and put them on again and gave the neighborhood the once over again. Then he said:

"I figured we could maybe make a deal. Pool our resources, as they say. I saw the guy go into your office, so I figured he had hired you."

"You knew who he was?"

"I'm working on him," he said, and his voice sounded flat and discouraged. "And where I am getting is no place at all."

"What did he do to you?"

"Well, I'm working for his wife."

"Divorce?"

He looked all around him carefully and said in a small voice: "So she says. But I wonder."

"They both want one," I said. "Each trying to get something on the other. Comical, isn't it?"

"My end I don't like so well. A guy is tailing me around

some of the time. A very tall guy with a funny eye. I shake
him but after a while I see him again. A very tall guy. Like a
lamppost."

A very tall man with a funny eye. I smoked thoughtfully.

"Anything to do with you?" the blond man asked me a
little anxiously.

I shook my head and threw my cigarette into the sand jar.
"Never saw him that I know of." I looked at my strap watch.
"We better get together and talk this thing over properly, but
I can't do it now. I have an appointment."

"I'd like to," he said. "Very much."

"Let's then. My office, my apartment, or your office, or
where?"

He scratched his badly shaved chin with a well-chewed
thumbnail.

"My apartment," he said at last. "It's not in the phone
book. Give me that card a minute."

He turned it over on his palm when I gave it to him and
wrote slowly with a small metal pencil, moving his tongue
along his lips. He was getting younger every minute. He
didn't seem much more than twenty by now, but he had to
be, because the Gregson case had been six years back.

He put his pencil away and handed me back the card. The
address he had written on it was 204 Florence Apartments,
128 Court Street.

I looked at him curiously. "Court Street on Bunker Hill?"

He nodded, flushing all over his blond skin. "Not too
good," he said quickly. "I haven't been in the chips lately. Do
you mind?"

"No, why would I?"

I stood up and held a hand out. He shook it and dropped it
and I pushed it down into my hip pocket and rubbed the
palm against the handkerchief I had there. Looking at his face
more closely I saw that there was a line of moisture across his
upper lip and more of it along the side of his nose. It was not
as hot as all that.

I started to move off and then I turned back to lean down
close to his face and say: "Almost anybody can pull my leg,
but just to make sure, she's a tall blond with careless eyes,
huh?"

"I wouldn't call them careless," he said.

I held my face together while I said: "And just between the two of us this divorce stuff is a lot of hooey. It's something else entirely, isn't it?"

"Yes," he said softly, "and something I don't like more every minute I think about it. Here."

He pulled something out of his pocket and dropped it into my hand. It was a flat key.

"No need for you to wait around in the hall, if I happen to be out. I have two of them. What time would you think you would come?"

"About four-thirty, the way it looks now. You sure you want to give me this key?"

"Why, we're in the same racket," he said, looking up at me innocently, or as innocently as he could look through a pair of dark glasses.

At the edge of the lobby I looked back. He sat there peacefully, with the half-smoked cigarette dead between his lips and the gaudy brown and yellow band on his hat looking as quiet as a cigarette ad on the back page of the Saturday Evening Post.

We were in the same racket. So I wouldn't chisel him. Just like that. I could have the key to his apartment and go in and make myself at home. I could wear his slippers and drink his liquor and lift up his carpet and count the thousand dollar bills under it. We were in the same racket.

7

The Belfont Building was eight stories of nothing in particular that had got itself pinched off between a large green and chromium cut rate suit emporium and a three-story and basement garage that made a noise like lion cages at feeding time. The small dark narrow lobby was as dirty as a chicken yard. The building directory had a lot of vacant space on it. Only one of the names meant anything to me and I knew that one already. Opposite the directory a large sign tilted against the fake marble wall said: *Space for Renting Suitable for Cigar Stand. Apply Room 316.*

There were two open-grill elevators but only one seemed to be running and that not busy. An old man sat inside it slack-jawed and watery-eyed on a piece of folded burlap on top of a wooden stool. He looked as if he had been sitting there since the Civil War and had come out of that badly.

I got in with him and said eight, and he wrestled the doors shut and cranked his buggy and we dragged upwards lurching. The old man breathed hard, as if he was carrying the elevator on his back.

I got out at my floor and started along the hallway and behind me the old man leaned out of the car and blew his nose with his fingers into a carton full of floor sweepings.

Elisha Morningstar's office was at the back, opposite the firedoor. Two rooms, both lettered in flaked black paint on pebbled glass. *Elisha Morningstar. Numismatist.* The one farthest back said: *Entrance.*

I turned the knob and went into a small narrow room with two windows, a shabby little typewriter desk, closed, a number of wall cases of tarnished coins in tilted slots with yellowed typewritten labels under them, two brown filing cases at the back against the wall, no curtains at the windows, and a dust gray floor carpet so threadbare that you wouldn't notice the rips in it unless you tripped over one.

An inner wooden door was open at the back across from the filing cases, behind the little typewriter desk. Through the door came the small sounds a man makes when he isn't doing anything at all. Then the dry voice of Elisha Morningstar called out:

"Come in, please. Come in."

I went along and in. The inner office was just as small but had a lot more stuff in it. A green safe almost blocked off the front half. Beyond this a heavy old mahogany table against the entrance door held some dark books, some flabby old magazines, and a lot of dust. In the back wall a window was open a few inches, without effect on the musty smell. There was a hatrack with a greasy black felt hat on it. There were three long-legged tables with glass tops and more coins under the glass tops. There was a heavy dark leather-topped desk midway of the room. It had the usual desk stuff on it, and in addition a pair of jeweller's scales under a glass dome and two large nickel-framed magnifying glasses and a jeweller's eyepiece lying on a buff scratch pad, beside a cracked yellow silk handkerchief spotted with ink.

In the swivel chair at the desk sat an elderly party in a dark gray suit with high lapels and too many buttons down the front. He had some stringy white hair that grew long enough to tickle his ears. A pale gray bald patch loomed high up in the middle of it, like a rock above timberline. Fuzz grew out of his ears, far enough to catch a moth.

He had sharp black eyes with a pair of pouches under each eye, brownish purple in color and traced with a network of wrinkles and veins. His cheeks were shiny and his short sharp nose looked as if it had hung over a lot of quick ones in its time. A Hoover collar which no decent laundry would have allowed on the premises nudged his Adam's apple and a black string tie poked a small hard knot out at the bottom of the collar, like a mouse getting ready to come out of a mousehole.

He said: "My young lady had to go to the dentist. You are Mr. Marlowe?"

I nodded.

"Pray, be seated." He waved a thin hand at the chair across the desk. I sat down. "You have some identification, I presume?"

I showed it to him. While he read it I smelled him from across the desk. He had a sort of dry musty smell, like a fairly clean Chinaman.

He placed my card face down on top of his desk and folded his hands on it. His sharp black eyes didn't miss anything in my face.

"Well, Mr. Marlowe, what can I do for you?"

"Tell me about the Brasher Doubloon."

"Ah, yes," he said. "The Brasher Doubloon. An interesting coin." He lifted his hands off the desk and made a steeple of the fingers, like an old time family lawyer getting set for a little tangled grammar. "In some ways the most interesting and valuable of all early American coins. As no doubt you know."

"What I don't know about early American coins you could almost crowd into the Rose Bowl."

"Is that so?" he said. "Is that so? Do you want me to tell you?"

"What I'm here for, Mr. Morningstar."

"It is a gold coin, roughly equivalent to a twenty-dollar gold piece, and about the size of a half dollar. Almost exactly. It was made for the State of New York in the year 1787. It was not minted. There were no mints until 1793, when the first mint was opened in Philadelphia. The Brasher Doubloon was coined probably by the pressure molding process and its maker was a private goldsmith named Ephraim Brasher, or Brashear. Where the name survives it is usually spelled Brashear, but not on the coin. I don't know why."

I got a cigarette into my mouth and lit it. I thought it might do something to the musty smell. "What's the pressure molding process?"

"The two halves of the mold were engraved in steel, in intaglio, of course. These halves were then mounted in lead. Gold blanks were pressed between them in a coin press. Then the edges were trimmed for weight and smoothed. The coin was not milled. There were no milling machines in 1787."

"Kind of a slow process," I said.

He nodded his peaked white head. "Quite. And, since the surface-hardening of steel without distortion could not be accomplished at that time, the dies wore and had to be re-made from time to time. With consequent slight variations in design which would be visible under strong magnification. In fact it would be safe to say no two of the coins would be identical, judged by modern methods of microscopic examination. Am I clear?"

"Yeah," I said. "Up to a point. How many of these coins are there and what are they worth?"

He undid the steeple of fingers and put his hands back on the desk top and patted them gently up and down.

"I don't know how many there are. Nobody knows. A few hundred, a thousand, perhaps more. But of these very few indeed are uncirculated specimens in what is called mint condition. The value varies from a couple of thousand on up. I should say that at the present time, since the devaluation of the dollar, an uncirculated specimen, carefully handled by a reputable dealer, might easily bring ten thousand dollars, or even more. It would have to have a history, of course."

I said: "Ah," and let smoke out of my lungs slowly and waved it away with the flat of my hand, away from the old party across the desk from me. He looked like a non-smoker. "And without a history and not so carefully handled—how much?"

He shrugged. "There would be the implication that the coin was illegally acquired. Stolen, or obtained by fraud. Of course it might not be so. Rare coins do turn up in odd places at odd times. In old strong boxes, in the secret drawers of desks in old New England houses. Not often, I grant you. But it happens. I know of a very valuable coin that fell out of the stuffing of a horsehair sofa which was being restored by an antique dealer. The sofa had been in the same room in the same house in Fall River, Massachusetts, for ninety years. Nobody knew how the coin got there. But generally speaking, the implication of theft would be strong. Particularly in this part of the country."

He looked at the corner of the ceiling with an absent stare. I looked at him with a not so absent stare. He looked like a man who could be trusted with a secret—if it was his own secret.

He brought his eyes down to my level slowly and said: "Five dollars, please."

I said: "Huh?"

"Five dollars, please."

"What for?"

"Don't be absurd, Mr. Marlowe. Everything I have told you is available in the public library. In Fosdyke's Register, in particular. You choose to come here and take up my time relating it to you. For this my charge is five dollars."

"And suppose I don't pay it," I said.

He leaned back and closed his eyes. A very faint smile twitched at the corners of his lips. "You will pay it," he said.

I paid it. I took the five out of my wallet and got up to lean over the desk and spread it out right in front of him, carefully. I stroked the bill with my fingertips, as if it was a kitten.

"Five dollars, Mr. Morningstar," I said.

He opened his eyes and looked at the bill. He smiled.

"And now," I said, "let's talk about the Brasher Doubloon that somebody tried to sell you."

He opened his eyes a little wider. "Oh, did somebody try to sell me a Brasher Doubloon? Now why would they do that?"

"They needed the money," I said. "And they didn't want too many questions asked. They knew or found out that you were in the business and that the building where you had your office was a shabby dump where anything could happen. They knew your office was at the end of a corridor and that you were an elderly man who would probably not make any false moves—out of regard for your health."

"They seem to have known a great deal," Elisha Morningstar said dryly.

"They knew what they had to know in order to transact their business. Just like you and me. And none of it was hard to find out."

He stuck his little finger in his ear and worked it around and brought it out with a little dark wax on it. He wiped it off casually on his coat.

"And you assume all this from the mere fact that I called up Mrs. Murdock and asked if her Brasher Doubloon was for sale?"

"Sure. She had the same idea herself. It's reasonable. Like I said over the phone to you, you would know that coin was not for sale. If you knew anything about the business at all. And I can see that you do."

He bowed, about one inch. He didn't quite smile but he looked about as pleased as a man in a Hoover collar ever looks.

"You would be offered this coin for sale," I said, "in suspicious circumstances. You would want to buy it, if you could get it cheap and had the money to handle it. But you would want to know where it came from. And even if you were quite sure it was stolen, you could still buy it, if you could get it cheap enough."

"Oh, I could, could I?" He looked amused, but not in a large way.

"Sure you could—if you are a reputable dealer. I'll assume

you are. By buying the coin—cheap—you would be protecting the owner or his insurance carrier from complete loss. They'd be glad to pay you back your outlay. It's done all the time."

"Then the Murdock Brasher has been stolen," he said abruptly.

"Don't quote me," I said. "It's a secret."

He almost picked his nose this time. He just caught himself. He picked a hair out of one nostril instead, with a quick jerk and a wince. He held it up and looked at it. Looking at me past it he said:

"And how much will your principal pay for the return of the coin?"

I leaned over the desk and gave him my shady leer. "One grand. What did you pay?"

"I think you are a very smart young man," he said. Then he screwed his face up and his chin wobbled and his chest began to bounce in and out and a sound came out of him like a convalescent rooster learning to crow again after a long illness.

He was laughing.

It stopped after a while. His face came all smooth again and his eyes opened, black and sharp and shrewd.

"Eight hundred dollars," he said. "Eight hundred dollars for an uncirculated specimen of the Brasher Doubloon." He chortled.

"Fine. Got it with you? That leaves you two hundred. Fair enough. A quick turnover, a reasonable profit and no trouble for anybody."

"It is not in my office," he said. "Do you take me for a fool?" He reached an ancient silver watch out of his vest on a black fob. He screwed up his eyes to look at it. "Let us say eleven in the morning," he said. "Come back with your money. The coin may or may not be here, but if I am satisfied with your behavior, I will arrange matters."

"That is satisfactory," I said, and stood up. "I have to get the money anyhow."

"Have it in used bills," he said almost dreamily. "Used twenties will do. An occasional fifty will do no harm."

I grinned and started for the door. Halfway there I turned around and went back to lean both hands on the desk and push my face over it.

"What did she look like?"

He looked blank.

"The girl that sold you the coin."

He looked blanker.

"Okay," I said. "It wasn't a girl. She had help. It was a man. What did the man look like?"

He pursed his lips and made another steeple with his fingers. "He was a middle-aged man, heavy set, about five feet seven inches tall and weighing around one hundred and seventy pounds. He said his name was Smith. He wore a blue suit, black shoes, a green tie and shirt, no hat. There was a brown bordered handkerchief in his outer pocket. His hair was dark brown sprinkled with gray. There was a bald patch about the size of a dollar on the crown of his head and a scar about two inches long running down the side of his jaw. On the left side, I think. Yes, on the left side."

"Not bad," I said. "What about the hole in his right sock?"

"I omitted to take his shoes off."

"Darn careless of you," I said.

He didn't say anything. We just stared at each other, half curious, half hostile, like new neighbors. Then suddenly he went into his laugh again.

The five dollar bill I had given him was still lying on his side of the desk. I flicked a hand across and took it.

"You won't want this now," I said. "Since we started talking in thousands."

He stopped laughing very suddenly. Then he shrugged.

"At eleven a.m.," he said. "And no tricks, Mr. Marlowe. Don't think I don't know how to protect myself."

"I hope you do," I said, "because what you are handling is dynamite."

I left him and tramped across the empty outer office and opened the door and let it shut, staying inside. There ought to be footsteps outside in the corridor, but his transom was closed and I hadn't made much noise coming on crepe rubber soles. I hoped he would remember that. I sneaked back across the threadbare carpet and edged in behind the door,

between the door and the little closed typewriter desk. A kid
trick, but once in a while it will work, especially after a lot of
smart conversation, full of worldliness and sly wit. Like a
sucker play in football. And if it didn't work this time, we
would just be there sneering at each other again.

It worked. Nothing happened for a while except that a nose
was blown. Then all by himself in there he went into his sick
rooster laugh again. Then a throat was cleared. Then a swivel
chair squeaked, and feet walked.

A dingy white head poked into the room, about two inches
past the end of the door. It hung there suspended and I went
into a state of suspended animation. Then the head was
drawn back and four unclean fingernails came around the
edge of the door and pulled. The door closed, clicked, was
shut. I started breathing again and put my ear to the wooden
panel.

The swivel chair squeaked once more. The threshing sound
of a telephone being dialed. I lunged across to the instrument
on the little typewriter desk and lifted it. At the other end of
the line the bell had started to ring. It rang six times. Then a
man's voice said: "Yeah?"

"The Florence Apartments?"

"Yeah."

"I'd like to speak to Mr. Anson in Apartment two-o-four."

"Hold the wire. I'll see if he's in."

Mr. Morningstar and I held the wire. Noise came over it,
the blaring sound of a loud radio broadcasting a baseball
game. It was not close to the telephone, but it was noisy
enough.

Then I could hear the hollow sound of steps coming nearer
and the harsh rattle of the telephone receiver being picked up
and the voice said:

"Not in. Any message?"

"I'll call later," Mr. Morningstar said.

I hung up fast and did a rapid glide across the floor to the
entrance door and opened it very silently, like snow falling,
and let it close the same way, taking its weight at the last
moment, so that the click of the catch would not have been
heard three feet away.

I breathed hard and tight going down the hall, listening to

myself. I pushed the elevator button. Then I got out the card
which Mr. George Anson Phillips had given me in the lobby of
the Hotel Metropole. I didn't look at it in any real sense. I
didn't have to look at it to recall that it referred to Apartment
204, Florence Apartments, 128 Court Street. I just stood there
flicking it with a fingernail while the old elevator came heaving
up in the shaft, straining like a gravel truck on a hairpin turn.

The time was three-fifty.

8

Bunker Hill is old town, lost town, shabby town, crook town.
Once, very long ago, it was the choice residential district of
the city, and there are still standing a few of the jigsaw Gothic
mansions with wide porches and walls covered with round-
end shingles and full corner bay windows with spindle turrets.
They are all rooming houses now, their parquetry floors are
scratched and worn through the once glossy finish and the
wide sweeping staircases are dark with time and with cheap
varnish laid on over generations of dirt. In the tall rooms
haggard landladies bicker with shifty tenants. On the wide
cool front porches, reaching their cracked shoes into the sun,
and staring at nothing, sit the old men with faces like lost
battles.

In and around the old houses there are flyblown restaurants
and Italian fruitstands and cheap apartment houses and little
candy stores where you can buy even nastier things than their
candy. And there are ratty hotels where nobody except people
named Smith and Jones sign the register and where the night
clerk is half watchdog and half pander.

Out of the apartment houses come women who should be
young but have faces like stale beer; men with pulled-down
hats and quick eyes that look the street over behind the
cupped hand that shields the match flame; worn intellectuals
with cigarette coughs and no money in the bank; fly cops
with granite faces and unwavering eyes; cokies and coke ped-
dlers; people who look like nothing in particular and know it,

and once in a while even men that actually go to work. But they come out early, when the wide cracked sidewalks are empty and still have dew on them.

I was earlier than four-thirty getting over there, but not much. I parked at the end of the street, where the funicular railway comes struggling up the yellow clay bank from Hill Street, and walked along Court Street to the Florence Apartments. It was dark brick in front, three stories, the lower windows at sidewalk level and masked by rusted screens and dingy net curtains. The entrance door had a glass panel and enough of the name left to be read. I opened it and went down three brass bound steps into a hallway you could touch on both sides without stretching. Dim doors painted with numbers in dim paint. An alcove at the foot of the stairs with a pay telephone. A sign: *Manager Apt. 106.* At the back of the hallway a screen door and in the alley beyond it four tall battered garbage pails in a line, with a dance of flies in the sunlit air above them.

I went up the stairs. The radio I had heard over the telephone was still blatting the baseball game. I read numbers and went up front. Apartment 204 was on the right side and the baseball game was right across the hall from it. I knocked, got no answer and knocked louder. Behind my back three Dodgers struck out against a welter of synthetic crowd noise. I knocked a third time and looked out of the front hall window while I felt in my pocket for the key George Anson Phillips had given me.

Across the street was an Italian funeral home, neat and quiet and reticent, white painted brick, flush with the sidewalk. Pietro Palermo Funeral Parlors. The thin green script of a neon sign lay across its façade, with a chaste air. A tall man in dark clothes came out of the front door and leaned against the white wall. He looked very handsome. He had dark skin and a handsome head of iron-gray hair brushed back from his forehead. He got out what looked at that distance to be a silver or platinum and black enamel cigarette case, opened it languidly with two long brown fingers and selected a gold-tipped cigarette. He put the case away and lit the cigarette with a pocket lighter that seemed to match the case. He put that away and folded his arms and stared at nothing with half-closed eyes. From the tip of his motionless cigarette a thin wisp of smoke rose straight up past his face, as thin and straight as the smoke of a dying campfire at dawn.

Another batter struck out or flied out behind my back in the recreated ball game. I turned from watching the tall Italian, put the key into the door of Apartment 204 and went in.

A square room with a brown carpet, very little furniture and that not inviting. The wall bed with the usual distorting mirror faced me as I opened the door and made me look like a two-time loser sneaking home from a reefer party. There was a birchwood easy chair with some hard looking upholstery beside it in the form of a davenport. A table before the window held a lamp with a shirred paper shade. There was a door on either side of the bed.

The door to the left led into a small kitchenette with a brown woodstone sink and a three-burner stove and an old electric icebox that clicked and began to throb in torment just as I pushed the door open. On the woodstone drain board stood the remains of somebody's breakfast, mud at the bottom of a cup, a burnt crust of bread, crumbs on a board, a yellow slime of melted butter down the slope of a saucer, a smeared knife and a granite coffee pot that smelled like sacks in a hot barn.

I went back around the wall bed and through the other door. It gave on a short hallway with an open space for clothes and a built-in dresser. On the dresser was a comb and a black brush with a few blond hairs in its black bristles. Also a can of talcum, a small flashlight with a cracked lens, a pad of writing paper, a bank pen, a bottle of ink on a blotter, cigarettes and matches in a glass ashtray that contained half a dozen stubs.

In the drawers of the dresser were about what one suitcase would hold in the way of socks and underclothes and handkerchiefs. There was a dark gray suit on a hanger, not new but still good, and a pair of rather dusty black brogues on the floor under it.

I pushed the bathroom door. It opened about a foot and then stuck. My nose twitched and I could feel my lips stiffen and I smelled the harsh sharp bitter smell from beyond the door. I leaned against it. It gave a little, but came back, as though somebody was holding it against me. I poked my head through the opening.

The floor of the bathroom was too short for him, so his knees were poked up and hung outwards slackly and his head was pressed against the woodstone baseboard at the other end, not tilted up, but jammed tight. His brown suit was rumpled a little and his dark glasses stuck out of his breast pocket at an unsafe angle. As if that mattered. His right hand was thrown across his stomach, his left hand lay on the floor, palm up, the fingers curled a little. There was a blood-caked bruise on the right side of his head, in the blond hair. His open mouth was full of shiny crimson blood.

The door was stopped by his leg. I pushed hard and edged around it and got in. I bent down to push two fingers into the side of his neck against the big artery. No artery throbbed there, or even whispered. Nothing at all. The skin was icy. It couldn't have been icy. I just thought it was. I straightened up and leaned my back against the door and made hard fists in my pockets and smelled the cordite fumes. The baseball game was still going on, but through two closed doors it sounded remote.

I stood and looked down at him. Nothing in that, Marlowe, nothing at all. Nothing for you here, nothing. You didn't even know him. Get out, get out fast.

I pulled away from the door and pulled it open and went back through the hall into the living room. A face in the mirror looked at me. A strained, leering face. I turned away from it quickly and took out the flat key George Anson Phillips had given me and rubbed it between my moist palms and laid it down beside the lamp.

I smeared the doorknob opening the door and the outside knob closing the door. The Dodgers were ahead seven to three, the first half of the eighth. A lady who sounded well on with her drinking was singing Frankie and Johnny, the roundhouse version, in a voice that even whiskey had failed to improve. A deep man's voice growled at her to shut up and she kept on singing and there was a hard quick movement across the floor and a smack and a yelp and she stopped singing and the baseball game went right on.

I put the cigarette in my mouth and lit it and went back

down the stairs and stood in the half dark of the hall angle looking at the little sign that read: *Manager, Apt. 106.*

I was a fool even to look at it. I looked at it for a long minute, biting the cigarette hard between my teeth.

I turned and walked down the hallway towards the back. A small enameled plate on a door said: *Manager*. I knocked on the door.

9

A chair was pushed back, feet shuffled, the door opened.

"You the manager?"

"Yeah." It was the same voice I had heard over the telephone. Talking to Elisha Morningstar.

He held an empty smeared glass in his hand. It looked as if somebody had been keeping goldfish in it. He was a lanky man with carroty short hair growing down to a point on his forehead. He had a long narrow head packed with shabby cunning. Greenish eyes stared under orange eyebrows. His ears were large and might have flapped in a high wind. He had a long nose that would be into things. The whole face was a trained face, a face that would know how to keep a secret, a face that held the effortless composure of a corpse in the morgue.

He wore his vest open, no coat, a woven hair watchguard, and round blue sleeve garters with metal clasps.

I said: "Mr. Anson?"

"Two-o-four."

"He's not in."

"What should I do—lay an egg?"

"Neat," I said. "You have them all the time, or is this your birthday?"

"Beat it," he said. "Drift." He started to close the door. He opened it again to say: "Take the air. Scram. Push off." Having made his meaning clear he started to close the door again.

I leaned against the door. He leaned against it on his side. That brought our faces close together. "Five bucks," I said.

It rocked him. He opened the door very suddenly and I had to take a quick step forward in order not to butt his chin with my head.

"Come in," he said.

A living room with a wallbed, everything strictly to specifications, even to the shirred paper lampshade and the glass ashtray. This room was painted egg-yolk yellow. All it needed was a few fat black spiders painted on the yellow to be anybody's bilious attack.

"Sit down," he said, shutting the door.

I sat down. We looked at each other with the clear innocent eyes of a couple of used car salesmen.

"Beer?" he said.

"Thanks."

He opened two cans, filled the smeared glass he had been holding, and reached for another like it. I said I would drink out of the can. He handed me the can.

"A dime," he said.

I gave him a dime.

He dropped it into his vest and went on looking at me. He pulled a chair over and sat in it and spread his bony up-jutting knees and let his empty hand droop between them.

"I ain't interested in your five bucks," he said.

"That's fine," I said. "I wasn't really thinking of giving it to you."

"A wisey," he said. "What gives? We run a nice respectable place here. No funny stuff gets pulled."

"Quiet too," I said. "Upstairs you could almost hear an eagle scream."

His smile was wide, about three quarters of an inch. "I don't amuse easy," he said.

"Just like Queen Victoria," I said.

"I don't get it."

"I don't expect miracles," I said. The meaningless talk had a sort of cold bracing effect on me, making a mood with a hard gritty edge.

I got my wallet out and selected a card from it. It wasn't my card. It read: *James B. Pollock, Reliance Indemnity Company, Field Agent*. I tried to remember what James B. Pollock looked like and where I had met him. I couldn't. I handed the carroty man the card.

He read it and scratched the end of his nose with one of the corners. "Wrong john?" he asked, keeping his green eyes plastered to my face.

"Jewelry," I said and waved a hand.

He thought this over. While he thought it over I tried to make up my mind whether it worried him at all. It didn't seem to.

"We get one once in a while," he conceded. "You can't help it. He didn't look like it to me, though. Soft looking."

"Maybe I got a bum steer," I said. I described George Anson Phillips to him, George Anson Phillips alive, in his brown suit and his dark glasses and his cocoa straw hat with the brown and yellow print band. I wondered what had happened to the hat. It hadn't been up there. He must have got rid of it, thinking it was too conspicuous. His blond head was almost, but not quite, as bad.

"That sound like him?"

The carroty man took his time making up his mind. Finally he nodded yes, green eyes watching me carefully, lean hard hand holding the card up to his mouth and running the card along his teeth like a stick along the palings of a picket fence.

"I didn't figure him for no crook," he said. "But hell, they come all sizes and shapes. Only been here a month. If he looked like a wrong gee, wouldn't have been here at all."

I did a good job of not laughing in his face. "What say we frisk the apartment while he's out?"

He shook his head. "Mr. Palermo wouldn't like it."

"Mr. Palermo?"

"He's the owner. Across the street. Owns the funeral parlors. Owns this building and a lot of other buildings. Practically owns the district, if you know what I mean." He gave me a twitch of the lip and a flutter of the right eyelid. "Gets the vote out. Not a guy to crowd."

"Well, while he's getting the vote out or playing with a stiff or whatever he's doing at the moment, let's go up and frisk the apartment."

"Don't get me sore at you," the carroty man said briefly.

"That would bother me like two per cent of nothing at

all," I said. "Let's go up and frisk the apartment." I threw my empty beer can at the waste basket and watched it bounce back and roll half way across the room.

The carroty man stood up suddenly and spread his feet apart and dusted his hands together and took hold of his lower lip with his teeth.

"You said something about five," he shrugged.

"That was hours ago," I said. "I thought better of it. Let's go up and frisk the apartment."

"Say that just once more—" his right hand slid towards his hip.

"If you're thinking of pulling a gun, Mr. Palermo wouldn't like it," I said.

"To hell with Mr. Palermo," he snarled, in a voice suddenly furious, out of a face suddenly charged with dark blood.

"Mr. Palermo will be glad to know that's how you feel about him," I said.

"Look," the carroty man said very slowly, dropping his hand to his side and leaning forward from the hips and pushing his face at me as hard as he could. "Look. I was sitting here having myself a beer or two. Maybe three. Maybe nine. What the hell? I wasn't bothering anybody. It was a nice day. It looked like it might be a nice evening—Then you come in." He waved a hand violently.

"Let's go up and frisk the apartment," I said.

He threw both fists forward in tight lumps. At the end of the motion he threw his hands wide open, straining the fingers as far as they would go. His nose twitched sharply.

"If it wasn't for the job," he said.

I opened my mouth. "Don't say it!" he yelled.

He put a hat on, but no coat, opened a drawer and took out a bunch of keys, walked past me to open the door and stood in it, jerking his chin at me. His face still looked a little wild.

We went out into the hall and along it and up the stairs. The ball game was over and dance music had taken its place. Very loud dance music. The carroty man selected one of his keys and put it in the lock of Apartment 204. Against the booming of the dance band behind us in the apartment across the way a woman's voice suddenly screamed hysterically.

The carroty man withdrew the key and bared his teeth at me. He walked across the narrow hallway and banged on the opposite door. He had to knock hard and long before any attention was paid. Then the door was jerked open and a sharp-faced blond in scarlet slacks and a green pullover stared out with sultry eyes, one of which was puffed and the other had been socked several days ago. She also had a bruise on her throat and her hand held a tall cool glass of amber fluid.

"Pipe down, but soon," the carroty man said. "Too much racket. I don't aim to ask you again. Next time I call some law."

The girl looked back over her shoulder and screamed against the noise of the radio: "Hey, Del! The guy says to pipe down! You wanna sock him?"

A chair squeaked, the radio noise died abruptly and a thick bitter-eyed dark man appeared behind the blond, yanked her out of the way with one hand and pushed his face at us. He needed a shave. He was wearing pants, street shoes and an undershirt.

He settled his feet in the doorway, whistled a little breath in through his nose and said:

"Buzz off. I just come in from lunch. I had a lousy lunch. I wouldn't want nobody to push muscle at me." He was very drunk, but in a hard practised sort of way.

The carroty man said: "You heard me, Mr. Hench. Dim that radio and stop the roughhouse in here. And make it sudden."

The man addressed as Hench said: "Listen, picklepuss—" and heaved forward with his right foot in a hard stamp.

The carroty man's left foot didn't wait to be stamped on. The lean body moved back quickly and the thrown bunch of keys hit the floor behind, and clanked against the door of Apartment 204. The carroty man's right hand made a sweeping movement and came up with a woven leather blackjack.

Hench said: "Yah!" and took two big handfuls of air in his two hairy hands, closed the hands into fists and swung hard at nothing.

The carroty man hit him on the top of his head and the girl

screamed again and threw a glass of liquor in her boy friend's face. Whether because it was safe to do it now or because she made an honest mistake, I couldn't tell.

Hench turned blindly with his face dripping, stumbled and ran across the floor in a lurch that threatened to land him on his nose at every step. The bed was down and tumbled. Hench made the bed on one knee and plunged a hand under the pillow.

I said: "Look out—gun."

"I can fade that too," the carroty man said between his teeth and slid his right hand, empty now, under his open vest.

Hench was down on both knees. He came up on one and turned and there was a short black gun in his right hand and he was staring down at it, not holding it by the grip at all, holding it flat on his palm.

"Drop it!" the carroty man's voice said tightly and he went on into the room.

The blond promptly jumped on his back and wound her long green arms around his neck, yelling lustily. The carroty man staggered and swore and waved his gun around.

"Get him, Del!" the blond screamed. "Get him good!"

Hench, one hand on the bed and one foot on the floor, both knees doubled, right hand holding the black gun flat on his palm, eyes staring down at it, pushed himself slowly to his feet and growled deep in his throat:

"This ain't my gun."

I relieved the carroty man of the gun that was not doing him any good and stepped around him, leaving him to shake the blond off his back as best he could. A door banged down the hallway and steps came along toward us.

I said: "Drop it, Hench."

He looked up at me, puzzled dark eyes suddenly sober.

"It ain't my gun," he said and held it out flat. "Mine's a Colt .32—belly gun."

I took the gun off his hand. He made no effort to stop me. He sat down on the bed, rubbed the top of his head slowly, and screwed his face up in difficult thought. "Where the hell—" his voice trailed off and he shook his head and winced.

I sniffed the gun. It had been fired. I sprang the magazine out and counted the bullets through the small holes in the side. There were six. With one in the magazine, that made seven. The gun was a Colt .32, automatic, eight shot. It had been fired. If it had not been reloaded, one shot had been fired from it.

The carroty man had the blond off his back now. He had thrown her into a chair and was wiping a scratch on his cheek. His green eyes were baleful.

"Better get some law," I said. "A shot has been fired from this gun and it's about time you found out there's a dead man in the apartment across the hall."

Hench looked up at me stupidly and said in a quiet, reasonable voice: "Brother, that simply ain't my gun."

The blond sobbed in a rather theatrical manner and showed me an open mouth twisted with misery and ham acting. The carroty man went softly out of the door.

10

"Shot in the throat with a medium caliber gun and a soft-nosed bullet," Detective-Lieutenant Jesse Breeze said. "A gun like this and bullets like is in here." He danced the gun on his hand, the gun Hench had said was not his gun. "Bullet ranged upwards and probably hit the back of the skull. Still inside his head. The man's dead about two hours. Hands and face cold, but body still warm. No rigor. Was sapped with something hard before being shot. Likely with a gun butt. All that mean anything to you boys and girls?"

The newspaper he was sitting on rustled. He took his hat off and mopped his face and the top of his almost bald head. A fringe of light colored hair around the crown was damp and dark with sweat. He put his hat back on, a flat-crowned panama, burned dark by the sun. Not this year's hat, and probably not last year's.

He was a big man, rather paunchy, wearing brown and white shoes and sloppy socks and white trousers with thin black stripes, an open neck shirt showing some ginger-colored hair at the top of his chest, and a rough sky-blue sports coat not wider at the shoulders than a two-car garage. He would be about fifty years old and the only thing about him that very much suggested cop was the calm, unwinking unwavering stare of his prominent pale blue eyes, a stare that had no thought of being rude, but that anybody but a cop would feel to be rude. Below his eyes across the top of his cheeks and the bridge of his nose there was a wide path of freckles, like a mine field on a war map.

We were sitting in Hench's apartment and the door was shut. Hench had his shirt on and he was absently tying a tie with thick blunt fingers that trembled. The girl was lying on the bed. She had a green wrap-around thing twisted about her head, a purse by her side and a short squirrel coat across her feet. Her mouth was a little open and her face was drained and shocked.

Hench said thickly: "If the idea is the guy was shot with the gun under the pillow, okay. Seems like he might have been. It ain't my gun and nothing you boys can think up is going to make me say it's my gun."

"Assuming that to be so," Breeze said, "how come? Somebody swiped your gun and left this one. When, how, what kind of gun was yours?"

"We went out about three-thirty or so to get something to eat at the hashhouse around the corner," Hench said. "You can check that. We must have left the door unlocked. We were kind of hitting the bottle a little. I guess we were pretty noisy. We had the ball game going on the radio. I guess we shut it off when we went out. I'm not sure. You remember?" He looked at the girl lying white-faced and silent on the bed. "You remember, sweet?"

The girl didn't look at him or answer him.

"She's pooped," Hench said. "I had a gun, a Colt .32, same caliber as that, but a belly gun. A revolver, not an automatic. There's a piece broken off the rubber grip. A Jew named Morris gave it to me three four years ago. We worked together in a bar. I don't have no permit, but I don't carry the gun neither."

Breeze said: "Hitting the hooch like you birds been and

having a gun under the pillow sooner or later somebody was going to get shot. You ought to know that."

"Hell, we didn't even know the guy," Hench said. His tie was tied now, very badly. He was cold sober and very shaky. He stood up and picked a coat off the end of the bed and put it on and sat down again. I watched his fingers tremble lighting a cigarette. "We don't know his name. We don't know anything about him. I see him maybe two three times in the hall, but he don't even speak to me. It's the same guy, I guess. I ain't even sure of that."

"It's the fellow that lived there," Breeze said. "Let me see now, this ball game is a studio re-broadcast, huh?"

"Goes on at three," Hench said. "Three to say four-thirty, or sometimes later. We went out about the last half the third. We was gone about an inning and a half, maybe two. Twenty minutes to half an hour. Not more."

"I guess he was shot just before you went out," Breeze said. "The radio would kill the noise of the gun near enough. You must of left your door unlocked. Or even open."

"Could be," Hench said wearily. "You remember, honey?"

Again the girl on the bed refused to answer him or even look at him.

Breeze said: "You left your door open or unlocked. The killer heard you go out. He got into your apartment, wanting to ditch his gun, saw the bed down, walked across and slipped his gun under the pillow, and then imagine his surprise. He found another gun there waiting for him. So he took it along. Now if he meant to ditch his gun, why not do it where he did his killing? Why take the risk of going into another apartment to do it? Why the fancy pants?"

I was sitting in the corner of the davenport by the window. I put in my nickel's worth, saying: "Suppose he had locked himself out of Phillips' apartment before he thought of ditching the gun? Suppose, coming out of the shock of his murder, he found himself in the hall still holding the murder gun. He would want to ditch it fast. Then if Hench's door was open and he had heard them go out along the hall—"

Breeze looked at me briefly and grunted: "I'm not saying it isn't so. I'm just considering." He turned his attention back to Hench. "So now, if this turns out to be the gun that killed Anson, we got to try and trace *your* gun. While we do that we got to have you and the young lady handy. You understand that, of course?"

Hench said: "You don't have any boys that can bounce me hard enough to make me tell it different."

"We can always try," Breeze said mildly. "And we might just as well get started."

He stood up, turned and swept the crumpled newspapers off the chair on to the floor. He went over to the door, then turned and stood looking at the girl on the bed. "You all right, sister, or should I call for a matron?"

The girl on the bed didn't answer him.

Hench said: "I need a drink. I need a drink bad."

"Not while I'm watching you," Breeze said and went out of the door.

Hench moved across the room and put the neck of a bottle into his mouth and gurgled liquor. He lowered the bottle, looked at what was left in it and went over to the girl. He pushed her shoulder.

"Wake up and have a drink," he growled at her.

The girl stared at the ceiling. She didn't answer him or show that she had heard him.

"Let her alone," I said. "Shock."

Hench finished what was in the bottle, put the empty bottle down carefully and looked at the girl again, then turned his back on her and stood frowning at the floor. "Jeeze, I wish I could remember better," he said under his breath.

Breeze came back into the room with a young fresh-faced plainclothes detective. "This is Lieutenant Spangler," he said. "He'll take you down. Get going, huh?"

Hench went back to the bed and shook the girl's shoulder. "Get on up, babe. We gotta take a ride."

The girl turned her eyes without turning her head, and looked at him slowly. She lifted her shoulders off the bed and put a hand under her and swung her legs over the side and stood up, stamping her right foot, as if it was numb.

"Tough, kid—but you know how it is," Hench said.

The girl put a hand to her mouth and bit the knuckle of

her little finger, looking at him blankly. Then she swung the hand suddenly and hit him in the face as hard as she could. Then she half ran out of the door.

Hench didn't move a muscle for a long moment. There was a confused noise of men talking outside, a confused noise of cars down below in the street. Hench shrugged and cocked his heavy shoulders back and swept a slow look around the room, as if he didn't expect to see it again very soon, or at all. Then he went out past the young fresh-faced detective.

The detective went out. The door closed. The confused noise outside was dimmed a little and Breeze and I sat looking at each other heavily.

II

After a while Breeze got tired of looking at me and dug a cigar out of his pocket. He slit the cellophane band with a knife and trimmed the end of the cigar and lit it carefully, turning it around in the flame, and holding the burning match away from it while he stared thoughtfully at nothing and drew on the cigar and made sure it was burning the way he wanted it to burn.

Then he shook the match out very slowly and reached over to lay it on the sill of the open window. Then he looked at me some more.

"You and me," he said, "are going to get along."

"That's fine," I said.

"You don't think so," he said. "But we are. But not because I took any sudden fancy to you. It's the way I work. Everything in the clear. Everything sensible. Everything quiet. Not like that dame. That's the kind of dame that spends her life looking for trouble and when she finds it, it's the fault of the first guy she can get her fingernails into."

"He gave her a couple of shiners," I said. "That wouldn't make her love him too much."

"I can see," Breeze said, "that you know a lot about dames."

"Not knowing a lot about them has helped me in my business," I said. "I'm open-minded."

He nodded and examined the end of his cigar. He took a piece of paper out of his pocket and read from it. "Delmar B. Hench, 45, bartender, unemployed. Maybelle Masters, 26, dancer. That's all I know about them. I've got a hunch there ain't a lot more to know."

"You don't think he shot Anson?" I asked.

Breeze looked at me without pleasure. "Brother, I just got here." He took a card out of his pocket and read from that. "James B. Pollock, Reliance Indemnity Company, Field Agent. What's the idea?"

"In a neighborhood like this it's bad form to use your own name," I said. "Anson didn't either."

"What's the matter with the neighborhood?"

"Practically everything," I said.

"What I would like to know," Breeze said, "is what you know about the dead guy?"

"I told you already."

"Tell me again. People tell me so much stuff I get it all mixed up."

"I know what it says on his card, that his name is George Anson Phillips, that he claimed to be a private detective. He was outside my office when I went to lunch. He followed me downtown, into the lobby of the Hotel Metropole. I led him there. I spoke to him and he admitted he had been following me and said it was because he wanted to find out if I was smart enough to do business with. That's a lot of baloney, of course. He probably hadn't quite made up his mind what to do and was waiting for something to decide him. He was on a job—he said—he had got leery of and he wanted to join up with somebody, perhaps somebody with a little more experience than he had, if he had any at all. He didn't act as if he had."

Breeze said: "And the only reason he picked on you is that six years ago you worked on a case in Ventura while he was a deputy up there."

I said, "That's my story."

"But you don't have to get stuck with it," Breeze said calmly. "You can always give us a better one."

"It's good enough," I said. "I mean it's good enough in the sense that it's bad enough to be true."

He nodded his big slow head.

"What's your idea of all this?" he asked.

"Have you investigated Phillips' office address?"

He shook his head, no.

"My idea is you will find out he was hired because he was simple. He was hired to take this apartment here under a wrong name, and to do something that turned out to be not what he liked. He was scared. He wanted a friend, he wanted help. The fact that he picked me after so long a time and such little knowledge of me showed he didn't know many people in the detective business."

Breeze got his handkerchief out and mopped his head and face again. "But it don't begin to show why he had to follow you around like a lost pup instead of walking right up to your office door and in."

"No," I said, "it doesn't."

"Can you explain that?"

"No. Not really."

"Well, how would you try to explain it?"

"I've already explained it in the only way I know how. He was undecided whether to speak to me or not. He was waiting for something to decide him. I decided by speaking to him."

Breeze said: "That is a very simple explanation. It is so simple it stinks."

"You may be right," I said.

"And as the result of this little hotel lobby conversation this guy, a total stranger to you, asks you to his apartment and hands you his key. Because he wants to talk to you."

I said, "Yes."

"Why couldn't he talk to you then?"

"I had an appointment," I said.

"Business?"

I nodded.

"I see. What you working on?"

I shook my head and didn't answer.

"This is murder," Breeze said. "You're going to have to tell me."

I shook my head again. He flushed a little.

"Look," he said tightly, "you got to."

"I'm sorry, Breeze," I said. "But so far as things have gone, I'm not convinced of that."

"Of course you know I can throw you in the can as a material witness," he said casually.

"On what grounds?"

"On the grounds that you are the one who found the body, that you gave a false name to the manager here, and that you don't give a satisfactory account of your relations with the dead guy."

I said: "Are you going to do it?"

He smiled bleakly. "You got a lawyer?"

"I know several lawyers. I don't have a lawyer on a retainer basis."

"How many of the commissioners do you know personally?"

"None. That is, I've spoken to three of them, but they might not remember me."

"But you have good contacts, in the mayor's office and so on?"

"Tell me about them," I said. "I'd like to know."

"Look, buddy," he said earnestly, "you must got some friends somewhere. Surely."

"I've got a good friend in the Sheriff's office, but I'd rather leave him out of it."

He lifted his eyebrows. "Why? Maybe you're going to need friends. A good word from a cop we know to be right might go a long way."

"He's just a personal friend," I said. "I don't ride around on his back. If I get in trouble, it won't do him any good."

"How about the homicide bureau?"

"There's Randall," I said. "If he's still working out of Central Homicide. I had a little time with him on a case once. But he doesn't like me too well."

Breeze sighed and moved his feet on the floor, rustling the newspapers he had pushed down out of the chair.

"Is all this on the level—or are you just being smart? I mean about all the important guys you don't know?"

"It's on the level," I said. "But the way I am using it is smart."

"It ain't smart to say so right out."

"I think it is."

He put a big freckled hand over the whole lower part of his face and squeezed. When he took the hand away there were round red marks on his cheeks from the pressure of thumb and fingers. I watched the marks fade.

"Why don't you go on home and let a man work?" he asked crossly.

I got up and nodded and went towards the door. Breeze said to my back: "Gimme your home address."

I gave it to him. He wrote it down. "So long," he said drearily: "Don't leave town. We'll want a statement—maybe tonight."

I went out. There were two uniformed cops outside on the landing. The door across the way was open and a fingerprint man was still working inside. Downstairs I met two more cops in the hallway, one at each end of it. I didn't see the carroty manager. I went out the front door. There was an ambulance pulling away from the curb. A knot of people hung around on both sides of the street, not as many as would accumulate in some neighborhoods.

I pushed along the sidewalk. A man grabbed me by the arm and said: "What's the damage, Jack?"

I shook his arm off without speaking or looking at his face and went on down the street to where my car was.

12

It was a quarter to seven when I let myself into the office and clicked the light on and picked a piece of paper off the floor. It was a notice from the Green Feather Messenger Service saying that a package was held awaiting my call and would be delivered upon request at any hour of the day or night. I put it on the desk, peeled my coat off and opened the windows. I got a half bottle of Old Taylor out of the deep drawer of the desk and drank a short drink, rolling it around on my tongue. Then I sat there holding the neck of the cool bottle and wondering how it would feel to be a homicide dick and find bodies lying around and not mind at all, not have to sneak out wiping doorknobs, not have to ponder how much I could tell without hurting a client and how little I could tell without too badly hurting myself. I decided I wouldn't like it.

I pulled the phone over and looked at the number on the slip and called it. They said my package could be sent right over. I said I would wait for it.

It was getting dark outside now. The rushing sound of the traffic had died a little and the air from the open window, not yet cool from the night, had that tired end-of-the-day smell of dust, automobile exhaust, sunlight rising from hot walls and sidewalks, the remote smell of food in a thousand restaurants, and perhaps, drifting down from the residential hills above Hollywood—if you had a nose like a hunting dog—a touch of that peculiar tomcat smell that eucalyptus trees give off in warm weather.

I sat there smoking. Ten minutes later the door was knocked on and I opened it to a boy in a uniform cap who took my signature and gave me a small square package, not more than two and a half inches wide, if that. I gave the boy a dime and listened to him whistling his way back to the elevators.

The label had my name and address printed on it in ink, in a quite fair imitation of typed letters, larger and thinner than pica. I cut the string that tied the label to the box and unwound the thin brown paper. Inside was a thin cheap cardboard box pasted over with brown paper and stamped *Made in Japan* with a rubber stamp. It would be the kind of box you would get in a Jap store to hold some small carved animal or a small piece of jade. The lid fitted down all the way and tightly. I pulled it off and saw tissue paper and cotton wool.

Separating these I was looking at a gold coin about the size of a half dollar, bright and shining as if it had just come from the mint.

The side facing me showed a spread eagle with a shield for a breast and the initials E.B. punched into the left wing. Around these was a circle of beading, between the beading and the smooth unmilled edge of the coin, the legend E PLURIBUS UNUM. At the bottom was the date 1787.

I turned the coin over on my palm. It was heavy and cold and my palm felt moist under it. The other side showed a sun rising or setting behind a sharp peak of mountain, then a double circle of what looked like oak leaves, then more Latin, NOVA EBORACA COLUMBIA EXCELSIOR. At the bottom of this side, in smaller capitals, the name BRASHER.

I was looking at the Brasher Doubloon.

There was nothing else in the box or in the paper, nothing on the paper. The handwritten printing meant nothing to me. I didn't know anybody who used it.

I filled an empty tobacco pouch half full, wrapped the coin up in tissue paper, snapped a rubber band around it and tucked it into the tobacco in the pouch and put more in on top. I closed the zipper and put the pouch in my pocket. I locked the paper and string and box and label up in a filing cabinet, sat down again and dialed Elisha Morningstar's number on the phone. The bell rang eight times at the other end of the line. It was not answered. I hardly expected that. I hung up again, looked Elisha Morningstar up in the book and saw that he had no listing for a residence phone in Los Angeles or the outlying towns that were in the phone book.

I got a shoulder holster out of the desk and strapped it on and slipped a Colt .38 automatic into it, put on hat and coat, shut the windows again, put the whiskey away, clicked the lights off and had the office door unlatched when the phone rang.

The ringing bell had a sinister sound, for no reason of itself, but because of the ears to which it rang. I stood there braced and tense, lips tightly drawn back in a half grin. Beyond the closed window the neon lights glowed. The dead air didn't move. Outside the corridor was still. The bell rang in darkness, steady and strong.

I went back and leaned on the desk and answered. There was a click and a droning on the wire and beyond that nothing. I depressed the connection and stood there in the dark, leaning over, holding the phone with one hand and holding the flat riser on the pedestal down with the other. I didn't know what I was waiting for.

The phone rang again. I made a sound in my throat and put it to my ear again, not saying anything at all.

So we were there silent, both of us, miles apart maybe, each one holding a telephone and breathing and listening and hearing nothing, not even the breathing.

Then after what seemed a very long time there was the quiet remote whisper of a voice saying dimly, without any tone:

"Too bad for you, Marlowe."

Then the click again and the droning on the wire and I hung up and went back across the office and out.

13

I drove west on Sunset, fiddled around a few blocks without making up my mind whether anyone was trying to follow me, then parked near a drugstore and went into its phone booth. I dropped my nickel and asked the O-operator for a Pasadena number. She told me how much money to put in.

The voice which answered the phone was angular and cold. "Mrs. Murdock's residence."

"Philip Marlowe here. Mrs. Murdock, please."

I was told to wait. A soft but very clear voice said: "Mr. Marlowe? Mrs. Murdock is resting now. Can you tell me what it is?"

"You oughtn't to have told him."

"I—who—?"

"That loopy guy whose handkerchief you cry into."

"How dare you?"

"That's fine," I said. "Now let me talk to Mrs. Murdock. I have to."

"Very well. I'll try." The soft clear voice went away and I waited a long wait. They would have to lift her up on the pillows and drag the port bottle out of her hard gray paw and feed her the telephone. A throat was cleared suddenly over the wire. It sounded like a freight train going through a tunnel.

"This is Mrs. Murdock."

"Could you identify the property we were talking about this morning, Mrs. Murdock? I mean could you pick it out from others just like it?"

"Well—are there others just like it?"

"There must be. Dozens, hundreds for all I know. Anyhow dozens. Of course I don't know where they are."

She coughed. "I don't really know much about it. I suppose I couldn't identify it then. But in the circumstances——"

"That's what I'm getting at, Mrs. Murdock. The identification would seem to depend on tracing the history of the article back to you. At least to be convincing."

"Yes. I suppose it would. Why? Do you know where it is?"

"Morningstar claims to have seen it. He says it was offered to him for sale—just as you suspected. He wouldn't buy. The seller was not a woman, he says. That doesn't mean a thing, because he gave me a detailed description of the party which was either made up or was a description of somebody he knew more than casually. So the seller may have been a woman."

"I see. It's not important now."

"Not important?"

"No. Have you anything else to report?"

"Another question to ask. Do you know a youngish blond fellow named George Anson Phillips? Rather heavy set, wearing a brown suit and a dark pork pie hat with a gay band. Wearing that today. Claimed to be a private detective."

"I do not. Why should I?"

"I don't know. He enters the picture somewhere. I think he was the one who tried to sell the article. Morningstar tried to call him up after I left. I snuck back into his office and overheard."

"You what?"

"I snuck."

"Please do not be witty, Mr. Marlowe. Anything else?"

"Yes, I agreed to pay Morningstar one thousand dollars for the return of the—the article. He said he could get it for eight hundred . . ."

"And where were you going to get the money, may I ask?"

"Well, I was just talking. This Morningstar is a downy bird. That's the kind of language he understands. And then again you might have wanted to pay it. I wouldn't want to persuade you. You could always go to the police. But if for any reason you didn't want to go to the police, it might be the only way you could get it back—buying it back."

I would probably have gone on like that for a long time,

not knowing just what I was trying to say, if she hadn't stopped me with a noise like a seal barking.

"This is all very unnecessary now, Mr. Marlowe. I have decided to drop the matter. The coin has been returned to me."

"Hold the wire a minute," I said.

I put the phone down on the shelf and opened the booth door and stuck my head out, filling my chest with what they were using for air in the drugstore. Nobody was paying any attention to me. Up front the druggist, in a pale blue smock, was chatting across the cigar counter. The counter boy was polishing glasses at the fountain. Two girls in slacks were playing the pinball machine. A tall narrow party in a black shirt and a pale yellow scarf was fumbling magazines at the rack. He didn't look like a gunman.

I pulled the booth shut and picked up the phone and said: "A rat was gnawing my foot. It's all right now. You got it back, you said. Just like that. How?"

"I hope you are not too disappointed," she said in her uncompromising baritone. "The circumstances are a little difficult. I may decide to explain and I may not. You may call at the house tomorrow morning. Since I do not wish to proceed with the investigation, you will keep the retainer as payment in full."

"Let me get this straight," I said. "You actually got the coin back—not a promise of it, merely?"

"Certainly not. And I'm getting tired. So, if you—"

"One moment, Mrs. Murdock. It isn't going to be as simple as all that. Things have happened."

"In the morning you may tell me about them," she said sharply, and hung up.

I pushed out of the booth and lit a cigarette with thick awkward fingers. I went back along the store. The druggist was alone now. He was sharpening a pencil with a small knife, very intent, frowning.

"That's a nice sharp pencil you have there," I told him.

He looked up, surprised. The girls at the pinball machine looked at me, surprised. I went over and looked at myself in the mirror behind the counter. I looked surprised.

I sat down on one of the stools and said: "A double Scotch, straight."

The counter man looked surprised. "Sorry, this isn't a bar, sir. You can buy a bottle at the liquor counter."

"So it is," I said. "I mean, so it isn't. I've had a shock. I'm a little dazed. Give me a cup of coffee, weak, and a very thin ham sandwich on stale bread. No, I better not eat yet either. Good-by."

I got down off the stool and walked to the door in a silence that was as loud as a ton of coal going down a chute. The man in the black shirt and yellow scarf was sneering at me over the New Republic.

"You ought to lay off that fluff and get your teeth into something solid, like a pulp magazine," I told him, just to be friendly.

I went on out. Behind me somebody said: "Hollywood's full of them."

14

The wind had risen and had a dry taut feeling, tossing the tops of trees, and making the swung arc light up the side street cast shadows like crawling lava. I turned the car and drove east again.

The hock shop was on Santa Monica, near Wilcox, a quiet old-fashioned little place, washed gently by the lapping waves of time. In the front window there was everything you could think of, from a set of trout flies in a thin wooden box to a portable organ, from a folding baby carriage to a portrait camera with a four-inch lens, from a mother-of-pearl lorgnette in a faded plush case to a Single Action Frontier Colt, .44 caliber, the model they still make for Western peace officers whose grandfathers taught them how to file the trigger and shoot by fanning the hammer back.

I went into the shop and a bell jangled over my head and somebody shuffled and blew his nose far at the back and steps came. An old Jew in a tall black skull cap came along behind the counter, smiling at me over cut out glasses.

I got my tobacco pouch out, got the Brasher Doubloon

out of that and laid it on the counter. The window in front was clear glass and I felt naked. No paneled cubicles with hand-carved spittoons and doors that locked themselves as you closed them.

The Jew took the coin and lifted it on his hand. "Gold, is it? A gold hoarder you are maybe," he said, twinkling.

"Twenty-five dollars," I said. "The wife and the kiddies are hungry."

"Oi, that is terrible. Gold, it feels, by the weight. Only gold and maybe platinum it could be." He weighed it casually on a pair of small scales. "Gold it is," he said. "So ten dollars you are wanting?"

"Twenty-five dollars."

"For twenty-five dollars what would I do with it? Sell it, maybe? For fifteen dollars worth of gold is maybe in it. Okay. Fifteen dollars."

"You got a good safe?"

"Mister, in this business are the best safes money can buy. Nothing to worry about here. It is fifteen dollars, is it?"

"Make out the ticket."

He wrote it out partly with his pen and partly with his tongue. I gave my true name and address. Bristol Apartments, 1634 North Bristol Avenue, Hollywood.

"You are living in that district and you are borrowing fifteen dollars," the Jew said sadly, and tore off my half of the ticket and counted out the money.

I walked down to the corner drugstore and bought an envelope and borrowed a pen and mailed the pawnticket to myself.

I was hungry and hollow inside. I went over to Vine to eat, and after that I drove downtown again. The wind was still rising and it was drier than ever. The steering wheel had a gritty feeling under my fingers and the inside of my nostrils felt tight and drawn.

The lights were on here and there in the tall buildings. The green and chromium clothier's store on the corner of Ninth and Hill was a blaze of it. In the Belfont Building a few windows glowed here and there, but not many. The same old plowhorse sat in the elevator on his piece of folded burlap, looking straight in front of him, blank-eyed, almost gathered to history.

I said: "I don't suppose you know where I can get in touch with the building superintendent?"

He turned his head slowly and looked past my shoulder. "I hear how in Noo York they got elevators that just whiz. Go thirty floors at a time. High speed. That's in Noo York."

"The hell with New York," I said. "I like it here."

"Must take a good man to run them fast babies."

"Don't kid yourself, dad. All those cuties do is push buttons, say 'Good Morning, Mr. Whoosis,' and look at their beauty spots in the car mirror. Now you take a Model T job like this—it takes a man to run it. Satisfied?"

"I work twelve hours a day," he said. "And glad to get it."

"Don't let the union hear you."

"You know what the union can do?" I shook my head. He told me. Then he lowered his eyes until they almost looked at me. "Didn't I see you before somewhere?"

"About the building super," I said gently.

"Year ago he broke his glasses," the old man said. "I could of laughed. Almost did."

"Yes. Where could I get in touch with him this time of the evening?"

He looked at me a little more directly.

"Oh, the building super? He's home, ain't he?"

"Sure. Probably. Or gone to the pictures. But where is home? What's his name?"

"You want something?"

"Yes." I squeezed a fist in my pocket and tried to keep from yelling. "I want the address of one of the tenants. The tenant I want the address of isn't in the phone book—at his home. I mean where he lives when he's not in his office. You know, home." I took my hands out and made a shape in the air, writing the letters slowly, h o m e.

The old man said: "Which one?" It was so direct that it jarred me.

"Mr. Morningstar."

"He ain't home. Still in his office."

"Are you sure?"

"Sure I'm sure. I don't notice people much. But he's old like me and I notice him. He ain't been down yet."

I got into the car and said: "Eight."

He wrestled the doors shut and we ground our way up. He didn't look at me anymore. When the car stopped and I got out he didn't speak or look at me again. He just sat there blank-eyed, hunched on the burlap and the wooden stool. As I turned the angle of the corridor he was still sitting there. And the vague expression was back on his face.

At the end of the corridor two doors were alight. They were the only two in sight that were. I stopped outside to light a cigarette and listen, but I didn't hear any sound of activity. I opened the door marked *Entrance* and stepped into the narrow office with the small closed typewriter desk. The wooden door was still ajar. I walked along to it and knocked on the wood and said: "Mr. Morningstar."

No answer. Silence. Not even a sound of breathing. The hairs moved on the back of my neck. I stepped around the door. The ceiling light glowed down on the glass cover of the jeweller's scales, on the old polished wood around the leather desk top, down the side of the desk, on a square-toed, elastic-sided black shoe, with a white cotton sock above it.

The shoe was at the wrong angle, pointing to the corner of the ceiling. The rest of the leg was behind the corner of the big safe. I seemed to be wading through mud as I went on into the room.

He lay crumpled on his back. Very lonely, very dead.

The safe door was wide open and keys hung in the lock of the inner compartment. A metal drawer was pulled out. It was empty now. There may have been money in it once.

Nothing else in the room seemed to be different.

The old man's pockets had been pulled out, but I didn't touch him except to bend over and put the back of my hand against his livid, violet-colored face. It was like touching a frog's belly. Blood had oozed from the side of his forehead where he had been hit. But there was no powder smell on the air this time, and the violet color of his skin showed that he had died of a heart stoppage, due to shock and fear, probably. That didn't make it any less murder.

I left the lights burning, wiped the doorknobs, and walked down the fire stairs to the sixth floor. I read the names on the doors going along, for no reason at all. *H. R. Teager Dental Laboratories, L. Pridview, Public Accountant, Dalton and Rees Typewriting Service, Dr. E. J. Blaskowitz,* and underneath the name in small letters: *Chiropractic Physician.*

The elevator came growling up and the old man didn't look at me. His face was as empty as my brain.

I called the Receiving Hospital from the corner, giving no name.

15

The chessmen, red and white bone, were lined up ready to go and had that sharp, competent and complicated look they always have at the beginning of a game. It was ten o'clock in the evening, I was home at the apartment, I had a pipe in my mouth, a drink at my elbow and nothing on my mind except two murders and the mystery of how Mrs. Elizabeth Bright Murdock had got her Brasher Doubloon back while I still had it in my pocket.

I opened a little paper-bound book of tournament games published in Leipzig, picked out a dashing-looking Queen's Gambit, moved the white pawn to Queen's four, and the bell rang at the door.

I stepped around the table and picked the Colt .38 off the drop leaf of the oak desk and went over to the door holding it down beside my right leg.

"Who is it?"

"Breeze."

I went back to the desk to lay the gun down again before I opened the door. Breeze stood there looking just as big and sloppy as ever, but a little more tired. The young, fresh-faced dick named Spangler was with him.

They rode me back into the room without seeming to and Spangler shut the door. His bright young eyes flicked this way and that while Breeze let his older and harder ones stay on my face for a long moment, then he walked around me to the davenport.

"Look around," he said out of the corner of his mouth.

Spangler left the door and crossed the room to the dinette, looked in there, recrossed and went into the hall. The bathroom door squeaked, his steps went farther along.

Breeze took his hat off and mopped his semi-bald dome. Doors opened and closed distantly. Closets. Spangler came back.

"Nobody here," he said.

Breeze nodded and sat down, placing his panama beside him.

Spangler saw the gun lying on the desk. He said: "Mind if I look?"

I said: "Phooey on both of you."

Spangler walked to the gun and held the muzzle to his nose, sniffing. He broke the magazine out, ejected the shell in the chamber, picked it up and pressed it into the magazine. He laid the magazine on the desk and held the gun so that light went into the open bottom of the breech. Holding it that way he squinted down the barrel.

"A little dust," he said. "Not much."

"What did you expect?" I said. "Rubies?"

He ignored me, looked at Breeze and added: "I'd say this gun has not been fired within twenty-four hours. I'm sure of it."

Breeze nodded and chewed his lip and explored my face with his eyes. Spangler put the gun together neatly and laid it aside and went and sat down. He put a cigarette between his lips and lit it and blew smoke contentedly.

"We know damn well it wasn't a long .38 anyway," he said. "One of those things will shoot through a wall. No chance of the slug staying inside a man's head."

"Just what are you guys talking about?" I asked.

Breeze said: "The usual thing in our business. Murder. Have a chair. Relax. I thought I heard voices in here. Maybe it was the next apartment."

"Maybe," I said.

"You always have a gun lying around on your desk?"

"Except when it's under my pillow," I said. "Or under my arm. Or in the drawer of the desk. Or somewhere I can't just remember where I happened to put it. That help you any?"

"We didn't come here to get tough, Marlowe."

"That's fine," I said. "So you prowl my apartment and handle my property without asking my permission. What do you do when you get tough—knock me down and kick me in the face?"

"Aw hell," he said and grinned. I grinned back. We all grinned. Then Breeze said: "Use your phone?"

I pointed to it. He dialed a number and talked to someone named Morrison, saying: "Breeze at—" He looked down at the base of the phone and read the number off— "Anytime now. Marlowe is the name that goes with it. Sure. Five or ten minutes is okay."

He hung up and went back to the davenport.

"I bet you can't guess why we're here."

"I'm always expecting the brothers to drop in," I said.

"Murder ain't funny, Marlowe."

"Who said it was?"

"Don't you kind of act as if it was?"

"I wasn't aware of it."

He looked at Spangler and shrugged. Then he looked at the floor. Then he lifted his eyes slowly, as if they were heavy, and looked at me again. I was sitting down by the chess table now.

"You play a lot of chess?" he asked, looking at the chessmen.

"Not a lot. Once in a while I fool around with a game here, thinking things out."

"Don't it take two guys to play chess?"

"I play over tournament games that have been recorded and published. There's a whole literature about chess. Once in a while I work out problems. They're not chess, properly speaking. What are we talking about chess for? Drink?"

"Not right now," Breeze said. "I talked to Randall about you. He remembers you very well, in connection with a case down at the beach." He moved his feet on the carpet, as if they were very tired. His solid old face was lined and gray with fatigue. "He said you wouldn't murder anybody. He says you are a nice guy, on the level."

"That was friendly of him," I said.

"He says you make good coffee and you get up kind of late

in the mornings and are apt to run to a very bright line of chatter and that we should believe anything you say, provided we can check it by five independent witnesses."

"To hell with him," I said.

Breeze nodded exactly as though I had said just what he wanted me to say. He wasn't smiling and he wasn't tough, just a big solid man working at his job. Spangler had his head back on the chair and his eyes half closed and was watching the smoke from his cigarette.

"Randall says we should look out for you. He says you are not as smart as you think you are, but that you are a guy things happen to, and a guy like that could be a lot more trouble than a very smart guy. That's what he says, you understand. You look all right to me. I like everything in the clear. That's why I'm telling you."

I said it was nice of him.

The phone rang. I looked at Breeze, but he didn't move, so I reached for it and answered it. It was a girl's voice. I thought it was vaguely familiar, but I couldn't place it.

"Is this Mr. Philip Marlowe?"

"Yes."

"Mr. Marlowe, I'm in trouble, very great trouble. I want to see you very badly. When can I see you?"

I said: "You mean tonight? Who am I talking to?"

"My name is Gladys Crane. I live at the Hotel Normandy on Rampart. When can you—"

"You mean you want me to come over there tonight?" I asked, thinking about the voice, trying to place it.

"I—" The phone clicked and the line was dead. I sat there holding it, frowning at it, looking across it at Breeze. His face was quietly empty of interest.

"Some girl says she's in trouble," I said. "Connection broken." I held the plunger down on the base of the phone waiting for it to ring again. The two cops were completely silent and motionless. Too silent, too motionless.

The bell rang again and I let the plunger up and said: "You want to talk to Breeze, don't you?"

"Yeah." It was a man's voice and it sounded a little surprised.

"Go on, be tricky," I said, and got up from the chair and

went out to the kitchen. I heard Breeze talking very briefly then the sound of the phone being returned to the cradle.

I got a bottle of Four Roses out of the kitchen closet and three glasses. I got ice and ginger ale from the icebox and mixed three highballs and carried them in on a tray and sat the tray down on the cocktail table in front of the davenport where Breeze was sitting. I took two of the glasses, handed one to Spangler, and took the other to my chair.

Spangler held the glass uncertainly, pinching his lower lip between thumb and finger, looking at Breeze to see whether he would accept the drink.

Breeze looked at me very steadily. Then he sighed. Then he picked the glass up and tasted it and sighed again and shook his head sideways with a half smile; the way a man does when you give him a drink and he needs it very badly and it is just right and the first swallow is like a peek into a cleaner, sunnier, brighter world.

"I guess you catch on pretty fast, Mr. Marlowe," he said, and leaned back on the davenport completely relaxed. "I guess now we can do some business together."

"Not that way," I said.

"Huh?" He bent his eyebrows together. Spangler leaned forward in his chair and looked bright and attentive.

"Having stray broads call me up and give me a song and dance so you can say they said they recognized my voice somewhere sometime."

"The girl's name is Gladys Crane," Breeze said.

"So she told me. I never heard of her."

"Okay," Breeze said. "Okay." He showed me the flat of his freckled hand. "We're not trying to pull anything that's not legitimate. We only hope you ain't, either."

"Ain't either what?"

"Ain't either trying to pull anything not legitimate. Such as holding out on us."

"Just why shouldn't I hold out on you, if I feel like it?" I asked. "You're not paying my salary."

"Look, don't get tough, Marlowe."

"I'm not tough. I don't have any idea of being tough. I know enough about cops not to get tough with them. Go ahead and speak your piece and don't try to pull any more phonies like that telephone call."

"We're on a murder case," Breeze said. "We have to try to run it the best we can. You found the body. You had talked to the guy. He had asked you to come to his apartment. He gave you his key. You said you didn't know what he wanted to see you about. We figured that maybe with time to think back you could have remembered."

"In other words I was lying the first time," I said.

Breeze smiled a tired smile. "You been around enough to know that people always lie in murder cases."

"The trouble with that is how are you going to know when I stop lying?"

"When what you say begins to make sense, we'll be satisfied."

I looked at Spangler. He was leaning forward so far he was almost out of his chair. He looked as if he was going to jump. I couldn't think of any reason why he should jump, so I thought he must be excited. I looked back at Breeze. He was about as excited as a hole in the wall. He had one of his cellophane-wrapped cigars between his thick fingers and he was slitting the cellophane with a penknife. I watched him get the wrapping off and trim the cigar end with the blade and put the knife away, first wiping the blade carefully on his pants. I watched him strike a wooden match and light the cigar carefully, turning it around in the flame, then hold the match away from the cigar, still burning, and draw on the cigar until he decided it was properly lighted. Then he shook the match out and laid it down beside the crumpled cellophane on the glass top of the cocktail table. Then he leaned back and pulled up one leg of his pants and smoked peacefully. Every motion had been exactly as it had been when he lit a cigar in Hench's apartment, and exactly as it always would be whenever he lit a cigar. He was that kind of man, and that made him dangerous. Not as dangerous as a brilliant man, but much more dangerous than a quick excitable one like Spangler.

"I never saw Phillips before today," I said. "I don't count that he said he saw me up in Ventura once, because I don't remember him. I met him just the way I told you. He tailed me around and I braced him. He wanted to talk to me, he gave me his key, I went to his apartment, used the key to let myself in when he didn't answer—as he had told me to do. He was dead. The police were called and through a set of events or incidents that had nothing to do with me, a gun was found under Hench's pillow. A gun that had been fired. I told you this and it's true."

Breeze said: "When you found him you went down to the apartment manager, guy named Passmore, and got him to go up with you without telling him anybody was dead. You gave Passmore a phony card and talked about jewelry."

I nodded. "With people like Passmore and apartment houses like that one, it pays to be a little on the cagey side. I was interested in Phillips. I thought Passmore might tell me something about him, if he didn't know he was dead, that he wouldn't be likely to tell me, if he knew the cops were going to bounce in on him in a brief space of time. That's all there was to that."

Breeze drank a little of his drink and smoked a little of his cigar and said: "What I'd like to get in the clear is this. Everything you just told us might be strictly the truth, and yet you might not be telling us the truth. If you get what I mean."

"Like what?" I asked, getting perfectly well what he meant.

He tapped on his knee and watched me with a quiet up from under look. Not hostile, not even suspicious. Just a quiet man doing his job.

"Like this. You're on a job. We don't know what it is. Phillips was playing at being a private dick. He was on a job. He tailed you around. How can we know, unless you tell us, that his job and your job don't tie in somewhere? And if they do, that's our business. Right?"

"That's one way to look at it," I said. "But it's not the only way, and it's not my way."

"Don't forget this is a murder case, Marlowe."

"I'm not. But don't you forget I've been around this town a long time, more than fifteen years. I've seen a lot of murder cases come and go. Some have been solved, some couldn't be solved, and some could have been solved that were not solved. And one or two or three of them have been solved wrong. Somebody was paid to take a rap, and the chances are it was known or strongly suspected. And winked at. But skip that. It happens, but not often. Consider a case like the Cassidy case. I guess you remember it, don't you?"

Breeze looked at his watch. "I'm tired," he said. "Let's forget the Cassidy case. Let's stick to the Phillips case."

I shook my head. "I'm going to make a point, and it's an important point. Just look at the Cassidy case. Cassidy was a very rich man, a multimillionaire. He had a grown up son. One night the cops were called to his home and young Cassidy was on his back on the floor with blood all over his face and a bullet hole in the side of his head. His secretary was lying on *his* back in an adjoining bathroom, with his head against the second bathroom door, leading to a hall, and a cigarette burned out between the fingers of his left hand, just a short burned out stub that had scorched the skin between his fingers. A gun was lying by his right hand. He was shot in the head, not a contact wound. A lot of drinking had been done. Four hours had elapsed since the deaths and the family doctor had been there for three of them. Now, what did you do with the Cassidy case?"

Breeze sighed. "Murder and suicide during a drinking spree. The secretary went haywire and shot young Cassidy. I read it in the papers or something. Is that what you want me to say?"

"You read it in the papers," I said, "but it wasn't so. What's more you knew it wasn't so and the D.A. knew it wasn't so and the D.A.'s investigators were pulled off the case within a matter of hours. There was no inquest. But every crime reporter in town and every cop on every homicide detail knew it was Cassidy that did the shooting, that it was Cassidy that was crazy drunk, that it was the secretary who tried to handle him and couldn't and at last tried to get away from him, but wasn't quick enough. Cassidy's was a contact wound and the secretary's was not. The secretary was left-handed and he had a cigarette in his left hand when he was shot. Even if you are right-handed, you don't change a cigarette over to your other hand and shoot a man while casually holding the cigarette. They might do that on *Gang Busters*, but rich men's secretaries don't do it. And what were the family and the family doctor doing during the four hours they didn't call the cops? Fixing it so there would only be a superficial investigation. And why were no tests of the hands made for nitrates? Because you didn't want the truth. Cassidy was too big. But this was a murder case too, wasn't it?"

"The guys were both dead," Breeze said. "What the hell difference did it make who shot who?"

"Did you ever stop to think," I asked, "that Cassidy's secretary might have had a mother or a sister or a sweetheart—or all three? That they had their pride and their faith and their love for a kid who was made out to be a drunken paranoiac because his boss's father had a hundred million dollars?"

Breeze lifted his glass slowly and finished his drink slowly and put it down slowly and turned the glass slowly on the glass top of the cocktail table. Spangler sat rigid, all shining eyes and lips parted in a sort of rigid half smile.

Breeze said: "Make your point."

I said: "Until you guys own your own souls you don't own mine. Until you guys can be trusted every time and always, in all times and conditions, to seek the truth out and find it and let the chips fall where they may—until that time comes, I have a right to listen to my conscience, and protect my client the best way I can. Until I'm sure you won't do him more harm than you'll do the truth good. Or until I'm hauled before somebody that can make me talk."

Breeze said: "You sound to me just a little like a guy who is trying to hold his conscience down."

"Hell," I said. "Let's have another drink. And then you can tell me about that girl you had me talk to on the phone."

He grinned: "That was a dame that lives next door to Phillips. She heard a guy talking to him at the door one evening. She works days as an usherette. So we thought maybe she ought to hear your voice. Think nothing of it."

"What kind of voice was it?"

"Kind of a mean voice. She said she didn't like it."

"I guess that's what made you think of me," I said.

I picked up the three glasses and went out to the kitchen with them.

16

When I got out there I had forgotten which glass was which, so I rinsed them all out and dried them and was starting to make more drinks when Spangler strolled out and stood just behind my shoulder.

"It's all right," I said. "I'm not using any cyanide this evening."

"Don't get too foxy with the old guy," he said quietly to the back of my neck. "He knows more angles than you think."

"Nice of you," I said.

"Say, I'd like to read up on that Cassidy case," he said. "Sounds interesting. Must have been before my time."

"It was a long time ago," I said. "And it never happened. I was just kidding." I put the glasses on the tray and carried them back into the living room and set them around. I took mine over to my chair behind the chess table.

"Another phony," I said. "Your sidekick sneaks out to the kitchen and gives me advice behind your back about how careful I ought to keep on account of the angles you know that I don't think you know. He has just the right face for it. Friendly and open and an easy blusher."

Spangler sat down on the edge of his chair and blushed. Breeze looked at him casually, without meaning.

"What did you find out about Phillips?" I asked.

"Yes," Breeze said. "Phillips. Well, George Anson Phillips is a kind of pathetic case. He thought he was a detective, but it looks as if he couldn't get anybody to agree with him. I talked to the sheriff at Ventura. He said George was a nice kind, maybe a little too nice to make a good cop, even if he had any brains. George did what they said and he would do it pretty well, provided they told him which foot to start on and how many steps to take which way and little things like that. But he didn't develop much, if you get what I mean. He was the sort of cop who would be likely to hang a pinch on a chicken thief, if he saw the guy steal the chicken and the guy fell down running away and hit his head on a post or something and knocked himself out. Otherwise it might get a little tough and George would have to go back to the office for instructions. Well, it wore the sheriff down after a while and he let George go."

Breeze drank some more of his drink and scratched his chin with a thumbnail like the blade of a shovel.

"After that George worked in a general store at Simi for a man named Sutcliff. It was a credit business with little books for each customer and George would have trouble with the books. He would forget to write the stuff down or write it in the wrong book and some of the customers would straighten him out and some would let George forget. So Sutcliff thought maybe George would do better at something else, and George came to L.A. He had come into a little money, not much, but enough for him to get a license and put up a bond and get himself a piece of an office. I was over there. What he had was desk room with another guy who claims he is selling Christmas cards. Name of Marsh. If George had a customer, the arrangement was Marsh would go for a walk. Marsh says he didn't know where George lived and George didn't have any customers. That is, no business came into the office that Marsh knows about. But George put an ad in the paper and he might have got a customer out of that. I guess he did, because about a week ago Marsh found a note on his desk that George would be out of town for a few days. That's the last he heard of him. So George went over to Court Street and took an apartment under the name of Anson and got bumped off. And that's all we know about George so far. Kind of a pathetic case."

He looked at me with a level uncurious gaze and raised his glass to his lips.

"What about this ad?"

Breeze put the glass down and dug a thin piece of paper out of his wallet and put it down on the cocktail table. I went over and picked it up and read it. It said:

Why worry? Why be doubtful or confused? Why be gnawed by suspicion? Consult cool, careful, confidential, discreet investigator. George Anson Phillips. Glenview 9521.

I put it down on the glass again.

"It ain't any worse than lots of business personals," Breeze said. "It don't seem to be aimed at the carriage trade."

Spangler said: "The girl in the office wrote it for him. She said she could hardly keep from laughing, but George thought it was swell. The Hollywood Boulevard office of the *Chronicle*."

"You checked that fast," I said.

"We don't have any trouble getting information," Breeze said. "Except maybe from you."

"What about Hench?"

"Nothing about Hench. Him and the girl were having a liquor party. They would drink a little and sing a little and scrap a little and listen to the radio and go out to eat once in a while, when they thought of it. I guess it had been going on for days. Just as well we stopped it. The girl has two bad eyes. The next round Hench might have broken her neck. The world is full of bums like Hench—and his girl."

"What about the gun Hench said wasn't his?"

"It's the right gun. We don't have the slug yet, but we have the shell. It was under George's body and it checks. We had a couple more fired and comparisoned the ejector marks and the firing pin dents."

"You believe somebody planted it under Hench's pillow?"

"Sure. Why would Hench shoot Phillips? He didn't know him."

"How do you know that?"

"I know it," Breeze said, spreading his hands. "Look, there are things you know because you have them down in black and white. And there are things you know because they are reasonable and have to be so. You don't shoot somebody and then make a lot of racket calling attention to yourself, and all the time you have the gun under your pillow. The girl was with Hench all day. If Hench shot anybody, she would have some idea. She doesn't have any such idea. She would spill, if she had. What is Hench to her? A guy to play around with, no more. Look, forget Hench. The guy who did the shooting hears the loud radio and knows it will cover a shot. But all the same he saps Phillips and drags him into the bathroom and shuts the door before he shoots him. He's not drunk. He's minding his own business, and careful. He goes out, shuts the bathroom door, the radio stops, Hench and the girl go out to eat. Just happens that way."

"How do you know the radio stopped?"

"I was told," Breeze said calmly. "Other people live in that dump. Take it the radio stopped and they went out. Not quiet. The killer steps out of the apartment and Hench's door is open. That must be because otherwise he wouldn't think anything about Hench's door."

"People don't leave their doors open in apartment houses. Especially in districts like that."

"Drunks do. Drunks are careless. Their minds don't focus well. And they only think of one thing at a time. The door was open—just a little maybe, but open. The killer went in and ditched his gun on the bed and found another gun there. He took that away, just to make it look worse for Hench."

"You can check the gun," I said.

"Hench's gun? We'll try to, but Hench says he doesn't know the number. If we find it, we might do something there. I doubt it. The gun we have we will try to check, but you know how those things are. You get just so far along and you think it is going to open up for you, and then the trail dies out cold. A dead end. Anything else you can think of that we might know that might be a help to you in your business?"

"I'm getting tired," I said. "My imagination isn't working very well."

"You were doing fine a while back," Breeze said. "On the Cassidy case."

I didn't say anything. I filled my pipe up again but it was too hot to light. I laid it on the edge of the table to cool off.

"It's God's truth," Breeze said slowly, "that I don't know what to make of you. I can't see you deliberately covering up on any murder. And neither can I see you knowing as little about all this as you pretend to know."

I didn't say anything, again.

Breeze leaned over to revolve his cigar butt in the tray until he had killed the fire. He finished his drink, put on his hat and stood up.

"How long you expect to stay dummied up?" he asked.

"I don't know."

"Let me help you out. I give you till tomorrow noon, a little better than twelve hours. I won't get my post mortem report before that anyway. I give you till then to talk things over with your party and decide to come clean."

"And after that?"

"After that I see the Captain of Detectives and tell him a private eye named Philip Marlowe is withholding information which I need in a murder investigation, or I'm pretty sure he is. And what about it? I figure he'll pull you in fast enough to singe your breeches."

I said: "Uh-huh. Did you go through Phillips' desk?"

"Sure. A very neat young feller. Nothing in it at all, except a little kind of diary. Nothing in that either, except about how he went to the beach or took some girl to the pictures and she didn't warm up much. Or how he sat in the office and no business come in. One time he got a little sore about his laundry and wrote a whole page. Mostly it was just three or four lines. There was only one thing about it. It was all done in a kind of printing."

I said: "Printing?"

"Yeah, printing in pen and ink. Not big block caps like people trying to disguise things. Just neat fast little printing as if the guy could write that way as fast and easy as any way."

"He didn't write like that on the card he gave me," I said.

Breeze thought about that for a moment. Then he nodded. "True. Maybe it was this way. There wasn't any name in the diary either, in the front. Maybe the printing was just a little game he played with himself."

"Like Pepys' shorthand," I said.

"What was that?"

"A diary a man wrote in a private shorthand, a long time ago."

Breeze looked at Spangler, who was standing up in front of his chair, tipping the last few drops of his glass.

"We better beat it," Breeze said. "This guy is warming up for another Cassidy case."

Spangler put his glass down and they both went over to the door. Breeze shuffled a foot and looked at me sideways, with his hand on the doorknob.

"You know any tall blonds?"

"I'd have to think," I said. "I hope so. How tall?"

"Just tall. I don't know how tall that is. Except that it

would be tall to a guy who is tall himself. A wop named Palermo owns that apartment house on Court Street. We went across to see him in his funeral parlors. He owns them too. He says he saw a tall blond come out of the apartment house about three-thirty. The manager, Passmore, don't place anybody in the joint that he would call a tall blond. The wop says she was a looker. I give some weight to what he says because he give us a good description of you. He didn't see this tall blond go in, just saw her come out. She was wearing slacks and a sports jacket and a wrap-around. But she had light blond hair and plenty of it under the wrap-around."

"Nothing comes to me," I said. "But I just remembered something else. I wrote the license number of Phillips' car down on the back of an envelope. That will give you his former address, probably. I'll get it."

They stood there while I went to get it out of my coat in the bedroom. I handed the piece of envelope to Breeze and he read what was on it and tucked it into his billfold.

"So you just thought of this, huh?"

"That's right."

"Well, well," he said. "Well, well."

The two of them went along the hallway towards the elevator, shaking their heads.

I shut the door and went back to my almost untasted second drink. It was flat. I carried it to the kitchen and hardened it up from the bottle and stood there holding it and looking out of the window at the eucalyptus trees tossing their limber tops against the bluish dark sky. The wind seemed to have risen again. It thumped at the north window and there was a heavy slow pounding noise on the wall of the building, like a thick wire banging the stucco between insulators.

I tasted my drink and wished I hadn't wasted the fresh whiskey on it. I poured it down the sink and got a fresh glass and drank some ice water.

Twelve hours to tie up a situation which I didn't even begin to understand. Either that or turn up a client and let the cops go to work on her and her whole family. Hire Marlowe and get your house full of law. Why worry? Why be doubtful and confused? Why be gnawed by suspicion? Consult cock-eyed, careless, clubfooted, dissipated investigator. Philip Marlowe, Glenview 7537. See me and you meet the best cops in town. Why despair? Why be lonely? Call Marlowe and watch the wagon come.

This didn't get me anywhere either. I went back to the living room and put a match to the pipe that had cooled off now on the edge of the chess table. I drew the smoke in slowly, but it still tasted like the smell of hot rubber. I put it away and stood in the middle of the floor pulling my lower lip out and letting it snap back against my teeth.

The telephone rang. I picked it up and growled into it.

"Marlowe?"

The voice was a harsh low whisper. It was a harsh low whisper I had heard before.

"All right," I said. "Talk it up whoever you are. Whose pocket have I got my hand in now?"

"Maybe you're a smart guy," the harsh whisper said. "Maybe you would like to do yourself some good."

"How much good?"

"Say about five C's worth of good."

"That's grand," I said. "Doing what?"

"Keeping your nose clean," the voice said. "Want to talk about it?"

"Where, when, and who to?"

"Idle Valley Club. Morny. Any time you get here."

"Who are you?"

A dim chuckle came over the wire. "Just ask at the gate for Eddie Prue."

The phone clicked dead. I hung it up.

It was near eleven-thirty when I backed my car out of the garage and drove towards Cahuenga Pass.

17

About twenty miles north of the pass a wide boulevard with flowering moss in the parkways turned towards the foothills. It ran for five blocks and died—without a house in its entire length. From its end a curving asphalt road dove into the hills. This was Idle Valley.

Around the shoulder of the first hill there was a low white building with a tiled roof beside the road. It had a roofed porch and a floodlighted sign on it read: *Idle Valley Patrol.* Open gates were folded back on the shoulders of the road, in the middle of which a square white sign standing on its point said STOP in letters sprinkled with reflector buttons. Another floodlight blistered the space of road in front of the sign.

I stopped. A uniformed man with a star and a strapped-on gun in a woven leather holster looked at my car, then at a board on a post.

He came over to the car. "Good evening. I don't have your car. This is a private road. Visiting?"

"Going to the club."

"Which one?"

"Idle Valley Club."

"Eighty-seven Seventy-seven. That's what we call it here. You mean Mr. Morny's place?"

"Right."

"You're not a member, I guess."

"No."

"I have to check you in. To somebody who is a member or to somebody who lives in the valley. All private property here, you know."

"No gate crashers, huh?"

He smiled. "No gate crashers."

"The name is Philip Marlowe," I said. "Calling on Eddie Prue."

"Prue?"

"He's Mr. Morny's secretary. Or something."

"Just a minute, please."

He went to the door of the building, and spoke. Another uniformed man inside, plugged in on a PBX. A car came up behind me and honked. The clack of a typewriter came from the open door of the patrol office. The man who had spoken to me looked at the honking car and waved it in. It slid around me and scooted off into the dark, a green long open convertible sedan with three dizzy-looking dames in the front seat, all cigarettes and arched eyebrows and go-to-hell expressions. The car flashed around a curve and was gone.

The uniformed man came back to me and put a hand on the car door. "Okay, Mr. Marlowe. Check with the officer at the club, please. A mile ahead on your right. There's a lighted parking lot and the number on the wall. Just the number. Eighty-seven Seventy-seven. Check with the officer there, please."

I said: "Why would I do that?"

He was very calm, very polite, and very firm. "We have to know exactly where you go. There's a great deal to protect in Idle Valley."

"Suppose I don't check with him?"

"You kidding me?" His voice hardened.

"No. I just wanted to know."

"A couple of cruisers would start looking for you."

"How many are you in the patrol?"

"Sorry," he said. "About a mile ahead on the right, Mr. Marlowe."

I looked at the gun strapped to his hip, the special badge pinned to his shirt. "And they call this a democracy," I said.

He looked behind him and then spat on the ground and put a hand on the sill of the car door. "Maybe you got company," he said. "I knew a fellow belonged to the John Reed Club. Over in Boyle Heights, it was."

"Tovarich," I said.

"The trouble with revolutions," he said, "is that they get in the hands of the wrong people."

"Check," I said.

"On the other hand," he said, "could they be any wronger than the bunch of rich phonies that live around here?"

"Maybe you'll be living in here yourself someday," I said.

He spat again. "I wouldn't live in here if they paid me fifty thousand a year and let me sleep in chiffon pajamas with a string of matched pink pearls around my neck."

"I'd hate to make you the offer," I said.

"You make me the offer any time," he said. "Day or night. Just make me the offer and see what it gets you."

"Well, I'll run along now and check with the officer of the club," I said.

"Tell him to go spit up his left pants leg," he said. "Tell him I said so."

"I'll do that," I said.

A car came up behind and honked. I drove on. Half a block of dark limousine blew me off the road with its horn and went past me making a noise like dead leaves falling.

The wind was quiet out here and the valley moonlight was so sharp that the black shadows looked as if they had been cut with an engraving tool.

Around the curve the whole valley spread out before me. A thousand white houses built up and down the hills, ten thousand lighted windows and the stars hanging down over them politely, not getting too close, on account of the patrol.

The wall of the club building that faced the road was white and blank, with no entrance door, no windows on the lower floor. The number was small but bright in violet-colored neon. 8777. Nothing else. To the side, under rows of hooded, downward-shining lights, were even rows of cars, set out in the white lined slots on the smooth black asphalt. Attendants in crisp clean uniforms moved in the lights.

The road went around to the back. A deep concrete porch there, with an overhanging canopy of glass and chromium, but very dim lights. I got out of the car and received a check with the license number on it, carried it over to a small desk where a uniformed man sat and dumped it in front of him.

"Philip Marlowe," I said. "Visitor."

"Thank you, Mr. Marlowe." He wrote the name and number down, handed me back my check and picked up a telephone.

A Negro in a white linen doublebreasted guards uniform, gold epaulettes, a cap with a broad gold band, opened the door for me.

The lobby looked like a high-budget musical. A lot of light and glitter, a lot of scenery, a lot of clothes, a lot of sound, an all-star cast, and a plot with all the originality and drive of a split fingernail. Under the beautiful soft indirect lighting the walls seemed to go up forever and to be lost in soft lascivious stars that really twinkled. You could just manage to walk on

the carpet without waders. At the back was a free-arched stairway with a chromium and white enamel gangway going up in
wide shallow carpeted steps. At the entrance to the dining
room a chubby captain of waiters stood negligently with a
two-inch satin stripe on his pants and a bunch of gold-plated
menus under his arm. He had the sort of face that can turn
from a polite simper to cold-blooded fury almost without
moving a muscle.

The bar entrance was to the left. It was dusky and quiet
and a bartender moved mothlike against the faint glitter of
piled glassware. A tall handsome blond in a dress that looked
like seawater sifted over with gold dust came out of the
Ladies' Room touching up her lips and turned toward the
arch, humming.

The sound of rhumba music came through the archway
and she nodded her gold head in time to it, smiling. A short
fat man with a red face and glittering eyes waited for her with
a white wrap over his arm. He dug his thick fingers into her
bare arm and leered up at her.

A check girl in peach-bloom Chinese pajamas came over to
take my hat and disapprove of my clothes. She had eyes like
strange sins.

A cigarette girl came down the gangway. She wore an egret
plume in her hair, enough clothes to hide behind a toothpick,
one of her long beautiful naked legs was silver, and one was
gold. She had the utterly disdainful expression of a dame who
makes her dates by long distance.

I went into the bar and sank into a leather bar seat packed
with down. Glasses tinkled gently, lights glowed softly, there
were quiet voices whispering of love, or ten per cent, or
whatever they whisper about in a place like that.

A tall fine-looking man in a gray suit cut by an angel suddenly stood up from a small table by the wall and walked over
to the bar and started to curse one of the barmen. He cursed
him in a loud clear voice for a long minute, calling him about
nine names that are not usually mentioned by tall fine-looking
men in well cut gray suits. Everybody stopped talking and
looked at him quietly. His voice cut through the muted
rhumba music like a shovel through snow.

The barman stood perfectly still, looking at the man. The

barman had curly hair and a clear warm skin and wide-set careful eyes. He didn't move or speak. The tall man stopped talking and stalked out of the bar. Everybody watched him out except the barman.

The barman moved slowly along the bar to the end where I sat and stood looking away from me, with nothing in his face but pallor. Then he turned to me and said:

"Yes, sir?"

"I want to talk to a fellow named Eddie Prue."

"So?"

"He works here," I said.

"Works here doing what?" His voice was perfectly level and as dry as dry sand.

"I understand he's the guy that walks behind the boss. If you know what I mean."

"Oh. Eddie Prue." He moved one lip slowly over the other and made small tight circles on the bar with his bar cloth. "Your name?"

"Marlowe."

"Marlowe. Drink while waiting?"

"A dry martini will do."

"A martini. Dry. Veddy, veddy dry."

"Okay."

"Will you eat it with a spoon or a knife and fork?"

"Cut it in strips," I said. "I'll just nibble it."

"On your way to school," he said. "Should I put the olive in a bag for you?"

"Sock me on the nose with it," I said. "If it will make you feel any better."

"Thank you, sir," he said. "A dry martini."

He took three steps away from me and then came back and leaned across the bar and said: "I made a mistake in a drink. The gentleman was telling me about it."

"I heard him."

"He was telling me about it as gentlemen tell you about things like that. As big shot directors like to point out to you your little errors. And you heard him."

"Yeah," I said, wondering how long this was going to go on.

"He made himself heard—the gentleman did. So I come over here and practically insult you."

"I got the idea," I said.

He held up one of his fingers and looked at it thoughtfully. "Just like that," he said. "A perfect stranger."

"It's my big brown eyes," I said. "They have that gentle look."

"Thanks, chum," he said, and quietly went away.

I saw him talking into a phone at the end of the bar. Then I saw him working with a shaker. When he came back with the drink he was all right again.

18

I carried the drink over to a small table against the wall and sat down there and lit a cigarette. Five minutes went by. The music that was coming through the fret had changed in tempo without my noticing it. A girl was singing. She had a rich deep down around the ankles contralto that was pleasant to listen to. She was singing Dark Eyes and the band behind her seemed to be falling asleep.

There was a heavy round of applause and some whistling when she ended.

A man at the next table said to his girl: "They got Linda Conquest back with the band. I heard she got married to some rich guy in Pasadena, but it didn't take."

The girl said: "Nice voice. If you like female crooners."

I started to get up but a shadow fell across my table and a man was standing there.

A great long gallows of a man with a ravaged face and a haggard frozen right eye that had a clotted iris and the steady look of blindness. He was so tall that he had to stoop to put his hand on the back of the chair across the table from me. He stood there sizing me up without saying anything and I sat there sipping the last of my drink and listening to the contralto voice singing another song. The customers seemed to like corny music in there. Perhaps they were all tired out trying to be ahead of the minute in the place where they worked.

"I'm Prue," the man said in his harsh whisper.

"So I gathered. You want to talk to me, I want to talk to you, and I want to talk to the girl that just sang."

"Let's go."

There was a locked door at the back end of the bar. Prue unlocked it and held it for me and we went through that and up a flight of carpeted steps to the left. A long straight hallway with several closed doors. At the end of it a bright star cross-wired by the mesh of a screen. Prue knocked on a door near the screen and opened it and stood aside for me to pass him.

It was a cozy sort of office, not too large. There was a built-in upholstered corner seat by the french windows and a man in a white dinner jacket was standing with his back to the room, looking out. He had gray hair. There was a large black and chromium safe, some filing cases, a large globe in a stand, a small built-in bar, and the usual broad heavy executive desk with the usual high-backed padded leather chair behind it.

I looked at the ornaments on the desk. Everything standard and all copper. A copper lamp, pen set and pencil tray, a glass and copper ashtray with a copper elephant on the rim, a copper letter opener, a copper thermos bottle on a copper tray, copper corners on the blotter holder. There was a spray of almost copper-colored sweet peas in a copper vase.

It seemed like a lot of copper.

The man at the window turned around and showed me that he was going on fifty and had soft ash gray hair and plenty of it, and a heavy handsome face with nothing unusual about it except a short puckered scar in his left cheek that had almost the effect of a deep dimple. I remembered the dimple. I would have forgotten the man. I remembered that I had seen him in pictures a long time ago, at least ten years ago. I didn't remember the pictures or what they were about or what he did in them, but I remembered the dark heavy handsome face and the puckered scar. His hair had been dark then.

He walked over to his desk and sat down and picked up his letter opener and poked at the ball of his thumb with the point. He looked at me with no expression and said: "You're Marlowe?"

I nodded.

"Sit down." I sat down. Eddie Prue sat in a chair against the wall and tilted the front legs off the floor.

"I don't like peepers," Morny said.

I shrugged.

"I don't like them for a lot of reasons," he said. "I don't like them in any way or at any time. I don't like them when they bother my friends. I don't like them when they bust in on my wife."

I didn't say anything.

"I don't like them when they question my driver or when they get tough with my guests," he said.

I didn't say anything.

"In short," he said. "I just don't like them."

"I'm beginning to get what you mean," I said.

He flushed and his eyes glittered. "On the other hand," he said, "just at the moment I might have a use for you. It might pay you to play ball with me. It might be a good idea. It might pay you to keep your nose clean."

"How much might it pay me?" I asked.

"It might pay you in time and health."

"I seem to have heard this record somewhere," I said. "I just can't put a name to it."

He laid the letter opener down and swung open a door in the desk and got a cut glass decanter out. He poured liquid out of it in a glass and drank it and put the stopper back in the decanter and put the decanter back in the desk.

"In my business," he said, "tough boys come a dime a dozen. And would-be tough boys come a nickel a gross. Just mind your business and I'll mind my business and we won't have any trouble." He lit a cigarette. His hand shook a little.

I looked across the room at the tall man sitting tilted against the wall, like a loafer in a country store. He just sat there without motion, his long arms hanging, his lined gray face full of nothing.

"Somebody said something about some money," I said to Morny. "What's that for? I know what the bawling out is for. That's you trying to make yourself think you can scare me."

"Talk like that to me," Morny said, "and you are liable to be wearing lead buttons on your vest."

"Just think," I said. "Poor old Marlowe with lead buttons on his vest."

Eddie Prue made a dry sound in his throat that might have been a chuckle.

"And as for me minding my own business and not minding yours," I said, "it might be that my business and your business would get a little mixed up together. Through no fault of mine."

"It better not," Morny said. "In what way?" He lifted his eyes quickly and dropped them again.

"Well, for instance, your hard boy here calling me up on the phone and trying to scare me to death. And later in the evening calling me up and talking about five C's and how it would do me some good to drive out here and talk to you. And for instance that same hard boy or somebody who looks just like him—which is a little unlikely—following around after a fellow in my business who happened to get shot this afternoon, on Court Street on Bunker Hill."

Morny lifted his cigarette away from his lips and narrowed his eyes to look at the tip. Every motion, every gesture, right out of the catalogue.

"Who got shot?"

"A fellow named Phillips, a youngish blond kid. You wouldn't like him. He was a peeper." I described Phillips to him.

"I never heard of him," Morny said.

"And also for instance, a tall blond who didn't live there was seen coming out of the apartment house just after he was killed," I said.

"What tall blond?" His voice had changed a little. There was urgency in it.

"I don't know that. She was seen and the man who saw her could identify her, if he saw her again. Of course she need not have anything to do with Phillips."

"This man Phillips was a shamus?"

I nodded. "I told you that twice."

"Why was he killed and how?"

"He was sapped and shot in his apartment. We don't know why he was killed. If we knew that, we would likely know who killed him. It seems to be that kind of a situation."

"Who is 'we'?"

"The police and myself. I found him dead. So I had to stick around."

Prue let the front legs of his chair down on the carpet very quietly and looked at me. His good eye had a sleepy expression I didn't like.

Morny said: "You told the cops what?"

I said: "Very little. I gather from your opening remarks to me here that you know I am looking for Linda Conquest. Mrs. Leslie Murdock. I've found her. She's singing here. I don't know why there should have been any secret about it. It seems to me that your wife or Mr. Vannier might have told me. But they didn't."

"What my wife would tell a peeper," Morny said, "you could put in a gnat's eye."

"No doubt she has her reasons," I said. "However that's not very important now. In fact it's not very important that I see Miss Conquest. Just the same I'd like to talk to her a little. If you don't mind."

"Suppose I mind," Morny said.

"I guess I would like to talk to her anyway," I said. I got a cigarette out of my pocket and rolled it around in my fingers and admired his thick and still-dark eyebrows. They had a fine shape, an elegant curve.

Prue chuckled. Morny looked at him and frowned and looked back at me, keeping the frown on his face.

"I asked you what you told the cops," he said.

"I told them as little as I could. This man Phillips asked me to come and see him. He implied he was too deep in a job he didn't like and needed help. When I got there he was dead. I told the police that. They didn't think it was quite the whole story. It probably isn't. I have until tomorrow noon to fill it out. So I'm trying to fill it out."

"You wasted your time coming here," Morny said.

"I got the idea that I was asked to come here."

"You can go to hell back any time you want to," Morny said. "Or you can do a little job for me—for five hundred dollars. Either way you leave Eddie and me out of any conversations you might have with the police."

"What's the nature of the job?"

"You were at my house this morning. You ought to have an idea."

"I don't do divorce business," I said.

His face turned white. "I love my wife," he said. "We've only been married eight months. I don't want any divorce. She's a swell girl and she knows what time it is, as a rule. But I think she's playing with a wrong number at the moment."

"Wrong in what way?"

"I don't know. That's what I want found out."

"Let me get this straight," I said. "Are you hiring me on a job—or off a job I already have."

Prue chuckled again against the wall.

Morny poured himself some more brandy and tossed it quickly down his throat. Color came back into his face. He didn't answer me.

"And let me get another thing straight," I said. "You don't mind your wife playing around, but you don't want her playing with somebody named Vannier. Is that it?"

"I trust her heart," he said slowly. "But I don't trust her judgment. Put it that way."

"And you want me to get something on this man Vannier?"

"I want to find out what he is up to."

"Oh. Is he up to something?"

"I think he is. I don't know what."

"You think he is—or you want to think he is?"

He stared at me levelly for a moment, then he pulled the middle drawer of his desk out, reached in and tossed a folded paper across to me. I picked it up and unfolded it. It was a carbon copy of a gray billhead. *Cal-Western Dental Supply Company*, and an address. The bill was for *30 lbs. Kerr's Crystobolite $15.75*, and *25 lbs. White's Albastone, $7.75*, plus tax. It was made out to *H. R. Teager, Will Call*, and stamped *Paid* with a rubber stamp. It was signed for in the corner: *L. G. Vannier*.

I put it down on the desk.

"That fell out of his pocket one night when he was here," Morny said. "About ten days ago. Eddie put one of his big feet on it and Vannier didn't notice he had dropped it."

I looked at Prue, then at Morny, then at my thumb. "Is this supposed to mean something to me?"

"I thought you were a smart detective. I figured you could find out."

I looked at the paper again, folded it and put it in my pocket. "I'm assuming you wouldn't give it to me unless it meant something," I said.

Morny went to the black and chromium safe against the wall and opened it. He came back with five new bills spread out in his fingers like a poker hand. He smoothed them edge to edge, riffled them lightly, and tossed them on the desk in front of me.

"There's your five C's," he said. "Take Vannier out of my wife's life and there will be the same again for you. I don't care how you do it and I don't want to know anything about how you do it. Just do it."

I poked at the crisp new bills with a hungry finger. Then I pushed them away. "You can pay me when—and if—I deliver," I said. "I'll take my payment tonight in a short interview with Miss Conquest."

Morny didn't touch the money. He lifted the square bottle and poured himself another drink. This time he poured one for me and pushed it across the desk.

"And as for this Phillips murder," I said, "Eddie here was following Phillips a little. You want to tell me why?"

"No."

"The trouble with a case like this is that the information might come from somebody else. When a murder gets into the papers you never know what will come out. If it does, you'll blame me."

He looked at me steadily and said: "I don't think so. I was a bit rough when you came in, but you shape up pretty good. I'll take a chance."

"Thanks," I said. "Would you mind telling me why you had Eddie call me up and give me the shakes?"

He looked down and tapped on the desk. "Linda's an old friend of mine. Young Murdock was out here this afternoon to see her. He told her you were working for old lady Murdock. She told me. I didn't know what the job was. You say you don't take divorce business, so it couldn't be that the old lady hired you to fix anything like that up." He raised his eyes on the last words and stared at me.

I stared back at him and waited.

"I guess I'm just a fellow who likes his friends," he said. "And doesn't want them bothered by dicks."

"Murdock owes you some money, doesn't he?"

He frowned. "I don't discuss things like that."

He finished his drink, nodded and stood up. "I'll send Linda up to talk to you. Pick your money up."

He went to the door and out. Eddie Prue unwound his long body and stood up and gave me a dim gray smile that meant nothing and wandered off after Morny.

I lit another cigarette and looked at the dental supply company's bill again. Something squirmed at the back of my mind, dimly. I walked to the window and stood looking out across the valley. A car was winding up a hill towards a big house with a tower that was half glass brick with light behind it. The headlights of the car moved across it and turned in toward a garage. The lights went out and the valley seemed darker.

It was very quiet and quite cool now. The dance band seemed to be somewhere under my feet. It was muffled, and the tune was indistinguishable.

Linda Conquest came in through the open door behind me and shut it and stood looking at me with a cold light in her eyes.

19

She looked like her photo and not like it. She had the wide cool mouth, the short nose, the wide cool eyes, the dark hair parted in the middle and the broad white line between the parting. She was wearing a white coat over her dress, with the collar turned up. She had her hands in the pockets of the coat and a cigarette in her mouth.

She looked older, her eyes were harder, and her lips seemed to have forgotten to smile. They would smile when she was singing, in that staged artificial smile. But in repose they were thin and tight and angry.

She moved over to the desk and stood looking down, as if counting the copper ornaments. She saw the cut glass decanter, took the stopper out, poured herself a drink and tossed it down with a quick flip of the wrist.

"You're a man named Marlowe?" she asked, looking at me. She put her hips against the end of the desk and crossed her ankles.

I said I was a man named Marlowe.

"By and large," she said, "I am quite sure I am not going to like you one damned little bit. So speak your piece and drift away."

"What I like about this place is everything runs so true to type," I said. "The cop on the gate, the shine on the door, the cigarette and check girls, the fat greasy sensual Jew with the tall stately bored showgirl, the well-dressed, drunk and horribly rude director cursing the barman, the silent guy with the gun, the night club owner with the soft gray hair and the B-picture mannerisms, and now you—the tall dark torcher with the negligent sneer, the husky voice, the hard-boiled vocabulary."

She said: "Is that so?" and fitted her cigarette between her lips and drew slowly on it. "And what about the wise-cracking snooper with the last year's gags and the come-hither smile?"

"And what gives me the right to talk to you at all?" I said.

"I'll bite. What does?"

"She wants it back. Quickly. It has to be fast or there will be trouble."

"I thought—" she started to say and stopped cold. I watched her remove the sudden trace of interest from her face by monkeying with her cigarette and bending her face over it. "She wants what back, Mr. Marlowe?"

"The Brasher Doubloon."

She looked up at me and nodded, remembering—letting me see her remembering.

"Oh, the Brasher Doubloon."

"I bet you completely forgot it," I said.

"Well, no. I've seen it a number of times," she said. "She wants it back, you said. Do you mean she thinks I took it?"

"Yeah. Just that."

"She's a dirty old liar," Linda Conquest said.

"What you think doesn't make you a liar," I said. "It only sometimes makes you mistaken. Is she wrong?"

"Why would I take her silly old coin?"

"Well—it's worth a lot of money. She thinks you might need money. I gather she was not too generous."

She laughed, a tight sneering little laugh. "No," she said. "Mrs. Elizabeth Bright Murdock would not rate as very generous."

"Maybe you just took it for spite, kind of," I said hopefully.

"Maybe I ought to slap your face." She killed her cigarette in Morny's copper goldfish bowl, speared the crushed stub absently with the letter opener and dropped it into the wastebasket.

"Passing on from that to perhaps more important matters," I said, "will you give him a divorce?"

"For twenty-five grand," she said, not looking at me, "I should be glad to."

"You're not in love with the guy, huh?"

"You're breaking my heart, Marlowe."

"He's in love with you," I said. "After all you did marry him."

She looked at me lazily. "Mister, don't think I didn't pay for that mistake." She lit another cigarette. "But a girl has to live. And it isn't always as easy as it looks. And so a girl can make a mistake, marry the wrong guy and the wrong family, looking for something that isn't there. Security, or whatever."

"But not needing any love to do it," I said.

"I don't want to be too cynical, Marlowe. But you'd be surprised how many girls marry to find a home, especially girls whose arm muscles are all tired out fighting off the kind of optimists that come into these gin and glitter joints."

"You had a home and you gave it up."

"It got to be too dear. That port-sodden old fake made the bargain too tough. How do you like her for a client?"

"I've had worse."

She picked a shred of tobacco off her lip. "You notice what she's doing to that girl?"

"Merle? I noticed she bullied her."

"It isn't just that. She has her cutting out dolls. The girl had a shock of some kind and the old brute has used the effect of it to dominate the girl completely. In company she yells at her but in private she's apt to be stroking her hair and whispering in her ear. And the kid sort of shivers."

"I didn't quite get all that," I said.

"The kid's in love with Leslie, but she doesn't know it. Emotionally she's about ten years old. Something funny is going to happen in that family one of these days. I'm glad I won't be there."

I said: "You're a smart girl, Linda. And you're tough and you're wise. I suppose when you married him you thought you could get your hands on plenty."

She curled her lip. "I thought it would at least be a vacation. It wasn't even that. That's a smart ruthless woman, Marlowe. Whatever she's got you doing, it's not what she says. She's up to something. Watch your step."

"Would she kill a couple of men?"

She laughed.

"No kidding," I said. "A couple of men have been killed and one of them at least is connected with rare coins."

"I don't get it," she looked at me levelly. "Murdered, you mean?"

I nodded.

"You tell Morny all that?"

"About one of them."

"You tell the cops?"

"About one of them. The same one."

She moved her eyes over my face. We stared at each other. She looked a little pale, or just tired. I thought she had grown a little paler than before.

"You're making that up," she said between her teeth.

I grinned and nodded. She seemed to relax then.

"About the Brasher Doubloon?" I said. "You didn't take it. Okay. About the divorce, what?"

"That's none of your affair."

"I agree. Well, thanks for talking to me. Do you know a fellow named Vannier?"

"Yes." Her face froze hard now. "Not well. He's a friend of Lois."

"A very good friend."

"One of these days he's apt to turn out to be a small quiet funeral too."

"Hints," I said, "have sort of been thrown in that direction. There's something about the guy. Every time his name comes up the party freezes."

She stared at me and said nothing. I thought that an idea was stirring at the back of her eyes, but if so it didn't come out. She said quietly:

"Morny will sure as hell kill him, if he doesn't lay off Lois."

"Go on with you. Lois flops at the drop of a hat. Anybody can see that."

"Perhaps Alex is the one person who can't see it."

"Vannier hasn't anything to do with my job anyway. He has no connection with the Murdocks."

She lifted a corner of her lip at me and said: "No? Let me tell you something. No reason why I should. I'm just a great big open-hearted kid. Vannier knows Elizabeth Bright Murdock and well. He never came to the house but once while I was there, but he called on the phone plenty of times. I caught some of the calls. He always asked for Merle."

"Well—that's funny," I said. "Merle, huh?"

She bent to crush out her cigarette and again she speared the stub and dropped it into the wastebasket.

"I'm very tired," she said suddenly. "Please go away."

I stood there for a moment, looking at her and wondering. Then I said: "Good night and thanks. Good luck."

I went out and left her standing there with her hands in the pockets of the white coat, her head bent and her eyes looking at the floor.

It was two o'clock when I got back to Hollywood and put the car away and went upstairs to my apartment. The wind was all gone but the air still had that dryness and lightness of the desert. The air in the apartment was dead and Breeze's cigar butt had made it a little worse than dead. I opened windows and flushed the place through while I undressed and stripped the pockets of my suit.

Out of them with other things came the dental supply company's bill. It still looked like a bill to one H. R. Teager for 30 lbs. of crystobolite and 25 lbs. of albastone.

I dragged the phone book up on the desk in the living

room and looked up Teager. Then the confused memory clicked into place. His address was 422 West Ninth Street. The address of the Belfont Building was 422 West Ninth Street.

H. R. Teager Dental Laboratories had been one of the names on doors on the sixth floor of the Belfont Building when I did my backstairs crawl away from the office of Elisha Morningstar.

But even the Pinkertons have to sleep, and Marlowe needed far, far more sleep than the Pinkertons. I went to bed.

20

It was just as hot in Pasadena as the day before and the big dark red brick house on Dresden Avenue looked just as cool and the little painted Negro waiting by the hitching block looked just as sad. The same butterfly landed on the same hydrangea bush — or it looked like the same one — the same heavy scent of summer lay on the morning, and the same middle-aged sourpuss with the frontier voice opened to my ring.

She led me along the same hallways to the same sunless sunroom. In it Mrs. Elizabeth Bright Murdock sat in the same reed chaise-longue and as I came into the room she was pouring herself a slug from what looked like the same port bottle but was more probably a grandchild.

The maid shut the door, I sat down and put my hat on the floor, just like yesterday, and Mrs. Murdock gave me the same hard level stare and said:

"Well?"

"Things are bad," I said. "The cops are after me."

She looked as flustered as a side of beef. "Indeed. I thought you were more competent than that."

I brushed it off. "When I left here yesterday morning a man followed me in a coupé. I don't know what he was doing here or how he got here. I suppose he followed me here, but I feel doubtful about that. I shook him off, but he turned up again in the hall outside my office. He followed me again, so I invited him to explain why and he said he knew who I was and he needed help and asked me to come to his apartment on Bunker Hill and talk to him. I went, after I had seen Mr. Morningstar, and found the man shot to death on the floor of his bathroom."

Mrs. Murdock sipped a little port. Her hand might have shaken a little, but the light in the room was too dim for me to be sure. She cleared her throat.

"Go on."

"His name is George Anson Phillips. A young, blond fellow, rather dumb. He claimed to be a private detective."

"I never heard of him," Mrs. Murdock said coldly. "I never saw him to my knowledge and I don't know anything about him. Did you think I employed him to follow you?"

"I didn't know what to think. He talked about pooling our resources and he gave me the impression that he was working for some member of your family. He didn't say so in so many words."

"He wasn't. You can be quite definite on that." The baritone voice was as steady as a rock.

"I don't think you know quite as much about your family as you think you do, Mrs. Murdock."

"I know you have been questioning my son—contrary to my orders," she said coldly.

"I didn't question him. He questioned me. Or tried to."

"We'll go into that later," she said harshly. "What about this man you found shot? You are involved with the police on account of him?"

"Naturally. They want to know why he followed me, what I was working on, why he spoke to me, why he asked me to come to his apartment and why I went. But that is only the half of it."

She finished her port and poured herself another glass.

"How's your asthma?" I asked.

"Bad," she said. "Get on with your story."

"I saw Morningstar. I told you about that over the phone. He pretended not to have the Brasher Doubloon, but admitted it had been offered to him and said he could get it. As I told you. Then you told me it had been returned to you, so that was that."

I waited, thinking she would tell me some story about how the coin had been returned, but she just stared at me bleakly over the wine glass.

"So, as I had made a sort of arrangement with Mr. Morningstar to pay him a thousand dollars for the coin — "

"You had no authority to do anything like that," she barked.

I nodded, agreeing with her.

"Maybe I was kidding him a little," I said. "And I know I was kidding myself. Anyway after what you told me over the phone I tried to get in touch with him to tell him the deal was off. He's not in the phone book except at his office. I went to his office. This was quite late. The elevator man said he was still in his office. He was lying on his back on the floor, dead. Killed by a blow on the head and shock, apparently. Old men die easily. The blow might not have been intended to kill him. I called the Receiving Hospital, but didn't give my name."

"That was wise of you," she said.

"Was it? It was considerate of me, but I don't think I'd call it wise. I want to be nice, Mrs. Murdock. You understand that in your rough way, I hope. But two murders happened in a matter of hours and both the bodies were found by me. And both the victims were connected — in some manner — with your Brasher Doubloon."

"I don't understand. This other, younger man also?"

"Yes. Didn't I tell you over the phone? I thought I did." I wrinkled my brow, thinking back. I knew I had.

She said calmly: "It's possible. I wasn't paying a great deal of attention to what you said. You see, the doubloon had already been returned. And you sounded a little drunk."

"I wasn't drunk. I might have felt a little shock, but I wasn't drunk. You take all this very calmly."

"What do you want me to do?"

I took a deep breath. "I'm connected with one murder already, by having found the body and reported it. I may presently be connected with another, by having found the body and not reported it. Which is much more serious for me. Even as far as it goes, I have until noon today to disclose the name of my client."

"That," she said, still much too calm for my taste, "would be a breach of confidence. You are not going to do that, I'm sure."

"I wish you'd leave that damn port alone and make some effort to understand the position," I snapped at her.

She looked vaguely surprised and pushed her glass away— about four inches away.

"This fellow Phillips," I said, "had a license as a private detective. How did I happen to find him dead? Because he followed me and I spoke to him and he asked me to come to his apartment. And when I got there he was dead. The police know all this. They may even believe it. But they don't believe the connection between Phillips and me is quite that much of a coincidence. They think there is a deeper connection between Phillips and me and they insist on knowing what I am doing, who I am working for. Is that clear?"

"You'll find a way out of all that," she said. "I expect it to cost me a little more money, of course."

I felt myself getting pinched around the nose. My mouth felt dry. I needed air. I took another deep breath and another dive into the tub of blubber that was sitting across the room from me on the reed chaise-longue, looking as unperturbed as a bank president refusing a loan.

"I'm working for you," I said, "now, this week, today. Next week I'll be working for somebody else, I hope. And the week after that for still somebody else. In order to do that I have to be on reasonably good terms with the police. They don't have to love me, but they have to be fairly sure I am not cheating on them. Assume Phillips knew nothing about the Brasher Doubloon. Assume, even, that he knew about it, but that his death had nothing to do with it. I still have to tell the cops what I know about him. And they have to question anybody they want to question. Can't you understand that?"

"Doesn't the law give you the right to protect a client?" she snapped. "If it doesn't, what is the use of anyone's hiring a detective?"

I got up and walked around my chair and sat down again. I leaned forward and took hold of my kneecaps and squeezed them until my knuckles glistened.

"The law, whatever it is, is a matter of give and take, Mrs. Murdock. Like most other things. Even if I had the legal right to stay clammed up—refuse to talk—and got away with it once, that would be the end of my business. I'd be a guy marked for trouble. One way or another they would get me. I value your business, Mrs. Murdock, but not enough to cut my throat for you and bleed in your lap."

She reached for her glass and emptied it.

"You seem to have made a nice mess of the whole thing," she said. "You didn't find my daughter-in-law and you didn't find my Brasher Doubloon. But you found a couple of dead men that I have nothing to do with and you have neatly arranged matters so that I must tell the police all my private and personal business in order to protect you from your own incompetence. That's what I see. If I am wrong, pray correct me."

She poured some more wine and gulped it too fast and went into a paroxysm of coughing. Her shaking hand slid the glass on to the table, slopping the wine. She threw herself forward in her seat and got purple in the face.

I jumped up and went over and landed one on her beefy back that would have shaken the City Hall.

She let out a long strangled wail and drew her breath in rackingly and stopped coughing. I pressed one of the keys on her dictaphone box and when somebody answered, metallic and loud, through the metal disk I said: "Bring Mrs. Murdock a glass of water, quick!" and then let the key up again.

I sat down again and watched her pull herself together. When her breath was coming evenly and without effort, I said: "You're not tough. You just think you're tough. You been living too long with people that are scared of you. Wait'll you meet up with some law. Those boys are professionals. You're just a spoiled amateur."

The door opened and the maid came in with a pitcher of ice water and a glass. She put them down on the table and went out.

I poured Mrs. Murdock a glass of water and put it in her hand.

"Sip it, don't drink it. You won't like the taste of it, but it won't hurt you."

She sipped, then drank half of the glass, then put the glass down and wiped her lips.

"To think," she said raspingly, "that out of all the snoopers for hire I could have employed, I had to pick out a man who would bully me in my own home."

"That's not getting you anywhere either," I said. "We don't have a lot of time. What's our story to the police going to be?"

"The police mean nothing to me. Absolutely nothing. And if you give them my name, I shall regard it as a thoroughly disgusting breach of faith."

That put me back where we started.

"Murder changes everything, Mrs. Murdock. You can't dummy up on a murder case. We'll have to tell them why you employed me and what to do. They won't publish it in the papers, you know. That is, they won't if they believe it. They certainly won't believe you hired me to investigate Elisha Morningstar just because he called up and wanted to buy the doubloon. They may not find out that you couldn't have sold the coin, if you wanted to, because they might not think of that angle. But they won't believe you hired a private detective just to investigate a possible purchaser. Why should you?"

"That's my business, isn't it?"

"No. You can't fob the cops off that way. You have to sat-isfy them that you are being frank and open and have nothing to hide. As long as they think you are hiding something they never let up. Give them a reasonable and plausible story and they go away cheerful. And the most reasonable and plausible story is always the truth. Any objection to telling it?"

"Every possible objection," she said. "But it doesn't seem to make much difference. Do we have to tell them that I suspected my daughter-in-law of stealing the coin and that I was wrong?"

"It would be better."

"And that it has been returned and how?"

"It would be better."

"That is going to humiliate me very much."

I shrugged.

"You're a callous brute," she said. "You're a cold-blooded fish. I don't like you. I deeply regret ever having met you."

"Mutual," I said.

She reached a thick finger to a key and barked into the talking box. "Merle. Ask my son to come in here at once. And I think you may as well come in with him."

She released the key, pressed her broad fingers together and let her hands drop heavily to her thighs. Her bleak eyes went up to the ceiling.

Her voice was quiet and sad saying: "My son took the coin. Mr. Marlowe. My son. My own son."

I didn't say anything. We sat there glaring at each other. In a couple of minutes they both came in and she barked at them to sit down.

21

Leslie Murdock was wearing a greenish slack suit and his hair looked damp, as if he had just been taking a shower. He sat hunched forward, looking at the white buck shoes on his feet, and turning a ring on his finger. He didn't have his long black cigarette holder and he looked a little lonely without it. Even his mustache seemed to droop a little more than it had in my office.

Merle Davis looked just the same as the day before. Probably she always looked the same. Her copper blond hair was dragged down just as tight, her shell-rimmed glasses looked just as large and empty, her eyes behind them just as vague. She was even wearing the same one-piece linen dress with short sleeves and no ornament of any kind, not even earrings.

I had the curious feeling of reliving something that had already happened.

Mrs. Murdock sipped her port and said quietly:

"All right, son. Tell Mr. Marlowe about the doubloon. I'm afraid he has to be told."

Murdock looked up at me quickly and then dropped his eyes again. His mouth twitched. When he spoke his voice had the toneless quality, a flat tired sound, like a man making a confession after an exhausting battle with his conscience.

"As I told you yesterday in your office I owe Morny a lot of money. Twelve thousand dollars. I denied it afterwards, but it's true. I do owe it. I didn't want mother to know. He was pressing me pretty hard for payment. I suppose I knew I would have to tell her in the end, but I was weak enough to want to put it off. I took the doubloon, using her keys one afternoon when she was asleep and Merle was out. I gave it to Morny and he agreed to hold it as security because I explained to him that he couldn't get anything like twelve thousand dollars for it unless he could give its history and show that it was legitimately in his possession."

He stopped talking and looked up at me to see how I was taking it. Mrs. Murdock had her eyes on my face, practically puttied there. The little girl was looking at Murdock with her lips parted and an expression of suffering on her face.

Murdock went on. "Morny gave me a receipt, in which he agreed to hold the coin as collateral and not to convert it without notice and demand. Something like that. I don't profess to know how legal it was. When this man Morningstar called up and asked about the coin I immediately became suspicious that Morny either was trying to sell it or that he was at least thinking of selling it and was trying to get a valuation on it from somebody who knew about rare coins. I was badly scared."

He looked up and made a sort of face at me. Maybe it was the face of somebody being badly scared. Then he took his handkerchief out and wiped his forehead and sat holding it between his hands.

"When Merle told me mother had employed a detective— Merle ought not to have told me, but mother has promised not to scold her for it—" He looked at his mother. The old warhorse clamped her jaws and looked grim. The little girl had her eyes still on his face and didn't seem to be very worried about the scolding. He went on: "—then I was sure she had missed the doubloon and had hired you on that account. I didn't really believe she had hired you to find Linda. I knew where Linda was all the time. I went to your office to see what I could find out. I didn't find out very much. I went to see Morny yesterday afternoon and told him about it. At first he laughed in my face, but when I told him that even my mother couldn't sell the coin without violating the terms of

Jasper Murdock's will and that she would certainly set the police on him when I told her where the coin was, then he loosened up. He got up and went to the safe and got the coin out and handed it to me without a word. I gave him back his receipt and he tore it up. So I brought the coin home and told mother about it."

He stopped talking and wiped his face again. The little girl's eyes moved up and down with the motions of his hand.

In the silence that followed I said: "Did Morny threaten you?"

He shook his head. "He said he wanted his money and he needed it and I had better get busy and dig it up. But he wasn't threatening. He was very decent, really. In the circumstances."

"Where was this?"

"At the Idle Valley Club, in his private office."

"Was Eddie Prue there?"

The little girl tore her eyes away from his face and looked at me. Mrs. Murdock said thickly: "Who is Eddie Prue?"

"Morny's bodyguard," I said. "I didn't waste *all* my time yesterday, Mrs. Murdock." I looked at her son, waiting.

He said: "No, I didn't see him. I know him by sight, of course. You would only have to see him once to remember him. But he wasn't around yesterday."

I said: "Is that all?"

He looked at his mother. She said harshly: "Isn't it enough?"

"Maybe," I said. "Where is the coin now?"

"Where would you expect it to be?" she snapped.

I almost told her, just to see her jump. But I managed to hold it in. I said: "That seems to take care of that, then."

Mrs. Murdock said heavily: "Kiss your mother, son, and run along."

He got up dutifully and went over and kissed her on the forehead. She patted his hand. He went out of the room with his head down and quietly shut the door. I said to Merle: "I think you had better have him dictate that to you just the way he told it and make a copy of it and get him to sign it."

She looked startled. The old woman snarled:

"She certainly won't do anything of the sort. Go back to

your work, Merle. I wanted you to hear this. But if I ever again catch you violating my confidence, you know what will happen."

The little girl stood up and smiled at her with shining eyes. "Oh yes, Mrs. Murdock. I never will. Never. You can trust me."

"I hope so," the old dragon growled. "Get out."

Merle went out softly.

Two big tears formed themselves in Mrs. Murdock's eyes and slowly made their way down the elephant hide of her cheeks, reached the corners of her fleshy nose and slid down her lip. She scrabbled around for a handkerchief, wiped them off and then wiped her eyes. She put the handkerchief away, reached for her wine and said placidly:

"I'm very fond of my son, Mr. Marlowe. Very fond. This grieves me deeply. Do you think he will have to tell this story to the police?"

"I hope not," I said. "He'd have a hell of a time getting them to believe it."

Her mouth snapped open and her teeth glinted at me in the dim light. She closed her lips and pressed them tight, scowling at me with her head lowered.

"Just what do you mean by that?" she snapped.

"Just what I said. The story doesn't ring true. It has a fabricated, over-simple sound. Did he make it up himself or did you think it up and teach it to him?"

"Mr. Marlowe," she said in a deadly voice, "you are treading on very thin ice."

I waved a hand. "Aren't we all? All right, suppose it's true. Morny will deny it, and we'll be right back where we started. Morny will have to deny it, because otherwise it would tie him to a couple of murders."

"Is there anything so unlikely about that being the exact situation?" she blared.

"Why would Morny, a man with backing, protection and some influence, tie himself to a couple of small murders in order to avoid tying himself to something trifling, like selling a pledge? It doesn't make sense to me."

She stared, saying nothing. I grinned at her, because for the first time she was going to like something I said.

"I found your daughter-in-law, Mrs. Murdock. It's a little strange to me that your son, who seems so well under your control, didn't tell you where she was."

"I didn't ask him," she said in a curiously quiet voice, for her.

"She's back where she started, singing with the band at the Idle Valley Club. I talked to her. She's a pretty hard sort of girl in a way. She doesn't like you very well. I don't find it impossible to think that she took the coin all right, partly from spite. And I find it slightly less impossible to believe that Leslie knew it or found it out and cooked up that yarn to protect her. He says he's very much in love with her."

She smiled. It wasn't a beautiful smile, being on slightly the wrong kind of face. But it was a smile.

"Yes," she said gently. "Yes. Poor Leslie. He would do just that. And in that case —" she stopped and her smile widened until it was almost ecstatic, "in that case my dear daughter-in-law may be involved in murder."

I watched her enjoying the idea for a quarter of a minute. "And you'd just love that," I said.

She nodded, still smiling, getting the idea she liked before she got the rudeness in my voice. Then her face stiffened and her lips came together hard. Between them and her teeth she said:

"I don't like your tone. I don't like your tone at all."

"I don't blame you," I said. "I don't like it myself. I don't like anything. I don't like this house or you or the air of repression in the joint, or the squeezed down face of the little girl or that twerp of a son you have, or this case or the truth I'm not told about it and the lies I am told about it and —"

She started yelling then, noise out of a splotched furious face, eyes tossing with fury, sharp with hate:

"Get out! Get out of this house at once! Don't delay one instant! Get out!"

I stood up and reached my hat off the carpet and said: "I'll be glad to."

I gave her a sort of a tired leer and picked my way to the door and opened it and went out. I shut it quietly, holding the knob with a stiff hand and clicking the lock gently into place.

For no reason at all.

22

Steps gibbered along after me and my name was called and I
kept on going until I was in the middle of the living room.
Then I stopped and turned and let her catch up with me, out
of breath, her eyes trying to pop through her glasses and her
shining copper-blond hair catching funny little lights from the
high windows.

"Mr. Marlowe? Please! Please don't go away. She wants
you. She really does!"

"I'll be darned. You've got Sub-deb Bright on your mouth
this morning. Looks all right too."

She grabbed my sleeve. "Please!"

"The hell with her," I said. "Tell her to jump in the lake.
Marlowe can get sore too. Tell her to jump in two lakes, if
one won't hold her. Not clever, but quick."

I looked down at the hand on my sleeve and patted it. She
drew it away swiftly and her eyes looked shocked.

"Please, Mr. Marlowe. She's in trouble. She needs you."

"I'm in trouble too," I growled. "I'm up to my ear flaps in
trouble. What are you crying about?"

"Oh, I'm really very fond of her. I know she's rough and
blustery, but her heart is pure gold."

"To hell with her heart too," I said. "I don't expect to get
intimate enough with her for that to make any difference.
She's a fat-faced old liar. I've had enough of her. I think she's
in trouble all right, but I'm not in the excavating business. I
have to get told things."

"Oh, I'm sure if you would only be patient——"

I put my arm around her shoulders, without thinking. She
jumped about three feet and her eyes blazed with panic.

We stood there staring at each other, making breath noises,
me with my mouth open as it too frequently is, she with her
lips pressed tight and her little pale nostrils quivering. Her
face was as pale as the unhandy makeup would let it be.

"Look," I said slowly, "did something happen to you when
you were a little girl?"

She nodded, very quickly.

"A man scared you or something like that?"

She nodded again. She took her lower lip between her little white teeth.

"And you've been like this ever since?"

She just stood there, looking white.

"Look," I said, "I won't do anything to you that will scare you. Not ever."

Her eyes melted with tears.

"If I touched you," I said, "it was just like touching a chair or a door. It didn't mean anything. Is that clear?"

"Yes." She got a word out at last. Panic still twitched in the depths of her eyes, behind the tears. "Yes."

"That takes care of me," I said. "I'm all adjusted. Nothing to worry about in me any more. Now take Leslie. He has his mind on other things. You know he's all right—in the way we mean. Right?"

"Oh, yes," she said. "Yes, indeed." Leslie was aces. With her. With me he was a handful of bird gravel.

"Now take the old wine barrel," I said. "She's rough and she's tough and she thinks she can eat walls and spit bricks, and she bawls you out, but she's fundamentally decent to you, isn't she?"

"Oh, she is, Mr. Marlowe. I was trying to tell you—"

"Sure. Now why don't you get over it? Is he still around—this other one that hurt you?"

She put her hand to her mouth and gnawed the fleshy part at the base of the thumb, looking at me over it, as if it was a balcony.

"He's dead," she said. "He fell out of a—out of a—a window."

I stopped her with my big right hand. "Oh, that guy. I heard about him. Forget it, can't you?"

"No," she said, shaking her head seriously behind the hand. "I can't. I can't seem to forget it at all. Mrs. Murdock is always telling me to forget it. She talks to me for the longest times telling me to forget it. But I just can't."

"It would be a darn sight better," I snarled, "if she would keep her fat mouth shut about it for the longest times. She just keeps it alive."

She looked surprised and rather hurt at that. "Oh, that isn't all," she said. "I was his secretary. She was his wife. He was her first husband. Naturally she doesn't forget it either. How could she?"

I scratched my ear. That seemed sort of non-committal. There was nothing much in her expression now except that I didn't really think she realized that I was there. I was a voice coming out of somewhere, but rather impersonal. Almost a voice in her own head.

Then I had one of my funny and often unreliable hunches. "Look," I said, "is there someone you meet that has that effect on you? Some one person more than another?"

She looked all around the room. I looked with her. Nobody was under a chair or peeking at us through a door or a window.

"Why do I have to tell you?" she breathed.

"You don't. It's just how you feel about it."

"Will you promise not to tell anybody—anybody in the whole world, not even Mrs. Murdock?"

"Her last of all," I said. "I promise."

She opened her mouth and put a funny little confiding smile on her face, and then it went wrong. Her throat froze up. She made a croaking noise. Her teeth actually rattled.

I wanted to give her a good hard squeeze but I was afraid to touch her. We stood. Nothing happened. We stood. I was about as much use as a hummingbird's spare egg would have been.

Then she turned and ran. I heard her steps going along the hall. I heard a door close.

I went after her along the hall and reached the door. She was sobbing behind it. I stood there and listened to the sobbing.

There was nothing I could do about it. I wondered if there was anything anybody could do about it.

I went back to the glass porch and knocked on the door and opened it and put my head in. Mrs. Murdock sat just as I had left her. She didn't seem to have moved at all.

"Who's scaring the life out of that little girl?" I asked her.

"Get out of my house," she said between her fat lips.

I didn't move. Then she laughed at me hoarsely.

"Do you regard yourself as a clever man, Mr. Marlowe?"

"Well, I'm not dripping with it," I said.

"Suppose you find out for yourself."

"At your expense?"

She shrugged her heavy shoulders. "Possibly. It depends. Who knows?"

"You haven't bought a thing," I said. "I'm still going to have to talk to the police."

"I haven't bought anything," she said, "and I haven't paid for anything. Except the return of the coin. I'm satisfied to accept that for the money I have already given you. Now go away. You bore me. Unspeakably."

I shut the door and went back. No sobbing behind the door. Very still. I went on.

I let myself out of the house. I stood there, listening to the sunshine burn the grass. A car started up in back and a gray Mercury came drifting along the drive at the side of the house. Mr. Leslie Murdock was driving it. When he saw me he stopped.

He got out of the car and walked quickly over to me. He was nicely dressed; cream colored gabardine now, all fresh clothes, slacks, black and white shoes, with polished black toes, a sport coat of very small black and white check, black and white handkerchief, cream shirt, no tie. He had a pair of green sun glasses on his nose.

He stood close to me and said in a low timid sort of voice: "I guess you think I'm an awful heel."

"On account of that story you told about the doubloon?"

"Yes."

"That didn't affect my way of thinking about you in the least," I said.

"Well—"

"Just what do you want me to say?"

He moved his smoothly tailored shoulders in a deprecatory shrug. His silly little reddish brown mustache glittered in the sun.

"I suppose I like to be liked," he said.

"I'm sorry, Murdock. I like your being that devoted to your wife. If that's what it is."

"Oh. Didn't you think I was telling the truth? I mean, did you think I was saying all that just to protect her?"

"There was that possibility."

"I see." He put a cigarette into the long black holder, which he took from behind his display handkerchief. "Well—I guess I can take it that you don't like me." The dim movement of his eyes was visible behind the green lenses, fish moving in a deep pool.

"It's a silly subject," I said. "And damned unimportant. To both of us."

He put a match to the cigarette and inhaled. "I see," he said quietly. "Pardon me for being crude enough to bring it up."

He turned on his heel and walked back to his car and got in. I watched him drive away before I moved. Then I went over and patted the little painted Negro boy on the head a couple of times before I left.

"Son," I said to him, "you're the only person around this house that's not nuts."

23

The police loudspeaker box on the wall grunted and a voice said: "KGPL. Testing." A click and it went dead.

Detective-Lieutenant Jesse Breeze stretched his arms high in the air and yawned and said: "Couple of hours late, ain't you?"

I said: "Yes. But I left a message for you that I would be. I had to go to the dentist."

"Sit down."

He had a small littered desk across one corner of the room. He sat in the angle behind it, with a tall bare window to his left and a wall with a large calendar about eye height to his right. The days that had gone down to dust were crossed off carefully in soft black pencil, so that Breeze glancing at the calendar always knew exactly what day it was.

Spangler was sitting sideways at a smaller and much neater desk. It had a green blotter and an onyx pen set and a small brass calendar and an abalone shell full of ashes and matches and cigarette stubs. Spangler was flipping a handful of bank pens at the felt back of a seat cushion on end against the wall, like a Mexican knife thrower flipping knives at a target. He wasn't getting anywhere with it. The pens refused to stick.

The room had that remote, heartless, not quite dirty, not quite clean, not quite human smell that such rooms always have. Give a police department a brand new building and in three months all its rooms will smell like that. There must be something symbolic in it.

A New York police reporter wrote once that when you pass in beyond the green lights of a precinct station you pass clear out of this world, into a place beyond the law.

I sat down. Breeze got a cellophane-wrapped cigar out of his pocket and the routine with it started. I watched it detail by detail, unvarying, precise. He drew in smoke, shook his match out, laid it gently in the black glass ashtray, and said: "Hi, Spangler."

Spangler turned his head and Breeze turned his head. They grinned at each other. Breeze poked the cigar at me.

"Watch him sweat," he said.

Spangler had to move his feet to turn far enough around to watch me sweat. If I was sweating, I didn't know it.

"You boys are as cute as a couple of lost golf balls," I said. "How in the world do you do it?"

"Skip the wisecracks," Breeze said. "Had a busy little morning?"

"Fair," I said.

He was still grinning. Spangler was still grinning. Whatever it was Breeze was tasting he hated to swallow it.

Finally he cleared his throat, straightened his big freckled face out, turned his head enough so that he was not looking at me but could still see me and said in a vague empty sort of voice:

"Hench confessed."

Spangler swung clear around to look at me. He leaned forward on the edge of his chair and his lips were parted in an ecstatic half smile that was almost indecent.

I said: "What did you use on him—a pickax?"

"Nope."

They were both silent, staring at me.

"A wop," Breeze said.

"A what?"

"Boy, are you glad?" Breeze said.

"You are going to tell me or are you just going to sit there looking fat and complacent and watch me being glad?"

"We like to watch a guy being glad," Breeze said. "We don't often get a chance."

I put a cigarette in my mouth and jiggled it up and down.

"We used a wop on him," Breeze said. "A wop named Palermo."

"Oh. You know something?"

"What?" Breeze asked.

"I just thought of what is the matter with policemen's dialogue."

"What?"

"They think every line is a punch line."

"And every pinch is a good pinch," Breeze said calmly. "You want to know—or you want to just crack wise?"

"I want to know."

"Was like this, then. Hench was drunk. I mean he was drunk deep inside, not just on the surface. Screwy drunk. He'd been living on it for weeks. He'd practically quit eating and sleeping. Just liquor. He'd got to the point where liquor wasn't making him drunk, it was keeping him sober. It was the last hold he had on the real world. When a guy gets like that and you take his liquor away and don't give him anything to hold him down, he's a lost cuckoo."

I didn't say anything. Spangler still had the same erotic leer on his young face. Breeze tapped the side of his cigar and no ash fell off and he put it back in his mouth and went on.

"He's a psycho case, but we don't want any psycho case made out of our pinch. We make that clear. We want a guy that don't have any psycho record."

"I thought you were sure Hench was innocent."

Breeze nodded vaguely. "That was last night. Or maybe I was kidding a little. Anyway in the night, bang, Hench is bugs. So they drag him over to the hospital ward and shoot him full of hop. The jail doc does. That's between you and me. No hop in the record. Get the idea?"

"All too clearly," I said.

"Yeah." He looked vaguely suspicious of the remark, but

he was too full of his subject to waste time on it. "Well, this a.m. he is fine. Hop still working, the guy is pale but peaceful. We go see him. How you doing, kid? Anything you need? Any little thing at all? Be glad to get it for you. They treating you nice in here? You know the line."

"I do," I said. "I know the line."

Spangler licked his lips in a nasty way.

"So after a while he opens his trap just enough to say 'Palermo'. Palermo is the name of the wop across the street that owns the funeral home and the apartment house and stuff. You remember? Yeah, you remember. On account of he said something about a tall blond. All hooey. Them wops got tall blonds on the brain. In sets of twelve. But this Palermo is important. I asked around. He gets the vote out up there. He's a guy that can't be pushed around. Well, I don't aim to push him around. I say to Hench, 'You mean Palermo's a friend of yours?' He says, 'Get Palermo.' So we come back here to the hutch and phone Palermo and Palermo says he will be right down. Okay. He is here very soon. We talk like this: Hench wants to see you, Mr. Palermo. I wouldn't know why. He's a poor guy, Palermo says. A nice guy. I think he's okay. He wanta see me, that'sa fine. I see him. I see him alone. Without any coppers. I say, Okay, Mr. Palermo, and we go over to the hospital ward and Palermo talks to Hench and nobody listens. After a while Palermo comes out and he says, Okay, copper. He make the confess. I pay the lawyer, maybe. I like the poor guy. Just like that. He goes away."

I didn't say anything. There was a pause. The loudspeaker on the wall put out a bulletin and Breeze cocked his head and listened to ten or twelve words and then ignored it.

"So we go in with a steno and Hench gives us the dope. Phillips made a pass at Hench's girl. That was day before yesterday, out in the hall. Hench was in the room and he saw it, but Phillips got into his apartment and shut the door before Hench could get out. But Hench was sore. He socked the girl in the eye. But that didn't satisfy him. He got to brooding, the way a drunk will brood. He says to himself, that guy can't make a pass at my girl. I'm the boy that will give him something to remember me by. So he keeps an eye open for Phillips. Yesterday afternoon he sees Phillips go into his apartment.

He tells the girl to go for a walk. She don't want to go for a walk, so Hench socks her in the other eye. She goes for a walk. Hench knocks on Phillips' door and Phillips opens it. Hench is a little surprised at that, but I told him Phillips was expecting you. Anyway the door opens and Hench goes in and tells Phillips how he feels and what he is going to do and Phillips is scared and pulls a gun. Hench hits him with a sap. Phillips falls down and Hench ain't satisfied. You hit a guy with a sap and he falls down and what have you? No satisfaction, no revenge. Hench picks the gun off the floor and he is very drunk there being dissatisfied and Phillips grabs for his ankle. Hench doesn't know why he did what he did then. He's all fuzzy in the head. He drags Phillips into the bathroom and gives him the business with his own gun. You like it?"

"I love it," I said. "But what is the satisfaction in it for Hench?"

"Well, you know how a drunk is. Anyway he gives him the business. Well it ain't Hench's gun, you see, but he can't make a suicide out of it. There wouldn't be any satisfaction for him in that. So Hench takes the gun away and puts it under his pillow and takes his own gun out and ditches it. He won't tell us where. Probably passes it to some tough guy in the neighborhood. Then he finds the girl and they eat."

"That was a lovely touch," I said. "Putting the gun under his pillow. I'd never in the world have thought of that."

Breeze leaned back in his chair and looked at the ceiling. Spangler, the big part of the entertainment over, swung around in his chair and picked up a couple of bank pens and threw one at the cushion.

"Look at it this way," Breeze said. "What was the effect of that stunt? Look how Hench did it. He was drunk, but he was smart. He found that gun and showed it before Phillips was found dead. First we get the idea that a gun is under Hench's pillow that killed a guy—been fired anyway—and then we get the stiff. We believed Hench's story. It seemed reasonable. Why would we think any man would be such a sap as to do what Hench did? It doesn't make any sense. So we believed somebody put the gun under Hench's pillow and took Hench's gun away and ditched it. And suppose Hench ditched the death gun instead of his own, would he have been any better off? Things being what they were we would be bound to suspect him. And that way he wouldn't have started our minds thinking any particular way about him. The way he did he got us thinking he was a harmless drunk that went out and left his door open and somebody ditched a gun on him."

He waited, with his mouth a little open and the cigar in front of it, held up by a hard freckled hand and his pale blue eyes full of dim satisfaction.

"Well," I said, "if he was going to confess anyway, it wouldn't have made very much difference. Will he cop a plea?"

"Sure. I think so. I figure Palermo could get him off with manslaughter. Naturally I'm not sure."

"Why would Palermo want to get him off with anything?"

"He kind of likes Hench. And Palermo is a guy we can't push around."

I said: "I see." I stood up. Spangler looked at me sideways along glistening eyes. "What about the girl?"

"Won't say a word. She's smart. We can't do anything to her. Nice neat little job all around. You wouldn't kick, would you? Whatever your business is, it's still your business. Get me?"

"And the girl is a tall blond," I said. "Not of the freshest, but still a tall blond. Although only one. Maybe Palermo doesn't mind."

"Hell, I never thought of that," Breeze said. He thought about it and shook it off. "Nothing in that, Marlowe. Not enough class."

"Cleaned up and sober, you never can tell," I said. "Class is a thing that has a way of dissolving rapidly in alcohol. That all you want with me?"

"Guess so." He slanted the cigar up and aimed it at my eye. "Not that I wouldn't like to hear your story. But I don't figure I have an absolute right to insist on it the way things are."

"That's white of you, Breeze," I said. "And you too, Spangler. A lot of the good things in life to both of you."

They watched me go out, both with their mouths a little open.

I rode down to the big marble lobby and went and got my car out of the official parking lot.

24

Mr. Pietro Palermo was sitting in a room which, except for a mahogany roll-top desk, a sacred triptych in gilt frames and a large ebony and ivory crucifixion, looked exactly like a Victorian parlor. It contained a horseshoe sofa and chairs with carved mahogany frames and antimacassars of fine lace. There was an ormolu clock on the gray green marble mantel, a grandfather clock ticking lazily in the corner, and some wax flowers under a glass dome on an oval table with a marble top and curved elegant legs. The carpet was thick and full of gentle sprays of flowers. There was even a cabinet for bric-a-brac and there was plenty of bric-a-brac in it, little cups in fine china, little figurines in glass and porcelain, odds and ends of ivory and dark rosewood, painted saucers, an early American set of swan salt cellars, stuff like that.

Long lace curtains hung across the windows, but the room faced south and there was plenty of light. Across the street I could see the windows of the apartment where George Anson Phillips had been killed. The street between was sunny and silent.

The tall Italian with the dark skin and the handsome head of iron gray hair read my card and said:

"I got business in twelve minutes. What you want, Meester Marlowe?"

"I'm the man that found the dead man across the street yesterday. He was a friend of mine."

His cold black eyes looked me over silently. "That'sa not what you tell Luke."

"Luke?"

"He manage the joint for me."

"I don't talk much to strangers, Mr. Palermo."

"That'sa good. You talk to me, huh?"

"You're a man of standing, an important man. I can talk to

you. You saw me yesterday. You described me to the police. Very accurately, they said."

"Si. I see much," he said without emotion.

"You saw a tall blond woman come out of there yesterday."

He studied me. "Not yesterday. Wasa two three days ago. I tell the coppers yesterday." He snapped his long dark fingers. "The coppers, bah!"

"Did you see any strangers yesterday, Mr. Palermo?"

"Is back way in and out," he said. "Is stair from second floor also." He looked at his wrist watch.

"Nothing there then," I said. "This morning you saw Hench."

He lifted his eyes and ran them lazily over my face. "The coppers tell you that, huh?"

"They told me you got Hench to confess. They said he was a friend of yours. How good a friend they didn't know, of course."

"Hench make the confess, huh?" He smiled, a sudden brilliant smile.

"Only Hench didn't do the killing," I said.

"No?"

"No."

"That'sa interesting. Go on, Meester Marlowe."

"The confession is a lot of baloney. You got him to make it for some reason of your own."

He stood up and went to the door and called out: "Tony."

He sat down again. A short tough-looking wop came into the room, looked at me and sat down against the wall in a straight chair.

"Tony, thees man a Meester Marlowe. Look, take the card."

Tony came to get the card and sat down with it. "You look at thees man very good, Tony. Not forget him, huh?"

Tony said: "Leave it to me, Mr. Palermo."

Palermo said: "Was a friend to you, huh? A good friend, huh?"

"Yes."

"That'sa bad. Yeah. That'sa bad. I tell you something. A man's friend is a man's friend. So I tell you. But you don' tell anybody else. Not the damn coppers, huh?"

"No."

"That'sa promise, Meester Marlowe. That'sa something not to forget. You not forget?"

"I won't forget."

"Tony, he not forget you. Get the idea?"

"I gave you my word. What you tell me is between us here."

"That'sa fine. Okay. I come of large family. Many sisters and brothers. One brother very bad. Almost so bad as Tony."

Tony grinned.

"Okay, thees brother live very quiet. Across the street. Gotta move. Okay, the coppers fill the joint up. Not so good. Ask too many questions. Not good for business, not good for thees bad brother. You get the idea?"

"Yes," I said. "I get the idea."

"Okay, thees Hench no good, but poor guy, drunk, no job. Pay no rent, but I got lotsa money. So I say, Look, Hench, you make the confess. You sick man. Two three weeks sick. You go into court. I have a lawyer for you. You say to hell with the confess. I was drunk. The damn coppers are stuck. The judge he turn you loose and you come back to me and I take care of you. Okay? So Hench say okay, make the confess. That'sa all."

I said: "And after two or three weeks the bad brother is a long way from here and the trail is cold and the cops will likely just write the Phillips killing off as unsolved. Is that it?"

"Si." He smiled again. A brilliant warm smile, like the kiss of death.

"That takes care of Hench, Mr. Palermo," I said. "But it doesn't help me much about my friend."

He shook his head and looked at his watch again. I stood up. Tony stood up. He wasn't going to do anything, but it's better to be standing up. You move faster.

"The trouble with you birds," I said, "is you make mystery of nothing. You have to give the password before you bite a piece of bread. If I went down to headquarters and told the boys everything you have told me, they would laugh in my face. And I would be laughing with them."

"Tony don't laugh much," Palermo said.

"The earth is full of people who don't laugh much, Mr. Palermo," I said. "You ought to know. You put a lot of them where they are."

"Is my business," he said, shrugging enormously.

"I'll keep my promise," I said. "But in case you should get to doubting that, don't try to make any business for yourself out of me. Because in my part of town I'm a pretty good man and if the business got made out of Tony instead, it would be strictly on the house. No profit."

Palermo laughed. "That'sa good," he said. "Tony. One funeral—on the house. Okay."

He stood up and held his hand out, a fine strong warm hand.

25

In the lobby of the Belfont Building, in the single elevator that had light in it, on the piece of folded burlap, the same watery-eyed relic sat motionless, giving his imitation of the forgotten man. I got in with him and said: "Six."

The elevator lurched into motion and pounded its way upstairs. It stopped at six, I got out, and the old man leaned out of the car to spit and said in a dull voice:

"What's cookin'?"

I turned around all in one piece, like a dummy on a revolving platform. I stared at him.

He said: "You got a gray suit on today."

"So I have," I said. "Yes."

"Looks nice," he said. "I like the blue you was wearing yesterday too."

"Go on," I said. "Give out."

"You rode up to eight," he said. "Twice. Second time was late. You got back on at six. Shortly after that the boys in blue came bustlin' in."

"Any of them up there now?"

He shook his head. His face was like a vacant lot. "I ain't

told them anything," he said. "Too late to mention it now. They'd eat my ass off."

I said: "Why?"

"Why I ain't told them? The hell with them. You talked to me civil. Damn few people do that. Hell, I know you didn't have nothing to do with that killing."

"I played you wrong," I said. "Very wrong." I got a card out and gave it to him. He fished a pair of metal-framed glasses out of his pocket, perched them on his nose and held the card a foot away from them. He read it slowly, moving his lips, looked at me over the glasses, handed me back the card.

"Better keep it," he said. "Case I get careless and drop it. Mighty interestin' life yours, I guess."

"Yes and no. What was the name?"

"Grandy. Just call me Pop. Who killed him?"

"I don't know. Did you notice anybody going up there or coming down—anybody that seemed out of place in this building, or strange to you?"

"I don't notice much," he said. "I just happened to notice you."

"A tall blond, for instance, or a tall slender man with sideburns, about thirty-five years old."

"Nope."

"Everybody going up or down about then would ride in your car."

He nodded his worn head. "'Less they used the fire stairs. They come out in the alley, bar-lock door. Party would have to come in this way, but there's stairs back of the elevator to the second floor. From there they can get to the fire stairs. Nothing to it."

I nodded. "Mr. Grandy, could you use a five dollar bill— not as a bribe in any sense, but as a token of esteem from a sincere friend?"

"Son, I could use a five dollar bill so rough Abe Lincoln's whiskers would be all lathered up with sweat."

I gave him one. I looked at it before I passed it over. It was Lincoln on the five, all right.

He tucked it small and put it away deep in his pocket. "That's right nice of you," he said. "I hope to hell you didn't think I was fishin'."

I shook my head and went along the corridor, reading the names again. *Dr. E. J. Blaskowitz, Chiropractic Physician. Dalton and Rees, Typewriting Service. L. Pridview, Public Accountant.* Four blank doors. *Moss Mailing Company.* Two more blank doors. *H. R. Teager, Dental Laboratories.* In the same relative position as the Morningstar office two floors above, but the rooms were cut up differently. Teager had only one door and there was more wall space in between his door and the next one.

The knob didn't turn. I knocked. There was no answer. I knocked harder, with the same result. I went back to the elevator. It was still at the sixth floor. Pop Grandy watched me come as if he had never seen me before.

"Know anything about H. R. Teager?" I asked him.

He thought. "Heavy-set, oldish, sloppy clothes, dirty fingernails, like mine. Come to think I didn't see him in today."

"Do you think the super would let me into his office to look around?"

"Pretty nosey, the super is. I wouldn't recommend it."

He turned his head very slowly and looked up the side of the car. Over his head on a big metal ring a key was hanging. A pass-key. Pop Grandy turned his head back to normal position, stood up off his stool and said: "Right now I gotta go to the can."

He went. When the door had closed behind him I took the key off the cage wall and went back along to the office of H. R. Teager, unlocked it and went in.

Inside was a small windowless anteroom on the furnishings of which a great deal of expense had been spared. Two chairs, a smoking stand from a cut rate drugstore, a standing lamp from the basement of some borax emporium, a flat stained wood table with some old picture magazines on it. The door closed behind me on the door closer and the place went dark except for what little light come through the pebbled glass panel. I pulled the chain switch of the lamp and went over to the inner door in a wall that cut across the room. It was marked: *H. R. Teager. Private.* It was not locked.

Inside it there was a square office with two uncurtained east windows and very dusty sills. There was a swivel chair and two straight chairs, both plain hard stained wood, and there was a squarish flat-topped desk. There was nothing on the top of it except an old blotter and a cheap pen set and a round glass ash tray with cigar ash in it. The drawers of the desk contained some dusty paper linings, a few wire clips, rubber bands, worn down pencils, pens, rusty pen points, used blotters, four uncancelled two-cent stamps, and some printed letterheads, envelopes and bill forms.

The wire paper basket was full of junk. I almost wasted ten minutes going through it rather carefully. At the end of that time I knew what I was pretty sure of already: that H. R. Teager carried on a small business as a dental technician doing laboratory work for a number of dentists in unprosperous sections of the city, the kind of dentists who have shabby offices on second floor walk-ups over stores, who lack both the skill and the equipment to do their own laboratory work, and who like to send it out to men like themselves, rather than to the big efficient hard-boiled laboratories who wouldn't give them any credit.

I did find one thing. Teager's home address at 1354B Toberman Street on the receipted part of a gas bill.

I straightened up, dumped the stuff back into the basket and went over to the wooden door marked *Laboratory*. It had a new Yale lock on it and the pass-key didn't fit it. That was that. I switched off the lamp in the outer office and left.

The elevator was downstairs again. I rang for it and when it came up I sidled in around Pop Grandy, hiding the key, and hung it up over his head. The ring tinkled against the cage. He grinned.

"He's gone," I said. "Must have left last night. Must have been carrying a lot of stuff. His desk is cleaned out."

Pop Grandy nodded. "Carried two suitcases. I wouldn't notice that, though. Most always does carry a suitcase. I figure he picks up and delivers his work."

"Work such as what?" I asked as the car growled down. Just to be saying something.

"Such as makin' teeth that don't fit," Pop Grandy said. "For poor old bastards like me."

"You wouldn't notice," I said, as the doors struggled open on the lobby. "You wouldn't notice the color of a hummingbird's eye at fifty feet. Not much you wouldn't."

He grinned. "What's he done?"

"I'm going over to his house and find out," I said. "I think most likely he's taken a cruise to nowhere."

"I'd shift places with him," Pop Grandy said. "Even if he only got to Frisco and got pinched there, I'd shift places with him."

26

Toberman Street. A wide dusty street, off Pico. No. 1354B was an upstairs flat, south, in a yellow and white frame building. The entrance door was on the porch, beside another marked 1352B. The entrances to the downstairs flats were at right angles, facing each other across the width of the porch. I kept on ringing the bell, even after I was sure that nobody would answer it. In a neighborhood like that there is always an expert window-peeker.

Sure enough the door of 1354A was pulled open and a small bright-eyed woman looked out at me. Her dark hair had been washed and waved and was an intricate mass of bobby pins.

"You want Mrs. Teager?" she shrilled.

"Mr. or Mrs."

"They gone away last night on their vacation. They loaded up and gone away late. They had me stop the milk and the paper. They didn't have much time. Kind of sudden, it was."

"Thanks. What kind of car do they drive?"

The heartrending dialogue of some love serial came out of the room behind her and hit me in the face like a wet dish-towel.

The bright-eyed woman said: "You a friend of theirs?" In her voice, suspicion was as thick as the ham in her radio.

"Never mind," I said in a tough voice. "All we want is our money. Lots of ways to find out what car they were driving."

The woman cocked her head, listening. "That's Beula May," she told me with a sad smile. "She won't go to the dance with Doctor Myers. I was scared she wouldn't."

"Aw hell," I said, and went back to my car and drove on home to Hollywood.

The office was empty. I unlocked my inner room and threw the windows up and sat down.

Another day drawing to its end, the air dull and tired, the heavy growl of homing traffic on the boulevard, and Marlowe in his office nibbling a drink and sorting the day's mail. Four ads; two bills; a handsome colored postcard from a hotel in Santa Rosa where I had stayed for four days last year, working on a case; a long, badly typed letter from a man named Peabody in Sausalito, the general and slightly cloudly drift of which was that a sample of the handwriting of a suspected person would, when exposed to the searching Peabody examination, reveal the inner emotional characteristics of the individual, classified according to both the Freudian and Jung systems.

There was a stamped addressed envelope inside. As I tore the stamp off and threw the letter and envelope away I had a vision of a pathetic old rooster in long hair, black felt hat and black bow tie, rocking on a rickety porch in front of a lettered window, with the smell of ham hocks and cabbage coming out of the door at his elbow.

I sighed, retrieved the envelope, wrote its name and address on a fresh one, folded a dollar bill into a sheet of paper and wrote on it: "This is positively the last contribution." I signed my name, sealed the envelope, stuck a stamp on it and poured another drink.

I filled and lit my pipe and sat there smoking. Nobody came in, nobody called, nothing happened, nobody cared whether I died or went to El Paso.

Little by little the roar of the traffic quieted down. The sky lost its glare. Over in the west it would be red. An early neon light showed a block away, diagonally over roofs. The ventilator churned dully in the wall of the coffee shop down in the alley. A truck filled and backed and growled its way out on to the boulevard.

Finally the telephone rang. I answered it and the voice said: "Mr. Marlowe? This is Mr. Shaw. At the Bristol."

"Yes, Mr. Shaw. How are you?"

"I'm very well thanks, Mr. Marlowe. I hope you are the

same. There's a young lady here asking to be let into your apartment. I don't know why."

"Me neither, Mr. Shaw. I didn't order anything like that. Does she give a name?"

"Oh yes. Quite. Her name is Davis. Miss Merle Davis. She is—what shall I say?—quite verging on the hysterical."

"Let her in," I said, rapidly. "I'll be there in ten minutes. She's the secretary of a client. It's a business matter entirely."

"Quite. Oh yes. Shall I—er—remain with her?"

"Whatever you think," I said and hung up.

Passing the open door of the wash cabinet I saw a stiff excited face in the glass.

27

As I turned the key in my door and opened it Shaw was already standing up from the davenport. He was a tall man with glasses and a high domed bald head that made his ears look as if they had slipped down on his head. He had the fixed smile of polite idiocy on his face.

The girl sat in my easy chair behind the chess table. She wasn't doing anything, just sitting there.

"Ah, there you are, Mr. Marlowe," Shaw chirped. "Yes. Quite. Miss Davis and I have been having such an interesting little conversation. I was telling her I originally came from England. She hasn't—er—told me where she came from." He was halfway to the door saying this.

"Very kind of you, Mr. Shaw," I said.

"Not at all," he chirped. "Not at all. I'll just run along now. My dinner, possibly—"

"It's very nice of you," I said, "I appreciate it."

He nodded and was gone. The unnatural brightness of his smile seemed to linger in the air after the door closed, like the smile of the Cheshire Cat.

I said: "Hello, there."

She said: "Hello." Her voice was quite calm, quite serious. She was wearing a brownish linen coat and skirt, a broad-brimmed low-crowned straw hat with a brown velvet band that exactly matched the color of her shoes and the leather trimming on the edges of her linen envelope bag. The hat was tilted rather daringly, for her. She was not wearing her glasses.

Except for her face she would have looked all right. In the first place her eyes were quite mad. There was white showing all around the iris and they had a sort of fixed look. When they moved the movement was so stiff that you could almost hear something creak. Her mouth was in a tight line at the corners, but the middle part of her upper lip kept lifting off her teeth, upwards and outwards as if fine threads attached to the edge of the lip were pulling it. It would go up so far that it didn't seem possible, and then the entire lower part of her face would go into a spasm and when the spasm was over her mouth would be tight shut, and then the process would slowly start all over again. In addition to this there was something wrong with her neck, so that very slowly her head was drawn around to the left about forty-five degrees. It would stop there, her neck would twitch, and her head would slide back the way it had come.

The combination of these two movements, taken with the immobility of her body, the tight-clasped hands in her lap, and the fixed stare of her eyes, was enough to start anybody's nerves backfiring.

There was a can of tobacco on the desk, between which and her chair was the chess table with the chessmen in their box. I got the pipe out of my pocket and went over to fill it at the can of tobacco. That put me just on the other side of the chess table from her. Her bag was lying on the edge of the table, in front of her and a little to one side. She jumped a little when I went over there, but after that she was just like before. She even made an effort to smile.

I filled the pipe and struck a paper match and lit it and stood there holding the match after I had blown it out.

"You're not wearing your glasses," I said.

She spoke. Her voice was quiet, composed. "Oh, I only wear them around the house and for reading. They're in my bag."

"You're in the house now," I said. "You ought to be wearing them."

I reached casually for the bag. She didn't move. She didn't watch my hands. Her eyes were on my face. I turned my body a little as I opened the bag. I fished the glass case out and slid it across the table.

"Put them on," I said.

"Oh, yes, I'll put them on," she said. "But I'll have to take my hat off, I think . . ."

"Yes, take your hat off," I said.

She took her hat off and held it on her knees. Then she remembered about the glasses and forgot about the hat. The hat fell on the floor while she reached for the glasses. She put them on. That helped her appearance a lot, I thought.

While she was doing this I got the gun out of her bag and slid it into my hip pocket. I didn't think she saw me. It looked like the same Colt .25 automatic with the walnut grip that I had seen in the top right hand drawer of her desk the day before.

I went back to the davenport and sat down and said: "Well, here we are. What do we do now? Are you hungry?"

"I've been over to Mr. Vannier's house," she said.

"Oh."

"He lives in Sherman Oaks. At the end of Escamillo Drive. At the very end."

"Quite, probably," I said without meaning, and tried to blow a smoke ring, but didn't make it. A nerve in my cheek was trying to twang like a wire. I didn't like it.

"Yes," she said in her composed voice, with her upper lip still doing the hoist and flop movement and her chin still swinging around at anchor and back again. "It's very quiet there. Mr. Vannier has been living there three years now. Before that he lived up in the Hollywood hills, on Diamond Street. Another man lived with him there, but they didn't get along very well, Mr. Vannier said."

"I feel as if I could understand that too," I said. "How long have you known Mr. Vannier?"

"I've known him eight years. I haven't known him very well. I have had to take him a—a parcel now and then. He liked to have me bring it myself."

I tried again with a smoke ring. Nope.

"Of course," she said, "I never liked him very well. I was afraid he would—I was afraid he—"

"But he didn't," I said.

For the first time her face got a human natural expression—surprise.

"No," she said. "He didn't. That is, he didn't really. But he had his pajamas on."

"Taking it easy," I said. "Lying around all afternoon with his pajamas on. Well, some guys have all the luck, don't they?"

"Well you have to know something," she said seriously. "Something that makes people pay you money. Mrs. Murdock has been wonderful to me, hasn't she?"

"She certainly has," I said. "How much were you taking him today?"

"Only five hundred dollars. Mrs. Murdock said that was all she could spare, and she couldn't really spare that. She said it would have to stop. It couldn't go on. Mr. Vannier would always promise to stop, but he never did."

"It's a way they have," I said.

"So there was only one thing to do. I've known that for years, really. It was all my fault and Mrs. Murdock has been so wonderful to me. It couldn't make me any worse than I was already, could it?"

I put my hand up and rubbed my cheek hard, to quiet the nerve. She forgot that I hadn't answered her and went on again.

"So I did it," she said. "He was there in his pajamas, with a glass beside him. He was leering at me. He didn't even get up to let me in. But there was a key in the front door. Somebody had left a key there. It was—it was—" her voice jammed in her throat.

"It was a key in the front door," I said. "So you were able to get in."

"Yes." She nodded and almost smiled again. "There wasn't anything to it, really. I don't even remember hearing the noise. But there must have been a noise, of course. Quite a loud noise."

"I suppose so," I said.

"I went over quite close to him, so I couldn't miss," she said.

"And what did Mr. Vannier do?"

"He didn't do anything at all. He just leered, sort of. Well, that's all there is to it. I didn't like to go back to Mrs. Murdock and make any more trouble for her. And for Leslie." Her voice hushed on the name, and hung suspended, and a little shiver rippled over her body. "So I came here," she said. "And when you didn't answer the bell, I found the office and asked the manager to let me in and wait for you. I knew you would know what to do."

"And what did you touch in the house while you were there?" I asked. "Can you remember at all? I mean, besides the front door. Did you just go in at the door and come out without touching anything in the house?"

She thought and her face stopped moving. "Oh, I remember one thing," she said. "I put the light out. Before I left. It was a lamp. One of these lamps that shine upwards, with big bulbs. I put that out."

I nodded and smiled at her. Marlowe, one smile, cheerful.

"What time was this—how long ago?"

"Oh just before I came over here. I drove. I had Mrs. Murdock's car. The one you asked about yesterday. I forgot to tell you that she didn't take it when she went away. Or did I? No, I remember now I did tell you."

"Let's see," I said. "Half an hour to drive here anyway. You've been here close to an hour. That would be about five-thirty when you left Mr. Vannier's house. And you put the light off."

"That's right." She nodded again, quite brightly. Pleased at remembering. "I put the light out."

"Would you care for a drink?" I asked her.

"Oh, no." She shook her head quite vigorously. "I never drink anything at all."

"Would you mind if I had one?"

"Certainly not. Why should I?"

I stood up, gave her a studying look. Her lip was still going up and her head was still going around, but I thought not so far. It was like a rhythm which is dying down.

It was difficult to know how far to go with this. It might be that the more she talked, the better. Nobody knows very much about the time of absorption of a shock.

I said: "Where is your home?"

"Why—I live with Mrs. Murdock. In Pasadena."

"I mean, your real home. Where your folks are."

"My parents live in Wichita," she said. "But I don't go there—ever. I write once in a while, but I haven't seen them for years."

"What does your father do?"

"He has a dog and cat hospital. He's a veterinarian. I hope they won't have to know. They didn't about the other time. Mrs. Murdock kept it from everybody."

"Maybe they won't have to know," I said. "I'll get my drink."

I went out around the back of her chair to the kitchen and poured it and I made it a drink that was a drink. I put it down in a lump and took the little gun off my hip and saw that the safety was on. I smelled the muzzle, broke out the magazine. There was a shell in the chamber, but it was one of those guns that won't fire when the magazine is out. I held it so that I could look into the breech. The shell in there was the wrong size and was crooked against the breech block. It looked like a .32. The shells in the magazine were the right size, .25's. I fitted the gun together again and went back to the living room.

I hadn't heard a sound. She had just slid forward in a pile in front of the chair, on top of her nice hat. She was as cold as a mackerel.

I spread her out a little and took her glasses off and made sure she hadn't swallowed her tongue. I wedged my folded handkerchief into the corner of her mouth so that she wouldn't bite her tongue when she came out of it. I went to the phone and called Carl Moss.

"Phil Marlowe, Doc. Any more patients or are you through?"

"All through," he said. "Leaving. Trouble?"

"I'm home," I said. "Four-o-eight Bristol Apartments, if you don't remember. I've got a girl here who has pulled a faint. I'm not afraid of the faint, I'm afraid she may be nuts when she comes out of it."

"Don't give her any liquor," he said. "I'm on my way."

I hung up and knelt down beside her. I began to rub her

temples. She opened her eyes. The lip started to lift. I pulled the handkerchief out of her mouth. She looked up at me and said: "I've been over to Mr. Vannier's house. He lives in Sherman Oaks. I—"

"Do you mind if I lift you up and put you on the davenport? You know me—Marlowe, the big boob that goes around asking all the wrong questions."

"Hello," she said.

I lifted her. She went stiff on me, but she didn't say anything. I put her on the davenport and tucked her skirt down over her legs and put a pillow under her head and picked her hat up. It was as flat as a flounder. I did what I could to straighten it out and laid it aside on the desk.

She watched me sideways, doing this.

"Did you call the police?" she asked softly.

"Not yet," I said. "I've been too busy."

She looked surprised. I wasn't quite sure, but I thought she looked a little hurt, too.

I opened up her bag and turned my back to her to slip the gun back into it. While I was doing that I took a look at what else was in the bag. The usual oddments, a couple of handkerchiefs, lipstick, a silver and red enamel compact with powder in it, a couple of tissues, a purse with some hard money and a few dollar bills, no cigarettes, no matches, no tickets to the theater.

I pulled open the zipper pocket at the back. That held her driver's license and a flat packet of bills, ten fifties. I riffled them. None of them brand new. Tucked into the rubber band that held them was a folded paper. I took it out and opened it and read it. It was neatly typewritten, dated that day. It was a common receipt form and it would, when signed, acknowledge the receipt of $500. "Payment on Account."

It didn't seem as if it would ever be signed now. I slipped money and receipt into my pocket. I closed the bag and looked over at the davenport.

She was looking at the ceiling and doing that with her face again. I went into my bedroom and got a blanket to throw over her.

Then I went to the kitchen for another drink.

28

Dr. Carl Moss was a big burly Jew with a Hitler mustache, pop eyes and the calmness of a glacier. He put his hat and bag in a chair and went over and stood looking down at the girl on the davenport inscrutably.

"I'm Dr. Moss," he said. "How are you?"

She said: "Aren't you the police?"

He bent down and felt her pulse and then stood there watching her breathing. "Where does it hurt, Miss—"

"Davis," I said. "Miss Merle Davis."

"Miss Davis."

"Nothing hurts me," she said, staring up at him. "I—I don't even know why I'm lying here like this. I thought you were the police. You see, I killed a man."

"Well, that's a normal human impulse," he said. "I've killed dozens." He didn't smile.

She lifted her lip and moved her head around for him.

"You know you don't have to do that," he said, quite gently. "You feel a twitch of the nerves here and there and you proceed to build it up and dramatize it. You can control it, if you want to."

"Can I?" she whispered.

"If you want to," he said. "You don't have to. It doesn't make any difference to me either way. Nothing pains at all, eh?"

"No." She shook her head.

He patted her shoulder and walked out to the kitchen. I went after him. He leaned his hips against the sink and gave me a cool stare. "What's the story?"

"She's the secretary of a client. A Mrs. Murdock in Pasadena. The client is rather a brute. About eight years ago a man made a hard pass at Merle. How hard I don't know. Then—I don't mean immediately—but around that time he fell out of a window or jumped. Since then she can't have a man touch her—not in the most casual way, I mean."

"Uh-huh." His pop eyes continued to read my face. "Does she think he jumped out of the window on her account?"

"I don't know. Mrs. Murdock is the man's widow. She

married again and her second husband is dead too. Merle has stayed with her. The old woman treats her like a rough parent treats a naughty child."

"I see. Regressive."

"What's that?"

"Emotional shock, and the subconscious attempt to escape back to childhood. If Mrs. Murdock scolds her a good deal, but not too much, that would increase the tendency. Identification of childhood subordination with childhood protection."

"Do we have to go into that stuff?" I growled.

He grinned at me calmly. "Look, pal. The girl's obviously a neurotic. It's partly induced and partly deliberate. I mean to say that she really enjoys a lot of it. Even if she doesn't realize that she enjoys it. However, that's not of immediate importance. What's this about killing a man?"

"A man named Vannier who lives in Sherman Oaks. There seems to be some blackmail angle. Merle had to take him his money, from time to time. She was afraid of him. I've seen the guy. A nasty type. She went over there this afternoon and she says she shot him."

"Why?"

"She says she didn't like the way he leered at her."

"Shot him with what?"

"She had a gun in her bag. Don't ask me why. I don't know. But if she shot him, it wasn't with that. The gun's got a wrong cartridge in the breech. It can't be fired as it is. Also it hasn't been fired."

"This is too deep for me," he said. "I'm just a doctor. What did you want me to do with her?"

"Also," I said, ignoring the question, "she said the lamp was turned on and it was about five-thirty of a nice summery afternoon. And the guy was wearing his sleeping suit and there was a key in the lock of the front door. And he didn't get up to let her in. He just sort of sat there sort of leering."

He nodded and said: "Oh." He pushed a cigarette between his heavy lips and lit it. "If you expect me to tell you whether she really thinks she shot him, I can't do it. From your description I gather that the man is shot. That so?"

"Brother, I haven't been there. But that much seems pretty clear."

"If she thinks she shot him and isn't just acting—and God, how these types do act!—that indicates it was not a new idea to her. You say she carried a gun. So perhaps it wasn't. She may have a guilt complex. Wants to be punished, wants to expiate some real or imaginary crime. Again I ask what do you want me to do with her? She's not sick, she's not loony."

"She's not going back to Pasadena."

"Oh." He looked at me curiously. "Any family?"

"In Wichita. Father's a vet. I'll call him, but she'll have to stay here tonight."

"I don't know about that. Does she trust you enough to spend the night in your apartment?"

"She came here of her own free will, and not socially. So I guess she does."

He shrugged and fingered the sidewall of his coarse black mustache. "Well, I'll give her some nembutal and we'll put her to bed. And you can walk the floor wrestling with your conscience."

"I have to go out," I said. "I have to go over there and see what has happened. And she can't stay here alone. And no man, not even a doctor is going to put her to bed. Get a nurse. I'll sleep somewhere else."

"Phil Marlowe," he said. "The shop-soiled Galahad. Okay. I'll stick around until the nurse comes."

He went back into the living room and telephoned the Nurses' Registry. Then he telephoned his wife. While he was telephoning, Merle sat up on the davenport and clasped her hands primly in her lap.

"I don't see why the lamp was on," she said. "It wasn't dark in the house at all. Not that dark."

I said: "What's your dad's first name?"

"Dr. Wilbur Davis. Why?"

"Wouldn't you like something to eat?"

At the telephone Carl Moss said to me: "Tomorrow will do for that. This is probably just a lull." He finished his call, hung up, went to his bag and came back with a couple of yellow capsules in his hand on a fragment of cotton. He got a glass of water, handed her the capsules and said: "Swallow."

"I'm not sick, am I?" she said, looking up at him.

"Swallow, my child, swallow."

She took them and put them in her mouth and took the glass of water and drank.

I put my hat on and left.

On the way down in the elevator I remembered that there hadn't been any keys in her bag, so I stopped at the lobby floor and went out through the lobby to the Bristol Avenue side. The car was not hard to find. It was parked crookedly about two feet from the curb. It was a gray Mercury convertible and its license number was 2X1111. I remembered that this was the number of Linda Murdock's car.

A leather keyholder hung in the lock. I got into the car, started the engine, saw that there was plenty of gas, and drove it away. It was a nice eager little car. Over Cahuenga Pass it had the wings of a bird.

29

Escamillo Drive made three jogs in four blocks, for no reason that I could see. It was very narrow, averaged about five houses to a block and was overhung by a section of shaggy brown foothill on which nothing lived at this season except sage and manzanita. In its fifth and last block, Escamillo Drive did a neat little curve to the left, hit the base of the hill hard, and died without a whimper. In this last block were three houses, two on the opposite entering corners, one at the dead end. This was Vannier's. My spotlight showed the key still in the door.

It was a narrow English type bungalow with a high roof, leaded front windows, a garage to the side, and a trailer parked beside the garage. The early moon lay quietly on its small lawn. A large oak tree grew almost on the front porch. There was no light in the house now, none visible from the front at least.

From the lay of the land a light in the living room in the daytime did not seem utterly improbable. It would be a dark house except in the morning. As a love nest the place had its points, but as a residence for a blackmailer I didn't give it very high marks. Sudden death can come to you anywhere, but Vannier had made it too easy.

I turned into his driveway, backed to get myself pointed out of the dead end, and then drove down to the corner and parked there. I walked back in the street because there was no sidewalk. The front door was made of ironbound oak planks, bevelled where they joined. There was a thumb latch instead of a knob. The head of the flat key projected from the lock. I rang the bell, and it rang with that remote sound of a bell ringing at night in an empty house. I walked around the oak tree and poked the light of my pencil flash between the leaves of the garage door. There was a car in there. I went back around the house and looked at a small flowerless yard, walled in by a low wall of fieldstone. Three more oak trees, a table and a couple of all metal chairs under one of them. A rubbish burner at the back. I shone my light into the trailer before I went back to the front. There didn't seem to be anybody in the trailer. Its door was locked.

I opened the front door, leaving the key in the lock. I wasn't going to work any dipsy-doodle in this place. What ever was, was. I just wanted to make sure. I felt around on the wall inside the door for a light switch, found one and tilted it up. Pale flame bulbs in pairs in wall brackets went on all around the room, showing me the big lamp Merle had spoken of, as well as other things. I went over to switch the lamp on, then back to switch the wall light off. The lamp had a big bulb inverted in a porcelain glass bowl. You could get three different intensities of light. I clicked the button switch around until I had all there was.

The room ran from front to back, with a door at the back and an arch up front to the right. Inside that was a small dining room. Curtains were half drawn across the arch, heavy pale green brocade curtains, far from new. The fireplace was in the middle of the left wall, bookshelves opposite and on both sides of it, not built in. Two davenports angled across the corners of the room and there was one gold chair, one pink chair, one brown chair, one brown and gold jacquard chair with footstool.

Yellow pajama legs were on the footstool, bare ankles, feet in dark green morocco leather slippers. My eyes ran up from the feet, slowly, carefully. A dark green figured silk robe, tied with a tasseled belt. Open above the belt showing a monogram on the pocket of the pajamas. A handkerchief neat in the pocket, two stiff points of white linen. A yellow neck, the face turned sideways, pointed at a mirror on the wall. I walked around and looked in the mirror. The face leered all right.

The left arm and hand lay between a knee and the side of the chair, the right arm hung outside the chair, the ends of the fingers touching the rug. Touching also the butt of a small revolver, about .32 caliber, a belly gun, with practically no barrel. The right side of the face was against the back of the chair, but the right shoulder was dark brown with blood and there was some on the right sleeve. Also on the chair. A lot of it on the chair.

I didn't think his head had taken that position naturally. Some sensitive soul had not liked the right side of it.

I lifted my foot and gently pushed the footstool sideways a few inches. The heels of the slippers moved reluctantly over the jacquard surface, not with it. The man was as stiff as a board. So I reached down and touched his ankle. Ice was never half as cold.

On a table at his right elbow was half of a dead drink, an ashtray full of butts and ash. Three of the butts had lipstick on them. Bright Chinese red lipstick. What a blond would use.

There was another ashtray beside another chair. Matches in it and a lot of ash, but no stubs.

On the air of the room a rather heavy perfume struggled with the smell of death, and lost. Although defeated, it was still there.

I poked through the rest of the house, putting lights on and off. Two bedrooms, one furnished in light wood, one in red maple. The light one seemed to be a spare. A nice bathroom with tan and mulberry tiling and a stall shower with a glass door. The kitchen was small. There were a lot of bottles on the sink. Lots of bottles, lots of glass, lots of fingerprints, lots of evidence. Or not, as the case may be.

I went back to the living room and stood in the middle of the floor breathing with my mouth as far as possible and wondering what the score would be when I turned this one in. Turn this one in and report that I was the fellow who had found Morningstar and run away. The score would be low, very low. Marlowe, three murders. Marlowe practically knee-deep in dead men. And no reasonable, logical, friendly account of himself whatsoever. But that wasn't the worst of it. The minute I opened up I would cease to be a free agent. I would be through with doing whatever it was I was doing and with finding out whatever it was I was finding out.

Carl Moss might be willing to protect Merle with the mantle of Aesculapius, up to a point. Or he might think it would do her more good in the long run to get it all off her chest, whatever it was.

I wandered back to the jacquard chair and set my teeth and grabbed enough of his hair to pull the head away from the chair back. The bullet had gone in at the temple. The set-up could be for suicide. But people like Louis Vannier do not commit suicide. A blackmailer, even a scared blackmailer, has a sense of power, and loves it.

I let the head go back where it wanted to go and leaned down to scrub my hand on the nap of the rug. Leaning down I saw the corner of a picture frame under the lower shelf of the table at Vannier's elbow. I went around and reached for it with a handkerchief.

The glass was cracked across. It had fallen off the wall. I could see the small nail. I could make a guess how it had happened. Somebody standing at Vannier's right, even leaning over him, somebody he knew and had no fear of, had suddenly pulled a gun and shot him in the right temple. And then, startled by the blood or the recoil of the shot, the killer had jumped back against the wall and knocked the picture down. It had landed on a corner and jumped under the table. And the killer had been too careful to touch it, or too scared.

I looked at it. It was a small picture, not interesting at all. A guy in doublet and hose, with lace at his sleeve ends, and one of those round puffy velvet hats with a feather, leaning

"N-nothing. Oh Alex. Please don't be so brutal."

"Stop it. *Stop it!* Show me how you did it, how you were standing, how you held the gun."

She didn't move.

"Never mind about the prints," Morny said. "I'll put better ones on. Much better ones."

She moved slowly across the opening of the curtains and I saw her. She was wearing pale green gabardine slacks, a fawn-colored leisure jacket with stitching on it, a scarlet turban with a gold snake in it. Her face was smeared with tears.

"Pick it up," Morny yelled at her. "Show me!"

She bent beside the chair and came up with the gun in her hand and her teeth bared. She pointed the gun across the opening in the curtains, towards the space of room where the door was.

Morny didn't move, didn't make a sound.

The blond's hand began to shake and the gun did a queer up and down dance in the air. Her mouth trembled and her arm fell.

"I can't do it," she breathed. "I ought to shoot you, but I can't."

The hand opened and the gun thudded to the floor.

Morny went swiftly past the break in the curtains, pushed her out of the way and with his foot pushed the gun back to about where it had been.

"You couldn't do it," he said thickly. "You couldn't do it. Now watch."

He whipped a handkerchief out and bent to pick the gun up again. He pressed something and the gate fell open. He reached his right hand into his pocket and rolled a cartridge in his fingers, moving his fingertips on the metal, pushed the cartridge into a cylinder. He repeated the performance four times more, snapped the gate shut, then opened it and spun it a little to set it in a certain spot. He placed the gun down on the floor, withdrew his hand and handkerchief and straightened up.

"You couldn't shoot me," he sneered, "because there was nothing in the gun but one empty shell. Now it's loaded

far out of a window and apparently calling out to somebody downstairs. Downstairs not being in the picture. It was a color reproduction of something that had never been needed in the first place.

I looked around the room. There were other pictures, a couple of rather nice water colors, some engravings—very old-fashioned this year, engravings, or are they? Half a dozen in all. Well, perhaps the guy liked the picture, so what? A man leaning out of a high window. A long time ago.

I looked at Vannier. He wouldn't help me at all. A man leaning out of a high window, a long time ago.

The touch of the idea at first was so light that I almost missed it and passed on. A touch of a feather, hardly that. The touch of a snowflake. A high window, a man leaning out—a long time ago.

It snapped in place. It was so hot it sizzled. Out of a high window a long time ago—eight years ago—a man leaning—too far—a man falling—to his death. A man named Horace Bright.

"Mr. Vannier," I said with a little touch of admiration, "you played that rather neatly."

I turned the picture over. On the back dates and amounts of money were written. Dates over almost eight years, amounts mostly of $500, a few $750's, two for $1000. There was a running total in small figures. It was $11,100. Mr. Vannier had not received the latest payment. He had been dead when it arrived. It was not a lot of money, spread over eight years. Mr. Vannier's customer had bargained hard.

The cardboard back was fastened into the frame with steel victrola needles. Two of them had fallen out. I worked the cardboard loose and tore it a little getting it loose. There was a white envelope between the back and the picture. Sealed, blank. I tore it open. It contained two square photographs and a negative. The photos were just the same. They showed a man leaning far out of a window with his mouth open yelling. His hands were on the brick edges of the window frame. There was a woman's face behind his shoulder.

He was a thinnish dark-haired man. His face was not very clear, nor the face of the woman behind him. He was leaning out of a window and yelling or calling out.

There I was holding the photograph and looking at it. And so far as I could see it didn't mean a thing. I knew it had to. I just didn't know why. But I kept on looking at it. And in a little while something was wrong. It was a very small thing, but it was vital. The position of the man's hands, lined against the corner of the wall where it was cut out to make the window frame. The hands were not holding anything, they were not touching anything. It was the inside of his wrists that lined against the angle of the bricks. The hands were in air.

The man was not leaning. He was falling.

I put the stuff back in the envelope and folded the cardboard back and stuffed that into my pocket also. I hid frame, glass and picture in the linen closet under towels.

All this had taken too long. A car stopped outside the house. Feet came up the walk.

I dodged behind the curtains in the archway.

30

The front door opened and then quietly closed.

There was a silence, hanging in the air like a man's breath in frosty air, and then a thick scream, ending in a wail of despair.

Then a man's voice, tight with fury, saying: "Not bad, not good. Try again."

The woman's voice said: "My God, it's Louis! He's dead!"

The man's voice said: "I may be wrong, but I still think it stinks."

"My God! He's dead, Alex. Do something—for God's sake—*do* something!"

"Yeah," the hard tight voice of Alex Morny said. "I ought to. I ought to make you look just like him. With blood and everything. I ought to make you just as dead, just as cold, just as rotten. No, I don't have to do that. You're that already. Just as rotten. Eight months married and cheating on me with a piece of merchandise like that. My

God! What did I ever think of to put in with a chippy like you?"

He was almost yelling at the end of it.

The woman made another wailing noise.

"Quit stalling," Morny said bitterly. "What do you think I brought you over here for? You're not kidding anybody. You've been watched for weeks. You were here last night. I've been here already today. I've seen what there is to see. Your lipstick on cigarettes, your glass that you drank out of. I can see you now, sitting on the arm of his chair, rubbing his greasy hair, and then feeding him a slug while he was still purring. Why?"

"Oh, Alex—darling—don't say such awful things."

"Early Lillian Gish," Morny said. "Very early Lillian Gish. Skip the agony, toots. I have to know how to handle this. What the hell you think I'm here for? I don't give one little flash in hell about you any more. Not any more, toots, not any more, my precious darling angel blond mankiller. But I do care about myself and my reputation and my business. For instance, did you wipe the gun off?"

Silence. Then the sound of a blow. The woman wailed. She was hurt, terribly hurt. Hurt in the depths of her soul. She made it rather good.

"Look, angel," Morny snarled. "Don't feed me the ham. I've been in pictures. I'm a connoisseur of ham. Skip it. You're going to tell me how this was done if I have to drag you around the room by your hair. Now—did you wipe off the gun?"

Suddenly she laughed. An unnatural laugh, but clear and with a nice tinkle to it. Then she stopped laughing, just as suddenly.

Her voice said: "Yes."

"And the glass you were using?"

"Yes." Very quiet now, very cool.

"And you put his prints on the gun?"

"Yes."

He thought in the silence. "Probably won't fool them," he said. "It's almost impossible to get a dead man's prints on a gun in a convincing way. However. What else did you wipe off."

"N-nothing. Oh Alex. Please don't be so brutal."

"Stop it. *Stop it!* Show me how you did it, how you were standing, how you held the gun."

She didn't move.

"Never mind about the prints," Morny said. "I'll put better ones on. Much better ones."

She moved slowly across the opening of the curtains and I saw her. She was wearing pale green gabardine slacks, a fawn-colored leisure jacket with stitching on it, a scarlet turban with a gold snake in it. Her face was smeared with tears.

"Pick it up," Morny yelled at her. "Show me!"

She bent beside the chair and came up with the gun in her hand and her teeth bared. She pointed the gun across the opening in the curtains, towards the space of room where the door was.

Morny didn't move, didn't make a sound.

The blond's hand began to shake and the gun did a queer up and down dance in the air. Her mouth trembled and her arm fell.

"I can't do it," she breathed. "I ought to shoot you, but I can't."

The hand opened and the gun thudded to the floor.

Morny went swiftly past the break in the curtains, pushed her out of the way and with his foot pushed the gun back to about where it had been.

"You couldn't do it," he said thickly. "You couldn't do it. Now watch."

He whipped a handkerchief out and bent to pick the gun up again. He pressed something and the gate fell open. He reached his right hand into his pocket and rolled a cartridge in his fingers, moving his fingertips on the metal, pushed the cartridge into a cylinder. He repeated the performance four times more, snapped the gate shut, then opened it and spun it a little to set it in a certain spot. He placed the gun down on the floor, withdrew his hand and handkerchief and straightened up.

"You couldn't shoot me," he sneered, "because there was nothing in the gun but one empty shell. Now it's loaded again. The cylinders are in the right place. One shot has been fired. And your fingerprints are on the gun."

The blond was very still, looking at him with haggard eyes.

"I forgot to tell you," he said softly, "*I* wiped the gun off. I thought it would be so much nicer to be *sure* your prints were on it. I was pretty sure they were—but I felt as if I would like to be *quite* sure. Get it?"

The girl said quietly: "You're going to turn me in?"

His back was towards me. Dark clothes. Felt hat pulled low. So I couldn't see his face. But I could just about see the leer with which he said:

"Yes, angel, I am going to turn you in."

"I see," she said, and looked at him levelly. There was a sudden grave dignity in her over-emphasized chorus girl's face.

"I'm going to turn you in, angel," he said slowly, spacing his words as if he enjoyed his act. "Some people are going to be sorry for me and some people are going to laugh at me. But it's not going to do my business any harm. Not a bit of harm. That's one nice thing about a business like mine. A little notoriety won't hurt it at all."

"So I'm just publicity value to you, now," she said. "Apart, of course, from the danger that you might have been suspected yourself."

"Just so," he said. "Just so."

"How about my motive?" she asked, still calm, still level-eyed and so gravely contemptuous that he didn't get the expression at all.

"I don't know," he said. "I don't care. You were up to something with him. Eddie tailed you downtown to a street on Bunker Hill where you met a blond guy in a brown suit. You gave him something. Eddie dropped you and tailed the guy to an apartment house near there. He tried to tail him some more, but he had a hunch the guy spotted him, and he had to drop it. I don't know what it was all about. I know one thing, though. In that apartment house a young guy named Phillips was shot yesterday. Would you know anything about that, my sweet?"

The blond said: "I wouldn't know anything about it. I

don't know anybody named Phillips and strangely enough I didn't just run up and shoot anybody out of sheer girlish fun."

"But you shot Vannier, my dear," Morny said almost gently.

"Oh yes," she drawled. "Of course. We were wondering what my motive was. You get it figured out yet?"

"You can work that out with the johns," he snapped. "Call it a lover's quarrel. Call it anything you like."

"Perhaps," she said, "when he was drunk he looked just a little like you. Perhaps that was the motive."

He said: "Ah," and sucked his breath in.

"Better looking," she said. "Younger, with less belly. But with the same goddamned self-satisfied smirk."

"Ah," Morny said, and he was suffering.

"Would that do?" she asked him softly.

He stepped forward and swung a fist. It caught her on the side of the face and she went down and sat on the floor, a long leg straight out in front of her, one hand to her jaw, her very blue eyes looking up at him.

"Maybe you oughtn't to have done that," she said. "Maybe I won't go through with it, now."

"You'll go through with it, all right. You won't have any choice. You'll get off easy enough. Christ, I know that. With your looks. But you'll go through with it, angel. Your fingerprints are on that gun."

She got to her feet slowly, still with the hand to her jaw.

Then she smiled. "I knew he was dead," she said. "That is my key in the door. I'm quite willing to go downtown and say I shot him. But don't lay your smooth white paw on me again—if you want my story. Yes. I'm quite willing to go to the cops. I'll feel a lot safer with them than I feel with you."

Morny turned and I saw the hard white leer of his face and the scar dimple in his cheek twitching. He walked past the opening in the curtains. The front door opened again. The blond stood still a moment, looked back over her shoulder at the corpse, shuddered slightly, and passed out of my line of vision.

The door closed. Steps on the walk. Then car doors opening and closing. The motor throbbed, and the car went away.

31

After a long time I moved out from my hiding place and stood looking around the living room again. I went over and picked the gun up and wiped it off very carefully and put it down again. I picked the three rouge-stained cigarette stubs out of the tray on the table and carried them into the bathroom and flushed them down the toilet. Then I looked around for the second glass with her fingerprints on it. There wasn't any second glass. The one that was half full of a dead drink I took to the kitchen and rinsed out and wiped on a dish towel.

Then the nasty part. I kneeled on the rug by his chair and picked up the gun and reached for the trailing bone-stiff hand. The prints would not be good, but they would be prints and they would not be Lois Morny's. The gun had a checked rubber grip, with a piece broken off on the left side below the screw. No prints on that. An index print on the right side of the barrel, two fingers on the trigger guard, a thumb print on the flat piece on the left side, behind the chambers. Good enough.

I took one more look around the living room.

I put the lamp down to a lower light. It still glared too much on the dead yellow face. I opened the front door, pulled the key out and wiped it off and pushed it back into the lock. I shut the door and wiped the thumblatch off and went my way down the block to the Mercury.

I drove back to Hollywood and locked the car up and started along the sidewalk past the other parked cars to the entrance of the Bristol.

A harsh whisper spoke to me out of darkness, out of a car. It spoke my name. Eddie Prue's long blank face hung somewhere up near the roof of a small Packard, behind its wheel. He was alone in it. I leaned on the door of the car and looked in at him.

"How you making out, shamus?"

I tossed a match down and blew smoke at his face. I said: "Who dropped that dental supply company's bill you gave me last night? Vannier, or somebody else?"

"Vannier."

"What was I supposed to do with it—guess the life history of a man named Teager?"

"I don't go for dumb guys," Eddie Prue said.

I said: "Why would he have it in his pocket to drop? And if he did drop it, why wouldn't you just hand it back to him? In other words, seeing that I'm a dumb guy, explain to me why a bill for dental supplies should get anybody all excited and start trying to hire private detectives. Especially gents like Alex Morny, who don't like private detectives."

"Morny's a good head," Eddie Prue said coldly.

"He's the fellow for whom they coined the phrase, 'as ignorant as an actor.'"

"Skip that. Don't you know what they use that dental stuff for?"

"Yeah. I found out. They use albastone for making molds of teeth and cavities. It's very hard, very fine grain and retains any amount of fine detail. The other stuff, crystobolite, is used to cook out the wax in an invested wax model. It's used because it stands a great deal of heat without distortion. Tell me you don't know what I'm talking about."

"I guess you know how they make gold inlays," Eddie Prue said. "I guess you do, huh?"

"I spent two of my hours learning today. I'm an expert. What does it get me?"

He was silent for a little while, and then he said: "You ever read the paper?"

"Once in a while."

"It couldn't be you read where an old guy named Morningstar was bumped off in the Belfont Building on Ninth Street, just two floors above where this H. R. Teager had his office. It couldn't be you read that, could it?"

I didn't answer him. He looked at me for a moment longer, then he put his hand forward to the dash and pushed the starter button. The motor of his car caught and he started to ease in the clutch.

"Nobody could be as dumb as you act," he said softly. "Nobody ain't. Good night to you."

The car moved away from the curb and drifted down the hill towards Franklin. I was grinning into the distance as it disappeared.

I went up to the apartment and unlocked the door and pushed it open a few inches and then knocked gently. There was movement in the room. The door was pulled open by a strong-looking girl with a black stripe on the cap of her white nurse's uniform.

"I'm Marlowe. I live here."

"Come in, Mr. Marlowe. Dr. Moss told me."

I shut the door quietly and we spoke in low voices. "How is she?" I asked.

"She's asleep. She was already drowsy when I got here. I'm Miss Lymington. I don't know very much about her except that her temperature is normal and her pulse still rather fast, but going down. A mental disturbance, I gather."

"She found a man murdered," I said. "It shot her full of holes. Is she hard enough asleep so that I could go in and get a few things to take to the hotel?"

"Oh, yes. If you're quiet. She probably won't wake. If she does, it won't matter."

I went over and put some money on the desk. "There's coffee and bacon and eggs and bread and tomato juice and oranges and liquor here," I said. "Anything else you'll have to phone for."

"I've already investigated your supplies," she said, smiling. "We have all we need until after breakfast tomorrow. Is she going to stay here?"

"That's up to Dr. Moss. I think she'll be going home as soon as she is fit for it. Home being quite a long way off, in Wichita."

"I'm only a nurse," she said. "But I don't think there is anything the matter with her that a good night's sleep won't cure."

"A good night's sleep and a change of company," I said, but that didn't mean anything to Miss Lymington.

I went along the hallway and peeked into the bedroom. They had put a pair of my pajamas on her. She lay almost on her back with one arm outside the bedclothes. The sleeve of the pajama coat was turned up six inches or more. The small hand below the end of the sleeve was in a tight fist. Her face looked drawn and white and quite peaceful. I poked about in the closet and got a suitcase and put some junk in it. As I started back out I looked at Merle again. Her eyes opened and looked straight up at the ceiling. Then they moved just enough to see me and a faint little smile tugged at the corners of her lips.

"Hello." It was a weak spent little voice, a voice that knew its owner was in bed and had a nurse and everything.

"Hello."

I went around near her and stood looking down, with my polished smile on my clear-cut features.

"I'm all right," she whispered. "I'm fine. Amn't I?"

"Sure."

"Is this your bed I'm in?"

"That's all right. It won't bite you."

"I'm not afraid," she said. A hand came sliding towards me and lay palm up, waiting to be held. I held it. "I'm not afraid of you. No woman would ever be afraid of you, would she?"

"Coming from you," I said, "I guess that's meant to be a compliment."

Her eyes smiled, then got grave again. "I lied to you," she said softly. "I—I didn't shoot anybody."

"I know. I was over there. Forget it. Don't think about it."

"People are always telling you to forget unpleasant things. But you never do. It's so kind of silly to tell you to, I mean."

"Okay," I said, pretending to be hurt. "I'm silly. How about making some more sleep?"

She turned her head until she was looking into my eyes. I sat on the edge of the bed, holding her hand.

"Will the police come here?" she asked.

"No. And try not to be disappointed."

She frowned. "You must think I'm an awful fool."

"Well—maybe."

A couple of tears formed in her eyes and slid out at the corners and rolled gently down her cheeks.

"Does Mrs. Murdock know where I am?"

"Not yet. I'm going over and tell her."

"Will you have to tell her—everything?"

"Yeah, why not?"

She turned the head away from me. "She'll understand," her voice said softly. "She knows the awful thing I did eight years ago. The frightful terrible thing."

"Sure," I said. "That's why she's been paying Vannier money all this time."

"Oh dear," she said, and brought her other hand out from under the bedclothes and pulled away the one I was holding so that she could squeeze them tightly together. "I wish you hadn't had to know that. I wish you hadn't. Nobody ever knew but Mrs. Murdock. My parents never knew. I wish you hadn't."

The nurse came in at the door and looked at me severely.

"I don't think she ought to be talking like this, Mr. Marlowe. I think you should leave now."

"Look, Miss Lymington, I've known this little girl two days. You've only known her two hours. This is doing her a lot of good."

"It might bring on another—er—spasm," she said severely, avoiding my eyes.

"Well, if she has to have it, isn't it better for her to have it now, while you're here, and get it over with? Go on out to the kitchen and buy yourself a drink."

"I never drink on duty," she said coldly. "Besides somebody might smell my breath."

"You're working for me now. All my employees are required to get liquored up from time to time. Besides, if you had a good dinner and were to eat a couple of the Chasers in the kitchen cabinet, nobody would smell your breath."

She gave me a quick grin and went back out of the room. Merle had been listening to this as if it was a frivolous interruption to a very serious play. Rather annoyed.

"I want to tell you all about it," she said breathlessly. "I—"

I reached over and put a paw over her two locked hands. "Skip it. I know. Marlowe knows everything—except how to make a decent living. It doesn't amount to beans. Now you're going back to sleep and tomorrow I'm going to take you on the way back to Wichita—to visit your parents. At Mrs. Murdock's expense."

"Why, that's wonderful of her," she cried, her eyes opening wide and shining. "But she's always been wonderful to me."

I got up off the bed. "She's a wonderful woman," I said, grinning down at her. "Wonderful. I'm going over there now and we're going to have a perfectly lovely little talk over the teacups. And if you don't go to sleep right now, I won't let you confess to any more murders."

"You're horrid," she said. "I don't like you." She turned her head away and put her arms back under the bedclothes and shut her eyes.

I went towards the door. At the door I swung around and looked back quickly. She had one eye open, watching me. I gave her a leer and it snapped shut in a hurry.

I went back to the living room, gave Miss Lymington what was left of my leer, and went out with my suitcase.

I drove over to Santa Monica Boulevard. The hockshop was still open. The old Jew in the tall black skullcap seemed surprised that I was able to redeem my pledge so soon. I told him that was the way it was in Hollywood.

He got the envelope out of the safe and tore it open and took my money and pawnticket and slipped the shining gold coin out on his palm.

"So valuable this is I am hating to give it back to you," he said. "The workmanship, you understand, the workmanship, is beautiful."

"And the gold in it must be worth all of twenty dollars," I said.

He shrugged and smiled and I put the coin in my pocket and said goodnight to him.

32

The moonlight lay like a white sheet on the front lawn except under the deodar where there was the thick darkness of black velvet. Lights in two lower windows were lit and in one upstairs room visible from the front. I walked across the stumble stones and rang the bell.

I didn't look at the little painted Negro by the hitching block. I didn't pat his head tonight. The joke seemed to have worn thin.

A white-haired, red-faced woman I hadn't seen before

opened the door and I said: "I'm Philip Marlowe. I'd like to see Mrs. Murdock. Mrs. Elizabeth Murdock."

She looked doubtful. "I think she's gone to bed," she said. "I don't think you can see her."

"It's only nine o'clock."

"Mrs. Murdock goes to bed early." She started to close the door.

She was a nice old thing and I hated to give the door the heavy shoulder. I just leaned against it.

"It's about Miss Davis," I said. "It's important. Could you tell her that?"

"I'll see."

I stepped back and let her shut the door.

A mockingbird sang in a dark tree nearby. A car tore down the street much too fast and skidded around the next corner. The thin shreds of a girl's laughter came back along the dark street as if the car had spilled them out in its rush.

The door opened after a while and the woman said: "You can come in."

I followed her across the big empty entrance room. A single dim light burned in one lamp, hardly reaching to the opposite wall. The place was too still, and the air needed freshening. We went along the hall to the end and up a flight of stairs with a carved handrail and newel post. Another hall at the top, a door open towards the back.

I was shown in at the open door and the door was closed behind me. It was a big sitting room with a lot of chintz, a blue and silver wallpaper, a couch, a blue carpet and french windows open on a balcony. There was an awning over the balcony.

Mrs. Murdock was sitting in a padded wing chair with a card table in front of her. She was wearing a quilted robe and her hair looked a little fluffed out. She was playing soli-taire. She had the pack in her left hand and she put a card down and moved another one before she looked up at me.

Then she said: "Well?"

I went over by the card table and looked down at the game. It was Canfield.

"Merle's at my apartment," I said. "She threw an ing-bing."

Without looking up she said: "And just what is an ing-bing, Mr. Marlowe?"

She moved another card, then two more quickly.

"A case of the vapors, they used to call it," I said. "Ever catch yourself cheating at that game?"

"It's no fun if you cheat," she said gruffly. "And very little if you don't. What's this about Merle? She has never stayed out like this before. I was getting worried about her."

I pulled a slipper chair over and sat down across the table from her. It put me too low down. I got up and got a better chair and sat in that.

"No need to worry about her," I said. "I got a doctor and a nurse. She's asleep. She was over to see Vannier."

She laid the pack of cards down and folded her big gray hands on the edge of the table and looked at me solidly.

"Mr. Marlowe," she said, "you and I had better have something out. I made a mistake calling you in the first place. That was my dislike of being played for a sucker, as you would say, by a hardboiled little animal like Linda. But it would have been much better, if I had not raised the point at all. The loss of the doubloon would have been much easier to bear than you are. Even if I had never got it back."

"But you did get it back," I said.

She nodded. Her eyes stayed on my face. "Yes. I got it back. You heard how."

"I didn't believe it."

"Neither did I," she said calmly. "My fool of a son was simply taking the blame for Linda. An attitude I find childish."

"You have a sort of knack," I said, "of getting yourselves surrounded with people who take such attitudes."

She picked her cards up again and reached down to put a black ten on a red jack, both cards that were already in the layout. Then she reached sideways to a small heavy table on which was her port. She drank some, put the glass down and gave me a hard level stare.

"I have a feeling that you are going to be insolent, Mr. Marlowe."

I shook my head. "Not insolent. Just frank. I haven't done so badly for you, Mrs. Murdock. You did get the doubloon back. I kept the police away from you—so far. I didn't do anything on the divorce, but I found Linda—your son knew where she was all the time—and I don't think you'll have any trouble with her. She knows she made a mistake marrying Leslie. However, if you don't think you got value—"

She made a humph noise and played another card. She got the ace of diamonds up to the top line. "The ace of clubs is buried, darn it. I'm not going to get it out in time."

"Kind of slide it out," I said, "when you're not looking."

"Hadn't you better," she said very quietly, "get on with telling me about Merle? And don't gloat too much, if you have found out a few family secrets, Mr. Marlowe."

"I'm not gloating about anything. You sent Merle to Vannier's place this afternoon, with five hundred dollars."

"And if I did?" She poured some of her port and sipped, eyeing me steadily over the glass.

"When did he ask for it?"

"Yesterday. I couldn't get it out of the bank until today. What happened?"

"Vannier's been blackmailing you for about eight years, hasn't he? On account of something that happened on April 26th, 1933?"

A sort of panic twitched in the depths of her eyes, but very far back, very dim, and somehow as though it had been there for a long time and had just peeped out at me for a second.

"Merle told me a few things," I said. "Your son told me how his father died. I looked up the records and the papers today. Accidental death. There had been an accident in the street under his office and a lot of people were craning out of windows. He just craned out too far. There was some talk of suicide because he was broke and had fifty thousand life insurance for his family. But the coroner was nice and slid past that."

"Well?" she said. It was a cold hard voice, neither a croak nor a gasp. A cold hard utterly composed voice.

"Merle was Horace Bright's secretary. A queer little girl in a way, overtimid, not sophisticated, a little girl mentality, likes to dramatize herself, very old-fashioned ideas about men, all that sort of thing. I figure he got high one time and made a pass at her and scared her out of her socks."

"Yes?" Another cold hard monosyllable prodding me like a gun barrel.

"She brooded and got a little murderous inside. She got a chance and passed right back at him. While he was leaning out of a window. Anything in it?"

"Speak plainly, Mr. Marlowe. I can stand plain talk."

"Good grief, how plain do you want it? She pushed her employer out of a window. Murdered him, in two words. And got away with it. With your help."

She looked down at the left hand clenched over her cards. She nodded. Her chin moved a short inch, down, up.

"Did Vannier have any evidence?" I asked. "Or did he just happen to see what happened and put the bite on you and you paid him a little now and then to avoid scandal—and because you were really very fond of Merle?"

She played another card before she answered me. Steady as a rock.

"He talked about a photograph," she said. "But I never believed it. He couldn't have taken one. And if he had taken one, he would have shown it to me—sooner or later."

I said: "No, I don't think so. It would have been a very fluky shot, even if he happened to have the camera in his hand, on account of the doings down below in the street. But I can see he might not have dared to show it. You're a pretty hard woman, in some ways. He might have been afraid you would have him taken care of. I mean that's how it might look to him, a crook. How much have you paid him?"

"That's none—" she started to say, then stopped and shrugged her big shoulders. A powerful woman, strong, rugged, ruthless and able to take it. She thought. "Eleven thousand one hundred dollars, not counting the five hundred I sent him this afternoon."

"Ah. It was pretty darn nice of you, Mrs. Murdock. Considering everything."

She moved a hand vaguely, made another shrug. "It was my husband's fault," she said. "He was drunk, vile. I don't think he really hurt her, but, as you say, he frightened her out of her wits. I—I can't blame her too much. She has blamed herself enough all these years."

"She had to take the money to Vannier in person?"

"That was her idea of penance. A strange penance."

I nodded. "I guess that would be in character. Later you married Jasper Murdock and you kept Merle with you and took care of her. Anybody else know?"

"Nobody. Only Vannier. Surely he wouldn't tell anybody."

"No. I hardly think so. Well, it's all over now. Vannier is through."

She lifted her eyes slowly and gave me a long level gaze. Her gray head was a rock on top of a hill. She put the cards down at last and clasped her hands tightly on the edge of the table. The knuckles glistened.

I said: "Merle came to my apartment when I was out. She asked the manager to let her in. He phoned me and I said yes. I got over there quickly. She told me she had shot Vannier."

Her breath was a faint swift whisper in the stillness of the room.

"She had a gun in her bag, God knows why. Some idea of protecting herself against men, I suppose. But somebody—Leslie, I should guess—had fixed it to be harmless by jamming a wrong size cartridge in the breech. She told me she had killed Vannier and fainted. I got a doctor friend of mine. I went over to Vannier's house. There was a key in the door. He was dead in a chair, long dead, cold, stiff. Dead long before Merle went there. She didn't shoot him. Her telling me that was just drama. The doctor explained it after a fashion, but I won't bore you with it. I guess you understand all right."

She said: "Yes. I think I understand. And now?"

"She's in bed, in my apartment. There's a nurse there. I phoned Merle's father long distance. He wants her to come home. That all right with you?"

She just stared.

"He doesn't know anything," I said quickly. "Not this or the other time. I'm sure of that. He just wants her to come home. I thought I'd take her. It seems to be my responsibility now. I'll need that last five hundred that Vannier didn't get—for expenses."

"And how much more?" she asked brutally.

"Don't say that. You know better."

"Who killed Vannier?"

"Looks like he committed suicide. A gun at his right hand. Temple contact wound. Morny and his wife were there while I was. I hid. Morny's trying to pin it on his wife. She was playing games with Vannier. So she probably thinks he did it, or had it done. But it shapes up like suicide. The cops will be there by now. I don't know what they will make of it. We just have to sit tight and wait it out."

"Men like Vannier," she said grimly, "don't commit suicide."

"That's like saying girls like Merle don't push people out of windows. It doesn't mean anything."

We stared at each other, with that inner hostility that had been there from the first. After a moment I pushed my chair back and went over to the french windows. I opened the screen and stepped out on to the porch. The night was all around, soft and quiet. The white moonlight was cold and clear, like the justice we dream of but don't find.

The trees down below cast heavy shadows under the moon. In the middle of the garden there was a sort of garden within a garden. I caught the glint of an ornamental pool. A lawn swing beside it. Somebody was lying in the lawn swing and a cigarette tip glowed as I looked down.

I went back into the room. Mrs. Murdock was playing solitaire again. I went over to the table and looked down.

"You got the ace of clubs out," I said.

"I cheated," she said without looking up.

"There was one thing I wanted to ask you," I said. "This doubloon business is still cloudy, on account of a couple of murders which don't seem to make sense now that you have the coin back. What I wondered was if there was anything about the Murdock Brasher that might identify it to an expert—to a man like old Morningstar."

She thought, sitting still, not looking up. "Yes. There might be. The coinmaker's initials, E. B., are on the left wing of the eagle. Usually, I'm told, they are on the right wing. That's the only thing I can think of."

I said: "I think that might be enough. You did actually get the coin back, didn't you? I mean that wasn't just something said to stop my ferreting around?"

She looked up swiftly and then down. "It's in the strong room at this moment. If you can find my son, he will show it to you."

"Well, I'll say good night. Please have Merle's clothes packed and sent to my apartment in the morning."

Her head snapped up again and her eyes glared. "You're pretty highhanded about all this, young man."

"Have them packed," I said. "And send them. You don't need Merle any more—now that Vannier is dead."

Our eyes locked hard and held locked for a long moment. A queer stiff smile moved the corners of her lips. Then her head went down and her right hand took the top card off the pack held in her left hand and turned it and her eyes looked at it and she added it to the pile of unplayed cards below the layout, and then turned the next card, quietly, calmly, in a hand as steady as a stone pier in a light breeze.

I went across the room and out, closed the door softly, went along the hall, down the stairs, along the lower hall past the sun room and Merle's little office, and out into the cheerless stuffy unused living room that made me feel like an embalmed corpse just to be in it.

The french doors at the back opened and Leslie Murdock stepped in and stopped, staring at me.

33

His slack suit was rumpled and also his hair. His little reddish mustache looked just as ineffectual as ever. The shadows under his eyes were almost pits.

He was carrying his long black cigarette holder, empty, and tapping it against the heel of his left hand as he stood not liking me, not wanting to meet me, not wanting to talk to me.

"Good evening," he said stiffly. "Leaving?"

"Not quite yet. I want to talk to you."

"I don't think we have anything to talk about. And I'm tired of talking."

"Oh yes we have. A man named Vannier."

"Vannier? I hardly know the man. I've seen him around. What I know I don't like."

"You know him a little better than that," I said.

He came forward into the room and sat down in one of the I-dare-you-to-sit-in-me chairs and leaned forward to cup his chin in his left hand and look at the floor.

"All right," he said wearily. "Get on with it. I have a feeling you are going to be very brilliant. Remorseless flow of logic and intuition and all that rot. Just like a detective in a book."

"Sure. Taking the evidence piece by piece, putting it all together in a neat pattern, sneaking in an odd bit I had on my hip here and there, analyzing the motives and characters and making them out to be quite different from what anybody—or I myself for that matter—thought them to be up to this golden moment—and finally making a sort of world-weary pounce on the least promising suspect."

He lifted his eyes and almost smiled. "Who thereupon turns as pale as paper, froths at the mouth, and pulls a gun out of his right ear."

I sat down near him and got a cigarette out. "That's right. We ought to play it together sometime. You got a gun?"

"Not with me. I have one. You know that."

"Have it with you last night when you called on Vannier?"

He shrugged and bared his teeth. "Oh. Did I call on Vannier last night?"

"I think so. Deduction. You smoke Benson and Hedges Virginia cigarettes. They leave a firm ash that keeps its shape. An ashtray at his house had enough of those little gray rolls to account for at least two cigarettes. But no stubs in the tray. Because you smoke them in a holder and a stub from a holder looks different. So you removed the stubs. Like it?"

"No." His voice was quiet. He looked down at the floor again.

"That's an example of deduction. A bad one. For there might not have been any stubs, but if there had been and they had been removed, it might have been because they had lipstick on them. Of a certain shade that would at least indicate the coloring of the smoker. And your wife has a quaint habit of throwing her stubs into the waste basket."

"Leave Linda out of this," he said coldly.

"Your mother still thinks Linda took the doubloon and that your story about taking it to give to Alex Morny was just a cover-up to protect her."

"I said leave Linda out of it." The tapping of the black holder against his teeth had a sharp quick sound, like a telegraph key.

"I'm willing to," I said. "But I didn't believe your story for a different reason. This." I took the doubloon out and held it on my hand under his eyes.

He stared at it tightly. His mouth set.

"This morning when you were telling your story this was hocked on Santa Monica Boulevard for safekeeping. It was sent to me by a would-be detective named George Phillips. A simple sort of fellow who allowed himself to get into a bad spot through poor judgment and over-eagerness for a job. A thickset blond fellow in a brown suit, wearing dark glasses and a rather gay hat. Driving a sand-colored Pontiac, almost new. You might have seen him hanging about in the hall outside my office yesterday morning. He had been following me around and before that he might have been following you around."

He looked genuinely surprised. "Why would he do that?"

I lit my cigarette and dropped the match in a jade ashtray that looked as if it had never been used as an ashtray.

"I said he might have. I'm not sure he did. He might have just been watching this house. He picked me up here and I don't think he followed me here." I still had the coin on my hand. I looked down at it, turned it over by tossing it, looked at the initials E. B. stamped into the left wing, and put it away. "He might have been watching the house because he had been hired to peddle a rare coin to an old coin dealer named Morningstar. And the old coin dealer somehow suspected where the coin came from, and told Phillips, or hinted to him, and that the coin was stolen. Incidentally, he was wrong about that. If your Brasher Doubloon is really at this moment upstairs, then the coin Phillips was hired to peddle was not a stolen coin. It was a counterfeit."

His shoulders gave a quick little jerk, as if he was cold. Otherwise he didn't move or change position.

"I'm afraid it's getting to be one of those long stories after all," I said, rather gently. "I'm sorry. I'd better organize it a little better. It's not a pretty story, because it has two murders in it, maybe three. A man named Vannier and a man named Teager had an idea. Teager is a dental technician in the Belfont Building, old Morningstar's building. The idea was to counterfeit a rare and valuable gold coin, not too rare to be marketable, but rare enough to be worth a lot of money. The method they thought of was about what a dental technician uses to make a gold inlay. Requiring the same materials, the same apparatus, the same skills. That is, to reproduce a model exactly, in gold, by making a matrix in a hard white fine cement called albastone, then making a replica of the model in that matrix in molding wax, complete in the finest detail, then investing the wax, as they call it, in another kind of cement called crystobolite, which has the property of standing great heat without distortion. A small opening is left from the wax to outside by attaching a steel pin which is withdrawn when the cement sets. Then the crystobolite casting is cooked over a flame until the wax boils out through this small opening, leaving a hollow mold of the original model. This is clamped against a crucible on a centrifuge and molten gold is shot into it by centrifugal force from the crucible. Then the crystobolite, still hot, is held under cold water and it disintegrates, leaving the gold core with a gold pin attached, representing the small opening. That is trimmed off, the casting is cleaned in acid and polished and you have, in this case, a brand new Brasher Doubloon, made of solid gold and exactly the same as the original. You get the idea?"

He nodded and moved a hand wearily across his head.

"The amount of skill this would take," I went on, "would be just what a dental technician would have. The process would be of no use for a current coinage, if we had a gold coinage, because the material and labor would cost more than the coin would be worth. But for a gold coin that was valuable through being rare, it would fit fine. So that's what they did. But they had to have a model. That's where you came in. You took the doubloon all right, but not to give to Morny. You took it to give to Vannier. Right?"

He stared at the floor and didn't speak.

"Loosen up," I said. "In the circumstances it's nothing very awful. I suppose he promised you money, because you needed it to pay off gambling debts and your mother is close. But he had a stronger hold over you than that."

He looked up quickly then, his face very white, a kind of horror in his eyes.

"How did you know that?" he almost whispered.

"I found out. Some I was told, some I researched, some I guessed. I'll get to that later. Now Vannier and his pal have made a doubloon and they want to try it out. They wanted to know their merchandise would stand up under inspection by a man supposed to know rare coins. So Vannier had the idea of hiring a sucker and getting him to try to sell the counterfeit to old Morningstar, cheap enough so the old guy would think it was stolen. They picked George Phillips for their sucker, through a silly ad he was running in the paper for business. I think Lois Morny was Vannier's contact with Phillips, at first anyway. I don't think she was in the racket. She was seen to give Phillips a small package. This package may have contained the doubloon Phillips was to try to sell. But when he showed it to old Morningstar he ran into a snag. The old man knew his coin collections and his rare coins. He probably thought the coin was genuine enough—it would take a lot of testing to show it wasn't—but the way the maker's initials were stamped on the coin was unusual and suggested to him that the coin might be the Murdock Brasher. He called up here and tried to find out. That made your mother suspicious and the coin was found to be missing and she suspected Linda, whom she hates, and hired me to get it back and put the squeeze on Linda for a divorce, without alimony."

"I don't want a divorce," Murdock said hotly. "I never had any such idea. She had no right—" he stopped and made a despairing gesture and a kind of sobbing sound.

"Okay, I know that. Well, old Morningstar threw a scare into Phillips, who wasn't crooked, just dumb. He managed to get Phillips' phone number out of him. I heard the old man call that number, eavesdropping in his office after he thought I had left. I had just offered to buy the doubloon back for a thousand dollars and Morningstar had taken up the offer, thinking he could get the coin from Phillips, make himself some money and everything lovely. Meantime Phillips was watching this house, perhaps to see if any cops were coming and going. He saw me, saw my car, got my name off the registration and it just happened he knew who I was.

"He followed me around trying to make up his mind to ask me for help until I braced him in a downtown hotel and he mumbled about knowing me from a case in Ventura when he was a deputy up there, and about being in a spot he didn't like and about being followed around by a tall guy with a funny eye. That was Eddie Prue, Morny's sidewinder. Morny knew his wife was playing games with Vannier and had her shadowed. Prue saw her make contact with Phillips near where he lived on Court Street, Bunker Hill, and then followed Phillips until he thought Phillips had spotted him, which he had. And Prue, or somebody working for Morny, may have seen me go to Phillips' apartment on Court Street. Because he tried to scare me over the phone and later asked me to come and see Morny."

I got rid of my cigarette stub in the jade ashtray, looked at the bleak unhappy face of the man sitting opposite me, and plowed on. It was heavy going, and the sound of my voice was beginning to sicken me.

"Now we come back to you. When Merle told you your mother had hired a dick, that threw a scare into *you*. You figured she had missed the doubloon and you came steaming up to my office and tried to pump me. Very debonair, very sarcastic at first, very solicitous for your wife, but very worried. I don't know what you think you found out, but you got in touch with Vannier. You now had to get the coin back to your mother in a hurry, with some kind of story. You met Vannier somewhere and he gave you a doubloon. Chances are it's another counterfeit. He would be likely to hang on to the real one. Now Vannier sees his racket in danger of blowing up before it gets started. Morningstar has called your mother and I have been hired. Morningstar has spotted something. Vannier goes down to Phillips' apartment, sneaks in the back way, and has it out with Phillips, trying to find out where he stands.

"Phillips doesn't tell him he has already sent the counterfeit doubloon to me, addressing it in a kind of printing afterwards found in a diary in his office. I infer that from the fact Vannier didn't try to get it back from me. I don't know what Phillips told Vannier, of course, but the chances are he told him the job was crooked, that he knew where the coin came from, and that he was going to the police or to Mrs. Murdock. And Vannier pulled a gun, knocked him on the head and shot him. He searched him and the apartment and didn't find the doubloon. So he went to Morningstar. Morningstar didn't have the counterfeit doubloon either, but Vannier probably thought he had. He cracked the old man's skull with a gun butt and went through his safe, perhaps found some money, perhaps found nothing, at any rate left the appearance of a stickup behind him. Then Mr. Vannier breezed on home, still rather annoyed because he hadn't found the doubloon, but with the satisfaction of a good afternoon's work under his vest. A couple of nice neat murders. That left you."

34

Murdock flicked a strained look at me, then his eyes went to the black cigarette holder he still had clenched in his hand. He tucked it in his shirt pocket, stood up suddenly, ground the heels of his hands together and sat down again. He got a handkerchief out and mopped his face.

"Why me?" he asked in a thick strained voice.

"You knew too much. Perhaps you knew about Phillips, perhaps not. Depends how deep you were in it. But you knew about Morningstar. The scheme had gone wrong and Morningstar had been murdered. Vannier couldn't just sit back and hope you wouldn't hear about that. He had to shut your mouth, very, very tight. But he didn't have to kill you to do it. In fact killing you would be a bad move. It would break his hold on your mother. She's a cold ruthless grasping woman, but hurting you would make a wildcat of her. She wouldn't care what happened."

Murdock lifted his eyes. He tried to make them blank with astonishment. He only made them dull and shocked.

"My mother—what—?"

"Don't kid me any more than you have to," I said. "I'm tired to death of being kidded by the Murdock family. Merle came to my apartment this evening. She's there now. She had been over to Vannier's house to bring him some money. Blackmail money. Money that had been paid to him off and on for eight years. I know why."

He didn't move. His hands were rigid with strain on his knees. His eyes had almost disappeared into the back of his head. They were doomed eyes.

"Merle found Vannier dead. She came to me and said she had killed him. Let's not go into why she thinks she ought to confess to other people's murders. I went over there and he had been dead since last night. He was as stiff as a wax dummy. There was a gun lying on the floor by his right hand. It was a gun I had heard described, a gun that belonged to a man named Hench, in an apartment across the hall from Phillips' apartment. Somebody ditched the gun that killed Phillips and took Hench's gun. Hench and his girl were drunk and left their apartment open. It's not proved that it was Hench's gun, but it will be. If it is Hench's gun, and Vannier committed suicide, it ties Vannier to the death of Phillips. Lois Morny also ties him to Phillips, in another way. If Vannier didn't commit suicide—and I don't believe he did—it might still tie him to Phillips. Or it might tie some-body else to Phillips, somebody who also killed Vannier. There are reasons why I don't like that idea."

Murdock's head came up. He said: "No?" in a suddenly clear voice. There was a new expression on his face, some-thing bright and shining and at the same time just a little silly. The expression of a weak man being proud.

I said: "I think you killed Vannier."

He didn't move and the bright shining expression stayed on his face.

"You went over there last night. He sent for you. He told you he was in a jam and that if the law caught up with him, he would see that you were in the jam with him. Didn't he say something like that?"

"Yes," Murdock said quietly. "Something exactly like that. He was drunk and a bit high and he seemed to have a sense of power. He gloated, almost. He said if they got him in the gas chamber, I would be sitting right beside him. But that wasn't all he said."

"No. He didn't want to sit in the gas chamber and he didn't at the time see any very good reason why he should, if you kept your mouth good and tight. So he played his trump card. His first hold on you, what made you take the doubloon and give it to him, even if he did promise you money as well, was something about Merle and your father. I know about it. Your mother told me what little I hadn't put together already. That was his first hold and it was pretty strong. Because it would let you justify yourself. But last night he wanted something still stronger. So he told you the truth and said he had proof."

He shivered, but the light clear proud look managed to stay on his face.

"I pulled a gun on him," he said, almost in a happy voice. "After all she is my mother."

"Nobody can take that away from you."

He stood up, very straight, very tall. "I went over to the chair he sat in and reached down and put the gun against his face. He had a gun in the pocket of his robe. He tried to get it, but he didn't get it in time. I took it away from him. I put my gun back in my pocket. I put the muzzle of the other gun against the side of his head and told him I would kill him, if he didn't produce his proof and give it to me. He began to sweat and babble that he was just kidding me. I clicked back the hammer on the gun to scare him some more."

He stopped and held a hand out in front of him. The hand shook but as he stared down at it it got steady. He dropped it to his side and looked me in the eye.

"The gun must have been filed or had a very light action. It went off. I jumped back against the wall and knocked a picture down. I jumped from surprise that the gun went off, but it kept the blood off me. I wiped the gun off and put his fingers around it and then put it down on the floor close to his hand. He was dead at once. He hardly bled except the first spurt. It was an accident."

"Why spoil it?" I half sneered. "Why not make it a nice clean honest murder?"

"That's what happened. I can't prove it, of course. But I think I might have killed him anyway. What about the police?"

I stood up and shrugged my shoulders. I felt tired, spent, drawn out and sapped. My throat was sore from yapping and my brain ached from trying to keep my thoughts orderly.

"I don't know about the police," I said. "They and I are not very good friends, on account of they think I am holding out on them. And God knows they are right. They may get to you. If you weren't seen, if you didn't leave any fingerprints around, and even if you did, if they don't have any other reason to suspect you and get your fingerprints to check, then they may never think of you. If they find out about the doubloon and that it was the Murdock Brasher, I don't know where you stand. It all depends on how well you stand up to them."

"Except for mother's sake," he said, "I don't very much care. I've always been a flop."

"And on the other hand," I said, ignoring the feeble talk, "if the gun really has a very light action and you get a good lawyer and tell an honest story and so on, no jury will convict you. Juries don't like blackmailers."

"That's too bad," he said. "Because I am not in a position to use that defense. I don't know anything about blackmail. Vannier showed me where I could make some money, and I needed it badly."

I said: "Uh-huh. If they get you where you need the blackmail dope, you'll use it all right. Your old lady will make you. If it's her neck or yours, she'll spill."

"It's horrible," he said. "Horrible to say that."

"You were lucky about that gun. All the people we know have been playing with it, wiping prints off and putting them on. I even put a set on myself just to be fashionable. It's tricky when the hand is stiff. But I had to do it. Morny was over there having his wife put hers on. He thinks she killed Vannier, so she probably thinks he did."

He just stared at me. I chewed my lip. It felt as stiff as a piece of glass.

"Well, I guess I'll just be running along now," I said.

"You mean you are going to let me get away with it?" His voice was getting a little supercilious again.

"I'm not going to turn you in, if that's what you mean. Beyond that I guarantee nothing. If I'm involved in it, I'll have to face up to the situation. There's no question of morality involved. I'm not a cop nor a common informer nor an officer of the court. You say it was an accident. Okay, it was an accident. I wasn't a witness. I haven't any proof either way. I've been working for your mother and whatever right to my silence that gives her, she can have. I don't like her, I don't like you, I don't like this house. I didn't particularly like your wife. But I like Merle. She's kind of silly and morbid, but she's kind of sweet too. And I know what has been done to her in this damn family for the past eight years. And I know she didn't push anybody out of any window. Does that explain matters?"

He gobbled, but nothing came that was coherent.

"I'm taking Merle home," I said. "I asked your mother to send her clothes to my apartment in the morning. In case she kind of forgets, being busy with her solitaire game, would you see that that is done?"

He nodded dumbly. Then he said in a queer small voice: "You are going—just like that? I haven't—I haven't even thanked you. A man I hardly know, taking risks for me—I don't know what to say."

"I'm going the way I always go," I said. "With an airy smile and a quick flip of the wrist. And with a deep and heartfelt hope that I won't be seeing you in the fish bowl. Good night."

I turned my back on him and went to the door and out. I shut the door with a quiet firm click of the lock. A nice smooth exit, in spite of all the nastiness. For the last time I went over and patted the little painted Negro on the head and then walked across the long lawn by the moon-drenched shrubs and the deodar tree to the street and my car.

I drove back to Hollywood, bought a pint of good liquor, checked in at the Plaza, and sat on the side of the bed staring at my feet and lapping the whiskey out of the bottle.

Just like any common bedroom drunk.

When I had enough of it to make my brain fuzzy enough to stop thinking, I undressed and got into bed and after a while, but not soon enough, I went to sleep.

35

It was three o'clock in the afternoon and there were five pieces of luggage inside the apartment door, side by side on the carpet. There was my yellow cowhide, well scraped on both sides from being pushed around in the boots of cars. There were two nice pieces of airplane luggage both marked L.M. There was an old black imitation walrus thing marked M.D. and there was one of these little leatherette overnight cases which you can buy in drugstores for a dollar forty-nine.

Dr. Carl Moss had just gone out of the door cursing me because he had kept his afternoon class of hypochondriacs waiting. The sweetish smell of his Fatima poisoned the air for me. I was turning over in what was left of my mind what he had said when I asked him how long it would take Merle to get well.

"It depends what you mean by well. She'll always be high on nerves and low on animal emotion. She'll always breathe thin air and smell snow. She'd have made a perfect nun. The religious dream, with its narrowness, its stylized emotions and it grim purity, would have been a perfect release for her. As it is she will probably turn out to be one of these acid-faced virgins that sit behind little desks in public libraries and stamp dates in books."

"She's not that bad," I had said, but he had just grinned at me with his wise Jew face and gone out of the door. "And besides how do you know they are virgins?" I added to the closed door, but that didn't get me any farther.

I lit a cigarette and wandered over to the window and after a while she came through the doorway from the bedroom part of the apartment and stood there looking at me with her eyes dark-ringed and a pale composed little face without any makeup except on the lips.

"Put some rouge on your cheeks," I told her. "You look like the snow maiden after a hard night with the fishing fleet."

So she went back and put some rouge on her cheeks. When she came back again she looked at the luggage and said softly: "Leslie lent me two of his suitcases."

I said: "Yeah," and looked her over. She looked very nice.

She had a pair of long-waisted rust-colored slacks on, and Bata shoes and a brown and white print shirt and an orange scarf. She didn't have her glasses on. Her large clear cobalt eyes had a slightly dopey look, but not more than you would expect. Her hair was dragged down tight, but I couldn't do anything much about that.

"I've been a terrible nuisance," she said. "I'm terribly sorry."

"Nonsense. I talked to your father and mother both. They're tickled to death. They've only seen you twice in over eight years and they feel as if they had almost lost you."

"I'll love seeing them for a while," she said, looking down at the carpet. "It's very kind of Mrs. Murdock to let me go. She's never been able to spare me for long." She moved her legs as if she wondered what to do with them in slacks, although they were her slacks and she must have had to face the problem before. She finally put her knees close together and clasped her hands on top of them.

"Any little talking we might have to do," I said, "or anything you might want to say to me, let's get it over with now. Because I'm not driving halfway across the United States with a nervous breakdown in the seat beside me."

She bit a knuckle and sneaked a couple of quick looks at me around the side of the knuckle. "Last night—" she said, and stopped and colored.

"Let's use a little of the old acid," I said. "Last night you told me you killed Vannier and then you told me you didn't. I know you didn't. That's settled."

She dropped the knuckle, looked at me levelly, quiet, composed and the hands on her knees now not straining at all.

"Vannier was dead a long time before you got there. You went there to give him some money for Mrs. Murdock."

"No—for me," she said. "Although of course it was Mrs. Murdock's money. I owe her more than I'll ever be able to repay. Of course she doesn't give me much salary, but that would hardly—"

I said roughly: "Her not giving you much salary is a characteristic touch and your owing her more than you can ever repay is more truth than poetry. It would take the Yankee outfield with two bats each to give her what she has coming from you. However, that's unimportant now. Vannier committed suicide because he had got caught out in a crooked job. That's flat and final. The way you behaved was more or less an act. You got a severe nervous shock seeing his leering dead face in a mirror and that shock merged into another one a long time ago and you just dramatized it in your screwy little way."

She looked at me shyly and nodded her copper-blond head, as if in agreement.

"And you didn't push Horace Bright out of any window," I said.

Her face jumped then and turned startlingly pale. "I—I—" her hand went to her mouth and stayed there and her shocked eyes looked at me over it.

"I wouldn't be doing this," I said, "if Dr. Moss hadn't said it would be all right and we might as well hand it to you now. I think maybe you think you killed Horace Bright. You had a motive and an opportunity and just for a second I think you might have had the impulse to take advantage of the opportunity. But it wouldn't be in your nature. At the last minute you would hold back. But at that last minute probably something snapped and you pulled a faint. He did actually fall, of course, but you were not the one that pushed him."

I held it a moment and watched the hand drop down again to join the other one and the two of them twine together and pull hard on each other.

"You were made to think you had pushed him," I said. "It was done with care, deliberation and the sort of quiet ruthlessness you only find in a certain kind of woman dealing with another woman. You wouldn't think of jealousy to look at Mrs. Murdock now—but if that was a motive, she had it. She had a better one—fifty thousand dollars' life insurance—all that was left from a ruined fortune. She had the strange wild possessive love for her son such women have. She's cold, bitter, unscrupulous and she used you without mercy or pity, as insurance, in case Vannier ever blew his top. You were just a scapegoat to her. If you want to come out of this pallid sub-emotional life you have been living, you have got to realize and believe what I am telling you. I know it's tough."

"It's utterly impossible," she said quietly, looking at the

bridge of my nose, "Mrs. Murdock has been wonderful to me always. It's true I never remembered very well—but you shouldn't say such awful things about people."

I got out the white envelope that had been in the back of Vannier's picture. Two prints in it and a negative. I stood in front of her and put a print on her lap.

"Okay, look at it. Vannier took it from across the street."

She looked at it. "Why that's Mr. Bright," she said. "It's not a very good picture, is it? And that's Mrs. Murdock—Mrs. Bright she was then—right behind him. Mr. Bright looks mad." She looked up at me with a sort of mild curiosity.

"If he looks mad there," I said, "you ought to have seen him a few seconds later, when he bounced."

"When he what?"

"Look," I said, and there was a kind of desperation in my voice now, "that is a snapshot of Mrs. Elizabeth Bright Murdock giving her first husband the heave out of his office window. He's falling. Look at the position of his hands. He's screaming with fear. She is behind him and her face is hard with rage—or something. Don't you get it at all? This is what Vannier has had for proof all these years. The Murdocks never saw it, never really believed it existed. But it did. I found it last night, by a fluke of the same sort that was involved in the taking of the picture. Which is a fair sort of justice. Do you begin to understand?"

She looked at the photo again and laid it aside. "Mrs. Murdock has always been lovely to me," she said.

"She made you the goat," I said, in the quietly strained voice of a stage manager at a bad rehearsal. "She's a smart tough patient woman. She knows her complexes. She'll even spend a dollar to keep a dollar, which is what few of her type will do. I hand it to her. I'd like to hand it to her with an elephant gun, but my polite breeding restrains me."

"Well," she said, "that's that." And I could see she had heard one word in three and hadn't believed what she had heard. "You must never show this to Mrs. Murdock. It would upset her terribly."

I got up and took the photo out of her hand and tore it into small pieces and dropped them in the wastebasket.

"Maybe you'll be sorry I did that," I told her, not telling

her I had another and the negative. "Maybe some night—three months—three years from now—you will wake up in the night and realize I have been telling you the truth. And maybe then you will wish you could look at that photograph again. And maybe I am wrong about this too. Maybe you would be very disappointed to find out you hadn't really killed anybody. That's fine. Either way it's fine. Now we are going downstairs and get in my car and we are going to drive to Wichita to visit your parents. And I don't think you are going back to Mrs. Murdock, but it may well be that I am wrong about that too. But we are not going to talk about this any more. Not any more."

"I haven't any money," she said.

"You have five hundred dollars that Mrs. Murdock sent you. I have it in my pocket."

"That's really awfully kind of her," she said.

"Oh hell and fireflies," I said and went out to the kitchen and gobbled a quick drink, before we started. It didn't do me any good. It just made me want to climb up the wall and gnaw my way across the ceiling.

36

I was gone ten days. Merle's parents were vague kind patient people living in an old frame house in a quiet shady street. They cried when I told them as much of the story as I thought they should know. They said they were glad to have her back and they would take good care of her and they blamed themselves a lot, and I let them do it.

When I left Merle was wearing a bungalow apron and rolling pie crust. She came to the door wiping her hands on the apron and kissed me on the mouth and began to cry and ran back into the house, leaving the doorway empty until her mother came into the space with a broad homey smile on her face to watch me drive away.

I had a funny feeling as I saw the house disappear, as

though I had written a poem and it was very good and I had lost it and would never remember it again.

I called Lieutenant Breeze when I got back and went down to ask him how the Phillips case was coming. They had cracked it very neatly, with the right mixture of brains and luck you always have to have. The Mornys never went to the police after all, but somebody called and told about a shot in Vannier's house and hung up quickly. The fingerprint man didn't like the prints on the gun too well, so they checked Vannier's hand for powder nitrates. When they found them they decided it was suicide after all. Then a dick named Lackey working out of Central Homicide thought to work on the gun a little and he found that a description of it had been distributed, and a gun like it was wanted in connection with the Phillips killing. Hench identified it, but better than that they found a half print of his thumb on the side of the trigger, which, not ordinarily being pulled back, had not been wiped off completely.

With that much in hand and a better set of Vannier's prints than I could make they went over Phillips' apartment again and also over Hench's. They found Vannier's left hand on Hench's bed and one of his fingers on the underside of the toilet flush lever in Phillips' place. Then they got to work in the neighborhood with photographs of Vannier and proved he had been along the alley twice and on a side street at least three times. Curiously, nobody in the apartment house had seen him, or would admit it.

All they lacked now was a motive. Teager obligingly gave them that by getting himself pinched in Salt Lake City trying to peddle a Brasher Doubloon to a coin dealer who thought it was genuine but stolen. He had a dozen of them at his hotel, and one of them turned out to be genuine. He told them the whole story and showed a minute mark that he had used to identify the genuine coin. He didn't know where Vannier got it and they never found out because there was enough in the papers to make the owner come forward, if it had been stolen. And the owner never did. And the police didn't care any more about Vannier once they were convinced he had done murder. They left it at suicide, although they had a few doubts.

They let Teager go after a while, because they didn't think he had any idea of murder being done and all they had on him was attempted fraud. He had bought the gold legally and counterfeiting an obsolete New York State coin didn't come under the federal counterfeiting laws. Utah refused to bother with him.

They never believed Hench's confession. Breeze said he just used it for a squeeze on me, in case I was holding out. He knew I couldn't keep quiet if I had proof that Hench was innocent. It didn't do Hench any good either. They put him in the lineup and pinned five liquor store holdups on him and a wop named Gaetano Prisco, in one of which a man was shot dead. I never heard whether Prisco was a relative of Palermo's, but they never caught him anyway.

"Like it?" Breeze asked me, when he had told me all this, or all that had then happened.

"Two points not clear," I said. "Why did Teager run away and why did Phillips live on Court Street under a phony name?"

"Teager ran away because the elevator man told him old Morningstar had been murdered and he smelled a hookup. Phillips was using the name of Anson because the finance company was after his car and he was practically broke and getting desperate. That explains why a nice young boob like him could get roped in to something that must have looked shady from the start."

I nodded and agreed that could be so.

Breeze walked to his door with me. He put a hard hand on my shoulder and squeezed.

"Remember that Cassidy case you were howling about to Spangler and me that night in your apartment?"

"Yes."

"You told Spangler there wasn't any Cassidy case. There was—under another name. I worked on it."

He took his hand off my shoulder and opened the door for me and grinned straight into my eyes.

"On account of the Cassidy case," he said, "and the way it made me feel, I sometimes give a guy a break he could perhaps not really deserve. A little something paid back out of the dirty millions to a working stiff—like me—or like you. Be good."

It was night. I went home and put my old house clothes on and set the chessmen out and mixed a drink and played over another Capablanca. It went fifty-nine moves. Beautiful cold remorseless chess, almost creepy in its silent implacability.

When it was done I listened at the open window for a while and smelled the night. Then I carried my glass out to the kitchen and rinsed it and filled it with ice water and stood at the sink sipping it and looking at my face in the mirror.

"You and Capablanca," I said.

CHRONOLOGY

NOTE ON THE TEXTS

NOTES

Chronology

1888   Born Raymond Thornton Chandler on July 23 in Chicago, only child of Florence Dart Thornton Chandler and Maurice Benjamin Chandler. (Mother was immigrant from Waterford, Ireland, to Nebraska. Father, born in Philadelphia in 1859, studied engineering at the University of Pennsylvania before moving to Nebraska to work for a railroad company. Parents were married in Laramie, Wyoming, in July 1887.)

1889–94   Father drinks heavily and is often absent. Chandler spends summers with mother in Plattsmouth, Nebraska, as guests of aunt Grace Thornton Fitt and her family. Parents eventually divorce. Father disappears and provides no support.

1895–99   Moves to England with mother in 1895. Lives with mother, grandmother Annie Thornton, and aunt Ethel Thornton in Upper Norwood, suburb south of London (later recalls that he and his mother were treated coldly by his grandmother and aunt). Spends summers in Waterford, Ireland, with uncle Ernest Thornton. Attends Church of England and goes to local school.

1900   Household moves to nearby Dulwich. Chandler enters Dulwich College as day student. Studies mathematics, music, Latin, French, divinity, and English history.

1901–2   Plays rugby and cricket. Studies French, German, and Spanish in preparation for career in business. Ranks at top of his form and wins prizes for general achievement and mathematics.

1903–4   Resumes study of classics, reading Virgil, Cicero, Caesar, Livy, and Ovid in Latin and Thucydides, Plato, Aristophanes, and the Gospel of St. Mark in Greek.

1905–6   Leaves Dulwich in April 1905 when family decides to send him abroad for further study in foreign languages. Studies commercial French at business college in Paris, then goes to Munich and studies German with a tutor. Visits Nuremberg and Vienna.

1907–8 Returns to England and lives with mother in Streatham in southwest London, where she had moved following death of her mother. Becomes naturalized British subject on May 20, 1907, in order to qualify for civil service examination. Takes examination in June 1907 and places third among six hundred candidates. Works as clerk in naval supplies office of the Admiralty. Resigns after six months.

1909–11 Works briefly as journalist for the *Daily Express,* then joins staff of the *Westminster Gazette.* Writes articles on European affairs and contributes sketches and poems. Lives with mother in Forest Hill in southeast London. Begins contributing literary essays to *The Academy* in 1911.

1912 Borrows £500 from uncle Ernest Thornton and returns to America. Becomes friends with Warren Lloyd, a Los Angeles attorney, during Atlantic crossing. Stays with aunt Grace Thornton Fitt in Nebraska before settling in Los Angeles. Works on apricot ranch and strings tennis racquets for sporting goods store. Lives in furnished rooms.

1913–14 Studies bookkeeping. Obtains job as accountant and bookkeeper for the Los Angeles Creamery with help of Warren Lloyd. Spends time with the Lloyd family and their friends, who are interested in literature, music, psychology, and the occult. Meets pianist and composer Julian Pascal and his wife Cecilia (Cissy), also a pianist, through Lloyd.

1915–16 Lives at 311 Loma Drive near Pershing Square with his mother, who has returned to America.

1917 Goes to Victoria, British Columbia, in August and enlists in the Canadian Army. Sails for England in November after three months of training.

1918 Assigned on March 18 to 7th Battalion, 2nd Infantry Brigade, 1st Canadian Division, and is sent to France. Serves in trenches in Lens-Arras sector (later writes: "Once you have had to lead a platoon into direct machine-gun fire, nothing is ever the same again"). Returned to England with rank of acting sergeant after receiving concussion during German artillery bombardment. Transfers in July to Royal Air Force and is in training school when war ends on November 11.

1919   Returns to Vancouver and is discharged from military service on February 20. Takes job in San Francisco office of an English bank. Returns to Los Angeles and works for the *Daily Express* for six weeks. Begins love affair with Cissy Pascal (born Pearl Eugenie Hurlburt in Perry, Ohio, in 1870). Cissy files for divorce from Julian Pascal in July.

1920–23   Settles with mother in Redondo Beach (later moves with her to Santa Monica), while Cissy lives in Hermosa Beach. Pascal divorce becomes final in October 1920, but Chandler delays marriage with Cissy because of his mother's disapproval of the difference in their ages. Begins working as bookkeeper for Dabney Oil Syndicate, company owned by Joseph Dabney and Ralph Lloyd, Warren Lloyd's brother.

1924   Mother dies of cancer in January. Chandler marries Cissy Pascal on February 6. Becomes auditor of Dabney Oil Syndicate (later South Basin Oil Company) and is soon promoted to vice-president in charge of Los Angeles office.

1925–31   Lives with Cissy in various apartments around Los Angeles, moving frequently. Enjoys playing tennis and attending college football games with friends. Becomes increasingly aware of his age difference with Cissy. Drinks heavily, behaves erratically (sometimes threatening suicide), and has affairs with younger women working in oil company office.

1932   Fired from South Basin Oil Company for drunkenness and absenteeism. Goes to Seattle and stays with army friends, then returns to Los Angeles when Cissy is hospitalized with pneumonia. After her recovery, they move to an apartment in Hollywood Hills. Chandler assists Edward Lloyd, son of Warren Lloyd, in lawsuit against South Basin Oil Company for misappropriation of revenues from Ventura Avenue oil fields once owned by Lloyd family. Receives allowance from Edward Lloyd of $100 a month, which allows him to devote himself to writing. Stops excessive drinking.

1933   Decides to write for pulp magazines. Spends five months
            writing first detective story, "Blackmailers Don't Shoot,"
            which is published in *Black Mask* in December. (Edited
            by Joseph T. Shaw, *Black Mask* is the leading pulp crime
            magazine; its contributors include Dashiell Hammett,
            Paul Cain, Carroll John Daly, Horace McCoy, Erle Stan-
            ley Gardner, Frederick Nebel, and Raoul Whitfield.)
            Chandler receives $180 for the story.

1934–37   Continues to write stories for pulp crime magazines. Pub-
            lishes ten stories in *Black Mask* (1934–37), seven in *Dime
            Detective* (1937–39) following Shaw's dismissal as editor
            of *Black Mask,* and one in *Detective Fiction Weekly* (1936).
            Chandler and Cissy move frequently (sometimes two or
            three times a year) throughout southern California, living
            in furnished apartments in Los Angeles, Riverside, La
            Jolla, Cathedral City, and Pacific Palisades, and sometimes
            renting a cabin at Big Bear Lake in the San Bernardino
            Mountains. (Later writes: "I never slept in the park but I
            came damn close to it. I went five days without anything
            to eat but soup once, and I had just been sick at that.")
            Socializes occasionally with other pulp writers, including
            Erle Stanley Gardner, Cleve Adams, Norbert Davis, and
            W. T. Ballard. Meets Dashiell Hammett at dinner for
            Black Mask contributors in January 1936 (their only
            encounter).

1938   Begins writing *The Big Sleep,* his first novel, in the spring.
            Makes private detective Philip Marlowe the protagonist
            and incorporates material from his previously published
            pulp stories "Killer in the Rain" and "The Curtain" (will
            employ the same method, which he calls "cannibalizing,"
            when writing *Farewell, My Lovely* and *The Lady in the
            Lake*).

1939   *The Big Sleep* published in the United States by Alfred A.
            Knopf in February and in Britain by Hamish Hamilton in
            March. Book receives good reviews and sells well. Chan-
            dler begins writing novel that becomes *The Lady in the
            Lake,* then puts it aside and begins work on another
            novel, which becomes *Farewell, My Lovely.* Meets Alfred
            and Blanche Knopf when they visit California in May.
            After outbreak of World War II in September, Chandler
            volunteers for officers' training in the Canadian Army but

is rejected because of his age. Crime story "I'll Be Waiting" is published in *The Saturday Evening Post* in October, and supernatural story "The Bronze Door" appears in *Unknown* in November.

1940   Finishes *Farewell, My Lovely* in late April. Novel is published in October by Knopf in the United States and Hamish Hamilton in Britain. Sales are disappointing. Works on *The High Window*.

1941   Continues to work on *The High Window* and *The Lady in the Lake*. "No Crime in the Mountains," the last of his stories for the pulps, published in *Detective Story Magazine* in September. Sells film rights to *Farewell, My Lovely* to RKO for $2,000 (film *The Falcon Takes Over*, with Philip Marlowe replaced by series character The Falcon, played by George Sanders, is released in 1942).

1942   Finishes *The High Window* in March. Sells film rights to Twentieth Century–Fox for $3,500 (film *Time to Kill*, with Philip Marlowe replaced by series character Michael Shayne, played by Lloyd Nolan, is released in 1943). Novel is published by Knopf in August (Hamish Hamilton publishes British edition in February 1943).

1943   Chandler is hired by Paramount to collaborate with director Billy Wilder on screen adaptation of James M. Cain's novella *Double Indemnity*. (Later describes collaboration as "an agonizing experience" in which he "learned . . . as much about screen writing as I am capable of learning, which is not much.") Earns $750 a week for 13 weeks' work on film. Resumes heavy drinking. Moves with Cissy into rented house at 6520 Drexel Avenue in Los Angeles. *The Lady in the Lake* is published by Knopf in November and sells well (Hamish Hamilton publishes British edition in October 1944).

1944   *Double Indemnity* is released in April. Film is a critical and popular success, and screenplay receives Academy Award nomination. Chandler works as contract writer at Paramount until September, sharing screen credit with Frank Partos for *And Now Tomorrow* (directed by Irving Pichel) and with Hager Wilde for *The Unseen* (directed by Lewis Allen and released in 1945). *Murder, My Sweet*, second film version of *Farewell, My Lovely,* directed by Edward Dmytryk and starring Dick Powell as Philip Marlowe, is released by RKO. Consulted during filming of *The Big Sleep* at Warner Brothers by director Howard Hawks. Publishes essay "The Simple Art of Murder" in December *Atlantic Monthly.*

1945   Begins writing original screenplay *The Blue Dahlia* for Paramount, which wants to make a film starring Alan Ladd before Ladd enters military service. Shooting begins before screenplay is finished; when Chandler falls seriously behind schedule, he proposes to producer John Houseman that he finish the script while drunk. Houseman agrees, and Chandler completes the screenplay in eight days, dictating to secretaries provided by the studio while receiving regular glucose injections from his doctor. (Film, directed by George Marshall, is released in 1946; Chandler receives Academy Award nomination and Edgar award from Mystery Writers of America for his screenplay.) Works for MGM on screenplay for *The Lady in the Lake,* directed by actor Robert Montgomery, who also plays Philip Marlowe. Leaves after disagreements with studio, and screenplay is completed by Steve Fisher with Chandler receiving no screen credit. Article "Writers in Hollywood" published in November *Atlantic Monthly.*

1946   Film version of *The Big Sleep* is released; Chandler is pleased by Humphrey Bogart's performance as Philip Marlowe ("so much better than any other tough-guy actor"). Works for Paramount on adaptation of novel *The Innocent Mrs. Duff* by Elisabeth Sanxay Holding, but ends relationship with studio before screenplay is completed. Angered by inclusion of story "The Man Who Liked Dogs," which he had "cannibalized" for *Farewell, My Lovely,* by Joseph T. Shaw in his anthology *The Hard-Boiled Omnibus.* Buys house for $40,000 at 6005 Camino de la Costa in La Jolla, where he and Cissy, who is increasingly frail, live in relative seclusion. Stops excessive drinking. Purchases dictation machine which he uses to carry on extensive correspondence (his frequent correspondents include mystery writer Erle Stanley Gardner; James Sandoe, book reviewer and librarian at University of Colorado; British publisher Hamish Hamilton; and Dale Warren, publicity director of Houghton Mifflin).

Ends connection with long-time literary agent Sydney Sanders in November.

1947   Begins writing original screenplay *Playback*, set in Vancouver, for Universal. Radio program featuring Van Heflin as Philip Marlowe is broadcast on NBC. *The Brasher Doubloon*, film version of *The High Window* directed by John Brahm and starring George Montgomery as Philip Marlowe, is released.

1948   Chandler completes *Playback* screenplay, but studio decides that filming in Vancouver is too expensive, and film is not produced. Works on novel *The Little Sister*. Becomes client of literary agency Brandt and Brandt in New York, and conducts extensive correspondence with agent Carl Brandt and his associate Bernice Baumgarten. Essay "Oscar Night in Hollywood" published in June *Atlantic Monthly*. Leaves Knopf over disagreements about copyrights, earnings from paperback editions, and other issues, and signs contract with Houghton Mifflin for *The Little Sister*. Finishes novel in September. Offers guidelines to scriptwriters for CBS radio series "The Adventures of Philip Marlowe," starring Gerald Mohr, but is otherwise uninvolved with program.

1949   Suffers from ailments, including bronchitis, skin allergies, and shingles, that become chronic conditions. *The Little Sister* is published in Britain by Hamish Hamilton in June and in the U.S. by Houghton Mifflin in September. Agrees to publication of collection of his pulp magazine stories proposed by Houghton Mifflin, but writes to editor Paul Brooks: "I am going to have to revise and edit this trash. There are crudities here and there which I can no longer tolerate."

1950   Works with director Alfred Hitchcock on screen adaptation of Patricia Highsmith's novel *Strangers on a Train* for Warner Brothers. Fantasy story "Professor Bingo's Snuff" published in *Park East* in August. Hitchcock becomes unhappy with Chandler's work on screenplay, and he is replaced by Czenzi Ormonde (Chandler and Ormonde share screenwriting credit when film is released in 1951, though little of Chandler's work remains in final version). *The Simple Art of Murder*, collection of early stories, published by Houghton Mifflin in September and by Hamish Hamilton in November. Chandler and Cissy are saddened by death of their black Persian cat Taki ("so much a part of our lives that even now we dread to come into the silent empty house after being out at night").

1951   Works on new novel, *Summer in Idle Valley* (later retitled *The Long Goodbye*). Visited in February by English novelist and playwright J. B. Priestley and during the summer by American humorist S. J. Perelman.

1952   Publishes "Ten Per Cent of Your Life," article on literary agents, in February *Atlantic Monthly*. Sends draft of *The Long Goodbye* to agents Carl Brandt and Bernice Baumgarten in May, and is troubled when they criticize "softness" of Marlowe in the novel. Begins making extensive revisions. Sails to England with Cissy in August, and sees publisher Hamish Hamilton, J. B. Priestley, film critic Dilys Powell, etymologist Eric Partridge, and others in London. Returns to United States in October. Breaks off relations with Brandt and Brandt agency in November. Cissy's health worsens.

1953   Works on novel loosely based on *Playback* screenplay but puts it aside. Resumes heavy drinking. Finishes *The Long Goodbye* in July. Cissy is acutely ill with respiratory and heart trouble. *The Long Goodbye* published in Britain by Hamish Hamilton in November.

1954   Houghton Mifflin publishes *The Long Goodbye* in the U.S. in March. After repeated hospitalizations throughout the year, Cissy dies on December 12.

1955   Chandler writes to Hamilton in January: "For thirty years, ten months and four days, she was the light of my life, my whole ambition. Anything else I did was just the fire for her to warm her hands at. That is all there is to say." Drinks heavily and suffers from deep depression. Attempts suicide with revolver while drunk on February 22; fires bullet into bathroom ceiling, then surrenders gun when police arrive. After being placed in county hospital for psychiatric observation, spends six days in a private sanitarium. Sells La Jolla house in March and leaves California. Visits friends in Chicago and Old Chatham, New

York. Drinks heavily while in New York City and recovers in New York Hospital. Sails to England in April. Learns onboard ship that he has won Edgar award from the Mystery Writers of America for *The Long Goodbye*. In London receives attention from press and other writers. Forms friendships with pianist Natasha Spender (wife of poet Stephen Spender), Helga Greene (who becomes his literary agent), and thriller writer Ian Fleming. Returns to America in September, then goes back to London in November after learning that Natasha Spender is ill. Visits Spain and Morocco with her and then returns to London, where she undergoes a successful operation. Chandler drinks heavily and is hospitalized for two weeks in a London clinic, where he is diagnosed as having malaria.

1956   Rents small apartment in St. John's Wood, London. Suffers from infatuation with Natasha Spender. Returns to America in May to avoid British taxes. Drinks heavily in New York, collapses, and is hospitalized for exhaustion and malnutrition. Returns to La Jolla in June and rents an apartment. Continues heavy drinking. Briefly considers marrying Louise Landis Loughner, San Francisco woman who had written him an admiring letter in 1955. Sees Natasha Spender in Arizona and California in December.

1957   Becomes involved in personal life of his divorced Australian secretary and her two children. Revises "English Summer," short story written in the 1930s, but abandons plans to expand it into a novel or play. Becomes involved in complex dispute with British authorities over taxes owed because of extended residence in England in 1955. Resumes work on *Playback* with encouragement from Helga Greene. Hospitalized again for drinking in August. Visited in November by Helga Greene. Completes *Playback* in late December.

1958   Begins novel "Poodle Springs," in which Philip Marlowe marries Linda Loring from *The Long Goodbye* (completes only a few chapters). Travels to England in February. At suggestion of Ian Fleming, goes to Capri with Helga Greene to interview deported American Mafia leader "Lucky" Luciano for the London *Sunday Times* (resulting article "My Friend Luco" is not published for legal reasons). Hospitalized in London for drinking in May.

Playback is published by Hamish Hamilton in July and by Houghton Mifflin in October. Returns to La Jolla in August and is rejoined by his Australian secretary. Works on "The Pencil," short story featuring Philip Marlowe. Chandler's health declines from his continued drinking; he is cared for by Kay West, a former neighbor in London.

1959   Visited in February by Helga Greene, who has him hospitalized. While in the hospital Chandler proposes marriage to Greene; she accepts. Visits New York at beginning of March with Greene to accept presidency of Mystery Writers of America. Returns alone to La Jolla while Greene goes on to London, where they intend to live. Drinks heavily, develops pneumonia, and is hospitalized on March 23. Dies in Scripps Clinic at 3:50 P.M. on March 26. Buried on March 30 at Mount Hope Cemetery in San Diego.

Note on the Texts

This volume contains thirteen stories by Raymond Chandler originally published between 1933 and 1939 in *Black Mask, Detective Fiction Weekly, Dime Detective,* and *The Saturday Evening Post,* and three novels, *The Big Sleep, Farewell, My Lovely,* and *The High Window,* published between 1939 and 1942.

Chandler was a slow and careful writer; he spent far longer on his stories for *Black Mask* and *Dime Detective* than was typical of writers for the pulps, who tended to turn out stories rapidly in order to earn a decent income. "I have never made any money out of writing," Chandler said in a letter to fellow pulp writer George Harmon Coxe. "I work too slowly, throw away too much." To another correspondent, Mrs. Robert Hogan, he wrote: "Mine was of course a losing game, on the surface. I wrote pulp stories with as much care as slick stories. It was very poor pay for the work I put into them."

Chandler's pulp stories were anthologized during the 1940s in a number of inexpensive collections: *Five Murderers* (New York: Avon Book Company, 1944), *Five Sinister Characters* (New York: Avon Book Company, 1945), *Red Wind* (Cleveland and New York: World Publishing Company, 1946), *Spanish Blood* (Cleveland and New York: World Publishing Company, 1946), and *Finger Man and Other Stories* (New York: Avon Book Company, 1947). For the most part these anthologies reproduced the periodical texts with only minor variations that probably were the result of house style, although in the case of "Smart-Aleck Kill" a passage occurs that is not present in the periodical version.

When approached by an editor at Houghton Mifflin with a proposal for the collection of stories that was published in 1950 as *The Simple Art of Murder,* Chandler responded: "You realize probably that I am going to have to revise and edit this trash. There are crudities here and there which I can no longer tolerate. The worst thing about them, the vast number of murders, I cannot change." In a number of the stories reprinted in *The Simple Art of Murder,* Chandler changed the name of the detective protagonist, and he interpolated expletives that in the periodical versions had been indicated by dashes. He did not, however, carry out a sweeping revision of his old stories; such changes and deletions that he made were cursory and occasionally created minor inconsistencies by leaving gaps in the narrative.

The texts of the stories printed here are therefore those of the original periodical publications, with two exceptions noted below. The following is a list of the sources:

Blackmailers Don't Shoot. *Black Mask,* December 1933.

Smart-Aleck Kill. *Finger Man and Other Stories* (New York: Avon Books, 1947). Because the *Black Mask* publication of "Smart-Aleck Kill" does not include a passage that was probably present in Chandler's original manuscript, the text printed here is taken from its first book appearance.

Finger Man. *Black Mask,* October 1934.

Nevada Gas. *Black Mask,* June 1935.

Spanish Blood. *Black Mask,* November 1935.

Guns at Cyrano's. *Black Mask,* January 1936.

Pick-Up on Noon Street. *The Simple Art of Murder* (Boston: Houghton Mifflin, 1950). The story first appeared in *Detective Fiction Weekly,* May 1936, under the title "Noon Street Nemesis"; this version deleted, against Chandler's wishes, references to the race of the characters. For the version printed in *The Simple Art of Murder* Chandler reconstructed the deleted passages from memory, the original manuscript having been lost in the interim.

Goldfish. *Black Mask,* June 1936.

Red Wind. *Dime Detective,* January 1938.

The King in Yellow. *Dime Detective,* March 1938.

Pearls Are a Nuisance. *Dime Detective,* April 1939.

Trouble Is My Business. *Dime Detective,* August 1939.

I'll Be Waiting. *Saturday Evening Post,* October 14, 1939.

In the case of stories that appeared originally in *Dime Detective,* chapter headings introduced in order to conform to the magazine's house style, and which were contrary to Chandler's usual practice, are omitted here. The name changes and some of the other revisions that Chandler made for *The Simple Art of Murder* are identified in the notes.

Besides the thirteen stories included in this volume, Chandler published eight other crime stories between 1935 and 1941 which have not been included because Chandler (in a practice he called "cannibalizing") used them as the basis for novels. These stories (which provided elements of *The Big Sleep, Farewell, My Lovely,* and *The Lady in the Lake*) are: "Killer in the Rain" (*Black Mask,* January 1935), "The Man Who Liked Dogs" (*Black Mask,* March 1936), "The Curtain" (*Black Mask,* September 1936), "Try the Girl" (*Black Mask,* January 1937), "Mandarin's Jade" (*Dime Detective,* November 1937), "Bay City Blues" (*Dime Detective,* June 1938), "The Lady in the Lake" (*Dime Detective,* January 1939), and "No Crime in the Mountains" (*Detective Story*, September 1941). He did not allow these stories to be reprinted in his lifetime, and when one was published in an anthology without his permission, he protested forcefully.

The novels in this volume— *The Big Sleep* (1939), *Farewell, My Lovely* (1940), and *The High Window* (1942)—were published in New York by Alfred A. Knopf; Chandler did not revise them after publication. The texts printed here are those of the first American editions.

This volume presents the texts of the original printings chosen for inclusion here, but it does not attempt to reproduce features of their typographic design, such as display capitalization of chapter openings. The texts are printed without change, except for the correction of typographical errors. Spelling, punctuation, and capitalization are often expressive features, and they are not altered, even when inconsistent or irregular. The following is a list of typographical errors corrected, cited by page and line number: 5.4, thin,; 49.2, worts; 80.25, yelled.; 160.7, Yes,; 242.13, said "Is; 245.33, You'r'a; 254.26, didn't; 278.17, I'd; 303.21, touched; 307.11, aroung; 320.25, livingly; 323.14, dreamily; 334.19, it you; 385.26, gasping his; 387.15, got .22; 395.2, on; 434.37, fanny,; 453.11, murdered!; 467.37, amigi; 490.27, breach; 498.15, blood son; 505.23, Reviera; 510.20, pockets; 534.6, George you; 555.37, laying; 558.36, no; 583.16, answered,; 631.7, come; 648.40, off; 662.13, it you; 670.25, I I; 693.24, coupier; 712.15, Mars; 738.7, Let's; 744.27, unindentified; 746.2, Rialito; 796.39, window-peaker; 824.21, at bit; 831.40, "Why."; 838.31, that,'; 850.30, known; 865.22, fast,"; 871.32, The; 877.38, sent; 884.10, I; 905.5–6, fine toothcomb; 910.37, you're; 979.18, ransome; 1010.13, sellling; 1053.9, acccount; 1114.13, dialogue.'; 1123.3–4, *Account*; 1144.39, its; 1168.16, said.; 1171.2, B ata.

Notes

In the notes below, the reference numbers denote page and line of this volume (the line count includes headings). No note is made for material included in standard desk-reference books such as Webster's *Collegiate, Biographical,* and *Geographical* dictionaries. For references to other studies and further biographical background than is contained in the Chronology, see Frank MacShane, *The Life of Raymond Chandler* (New York: E. P. Dutton, 1976); *Selected Letters of Raymond Chandler* (New York: Columbia University Press, 1981), edited by Frank MacShane; *Raymond Chandler Speaking* (Boston: Houghton Mifflin, 1962), edited by Dorothy Gardiner and Kathrine Sorley Walker; and *The Notebooks of Raymond Chandler and English Summer: A Gothic Romance* (New York: Ecco Press, 1976), edited by Frank MacShane.

PULP STORIES

9.20   red hot!] Gunman.

17.18   McNeil's Island} McNeil Island, a federal penitentiary in Puget Sound, about 10 miles southwest of Tacoma, Washington.

20.38   wiper] Gunman; hired killer.

32.37   beezer] Nose.

43.12   flattie] Police officer.

46.28   loogan] Thug; gunman.

52.6   Mallory] In the 1950 collection *The Simple Art of Murder,* Chandler changed the protagonist's name to Johnny Dalmas.

61.36   "Sweet Madness."] Song by Ned Washington and Victor Young, featured in the film *Murder at the Vanities* (1933).

64.21   Hays office] Popular name for the Motion Picture Producers and Distributors of America, Inc., after Will Hays (1879–1954), its president from 1922 to 1945. In 1930 the MPPDA adopted a production code regulating the moral content of movies, which remained in effect until 1966.

69.21   Lingle killing] Jake Lingle, a *Chicago Tribune* police reporter involved with Al Capone and other gangsters, was murdered by an unidentified gunman on June 9, 1930.

95.10   my private office.] In *The Simple Art of Murder,* the passage reads: "my private office, lettered '*Philip Marlowe . . . Investigations.*' "

96.19   ———] In *Finger Man and Other Stories* (1946) and later editions: "sonofabitch."

98.19–20   for ——— sake] In *Finger Man and Other Stories* and later editions: "for Pete's sake."

99.8–18   It was . . . chandeliers.] Since Chandler adapted this description for use in *The Big Sleep,* he condensed the passage in the text printed in *Finger Man and Other Stories* and later editions.

99.21   Bacardi} In *Finger Man and Other Stories* and later editions: "tequila."

100.1–9   "I like . . . roulette."] In *Finger Man and Other Stories* and later editions, the passage reads:

> "Smooth it out with what?" I said. "You got a wood rasp handy?"
> He grinned. I drank a little more of the tequila and made a face.
> "Did somebody invent this stuff on purpose?"
> "I wouldn't know, mister."
> "What's the limit over there?"
> "I wouldn't know that either. How the boss feels, I guess."

123.12   the little ———] In *Finger Man and Other Stories* and later editions: "the little bastard."

132.38   them ———'s!] In *Finger Man and Other Stories* and later editions: "them bastards!"

135.36   the fat ———] In *Finger Man and Other Stories* and later editions: "the fat louse."

136.13   highball] Leave town; run away.

160.38   *Skaters' Waltz*] "The Skaters" (1882), waltz composed by Emile Waldteufel.

167.23   For ——— sake] In *The Simple Art of Murder:* "For Christ sake."

169.15   Jesse Livermore,"] Livermore (1877–1940), speculator and author of books on how to play the stock market.

172.8   *mensur*] Form of dueling prevalent at German universities before World War I.

175.5   Holy ———!] In *The Simple Art of Murder:* "Holy Christ!"

175.14   the ———'s gun!] In *The Simple Art of Murder:* "the bastard's gun!"

176.14   For ——— sake] In *The Simple Art of Murder:* "For Pete's sake."

185.32   you ——— ———] In *The Simple Art of Murder:* "you bastard."

191.36   for ———'s sake?] In *The Simple Art of Murder:* "for Pete's sake?"

192.1–10   Aage said . . . highbinder!"] Omitted in *The Simple Art of Murder*.

206.19   —— damn'] In *The Simple Art of Murder*: "goddamn."

209.28   "—— . . . throatily.] Omitted in *The Simple Art of Murder*.

209.40   —— damn'] In *The Simple Art of Murder*: "goddamn."

216.27   —— damn'] In *The Simple Art of Murder*: "goddamn."

216.39   yard] One hundred dollars.

228.5   by ——] In *The Simple Art of Murder*: "by God."

235.2   TED MALVERN] In *The Simple Art of Murder* Chandler changed the protagonist's name to Ted Carmady.

239.31   ducat] Admission ticket.

242.22   yards] See note 216.39.

255.35   redhot] See note 9.20.

293.4   keister] Suitcase.

297.3   vag] Arrest on a vagrancy charge.

328.18   brace] Confront.

333.10   Carmady] In *The Simple Art of Murder*, Chandler changed the protagonist's name to Marlowe.

342.9–16   The first . . . ain't neither."] Omitted in *The Simple Art of Murder*.

353.34   "Chloe,"] "Chloe: The Song of the Swamp" (1927) by Gus Kahn and Charles N. Daniels.

354.3   repeal] The 18th Amendment, which established Prohibition, went into effect on January 16, 1920. It was repealed by the 21st Amendment, proposed to the states by Congress on February 20, 1933, and ratified on December 5, 1933.

368.28   John Dalmas] In *The Simple Art of Murder* Chandler changed the protagonist's name to Philip Marlowe.

378.38   Joseph Choate] In *The Simple Art of Murder* Chandler changed this character's name to Joseph Coates.

381.24–25   Her face . . . moment.] Omitted in *The Simple Art of Murder*.

381.27–29   "Scream . . . trap.] Omitted in *The Simple Art of Murder*.

386.16–17   "I'm sorry . . . killer.] Omitted in *The Simple Art of Murder*.

386.39   Holy ——!]   In *The Simple Art of Murder*: "Holy Christ!"

387.36   you ——]   In *The Simple Art of Murder*: "you bastard."

393.23   that story,"]   "Mr. Know-All" by W. Somerset Maugham.

393.25   "I've read it," I said.]   In *The Simple Art of Murder*, the passage reads: " 'I've read it,' I said. 'Maugham.' "

412.13   The back . . . dog's nose.]   Omitted in *The Simple Art of Murder*.

418.5   PBX]   Private Branch Exchange, a telephone facility handling communications within an office.

420.21   vagged]   See note 297.3.

429.12   *Solitude*]   Song (1934) composed by Duke Ellington, with lyrics by Eddie De Lange and Irving Mills.

429.22   E in Alt]   In *The Simple Art of Murder*: "E above high C."

434.25   bump]   Death.

434.25   Dutch]   Suicide.

438.17–18   —— — - ——!]   In *The Simple Art of Murder*: "Son of a bitch!"

438.35   —— — - ——!]   In *The Simple Art of Murder*: "Son of a bitch!"

448.37–38   "The King in Yellow]   Title of Robert W. Chambers' linked collection of fantastic tales (1895) involving the sinister influence of a mysterious book on whoever reads it.

486.21–23   The man . . . glass]   Because this description duplicates a passage in "Guns at Cyrano's," Chandler revised it in *The Simple Art of Murder* to read: "The man sat with a small glass . . ."

493.23   enough hot . . . Mae West's hips.]   In *The Simple Art of Murder*: "enough phony pearls to cover an elephant's caboose."

496.8   Abyssinia."]   "I'll be seeing you."

506.32   pills]   Cigarettes.

508.4   The —— — ——!]   In *The Simple Art of Murder*: "The son of a bitch!"

509.7   Baby Leroy]   Film name of LeRoy Winebrenner (b. 1932), who appeared in comedies including *Tillie and Gus* (1933), *It's a Gift* (1934), *The Old-Fashioned Way* (1934), and *The Lemon Drop Kid* (1934).

514.20   Robert Donat . . . Yacht Club Boys."]   Robert Donat (1905–58), English star of *The 39 Steps* (1935) and *Goodbye, Mr. Chips* (1939); the Yacht Club Boys, harmony group featured in musicals such as *Pigskin Parade* (1936).

516.22   Johnny Dalmas] In *The Simple Art of Murder* Chandler changed the protagonist's name to Philip Marlowe.

517.7   the Jeeter of *Tobacco Road*] Jeeter Lester, shiftless Georgia share-cropper in Erskine Caldwell's 1932 novel.

524.34   darb] Beaut; lulu.

530.32   you ——] In *The Simple Art of Murder*: "you bastard."

535.26   you ——!] In *The Simple Art of Murder*: "you bastards!"

535.33   you —— — ——!] In *The Simple Art of Murder*: "you sons of bitches!"

542.11   dummy-chucker] Someone who pretends to be deaf and dumb for criminal purposes.

553.34   —— — - ——] In *The Simple Art of Murder*: "son of a bitch."

560.39   put the bee on] Ask for money.

565.9–16   A shiny . . . the room.] Since Chandler adapted this and the paragraph below into *Farewell, My Lovely,* he omitted them in *The Simple Art of Murder*.

565.29–36   The loudspeaker . . . Mexican.)] See note 565.9–16.

572.12   The Last Laugh. Emil Jannings.] F. W. Murnau's film *The Last Laugh* (1924) stars Emil Jannings.

572.14   "Spring, Beautiful Spring,"] Song ("O Frühling, Wie Bist Du So Schön") written in 1903 by Paul Lincke; also known as "Chimes of Spring."

572.30–31   The Blue Bird] Allegorical play (1909) by Maurice Maeter-linck, filmed in 1918 and 1940.

THE BIG SLEEP

605.32   pin-seal] Sealskin.

624.38   Mann Act] Passed in 1910, the act made it a federal offense to aid or participate in the transportation of a woman for immoral purposes across a state line.

629.34   the Quints] The Dionne quintuplets, born in Ontario in 1934, who became objects of intense public interest.

634.21   flash gambling] Crooked gambling.

647.36   check raiser] Someone who alters checks for fraudulent purposes.

663.26–27   like Caesar . . . to men] Cf. Suetonius, *The Twelve Caesars,* Bk. I: "And to emphasize the bad name Caesar had won alike for unnatural and natural vice, I may here record that the Elder Curio referred to him in a speech as: 'Every woman's husband and every man's wife.'" The subject of the passage is Gaius Julius Caesar.

664.10   took it into chancery] Held it under his arm.

750.32   Philo Vance] Fastidious and erudite hero of a series of detective novels by S. S. Van Dine (Willard Huntington Wright, 1888–1939), including *The Canary Murder Case* (1928), *The Greene Murder Case* (1928), and *The Kennel Murder Case* (1933).

FAREWELL, MY LOVELY

788.36   Will Hays] See note 64.21.

837.6   gowed-up] Under the influence of an opiate.

939.3   Moral Rearmament] Organization promulgating absolute standards of morality and "the dictatorship of God," founded by American evangelist Frank Buchman (1878–1961).

945.17   Roses of Picardy] Song (1916) by Frederick Edward Weatherly and Haydn Wood.

THE HIGH WINDOW

1006.21   Lombardos] Guy Lombardo and His Royal Canadians, a popular orchestra featuring Lombardo's brothers Carmen and Lebert.

1030.40–1031.1   devaluation . . . dollar] Measures taken by the Roosevelt administration and Congress in 1933–34 resulted in the gold value of the dollar falling from par to 59.06 cents.

1056.5   NOVA. . . EXCELSIOR] "New York Columbia Ever Upward."

1061.6   gold hoarder] Gold hoarding was a criminal offense under the Emergency Banking Relief Act of 1933.

1070.2   braced] See note 328.18.

1071.39   *Gang Busters*] Radio crime drama.

1080.35   PBX] See note 418.5.

1081.24–25   John Reed Club] The John Reed Club was started in 1929 by the editorial board of *New Masses*. The club was named in honor of John Reed (1887–1920), author of *Ten Days That Shook the World*, and had as its major aim the broadening of the cultural appeal of radical socialism. By 1934, there were some 30 clubs in cities and towns across the United States.

1085.16   Dark Eyes] Adaptation (1926) by Harry Horlick and Gregory Stone of Russian Gypsy song *Otchi Tchorniya*.

CATALOGING INFORMATION

Chandler, Raymond, 1888–1959
  (Selections)
  Stories and early novels / Raymond Chandler.
    p. cm. — (The Library of America ; 79)
    Contents: Pulp stories—The big sleep—Farewell, my lovely—
The high window.
    1. Marlowe, Philip (Fictitious character)—Fiction. 2. Private
investigators—California—Los Angeles—Fiction. 3. Detective
and mystery stories, American. 4. Los Angeles (Calif.)—Fiction.
I. Title. II. Title. The big sleep III. Title. Farewell, my lovely.
IV. Title. The high window. V. Series.
PS3505.H3224A6   1995b   94–45462
813'.52—dc20
ISBN 1–883011–07–8

THE LIBRARY OF AMERICA SERIES

This book is set in 10 point Linotron Galliard,
a face designed for photocomposition by Matthew Carter
and based on the sixteenth-century face Granjon. The paper is
acid-free Ecusta Nyalite and meets the requirements for permanence
of the American National Standards Institute. The binding
material is Brillianta, a woven rayon cloth made by
Van Heek-Scholco Textielfabrieken, Holland.
The composition is by The Clarinda
Company. Printing and binding by
R.R.Donnelley & Sons Company.
Designed by Bruce Campbell.